THE BURNING CITY

Larry Niven

TALES OF KNOWN SPACE
THE INTEGRAL TREES
WORLD OF PTAVVS
RINGWORLD
PROTECTOR
THE SMOKE RING
N-SPACE
PLAYGROUNDS OF THE
  MIND
CRASHLANDER
FLATLANDER
THE RINGWORLD THRONE
DESTINY'S ROAD
RAINBOW MARS

Jerry Pournelle

JANISSARIES
HIGH JUSTICE
KING DAVID'S SPACESHIP
EXILES TO GLORY
RED HEROIN
PRINCE OF MERCENARIES
FALKENBERG'S LEGION
STARSWARM

Larry Niven & Jerry Pournelle

INFERNO
OATH OF FEALTY
THE MOTE IN GOD'S EYE
LUCIFER'S HAMMER
FOOTFALL
THE GRIPPING HAND
THE BURNING CITY

Larry Niven & Steven Barnes

DREAM PARK
THE BARSOOM PROJECT
THE CALIFORNIA VOODOO
  GAMES
DESCENT OF ANANSI
ACHILLES' CHOICE
SATURN'S RACE

Larry Niven, Jerry Pournelle & Steven Barnes

LEGACY OF HEOROT
BEOWULF'S CHILDREN

Larry Niven, Jerry Pournelle & Michael Flynn

FALLEN ANGELS

Jerry Pournelle & S. M. Stirling

GO TELL THE SPARTANS
PRINCE OF SPARTA

Jerry Pournelle & Charles Sheffield

HIGHER EDUCATION

LARRY NIVEN & JERRY POURNELLE

THE BURNING CITY

POCKET BOOKS
New York   London   Toronto   Sydney   Singapore

This book is a work of fiction. Names, characters, places and incidents are products of the authors' imagination or are used fictitiously. Any resemblance to actual events or locales or persons, living or dead, is entirely coincidental.

POCKET BOOKS, a division of Simon & Schuster Inc.
1230 Avenue of the Americas, New York, NY 10020

ISBN:0-671-03660-2

First Pocket Books hardcover printing March 2000

POCKET and colophon are registered trademarks of Simon & Schuster Inc.

Printed in the U.S.A.

For Roberta and Marilyn

Editor's Acknowledgment

The editor would like to thank Larry Niven
and Jerry Pournelle for that rarest of all novels,
one with something to say.

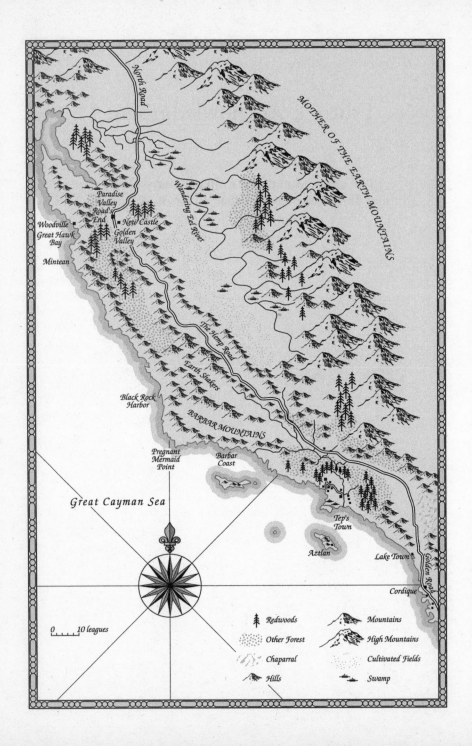

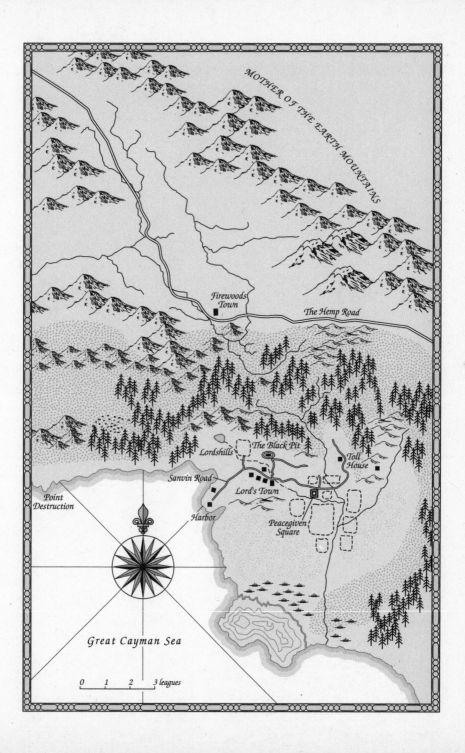

"It is not God who kills the children. Not fate that
butchers them or destiny that feeds them
to the dogs. It's us. Only us."
From *Watchmen* by Alan Moore

CAST

Gods

YANGIN-ATEP (TEP, FIREBRINGER)
ZOOSH
COYOTE
BEHEMOTH
LOKI
PROMETHEUS

Lordkin

Placehold

WHANDALL PLACEHOLD (Seshmarl)
POTHEFIT: Whandall's father
SHASTERN: Whandall's younger brother
SHIG: Whandall's younger brother
MOTHER'S MOTHER: Dargramnet
WANSHIG: Whandall's older half brother
RESALET: Whandall's father's brother and leader of the Placehold
WESS: a girl about Whandall's age
LENORBA
VINSPEL
ILYESSA: Whandall's sister
THOMER
TOTTO
TRIG: Whandall's brother
ELRISS
RUBYFLOWER
ILTHERN

SHARLATTA
FREETHSPAT

Serpent's Walk

LORD PELZED
GERAVIM
TUMBANTON
TRAZALAC
STANT CORLES
DUDDIGRACT
RENWILDS
COSCARTIN
SHEALOS
THE FORIGAFT BROTHERS
KRAEMAR
ROUPEND
CHAPOKA
MIRACOS
HARTANBATH

Other Bands

BANSH
ILTHER
ALFERTH
TARNISOS
ILSERN: a tough, athletic woman
CHIEF WULLTID
IDREEPUCT
FALCONS: called Dirty Birds by most but not to their faces
STAXIR

Kinless

KREEG MILLER
RIGMASTER
WILLOW ROPEWALKER
CARVER ROPEWALKER
CARTER ROPEWALKER

HAMMER MILLER
IRIS MILLER
HYACINTH MILLER
OPAL MILLER
DREAM-LOTUS INNKEEP

Lords

LORD CHIEF WITNESS SAMORTY
LORD CHANTHOR
LORD QIRINTY: a lord fascinated by magic
LADY RAWANDA: first lady of Lordshills
LORD JERREFF
SHANDA
RABBLIE (LORD RABILARD)
LORD QUINTANA: later becomes Lord Chief Witness
MORTH OF ATLANTIS
LORD QUIRINTHAL THE FIRST
ROWENA
LADY SIRESEE

Their Servants

SERANA: a cook; later, chief cook
ANTANIO
BERTRANA (MISS BATTY): governess
PEACEVOICE WATERMAN

Turf

PLACEHOLD
SERPENT'S WALK
PEACEGIVEN SQUARE
BULL PIZZLE
FALCON LAIR: generally called Dirty Bird
THE WEDGE: the meadow at the top of Deerpiss River
CONDIGEO

LORD'S TOWN
THE LORDSHILLS
WOLVERINES
TEP'S TOWN (VALLEY OF SMOKES, BURNING CITY)
WATER DEVILS
SANVIN STREET: winds over the low hills that separate Serpent's Walk
    from the harbor
THE BLACK PIT
ATLANTIS
BARBAR MOUNTAINS
TOROV
MAZE WALKERS
EASTERN ARC
GOOD HAND HARBOR
OWL BEAK
MARKET ROUND
SERPENT STREET
COLDWATER
DARK MAN'S CUP STREET
DEAD TOWN
THE TORONEXTI
LION'S ATTIC
STRAIGHT STREET
ANGLE STREET

Lookers

TRAS PREETROR
ARSHUR THE MAGNIFICENT

Seamen

JACK RIGENLORD
ETIARP
MANOCANE
SABRIOLOY

Water Devils

LATTAR

Beyond Tep's Town

Turf

FIREWOODS TOWN
WALUU PORT
THE HEMP ROAD
MOUNT JOY
PARADISE VALLEY
STONE NEEDLES
GORMAN
GOLDEN VALLEY
LAST PINES
MARSYL TOWN
ORANGETOWN
COYOTE'S DEN
GREAT HAWK BAY

Clan Members and Others

SPOTTED COYOTES
RORDRAY
BLACK KETTLE (KETTLE BELLY)
NUMBER THREE
NUMBER FOUR
HAJ FISHHAWK
RUBY FISHHAWK
ORANGE BLOSSOM
BISON CLAN
MIRIME
LONESOME CROW
GREATHAND: the blacksmith
HICKAMORE
FAWN
MOUNTAIN CAT
STARFALL

RUTTING DEER
TWISTED CLOUD
STAG RAMPANT

Book Two

Turf

ROAD'S END
DEAD SEAL FLATS
GRANITE KNOB
LONG AVENUE
NORTH QUARTER
NEW CASTLE
HIGH PINES
GREAT VALLEY
RORDRAY'S ATTIC
MOUNT CARLEM
WARBLER FLATS
DRYLANDS
FARTHEST LAND
STONE NEEDLES
MINTERL
CASTLE MINTERL
HIP HIGH SPRING
VEDASIRAS RANGE
FAIR CHANCE
THE ESTATES
CARLEM MARCLE
NEO WRASELN
QUAKING ASPEN
THE SPRINGS

Travelers

WHANDALL FEATHERSNAKE
GREEN STONE
LARKFEATHERS
SABER TOOTH
CHIEF FARTHEST LAND

HAWK IN FLIGHT
WOLF TRIBE
MOUNTAIN CAT
SESHMARLS THE BIRD
TERROR BIRDS
LILAC
WHITECAP MOUNTAIN
PUMA TRIBE
PASSENGER PIGEON
THONE
KING TRANIMEL
GLINDA
DREAM OF FLYING
WHITE LIGHTNING
STONE NEEDLES MAN (CATLONY, TUMBLEWEED, HERMIT)
HIDDEN SPICE
CLEVER SQUIRREL (SQUIRRELLY)
LURK (NOTHING WAS SEEN)
STARFALL ROPEWALKER
FIGHTING CAT FISHHAWK
BURNING TOWER
INSOLENT LIZARD
FALLEN WOLF

Returning

HALF HAND
EGON FORIGAFT
MASTER PEACEVOICE WATERMAN
LORD CHIEF WITNESS QUINTANA
WITNESS CLERK SANDRY
ADZ WEAVER
FUBGIRE
RONI
HEROUL
FIREGIFT
SILLY RABBITS
SADESP
LEATHERSMITH MILLER (SMITTY)
SAPPHIRE CARPENTER

SWABOTT
REBLAY OF SILLY RABBITS
HEJAK
LAGDRET

PREFACE

There was fire on Earth before the fire god came. There has always been fire. What Yangin-Atep gave to humankind was madness.

Yangin-Atep's children will play with fire even after they burn their fingers.

It was only Yangin-Atep's joke, then and for unmeasured time after. But a greater god called down the great cold, and Yangin-Atep's joke came into its own. In the icy north people could not survive unless the fire god favored one of their number.

Cautious men and women never burned themselves twice; but their people died of the cold. Someone must tend the fire during the terrible winters. Twelve thousand years before the birth of Christ, when most of the gods had gone mythical and magic was fading from the world, Yangin-Atep's gift remained.

BOOK ONE

WHANDALL PLACEHOLD

PART ONE

Childhood

CHAPTER

1

They burned the city when Whandall Placehold was two years old, and again when he was seven.

At seven he saw and understood more. The women waited with the children in the courtyard through a day and a night and another day. The day sky was black and red. The night sky glowed red and orange, dazzling and strange. Across the street a granary burned like a huge torch. Strangers trying to fight the fire made shadow pictures.

The Placehold men came home with what they'd gathered: shells, clothing, cookware, furniture, jewelry, magical items, a cauldron that would heat up by itself. The excitement was infectious. Men and women paired off and fought over the pairings.

And Pothefit went out again with Resalet, but only Resalet came back.

Afterward Whandall went with the other boys to watch the loggers cutting redwoods for the rebuilding.

The forest cupped Tep's Town like a hand. There were stories, but nobody could tell Whandall what was beyond the forest where redwoods were pillars big enough to support the sky, big enough to replace a dozen houses. The great trees stood well apart, each guarding its turf. Lesser vegetation gathered around the base of each redwood like a malevolent army.

The army had many weapons. Some plants bristled with daggers;

some had burrs to anchor seeds in hair or flesh; some secreted poison; some would whip a child across the face with their branches.

Loggers carried axes, and long poles with blades at the ends. Leather armor and wooden masks made them hard to recognize as men. With the poles they could reach out and under to cut the roots of the spiked or poisoned lesser plants and push them aside, until one tall redwood was left defenseless.

Then they bowed to it.

Then they chopped at the base until, in tremendous majesty and with a sound like the end of the world, it fell.

They never seemed to notice that they were being watched from cover by a swarm of children. The forest had dangers for city children, but being caught was not one of them. If you were caught spying in town you would be lucky to escape without broken bones. It was safer to spy on the loggers.

One morning Bansh and Ilther brushed a vine.

Bansh began scratching, and then Ilther; then thousands of bumps sprouted over Ilther's arm, and almost suddenly it was bigger than his leg. Bansh's hand and the ear he'd scratched were swelling like nightmares, and Ilther was on the ground, swelling everywhere and fighting hard to breathe.

Shastern wailed and ran before Whandall could catch him. He brushed past leaves like a bouquet of blades and was several paces beyond before he slowed, stopped, and turned to look at Whandall. *What should I do now?* His leathers were cut to ribbons across his chest and left arm, the blood spilling scarlet through the slashes.

The forest was not impenetrable. There were thorns and poison plants, but also open spaces. Stick with those, you could get through . . . it *looked* like you could get through without touching anything . . . almost. And the children were doing that, scattering, finding their own paths out.

But Whandall caught the screaming Shastern by his bloody wrist and towed him toward the loggers, because Shastern was his younger brother, because the loggers were close, because somebody would help a screaming child.

The woodsmen saw them—saw them and turned away. But one dropped his ax and jogged toward the child in zigzag fashion, avoiding . . . what? Armory plants, a wildflower bed—

Shastern went quiet under the woodsman's intense gaze. The woodsman pulled the leather armor away and wrapped Shastern's wounds in strips of clean cloth, pulling it tight. Whandall was trying to tell him about the other children.

The woodsman looked up. "Who are you, boy?"

"I'm Whandall of Serpent's Walk." Nobody gave his family name.

"I'm Kreeg Miller. How many—"

Whandall barely hesitated. "Two tens of us."

"Have they all got"—he patted Shastern's armor—"leathers?"

"Some."

Kreeg picked up cloth, a leather bottle, some other things. Now one of the others was shouting angrily while trying not to look at the children. "Kreeg, what do you want with those candlestubs? We've got work to do!" Kreeg ignored him and followed the path as Whandall pointed it out.

There were hurt children, widely scattered. Kreeg dealt with them. Whandall didn't understand, until a long time later, why other loggers wouldn't help.

Whandall took Shastern home through Dirty Birds to avoid Bull Pizzles. In Dirty Birds a pair of adolescent Lordkin would not let them pass.

Whandall showed them three gaudy white blossoms bound up in a scrap of cloth. Careful not to touch them himself, he gave one to each of the boys and put the third away.

The boys sniffed the womanflowers' deep fragrance. "Way nice. What else have you got?"

"Nothing, Falcon brother." Dirty Birds liked to be called Falcons, so you did that. "Now go and wash your hands and face. Wash hard or you'll swell up like melons. We have to go."

The Falcons affected to be amused, but they went off toward the fountain. Whandall and Shastern ran through Dirty Birds into Serpent's Walk. Marks and signs showed when you passed from another district to Serpent's Walk, but Whandall would have known Serpent's Walk without them. There weren't as many trash piles, and burned-out houses were rebuilt faster.

The Placehold stood alone in its block, three stories of gray stone. Two older boys played with knives just outside the door. Inside, Uncle Totto lay asleep in the corridor where you had to step over him to get in. Whandall tried to creep past him.

"Huh? Whandall, my lad. What's going on here?" He looked at Shastern, saw bloody bandages, and shook his head. "Bad business. What's going on?"

"Shastern needs help!"

"I see that. What happened?"

Whandall tried to get past, but it was no use. Uncle Totto wanted to hear the whole story, and Shastern had been bleeding too long. Whandall started screaming. Totto raised his fist. Whandall pulled his brother upstairs. A sister was washing vegetables for dinner, and she shouted too. Women came yelling. Totto cursed and retreated.

Mother wasn't home that night. Mother's Mother—Dargramnet, if you were speaking to strangers—sent Wanshig to tell Bansh's family. She put Shastern in Mother's room and sat with him until he fell asleep. Then she came into the big second-floor Placehold room and sat in her big chair. Often that room was full of Placehold men, usually playful, but sometimes they shouted and fought. Children learned to hide in the smaller rooms, cling to women's skirts, or find errands to do. Tonight Dargramnet asked the men to help with the injured children, and they all left so that she was alone with Whandall. She held Whandall in her lap.

"They wouldn't help," he sobbed. "Only the one. Kreeg Miller. We could have saved Ilther—it was too late for Bansh, but we could have saved Ilther, only they wouldn't help."

Mother's Mother nodded and petted him. "No, of course they wouldn't," she said. "Not now. When I was a girl, we helped each other. Not just kin, not just Lordkin." She had a faint smile, as if she saw things Whandall would never see, and liked them. "Men stayed home. Mothers taught girls and men taught boys, and there wasn't all this fighting."

"Not even in the Burnings?"

"Bonfires. We made bonfires for Yangin-Atep, and he helped us. Houses of ill luck, places of illness or murder, we burned those too. We knew how to serve Yangin-Atep then. When I was a girl there were wizards, real wizards."

"A wizard killed Pothefit," Whandall said gravely.

"Hush," Mother's Mother said. "What's done is done. It won't do to think about Burnings."

"The fire god," Whandall said.

"Yangin-Atep sleeps," Mother's Mother said. "The fire god was stronger when I was a girl. In those days there were real wizards in Lord's Town, and they did real magic."

"Is that where Lords live?"

"No, Lords don't live there. Lords live in Lordshills. Over the hills, past the Black Pit, nearly all the way to the sea," Mother's Mother said, and smiled again. "And yes, it's beautiful. We used to go there sometimes."

He thought about the prettiest places he had seen. Peacegiven Square, when the kinless had swept it clean and set up their tents. The Flower Market, which he wasn't supposed to go to. Most of the town was dirty, with winding streets, houses falling down, and big houses that had been well built but were going to ruin. Not like Placehold. Placehold was stone, big, orderly, with roof gardens. Dargramnet made the women and children work to keep it clean, even bullied the men until they fixed the roof or broken stairs. Placehold was orderly, and that made it pretty to Whandall.

He tried to imagine another place of order, bigger than Placehold. It would have to be a long way, he thought. "Didn't that take a long time?"

"No, we'd go in a wagon in the morning. We'd be home that same night. Or sometimes the Lords came to our city. They'd come and sit in Peacegiven Square and listen to us."

"What's a Lord, Mother's Mother?"

"You always were the curious one. Brave too," she said, and petted him again. "The Lords showed us how to come here when my grandfather's father was young. Before that, our people were wanderers. My grandfather told me stories about living in wagons, always moving on."

"Grandfather?" Whandall asked.

"Your mother's father."

"But—how could she know?" Whandall demanded. He thought that Pothefit had been his father, but he was never sure. Not *sure* the way Mother's Mother seemed to be.

Mother's Mother looked angry for a moment, but then her expression softened. "She knows because I know," Mother's Mother said. "Your grandfather and I were together a long time, years and years, until he was killed, and he was the father of all my children."

Whandall wanted to ask how she knew that, but he'd seen her angry look, and he was afraid. There were many things you didn't talk about. He asked, "Did he live in a wagon?"

"Maybe," Mother's Mother said. "Or maybe it was his grandfather. I've forgotten most of those stories now. I told them to your mother, but she didn't listen."

"I'll listen, Mother's Mother," Whandall said.

She brushed her fingers through his freshly washed hair. She'd used three days' water to wash Whandall and Shastern, and when Resalet said something about it she had shouted at him until he ran out of the Placehold. "Good," she said. "Someone ought to remember."

"What do Lords do?"

"They show us things, give us things, tell us what the law is," Mother's Mother said. "You don't see them much anymore. They used to come to Tep's Town. I remember when we were both young— they chose your grandfather to talk to the Lords for the Placehold. I was so proud. And the Lords brought wizards with them, and made rain, and put a spell on our roof gardens so everything grew better." The dreamy smile came back. "Everything grew better; everyone helped each other. I'm so proud of you, Whandall; you didn't run and leave your brother—you stayed to help." She stroked him, petting him the way his sisters petted the cat. Whandall almost purred.

She dozed off soon after. He thought about her stories and won-dered how much was true. He couldn't remember when anyone helped anyone who wasn't close kin. Why would it have been different when Mother's Mother was young? And could it be that way again?

But he was seven, and the cat was playing with a ball of string. Whandall climbed off Mother's Mother's lap to watch.

Bansh and Ilther died. Shastern lived, but he kept the scars. In later years they passed for fighting scars.

Whandall watched them rebuild the city after the Burning. Stores and offices rose again, cheap wooden structures on winding streets. The kinless never seemed to work hard on rebuilding.

Smashed water courses were rebuilt. The places where people died—kicked to death or burned or cut down with the long Lordkin knives—remained empty for a time. Everybody was hungry until the Lords and the kinless could get food flowing in again.

None of the other children would return to the forest. They took to spying on strangers, ready to risk broken bones rather than the terri-ble plants. But the forest fascinated Whandall. He returned again and again. Mother didn't want him to go, but Mother wasn't there much. Mother's Mother only told him to be careful.

Old Resalet heard her. Now he laughed every time Whandall left the Placehold with leathers and mask.

Whandall went alone. He always followed the path of the logging, and that protected him a little. The forest became less dangerous as Kreeg Miller taught him more.

All the chaparral was dangerous, but the scrub that gathered round the redwoods was actively malevolent. Kreeg's father had told him that it was worse in his day: the generations had tamed these plants. There were blade-covered morningstars and armory plants, and lord-kin's-kiss, and lordkiss with longer blades, and harmless-looking vines and flower beds and bushes all called touch-me and marked by five-bladed red or red-and-green leaves.

Poison plants came in other forms than touch-me. Any plant might take a whim to cover itself with daggers and poison them too. Nettles covered their leaves with thousands of needles that would burrow into flesh. Loggers cut under the morningstar bushes and touch-me flower beds with the bladed poles they called severs. Against lordwhips the only defense was a mask.'

The foresters knew fruit trees the children hadn't found. "These yellow apples *want* to be eaten," Kreeg said, "seeds and all, so in a day or two the seeds are somewhere else, making more plants. If you don't eat the core, at least throw it as far as you can. But these red death bushes you stay away from—far away—because if you get close you'll eat the berries."

"Magic?"

"Right. And they're poison. They want their seeds in your belly when you die, for fertilizer."

One wet morning after a lightning storm, loggers saw smoke reaching into the sky.

"Is that the city?" Whandall asked.

"No, that's part of the forest. Over by Wolverine territory. It'll go out," Kreeg assured the boy. "They always do. You find black patches here and there, big as a city block."

"The fire wakes Yangin-Atep," the boy surmised. "Then Yangin-Atep takes the fire for himself? So it goes out . . ." But instead of confirming, Kreeg only smiled indulgently. Whandall heard snickering.

The other loggers didn't believe, but . . . "Kreeg, don't you believe in Yangin-Atep either?"

"Not really," Kreeg said. "Some magic works, out here in the woods, but in town? Gods and magic, you hear a lot about them, but you see damn little."

"A magician killed Pothefit!"

Kreeg Miller shrugged.

Whandall was near tears. Pothefit had vanished during the Burning, just ten weeks ago. Pothefit was his father! But you didn't say that outside the family. Whandall cast about for better arguments. "You *bow* to the redwood before you cut it. I've seen you. Isn't that magic?"

"Yeah, well . . . why take chances? Why do the morningstars and laurel whips and touch-me and creepy-julia all protect the redwoods?"

"Like house guards," Whandall said, remembering that there were always men and boys on guard at Placehold.

"Maybe. Like the plants made some kind of bargain," Kreeg said, and laughed.

Mother's Mother had told him. Yangin-Atep led Whandall's ancestors to the Lords, and the Lords had led Whandall's ancestors through the forest to the Valley of Smokes where they defeated the kinless and built Tep's Town. Redwood seeds and firewands didn't sprout unless fire had passed through. Surely these woods belonged to the fire god!

But Kreeg Miller just couldn't see it.

They worked half the morning, hacking at the base of a vast redwood, ignoring the smoke that still rose northeast of them. Whandall carried water to them from a nearby stream. The other loggers were almost used to him now. They called him Candlestub.

When the sun was overhead, they broke for lunch.

Kreeg Miller had taken to sharing lunch with him. Whandall had managed to gather some cheese from the Placehold kitchen. Kreeg had a smoked rabbit from yesterday.

Whandall asked, "How many trees does it take to build the city back?"

Two loggers overheard and laughed. "They never burn the whole city," Kreeg told him. "Nobody could live through that, Whandall. Twenty or thirty stores and houses, a few blocks solid and some other places scattered, then they break off."

The Placehold men said that they'd burned down the whole city, and all of the children believed them.

A logger said, "We'll cut another tree after this one. We wouldn't need all four if Lord Qirinty didn't want a wing on his palace. Boy, do you remember your first Burning?"

"Some. I was only two years old." Whandall cast back in his mind. "The men were acting funny. They'd lash out if any children got too close. They yelled a lot, and the women yelled back. The women tried to keep the men away from us.

"Then one afternoon it all got very scary and confusing. There was shouting and whooping and heat and smoke and light. The women all huddled with us on the second floor. There were smells—not just smoke, but stuff that made you gag, like an alchemist's shop. The men came in with things they'd gathered. Blankets, furniture, heaps of shells, stacks of cups and plates, odd things to eat.

"And afterward everyone seemed to calm down." Whandall's voice trailed off. The other woodsmen were looking at him like . . . like an enemy. Kreeg wouldn't look at him at all.

CHAPTER
2

The world had moved on, and Whandall had hardly noticed.

His brothers and cousins all seemed to have disappeared. Mostly the girls and women stayed home, but on Mother's Day each month the women went to the corner squares where the Lordsmen gave out food and clothing and shells, presents from the Lords. There were always men around that day and the next. Later, they might be around or they might be gone.

But boys appeared only for meals and sleep, and not always then. Where did they go?

He followed a cluster of cousins one afternoon. As in the forest, he took pride in being unseen. He got four blocks before four younger men challenged him. They'd beaten him half senseless before Shastern turned around, saw what was happening, and came running.

Shastern showed the tattoos on his hands and arms. Whandall had once asked about those, but Shastern had put off answering. They blended in with the terrible scars Shastern carried from the forest, but many of his cousins had them too. He never asked that kind of question of his cousins. Now Whandall did not quite hear what Shastern and his cousins said to them, but the strangers turned him loose and his cousins carried him home.

He woke hurting. Shastern woke around noon and sought him out. Shastern was barred from speaking certain secrets, but some things he could say . . .

Serpent's Walk wasn't just this region of the city.

Serpent's Walk was the young men who held it. These streets belonged to Serpent's Walk. Other streets, other bands. The region grew or shrank, streets changed hands, with the power of the bands. They put up signs on walls and other places.

Whandall had been able to read them for years. Serpent's Walk had a squiggle sign, easy to draw. Dirty Birds was a falcon drawn wild and sloppy. Shastern showed him a boundary, a wall with the Serpent's Walk squiggle at one end and a long thin phallus to mark Bull Pizzle territory at the other. Unmarked, one did not walk in Serpent's Walk, or in Bull Pizzle or Dirty Bird either, if one did not belong. As a child Whandall had wandered the streets without hindrance, but a ten-year-old was no longer a child.

"But there are places with no signs at all," Whandall protested.

"That's Lord territory. You can go there until one of the Lordsmen tells you not to. Then you leave."

"Why?"

"Because everyone is scared of the Lordsmen."

"Why? Are they so strong?"

"Well, they're big, and they're mean, and they wear that armor."

"They walk in pairs too," Whandall said, remembering.

"Right. And if you hurt one of them, a lot more will come looking for you."

"What if they don't know who did it?"

Shastern shrugged expressively. "Then a bunch of them come and beat up on everybody they can find until someone confesses. Or we kill someone and say he confessed before we killed him. You stay away from Lordsmen, Whandall. Only good they do is when they bring in the presents on Mother's Day."

Whandall found it strange to have his one-year-younger brother behaving as his elder.

He must have spoken to Wanshig too. Wanshig was Whandall's eldest brother. Wanshig had the tattoos, a snake in the web of his left thumb, a rattlesnake that ran up his right arm from the index finger to the elbow, a small snake's eye at the edge of his left eye. The next night Wanshig took him into the streets. In a ruin that stank of old smoke, he introduced his younger brother to men who carried knives and never smiled.

"He needs protection," Wanshig said. The men just looked at him. Finally one asked, "Who speaks for him?"

Whandall knew some of these faces. Shastern was there too, and he said, "I will." Shastern did not speak to his brothers, but he spoke of Whandall in glowing terms. When the rest fled the forest in terror,

Whandall had stayed to help Shastern. If he'd learned little of the customs of Serpent's Walk, it was because he was otherwise occupied. When none of the boys would return to the wood but took to the streets instead, Whandall Placehold continued to brave the killer plants, to spy on the woodsmen.

The room was big enough to hold fifty people or more. It was dark outside now, and the only light in the room came from the moon shining through holes in the roof, and from torches. The torches were outside, stuck into holes in the windowsills. Yangin-Atep wouldn't allow fires inside, except during a Burning. You could build an outside cookfire under a lean-to shelter, but never inside, and if you tried to enclose a fire with walls, the fire went out. Whandall couldn't remember anyone telling him this. He just knew it, as he knew that cats had sharp claws and that boys should stay away from men when they were drinking beer.

There was a big chair on a low platform at one end of the room. The chair was wooden, with arms and a high back, and it was carved with serpents and birds. Some kinless must have worked hard to make that chair, but Whandall didn't think it would be very comfortable, not like the big ponyhair-stuffed chair Mother's Mother liked.

A tall man with no smile sat in that chair. Three other men stood in front of him holding their long Lordkin knives across their chests. Whandall knew him. Pelzed lived in a two-story stone house at the end of a block of well-kept kinless houses. Pelzed's house had a fenced-in garden and there were always kinless working in it.

"Bring him," Pelzed said.

His brothers took Whandall by the arms and pulled him to just in front of Pelzed's chair, then forced him down on his knees.

"What good are you?" Pelzed demanded.

Shastern began to speak, but Pelzed held up a hand. "I heard you. I want to hear him. What did you learn from the woodsmen?"

"Say something," Wanshig whispered. There was fear in his voice.

Whandall thought furiously. "Poisons. I know the poisons of the forest. Needles. Blades. Whips."

Pelzed gestured. One of the men standing in front of Pelzed's chair raised his big knife and struck Whandall hard across the left shoulder.

It stung, but he had used the flat of the blade. "Call him Lord," the man said. His bared chest was a maze of scars; one ran right up his cheek into his hair. Whandall found him scary as hell.

"Lord," Whandall said. He had never seen a Lord. "Yes, Lord."

"Good. You can walk in the forest?"

"Much of it, Lord. Places where the woodsmen have been."

"Good. What do you know of the Wedge?"

"The meadow at the top of the Deerpiss River?" What did Pelzed *want* to hear? "Woodsmen don't go there, Lord. I've never seen it. It is said to be guarded."

Pause. Then, "Can you bring us poisons?"

"Yes, Lord, in the right season."

"Can we use them against the enemies of Serpent's Walk?"

Whandall had no idea who the enemies of Serpent's Walk might be, but he was afraid to ask. "If they're fresh, Lord."

"What happens if they aren't fresh?"

"After a day they only make you itch. The nettles stop reaching out for anyone who passes."

"Why?"

"I don't know." The man raised his knife. "Lord."

"You're a sneak and a spy."

"Yes, Lord."

"Will you spy for us?"

Whandall hesitated. "Of course he will, Lord," Shastern said.

"Take him out, Shastern. Wait with him."

Shastern led him through a door into a room with no other doors and only a small dark window that let in a little moonlight. He waited until they were closed in before letting go of Whandall's arm.

"This is dangerous, isn't it?" Whandall asked.

Shastern nodded.

"So what's going to happen?"

"They'll let you in. Maybe."

"If they don't?"

Shastern shook his head. "They will. Lord Pelzed doesn't want a blood feud with the Placehold family."

Blood feuds meant blood. "Is he really a Lord—"

"He is here," Shastern said. "And don't forget it."

When they brought him back in, the room was dark except for a few candles near Pelzed's chair. Shastern whispered, "I knew they'd let you in. Now whatever happens, don't cry. It's going to hurt."

They made him kneel in front of Pelzed again. Two men took turns asking him questions and hitting him.

"We are your father and your mother," Pelzed said.

Someone hit him.

"Who is your father?" a voice asked from behind.

"You are—"

Someone hit him harder.

"Serpent's Walk," Whandall guessed.

"Who is your mother?"

"Serpent's Walk."

"Who is your Lord?"

"Pelzed. . . . Argh. Lord Pelzed. Aagh! Serpent's Walk?"

"Who is Lord of Serpent's Walk?"

"Lord Pelzed."

It went on a long time. Usually they didn't hit him if he guessed the right answer, but sometimes they hit him anyway. "To make sure you remember," they said.

Finally that was over. "You can't fight," Pelzed said. "So you won't be a full member. But we'll take care of you. Give him the mark."

They stretched his left hand out and tattooed a small serpent on the web of his thumb. He held his arm rigid against the pain. Then everyone said nice things about him.

After that it was easier. Whandall was safe outside the house as long as he was in territory friendly to Serpent's Walk. Wanshig warned him not to carry a knife until he knew how to fight. It would be taken as a challenge.

He didn't know the rules. But one could keep silent, watch, and learn.

Here he remembered a line of black skeletons of buildings. The charred remains had come down and been carried away. Whandall and others watched from cover, from the basement of a house that hadn't been replaced yet. Kinless were at work raising redwood beams into skeletons of new buildings. Four new stores stood already, sharing common walls.

You knew the kinless by their skin tone, or their rounder ears and pointed noses, but that was chancy; a boy could make mistakes. Better to judge by clothing or by name.

Kinless were not allowed to wear Lordkin's hair styles or vivid colors. On formal occasions the kinless men wore a noose as token of their servitude. They were named for things or for skills, and they spoke their family names, where a Lordkin never would.

There were unspoken rules for gathering. There were times when you could ask a kinless for food or money. A man and woman together might accept that. Others would not. Kinless men working to replace blackened ruins with new buildings did not look with favor on Lordkin men or boys. Lordkin at their gatherings must be wary of the kinless who kept shops or sold from carts. The kinless had no rights, but the Lords had rights to what the kinless made.

The kinless did the work. They made clothing, grew food, made and used tools, transported it all. They made rope for export. They harvested rope fibers from the hemp that grew in vacant lots and anywhere near the sluggish streams that served as storm drains and sewers alike. They built. They saw to it that streets were repaired, that water flowed, that garbage reached the dumps. They took the blame if things went wrong. Only the kinless paid taxes, and taxes were whatever a Lordkin wanted, unless a Lord said otherwise. But you had to learn what you could take. The kinless only had so much to give, Mother's Mother said.

Suddenly it was all so obvious, so embarrassing. Loggers were kinless! *Of course* they wouldn't help a Lordkin child. The loggers thought Kreeg Miller was strange, as the Placehold thought Whandall was strange, each to be found in the other's company.

Whandall had been letting a kinless teach him! He had carried water for them, working like a kinless!

Whandall stopped visiting the forest.

The Serpent's Walk men spent their time in the streets. So did the boys of the Placehold, but their fathers and uncles spent most of their time at home.

Why?

Whandall went to old Resalet. One could ask.

Resalet listened and nodded, then summoned *all* the boys and led them outside. He pointed to the house, the old stone three-story house with its enclosed courtyard. He explained that it had been built by kinless for themselves, two hundred years ago. Lordkin had taken it from them.

It was a roomy dwelling desired by many. The kinless no longer built houses to last centuries. Why should they, when a Lordkin family would claim it? Other Lordkin had claimed this place repeatedly, until it fell to the Placehold family. It would change hands again unless the men kept guard.

The boys found the lecture irritating, and they let Whandall know that afterward.

Mother never had time for him. There was always a new baby, new men to see and bring home, new places to go, never time for the older boys. Men hung out together. They chewed hemp and made plans or went off at night, but they never wanted boys around them, and most of the boys were afraid of the men. With reason.

Whandall saw his city without understanding. The other boys hardly realized there was anything to understand and didn't care to know more. It was safe to ask Mother's Mother, but her answers were strange.

"Everything has changed. When I was a girl the kinless didn't hate us. They were happy to do the work. Gathering was easy. They gave us things."

"Why?"

"We served Yangin-Atep. Tep woke often and protected us."

"But didn't the kinless hate the Burnings?"

"Yes, but it was different then," Mother's Mother said. "It was arranged. A house or building nobody could use, or a bridge ready to fall down. We'd bring things to burn. Kinless, Lordkin, everyone would bring something for Yangin-Atep. *Mathoms,* we called them. The Lords came, too, with their wizards. Now it's all different, and I don't understand it at all."

One could keep silence, watch, and learn.

Barbarians were the odd ones. Their skins were of many shades, their noses of many shapes; even their eye color varied. They sounded odd, when they could talk at all.

Some belonged in the city, wherever they had come from. They traded, taught, doctored, cooked, or sold to kinless and Lordkin alike. They were to be treated as kinless who didn't understand the rules. Their speech could generally be understood. They might travel with guards of their own race or give tribute to Lordkin to protect their shops. A few had the protection of Lords. You could tell that by the symbols displayed outside their shops and homes.

Most barbarians avoided places where violence had fallen. But lookers sought those places out. The violence of the Burning lured them across the sea to Tep's Town.

Boys who gave up the forest had taken to spying on lookers instead. Whandall would do as they did: watch the watchers. But they were far ahead of him at that game, and Whandall had some catching up to do.

Watch, listen. From under a walk, from behind a wall. Lookers took refuge in the parts of the city where kinless lived, or in the harbor areas where the Lords ruled. Lordkin children could sometimes get in those places. Lookers spoke in rapid gibberish that some of the older boys claimed to understand.

At first they looked merely strange. Later Whandall saw how many kinds of lookers there were. You could judge by their skins or their features or their clothing. These pale ones were Torovan, from the east. These others were from the south, from Condigeo. These with noses like an eagle's beak came from farther yet: Atlantean refugees. Each spoke his own tongue, and each mangled the Lordkin speech in a different fashion. And others, from places Whandall had never heard of.

Serpent's Walk watched, and met afterward in the shells of burned buildings. They asked themselves and each other, *What does this one have that would be worth gathering?* But Whandall sometimes wondered, *Does that one come from a more interesting place than here? or more exciting? or better ruled? or seeking a ruler?*

CHAPTER
3

When he was eleven years old, Whandall asked Wanshig, "Where can I find a Lord?"

"You know where Pelzed lives—"

"A real Lord."

"Don't talk like that," Wanshig said, but he grinned. "Do you remember when those people came to the park? And made speeches? Last fall."

"Sure. You gathered some money in the crowd and bought meat for dinner."

"That was a Lord. I forgot his name."

"Which one? There were a lot of people—"

"Guards, mostly. And lookers, and storytellers. The one that stood on the wagon and talked about the new aqueduct they're building."

"Oh."

"The Lords live on the other side of the valley, in the Lordshills mostly. It's a long way. You can't go there."

"Do they have a band?"

"Sort of. They have guards, big Lordsmen. And there's a wall."

"I'd like to see one. Up close."

"Sometimes Lords go to the docks. But you don't want to go there alone," Wanshig said.

"Why not?"

"It's Water Devils territory. The Lords say anyone can go there, and the Devils have to put up with that, but they don't like it. If they catch you alone with no one to come back and tell what happened, they may throw you in the harbor."

"But Water Devils don't go into the Lordshills, do they?"

"I don't know. Never needed to find out."

How do you know what you need to find out until you know it? Whandall wondered, but he didn't say anything. "Is there a safe way to the harbor?"

Wanshig nodded. "Stay on Sanvin Street until you get past those hills." He pointed northwest. "After that there aren't any bands until you get to the harbor. Didn't used to be. Now, who knows?"

The forest had fingers: hilltop ridges covered with touch-me and lordkin's-kiss that ran from the sea back into the great trees with their deadly guards. There were canyons and gaps through the hills, but they were filled with more poisonous plants that grew back faster than anyone could cut them. Only the hills above the harbor were cleared. Lords lived up there. When the winds blew hard so that the day was clear, Whandall could see their big houses. The adults called them palaces.

Whandall pointed toward the Lordshills. "Does anyone gather there during a Burning?"

Wanshig squinted. "Where? On Sanvin Street?"

"No, up there. The palaces."

"That's where the Lords live. You can't gather from Lords!"

"Why not?"

"Yangin-Atep," Wanshig said. "Yangin-Atep protects them. People who go up there to gather just don't come back. Whandall, they're Lords. We're Lordkin. You just don't. There's no Burning up there either. Yangin-Atep takes care of them."

At dawn he snatched half a loaf from the Placehold kitchen and ate it as he ran. The energy boiling in him was half eagerness, half fear. When it faded, he walked. He had a long way to go.

Sanvin Street wound over the low hills that separated Tep's Town from the harbor. At first there were burned-out shells of houses, with some of the lots gone back to thorns and worse. The plants gradually closed in on the old road. When he reached the top of the hills, all was thorns and chaparral and touch-me, just sparse enough to permit passage. It was nearly dark when he reached a crest of a ridge. There were lights ahead, the distance enough that he didn't want to walk farther. He used the dying twilight to find a way into the chaparral.

He spent the night in chaparral, guarded by the malevolent plants he knew how to avoid. It was better than trying to find a safe place among people he didn't know.

The morning sun was bright, but there was a thin haze on the ground. Sanvin Street led down the ridge, then up across another. It took him half an hour to get to the top of the second ridge. When he reached it, he could see a highlight sun glare, the harbor, off ahead and to the left.

He had reached the top. He knew of no band who ruled here, and that was ominous enough. He crouched below the chaparral until he was sure no eyes were about.

He stood on a barren ridge, but the other side of the hill was— different. Sanvin Street led down the hills. Partway down, it divided into two parallel streets with olive trees growing in the grassy center strip, and to each side of the divided street there were houses, wood as well as stone.

He was watching from the chaparral when a wagon came up from the harbor. He had plenty of time to move, but close to the road the chaparral was too sparse to hide him, and farther in were the thorns. He stood in the sparse brush and watched the wagon come up the hill. As it passed him the kinless driver and his companion exchanged glances with Whandall and drove on. They seemed curious rather than angry, as if Whandall were no threat at all.

Couldn't they guess that he might bring fathers or older brothers?

He went back to the road and started down the hill, openly now, past the houses. He guessed this was Lord's Town, where Mother's Mother used to go when she was a girl.

Each set of houses was banded around a small square, and in the center of each square was a small stone cairn above a stone water basin, like Peacegiven Square but smaller. Water trickled down the cairn into the basin, and women, Lordkin and kinless alike, came to dip water into stone and clay jars. Down toward the harbor was a larger square, with a larger pool, and a grove of olive trees. Instead of houses, there were shops around the square. Kinless merchants sat in front of shops full of goods openly displayed, free for the gathering, it seemed. In the olive grove people sat in the shade at tables and talked or did mysterious things with small rock markers on the tables. Shells—and even bits of gold and silver—changed hands.

Were these Lords? They looked like no one he had ever seen. They were better dressed than the kinless of Serpent's Walk, better dressed than most Lordkin, but few had weapons. One armed man sat at a table honing a big Lordkin knife. No one seemed to notice him; then a merchant spoke to him. Whandall didn't hear what was said, but the merchant seemed friendly, and the armed Lordkin grinned. Whandall watched as a girl brought a tray of cups to a table. She looked like a Lordkin.

No one paid him any attention as he walked past. They would glance at him and look away, even if he stared at them. He wasn't dressed like they were, and that began to bother him. Back of the houses, he could sometimes see clothes hanging on lines, but gathering those might be riskier than remaining as he was, and how could he know that he was wearing them right?

He went on to the bottom of the hills, nearer yet to the Lords' domain. Soon there was black, barren land in the distance to his right, with a gleam of water and a stench of magic. It had to be magic; it was no natural smell. Breathing through his mouth seemed to help.

The place drew him like any mystery.

Whandall knew the Black Pit by repute. Scant and scrawny alien scrub grew along the edges of black water a quarter of a mile on a side, and nobody lived there at all. He'd heard tales of shadowy monsters here. All he saw were pools that gleamed like water, darker than any water he'd ever seen.

A palisade fence surrounded the Pit, more a message than a barrier. A graveled wagon road led into it through a gate that Whandall was sure he could open. The fence was regular, flawless, too fine even for kinless work. Kinless working under the eyes of Lords might make such a thing.

Such offensive perfection made it a target. Whandall wondered why Lordkin hadn't torn it down. And why did Lords want people kept away? He saw no monsters, but he sensed a malevolent power here.

The distant harbor drew him more powerfully yet. He saw a ship topped by a forest of masts. That was escape, that was the way to better places, if he could learn of a way past the Water Devils.

Ahead and to the right was a wall taller than any man. Houses two and three stories tall showed above the wall. Palaces! They were larger than he'd dreamed.

The street went past an open gate where two armed men stood guarding a barrier pole. They looked strange. Their clothing was good but drab and they were dressed nearly alike. They wore daggers with polished handles. Helmets hid their ears. Spears with dark shafts and gleaming bronze spearheads hung on brackets near where they stood. Were they armed kinless? But they might be Lordkin.

A wagon came up from the harbor and went to the gate. The horses seemed different, taller and more slender than the ponies he saw in

Tep's Town. When it reached the gate, the guards spoke to the driver, then lifted the barrier to let the wagon in. Whandall couldn't hear what they said to each other.

If the guards were kinless, they wouldn't try to stop a Lordkin. Would they? He couldn't tell what they were. They acted relaxed. One drank from a stone jar and passed it to the other. They watched Whandall without much curiosity.

The gate was near a corner of the wall. Whandall became worried when he saw the guards were looking at him. There was a path that led along the wall and around the corner out of sight of the guards, and he went along that, shuffling as boys do. The guards stopped watching him when he turned away from the gate, and soon he was out of sight around the corner.

The wall was too high to climb. The path wasn't much used, and Whandall had to be careful to avoid the weeds and thorns. He followed the path until it led between the wall and a big tree.

When he climbed into the tree he was glad he hadn't tried to get over the wall. There were sharp things, thorns and broken glass, embedded in its top. One bough of the tree not only grew over the wall but was low enough that it had scraped the top smooth. That must have taken a long time, and no one had bothered to fix it.

Mother's Mother had told him that kinless believed in a place they called Gift of the King, a place across the sea where they never had to work and no Lordkin could gather from them. The other side of the wall looked like that. There were gardens and big houses. Just over the wall was a pool of water. A big stone fish stood above the pool. Water poured from the fish's mouth into the pool and flowed out of the pool into a stream that fed a series of smaller pools. Green plants grew in those pools. There were both vegetable and flower gardens alongside the stream. They were arranged in neat little patterns, square for the vegetable gardens, complex curved shapes along curved paths for the flower beds. The house was nearly a hundred yards from the wall, two stories tall, square and low with thick adobe walls, as large as the Placehold. The Gift of the King, but this was no myth. The Lords lived better than Whandall could have imagined.

It was late afternoon, and the sun was hot. There was no one around. Whandall had brought a dried crabapple to eat, but he didn't have any way to carry water, and he was thirsty. The fountain and stream invited him. He watched while his thirst grew. No one came out of the house.

He wondered what they would do to him if they caught him. He was only a thirsty boy; he hadn't gathered anything yet. The people outside the walls had glanced at him, then glanced away, as if they didn't want to see him. Would the people in here do the same? He didn't know, but his thirst grew greater.

He crawled along the tree branch until he was past the wall, then dropped into the grass. He crouched there waiting, but nothing happened, and he crept to the edge of the fountain.

The water was sweet and cool, and he drank for a long time.

"What's it like outside?"

Whandall jumped up, startled.

"They don't let me go outside. Where do you live?"

The girl was smaller than he was. She'd be eight years old or so, where Whandall was already eleven. She wore a skirt with embroidered borders, and her blouse was a shiny cloth that Whandall had seen only once, when Pelzed's wife had dressed up for a party. No one in Whandall's family owned anything like that, or ever would.

"I was thirsty," Whandall said.

"I can see that. Where do you live?"

She was only a girl. "Out there," he said. He pointed east. "Beyond the hills."

Her eyes widened. She looked at his clothing, at his eyes and ears. "You're Lordkin. Can I see your tattoos?"

Whandall held out his hand to show the serpent on the web of his thumb.

She came closer. "Wash your hands," she said. "Not there; that's where we get drinking water. Down there." She pointed at the basin below the fountain pool. "Don't you have fountains where you live?"

"No. Wells." Whandall bent to wash his hands. "Rivers after it rains."

"Your face too," she said. "And your feet. You're all dusty."

It was true, but Whandall resented being told that. She was only a girl, smaller than he, and there was nothing to be afraid of, but she might call someone. He would have to run. There wasn't any way out of here. The branch was too high to reach without a rope. The water felt cool on his face and wonderful on his feet.

"You don't need to be afraid of me," she said. "Now let me see your tattoo."

He held out his hand. She turned it in both her hands and pulled his fingers apart to bare his serpent tattoo to the sun.

Then she looked closely at his eyes. "My stepfather says that wild Lordkin have tattoos on their faces," she said.

"My brothers do," Whandall said. "But they carry knives and can fight. I haven't learned yet. I don't know what you mean by 'wild.' We're not wild."

She shrugged. "I don't really know what he means either. My name is Shanda. My stepfather is Lord Samorty."

Whandall thought for a moment, then said, "My name is Whandall. What does a stepfather do?"

"My father's dead. Lord Samorty married my mother."

She'd spoken of her father to a stranger, without hesitation, without embarrassment. Whandall tasted words on his tongue: *My father is dead; we have many stepfathers.* But he didn't speak them.

"Do you want something to eat?"

Whandall nodded.

"Come on." She led him toward the house. "Don't talk much," she said. "If anyone asks you where you live, point west, and say 'Over there, sir.' But no one will. Just don't show that tattoo. Oh, wait." She looked at him again. "You look like someone threw clothes at you in the dark."

Huh?

"Miss Batty would say that," she said, leading him south around the house. "Here." Clothes were hanging on long lines above a vegetable patch. The lines were thin woven hemp, not tarred. "Here, take this, and this—"

"Shanda, who wears this stuff?"

"The chief gardener's boy. He's my friend, he won't mind. Put your stuff in that vat—"

"Is anyone going to see me who knows who we gathered it from?"

She considered. "Not inside. Maybe Miss Batty, but she never goes to the kitchen. Wouldn't eat with the staff if she was starving."

A band of men carrying shovels came around the house. One waved to Shanda. They began digging around the vegetables.

The gardeners were kinless, but they were better dressed than Lordkin. They had water bottles, and one had a box with bread and meat. A lot of meat, more than Whandall got for lunch except on Mother's Day, and often not then. If kinless lived this well, how did Lordkin live here?

A Lordkin should have guile. Watch and learn . . .

Shanda led him into the back of the house.

CHAPTER
4

The house was cool. Shanda led him through corridors to a room
that smelled of cooking. A fat woman with ears like a Lordkin's
stood at a counter stirring a kettle. The kettle frothed with
boiling liquid. Whandall stared. The smells went straight to his hunger.

The counter she stood over was a big clay box. The top was an iron
grill, and flames licked up through it, under a copper pot.

A fire, *indoors,* that didn't go out. Squinting, he approached the
yellow-white glare and lifted his hands to it. *Hot.* Yes, fire.

Shanda gave him the funniest look.

The fat woman looked at them with an expression that might have
been menacing but wasn't. "Miss Shanda, I got no time just now. Your
daddy is having visitors. There's a wizard coming to dinner, and we
have to get ready."

A wizard! But Shanda didn't act surprised or excited. She said, "Serana, this is Whandall, and he's hungry."

The fat woman smiled. "Sure he's hungry. He's a boy, isn't he? A
boy's nothing but an appetite and trouble," she said, but she was still
smiling. "Sit over there. I'll get you something in a minute. Where do
you live?"

Whandall pointed vaguely west. "Over there . . . ma'am."

Serana nodded to herself and went back to the stove, but then she
brought out a bowl and a spoon. "Have some of my pudding," she
said. "Bet your cook can't make pudding like that."

Whandall tasted the pudding. It was smooth and creamy. "No, ma'am," Whandall said.

Serana beamed. "Miss Shanda, this is a nice boy," she said. "Now scoot when you get done. I've got my work to do."

After he finished the pudding, he followed Shanda down another corridor. The house was built around an interior courtyard, and they went upstairs to a long outside balcony over the atrium. There was a small fountain in the center of the courtyard.

There were half a dozen doors along the balcony. Shanda led him to one of them. "This is my room." She looked up at the sun. "It won't be long until dark. Can you get home before night?"

"I don't think so," Whandall said.

"Where will you stay?"

"I can stay out in the chaparral."

"In the thorns?" She sounded impressed. "You know how to go into those?"

"Yes." He grinned slightly. "But I don't know how to get out of here. Will the guards stop me?"

"Why should they?" she asked. "But if you don't come home tonight, won't someone worry about you?"

"Who?"

"Your nurse . . . oh. Well, come on in."

The room was neat. There was a closet with a door, and there were more clothes hung up in it than any of Whandall's sisters had. There was a chest against one wall, and the bed had a wool blanket on it. Another blanket with pictures woven into it hung above the bed. There was a window that faced out on the balcony, and another on the opposite wall. That looked out on a smaller interior courtyard crisscrossed with clotheslines and drying clothes, more rope than Whandall had ever seen in one place. He eyed the clothesline with satisfaction. It looked strong, and there was so much they might not miss one piece. It would get him up to the tree branch. If he could take it home, it would make Resalet happy. They always needed rope at the Placehold. But he didn't know the rules here.

"Could you really sleep in the thorns?" she asked. "How?"

"Without leathers you can't go far into the chaparral," Whandall said. "There's a lot worse than thorn. You have to know what plants are safe. Most aren't."

"What are leathers? Where do you get them?"

"You need a leather mask and leggings, at least. Some kinless have them, and the foresters use sleeves and vests. I don't know where my uncles got them. They must have gathered them."

"But you don't have any with you. There's nobody in the room next to this. You can sleep there tonight."

They ate in the kitchen at a small table in the corner. Serana put food in front of them, then went back to her stove. Other servants came in and Serana gave them instructions on what to do. Everyone seemed to be in a hurry, but there was no shouting, and no one was frantic.

There were more *kinds* of food than Whandall had ever seen for one meal. Serana arranged trays of food, eyed them critically, sometimes changed the arrangements. When she was satisfied, the servants came and took the trays out to another room where the adults ate. It was like . . . the gardens here, and the neat little fence around the Black Pit . . . it was *orderly*. Serana was making *patterns* with her cooking.

Whandall couldn't take his eyes off the stove.

Once during dinner a tall woman with serious eyes and dark clothing looked into the kitchen. She nodded in satisfaction when she saw Shanda. "Did you study your lessons?" she demanded.

"Yes, ma'am," Shanda said.

She fixed Whandall with a critical eye. "Neighbor boy?" she asked.

"From down the road," Shanda said quickly.

"You behave yourself," the woman said. She turned to the cook. "Did she get a good dinner?"

"I always make a good dinner for Miss Shanda, even when I've got guests to cook for," Serana said huffily. "Don't you worry about that."

"All right. Good night."

After she left, Shanda giggled. "Miss Batty's not happy," she said. "She wants to eat with the family, but they didn't invite her tonight."

"That's as it may be," Serana said. "Miss Bertrana's all right. Not like that other nurse you had. You be nice to her."

Miss Batty was kinless. Whandall was certain of it. He wasn't quite as certain that Serana was Lordkin. And neither seemed to care much.

A servant came carrying a tray of dirty dishes. Some were piled high with uneaten food.

After dinner they went back to the balcony. The adults came out to the atrium to finish their own dinner. Whandall and Shanda lay on the balcony outside her room and listened to them.

The courtyard was lit by a central fire and by candles in vellum cylinders. There were four men and three women in the courtyard. Lazy wisps of steam curled up from the cups they were holding. One of the men said, "I thought that wizard was coming to dinner."

"He was invited, Qirinty. I don't know what happened to him."

"Stood you up, did he, Samorty?"

Samorty had a deep and resonant voice, and his chuckle was loud. "Maybe. I'd be surprised, but maybe."

When Placehold men talked in the evenings, there were usually fights. These men smiled, and if anyone was angry, it was well hidden. Whandall came to believe that he was watching a dance. They were dancing with the rhythm of speech and gestures.

It was a thing he could learn. A Lordkin should have guile.

Qirinty's voice was feeble; Whandall had to listen hard. "We need a wizard. The reservoir's getting low again. If it doesn't rain pretty soon we could be in trouble, Samorty."

Samorty nodded sagely. "What do you propose we do?"

"It's more your problem than mine, Samorty," the other man said. He picked up two cups, interchanged them, tossed them lightly in the air. The cups were chasing each other in a loop, and now he'd added a third cup.

"Lord Qirinty has such wonderful hands!" Shanda said.

It enchanted Whandall that Shanda already knew how to lurk. He asked, "Are those Lords?"

Shanda giggled. "Yes. The big man there at the end is Lord Samorty. He's my stepfather."

"Is that your mother with him?"

"Rawanda's not my mother! Stepmother," Shanda said. "My mother's dead too. She died when Rabblie was born."

"Rabblie?"

"My little brother. There. With her. He's five. She doesn't like him any more than she likes me, but he gets to eat with them because he's the heir. If she ever has a boy, he's dead meat, but I don't think she can have children. She had one, my sister, and that took a week. It was almost two years ago—"

Whandall tapped her arm to shut her up, because Lord Samorty was talking: ". . . Wizard. Can he do it again?"

"Would you want him to?" one of the others asked. "The iceberg damn near wiped out the city!"

The women shouted with laughter. The man with the clever hands said, "It did not, Chanthor! It crossed *your* farm."

Samorty chuckled. "Well, and mine too, and left nothing but a plowed line three hundred paces wide and longer than any man has traveled. That cost me, I admit, but it didn't cross much of the city, and it sure solved the water problem."

Chanthor snorted.

Qirinty snatched his cup and added it to the dance.

Samorty said, "A mountain of ice from the farthest end of the Earth. Don't you sometimes wish you could do that?"

"That, or *any* real magic. But he said he could do it only once," Lord Qirinty said.

"He said that after we paid him. Did you believe him? I'd say he wants a better price."

Qirinty set the cups down without spilling a drop. "I don't know if I believed him or not."

One of the servants came in. "Morth of Atlantis," he announced.

Morth? Whandall knew that name . . .

He stood tall and straight, but Morth was older than any of the Lords, fragile and perhaps blind. His face was all wrinkles; his hair was long and straight and thick but pure white. He tottered very carefully into the circle of firelight. "My Lords," he said formally. "You will have to forgive me. It has been twenty years since I was last here."

"I would think Lordshills is easy enough to find," Samorty said. "Even if you had never been here before."

"Yes, yes, of course," Morth said. "To find, yes. To get to, perhaps not so easy for one in my profession. I came by the back roads. The ponies I hired could not climb your hill, and as I walked up, this change came on me. But you must know all this."

"Perhaps we know less than you think. A dozen years ago a Condigeano wizard offered us a spell that would let cook fires burn indoors," Samorty said. "Cheap too. He didn't have to cast it himself. Sent an apprentice up to do it. It worked, but since then the only horses that can get up the hill are our big ones. The Lordkin ponies can't make it. We don't know why."

Morth nodded. He was amused without making a point of it. "But surely this—spell—has not lasted a dozen years?"

"No, he sends an apprentice to renew it. He's done that twice since. We've discussed having him cast it for other areas, but we decided not to."

"Oh, good," Morth said. "Very wise. May I be seated?"

"Yes, yes, of course. Dinner's finished, but would you like tea and dessert?" Samorty's wife said.

"Thank you, yes, my lady."

Rawanda waved to a servant as Morth sat with an effort.

The fourth Lord was older than the rest. The others had come out with women, but he reclined alone on his couch. The servants treated him with as much respect as they treated Samorty. He had been quiet, but now he spoke. "Tell us, Sage, why is it wise not to cast this spell in the other parts of the city? Why not in Tep's Town?"

"Side effects," Qirinty said. "The Lordkin need their ponies."

"Yes, that and the fires, Lord Jerreff," Morth said. His voice had changed slightly. There was less quaver.

"Could you cast such a spell if we asked you to?"

Morth cut off a laugh. "No, Lord. No wizard could do that. Only apprentices cast *that* spell, and I'll wager that it's never the same apprentice twice, either."

"You'd win that wager," Samorty said. "Is this spell dangerous?"

"Confined to a small area, no," Morth said. "Cast throughout Tep's Town? I am certain you would regret it."

"Fires," Lord Jerreff said. "There would be fires inside houses, anytime, not just during a Burning. That's what our Condigeano wizard told us. He wouldn't tell us what the spell was. Just that it would keep Yangin-Atep at a distance. Sage, I don't suppose you will tell us either?"

Morth solemnly shook his head. "No, Lord, I cannot."

"But you do know what the spell is."

"Yes, Lord, I know," Morth said. "And frankly I am concerned that a hedge wizard from Condigeo would know about—about that spell. I am also surprised that you would employ powerful magic you do not understand."

"Oh, we know what it does," Qirinty said. "It uses up the power in magic, the manna. Gods can't live where there's no manna."

"I didn't know that," Lord Chanthor said. "Did you know, Samorty?"

Lord Samorty shook his head. "All I bargained for was a way to let the cooks work inside. Does that mean the fountains aren't magic?"

"Just good plumbing, Samorty," Lord Qirinty said. "But there is magic in running water—I suppose that's why our Sage looks better now. He found some manna in the fountains."

"Astute, Lord. But very little, I fear." He chuckled mirthlessly. "I do not believe you need pay to renew the spell this year."

"Is that why the wizards can't bring rain?" Samorty demanded. "No manna?"

"Yes," Morth said. "The manna is dying all over the world, but especially here in Tep's Town. The void you have created here isn't helping."

"Where can we find more manna?" Chanthor asked.

"The water comes from the mountains," Qirinty said. "Look there, if we can find the way."

"There are maps," Chanthor said. "I recall my father telling me of an expedition to the mountains. They brought back manna—"

"Gold. Wild manna. Unpredictable," Samorty said. "Some of the effects were damned odd."

"Yes, Samorty, and anyway, they got all they could find," Chanthor said. "We wouldn't do better. But there was water. Can we get water from the mountains?"

"*We* can't. Maybe nobody can."

"We did once."

"Yes, Jerreff, and long ago the kinless were warriors," Chanthor said.

"Do you believe that?" Samorty asked.

"Oh, it's true," Jerreff said.

"My Lords, we are neglecting our guest," Samorty said. He turned to Morth. The wizard was quietly sipping tea. He looked less ill than when he had come to the table.

"Sage, if we don't have water, there'll be a Burning, sure as anything. How can we stop it?" Qirinty asked. "Can you bring more water?"

Morth shook his head. He spoke solemnly. "No, my Lords. There is not enough manna to bring rain. As for the gold in the mountains, you don't want it."

"Isn't it magic?"

"Wild magic. I've heard some very funny stories about gold's effect on men and magicians, but in any case, I would not survive the rigors of the trip."

"There are other mountains," Jerreff said. "The Barbar Mountains remain. Too far to go by land, but we could take ship."

Morth smiled thinly. "I fear I must decline that as well," he said.

"The ice. Can you bring more ice?" Qirinty demanded. "We will pay well. Very well, won't we, Samorty?"

"We would pay to have the reservoirs filled again, yes," Samorty said. "You would not find us ungenerous."

"Alas, as I told you then, I could do that only once. Loan me a charioteer and I could fill your reservoirs, but I do not believe you would care for salt water."

"Salt water?" Samorty demanded. "What would we want with reservoirs full of salt water?"

"I can't imagine," Morth said. "But it is the only kind I control just at the moment." His smile was thin and there was a tiny edge to his voice. "It would be difficult but not impossible to drown the city and even parts of the Lordshills, but the water would be sea water."

"Are you threatening to do that?" Samorty demanded.

"Oh no, Lord. I have worked for many years to prevent that,"

Morth said. Mother's Mother's humor sometimes matched this old man's: they laughed at things nobody else understood. "But do not be deceived, it could happen. For example, if you were to use in Tep's Town the spell that that idiot Condigeano used here, you might well find the sea walking across the city. May I have some more tea?"

"Certainly, but it is a long way back, Sage, and I perceive you are not comfortable here," Samorty said. "With your permission I will arrange transportation with our horses, and an escort of guards."

"Your generosity is appreciated," Morth said.

Morth. "He's too old," Whandall murmured.

The girl asked, "Too old for what?"

"He's not who I thought." *Too old to be the Morth who killed my father and put my uncle to flight.* But wasn't that also Morth of drowned Atlantis? Mother's Mother had told another tale. "The wizard who wouldn't bless a ship?"

"Yes, that's him," Shanda said.

Samorty clapped his hands for a servant. "Have the cooks prepare a traveler's meal for the wizard. We will need a team and wagon from the stables, and two guardsmen to accompany Morth of Atlantis to the city."

"At once, Lord," the servant said.

"He will see to your needs, Sage," Samorty said. "It has been our honor."

"My thanks, Lords." Morth followed the servant out. He leaned heavily on his staff as he walked. They watched in silence until he was gone.

This powerless wizard couldn't be the Morth who had killed Pothefit. Was it a common name in Atlantis?

"Well, he wasn't any use," Chanthor said.

"Perhaps. I want to think about what he *didn't* say," Jerreff said.

"What I learned is that he can't get us any water. So what do we do now?" Samorty demanded.

"The usual. Give out more. Increase the Mother's Day presents," Chanthor said.

Whandall's ears twitched. More Mother's Day presents was good news for the Placehold, for Serpent's Walk, for everyone! But Lord Qirinty said, "The warehouses are getting empty. We need rain!"

"There's a ship due with some sea dragon bones," Chanthor said. "Magic to make rain, if Morth is as good as he says he is."

"It won't happen," Jerreff said, "and you know it. Do you remember the last time you bought dragon bones? Ebony box, lined with velvet, wrapped in silk, and nothing but rocks inside."

"Well, yes, but that merchant is crab dung now," Chanthor said, "and I keep my hemp gum in that box. This time the promise comes from a more reputable ship captain."

"He'll have a good excuse for not having any dragon bones in stock," Jerreff said. "Chanthor, Morth wasn't revealing secrets; he was speaking common magicians' gossip. Magic fades everywhere, but *here*. . . . Why would anyone send objects of power *here*? What can we pay compared to the Incas? Or Torov? Even Condigeo could pay more than we can!"

"All true," Qirinty said. "Which brings us to the question, why does Morth of Atlantis stay here? We all saw him move a mountain of ice!"

"Forget Morth. He has no power," Samorty said.

"It is a puzzle worth contemplation, even so," Jerreff said. "Here he is weak. He would be more powerful in a land better blessed with magic. An Atlantis wizard could command respect anywhere."

"They're rare, all right," Lady Rawanda said. "And there won't be any more."

A ripple of response ran around the table. Horror brushed its hand along Whandall's hair. Tellers even in Tep's Town spoke of the sinking of Atlantis.

Chanthor said, "Ship captains are still telling stories about the waves. Wiped out whole cities. Do you suppose that's what Morth is talking about? Salt water. Can he raise big waves? That might be useful, if anyone attacked us from the sea."

"Who'd attack us?" Qirinty asked.

"We've been raided a few times," Chanthor said. "The last one was interesting, wasn't it, Samorty?"

Lord Samorty nodded. "Nine dead, though."

"Nine dead, we sold six more to Condigeo, and we got a ship out of it," Chanthor said.

"Oh, what happened?" Rawanda asked.

"Ship's captain ran out of luck," Chanthor said. "Lost his cargo; talked the crew into raiding in our harbor for their pay. Water Devils saw them coming. Happened to be my watch. I took Waterman and his ready squad down. All over in an hour. As Samorty said, nine dead, four of them Water Devils. No Lordsmen hurt, and we made a pretty good profit selling the survivors even after we paid off the Water Devils."

"What about the captain?" Jerreff asked.

"He owes us," Samorty said. "I let him recruit crew from unemployed kinless. Seems to be working well. The kinless bring money

back for their relatives to spend here, and we have a merchant ship—
not that I've thought of any use for it. It can't bring us rain."

"We're due for rain, though," Chanthor said.

"If Yangin-Atep doesn't chase it away," Qirinty's wife said.

"There's no predicting that," Qirinty said. "But, you know, I think
he's less powerful when it rains. Fire god, after all: why not?"

Yangin-Atep. The Lords knew of Yangin-Atep. And they had fires
indoors. Yangin-Atep never permitted fires indoors. And they'd
hosted Morth of Atlantis, who had killed Pothefit, but he seemed too
frail to defend himself at all.

They talked so fast, and it was all hard to remember, but that was
part of a Lordkin's training. Whandall listened.

"We need a small Burning," Jerreff said. "If we stop the Burnings
altogether, the lookers won't come here anymore, and we'll all die of
boredom. A little Burning, just enough to get it out of their system."

"You're a cynic, Jerreff," Samorty said.

"No, just practical."

"If we don't get some rain soon, there'll be more kinless wanting to
move out of the city and into our town," Chanthor said sourly.

"Can't blame them. But we have no place to put them," Qirinty
said. "No jobs, either. I've got more servants and gardeners than I
need, and without water there won't be enough crops to feed the
people we have, Samorty."

"Tell me the last time you didn't see a real problem coming," Rawanda said.

Qirinty shrugged and produced a dagger from thin air. "Someone
has to worry about the future."

"And you do it well. Just as Jerreff worries about the past. I'm
grateful to you both." Samorty stood. "Now, I'm afraid you'll have to
excuse me. I'm on watch tonight." He raised his voice. "Antanio, bring
my armor, please."

"Yes, Lord," someone called from the house. A moment later two
men came out struggling under a load. They dressed Samorty in a
bronze back-and-breastplate. They hung a sword longer than two
Lordkin knives on a strap over one shoulder and handed him a helmet.

"Is the watch ready?" Samorty asked.

"Yes, Lord; they're waiting at the gate."

"Armor all polished?"

"Yes, Lord."

"Fine." To his guests, he said, "Enjoy yourselves. If there's anything you need, just ask. Rawanda, I'll be late tonight. I have a double watch."

"Oh, I'm sorry to hear that," the lady said.

"She's not sorry," Shanda whispered. "She doesn't even like him."

"Do you?" Whandall asked.

"Samorty's not so bad," Shanda said. "He was very nice to my mother after my father was killed in the Burning."

There was so much to learn! The Lords who controlled Mother's Day knew supplies were running out. They needed water. Whandall had never thought about water before. There were the wells, and sometimes rivers, and the fountain at Peacegiven Square, and sometimes those were nearly dry. Water was important, but Whandall didn't know anyone who could control water.

But this wizard had brought water once, and he was welcome here now. Because he was a wizard, or because he brought water? And how did you become a Lord in the first place?

"Was your father a Lord, Shanda?"

"Yes. Lord Horthomew. He was a politician and an officer of the watch, like Samorty."

"How was he killed?"

"I don't know," she said.

CHAPTER
5

When it was light, he waited outside Shanda's door. It seemed like a long time until she came out, but the sun was still very low in the east. He fidgeted, and finally said, "I have to piss, and I don't know where, and—"

She giggled. "I told you—the room is at the far end of the hall under the stairs. Didn't I tell you?"

He didn't remember. Certainly he hadn't understood. He thanked her and ran toward the stairs.

"Lock the door when you're inside," she whisper-called.

The room below the stairs had windows too high up to look out, and a door with a latch. Inside a stream washed into a basin at his chest level, then spilled over into a trough on the floor. It was all clean, and nothing smelled. When he came out, there was a man waiting outside the door. He had the round ears of a kinless, and he looked like the man who had brought Samorty's armor. He didn't say anything to Whandall as he went inside.

They ate in the kitchen. Serana fussed over them and didn't seem surprised to find Whandall was still there.

"We're going to play in the big park," Shanda told Serana. "Will you tell Miss Batty for me?"

Serana made disapproving sounds. "I'll tell Miss Bertrana you called her that." She didn't sound like she meant it. "You'll need a lunch. I'll fix up something. You be back by suppertime."

They went to the courtyard where the clothes were drying, and

Whandall selected a length of rope. He went to the tree branch and threw the rope over it and tied knots in the rope. With the rope there, he felt safer, because he thought that once he was over the wall no one could catch him in the chaparral. Not without magic.

The Lords did magic. Everyone said so. Lord Qirinty made cups dance and pulled a dagger from thin air, but it was Lord Qirinty who had wished they could do real magic. But the *stove* was magic. It all made Whandall's head hurt. Learning things was not the same as understanding them . . .

He started to climb the rope. When he got on the branch, he saw Shanda was climbing up. She wasn't good at climbing.

"Help me up," she said.

He reached down and took her hand and pulled her up to the branch. Then he looked around. One of the men with shovels had seen them climb up, but he only went back to work.

"Can I get back in this way?" she asked.

"You're not going out."

"Yes, I am."

"Shanda, the chaparral is dangerous. You'll get hurt and your stepfather will kill me."

"I won't get hurt if you show me what to do."

"No." He crawled along the tree limb until he was over the wall. She came right behind him. "No," he said again, but he knew it was no use. "Go back and pull the rope to the outside of the wall."

Just near the wall the plants seemed weak and almost lifeless, but farther away they grew thicker. In a mile they'd be luxurious. Two miles farther were the first of the redwoods. "Those are wonderful," he told her. "Wait till you see them close."

But she wasn't avoiding the plants. He stopped her. He showed her lord's-kiss and nettles and thorn bushes, and three kinds of touch-me. "Three leaves," he said. "Three leaves and white berries, and it doesn't just sit there. Watch." He saw a stick on the ground and examined it carefully before he picked it up. Then he rubbed his hands on one end and held it by the other end, moving it closer and closer to a large vine. At a hand's distance, the vine moved just enough to brush the stick.

Whandall showed her an oily smear on the stick. "You wouldn't want to touch that."

"Would it kill you?"

"No, it just makes you swell up in bumps. The vine can kill you. Things it touches only hurt you."

She still wanted to move too fast. He showed her some of the scars the plants had left on him when he was with the foresters. He made her follow just in his footsteps, and whenever she wanted to look at something, he stopped.

There wasn't the ghost of a chance they would reach the redwoods today.

At noon they stopped and ate lunch, then started back. Whandall took his time, pointing out plants even if she'd seen them before. *He'd* forgotten often enough, and Kreeg had had to remind him . . .

She held a branch at the broken end. Glossy red-and-green leaves grew at the tip. "What would happen if I rub that stick on my stepmother's chair?"

"Not the stick, the leaves. Shanda, really?"

She nodded, grinning.

"Well, she won't die. She'll itch and scratch."

"It's magic?" Shanda asked. "If it's magic it won't work at all inside the walls. That's what my stepfather says."

That would explain the cook fires, Whandall thought. But not Qirinty's dancing cups.

"I'm going to try it," she said.

He stood under the rope as she climbed it, in case she fell. She waved from the top and was gone.

It had been a glorious day.

He was out of the chaparral before the light of sunset died, but the night was turning misty. When Whandall reached the hilltops, he could see fog curling in from where the harbor had been. He watched it for a time, humped above the land. Then he heard shouts. Had someone seen him? Water Devils, perhaps someone worse. He couldn't see anyone, but he ran into the fog, running as hard as he could until he was exhausted.

Fog was all around him as he caught the stench of the Black Pit. The Pit itself was not to be seen. What he saw was dark shadows racing toward him.

He ran back the way he had come, but he was too tired to run far. When his breath ran out he trailed to a stop.

He hadn't heard a sound.

He'd seen . . . what had he seen? Dogs or wolves, but *huge*. But nothing chased him now. He had to get past the Pit to get home, and someone had chased him up the hill. A band was more dangerous than shadows.

The shadows came again as he crested the hill. This time he watched. Bent to pick up a sharp-edged rock in each fist, and watched again. He wished with all his heart that he already had his Lordkin knife. He had outrun them before and he could again . . . but they were only shadows. Wolf-shaped shadows, and something much larger, racing silently toward him.

They were less real as they came near. Whandall yelled and swung his rocks to smash skulls, and then he was among them, in them, and breathless with wonder. They were pockets in the fog: half a dozen wolf shapes all merged now into one thrashing bubble of clear air. The larger shape was a cat as big as Placehold's communal bedroom, armed with a pair of fangs very like Lordkin knives. Then that too was part of the bubble, thrashing as it fought the wolves, and Whandall could watch the shadow shapes of huge birds wheeling above the misty slaughter.

They'll never believe me. But what a day!

CHAPTER
6

He had carried his own clothes in a bundle. Now he put them on over his new ones, so that he could get back to Placehold safely. It took all day. After noon, he ate the roll that Serana had given him.

The waning moon was high when he got back home. Hungry, he checked out the tables and cookpot for leftovers. That got him nothing but sticky feet. He crept into the sleeping room and fell asleep at once.

In the morning his toes remembered the clean blond wood that floored Lord Samorty's kitchen as they squished across Placehold's sticky flagstones. In the roar of Placehold's shouts and laughter and curses he remembered the busy quiet around Serana.

He tore a piece of bread off what Wanshig had gathered. Wanshig jumped, then laughed. "Where did you gather the new clothes?"

His sisters and cousins all looked at him. "Pretty," Rutinda said. "Are there more?"

A Lordkin should have guile, even with his own kin. Whandall wanted to think about what he had seen before he talked about it. There was no way to explain that gathering was not a way of life to the Lords and those who worked with them.

So . . . "Clothesline at a house off of Sanvin Street," Whandall said. "Kinless house, nobody looking, but there wasn't anything else worth gathering."

"Too bad," Wanshig said. "Ready for knife lessons?"

"Sure."

They practiced with sticks. Whandall was still clumsy. He'd have been killed a dozen times if they'd used real knives.

"Next year." The uncles who'd been watching the lessons were sure about it. "Next year."

The Lordsmen fought with spears and swords, not with the big Lordkin knives. Whandall thought about the Lordshills, where even the gardeners lived as well as Pelzed and Resalet did. The Lordsmen would live even better than gardeners. Fighters always did. His uncles would never be able to teach him to fight the way Lordsmen did. But someone might. He knew he had to go back.

He washed his new clothes, but he could think of no place to dry them where they would not be stolen. He carried them as a damp bundle when he took to the roads four days later. They smelled of damp.

His path ran through Flower Market. He kept to shadow when he could, and the windowless sides of buildings, and was still surprised to get through untouched.

Beyond Flower Market nobody lived, or so he'd been told. He saw occasional dwellings but was able to avoid them. When he reached the ridge it was nearly dark. He thought of staying in the chaparral, then laughed. He knew a better place.

The Black Pit was stench and mist and darkness, and a misty blur of a full moon overhead. The moon lit shadows that came bounding to greet him. Wolves as big as Whandall himself, all in a leaping pack. Birds big enough to pluck him from the ground. Two cats bigger than Whandall's imagination. Bubbles in the fog, they merged in a frantic seething bubble, and Whandall laughed and tried to play with them, but he touched nothing but fog.

Rumor spoke that the Black Pit had swallowed people. He shied from going too deep into it. He didn't want any more of that alien stench, either. He spread some marsh grass over a flat rock and lay down on that. With two layers of clothes around him, he wasn't even particularly cold.

Half asleep, he watched another shadow edging toward him several feet above the black swamp. It was rounded and almost featureless, and the ghosts already around him made shadows to interfere with what approached. It was even bigger than the cats. Sleepily he watched it come and tried to guess its shape, then fell asleep still wondering.

The gardener's boy's clothes were still damp when he put them on at dawn. His own Serpent's Walk garments were underneath. He wasn't cold, just sodden. He walked his clothes dry before he reached the broad wagon path that must be Sanvin Street.

When he got to the barren lands, a wagon came up behind him. The kinless driver looked at Whandall and stopped. "Need a ride?"

"Yes, thank you." He hesitated only a moment. "Sir."

"Climb on. I'm going to the harbor. Where are you headed?"

"To see . . . friends. At Lord Samorty's house."

"Inside, eh? Well, I'll let you off at the fork. Hup. Gettap." The two ponies drew the cart at a pace faster than Whandall would walk. The kinless driver whistled some nameless tune. He was a young man, not much over twenty.

The cart was filled with baskets with the lids tied on them. "What is that?" Whandall asked.

The driver eyed Whandall carefully. "Who did you say your friend was?"

"Shanda."

"Samorty's daughter?"

"Stepdaughter," Whandall said. "Sir."

"Right. Your father work for Samorty?"

"Yes, sir."

"Explains the shirt," the driver said.

Whandall widened his eyes and looked up at him.

The driver grinned. "If you was to look in one of those baskets you'd see cloth just like what you're wearing. My cousin Hallati has a loom in his basement. Weaves that cloth, he and his wives and daughters. We sold a stack of it to Samorty last month."

Hallati. Whandall had never heard the name, but he would remember it. How many other kinless were hiding valuables?

"Hope we can move Hallati out soon. I don't like this drought much. Gets dry and those Lordkin jackals get ugly. Almost got my cousin's place last time. Almost," the cart driver said, and pulled the animals to a stop. This was the road to the Lordshills. Whandall got out and waved a good-bye.

There were different guards when he got to the gate. They didn't pay much attention to Whandall as he came up the road.

"Don't remember you," one of the guards said. "Where do you live, boy?"

"Lord Samorty's house—"

"Oh. Gardening crew?"

"Yes, sir."

The guard nodded. They didn't bother to raise the barrier, but it was easy to walk around it, and the guards were already talking about the weather by the time Whandall was inside.

There were big houses and wide streets. Palm trees grew at regular intervals, in patterns. The houses were grand. Something more, something weird. Thirty houses shouldn't be quite so similar, though no two were identical; but neither should they remind a boy of a stand of redwoods or a range of hills.

Like a redwood, like a granite hill, each house looked like it had been in place forever. Like . . . Whandall stepped back and looked around him, because he could feel how the shock changed his face. Anyone who saw him would know he was a stranger, staring as if he'd *never* seen a long street lined on both sides with houses, *none* of which had ever been burned and replaced. The flower beds—they were shaped and arranged to fit around the houses! Not one structure showed any sign of haste, of *Get a roof on that before the rain starts!* Or *Use the beams from the Tanner house—they don't quite fit, but the Tanners won't need them anymore.* Or *Just do something to shelter us—don't bother me; can't you see I'm grieving?*

It made him uneasy.

He didn't know what Lord Samorty's house would look like from the front, but it had to be near the wall. He worked his way eastward until he was sure there was only the one layer of houses between him and the wall, then north until he could see the big tree. After that it was no problem finding his way around the back of the house to the fountain. He washed his hands and face and feet without waiting to be told to.

"I didn't really think you would come back," Shanda said.

"I said I would . . ."

"A Lordkin's promise." There was not much warmth in her smile, but then it brightened. "You promised to show me the redwoods."

He thought about that.

"I have leathers. For both of us." She showed him a box hidden under the bed in her room. "I got them from the gardeners. They don't use them anymore."

Whandall examined the gear.

"It's good, isn't it?" Shanda demanded.

"It's good enough," he admitted. "But we'd be out all night."

"That's all right; Miss Batty will think I'm visiting," Shanda said.

"I'll tell her I'm staying with Lord Flascatti's daughter. Miss Batty will never check."

"But—"

"And my stepmother wouldn't care if I never came back. We'll take lunch and dinner and—"

Whandall looked up at the sun, low in the west. "It's way too late—"

"Not today, silly. In the morning. Or next day. You don't have to get back today, do you?"

He shook his head. If he never came back, his mother would worry about him a little, but she wouldn't do anything, and no one else would care much. Not unless they thought he'd been killed by kinless.

"Did you try that stick?"

Shanda grinned. "That same night. On Rawanda's chair! Yes! It gave her a little red rash, and it itched her for two days. I think it still does." Her face fell a bit. "Samorty must have got some on his arm, because he got a rash too. I guess he knew what made it, because he yelled at the gardeners about it, and the gardeners yelled back, and they all went out to look for a poison plant, but they didn't find any. I didn't want to hurt Samorty."

Good, Whandall thought. And better that she hadn't been caught, and no one knew where she had been. Or who she had been with . . .

A little red rash. Whandall had given leaves of that same plant to Lord Pelzed, and they'd used them on Bull Pizzle boys. No one died, but a dozen of them were useless for a week, and Pelzed and the Bull Pizzle Lord had made a treaty not to do that again. Pelzed had been pleased. But here it was just a little red rash. Plants lost power here.

"Let's get something to eat," Shanda was saying. "Serana doesn't think I eat enough. She'll be glad to see you."

The kitchen was warm and dry and smelled of foods Whandall could only guess at. Serana filled his bowl with soup and heaped bread on the table, then apologized for not having anything for him. "Will you be staying for dinner?"

"If that's all right," Whandall said. "Ma'am. This sure is good."

Serana smiled happily.

They watched the gardeners, but they avoided everyone else. Shanda showed him the carp pools, with bright colored fish. A pair of servants got too curious, and Whandall was frantically trying to find answers when Shanda laughed and ran away with Whandall following. She led him to another part of the yard.

There was a small, queer house, too small for Shanda and way too small for Whandall. There were rooms no bigger than a big man, and

tiny passages they could crawl through, and open walls. The curious
servants had followed. Whandall had to wriggle like an earthworm,
but he followed Shanda deeper into the maze, into twists and shadows, until no eyes could reach them.

He felt a moment of panic then. If this place should burn! They'd
be trapped, wriggling through flaming twists. But the gardeners were
all kinless, weren't they? And he wouldn't show the little girl his fear.
He followed Shanda deeper yet.

There was a small room at the center, just big enough for both of
them to sit up.

"Why is it so small?" Whandall asked.

"It's a playhouse. It was built for my little brother, but he doesn't
like it much, so I get to play in it."

A playhouse. Whandall could understand the notion, but he would
never have thought of it. An entire extra house, just for fun!

After dinner they lay on the balcony above the courtyard and listened to the Lords talk.

Four men and three women lolled on couches that would have
looked really nice in the Placehold courtyard. No one said anything
until an elderly kinless brought out a tray of steaming cups. Lady
Rawanda passed them to the others.

Qirinty's wife sipped, then smiled. "Really, Rawanda, you must tell
us where you get such excellent tea root."

"Thank you, Cliella. It is good, isn't it?" Rawanda said. There was
another silence.

"Quiet lately," Jerreff said. "I don't like it."

"Then you should be pleased," Samorty said. "We caught a sneaker
last night."

"Any problems?" Jerreff asked.

"No, there was a Jollmic ship in port. We got a nice burning glass
for him. Quintana, isn't it your watch tonight?"

"I traded."

"Traded with who?"

"Well, actually—"

"He paid Peacevoice Waterman extra," Qirinty said. He produced a
grapefruit from thin air and inspected it.

Samorty shook his head sadly. "Bad practice," he said.

Quintana laughed. He was round and pudgy and looked very con-
tented on his couch. "What can it hurt? Samorty, you may like parad-
ing around all night in armor, but I don't! If there's need, I'll turn
out—"

"If there's need, the watchmen will be taking orders from Waterman, not you," Samorty said.

"Not to mention that Waterman will get any loot they find," Jerreff said dryly.

"You worry too much, Samorty," Rawanda said. "You think the city will fall if you don't hold it up—"

Samorty laughed thinly. "It fell once. To us! But peace. It won't fall tonight. More wine?" He poured from a pitcher on the table.

Shanda stirred and whispered, "That's you they're talking about."

"Sneaker?"

"No, the *Lordkin!*"

Whandall nodded. His family, street, city, in the hands of these dithering, bickering Lords. . . . Was he too young to be sold onto some foreign ship? For an instant the idea was indecently attractive . . .

"Yangin-Atep's still asleep," Quintana said. "Watchmen told me there were three fires over in the benighted areas."

"I didn't hear about any fires. Have trouble?"

"Just brush fires. The kinless must have put them out."

"This time," Samorty muttered. "What I worry about is when the Lordkin won't let the kinless put out the fires."

"Yangin-Atep protects houses," Quintana said.

"But not brush. Suppose all the chaparral burned at once?" Jerreff asked. "Would that wake Yangin-Atep? Half the city could burn if Yangin-Atep wakes while the hills are burning!"

"Now that would be something to worry about," Rowena said.

"Sure would. You're too young to remember the last time," Samorty said. "I was only ten or so myself."

"We don't know what wakes the god," Qirinty's wife said.

"Sure we do. Hot weather. No rain. That hot, dry wind from the east," Qirinty said.

"Sometimes." Samorty sounded doubtful. "I grant you that's usually what things are like when the Burning starts. But not always."

"Get us some rain and things will be all right." Qirinty toyed nervously with a salt shaker, then caused it to whirl about.

"Sure," Rowena said.

"If we can't get rain, maybe we ought to do something else," Qirinty said carefully. He put the salt shaker down.

"What?"

"Finish the aqueduct. Get more water into the benighted areas—"

"Be real," Samorty said. "That's no easier than getting rain!"

"They have a new aqueduct in South Cape," Quintana said. "One of the ship captains told me."

"Sure, and they have wizards in South Cape," Qirinty said. "And dragon bones for manna. We don't. But we could still build the aqueduct—"

"There's no money," Samorty said.

"Raise taxes."

"We just raised taxes," Jerreff said. "You can't squeeze the kinless much more."

"Borrow the money. We have to do something! If there's another Burning it will cost even more to rebuild and we'll *still* have to finish the aqueduct." At the word *still*, Qirinty made a dagger vanish. From his vantage above, Whandall saw how he did it. He might have learned it from a pickpocket. "Doesn't Nico owe us?"

"Sure he does, and maybe he can talk his masons into working with him as a favor, but it would still take two hundred laborers to finish that job. They'd all have to be fed."

"I suppose," Qirinty said sadly.

"Maybe we can talk the Lordkin into finishing the aqueduct." Rowena laughed sourly. "After all, they're the ones who need it."

"Yeah, sure," Quintana said. He poured himself another glass of wine. "But Qirinty's right. We should do something . . ."

Lord Quintana's wife was slim and long, with sculpted hair. She'd arranged herself on the couch so that everyone would see her legs and painted toenails, and she seldom spoke. "I don't see why everyone worries so much about the Lordkin," she said. "We don't need them. What do we care what they do?"

Quintana ignored her.

"No, I mean really," she said. There was a hard edge to her voice. "They need the aqueduct, but they won't work on it. The very idea that they might makes us laugh."

"And when Yangin-Atep wakes and they burn the city?" Samorty said gently. He liked Lady Siresee.

"Kill them."

"Not easy," Qirinty laughed. "There are a lot of them, and after all they won last time."

"Squeeze the kinless much harder and you'll get another war," Jerreff said. "Some of them are getting desperate."

"Yes," Samorty said. "But they'd really be in bad shape after a Burning."

"There are stories," Jerreff said. "Whole city burned down. Even our town."

"Where did you hear that?" Samorty asked.

"At the Memory Guild. Yangin-Atep used to be more powerful," Jerreff said. "He could seize everyone, Lordkin and Lords too. Burnings were really bad in those days. Didn't your father tell you that, Samorty?"

"Yangin-Atep has no power in here." Samorty waved at the sculpted gardens and too-perfect houses. "And damned little in town."

"Sure, and you know why," Qirinty said. "We can fence him out, but we can't control him."

"Gods have gone mythical," Jerreff said.

"Don't be a fool," Samorty said. "You heard what Morth said. And suppose we *could* send Yangin-Atep into myth—what happens then?"

"No more Burnings," Jerreff said.

"At what cost?"

"I don't know," Qirinty said.

"Neither do I, and that's the point," Samorty said. "Right now we've got things under control—"

"Sort of," Jerreff said.

"Enough." Samorty clapped his hands. The kinless servants brought in new trays of mugs. "We have a performance tonight."

"Oh, what?" Qirinty's wife asked.

"Jispomnos."

"No, no, that's long," Quintana said.

"Not all of it—scenes from part one," Rawanda said. "Nobody does the whole thing."

"Even so," Quintana said. "I'll be back . . ." He went off toward the small room under the stairs.

CHAPTER
7

P*erformance* was a way of telling a story. Several people acted out lives that weren't theirs, on a platform with moveable furniture. A man with a booming voice spoke as storyteller. Whandall had never seen anything like it.

The performance was long, and Whandall didn't understand a lot of the words. Jispomnos had beaten his woman, had tracked her down after she fled from him, had killed her and the man he found with her. Whandall understood that well enough. Whandall's uncle Napthefit had killed Aunt Ralloop when he found her with a Water Devil. He'd tried to kill the man too, but the Water Devil had run to his kin.

But Jispomnos's woman was kinless!

The killing wasn't shown.

Guards took Jispomnos away. He walked away when they turned their backs. The guards chased Jispomnos around and around the stage in excruciating slow motion and all sang in a harmony that Whandall found beautiful, but they sang so *slowly!*—in time to somnolent music that ran on forever. . . .

Shanda pulled his ear to wake him. "You were snoring."

"What's going on now?"

"Trial."

He watched for a time. "I don't understand anything at all! What's the trial about?"

She looked at him with wide eyes. "There was a murder," she rebuked him. "It's about whether he did it or not."

"Jispomnos is a Lordkin, isn't he?" Or was the *actor* a Lordkin *playing* Jispomnos?

But Shanda only looked at him strangely.

Whandall swallowed what he was about to say. Shanda wasn't Lordkin. Instead he pointed and said, "The kinless woman and the two men, who are they? They're doing all the talking."

"The men, they speak for Jispomnos. Clarata speaks for the court."

"Jispomnos won't speak for himself?" Cowardice or pride? "Why *two* men?"

"I don't know. I'll be back," she whispered.

Whandall nodded. It had been a long performance.

He watched. It was difficult to untangle. The kinless woman Clarata told of the killing, questioned any who had been nearby, showed bloody clothing. Of the men who spoke for Jispomnos, the little kinless man demanded that Clarata produce Jispomnos's knife. Whandall nodded: no Lordkin would throw away his knife. He argued that the clothing wasn't his, didn't fit. Jispomnos was elsewhere during the killing—in the Eastern Arc, in the woods, in a dockside winery with Water Devils to vouch for him, and on a boat bound for Condigeo—until the audience roared with laughter, covering Whandall's own giggles.

But the Lordkin advocate spoke of Jispomnos's prowess as a fighter, his standing in the bands . . .

Shanda came back. "What did I miss?"

"I think I get it."

"Well?"

"They're not talking to the same people. The little kinless, he's funny, but two of the judges are kinless, so he's talking to them. He tells them Jispomnos didn't do it. But Jispomnos took a kinless as his woman. He lives like a kinless. What the Lordkin judges want to know is, did Jispomnos make himself kinless? The Lordkin advocate, he's telling them that Jispomnos is still a Lordkin. He had the right to track his woman down and kill her."

"The *right?*" Her eyes bugged. *"Why?"*

He had no way to tell her that. It just *was.*

So he lied. "I don't understand that either."

Shanda whispered, "I don't think anyone does. It's based on something that really happened in Maze Walkers. A Condigeo teller wrote this opera. The grownups like it."

The trial was still going on when part one ended and everyone applauded.

The lords and ladies drifted apart. Samorty and Qirinty walked under the balcony. Samorty was saying, "And that's the *best* part. Greatest argument for getting rid of that arts committee I ever saw."

"Let *me* run the arts committee. Or you. Or Chondor. At least we'll have shows that satisfy someone." Qirinty stopped in his tracks. "That's what we need! A show! Not for us. For the Lordkin!"

"Not Jispomnos!" Samorty said. "You'd start the next Burning!"

"No, no, I mean, give them a parade," Qirinty said. "Get their attention and tell them about the aqueduct. Tell them we'll have it done . . . before the rains?" He went back to his couch, looked up at the night sky. "It's the season. Why doesn't it rain?"

"Not a bad idea," Jerreff said. "While all the Lordkin are off at the parade, Samorty here can meet with the kinless association council. Explain what we're really doing with their taxes."

"Find out if they're ready to join the Guard," Siresee said.

Quintana said, "Lordkin hear you're meeting with kinless and not them, there'll be trouble."

Jerreff waved it off. "We'll meet with some Lordkin too."

"Who?" Qirinty asked.

"Who cares? Get the word out, we're meeting their leaders. Somebody will show up."

"Now that's disrespectful," Samorty said. "And the Lordkin want respect."

"No, they don't. They demand it." Siresee's words were meant to cut.

"Well, they say they want it, and they certainly demand it," Samorty said placidly. "I agree, Jerreff, it doesn't matter a lot which Lordkin we talk to. They don't keep their own promises, and none of them can make promises for Yangin-Atep. But we have to talk to them."

"Why?" Siresee asked.

"Time you children went to bed."

Behind him! Whandall jumped, but it was only Serana the cook. "Before Miss Bertrana catches you up so late," she said.

Morning was cloudy, and just after breakfast Miss Bertrana came into the kitchen and took Shanda by the hand. "Your father wants you," she said. "In your pink dress. There are visitors."

Shanda looked pained. She turned to Whandall. "I'm sorry . . ."

"That's all right," Whandall said. "I'd better go home."

"Yes, but have some of my corn cake," Serana said. "I like to see a boy with a good appetite."

"Where did you say you lived?" Miss Bertrana asked.

Whandall pointed vaguely to the west. "Over near the wall, ma'am . . ."

"Well. Miss Shanda will be busy all day. Tomorrow too."

"Yes, ma'am. Too bad, Shanda."

"Are they showing me off?" the little girl asked.

"I wouldn't put it that way, but it's Lord Wyona's family." Miss Bertrana said the name reverently. "Come on; you'll have to change."

Shanda hesitated a moment. "You'll come back?"

Serana was at the stove rattling pans. "It takes two days each way," Whandall whispered.

"Please?"

"I'll be back," he said. "Really. I just don't know when."

"Next time we'll get to the forest." Shanda lowered her voice. "I'll leave some things for you in my room, in the chest. You can have all the boys' clothes there."

The chest was nearly full, and Whandall couldn't tell the boys' clothes from the girls. Most of the things were too small anyway. Shoes: fancy, not sturdy. They wouldn't last a week in Serpent's Walk. There was far more stuff here than he could carry, and even if he could carry it, what then? He'd look like a gatherer. If the Lordsmen didn't catch him, his own people would.

There were boys in the yard playing a complicated game. Hide and run, track and pounce. Imitation Lordkin. Pitiful. Whandall watched them while he thought.

He'd need an outfit, a way to blend in here when he returned. But anything that would blend in here would stand out in Serpent's Walk.

A Lordkin had to be crafty.

It came to him that he could wear his own clothes underneath, then two more layers of Lord's clothing topped by the loose jacket, and still not look too odd. Those boys were all bulkier than he was. They ate better—and more often.

When he was dressed, he felt bulky. He left Shanda's room carefully, with a twinge of regret for all the stuff he was leaving behind, too much to gather. He left by going over the wall. Guards might notice how much he was wearing.

No one paid any attention to him while he was in the area near the Lordshills. There were people and carts on the road. No one offered him a ride, but no one stopped him either. At the top of the ridge he stopped and looked back at the Lordshills and their wall. Then went on. He knew where he could sleep safely.

The Pit was beginning to seem a friendly place. The moon was still near full. The light picked up the shadows of predators coming to

greet him while he made himself comfortable. Through the ghosts'
restless pockets in the fog he watched some larger shadow. He
couldn't see it move, but every time he dozed and woke, it was nearer
yet.

Then he saw something swing above it—a limb—and he knew its
shape.

It was twice the size of one of the giant cats, with a rounded body,
and it was upside down. It was hanging from an imaginary cylinder,
perhaps the branch of a tree eons dead, by its four inward-curving
hands. Its head hung, possibly watching Whandall himself. One of the
tremendous cats suddenly discovered it, turned, and sprang, and then
the horde of beasts was tearing it into wisps. The creature fought
back, and birds and giant wolves too became drifting shreds of fog.

In the morning he put on everything he had, with his old clothes on
top of it all. He looked bulky and he couldn't run, but he might get
through . . .

CHAPTER
8

He had reached Bull Pizzle territory when he heard shouts. Sanvin Street was supposed to be safe, outside the jurisdiction of any band, but five older boys were coming toward him. Whandall began to run. They chased him down and tackled him.

"Hoo!" one of them shouted. "Look what all he's got!"

"Where?" another demanded. "Where'd you gather stuff like this?" When Whandall didn't answer, he hit him on the head with his fist. "Where?"

"Lordshills," Whandall said.

"Yeah, sure. Now where?" They hit him some more and sat on his head.

"Leave me alone!" Whandall shouted. He wanted to scream for help, but it wouldn't do any good. They'd just call him a coward and crybaby. But he could shout defiance . . .

"Serpents!" He heard the cry from down the street. "Serpent's Walk!" A dozen older boys, led by his brother Wanshig, were coming.

"Bull Pizzle!" his tormentor shouted. Then the others were there. Whandall felt the weight lift from his head. There were the sounds of blows.

"You all right?" Wanshig asked. "Come on, let's get out of here."

When they were back at Placehold, Wanshig thanked the others. "Somebody'd better tell Lord Pelzed," Wanshig said. "We may have trouble with Bull Pizzle."

"I never left Sanvin Street," Whandall protested.

Wanshig shrugged. "So what happened? Get anything good?"

"Just some clothes, and look, they tore them, and they gathered my jacket and shoes." Whandall felt bitter disappointment. Nothing had gone right this time. "This stuff is too small for them anyway—"

"Nice, though." Wanshig fingered the shirt Whandall was inspecting. "Nice. You just need a way to get stuff back to Placehold. Take one of us next time."

Even his own family lusted for what the Lords threw away!

"It wouldn't work," Whandall said. "It was . . . sort of an accident that I got in and made friends inside." They'd never believe him if he said that Shanda had given him all those things. Or they'd want to know why. "Nobody notices me. But the Lordsmen wouldn't let a bunch of us in."

"How many Lordsmen?"

"Lots," Whandall said. "Two at the gate, but there are others just inside."

"Yeah, we heard that," Wanshig said. "And they have magic too. Did you see any magic?"

"Maybe a little."

"Ten, twenty years ago, before I was born, three bands got together and went to the Lordshills to gather. None of them ever came back," Wanshig said. "None."

Maybe magic, Whandall thought. *And maybe it was only guards with armor and spears fighting together with the Lords to tell them what to do, and a ship to carry the losers away.* But he could never explain that to Wanshig.

He said, "Wan, there's going to be a big show. The Lords will have a show in the park, and give away some presents, maybe do some magic."

"When?"

"Five days, I think," Whandall said. He counted on his fingers. "Five days counting today."

Wanshig smiled. "Good. Don't tell anyone. *Anyone.* We'll keep this for the family."

"What will you do?"

"I'll have every Placeholder who can pick a pocket ready for them. We'll have first pick of the crowd." Wanshig nibbled his lip, considering. "We can't keep Bull Pizzle out of the park. Can we make them go somewhere else? Something to get them to the other side of town . . ."

Whandall watched his brother think.

Wanshig grinned. "Did they go through your pockets?"

"You got there first."

Wanshig's grin got bigger. "So they don't know you weren't carrying gold. Whandall, Iscunie has been seeing a Bull Pizzle boy. She can tell him you gathered some gold in the harbor town and ten of us are going back for more. We'll be coming back the morning of the parade, on the south side. That'll get every Bull Pizzle down there, and we'll have the park to ourselves."

There were drums and flutes, and five wagons. Thirty Lordsmen in shiny bronze armor marched with spears and shields, and when they got to the park they did a complicated thing of marching in a circle. Then more Lordsmen came and filled in between them so that the circle was protected, and the wagons came in.

A family of kinless strung a rope between two thick trees, as high as a man could reach and so taut that it hung almost straight. A kinless boy younger than Whandall walked from one tree to the other along the rope, turned and walked back, perfectly balanced, while kinless and a few Lordkin whistled and applauded. Whandall realized that these must be the Ropewalker family, who sold rope near the Black Pit.

The Lordsmen were still at work. A portable stage unfolded out of one of the wagons. Another wagon was covered by a tent. When the stage was up a man came out costumed in feathers like an eagle.

The kinless gathered around the wagons. More Lordsmen walked through the crowds. Flutes played, and drums, and someone passed out little cookies to the children. There was a little round platform that turned, with wooden dragons on it for children to ride.

At first it was turned by kinless running around it. When the Lordkin pushed all the kinless children off and took their places, the kinless drifted away into the crowd. A couple of Lordkin fathers tried to get older boys to push it, but nobody would, so after a while it sat there unused while people watched the show.

Most Lordkin kept to themselves in one corner of the park, but Placehold pickpockets moved among kinless and Lordkin alike. One was caught. The kinless man shouted curses at him, but when Lordkin men moved toward him, he let him go with more curses.

A troupe of acrobats came out onto the stage. They flew for short distances with the aid of a seesaw. Another climbed a long pole and hung by his teeth. A man and a woman, both Lordkin, ate fire, and a burly kinless man swallowed a long thin sword. The Ropewalkers danced on their tightrope, this time the boy and a younger girl, who did a backward somersault while an older man stood under her as if to catch her if she fell. She was very steady and he wasn't needed.

Whandall moved closer to where they were passing out cookies. One of the girls . . .

"Shanda," he said.

She looked startled. "Oh. I didn't recognize you."

Whandall saw her look nervously up at her stepfather on the platform, where he was about to make a speech. Whandall took a cookie. "Are they still looking for Lordkin to talk to?"

"I think so, but they haven't," she said.

Lord Samorty began his speech about the new aqueduct and how it would bring fresh water from the mountains. The kinless cheered in places.

"Will you take me to the redwoods?" Shanda asked. "Not for a while. We'll be doing this show in other parts of town."

"I'll try. Before the rain if I can. Rain makes everything grow and it's harder."

Something bright appeared on the stage, then vanished. "An evil wizard is keeping the rain for himself," Samorty was saying. "We'll beat him. There'll be rain!"

Kinless and Lordkin alike cheered.

"But now there's a water shortage, and it's very hard on the horses and oxen," Samorty was saying. "Delivery is difficult. So next Mother's Day will be special. There'll be nine weeks' rations and some other extras."

The Lordkin cheered.

"And that will have to last for two Mother's Days," Samorty was saying. "And you'll all have to come to Peacegiven Square to get it, because we won't be able to bring everything to the usual distribution places."

Crowd noises were drowning out Samorty. He waved, and three magicians came on the stage. They made things appear and disappear. One called Shanda up on the stage and put her in a box, and when it was opened, she was gone. Whandall looked for her, but he couldn't see her.

Wanshig came up behind him. "Lord Pelzed isn't happy," he said, but there was a laugh in his voice. "He's got all of Serpent's Walk out picking pockets now, but we got the best. Good work."

The magicians made a vine grow.

"I know how to make Pelzed happy," Whandall said.

"How?"

"He can meet the Lords."

"You don't know any Lords."

"I know who they are," Whandall said. "That was Lord Samorty who made the speech—"

"Everybody knows that."

"And the man over there talking to the magicians is Lord Qirinty. He's a magician himself, or at least a pickpocket, and the fat one in armor with the Lordsmen, that's Lord Quintana. The pretty lady serving soup is his wife."

"So you know who they are."

Whandall hadn't heard Pelzed come up behind them. "What else do you know?" Pelzed demanded. "Wanshig, you didn't share. We'll have to talk about that."

Wanshig looked worried.

"Lord Pelzed, I heard the Lords wanted a Lordkin leader to talk to," Whandall said.

Pelzed looked crafty. "Say more."

"They want the most powerful leader in this part of the city," Whandall said. "But I don't know what they want from him."

"That's me," Pelzed said. "Go tell them."

Whandall hadn't thought this out far enough. "Uh . . ."

"Do this for me and we'll forget what happened this morning," Pelzed said. He pointed up on the stage. "See that guy?"

"Foreigner," Wanshig said. "I've seen him before—"

"He's a teller," Pelzed said. "If I meet the Lords he'll tell everyone else. Whandall, how sure are you about their wanting to talk to us?"

Whandall thought about it. They hadn't wanted to talk to the Lordkin, but they thought they'd have to, only Whandall didn't dare tell Pelzed that. "I heard them plan it out over dinner," Whandall said.

"Whandall's a great sneak," Wanshig said.

"I remember," Pelzed said. "Well, go tell them I'm here."

"No, you come with me, Lord Pelzed," Whandall said. "Shig, you come too." He led them back behind the tent. As he'd hoped, Shanda was there. Whandall bowed as he'd seen kinless do. "Lady, this is Pelzed, the leader of Serpent's Walk."

The little girl looked surprised, then smiled. For a moment Whandall was afraid she'd wink or grin, but she just said, "Pleased to meet you. I'll go tell my father you're here."

She came back with Samorty, who invited Pelzed past the guards. No one invited Whandall and Wanshig, so they went back to watch the show. When Pelzed came out, he had a new burning glass and was very proud. He showed it to everyone. Then he found Whandall.

"You called me Pelzed. Not Lord Pelzed," he said.

Whandall had thought that through. "I thought the Lords might not like hearing you called Lord. They can make you disappear, Lord Pelzed," he said.

"You really have been in Lords' houses."

Whandall nodded. He already regretted letting them know.

"What did they want?" Wanshig asked.

Pelzed waved his hands. "It was important. Labor peace. How to organize for the new distribution on Mother's Day. They're going to let more female hemp plants grow in some of the fields. Important stuff I can't talk about. There'll be a meeting tonight. Be there, Wanshig . . . Whandall. Be there."

The meetinghouse had stone walls but no roof. There had been a roof, but it hadn't been strong enough. One night the men of Serpent's Walk had climbed onto the roof; no one remembered why. The beams broke. The kinless family who had once lived in the house couldn't be found, so Serpent's Walk couldn't meet there when it rained. It didn't rain much anyway.

Whandall and Wanshig had to tell everyone how Lord Pelzed was summoned to meet with the Lords, while no one from Bull Pizzle or any other band had been called. Only Pelzed.

They spoke of the new Mother's Day. Everyone would be in one place. They'd need all the women to collect and carry, and all the men to protect the women and their gifts.

"It'll be safe in the square," Pelzed's advisors said. "Lordsmen will see to that. But outside—"

"We need two bands," Pelzed said. "One to protect our stuff. Another to see what we can gather from Bull Pizzle."

Bull Pizzle will be doing the same thing, Whandall thought.

Pelzed appointed leaders. Wanshig would be one of them. Whandall thought he'd be in Wanshig's band, but he wasn't. He couldn't fight yet, so he was afraid he'd be assigned to help the women carry. That would be shameful. But the meeting was over before anyone told him what to do.

When everyone else was leaving, Pelzed made Whandall and Wanshig stay behind. Pelzed sat at the head of the table, with guards standing behind him. "Sit down," he invited. "We'll have some tea."

Everyone knew about Pelzed's tea. It was made with hemp leaves, and enough of it left you babbling. Pelzed sipped at the hot brew. Wanshig gulped his. Whandall sipped, just keeping up with Pelzed. It made his head spin, just a little.

"So. You have been to Lord's Town."

"Yes, Lord," Whandall admitted.

"And you brought back fine clothes. What else is there that we can gather?"

"Everything," Whandall said. "But you'll die of it. They have magic. Lord Pelzed, they have stoves inside their houses! The fires don't go out. Yangin-Atep . . ." He didn't want to say it, not here where Yangin-Atep ruled.

"I saw the Lordsmen in their armor," Whandall said. "And big swords, and spears. Every night a Lord puts on armor like that, and so do the Lordsmen, and they go on watch."

"Where do they go?" Pelzed demanded.

"Everywhere. They call it the watch, because they watch for gatherers. Not just in the Lordshills. There's a village outside the walls, and they watch there too. And they have magicians." How much could he tell Pelzed? Whandall was trapped between loyalties. He owed Pelzed, he *belonged* to the Placehold, but the future he longed for might be with the Lords.

"We saw the magic," Miracos said. He was the advisor who stood at Pelzed's right. Sometimes he spoke aloud and sometimes he whispered in Pelzed's ear. "Vines growing. Fireballs."

"And I saw the Black Pit," Whandall said.

Everyone wanted to know about the Pit. Whandall told them as much as he dared. No one believed him.

"There's a wall around Lordshills," Miracos said. "But there's no wall around those big kinless houses? Lord's Town?"

"There is in back." Whandall tried to explain about the little squares, tables and plants in the middle, houses around them, walls behind the houses. "And the watch is there."

"This watch," Pelzed asked. "Swords. Armor. *Kinless?*"

"I think so. It's hard to tell with those helmets."

"Kinless with armor. Weapons," Miracos said. "Bad."

"They never come here," Pelzed said. "Lords do what Lords do." He made it sound profound. "But tell us more about those kinless homes. What's there? What can we gather?"

Whandall described some of what he had seen, shops with pots and beads and cloth, clothing hung on lines, people sitting in the squares drinking from cups and talking.

"No Lordkin there," Miracos said. "Maybe we could go live there."

"Lords won't let us," Pelzed said.

"Lords always telling us what to do," one of the guards said. "Like to show them my knife. Right up them."

"Lords make the kinless work," Pelzed said. "If you could do that, if

I could, we'd have a roof! Whandall, go back. Take someone with you. Wanshig. Take Wanshig; bring me back something. Go learn the way."

"I heard three bands went to the Lordshills together to gather," Wanshig said. "Three together, and none of them ever came back. Dirty Bird was powerful before that happened."

"You scared to go with Whandall?" Pelzed demanded.

"Yes, Lord. Anybody would be scared. Whandall's the only one I ever met who went into Lord's Town and came out. Only one I ever *heard of* doing it."

"Not talking about inside the walls," Pelzed said. "Lords are Lords. Leave Lords alone. But those kinless houses out there, that's different. Go look, Whandall. When everyone's carrying stuff, the way will be clear; you can bring things back. Go see what you can find. I'd like me a shirt like yours . . ."

Whandall was glad of being small. His shirt wouldn't fit Pelzed. But if a little Lord's girl could keep what was hers, maybe a Lordsman could too.

CHAPTER
9

Serpent's Walk was coming to know a certain visiting looker. After the carnival, everyone knew his face.

The boys knew his names: he was Tras Preetror of Condigeo. Tras fascinated them. He spent the whole day in idleness, like a Lordkin. The kinless liked him even when he was with Lordkin, because Tras paid for what he took.

Not always, though. Sometimes he told stories instead.

He would walk away from a fight, or run, but sometimes he *talked* his way out. Wanshig got close enough to see Zatch the Knife accost Tras. He reported that they were presently talking like brothers long separated; that Tras Preetror shared a flask with Zatch. Zatch took nothing else.

Everything about Tras Preetror was exotic, peculiar. Whandall knew he had to see more.

The boys of Serpent's Walk kept getting caught because they went in bands. Bands could hide in the forest, because the forest was roomy. In the city people occupied what space there was. Getting caught got you laughed at. Whandall preferred to lurk alone.

Others learned that Tras Preetror was staying with a kinless family in the Eastern Arc. The kinless had bought protection from the Bonechewers who owned that area, so the house was nicer than most. It also meant that Whandall risked more than being laughed at if he got caught.

Three days after the carnival, the morning's light found eleven-year-old Whandall on the roof, just above Tras's curtained window. He'd slept there, flattened on the slope of the roof.

He heard Tras wake, piss, and dress himself, all while singing in the rolling Condigeano tongue. Tras's footsteps went straight to the curtained window. His arm reached through with something in his hand.

"Come down, boy," he said, tormenting the syllables of normal speech. "I've got something for you. Talk to me."

Whandall flattened against the roof while he thought it over. He hadn't gathered anything from the room. The teller couldn't be angry about *that*. He was singing again . . .

Whandall joined in the chorus and swung on in.

"You sing pretty," Tras said. "Who are you?" He held out his gift. Whandall tasted orange wedges in honey for the first time.

"Name Whandall of Serpent's Walk. Happy meet you, Tras," he said in Condigeano. He'd practiced the words while he and others eavesdropped on the lookers.

"Happy meet you, Whandall," Tras said in bad talk-to-strangers speech. "I talk to other . . . you call *Lordkin?*"

"Lordkin, yes, of Serpent's Walk."

"Tell me how you live."

He understood the words *how you live,* but Whandall couldn't make sense of them. "How I guard my self? My brothers teach—*will* teach me how to use a knife. I walk without one until I know."

"What you do yesterday?"

"Hid in the . . . hid. Watched this house. Can't see roof. No Lordkin around. Climb house next door, look at roof. Go for blanket, come back, sleep on roof. Wait for you. Tras, speak Condigeo."

Tras said in his own speech, "Are a lot of your days like that?"

"Some."

"Maybe. . . . Tell me how the *kinless* live."

"I don't know."

"Mmm." Disappointed.

Whandall said, "I know how woodsmen live. Woodsmen are kinless."

"Tell me."

Whandall began to speak of what he'd learned. The dangerous plants, their names, how to recognize and avoid them. The rite that woodsmen performed before they felled a redwood and cut it up. What they ate. How they talked. Why none but Kreeg Miller would help injured Lordkin children. How they came to accept Whandall.

Tras listened intently, nodding, smiling. When Whandall ran down he said, "There, now, you've told me a lot about yourself. You rescued your brother. Lordkin don't work, but you carried water when you saw there was need. Lordkin don't learn about the forest, even the ones who go in as children. Lordkin like to watch without being seen. You gather, but the kinless try to stop you, because what you gather is what they make or sell or use. You don't worship trees, but you worship Yangin-Atep. You see?"

"Tras? Show me what you say. Tell me how you live."

Tras Preetror talked.

He had come to watch the Burning, to travel afterward and tell what he'd seen. "If you want to see the world, a teller is what you want to be. Wherever you go, they want to know what it's like where you came from. Of course you should know the speech. My family could afford a woman of the Incas to teach me and my brothers and sisters and cousins. We learned geometry and numbers and incantations, but I learned Inca speech too. . . ."

Tras mangled the words and rhythms of normal speech until Whandall's head hurt. Sometimes he didn't have the words. Finding them turned into lessons in Condigeano speech.

". . . *Rich.* If I was rich, I could get my own ship and take it where I wanted."

"Tras, someone could take it away and go where *he* wants."

"Pirates? Sure. You have to be better armed than they are or carry a better wizard or somehow persuade a pirate that you do.

"Once upon a time, two Torovan privateers had us bracketed far from shore. Privateers are pirates, but a government gives them a license to steal—I mean gather. Who has a better right?" Tras laughed and said, "But *Wave Walker* carried a wizard that trip.

"We watched. Acrimegus—he was *our* wizard—sent a beam of orange light from his hand down into the water near one of the other ships. It was just bright enough to see in twilight. He held it there, on and on, while we maneuvered and the two ships countermaneuvered and came closer and closer. Then the water boiled at that one spot. When Acrimegus gave us the signal, we all pulled the sails down and then crowded along the rail. The privateers must have thought we were crazy.

"A head broke the surface. It was almost the same size as the nearest ship. All of us shrieked and went running below, all but Acrimegus. I stuck my head back out to see the rest. The head was rising and rising on what looked like leagues of neck. It turned toward *us*. Acrimegus waved and danced and shouted, 'No, no, you massive great fool,' until it turned toward the privateer and started to dip—"

"What *was* it?"

"Well, an illusion, of course, but the privateers turned about and ran. What made it work wasn't just Acrimegus's light effects, but the details, the way he acted, the way *we* were acting."

"Were you frightened?"

"I pissed in my kilt. But what a story! I'd travel again with Acrimegus any day. Now you tell me something."

"I've seen a Lord."

"So have I. Where was your Lord?"

"At home, in Lordshills. He had a fountain. And a room inside where they can cook. A room to piss in, with running water. And a room where kinless wrote things on paper and put them in jars, but I couldn't go in there." Whandall decided not to speak Samorty's name. He would hold that in reserve.

"Can you read?"

"No. I don't know anyone who can read." Except the Lords could read. And Shanda.

"You do now. What did your Lord do?"

Whandall was still trying to understand what he'd seen on two visits. "He had other Lords to dinner, and a magician. People who weren't Lords brought the food and took it away, and all the Lords did was talk and ask each other questions. At the end they acted like they'd fixed something broken, only . . . only it was the next Burning. They think if they can make people talk to each other, they can miss the next Burning. And at the end he put on armor and went out with some other armed men."

"Did they . . . do *you* think they put off the next Burning?"

No grown man or woman could answer that question. Whandall didn't think even Lord Samorty knew that. Whandall said, "No."

"Then when will it happen?"

"Nobody knows," Whandall said. "There was another Lord who made cups move in a circle. Like this—"

"Yes, that's called juggling."

"How do you do it?"

"Years of practice. It isn't magic, Whandall."

"It isn't?"

"No."

"There was a . . ." Whandall couldn't remember the word. "People pretending to be other people. Telling each other a story like they don't know they're being watched. *Jispomnos,* they called it."

"I've seen *Jispomnos.* It's too long for after dinner. It runs on forever! You saw just pieces, I bet. Was there a part where the wife's parents want blood money?"

* * *

They talked through the morning and deep into afternoon. Whandall practiced his scanty Condigeano from time to time, but usually they were each speaking their own language.

Tras spoke of his own affairs without hesitation. Still, it was hard for even a teller to tell how he lived . . . to see it from inside . . . to see what a stranger must miss. They had to walk circles around their lives, to sneak up on the truth.

"Do you know who your father was?"

Whandall said, "Yes. Do you?"

"Yes, of course," Tras said.

"What you did with your face. It looked like you wanted to fight."

Tras shrugged uncomfortably. "Maybe for just a moment. Sorry. Whandall, it's an insult to ask if anyone but my father is my father." Tras changed to local speech. "This not Condigeo. *You* feel I still respect you?"

"Yes, but we don't say *father*. Resalet—" Tras lofted one eyebrow. Whandall explained, "Resalet is father to my brothers Wanshig and Shastern and two of my sisters. He tells us, '*I* know who *my* father is. So do you. But maybe I'm talking to one who isn't so lucky. I don't throw it in his teeth. You don't either. You say *Pothefit*. You and I and he know who I mean. Even if we're wrong.' "

"Pothefit. Your father. Have other name?"

"Not to tell."

"Live with you?"

"Pothefit was killed by a wizard."

Tras's face twisted. The man's face was so alien, it was hard to tell just what he was showing. He said, "When was that?"

"My second Burning. I was seven. Five years ago." *Almost five,* Whandall thought.

"I missed it. My ship left late. Now nobody seems to know when the next Burning will start," Tras said.

"Nobody knows," Whandall agreed.

Tras Preetror sighed. "But someone has to know. Someone has to set a fire."

An odd viewpoint, Whandall thought. "Yangin-Atep sets fire."

"They used to know, here in Tep's Town. In late spring, every spring, you'd burn the city. Now it's been . . . three years? What do you remember of the Burning?"

Whandall tried to tell him. Tras listened for a bit, then asked in Condigeano, "A wizard killed this Pothefit?"

"It was said."

"Odd. *I'd* know if there was a powerful wizard in Tep's Town."

"He's here. I've seen him. Someday I'll see him again. I don't know enough about magic yet. I don't even have my knife."

Tras said, "I've seen those knives. Half a pace long, plain handles, maybe a little crude?"

"Crude?"

"A Condigeano merchant would spend more effort. Inca smiths get *very* fancy. Here, someone would just take it away from him."

Whandall frowned, remembering something. "Why did you laugh?"

Tras looked guilty. "You caught that? I'm sorry."

"Yes, but why?"

"Magic wears out. It wears out faster in cities because there are more people. Everybody knows a *little* magic. You ever try to work a spell near a courthouse? It's bad enough in Condigeo.

"But here! There's something about Tep's Town that eats the magic right out of spells and potions and prayers. Here, it's hard to imagine what a wizard could do that would hurt a careful man. He must have taken your f—taken Pothefit by surprise."

How? A man so old that he might die before Whandall had his knife! A gatherer must be wary, ready to run or fight. What could Morth of Atlantis have done to surprise Pothefit?

But Whandall only asked, "Have you been where magic is strong?"

"They're dangerous places. Deserts, the ocean, mountain peaks. Anywhere magicians have a hard time getting to, that's where magic can still leap out and bite you. But I like to go look," Tras said. "I'm a teller. I have to go to where I can find stories to tell."

"What will happen when all the magic is gone?"

Tras looked grave. "I don't know. I don't think anyone knows, but some magicians say they have visions of a time when there is no magic, and everyone lives like animals. Others say that after a long time there'll be a new age that doesn't need magic."

Whandall's mind's eye showed him Tep's Town spreading to cover the world . . . just for a moment, before he blinked the image away.

What Whandall remembered best of that afternoon was how little he understood of what he'd seen of his world. But he'd learned just by talking, and the teller didn't seem disappointed.

CHAPTER
10

Of course Whandall asked Tras Preetror about Lords. Strangely, Tras wanted *him* to find out more.

"Tras, we saw you with them on the wagon. You spoke to them," Whandall said.

"We see them when they want to be seen," Tras said. "A show for tellers. But you've seen Lords when they didn't know. Whandall, everyone is curious about your Lords. Who are they? Where do they come from? How do they get their power?"

"Don't other people have Lords?"

"Lords, Kings, and a hundred other ways to keep chaos imprisoned," Tras said. "But Tep's Town is different. You burn down your city, the kinless rebuild, and everyone thinks it won't happen without the Lords. Maybe everyone's right. I want to *know*. Whandall, don't you want to go back?"

Whandall was learning how to survive in the streets of Serpent's Walk. In the "benighted sections" he had enemies but also friends and guides. He was actually getting good at it. In the Lordshills were dangers he didn't understand. No, he didn't really want to go back; not now. Not until he understood better what he might do there.

He had no place in Lordshills. Or in Lord's Town nearby, where kinless and Lordkin lived together and hung clothes out to dry. But he might learn, in time. The kinless in the pony cart had spoken of moving his relatives to Lord's Town. And there were gardeners, and Lordsmen living inside the walls of Lordshills. They had to come from

somewhere. He had to learn these things. But where? Going to Lordshills without knowing more could be dangerous.

There was his promise to Shanda. But he'd *told* her it might take
time.

He tried avoiding the teller. It made life less interesting, and Tras
sought him out anyway. Whandall began to wonder: what would the
teller *do* to persuade him?

Whandall hadn't looked at the clothes Shanda had given him in a
third of a year. When he saw their condition, he put a kilt and shirt on
under his Serpent's Walk gear and took them to show the teller.

They were torn. They stank. "It's all like this," he told Tras.

"Dry rot. And how did they get ripped?"

"Bull Pizzle caught me. And afterward I couldn't hang them up to
dry without somebody gathering them."

Tras offered to get him some soap.

Whandall explained that soap was unheard-of treasure. His family
would gather it from him, if he could get it *that* far. Unless . . .

Tras grumbled at the price, but he paid.

Whandall went home by hidden ways, concealing a whole bag of
soap. Guile and a brisk breeze hid him through Dirty Bird to Serpent's
Walk, and from there a cake of soap bought him an escort back to the
Placehold.

He could think of only one way to hide so much soap. He started
giving it away.

His mother praised him extravagantly. Brothers took a few cakes to
give to their women. He spoke to Wess, a girl two years older than
Whandall, the daughter of his aunt's new lover. For the luck that was
in his words or because she liked him or for the soap she knew he had,
she lay with him and took his virginity.

Now Placehold reeked of soap, and Whandall could safely use the
rest. He cleaned the clothes Shanda had given him. Pants and two
shirts had rotted too badly; they came apart. He found he could still
assemble a full outfit.

He went back to Wess and begged her to sew up the rips. They
didn't have to hold long, or to stand up to more than a second glance.
When Wess agreed, he gave her another cake of soap.

It would not do to trade with a Lordkin, man or woman. But a gift
would persuade Wess not to forget her promise or keep it badly. He
could see himself in the Lordshills, trying to get into pants that had
been sewn shut at the cuffs!

* * *

His clothes must have been good enough, because the guards paid no attention to him at all. This time he knew the way to Samorty's house.

Dinner in Serana's kitchen was as good as he remembered. There was always more than enough food in a Lord's house. Whandall thought that must be the best thing about living here. You could never be hungry.

Shanda had new clothes for him.

"When did you get these?" Whandall asked.

"Just after the carnival," she said. "When you didn't come back, I thought about giving them to the gardeners, but you said it might be a long time."

Whandall was impressed: not that she had saved them for him, though that was nice, but that she could keep things a long time. No one gathered from her room. He'd seen clothes hung to dry, unguarded.

The Lords had gone to someone else's house, so there was nothing to do. Whandall slept in the empty room next to Shanda's.

In the morning they went over the wall with a lunch Serana had packed. Whandall inspected Shanda in her leathers before he let her go further. He was no less careful with his own.

The hills near the Lords' wall were ablaze with flowers. It was glorious, but Whandall had never seen the chaparral like this. All the patterns and paths he remembered were gone.

The chaparral seemed well behaved this near the Lords' wall. Whandall tried to urge caution, but Shanda was entranced by the beauty. The farther they went, the more vicious it all became. Yet the hills still flared in every conceivable color! Every bouquet of swords had a great scarlet flower at the tip. Touch-me displayed tiny white berries and pale green flowers with red streaks. Hemp plants grew taller than Whandall. They looked inviting, but Whandall wouldn't touch them.

"I've never seen the woods like this," he confessed. "Don't pick anything, okay? Please?"

There were few paths, and animals had made those. At least Shanda seemed to be taking the plants seriously. The whips and morningstars were visibly dangerous, and she'd seen what touch-me did to her stepmother. He watched her weave her way through a patch of creepy-julia, very cautious, very graceful, very pretty among the black-edged lavender flowers. But she kept stopping to look.

He wove a path through touch-me and bouquets of swords to an apple tree. She followed carefully in his footsteps. They ate a dozen tiny apples and, in a field of high yellow grass, threw the cores at each other.

It was well past noon and they were ravenous again before they reached the redwoods. They were a thousand paces outside Lord's Town.

These trees seemed different. They were not taller or larger, but none of them had ever been cut. Perhaps the Lords protected their view of the forest from the woodsmen.

At Shanda's urging he kept moving until the city couldn't be seen at all. All was shadows and wilderness and the huge and ancient pillars.

"This won't hurt you," he said. "Watch your feet!" He walked a crooked path to a twisted trunk that was half bark, half glossy red wood.

"Freaky."

"Yeah. Firewand. This's all right too." A pine tree loomed huge next to children, but tiny beneath the redwoods. Whandall plucked a pine cone and gave it to her. "You can eat parts of this." And he showed her.

Pelzed had been impressed with his knowledge of the forest. Would Shanda's father?

Serana's packed lunch was clearly superior, but Shanda picked another pine cone to keep.

They were late starting home. Whandall didn't worry at first. He only gradually saw that as shadows grew long, the world lost detail. The sun was still up there somewhere, but not for them. You couldn't quite tell where anything was: paths, morningstars, touch-me, a sudden drop.

He found them a patch of clear ground while he still could.

There was a bit of lunch left over. No water. The leathers had been too hot during the day, but they were glad of them now. He and Shanda still had to curl up together for warmth.

He felt stirrings, remembering the clumsy coupling with Wess. Wess was older. He'd thought she would know more than he did. He might have been her first—she wouldn't say—and he still didn't really know how.

The plants were very close—the thought of getting touch-me between his legs made him shudder—and Shanda wasn't at all interested. Instead they lay looking at stars. A meteor flashed overhead.

"Lord Qirinty keeps hoping one of those will fall where he can find it," Shanda said. "But they never do."

Deep into the black night, when he felt her uncoiling from him, he made her piss right next to him where he knew it was safe. He held his own water until the first moments of daylight.

They could take off the masks when they got closer to the wall, but it wasn't safe to remove the leathers.

When they came in over the wall, Miss Bertrana was waiting by the rope. She took Shanda's hand. Whandall tried to run away, but two gardeners grabbed him. They didn't hurt him, but he couldn't get away. They followed Miss Bertrana and Shanda into the house.

Lord Samorty was sitting at a table talking to two guardsmen. Miss Bertrana brought Shanda to the table. Samorty eyed Shanda's leather leggings. "Where did you sleep?" he asked.

"In a clearing."

"Do you itch?"

"No, sir."

He turned to Whandall. "So you know the chaparral." He got up to inspect Whandall's earlobes. "Interesting. Who did you learn from?"

"Woodsmen."

"They taught you?" Disbelieving.

"No, Lord; we lurked."

Samorty nodded. "I've seen you before. Sit down. Miss Bertrana, I'll thank you to take Miss Shanda to your rooms and discover her condition."

"Sir?"

"You know very well what I mean."

"Oh. Yes sir," Miss Bertrana said.

Shanda started to protest. "Father—"

"Just go," Samorty said. He sounded weary and resigned to problems, and his voice was enough to cut Shanda's next protest off before it began. She followed Miss Bertrana out.

"Where have I seen you, boy?" Samorty demanded. He didn't seem angry, just annoyed by the distractions, and very weary.

Whandall didn't know what to say, so he stared at the table and said nothing. There was something carved into the table, lines, some curved, a big square shape with smaller square shapes in it . . .

"You like maps?" Samorty asked.

"I don't know," Whandall said.

"No, I guess you wouldn't," Samorty said. "Look. Think of this as a picture of the way the city would look if you were high above it. This is the Lord's Town wall." He indicated the square. "This is this house, and right here is where you two went over the wall."

Whandall's terror warred with curiosity. He bent over the carving to study it. "Is it magic, Lord?"

"Not now."

Whandall stared again. "Then—that's the sea?" he asked.

"Right. Now, how far from the wall before the chaparral gets really nasty?"

"Two hundred paces?" Whandall said. "Two hundred and it will hurt you. Five hundred and it kills."

"How far did you take my daughter?"

Whandall's voice caught in his throat.

"We know it was a long way because we saw you coming back," Samorty said. "And you were a lot more than five hundred paces out, far enough that nobody would go out after you. Where did you take her? Show me on this map."

"We had to go around a lot of . . . bad places," Whandall said. "So I'm not sure. Are these the trees?"

"Yes."

He put his finger into the forest. "About that far."

Samorty looked at him with new respect. "Is there hemp out there?"

"Yes, Lord, but it's dangerous."

"How?"

Kreeg Miller had told him a tale. "We heard the woodsmen say that once they found four men dead with smiles on their faces. They'd let one of the hemp plants catch them. They went to sleep and it strangled them."

Miss Bertrana came in without Shanda. "She's fine," she said.

"You're certain."

"Oh, yes sir, intact—no question about it. And there's no rash either."

"Good. Thank you. You may go."

"Yes, sir." Miss Bertrana escaped happily.

"Let me see your hands," Samorty said. He recoiled from the dirt and clapped his hands. "Washbasin," he said to the kinless who came in answer. "Now. Wash up," he told Whandall. His voice was almost friendly now.

Whandall washed his hands carefully. Whatever Miss Bertrana had said seemed to have calmed Samorty and given him some new energy, as if one of his problems didn't matter anymore. When Whandall was done washing, Samorty inspected his tattoo.

"Serpent's Walk," he said almost to himself. "I remember you. You brought Pelzed to see me."

"Yes, sir—"

"For which I thank you. What's your name?"

Whandall was too afraid to lie. "Whandall Placehold."

"Well, Whandall Placehold, there's no harm done here. You want those leathers? Keep them. And here." He went to a box on a table in the corner, and came back with a dozen shells. "Take these."

"Thank you, sir—"

"Now don't come back," Samorty said.

Whandall had never had a dream ripped out of him. It hurt more than he thought anything could.

Samorty clapped his hands and told the kinless servant, "Bring me Peacevoice Waterman. He should be just outside."

Peacevoice Waterman was big and almost certainly Lordkin.

"Peacevoice, this is Whandall Placehold. Take Whandall Placehold to the gate. Show him to the watch, and tell them he's not welcome here any longer."

"Sir."

"Tell him too," Samorty said.

When they reached the gate, Waterman took out his sword. "Easy or hard way, boy?" he demanded.

"I don't know what you mean—"

"Don't you? It's simple. Bend over, or I'll bend you over."

Whandall bent. Waterman raised the sword . . .

The flat of the sword made a loud whack as it hit Whandall's buttocks, but he was still wearing the leathers and it didn't really hurt at all. Not compared to the loss he felt. Waterman hit him five times more.

"All right. Get," Waterman said. "Go gather somewhere else."

"This was all given to me!"

"Good thing too," Waterman said. "Boy, you don't know how lucky you are. Now get out of here. Don't come back."

CHAPTER
11

Tras Preetror was both disappointed and intrigued. "For what that soap cost me," he said, "I could have got a dozen stories from that wizard. From you it's all hints at something bigger."

Whandall had not spoken of the map. He had to keep *something* back. He asked, "Wizard, Tras?"

"Morth of Atlantis. You must know him."

"Yes." Whandall didn't say that it was Morth of Atlantis he had seen at Lord Samorty's dinner.

"You have to go back, you know," Tras said.

Whandall felt his buttocks. He wasn't hurt this time. The leathers hadn't been interesting enough to attract attention from the Bull Pizzles, so he'd gotten home safely with the shells Lord Samorty had given him. Would woodsman's leathers help him win a fight or only hamper his swordplay?

But he remembered the sound of that sword hitting him. It was sharp, and if it hadn't been turned to hit him flat, he'd have lost a leg. Whandall was sure that even the flat would hurt dreadfully without the leathers. "No."

"Think of the stories," Tras said.

"They know me. They won't let me in."

"The tree—"

"They *know* about the *tree*, Tras," Whandall said.

"There has to be a way," Tras said. "Nobody talks about the Lordshills. Not the Lords, not the people who live there. There have to be stories."

"Morth has been to Lordshills, and he knows things he's never told the Lords. He brought water to Tep's Town," Whandall said. Maybe he could interest Tras in Morth and then he'd leave Whandall alone.

Whandall had forgotten Pelzed.

Ten days later he was summoned to the Serpent's Walk meetinghouse.

Pelzed was all smiles. He poured from a teapot and slid hot hemp tea over to Whandall. His eyes commanded. Whandall drank.

They drank hemp tea at Serpent's Walk meetings, but it was never as strong as this. Whandall was sweating and hungry before he drank half of it. His head—he heard things, pleasant sounds.

"The teller says you won't go back to Lord's Town," Pelzed said.

"Lord? You talk to Tras Preetror?"

"That's not your business."

"Did he tell you I got caught?" Whandall demanded.

"No. You look all right. Any broken bones?"

"No, Lord, b—"

Pelzed waved it away. "What did you see?"

"Redwoods," Whandall said. "The inside of a Lord's house, a big room where he calls people and gives orders." And a map. If he told Pelzed about maps he'd have to draw them for him. "A big Lordsman with a sword beat me and told me never to come back. So I won't, Lord." They would beat him, but worse, they would send him away again. Whandall had tried to forget Lordshills and the Gift of the King.

"Tras says he will pay for a new roof on the meetinghouse," Pelzed said.

"Tras is generous."

"If you take him to Lord's Town. Have some more tea."

"I can't go there!"

"Sure you can. Tell them I sent you," Pelzed said. "Tell them you have a message from Lord Pelzed of Serpent's Walk. They know me!" he said proudly.

A Lordkin should have guile. "They won't believe me," Whandall said. "You're important, but I'm just a boy they already threw out." Inspiration. "Why don't you go instead, Lord?"

Pelzed grinned. "No. But they'll believe Tras Preetror," he said. "He'll tell them. Have some more tea."

They'd told him never to come back. Maybe this way would work, Whandall thought. His head buzzed pleasantly. This time he would watch, do nothing, learn the rules and customs.

The gardener's clothing wasn't fine enough for an emissary of Lord Pelzed. Pelzed sent gatherers to inspect the kinless shops. When they found something Tras Preetror thought might do, Serpent's Walk built a bonfire at the street corner nearest the shop. Others began making torches. Then Pelzed offered a trade: new clothes, and there wouldn't be a burning. The kinless were happy to accept.

Tras hired a wagon to take them to the Lord's Town gate. The kinless driver was astonished but willing so long as he didn't have to go further into Tep's Town than Ominous Hill.

Whandall took the opportunity to examine the ponies that pulled the wagon. The beasts tolerated Whandall's gaze but shied from his touch. Bony points protruded from the centers of their foreheads.

They passed the Black Pit. "You want to be a teller, you have to look for stories," Tras said. "There must be stories about the Black Pit."

Whandall gaped as if he'd never noticed the place before.

"Fire," the kinless wagoneer said. "Used to be fire pits, my grandfather said." His voice took on the disbelieving tone kinless used. "Fires and ghost monsters, until Yangin-Atep took the fires away. Now the Lords've put up a fence."

The guards watched with interest as they came up the hill. A quarter of the way up, the ponies slowed. The driver let them go on a few more paces, then stopped. "Far as I go."

"Why?" Tras Preetror asked.

"Bad on the ponies. Can't you see? Look at their foreheads."

Horns as long as a finger joint had shrunk to mere thorns. The beasts actually seemed to have *shrunk*.

Tras said, "But the hill's not that steep."

"Just the way it is here," the driver said.

"I saw horses go in the gate!" Whandall said. But they hadn't borne these bony nubs.

"Lord's horses. Bigger than my ponies." The driver shrugged. "Lord's horses can go up that hill. Mine can't."

"You were paid to take us to the gate!" Tras said.

The driver shrugged again.

"We'll have to walk, then," Tras said. "Not so dignified. Here, Whandall, stand straight. Look proud."

They walked the rest of the way up. "Let me do the talking," Tras said. He walked up to the guard. "We're emissaries from Serpent's Walk. That's Whandall, nephew to Lord Pelzed of Serpent's Walk. We'd like to speak to Lord Samorty."

"Would you now?" the guard asked. "Daggett, I think you'd better go get the officer."

Tras began another speech. "Don't do you no good to talk to me," the guard said. "I sent for the officer. Save it for him. But you do talk pretty."

Whandall recognized the officer as Lord Qirinty. Peacevoice Waterman was with him.

"You, lad," Waterman said. "Didn't we tell you to stay away from here?" He turned to Qirinty and spoke rapidly, too low for Whandall to hear. Qirinty's eyes narrowed.

"We are emissaries from Lord Pelzed of Serpent's Walk, to talk about the new aqueduct," Tras said.

"And what would Lord Pelzed of Serpent's Walk have to do with the new aqueduct?" Qirinty asked. His voice was pleasant enough, but there was more curiosity than friendliness in it.

"He can get you some workers—"

Qirinty laughed. "Sure he can. Peacevoice, I don't think we need any more of this."

Waterman's badge of office was a large stick. He smiled pleasantly as he walked over to Tras Preetror and eyed his head expertly.

"Your superiors won't like—"

Waterman whacked Tras just over the right ear, and Tras dropped like a stone. Waterman nodded in satisfaction. "Mister Daggett, this one's for you," he said. "Sort of a bonus, like." He turned to Qirinty. "Now, about this lad—"

"Well, he doesn't learn very well, does he?" Qirinty asked. "He's done us no harm, and I believe you said Samorty's daughter likes him?"

"Yes, sir, I expect Miss Shanda won't like it a bit when we feed him to the crabs."

"That may be a bit drastic," Qirinty said. "But do see that he understands this time."

"Yes, sir."

This time Whandall wasn't offered a choice of hard or easy. Waterman swung the stick. When Whandall put his hands up to protect his head, the stick swung in an arc to his legs, hitting him just behind the knee. Whandall yelled in pain as he fell to the ground. He doubled over to protect himself.

The other guard kicked him in the back, just above the waist. Nothing that had ever happened to him hurt that bad.

"Now, now, Wergy," Waterman said to the guard. "He's going to need them kidneys to pee with."

"They didn't give me a choice!" Most of that came out as a scream as the stick descended, this time on Whandall's upper left arm, then swung instantly to hit his buttocks from behind. "They didn't. I had to come!" Another blow to his left arm. After that Whandall didn't notice who hit him or where. He just knew it went on for a long time.

CHAPTER

12

When he woke, it was dark. He felt a jolt and closed his eyes tightly, afraid he was being beaten again, but finally he opened them to see that he was in the back of the cart. They were just passing the Black Pit.

The kinless driver turned when he stirred. "You going to live?" he asked without much interest.

"Yes . . . thank you—"

"Had to come this way anyway," the driver said. "Here, have some water." He passed back a flask. Whandall's left arm wasn't working at all. He was surprised to find that his right would lift the flask to his lips. Every muscle of his body seemed to be throbbing in unison.

It was nearly dawn when they reached Peacegiven Square. The driver lifted him down from the wagon and left him lying by the fountain. His brothers found him just before noon.

It was late afternoon before Whandall remembered that Tras Preetror wasn't with him. He spent some hours wondering what might have happened to him. Maimed, flayed, impaled . . . were there cannibals among the ships of the harbor, to whom Tras Preetror might have been sold? Such thoughts gave him some comfort.

His left arm was broken. Other agonies masked the pain, and nobody ever set it. He cradled it, held it straight as best he could, and finally Mother's Mother used a strip of cloth to bind it rigidly against his chest. It healed a little crooked.

While Whandall lay healing in his room, his mind roamed free of probability and logic. Mad dreams, mad schemes chased each other through his head. Rescue Shanda from her unparents. Kill Pelzed, take his place, increase his power until he was the equal of a Lord. Become a teller, roam the world . . . which in his mind was a great foggy swirling wall of rainbow colors.

His mother had him moved to a room closer to hers, shared with her latest infant and three others. Mother's Mother brought him soup. It was all he was able to eat. Two days passed before he could get to a window to piss. A week before he could walk around Placehold.

A cousin and her man had gathered his room while he healed in the nursery.

He couldn't lift or gather. They set him to cleaning the kitchen and the public areas alongside much younger girls and boys.

Wess was with Vinspel, a dark man of Serpent's Walk who had been visiting Whandall's sister Ilyessa but found Wess more attractive. She avoided being caught talking to Whandall alone. When he ran her down, he saw a look in her eyes that made him wonder what he looked like. Crippled. Marred. He took to avoiding Wess. She didn't need more soap.

It was bad to be a weakling in Placehold, but the street would have killed him. When he could climb to the roof, they set him to working on the rooftop garden. It was less shameful than cleaning, and he couldn't be seen by anyone outside Placehold.

The Placehold had a large flat roof strong enough to support a foot of dirt and buckets of water. Rabbits couldn't get up there, and most insects didn't. Picking bugs off carrots was work for girls and young boys. Whandall resented having to do it, but there wasn't anything else for a one-armed boy who couldn't use a knife.

Like the plants of the forest, the crops fought back.

If they were attacked by rabbits or insects or pulled up when young, they developed poisons. You could pluck a young carrot or an ear of corn and cook it quickly and it wouldn't be deadly, but leave it a day and it would bring tumors and painful death. Traders sometimes bought Tep's Town root vegetables, and Whandall had once asked Tras Preetror what they did with them.

"Sell them to wizards," Tras had told him. "Most places, they'll kill even a wizard, but Tep's Town doesn't have so much magic. The plants still fight back, but not so hard. Wizards eat Tep's Town carrots to gain strength."

"Tras?"

"Anything that doesn't kill you makes you stronger," Tras had said in the voice he used when quoting somebody dead. Now Whandall remembered and hoped it was true.

Mostly, garden workers protected crops from rabbits and insects until they were big and old and tough. Plants gone to seed didn't care whether they were eaten. These they pulled up for food. Old carrots, onions, and potatoes would keep a long time.

It was work for kinless, but no kinless could be allowed up on the Placehold roof. Whandall found it a pleasant way to pass time. The work wasn't hard, except for carrying buckets of water up the stairs, and that was done in an hour each day. The rest was only tedious. He had to crawl along the vegetable rows looking for insects to kill. The view from the roof was wonderful.

Whandall remembered the carving on Lord Samorty's table. A "map." From the roof Whandall could see all of Serpent's Walk and some of the other band territories and could see where people went on Mother's Day and afterward. He tried to draw the patterns.

A room opened up for him just when living with crying and crawling infants was about to drive him crazy. Shastern led him to a tiny room just below the roof. He'd have to do something about the unwashed smell . . . which suddenly struck him as familiar.

"Lenorba's room," he said.

"Was."

"Where is she?"

"Nobody knows. We needed an extra woman at the last Mother's Day. We took Lenorba. Of course we stopped at the border of Peacegiven Square and the women went on. Lenorba never came back. They got her."

Whandall nodded. It was thirteen years ago, and most people must have forgotten what Lenorba had done . . . yet he could feel no surprise.

His arm stopped hurting, and eventually he took off the swaddling strip Mother's Mother had used to bind it up. The arm was crooked, but he could use it. Hauling water up the stairs helped strengthen it. Picking insects off carrots gave him skill in small movements.

After Whandall's arm healed, he took his knife lessons seriously, although the instruction was haphazard. Whandall thought about each lesson and practiced on the roof. He wondered why you did things a certain way. Then he discovered that if he practiced foot movements with no knife, his arms just held out defensively, he could concentrate on getting the steps exactly right. Then he thought about the cloak over his left arm, moving that as a shield, and learned precisely where his arm should be to protect against a thrust or a slash. Then he

learned knife movements, standing still and concentrating on his hand
and arm. Each time he thought about getting one thing right.

His uncles and cousins had nearly given up in disgust, thinking
Whandall slow and simple. "Must have got hit in the head," one of his
uncles said, not bothering to lower his voice so Whandall wouldn't
hear. Whandall went on practicing, one move at a time, concentrating
on getting each one just right.

When Whandall thought he had learned all the moves they would
teach him, he put them all together.

His uncles were astonished at the result. Suddenly he could best his
cousins, younger and older, in mock duels with wooden knives. He
was growing stronger, and now he was quick and deceptively fast, and
he used his limbs effectively. One day he bested Resalet. The next,
Resalet and his grandson working together. That was the day they
pronounced him ready to go to the streets again and gave him a knife
of his own. They said it had belonged to Pothefit. Whandall knew
better, but the lie pleased him.

Even so, he was wary on the streets. Rumor said that Pelzed was
most unhappy with him. His first foray was a walk with his brothers, a
seeking for conversation . . . and he found he was treated with respect. He was Whandall of Serpent's Walk, and so long as he stayed in
the Walk or allied territory, he was safe. He thought of asking for a
face tattoo, but he put that off. He still had sores on his head, and a
scar at his left eye. It was an angry red ring with a white center, painful
to touch. His left arm was shorter than his right. In time the pain
faded, but he grew slowly.

PART TWO

Adolescent

CHAPTER
13

irls. Suddenly they snagged at Whandall's eyes. The sight of a pretty girl held all of his attention. If he was talking to Lordkin or gathering from a kinless, a clout across the head might be his first return to sanity.

What had changed? Whandall's loins worried at him like a bad tooth.

Girls weren't eager to go with a scarred thirteen-year-old with no tattoo.

He'd avoided Wess while he was healing. He didn't want her to see him that way. Now Wess was avoiding *him,* and Vinspel wouldn't let a man near her anyway. The other boys found ribald amusement in the ring-shaped scar at his eye. Maybe it was even worse than he'd guessed.

Other boys talked about girls they'd had, and Whandall joined in, telling stories as Tras Preetror had taught him. You didn't doubt another boy's story. If he needed to prove himself a man, he might do it with a knife.

Whandall could do that. The first time a Bull Pizzle challenged him, Whandall had startled him and everyone else. The fight was over before it started, the Pizzle disarmed with a cut across the back of his hand. Whandall could have killed him easily, but that would start a blood feud. Instead he took his knife. The next day two more Bull Pizzles challenged him. They were both young, with knives but no face tattoos. In minutes Whandall had two more knives. Then Lord Pelzed and the Bull Pizzles met, and Whandall was told to stay out of Pizzle territory, and everyone left him alone.

His skill impressed his uncles but not the girls. What did impress them? No man knew.

Girls were never found alone. They were with older, tougher boys, or even men; a few had brothers who guarded them fiercely. Whandall spoke of trying his new skill with a knife. The next night he was summoned to speak with Resalet.

"So you're able to fight all of Bull Pizzle, and possibly Owl Beak as well," Resalet said. "Alone, without help. It seems we taught you well."

Whandall at thirteen thought he was immortal, but part of him knew better. There was a black pit in his stomach when he said, "Only kinless are abandoned by their kin."

Resalet said, "Now think on this. You will fight for a woman. You will win, and her man, or his brothers, or *her* brothers, or all of those, will fight you. You are skilled, but you're small. Blood will flow. Someone will die. When you are killed, the Placehold will demand blood money from those who killed you." He eyed Whandall carefully. "For fools we don't need *much* blood money."

Whandall shuffled his feet, unable to reply.

"You're too young to fight for a woman," Resalet told him.

"I feel like I could," Whandall said.

Resalet grinned, showing wide gaps in his teeth. "Know what you mean. But the Placehold can't start a war over getting you a woman. Shall we buy you a woman for a night?"

Whandall understood that the word *buy* was an insult. Still, he considered the offer. . . .

There were women who lived with their children but no men. Some were always popular. Others might have a suitor for a few days after Mother's Day; then they were around for a jewel or a shell or a skirt, or a shared meal and a place to sleep, or for nothing. What would any of them do for soap? But Tras's soap had near killed Whandall, and Tras was dead or gone, and what kind of woman would look at a strange, scarred boy this soon after Mother's Day?

"Not just yet," he said, "but thanks."

Resalet nodded sagely. "You'll be a good Lordkin, someday. But you're not one yet. Grow more before you take a tattoo."

"You won't take my knife!"

"No. But carry it softly while you grow."

* * *

Ask! But who could he talk to? Boys his age were afraid of him, and older boys laughed because he knew so little. His mother had no time for him.

He used a shell Samorty had given him to buy a melon—fruit soft enough to eat without teeth—and brought it to Mother's Mother. Dargramnet hacked it with her sleeve knife and ate it noisily.

"Girls," Whandall prompted, and waited.

The thin lips parted in a smile. "Yes, yes, I see them now. Not like they were when I was a girl. Go with anyone now. They'll learn. Too late, they'll learn too late. I warned them, I warned them all. It's very hot today, isn't it?"

She didn't always hear or remember what Whandall said. Whandall wasn't sure she knew who he was. Still, the stretch of years within her mind must be worth exploring. What had the girl Dargramnet wanted in a man?

He asked, "What were the men like?"

Mother's Mother spoke of the men she'd known. Strif, Bloude, Gliraten—old lovers came and went in Dargramnet's mind as they must have in life, interchangeable inside broken stories, until Whandall couldn't tell one from another. Her second son Pothefit, strong enough to lift a wagon, stubborn as a Lord. Wanshig and Whandall, her first grandsons, Thomer's sons by Pothefit and Resalet, cousins who shared everything. "Most of them dead, now. Killed in knife fights. Burnings. Just gone."

Whandall nodded. Many of the boys he'd grown up with were dead. They'd survived the forest, but not the city. Tep's Town killed boys. Did other cities? Did boys die so young in Lord's Town or in the Lordshills or Condigeo?

One could watch and try to learn.

Unattached women without kin to protect them were hard to find, and they wanted big men to be with . . . except on Mother's Day. The Lords didn't give their gifts to women who had men. Women went to Peacegiven Square alone, and one need only listen to learn who had a man waiting.

Most girls wanted to marry. Most men didn't, but they wanted their sisters married. One or two of Whandall's sisters' friends might be ready to marry, but that was too big a bite for Whandall at thirteen.

Not that he'd reasoned any of this out, exactly. But every Lordkin knew that there was a time when a man need not ask. Whandall remembered a high optimism, a firelight feast for eyes grown bored

with daylight, frenzy and excitement, couples pairing off, when he was
seven years old. . . .

"Shig, when will the Burning come?"

Wanshig laughed. "You're a looker now?"

They were at dinner in the Placehold courtyard. The sky was red
with sunset. Speech ran softly round the circle of adults and the
smaller circle of children.

Wanshig was eighteen now. He'd watched Whandall practicing with
his knife and twice had joined him on the roof, not ashamed to learn
from his younger brother. Whandall liked him best of all his kin.

Now Wanshig set his spoon down and said, "Nobody knows. Long
ago it was once a year. Now, every four or five. Even when Mother
was a little girl, they couldn't tell anymore. Maybe gods sleep, like
your Uncle Cartry after a Lordsman whacked his head. Maybe
Yangin-Atep isn't dead—he just never wakes up."

"Did Yangin-Atep take you?"

Wanshig laughed again. "No! I was only . . . twelve, I think."

"*Someone,* then."

"They say Yangin-Atep possessed Alferth and Tarnisos. You don't
know them, Whandall. They're crazy enough without help. All I know
is, we see fires south of us, smoke blowing our way. Resalet whoops
and dives into Carraland's Fine Clothes, and we all follow. Carraland
runs away shouting out looker gibberish—"

"What happened to Pothefit?"

That snapped Wanshig out of his wistful nostalgia. "Whandall, do
you remember when they came in with the cook pot?"

"Yes, Shig."

*Pothefit and Resalet were shadows against the dancing blaze from the
granary, carrying the cauldron through Placehold's main door while Wanshig and another brother pretended to help.*

"We gathered it out of a wizard's shop on Market Round. We piled
stuff in the cook pot too, but we went back for more, and to burn the
place. An Atlantis wizard, a stranger, he didn't know any better than
to come back to his shop during the Burning. He found us. Pothefit
was trying to set the shelves alight. The wizard waved his hand and
said something, and Pothefit just fell over. Rest of us got away."

Lord Samorty's courtyard . . . "I saw him. Morth of Atlantis."

"Me too. That shop on Market Round, he built it again after the
Burning."

"No, Shig, Morth of Atlantis was too old for that. He was almost
dead."

"Right, and cook fires burn inside. Whandall, that is Morth of Atlantis, the shop on Market Round."

"Where does he go at night?"

Wanshig cuffed him hard enough to make the point. "Don't even think it. Never remember a killing after the Burning."

Whandall rubbed his ear. "Shig, you've killed."

"Barbarians, lookers, kinless, uglies, anyone who's insulted you
. . . you can kill. But that's only during the Burning, Whandall, and it's not a big part of it. It's only . . . it's bad to hold your anger locked in your belly for too long. You have to let it go."

Something in the conversation had attracted Resalet's attention. "Whandall, how do you reckon we keep the Placehold when everybody wants it?"

"We watch. We can fight—"

"We can fight," Resalet said. "But we couldn't fight everyone."

"Serpent's Walk," Whandall said.

Resalet nodded gravely. "But Serpent's Walk can't fight Bull Pizzle and Owl Beak and Maze Walkers all together. And what happens if Lord Pelzed wants to live *here?*"

Whandall had never thought of *that.*

Resalet grinned, showing as many black spaces as teeth. "We're smarter than they are. We have rules," he said. "And the first one is, don't start fights you can't win. Don't even start fights that will cost you strength. But once you do get in a fight, win it no matter what happens, no matter what it costs. Always win! Always win big. Make an example of your enemies, every time."

"Lords do that too." They'd done it to Whandall. "What if you can't win?"

Resalet's grin widened. "You never think about that once it's started." He went back to his soup.

Whandall was about to say something, but Wanshig put his bowl aside and stood up. "Show you something."

"What?"

"Come on." Wanshig pulled a burning stick from the cook fire and ran, whirling it round his head.

He was through the courtyard's narrow entrance with Whandall just behind him. The flame gleamed pale in the dusk. Wanshig skidded around another corner, crossed the street diagonally, and . . .

Whandall, running behind him, saw Wanshig hurl the torch through the window of Goldsmith's wire jewelry shop. The owner was just about to pull the shutter down for the night. He screeched as the torch went past his ear—

And the flame snuffed out.

Wanshig kept running past the store, whooping. Whandall followed. In the shadow of an alley they stopped to breathe, then to laugh.

"See? If the Burning isn't on us, indoor fires just go out. Then maybe you get laughed at and maybe you get beat up, depending. *So don't be the one to start the Burning.* Let someone else do it." Wanshig grinned. "You were about to get a beating," he said.

"I just wanted to know—"

"You wanted to know what happens if so many come after us that we can't win," Wanshig said. "Whandall, you know what would happen. We'd run away. But Resalet can't say that! Not even inside the Placehold. If the story got out that you could take the Placehold without killing every one of us, that any of us even thinks that way—we're gone."

CHAPTER
14

One day a fire began in the brush behind a kinless house just outside Serpent's Walk territory. All the kinless in that area turned out. They brought a big wagon pulled by the small kinless ponies. It had a tank on it, and kinless men dipped water from it and threw it on the fire until it was out.

Whandall watched from behind a flowering hedge. On the way home he gathered an apple to give Resalet.

"Why do they bother? The fire would go out. Wouldn't it?" Whandall asked.

Resalet was in a mellow mood. "Kinless don't believe in Yangin-Atep," he said. "So Yangin-Atep doesn't always protect them. Against *us,* yes, unless there's a Burning. Sometimes against accidents. Not always, and the kinless don't wait to find out."

"Those wagons—"

"They keep them in the stable area," Resalet said.

"What if the fire is too far away?"

Resalet shrugged. "I've seen them turn out with buckets when there's water in the River of Spirits."

The River of Spirits flowed out of the forest and down through Lordkin territory before it reached the kinless area. It stank. Whandall thought he'd rather see Placehold burn than have a fire put out with what was in that river.

There was much to learn about Yangin-Atep, and one could ask. Mother's Mother told him some. When she was a girl she had heard a tale that the kinless had once been warriors with a god of their own, before Yangin-Atep and the Lords brought the Lordkin to Tep's Town. She couldn't remember who had told her the story, and she thought the days were hotter than they used to be.

Days were long for Whandall. He was smaller than other boys his age, and the months spent healing, and afterward doing children's work, had lost him what friends he might have had. His best friend was his older brother Wanshig, and Shig didn't always want a smaller boy hanging around with him.

There was little to do. His uncles were content to have him hang around Placehold in case of need, but that was no life.

His younger brother Shastern had grown while Whandall was recovering. Now anyone seeing them together took Shastern for the elder. Shastern was deeply involved in Serpent's Walk activities. He was leader of a band that gathered from the kinless in Owl Beak.

"Come with us, Whandall," Shastern urged. "Lord Pelzed wants us to look at a street in Bull Pizzle territory."

"Why? I can't run fast."

"No, but you can lurk. If you don't do it, I'll have to."

Whandall thought about that. "You didn't used to be very good at lurking."

"I'm learning. But you're better."

"What are we looking for?" Whandall asked.

"Dark Man's Cup Street. It's right at the border—"

"I know where it is," Whandall said. "There's nothing there! Shaz, there's nothing to gather. What would Lord Pelzed want with that place?"

Shastern shook his head. "He didn't tell me. He said to find who's living there now. When was the last time you were there?"

Whandall thought back. "Six weeks? I was following a kinless, but maybe he knew I was behind him." Whandall shrugged. "I lost him in the trash on that street. It's that bad."

"Come tell Lord Pelzed."

"I think he's mad at me—"

Shastern shook his head. "Not that I know of. Whandall, you have to see him sometime. This way you can do him a favor."

"All right." Whandall felt his heart beat faster. Suppose Pelzed—Lord Pelzed!—wanted him to pay for the cart and clothes? Or the roof Tras Preetror had promised? But Shastern was right—he had to know sometime.

Pelzed found time for the boys that afternoon. "Shastern says you followed a kinless to Dark Man's Cup," he said. "Have some tea."

The tea was weak and didn't do anything to Whandall's head. He sipped and found it good. "He was kinless," Whandall said, "but he didn't live there."

"Who does?"

"I only saw some women."

"Lordkin?"

"Yes. I think so," Whandall said. "Lord Pelzed, Dark Man's Cup looks like there hasn't been a kinless there for years! It's all trash and weeds in the street, and it stinks."

"Children?"

"Two babies," Whandall said. "Dirty, like their mothers."

"No men?"

"I didn't see any."

"Go find out," Pelzed said.

"Lord—"

"Go find out. There'll be men. Find out who they are."

"Lord, why? There's nothing there!"

"But there could be," Pelzed said. "And I'll send Tumbanton with you. Have some more tea."

Dark Man's Cup lay on the other side of a small gully that had running water during the rainy season but was usually dry. The creek bed was filled with trash and sewage, and there was no bridge. Three boys and an older man picked their way through the trash, with Whandall in the lead.

Tumbanton was usually seen at Pelzed's right hand. He was the whip hand, the trainer, when a boy joined Serpent's Walk. He'd saved Pelzed's life twenty-six years ago, when they were both no more than gatherers. He'd defended their retreat when a raid on Maze Walkers went disastrously wrong. Six had died. Tumbanton and Pelzed had escaped. Tumbanton usually went without a shirt to show the maze of scars from that event. He loved to tell the story.

But he'd picked up a trace of a limp too, and a noisy, wobbly walk. His son Geravim, with no scars to speak of, seemed as clumsy as his father.

"What's Pelzed want with this place anyway?" Geravim asked as he shook filth off his sandals.

Tumbanton must know that, but he didn't speak.

"Maybe he thinks he can get the kinless to build a bridge," Shastern said.

"Wish they'd done it already," Geravim muttered.

And why would they, when the Lords and Lordkin would only gather what they built? But they did. Kinless did work, sometimes, and only men like Pelzed knew why.

Pelzed's family had never been important. How *had* he become Lord Pelzed?

Whandall caught a whiff of cooking meat. It was faint, nearly masked by the smells of sewage and decay, but it was there.

"Something?" Shastern asked.

"Probably not," Whandall said. "Wait here, I'll be right back."

There was no wind, but when he'd smelled the cook fire there had been a puff of air from the south. Whandall went that way, downstream if there had been any water in the gully. There were thickets of greasewood and sharp plants like lordswords except these were smaller and didn't move to strike at him. Another patch looked like a variety of lordkiss, three leaves and white berries, but the leaves were sickly red. Ahead was a patch of holly, thorns, and berries. There was a tunnel in the thorns and rabbit droppings on the path. He sniffed. Fresh.

The way led steeply down. The center of the gully was deep, a dry streambed, but on the sides there were shelves of flat land fifty feet wide and nearly that far above the streambed. Above them were thickets all the way to the top of the gully and beyond, but the shelves themselves had clear patches among the weeds and chaparral. The smell of cooking meat got stronger as he went south. When he reached the end of the narrow twisting passage through the holly bushes he stayed prone and used his knife to part the weeds ahead of him so he could look without being seen.

He saw a cook fire. A slab of meat roasted on a spit above it. Behind the fire was a cave into the gully bank. The entrance was hidden from above and most other directions by holly bushes and scrub oak.

Three kinless men sat by the fire. They were sharpening axes. A kinless girl came out of the cave and put sticks on the fire.

A patch of hemp grew just beyond the camp area. These plants seemed different from the hemp that grew in the fields between Tep's Town and the Lordshills, taller and more lushly green. As the girl passed, Whandall saw the plants stir in a breeze he couldn't feel. Wild plants would have done that too.

Whandall couldn't make out what the kinless men were saying. He wriggled backward until he could turn around, then went back to Shastern and the others.

"Find something?" Shastern asked.

Whandall shook his head. He might have spoken, but Geravim and Tumbanton weren't relatives. The rogue kinless wouldn't have much worth gathering, but he'd keep this a secret for the family.

The gully had always been a no-man's-land, used as a garbage dump by Serpent's Walk and Bull Pizzle alike and serving as an easily recognized boundary. Dark Man's Cup was the first street on the other side, about a hundred feet from the gully. Beyond it was a tangle of streets and thistle fields mixed together before the town proper started again.

There were nine houses on Dark Man's Cup. Five had roofs. One of the roofless houses was stone and would be a good house if someone could make the kinless build a roof. Two of the roofless structures had been used as garbage dumps and outhouses, and only three of the houses with roofs seemed to be inhabited. Those stood apart, three houses together along a field partially cleared of weeds.

Every wall of every house, inhabited or not, had a Bull Pizzle mark. They watched a boy about Shastern's age repainting the Bull Pizzle mark on his front wall.

Whandall left Shastern and the others at the edge of the gully and crept through the trash piles in the yards behind the houses. Each household had a small cleared patch in back where they built the cook fires and another small area where children played. Weeds grew everywhere, even in the cleared patches. Everything stank. One house had a dog, but it didn't seem interested in anything outside its own yard.

There were snares in the animal paths behind the houses. Whandall automatically avoided them as he crept toward the inhabited area. He moved quickly but silently, and no one noticed him. Whandall grinned to himself. Watching the kinless woodsmen had been good practice.

Whandall saw only four men. Two were ancient and sat in toothless conversation near a cook fire in one of the yards. One was about twenty. The other was the boy who had repainted the Bull Pizzle sign.

Whandall watched to see if anyone else would come. Then he heard a rustling behind him.

He turned to see Shastern coming. Shaz walked carelessly along a game path—

"Watch out! Traps," Whandall said. He tried to keep his voice low, but one of the old men must have kept his hearing.

"Spies!" the old man shouted. "Spies! Bull Pizzle! Spies!"

And the warning had done no good. Shastern was entangled in a snare. When it tripped him another snare caught his arm.

There were shouts from somewhere to the east.

Whandall ran back to Shastern. When he reached him, there were more shouts, louder.

"Bull Pizzles coming," Shastern said. "Cut me loose!"

It was hard to cut the leather thongs without hurting Shastern. Finally Whandall had his brother's arm free. Together they freed his legs. Shastern stood and grinned feebly.

"Now what?" Whandall asked.

"Now we run like hell, big brother!" Shastern said. He ran for a few yards, then went down as another snare caught him. By the time Whandall had helped cut him free, the shouts of the Bull Pizzle warriors were much closer. They couldn't see anyone, but it sounded like the warriors were just behind them. Shastern ran in bounding leaps, hoping to avoid the snares. Whandall ran behind him, watching for traps, as Shastern got farther and farther ahead.

Geravim and Tumbanton were gone. Shastern was far ahead, and Whandall heard shouts behind him. He was nearly winded. They would catch him soon. Better to stop while he could still fight.

He looked for a place to stop. A corner would be best, but there weren't any. There weren't even walls here. The best refuge he could see was a holly bush. It would be useless against a spear but it would protect his back from knives. He ran to the holly bush, scooped a handful of dirt, jacket over his left arm, turned. The big Lordkin knife felt good in his hand and he tried to grin as he'd seen big Lordkin men do when they were menacing kinless.

There were only three of the Bull Pizzles. All were bigger than Whandall, the oldest probably twenty. He had seen none of them before. Whoever lived on Dark Man's Cup was content to let others defend it for them.

One had a knife. That didn't worry Whandall, but another had a big club studded with obsidian blades. The third boy had a rock tied onto a long rawhide thong. He swung it around his head in a lazy circle, the rock still moving fast enough that if it hit Whandall it would brain him.

As the first Bull Pizzle came toward him Whandall threw dirt into his face, then lunged forward, slashing, before retreating to his bush. Blood flowed from the Bull Pizzle's chest and the knifeman howled in pain.

The older boy had the club. He gestured to his companions to spread out. "He's fast, but he can't get us all." The Bull Pizzle leader grinned. A tattoo marked his left eye. "What you doing here, boy? Looking to get killed? What band marks itself with a *target?*"

Target? Oh, he meant the scar around Whandall's eye.

Whandall looked for a way out. There didn't seem to be one. "We were following a kinless for shells," Whandall said. "But we lost him, then my . . . friend was caught in a snare. We did you no harm."

"You're in Pizzle territory," the older boy said, then glanced expertly at Whandall's hand. "We don't want Snakes here!" He gestured again, to spread the other two out farther. The boy with a knife had stopped snuffling when he found that his cut wasn't serious. Now he tried to rub the dirt from his eyes. He moved over to Whandall's left side, away from Whandall's knife. His knife was held clumsily. A beginner, Whandall thought. He'd be no problem at all.

The club worried him. It was long enough to reach him before he could strike. Whandall had never faced a club before. "You scared to use a knife?" Whandall taunted.

"No, just careful," the older boy said. "You want to give up?"

"What happens if I do?"

The club man shrugged. "Up to our chief," he said. "Don't know what Wulltid will want to do with you. Can't be worse than what we'll do if you don't give up!"

The problem was, it could be. On the other hand, Pelzed might ransom him, since he'd been sent by Pelzed. There wasn't an active war with Bull Pizzle. But Pelzed wouldn't be happy . . .

"You going to give up?" the club wielder asked. "Running out of time—"

"I have lots of time," Whandall said. He'd caught his breath now. The situation was bad. The boy with the bola had moved well off to Whandall's right and was swinging it faster now.

The club man raised his weapon. "Last chance."

"Yangin-Atep!" Whandall shouted. "Yangin-Atep!"

The Bull Pizzle leader was startled for a moment. He looked around as if expecting the fire god to appear. Then he laughed. "Yangin-Atep loves Bull Pizzle as much as Snake Shit!" he roared.

"Which is not at all," the knifeman said. "Maddog, I don't care if he gives up—I get to cut him!"

"Yeah, I think so. Yangin-Atep! Yangin-Atep isn't going to wake for you."

Whandall didn't think so either, but it had been worth trying.

"Serpent's Walk!" The shout came from the gully.

"Snake Feet!" Whandall answered.

"Coming!" It was Shastern's voice. There was wild thrashing in the gully. "We're coming!"

Maddog listened. It sounded like half a dozen Serpent's Walk warriors, and he didn't like the odds. "Stay out of Pizzle territory!" he shouted. He gestured to the others, and they withdrew toward the east.

As soon as they were away, Whandall ran toward the gully and over the lip. Shastern was there alone. He had a tree branch and was bashing at the chaparral. "We're coming!"

"Good to see you, Shaz," Whandall said.

Shastern grinned. "Good to see you, big brother. Now let's run before they find out it's just me!"

"Geravim and Tumbanton?"

"Ran."

CHAPTER
15

Pelzed listened carefully to Whandall's account. "No one important living there," he said. "None of the people who chased you live there. You're sure?"

"Yes, Lord." Whandall hesitated. "Lord, may I ask—"

Pelzed's eyes narrowed. "Thinking of taking my place?"

"No, Lord. I couldn't do it," Whandall said.

Pelzed considered that. "I think you're smart enough to believe that," he said. "Whandall, what I'm looking for is territory we can claim."

"But it's not worth claiming!" Whandall exclaimed.

Pelzed smiled. "Glad you think so. If you think it's worthless, Wulltid of Bull Pizzle will be sure of it."

Pelzed and Wulltid met in Peacegiven Square under the watchful eye of the patrolling Lordsmen. They had agreed to bring only four men each. Wulltid brought four great hulking bodyguards. Pelzed had two of his regular guards, but he also brought Whandall and Shastern.

"You raided my territory," Wulltid began abruptly.

"Calm," Pelzed said. "Have some tea." He poured from a stone jug wrapped in straw to keep it hot. The cups had been kept warm the same way. Pelzed lifted his cup, sipped, and nodded. "So. Greetings, Chief Wulltid."

Wulltid stared sourly at Pelzed, lifted his cup, and drank. "That's pretty good," he admitted. "Greetings, Lord Pelzed. But you still raided my territory."

Pelzed swept his hand to indicate Whandall and Shastern. "I sent these two boys to see what you've made of Dark Man's Cup," Pelzed said. "Which is nothing at all. Two boys, to a street you don't care about. Now how's that a raid?"

"Still my territory," Wulltid said.

"Let's talk about that. What will you take for it? Hemp? How much hemp? Maybe some tar?"

"Hemp? Tar?" Wulltid glared at Whandall. "Boy, what did you find there? Gold?"

"Trash. It's a trash heap, Chief Wulltid," Whandall said. He turned to Pelzed and repeated, "A trash heap, Lord!"

"So why does your boss want that place?" Wulltid demanded.

Whandall's perplexity was genuine.

"It's simple enough," Pelzed said. "I've got some relatives who need homes, and some kinless who'll build for them. Need a place. Dark Man's Cup won't be too bad once all the trash is thrown in the gully."

"That's what I thought," Wulltid said. "But the kinless I put in there wouldn't stay. Yours won't either."

"That's my problem," Pelzed said. "Now just what do you want for the Cup? It's not like it's worth much."

"What if I said I don't believe you?" Wulltid said pleasantly. "There's more to this."

"They're not close kin. . . ." Pelzed smiled. "Lord Samorty asked me. The Lords want that area cleaned up."

"Why?"

"Who knows why Lords want things? But they asked me."

"What did they offer?"

Pelzed sighed. "Five bales of hemp."

"Five! They only gave me three!"

"You took it? But you didn't get it clean," Pelzed said.

Wulltid scratched his head. "I tried. I could have kept that place clear for two years. Three, even. But that Gemwright wanted five years! I had to promise five! Gemwright—he's one crazy kinless."

"You didn't even give him two years," Pelzed said cheerfully. "Bull Pizzles were gathering in the Cup a year after the kinless moved in."

Wulltid sipped tea without comment.

"So the work stopped. You couldn't keep your people from gathering, the kinless moved out, and now you're stuck protecting a place that nobody worth anything will live in! Chief, I'm doing you a favor taking that slum off your hands. But I'll give you half a bale."

"You're getting five bales," Wulltid said. "I want two for Dark Man's Cup."

"One," Pelzed said. "You have three already."

"Two."

"All right. Two," Pelzed said. "But we get a Lord's Witness to this deal."

Wulltid shrugged. "You'll pay him, then. I won't."

The Lord's Witness was accompanied by two Lordsmen guards and a kinless clerk no more than Whandall's age. The clerk dressed like servants Whandall had seen in Lordshills. The Witness wore a tight-fitting cap that completely covered his ears, and dark robes of office.

The clerk spoke in a high-pitched voice. "You wish the attention of a Lord's Witness? That will be ten shells in advance."

Pelzed laid them in a row, one smooth motion, ten shells marked by a Lord's Clerk. The clerk swept them into a leather pouch. He turned to the Witness. "They have paid, Honorable."

The Witness sat down to listen.

"An agreement between Lord Pelzed of Serpent's Walk and Chief Wulltid of Bull Pizzle," the clerk said. "Speak, Wulltid of Bull Pizzle."

"We give the street known as Dark Man's Cup to Serpent's Walk," Wulltid said. "Serpent's Walk will complete what's left of the work Bull Pizzle was paid to do. We will remove all Bull Pizzle people within two days and never return. Serpent's Walk has to repaint all the signs; we won't do that."

The clerk wrote on what looked like a sheet of thin white leather. When Pelzed tried to speak, the clerk held up a hand until he had finished writing. "Now. Speak, Pelzed of Serpent's Walk."

"We will complete the work offered by Lord Samorty's clerk. The Lords will pay us five bales of hemp and two buckets of tar. We will pay two bales of hemp to Bull Pizzle.

"In return, all trash will be removed from the street and yards, five houses of kinless will be established, and no one will gather in Dark Man's Cup for five years."

The clerk wrote again. "Do both of you accept this?" he demanded. "Then mark this vellum. Thank you. That will be twenty more shells."

Afterward, Pelzed was talkative and amused. "It was easy!" he crowed. "Wulltid never suspected a thing!"

Whandall didn't ask, but he *looked.* Pelzed laughed. "We had no way to expand in that area because of the gully," he said. "I've always wanted something on the other side. The gully may be worth something. Clean it up and a kinless could grow hemp there, I think."

Whandall remembered the hidden kinless camp.

"So I wanted it," Pelzed said. "I could have bought it, maybe, but this way is better. Look, Whandall—now the Lords know Bull Pizzle took their three bales, and two more of mine, and did nothing for it. Five bales for nothing. I'm getting the three Bull Pizzle got, and I'll get it cleaned up."

Whandall waited a respectful moment. "How, Lord?"

"My kinless believe me when I tell them they'll have five years with no gathering," Pelzed said. "Do you believe me, Whandall?"

Whandall didn't answer instantly. Pelzed asked, "You know Fawlith?"

"The beggar who babbles all the time?"

"That's him. We caught him and his brother gathering on a street where I promised the kinless we'd leave them alone."

"I didn't know he had a brother."

Pelzed just grinned. "Want to live in a house of your own?" he asked. "I'll need two Lordkin families in the Cup. To watch over the kinless there. Ready to start a family?"

Whandall thought about it for a moment. "Thank you, no, Lord, I have a home." He shrugged. "I don't have a woman."

"Fine house will get you a woman," Pelzed said. "Even with that eye. But you're young. Ask me when you're ready. I owe you for this."

"Three of them," Shastern said, much later. "And you held them off until I scared them away. Tell me how to do that."

Whandall tried to explain. He told Shastern how he'd practiced each move, thinking about that and nothing else, and how it had taken months.

Shastern didn't believe him. There had to be a secret that Whandall wasn't telling him. Shastern left in disgust, leaving Whandall more alone than ever.

CHAPTER
16

As the scars of Burning faded, the lookers dwindled. They never went away entirely. Though Tras Preetror was gone, other tellers remained.

A teller gave Shastern a handful of fruit to torch Carver's lumberyard. At a dead run and with a blood-curdling whoop, Shastern hurled paired torches past a heap of beam ends and into the work shed. The fires went out, of course. Shastern shared the fruit around afterward.

They never told the lookers what happened to fires outside the shed.

Whandall liked lookers. Like most kinless, they made little trouble when their things disappeared. A looker who made a fuss would be returned to the docks in bruised condition, and who would complain? Many—not just tellers—carried little flasks of wine as gifts in return for stories or guidance. Some carried preserved fruit for children. And, of course, they told stories.

In spring again, three years after the beating, Pelzed summoned Whandall to his roofless hall.

Tumbanton wasn't about. It came to Whandall that he hadn't seen Tumbanton or Geravim the last few times Pelzed summoned him. Tumbanton and his son might be avoiding Whandall, after leaving Whandall and Wanshig to the mercy of the Bull Pizzles.

These days Whandall had the status of a man, even though he had not selected his tattoo. Tentatively he opened conversation with some of Pelzed's men and found them speaking openly, treating him as an equal. But when he asked after Tumbanton, nobody wanted to hear that question. Whandall hid his amusement and, naively, asked after Geravim too.

Talk died. Whandall meandered casually toward Pelzed's rooms. He'd best not name those names again until he knew more.

The Serpent's Walk Lord offered hemp tea, and waited until Whandall had sipped before he spoke. "Tras Preetror is back."

Whandall stared. "I thought they'd fed him to the crabs!"

"Seems not. He owes me a new roof. Anyway, I'd like to hear his story. Wouldn't you?"

Whandall had learned caution. He only nodded, *Go on.*

"I want to meet him, but I hadn't decided who to send. Anyone else, he might not pay attention. If I send you, he'll try to explain what went wrong. Bring him here, right?"

"Lord, I am your messenger and no more. He comes or he doesn't. Where would I find him?"

"Nobody knows." Pelzed smiled; the tea was making him mellow. "Not in the Lordshills, I think."

Tumbanton thought Pelzed owed him. Pelzed might be tired of hearing it.

Tumbanton had heard Pelzed's prohibitions but might think himself an exception.

Tumbanton and his son had explored Dark Man's Cup. It gave them a proprietary interest. . . .

Whandall couldn't ask around Pelzed. He couldn't ask in Dark Man's Cup: stray Lordkin dared not be seen there. But Pelzed had set two Lordkin families, Corles and Trazalac, to guard the Cup. When Stant Corles came to the Long Mile Market to shop, Whandall was there with a cold baked potato.

Stant only knew that four Lordkin had tried to gather from the kinless in the Corles family's charge. They'd moved into the house under cover of night and held the family as terrorized prisoners. When it was over, the kinless were freed and three Lordkin had been given to the Lords. No telling what would happen to them. But the fourth, the older man with all the scars . . .

"We strung him up and played with him. He lasted two days. Not my idea. Long as he could talk at all, he kept trying to tell us he was friends with Lord Pelzed. Old man Trazalac, he thought that was *way* too funny. He never said why, and you know, I'm not inclined to ask twice."

Tras Preetror was in the village near the harbor. That was already too close to the Lordshills for Whandall.

Peacegiven Square was neutral territory and was the closest place to the hills and hemp fields separating the "benighted area"—most of Tep's Town—from Lord's Town, the harbor, and Lordshills. The Lords had changed the way things were done. Before the carnival, carts and guards came to local parks once each month. This year they gave out more, but the women had to go farther to get it.

All the women had to travel to Peacegiven Square each eight weeks. Thence the Lordsmen guards and kinless wagoneers brought baskets of grain and jars of oil. Sometimes there were fruits, and twice a year there might be cheese. The kinless clerks were protected by big Lordsmen with helmets and spears.

There were things the women had to say. "I am a widow." "I have no home." "My children are hungry!" "No man protects me."

Any men must hang back at the edges of the square. The clerks would give only to single mothers and to women too old to have children. Many a woman must borrow a child.

The Lordsmen and their kinless clerks passed out the goods and the women carried them out of the square. Then the fights started.

Men gathered from unprotected women. All the Placehold men would make a circle around Mother and Mother's Mother and the aunts and sisters and cousins. Placehold had a cart pulled by the younger boys. Some goods went into the cart, but not all, because another band might gather the cart.

Placehold was large enough, with enough women, that it was better to protect what they had than to try to gather more. They'd learned that the first Mother's Day after the carnival. Others were learning too.

They had finished packing everything in carts or hanging it on poles for the women to carry when Whandall saw Tras Preetror.

He told Resalet, "Pelzed wants me to talk to him."

Resalet eyed the crowd, then nodded. "We can spare you this time. It's well to keep peace with Pelzed. Come home when you can."

Tras looked older, thinner, more wiry. The sight of Tras made Whandall's bones ache with memories. "They told me they'd fed you to the crabs," he said.

"They told me they'd done that with you," Tras said.

Peacegiven Square was clearing fast, with households and families and bands moving rapidly away, trying to get home safely before someone gathered everything from them. Tras selected an outdoor table at the street corner and ordered honey tea for both of them. He inspected Whandall as they sat.

"Clearly they didn't. You've grown. Got your knife too."

"I thought I was crippled for life," Whandall said. "Tras, you said you could persuade them, but you can't persuade people who don't listen! What did they do to you?"

"Sold me as a deckhand," Tras said. "I was two years working off the price they got for me." He looked down at his callused hands. "Sea life is hard, but I'm in better shape than I've ever been. Got some good stories too."

"Lord Pelzed wants to hear them. He says you owe him a roof."

Tras Preetror laughed like a maniac.

Whandall found that irritating. He asked, "Been back to the Lordshills?"

The laugh caught in his throat. "You were right, of course. But they don't care what I do now. I saw that Peacevoice Waterman at the docks when my ship came in. He was surprised I was a passenger and not crew, but all he did was warn me to stay away from Lordshills. I didn't need that warning this time." Tras looked up at the olive tree sheltering them. "But, you know, maybe there's a way . . ."

"Not with me, Tras," Whandall said.

"Next Burning?" Tras asked. "Get your friends, relatives, everyone you know, and take Yangin-Atep to the Lords. That'll teach them—"

"Teach somebody, maybe," Whandall said. "But it won't be me." For a moment Whandall thought of life without the Lords. It would be vastly different. Better? He couldn't know.

The tea was pleasant, different from the hemp tea that Pelzed served. Tras must have seen that Whandall liked it, because he ordered more. He sipped carefully. "Touch of hemp and sage," he pronounced. "The bees must go to the hemp fields."

Whandall looked puzzled.

Tras asked, "Don't you know where honey comes from?"

Whandall shook his head.

"I guess loggers don't have honey," Tras mused. "Bees make honey. Then beekeepers collect it."

Worlds opened when Tras spoke. Beekeepers would be kinless, wouldn't they? Where did they keep the honey they had gathered? Did the bees protect them? Whandall asked, and Tras Preetror knew. . . .

"Other places, a beekeeper negotiates with the queen. He agrees to guard the hive, or maybe he grows them a garden. They like gold. Here the queen's magic won't protect the hive from animals and gatherers. I guess you can just take the honey, but so can anyone else. I'd guess some kinless has to guard the hives, drive off bears, hide the location from Lordkin. . . . Only . . . I heard something. What was it?"

Whandall was thirsty for knowledge. He had not guessed how much he missed Tras Preetror. He watched Tras wrestle with his memory. . . .

"D-daggers. The Tep's Town gatherer bees have started growing poisoned daggers like little teeny black-and-yellow Lordkin," Tras said gleefully. "Right. Your turn."

Whandall had missed that too. He told how he had been returned to the Placehold and tended in the Placehold nursery. How he had moved into the tiny room upstairs. "Lenorba's room. They finally got her, thirteen years late."

"Who?"

"I heard the tale when I was a little boy. You've seen *Jispomnos* played, Tras. You know that what a man does with his woman is nobody's business but theirs—"

"Even murder."

"Right. A woman who kills her man doesn't see much hassle either. Maybe he's slapped her around and everyone knows it, everyone sees the bruises. But it wasn't like that with Lenorba and Johon.

"Johon of Flower Market moved in with her because she was a little crazy, 'specially for sex. Then when he got tired of that, she didn't. She was with a lot of men. One of 'em beat Johon up. Johon went home and beat up Lenorba. Then they talked, and both said they were sorry, and they went to bed. She wore him out. He went to sleep beside her and she killed him in his sleep. Then she ran home to the Placehold.

"She really seemed to think that all she needed was a bruise to show. It's not like that. Flower Market let it be known that if they found Lenorba outside the walls they'd kill her. So she never left again.

"Wanshig told me the rest. There weren't enough women in the Placehold to get us what we needed on Mother's Day, unless they took Lenorba. They gave her a baby to hold . . . gave her my little brother Trig. The men escorted the women to Peacegiven Square, but they had to stop at the border, and all the women went on. Afterward they found Trig sitting on the dais, right on stage, sucking on a plum. They never found Lenorba."

The square was nearly deserted now.

Wanshig came across the square to stand beside Whandall. He eyed Tras Preetror suspiciously. "We got the cart home safe," Wanshig said. "So I came back to look out for you. Last time you went with him, you were a year healing. More," he added, looking at the bright red circle of inflammation by Whandall's left eye.

Tras looked pained. "They let him come home," he said. "I was two years buying my way off that ship!"

Wanshig sat without being invited. "You were on a ship?"

"Yes."

"Where did you go? Condigeo?"

Tras laughed. "The long bloody way! When we got back to Condigeo I bought my way free. But first we went north."

"Where?" Wanshig asked.

"Lordship Bay, first. They call it that because your Lords have kin there, or say they do. Then Woodworker Bay, then around the cape to Sugar Rock. North of that is Great Hawk Bay. One day I may go back there. Best fish restaurant anywhere, run by a burly merman called the Lion. Then we went south, but our wizard wasn't good enough; a storm drove us past Condigeo to Black Warrior Bay."

Whandall was surprised to see that Wanshig was listening in fascination. "I've never even seen the harbor up close," Wanshig said. "So you went to sea, and Whandall got his arm broken. I think you owe my brother."

"Pelzed says I owe him a roof."

"Pelzed knows you'll never pay," Wanshig said. "This is different. You owe Whandall."

Tras shrugged. "It may be, but how do I pay? It took nearly everything I had to buy myself away from the captain!"

"Why did you come here?" Whandall asked.

"Stories. It's a risk. If I stay away too long, I'll forget the Condigeano speech. You know how languages change. There'll be slang I don't know. What kind of teller would I be then? So I stayed in Condigeo long enough to learn, but I had to come back. It's time for a Burning, and I can't miss the next one. How long has it been, six years? Do you feel the Burning near?"

Wanshig said, "The next teller who asks that question dies."

Whandall asked, "Why is it so important?"

They were mixing Condigeano and common speech. Whandall was still the only Lordkin who could do that. Wanshig wasn't able to follow much of what they were saying. Tras said, "The fewer tellers watch the Burning, the better a story it makes. When the others go home, that's when it pays me to be here. But I wish your Yangin-Atep would stir himself."

"Alferth and Tarnisos started the last Burning," Whandall told him. "Shall I show them to you?"

"Man, those guys are weird," Wanshig said. He shifted to an accent used mostly inside Placehold and spoke too rapidly for Tras to understand. "And you don't know where they are."

"I can find them," Whandall said.

"Sure." He looked at Tras, who was trying to understand what they were saying. "You're really not mad at him, are you?"

Whandall shook his head. "Not anymore."

"Well, they're over in Flower Market Square."

"How do you know that?"

"It's where they hang out now. There's a truce between Flower Market and Serpent's Walk." Wanshig changed to common speech. "You want to talk to the Lordkin who started the last Burning, give my brother five shells. You can afford that. Some other time we'll talk about more."

Alferth was a surly, burly man near thirty. There was a distorted look to his nose and ears. Whandall wasn't old enough to work out what had him so angry all the time, but he could imagine what Alferth's meaty hand would feel like, swung with that much weight behind it. He had no urge to talk to Alferth himself. But he stayed close after pointing Alferth out to Tras Preetror.

Tras sat down at Alferth's table at the end of a meal, set a flask between them, and asked, "What was it like to be possessed by Yangin-Atep?"

Alferth expanded under the looker's interest. "I felt an anger too big to hold back. Tarnisos screamed like a wyvern and charged into old Weaver's place, and I charged after him. We kicked him and his wife—I never saw his kids—we took everything we could, and then Tarnisos set the place afire. By then there were too many of us to count. I had an armful of skirts. For half a year I had a skirt for every woman who—"

"Why Weaver?"

"I think the old kinless refused Tarnisos credit once."

Tras asked, "Why would *Yangin-Atep* start with Weaver?"

Alferth's laughter was a bellow, a roar. Whandall left with a gaping sense of loss, a pain in the pit of his belly.

CHAPTER
17

When Whandall was an infant, Morth of Atlantis had brought water to the Lords. He must have been paid well. Now he kept a shop in what the Lords called the benighted section, far from the docks and the Lordshills.

It was not right to be stalking the man who had killed Pothefit during a gathering. *Never remember a killing after the Burning.* But Morth was a knot of enigmas. . . .

Why would a wizard of power live in the benighted areas?

Why would a Lordkin of fourteen years' age visit a magic shop? Whandall had better have an answer ready for *that.*

He blocked the path of a dumpy woman in Straight Street. The kinless looked at him differently now he was near grown—no longer cute, not yet menacing while his knife was hidden—but still she fished in her purse and gave him money. Probably not enough. It didn't have to be.

He watched until the shop was empty of customers before he went in.

Morth of Atlantis was younger than he remembered from that night in Lordshills. Against all reason, Whandall had somehow expected that. It didn't even startle him that sparse hair white as salt was now sandy red. But he was still an old man of dubious humanity, tall and straight, with dry brown skin and a flat belly and an open, innocent face with a million wrinkles. A little silly, a little scary.

Whandall asked, "Can you cure pimples?"

The magician peered close. One quick straight thrust could have cut his throat, but what spells protected him? "You've got worse than pimples." He touched the inflammation by Whandall's eye. His hands were surprising: fingers widest at the tips! "That's ringworm. It'll never go away by itself. Thirty shells."

Whandall cursed mildly and showed the five the woman had given him. "Maybe later."

"As you wish."

A kinless would have bargained. Lordkin didn't, and maybe magicians didn't. Whandall asked, "You're from Atlantis?"

The man's face closed down.

"I'm Seshmarl of Serpent's Walk." Whandall knew better than to give his true name to a magician. "Savant, our younger street-brothers wonder about you. If you don't want to be asked over and over how you escaped Atlantis, tell it only once. I'm a good teller. I'll tell them."

"Are you?" Morth smiled at him. How could an old man have so many teeth? "Tell me a story."

Whandall hadn't expected this, but without a stammer he said, "Yangin-Atep was the god who brought the knowledge of fire to the world. But Zoosh beat him in a knife fight, so men began to serve Zoosh instead of tending fires for Yangin-Atep. Lifetimes later, only the Lordkin still serve Yangin-Atep. When we came south from the ice, Yangin-Atep traveled with us. Have you heard the tale?"

"Not from your view."

"We weren't finding enough wood until the Lords showed us the way to the forest. There we hunted during the day and built big fires at night. In the forest Yangin-Atep grew strong. We cut and burned our way through, and that was how we found Tep's Town. The kinless called it something else, of course."

"Valley of Smokes," the magician said.

Whandall was taken aback. *"Kinless* called it that?"

"Have you seen how red the sunsets are here? Or how hard it is to breathe after the Burning? Something about the shape of the land or the pattern of winds keeps fog and smoke from blowing away. It isn't your fire god. Something older. A kinless god, maybe."

During the Burning and after, Mother's Mother's breath rasped as if she were dying. Whandall nodded.

"But the harbor is Good Hand, for the look of curled fingers." Morth saw Whandall's unspoken *Huh?* and added, "You have to see it from the air."

Oh, right, from the air. The magician had him totally off balance. *Story,* he was in the middle of a story—

"The kinless couldn't fight us, because Yangin-Atep was strong again. So the kinless came to serve us. They still wear the noose, as we still hold their lives." Just as Mother's Mother had told the tale to her grandchildren, with no mention of alliance with the Lords.

"I never would have taken that for a noose," Morth said. "A strip of colored cloth around the neck? Hangs down the chest?"

"That's it."

"I've walked along the woods many times. Where is this wide path your folk burned their way through?"

"North from here, but it's been lifetimes . . . six lifetimes, anyway. Maybe the trees grew back?"

The magician nodded. "That's Lordkin and kinless. What of the Lords?"

"We met them before we found the forest. They showed us how to gather wood, taught us about Yangin-Atep and Zoosh—"

"Why would they know about Yangin-Atep and Zoosh?"

"I don't know. The Lords have not always been with us, but they were with us when we took this land. They spoke to the kinless. They keep the kinless working."

"But you are Lordkin. Are you kin to the Lords?"

Whandall shook his head. "I've asked that. No one says different, but no one says so either."

The magician smiled thinly. "I see. So now you take what you want from the kinless, and the Lords gather from you."

"No, the Lords gather from the kinless, seldom from us. They have their own lands, and the harbor. And . . . ?"

The magician nodded. "All right. You know the story of Atlantis?"

"The land that sank. A long way from here."

"Right on both. A very large land mass a very long way from here, and it sank because the swordsmen came."

Whandall just looked at him.

"I was wizard to the fishing folk, human and mer. I was blessing a new ship at the docks. Attic warships came into sight, east of us. Hundreds. The captain decided I could finish my spells while we sailed for safety. I could have stayed and fought alongside the priests, but . . . it was too late."

"Did you know Atlantis was going to sink?"

"Yes and no. Something was coming sometime; everyone knew that. A thousand years ago, priests of Atlantis were already making spells to keep the land quiet. The quakes were long postponed. We didn't know they would come that *day*. The Attic soldiers must have reached the priests during the Lifting of Stone ceremony.

"After sunset we saw waves like black mountains marching toward us. Our ship floated above the water, but the waves below and the wind they took with them tossed our ship like a child's toy."

"And you brought water to Tep's Town?"

"Wh—? Yes. Yes, that was me. It's a good story. I'll tell you another time."

Nobody but Tras Preetror did that: traded information for information.

Whandall smiled. *A mountain of ice had come from the end of the Earth at Morth's bidding, scouring across lands belonging to the Lords.* Whandall would know if Morth told the story right, and Morth had no way to know that Whandall knew.

A long city block away, Tras Preetror stepped out of a shadow to intercept him. He wanted to talk about Morth of Atlantis. Did Lordkin deal much with magicians? with barbarians? with magic, other than their own peculiar fire magic? What was Whandall doing in Morth's shop, anyway?

What was Tras doing waiting for him here? Whandall didn't ask that. He said, "Morth is funny. He trades what he knows for what you know, like kinless trade shells for goods. Tras, what's it like to sail on a trader?"

Tras offered strips of jerked meat. "I expect all magicians do that. Information is what they sell, in a way. What did you trade with him?"

Whandall ate. "Yes, Tras, but what's it like to sail on a trader?"

"I prefer not to be reminded of my experience . . ."

Whandall waved and turned away.

"All right." Tras Preetror looked at him hard. "It's no fun as a deckhand. It's different as a passenger, as a teller. Tellers do a lot of traveling. We get over being seasick quick, or we quit, or travel on land instead."

"What's seasick?"

How to survive seasickness, and how to survive a storm, and what you ate at sea—it was different for passengers and crew—and what you'd better eat on land to get healthy again. Weather magic and how it could kill you. Tras was skilled at telling. "You never know how strong the magic is when you're on the ocean. The manna—you understand manna?"

Whandall shook his head. He'd heard that word. Where? On Shanda's balcony!

"Boy, you're going to owe me. Manna is the power behind magic. Manna can be used up. The man who learned *that* ranks with the woman who learned what makes babies. At sea there are currents, and manna moves with those. A spell to summon wind might do nothing at all, or raise a tempest to tear your ship apart. There are water elementals and merfolk."

"Does Morth know about this?"

"Have you ever seen an *old* Atlantis ship?" Whandall shook his head, and Tras said, "The bottom has windows and hatches. It floats above the water."

"Above the water. Above land too?"

"The most powerful did. No longer, I think. And the ships they built in this last hundred years, before Atlantis sank, they're ship shaped. If some ocean current swirls away the manna, down comes the ship, *splash,* and then you don't want windows breaking below the water.

"*Sure,* Morth knows about manna. Likely he thinks it's his most secret secret. So, Whandall, are you thinking of taking up sailing?"

"Tras, we never see the docks. The Water Devils don't want anyone else there."

"That's all that's stopping you?"

Whandall had seen ships, but only from the top of Wheezing Hill. He'd be guessing. Well . . . "I can't see why a ship's captain would let a Lordkin on. Wouldn't it be dangerous? What if a sail disappeared, or that tube they look through, or that big board at the back—"

Tras was laughing. "Rudder. Damn right it would. Whandall, you couldn't buy or beg your way aboard a boat, and kinless can't either, because most barbarians can't tell kinless from Lordkin. You'll never learn enough to *steal* a ship, and the dockside Lordkin won't help you do that because they'd lose the trade, such as it is."

"Do you think I could become a teller?"

Again Whandall was subjected to intense scrutiny. "Whandall, I think you could. You've got the knack already, trading information with me like a kinless sweets merchant. But anyplace these boats go, they know about Lordkin, and you have the look. You'd never be welcome—anywhere."

Whandall nodded, trying to swallow his disappointment. He said, "Morth was blessing a new ship at the Atlantis docks when . . ."

CHAPTER
18

On a later day Whandall returned to Morth of Atlantis.
He lurked a bit before he went in. Tras Preetror seemed to
be following him around, and he didn't like that. How could
anyone lurk, hide, spy, gather, with a *teller* hovering at his elbow? But
Tras wasn't about, and Whandall—*Seshmarl* went in and bought an
acne cure for fourteen (not thirty) shells. It was an evil-smelling cream
altered by gestures. It hurt when he rubbed it in, but three days later
the ring-shaped inflammation was fading from his eye, and his pimples
were smaller too. In a week his skin was clear except for the ringworm,
and that was smaller. Morth gave value for money.

He came again and asked about love potions. Morth wouldn't sell
those. He considered it wrong to tamper with another's mind.
Whandall nodded and pretended to find that sensible, and wondered
who the man thought he was befooling.

"I could have used a love potion a time or two," the wizard said.
"Can you guess how lonely it's been for the last Atlantis wizard in a
town of no magic?"

"You're talking to a Lordkin. That's lonely."

"Yes. Come any time, Seshmarl, even if you can't afford to buy.
Wait now, I can do tattoos," Morth said suddenly. "You're Serpent's
Walk? Would you like a serpent tattoo?" He waved at an elaborate
golden-feathered serpent, somewhat faded, displayed on one wall.

"Beautiful." He'd never find money for that! "I have a tattoo,"

Whandall said, and gave Morth a glimpse of the tiny serpent in the web of his thumb. "I haven't asked for another yet."

Morth looked down at Whandall's hand. His brows furrowed . . . but he only looked up after a moment and leaned close into Whandall's face. "A tattoo would be painful over ringworm and look odd too. But I see my cure is working."

"Yes." Whandall pointed at the feathered serpent and asked anyway. "How much for that? Where the ringworm was?"

Morth laughed. "I'd ask enough to put a new room on my house, normally. Here . . . where would I find a client? Seshmarl—no, wait." Morth took Whandall's right hand, the knife hand, in both his hands. Bad manners. He spread the fingers wide. Morth wasn't just staring at Whandall's hand now; he was pulling it toward the oil lamp above them. Astonished, Whandall let him do that.

Light fell on his hand. Morth had an open face, not used to hiding things, but now Whandall couldn't tell what he was thinking. He said, "You're going to leave Tep's Town."

"Why would I want to do that?"

"Can't tell. Maybe you *don't* want to. Will you take a word from me?" Morth was still studying . . . *reading* Whandall's hand. "Never go near rivers or the ocean. If you depart by land, it's likely your own idea. But you might visit the docks and travel the rest of the world as an oarsman with a bump on his head or be carried in the bellies of a school of fish."

Whandall had to clear his throat to speak. "We can't go to the docks anyway. Water Devils don't like people from outside. Morth, do you know your future?"

"No."

"What can I give you to put that tattoo on my face?"

". . . Yes. Seshmarl, I have some errands for you. And one day, when you are fully healed and your, um, bandlord has given permission, come to me. The tattoo will be my gift."

There were days he came with no excuse but the whim to talk. He would watch Morth and his customers discuss their needs. Then Morth would hand them something from under the counter; or step to a shelf and mumble and wave, or only stand watching for several seconds before snatching up some box or tiny flask, as if avoiding invisible teeth, and give it to the customer with elaborate instructions.

One could ask.

Medicines for pain? Yes, Morth had those (but his hands stayed still and his eyes didn't move from Seshmarl's). For wheezing, shortness of breath? Morth sold a lot of that, especially after the Burning. He bought herbs from loggers.

Philosopher's stone? Unicorn's horn? Boy, you've got to be joking! Magical cold torch? Spell of glamour? Invisibility? Levitation? Those didn't work here either. "I had a cook pot once that would cook without fire. Never knew what to do with it. Didn't use it because I would wear it out. I couldn't sell it because it wouldn't work very long. Finally it was stolen, not that it will have done the thieves any good. Magic is weak in the Valley of Smokes."

"Well, it would still be a pot," Seshmarl said.

"True."

"Is it that way everywhere?"

"Less so some places." Morth's eyes went dreamy.

"Why here?"

Morth shrugged. "Yangin-Atep. Magic is the life of a god. It's like you can't keep honey where there are ants. Atlantis had no god."

"Can you do prophecy?"

"Seshmarl, to know the future is to change it, so that time wriggles like a many-headed snake. What you see is false because you've seen it. Even if there were magic enough, how could I read the lines in my own hand? We student wizards couldn't even read each other's lines; our fates were bound up together, tangled." Morth shrugged as if great weight sat on his shoulders. "I read part of your fate because you might leave. See, time spreads ahead of us like this . . ." He reached above his head. "This fan. Your most likely future leads to places where magic still holds power. Traces of manna flow back through time to weave meaning into the lines on your hand."

"I'm going to leave?"

Morth took his hand again and spread it in the lamp glow. "Do you see? It's the pattern the lines make with the ambient magic, anywhere in the world but here. Yes, you still have the chance to leave, and you should still stay clear of water, except for bathing."

Bathing? Whandall saw only his hand. He asked, "Morth, why would a magician live where there's no magic?"

Morth smiled. "Seshmarl, that's not something I'd tell anyone."

Morth had said that Whandall would leave Tep's Town. In his present state that seemed desirable. Had he healed enough? Did he know enough?

He tried to beg money from Resalet. "Just suppose, now, suppose Morth sells me a potion of easy breathing for Mother's Mother. I might see where he takes it from. If it's where the pimple salve came from, then that's the medicines, and if he's lying about unicorn's horn, which is supposed to be *priceless*—"

"Stay out of that magician's shop." Resalet's finger stabbed Whandall's chest. "You don't know what he can do. Read minds? Make you die in a month? He's the man who killed your father."

"I know that."

"But does *he?* Stay away from Morth of Atlantis!"

If he couldn't *buy* from Morth, was there anything Morth might want from Seshmarl?

He asked. Morth said, "I want to know more about the forest."

"You buy your herbs from loggers. Ask them."

"That is a very strange situation," Morth said. "Lords tell the loggers where they can cut down trees. I mean, *exactly* where and which. They don't log themselves—"

Whandall suggested, "Maybe they're hiding something in the forest."

"Yes, and maybe they just like telling people how to live their lives!" Morth took dried leaves from a jar. "Here, smell this. Do you know it? Does it grow there?"

"Wait . . . yes. Sage. Grows where the trees open out. It doesn't kill, and it smells great when you walk through it. Hey, they use this for cooking at Samorty's house!"

"Yes, it's good for that and other things. What about this one?"

Whandall took the sheet of pale bark—rubbed it, sniffed it, held it to daylight in the doorway. "I don't think so."

Morth smiled. "Willow bark. I didn't think it grew around here. What about this?"

Long leaves. "Yes. Foxglove," Whandall said.

"It can be valuable. Do you know of poppies?" He showed a faded flower.

"I know where there are whole fields of them," Whandall said. "The loggers say they are dangerous." He didn't add that he had been to the poppy fields and nothing happened.

They whiled away an afternoon. Morth was dubious: he didn't want Whandall—*Seshmarl*—picking plants that were *not quite* what he wanted. That was dangerous. "Bring me the whole plant or a whole branch when you can, so I'll know what I have."

Morth sent him to where there were no loggers. Whandall didn't want to meet loggers anyway: he was no child, and he'd be on their turf. Kinless or not, they had axes and severs. He sought Morth's plants in the old growth and found them rarely.

On his second foray he approached the Lordshills from the forest side.

There was the blank wall back of Lord Samorty's house. The tree had been cut back, and there were marks on the top of the wall where it had been repaired. Whandall watched the hill for a time. No guards . . . and if they chased him into the wood he would outrun them or lead them into lordkiss. He half ran, half crawled within range of the wall, then hurled what he was carrying. He was in shadow when he heard the splash. He didn't wait for more.

But a pine cone had splashed into the laundry pond, and Shanda would know of it. She would know he was alive.

CHAPTER
19

Morth's plants were rare, but they both understood that Morth sought knowledge too. He was using Whandall's explorations to map the forest.

Morth wasn't stingy with his rewards. Whandall collected medicines to ease pain and reduce a swelling and bring sleep. Foxglove leaves made a powder that would send a man into jittery mania just before a fight. Poppies yielded a brown gum that gave good dreams. All of these lost their power if not used, and often Whandall had more than Morth and Placehold combined would need.

He began trading them for favors on the street.

Morth always told how to use the powdered leaves. Sniff carefully. Never more than once a week, and don't ever heat them first. Whandall was careful to do the same.

Then one day he was summoned to Pelzed.

Pelzed was angry. "Did you give Duddigract some of your foxglove?" he demanded.

Duddigract was one of Pelzed's advisors, a big man with a bad attitude, always muttering about what he'd like to do to the Lords. He was usually behind Pelzed. Today he wasn't anywhere to be seen.

"No, Lord. We don't get along."

"He's dead," Pelzed said. "Some Maze Runners raiders came into the Walk. I sent Duddigract to deal with them." He turned to one of the men behind him. "Renwilds, tell it again."

"Yes, Lord. Duddigract saw the Maze Runners. Five of them. There were only six of us, but Duddigract looked mean. The Maze Runners looked scared, and I was sure they'd run if we gave them a chance. We could chase them out. They'd run, they'd be gone with no blood shed, and they'd drop anything they gathered. I started to say that to Duddigract, and I saw he had a leaf full of white stuff. He took a big sniff of that, then he stuffed a wad of brown gum in his mouth and chewed, then he took another big sniff from the leaf. We tried to say something but he just grinned, said it would be a shame to waste it, now he was ready to fight."

Pelzed looked to Whandall. "You know what he's talking about," Pelzed said.

"Yes, Lord. I always tell people how dangerous the white foxglove powder is. The brown gum is safe enough, that just puts you to sleep, but the white is dangerous."

"What does the white do?" Pelzed demanded.

"Lord, I don't know. I just know that's what Morth of Atlantis tells his customers. He never sells them more than a pinch or two of white, and he makes them sniff it there in the shop. He won't sell them any more until it's been a week or more. Brown he'll sell any time, but not white."

"Say more, Renwilds," Pelzed ordered.

"I'd say that magician knows what he's talking about," Renwilds said. "Duddigract sniffed that stuff and got a big grin, and all of a sudden he was a wild man. He took out his knife and before any of us could say anything he was all over the Maze Runners. They were ready to talk, you know, brag a little before they ran, and we were all set to brag back, and there's Duddigract with his knife out. He cut down two with no warning; they didn't even get to draw. By then the others had their knives out and one of them cut Duddigract, and Lord, it was like he didn't even feel it. Duddigract yelled, but it wasn't like he was hurt, it was like the Burning had come. We were sure Yangin-Atep had him, but Duddigract didn't want to burn anything. He just wanted to kill! He killed another Maze Runner, and the others dropped everything and ran. They were really scared, but so were we, Lord. When the Maze Runners ran, Duddigract looked at us like he didn't know us!"

Pelzed nodded grimly. "Go on."

Renwilds shrugged. "It was that powder, Lord. It summons invisible monsters."

"Uh huh. Why didn't you chase the Maze Runners?"

"Too fast, Lord, and we'd have had to get around Duddigract! So we were trying to figure what to do when Duddigract screamed again and fell down, babbling about how monsters were after him, and he curled up like he was going to sleep, only he never woke up."

"Where did he get it?" Pelzed demanded.

"He wouldn't tell us, Lord. Said he'd gathered it, but he wouldn't say where."

Pelzed turned to Whandall. "Well?"

Whandall told what he knew. "Lord, about a week ago some Black Lotus warriors caught me near the east border. There were too many to fight, so I let them gather a bag of powders I was taking to Morth. Maybe there was enough in there to do that to Duddigract. Or maybe they mixed the powders. But I don't know how they got from Black Lotus to Duddigract!"

"You didn't tell me they gathered anything, Whandall. Just that they'd chased you."

"I was embarrassed, Lord."

Pelzed nodded thoughtfully. "I sent Duddigract to look into it," he said. "He must have caught up with the Lotus warriors. And he never told me! Never told me!" Pelzed grew visibly angry, but not with Whandall. "It's his own fault, then," Pelzed said. "But Whandall, be careful with those powders."

"I will, Lord."

But there were always more powders, and friends were always ready to accept them. There was so much he could buy with foxglove.

But some liked the stuff too much.

One day three followed him home. Resalet came out with two uncles and chased them away.

That evening Whandall was summoned to Resalet's big northeast room on the second floor. Resalet eyed him critically. "Dargramnet says you're smart," Resalet said. "Or used to say it."

Whandall nodded. It had been a year since Mother's Mother had recognized Whandall when she saw him. Now she sat by the window and talked of old days and old times to anyone who would listen. The stories were interesting, but she told the same ones over and over.

"So if you're smart, why are you acting like a fool?"

Whandall thought for a moment, then took a handful of shells from his pouch and laid them on Resalet's table.

"Yes, bigger fools than you will pay," Resalet said. "And if they think you keep that stuff here? They'll come to take it. We'll have to fight. We'll lose people; there'll be blood money. The Lords may get involved. We can't fight Lordsmen!"

"Lords don't care about hemp," Whandall said. "They keep hemp gum! In ebony boxes."

"Don't show off for me, boy," Resalet said. "I know you've been to Lordshills, and look what it got you! You came in beat up and useless, a lot more trouble than you were worth. Hadn't been that Dargramnet likes you, we'd have thrown you out to the coyotes. I don't know what the Lords do at home, but down here hemp trouble gets you Lordsmen. Enough Lordsmen and they tear your house down. This is Placehold! We've had Placehold longer than I've been alive, and we're not going to lose it because of you."

Whandall tried to change the subject. "The Bull Pizzles sell hemp. Pelzed serves hemp tea."

"Pelzed is damn careful with his tea," Resalet said. "And since when did Serpent's Walk learn from Bull Pizzle?" He shook his fists violently. "And I don't care if Serpent's Walk sells hemp; we're Placehold. Whandall, if you want to trade powders, do it somewhere else. Get your own house. Placehold doesn't want the trouble. Do you understand me?"

"Pelzed offered me a house in Dark Man's Cup," Whandall said. "Should I take it?"

"If you like."

Whandall was startled to realize that Resalet meant it. Up to then it was just a boy talking to adults, but Resalet meant it. He really could be thrown out of Placehold.

He thought about living alone. It might be fun. But the other boys his age who moved out of their households to live alone were mostly dead.

Coscartin wasn't dead. Coscartin had half a dozen other young men living with him, and that many women, and some kind of arrangement with Pelzed. The stuff he dealt in was supposed to come from the Water Devils.

"I'd rather stay here."

"Then give up the powder," Resalet said. "Give it up right out loud. Give away all your stock. Make sure everyone knows you won't have more."

"But why?"

"Because I tell you—"

"Yes, I understood that," Whandall said. "I mean—what do I tell them?"

Resalet chuckled with the first sign of amusement since Whandall had come into his room. "Tell them you had a vision from Yangin-Atep."

"No one will believe that!"

"Then tell them anything you want, but you bring more of that stuff here, you're going out."

They told stories about Whandall's party for years. He brought out everything, white powders and yellow foxglove leaves and brown gum. He parceled it out with care. Wanshig found some hemp. Tras Preetror wrote two songs and told stories, but as the night went on his speech became an endless stream of babbling.

Shealos managed to finesse three times his share of the brown poppy gum. Whandall let him do it: he was a noisy whiner when thwarted. Shealos went to sleep in a corner, where the Forigaft brothers must have found him.

No one was seriously hurt.

There would never be another party like it. But it left ripples. . . .

Two young Lordkin ended up in the river, unhurt but stinking.

Three girls became pregnant.

Shealos didn't wake until sunset the next day, in the middle of an intersection, stripped naked and painted with the wrong band signs and a short written message.

A blank wall in the kinless house Whandall had taken over for the party bore more words, written inside a pattern made from ten local band signs . . . kind of pretty, really, but any band would take it as a killing insult.

More messages were found scrawled in bright red paint on the long wall around Dead Town on the day after Whandall's party. Dead Town was where folk were buried if no family claimed them. Nobody painted band signs in Dead Town: all factions were welcome there.

Pelzed was asked to summon the Forigaft brothers.

These four brothers had somehow learned to read. It made them arrogant. The brothers painted messages on any clean surface. You couldn't tell what they said, not even by asking one of them, because they would lie. The night of Whandall's party they must have gone crazy on the powders. Whandall remembered their antics, howling and gymnastics and . . . wait now, he'd *seen* them doing that to his wall, and he'd laughed like a loon. He didn't remember seeing them leave.

The brothers were scattered about Serpent's Walk and Peacegiven Square. They were easy to spot. They mumbled to themselves. They shouted foul and cryptic threats and accusations into the faces of passersby. Two brothers tried to write something on Renwilds's burly belly, using yellow paint and their fingers. Renwilds let them finish, then knocked them both senseless.

They were all crazy as loons. Pelzed fed them for two weeks, then somehow traded them to the Wolverines, who lived below Granite Knob, for a wagonload of oranges.

Whandall copied some of their marks off a wall and brought them to Morth.

" 'I was not Lordkin! Zincfinder tattooed my corpse!' " Morth read. " 'Search the sand at Sea Cliffs for the treasure I died for.' 'She hid my knife!' " He looked up. "Your Dead Town must have its share of murder victims. When your mad readers were spraying the graveyard, the ghosts wrote messages on their minds. Justice carries its own manna."

Sometimes Whandall regretted his decision. He could have been living in a household of sycophants and women, like Coscartin. . . .

Coscartin and all his household were killed by rivals unknown, half a year after Whandall's party.

CHAPTER
20

When Wanshig reached fifteen he began working with Alferth. Alferth was a tax taker, which gave him avenues into kinless commerce. One afternoon Wanshig pulled Whandall away from his friends, back to the courtyard of the Placehold house.

"Taste this," Wanshig said. "Just a sip."

It was a small clay flask. The fluid inside had a fire in it. Whandall almost choked. "What—"

"Wine."

"Oh. I know about wine."

That made Wanshig laugh. "Well, you're clever in spots, little brother, and you know how to keep your mouth shut. Can you think of a way to make the kinless bring this stuff in to sell?"

They shared the bottle unequally. "Outside Tep's Town there are taverns," Wanshig said.

"How do you know this?"

"Tellers," Wanshig said. "And do you remember Marila? She was a Water Devil, and she listened at home. Stories of other lands. And of the docks."

"And what are these taverns?" Whandall asked.

Wanshig smiled dreamily. "Gathering places. For men, or even men and women together, to drink wine, be together with friends, celebrate. There are wine shops everywhere but here. Why not Tep's Town?"

But wine was doing a slow burn inside Whandall. "Yangin-Atep's fire," he pronounced. "Magic?"

"Yeah."

Wine felt good. *Whee,* Whandall thought, and he felt words bubbling to his partly numb lips. *Resalet ran away,* he thought. *He left my father to die.* Things he didn't want to say to any Placeholder, ever. *Lordkin don't work for anyone.*

Shig said, "I don't work *for* Alferth. I work *with* him."

He'd said it out loud! Whandall slapped his hand across his mouth. He tried to say—

"No, little brother. You have to work *with.* Otherwise you're all alone," Wanshig said. "Sometimes it's hard to tell which is which. It runs the other way too. Some Lordkin work. Some kinless take things."

"—said what?"

"Kinless loses his work, what can he do? Got to have food. Blanket. Shoes. He gathers them. We'd kill him, sure—he doesn't have the *right*—but why would anyone catch him? Something's missing, nobody asks who gathered it. Never mind that, little brother. Why don't the kinless keep wine shops?"

"Wine *shops?* If it feels this good?" Whandall gestured widely; Wanshig ducked. "Someone wants wine, just smash in the door! If it's too strong, go for help. If the winetender tries . . . we beat on him, kill him, maybe. Kinless would be crazy to keep this stuff around."

"Taverns, then. Make them sell drinks one at a time."

Whandall, with wine buzzing in his ears and his blood, could feel what was wrong with *that.* Kinless and barbarians might drink wine and keep their self-control. In the Burning City men would drink; then unguarded words would bubble through their lips and they would fight. No tavern would survive.

Shig said, "The most we ever get *here,* someone pops up on a street corner with maybe eight of these little flasks. When they're gone, he's gone. He's not there long enough to be robbed."

"Where's he get it?"

"The flasker? Lords and kinless get some wine through the docks, from Torov and Condigeo. If the rest of us find out, we take it, of course, so they give some to the Water Devils. And there's another place."

They wobbled as they stood, and Wanshig led him north. Whandall's head cleared quickly. The wine was gone. There hadn't been much, just enough for two.

The houses north of Tep's Town ended at the forest. Wanshig led off northwestward. Whandall was sober now and full of questions, but Wanshig only smiled.

Here the forest withdrew from the city, leaving a delta of meadow, the Wedge, with a slow stream, the Deerpiss, meandering down its center. Whandall had known of the Wedge all his life, and only began to wonder as Wanshig led him up the stream. Why hadn't the meadow filled with houses?

Where the Wedge converged to a point, a two-story stone house straddled the stream like a blockage in a funnel. On either side the road would be wide enough for wagons, but gates blocked both sides.

Two men emerged from a second-story door. One started down the ladder.

Whandall had seen Lordsmen's armor and lumbermen's leathers. Both men wore what lumbermen would wear, like what the boy Whandall himself had worn. Both men were masked in what might have been lumbermen's leathers, but were not.

Wanshig ran at the rightward gate. Whandall followed at speed. Wanshig climbed the gate like a monkey, with Whandall right behind him. Lordkin didn't ask permission; they went where they would.

The two armored men scrambled to the ground and lifted weapons. They carried . . . not quite severs. Hafts ended in straight blades sharpened on both sides.

Whandall didn't hear what words Wanshig spoke, but the men stepped aside, glancing incuriously at Whandall as he dropped to the ground. They were climbing back up as Wanshig led off along the stream. The forest had closed in at the banks.

Now out of earshot, Whandall asked, "What was that place?"

"Guardhouse," Wanshig said. "After our fathers took Tep's Town, we made the kinless build that across our path. The path is gone, but the Toronexti are still here. They let anyone through, but they take part of what they're carrying. It's custom. These days they guard something else too."

"The path. I could tell Morth—" He bit it off, eons late. Was it the wine, this long after? "I have to *see* him, Shig. Don't worry, I won't do anything stupid."

Wanshig seemed unsurprised. "How did he kill Pothefit?"

"I haven't asked yet."

"*Don't* ask. But find out."

Where the stream bent to the right, Wanshig walked straight into the forest.

The tall straight spikes must be young redwoods. Mature redwoods had been felled here; huge stumps remained. Wanshig led them a careful crooked path around morningstar plants, nettles, spear grass, red-and-green clumps of touch-me. Whandall was ready to snatch him to safety, but his older brother *had* learned.

They'd traveled a couple of hundred paces before the trees opened out. Here were croplands, a wide expanse of vines planted in straight rows. Kinless men and women were at work. There were Lordkin about too.

Wanshig and Whandall watched from their bellies. Wanshig said, "The Lords get some of their wine here, but of course they need somebody to protect it. That's where Alferth comes in. He got the Toronexti to do it. He leaves them half."

"What kind of half?"

"He cheats a little. They cheat a little." Wanshig began creeping backward. "I wanted you to know. If you've got any ideas—"

"Do we really want more wine in Tep's Town?"

"We do if it's *ours.*"

But wine makes us kill, Whandall thought, *and mostly we kill each other. Lords drink wine without problems. Kinless can handle it.* We *teach kinless to control themselves. Barbarians learn or die. With us, though . . .*

He said, "What we were drinking, did it come from here?"

"Right," said Wanshig.

"What the lookers give us, is it—"

"Better. Smoother."

"It's not the best, I bet." Wanshig glared, and Whandall said, "Lookers know we don't know the difference, so they buy cheap. Some barbarian somewhere *knows* how to make better than we've got. We should find him and talk him into working for us."

Wanshig shrugged his eyebrows. *Talk?* Barbarians brought in wealth. The Lords would spit fire if a barbarian was kidnapped. Alferth wouldn't dare.

But better wine would be better for the city than more wine, Whandall thought.

CHAPTER 21

Resalet had told him to avoid the magician and give up all his plants and powders. Whandall hadn't seen Morth in just under a year. The boy Seshmarl had grown older. Had he come to look too dangerous?

Two kinless customers looked at him nervously. The magician flickered a smile at him, then finished serving them. When they had left, the magician said, "Seshmarl! Tell me a story!"

Information for information. "If you follow the Deerpiss north out of the city, you get to a meadow, then a guardhouse with masked and armored men. They'll take some of what you're carrying. What they're guarding is the old path where my people cut their way through the forest to the Valley of Smokes. But don't go there, right? Just look."

"You *have* been busy," Morth said.

Whandall smiled.

"Is the path still open?"

"I don't think so."

"What if I want to *leave* Tep's Town?"

"The docks—"

"I can't go near the sea. I tried going south once, but it's all marshes."

"I don't know anything about that. Nobody goes that way."

"Seshmarl, the forest—"

"Not through the forest. Been two hundred years. The woods grow back. There's poison plants and lordkiss and morningstars and hemp and foxglove." He didn't intend to speak of the vineyard.

"Curse! And a guardhouse too?"

"You face *them,* you'd better have a story. But don't you have some spell for finding paths?"

The magician didn't answer. He told a story instead. "The fire god lost many battles. Sydon drowned his worshippers in Atlantis. Zoosh used the lightning against him in Attica, and is said to hold him in torment. Wotan and the ice giants battled him in the north, and again they torment him still. In many places the Firebringer bears a great wound in his side. Here too, I think. Your people must have fled Zoosh's people. You Lordkin may well be the last worshippers of Yangin-Atep."

"Yangin-Atep gave us everything. Heat, cooking—"

"Burning cities?"

"We don't burn the whole city, Morth. Only tellers say that. At any Burning we lose . . . Resalet says three or four hands of buildings."

"It's still crazy."

Whandall said, "Even a wizard might want to avoid Yangin-Atep's anger."

Morth smiled indulgently. "Yangin-Atep is near myth. His life uses the magical strength that would give my spells force, but there's little of that to start with. In these days magic works poorly everywhere. Yangin-Atep does not stir. I would sense him."

"Can you predict the Burnings?" Tras Preetror would pay well for that information.

"Sometimes," Morth said mysteriously.

He couldn't. But he knew when Yangin-Atep would wake. He had to. "Why did you want to know about the forest?"

"I want to get out," Morth said.

I can't go near the sea, he'd said. Whandall took a wild guess. "Will the ice chase you?"

Morth swallowed a laugh; it looked like a hiccup. "What do you know of that?"

"You brought a mountain of ice once. I wondered how. But if ice would chase you, the Lords would pay well, so it's not ice. Waves? Saltwater?"

"You know a lot," Morth said, no longer amused. The wizard took Whandall's hand again, stared, and nodded. "You have destinies. Most have only one, but you have choices. One choice may lead to glory. Be ready. Now tell me about the path through the forest."

Whandall persisted. "Why do you want to leave? Is it the elemental?" He still didn't know what the word meant.

"Last month I hired a wagon to take me to the harbor. I'd heard nothing of a water sprite in many years. As I crossed the last hill, a single wave rose and came toward me. The sprite is still out there in the harbor."

"Does Yangin-Atep protect you, then?"

"In a manner of speaking, yes, Seshmarl. The fire god won't permit a water sprite here. I'd heard about the Burning City all my life, but I never wanted to live here. Few do. Seshmarl, I came to *hide!*"

"The lookers come."

"Oh yes, tellers have made this city famous. Fools used to visit every spring to see the Burning. I suppose the lookers bring money that helps pay the cost of rebuilding. To me it all seems quite crazy. But it does make your city safer."

Whandall swallowed his anger. A Lordkin should have guile . . . never remember a killing after the Burning. . . . "Yangin-Atep protects us most of the time. Fires *don't* burn indoors." *Not here.* "Are there other cities where fires *can't* start by accident?"

"Oh, magic can protect a building," Morth said, "and I know a spell to douse a fire that works even in Tep's Town."

"The Lords cook indoors," Whandall said. "And they lit torches in the big room after dark. Not just candles, torches."

Morth said nothing.

It had been dry in Tep's Town for two years. "You brought water once."

"A water elemental chased me, embodied in an iceberg from the southernmost end of the earth. It hunted me, to kill me. Seshmarl, when things move, they want to keep on moving," Morth said. "The bigger and heavier it is, the harder it is to stop. The iceberg was the biggest and heaviest thing that ever came here."

"What stopped it? Yangin-Atep!" Whandall realized suddenly. "You used Yangin-Atep to turn that curse to an advantage."

"Destinies," Morth muttered to himself. "Yes, Seshmarl. That's a lot of what magic is, understanding how things work and turning them to your advantage. I let it chase me until there was no manna to move the iceberg farther."

"But you can't do it again."

"The elemental won't do it again," Morth said. "It would have to go far away to find ice. It won't go that far from me." The magician looked out the window, but he wasn't seeing the street outside. "This tale is not one to be told, Seshmarl. It might reach the Lords."

And that was valuable information, Whandall thought, though he didn't know how to use it. "My teacher says I can have a tattoo now," he said diffidently. "My brother wanted to do it, but I said I knew an artist."

For a breath he wasn't sure Morth had heard. Then the magician said, "Wonderful!" and wheeled around. "The same? The winged serpent of Atlantis? Let me show you."

He took a box from a shelf and reached inside. He unwrapped a fine cloth and let it hang from his fingers. It was a scarf in gold and scarlet and blue. "Here, do you like it?"

"Oh, yes." The scarf was *new*. It was far finer than the faded painting he'd once seen on Morth's wall . . . which had disappeared sometime in the past year.

Whandall couldn't take his eyes off the serpent in flight. It sported a crest of feathers, and little feathered wings on either side of its neck, like no serpent he'd ever heard of. The colors blazed.

But it was *big*. It would cover his face and shoulder and half his arm! Whandall remembered getting his thumb tattooed. "If it won't . . . how much does it hurt?"

"Hurt? No. Here, sit." He settled Whandall cross-legged on a rug.

Morth spread the scarf over the box and moved Whandall's arm until the scarf was under his upper arm and shoulder. The lines and colors of the scarf lifted and crawled along his skin. Whandall's eyes tried to cross. He felt a stirring as if a snake were settling on his arm, squeezing, sliding up his shoulder, his neck, his face. There was no pain, no swelling, no blood.

He hid out for a night and a morning. "I stayed the night. I didn't want to face anyone. It just hurt too much," he told Resalet.

Resalet's eyes were popping. He stripped off his tunic in one angry maneuver and moved against Whandall, arm to arm, to compare his own faded blue snake, fifteen years old, to Whandall's four-color god-thing. He cursed. "It's wonderful! How can I get one?"

"I'll ask."

"Ask who? Is it Morth again?"

Whandall admitted it. Resalet said, "Tell me all about it."

Whandall thought it prudent to describe near-unbearable pain, as if a snake's fangs had sunk into him.

"I don't care if it hurts. It just floated off the scarf and crawled up your shoulder? Did he say anything? Gesture?"

"Picked it up, put it down. Shall I ask if I can bring a . . . mmm . . . an uncle? It might cost a lot."

"No, don't bother. Does he know who you are?"

"Seshmarl. Of Serpent's Walk. He had to know that much."

"You be careful with Morth of Atlantis, Whandall. No more powders! No more hemp!"

Whandall went back on another day and waited until the shop was empty before he entered. He'd gathered a wine flask, and he set it on the counter. They sipped it together.

Then Whandall asked, "Is this magical?"

Morth laughed. "No. It's not very good either, but there's not enough here to hurt us. Can you tell me any more about how a man might leave Tep's Town?"

Whandall shook his head. "But I know of a safe place. Most of the city is afraid of the Black Pit."

Morth was astonished. "How did you come to know that?"

"I've slept near the Black Pit. Nobody bothers you there, and the monsters can't touch you."

Morth nodded. "If there was manna about they'd be dangerous enough. The cats of Isis, the hounds of Hel, the birds of Wotan, some tremendous war beasts, they all died by thousands of thousands in a war of gods. Only a tiny fraction wound up in the tar. Gods themselves went myth in that last battle," he said.

"Morth, tell me again about the iceberg."

Morth looked thoughtful. "You know the story."

"Yes, but I don't understand it all. Magic doesn't work here, but you make it work."

"And should I tell you?" Morth said, half to himself. "Let me see your hand again." He studied Whandall's palm. Then the magician sipped wine, and settled himself to tell the story.

"The wells of Atlantis dried up ages ago. We were too many for the rivers to support, and nobody *likes* rain. For a thousand years the people of Atlantis drew their water from the end of the world. Atlantis magic has ruled water for as long as we can remember. We send— sent—water sprites south to fetch icebergs and bring them to be melted for our water. When . . ." Morth considered, then went on. "When I left Atlantis instead of staying to fight, an iceberg was in sight of the harbor. The priests commanded the water sprite to hunt me down and kill me. I crossed an ocean and a continent and I reached the coast with a mountain of ice chasing me.

"At Great Hawk Bay the mers at Lion's Attic told me about Tep's Town. I was almost here before my ship sank down in the desert.

"I *knew* the elemental could get this far. I could hope it couldn't get any farther, not in the fire god's domain. To the Lords I swore I could bring an iceberg to that dry lake they call the Reservoir now, in the Lordshills. Yangin-Atep had power there in those days. I told the Lords to pay me on delivery, and I hoped that Yangin-Atep had the power to stop the ice."

Whandall nodded, then sipped the last half-swallow of wine.

That amused Morth. "Don't you wonder how I knew they'd pay? Never occurred to you? Lordkin! Two or three Lords were *very* irritated. That cursed sprite took a mountain of ice across land they owned."

Whandall nodded. "Samorty's turf. Chanthor's."

Now Morth looked surprised. "You knew?"

"That much. How did you make them pay?"

"I led them to wonder what their houses would look like if another iceberg crossed Blawind Hills."

"What about the water thing? Melted?"

"No. The damned elemental is waiting offshore. I can't ever go near water. But I spent the Lords' money long ago, and I can't pull that stunt again."

"Are you afraid of the Burning?"

"Oh, no. I'll sense when Yangin-Atep rises. I can see that much. There will be one, maybe two small Burnings, then a big one," Morth said. "Then I'll get out. I never want to see *that* again."

Whandall wondered if Morth wasn't whistling through Dead Town. Not Seshmarl's problem. He said, "The Toronexti—the tax guards—will take almost everything you own."

"Perhaps they won't see it all," Morth said.

"Were you here last time?" *When my father died!*

"Yes." The alien face turned haggard. "I could have been killed. There was nothing, *nothing* to tell me that Yangin-Atep was awake, not even after I saw smoke and fire pluming up. I went home to keep my house from burning. That night I went back to the shop. Stupid. Thieves—*gatherers*—had already stripped it bare. I was looking around and planning how to rebuild when more gatherers came in and saw me."

His mouth was very dry. Whandall asked, "What happened?"

"I used a calming spell."

"What?"

Belligerent and guilty, Morth said, "It's simple magic, so simple it even works here. It takes the anger out of a man, and puts out fires too. I've used it before. It isn't as if I wanted to hurt them. I threw a calming spell at the big one when he came at me with that knife. He went down like a handful of sticks. The others screamed and ran away."

"Dead?"

"Dead and *cold!* I pulled him outside and left him. A barbarian pulling a dead man by the ankles and nobody paid any attention! Seshmarl, does Yangin-Atep really possess people?"

"I think so." Shouldn't a wizard know?

"That thug was all anger, all fire. Yangin-Atep must have had him, and when I sucked the anger out of him, I think his life came with it." Morth looked up. "The Burning. What did you see?"

"I was only seven."

"Did you feel Yangin-Atep? I've sometimes wondered what that's like."

"No. Maybe next time."

Four kinless came in then. Whandall sensed their unease and left.

And maybe Yangin-Atep heard Morth's insults, sluggishly, in his coma.

PART THREE

The Burnings

CHAPTER
22

For three years rain had been sparse. Even the trees with their deep roots showed the dryness. The reservoirs went dry. Some said that the fountains in the Lordshills were still running, others said they weren't, and no one really knew.

A few kinless purchased rain. Weather wizards were rarely successful, but some sold the names of their clients: kinless who had money to throw away. There were beatings and robberies, leaving less to be spent on weather wizards.

The Deerpiss became a trickle, then dried up. Wells went dry. The Lords sent out a decree that water must be used only for drinking and washing. The kinless agreed, and demanded even stricter rationing. Lordkin didn't listen to such stuff. They used water to cool themselves and their homes, until even drinking water was a trickle, and there would be none to douse fires. It was a dry season, without water, and *that* might have been what wakened the fire god, twelve days after Morth belittled him.

Whandall alone wasn't big enough to get water when bigger men were thirsty. That morning Wanshig and Whandall escorted the women and younger children across the central city to a working well. Resalet stayed in with a hangover. The other Placehold men were not to be found.

Elriss was new. She stayed at the periphery, helping to keep the older women in place and moving. Wanshig hovered close to her. He'd brought Elriss home twenty days past, and she had his heart and mind.

Mother's Mother hadn't been outside the walls in many years. Whandall heard her muttering at everything she saw. The dirt. Bad manners among the Lordkin. Sullen faces among the kinless.

At least thirty kinless were using the well. At the sight of the approaching Lordkin family, they drifted away in little clumps.

The bucket brought up a scant mouthful.

The kinless had taken it all! And that alone might have started the Burning. But Whandall, waiting for his turn to scoop up a handful of water for Mother's Mother, smelled smoke on the windless air. Too early for a cook fire . . .

"Stay together," Wanshig snapped. "Get the women and children home."

The Burning had begun.

They had to go out of their way several times.

Fire was just catching in the message-service offices. Kinless were trying to get the horses out. Others were fighting the fire with wet blankets. The kinless fire wagon had just come when half a dozen Lordkin waded into the kinless with curses and long knives. Firefighters fell bleeding. Others ran. One Lordkin sat on a kinless man's head and beat on his chest with a rock. Another came over and kicked the kinless man and laughed.

Mother's Mother was leaning on Mother, gasping. "Monsters! We never killed! We only burned; we never killed!" Mother and Whandall led her rapidly away from the scene.

Whandall looked at Wanshig and didn't ask, *Is it true or is she crazy?*

"Maybe men didn't tell women everything. Even then," Wanshig said quietly.

It was peaceful on Angle Street, where the land humped a bit to hide the smoke southward. Faces turned curiously toward a crowd of women with only two men for escort, and Wanshig whispered, "Relax. Stroll. Just another dull morning, okay?"

And Whandall tried to feel that. Take it easy, nod at Mother's Mother's ranting and hope nobody hears. Elriss looks like she needs any strong man's help, but Mother's taking care of that, easing her back where she doesn't show.

Tras Preetror the teller hailed him. "Whandall! What are you doing? Don't you know what's happening?"

Wave at Tras Preetror, smile, walk toward him. "Hello, Tras." Breezy, a little bewildered: "What are you talking about?"

Tras made no effort to hide his delight. "Oh. Guarding the women, good idea. But why aren't"—he waved about him, voice rising—*"they* doing something? Isn't the Bur—"

Whandall slammed a quick punch at Preetror's heart. Shut off his breath! Tras was expecting it; he dodged and turned, sloughed the blow, backed out of reach. "Isn't the Burning supposed to happen all at once? Do you *feel* Yangin-Atep? Do you feel the rage?"

A teller's task isn't to keep the peace. All these years Whandall had known Tras Preetror without ever quite grasping that truth.

Too late now. Angle Street had heard his message. Lordkin were disappearing into shops. Kinless were fleeing, converging into a pack. Tras joined them, bubbling with news.

Wanshig had Whandall's arm. "Move *out,* Whandall. Through there. You lead; I'll trail. Elriss, follow Whandall."

Another street. Pelzed passed with nine Serpent's Walk men. "Whandall! Wanshig!" Pelzed shouted. "We're going to Lord's Town! Come with us."

Whandall waved to indicate the women.

Astonishingly, Pelzed nodded calmly, as if he understood the need. "We can't wait," he said, and gestured his Serpent's Walk warriors toward Sanvin Street. "You'll miss the best." Then they were gone, and the smell of smoke was thicker yet.

Three cross-streets later: the Burning had arrived before them. A handful of lookers confronted a pudgy Lordkin in his forties. Did he need help?

No, the barbarians were merely bewildered, and the Dirty Bird was shouting into their faces while his arms described expansive circles. "It's free! Take it—it's all ours!" Joyfully he tried to lead them into a shoemaker's shop, where a score of gatherers were already seated on the dirt floor, passing shoes back and forth, trying to find something to fit.

The party atmosphere called to Whandall, but Wanshig steered the Placehold women around that scene too.

And finally home, and upstairs to the more defensible second floor. Placehold had stone walls. The floors would burn, but they were thick wood, and it would take determined effort to get them blazing. No one in the past had ever taken the time. The women were as safe as they would ever be.

And Whandall asked, "Now?"

"Yes, O eager one—" Whandall was halfway down the stairs. All the fine loot would be gone! Wanshig shouted down at him. "Wait! Where are the rest of us?"

Whandall stopped himself with an effort. There was a surging in his blood and a heat in his loins. Both were familiar, but they had never been this strong. The Whandall who once sat on Mother's Mother's

lap and listened to stories of a better time watched the rest of himself
losing control and whispered its disapproval.

"Where are they?" Wanshig demanded. "Resalet, Shastern, the
other men? The boys?"

"Gathering!"

"Whandall, I thought Resalet would wait!" Wanshig clambered
down after him. "He's gone. All the men are gone."

"Shig, they're just out gathering and partying with everyone else."

"Resalet has been talking about Morth of Atlantis," Wanshig said.
He looked up the stairs to see Elriss staring down at him.

"Come back," Elriss said.

"I think they went to Morth's shop," Wanshig said. With an effort
he turned away from Elriss and followed Whandall outside. "I think
they went as soon as the fires started."

"What would he want there?" Whandall demanded.

"Powders. Hemp," Wanshig said.

"Resalet hates that stuff!"

Wanshig laughed.

"Resalet's afraid of Morth," Whandall said. "What about 'Never
remember a killing after the Burning?' "

They were back in the street. Where the granary had been, the new
restaurant was burning: a hard-luck site. Eastward, a shouting match
over who had first claim to an ornate desk was about to turn violent,
while someone disappeared with the matching chair.

Wanshig looked back to the Placehold. "Who'll watch the women?"
he demanded. "Someone has to stay." He looked at Whandall and
saw almost uncontrolled eagerness. "And I know, I know, it won't be
you, little brother."

A kinless hurried past pulling a cart. "Help me!" the kinless
shouted. A dozen youths, Serpent's Walk, Flower Market, Bull Pizzle
all mixed together, ran after him, shouting and laughing. The cart
overturned almost at Wanshig's feet, and the kinless merchant ran on
unencumbered. Rings with red stones spilled out of the wreckage and
Wanshig scooped up several. He handed one to Whandall.

"Ours!" a Bull Pizzle shouted, but he was laughing. He saw
Whandall's elaborate tattoo, looked up to the walls to see the Serpent's Walk signs, and eyed Whandall nervously. No one moved for a
moment. Then the Bull Pizzle laughed again and dove into the mob at
the cart. They tore the cart apart and left in a bunch, carrying dresses
and trousers and a coil of rope.

There was smoke to the west. Wanshig turned that way, hurrying.

"Whandall, you've been spying on Morth. Is there anything our fathers should know about him? Anything that might hurt them?"

That *was* why he'd gone to Morth, wasn't it? Months ago. Whandall thought he remembered other reasons. Morth was nearly a friend. But those memories conflicted with the fire in his veins. Whandall said, "He told me about the spell that killed Pothefit. He won't use that again. But you don't exactly ask a magician, 'Please tell me what you use to stop Lordkin from taking things.' "

"Then what exactly do you ask him?"

"I watch. I listen. Shig, some things he just picks up and sells. Other things he waves his hands or mutters under his breath. Some of those, it's never the same twice, so maybe he's bluffing. I can't tell you what to take." He stopped, remembering. "Shig, I don't think Morth will be there at all."

"He lives at the shop."

"He'll be afraid. He didn't mean to hurt Pothefit!"

They were jogging now, moving wide around gatherers staggering under loads of valuables or trash. Whandall stopped suddenly.

Men his own age were gathering a kinless woman. It looked like fun. More: he knew her, Dream-Lotus Innkeep of the western edge, four years his elder and very lovely. He'd never quite worked up the nerve to approach her, to learn if she would have the love of a young Lordkin, and now he need not ask.

Wanshig tried to pull him away. Whandall resisted. "Come *on*, Shig—"

"No. Elriss would kill me." He looked into Whandall's face and gave up. "I'll go on ahead. Maybe I can get them to hold up." His grip closed like a vise on Whandall's arm. "You *follow* me, yes? You don't stop again."

"Yes, Shig, yes."

CHAPTER
23

He was ready to follow Shig. Pulling his clothing on, checking his own belongings, trading jokes with the others, happy—when he saw that the man now on top of Dream-Lotus was strangling her!

Before the sight had quite registered, Whandall's knife was out and moving in a downward arc. Neatly, precisely, he sliced the man's left ear off.

The man bellowed. His rutting urge had his lower body in thrall, but his head and shoulders tried to turn, tried to reach his belt and knife.

The man who held Dream-Lotus's wrists had only begun to react. Horrified at the strangling, or horrified at Whandall's meddling: no way to tell. Someone else bellowed and snatched at him. Whandall rolled across the strangler's back, notched his other ear, then ran, slashing backhand at his nose and unexpectedly nicking the tip and upper lip. The strangler let go of Dream-Lotus's throat and stood up. Dream-Lotus sucked air in a whistling shriek while Whandall ran.

He'd once heard a man say that strangling a woman would make her react, that it was a greater kick. He'd thought that was disgusting; he thought so now.

There were too many following him to stop and make a stand. Skill was no use here. Run! The strangler himself was in the lead, legs pumping hard, barefoot to the hips. Big guy, and scarred, under a tattooed orchid.

But the knife, so quick! Maybe he could have talked? Persuaded the man to . . . what? Nobody plays at sweet reason during a Burning.

Through here! Rigmaster's ropewalk was a long building with no windows but plenty of hemp in storage. It had started to burn. Maybe the strangler would step on a live coal. Whandall caught a lungful of smoke, realized his mistake, and swerved away, rightward around the pall of pale smoke, then hard left. Someone ran out of the building, a kinless carrying a bundle. He saw Whandall, screamed, and ran hard, still carrying what looked like carved wooden blocks. They'd have burned, but what were they? If Whandall weren't running for his life he'd have found out—

When Yangin-Atep possessed a man, was this what he felt? It didn't feel divine. For that moment he'd felt so wonderful, he'd been so *grateful* to Dream-Lotus. Then someone was hurting her, and the chance to rescue her was all he could have desired. It felt very natural to cut the strangler, and not at all divine.

Feet pounding hard, Whandall completed his arc around the cloud of hemp smoke. The strangler was a trace of shadow, and yes! he was cutting across, through the rope factory itself! There were other shadows in there: the strangler's friends.

Maybe they'd all chase Whandall and let Dream-Lotus go. Maybe the strangler would outrun the rest, use all his strength catching up, to die under Whandall's knife. Would Dream-Lotus be pleased, grateful for such a gift?

Maybe not. They were squeamish, the kinless, and after all, Whandall too had raped her.

Behind Whandall the strangler ran out of the burning structure, choking and half blinded and reeling with the effects of hemp smoke. He slowed, hearing the laughter that followed him. He looked down, realized his nakedness, and began to laugh despite the blood that flowed from nose and ears. Those behind him staggered about in a giggling fit. They collapsed in laughter as more of the hemp smoke blew past them.

Whandall slowed too, to laugh and gesture, then ran on. Which way was Morth of Atlantis?

As the danger faded, Whandall remembered his thirst. Water was what he would be gathering if he dared stop. What would Resalet expect to find in Morth's shop, of all places? Wanshig must be wrong!

But Whandall kept running, because he knew in his gut that Wanshig was right.

As he ran, his mind caught up.

The scarf! Resalet thought he could gather a tattoo from Morth of Atlantis!

Tras Preetror was interviewing a handful of gatherers in Silda's Handmeals. The gatherers were preening, proud that their lives would be made legend in lands they'd never see. That son of a dog had helped to spread the Burning beyond its reasonable bounds. If Whandall could catch Tras alone—

You don't stop again. Whandall didn't stop. His head was clearing.

He should be nearing Morth's shop.

Morth's defenses might have preserved him—but might also be used up by now. Random looters wouldn't know what was safe to take. He hoped his brothers and uncles had waited. He should have come sooner.

Some landmarks were missing: the belfry, the Houses of Teaching. The tallest structures must have made the best torches.

That glare of light and heat to his left: Wood's lumberyard? Lordkin had piled beams into a tent shape to burn better. Just beyond it—

Morth's shop?

Matters were not as he expected. Buildings around the site were burned, charred, but the shop of Morth of Atlantis was a flat circle of gray ash. Whandall felt a fist closing in his chest. *Nothing* had survived.

Those were bones . . . skulls. Five skulls.

Maybe Morth was among them. Maybe Whandall's family was avenged.

Maybe Morth had bent the god's exuberant rage to his own will, to punish looters.

Whandall wouldn't know until he reached home. He couldn't make himself hurry. He couldn't go straight home: the strangler's Flower Market street-brothers hadn't had time to forget Whandall's face.

He saw a whooping Lordkin drop a howling dog into a well to die. That struck him as stupid, but there were four Lordkin and they were big. He left them alone. He found clumps of kinless holding off jeering Lordkin with makeshift weapons, and he left them alone too. In the back of his mind he could see himself and his kin, and in truth, the whole thing was beginning to look stupid.

Others might have thought so. Whandall saw more of caution than of Yangin-Atep's manic joy. The Burning was ending, though coals still burned.

The family cook pot had been stolen from the courtyard. The men hadn't come home.

They never came home. Even Wanshig had disappeared. Whandall at fifteen was the oldest man in the Placehold.

CHAPTER
24

The men were gone—and Mother's Mother never showed surprise. She'd lived in a world of her own for years. She came back to reality long enough to organize the household. The women took her orders, perhaps because they were terrified.

She took time to hold Whandall as she might have held a small child. "You're the oldest now," she said. "Keep the Placehold! I've always been proud of you. You saved your brothers before; now you have to do it again. Keep the Placehold!"

It was as if she had waited half her life for this. Now, tasks done, she slipped away, back to some pleasant place that no one else could see.

Elriss was pregnant. She wept for Wanshig and stayed in the women's rooms. Mother was more practical. In the first light of the morning after the burning she found Whandall.

"I have to leave."

"Why?" he asked. They had never been very close. With a new baby every year she had little time for him even though too many died. He'd spent more time with Mother's Mother. "Will you be back?"

"I'll come back if I can," Mother said. "Elriss will take care of the youngest. You and Shastern can take care of yourselves. Whandall, there's no food and no water."

"We need you to get food from the Lords," Whandall said.

"Elriss and Wess and Mother—three's enough. The Lords won't give any more than three can gather," Mother said. She lifted her carpet bag. "I'll be back if I can come back."

"But where will you be?"

She didn't answer. Whandall watched her go down the stairs. There she joined two other Placehold women, women who had both left babies in the Placehold's care. He watched them make their wary way out into the street, out into the Burning, and wondered if he'd ever see Mother again.

Three hours after first light Shastern and five younger boys came in pulling a cart. Each had an armful of stuff, clothing, enough rope to trade for a big cook pot if they could find someone who'd trade. There was a small cook pot in the cart. There was food amid the junk, but some of it was spoiled and the rest would have to be eaten in a hurry.

They traded whooping memories of the Burning. One by one they turned serious when they saw there were no men. The younger boys gathered around Whandall in the big room on the second floor. Girls came out to join them. They all stared at Whandall Placehold.

Shastern demanded, "Where are the men?"

"Gone," Whandall said. He didn't tell them what he suspected, that all including Wanshig had been blasted by Morth of Atlantis. Was there anything he could have done? If he'd stayed with Wanshig, would all the men have lived?

"But they'll be back," Shastern said. "They're just . . ." He saw Whandall's face. "What do we do?" Shastern asked. "When the word gets out, there'll be men come to gather the Placehold!"

"What do we eat?" Rubyflower asked. Her ten-year-old eyes were as big as dinner plates.

"How much food do we have?" Whandall asked.

Rubyflower shook her head. "I don't know. A week before Mother's Day we usually have more in the pantry than we have now."

"And it's two weeks to Mother's Day," Whandall mused. "Have you heard anything about Mother's Day? Will the Lords come? Will they bring the gifts?"

No one knew.

Whandall sent Ilthern to find out. "Don't talk," Whandall said. "Just listen. See what they're saying in Peacegiven Square. Listen to the Lordsmen and their clerks. Maybe they'll say something."

"It won't matter," Rubyflower said. "If they had Mother's Day tomorrow, we'd never get the cart back from Peacegiven Square! Someone would gather everything!"

The little girl was right, Whandall thought. Only four men in the Placehold carried knives; only two wore tattoos. Placehold itself might be defended by barricading the stairs. It wouldn't burn; the Burning was already fading. "Bring up rocks," Whandall told Rubyflower. "Get the other girls. Boys too. Ecohar, you go with them. Bring up rocks."

"Here?"

"Here and on the roof. Try not to look frantic."

"And what do we eat, Whandall?" Shastern asked quietly when the smaller children were gone for rocks. "Rubyflower's right—we'll never get a cart home."

"Whandall will think of something." Wess spoke from behind him, possession and pride in her voice.

Vinspel had been killed in a knife fight, ten days back. They'd had to tell Wess. No man would tell her, or tell any woman, that Vinspel had been fighting for another woman. The other Placehold women liked Wess too, but they *would* talk.

And now Whandall could only think that no man could keep her from him.

She was the oldest girl in the room. Mother's Mother was leader of the Placehold, but she was somewhere else inside her mind. Mother had been the real leader, usually, when she didn't have flasks and powders. But now she was gone. If Wanshig came back, Elriss would be leader. Now—

Now, Whandall's woman would have the job, honors and duties alike. It came to Whandall that he didn't really know what that meant. He knew that Mother's Mother, then Mother, had kept the keys to the pantry. Neither seemed to cook or sew or clean. Others did that. But without someone to make it happen, they didn't.

Two children began to wail. Wess grabbed the oldest, a six-year-old, and shook him. "Quiet. Let Whandall think," she said. "Go with Rubyflower and get some rocks. All of you, shoosh! Get rocks we can throw from the roof. Not you, Raimer. Get some water for the roof garden. Not drinking water; dirty water will do fine. Come on, all of you—let's get to work."

Whandall nodded. "Rocks. Good," he said. "Shastern, you help Wess. Find some way to barricade the stairway too. I'll be back as soon as I can."

"Where are you going?" Shastern asked.

"Pelzed."

He'd have to tell Pelzed how helpless the Placehold was. That would be dangerous, but Pelzed would find out anyway. Better to tell him straight off. Pelzed—Lord Pelzed—owed Whandall a favor. Would he remember? Would he care? But it was the only place Whandall could go.

Pelzed had led a band toward Lord's Town. Whandall couldn't follow there. He'd wait at Pelzed's roofless house.

But Pelzed was back.

Three of Pelzed's women were going through a stack of gatherings. Pelzed shouted when he saw Whandall. "Whandall! Come have some tea!"

Whandall approached warily. He waved to indicate the loot. "From Lord's Town? Lord."

Pelzed grinned. "Not exactly," he said. "Sit down."

"Yes, Lord Pelzed."

"Heard you'd had some trouble," Pelzed said. "Wanshig's gone? Some of the other men."

"Yes, Lord. Lord, you once said you owed me a favor. We need help, Lord."

Pelzed poured tea and pushed the cup over to Whandall. "Tell me."

"All the men are gone, Lord," Whandall said. "There's only me and the younger boys. The women will try to find men, but . . ."

Pelzed nodded. There was no expression in his eyes at all as he sat lost in thought. Finally he said, "Are you asking for my protection?"

"Yes, Lord."

"Why not ask the Lordsmen?"

"Lord, there are lines a hundred people long in front of every clerk in Peacegiven Square," Whandall said. "And what good would it do? Men come to gather the Placehold. We send for the Lordsmen, and maybe they come and maybe not, but they won't come in time to do us any good. We have our own Lord here. Why go to the Lords of Lordshills?"

"You learn fast," Pelzed said. "All right. We'll protect your cart on Mother's Day and I'll get the word out that anyone gathering at the Placehold will have to answer to me. And I'll speak to the Lord's clerks in the Square. You'll be all right."

"Thank you, Lord."

"You'll have to control the Placehold. Don't make any new enemies. I can't fight new enemies," Pelzed said. "You remember that."

"Yes, Lord."

"How many boys do you have at Placehold?"

"Eleven, Lord, not including Shastern."

"They'll all join Serpent's Walk," Pelzed said. "Join knowing they owe us."

"Yes, Lord."

"Good." Pelzed sipped more tea. A crafty smile came to his lips. "Don't you want to know what happened?" he asked.

"Oh, yes, Lord," Whandall said. "I saw you going toward the Lords-hills."

"So did the Bull Pizzles," Pelzed said. "They were following us. We couldn't shake them and there were too many to fight, so there we were, going out gathering with a bunch of Pizzles following right behind. I had a good plan—wear forester leathers. Wear leathers and make sure we didn't leave any dead behind. They'd never know it was us. But when we got closer we saw Lordsmen. Twenty, maybe more. They had armor, swords, spears, big shields, and we weren't about to get past them. Kraemar and Roupend were feeling Yangin-Atep's power. They wanted to run in and gather. I couldn't control them much longer."

"Is that where you got all that?" Whandall asked. "Lord's Town?"

"No, what I did was let the Bull Pizzles get past me, then go back to the Pizzle streets," Pelzed said. "With our leathers on. Struck a bargain with the kinless there. Kraemar and Roupend got to burn some old houses and stores, the rest of us gathered all this, and the Bull Pizzles never came back. I may even have a new street for Serpent's Walk."

"Lord—was Chief Wulltid killed, then, Lord?"

"No, you know what he's like; he didn't go with his men. He stayed to take his pleasures in his own houses." Pelzed laughed. "I hope he enjoyed himself. He won't like my new arrangements." The grin was wider. "But the Lords will. Bull Pizzle isn't very popular with the Lords right now."

Whandall sipped tea and listened. He tried to imagine himself as Lord Whandall of Serpent's Walk. It was a good picture, and the more he thought about it, the more he liked it. It was a big job and he didn't know how to do it, but he could watch Pelzed and learn.

Wess had moved all his things into the big northeast room. Resalet's clothes were gone. His other things, bronze mirror, drinking cup, were laid out for Whandall's approval.

Wess was wearing a short wool skirt and a thin blouse that opened down to her navel.

Where did you get that? He knew he shouldn't ask. *From Vinspel?* His hands were on her shoulders. "Nice," he said, and repeated himself: "Nice. Wess, you're beautiful." She must have used the mirror, he thought, and he reached out for the magical thing and looked into it.

There was no trace, now, of that ring-shaped scar. The serpent tattoo was magnificent . . . alien.

"What did I look like?" he asked. "I stayed clear of you while I was healing." He'd let her see him once. The look in her eyes.

"That scar. I never thought it would heal."

"I found magic," he said. "Wess, I've got to talk to the rest of the house, but first, what have you got done?"

The children were being taken care of.

There was food. This evening's dinner would be huge: they were cooking everything that wouldn't keep. They'd eat as much as they could. Tomorrow, who knew?

Stashes of rocks were on the roof, and children on guard. Invaders would expect rocks. There should be something else too, something to startle a gathering band. Boiling water? Too complicated; too much work, and where would they get water? *Think* of something. Fire would burn *on* a roof.

The Placehold was nearly empty. Was there some way the place could look busier? All that showed from the street was a blank wall and a wide gate. What men he had, he could move them through that gate more often.

"And I couldn't think of anything else," she said. "You?"

"I've got Pelzed's protection. The only idea I had. Dark Man's Cup will do us some good, I think. Pelzed killed some friends for not keeping his promises there."

CHAPTER
25

Whandall was busier than he had ever been in his life.
He'd forgotten that everyone went hungry following the
Burning. There wasn't enough food outside: too many
gatherers and not enough to gather. Hunger, then feasts when anyone
could gather food. They fought over the dishes, and everything tasted
so good, he remembered that. Now he knew why: they were starving.

Whandall's elder half sister Sharlatta came home with Chapoka.
Chapoka was an adult male, and there was no more to be said for him.
He never gathered except from a friend, he complained about everything, and he never shut up. Whandall knew him well enough to throw
him out.

Chapoka wouldn't be thrown, and Whandall was harassed and hungry. He decided his household of children could use entertainment.
The fight in the courtyard left Chapoka with scars he would have to
explain for the rest of his life. The gaudiest were on his back.

Afterward the Placehold's survivors treated Whandall like a Lord.
During this time, lack of respect was one complaint he never had.

He hadn't realized—he had to leaf back through his memories to
understand that *everyone always complained to a Lord all the time.*

Even Wess. Loving Wess was wonderful, and she held the Placehold
together as much as anyone. But . . . living with a woman took new
skills at accommodation and ate time he didn't have. It wasn't like
living with a roomful of brothers, and he hadn't *liked* that very much.

He saw his former life as a long dream of idleness. He came to understand why fathers disappeared. Maybe he wouldn't have stayed with it. But he knew. . . .

He knew where the men had gone. Whatever befell the Placehold now was his doing.

Whandall's mother brought Freethspat home four weeks after the Burning. Everyone was astonished. He was a heavily scarred man around thirty years old, from so far across town that nobody knew anything of his clan. "Sea Cliffs," he said, and he showed a finely tattooed sea gull in flight.

When Whandall came home that afternoon, Freethspat and Mother had the northeast room. Whandall's things were in the north room that Shastern had taken because no one wanted to move Elriss from the southeast room she had shared with Wanshig.

Wess moved in with Elriss. She was avoiding him again. Once they met on the stair, and Wess spoke rapidly, before he could open his mouth.

"You could have *asked* me to stay."

"What if I asked now?"

"Stay where? Whandall, I would have followed you. You never said anything. It's like I came with the northeast room, or with your being the oldest man!"

"I wasn't sure," Whandall said. She'd left him once before. She had come to him when his status changed, and it might change again. For those reasons and one other, he'd dithered.

That other reason . . . "Wess, if I had you *and* the Placehold to take care of, that would be my life. Guard you and the rest of them until I am dead. I know how to do that. Be Pelzed's right hand. When Pelzed wants to slack off a little, years from now, I'd *be* Lord Pelzed. Lord Whandall," he tasted the name, "except when Lords or Lordsmen can hear me. I . . . ."

She waited for him to go on, but he didn't know how to say it. He hadn't even tried until now. *I don't want to be Pelzed! Pelzed bows and scrapes and flatters, and sets his people against each other, and lies, and kills, and tells other people to kill friends. And with all that lives not a half as well as the real Lords in Lord's Town. What I want, it isn't here—*

Wess brushed past him and was gone.

Coals still burned.

The killing of firefighters had got up the kinless's noses. Now they wanted to carry knives.

For months after the Burning, the talk was of little else. There was no fundamental disagreement among the Lordkin. How could a conquered people be permitted weapons? Of course the firefighters shouldn't have been killed . . . not *killed*. But fire was Yangin-Atep's. Wait, now, Yangin-Atep suppressed fire too! So it wasn't blasphemy. Yes it was, but they could have been driven off . . . taught an unforgettable lesson, scarred or maimed, *then* driven off . . . but they'd *soaked* those blankets to smother the fires—that was *drinking* water. . . .

In the street-corner gatherings, Whandall tried to stay out of the arguments. They could get you killed. A teller from Begridseth was beaten for asking the wrong questions, and again Whandall didn't participate.

At home the women were in quiet mourning, but Mother's Mother left no doubt about how she felt. The Lordkin had become no better than animals.

The kinless couldn't see reason. They had been attacked while rescuing horses—yes, and fighting a fire too. Attacked and murdered. The kinless wanted the killers' heads. Hah! No hope of that, of course, even without the protection of their street-brothers. You'd have thought half the city had watched the firefighters die; they were willing to describe what they thought had happened in minute detail, but nobody could remember a face.

But the kinless wanted to carry knives or clubs, to fight back next time!

Many Lordkin would have offered them the chance, for amusement. A bad precedent, though, a reversal of ancient law.

But nothing was being built.

Lords and kinless were holding talks; Lordkin spoke at every intersection; and every mouth was dry. The Deerpiss carried water an uncertain distance and then stopped, because smashed aqueducts were still smashed.

Garbage wasn't moving. The Lordkin began to see that it would not move itself. Rats and other scavengers were growing numerous. Ash pits that had been stores and restaurants now began to serve the Lordkin as garbage dumps.

Mother's Day came and went. Nothing was distributed in Peacegiven Square because there was nothing to distribute. Scant food was coming into the city; too much was disappearing on the way. Great fire, would the Lordkin have to take up driving wagons themselves?

* * *

That, Whandall decided, was an interesting notion.

Now Freethspat and Whandall and Shastern were the only men in the Placehold. Freethspat fit in well enough. He didn't often beat the younger children and never seemed to beat the women at all. He was respectful to Pelzed and spoke well of Serpent's Walk. Mother never yelled at him, which was unusual.

A week after his arrival, Freethspat was gone all night. Whandall wondered if he'd disappeared. Mother had no doubts, and in the morning he brought home a pushcart full of food, some of it fresh. There was enough food to last a week and no one mentioned the blood on the cart.

Freethspat was a provider.

Freethspat might have had a little Lords' blood in him too. Over the next three weeks, rooms nobody would walk in barefoot became jarringly clean, and the Placehold girls smiled proudly when Freethspat praised them. Six Placehold boys who had been old enough to gather in the Burning, but too young for anything so serious as robbing a wizard, now brought home gold rings and wallets from looker pockets and produce from kinless markets. And Whandall—

"Now it's your turn," Freethspat said.

They were in the courtyard, gathered for dinner. Heads turned as Freethspat spoke. They'd heard this conversation before.

Whandall asked, "Mean what?"

"Mean it's time you earned your keep, Whandall," Freethspat said. "Sure, I can get more to eat, but what happens to your mother if they get me? And your sisters? Your turn."

"I don't know where to get food."

"I can show you, but your mother says you know a lot," Freethspat said. "You've been to Lordshills. Take me there."

Whandall shook his head. "The Lordsmen will kill us both. Me for sure. Lord Samorty told them last time I was there. Here, look at my arm—it grew back crooked." Whandall pulled off his shirt. "Here—"

"Then somewhere else. You know the forest, but there's nothing to be had there, is there? No. Then somewhere you went with your brother—what was his name?"

"Wanshig," Elriss said, glaring. She was nursing Wanshig's son.

"Wanshig," Freethspat said. "They tell me you hung around with him a lot, Whandall. He must have showed you something. They say Wanshig was smart."

"He was," Elriss said.

"So show me."

Whandall could have liked Freethspat. But the man was just an inch taller and just an inch wider than Whandall, just a little too obtrusive in his strength. He called him *Whandall,* as a brother would. He lived in Whandall's room.

There had been no need for Whandall's gathering skills in the time since the Burning. (Eleven weeks? *That* long?) There was no need now.

But Whandall was getting restless, and Wess was unobtrusively following the exchange, and it wouldn't take much of a coup to shut Freethspat up. "I did have a notion," Whandall said. "I just couldn't see a way to make it work. Freethspat, what do you know about wine?"

Well back from the road and screened by growths of touch-me vine, Whandall and Freethspat watched the vineyard. The noon sun was making the workers torpid. Their patient drudgery hadn't changed since he and Wanshig had watched them nearly a year ago. The grapevines were glossy green; the buildings behind them showed no sign of scorching. The Burning of two months back simply hadn't happened here.

The Lordkin guards did seem more alert. A youth passed Whandall walking upright and noisily, far from the comforts offered by that big house. Woodsman's leathers made him clumsy, and still he avoided the morningstar bushes and beds of touch-me, steering wide of the hiding place Wanshig had found for them.

Whandall had been surprised to see how much Freethspat knew about leathers and the chaparral. Freethspat knew about a lot of things.

And here came a pony, a local pony with a fleck of white bone on its forehead, pulling a wagon with a single driver.

"That one," Freethspat said. "No. It's empty."

"Wait," Whandall whispered. He watched the wagon go by. Just watched this time.

He was not bored. In Serpent's Walk, *there* he'd been bored. The same limp justifications—"What do the kinless want of us? When Yangin-Atep takes us, we do these things! It's not us; it's the rage!"—until they believed it themselves.

It was hard to believe in that empty wagon. Wasn't the bed a little high? Easy to picture a false floor with flasks of wine under the boards. The kinless driver tugged at his yellow silk noose. A little besotted, was he, rolling a little with the wagon's motion? A big one, he was, with shoulders like boulders; maybe you needed that to control a pony. It hardly mattered. A kinless wouldn't fight.

The guard was a Lordkin, Whandall's age, fifteen or sixteen. Older men had sent him out, and stayed to drink in comfort, no doubt. In armor he'd be helpless. Whandall could take him.

Then the wagon, much closer now—have to sprint to catch it—and the driver. Arms like a wrestler. The big hat shadowed his face, but the nose was flat. Hard to believe in him too. He was still tugging at the yellow silk tied loosely around his thick neck. He wasn't used to it.

Damn! The hat shadowed his nose and ears, but—

"That driver is Lordkin," Freethspat said. His voice was filled with disgust. "Working like a kinless!"

"You're right."

"What could you pay a Lordkin to make him work like a kinless? What could he gain that another Lordkin couldn't take away from him?"

Whandall thought about it while the wagon receded. "Wine, maybe, if he drank it right away. Secrets, things nobody else knows. This isn't going to be so easy, is it? We may have to kill the driver."

"Have to kill the guard anyway. Your turn, Whandall."

CHAPTER
26

The next wagon didn't appear until near sunset. The same guard had been out there for all that time, pushing through branches, wearing a path, sweating into his leathers, and bored into a stupor. The wagon distracted him.

"Now," Freethspat said without turning.

It was Whandall's scheme. All it needed for completion was some way to avoid killing. Freethspat was a skillful gatherer. He knew things. He had brains.

Freethspat turned to look at Whandall. "He's too far now. When he comes back, take him."

"I brought you here," Whandall protested. His voice never rose above the sound of the breeze in leaves. "Isn't that enough?"

Freethspat studied Whandall with interest. "You're not scared?" he whispered.

"No."

"I understand. But Whandall, this is what we are. This is what a Lordkin is. Here and now. Right now. With me watching."

Whandall took in a deep breath. The guard was coming toward him again. His forearm and wrist brushed a morningstar. He grunted in pain and shied back, and then Whandall slammed into his back. And cut his throat.

It was his first kill, and it went much better than he'd expected. Whandall had several seconds to get into place before the wagon arrived. He didn't look back at the corpse.

He thumped into the wagon bed while the wagoneer was scanning the trees for the guard. The wagoneer half stood, turning, slicing blind with his long knife in a move he must have practiced for years. Whandall blocked the blade with his own and threw with his other hand.

Pebbles spattered the pony's head and ears. The pony screamed and surged forward. The wagoneer stumbled, tried to stab out anyway, and was cursing as Whandall's blade slid in under his armpit.

The road curved wide around, down to the streambed. The turns weren't sharp and the pony knew the way. Whandall had time to put on the hat and coat—and figure out how to move the complicated knot to get the noose off the corpse and onto his own neck—before the gatehouse came in view. Bile was rising in his throat. He let the pony slow. It wouldn't do to be seen vomiting over the side.

He heard Freethspat climbing in behind him. There was a rustle as he hid under the tarp. "Well done," came the whisper. "Couldn't have done it better myself. Whandall, I'm proud of you."

Whandall didn't care to speak.

Freethspat examined the dead man, then cursed softly.

"What?"

"He's a Toronexti," Freethspat said. "So was the other one. Why didn't you tell me?"

"Tell you what?" Whandall demanded. Suddenly he remembered Wanshig's words: Alferth had hired Toronexti to guard the vineyards.

Freethspat sighed. "You have a lot to learn, boy. You don't gather from the Toronexti. Ever."

Whandall pointed to the dead man. "They're not so tough—"

"No, they're not. But there are a lot of them. You kill one, others come looking for you, and *you won't know who they are.*"

"So what do we do?"

"We get out of here with this stuff." Freethspat frowned. "We get rid of it as quick as we can. Maybe they gathered the wagon. No Toronexti marks on *that.*"

"What do they look like?"

"Never you mind."

It was tempting to think in terms of secrets: of hiding. The wine under the false bed was in little flasks. *Those* could be hidden. It was what you did with wine. But how would you hide a wagon?

They discussed it after they'd cleared the gatehouse. They reached home in a stony silence.

Whandall began moving garbage.

Friends offered suggestions: get shovels, line the wagon with hay. Some of the Serpent's Walk men helped him do that. Others helped move garbage away from where they lived, until they got bored. Freethspat stayed with it. If any part of the scheme had collapsed, Freethspat would have gotten Whandall out alive and then never let him forget it. But he became good with the shovel, and he stayed with it.

Four more were good enough at it, and stayed long enough, that Whandall and Freethspat shared wine with them. They stayed as a core, to gather other men.

Four days of that, and everyone was tired of it. Serpent's Walk was full of men from Alferth's quarter who knew very well where and how Whandall got that wagon. Whandall left the wagon abandoned. It disappeared, with a few flasks left under the boards as a gift.

There was wine for Mother and Mother's Mother; for his sister Sharlatta and the man she'd brought home after Whandall evicted Chapoka; for Elriss, who had known no man since Wanshig disappeared, and Wess, whose man had taken to vanishing at night. Wine served as a don't-kill-me gift for Hartanbath, the man he'd cut. That was Freethspat's suggestion. Whandall and Freethspat shared two bottles with Hartanbath and some of his Flower Market friends, and were gone before Hartanbath had drunk very much.

Dusk in Tep's Town. Whandall stood at the western edge of the Placehold roof garden to watch the sun fall into the sea. The landscape below softened, hiding the garbage and the filthy streets. A few kinless hurried home, eager to reach shelter before darkness gave the world over to gatherers and worse.

There were Lordkin with no place to go. Some found shelter with kinless. That could be tricky. Kinless had no rights, but some were protected. Pelzed and other Lordkin leaders put some streets off limits. The Lords didn't permit a breach of the peace, but they never said what that was. Armed Lordsmen might come to help a kinless house under siege. Sometimes Lordsmen squads swept through Tep's Town and rounded up any Lordkin unlucky enough to get their attention. They took their prisoners to camps where they were put to work on the roads and aqueducts for a year. That didn't seem to happen in Serpent's Walk. Pelzed? Luck? Yangin-Atep?

Probably not Yangin-Atep.

And you didn't steal from the Toronexti. But only Freethspat could recognize them, so now what? And how did he *do* that?

The day faded, and now the city was lit with a thousand backyard cook fires.

Whandall took out three flasks of wine. He drank the first in three gulps. He was halfway through the second when he heard the scream.

He listened long enough to be sure it didn't come from the Placehold. He sipped more wine. Not his business. The scream ended with a strangled gurgle. Someone had died of a cut throat. Whandall wondered who it might be. Someone he knew? A kinless who resisted? More likely a Lordkin knife fight.

Freethspat was proud of him. He'd killed the guard. His first kill. Some would add to their tattoos, or wear an earring. It was what Lordkin did. This was what it meant to be Lordkin.

His belly spasmed and spat the last swallow of wine straight up into his nose and sinuses. He doubled over, coughing and snorting and trying to get the acid out of his windpipe, and more wine came up. Stupid. He knew what wine did. He got himself under control and took another swallow.

There were torches over by the new ropewalk. The scream had come from that direction. Could someone be gathering there? Who'd be such a fool? The ropewalk was in Pelzed's forbidden zone. Two Lordkin families lived among the kinless rope makers. Whandall had been inside that area only once, during the Burning. Rebuilding of the ropewalk started the day after the Burning, and Pelzed himself came down to supervise and make it clear that the kinless working there were never to be molested. Rope was important, both to use and to sell. Once Whandall had been curious about how it was made, but no Lordkin knew that.

Hemp held many secrets. Where hemp was grown, how the fibers were stripped from it, always at dawn after a night of heavy dew, but no one knew why. Tar was brought from the Black Pit. Hemp fibers and tar were taken to a long narrow building, and later they came out as rope, some tarred, some not, to be used and sold. Ships used rope. Rope left Serpent's Walk, gold and shells came back, and every step of that was protected by Pelzed here and the Lordsmen elsewhere.

A dozen torches now. Whandall began the third flask of wine. It was his last. The screams had stopped. The torchbearers went out of sight. Whandall thought he saw shadows moving near the ropewalk.

The next morning a Lordkin from the Hook was found with his throat cut. Someone had gathered his clothes and shoes, leaving him naked on a trash heap.

CHAPTER
27

Thus Whandall—who already knew how to fight and how to run—learned how to gather a pony-drawn vehicle and *really* move out. One day he might be glad.

And he had a hell of a story to tell, if the chief flasker ever wanted to make something of it.

That was unlikely. Alferth worked with (never *for*) certain lords. Whandall had robbed *them*. Alferth would defend his status, but he would never defend property. To Alferth, Whandall and Freethspat had only demonstrated their skill.

A great many Lordkin were part kinless, as many kinless merchants were part Lordkin. Only kinless would defend property. And Alferth's nose was a little too pointed, and he didn't have enough earlobe, and in fact any fool could see (as any wise man would forget) that Alferth had kinless blood.

But somewhere a Lord had been robbed. Whandall wondered about *him,* and about the Toronexti that Lord had hired to guard and move his wine. What would *they* do? The Toronexti guarded a path to nowhere, and nobody knew who they were. Alferth knew who had killed two of them.

Whandall was coming to realize that no one ever felt safe in Tep's Town.

He stopped worrying about Alferth, though. Alferth wouldn't talk to the Toronexti *now.* They'd want to know why he hadn't spoken earlier. They'd lost a wagon they were guarding; they'd never want anyone to know that! If Alferth spoke, he would only embarrass himself and the Toronexti. Nobody did that.

They were still talking, somewhere in the higher circles no Lordkin had seen save Whandall, up there where the Lords set the taxes and the kinless made their futile protests. On the street corners there was talk of compromise. Whandall heard the rumors and wondered what to believe.

Tep's Town was to have a troop of guards.

Whandall laughed when he heard that, but the rumors piled up details, and the laughter faded. Someone in the councils was serious.

Several hands of kinless men would be given weapons, never to be concealed. Most would be allowed hardwood sticks and torches.

Torches? A mad suggestion. Fire belonged to Yangin-Atep. Darkness belonged to any gatherer in need.

Rigid rules were laid down. The guards might use their sticks in carefully described circumstances, but never otherwise. Only officers (their numbers restricted) might carry blades, and those no longer than a hand. Guards would wear conspicuous clothing. They must never approach a Lordkin by subterfuge. From time to time their behavior would be reviewed by the Lordkin and the Lords.

Whandall wondered what the kinless thought they had won. Hedged about with such rules, they'd be more helpless than ever. The Lords themselves, and the loudest voices among the Lordkin, might have agreed to this nonsense, but if Lordkin saw fit to take a stick away from some kinless guard, they would!

But water and food were moving again. Garbage was leaving the inner city, though a few of those ash pits turned garbage pits were being made to grow food. Structures began to rise to cover the scars of the Burning.

Everyone was happy about that, but Whandall remembered the Lordshills and wondered.

Rumor flowed down from Lord's Town. There, Lordkin and kinless lived together and worked for mutual benefit. Garbage still moved. The fountains were turned off, most of them, but the date and olive trees weren't dry. Flower gardens still grew.

How was it done? Who were these Lords to have a city and a life when Tep's Town was dying?

It was death to go and look.

There had been a living god who gave fire to men. Nobody could doubt that. But Alferth, who started the Burning when Whandall was seven, hadn't been possessed by Yangin-Atep. He'd laughed when Tras suggested such a thing. The fires he'd set didn't seem to be motivated by anything bigger than the whim to watch a fire.

Whandall was losing faith. Yangin-Atep must be mythical by now. Morth of Atlantis was gone.

The Placehold women didn't want Whandall to take a woman. He was the last man born in the Placehold. Yangin-Atep forbid he should leave—the house would have *no* trusted protector—but one more woman would be a hardship.

Wess came to share his bed sometimes, so he should not have been lonely. Wess had reconsidered. Freethspat wasn't interested in a second wife, and Whandall was as good a catch as Wess was likely to find. She made it clear to Whandall that she would move in anytime he asked.

Whandall refused. It rankled that she had moved out of his room when she thought Freethspat might be available. . . .

And other men came to visit. Wess was never unfriendly to any man who might have power. Freethspat was here, and his sister Ilyessa brought home a man . . . and it didn't feel like his family anymore.

One day Whandall would bring home a mate. The women would presently accept her. He would sire children. He was a fighter—or the rest of the city thought he was. He would rise in power among Pelzed's counselors, and a few would whisper that Pelzed thought of him as his heir. In later years he would sometimes collect taxed goods to supply a feast. He would speak with the Lords to shape civic policy. The Placehold and the city expected these things of him.

They didn't know that fire had claimed the Placehold men because Whandall stayed behind to get laid.

He was leery of making decisions for others. He held his opinions to himself and shied away from being too persuasive. And he watched the city rebuild.

PART FOUR

The Return

CHAPTER
28

Two years after the Burning, Elriss had blossomed into a very handsome woman, desired by nearly every man who saw her. She worked in the roof gardens and tended Arnimer, the son born months after the Burning. She taught all the Placehold children. She worked with the other women, and she was respectful to Freethspat; but except to go to Peacegiven Square on Mother's Day, she never left the Placehold, and she never spoke to men, visitors, or single Placeholders, except for Whandall.

She treated Whandall like Wanshig's little brother. Even wine hadn't tempted her. Presently even Whandall thought of her as a sister.

Whandall was dressing. Presently he would go to the meetinghouse to drink tea with Pelzed, carry out any errand Pelzed might have, watch how power was used . . .

Elriss came shouting to his door. "Wanshig is back!" she cried. "I see him! He's coming up the street."

And moments later Wanshig was there. He looked older, thinner, and a great deal stronger. Whandall had only moments to greet him before Elriss swept him into the room she had held from before he left. She showed him her son. Then the infant Arnimer was sent out to play with the other children, and no one saw Elriss or Wanshig for a long time.

Whandall went to the roof.

Wanshig knew! Whandall could have come to help the Placehold

men, but he stopped for Dream-Lotus. Wanshig was back, and Wanshig knew.

They sat drinking weak hemp tea after dinner. Everyone listened as
Wanshig told his story. He was looking at Whandall as he said, "I ran
just as fast as I could and I was still too late. I saw an old man running
away, looking back. I wondered if it was Morth."

Whandall realized he'd been holding his breath.

"The shop was full of Lordkin," Wanshig said. "I could see them
through the door and a big window: at least ten, and they were all
Placeholders, Whandall. Enough Placehold men to drive anyone else
away.

"Things were burning inside. Resalet was possessed of Yangin-
Atep! I saw him wave at a shelf, and a whole line of pots puffed into
flame. He picked up something big in both arms."

"What was that?"

"I never knew. Understand, I was moving at a dead run. Legs like
soggy wood. All I saw of anyone was a shadow backed by fire. I knew
Resalet by the way he moved, and his arms were wrapped around a
heavy round thing about as big as . . . as Arnimer."

The babe looked up on hearing his name. Wanshig stroked his back
and said, holding his voice to an icy calm, "I tried to scream 'Get out!
Get out!' I went, 'Whoosh!' No breath. I sucked in air to scream.
Whatever was burning in that shop caught in my throat. I went into a
coughing fit.

"Cousin Fiasoom staggered through the door, clawing at his throat,
and fell to his knees. Resalet was coughing too. I could see him hunch
over, just inside the doorway. He gestured the edge of his round thing
into a tiny white flame, very bright. He plucked off the lid.

"Everything went white."

"The box exploded?"

"No. I saw just that much. *Resalet* exploded. *Resalet* was one great
glare like looking into the sun at noon. It was like daggers in my eyes.
I screamed and threw my arms over my eyes and curled up around
myself. I felt Yangin-Atep *breathe* on my back, one long blast, and
then he went away.

"I was blind. When I could move, I waited a bit. Maybe someone
from the Placehold would see me, see? Nobody did, so I started feeling my way around. I stayed back from the heat that must have been
Morth's shop. I could hear the riot around me.

"My sight came back with edges and white spots. I could see people
around me gathering and burning. I wanted out. You understand?

Out. No more Burning. No more Serpent's Walk, no more Tep's Town."

"Sure, Shig."

"Nobody's called me that in a long time."

"What then? The women were guarding the Placehold—"

"I didn't even think of that. I went to the Black Pit. I couldn't see; I couldn't fight. I needed a place to hide, and you told me ghosts couldn't hurt me, remember? I thought they'd scare away anyone else, so I went there. Spent the night.

"In the morning I could see more. My good white tunic was charred all across the back where Yangin-Atep had breathed on me. My hair came off in handfuls. It was *crisp.* There were a lot of fires far away, east and south. Whandall, I never wanted to see fire again."

Whandall laughed.

Wanshig didn't. He said, "I went to the docks. I played sneak-and-spy past a few Water Devils. There were ships. I went to the biggest.

"The entrance to a ship, they call that a *gangplank.* Two men were on guard there, not Water Devils. I told the big one, the older one, 'I want to sail on a ship.'

"Both men laughed, but I could feel them separating a little, you know? To put one behind me. The big one said, 'Well, that's not a problem, boy,' and I turned fast and caught the other one's arm.

"He'd tried to hit me with a little wood club they call a *fishkiller.* You know, Whandall, we *practice* this kind of thing. I broke his arm and let him dangle over the water, holding him out with my one arm—you know, showing off. I told Manocane, the big guy, the officer, 'I want *his* job.'

"That was Sabrioloy. His job was guarding the Lordkin. When the Lordsmen wheel up a cart full of gatherers, Sabrioloy knocks them on the head, shows them who's boss. He tried that with me. After that, I was boss, boss over the Lordkin sailors, anyway. Sabrioloy showed me the rest of what I needed to know. He trained me, and I didn't throw him over. Whandall, he couldn't swim."

"A ship's man? I thought even Water Devils could swim."

"Most sailors can't swim."

Their doubt must have showed. Wanshig said, "We were just pulling out of the bay. The officers wanted more sails up, so Sabrioloy and I drove the men aloft to raise them. Jack Rigenlord was an old hand, and he was up there above us all. Then a *mountain* of water stood up out of the sea and hit us broadside. It must have been magic, Whandall. I never saw anything like it before or since. Waves come in lines, rows, but this just stood up and curled over and *wham.* The ship heeled over and the mainmast bowed like a whip. Jack flew into the sea. He waved once at us and was gone. That made me a believer.

"I made Etiarp teach me to swim, first time we docked near a beach. Etiarp was a Water Devil who tried to gather from a merchant ship. We taught a few of the Lordkin. If a Lordkin could swim, I promoted him. We taught Sabrioloy too."

CHAPTER
29

It was a night of storytelling, and it ran nearly to dawn.

Freethspat told how he and Whandall had gathered a wine wagon. He still had a flask to pass around; only Yangin-Atep might know where he'd hidden it all this time. Whandall let him describe the escape. Then he told how he'd turned himself and Freethspat and the wagon into a garbage hauling business. He much enjoyed Wanshig's open amazement and Freethspat's determined grin.

Wanshig let the flask pass him while he told a story of being chased by a snake-armed monster bigger than the ship. When Freethspat called him a liar, Wanshig only shook his head.

The old Wanshig would have had some clever riposte. The new one saw how they stared, puzzled, waiting.

He said, "We sailed into Waluu Port eighteen days after Jack Rigenlord drowned. A woman came down to the dock asking for Captain Jack.

"Now Jack, he didn't have more than one woman in any one port, and some of them thought he was captain, I guess. Fencia, she had a marriage contract. When Jack didn't appear, she found us at the nearest saloon.

"Manocane knew her. He made her sit down, and bought her a mulled ale and made her drink, and then he said, 'Jack married the mermaid.'"

Freethspat was delighted. "I've heard of mermaids when I was a boy—"

"Oh, the merfolk are real enough," Wanshig said. "They're wonderful! They like to pace a ship, ride the bow wave. Where the magic's weak they take the shape of a big fish, but they breathe air, not water. There's a nostril *right* on top. Where the magic's strong you see a man or woman with fishy hindquarters. We don't offend the mers. They can drive fish toward a fleet or away, and show you where the rocks are when it's thick with fog. We like the merfolk.

"But it's just a sailor's way of speaking, 'He married the mermaid.' Jack Rigenlord *drowned*. We don't like to say *drowned*. But Fencia of Waluu Port didn't know that. She was furious. 'He was going to marry me! I waited through six years and four voyages for him to get enough money, and now he's married a *mermaid?* How does he expect to get *children?*'

"We'd been drinking. She was *so* angry, you know, and I guess I thought it was funny. You know: *married!*" Laughter rippled. Wanshig didn't smile. "Manocane opened his mouth, but I cut in first. I said to Fencia, 'No, wait, they aren't married *yet*. He says he wants your permission.'

"I saw every head turn. I heard a lot of laughing choked back.

"'My permission!' she screams, and she makes me tell her all the details. What was he doing when she popped out of the water? What did the mermaid look like? Did she cover her breasts? Did she sing him down into the water or did he just see her and jump? Did Jack even remember Fencia? I made it up as I went along. By now we were surrounded. Sailors have a deadpan way of telling a story, so they kept straight faces. If Fencia heard any cackling she must have thought they were laughing at her because her man left her.

"I thought we were about to get some real entertainment. Sometimes an angry woman can remind a sailor why he left the land."

Whandall waited. When Wanshig didn't speak again, he asked, "Then what?"

"She gave it," Wanshig said.

"What?"

"She didn't do any more screaming that night. She just turned around and stalked out, head high. The next morning Fencia came to the dock and announced to a big crowd that her engagement to Jack Rigenlord was at an end and he was free to do as he liked. If she cried, it wasn't where anyone could see her. Manocane and I got all the other sailors to hold their tongues. I heard what they said afterward, but me, I thought she was brave.

"I've lied since," he told them all, "but I don't *like* it. People get hurt. And I'm home now, and I won't lie again."

* * *

On subsequent nights, Shastern listened quietly to Wanshig's tales of the sea. He concealed his thoughts, but when Wanshig spoke, Shastern always came to listen. Whandall noticed, and wondered if Shastern's thoughts resembled his own. If Whandall was fated to leave Tep's Town . . . despite Morth of Atlantis, might it be by sea?

CHAPTER
30

Wanshig found Whandall on the roof garden. Whandall had developed the habit of seeing to the health of the plants. Wanshig said, "I want you to know that two of us couldn't have done any more than I did. You could have got there in time to be blinded, that's all."

Whandall had found a few bugs already, so he finished inspecting the row of tomatoes. He stood up to find Wanshig watching the sun fall into the sea.

"What are you watching for, Shig?" Whandall asked.

"Green flash. Just as the sun vanishes, sometimes, when it's very clear, you can see a flash of green," Wanshig said.

"Have you seen it?"

"Twice, but never from shore," Wanshig said. "Just when we were at sea. It's very good luck. The weather is always great the next day." Wanshig stared westward, at the darkening hills. "Sunsets are better when the sun falls into the sea."

"You liked sailing," Whandall said.

"I loved it."

"So why did you come back? For Elriss?"

Wanshig looked around to be sure they were alone, and still he lowered his voice. "That's what I told her," he said. "But Whandall, they put me ashore."

"Why?"

Wanshig didn't answer that day.

He'd been home for nearly a week, then, and Whandall hadn't seen him taste wine.

Wanshig wobbled home long after dinnertime. Whandall found him washing in the courtyard tub, in the dark. "Shh," he said. "I don't want Elriss. To see me."

"What happened? You haven't had a drink—"

"Three weeks and a day. A teller found me, Whandall. Somehow he heard. A Lordkin went sailing and came back. He had some flasks."

Whandall nodded in the dark. "What did you tell him?"

"Stories."

"Why you came home?"

"Nonono! Not that."

Whandall waited.

"They liked me, Whandall. I did them some good. Taught most of the crew to swim. Protected the merchants. Nobody gathered from our passengers! They really liked me."

"B—"

"Shipmasters trade," Wanshig said. "They don't want to be known as pirates. Pirates aren't welcome. Condigeo keeps warships. They can afford them because they hire them out to other towns, to hunt pirates, so you never know when you sail into a harbor whether they might have pirate hunters ready to come inspect you. Ships get a reputation." He paused to stare at the first stars. "So they don't want gatherers on board."

Whandall thought about that. "And you didn't know this?"

"I knew it. They told me the first day I was aboard. No gathering in port. Ever. Of course I didn't believe them, until the first time they caught me. Took everything I had and gave it back, and gave my pay to the people I'd gathered from. Taught me a proper lesson, they did."

Whandall didn't say anything.

"But then I got drunk. There's a town below the Barbar Mountains, three days' sail west of here. Stuffy place, but lots of magic. Silks, arts, crafts. And I was coming home; I'd be here in three days! First time we'd put in here since I shipped out. Whandall, nobody wants to come here! Not often, anyway. So there was this shop, with a dress that would look terrific on Elriss."

"You thought she'd still be here?"

Wanshig looked around again. Elriss wasn't about.

"Her or someone. But I couldn't afford it. That was all right, I'd get it another time, but then I went down to the docks and some of my buddies had bought a whole keg of beer. We sat drinking all night, and come morning—" Wanshig shrugged. "Well, it seemed like a good idea to go get that dress. Of course they caught me. The captain didn't say anything about it, not then, but when we got here he put me ashore and told the other captains."

One morning Shastern was gone. When he didn't come back the next day, Whandall told Pelzed. Patrols were sent out, and a formal question was sent to Wulltid of Bull Pizzle. Shastern was a loyal soldier of Serpent's Walk.

Wulltid's answer was polite but brief. No one had seen Shastern of Serpent's Walk. If anyone did, he would be well treated and delivered to his home.

Three days after Shastern disappeared, Whandall sat with Pelzed in the Serpent's Walk meetinghouse. Pelzed had made a complicated trade of services and protection. Now a kinless crew showed up to put on a new roof. Whandall thought he recognized two of the older workmen as woodsmen he'd seen with Kreeg Miller, but he didn't speak to them. They'd never know him!

A runner came to the long table where Pelzed sat most days. "Shastern is back, Lord," he said.

"Where?"

"Peacegiven Square. There's a wagon with a Lordsman in armor and a Water Devil."

Pelzed frowned. "The Lords are bringing Water Devils to Serpent's Walk?"

"Lord, he's a boy. Small tattoo, no knife. He asks to speak to you, and there's a Lord's clerk there too. They ask you to come, Lord."

Pelzed looked around the meeting room. "Miracos. You'll stay here. Whandall, come with me." Pelzed selected two more guards. Whandall thought Miracos glared at him as they went out. Everyone wanted to stand near Pelzed when he spoke to the Lord's clerks, and Miracos thought of himself as Pelzed's chief advisor. Lately Whandall had been favored. . . .

Shastern lay on a litter in front of the Witness table. A helmeted Lordsman stood next to him. The wagon was nearby, driven by a kinless teamster and drawn by kinless ponies, not the big horses Lords used for their own business.

The Lord's Witness, with his tight-fitting cap and robes, sat at the table. He didn't rise when Pelzed arrived with his retinue, but the kinless clerk stood and bowed to Pelzed, then intoned formally "Witness, we see Pelzed of Serpent's Walk."

The Witness stood. His voice was thin and dry, very formal. "Pelzed of Serpent's Walk, I am instructed to convey the greetings of Lord Samorty of the Lordshills. Lord Samorty wishes you well." He sat again.

The clerk turned to the Water Devil, an unarmed boy of no more than sixteen with hand tattoo only. "Speak, Lattar of the Water Devils."

"Witness, we return Shastern of Serpent's Walk to his people," Lattar said. "He was cast onto the docks by ship's guards at *Womb of Pele*'s gangplank. Let the record show that his injuries are not of our making. We found him, we tended to his wounds, and he is now delivered to his people."

The clerk turned to Shastern. "Do you dispute this, Shastern of Serpent's Walk?"

Shastern mumbled something. The clerk frowned, and Whandall went over to his brother. He could see that Shastern's mouth was swollen, and there were bruises showing through his tattoos.

Shastern saw Whandall and tried to smile. "Greetings, big brother," was what he tried to say, but only Whandall understood it. "Lost a tooth."

"Did Water Devils do this?"

"No." Shastern tried to move his head. "Shif'sh crew," he managed to say. "Devils sen' me home. Not their fault."

Whandall turned to Pelzed. "He doesn't dispute it, Lord."

Pelzed nodded. "Serpent's Walk is satisfied. Return my thanks to Samorty of Lordshills."

The clerk smiled wryly. "Witness, all parties are satisfied," he said.

The Witness spoke without rising. "Read the proclamation."

The clerk took a parchment from under his robe. "Proclamation. To all those who hear this, take heed, for it is the law.

"Many shipmasters are unfamiliar with the customs of the Lordkin of Tep's Town. This has resulted in unfortunate incidents causing disrespect and injury to Lordkin. Therefore, for the protection of the Lordkin, henceforth all Lordkin who wish to approach any ship in the harbor of Tep's Town must first obtain permission from the Lordsmen officer of the harbor watch. We regret the necessity of this ruling, but it must be strictly enforced. By order of Samorty, Chief Witness of Tep's Town and Lordshills Territories."

The clerk turned to the Witness. "The proclamation has been read. We will read it again each hour this day and the next."

The Witness nodded.

The clerk turned back to Pelzed. "Pelzed of Serpent's Walk, you have heard the proclamation of the Lords. Take heed. Your kinsman

Shastern of Serpent's Walk has been returned to you. The wagon has been hired for the day and is at your disposal. Witness, our fees were paid in advance, and there is no more business to be done."

Shastern healed fast. One tooth was gone, and his sisters fed him soup for a week while the swelling in his jaw subsided, but no bones were broken. At dinner Shastern told everyone he'd tried to gather from a harbor tavern, met a crewman and went aboard, and was beaten when the other crewmen saw him.

But he spoke with Whandall on the roof, alone. "I thought if Shig could go to sea, so could I," Shastern said. "But they wouldn't let me on the ship at all. The whole crew beat me. I kept saying I knew they didn't want gatherers, that I'd never gather, I didn't come to gather, I just wanted to go to sea, and they kept kicking me. If the Lordsman hadn't come, they would have killed me, I think."

Shastern fingered his tattoo. "Whandall, Pelzed of Serpent's Walk is a name with power. They don't call him Lord, but the Lordsman knew his tattoo. There was some kind of meeting with the Devils chief and the Lordsmen, and then they sent for a Lord."

"Samorty?"

"Yes, they called him that."

Whandall nodded. "He goes on watch himself. What did they meet about?"

"About me," Shastern said. "I just wanted to get home. I was dripping blood, and I needed a drink. When the Lord saw me, he got angry. 'Clean him up,' he said. His voice was real low and mean. 'Are you blind? Don't you see that tattoo?' So they got me a basin of saltwater and another of fresh, and a cup of wine. Good wine. Then they went in another room, but the big Lordsman wouldn't let me go. He got me another cup of wine, but he went with me when I had to piss."

"Deciding what to do with you," Whandall said. "I'm guessing, but it's like them. They cleaned you up so if they let you go, you'd tell about that. Then they decided whether to let you go or feed you to the crabs." Whandall put his hand on his brother's shoulder.

"Maybe," Shastern said. "They were nice enough when they came out. Made the ship captain apologize. He gave me a bag of shells and two silvers." Shastern held out a coin stamped with a hummingbird. "Then the Lord said, real slow and careful, that he regretted it but Lordkin had to stay away from the ships, and they'd draw up a proclamation. That was when he said nice things about Pelzed and Serpent's Walk, like he didn't want Pelzed mad.

"But we can't ever go to sea."

Whandall nodded and looked out over the Valley of Smokes.

CHAPTER
31

He was twenty before the Burning came again. And this time *everyone* was ready.

Hartanbath was more bison than man. In the Serpent Street region of Tep's Town—Flower Market, Bull Pizzle, Serpent's Walk, and several lesser bands—he was the man a fighter must defeat.

His missing ear-and-a-half contributed to Whandall's own reputation. Whandall could never have hurt him if Hartanbath hadn't been powerfully distracted. Hartanbath seemed to have learned *that* lesson. He was never seen fornicating in public again, with or without a woman's consent.

Whandall did not want a rematch. Few did. Hartanbath didn't lose.

At seventeen Whandall had taken to driving Alferth's wine wagons. Two years later he was present when Alferth held a street-corner drinking party.

A half-naked, dark-skinned, heavily armed looker ambled up and took a flask of wine with each hand.

Hartanbath objected.

The looker mocked Hartanbath's ears.

The looker was younger. Hartanbath was an inch taller and a stone heavier. Both could hit like logging axes. But Hartanbath ran out of strength first, sat down, and covered his head until the looker was satisfied.

Then the looker finished the wine and consented to tell stories.

He was Arshur the Magnificent. Some tremendous mountain range east of the Valley of Smokes had birthed his people. To the child Arshur, all was vertical, and all vertical faces were slippery with snow and ice. Arshur could climb any wall, enter any building, bypass any trap a householder might set for a thief (as if kinless would dare!).

There were cities where a thief might be imprisoned, others where he might be hanged, and cities where no thief could escape the King's magicians. Arshur had gathered fortunes in these places and others. He had fought monsters and magicians with his good sword—a huge clumsy mass of spelled bronze, thrice the size of a decent knife. A seer had predicted that he would one day be a King. When Arshur explained what a king was, the laughter angered him.

"So tell us, *Majesty,*" Shastern asked, "what brings your magnificence to Tep's Town?"

Arshur's face clouded only a moment. Then he downed the last of the flask and struck a pose. "I spent my last gold coin on a party," he said. "This was up the coast, to the north and west, Great Hawk Bay they call it. They do have hawks, but mostly they have merfolk."

"Merfolk?" One of the younger onlookers was willing to admit ignorance.

"Werepeople," Arshur said. "You hear of were*wolves?* These are sea creatures. No? Shape changers. People who become animals."

"Old tales," Alferth said. "Not told much anymore. Are you saying they're *real?*"

Arshur nodded vigorously. "Real, yes. You would not doubt my word?"

No one did, of course.

Arshur said. "Bear men are the worst. Not as much sense as a wolf, and when they want to—" He made motions with his hips.

"Rut," someone shouted.

"Rut, yes. When they want to rut they rut anything. Anybody. They're big and hard to kill, so when they want to rut, most people get rutted. Sea people are easier to deal with. They like people. Especially the girls. *Great* rutting. And the merfolk at Great Hawk Bay set the best table in the universe. There's a restaurant in the harbor, an island with a bridge to it. Rordray, that's his name—Rordray owns the place. Sometimes cooks himself but usually leaves that to others. He built the place to look like the top of a castle because that's the way his last one looked, somewhere else where the sun rises out of the sea."

The sun rises out of the sea. Wanshig had *seen* that.

"You spent all your money, Your Magnificence," Shastern

prompted. It wasn't obvious to anyone but Whandall that Shastern was set to run if Arshur came after him.

Arshur laughed instead. "It's sad being in a place of magic with no money. Rordray didn't need me! Neither did anyone else. If you steal—"

"Gather."

"—gather, they have magic to catch you. Besides, I like the people at Great Hawk. I could steal—sure, I can steal from anyone—but they'd know who did it! Then Rordray said he'd pay me for hemp and sage leaves, and the best comes from a place he calls the Valley of Smokes. That's here."

Whandall asked, "Don't they have hemp and sage other places?"

The barbarian looked at Whandall. "Other places they grow too strong. Something to do with magic. Wizards can change the taste, but Rordray says they never get it as good as grows here naturally."

"Hemp tea," Alferth said. "I've been told that before—that you get good hemp tea here."

"You sure do," Arshur said. "Wish I had a cup. Storytelling is thirsty work."

"Later," someone shouted. "How'd you get here?"

"Took ship," Arshur said. "Fought off pirates, big canoes of them at the cape. They turned and ran after they saw what I did to the first canoe! More pirates out of Point Doom—fought them off too. So when we got here I figured I had some drinks coming. Only thing was, I hadn't been paid yet, and the tavernkeeper wouldn't give me any credit."

"Tavernkeeper?" someone asked.

"Boy, don't you know anything?" Arshur demanded. "But you know, I see how you wouldn't. No taverns here! Just down at the docks. It's a place where they sell hemp tea, ale, wine sometimes. Tables and benches. Good roaring fire at night, only not here; here, the fire's always outside.

"Anyway, I was drinking good ale in peace when the owner demanded his money. He called the watch when I couldn't pay. By the time I explained to them, they'd beaten me upside of the head. The ship captain gave my pay to the tavernkeeper for damages and sailed on before I woke up! So here I am. I'll ship out one day, but I thought I'd see the country."

"How do you like Tep's Town?" Alferth asked.

"Not so good. No magic. Not that I know much magic, but a little magic makes life slide by a little smoother. And the women! Down there by the harbor there's a nice town—Lord's Town, they call it.

They sure didn't want me there! Anyplace I'd go, they'd send for the watch. Chased me right out of town, they did. So I get here, and the women all run away when I try to talk to them! One of them pulled a knife on me! On *me!* I wasn't going to hurt her. They tell me you can rut anytime you want to here, whether the women want to or not, but I sure didn't find it that way."

"Burning," Shastern said. "That's during a Burning. You just missed it."

"Arse of Zoosh! I never have any luck. When do you do it again? Next year? Maybe I'll stay a year."

"Maybe in a year," Alferth said. "And maybe longer."

"It'll be longer," Hartanbath said. Tenderly he touched his remaining shred of ear, notched by Whandall and now torn by Arshur. "Maybe a lot longer. Seems like more years between Burnings than when I was a kid."

Alferth climbed unsteadily onto the wagon and stood on the seat. He swayed just a bit as he shouted to the crowd. "What say? Is Arshur a Lordkin?"

"Yeah, who says I'm not?" Arshur demanded.

There were shouts. "Not me!" "Lordkin he is!" "Hell, I don't care." "Hey, this could be fun!"

Arshur was treated as a Lordkin from that day. Hartanbath disappeared for a season—healing?—then came back to pound the first fool who referred to his loss. He and Arshur were seen drinking together. . . .

It was an endless, pointless dance; but you had to keep track of who was on top. Arshur fitted into Lordkin society. For a few months he stole what he willed and carried his loot about, until he realized what older children knew almost by instinct: that a kinless might as well tend and carry property until a Lordkin needed it.

And one day Arshur got in a fight with the town guard.

His companions chose not to involve themselves. "They just kept hitting him and hitting him with those sticks," Idreepuct told them later, with secondhand pride. "He never gave up. They had to knock him out; they never made him give up."

Idreepuct was speaking in an intersection of alleys, to people already angry. Voices thick with rage demanded, "What was he *doing* to make them do *that?*" and, "Are the Lords *crazy,* to give them those *sticks?*"

Doing? It seemed almost irrelevant, but the tellers kept asking, and Idreepuct presently confessed. Ilsern—a tough, athletic woman who had never admired a man until Arshur came—had heard somehow of Alferth's secret wine wagons. Of course she told Arshur and Idreepuct.

They snatched a wagon. It was piled with fruit and it didn't look much like Alferth's wagons, but they took it anyway. They drove down Straight Street, whipping the ponies into a frenzy. Ilsern pelted passersby with fruit while Dree tried to pull the floorboards up and the kinless driver clung to the side and made mewling sounds.

By now the town guard didn't just have sticks and vivid blue tunics. They had built themselves small, fast wagons to put them where there was trouble. Wagons weren't part of the Lords' agreement, but they weren't exactly weapons either.

A guard wagon chased them. Then another. Kinless scattered out of the way. Dree got the floorboards up. "Nothing but road down here," he told Arshur, and Arshur swore and drove the ponies even harder. They nicked a fat Lordkin lady carrying a heavy bag; she screamed curses as they sped away.

They were fire on wheels until one pony fell dead, pulling the other down too.

And that was the end. Idreepuct and Ilsern stayed where they had fallen in the road, kneeling in surrender, and that stopped the guard, of course. Rules were rules. You knelt, they had to freeze. It could be very funny to watch their frustration.

But Arshur was still jittering with berserker joy.

He broke one guard's ribs and another's shoulder, and a blow to his head left another unconscious for two days. When Whandall came on the scene, they were carrying Arshur away strapped to a plank, laughing and insulting the guards, with a broken leg and bruises beyond counting. "And one of 'em hit him in the head," Idreepuct complained. "They can't *do* that, can they?"

Tarnisos said, "Big deal. Arshur's got a head like a rock—" as Whandall strode briskly out of earshot, and then ran.

There was Mother's man Freethspat on a corner talking to Shangsler, the big-shouldered man who had moved in with Wess twenty days past. Whandall stopped to describe the situation. He ran on, gathering whatever Placehold men he recognized. All of them were near strangers. Some would defend the house; some would celebrate the Burning instead.

The Lordkin believed they could feel it when Yangin-Atep stirred. Whandall felt that now. He intended to be guarding the house when the Burning began.

* * *

Days later, nothing at all was burning, and the Placehold men were letting him know it.

Whandall felt foolish. He *might* have noticed that Idreepuct had spilled the secret of the wine wagons to a score of loose tongues. Some had seen Alferth's wagons moving regularly along the Deerpiss. . . .

The vineyard was said to be totally destroyed. Now the most excitable among the city's Lordkin were out of action, nursing their first real hangovers. A gray drizzle had driven them indoors. The town guard had virtually disappeared, tactfully or prudently, carts and sticks and all.

The Burning remained a smoldering potential. It was only a matter of time.

PART FIVE
The Last Burning

CHAPTER
32

It had been raining hard for two days.

The Placehold would have camped in the courtyard for safety, but you couldn't have a Burning in the rain, could you? So the women and children were inside and the men were guarding the door in rotation.

But twenty-year-old Whandall was elsewhere, dripping wet in a windless rain, surrounded by seven sullen Lordkin in their thirties. A very bitter Alferth described what followed Arshur's beating:

A gathering horde of Lordkin flowed upstream along the Deerpiss and through the meadow, the Wedge. They damaged the gatehouse but couldn't be bothered to take the bricks apart. No mention was made of Toronexti guards: they must have joined the crowd.

Laborers saw human figures straggling out of the forest. Ten; twenty. They alerted Alferth. All the vintners, Lordkin and kinless, prepared to protect their holding. Only Tarnisos on the roof noticed the dust plume as *hundreds* of invaders surged up from the gatehouse.

They stomped the vines into mush. A few stopped to taste grapes for the first time. The rest stormed the wine house. It was deserted: Alferth and his people were fleeing through the forest, weaving a path among the deadly guardians of the redwoods, guided by what they had learned from Whandall Placehold.

The invaders found the vats in the basement and drank everything that would flow.

Alferth waited two days before he took his people back.

In the woods they found corpses slashed and mottled and swollen. Many who took that shortcut never reached the vineyards. Two hands more of bodies lay among the vats, killed by bludgeons and Lordkin knives, by wine and each other. The living had returned to town.

Whandall wasn't sorry to have missed that! Still, he gave thought to his own status. Alferth had been important to Pelzed and Serpent's Walk. Pelzed might see Whandall as more than Alferth's man, but Pelzed might equally consider that Whandall had held the Placehold with Pelzed's help, that all debts were paid.

Alferth was in his midthirties. Most of the boys he'd grown up with must be dead by now. What would it take to put him back together?

Whandall raised his voice above the rattle of raindrops. "Alferth, they didn't take what you *know*. You've still got that."

Alferth only looked grim. He was thinking like a victim. Freethspat found that disgusting and was starting to show it. Tarnisos was ready to kill someone. Anyone.

"You know how to make vines grow," Whandall said. "Alferth, you know how to make juice turn into wine and the wine into . . . well, *respect*. I don't know any of that. Almost nobody does."

"Kinless. They know it all," Alferth said.

"Find some land somewhere else."

"Time, you kinless fool. It takes time and work to make wine. A *year* before there's anything to drink, and that's after you have vines. Longer to grow vines. I'll be forgotten by then. Without wine I'm nothing."

Alferth was thinking like a kinless. "That's how we grew up," Whandall pointed out. "We have nothing except what we gather." He looked for support and saw smiles flicker. Not enough, and it wasn't quite true either. The child Alferth had had nothing, but he hadn't been *old*.

It came to Whandall that he had done what he could. Leave now. . . .

A two-pony wagon came trotting up Straight Street.

Alferth and his men watched from the curb. It came near, through several silent minutes. The little bone-headed ponies were pulling hard: the wagon was heavy, though the bed held only a few coils of rope.

Whandall cursed in his mind. He smelled blood. They were next to a butcher shop, but Whandall could recognize an omen. *Go home; get everyone into the courtyard. It's still raining, but the Burning is on us, I feel it.* . . . But he'd shouted of the Burning six days ago, and *nothing*.

Tarnisos trotted a few paces west to an ash pit, a shop for farm gear five years ago. The rebuilding hadn't touched it. He came back with an arm's length of fence post charred at one end.

Alferth stepped casually into the road. Freethspat followed, then the rest. Whandall hadn't moved. Without willing it, he became the fixed end of an arc across Straight Street.

The driver might have been dozing or hiding his face from the rain. He looked up far too late. Pulled on the reins, tried to turn the ponies. Far too late, as seven Lordkin swarmed over his wagon and wrestled his ponies to the ground.

He fought. He shouldn't have done that. Alferth took a solid blow to the head, and then the rest were on the driver, beating him.

"Aye, enough!" Whandall said. Louder, "Enough!"

Nobody chose to hear.

Whandall couldn't watch, couldn't interfere, dared not show his anguish. He turned to the cart instead. The bed was high, maybe too high. It carried coils of tarred rope, but not a lot of that. Had someone else taken to driving wine? Wine would distract them. He felt for a loose board, found a corner and lifted.

Eyes.

Three small faces. One mouth opened to scream. A child's hand covered the smaller child's mouth. Whandall put a finger to his lips, then set back the board, having seen very little . . . but at least three children.

Tarnisos set himself as if in a whackball game and swung his fence post at the driver's head.

They were killing him. He'd been curled around himself on the ground, but at Tarnisos's blow he sprawled loose and sloppy. And Whandall felt a rage burning outward from his belly. Not since he'd cut Hartanbath had he felt like this . . . but he was helpless as Tarnisos wound up for another blow.

Whandall raised his hand and set Tarnisos's weapon afire.

Tarnisos dropped the flaming beam with a yell and a backward leap.

Yangin-Atep was real. Yangin-Atep was in Whandall as a jubilant rage. He pointed into the butcher shop and it caught with a flash and a roar. The men still kicking the wagoneer looked around at the sudden light, and knew.

The Burning had begun.

The butcher shop burned merrily in the rain, flames cradling the apartment above. Tarnisos picked up his torch and tried to set the shop next door alight. It was wet, and Whandall held his power back. The rest were kicking smoldering wooden walls into slats to make more torches.

The kinless driver looked dead. Moving him might kill him if he wasn't, but he wasn't safe here. Whandall crossed the man's arms and enclosed the man's elbows and torso with his own arms. Resalet taught his boys to do that, to hold in damaged innards. He eased the man into the wagon, nesting him in a coil of rope.

He got onto the seat, found the whip, and used it. The wagon lurched away.

Tarnisos yelled and came pelting after him.

The last Burning had happened in a drought. This time everyone had stored food. A handful of kinless children would not discommode the Placehold, Whandall thought. They could tend the house while the Burning lasted and then go home, if they still had a home.

But four strangers were now pelting along behind Tarnisos, and Tarnisos had caught the wagon and was pulling himself aboard. What did the man think he was doing?

Tarnisos pulled himself over the benchback and next to Whandall. "You felt it!" he crowed. "Yangin-Atep! Alferth thought I was crazy, but you *feel* it, right? Right?"

With the weight in children the ponies were pulling, Whandall wasn't going to outrun anything. He waved behind him. Six followed now, and one had swept up an armful of faggots. "Who're they?"

Tarnisos looked back. "Nobody. They saw you start the Burning, maybe."

Maybe. Maybe they recognized a false-bottomed wagon. They thought they were chasing wine! Better distract them.

It was like being drunk. Not words he never wanted to speak, but *fire* leaked from the joyful rage at his core. The bundle of sticks flamed at both ends, and the man carrying them whooped. He began passing them out in some haste.

This next turn would take him home, but Whandall drove straight on. Behind the running men, fires were catching. He could not lead this merry mob to his own front door! Let Freethspat warn them of what was coming.

"Why'd you take the—" Tarnisos rapped the probable corpse's skull. "Him?"

"Anything on him?" Best not to let Tarnisos know what he was hiding.

Tarnisos inspected the man. "Nothing anyone would want. He's dead. Why did you want the wagon?"

"I've got something in mind," Whandall said.

A much easier turn came up. He could follow it west and north toward the Black Pit, then north along the Coldwater until it branched into the Deerpiss—a route Whandall knew well. Two of the runners dropped back, and then all of the rest in a clump, barring one. They'd stopped to gather at a store, it looked like. But the last runner was pumping hard. Monumentally ugly, he was, a barbarian. Whandall picked him for a teller just arrived.

He kept driving.

Markets and large stores attracted unwanted attention; they were looted too often. Feller's Disenchanted Forest was big for Tep's Town. Now, ahead of the Burning and first of the local looters, Whandall pulled up in front and got out.

"Coming?"

"Whandall, what is it you *want?*"

"Dunno. I've never been in here before."

A squinting clerk approached them. Behind him, kinless customers were moving briskly out of the store. The nearsighted clerk lost his smile, turned, and ran.

Whandall ignored them all. He selected two big axes, two long poles tipped with blades, blankets. Rope was already in the wagon. Thick leather sheets loosely bound by laces: one size fits all, adult or child. Wooden masks with slits for sight. He piled some into Tarnisos's arms and some into his own and led the way out into the rain.

The teller had caught up. He blocked Whandall's path and tried to speak, but he could do nothing but heave for breath. Whandall's look sent him stumbling back.

Tarnisos stopped in the doorway. "Nobody would want this stuff, Whandall!"

"I said I had something in mind." He dropped his load into the wagon and returned.

Tarnisos pushed his own load into Whandall's arms. "There's a stash of shells somewhere in there, and I want it." He jogged back in, pushing past the gasping teller.

Whandall dumped the stuff into the wagon. He'd watched woodsmen at work, long years ago. What had he forgotten? He had rope, severs and axes, sleeping gear, armor . . .

Lightning played through the black clouds. In this light the driver looked very dead. Whandall lifted the man out of the wagon bed and set him under the awning. Poor kinless, he'd gotten in the way at the wrong time. Other kinless would heal him or bury him.

Whandall boarded the wagon. A clattering approached . . .

A wagon rounded the corner on two wheels. Voices hailed Whandall to halt.

Whandall reached for his rage. The guard wagon flapped one great sheet of flame. Town guards screamed and baled out, hit the dirt and rolled.

The teller tried to talk to a fallen guard. The guard's stick whacked his shin; the teller danced. Whandall laughed, a sound like a maddened bird, startling himself.

Two guards were on their feet, running toward Whandall, waving sticks. The ponies were running better now, but they still wouldn't outrun men on foot.

Whandall's wave turned their regulation sticks into torches.

He waved behind him, setting one end of Feller's Disenchanted Forest on fire. The stairs had been at the other end. Tarnisos would have his chance to get out. Whandall didn't want him hurt; he wanted only to be rid of him.

It was quiet beyond the houses. Lightning flickered in black-bellied clouds. Whandall listened for children rustling beneath the wagon bed, but he heard nothing. It worried him. They could be suffocating. Whandall cursed. Being wet bothered him unreasonably.

He made for the Black Pit.

CHAPTER
33

The Pit was changed. Only the stink was the same. The gate was open, but much of the fence was in ruins, half rebuilt, but not as neatly as Whandall remembered. As he pulled the ponies to a stop, he found no mist around him, and no misty monsters. He was alone but for the black and silver pools that made up the Pit, and a scrawny coyote pacing the shore not far away, eyeing him distrustfully.

Here was no protection at all. Whandall kept an eye for rioters and rivals and city guards. But the coyote would have fled such invaders.

He found the wagon bed's loose corner and pulled it up. He thought of the long knife he hadn't drawn, and the way he'd seen rats react to being trapped.

The children didn't move. By the wave of body odor, they'd been in there for some time. Their big eyes watched him in wariness and fear. They snorted at the alien stench of the Pit. Seven of them were packed in with hardly a wine flask's worth of empty space to share.

The youngest might be four and five. Two were hardly children at all. The older boy might have been a Lordkin of nineteen; the girl, sixteen; though Lordkin would have been at Whandall's throat by now. The girl was trying not to meet his eyes.

She was as beautiful as any woman he'd ever seen. She was slender, tall for a girl, her legs long and smooth. Surely there were Lordkin among her ancestors. The lines did blur between Lordkin and kinless. Sometimes the results were wonderful. His whole body and mind were ready to drown in the dark deeps of her eyes.

He held back. He could guess how he must look to a kinless. She was already terrified.

"I'm Whandall," he said. "The man who was driving you was killed."

The girl's shoulders slumped. "I knew it," she whispered.

Whandall couldn't take his eyes off her. She started to cry, tears welling despite her efforts at control. The man must have been her father, but of course Whandall couldn't ask. He desperately sought for something to say that wouldn't offend her, wouldn't scare her away. Nothing came to him so he turned to the boy.

"Who are you?"

"Carver Ropewalker," the boy said.

"Your sister?" Whandall asked.

Carver Ropewalker nodded and sat up. "What are you going to do?" He was trying to sound brave, but the fear came through in his voice, and he kept glancing at Whandall's big Lordkin knife.

"I'm not sure. I got you out of the Burning," Whandall said. *I saved you! You could at least thank me! But now what?* "You could wait here—"

"Here? This is the Black Pit!"

Whandall was listening to the boy, but he was watching the girl as both climbed out of the wagon. The younger children stayed in the compartment, their eyes enormous. The girl was crying but trying not to show it, afraid but not terrified. And who wouldn't be afraid of the Black Pit? "Stay here with me. I can't go back yet. I'm possessed of Yangin-Atep."

Carver Ropewalker looked at him in disbelief and a scorn he was trying to swallow. The girl seemed more frightened than ever. "We'll be all right here," she said. She wouldn't meet Whandall's eyes or even look at him.

Whandall realized she was more afraid of him than the Pit. A kinless girl, unmarried, her father dead, the city burning despite the rain. Now she faced a Lordkin babbling that he was possessed of the fire god!

"I didn't hurt the driver," he said, in case she feared that too. "I tried to save him, but he was dying before I could get him in the wagon." He didn't think they believed him. Yangin-Atep's anger rose in a surge. Who did they think they were? These were kinless, kinless at his mercy, and the Burning had begun!

"You can leave us here," Carver said. He wasn't quite demanding and not quite pleading. "Don't worry about us. We'll get back—"

"There'll be nothing to go back to!" the girl wailed. "I smelled hemp smoke after we got in the wagon compartment." She peered through the gloom and rain toward the city she couldn't see. "You should hurry back," she said. "You'll be missing the fun."

Yangin-Atep's fire rose higher in Whandall Placehold. She hated him. They all hated him. She was his if he wanted her, and he did, as he had never before wanted a woman.

They were all staring at Whandall now. Carver tried to get between Whandall and the girl. Brave and futile, a silly gesture. Carver Ropewalker was no threat, none at all. Yangin-Atep or someone laughed within him, and Whandall moved forward, his control stretched to its limits.

Something growled behind him. Whandall turned gladly to face a new threat.

There was no threat. There were only these pools of black water, and the snarling coyote.

Not water. It was waveless black stuff that didn't reflect, and scattered silver pools of water on top, and a deer's head . . . no, a terrified deer struggling neck deep, its antlers jittering. That was what held the coyote's attention: the coyote was trying to decide whether to go after the deer. It snarled at Whandall: *Mine!*

Yeah? Whandall focused on the far side of the black pool, where the coyote was glaring at him like a rival, and let a little of his rage leak out. He thought the coyote's fur might puff into flame. He wasn't expecting what happened.

An acre of black goo flamed and rose into a mushroom of fire.

The deer screamed and thrashed. The coyote ran. Shadows in the flame formed a pair of dagger-toothed cats who menaced the drowning deer.

Carver Ropewalker gaped at the fireball.

"I'm possessed of Yangin-Atep," Whandall repeated. "What will the Burning be like if I'm not there? It might—I don't—" Whandall's hands were trying to speak for him. He kept secrets better than he told them.

The girl wouldn't meet his eyes. Whandall felt the girl's fear. He suddenly understood what Arshur the Magnificent had tried to tell them: the women of Tep's Town wouldn't play at sex. They were afraid to be noticed.

He forced out, "I don't *like* burning down my *city* every few years. It makes a mess. People *die*. Mother's Mother says they never used to, but they do now." Again he was speaking to Carver, but he was watching the girl. Did she look just a little less afraid? But she still hated him.

"Father is dead, then?" Carver Ropewalker asked.

"The driver? Carver, I'm not sure. I left him where he could get help or burial."

He could see Carver swallowing that: dealing not just with his father's death but his own new responsibility and the ambiguous, dangerous presence of a fire-casting Lordkin. Presently he nodded.

"Father got in trouble," he said. "The Lordkin, you know what they've been like since the guards beat up that barbarian. We have a ropewalk in the Pond District—"

"Yeah?" The Pond had once belonged to the kinless. Now the populace was mostly Lordkin; the only kinless were those who couldn't afford to get out. They must have felt like mammoths in a roc nest.

"And Father lost his temper."

"How do I name you?" Whandall asked.

Willow Ropewalker was the older girl, Carver's sister. She finally elected to look at him but not to smile. Their brother Carter was twelve or so. His hand was hidden, certainly holding a weapon. The younger ones were children of Carver's father's sister: Hammer, Iris, Hyacinth, and Opal Miller.

Carver and Willow and Whandall got the younger children out of the wagon. Two were crying without sound. Willow looked around her and into the Pit.

The fire-cats had become shadow-cats in smoke. They were stalking a dead tree, like house cats the size of houses. Whandall said, "They won't hurt us. They're only ghosts, but they'll scare everyone else off. This is a good place to wait."

"This is the Black Pit!"

"Yes, Carver, I know."

Carver said, "All right, Whandall; it's nothing *I'd* have thought of. I guess those fences will keep the kids out of the tar—"

Oh, *that* was it. The Black Pit smelled ferociously of rope! It was *tar*, not magic, though there must be magic here.

"Tar," the boy Hammer said. "Carver, we—"

"*Stay away!* These ghosts—don't you know how they *died?*" Whandall didn't; he listened. Carver said, "The tar sucked them down! Prey and killer together. Thousands of skeletons all down there in the tar, their ghosts in battle until the end of time."

The rain fell more heavily. The tar fires went out, but black smoke hung over them, and the rain was sooty. Willow tried to cover the children.

Carver said urgently, "Hey, Whandall. These blankets, we can spread them for an awning? Tilt 'em so they can drip?"

"Go ahead."

For an instant Carver was at a loss. Then he and the children began to look along shore for dead trees, poles, props for blanket-awnings. His voice drifted back. "Then what, Lordkin? How long will the Burning last?"

Whandall didn't want to talk to them. It was enough to control the rage. But the boy deserved an answer. "There's no telling. Yangin-Atep could take someone else. You'll have to wait. If the sky clears up, look for smoke. If there's no smoke over Tep's Town, go home."

The boy Hammer Miller was still in the wagon. "The ponies have gotten bigger," he said.

Whandall had wondered if it was his imagination. The beasts had pulled more strongly as they ran toward the Black Pit. Now they shuffled with nervous energy. They'd eaten every plant in reach. They were bigger, yes, and the projections in their foreheads were horns long enough to hurt a man.

Hammer asked, "What *is* all this stuff you brought?"

Whandall spoke his heart's desire. "Or we could cut our way through the forest."

Carver said, "You're joking?" But Willow Ropewalker ran to the wagon bed and began running her hands through the loot.

"Carver, he isn't! Axes . . . saws . . . leathers . . . up the Coldwater would take us right to the forest edge. We *can*—we can *leave!* That's what Father wanted. The Burning was coming. He—" She glared at Whandall. "Oh, fine, and now we'll be taking the Burning with us! I don't suppose you know how to swing an ax?"

Whandall smiled at her. Her beauty would make him drunk if he let it. "I don't know, Willow. Kreeg Miller never let me hold an ax, but I watched. I can drive ponies, and I couldn't do that once."

But his plans—daydreams, really—hadn't run past this moment.

He said, "Lady." He tasted the word. Pelzed's woman liked to be called that. "Lady, there's a world out there. What do you think? Could we get through?"

"Father thought so," said Willow. "Your army came through the forest with the Lords leading you. Those old Lordkin must have chopped their way through. Whandall, you'd *better* learn to use an ax."

"You're both crazy," Carver said.

Whandall recognized the way Willow looked at her older brother: a contempt born of too much knowledge. "We can't stay, Carver! Whatever we have is all gone. There's a world out there—"

"I've been on the docks," Carver said.

Willow just looked. *Huh?* Whandall said, "My brother was a sailor. What's your point?"

"I've met sailors and lookers and tellers from all up and down the coast and farther yet. All they know is, this is the town they burn down. Willow—Whandall—they don't know kinless from Lordkin from Lords. *They can't tell the difference.* We go out there, we go as thieves. Forgive me—you say *gatherers,* don't you?"

It came to Whandall that he had never believed it in the first place. He wasn't disappointed, then, to know that Carver was right. That Wanshig had told him the same. Wanshig, who held a post for three years and was then put back on the docks in Tep's Town, because he couldn't stop gathering, because he was Lordkin.

But the blood was draining from his face, and he could only look at the ground and nod.

Morth asked, "What if a magician vouched for you?"

Whandall looked up. He felt that he should be startled, somehow.

Morth of Atlantis looked no older than the last time Whandall had seen him. His clothes were inconspicuous but finer than what he had worn in Tep's Town. His hair was going gray. White to gray, waves of orange-red running through it like cloud-shadows as Whandall watched.

"Morth," Whandall said.

"My word should be enough, I think," Morth said. "And it would be wise if we did not get closer together."

A magician. A water magician. Whandall felt Yangin-Atep's rage. Fear came back to Willow's eyes, and Whandall fought with Yangin-Atep. Morth must have felt the struggle. He moved away.

"So why would some random barbarian trust you?" Whandall shouted. "For that matter—" Something odd here. "Where did you *come* from?"

Bubbles in drifting smoke, a mere suggestion of huge dagger-toothed cats, were playing around Morth's feet.

"A lurking spell. It worked?" Morth looked around him, very pleased at the signs of astonishment. "There's still manna around this place. Good. We'll be safe here until we decide."

Whandall left his knife where it was, pushed through the leather sleeve in his belt, but he hadn't forgotten it. He said, "Morth, you don't just happen to be here."

"No, of course not. I came here because I thought you would. I almost followed you, but I guessed you must be in the middle of the Burning, so—" Smile, shrug. He saw no answering understanding, so he said, "The tattoo. I prepared it after I saw the lines in your hand. I can follow its pattern anywhere in the world. I'm hoping to follow you *out.*"

Willow exclaimed, "Out! Then you think so too! It's possible! Whandall—" She said his name almost defiantly. "Whandall, is he really a wizard?"

"Morth of Atlantis, meet the Ropewalkers and the Millers. Yes, Willow." Her name didn't come easily. "He's a wizard. Once a famous one. I mean, look at his hair. Did you ever see such a color on an ordinary man? Morth, where have you been since—since you lost your shop?"

"I moved to the edge of the Lordshills, as a teacher. It seemed to me that Yangin-Atep had cost me everything, Burning after Burning. I had better go to where a god could find no magic. I never built another shop."

"I saw the ash pit. Some burned skulls."

Morth must have sensed that there was more to this than curiosity. "Yes. And in the ashes did you see an iron pot with a lid?"

"No. Wait, my brother saw that. Is it important?"

"It was my plan to get out! It was my last treasure!" Morth's fists were clenched at his sides. "I thought cold iron was all I needed to protect it. The Burning City! It never crossed my mind that cold iron can be heated!"

The Ropewalkers and Millers were fascinated. Truly, so was Whandall.

"Well." Morth had regained control of himself. "I never sensed the Burning. I was fooling myself about that. That afternoon I was eating lunch at my counter when I looked out the door at eight Lordkin running straight at my shop! I saw the big one cast fire from his hand, and that was all *I* needed. I went out the back.

"My last treasure was two Atlantean gold coins rich in manna. Get those out of Tep's Town and I'm a wizard again. They would have lost all magic if I hadn't stored them in a cold iron pot with a spelled lid. It was too heavy for one man to carry. I cut the handles off and made myself believe that nobody could steal—sorry, Seshmarl—*gather* it."

Carver said, "Seshmarl?"

"It's Whandall," Whandall admitted.

Morth said, *"Whandall,* then. The Lordkin charged into my shop. I looked back. They weren't chasing me; I slowed and watched. The big man, he picked up my pot in his two arms. I just have trouble believing how *strong* you Lordkin are."

Whandall nodded. Morth said, "I'd seen him start fires. He was possessed of Yangin-Atep."

Carver and Willow looked at each other.

"I still didn't think he could get the pot open until he caused the iron to burn. Hot iron doesn't stop manna flow. I saw him lift the lid and look inside. Two gold coins must have been the last thing he ever saw."

He hardly needed to say, *And then all the magical power left behind by sunken Atlantis roared into a man possessed of the fire god.*

"You just don't seem to have very good luck," Whandall said, "with the Placehold men." And that was how he knew he was leaving: he had spoken his family's name among strangers.

CHAPTER

34

The rain stopped at evening, and by night the skyline had become a patchy red glow. The Burning continued without Whandall. The night seemed endless. Whandall made his bed on rock, wrapped in a blanket snatched from Feller's, far enough from the kinless children to make them stop *twitching*.

He half woke from a dream of agony and rage. His hands were fire that reached out to spread fire like a pestilence, by touch. The Placehold was burning. He was the Placehold, he was burning, and his shape was gone alien, a crab with a long trailing, looping tail and a terrible freezing, bleeding wound somewhere near his heart.

For a long moment he knew that fires were the nerves of Yangin-Atep. He sensed all of the fires in the Valley of Smokes and two ships offshore, one cooking breakfast, one aflame. He felt his life bleeding out through Lordshills where a Warlock's Wheel had eaten away all the magic. Then it all went away like any dream and left him chilled and wet.

He gestured and the half-dead fire flared into an inferno. At least it was easy to tend a fire!

He was very aware of Willow Ropewalker not far away. Desire rose and he held it back as he would hold a door, his weight on one side, enemies on the other.

Desire and excitement. They could leave, forever. Would they leave together? "Morth!"

The wizard was on the other side of the fire, and he stayed there. Whandall had to shout. Anyone might overhear. So be it.

"What will happen? You've seen my future. Is it with"—he gestured to Willow—"them?"

Morth considered what to say. "I haven't read their future," he said. "I don't know them well enough to do that. You may leave the Valley of Smokes. I don't know about the Millers and Ropewalkers. Further in the future, the line loops and blurs. You may return." He studied Whandall from the other side of the fire. "I can say this. You will have a more pleasant life with friends. With people who know who you are. Consider, Seshmarl—Whandall—you're choosing a new and unknown path. Easier to walk it with others."

"You know what I'm thinking, then?"

Morth shook his head sadly. "I know what *Lordkin* think. Actually, most Lordkin don't think at all. They just act. You're different."

"It's hard," Whandall said.

Morth smiled thinly. "I can't help. Anything I could do to calm you would probably kill you."

"As you—no, as *it,* your spell—killed my father," Whandall said.

Morth said nothing. Whandall wondered if he'd known all along. Wizard, liar, he'd killed Whandall's family. Yangin-Atep's rage boiled inside him, and Morth was gone.

Whandall heard a distant bush rustling. Flame shot high as greasewood ignited, and Whandall knew that *he'd* done that. He thought he saw a shadow beyond the flame.

"Morth!"

There was no answer.

"Whandall?" It was Carver, behind him.

"Stay away. I'm possessed of Yangin-Atep," Whandall said.

"Where's Morth?"

"I don't know. Running."

The night went on endlessly, and always there was the glow of fire over Tep's Town.

CHAPTER
35

Daylight. Whandall, dreaming fire, snapped awake as if he were guarding the Placehold with only children for defenders.

They were in the wagon, sleeping, most of them. One kinless boy was down by the fence.

Whandall went down to shore, walking wide of that black stuff that stuck to everything. The boy was Hammer Miller. Whandall hailed him from a safe distance.

Hammer turned without surprise, one hand hidden. The other held a milk pot. "I want to get some tar," he said.

"I can't let you go. Your sister would kill me."

"No, not Willow. Carver might. We can sell it."

"How do you know?"

"Everyone needs rope!"

"How much do you need?"

Hammer showed him a milk pot. "This much. I don't think I can lift it when it's full. I'll have to get Carver."

Whandall watched how they went about it.

First they talked the problem to death.

Carver and Willow tied a rope to Hammer's waist. Then, while Hammer danced with impatience, they tied another rope to the neck of the jar and let the rope trail.

Hammer went over the fence. He walked with some care and, twelve paces out, found his feet mired.

The coyote came out of nowhere, streaking for the mired boy.

Whandall touched the beast with flame. A ring of flame flashed outward. Hammer shouted and ducked. The flame just singed him before it puffed out.

Carver was cursing him. Whandall said, "Didn't think. Sorry."

The coyote was gone. Hammer was still mired.

They pulled on the rope. He shouted. They left off long enough for him to scoop a mass of sticky black stuff into the jar, waist deep now and still sinking. They pulled again. It was hard work. Whandall joined them on the rope. Hammer tried to drag the jar after him, lost it, then caught the rope that tethered the jar and dragged it a little farther. When he could stand he braced himself and began pulling. Carver went over the fence, treading in the shallow footprints Hammer had left before he sank. Together they pulled the jar out half full.

"Enough," Carver said.

It wasn't that much different from a raid on some shop in Maze Walkers. Lurk, spy out the territory, test the defenses. Then go for it, gathering what you can. Anything unexpected has to be fixed on the fly. Settle for what you can gather in one pass; don't go back for more.

And this awful stuff, which had already ruined every scrap of clothing he could see, could be made into wealth by moving it somewhere else. How did they *know? That* was the hard part.

Now the wagon stank of tar, not of bodies long confined. The ponies pulled more strongly as they moved northwest. Whandall waited until he was moving up the Deerpiss before he made the Ropewalkers and Millers get under the floorboards. Tar pot on top. A guard would think hard before he lifted *that.*

The brick guardhouse was in sight, its gates closed. Opening them wouldn't be complicated . . .

A guard popped out, saw him, shouted, "Staxir!" Two more stepped out to study his approach. They all wore armor, but on this hot day none of them were fully protected, though they all wore masks.

They swung the gate open and retreated back under an awning.

What were Toronexti doing here? Though they looked edgy, weapons drawn, it looked like he could just drive on through. . . .

Nah. He stopped alongside the awning and, before any of them could speak, asked, "Staxir? What are you doing here? The vineyard's nothing but muck."

They laughed. They were older Lordkin, and wiser. "We're not here for Alferth!"

"We'll miss the wine, though, Stax—"

"This is the *path*. The Toronexti have to be here if the kinless want to leave."

Another surprise? Whandall asked, "The path goes right through the forest? Really?"

"No, but kinless still try it," Staxir said. "The Burning could start any hour, and don't *they* know it!"

"So we look in their wagons and take what looks good, and in a day they come back, and we take—"

"What're *you* carrying?"

Whandall said, "Stuff for cutting trees."

"What is that *stink?*"

"Tar. The woodsmen, they cover their hands with it to stop plant poisons. There're kinless out past here getting lumber, aren't there?"

"No," Staxir said.

Whandall scratched his head. "Well, there will be. The Burning is on, so I took this stuff. I can keep it in the wine house, day or two."

Men who might have taken some of his good tools a moment ago thought again. Eyes turned toward Tep's Town. Staxir said, "We gotta be here. Kinless'll be trying to get out again with everything they own."

"You don't need us all, Stax."

"Safer here. Dryer."

Sounds of disgust.

Whandall waved and drove on. He could guess the unspoken: a wagoneer who came this way with heavy gear to sell would be back with shells for a tax man's pockets. But Whandall didn't plan to come back.

Weeds were starting to cover the trampled vineyard. Whandall pulled the wagon behind the brick wine house. The roof wasn't brick; it had been timber and thatch, and it had burned. Whandall cursed. He was tired of being wet.

He got the children out of the wagon. Two youngsters were beginning to cry without sound. Whandall helped Willow out. Carver rejected his hand. He was still looking at Whandall like a dangerous animal. It was getting on his nerves.

A stub of blackened timber poked from the wine house roof. Whandall let a little of his rage leak into it. Against the black-bellied clouds it made orange-white light and a bit of heat.

Willow looked around her and said, "We're at the forest."

"What is this place?" Carver asked.

"Wine house," Whandall said. "The roof's gone, but the walls are still up." Shelter. But it was not yet noon, and he didn't want to stop. He looked at the malevolent forest across his path. Could they really get through that?

Carver walked toward the woods and into them.

"Careful!" Whandall called. He followed, with Willow just behind him.

The redwoods towered over them. These were young trees, though tall enough to cut the force of wind-driven rain. Deeper in, they would be much bigger. A hundred varieties of thorns and poison plants clustered protectively around their bases.

Whandall spoke to Willow, hoping that Carver and the children would listen. You didn't lecture a grown man directly if you could avoid it. "Stay clear of this thorny stuff. It's too dark to see how close you are. At night you wouldn't move at all. These pine trees, they won't hurt you. Almost everything else will. Even the redwoods make you want to look up when you should be watching your feet—"

"Where did you learn about the forest?" the twelve-year-old asked.

"I used to watch the loggers, Carter. I carried water for them. Carver, do you think we can cut our way through here?"

"You brought those cutting things."

"Severs."

"Severs. We can use those," Carver said. "But the plants can always reach farther than you think. You think you've got clearance, but—I'm worried about the children."

"These leathers'll fit the older ones. And us." *We could cut a path for children,* Whandall thought, *or a wider path for a wagon.* But how far did the forest go? "It took an army half a year to get through, two hundred years ago," Whandall said.

"We only need enough for one wagon," Willow said briskly. "We go around what we can, cut when we have to. Sell the lumber gear when we get to the other side, and the tar, if there's anyone to buy. Did you bring a whetstone?"

"Whatever that is, I didn't bring it."

Whandall hadn't thought in terms of buying and selling. Kinless would know how to trade, how to work, how to *find* work. On the other side of the forest, *Lordkin would not have license to take what they wanted.*

He hadn't missed that point, but he was starting to feel its force.

But he felt the warmth stirring in his belly, not unlike lust, not unlike the heat that rose from wine. Alferth was wrong to call it *anger.*

"This was Yangin-Atep's path."

His arm reached forward and the heat ran through his fingertips, feeling out the old path, far beyond what his eyes could see. Yangin-Atep's trailing tail. The dream held for an instant and was gone again.

Brushwood caught. Vines and thorn plants burned in the rain. An eddy swirled the smoke around them and made them choke. Then the wind steadied, blowing it north ahead of them.

CHAPTER
36

The land ran generally uphill. The flame-path didn't cramp them, but it wasn't quite a road. There were stumps Whandall had to burn out. The horses were grown visibly stronger. They pulled with little effort, but they shied at Carver's touch on the reins.

Whandall tried it. Both ponies stopped and turned to look at him along spiral spears as long as a forearm. Willow took the reins from his unresisting hands, and the ponies turned and began to pull.

That first night they stripped a dozen crabapple trees for their dinner. Children didn't need to be instructed to hurl the cores away: they did it by instinct.

Carver suggested that Whandall sleep between the wagon and the vineyards. Lordkin might follow the scorched path, he said. Carver was trying to protect Willow. Whandall went along with that.

But in the morning he told Carver, "We don't need a guard at night. Only a madman would walk through the forest in the dark." He pointed back down the trail. A blackened ruin, ash and mud, with a few flecks of green growing into it. It wasn't straight, and it certainly wasn't inviting.

"That's odd," Carver said. He pointed ahead. The trail remained black, no traces of green at all.

The redwoods stood like pillars holding up the black-bellied clouds. Their shadows made a twilight even at noon.

Where Whandall's fire had gone, they saw nothing of predators and nothing of prey. They had to strike out sideways to their path to find anything to eat.

Willow picked an apronful of small red berries for them. Delicious. Whandall watched her mind wrestle with itself before she warned him. "Whandall, don't eat these berries if they're growing near a redwood."

"I know. We need to keep the kids away from any berry patch. The poison patches look too much like redberries."

Carver made slings, a weapon new to Whandall. It would send a stone flying at uncanny speed. Carver was good with a sling; Carter was even better; Whandall developed some skill. They were able to feed themselves and the children and to fend off coyotes.

Kinless with weapons. Kinless *skilled* with weapons. He half remembered the Lords talking of an old war fought against the kinless. How had kinless fought? Had they used slings? Why had they lost?

He dreamed that night, of Lords with helmets and armor and spears leading a horde of Lordkin with knives. They fought a smaller, slimmer people who used slings and small javelins. The stones rattled against the Lords' shields. A few mad Lordkin held their hands out, and sheets of fire flowed into the kinless ranks.

And every one of the fire-wielding Lordkin looked like Whandall.

In rain they had slept under the wagon. They'd left the rain behind, and now they could sleep in the wagon, off the ground. Fire was easy: half-burned charcoal was everywhere. They dug a midden and laid a ridge of dirt from the midden to the wagon. In the dark a child could follow it by feel.

Whandall watched them, studying how the kinless worked, how the kinless thought. How they talked. Always they talked.

Their third morning brought them to the crest of the mountains. Downhill, the land was blackened and almost bare. Plants were growing back. Whandall hadn't done this; it was half a year old. But the going looked easy and the path was clear. Whandall's new burn switchbacked through the half-grown plants like a black snake.

"Whandall, this is easy traveling, and we don't need your fire. Let's go back for another wagon."

"Who, Carver?" he asked, knowing Carver would never leave Whandall with Willow. Lordkin men (some, anyway) guarded their women no less than Carver did.

"You and me. Willow, you can keep the wagon moving, can't you? The ponies won't mind anyone else anyway. If you get into trouble, just stop."

* * *

Green creepers were sprouting everywhere along the path, poking through the ash of Whandall's burning. Between dawn and sunset Carver and Whandall retraced their path through the burned woods.

A wagon had been left near the loading dock. One of the mares had wandered into view. She was smaller than the stallion ponies, and her horn was just a nub.

They watched the wine house through sunset until midnight before they believed that it was deserted. Then Carver approached the mare and was able to put a bridle on her.

They found hundreds of little flasks heaped against a wall. "Empty," Whandall pointed out.

"Well made, though. They won't leak. Maybe we can sell them on the other side."

They heaped the wagon with flasks and cut some grass for the mare too. They slept in the ruined wine house.

In the morning Whandall rode facing backward, wary that something might follow, while Carver drove.

Carver grumbled, "We didn't see anyone following us!"

"Lordkin know how to lurk." Some half-suspected danger tapped at the floor of Whandall's mind. He watched their back path.

It wasn't black anymore; it was green. "This ash must make wonderful fertilizer," he said.

Carver turned around. "You can almost see it growing!"

Ahead of them was only blackened dirt.

"Yangin-Atep," Whandall said, "wants us gone."

Carver snapped, "When did your fire god become a fertility goddess?"

"Not Yangin-Atep, then, but *something* wants us gone. The forest?" Whandall remembered days in Morth's shop, Morth reading his palm, mumbling about Whandall's destiny. Could a god read destiny too? "I think that's it. I'm carrying fire through a forest."

"We're being expelled," Carver said.

Whandall shook his head, smiling. "You're escaping. I'm being expelled." And even as he watched the trail behind seemed to grow more creepers.

Travel went fast. The mare grew stronger as they traveled, and larger, but she wasn't giving them any trouble. Behind them the trail's outline blurred with green.

* * *

Coyotes had discovered the travelers' abandoned middens. That was scary. That evening Whandall and Carver crawled under the wagon to sleep, back to back and armed.

A voice in the dark. "This magician who killed your father. Did you try to kill him?"

"No, Carver."

"Good."

Whandall believed he had nothing to hide from Carver: nothing so monstrous as the open truth of what he was. Still, sharing secrets outside the family seemed unnatural.

Into the quiet dark Carver said, "Did you know that *plague* is a kind of living thing? Wizards can see it. Wizards can kill it and heal the client. Otherwise it grows. Without a wizard, other people get sick too, more and more. We need wizards. But wizards don't like the Valley of Smokes."

" 'Course not. No magic."

The dark was silent a while longer. Then Carver asked, "Why not?"

"Kill Morth? Why?"

"Your father."

"Morth did what kinless do. Sorry, *taxpayers.* What we do too. If Pothefit caught a looker taking the cook pot from the Placehold courtyard, he'd've killed him."

It was too dark to see Carver's expression. Whandall said, "The Burning killed Pothefit. In the Burning you can have anything you can take. They couldn't take Morth's shop."

Silence from Carver. The woods stirred: something died violently.

"That's what I was trying to remember," Whandall said suddenly. *"Morth* could follow us. I keep forgetting Morth. Carver, we wouldn't *see* him. That lurk spell."

Near sunset of the next day they reached the crest of the mountains and found two dead coyotes near a dead campfire.

Carver ran.

Whandall watched him disappear into the rocks. He almost followed. Coyotes might menace Willow and the children! But Whandall was trying to learn kinless ways, and what about the wagon?

Unhitching the mare wasn't easy. She tried to pull the rope out of his hands. He hung on long enough to tie it to a tree stump. The length of it would let her reach forage. She had her horn if coyotes came back.

Then—but wait. What had killed these beasts?

He stooped over one of the corpses. Not a mark on them. Wide blood-red eyes, mouths wide, tongues protruding. He touched the slicked-down fur, expecting to find it wet, but it wasn't.

He caught Carver far downslope at the next dead campfire. There they slowed to a walk, blowing hard. Willow and the wagon must have taken a full day to cover this distance. Carver's hands held his sling and a handful of rocks cracked to get sharp edges. He said, "I wish I had a knife."

Whandall said, "With *that* you don't have to let them so close. I wish I had a sever."

Day was dying. They smelled meat cooking, and they slowed.

They saw the fire first, and a young looker standing tall and straight, backlit, with orange-red hair falling to his shoulders. Willow had the horses tied and a fire going. Then a whiff of corruption showed an arc of dead coyotes at their feet.

Willow saw two men coming at a grim half-run, Whandall's knife point, Carver's whirling sling. She leaped up from her cooking and stepped quickly to the man's side.

"He saved us!" she shouted. "The coyotes would have torn us apart!"

Carver's sling drooped. He said, "Morth?"

Morth smiled faintly.

"Morth, you're young!"

"Yes, I found this!" Morth held out a handful of yellow lumps. Whandall had never before seen the magician *gleeful.* "Gold!" he said. "In the river!" He stepped forward past Whandall's knifepoint and pushed the gold into Whandall's unresisting hand.

Whandall said, "This is dangerous, isn't it? Wild magic."

"No, no, *this* gold is *refined.* I've taken the magic," Morth said. "Can't you see? Shall we race? Shall I stand on my head for you? *I'm young!*"

Carver backed up a bit, and so did Willow. Here was no lurking spell. Morth *wanted* to be noticed. He babbled, "Gold *is* magic. It reinforces other magic. Look!" He leaped straight up and kept rising until he could grasp a branch twice Whandall's height above him. He shouted down, "Not just young! I used to *fly!*"

He dropped lightly. "Give gold to a wizard, most of the power leaches from the gold. After that it's refined gold, harmless. People use it as if it has value, but the original meaning was, *I gave gold to a wizard to touch. A wizard owes me.* Whandall, keep the gold. Morth of Atlantis owes you."

Whandall put the nuggets in the pouch beneath his waistband. He asked, "Why?"

Morth laughed. "You're guiding me out."

Whandall's fingers brushed his cheek: the tattoo he couldn't see. "And every wizard in the world can track me?"

"Every Atlantean wizard," Morth said, and laughed like a lunatic.

CHAPTER
37

Willow had roasted a half-grown deer and some roots Morth had found. The adults held back—even Morth, even Whandall, ravenous but following their lead—until the children were fed. Then they dug in.

Carver suddenly cried out. "Lordkin! Did you do anything about the other wagon?"

Whandall told him what he'd done. "But the mare doesn't like me, so you'll have to go get her yourself. Unless you think we should both go?"

Whandall enjoyed what Carver's face did then. Leave Willow with Whandall? or leave the wizard with Willow and no Whandall to guard *him?* or take Willow, leaving the children alone with the wizard *and* the Lordkin and nobody who could handle bonehead stallions? . . .

"I'll go."

"It can wait till morning."

"I should hope so."

The night was black as the inside of a lion's belly. Whandall had to imagine: Carver, Willow, Morth, the gently snoring Carter, and himself, arrayed in a five-pointed star in the dirt near the wagon, feet pointing inward, severs ready to hand. The children in the wagon. Hyacinth dropping over the side, sleepy and clumsy, *thud,* crawling away to use the pit.

"It's the biggest burn patch we've seen. It took us all day to cross it, and half of yesterday." Willow's voice in the dark, wondering and content.

Joking, Whandall said, "This fire wasn't mine."

"Lightning," Willow said. "Lightning hits the highest tree. It burns. Afterward the redwood grows in two prongs. Sometimes coals fall and a patch of forest catches."

"Why doesn't the whole forest burn? Woodsmen just go home when they see a fire."

She said, "Patches burn, then they go out."

Morth said, "Yangin-Atep spends most of his time in a death-sleep, but a big fire wakes him. Feeds him. Fire is Yangin-Atep's life."

A companionable silence. Then Carver said sleepily, "What if you don't believe in Yangin-Atep?"

Whandall raised his voice above Morth's laugh. "Carver, firewand seeds don't sprout unless there's been a fire. Neither does redwood. This land is fire's *home*. Tep's Town—"

"Valley of Smokes."

"Smokes. Would have been burned out before I was ever born if some power weren't snuffing the fires. Yangin-Atep is the reason fire won't burn indoors. There's a truce between Yangin-Atep and the redwoods, so they don't burn. I tried to tell Kreeg Miller . . . a tax-payer woodsman?"

Willow said, "There are a lot of people named Miller."

Whandall had nursed a hope that he was helping Kreeg Miller's relatives. There was an old debt he'd never acknowledged.

Willow said, "Outside the forest there's no Yangin-Atep. You could cook indoors. Get your food still hot. Yes?"

"Yes," said Morth and Whandall.

"Well, I never heard of such a thing, but we'll see." Willow turned and was asleep.

Whandall rolled his blanket tighter around him, wishing he could get up and stroll around, knowing that a thorn plant or laurel branch would surely slash him if he did. They had left the rain behind. The sound of the night was wind and sometimes a tiny cry of mortal agony.

CHAPTER
38

For a time the wagon moved easily downhill with Willow at the reins. Then they had to use the severs, sliding the poles under nettles and morningstars and lordkin's-kiss to cut the roots with the blades, to shape a path wide enough for children and a wagon. They could have used Carver's help, but Carver had gone back for the mare and second wagon.

Willow spoke: "This yellow blanket, *this* we use to clean the severs, to get the poison sap off. Use the rough side only. *You* don't *ever* touch it, right, Hammer? Iris? Hyacinth? Opal?" The children nodded. "This one blanket, because there's nothing else that color. The blanket hangs here on the wagon tongue, never moves, so anyone can find it."

They saw problems before they happened. Looked for them. They lectured each other as easily as they lectured a Lordkin male.

Carter and Hammer were assigned to hold the other children together. They moved fairly rapidly. Half a morning later, Whandall remembered part of the deer left in the wagon from last night. He dropped the sever, stood up—

"Whandall. Don't try to save work. Touch-me venom can stay on a blade and brush off on the wagon and then on a child. Someone could sit on it. It's clean when it leaves your hands, every time," Willow said. "Understand?"

A blank face hid his rage. Whandall picked up the sever and wiped the blade clean. Willow had treated him like a child, a bad child, in front of Morth and the children. Carter and Morth both had the grace to be paying attention to something else. If Carver had been here, Whandall might have had to hurt him.

In a later, calmer moment, it came to him that she hadn't spoken by chance. Willow had been watching, waiting for him to do what he did.

A stand of lordkiss blocked Whandall's scorch-path, its leaves barely singed. Morth called, "Whandall! Don't burn it! You'd strangle us all. The smoke is poisonous."

Whandall had reached for Yangin-Atep's rage and found only a dying ember. The fire god was leaving him.

They had to dig a path around the lordkiss. He thought of it as showing off his strength, to make it feel less like work.

In early afternoon they broke through the undergrowth above running water.

Through sparse branches Whandall saw a far distant mass floating in the sky: a cone with its base in cloud, gray rock and green-tinged black capped with blazing white.

Morth gaped. "What is *that?*"

"The legends said it would be there," Carter mused. "Before the Lordkin came, there was a path through the forest."

"Mount Joy," Willow whispered. "But the story said you could only see it if you were worthy. One of the heroes—"

"Holaman," Carter said.

"Yes. He spent a lifetime searching for this vision," Willow said. "Are we blessed?"

"With good weather," Morth said. "But I think my path leads there." He held his arm out, palm down, and looked along it, first with his fingers together, then spread.

"Magic?" Carter asked.

"No, navigation. If your stories are right, we won't see this again, so I'm looking for landmarks in line with it."

"Looks hard to reach," Carter said. Whandall was thinking, *Impossible. But for a wizard?*

Morth said, "The world's most inaccessible places are the places where wizards have never used up the manna. I have to go there. Gold would keep me alive, but the magic in gold is chaotic. I was too long in Tep's Town." Morth ran his hand distractedly through his hair. "I need the magic in nature to fully heal. Too much gold would drive me crazy."

He looked at the fistful of red and white strands he was holding and whooped laughter. "Too little is bad too!"

Willow led the stallions. The wagon lurched, and sometimes the children had to heave up on the downside to keep it from rolling over. Still, matters had improved: nothing ahead of them seemed to need cutting. The vegetation grew right up against the shore, and it was touch-me all the way. But the river ran shallow at the edges, and the wagon wheels would only run a few hands deep.

Willow said, "We'll find easier traveling if we follow the river."

Whandall waited for Morth's reaction. He'd been treating Morth like a friend who sniffs white powder: a dubious ally. This might be the chance to be rid of him. But Morth only said, "You can't stay with the river long."

"No, of course not. Wagons don't go on water, do they, Whandall?"

Surprised to be asked his opinion, Whandall said, "Willow, people don't go on water either."

The way she looked at him, he flushed. She asked, "Whandall, can't you swim?"

"No. My brother can."

"I meant," Morth said gently, "that the sprite can't get to me right away, but he must know I'm here. Let's see how far we can get."

The river continued shallow. The wagon bumped over rocks. They had to run slow, where the still growing ponies wanted to *run*. Carter and Willow couldn't leave them without their becoming restive. They'd grown large and dangerous, as big as Lords' horses, with horns that would outreach Whandall's Lordkin knife.

"I could spell them," Morth said. "Gentle them."

"No." Morth was as twitchy as the ponies; Whandall didn't trust his magic.

"Well, at least I can dispel the stink of tar!" He gestured, but nothing happened. The smell was still there. Morth frowned, then danced ahead, vanished out of sight. A fat lot of help he was . . . but it could be said that he was scouting terrain, springing traps that would otherwise wait for children and a wagon.

The ponies and wagon plodded on, veering around deeper pools, rolling over rocks, wobbling, tilting, held from rolling over only by a Lordkin's strong shoulder, whenever Whandall hoped to leave this snail's trek and follow the magician.

Carver wouldn't have much trouble catching up, Whandall decided. He'd find a path carved ahead of him.

They were halfway down the mountain when Morth came bounding back, bellowing, "Don't any of you lordspawns get *hungry?*" He gestured and sang, and suddenly Whandall's clothes were clean. Even the tar stains were gone. "Now to eat!"

The children chorused their agreement. Morth roared laughter. "I could eat . . . the gods know what I could eat!" He faced the woods and raised his hands as if they held invisible threads. "Let's just see. Seshmarl, a fire!"

Whandall gathered an armful of dry brush and set a few fallen limbs on it. His touch raised no more than a wisp of smoke.

It was not that he enjoyed being ordered about like a kinless! But Whandall preferred to hide how weakly the power of Yangin-Atep ran in him. And Morth's hands still waved their messages into the forest, while white chased red in waves down Morth's luxuriant mane and beard. Whandall coaxed the smoldering kindling until flame rose toward his fingertips. When Morth turned from the woods, there was fire.

Animals came trooping out of the wood. A gopher, a turkey, a fawn, a red-tailed hawk, a half-starved cat as big as Hammer, and a family of six raccoons all filed up to Morth and sorted themselves by size. The cat was smaller than the ghosts of the Black Pit, and it didn't have those huge dagger teeth.

Whandall made a sound of disgust. An animal might be meat, but it should be hunted! Altering its mind was—

(Hadn't Morth said that once?)

But the animals were strangling. All but the raccoons were reaching for air and not finding it, thrashing, gaping, dying. The bird tried to reach Morth, and would have if he hadn't dodged, and then it was dead too.

Drowned. And a burbling chuckle leaked out of Morth.

Whandall reached for his knife. It wasn't needed. He and the kinless watched as two adult and four half-grown raccoons stripped the feathers from the bird and butchered the drowned animals with their clawed hands, skewered the meat and set it broiling. The children watched in fascination.

The raccoons all spasmed at once, *looked,* and instantly disappeared into the chaparral.

Hawk had a miserable taste, but everyone tried it. Willow convinced the children that they'd brag about this for the rest of their lives. Turkey and deer were very good, and gopher could be eaten. They had safe fruit Morth had found, with his ability to see poison. It struck

Whandall that he had not eaten this well since Lord Samorty's kitchen.

In early afternoon Morth suddenly said, "Here!" and waded into the stream.

Whandall was startled. "Morth? Aren't you afraid of water?"

"We've hours before the sprite can get here." Morth bent above the purling water with his arms elbow deep, fingers spread just above the river bed. Whandall saw golden sand flow toward him, merging into a lump.

"Ah," he said. He picked up a mass the size of his head as if it were no heavier than a ball of feathers. For a time he stood holding the gold against his chest, with his eyes half closed and the look of a man breathing brown powder smoke from a clay pot. Then he handed it to Whandall. "Again, for my debt. Put this in the wagon."

Whandall took it. He wasn't prepared for its weight. It would have smashed his toes and fingers if he'd been a bit less agile.

Morth was helpless on the ground, laughing almost silently, *Hk, hk, hk.*

With every eye on him, Whandall set himself, lifted, hugged the gold to his chest, and carried it toward the wagon.

Morth rolled over and stood up. Mud covered his sopping wet robe. He'd lost weight: his ribs showed through the cloth. His hair was red and thick and curly. His long, smooth, bony face wore a feral look, like a young Lordkin about to test his knife skills for the first time.

"That's better," he said. "Little more of that." He walked back into the river and began wading downstream.

Willow repacked the wagon, Whandall helping, while the children put out the fire and wrapped the remaining deer meat in grass. Whandall said, "He never helps."

Willow looked startled. "You don't either."

"I'm helping now."

"Well, yes, thank you. You don't do it often. Well, it's because the ponies don't like you."

"What I meant was, you don't seem to notice," Whandall said. "Morth has lived in Tep's Town longer than I've been alive, but he's a looker. Do you see him as a . . . ?"

"Yes. Maybe." Willow laughed uneasily. "He's a funny-looking Lordkin? Crazy and dangerous, and sometimes he can do something we can't."

They set off with the wagon. They saw Morth rock hopping downstream until the river turned.

* * *

Late afternoon. Whandall heaved upward while the ponies pulled. The wagon lurched, rolled, and was back into riverbed that was shallow and flat.

"I quit," Willow said.

Whandall looked up. She was riding, he was walking . . . but she was exhausted. The restive ponies had worn her out.

"We have to get the wagon on shore," he said.

"Do we really?"

"The water thing that hunts Morth, it's coming up the river. We don't want to be in the way. And there isn't any shore yet . . ."

So they wrestled the wagon through another eighty paces of rough water. Then there was a strip of sand and a sloping bank they could push the wagon up, and Willow could sleep forty feet above the water.

Whandall had worked hard too. Had worked. He was new to that.

It was good to lie down on warm earth. The children lay about him, all asleep. Willow was curled up with a tree root for a pillow, comfortably distant from the Lordkin, with ponies tethered on either side, one rope strung between two trees. Whandall watched her for a time, his mind adrift.

The ponies looked up at him. He felt the heat of their stare.

They stood. They pulled in opposite directions, a steady pressure. The rope parted silently. They walked directly toward him.

Whandall scrambled to his feet, already choosing a tree to climb, but a stallion trotted to block it. He picked another and that was blocked. The rocks? Yes, the rock slope behind him: he ran toward it ahead of a pair of ponies charging at full tilt, their horns lowered.

It all had a dreadful familiarity. He knew exactly what to do because the ponies behaved exactly like a pair of Bull Pizzle bullies, and if he couldn't get around them he'd be dead. He was climbing the rocks before they reached him, and then the rocks impeded their hooves. But the slope was steep. Stones rolled—a pony screamed—he kicked a few loose on purpose, and now he was high above them. He'd have taunted them like frustrated Bull Pizzle Lordkin—

But ponies didn't act like this!

Ensorcelled?

He reached into his pants, into the concealed pouch, and found Morth's handful of gold dust. He tossed a cloud of gold over them.

The ponies went mad, scrambling at the slope, risking their hooves and their bones and their lives. Then they paused . . . looked at each other . . . turned and trotted, then galloped back toward the wagon.

Wild magic would strengthen a spell but disrupt it too, Morth had said. But who could have spelled these ponies if not Morth of Atlantis? Whandall scrambled down the slope, chasing the bonehead ponies.

Willow was standing in the wagon bed holding a sever. Morth stood out of range, laughing, ignoring the ponies who were now menacing *him*. The air around him seemed to sizzle.

Whandall called, "Willow!"

She was near tears and glad to see him. "He wanted—I don't know what he wanted, I didn't let him get that far."

Morth was offended. "No woman would have reason to be insulted! I'd never have offered if I hadn't seen something of lost Atlantis in you. I have gold!" He held a yellow chunk the size of a child's head in each hand. He stood as if bracketed by suns.

"Willow Ropewalker, I have power! I can protect you from whatever dangers await us. Can you hold a man when you lose your youth? You don't *have* to get old! And I don't either!"

The heat rose up in Whandall, but only the merest flicker. He reached for Yangin-Atep, but Yangin-Atep was gone. He drew his knife. He saw Morth's hands rise. Willow raised the sever as if she would throw it. "Stop!" she commanded.

Morth turned toward her, his back toward Whandall. "What must I do to convince you I mean no harm? Willow, forget what I spoke—"

"Leave her mind alone!"

Morth laughed. His hands wove invisible threads. A great calm settled on Whandall. He knew that this was the spell that had killed his father.

Smiling gently, he strolled toward Morth. Morth watched with interest. Whandall was well within range. Now . . . but first he gave warning.

"Morth, do you think that I can't kill a man without getting angry first?"

"Seshmarl, you surprise me."

"Leave us. We've helped each other, but you don't need us anymore."

"Oh, you need me," Morth said. His eyes flicked away and back, and he laughed again. Whandall held his pose. Morth would be dead before he had spat out the first syllable of a spell.

"You need me elsewhere, Seshmarl! So, here is more gold, refined." Morth dropped the gold and danced away. He was ten paces uphill from Whandall's reflexive lunge, dancing between bouquets of swords and slashing laurels faster than the plants could move. In the gathering dusk he paused on the rocky crest and shouted downstream.

"You!"

A wave was rolling up the river.

Tidal bore, a later age would call such a thing. It followed the river's meandering path, growing taller as it came. It would drown this camp. Morth watched it and laughed.

"You! Aquarius!" Morth was tiny with distance, but they heard him clearly. "You great stupid wall of water, do you know that you've made me rich? Now see if you can follow me!" And Morth ran.

The fastest Lordkin chased by the most savage band had never run so fast as Morth. The wave left the river's course and tried to follow him, straight up a hillside and along the crest, dwindling, slumping. Morth's manic laughter followed him down a hill and up another, straight toward the distant white-topped cone of Mount Joy, until he was no more than a bright dot on the mind's eye.

They waited until evening before going to the river for drinking water. The river roiled with white froth and weird currents even where there were no rocks.

CHAPTER
39

At dusk Whandall tried to start a cook fire, but the power had left him. There was plenty of cooked meat from Morth's feast, but there would be no more cooking until they could learn to make fire.

The absence of Yangin-Atep was loss and gain, like a toothache gone and the tooth with it.

Carver rejoined them by the light of a setting half-moon.

Whandall was ready to kill him even after he knew that the sound of a mare and wagon thrashing through brush wasn't a dozen coyotes. Fool kinless! Maybe the mare's magic led him through that maze of death.

Willow spoke before Whandall could. "Brother, have you been traveling through chaparral by dark?"

"Willow! I was worried—"

Her voice was low and her speech was refined, and Whandall listened in awe and dread. He never wanted to hear her speak to *him* that way.

Carver lay between them. In the night, when Willow might be asleep, he rolled toward Whandall and said, "I was afraid for her. I was afraid."

Whandall whispered, "I hear you."

Silence.

"You missed all the excitement. I'll tell you tomorrow."

* * *

There were stretches of narrow beach. Elsewhere they could rock-hop or wade. But the moment came when they reached a deep pool with vertical walls on either side.

Carver said, "I'm going to teach you to swim."

At first it seemed the cold would kill him. Its bite eased quickly. The bottom was soft mud, a delight to the toes. The water came to his chin. He couldn't really drown. Still, for a time it felt like Carver and Willow had decided to drown him. Sweep your arms to *push* the water back and breathe in while the water isn't in your face. Breathe out anytime. . . .

He began to feel the how and why of it. But already the trees hid the sun, and he was exhausted and shaking with cold. And ahead was the river, with no way up the bank. They would have to go on. How far Whandall didn't know.

There was no fire. They ate cold meat and berries by the light of a growing moon.

The night closed down while the elders described their river trip, and the swimming lesson, amid much laughter.

Presently Whandall asked of nobody in particular, "What do you think is out there?"

"We never get lookers from the other side of the forest," Carver said. "Maybe there's nothing. Maybe nothing but farms or herdsmen."

"Or more forest, or nothing at all," Whandall said.

"No Lordkin, anyway," Willow said.

"Doesn't mean there can't be . . ."—Carver searched for a better word, then gave up—". . . thieves. Or old stories about Lordkin. We don't *know* that they don't know about Lordkin. Tomorrow you stay with the children, Whandall. They couldn't keep up anyway—"

"Carver, I can swim! You taught me!"

"You learned fast too," Willow assured him. Her hand was on his arm; she hadn't done that before. "Now you know how to swim in a pool, Whandall. If you ever fall in the water, you might even get out alive. But we'll be wading in a running river—"

"You shouldn't come anyway," Carver said. "You shouldn't be seen."

"We'll take Carter and the severs . . . better leave you one sever for the coyotes, Whandall. We'll come back when we know where the river goes."

Whandall wished he could see their faces. He was just as glad that they couldn't see his.

* * *

For two days Whandall kept himself and the children busy widening the path to the river, giving them more safe space to roam. Whandall and Hammer found unwary prey at the edges of the scorch. Hammer knew how to fish. He tried to teach Whandall, and Whandall caught two. They ate them raw.

Feeding the ponies was difficult. They couldn't be let loose to graze, because no one but Willow could catch them. Whandall gathered anything that looked like grass or straw, and the children carried the fodder up to where the ponies were tethered. They had to carry water as well. If Whandall came near the ponies, they menaced him with their horns and strained at the ropes holding them to trees. More than once Whandall was grateful that the Ropewalkers knew their craft.

But all three of the Ropewalker family were gone, leaving him with the four Miller children and one of the wagons. The wagon with the bottles and the gold.

Whandall knew nothing of kinless families, loyalties, infighting, grudges. It worried him.

Carver and Willow and Carter Ropewalker might cease to need him very soon. It might have happened already. A Lordkin with a knife would be all he was and all he had, for whatever that might mean to strangers on this side of the forest.

In Tep's Town, a Lordkin with a knife need be nothing more.

He could go back. What could stop him?

But strangers guarded the Placehold, men brought home by Placehold women during the past few years. They could protect the house if they had the nerve; they might have lost it already; they had little in common with Whandall Placehold. Elriss and Wanshig were friends, but they were together with their children most of the time. Wess had another man, and another after that, and never came back to Whandall. Other women were friends for a day or a week, never more. Alferth's wine wagons had nothing to carry. What was there to hold Whandall in Tep's Town?

Here on the other side of the forest, Lordkin might be unknown.

He did not know how he would survive where he could not simply gather what he needed. But kinless knew how to make things happen; it wasn't all luck and a Lordkin knife. They could teach Whandall, as they'd taught him to swim. He'd brought them out of the burning city. They owed him.

And there was Willow. If only. A Lordkin could have a kinless woman, but only by force, and he could not force Willow.

He could treat her—he *had* treated her—with the respect he would give a Lordkin woman. She seemed to have lost her fear of him, and he was glad of that. But why would Willow look at a Lordkin male?

It was not too late to go back. Take the Miller children. Give them over to the first kinless he met.

These thoughts played through his mind while he hunted food for the children and tried to keep them out of trouble.

At the next noon the Ropewalkers were back.

"A road," Willow told them. "And a long way up the road are some houses."

"How far?" Whandall asked.

"We can be to the road tomorrow afternoon if we start now."

Whandall thought about that. "What are the people like?"

"We didn't see any people," Willow said.

"We didn't want to be seen," Carver said. "So we didn't get very close."

"What are the houses like?" Whandall asked.

"Squarish, made of wood. Solid looking, well made. Roofs like this." He held his hands to indicate a peaked roof, unlike the flat roofs that were more usual in Tep's Town. "Very solid."

"Interesting," Whandall said. "Like Lords' houses? Made by people not afraid of burning?"

"Yes!" Willow clapped her hands. "I never thought of that, but yes!"

Whandall got up. "I'll load the wagon. You'll have to hitch the ponies."

PART SIX

The Bison Tribe

CHAPTER 40

The ponies were as big as Lords' horses now, and each had a spiral horn, larger than a Lordkin knife, growing from his forehead. Outside conditions had bleached them: they were as white as chalk, with long silky manes. They looked nothing like the kinless ponies they'd been. The mare was nearly as big as the stallions, but her horn was smaller, and she hadn't lost the gray coloring. She was tame.

The stallions were not tame. They went frantic when Whandall or Carver approached them. They wouldn't attack the children, but only Willow could bridle them and hitch them to the wagon. If she tried to ride on the wagon they stopped and waited until she walked ahead again.

One more night on the river. Whandall sat and stared at the water. What would they find ahead? What would Willow do? She lay asleep next to her brother. Her straight black hair was a tangle and she slept from exhaustion, and Whandall thought her the most beautiful woman he had ever seen. He wondered at that. Magic?

They started early the next day, and at noon they came to a bend in the river. Carter pointed excitedly. "The road is just up there." He pointed up the steep slope.

There were trees in the way. Whandall scouted out a route to the road. By going around they could avoid most of the trees, but finally there was no choice. They'd have to cut two trees to get through.

Neither tree seemed to be guarded by other plants. There were few plants in the forest, and those were just bushes and leafy plants, without thorns. They didn't move when approached.

This tree was broad-leafed, the trunk thinner than a man's body. Whandall bowed to it as he'd seen Kreeg Miller do, then chopped a deep notch on one side in the direction he wanted it to fall. Then he and Carver chopped on the other side until it fell, not quite where he wanted, but out of the way.

The other, larger tree dropped exactly where Whandall aimed it, and they were free to go to the road. Willow brought up the horses and wagon. "You bowed to the tree," she said.

Whandall shrugged. "Woodsmen do that."

Willow giggled. "To redwoods," she said. "Not to all the trees. Just redwoods."

"There aren't any redwoods here."

Willow's smile faded slightly. "I know."

"You care?"

She said, "Grandmother loved them. I think we protected each other, humans and redwoods, before the Lordkin came. Here they're gone."

"Maybe we'll find more," Whandall said. He looked at the trees he'd felled. "We won't run out of wood, anyway. Maybe someone will have a fire."

"I hope so," Willow said. "Bathing in cold water. Ugh."

Kinless women took baths every day, Whandall had learned, even when there wasn't soap or hot water, nothing but a stream. It seemed a strange custom. He'd jumped in himself, and whooped and thrashed like the others, to show that he too could stand cold.

The road was no more than a deeply rutted track, but while the river itself wandered in sweeping curves like a snake, the road was straight. Here and there the river had changed course to undermine the road. There the road curved away from the river, then straightened out again.

They had jerked meat, and bread they'd baked when they had fire. Evening found them on the road. Just after dusk Carver looked at the night sky. "We're going north," he said.

"How do you know that?" Whandall asked.

"Stars," Willow said. "Father taught Carver how to read stars."

"It's hard," Carver said. "I looked last night, and I couldn't tell. There are more stars here. Lots more, too many to recognize! This early in the evening it looks right. But when it's dark there are thousands and thousands of stars."

"What are stars?" Carter asked.

"Dargramnet . . ." Whandall hesitated. "My mother's mother. She said the stars are cook fires of our ancestors. Cook fires and bonfires to Yangin-Atep."

"You hesitated," Willow said. "You do that when you speak of your family. Why?"

"We—the Lordkin—don't talk about families to strangers," Whandall said. "Or even close friends."

"Why not?"

Whandall shook his head. "We just don't. I think part of it is certainty. You know who your mother is, but not always your father, and your mother might go off anytime. Even when you think you know— but *you* know, don't you? How?"

"Whandall, girls don't sleep with men until they're married," Willow said.

Sleeping wasn't what made babies, but this seemed to be a language thing. Did she *really* mean . . . ? Whandall asked, "What happens if they do?"

"No one will marry them," Willow said. Pink was flooding into her neck and cheeks. "Even if it's not their fault. There was a girl, the daughter of a friend of Mother's. Dream-Lotus was a few years older than me, old enough to be . . . attractive, during the last Burning. Some Lordkin men caught her. They almost killed her. Maybe it would have been better if they did."

Whandall's voice came out funny. "Why?"

"She had a baby," Willow said. "It wasn't her fault—everyone knew that—but she had a baby, and no man would have her. Her father died, and then her brother drank himself to death."

"What happened to her?" Whandall asked. He didn't dare ask about the baby.

"We don't know. After Mother died we lost track of Dream-Lotus. She always wanted a job in the Lordshills. Maybe she went there."

They came to the edge of the town at noon the next day.

First there were the dogs. They ran barking toward Willow. One got too close, and the rightside pony lowered his horn and lunged. The dog ran away howling. The barking and howling brought two townsmen.

They were big men, dark of complexion, each with long straight black hair braided in a queue hanging down his back. One held a leather sling in one hand and a rock in the other. The other man had an ax. They shouted something unintelligible, first at Whandall, then at the howling dog. The dog came over to them, and the man with the ax bent to examine it. He spoke without getting up, and the other man nodded. Whandall's thumbnail brushed the big Lordkin knife at his belt, just to know where it was.

The men looked from Whandall on the wagon to Willow walking ahead of the horses, frowned, and one said something to the other. Then they pointed to the horses and one laughed.

"Hello," Whandall said. "Where are we?" No response. He repeated himself in Condigeano.

The man with the leather sling said something, saw Whandall didn't understand, and pointed up the road. They called their dogs and watched until Willow had led the wagon out of sight.

Whandall counted twenty houses before he stopped trying to count them. There were at least that many more, strung along three parallel dusty streets. The largest house was about the size of a good Lordkin house in Tep's Town, but they had flower gardens in front, and a few had fenced yards. They didn't look as elegant as Lords' houses, but they were not crude, and they were clearly built to last a generation and more, some wood, some baked clay, none stone.

At the far end of town was a wagon camp, a dozen or more big covered wagons drawn into a circle. Just before the wagon circle there was a wooden rail corral holding a hundred or more great shaggy beasts. They seemed to have no necks. Their eyes stared out of a big collar of fur, and they had short curved horns and lashing tails. They stood in a circle, the biggest ones on the outside, smaller ones inside, and they munched on baled hay while staring malevolently at Whandall and his wagon.

When Willow tried to speak to a gaudily dressed lady on the dusty town main street, she didn't seem unfriendly, but she only laughed and pointed to the wagon circle.

"My feet hurt," Willow said.

Two boys came out of the wagon train circle and shouted something. Whandall gestured helplessly. They laughed and went back inside, and in a moment a large man of around forty came out. His face was weathered and he had a bit of a squint.

He was lighter of complexion than the men they'd seen earlier. He was dressed in leather, long trousers, long-sleeved pullover tunic, soft leather boots. A big red moon was painted on the left breast of his tunic. Red and blue animals chased each other in a circle around the moon. A dark red sun blazed on his back, and below it, warriors with spears chased a herd of the same ugly beasts they'd seen in the corral.

His hair was black with some gray at the temples, plaited into a queue that hung halfway down his back. There were feathers in his hair, and he wore a bright silver ring with a big blue-green stone. Another silver and blue-green design hung on a thong around his neck. His belt held a very serviceable-looking knife with a fancily carved bone handle. The blade was not as long as Whandall's Lordkin knife.

"Hiyo. Keenm hisho?"

Whandall shook his head. "Whandall," he said. "From Tep's Town."

The man considered that. "Know Condigeano?"

"I speak good Condigeano," Whandall said excitedly.

"Good. I don't speak your tongue. Not much contact with the Valley of Smokes," he said. "How'd you get here?"

"We cut a path through the forest," Whandall said.

"I'm impressed." He looked from Whandall to Willow, looked at the ponies, looked at the children on the wagon. "Don't think I ever met anyone who got out that way. There's a few harpies in Condigeo, but they got there by ship."

Willow looked back at Whandall. "Harpies?" she said.

"I guess he means us," Whandall said.

Willow shuddered. "Tell him—" She caught herself.

"Fine-looking one-horns," the man said. "Looking to sell them?"

"No, I don't think so," Whandall said.

"Well, all right. That your sister?"

Whandall choked back the automatic rage at the impertinent question. "No."

"Um. You hungry? My name's Black Kettle, by the way." He patted his ample paunch. "But everybody calls me Kettle Belly." He swept his hand to indicate the wagon train. "This is the Bison Clan."

"I am Whandall." Clan? That was too complicated. "And that's Willow. Her brothers Carver and Carter. The children are cousins," Whandall said.

"Ah. Your girl?"

I already told you more than you have to know! But the question seemed innocent enough. Maybe people here talked about such things. Tras Preetror had.

Willow wouldn't understand him. Whandall said, "I hope so."

Kettle Belly smiled. "Good. Fine-looking girl. Here, follow me. We'll get you something to eat."

"Thanks. We could use fire too."

Kettle Belly laughed heartily. "A Valley of Smokes harpy can't make fire?"

Whandall wanted to resent that, but Kettle Belly seemed so friendly and well intentioned that he couldn't. Instead he laughed. "Never learned how. Never needed to."

"Guess I understand that all right," Kettle Belly said. "You come on with me, then." He turned to one of the children. "Number Three—"

"I'm Four."

Kettle Belly roared laughter again, and gave instructions. He turned back to Whandall. "I told him to let Mother know we've got company. And he'll look up Haj Fishhawk's wife. She came from the Valley of Smokes; she'll be able to talk to your friends. When you're ready to trade those one-horns, let me know; I'll give you a good price and show you how to drive bison."

"Why would I want to sell them?"

Kettle Belly smiled indulgently. "Well . . . something might come up."

Ruby Fishhawk was at least fifty, a kinless woman with soft eyes and long fluffy hair gone white. As soon as she met Willow she began asking questions about family. Who was Willow's mother? Who was her father's mother? In minutes she found that Willow's father's mother had married Ruby's aunt's brother, and Willow's mother's brother was Ruby's cousin.

"But you're tired. Kettle Belly says you don't have fire! How long?"

"Three days," Willow said.

"You poor thing! Come with me; I have a bathtub. I love my husband, I love the trader folk, but they don't bathe properly! Sweat lodges are all very well, but there's nothing like a proper bath! Come on; I'll show you—"

"What about the horses?" Willow asked. "Whandall can't handle them . . ."

Ruby grinned as if Willow had made a good joke. "We'll take care of that." She spoke rapidly to Kettle Belly.

He nodded and pointed to a second and larger corral beyond the circle of wagons. There were two of the one-horned stallions. Each stood in his own part of the corral. One had the company of two gray shorthorn mares. The other was alone. They eyed Whandall's team and snuffled. Whandall's mare whinnied.

Girls younger than Willow carried fodder to the corral. One of the girls was watching the strangers with evident curiosity. Kettle Belly gestured and she came over to them. She was shapely, a little younger than Willow and just beginning to show as a woman. Whandall found her pretty in an exotic way. Her hair was long and straight, tied with a bow of orange ribbon, and she smiled at Whandall.

Kettle Belly spoke rapidly, finally saying "Whandall." The girl smiled, and nodded to Whandall. "Her name translates to Orange Blossom," Kettle Belly said. "You'll learn to say it, but not now. I think she likes you."

Orange Blossom smiled shyly.

"She'll take care of your one-horns. Your wagon will be safe enough here next to mine."

Orange Blossom began to unhitch the horses. Whandall watched, wondering what to do. The horses and wagon were all they owned. He saw that Kettle Belly was watching him with wry amusement.

"It'll be all right, lad," Kettle Belly said. "Think about it, we're Bison Clan wagon traders. Everyone knows who we are. If we were thieves, would any town trust us? It's not like we could run! Not with bison pulling the wagons!"

Orange Blossom slipped a bridle on the mare. She didn't bother with the stallions. She led the mare toward the corral, and the stallions followed docilely.

"Young colts," Kettle Belly said. "Give them another year, they'll fight. Right now they won't be any problem."

Ruby was still talking. "Well, that's all settled, then. Come, Willow." She led Willow off into the circle of wagons.

"She hasn't heard her own language since the last time we went to Condigeo," Kettle Belly said. "She has kinfolk there. Kinfolk as she reckons them, anyway. Well, come on, lad, there's better things than bathtubs! Tell the youngsters to go with Number Four there; he'll find them something to eat."

"Number Four?" Whandall asked.

"Ho, we don't give boys names like they do in the cities," Kettle Belly said. "When they're old enough, they find their names. Until then we just call them by their father's name, unless there's so many they have to have numbers. Anyway, Four will see the kids are fed. You come with me."

Whandall explained to the Ropewalkers and Millers who had been listening without comprehension.

Carver thought he should stay with the children. Carter had a different idea. He wanted to go with Whandall. Whandall was about to say it was all right with him when he saw that Carver didn't approve. "You'd better help your kin," Whandall said.

"All right, Whandall," Carter said.

Kettle Belly led Whandall to one of the big wagons. The wagons were roofed over with hoops covered with some kind of cloth. The roof was high enough that Whandall thought he would be able to stand under it, but they didn't go inside. Kettle Belly led him around the wagon and into the circle.

An awning had been attached to the top of the wagon and led out to poles, so that it made a high-roofed shed to shade them from the sun. Large boxes made low walls around the covered area. The area under the roof was carpeted, and there was a bench just outside it. Kettle Belly sat on the bench and began pulling off his boots. He indicated that Whandall should do the same.

"We mostly take off our shoes before we go in," he said. "Saves the women some work."

Whandall considered that. It was a new way of looking at things.

The carpet felt strange to his bare feet. He had seen carpets in Lordshills, but he'd never walked on one. These were brighter in color and seemed sturdy. He thought the Lords would pay well for one. "How are these made?" he asked.

"What, the carpets? Woven," Kettle Belly said. "From wool. This one was done by hill shepherds. They weave them in winter." He turned back a corner of the carpet. The underside was covered with thousands of small knots.

"It must take a long time."

"It does," Kettle Belly said. "This one probably took eight or ten years to make. You can get cheaper ones in towns. Weave won't be as close, flax and hemp threads in the wool. There may be some for sale here when the market opens tomorrow. Have a seat."

They sat on wool-stuffed pillows. The pillows were woven of a coarse material like the carpets, but they had different designs. Kettle Belly sat with his legs out, his back against one of the wagon boxes.

If you had to live out of a wagon, carpets were a good idea, Whandall thought. "Do they sell good carpets here?"

Kettle Belly smiled. "Well, I wouldn't want the Firewoods Town people to hear me say," he said. He watched Whandall react to that and grinned. "Marsyl carpets look all right, but Marsyl Town doesn't get cold enough in winter. Sheep here don't have the best wool. We buy Marsyl carpets when we're headed south and we don't have a full load. They sell all right down Condigeo way."

"You're not going south," Whandall guessed. Tras Preetror had said that Condigeo was six days' sail south of Tep's Town.

"Right."

Kettle Belly clapped his hands. A woman about his age came out from behind the wagon boxes. She was darker than Kettle Belly and considerably thinner. Her skirts were leather with designs tattooed on them in bright colors. Some of the tattoos were emphasized by colored thread sewn into patterns. Her dark hair was pulled back and tied with a ribbon but not plaited like the men wore theirs.

Kettle Belly stood when the woman came into the enclosed area, and after a moment Whandall did too.

"Whandall, my wife Mirime. I'm afraid she doesn't speak much Condigeano." Kettle Belly spoke rapidly in a tongue that meant nothing to Whandall, but he thought he heard the word *harpy*. Mirime didn't look happy with her new guest, but finally she nodded and went out between the boxes to what must have been another room. In a moment she returned carrying a tray with two cups and a bottle. She set it down on the carpet, bowed slightly, and left.

Kettle Belly waved Whandall to the cushions. He filled both cups and handed one of them to Whandall. The cup reminded Whandall of the thin-walled cups the Lords used, and like the Lords' cups it had figures painted on it. There was a ship on one side, and a woman with a fishtail on the other.

It was filled with a wine that smelled wonderful. Whandall was about to gulp it down when he saw that Kettle Belly sipped at his, then watched Whandall. Whandall sipped too. It was smooth and sweet, nothing like the wines he'd had in Tep's Town. He sipped again. In moments the cup was empty.

Kettle Belly refilled the cup from the stone jug. "We saw big smoke last week," he said. "Burning?"

Whandall nodded. "Yes."

Kettle Belly clucked. "Never did understand that. Why would you want to burn your city down?"

"Not everyone wants to," Whandall said.

"Sure. Ruby Fishhawk told me. There's two kinds of harpies, ones like her who put the fires out and the other kind."

"Kinless and Lordkin," Whandall said.

"Yep, that's what she called them."

"Lordkin follow Yangin-Atep," Whandall said. "When the fire god takes a man, the Burning starts." The wine cup was empty again. Kettle Belly filled it without being asked. Whandall drank more.

"Lordkin do other things," Whandall said morosely.

"Thieves, aren't they?"

"We gather. In Tep's Town that's not stealing. Not for Lordkin."

"It is here," Kettle Belly said.

"Willow is kinless," Whandall said. He hesitated. The wine burned in his stomach. "So are the others. But I'm Lordkin."

"Well, of course you are," Kettle Belly said. The laughter was back in his voice, and his smile was broad.

"You knew?"

Kettle Belly roared with laughter. "Whandall, Whandall, everybody knows."

Whandall frowned. "How?"

For answer, Kettle Belly called out, "Mirime! Bring the mirror."

The woman came back in carrying a bronze mirror that Kettle Belly polished with a clean soft cloth, then handed to Whandall. "You don't have a mirror, do you?"

Whandall looked.

He saw a bright feathered serpent with a man's face under it.

"Other places, other customs," Kettle Belly said. "Tep's Town isn't the only place that has tattoos. But they're said to be gaudier among the Lordkin harpies, and Whandall, no place have I seen anything like that! It's why no one was afraid of you, you know."

"I don't understand." Whandall found the wine buzzing in his head and heard his speech thicken. "The tattoo, it's prob'ly Atlantis."

"Atlantis! But you're not from Atlantis."

"No, no . . . made friends with an Atlantis wizard," Whandall said, wondering why he was talking so much to this stranger.

"Well, he did you proud. But Whandall, anyplace you go, anything you do, it'll be known all up and down the road in weeks," Kettle Belly said. "You're the easiest man to describe on the Hemp Road!"

"Is it ugly?" Whandall asked.

"Takes getting used to, I'll say that," Kettle Belly said. "But once you do, it's sort of pretty."

Whandall drained his cup and held it out again. Kettle Belly leaned over to fill it, then stopped. "Sure?"

"No. Dumb." Whandall's fist closed, hiding the cup. "But this, my brother was looking for this."

"Meaning?"

"Good wine. Wanshig was *sure.* Never tasted anything like this, but he was *sure.* Like I was *sure* there's a way out an' I finally found it."

Kettle Belly nodded understanding. "Question is, can you hold it?"

It wasn't a familiar term to Whandall. It? Wine. "Sure."

"I hope so," Kettle Belly said. "Lad, I hope so. You're not the first, you know."

Whandall frowned the question.

"Other Lordkin harpies come out. Why do you think we call you harpies? Most don't last. The lucky ones get put back. Most get killed when it's too much trouble to put them back."

"What happens to the rest?"

"There aren't many. You met Ruby Fishhawk. There are two harpy guards with Lonesome Crow's wagon train, and I hear tell of a harpy leathersmith up in Paradise Valley. Not sure I know of any others. Maybe a few more women."

Whandall thought about that. "There's no way to put me back."

"I knew you were smart. You can control yourself too. Sober, you can, anyway."

How would he know that? What magic did they have here?

"Tell you what, let's have some water," Kettle Belly said. "More wine with dinner. First let me show you around."

CHAPTER
41

The wagons weren't like Whandall's. They were well designed and bigger. There were cargo wagons and wagons to hold bales of hay and fodder, but every family had one that was like a house on wheels. Those were covered by a roof of closely woven cloth held up by metal hoops, and they had a complicated harness arrangement to attach them to the weirdly shaped bison.

"Keeps our Greathand busy," Kettle Belly said. "The blacksmith. And lots of leatherwork. But there's no magic needed. Lots of people on the road. Magic runs thin along the Hemp Road. Best not to depend on magic too much."

Whandall nodded. "There's not much magic in Tep's Town."

"That's what they tell me," Kettle Belly said.

"You call it the Hemp Road."

Kettle Belly shrugged. "There's other commerce. Probably as much wool as anything else. But hemp's a stable product. Always a demand for good hemp. Fiber, rope, smoking flowers, hemp tea, hemp flower gum. You can always get a good price for good hemp."

"Doesn't it try to kill you?" Whandall asked.

"What, *hemp?*"

"Maybe it forgot how," Whandall muttered. Kettle Belly looked at him strangely but didn't say anything.

The wagons they lived out of were bare inside. Kettle Belly explained, "We don't so much live in the wagons as just outside of them. The wagon boxes nearly fill the wagons when we're on the road, and make the walls when we're in camp. See, some of the boxes open from the side, some from the top. Stack the boxes, spread the canopy roof, spread the carpets, lash everything down, and you've got your travel nest. We can be done an hour after we make camp if everyone works together."

It was all new to Whandall. No Lordkin, no kinless. Just people who worked like kinless but kept what they made. . . .

"Who owns all this?" Whandall asked.

"Well, that's complicated," Kettle Belly said. "Lot of this stuff is owned by the wagon train. Most families own a cargo wagon; a few own two; I own three. And every family owns a housewagon and team of bison. That's the bride's dowry." He grimaced. "Five girls I've had. Married off two. Three to go, three more outfits to buy! But my girls get the best. You should see what I'm having made for Orange Blossom. There's a smithy fifty leagues up the road, makes great wagons. Like this one. We'll collect hers next time we're through there, sometime this summer. She'll have to beat the boys away with a stick after they see that rig!"

Like kinless, Whandall thought. Kinless men took care of their daughters. Lordkin men seldom knew who their children were. A boy could look like his mother's man, and then it was pretty clear, but you never knew with girls.

Dowry. A new word, and Kettle Belly talked so fast Whandall wasn't sure of everything he had said. There was too much to learn. And yet. Whandall grinned broadly. He had learned one thing—he had a chance here. A real chance.

The market area was a field beyond the town. There were tents and wagons with platforms, and an air of messiness as townsfolk and wagoneers hastened to set up the fairgrounds. "It'll look pretty good in the morning," Kettle Belly said. He led the way to a large tent at one corner of the field. Orange Blossom supervised as four children worked to lay out carpets, set up tables, and generally make preparations.

"So, Whandall, got anything to sell?" Kettle Belly asked.

"You can see the wagon's empty—"

"Mostly I see it's got a false bottom." Kettle Belly chuckled. "No telling what you've got in there. Of course that's the idea. Anyway, I won't charge you much to set you up a table in my tent."

"Is this a good place to sell?" Whandall asked.

Kettle Belly shook his head. "Depends on what you're selling. Oh, well, not really. Not a lot to buy here, either, other than food and hay, leastways not going north in spring. We'll buy some berries. Crops ripen here quicker than they do up north; sometimes you can turn a good profit moving berries north while people are sick of winter food. But they won't have much, and you have to be careful. Berries spoil fast if you hit a stretch where the magic's weak."

"Then why do you stop here?"

"Heh, lad, we don't have any choice. The bison go only so far, then they stop for a couple of days. Have to let them rest up and fill their bellies. That's most of this town's excuse for existence, wagon stop on the Hemp Road." He eyed Whandall critically. "And now we have to come to some agreement."

"What does that mean?" Whandall turned wary, and crouched slightly.

"Knife fighter. Lonesome Crow tells me you harpies are good at knife fighting," Kettle Belly said.

"Good enough," Whandall said. "What kind of agreement?"

"Boy, you keep asking for information. It cost me to learn what you want to know. Should I tell you for free?"

Whandall considered that. "Wizards trade information," he said. "Tellers trade stories. I studied with a teller."

"Yes, but you don't know anything I need to know," Kettle Belly said. "Leastwise I doubt you do. Stories are good. You can eat off good stories. Any night you have a good story, dinner's free. But what do you know that I need to know?" By now he must have seen Whandall's grin.

"Great Hawk Bay," Whandall said. "They'll pay well for herbs and spices."

"Depends on the spices," Kettle Belly said. "We don't get that far west. There's a market in Golden Valley that pays better than Great Hawk, for that matter. Great Hawk's on the sea, they get ship trade. Whandall, do you have Valley of Smokes spices in that wagon bottom?"

Whandall considered his options. None of them seemed very good. Might as well tell the truth. "Some."

"Hold on to them. Golden Valley's the place to sell those. If you can get there."

"Why would that be a problem?" Whandall asked.

Orange Blossom giggled behind them. "It won't, if you stay with us," she said. She was using a broom to sweep off the carpet.

"It can get tricky," Kettle Belly said. "Bandits. Maybe you can fight them off, but generally there's more than one. Then there's the tax collectors. Every town wants a cut. They'll take all they can get from a lone traveler. You go alone, you won't get two hundred miles."

Whandall didn't say anything.

"You're tough," Kettle Belly said. "And damned mean looking to boot. But one man alone isn't enough to fight off tax collectors."

Whandall thought of the Toronexti. "Are you making an offer?"

"I'm thinking about it."

"Do, Father," Orange Blossom said.

"Yep. Whandall, you travel with us to Golden Valley. If there's fighting to do, you'll fight on our side. You pay your own travel expenses, that's food and fodder. We pay the taxes. You keep up with us. It costs you a third."

"Father!" Orange Blossom said.

"Hush, child!"

"A third of what?"

"Of the value of everything you have when we get to Golden Valley."

"What does everyone else pay?" Whandall asked.

"A fifth. But you'll be a lot more trouble than they are."

"Starting from Condigeo," Whandall guessed. "They pay that starting from Condigeo." He wasn't used to bargaining. But a Lordkin must have guile. . . .

"Well, you have a point," Kettle Belly said. "And besides, my daughter likes you. A quarter, Whandall, and that's my best offer. A quarter of what you're worth when we get to Golden Valley." He paused. "You won't get a better offer."

Supper was a big affair. A huge pot of stew bubbled over an open fire in the middle of the wagon camp. Carpets and cushions were spread out around it. Men and older women sat while children and younger women served out bowls of stew and small pots of a thin wine generously watered.

Kettle Belly waited until Whandall had finished a bowl of stew, then came over to introduce him around the wagon circle.

First he was taken to a wagon with a cover painted like the sky. An odd funnel-shaped cloud reached from the top of the canopy to the bottom of the wagon bed. It was so real that Whandall thought he could see it move if he looked away from it. If he stared at it, it stayed still.

The wagon was tended by two women as old as Ruby Fishhawk, and a girl about Willow's age. The girl stared at Whandall until Kettle Belly spoke rapidly, and one of the women went inside. She came out with a man.

"Hickamore," Kettle Belly said. He spoke rapidly, then turned to

Whandall. "This is Hickamore, shaman of this wagon train. I've told him that I have invited you to join the wagon train."

Hickamore was ageless, his dark skin like the leather he was dressed in, his eyes set deep in his head. He might have been thirty or ninety. He stared at Whandall, then looked *past* him into the distant hills. Whandall started to say something, but Kettle Belly gestured impatiently for silence. They stood and waited while Hickamore stared at nothing. Finally the shaman spoke in Condigeano.

"Whandall Placehold," he said.

Whandall jumped.

"This is your name?" Hickamore made it a question.

"Yes, Sage, but I have not told it to anyone here."

Hickamore nodded. "I was not sure. You will have other names, all known to the world. You will not again have or need a secret name."

"You see the future."

"Sometimes, when it is strong enough."

"Will I meet Morth of Atlantis again?"

Hickamore stared into the distance. "So the story is true. An Atlantis wizard lives! I met one long ago, before Atlantis sank, but I know little of Atlantis. I would know more."

Whandall said nothing. A shrewd light came into the old shaman's eyes. "Black Kettle, am I an honest man?"

"None more so," Kettle Belly said.

"None here, anyway. Whandall Placehold, I make you a trade. Black Kettle will charge you half the traveler fee he demands, and you will tell me all you know of Morth of Atlantis."

"Now, Hickamore—"

"Black Kettle, do you dispute my right?"

"No, Sage." Kettle Belly shrugged. "He hadn't accepted my offer."

"He does now," Hickamore said. "One part in ten."

Kettle Belly howled. "One in eight is half what I offered!"

Hickamore stared at him.

"Robbery," Kettle Belly said. "Robbery. You'll ruin us all! Oh, all right, one part in ten, but you must satisfy the Sage, Whandall!"

It was all happening too fast, and Whandall still felt the effects of the wine. Were they stealing from him? Was all this staged? Pelzed had done that. And the Lords, with their circuses and shows. They were certainly treating him like a child, arguing over his goods.

His and Willow's. And the children. One part in ten would be half what anyone else paid. And they didn't know about the gold. A Lordkin must have guile. . . . "Thank you," Whandall said. "We accept."

Greathand the blacksmith was nearly as big as Whandall, much bigger than anyone else in the wagon train, with arms as big as Black Kettle's thighs. He eyed Whandall suspiciously and spoke mostly in grunts, but he didn't object to Whandall's joining the wagon train.

After Black Kettle introduced Whandall around the circle of wagons, Ruby Fishhawk took Willow and the others on the same tour. The evening ended with wine and singing, and Whandall fell asleep staring at the blaze of stars overhead.

The market tents were set up in a field next to the wagon camp. Not all the Bison Clan families had tents. Some shared, two families with tables in one tent. Everyone displayed something for sale; that was a rule Kettle Belly insisted on. Even overpriced goods made the fair look larger.

Across the field from the wagon train tents the townsfolk set up their own market. Their tents were less colorful than the Bison Clan's, and there were not many goods for sale. Mostly the town dealt in food stocks and fodder.

Kettle Belly went with Whandall to inspect the town's goods.

One tent sold rugs. Warned by Kettle Belly, Whandall inspected these closely. There were fewer knots on the underside of the carpet, and the patterns were not as bright or as well done.

As they walked away Kettle Belly muttered, "Overpriced. Far too high for this time of year. I wonder if they know something."

"What might that be?"

"Cold winter. Wind off the high glaciers. Have to ask Hickamore."

"We need rugs," Whandall said. "I don't mind sleeping on the ground, but Willow isn't used to it. The children aren't."

"Tell her to hold on a couple of weeks," Kettle Belly said. He pointed north. "Beyond the pass at the end of this valley we start up into the mountains. Not the real mountains, but they're high enough that the wool's better. We'll be in Gorman in two weeks. Look for rugs there. They won't be as good as mine, but they'll do. Use them on the road, buy better in Golden Valley, and sell the Gorman rugs in Last Pines next year. You'll get at least what you paid for them."

Orange Blossom had harnessed and bridled two pony stallions. Streamers flowed from their horns. In the scantiest of clothing Orange Blossom stood on their backs, one foot on each, and rode through the town to bring the townsfolk to the market field. A stream of young men followed her back to the market.

Willow caught him gaping. "She does that well," Whandall said.

Willow only nodded. Then she went to find her brother, and together they went to the Fishhawk tent. They came back with two of the Fishhawk boys and two posts twice as long as Whandall was tall. Carter dived into the hidden compartment of their wagon and came out with ropes. They stood the posts eight paces apart, and used ropes and stakes to hold them upright. Then they strung a rope from one post to the next and tightened it with a stick twisted into the rope.

Willow vanished into their tent. She came out wearing skintight trousers and tunic. "Catch me," she shouted to Whandall. Then she climbed agilely to the top of one of the poles and stood on it. "Catch me!" she shouted again.

Carter moved beside Whandall. "She wants you to stand beneath her in case she falls. If she falls, you catch her."

"Oh." Memories came back. "You're the ropewalkers!"

Carter stared.

"I mean I saw you before, before I knew what your name was," Whandall said. He remembered the man who had stood beneath the ropewalking girl during Pelzed's show. That must have been her father! Whandall moved out under the rope, his eyes fixed on Willow. She was both beautiful and vulnerable.

Willow smiled down at him. "I'll probably fall. I haven't done this in a long time," she said. "But you're strong."

"I'd suit up," Carter said, "only there's nothing to wear."

"Next time," Willow said. "I'll work alone today." She walked out onto the rope.

Whandall stayed under her. It wasn't easy. She did backward somersaults, stood on her hands on the rope, jumped and caught herself. She seemed less graceful than the little girl Whandall remembered, but she got the attention of the spectators.

A mixed crowd of villagers and wagon train boys gathered to watch. They all stared at Willow. She smiled back at them and did a forward somersault.

Carver was standing by one of the posts. "Wow."

Whandall looked at him.

"Forward's a lot harder than backward. You can't *see,*" Carver said. "She's still the best—"

Willow attempted something complicated. She was falling before he quite realized that it wasn't an act. She had the rope and lost it, but it slowed her for a moment, and then Whandall was under her. Whandall braced himself.

She fell limply into his arms. He caught her and they both went down, knocking the wind out of his chest. They lay on the ground, Willow atop him. Despite the pain, it felt good to Whandall. She was well muscled, soft at the shoulders—his hands moved involuntarily.

Willow smiled and deftly got up. "Thanks. My hero." She said it half mockingly—but only half—and she smiled. Then she bowed to the crowd and went into their tent.

Kettle Belly came over to their wagon after dinner. "I feel better about the deal you made," he told Whandall. "You didn't tell me Willow could perform."

"Carter can too," Whandall said, remembering. "He needs practice, though."

"They'll have the chance. A good show is worth a lot, Whandall. They'll draw crowds out in Stone Needles country. Golden Valley too. Whandall, we're moving out tomorrow. How will you move your wagons?"

"The ponies—"

"They'll be slow. Willow can still lead them?"

"Well, I suppose so, I don't know why she couldn't."

Kettle Belly grinned knowingly. "Good. But it won't do. They won't move faster than the girls can walk. Most of the way is uphill. The girls will get tired and slow us down, even if Orange Blossom takes turns with Willow. Willow will be too tired to practice. And what about your mare?"

"Carver can still handle her. She'll pull a cart if he drives it." Whandall shrugged. "Not me. That mare wants me dead."

Kettle Belly grinned again. "Okay. Good. Carver drives the wagon with the mare. The other wagon's a different matter. I'll bring over some bison in the morning, and Number Three will show you how to hitch them up."

"What about our ponies?"

"They'll follow the girls. Willow and Orange Blossom can ride at the tailgate of your wagon, and all the one-horns will follow them. Darned things are more trouble than they're worth, but they're popular in Golden Valley."

CHAPTER
42

After dinner he left the Ropewalkers and Millers working on the wagon. Carver sent a dirty look after him, a look he was meant to catch. He stopped. He said, "Carter, maybe you'd better come with me."

Carter trotted to Whandall's side, but, "This is work," Carver said, as if Whandall might not recognize it on sight. "We need all the hands we can get."

"I made a bargain with Hickamore, the wizard," Whandall informed them all. "If I don't keep it, we'll be paying Kettle Belly a fourth of what we own. So I'm going to tell him stories about Morth—"

"But why Carter? He doesn't speak Condigeano!"

"Carter might have seen things about Morth that I didn't. The younger children would miss anything subtle, and you weren't *there*, Carver. While Willow and I were dealing with Morth, you were a day's walk away dealing with a cart and mare that you had left behind. But I could take Willow instead."

"Oh, Whandall, I think they need me here," Willow said with apparent regret. "Take Carter."

Carver began pounding a post into the ground. Carter and Whandall went to Hickamore's wagon.

The shaman and his family sat under the stars. They must have had first choice of campsites; the circle of rocks around his fire was almost too convenient as a conversation pit.

"My children, these are Whandall and Carter, surely the most unusual of visitors to our home." How had Hickamore known Carter's name? Magic. "Folk, greet my daughters Rutting Deer and Twisted Cloud, and their friends Fawn and Mountain Cat."

Twisted Cloud was just turned fourteen, quite pretty in the local fashion, high cheekbones and arched brows and straight dark hair. She had Carter's full attention. Running Deer (the shaman *couldn't* have said *Rutting Deer,* could he?) was seventeen, with that same look, exotic to Whandall. Fawn didn't say, but she looked to be the same age. Fawn was pretty enough, but Running Deer was Twisted Cloud made mature: tall and lovely, with dark straight hair sculpted into a single braid. Mountain Cat was eighteen or nineteen and finely dressed. He was with Fawn or with Twisted Cloud—it was difficult to tell which—but he didn't want the barbarians near either of them.

Whandall sat aside. Even among lookers he knew how to avoid knifeplay.

The girls chattered. "Willow," Twisted Cloud said. "Why is she named Willow?"

"It's their way," Fawn said. "Like Ruby. Something precious."

Twisted Cloud nodded understanding. "It's hard to find. Maybe they don't have any in the Valley of Smokes?"

The old man offered Whandall wine. Whandall asked for river water instead. Twisted Cloud scowled, knowing she'd be sent to the cistern to fetch it, and she was.

Hickamore asked, "When did you first see Morth of Atlantis?"

"He was in Lord Samorty's courtyard below Shanda's balcony, talking to the Lords. He looked decrepit, then, and amused. I was only a little boy, but even I could see that he thought they were all fools. They saw it too, I think, but they thought he was *wearing* it. A wizard's attitude, like the Lords' attitudes they all wore like masks. But it wasn't."

"He did think they were fools, then. Why?"

"They used something that burned up all the magic right through their whole town. Magic didn't work there. Morth was dying for lack of magic—"

"A Warlock's Wheel?"

Whandall shrugged.

Hickamore was excited. "What did it look like?"

"I never saw it. What's it supposed to look like?"

But in the distraction of Twisted Cloud's return, the question got lost. Whandall drank, then thanked her, and Hickamore asked, "What was a Lordkin boy doing on a Lord's balcony?"

Whandall told of crawling over the wall, meeting Shanda, the exchange of clothes. . . . Running Deer, Fawn, and Twisted Cloud were listening, rapt. Mountain Cat had forgotten all his suspicions under the lure of a good story.

Hiding on the balcony watching an opera. The Black Pit at night. The magic forest: Hickamore wanted to know more about hemp.

"It wants to kill you," Whandall said. "Everyone knows that. You can't walk through a hemp field without falling asleep, and it will strangle you by morning."

"Not here," Mountain Cat said.

"Ropewalkers," Hickamore said. "How do they make rope if the hemp tries to kill them?"

Whandall looked to Carter. "Carter, the shaman asks—"

Carter said in broken Condigeano, "Old men know. Never teach me."

At Hickamore's urging, Whandall described taking Shanda through the chaparral, being caught by Samorty's people, the mock beating. Hickamore wanted to know more about maps. Whandall drew Tep's Town in the dust, by firelight. Hickamore gave him colored sand to improve it.

Then Hickamore added Whandall's improvements to a map he must have drawn earlier. Grinning, he watched Whandall's face as the map came to life. A green-sand forest bowed and rippled to a yellow windstorm. Cobalt river tracks glittered. Bison no bigger than ants ran before the orange sparkle of a prairie fire. Within the fire a bird's beak showed for an instant, there and gone, and something else, a bird as large as a bison, ran ahead of the fire and vanished.

Carter was yawning, and that gave Whandall his excuse to depart. Bringing Carter had been a good idea.

Hitching up bison was a pain, but driving them turned out to be easier. The beasts were not very smart. They wanted to follow their leaders. They were hitched four to a wagon. As long as a team of bison could see the team in front of them they followed docilely. Kettle Belly drove the lead wagon.

The road took them steadily north. They crossed two small streams, then the road led steadily upward.

The first sign of the terror bird was a high, piercing shriek. Then a scream from a woman in the lead wagon. Then more of the alien shrieking. Then a coyote burst from the chaparral, followed by something bright green and orange, and big.

Whandall had never seen its like. It ran on two legs like a chicken, but the eyes were a head higher than Whandall's and it hadn't even straightened up! The head was too big for its body, mounted on a thick and powerful neck. The beak was most of the head, and it wasn't shaped like a chicken's. It was curved and hooked, built for murder. The legs were thick and stumpy, thighs nearly as big around as Whandall's, and covered with feathers. A plume of tail feathers fanned out behind it.

Whandall gaped. It was clearly a bird, but those weren't wings! The forearms ended in what looked like Lordkin knives, with no pretense at flight.

The coyote ran in terror. An astonished camp dog sprang after it just too late, and the beast shrieked again and charged the dog. The dog dodged by a hairbreadth. The beak snapped shut on nothing, striking timber from a wagon's side. The howling dog dove under the wagon.

The apparition darted after it.

Bison panicked. The lead wagon jolted as the bison broke into a cumbersome canter. Others followed. In seconds the orderly wagon train was a mass of stampeding bison pulling wagons, and the bird was in the middle of it.

Willow and Orange Blossom were seated on the tailgate of their wagon, clinging to ropes as the wagon lurched away. The bird hesitated, then charged them.

Whandall snatched a blanket from a wagon seat and ran forward, waving his Lordkin knife, shouting a wordless challenge.

Ponies tried to block the thing, but it evaded their horns and aimed a kick powerful enough to stagger the larger stallion. Then it ran toward Willow. It was faster than Whandall. Whandall flapped the blanket at its eye.

The bright blanket got the terror bird's attention. It turned to charge Whandall, its eyes fixed on the blanket. Whandall kept the blanket in front of him until it was nearly on him, then stretched out his blanket-covered left arm and raised it while turning to his left. The bird stretched out its neck and dove into the blanket. Whandall brought down the big Lordkin knife at the base of its neck.

The neck was too thick. The bird ran a circle around Whandall, blinded and trying to tear through the blanket, while Whandall sawed at the neck with his knife. Turning the edge forward got it under the feathers. Round and round, but that *had* to be bone, and he was getting through it, and then the head was bent back but the bird was still running. It ran Whandall into the side of a wagon. He spun off and lay dazed.

The bird was hellishly fast, but its head flopped loose now, and here came Carter and Carver with a rope stretched between them. The bird's random path veered toward them. They pulled the rope taut and tripped it. As it thrashed they ran round it, wrapping the legs so it couldn't get up.

The spear-claw forearms thrashed for ten minutes. By the time the beast was still, Kettle Belly and the other drivers had halted the wagon train. Now they all gathered around Whandall and the Ropewalkers and the dead bird.

"What in the hell is that?" Whandall demanded.

"Terror bird," Kettle Belly said. "They're rare."

"Let's keep it that way," Whandall said, but he was grinning. Victory felt good. And Willow was looking at him in a way she never had before. So were the other girls of the wagon train, all of them. That felt good too.

The terror bird made soup to feed the whole train, in a row of the big bronze pots that most of the wagons carried. The train gathered around Hickamore's ring of rocks to share it. The meat was tough, and *red*, less like bird than bison.

As they ate, Hickamore asked Whandall about his tattoo. Whandall had learned some of the local speech by now, but it went better with Ruby Fishhawk to translate from his own language.

"I know now that Morth of Atlantis made it for me, and enchanted it, so that he could follow me out of the Burning City. I believe it killed all the men in my family. . . ."

Gradually the folk around them went silent. Hickamore's daughters listened, and the Ropewalkers and Millers too, and Willow. They'd never asked him about the feathered snake tattoo. What had they known of Lordkin? They might not know *this* tattoo was unusual.

Whandall felt good. If Willow hadn't been there he might not have stuck to river water. The party broke up far too early.

The road led up to another pass. Orangetown was in a vale there, and unlike Marsyl, Orangetown had walls.

The town gates were set into stone gate towers, and the walls were stone for a hundred paces to each side of the gates. Elsewhere they became a wooden palisade, logs sharpened at the top and set into low stone walls, chest high to Whandall. Whandall thought Orangetown was smaller than Lordstown. It was certainly tiny compared to Tep's Town.

There were permanent corrals outside the walls, with pens for the bison and another fenced area for the ponies. A steady wind blew from the northeast and the pens were downwind of both the town and the campground. The campground itself had wells and fountains and stone-lined walks. There were feed stores and warehouses adjacent to the animal pens. A large field with wooden seats filled the area between the campgrounds and the animal pens.

Kettle Belly and a dozen of his younger relatives—sons, daughters, nieces, nephews, and cousins—came to help Whandall and the Ropewalkers unhitch their animals and set up camp. "You'll be here," Kettle Belly said, indicating an area among the low trees. "That's your well. The toilet trench is in the grove there. Use it, and clean up any animal droppings. They're sticky about that here."

Whandall smiled to himself. Not everyone had a well and a fireplace at his campsite. The area Kettle Belly picked for Whandall was nearly as large as Hickamore's, and certainly nicer than what the Fishhawks got. "The town looks organized," Whandall said.

"We'll pay for it, but yes, they're organized. One thing. Catch up on sleep. It's safe here. When we set out north again we'll stand night watches until we get to the Big Valley." He eyed Whandall's big Lordkin knife. "Wouldn't surprise me if you got a chance to use that again."

"More of those birds?"

"I'm hearing rumors of two bandit tribes in the hills."

Carter fingered the sling he wore openly around his neck and displayed a bag of stream-rounded stones. "We'll be ready!"

Whandall smiled thinly. He'd never seen a kinless with a sling until Carter took to wearing one. Carter had a knife too. He was clumsy with it, but the kinless were good with slings. More than ever, Whandall thought he knew why Lordkin turned up missing from time to time back in Tep's Town. . . .

"Bandits have seen slings before," Kettle Belly said.

"Bet they never saw anyone like Whandall before!"

Kettle Belly eyed the orange feathers Whandall wore in his plaited hair and the gaudy feathered serpent crawling up his arm and across his cheek and eye. "Now there you may be right."

"I heard Morth say, 'What if a magician vouched for you?' I had no idea he was there, and I wasn't even surprised. Morth called it a lurk spell," Whandall said.

He took a strawberry. The shaman had set out a platter of big red strawberries. Whandall hadn't seen anyone picking them. "Shaman, where did you get these?"

"Treeswinger Town, before we met you," Hickamore said. He saw Whandall's astonishment. "My magic preserves many kinds of food. One of the ways in which I earn my keep."

Whandall ate another strawberry, then drank. He lifted the water bottle to show Twisted Cloud. "Brought my own. You won't have to leave this time."

The girl giggled.

She did too much of that. Whandall didn't know how to deal with a giggler. He continued, "Two huge dagger-toothed cats made of fog and smoke were playing around Morth's feet. His hair was going white to pink and back again, like cloud shadows. He had magic to make him young, but it wanted power.

"I had to hold back. I wanted to kill him. No reason at all. Yangin-Atep was in me, and Yangin-Atep is a fire god, and Morth is a water wizard. Morth backed away. The kinless children were still giving me plenty of room . . ."

Hickamore held out the wine flask.

He had only made that gesture once, the first night of storytelling. After that, he'd kept the bottle. Whandall took the bottle and drank.

It wasn't watered. Better not do that again!

Mountain Cat reached. Whandall passed the bottle.

Whandall asked Carter for his own memories of Morth, and then Willow's and Carver's. Carter laughed. He said that Willow had thought Morth might protect them from the Lordkin who threw fire. Hammer had found Whandall awesome, because he frightened Carver; but Morth tended to lecture, like his father.

Whandall didn't take the bottle again, but he could feel its effect burning in his blood. He spoke on. The fire track through the forest, Morth suddenly among them . . . Tell them about gold in the riverbed? Not yet.

Twisted Cloud went to bed. Mountain Cat made his excuses and departed. Carter was asleep.

Whandall picked the boy up in his arms and made his farewells.

The campfire lit his way, barely. He became aware that both older girls were walking with him. One spoke in a teasing voice. "Mountain cats made of smoke? Is any of that true?"

Whandall kept walking, because Carter was heavy. He said, "I wouldn't lie. Also, I wouldn't lie to a shaman until I knew his power."

"Why do you bring the boy with you? You almost never ask him anything. Is he your ———?"

"He is under my protection. What was that word?"

"Stays with you so that a woman can't get you in trouble, so that another woman's dowry is safe. Does Willow Ropewalker fear for her dowry? She doesn't have one!"

"Running Deer, what *is* that word, *dowry*?"

But the girls were gone, so abruptly that Whandall wondered just how much wine he'd taken. One full swallow; it had burned his throat going down. Maybe some wines were stronger than others.

CHAPTER
43

The water in their camp well was cool and sweet. Whandall drank his fill, then splashed himself clean in the washing pool next to the well. The afternoon was hot. It had been a long day, starting before the sun came up.

He found shade in a thicket near the wagon and stretched out for a nap.

The sun was still high when he was awakened by someone moving. He looked out through the thicket, moving just his head. Old habits die hard.

Willow was tightening a rope four feet above the ground. For practice she liked it high enough that a fall would hurt, but not so high that she'd break bones. She tugged on the rope, nodded in satisfaction, and went into the wagon. Whandall waited for her to come out. He liked to watch her, although Willow didn't want anyone to watch her practice.

She came out wearing bright feathers. When they'd skinned the terror bird, Whandall had given the feathers to Willow. He hadn't known she had made a costume from them. It looked good on her, gold and green and orange feathers sewed into the cotton and linen cloth most townspeople wove and sold. It fit her tightly, showing the curve of her hips and breasts, and stopped short at the knees to show her perfect calves. Whandall stifled his approval. She might be angry with him for watching her. When Willow got angry, she got more and more quiet, and if he asked her what was wrong, she would mutter, "Nothing." It drove him crazy.

She vaulted onto the rope and did a quick back somersault, then a handstand, the feathered skirt tumbling down to show more feathers and a few inches of thighs. Wagon train women and townswomen never allowed anyone to see them when they weren't fully clothed . . . unless they were performing, like Orange Blossom riding the ponies. Then they wanted everyone to see them. Girls were confusing.

Willow came off the handstand and dove forward. Whatever she attempted, she missed, and nearly fell, just catching the rope. She used it to swing upward and back onto it, then did a forward somersault.

"Bravo!" Carver came around the side of the wagon.

"You startled me," Willow said. "Coming up?"

"No. I've lost the knack," Carver said.

"Brother, you just need practice."

"No, I've really lost it. Besides, no one wants to see me do ropewalking. They want to see pretty girls."

"That was nice. Do you really think I'm pretty?"

"Yes. Whandall thinks so too."

"Maybe." She jumped lightly to the ground. "Well, if you aren't going to be part of the act, I'll have to work out a new routine."

"You'll do fine," Carver said. "Mother always said you were really good."

"I miss her," Willow said.

"Dad too."

"Well, sure, but—yeah, Dad too."

Carter and Hammer came out of the wagon. "Hi. Hey, you look great," Carter said. "Did you make that?"

"Well, I sewed it," Willow said. "Ruby Fishhawk helped."

Carter fingered the feathered skirt. "That sure was something to see. Whandall saw that bird looking at you and *pow!* He was right there, that big knife out, that blanket—did you see what that bird did to the blanket? It would have torn Whandall the same way, only he was too fast for it. And strong. You ever seen anyone stronger?"

"Will you stop with that?" Carver said.

"Why should I?"

Whandall lay still, wondering what to do now. Lurking was natural, but *this* . . .

"Wasn't he, Willow?" Carter demanded. "Wasn't he wonderful?"

Willow nodded but didn't say anything.

"Ah, you think Whandall can't do anything wrong," Carver said.

"But what does he really know how to do? He can't tame ponies. Even my mare runs away from him. He can't make rope. What can he do?"

"He can fight!"

"Lordkin can fight," Carver said. "And he's a Lordkin."

"He's not," Carter said. "He's not Lordkin and we're not kinless! Not out here."

"Then what are we?" Hammer asked.

"I guess we're just people," Carter said. "Rich people."

"Whandall's rich," Carver said. "We're not. Morth gave that gold to Whandall, not us. We don't even own the wagon, not if Whandall says we don't."

Hammer had been listening with attention. "But it's ours," Hammer said. "Well, yours. But one of the ponies was my dad's, so that makes it mine."

"Yours if Whandall says it is," Carver said.

"It's mine anyway!" Hammer said. "If that Lordkin harpy won't give it to me, I'll—"

Carter laughed. "You won't do anything!"

"I'll get help," Hammer said. "Carver will help. And the wagonmaster. And the blacksmith. They'll make him give me my pony!"

Carter laughed again. "You think everyone in this wagon train could take something away from Whandall if he didn't want to give it? He could kill everyone here!"

"Well, maybe not," Carver said. "But you're right—he'd be pretty hard to take out. They won't try it. The wagon train can't afford to lose that many people dead or hurt. Unless we get him in his sleep."

"You won't do that!" Carter said. "Why are you all mad at Whandall? He saved Willow from that bird! He saved us all. We'd never have got out of that forest. We'd still be in Tep's Town if it wasn't for Whandall, and he never did any of us any harm. Willow, you're the oldest; make him stop talking like that."

"We still don't know what happened to Father," Carver said.

"Whandall didn't hurt him," Carter said.

"He says he didn't," Willow said.

"You believe him?" Carver demanded.

"Yes. Yes, I do. Anyway, he was possessed of Yangin-Atep," Willow said slowly. "Yangin-Atep could do anything. It wouldn't be Whandall's fault."

"You believe in Yangin-Atep now?" Carver asked.

"Don't you? Morth does. You saw what Morth could do with magic, and Morth was afraid of Yangin-Atep!"

"Yangin-Atep can't take Whandall again," Carter said. "We're safe here."

"We don't know that," Willow said. "We don't know what gods there are, or what they'll take a whim to do. But I think we're safe from Whandall."

"He's still Lordkin," Carver said.

"Why do you keep saying that?" Carter asked.

"Because that's what everyone says. Everyone in the wagon train."

"Does Kettle Belly say it?" Willow asked.

"No—"

"Hickamore?" She was holding back a laugh.

"I never asked him."

"Who *have* you been listening to?" Willow asked.

"Yeah, who's everybody?" Hammer chimed in.

Carver was turning belligerent. "Rutting Deer. And Fawn, the blacksmith's older daughter. They say he's a Lordkin boor."

Willow laughed merrily, and Whandall's heart danced inside him. She said, "You don't know much about girls, do you, little brother?"

Carver gaped at his sister. That *hurt*.

"I already heard that story," Willow said. "Ruby Fishhawk told me. Rutting Deer—"

"Her mother had a vision," Hammer snickered. "Can you picture it?"

"Hush. Rutting Deer and Fawn are together all the time, and they both had their eyes on Whandall after he killed the terror bird—"

"So did you!" Carter laughed. "I saw you."

"So they tried to flirt with him." Willow forged on: "Carver, Fawn's not as good looking as Rutting Deer, is she? But she's not promised. Rutting Deer is promised to a boy in another wagon train. They both think it's fun to flirt. That poor boy, Mountain Cat—anyway, Whandall just couldn't believe that name!"

"I can understand that," Carver said. "I can hardly make myself say that in front of a girl. Even if it's her name."

"He thought he'd heard wrong. Whandall called her Running Deer. But he got them mixed up and called *Fawn* Running Deer. Now they both want his liver," Willow said.

"He's still a Lordkin," Carver said stubbornly.

"And Mountain Cat is still their toy doll, but you could take his place if you say what they want."

Whandall would have paid a high price to be somewhere else. No outsider should hear any of this.

"Us. The wagon," Carver said. His face was very red, and he was forcing the words out. "The team. Who owns any of this? Whandall already gave away one part in ten—"

"That was a good deal!" Carter said. "Everyone else pays more."

"Yes, but he made the deal for all of us," Carver said. "He didn't ask us. Like it's all his."

"So you'd give Kettle Belly twice as much. More. He wanted a quarter! You're very free with the family goods." Willow turned away. "It's time to start dinner. Whandall will be hungry. Carter, Hammer, go find us some wood."

Whandall crawled out through the thicket, staying with the shadows, sliding through branches without bending them. He knew how to hide from kinless. There was a lot to think about as he walked back to the main camp.

Rutting Deer. Fawn. Got them mixed up in the dark, Whandall thought. Names were important. In Tep's Town you never let anyone know your true name, so whatever name people called you wasn't real to begin with. Out here, your name was your *self. Rutting* Deer?

Flirting. Willow said Rutting Deer and Fawn were flirting. He didn't know that word. What had they been doing before they turned cold?

They'd been talking about dowries.

What's a dowry?

Whandall glanced up at the sun. Still high. Hours to dinner. Time to find out. There was a person he could ask. . . .

He bought half a dozen ripe tangerines in the Orangetown market. Mother's Mother had liked those when she could get them. He took them to Ruby Fishhawk's wagon. She didn't hesitate before inviting him into the wagon box tent for tea. It was automatic to take off his boots before going in. He'd learned that much.

Ruby fussed with tea things, poured a cup, and sat on a cushion across from Whandall. "Now. What is this about?"

"I need help," Whandall said. "I don't know anything about girls."

"A boy your age? I don't believe it," Ruby said. She grinned to make it clear what she thought.

"Girls *here,*" Whandall said. "And Willow."

"Willow. Oh. Yes, of course. I keep forgetting that you're Lordkin."

"Forgetting?" Whandall leered out of a rainbow-colored snake.

"Well, it's more I forget what Lordkin are," Ruby said. "And you're not like the ones I remember. Well, usually you aren't. The way you went after that terror bird, now that's how I remember Lordkin. Fearless. Strong. When I was a girl I used to wonder about Lordkin men, what it would be like to have a protector like you." She grinned. "That was a long time ago. You like Willow, do you?"

"Yes." Whandall found it hard to speak about Willow. What could he say? "She's the most beautiful woman I ever saw."

"My. Have you told her that?"

"No."

"Why don't you?"

"I don't know how."

"You just told *me*," Ruby said. She chuckled. "Whandall, are you asking me how to court her?"

"What does *court* mean? Like *flirt*?"

"Well, courting is serious flirting," Ruby said. "If a boy only wants a girl's attention, he flirts. If he's thinking of marriage, he goes courting."

Whandall digested that. "Is that what girls do too? Flirting isn't serious? Courting is?"

"Well, yes. It's a little more complicated than that, but yes."

"Then I want to know how to court her."

"You can't," Ruby said. "No, wait, you're the *only* one who could, and she knows that, and girls like to think they have a choice. They usually don't, but they like to think they do."

Whandall repeated what he almost understood. "Why am I the only one who can court her?"

"She doesn't have a dowry." Ruby reached over and poured more tea. "That won't matter to you, but it will to all the other boys."

"Yes! What's a dowry?"

Ruby grinned mysteriously. "A dowry is a fortune. Money. A wagon. Rugs. Things girls bring to a marriage, Whandall."

"You mean boys court girls for what they *own?*" Whandall was being shown a whole new evil. "Lordkin would never do that!"

"They wouldn't, would they?" Ruby said, "I'd forgotten that too. The boys here don't think that way. Think on it, Whandall. A dowry belongs to the woman! If her husband mistreats her or throws her out, she takes it back with her. Ideally it will be enough to live on, to support any children she might have. And a husband thinks hard about getting rid of his wife if it means he has to hire out as a laborer." She laughed. "I had to have it explained to me, you know. Kinless don't think that way either. A girl's dowry in Tep's Town, some Lordkin buck would gather it."

"Oh—"

"Not you, dear. We don't have kinless and Lordkin here."

"That's what Carter says." Whandall mused. "What does Willow need to make a dowry?"

"A wagon and team, if she's going to live on the road. Money. Clothes. Rugs. The more the better, Whandall."

"The wagon is hers," Whandall said. "It always was, but I guess she doesn't know that. If she has a dowry, anyone can court her?"

"Well," Ruby said, looking at Whandall's thick arms and bulging muscles, "they can, but some will be afraid to as long as they think you're involved. But that's all right, Whandall. Willow will understand that." She chuckled. "Of course any boy might find his courage. And Willow is a lovely girl."

"What do I do after she has her dowry?"

"Give her presents—"

"I did. A dress, and a necklace. She thanked me, but she never wore them."

"Did you ask her to wear them for you?"

"No—"

"Land's sake, boy!"

"But—"

"You want her to wear them for someone else?"

"No!"

"Well, then, you have to ask her," Ruby said. "Whandall, Willow grew up kinless. Kinless never show anyone what they have. It took me a year before I wore my nicest clothes outside the wagon tent! It's not something you think about; it's just the way kinless live."

Kinless were drab; he'd thought it was their nature. Now he began to understand. "And if I ask her to wear the things I bought her, and she says no?"

"You'll know you need to do some more courting," Ruby said. She winked. "Give her a little time, Whandall."

"I will," Whandall said, but as he walked back to his—Willow's— wagon, he saw Orange Blossom smiling at him, and two other girls sat with their legs showing, and he wondered just how long he could wait. It had been hard, learning to be a Lordkin, but at least he'd understood what he wanted to be.

Supper was ready when he got to the wagon, and then Hickamore wanted a story. There was no chance to talk to the Ropewalkers and Millers.

CHAPTER
44

Orangetown wasn't truly a pass, but more a level spot on the way up to the high country beyond. The next two days led steeply up, with no good place to make camp. Everyone had to help ease the wagons through stony fields. The hills rose steeply to each side and ahead, and all were covered with brilliant orange flowers. Whandall had never seen anything like them.

"Beautiful," he said.

Kettle Belly grunted and put his shoulder to the other wheel of the Fishhawk wagon. "Ready! Heave!" Together they lifted the wagon wheel out of the hole. "The flowers are pretty enough, but there's another thing I like about them," Kettle Belly said. "They're too low to hide anyone sneaking up on us. Out here we don't have to worry too much about bandits, and tonight we can be in a safe campsite. I think we'll stop there to rest up." He waved his arm to indicate the trail ahead. "After that, though, we'll be back in scrub oak and chaparral, and rocks. There's bandits out there—I can smell them."

"You can *smell* bandits?" Whandall could have used that talent in Tep's Town!

"Well, maybe not. But Hickamore can. A good wizard can give warning, and Hickamore's good. Blast! Now Ironfoot's wagon is stuck—"

"Kettle Belly!"

The caravan chief looked around at Whandall's horrified shout. He said, "Ah."

Moving among the mountains, grayed by distance, was a vastness built to their mountains' own scale. Its legs were as tall as redwoods, but so wide that they looked stumpy. Its torso was another mountain. A forest of hair, piebald brown and white, hung down all around it. Ears bigger than any sail. An arm . . . a boneless arm where a nose might have been, lifted and fell as the . . . god turned to study them.

"It's Behemoth," Kettle Belly said. "It won't come any closer. Nobody's ever seen Behemoth close. Give me a shoulder here, Whandall."

Whandall set back to work. From time to time he looked up at Behemoth moving among the mountains, until the moment when he looked up and the beast god was gone.

The road became steeper, then leveled off. Whandall was glad of it. He and the blacksmith and Kettle Belly were the strongest men in the wagon train, and sometimes it took all three of them to get a heavy wagon over a bad place. "I'll be glad when this day is over," Whandall told Kettle Belly.

Kettle Belly glanced up at the sun. "Two hours and a little more. Only one place to camp tonight," he said. "Four! Run ahead and tell the scouts we'll camp at Coyote's Den. Not that they won't know it."

"All right, Dad!"

"Coyote's Den?" Whandall asked.

"The road forks just up ahead. The right-hand branch goes uphill. We'll take that one." Kettle Belly grinned as Whandall groaned. "Not too steep, and it's a good road. The Spotted Coyotes see to that. They've made a good place to camp, too. Of course they had to."

Whandall frowned the question Kettle Belly had expected.

"They had to because there aren't enough of them to be tax collectors without giving some service," Kettle Belly said. "Look around you. Nothing here but some pasturage, and not a lot of that. Over there, beyond that ridge, there's some better land, but no one ever goes that far off the Hemp Road. For some reason the Spotted Coyote tribe has to live here, something about instructions from their god."

"He told them to live here but he didn't give them anything to live on?" Whandall asked. "What does he do for them?"

"Beats me," Kettle Belly said. "Coyote's a strange one. Nobody really knows what he wants. Anyway, the Spotted Coyotes made the best of it. They found a big ring of boulders, and over the years they've made it into a rest stop. Here we go; that's the fork."

Kettle Belly's number three son ran out with a long curved cow horn. "Can I do it?" he asked excitedly.

"Sure."

Number Three blew six long blasts on the horn.

"That tells the Spotted Coyotes how many of us to fix dinner for," Kettle Belly said. "That's how it works. You tell them you're coming, and they cook up stew to be ready when we get up to the top. They feed us and watch out for us." Kettle Belly's lips pursed into a small tight grin. "And they don't charge any more than they ask for just to pass through their territory."

"Are there a lot?" Whandall asked.

"No, not really, but enough you wouldn't want to fight them, and you *really* wouldn't want them making the road worse than the winter rains do."

"Toronexti," Whandall said. When Kettle Belly gave him a blank look, Whandall tried to explain. "Tax collectors. Toll takers. But *they* never give you anything for what they take."

"So you organize a lot of people and go kill them," Kettle Belly said. "That's what we do. If a town gets mean enough, we get all the wagoneers together and go burn them out."

Whandall thought about trying to organize enough Lordkin to destroy the Toronexti. Nobody knew how many they were, where they lived, nor even who they were behind those masks. They were backed by the Lords, it was said. Nobody could fight the Lordsmen.

The top of the hill was a natural fortress. A spring bubbled up in the center of a ring of boulders that formed a natural castle large enough to enclose a wagon train and all the livestock. Over the years the Spotted Coyote clan had smoothed out the area inside the boulder circle and built corrals and pens and shelters, and big cook fire rings. The smells of bison stew wafted to the wagon train.

Kettle Belly and a small dark man about his age shouted and gesticulated at each other. Whandall thought they were pretending at passion as they went through a ritual. Kettle Belly would throw up his hands in disgust, and the Spotted Coyote leader would gesture outside the circle, grinning as he pointed out a small column of smoke a couple of miles away. Kettle Belly looked worried, then shouted again. . . . Eventually they came to some agreement, and money changed hands. By then dusk was falling and the stew was done.

They ate dinner around a big campfire. Logs had been arranged in a circle to form seats and backrests. It was pleasant to sit back and relax with the prospect of a night's sleep without need for guard duty.

Whandall pleaded exhaustion when Hickamore wanted to talk about Morth of Atlantis, and soon the wizard was deep in conversation with a man twice his age who wore a mantle of wolf skin. A

Spotted Coyote boy came around to fill everyone's cup from a goat-skin of wine. Whandall sipped appreciatively. It was not as good as the wine Kettle Belly kept in his wagon, but it was smoother and more pleasant than anything that made its way to Tep's Town.

A pleasant evening. Willow sat next to him, tired because the girls had been hopping on and off the wagon all day as the hills became steeper and they had to get out and push.

Flirting. Courtship is serious flirting. Flirting meant being amusing and funny, and Whandall didn't know how. He looked around to see how others were doing it.

Not far away Carver sat with Starfall, the blacksmith's dark-haired daughter. They sat very close together. Whandall couldn't hear what they were saying, but Starfall seemed to be doing all the talking as Carver sat listening attentively. That seemed like something Whandall could do, but Willow wasn't saying anything!

"Did you like the dress I bought you?" Whandall asked.

"Yes, very much. Thank you."

"You don't ever wear it."

"Well, I wouldn't want to wear it here, with all these strangers," Willow said.

"Kettle Belly says they're safe," Whandall said. "They're not—" He cut himself off.

"Thieves?"

"I was going to say 'gatherers.' "

"Oh." She looked at him with wide eyes. "I keep forgetting," she said.

"That's good."

She smiled softly. "Be right back."

Carver was still listening to Starfall. She moved closer to him. Whandall had no trouble imagining her warmth against his side. The boy said something, and Starfall laughed appreciatively. Other couples were talking softly, boys smiling, girls laughing. If only he could hear what they were saying!

Willow returned. She was wearing the blue dress Whandall had bought, and the gold-and-black onyx necklace.

"That's—wonderful," he said, settling for that, although he wanted better words. "I knew it would look good on you."

"And it does?"

"Better than I thought," Whandall said.

Her smile was haunting. She sat next to him, not as close as Carver was sitting to Starfall, but she had never been so close. He could feel her warmth radiating against his side, warmer than the fire. They didn't talk for a long time. Whandall kept trying to think of something clever to say, but nothing came to mind, and it was enough just to be close to her.

When Carver and Starfall left the firelight circle and went off into darkness, Whandall thought Willow was about to say something, but she didn't. He imagined standing up, taking her hand and leading her to privacy and secret places, but he did nothing, and he wondered if his legs had forgotten how to obey him.

Suddenly she smiled at him and touched his face. Her touch was light and smooth, as she ran her fingers along his tattoo, down his arm, still smiling. Then she sat close to him, and they stared at the fire.

Carver had a sappy grin at breakfast. It faded when he went to hitch up the mare. The pony reared and tried to trample him. Whandall watched, frowning, as Carver shouted at the pony. Someone in the next wagon party laughed loudly.

A few minutes later, Greathand the blacksmith came to Whandall's wagon. He wasn't unfriendly, but he seemed preoccupied. "Need a favor," he said. "Like to have Willow bring one of your ponies over to my wagon."

"Sure. Why?"

"Rather not say until I know," Greathand said. "If you don't mind." The blacksmith seldom asked favors. Whandall was pretty sure no one ever refused him when he did ask. And there was no reason not to do it. Was there?

Willow had heard. She led the smaller of the horned ponies over to them. Whandall had to look twice: it was as large as the larger one had been the day before, and without the black star marking on its forehead Whandall would not have known which one it was.

The ponies changed size sometimes. Whandall had asked Hickamore about it. "Magic changes along the road," the wizard had told him, then asked how Morth cured skin diseases.

Willow followed Greathand toward his wagon. Whandall watched her lead the pony for a moment and remembered her smiles last night. But there was work to do loading the wagon.

When Willow came back, Greathand and Kettle Belly were behind her. They waited until she led the pony back to join the others. Greathand stood back and let Kettle Belly talk for him. "These aren't your kin, but it's your wagon," he said.

"Willow's wagon," Whandall said.

"You're in charge," Greathand said. "That boy Carver doesn't have a father, and he's in your wagon!"

"Yes," Whandall said. It sounded like an admission but Whandall didn't know why.

"So we can talk to you about him," Kettle Belly said. "What's his situation? Profession?"

"He knows how to make rope, and sell it," Whandall said. "Why?"

Greathand frowned. "Why are you—?"

Kettle Belly held up a hand. "Ropewalking. Expensive to set up, but a ropewalk makes good money," he said. "Have to have a place to do it, though. Not on a wagon train." He turned to Greathand. "Starfall doesn't have a wagon yet. Want to think about a different dowry?"

"She can't take back a ropewalk!" Greathand said. "But she didn't want a wagon anyway. She's always talked about living in a town year-round."

"Well, we can work that out, then," Kettle Belly said. "How old is the boy?"

"Sixteen, I think," Whandall said.

"Little young," Kettle Belly said.

"Starfall's only fifteen," Greathand growled. "If the damn fool hadn't made such a big thing about not being able to harness that mare, maybe—anyway, Starfall's all excited, so I guess it's got to be. Whandall, we'll talk when we're over the pass, discuss arrangements, where the kids want to live, what it takes to set up a ropewalk. You tell Carver he's a damn lucky boy." The blacksmith went away, still muttering under his breath.

Whandall frowned at Kettle Belly. "I saw Carver and Starfall go off together, but they weren't the only ones last night!"

"They're the only ones that all of a sudden can't harness one-horns," Kettle Belly said. He grinned. "I always thought you were putting me on, but you really don't know!" He laughed at his enormous joke. "Whandall, *everyone* knows it! Nobody but a virgin can harness a one-horn. Yesterday Carver could harness the mare and Starfall didn't have any trouble with the stallions. This morning—"

"I've been stupid." Many cryptic things were becoming plain.

"Doesn't work that way in the Valley of Smokes, then?"

"No." Whandall thought about it. "Ponies are smaller, don't have real horns. It surprised us when ours grew those big horns. Magic! Kettle Belly, what happens now?"

"Well, you heard. Greathand will have to come up with another kind of dowry. I don't know if he can afford a ropewalk—he's got Fawn to marry off too—but he'll do what he can. Carver have any shares in your stock?"

Whandall nodded. "He's not poor. This is all new to me. What happens if they don't want to marry?"

"Come on—they knew there were one-horns in the wagon train!"

"Carver didn't know what that means."

"Starfall did," Kettle Belly said. "You trying to tell me that it's different in the Valley of Smokes?"

Whandall remembered Willow's story of what happened to Dream-Lotus. "No. Not for kinless," he said. Carver must have known what he was getting into. Whandall remembered incidents with Fawn and Rutting Deer, chances he had, things he might have done.

It was different here, because there weren't Lordkin here, and he could never explain that. "No," he repeated.

Kettle Belly squinted up at the rising sun. "Burning daylight," he said. "We have to get moving. Whandall, you'd better explain this to Carver."

"Yes. Does he have any choices?"

"Well, he can take a wagon as dowry, if he wants to learn this life. Being married to Greathand's daughter won't hurt him a bit."

"What if he runs away?"

"He'd better run damn far from the Hemp Road. Forever."

CHAPTER
45

They made camp in a boulder field. Large rocks helped form a natural rectangular fortress, nothing so refined as the place the Spotted Coyotes had built. Wagons filled in gaps among the big rocks. Whandall watched their placement—all wagons in sight of each other. They'd traveled until near sunset to find such an open place . . . an easy trek down the gorge to the river . . . but wouldn't any bandit know just where wagons would stop? And the boulders and the rising and falling ground around them could hide all of Serpent's Walk and Bull Pizzle together.

But Hickamore drank strong hemp tea and sang, and when he came out of his trance was satisfied. There were bandits near, but they only watched. They had no plan, no purpose, only their envy.

The sun had set, but the west was still red and orange. Whandall sent two of the Miller children to keep watch outside the wagon circle. "Stay very still, and if you hear anything, shout and run under the wagon. But yell first!"

Then he had Willow, Carver, Carter, and Hammer sit down around the fire.

"We need to talk," Whandall said. "Carver, you knew what was expected when you went off with Starfall."

Carver looked very solemn. "Yes. Well, I knew it in my head," he said. "I wasn't thinking much, though."

"Starfall was," Willow said.

"How are you so sure?" Carter demanded.

She shrugged. "Girls always are. In Tep's Town you might get away with being careful, but it's a big risk. Out here—believe me, Starfall knew what she was doing. So did you, I think."

"It's so—permanent," Carver said. "That's what I'm having trouble with."

Carter nodded in sympathy.

"So what do you want to do?" Whandall insisted. "I think I'm supposed to negotiate for you. Where do you want to live?"

"I can make rope," Carver said. "Well, if Carter will help. Carter, I'll teach you my part if you'll teach me yours."

"Greathand can't afford a ropewalk," Carter said.

They all looked at the wagon. Then they looked at Whandall. No one said anything.

Whandall grinned. "Depends on Willow," he said.

"Me! I don't have anything, except the dress you bought me. I don't have anything at all!"

And she was near tears. Dowries. Was that the problem? "The wagon. The ponies. Willow, they're all yours." He'd been thinking how to say that. He'd waited too long.

"One of the ponies is mine!" Hammer protested.

Whandall shrugged. "Argue that with Willow," he said. "But Kettle Belly says one pony is worth a team of bison, so Willow has a wagon and team."

"And the mare?" Carver demanded.

"I have a claim," Whandall said. "I helped catch her. The hemp and tar too—part of that's mine. I won't claim it, though. Willow can have my share."

"Why?" Willow asked. "It's very nice of you, Whandall, but why?"

"I know why," Carver said. "Don't you?"

She didn't answer, but she had the same vague smile that had appeared when Whandall said she owned the wagon and ponies. She looked quickly at Whandall, then looked away again.

"Don't forget, the wagonmaster gets a tenth," Whandall said. "Now about the gold."

"Morth gave that gold to you," Carter said. And Carver said, firmly, "Yes."

Whandall nodded. "I'll share. I needed you to move it for me. Still do. There's enough for your ropewalk, I think, if you and Carter stay together. I keep half. You, all of you, share the rest any way you decide." Half would still be a lot. "Half after the wagonmaster gets his share."

"Kettle Belly doesn't know about that gold," Carver said. "No way he could know."

"We could hide it," Carter said eagerly.

"No."

"Whandall—"

"No," he repeated. "We tell the wagonmaster."

"Why?" Carter demanded. "He doesn't know—he can't know."

Whandall tried, but words came slowly. "I said. I promised."

"A Lordkin's promise," Carter said. "Made to a thief!"

"Kettle Belly's not gathering," Whandall said. "He's—he's working with us."

Carter looked to the others. Some understanding flowed among them. Carver said, "All right," and shrugged.

Whandall felt like an outsider. There was a long silence. Finally Whandall got up and left the wagon. No one spoke until he was too far away to make out words, then Carter and Carver began speaking excitedly.

CHAPTER
46

"Come in," Kettle Belly said in invitation. "Have some wine."

"No, thank you," Whandall said. "I have something to show you."

"Yes?"

"Not here. At Willow's wagon."

Kettle Belly frowned at the setting sun. "Time to set the watch," he said. He began pulling on his boots. "Willow's wagon, you said? Not yours?"

"Hers after her father died," Whandall said. "In the Burning."

"Makes sense," Kettle Belly said. "I keep forgetting about the one-horns."

"The ponies are hers too."

"Well, of course." Kettle Belly tied off his boot laces and held out his hand for Whandall to help him up. They set off at a brisk pace with two of Kettle Belly's nameless sons following. "Good. Let's go. You and Willow getting along all right, then?"

Whandall didn't answer.

"And it is my business," Kettle Belly said. His tone was serious now. "Everything that happens in this wagon train is my business until we get to Paradise Valley."

"Pelzed used to say things like that."

"Who's Pelzed?"

"Someone I used to know. I think we ought to hurry."

Kettle Belly was taking two steps to Whandall's one and didn't have breath for an answer.

"Leave that alone," Willow shouted.

"Why?" Carver demanded.

"Because—"

"Hello, Willow," Kettle Belly said.

Carver turned quickly. He was holding a gold nugget in both hands. It was pulling him to the ground.

"That's what we wanted to show you," Whandall said. "We have gold."

"I see that," Kettle Belly said. "More than that?"

"What's in the wagon."

The wagon bed was open, and Kettle Belly looked. He said, "That's a lot of gold."

"I know. It's refined gold too."

"Where did you get it?" The shaman's voice. They turned to see Hickamore come out of the shadows.

"Damn that lurking spell!" Whandall shouted.

Hickamore grinned. "I wondered if you would tell the wagon-master." He turned to Kettle Belly. "Now, Black Kettle, behold the skill of your shaman and the value of our bargain. Dowries for all your daughters in your share alone!" Hickamore cackled. Suddenly he stiffened. He went past Carver and reached into the false compartment of the wagon, now open.

"Stop that!" Carter shouted.

Hickamore ignored them. His skinny arms lifted, holding two nuggets both as big as his head, as if they floated up under his palms. "Refined, you said. A wizard absorbed its power. Morth? Is that who you meant? He didn't take it all, boy!" The old man's voice had gained in timbre and volume: it must have been audible throughout the camp. "Here." He handed a nugget to Carter (who dropped it) and one to Hammer (who staggered), took the nugget Carver was holding, and lifted it high. His face twisted in joy. His eyes rolled back into his head, and he stood entranced.

"Now what have you done?" Kettle Belly demanded of Whandall. His two sons stared at the shaman. In the shadows were Bison folk who had followed Hickamore's voice toward possible entertainment.

Carver and Carter had given over shouting at Kettle Belly. They watched the shaman. Willow ignored Hickamore to stare at Whandall, looking at him in a way she never had before, not unfriendly, certainly not angry, but as if she'd never really seen him. Before Whandall could speak to her, Hickamore recovered. He grinned wildly. "More gold calls. It's kin to this," he said.

"We're a long way from the river," Whandall said.

"Yes, yes, it was washed down to the river from above," Hickamore said. "The hills are alive with its music; I feel the power of it calling me. We must find it."

"Now?" Kettle Belly demanded. Hickamore nodded ecstatically.

"Is this wise?" Kettle Belly said. "There are bandits all about us."

"With the power in the gold, I will find and destroy them all!" Years had fallen from Hickamore's face, but they were creeping back again. His voice must have carried for miles; any bandit spy would hear him.

"You made a spell so you wouldn't get old," Whandall guessed.

Hickamore grinned craftily. "I have spoken many spells in my life, Lordkin. Kettle Belly, I must find that gold tonight. It wants me."

"How much gold?"

Hickamore shook his head. "As much as this, perhaps more. You want refined gold. I want—"

"The gold changed Morth," Whandall said slowly. "He became someone else."

"Younger, you told me," Hickamore said.

"Yes, and crazy!"

"I am already crazy," Hickamore said with casual conviction. "Whandall, come. We will search together, and you can tell me more of Morth of Atlantis."

"But—"

"Recall our bargain," Hickamore said. "Black Kettle will count what is here. Come." Before Whandall could protest, the shaman took his hand and pulled him away from the wagon. Behind him Whandall could hear the others shouting as Kettle Belly inspected the false wagon bottom. He tried to go back. He'd left Kettle Belly surrounded by armed adolescents in an argument over wealth!

Missing the point entirely, the shaman said, "Your friends are safe with Black Kettle. He is an honest man. I have said so, and it is true. You!" He turned to one of Kettle Belly's sons. "Number Three. Run quickly to my wagon and tell Twisted Cloud that her father needs her instantly to go with him on a journey. Run!"

"Why Twisted Cloud?" Twisted Cloud was Hickamore's fifteen-year-old daughter, who giggled.

"We seek magic. Rutting Deer has no sense of magic. Her jawline is clearly mine, else I might be suspicious of my wife," Hickamore said.

Whandall looked sharply at Hickamore, but if the shaman noticed, he didn't react.

A half-moon peeked through scattered streamers of cloud, nearly overhead. The clouds stirred restlessly.

The older man strode on. Before they reached the wagon train, they saw Twisted Cloud running toward them, still fastening her skirt. Her black hair flew in the wind.

"You feel it?" Hickamore demanded.

"Something," she said. She wasn't giggling now. "Father, what is it?"

Hickamore seemed to sniff at the air. "This way, I think—"

"No," Twisted Cloud said. She cocked her head to one side. "More uphill, where the flood ran."

"Ah. Yes. It is very bright."

There was nothing bright ahead of them, but Whandall didn't say so. He'd seen Morth at work.

They were rushing ahead of him, running through poppies and scrub brush and over rocky ground. Whandall had trouble keeping up. A young girl and an old man were leaving Whandall in their dust. Hickamore might be enchanted—was enchanted—but how could Twisted Cloud outrun Whandall?

She saw him stumble—somehow, though she was far ahead— turned back and took his wrist, and ran again, pulling him.

She babbled breathlessly as she ran. "I squinted when I was little. My father made magic to strengthen my sight. It worked, a little. I've never seen so well as tonight! There are spirits about, but nothing dangerous. Follow me!"

"Oh, that's it. You're seeing—in the dark. Did Hickamore make himself—young too?"

A laugh in her voice. "Yes, but when he was younger . . . ." She stopped talking.

The ground wasn't tripping him anymore. They were climbing a steep hill of bare pale rock. Twisted Cloud was steering him aright; but Hickamore was far above them now, outrunning them both. Power in the half-refined gold was taking him back through time; or else he was running over raw gold left by a flood.

Whandall gasped, "He doesn't need me . . . as much as he thought!"

Her answer was not to the point. "Rutting Deer is promised, you know."

"Doesn't like me."

"My dowry isn't the equal of hers, but—"

Whandall laughed. "Hickamore wants *us* together?"

"Just to *see* each other, it may be. To notice."

A man could be knifed for lusting after a girl this young. *Change the subject.* "When he was younger. What kind of magic . . . does a shaman cast?"

She laughed. "I'll tell you one he told *me.* Piebald Behemoth was dying. Father was his apprentice. A shaman must not be seen to grow ill and die. Father took the aspect of Piebald Behemoth and became our shaman." Twisted Cloud was pulling him uphill and chattering as if a fifteen-year-old girl had no need to draw breath. She'd never spoken so much in her older sister's presence. "The Bisons *wanted* to be fooled, you understand. Father let himself get well over the next year. Took a new name. And of course he blesses crops for the villages we pass and makes weather magic that sometimes works. The twisted cloud that was tearing up the camp the day I was born, Father dispersed it before it reached our wagon. Mother told me about that."

Their path converged with a small and narrow, swift-running stream. Hickamore was far ahead. Twisted Cloud raised her voice above the sound of rushing water. "And once he tried to summon Coyote, but the god wouldn't come."

The stream narrowed and was partially dammed, so that it formed a falls as high as a tall man. Twisted Cloud and Whandall reached the stream just as Hickamore was emerging from the pool behind the boulder. He was holding a nugget the size of his fist and grinning like a fool. Lean as a snake he was, and muscled like a Lordkin. Black hair fell to his shoulders. His eyes were ecstatic and mad.

All in a moment his black hair curled; a wave of gold ran through it, and then a wave of dirty white. Then most of the white mane was dripping into the stream, leaving bald and mottled scalp. Hickamore's face contorted. Gaunt and hollow, jaw more square, brows more prominent, it was not his face at all but the face of a dying stranger.

Hickamore fell backward into the water. His twisted features were a grimace of pain and horror. One eye turned milky, the other stared wildly.

"Father!" Twisted Cloud screamed. She held two smaller nuggets. When she ran to her father with them, he writhed in pain. She threw the gold into the water and reached to wrest the larger nugget from Hickamore's fingers. "It's the old spells!" she shouted over her shoulder. "Take the gold!"

Whandall ran to help.

The old man's arms had gone slack, but the gold would not release his fingers. Twisted Cloud touched it and yelped. She pulled her hands loose as if the gold were sticky and lurched back into Whandall, shouting an unfamiliar phrase.

He tried to get around her. Then his mind caught up: she'd shouted, "Don't touch it!"

Hickamore whimpered and spat teeth. The sound in his throat was a death rattle. Then he was still. The current dribbled water into his mouth.

Whandall asked, "Are *you* all right?" For Twisted Cloud was looking around her like a blind woman. This wasn't mourning; this was something else.

Her eyes found him and pinned him to reality. "I can *see*. I think I never saw before. Whandall Feath—"

"Girl, what happened to your father?"

"All the old spells. Did Morth of Atlantis know how to make a failed spell go away?"

"I have no idea."

"Father didn't know. Piebald Behemoth didn't know. Father took the old shaman's aspect on the night Piebald Behemoth died, before I was born. Stay *here*, Whandall."

The stream was icy on his shins. The shaman's daughter spoke *before* he started to wade to shore. He stopped, and looked, and saw the merest shadow of what was happening on shore.

Both sides of the stream were thickly overgrown with plants. It hadn't been like this earlier. You could almost see them growing. Whandall hissed between his teeth. He was not a man to take such a thing lightly.

"Father blessed crops," the girl said, "and made rain during drought. That didn't always work either."

Clouds were forming knots in the half moonlight, gearing up for rainstorms decades postponed.

"Should we be in a riverbed when the rains come?"

"No." Twisted Cloud turned and began to wade downstream. "We have a few minutes. It won't be like this farther down."

Whandall had lost all feeling in his feet. The bushes on both shores were closing above them. Behind their backs, the voice of a god laughed.

They whirled around.

The dead shaman was sitting up. His voice was strong, and louder than the falling water. "Cloud, dear, your father is dead. He lived a life very much to his liking, and no more can be done for him. Harpy–Seshmarl–Whandall?"

"Coyote."

"Hickamore once mimicked a shaman freshly dead. His spells have succeeded beyond his maddest dreams. And I am Coyote, yes." The voice of a god. Hickamore had tried to call Coyote. "But do you know who Coyote is?"

"A god among the Bison People. I've heard stories. My people may have known of you, Coyote. The stories make you sound like a clever Lordkin."

Coyote laughed. His throat was drying out in death. Whandall glanced aside: Twisted Cloud was basking in a state of worship. He'd get no help from her. *Don't offend a god,* he thought, and hoped it could be that simple.

Coyote said, "I must know more of this Morth. I see that you understand the notion of trading knowledge, trading stories. Will you trade with me?"

"That would delight me," Whandall said; and Whandall was gone.

CHAPTER
47

Whandall Placehold came to himself in black night, shadowed by a boulder, kneeling in pooled blood above a dead man. He was holding his Lordkin knife, and it dripped. He stayed quite still—more still than the dead man, whose heel still jittered against the rock—and listened.

He heard not city noise but campground noise. Running water. Forty beasts and a hundred children and elders and men and women settled down for bed. The campground must be just the far side of this rock. Sounds announced a dozen Bison gone to gather water. Nobody did that alone; there might be bandits about.

A smallish bandit lay right at Whandall's feet. His throat had been cut. His knife was better than Whandall's, and he wore a sheath too. Whandall took both. The moon wasn't up yet, but there was starlight and campfire light, and in the west a wall of black clouds sputtered with continuous lightning. In that near darkness he could see lurkers who moved too often. In just these few breaths he'd seen too many to be mere spies.

Would they attack the caravan directly? Or the little water-gathering party? Where was Twisted Cloud? Safe? *Where was Willow?*

How had he come here? Memory was there to be fished up if he could find any kind of bait.

So. The dead man . . . and a chest-high rock. Rocks everywhere, hiding places everywhere, but Coyote must have . . . *had* seen this rock as the best. A bandit or two *must* be hiding there, so Coyote had crept from shadow to shadow until this shadow gave up its lurker. Coyote cut his throat, and now it was *his* hiding place. Then—

Then nothing. Only Whandall blinking in the dark.

Ah. He'd been counting on the gold! And it all came flooding back. ·. . .

Coyote had become Whandall. Whandall had become Coyote. Whandall was gone.

Coyote held out his hand. Twisted Cloud took it and came into his arms with a laugh, her joy a near-intolerable glare.

Whandall shied back. That memory was too intense. It blinded him to the danger in the lightning-lit night. Women had loved Whandall for gifts, or for status, or for love alone, and one he had gathered; but he had never been *adored*.

Coyote expected it. He knew how to treat a worshipper.

Sending the girl into ecstasy was not the point. She might remain rapt, wandering in enlightenment while she grew old. He had to keep bringing her back, with humor, with sudden bursts of startling selfishness, or, for minutes at a time, by becoming Whandall Placehold, ignorant and lost, puzzled and horny. This Whandall was a mocking graffito, and the memory made Whandall's ears burn, but it snapped Twisted Cloud from nirvana into postcoital laughter.

Everything was funny to Coyote.

They'd loved in the freezing stream, an hour ahead of a flash flood, while plants went crazy all around the old shaman's body. Coyote loved the danger. Then they'd run downstream ahead of hard rain and a flurry of hail.

And while they ran, Coyote had run barefoot through Whandall's memories. Tracing Morth. Matching Whandall's life to sketchy tales he'd found in Hickamore's dying brain. Seeking more.

Whandall had guessed right. The shaman didn't know of a lurking spell. He hid in shadows like any Lordkin gatherer.

Coyote lurked in the same fashion, hiding in shadows, risking a too-keen eye. *Of course* a god need not be seen. But that was a cheat, as Morth's lurking spell was a cheat, Coyote thought contemptuously, even as he yearned to try Atlantean magic.

Whandall, remembering, saw what Coyote had forgotten: he must *teach* his skills. A god can't teach a god's power to his worshippers!

In Whandall only a trace remained of Yangin-Atep the torpid fire god, but Coyote sensed kinship. He saw a city of thieves and arsonists! And himself barred forever by his nature!

The stories. Coyote loved stories. He learned Wanshig's tale of Jack

Rigenlord and the Port Waluu woman, and Tras Preetror confronting Lord Pelzed's men, and others. The story he'd told Hickamore of a boy and girl on Samorty's balcony, Coyote balanced against Whandall's own memory.

He reveled in the *performance,* story and music and people pretending to be what they were not. He lived it again while his body ran blind. Plants lashed Coyote, unnoticed, and now Whandall felt scratches and swellings across every exposed square inch of skin.

What he left behind . . .

Coyote remembered walking from the frozen east across a wilderness of ice that had been ocean, crossing stretches of water he ensorcelled to buoy his followers. Then south toward the sun, he and his people, six hundred years moving south under pressure of starvation. Setting fires to drive game into reach and to leave the forests free of undergrowth afterward. He had become Coyote while they wandered, but he bore other names elsewhere, and he was there still. Tribes encircling the world's cap of ice shared a trickster god, and another lived in the tundra, and in Atlantis another. In the Norse lands he was Loki, who was also a god of fire.

Gods of a same nature shared a life, and memories and experience were contagious. Loki the fire god was being tormented. Prometheus gave fire and knowledge to men and was punished by Zoosh. Birds tore at his liver. Yangin-Atep felt the same agony: his life leaked through the gash that was Lord's Town, an emptiness made by Lords with a Warlock's Wheel. Whandall Placehold had felt their agony in his sleep.

Coyote had kept his bargain. Story for story.

Urgency added spice. Coyote had never forgotten the bandits. He and Twisted Cloud stopped and spread their clothes on bare rock and loved again, and again lower down.

He said presently, "They've come to attack your caravan. They'll do it while the shaman's gone. Twisted Cloud, return to your folk. I will stop them."

"Please," Twisted Cloud said, "don't let Whandall be killed."

"I won't," Coyote promised. He had no idea whether the Lordkin would live.

Neither did Whandall. Lordkin's promise! Still, Twisted Cloud's last thought for him made him warm inside.

Every few breaths he saw more bandits in the rocks, in the dark. They had some skill, he decided. Whandall alone would have seen less of these lurkers in their native turf, and they'd have seen him. But something of Coyote's skills stayed with him.

Coyote had intended more. He moved ahead of Twisted Cloud, lurking shadow to shadow.

Twisted Cloud moved toward the camp, slowing as she came. With skills taught by her father, she would remain hidden from bandits; but Coyote knew what would happen when she reached the caravan. Perhaps she did too.

Coyote passed lurking bandits and left them alive, save one who just wouldn't get out of the way. He passed through the caravan's ring of guards. They patrolled in pairs. The boy Hammer and the young man Carver were on duty.

The rest of the Miller and Ropewalker families were on guard around their own wagon.

By now most of them should have been asleep. Little Iris Miller was out like a doused flame, but the rest were up and edgy. This was going to be difficult. Twisted Cloud was perhaps twenty-five minutes away; Coyote would have that long.

He needn't escape with gold! Coyote only needed to touch it, but for several seconds. He needed a disguise . . . wait. Why not pass himself off as *Whandall Placehold?*

He slid out of their vicinity, circled and came back from the uphill direction, a Lordkin stumbling just a bit in the wild sputtering dark. "Willow, you still up? Carter? I saw Hammer on sentry duty."

She said, "Whandall, *good—*"

Carter broke in. "Yeah, well, the entire *caravan* knows what we're carrying, thanks to *you.* We don't just have bandits to worry about— it's *everyone.*"

Carter was disappointed in Whandall. Coyote was enjoying himself immensely.

"My first good chance to teach you how to hide what you've gathered, and I failed you. Poor child. *Now hear this,*" he said with the authoritative rasp Whandall Placehold had spent years perfecting. Heads snapped up. "We are not gatherers. If we were gatherers, we wouldn't know what to gather and what to leave alone, because we're among strangers. Town or caravan, we'd be caught and hanged the first time we tried. But none of that matters, because *we are not gatherers.*"

Willow was smiling radiantly; Coyote saw that without looking at her. The smaller children looked mutinous, but Carter's jaw hung

slack. Coyote held his eye until he nodded. Then he went to the
wagon.

They'd closed up the floor. Coyote made as if to inspect it. "Did
Kettle Belly count this?"

"Yes, Whandall," Willow said.

"Good!" But he was reaching for the manna. No need to open the
false bed. Wood planks wouldn't stop the flow.

No need indeed. Two wizards had sucked all the power out of all
that gold. It was as dead inside the wagon bed as so many rocks.

Twisted Cloud was ten minutes away.

Any attempt to delay her would eat his time too, and *he* didn't have
time. Coyote-as-Whandall stalked away saying, "I'll go patrol. I bet
Hammer's ready for a nap."

Willow stared after him. "Be careful," she called. "Be careful."

Out beyond the firelight, he melted into the shadows. He'd needed
wild gold! Coyote was going to miss the battle! And all he could do
now was set this fool Lordkin in place.

CHAPTER
48

By now Whandall knew where most of the bandits were, at least those nearby. Fifty or so. There might be many more. A messenger was moving among them, but whatever his words, they were not "Attack!" Even a stranger's body language told him that.

They weren't waiting for anything in particular. They watched and envied. The shaman had known that in hours, or a day, they would run out of patience.

But Coyote had been waiting, and now Whandall knew why.

A pony whinnied. Then the others. Then the firelight showed Twisted Cloud walking proud and erect, with nothing to hide.

The ponies would have screamed their anger if she had lain with a man . . . with, say, Whandall Placehold. But Twisted Cloud had lain with Coyote. She was carrying Coyote's child, freshly conceived.

The ponies went mad. They began to destroy the corral.

The bandits knew a distraction when they saw it. Without Twisted Cloud, their attack might have come at any time. They'd already marked the locations of most of the caravan's guards. They charged in a scuffling run. The scouts ran about whacking laggards to get them moving.

And Whandall was behind them.

First things first. The nearest man was slow, and his back was turned. Whandall could have swung wide, but the man ahead of *him* had a fine knife with a big shiny leaf-shaped blade. Whandall would have to kill the first man before he fought the second.

The bandit never heard him. A backhand slash at a leg, draw across the thigh until it spurted blood, then bring the knife around and high and straight down to the join of neck and shoulder. He barely croaked as he fell.

But the second must have glimpsed something. He whirled around to see in the half moonlight a silent giant with a dripping knife. He screamed when he should have fought, and then the point was in his throat.

But Whandall's knife stuck in the bone. And again he'd been seen! The bandit to his left turned and charged and ran himself on the knife Whandall had taken from the man Coyote had killed. Whandall left his own knife where it stuck. He had two bandits' knives, each long and heavy, the hilt grooved for fingers, and with a guard! Treasure indeed in Serpent's Walk, and worth his life out here, maybe, because four or five bandits were spreading through the boulders to surround him.

Again! What were they seeing? A Lordkin should know how to lurk!

Elsewhere the bandits were converging on the wagons, yelling like Lordkin, each pretending he was a mob. Whandall had been told they would do this. Among the rocks, who could know how many there were?

Kettle Belly stood in the center of the wagon camp, surrounded by his sons and a dozen others, the trained young men he called his army. Others, men and women and adolescent children, went to defend their own wagons. Younger children scrambled under wagons.

Kettle Belly shouted orders—and was obeyed. At his command fifteen young men with spears and javelins formed a line and threw their javelins at the bandits they could see. The wrong band, the disorganized gatherers. Kettle Belly couldn't see the bandit lord, but Whandall could.

That one. His brighter colors flashing in moonlight, a burly bandit shouted orders to twenty companions who wore colorful sashes. Those hesitated, awaiting his word. The equivalent of Pelzed's guard, Whandall thought. But most of the horde were rushing toward the wagons, paying no attention to the big man.

Those were no threat. They were gatherers who would run if faced with real force. It was the bandit chief and his henchmen that the Bisons ought to fear.

Memories flooded through Whandall, riding the shouts of the bandits. Coyote had run with bandits too, and he knew them. Bandits didn't want to destroy a wagon train. They wanted loot, women, and a wagon to carry it all. Eight or ten bandits could snatch a wagon and pull it into the dark, if other bandits stayed to harry pursuit. Men could outrun a bison team.

Five bandits were coming at Whandall, spreading out to surround him. Not enough to slow the horde. Yelling wouldn't even be noticed, but—"Snake feet! Snake feet!" he screamed. He danced between two men and turned on one with slashing doubled blades and left him with both arms bleeding, then whirled to find the other *much* too close, stabbed him through the heart, and delicately plucked his blade. "Serpent's Walk, you ignorant lookers!" and he ran.

Three still chased him. He was lucky to get any attention at all! He was only one man with a few corpses around him; over there was a wagon train rich with loot. These savages were going to kill a lot of people unless he could distract them.

Four of the front rank of gatherers went down before Bison Clan's spears. Two got up and limped away from the battle. Kettle Belly's army hefted spears in both hands and advanced toward the charging bandits. They hadn't seen the bandit chief and his guard moving toward the caravan at a jog, holding formation.

Whandall ran to intercept them. He'd guessed their target.

He could hear panting behind him. He turned once and slashed and was running again. Three behind him now, one wounded, and none of them really wanted to catch him. In the caravan, some of the defenders had noticed Whandall.

From somewhere behind them came a high-pitched song that sounded of rushing wind, of storms and joy and death. Twisted Cloud! Her voice carried courage to her friends, fear to her enemies, and more.

Gold! She would be carrying some of the river gold, empowered by its wild magic. What had she learned from her father? Her spells would be uncontrolled in the best of times, and now—Whandall didn't think he should put much trust in Twisted Cloud's spells. Still her song rang out, and a few of the rear rank of bandits melted away into the night behind them.

A wind was rising. The storm that had gathered above Hickamore was coming to Bison Clan.

Carver stood on Willow's wagon, Carter just behind him, their slings whirling. There wasn't much light, and if their stones hit anyone there was no sign of it.

It was a game. Coyote would call it a dance. The bandits wanted loot, women if they could get them. The wagonmaster wanted to limit his losses, keep his people safe, inflict enough damage to make the bandits think again before attacking his wagon train. He would risk men to save women. He would risk all to save all the wagons, but he would not risk many men to save only one.

The bandits would choose the wagon least guarded, the lightest and easiest to move. Willow Ropewalker's wagon was small and near, defended by children.

And Whandall Placehold was behind them.

Coyote memories and Kettle Belly's training were overlaid on what he could see. What Coyote knew of bandits and raids was all scrambled up with memories of possession by Yangin-Atep. That was different. He'd been possessed of Yangin-Atep, but he had *been* Coyote. Coyote had opened his memory and doused him with knowledge and stories. Whandall would be days sorting out his own memories from Coyote's.

Three of the chieftain's score had been cut down by the caravan's defenders, but other freelance bandits were gathering around that core of men, increasing their number.

The corral splintered. The bonehead stallions ran mad through the camp, horns flashing in moonlight. Twisted Cloud ran behind them, flapping her arms, howling like a coyote, guiding them into the attackers. Bandits scattered ahead of them. One rose on a horn and was thrown flying, and one ran straight into Whandall's knife, stopped in mortal shock, and screamed only when he saw Whandall's face. Whandall moved among them, slashing. The ponies broke free and ran screaming from Twisted Cloud.

The bandit chief shouted more orders. Five of his guard and half a dozen other bandits heard, thought it over, and converged toward Whandall Placehold. About time they noticed him! Whandall backed away from the horde that was coming at him; whirled and struck down the tired man at his back; turned back and saw them stop as if they'd hit a wall. Then half of them came on.

Too many. Too many were coming at him at once. If they swarmed ahead, they'd have him before he could deal with more than two.

The bandits knew that. No one wanted to be one of the two.

Whandall snatched up a cloak that a dead bandit had gathered from a wagon. He wound it around his arm with the skirt dangling, just in time to shield himself from a knife thrown from the shadows. It was still turning, and struck the cloak without penetration. Whandall leaped forward to slash and felt the *chuk!* of his blade striking bone.

Then he leaped atop a boulder.

Kettle Belly shouted orders. His spearmen moved forward at a trot, spears held waist high in an underhand grip. The bandit chief was between Kettle Belly's spears and a maniac dripping blood and marked with a serpent. His companions closed around their chief and shouted in a language Whandall had never heard before. He understood every word.

"Look what I got, Prairie Dog!"

"Fool! My brother is dead. It's not loot I want, it's blood."

"Drink alone, then."

"His *face!* His *face!* You said their shaman was dead!"

"Run away!"

They were pursued by worse than Kettle Belly's laughter.

Some had snatched clothing that Ropewalker wagon had set out to dry. A gale wind pulled at the cloth like sails, and they ran off balance and half blind. Whandall ran after them, striking down the slowest, who fell with a scream.

Two others turned, releasing what they carried, drawing knives as their loot flapped away like ghosts. Then one fell without a sound. The other dithered an instant, then came on alone. Whandall killed him.

He looked around to see a whirling sling, a triumphant grin. "The moon's come out!" Carver shouted.

His sling whirled. A bandit with a wooden chest in his arms cursed as the stone hit his back. He turned, dropping the chest. It shattered. Whandall caught up to him. Slash the leg, chop to the shoulder, run past, take another.

"Whandall!" Kettle Belly's voice, well behind, too far behind to be any help.

Carver laughed beside him. "Whandall! Do you know what your *face* is like?"

He'd seen himself in Morth's mirror. But Carver didn't wait for an answer. "You light up! Every time . . . you kill a man . . . the snake lights up . . . in blue fire! Just for a breath, but . . . it scares them out of their *minds!*"

There must be magical power—*manna*—in murder. It was lighting up his magical tattoo. But only for an instant, and now each running man perceived Whandall in the dark behind him. A man clutching a big wood bucket with a handle turned and saw him, and shrieked. Whandall's utmost burst of speed still couldn't catch him, though his staccato scream was announcing his location all across the plain . . .

Enough. "Carver!"

"They're getting away!"

"Leave some to tell the *tale,* Carver," Whandall commanded. "Come back to the wagons."

He had two fine new knives. He'd left his crude Lordkin knife somewhere on the plain, stuck in a man's throat. Coyote spoke to him, from memory or from the shadows, not in words but in pictures, of a pack of coyotes running away to regroup and fall on a pair of pursuing dogs. He urged Carver into a run.

CHAPTER
49

Nobody slept. Conversations clustered around the wounded. There was wine. Whandall was treated as a hero, except that nobody offered him wine. He said nothing, and looked.

Many were heroes that night, and great was the praise they received, but only the wounded were drinking wine. That actually made sense, he thought. Wine dulls pain.

Everybody had a story. They all wanted to hear Whandall's, but they didn't want to shut up.

"We've been counting on you, you know. We wanted to see how a harpy would fight." This from a man who remained cheerful as his wife bound up a deep slash across his back. He'd never spoken to Whandall before. "After Hickamore went off with you, we were all twitchy, waiting for the attack, wondering when it would come, why Hickamore would leave us *now,* why he'd taken the harpy. Thinking he must be crazy."

"He was crazy," Whandall affirmed.

"Yeah?"

"Gold fever."

"Ah." The wounded man found his train of thought. "Then the *ponies* all went crazy. We near jumped out of our skins. We saw Twisted Cloud come back alone, and bandits running out of the dark, and guards running ahead of them to get into position. Everyone armed was running somewhere; anyone else was looking for weapons.

Twisted Cloud saw what was happening, and she ran around flapping her arms at the ponies—"

"They were running away from me," Twisted Cloud said, "and I thought I could steer them into the bandits. It worked, a little, but they wrecked a lot too, and I wouldn't count on their coming back." She seemed unhurt. She smiled at Whandall, a sudden bedroom smile, and he couldn't help leering back. She told Kettle Belly, "I carry Coyote's child. That's what they were afraid of."

Fawn and Rutting Deer were tending Mountain Cat. That looked like a near miss, a wide bloody knife stroke across his ribs and chest, an inch above cutting his belly open. His arm was bleeding too. Fawn glared at Whandall (and, interestingly, Rutting Deer didn't) but Mountain Cat didn't notice.

"You saved me," he said, "know it or not. That son of a broke-horned pony cut me and was going into his backslash. That would have opened me like a salmon. Then, out there on the desert, you pulled your knife out of some poor bastard and looked at us like a hell-blue glowing snake, and he just couldn't look away. And I did! I think I sliced up his eye. Anyway, he ran."

Rutting Deer seemed bewildered. She caught Whandall looking and shrugged helplessly. "I never saw anything. Just you killing someone in the dark, and poor Mountain Cat fighting for us."

"I can't see it either," Whandall told her.

By midnight it was over. Kettle Belly's men took a tally by dim firelight and intermittent moonlight, not straying too far and never separating.

The score was twenty dead bandits against one old man who died of a heart attack and one young boy who was out after stream water. They found him facedown in the water, his head bashed in and his bucket missing. Some rope, clothing, a few pots, one mirror, some harnesses, a couple of spears; they lost very little and got some of it back. Most agreed that it would be a while before *these* bandits attacked the Bison Clan again.

"But there are other bandits," Kettle Belly said, "All along the trail." As Whandall crossed between fires, the man had moved smoothly into place beside him. "Winning this kind of fight can be really expensive. It wasn't, but it could have been."

Whandall waited.

"Hammer saw you and Carver running into the dark and out of sight! We thought they'd killed you!"

"We chased them."

"You have wagons to defend. You could get lost. They could double back around you!" Kettle Belly studied him. "It doesn't make *sense* to risk everything like that. We couldn't go after you, you know, and then you wouldn't be there next time.

"Look, harpy, this is how it's supposed to work. The bandits give up trying to get a wagon as soon as we show them some blood. Then they grab anything they can and run. Typically you'll see a couple of bandits facing off against a wagon family, and nobody really wants a fight. The owners shout for help. A couple of neighbors come, and the bandits run away and hit some other wagon."

Whandall began to doubt. Had he broken some law? "Kettle Belly, do we have some kind of bargain with them? A treaty?"

"With bandits? No!"

"Then it doesn't make sense to follow *their* rules. We gave them no guarantees, right? They're not holding back to keep some bargain, are they? Let's shake them up a little. They want rules? Let them come and ask for rules."

Kettle Belly sighed. "Hickamore said bandits wouldn't know what to make of you. He was right. You're more interested in killing them than in protecting the wagons. Now you're telling me you were following a *plan?*"

"Plan. Well. I did what I've been taught. The Placehold never makes half of a war."

Whandall dreaded the moment when he must face Willow . . . but when the moment came it didn't matter.

Hickamore's storm swept over Bison Clan. They were soaked and blinded. The rain was gone as quickly as it came, leaving them in a howling hot wind.

Kettle Belly and Twisted Cloud drove them to work. The flood was coming just behind!

The wagons were already on high ground, trust Kettle Belly for that, but everything had to be tied down, anchored. There was the risk that bandits would strike again under cover of the storm . . . and in the midst of all that, he and Willow could only glimpse each other at a half-blind run.

In a moon-shrouded moment they almost ran into each other. Willow blinked, then gripped his shoulders and bellowed, "Was it the fire god?"

"No, it was Coyote! You heard—"

"I was afraid she might be wrong!" She was gone.

Dawn showed the wagons on islands in a flood. Bandits would drown before they could gather anything. It seemed safe to sleep . . . and everyone posted a guard anyway.

Iris Miller had slept. She started to complain, but Willow touched her cheek and asked, "Who else could we trust?" and Iris went.

And they slept.

Whandall woke near noon. Traces of breakfast remained: the rest of the caravan hadn't been up long. He could see several of them out on the damp plain finding treasure the bandits had dropped.

Whandall had been thinking. Willow certainly knew, as the whole caravan knew, that Twisted Cloud was pregnant by Coyote where the only living man-shape was Whandall's. Whandall was prepared to spend months or years explaining to Willow that it was Willow he loved. He would be patient. He must satisfy her brothers too: not just Carver—who had fought beside him joyfully, who might be ready to accept him—but Carter too. It might take forever. So be it . . .

But Twisted Cloud was pregnant by his doing, and that was another matter. Whandall had heard too many Lordkin say "possessed" and known it for a threadbare excuse. If Twisted Cloud claimed him, he must marry her.

Two wives were rare among the Bison people.

But while Whandall was thinking, Kettle Belly acted.

At high noon Kettle Belly led Twisted Cloud to a table, helped her up, and joined her. Whandall saw no other signal, but conversations chopped off. Bison Clan gathered around them.

Kettle Belly's voice rolled like a Lord's. "Twisted Cloud will bear the grandchild of our shaman and the child of Coyote himself!"

Twisted Cloud glowed with pride.

Willow Ropewalker stepped up beside Whandall.

"What man is worthy of raising such a child? Coyote's son or daughter—"

"Daughter," Twisted Cloud shouted happily.

"—will be powerful and willful and prone to mischief. Twisted Cloud's man must control the child long enough to teach her—"

Willow called, "Kettle Belly? Wagonmaster?"

A ripple of discontent. Kettle Belly looked down, displeased.

"I claim Whandall Placehold as mine."

Whandall turned to look at her. Willow met his eyes, forcing herself.

Kettle Belly said, "Fine," and dismissed her.

Whandall couldn't think of an intelligent question. But if she didn't mean it, he was going to die.

"Women talk about being *courted,*" Willow told him carefully, "and I liked that. And you gave me a dowry so I'd have a choice. And it's been fun, Whandall," she held both of his hands now, "you courting me and not knowing how, and of course my *brothers* had to get used to you, but—"

"Willow—"

"—but I thought she might claim you! You made her pregnant!"

"Listen, that was—"

"So I got in first."

Whandall couldn't stop grinning. He dared squeeze her hands, then pull her into his arms. They turned thus to watch the ceremony. She clung to him, stroked his tattoo, ran her hand down his left arm to touch the misshapen wrist bones. Then she looked at him and smiled again.

After a long time, Whandall became aware of the rest of the world. What was Kettle Belly doing? Holding an auction?

"She does *not* seem eager to claim me," he observed.

"You're disappointed? Because I just—"

"No!"

"—just realized. You can't see your own tattoo glowing? Rutting Deer can't see it either, but anyone else must be keeping his mouth shut, because it means he doesn't have shaman's blood. *You* can't raise Coyote's child."

"Oops."

"But Orange Blossom— Hello, Carter. Did you—"

"I heard. My shy sister. Now I suppose you never will teach us how to gather," Carter said to Whandall.

Whandall said, "No."

"But you can teach us how to fight."

"You do fine."

Stag Rampant, a young man of Leathersmith Wagon, claimed Twisted Cloud. Whandall had seen the man's doubts, but they were gone now.

She would certainly be Bison Clan's religious leader until her daughter had gained maturity, and maybe beyond. And the rustle of activity was Bison Clan gearing up to travel. Late as it was, they could still make First Pines by evening.

BOOK TWO

WHANDALL FEATHERSNAKE

Twenty-two years pass . . .

PART ONE

The Raven

CHAPTER
50

Whandall just missed the bird. He was rooting around in the back of the cart while Green Stone drove. He heard Green Stone cry out. He wriggled backward out of the luggage space.

Whandall's second son was lean and rangy, taller than his father. He was standing precariously on the wobbling bench while the bison plodded ahead. "There! Did you see it? It was wonderful, a bird colored just like your tattoo, Father! It's behind those trees now."

"Watch where you're driving, Stone." The trees were bare, but Whandall still saw nothing. He didn't stand up. The winter wind cut like a forest of knives.

The Hemp Road continued north and east along the base of the low western hills. Whandall had set New Castle on one of those. Ahead was an open plain and river valley, where the Hemp Road ended.

Whandall fished out bread and cheese for their lunch. He could see dust ahead, at the horizon or beyond. He would not see more for another hour.

There was a fair-size town at the far end of the Hemp Road, a place for supplies and refitting, a market center for all of the caravans. Roads came together there, the coast road that led west to Great Hawk Bay, and another that wound through mountain passes north and east to valleys Whandall never expected to see.

In midwinter Road's End was six hours' travel from the New Castle.

It would be faster in summer, slower in the spring mud. Nobody would travel that distance twice in one day. Willow wouldn't expect him back for three or four.

There were just under a hundred wagons in the wagon yard. Forty bore the fiery feathered serpent that had become the sign of Whandall Feathersnake. The count was uncertain: some wagons were only components. Wheels lay everywhere.

Mountain Cat lifted an axle into place for a Feathersnake wagon that had come home on skids. He'd have used the pulleys, but with Whandall watching, he preferred to show off his strength. "Whandall Feathersnake," he asked, "how runs your life?"

Whandall hefted the other end of the heavy beam. "No excitement."

"We want to thank you for the rug. Rutting Deer set it in our gossip den."

"Good." The public area. Unspoken: he would never see it there. Though the women stayed polite, Willow did not visit Rutting Deer.

Sometimes Whandall wondered. Had Rutting Deer gone to Mountain Cat's tent in fury because Whandall misused her name? Or was it the night of the battle, with Mountain Cat a wounded hero and the bonehead ponies all fled into the dark? Did she expect her father to bargain with unicorns for her? But Hickamore died, and still she might have married the man she was promised to; but one of the ponies had come back after the battle. . . .

So she'd married Mountain Cat. Without a wagon for a dowry, they'd settled in Road's End and found what work was there.

He could never ask. The Feathersnake family had to get along with a man who built their wheels and a woman who served their food. He said, "I just got here. What are the hot stories?"

"Plenty of work." Mountain Cat waved around. He told what he'd heard, a Bison Clan wagon lost to bandits this year and found in pieces. Pigeon's Wagon had lost control on the long hill from High Pines to the Great Valley and disintegrated; only the metal parts had come home.

"Did you see the bird? Rainbow colored. It circled us for hours. Looking for something, I think."

"No."

"Are you in a hurry for anything?"

"No, but tell me what's finished."

Whandall spent three days inspecting his own wagons, trading goods and tools and lore, trading stories too, as he had for a dozen years, and planning the summer's route with his firstborn son. Saber

Tooth was just twenty. He'd been leading the wagons for three years now.

Whandall found himself wishing he were going too.

He had long since given up traveling to raise and guard his family, to build and maintain the New Castle, and to manage the details of trade. All of these matters he delighted in, but . . . if only he could be two men. Let him set *Seshmarl* in charge of the New Castle while *Whandall* ran off down the Hemp Road with the caravan for one more summer.

They kept telling Whandall about the flame-colored bird. It had circled the sprawl of partly repaired wagons at Road's End three times, then flown off down the road. Whandall grew tired of hearing about the bird. Everyone had seen it but him.

Past the New Castle's entry sign, a horde of younger children came running to greet him: not just his and Willow's children and grandchildren, but Millers and Ropewalkers and servants' children too. The New Castle was getting crowded, Whandall thought, and then he heard what they were calling.

"The bird! The bird!"

"Well, what?" He scooped up Larkfeathers, Hammer Ropewalker's girl, who named herself for the startling yellow hair she had seen in a trader's mirror. "Did I miss the cursed thing again?"

"No, no, look up!"

Nothing.

"At the sign, the sign!"

Behind him. He'd passed right underneath it.

The New Castle buildings were square-built, roomy but a bit drab. Willow didn't like to display their wealth. But she had let him sculpt and paint that sign, a great gaudy winged snake in all the colors of fire, and mount it high above the main gate as a signature and a warning.

The bird was perched on its head. Against those colors it was almost invisible. But the children were shouting, "Seshmarls! Come down, Seshmarls!"

The great bird took flight. It wheeled above them, flapping hard. Shadow-blackened with the sun behind it, it was clearly a crow. It cried, "I am Seshmarls!" in a voice that was eerily familiar.

It was too big to perch on a child's arm. It circled, thwarted, until Whandall lifted his own left arm, hardly believing. The bird settled crushingly.

The children cried, "Say it! Say it! 'I am Seshmarls!'"

By its shape, by its flight, it was a crow. Magic must have changed its colors. It could hardly be covered in paint and still fly! It turned its head to study Whandall, first with one eye, then the other.

It said, "Help me, Whandall Seshmarl! My hope lies in your shadow."

Whandall whispered, "Morth?"

The wizard's voice said, "Come to Rordray's Attic and Morth of Atlantis will make you rich!"

"I am rich," Whandall said.

The bird didn't have an answer for that. "I am Seshmarl's," it said. This time Whandall heard the possessive. The children gurgled in delight.

"What else does it say?" Whandall asked them.

"Anything we want it to!" Larkfeathers shouted. "And it knows us by name! I can tell it to carry messages, to my sisters or to Glacier Water's Daughter Two, and it does, in my voice!"

"Where does it sleep?"

"Here, mostly, but Aunt Willow lets it in the house if it wants to come in. It's ever so nice a bird, Uncle Whandall."

It would have to be, Whandall thought. He turned back to the bird. "Morth of Atlantis?"

"Help me, Whandall Seshmarl! My hope lies in your shadow."

"Help how?"

"Come to Rordray's Attic."

"Why should I?"

"Morth of Atlantis will give you wealth and adventure."

"How?"

"Help me, Whandall Seshmarl! My hope lies in your shadow. Come to Rordray's Attic."

Green Stone laughed. "Not very smart."

"It's a bird."

"I meant the wizard who sent it," Stone said. "Offering you wealth and adventure! You're almost as rich as Chief Farthest Land, and you've had more adventure than a man can stand!"

"I suppose," Whandall said. He'd said it himself often enough. He looked back to the bird. "When?"

"Another messenger comes," the bird said. "Wait."

The kinless didn't like to display their wealth. The wonderful dresses Whandall had bought her Willow had at first worn only for him; then only when playing hostess inside her own house. What wealth showed was in the private areas of the house.

Willow met him at the door. She led him through toward the back, the bird on his shoulder, Willow draped softly along his other side.

She'd set up a roost in the bedroom. She must consider the bird immensely valuable. And they both knew what would happen next, but in front of the bird? He said, "You know it can talk."

"Just what someone teaches it. *Oh.* Seshmarls, should we cover its ears? Love, do birds have ears?"

"Willow, I think you'd better hear this." To the bird he said, enunciating, *"Why should I?"*

The bird croaked, "Morth of Atlantis—"

"Morth!" Willow exclaimed.

"—will give you wealth and adventure. Help me, Whandall Seshmarl—"

Willow moved the roosting post out into the hall and they returned to the bedroom. A sense of priorities could be a valuable thing.

During the next few winter weeks their discussions formed a pattern.

Morth wanted to enter their lives again. Morth was not to be trusted! His wealth wasn't needed! As for Whandall leaving the New Castle, "Do you remember the last time you went with the caravan?"

"We nearly lost the New Castle," Whandall admitted. "I nearly lost you."

"Well, then."

During those first six years a legend had spread up and down the Hemp Road, of a grinning giant who wore a tattoo that flared with light when he killed. Then Whandall Feathersnake had retired. Three years later he'd led the summer caravan south. He returned to find invaders in the New Castle. A new tale joined the old, but Willow had extorted a promise.

Now he said, "Well then, they died. The story's all along the route. The farther you follow it back toward Tep's Town, the bigger the numbers get. Whandall Feathersnake was gone three years, seven, ten. Snuck back in as a beggar, covering *this* with mud," Whandall slapped his tattooed cheek, "depending on who's talking, or even shaved the skin off, leaving a hideous scar. Killed twenty, thirty, forty suitors who wanted to claim his wife and land—"

Nobody would dare try me now, he didn't say, but Willow heard the words between the words. She changed the subject. "I never liked it, you know. Sending you in *that* direction after I was pregnant. Back toward Tep's Town."

"Oh, that. No, love, I promised. But Rordray's Attic is on the coast, due west of us. Puma Tribe sends wagons every few years."

They'd told him of Rordray's Attic. It was a mythical place inhabited by shape changers, unreachable save by magic, the food touched with a glamour unequaled anywhere. That food was mostly fish, it seemed, and Whandall had not been much tempted.

Later, as the caravan route was extended, he met a few who had seen the place. Then a pair of Puma who had spent a few days there and been served from Rordray's kitchen. Sometimes another wagon's primary heir rode with Puma. They didn't go to make themselves rich. Despite the difficulties of crossing two ranges of jagged hills, it was a training exercise, a lark, an adventure.

Now Whandall said, "I'd add a wagon to their train and take just Green Stone. Bring back fish, spelled or just dried. I never liked fish myself, but some do. Take . . . mmm . . . rope, everyone wants rope—"

"Dear—"

"Maybe Carver's feet are itching too."

"Whandall!"

"*Yes,* my most difficult gathering."

"*I?* Do purses leap out to claim you the way I did? But you *do* remember Morth. Ready to make me immortal, his for eternity, like it or not? Crazy as a bat Morth? Running up Mount Joy with a fat frothy wave struggling uphill behind him?"

Whandall soothed her. "*Two* bats."

"But you got us away from him. Now let's keep it that way!"

"Yes, dear." Wagons couldn't move in the winter anyway.

CHAPTER
51

Two flaps and a space between made up the Placehold's front door. A man going in or out would not take all the Placehold's warm air with him. They didn't build that way in the Valley of Smokes because it never got that cold . . . and because too fine a house made too fine a gathering.

On a fine, clear, cold morning, Whandall stood in the double door and looked past the outer flap.

It looked like you could start *now,* take the wagons and *run.*

From the gate floated the voices of Saber Tooth and Green Stone. Whandall heard "Tattoo . . ." and tried to ignore the rest.

"Morth! Gave Father . . . us too!" That was Stone.

"Not us. You, if you like." Saber Tooth.

Whandall sipped from a dipper of orange juice. The air was clear and cold; the animals were not quite awake. Sound carried amazingly well.

"What if Morth . . ."

". . . wizard *wants* something. Know that. Pay with a tattoo?"

"Mother won't let him go."

Whandall grinned.

Willow spoke at his ear. "Our sons are misinformed. Whandall Feathersnake doesn't obey worth a curse."

Whandall didn't trust his voice. She'd startled him badly.

"Why does Stone want that tattoo so much?" Willow wondered.

He cleared his throat and said, "It's not just the tattoo. Stone would be my second in command on that trek. He could talk to a wizard. See the ocean. Taste food Saber Tooth has only heard about. At the end he'd have something his brother doesn't. Saber Tooth, now, *he* thinks he doesn't want a tattoo, but he *knows* he'll be riding toward the Firewoods with the caravan come spring, and nowhere near the ocean, wherever his brother might be."

"I wish he'd give it a rest. Talk to him?"

"And say what?"

"The only thing that ever scared Morth was water! And now he claims to be at a seaside inn? It's some kind of trap! *Seshmarls!*"

The bird was on her shoulder. "I am Seshmarl's," it responded.

"I finally remembered. Seshmarl is the name you used to lie to Morth! *Morth of Atlantis!*"

"Help me, Whandall Seshmarl! My hope lies in your shadow," the bird croaked. "Come to Rordray's Attic and Morth of Atlantis will make you rich!"

"He's afraid," Willow said.

"Sounds like it." Whandall sipped at his orange juice.

"Afraid of what?"

"It's hard not to wonder."

Wagons couldn't move in the spring mud, either. Two ranges of hills stood between New Castle and the sea, but the plain between was flat and well watered. Life was giving birth to life all up and down the Hemp Road. The tribes worked on the wagons and waited.

The Lion's messenger was a small man with an odd look to his jaw. He came alone, making his way downhill wearing nothing but a backpack. When the Placehold's men had come to meet him he had dressed in a breechcloth and a short-haired yellow hide.

"You're Puma Tribe, aren't you?" Green Stone asked him.

"That's right."

"Well, Puma's got five wagons in repair at Road's End. This's the New Castle. That higher hill south, that's Chief Farthest Land."

"New Castle, right. I'm to see Whandall Feathersnake," the stranger said. "Got a contract for him, and you ain't him."

"You're hard to fool. I'm his second son."

"You're not wearing his tattoo. I talked to the guy that gave it to him."

"Wait here at the gate," Stone said, and ran for the house.

* * *

The pack bore thick straps intricately knotted about his shoulders. It would be difficult to remove, Whandall thought, if you only had paws to work with. The tattoos on his cheeks—"Puma?"

The man grinned at the ambiguity. "Yes and yes."

The tribal names had been more than names once. From time to time a shape changer turned up. Saucer Clouds, Twisted Cloud's first son, was claimed to be a *were*bison. Wolf Tribe had thrown up a were-wolf; they were watching him grow with some unease.

"That'd explain why you travel alone . . . ?"

"Why *and* how. Name's Whitecap Mountain, and I'm here to offer a contract."

"With . . . ?"

"Rordray, called the Lion. He's a were too—they all are at the Attic, but they're seaweres, they're mers. Can you read?"

"No."

"Rordray sends refined gold." Whitecap Mountain reached into his pack.

"Hold up," Whandall said. "My wife should hear this." And others should not! Whandall led him down the path and through the main double door.

Willow greeted him and served hot lemon water. She was punctilious if not, perhaps, cordial.

Whitecap Mountain generally traveled with Puma wagons, he said, but this trip he'd been sent for Whandall Feathersnake. The refined gold in his pack was a flat sheet with the letters of a message pounded into it. "Yours. More on arrival; depends on what you bring. Shall I read it to you? Rordray wants a noonmarch of rope. Two sides of bison, smoked. Mammoth if you can get it anywhere near fresh. Black pepper, sage, basil, rosemary, and thyme. Wood for construction. He'll send back fish raw or cooked. Rordray's the best cook known to men, weres, or gods. Also, he has sea salt, and the mers sometimes bring him treasure from lost ships."

"Sea salt," Willow mused. "We're nearly out." She caught herself. "But—"

Whandall nodded, grinned slightly. Salt was rare enough on the Hemp Road, and the salt found in dry lakes didn't have the proper savor. Something was missing that was found in sea salt, according to Twisted Cloud. Without it your throat could swell up, or your children could grow up stupid or twisted.

It sounded like two wagons' worth of goods. *Better take four,* Whandall thought. Rordray was paying enough, and Whandall didn't know the traveling conditions. Two of his own traveling with two of

Puma's should be safe enough. Pay them whatever it takes. *If* he was going at all. He looked at Willow, but she wasn't sending any kind of signal.

So he negotiated. "But fish, now, what if I can't sell it? Not a lot of us eat fish, and those that do, they say they like it fresh."

"Absolutely fresh and spelled to stay that way," the Puma said.

"You've got a wizard?" *Innocent smile, think Seshmarl,* but cups rattled on Willow's tray.

The Puma said, "I only saw him once. He never comes down the mountain."

Green Stone made a nuisance of himself during dinner. The children had been hearing about Morth of Atlantis since they were little. Stone wanted to know *everything.* The Puma obliged.

"I went up with the talisman box filled with Rordray's cooking, and brought the box back down next morning with the spell renewed. I never slept at all that night. That wizard, he *really* wants to talk. And he's got stories! I can't figure why he stays up there."

Whandall only nodded. If Morth hadn't told him about the water sprite, the tale wasn't Whandall's to give away.

They took Whitecap Mountain to their guesthouse and settled him in. When they moved to the bedroom, Whandall expected to talk all night.

"Now we know," he said. "That poor looker. The water thing has him trapped on a mountain, all alone. He told me once how lonely it was to be the last Atlantis wizard in Tep's Town."

"Why would he think you can help?"

"Had a vision? Magic. No point trying to guess *that.*"

"You wouldn't miss Hawk In Flight's wedding?" The household was gearing up to marry their eldest daughter to the second son of Farthest Land: a major coup.

Whandall said, "That's in spring. We could leave right after. The ocean, it's only a third as far as the Firewoods . . ." at the other end of the Hemp Road.

Willow nodded.

Whandall said, "Daughters and sons are different problems. I think Night Horse will ask for Twisted Tree. Do we accept?"

"We'd best. She's ready."

"She's young."

"This isn't Tep's Town. Girls aren't afraid to be girls where people can see them. They grow up faster this way."

Whandall had never quite believed in this form of cause and effect.

He said, "Sons are easier. Saber Tooth will be wagonmaster. Green Stone is shaping up nicely. Twisted Tree is a little young—"

"You had a point?"

"Yes, dear. Fourteen Miller and Ropewalker boys, ten of 'em nephews. We may get more. Half of 'em work the Feathersnake wagons. Half of *them* are married already. The Ropewalk is only so big. So is the Hemp Road, love, though that's not so easy to see. There won't be work for everyone by . . . by the time we're fifty."

"They'll find lives. We raised them right." Willow looked at him coolly. "Or are you thinking of taking over some of Puma turf?"

"No! That's not the right answer, but I think I should look at extending the caravan route. Travel with Puma for guides. *See* another route. *See* if I could tell them how to do it better. It might give me ideas for cooperation."

"I suppose I'll have to let you go," Willow said. "Stone won't let me rest until I say yes."

"No, love, you don't have to put up with that. It would be very easy for me to say that this tattoo—*look* at me?—*this* tattoo is *mine,* and no other soul shall wear it. I could make that stick. Do you . . . you like it on me, right? You're used to it?"

She stroked his cheek as if smoothing feathers. He had to shave often or his beard would cover the tattoo. He said, "Because maybe Morth could take it off."

"No!"

"But maybe you just hate the thought of seeing it on Stone?"

"It's more like he's growing up too fast. I know that's silly. Men wear tattoos. But if he comes back with a tattoo that good, he'd better be bringing one for Saber Tooth, or there'll be trouble."

"Point taken."

"I asked Twisted Cloud about this."

"You did? What did she say?"

Willow's eyes unfocused as she tried to remember *exactly.* She said, " 'In the old drowned tower your people will find what they need of sustenance.' So she says you're going."

"Yes, dear."

CHAPTER
52

Whandall had heard of ancient highways built by magic to serve ancient empires in other lands. The Hemp Road was a wilderness compared to those; but it was a highway compared to the route to Great Hawk Bay.

It was hard work going uphill, harder going down, with everyone hanging back holding ropes to keep the wagons from plunging to their doom. The ground was rough in the valleys. They lost wheels.

The bird spent most of its days in flight and returned to the wagons at night.

Whandall had been a young man when last he guided a team of bison. He swung back into caravan routine with surprising ease. His Puma guide, Lilac, was a good driver and bison tender. There was work to be done, but in between you could be lazy as a Lordkin.

Along the Hemp Road they told stories of places where a simple summoning spell would bring all the game you wanted, meat every night. Partridges, rabbits, deer, they came when summoned, and old men remembered those times, or said they did.

Lilac sang in the evening dusk. Three rabbits came and sat on their haunches, waiting patiently for her to wring their necks. One short scream as the rabbit understood . . .

The track led through high grass, past stands of scrub oak trees. The air hung heavy in the mornings, heavy dew and swirling mists.

"No rain here," Lilac said. "The dew is all. Good for garlic and thistle, not much else."

From time to time they encountered a flock of crows. Seshmarls wheeled up to them, squawking in crow language, and they would fly away in terror. Sometimes the bird chased them, but he always returned to Whandall's arm in the evening.

On the Hemp Road even a lazy Lordkin had to watch for gatherers from other bands: for bandits. On this route, bandits couldn't survive. There weren't enough wagon trains to support them. Towns were few, little more than hunting camps. Farming and hunting communities could survive . . . and if a badly guarded caravan passed, why, farmers might gather some opportune treasure. One must still keep watch.

No one had ever heard of him here. The Feathersnake sign guarded his wagons on the Hemp Road, but not here.

On the tenth day he saw a restlessly stirring black mass ahead of the caravan.

He tried to guess what he was seeing.

He was driving. The bird Seshmarls perched beside his ear, gripping the edge of the roof above the driver's bench. From time to time it took wing to hunt. They were both enjoying themselves, and Whandall didn't want company. But after a time, reasoning that anything he couldn't identify might be dangerous, he called down into the covered wagon bed.

Lilac poked her head out. She was a pretty nineteen-year-old of Puma Tribe who had made this trip as a girl, twice. She traveled in Whandall's wagon rather than Green Stone's, at her mother's insistence. Those two found each other too interesting.

She watched for a time. She said, "Crows. Ravens. Something like that."

The bird rose from the roof and flapped toward the black mass. A crow colored like a flying bonfire, he had driven away half the flock when the wagons came in range. What the crows had hidden was the white-and-red bones of a beast bigger than any wagon.

Looking over Whandall's shoulder, Lilac said, "Mammoth."

"Are they common around here?"

She was awed. "Tribes around here dig pits for 'em. It's dinner for two days for a whole tribe and any guests. I heard of a war that stopped because Prairie Dog Tribe trapped a mammoth and invited the Terror Birds to share, but it doesn't happen often. No, they're not common. Nobody I know ever saw one alive. You?"

Fool Turkey, who drove the Wolf Tribe wagon for many years, told a tale of riding a mammoth for nearly the length of the road before slaughtering it to stave off a famine . . . but Fool Turkey was a champion liar. Whandall said, "No. You'd think they'd be too big to miss."

Lilac nodded.

"A pit could trap one, not just kill it."

"Got to dig them deep. If it lives through the fall it could climb out, and it comes out angry."

"So? I mean, it's big, but—" But the girl smiled and made an excuse to go back into the wagon.

Every tribe has its secrets, Whandall thought.

They rolled on toward the sunset. Then one night they could hear the sea, a sound Whandall had not heard for twenty-three years.

CHAPTER
53

A wave broke in white spume and rolled toward the children.
Lilac and Green Stone danced back, not quick enough. Foam
and seawater rolled over their legs. The wave receded and they
followed it.

Dancing with the ocean.

Whandall watched from well back. He could swim in a river, but
this . . . he could almost sense the mass of water ready to roll a
swimmer under.

Far across the calm waters of the bay, a score of boats bobbed about
a cluster of drowned towers.

"There's a fair-size city down there under the water," Lilac told
Green Stone. She turned and called to Whandall. "Wagonmaster? I
suppose you could find drowned cities along *any* coastline after Atlantis sank . . . ?"

"My brother would know." Whandall hadn't thought of Wanshig in
many years.

What poked above the waves was a handful of ruins solid enough to
moor boats to, and an extensive flat roof, crenellated, that stood four
stories above the water. Waves had smashed the southern edge; a new
wall had been bricked in.

Any storm would make the lower levels unusable, Whandall
thought, but that left two stories and an extensive floor plan. He could
see gardens on the roof, as with the Placehold.

It had been four years since Puma Tribe sent wagons.

He should stop thinking of these two as children. Lilac had proven an excellent guide. . . . "Lilac, we brought twice as many people as the Attic is used to. How do you think they'll handle it?"

"Simplest thing is just not to send a boat," Lilac said.

Green Stone asked, "Why didn't you send the bird ahead, Father?"

"I want to know if they fluster easily."

Behind them the sons and nephews and grandsons of Puma and Bison tribes were making camp, tending beasts, pulling the wagons into a defensive ring, working the spells that would give them safety and clean water, all under Carver Ropewalker's direction. Lilac and Green Stone went to join them. Whandall left them to it.

There were mountains in view. Any of those largest three . . .

"Are you really thinking of climbing a mountain?"

It was Carver. Whandall didn't answer.

Whandall was master of the caravans. Carver Ropewalker stayed home and made rope. This trip had firmed him up a bit. He bore marks of the kinless: round ears, pointy nose. Once these differences had been life itself. He looked across the water for a time before he spoke.

"Whandall, I've lost two belt knots and I'm stronger than I've been in years. I *am* glad I came. But do you believe Twisted Cloud?"

"Prophecy works as well as it ever did."

"The magic goes away. Prophecies go vague and cryptic. They tell you less. Twisted Cloud *didn't* say, 'Eat at Rordray's Attic and you'll be rich again.'" Carver closed his eyes to remember *exactly*. "'In the old drowned tower your people will find what they need of sustenance.' Whandall, it's fifty years since Atlantis went under. Can you imagine how many drowned towers there are along this coast?"

"Be fun to search them out."

"They're sending us a boat."

Rordray's Attic, kitchen and restaurant, was the top floor of the old Carlem Marcle Civic Center's south tower. The roof could house an overflow. The next floor down was all guest rooms, Lilac said.

The restaurant was full of fishermen. Rordray and his son directed some of them to push tables together to accommodate Puma's thirty-three travelers. The sudden influx hadn't bothered Rordray and they hadn't run out of food or drink.

Thone had met them with the boat: a big blond man, Rordray's son. His smooth round strength and perpetual smile suggested one or another sea mammal. He described what his father had prepared for the noon meal, as if it were a string of amazing discoveries.

Thone's enthusiasm was infectious. Whandall took a bite of swordfish with only the slightest of qualms. Lilac was watching him with a grin. She laughed loud at the look on Whandall's face.

"Good," Whandall said in amazement.

All the mers were watching him.

He said, "I don't think I've ever really tasted fish."

"Try the vegetables too."

In midafternoon the place was still half full, though most of Whandall's travelers had been rowed ashore. Rordray's customers liked to take their time. Many must be were creatures, Whandall thought. The huge, smoothly muscled guy *had* to be a mer whale. He had eaten twenty headsman crabs; he had picked up a table for ten all by himself.

Carver and Whandall loved the Attic on sight, but of course it was too small—

"Now, wait," Carver said. "You don't doubt Rordray can *feed* a caravan, do you?"

"After a meal like that? And I saw the size of his ovens. But—"

"Rooms? Most of a caravan would stay in the wagons anyway to save money. And he's got storage in those other buildings."

"Did you notice that everything came from the sea?"

"Spices. He's got spices from as far back as Beesh, and some root vegetables too."

Whandall said, "Caravan passengers demand every variety of diet known to man or beast. We get vegetarians. We get fat going for thin, thin going for fat, weird going for wizardry or lost youth or moral dominance games. Some won't touch fish. Some think fish is poisonous—Lion!" Their host was just emerging from the kitchen. Wait, now, Lion was a *nickname!* "Rordray, sir, can you favor us with a minute of your time?"

The Lion stopped by their table. The bird on Whandall's shoulder suddenly said, "Morth of Atlantis greets you, Rordray, and begs a favor."

Rordray laughed. "Whandall Feathersnake. I see the wizard's message reached you."

Whandall said, "Yes. Carver Ropewalker is my partner; Green Stone, my son. Lilac—"

"Good to see you again, Sir Lion," Lilac said.

"A pleasure, Lady Puma. You've grown well."

"Is Morth here?" asked Whandall.

Lion—Rordray—laughed. "Not likely! He was here twice. He loves the sea. He stayed a day too long, nineteen years ago—" Rordray's eyes questioned. What secrets should he spill here?

"The water sprite," Whandall said.

"It came on us here. Morth fled uphill. The wave washed away part of the restaurant." Shrug. "None of us drowned. Gentlemen, what have you brought me?"

Whandall showed him what spices would ride in a pouch. Rordray pinched, sniffed, tasted, approved. Carver described the rest. Cured deer meat, bison on the hoof, no mammoth. Sage. Rope. Brandy; the Puma scout hadn't asked for that. "Of course you can inspect all of this in the morning. What can we take back?"

They discussed it. Rordray could sell them sea salt. Morth needed a fishing net; Whandall was to pay for it—Rordray didn't know why. Rordray's crew could never get enough rope. Could the Bison Clan increase their shipments? But Puma had slacked off because of a dwindling market.

Perhaps a market could be developed along the Hemp Road, for fish? Shipping fresh and fresh-cooked fish east would require another talisman box. Morth of Atlantis would be the only possible source for that. *We do need another trade route,* Whandall told himself. "Is Morth hard to reach?"

"I wouldn't try it myself," Rordray said. "He settled on the peak of Mount Carlem, there to the south and east. No wagon can climb that. Whitecap Mountain can guide you, if you can climb."

Carver laughed. "What Whandall can't do is turn down a challenge."

Rosemary? Thyme? Bison Clan didn't know a source for those. Morth might. Whandall wouldn't even recognize these plants. Rordray fished out tiny brown paper pouches, pinched out samples, and rubbed them under his nose.

Lilac exclaimed, "Thyme? *I* know that. We passed it coming here. I've smelled it near the Stone Needles."

Meat of a terror bird? Puma had a hair-raising tale, and so did Whandall, but the point was made: Butchering a terror bird was a matter of happenstance . . . not a delicacy one could fully recommend, either, but as a curiosity . . . as jerky? Or carry Morth's back breaker of a cold iron talisman box.

"The Hemp Road runs from the Drylands near Condigeo north past Firewoods opposite Tep's Town, down into the Great Valley past Farthest Land to Road's End, and back," Carver said. "Now we want to extend the route."

"You're successful, then."

"Until recently," Carver said, and Whandall said, "Fire's *sake*, Carver!"

Carver glared at him. "Yes. Successful. Our problem is, shall we build up the route west to Carlem Marcle and the Attic, or northeast for whatever we find? The rumor of Rordray's Attic would bring us custom all by itself, but it's not enough. And there's a road to build."

Rordray nodded, unsurprised. "I would never have room downstairs for so many, not unless the sea sinks by a few floors."

That wasn't likely. Was it? Morth would know. Without Morth, there was no trade route. They would have to speak with the wizard.

A man and two women emerged from the kitchen, all built on Rordray's own heroic scale. The older woman reached past Carver, set down a tray with a pitcher and eight small cups. Rordray waved. "My wife and daughter, Arilta and Estrayle. You've met Thone." They were pulling up their own chairs. The table had been roomy a moment ago.

Carver poured for them all, then sipped. Whandall sipped from his own cup, carefully. It was the brandy they'd brought from Zantaar Tribe, and it was deadly stuff.

He said, "Well, Carver, the prophecy holds. We've found sustenance." He saw his partner's glare and made haste to change the subject. "Rordray, when I was a child I learned to trade information and stories. Shall we talk about Morth? If he led a water sprite to you, I'm surprised you're still friends."

"Well, you know," the Lion said, "it was Morth who warned us out of the old castle in Minterl. Do you recall that there were two sinkings of Atlantis?"

The caravaners looked at each other. Talk eased off a bit among the remaining customers.

"Where you've lived, maybe you never knew. The ground shakes, then stops? Near the sea, we notice that," the Lion said. "We knew of Atlantis in Minterl. We knew when the land shook and the wave covered whole towns. I set up my first inn in the tip of a sunken tower in what was once Castle Minterl.

"We have always traded with Atlantis. Naturally the ocean is no barrier to *us*. There is little of trade in goods, but stories travel along the whale path. Word of that side of the world comes half a year late. We heard that the east side of the island had settled, drowning beaches and beach cities a third of the way around the island. These were fishing communities, so there were mers to rescue land dwellers. Not many died. The King declared a disaster and raised taxes.

"The second quake came half a lifetime later," Rordray said, "when nobody remembered Castle Minterl as anything but Rordray's Attic.

"Mers still ran the fishing industry around Atlantis, but ashore we'd lose the shape of men. Fishing requires boats, harbors, warehouses, weather prediction, and a little judicious guiding of the currents. The fishers' local wizard was a man nearing his thirties, named Morth.

"Word came with a pod of whales. Morth had foreseen a tidal wave that would wash away whole civilizations. Morth's warning went to many more than just my little Attic, but he saw the Attic's doom."

"Did he know that Atlantis would sink to make that wave?"

"Wizards can't see their own fate. But *I* guessed."

"So you left."

"No, no. We had barely heard of Morth! We consulted local shamans and performed our own spells. We saw enough to convince us. When the wave and the quake came, we were facing a different ocean."

The Lion poured Zantaar brandy. Whandall put his cup in his pocket. Lion said, "The wave had to circle the world to reach us here at Great Hawk Bay. Then came Morth in a ship that floated above the land, but so low that it must circle trees. We made him welcome.

"He told us of the magical thing that hunted him. I recalled the Burning City. We were loading his ship with provisions when a mountain of ice came floating toward us. Morth sailed away inland, the ice sailed south, and we knew no more for half of a man's lifetime."

"I assume he filled you in later," Whandall said.

Rordray grinned. "He claims holes in his memory after he found gold in riverbeds. You may still have tales to tell."

The evening had grown dark, and it seemed to be story time. A pointy-eared fisher ordered a round of beer for the house. "I am Omarn," he told the newcomers. "When Atlantis sank I was near Minterl in dolphin form. I saw water humping up behind me. I swam like mad, and when the wave passed me I was going fast enough to ride it. The ride of my life! I rode the wave almost to the mountains. I saw the Lion's old Attic smashed all in an instant. Mers don't drown, but if anyone was still in there, Rordray, I think he must have been smashed under the rocks."

"No, we were all clear," the innkeeper said.

Whandall asked, "Shall I tell what Morth of Atlantis was doing in Tep's Town? I saw some of that."

"Wait now, Whandall Feathersnake," the innkeeper said. "A tale has come to us of a tattooed caravan lord who came home to find himself pronounced dead and his wife attended by a host of suitors. Can you tell us the truth of this?"

So, Rordray would trade tales with a stranger, but he wanted to name the tale. Whandall hesitated . . . and saw instantly how they would take that. He *must not* seem to be hiding old murders.

He said, "I used a protection. If I tell you what I had, do not ask where I kept it."

He had everyone's attention now. Carver and Green Stone had heard his tale, but the rest had not. Whitey guessed: "A dagger?"

"No, it was a handful of gold sand. Raw gold right out of a river. Once upon a time I used it to save us from . . . well, *Morth*. Raw gold turns Morth crazy. I always carry raw gold with me."

They sipped and listened.

"This was nine years after I married Willow Ropewalker, and three years since I rode with a caravan. I set up my life so I could stay home and raise my children. I visited nearby towns from time to time, and if anyone wanted me, he could find me.

"Burning Grass and Three Forks came to tell me that men on my wagon had cheated them. I asked around and decided it might be true. I told Willow I must ride with the caravan again.

"Angry Goose was running a game that uses a gold bead and three nut shells, and two friends sat in the game to protect him. It was a cheat. I threw them off and divided their goods. But Goose and his men should never have been allowed aboard.

"There was more. Everything went loose and sloppy when Black Kettle had to leave the caravan. I saw them camping in flood basins. I saw a man badger Twisted Cloud into changing a prediction. The guards held gambling parties.

"I saw that I'd have to ride the whole circuit. We were a long way back from the Firewoods at the southern end of the route before I was sure I'd straightened things out. I had some bruises. Caravaners are mighty fighters, and it must be easy to forget that what's given them to rule isn't theirs—"

"Did you have to kill anyone?"

"No."

"Good."

"Not then. I left the caravan at Warbler Flats. I stopped a couple of nights with friends, then rode on through Hip High Spring and home to the New Castle.

"My son Saber Tooth met me at the gate. He was only eight then. He carefully explained that the house was full of men who wanted to marry Mother, and Mother was afraid of them.

"I sent Saber Tooth in to find my wife and, if he could talk to her, tell her Father says to get ready to duck under something. Then come and tell me where everyone is. I told him where I'd be."

Whandall laughed and gestured at his cheek, shoulder, twisted arm. "I can't remember the last time I thought of disguising myself. There was nothing for it but to go right in, but I didn't have to go in the front door. I came by the hay chute—"

Rordray laughed. "What, is your house a barn too?"

"Yes. In by the hay chute, talk to the bison a bit so they don't raise a ruckus. I wasn't sure Saber Tooth could do it, so I wasn't going to wait very long. But he came to the hayrack and told me. Willow would be in the hidey closet with the four youngsters. Four men were terrorizing the kitchen staff.

"I gave Saber Tooth a knife and hid him in the hay. I went into the kitchen fast. Four men, right. Three were from Armadillo Wagon— Passenger Pigeon and his father and uncle—but the fourth was a stranger in Lordsman armor.

"I started to say, 'Welcome to the New Castle, gentlemen.' But they went for weapons as soon as they saw me. Not meaning to be surrounded, I slashed first at the ones who didn't have armor. Bussard's Shadow went down spraying blood everywhere, and I slashed Pigeon's knife arm. Then the armored man stepped between them and me. The ones still standing snatched Bussard's Shadow and ran backward pulling his arms, while the Lordsman came at me.

"That was scary. But Lordsman armor doesn't cover everything. I got a chopping block between him and me, thinking I'd jab at his ankles. But he pushed it over and ran after the others.

"I got outside, carefully, not wanting to be ambushed. They were running into the Ropewalk, the two Armadillo Wagon men carrying the third, and the armored man walking backward after them. I started to wonder who of the Ropewalker family was in there, but the only thing to do about that was run in and look.

"Rordray, my wife's family doesn't let me in there. I saw it once, when it was new and near empty. It looked no different from a barn.

"Years had passed since then. The place stank of hot tar. The Ropewalk was stacked to near the ceiling with spools of rope, each about as big as a man. The Ropewalkers stack them on end so they won't roll. The aisle ran down the center. Back of it, at least five Armadillo men were getting themselves out of the way. Somebody yelled like a Lordkin on wine. It was Carter Ropewalker. He was lying down and wriggling. I guessed he was tied up.

"But mostly, *three* men in Lordsman armor were facing me in that pose they use with the shields locked edge to edge. I saw that once during a fair in Tep's Town. *Nothing* can get through that.

"Rordray, I sure couldn't fight them. I could outrun them, even moving backward, but they had Carter. What I did was climb the bales of rope and hop to the back of the building. The Armadillo men were still just staying clear. The armored men ran toward me, got close, and lockstepped their shields again. That gave me time to cut Carter loose and send him up the spools. He got a rope anchored in the smoke hole to the roof. He was pretty battered and not climbing very fast. I waited until he was through, then climbed up after him.

"Then I sprinkled my gold sand down into the Ropewalk.

"I kept a hand on Carter to keep him from looking into the smoke hole. We could have gone down the outside then if Passenger Pigeon hadn't been below us with a long knife. Left-handed, though. He yelled up and threatened to burn down the Ropewalk if we didn't surrender. I told him he should move the rope-weaving device out first. That's the actual Ropewalk, the most valuable single thing at the New Castle.

"We got some of the story out of him while we all circled around and waited for developments.

"The way Pigeon tells it, this all happened because three Lordsmen took ship to escape the Lords in Tep's Town. Pigeon didn't know why. They took their armor with them. They offered to protect Armadillo Wagon on the Hemp Road, but Pigeon told them about a Lordkin gone missing, so they attacked the New Castle instead.

"Armadillo Wagon wouldn't have done this to anyone *but* a Lordkin. But, see, I'd been married nine years. Now I was going off. Lordkin don't come back! Everyone knows it. So Passenger Pigeon and his tribe set forth to marry the abandoned widow. Willow Feathersnake wasn't going anywhere until she agreed. There were the children for hostages. Pigeon told us he never threatened them. Later, Willow told me he did.

"By and by Carter and I decided that nobody was coming out of the Ropewalk. I went over the roof fast and slid down the other side and was in fighting stance before Pigeon could come around. He ran for the Ropewalk doors. They were closed. Carter and I blocked his path, but we let him pull a door open and look in.

"He backed away gobbling like a turkey."

Rordray's family were nodding. Mers were sophisticates in magic. And Whandall's family knew the tale, but horror looked out of Lilac's eyes.

"They were all strangled," Whandall said. "Pulled into shapes no sane man ever thought of. Nobody but Pigeon left to tell the tale. He sits at the south gate of Hip High Spring and warns you about hemp, even if you don't ask. Hemp is like that, you know? It wants to soothe you to sleep and lose you in dreams and then strangle you. And hemp rope on wild magic is a thing of nightmares."

Nobody seemed to want to top that story. It was full dark by now. The remaining fishers went up to the roof, and Whandall heard splashing. Then Estrayle led them down to their rooms.

The room was clean, the bed a bit damp. Still, it was luxury. He could not fall asleep at first, and could not think why.

Presently he realized that they didn't turn off the ocean at night. The *shh, sss* of the waves went on forever . . . and presently carried him away.

CHAPTER
54

They left for Morth's mountain after two days of feasting.

Whandall was inspired. "People come to Road's End tired and ready to be pampered. They want fish from Rordray's Attic. They just don't know it yet! If we can bring this to Road's End, we have goods to trade."

"Find Morth," Rordray said.

They took one of the wagons. Green Stone *had* to come, that became clear, so Whandall made him drive. Whitey couldn't drive because the bison didn't trust him. Lilac—Whandall wasn't sure why they were taking Lilac. He and Green Stone had decided sometime last night. Someone had to guard the wagon while the others were climbing. Why Lilac?

Willow would have his head.

Or not. Lilac might be just the girl—woman—for Green Stone. A link to Puma Tribe could solve some problems for the family, and the trade to Great Hawk Bay would never be vast, but it could be lucrative.

They hadn't brought a one-horn, but every woman knew she would confront one eventually.

They rode for four days, taking their time, hunting, letting the bison graze where they would, before the ground grew too rough to go nearer. Whitey spent an extra day leading them around the mountain to the shallower eastern slope. They stopped where bison could still forage.

Mount Carlem stood above them all that night, intimidating.

They started at dawn, leaving Lilac in charge of the wagon. They climbed in shirts, kilts, and packs. When the bird settled on Whandall's pack, Whandall chased him away. The bird rose with an angry squawk, found an updraft, and kept rising out of sight.

Green Stone carried a flat box of cold iron, a rectangle with the corners cut off, flat enough to ride a strong man's back. This one was empty and not yet ensorcelled. Whandall had the heavier talisman box loaded with provisions from the Attic kitchen. They left the heavy fishing net on the wagon. If Morth somehow needed that to get down, someone would have to go back for it.

The packs held water, blankets, and clothes. Why so many clothes? Because Whitey insisted.

The day grew hot. Shirts came off early. At noon Whitey let them stop to drink. By then Whandall knew he was an old man beyond his strength. He had never climbed like this. Everyone else was making his decisions for him . . . had been for years, without his realizing it . . . and he was just beginning to resent it.

When Whitey and Green Stone went on, Whandall made himself follow. He was at the edge of making his son trade burdens with him . . . but now the way became easier.

They'd found reserves of strength, Whandall thought, but it rapidly became ridiculous. They'd been climbing toward a scary, near vertical bare rock slope. The tilt seemed less now; it had flattened out. But the horizon eastward was tilted up like a dandy Lord's hat! It looked like anything loose should be sliding west toward the sea.

Green Stone said nothing of this. He must have thought he was going mad. Whitey watched them both with that Puma grin.

Whandall bellowed, "Mooorth!"

He just glimpsed a man-shaped streak zigzagging at amazing speed among tall stands of lordblades, near naked and all knobs, red braids flying. "Whandall Placehold!" Glimpsed and already here. "You came!"

Whandall looked him over. Morth wore only a sun-bleached and ragged kilt, and the bird now settling on his shoulder. He was tanned near black. His feet were bare and callused hard. The Morth of twenty years ago had dressed better but was otherwise little changed. Lean, with stringy muscles and prominent ribs; high cheekbones; long, curly red hair washed and braided. He was grinning and panting like a dog . . . and even so, he did not seem *mad*.

Whandall said, "Right. You know Whitey. Green Stone, this is Morth of Atlantis. Morth, my second son. Willow's second son."

The wizard gripped the boy's hand. "Green Stone, I'm very pleased you could come! May I see your palm?"

The boy looked at his father, got a nod, and let Morth turn his hand palm upward in the sunlight. Morth said, "I haven't done this since . . . Early marriage. Children branch off soon, here. Twins. Both girls." The wizard pointed with a fingernail that needed tending. "No, don't squint, you can't see your own future. More children down the line, I think, but your path gets fuzzy . . ." Morth looked up with satisfaction in his eyes. "Come. I live on the peak."

"Can you fly us?"

"Whandall, those days are long gone mythical! But I wove a spell for easier climbing so the Lion's people can visit me."

He babbled as they climbed. "The way I left you and the children, I'm embarrassed. Of course gold fever had my mind, and I still had to lead the water elemental away from you—"

"We saw that."

"—just kept going into the mountains. There's manna untouched by any wizard, but there's also wild magic, virgin gold. I have no idea how long I was out of my mind. I wound up on some tremendous height in the Vedasiras Range, with no gold around me, just a magical place with a view of half the world. Like this place, really, but even farther from any decent hunting. By the time I had my senses back—why do they always say that?—I was sensing *everything,* no path blocked within my mind, no way to concentrate on any one thing, like eating or bathing, digging a jakes, raising a shelter, tending a wound. Scatterminded. *That* was what had me so crazy.

"Where was I? I was stuck on a mountaintop, sane but starving and tanned like Sheban leather. Only my own spells were keeping me alive. I found meat and firewood downslope and spent some time building my strength back. Built a talisman to get me through, then set out north for Great Hawk Bay."

"Rordray told us."

"I thought I'd lost the sprite. All that wild gold should have had it totally confused. I was careless. When that wave humped itself, I just went up the nearest mountain as quick as I could. I've been stuck here ever since."

They put their shirts back on. It had grown cold. Morth didn't notice.

The mountain's peak was a fantastic lacework of stone castle. *In-*

defensible, was Whandall's first thought. Any Lordkin tribe could have pulled it down with their hands. *What's holding it up?*

He looked in vain for supporting beams. There was no wood to be seen anywhere. It was as if rock had melted and flowed into place. There were no corners, no straight lines. Rooms and chambers and corridors spilled over and under and between each other like the insides of a careless knifefighter, rising up into a bulb of clear glass, a wonderful wizard's crow's nest.

Morth led them in.

In a roomy ground-floor chamber the rock walls humped into chairs around a fire. Four people, four chairs, and a high ridge for a bird to perch. Dark rocks were burning in the fireplace.

Whitecap Mountain set out both talisman boxes. He didn't open them. The Attic's provisions were for Morth alone. But Morth had prepared a meal for four, a stew of mountain goat, herbs, and roots. Whandall realized that he was ravenous; he saw the look in Green Stone's eye and waved him on.

When they had slaked their hunger a bit, the wizard said, "You came at my asking. I can pay that debt now, in refined gold." He waved at the fireplace. "Take what you like."

Had Morth been using wild magic? But the gold he was pointing at had drained out of the fireplace and formed a flat pool before it froze. Whitey and Green Stone wiggled it loose, used an edge of rock to break it in roughly equal halves, and slid it into packs.

"Energy wants to be heat," Morth said. "The simplest thing you can do with any kind of manna is help it to become heat. I can burn gold ore without its hurting me, and the expended gold just flows out."

Whandall nodded. *Uh huh.*

The wizard pointed to Whandall's crotch. "What is that?" Morth caught himself. "Secret?"

"Supposed to be. I'm not surprised *you'd* see it." Whandall eased a flat metal flask out from just above his groin. "What does it look like to you?"

"A dead spot. I can show you how to see the blind spot in your eye, but this is a bit more obvious. Nothing else looks like cold iron."

Whandall held it up without opening it. "Coarse gold right out of a riverbed. You wouldn't remember when I threw gold at ensorcelled ponies? But—" Whandall waved away Morth's attempt at an old apology. "But it broke the spell. So I carry raw gold, just in case, and it did save me once."

"That must be an interesting tale," Morth said, "but I want to hear a different one. Whandall, tell me about the last time you did violence."

Whandall looked at him. "Violence?"

"We last saw each other twenty-one years ago. I don't quite remember, but I think I tried to take a girl you wanted. I think you tried to kill me," Morth said.

"No. Not tried. I thought I might have to."

"Now I hear tales of a wagonmaster whose sign is a feathered serpent. He keeps his oaths and enforces honesty with a knife of spelled bronze. Whandall, I have to know what you are."

"The last time I did violence."

"Was that it?"

They were all waiting. Whandall said, "No, it was the last time I saw Tras Preetror. Do you remember him?"

"The teller."

"Six years ago. I was up on the house with my sons, fixing the roof. A servant came to tell me I had a visitor.

"It was Tras Preetror and a big man in part Lordsman armor who stood behind him and didn't say anything. They'd got past the guards. Willow was serving him tea. I got her aside and she wanted *me* to explain what he was doing here."

"Hospitality," Morth said.

"He hadn't asked for food and fire and shelter from the night," Whandall said. "I made sure of that. He'd just barged in, invited himself as if he belonged there.

"I had tea with them. He told us his tale. He's a *good* teller, Morth, you remember. He'd taken ship up to Great Hawk Bay to get tales from the mers at Rordray's Attic. I'd heard of this place from the caravans, but Tras told us a lot more.

"He'd heard rumors from the Puma wagons about a new head man in the caravans. He tracked the tales of a snake tattoo, east and south. Morth, I *have* to know that a traveler can reach me if my wagons have cheated him. The caravan tribes guided Tras straight to my house.

"Now he's waiting for *my* story, right? I showed him my cold iron case, and opened it, and blew a bit of gold dust on him and his man. I didn't see any result, Morth, but I *hate* your damn lurking spell and I thought he might have used it on my gate guard.

" 'Raw gold,' I told him. 'It distorts magic spells.' "

Morth barked a laugh.

" 'And it saved my life once,' and I told him just enough of the fight with Armadillo Wagon to hook him. 'Come with me, if you like, I'll show you where the bodies are buried.' And I stood up and led him out, still talking. 'Tras, every time I think I've given up violence, something pops up.' That got him moving, and his man jumped up and went ahead of us.

"He didn't seem to speak the local tongue. I switched to Condigeo. Tras's man didn't know that either, but hey, I hadn't practiced in a while. I was just finishing the Tale of the Suitors when we reached the graveyard.

" 'We bury all our dead here,' I said, and I took them among the graves.

"The Armadillo wagon ghosts came out to play. They couldn't touch us, of course, but they tried to attack *me*. Tras was used to ghosts. He forgot that his Lordsman guard wouldn't be. The guard was shivering and whimpering and trying to back through a boulder. Tras tried to interview one of the ghosts. I drifted behind three trees growing together, went between them and up, and hid myself.

"I talked through the treetops. 'Tras, there's something I should tell you, because you'll have to translate for me.'

" 'Where are you?'

" 'Behind you, Tras, always behind you. We know how to lurk. Tras, do you remember starting a riot? I tried to shut you up—'

" 'No, Whandall Feathersnake, you can't blame me for that!' And he laughed.

"His man had his nerve back. Tras spoke to him and he began circling around. He had me placed pretty quick. He pulled more armor from his pack, shin guards and stuff. Morth, I think there must have been some kind of turnover in Tep's Town. There's too much armor floating around in the great wide world. The gatherers from Armadillo Tribe had armor too.

"I said, 'Let's test your memory again. You know how Lord Pelzed's men left me. Do you remember?'

" 'That's not my fault either!'

" 'Tras, you will be in the same condition when I leave here. If you tell your man to protect you now, there won't be any living man to carry you away. I'll bury you here in the graveyard. If you tell him to step aside, he can take you someplace to heal.' "

Morth asked, "Did you think he'd do it?"

Whandall shrugged. "I gave him the chance. I don't know what he told his guard. When I dropped from the tree, the guard moved on me. I thought I'd have to kill him. He took some cuts and some bruises, and then he backed away protecting himself, and then he ran. Tras was gone.

"I tracked Tras down to the crypt and, well. I kept my promise.

Then I slapped him awake and gave him some water, and I told him that if his man didn't come back for him by sunset of the next day, well. But if he did, there were stories I didn't want to hear. 'If I ever hear anyone describe how my household is arranged, or what kind of tea I serve, if I hear about a flask of gold sand' "—Whandall rapped his groin—" 'I will know who they heard it from.' I told him I travel everywhere, from Condigeo to Great Hawk Bay—I was lying, of course. I told him people are entitled to privacy, and some will kill for it. I'm not sure he heard any of that, Morth. I was raving. That diseased looker invaded my house. Nobody but the Armadillo Clan ever did that. Ask their ghosts."

Morth was silent.

"Tras wasn't hurt any worse than Samorty's men hurt me, but of course he's older. I don't know if he healed. He was gone at the next day's sunset."

And to hell with what Morth thought of him. Coming here wasn't Whandall's idea.

The night had turned cold, fire or no. They wore the cloaks Whitey had insisted they carry. Morth donned an impressive robe.

Whitecap Mountain broke the silence. "I know why the town of Fair Chance came to be deserted."

"That's a good story, but a partial truth," Morth said. "I sense a tribal secret at its heart. You won't tell *that*. As for me, my tale hasn't happened yet. My tale is that I must destroy the water sprite that wants my life. Living here is driving me mad."

"Go inland," Whitey said as if he was tired of repeating it.

"When I came here I was running from a wave. I climbed, thinking that water could not flow up so steep a slope. Water doesn't have to! A wave isn't a moving block of water, it's a pattern moving *through* water. The sprite can flow like a wave. It came to me through the ground water. It lives below me. When I go down to the spring, I go fast. I'll show you tomorrow, if you like."

Green Stone asked, "Is that safe?"

"Oh, you can watch from above. Get a view of the immediate danger. Whandall, what I want from you and your caravan is transport. Take me inland, out of its reach. Take me to the Hemp Road."

"You'd settle there?" Willow would love that!

"Oh, no," Morth said. "I'm going to *finish* this. I'm going to kill the water sprite. I think I have to return to the Burning City to do that."

Whandall said, "You've been trapped on a mountain for twenty years. This thing has hunted you for more than forty, and now you've decided to kill it. Is that about the size of it?"

Morth grinned in the yellow light of burning gold. "I can't tell you all of it."

"Morth, you can't even tell me *part* of it. You can't even get off this mountain!"

"That I might manage. I'd have to outrun the elemental. Water's natural path is downhill. I might run myself to death. But with transport to carry me farther, I might make it."

"And then you might just think you'd done all a man could do!"

"Once upon a time I thought I could rob Yangin-Atep's life. Steal the fire god's manna."

Nobody but Whandall laughed. The others had barely heard of Yangin-Atep; they couldn't know his power. Whandall asked, "What stopped you?"

"I saw less evidence of the god every decade. Yangin-Atep must be almost mythical by now, and I could never find where his life is centered. But the hope kept me there much longer than I should have stayed."

Whandall knew he was staring. "Why didn't you *ask?* Yangin-Atep lives in the cook fires!"

And he knew Carver's look: appalled and amused. Whandall had never learned to hoard information.

Morth paled. "In the fires. I'm a fool. I never asked the thieves!"

They were still arguing when it became impossible not to sleep. Whandall didn't remember whether he saw flowing rock, but the stone chairs were all stone couches in the morning.

CHAPTER
55

Morth stopped at a shallow rain-etched dip in the rock, damp at the bottom, to pick up a bucket. Then he led them to the edge of an abrupt drop. He pointed down along a bare rock face.

"See the streak where the rock changes color? That's overflow from the spring."

Whitey said, "Right."

Morth dropped over the edge.

Whandall could have caught his robe—would have, were he a child or a friend. But Morth wasn't falling. He was running down the mountain's side, weaving through the rubble. Once Whandall would not have believed what he saw. Morth dropped as fast as a falling man, zigzagging toward the gleam of water that marked the spring. He ran past it, dragging the bucket, and was already moving uphill, laughing like a maniac.

Water splashed up after him. Morth led it, still faster than a man, but he had been moving faster yesterday.

The men threw themselves backward as the wave came over the crest. Morth ran across the dip, emptying his bucket halfway, then turned and gestured. The wave crashed into the dip.

Morth was panting hard as they came up, but he was laughing too. Water half filled the dip. It lay almost still, rippling as if in a strong wind.

Whitey asked, "Wouldn't you love to be watching, *first* time he tried that?"

"I take it you can't trap it?" Whandall asked Morth.

"No, and enchanting the spring doesn't trap it either. A water elemental is a fundamental thing, and exceedingly slippery."

"All right. If this works, you'll owe Puma Tribe and my family too. Puma you can pay in refined gold," Whandall said. "Right, Whitey?"

Whitey nodded. "But ask Lilac. We change any oaths by mutual agreement only."

"My family might ask other things," Whandall said. "Tattoos, for instance. If we can get you as far as Road's End, the New Castle will ask three boons."

"I don't believe I can duplicate that tattoo."

Green Stone's disappointment didn't show at all. The boy was a natural trader. Whandall said, "We'll think of something. You pay in magic. Three tasks."

"I offered one."

"Did I accept? It got pretty sleepy last night."

Morth looked into Whandall's grin and decided not to make *that* claim. He said, "One when I'm free of the mountain. One at Road's End. One when the sprite is myth."

"Morth, you have no reason to think you can myth out a water elemental!"

Morth said nothing.

It's two wishes, then. "Done. It's . . . midmorning? And the sprite wouldn't stop us from going down? Whitey?"

"It stops Morth. Only trouble I ever had," the Puma said, "I tried to stop at the spring for a drink. Wagonmaster, I still think you should have taken gold. Wizard, we'll be down before nightfall. The wagon will move at first light, north to the trail and then east. *We don't stop.*"

"If I don't get down alive, the talisman box is yours, and the provisions in it. I renewed the spell. I'll enchant this one too before I go down."

Whandall said, "That's settled. Now tell the bird. Seshmarls?"

"Help me, Whandall Seshmarl—"

"Good bird. Morth, you tell the wagons—"

"Whandall, let me teach you how to make the bird carry your messages."

Whandall listened. He mimicked the bird's secret name, then spoke a few words. The bird looked at him in disgust.

Whandall grumbled, "My children learned all by themselves. Why don't I?"

"You have less magical talent than anyone I ever met," Morth said. "Interesting that your children don't share that disability."

"Disability."

Morth grinned. "You're an emptiness any god can fill. You just can't keep them out. Feathersnake Inn! And you'll never be a wizard, of course, but *this* you can learn."

Whandall practiced the bird's secret name, blowing the syllables out with puffed cheeks, then curling his tongue for the shrill whistle that ended it. He spoke his messages. "Tell the Puma wagons to return at their own pace. Whitecap Mountain has gold to pay them for their trouble. Rordray will get his boxes late. Late and loaded with red meat—mammoth if we can get it, elk or antelope or bison otherwise— and spices. Maybe we can find spices in the Stone Needles—"

"Keep messages *simple*," Morth said.

"Was that—"

"It's getting too long. Say, 'Message ends. Seshmarls, go.' "

"Message ends. Seshmarls, go."

"My hope lies in your shadow," the bird said, and took flight.

Whandall and the others began their descent. The sooner they were down, the better.

Lilac drove. Brush grew everywhere and the land was uneven. She had to be exceedingly careful until they reached flat ground, and wary after that. They wouldn't reach the trade road until after noon. A man on foot could run circles around them, Whandall figured, let alone a wizard.

They saw a column of mist drifting down the mountain and guessed at the waterfall within it.

Near the foot of the mountain Lilac made out a dot moving just enough to catch her attention. Whandall said, "Whitey? He might need help."

"Shall I hold his hand while he drowns?"

Whandall swung down from the wagon.

"I'll go. Tend your wagon." Whitecap Mountain dropped beside him and jogged away. Whandall lost track of him in some brush, and after that he was harder to see and moving faster.

There was something about weres, Whandall speculated. Did their magic—did *all* magic—work better when nobody watched? There must be things, processes, that an observer could not watch without altering them. . . .

Morth would know. Whandall jogged back to the wagon.

Sometime later Whitey strolled up carrying Morth's pack. Whitey stowed it and loped off to rejoin Morth.

Whandall wasn't sure they'd reached the trade road until late afternoon. Several times he was minded to ask Lilac to stop. The closer Morth got, the more those dots moved like a pair of cripples.

No danger showed. But Whandall could picture water flowing out of the ground into a mountainous bubble, over the wagon, bison drowning, Lilac and Green Stone drowning. . . . They should have brought a mer. A mer underwater could still act.

They came closer. Morth leaned heavily on Whitecap Mountain. Whitey wasn't enjoying this at all. Morth looked like an old man dying of exertion. Dirty gray hair and beard, skin like cured leather, eyes too weary to look up. He was still moving faster than the wagon, but enough was enough. Whandall told Lilac to stop and let the bison graze.

They laid Morth in the wagon bed.

The sun was setting, but a full moon had crested the horizon. Whandall remembered a stream within their reach if they could keep going by night.

They were trying to reach water while they fled a water elemental. The irony did not escape Whandall's attention. Men could carry water, but bison must have a pool or stream. The path to Great Hawk Bay followed the water sources.

Ask Morth. . . . Morth was looking better already, but best to let him sleep.

Rordray's massive dinner fed them all during the next day. Morth didn't eat much. His strength was slow returning even though he had packed *something* in the second cold iron box. *Talisman,* he said. *Don't look.* He reached in from time to time.

That night he slept like a dead man.

The next day he was fizzing with energy. Lilac taught him something of how to guide a bison team, just to keep him occupied. Later he went off with Whitey to hunt. They came back with half a dozen rabbits.

They camped and set the rabbits broiling while there was still light. Morth lifted a clay-capped vessel of wine, the last of what Rordray had packed, and offered it.

Whandall said, "Not for me. Morth, we should know more about what's chasing us. Who hates you that much? Where did they get something that powerful?"

"Oh, *that* was easy. They just diverted the nearest water sprite and sent it to kill me. It was moving an iceberg—" Morth laughed at their bewilderment. "The wells in Atlantis ran dry a thousand years ago. We used to send elementals south to break off mountains of ice and bring them to Atlantis for fresh water. The southland is all ice and untouched manna, because wizards can't survive there. Elementals gain immense power.

"But that's the real question, isn't it? *Why?* They were in a rage. They'd been in a rage for nearly a year. We all were."

"Why?"

"The Gift of the King." Morth carefully cracked the clay stopper and drank before he went on.

"We were the lords of magic. Our wealth made us targets for every barbarian who might hear tales of us, and the very land beneath us was trying to return to the sea. Every twenty, thirty years we'd lose a daywalk of beachfront. If Atlantis lost the skills of magic, it was all over.

"King Tranimel came to decide that the power of magic has no limit. It's as crazy as thinking a tribe of bandits can steal from each other forever—no offense, Whandall."

Whandall said, "After all, we don't *see* wealth being made. It just appears, always in somebody else's hands. We only need to gather it."

"You still say *we?*"

"*We Lordkin.* It's been a long time. So the King decided . . . ?"

"If wizards had held Atlantis above the waves for all these years, it must be that we can do anything. The King decided to make everything perfect."

Whandall could hear him grinding his teeth. Then, "Nothing is ever perfect, but Atlantis came closer than any nation on Earth. One day a King of Atlantis would achieve perfection. Tranimel would be that King.

"We wizards learn to use spells that do their work without showy side effects. Spells fail as time passes," Morth said. "A palace doesn't need to rise from the earth in a blaze of light. Better plows and crop rotation make fertility ceremonies more effective. You see? Less gets you more, if you do it right. But magic always looks too easy!

"The King, though willing to admit that water must run downhill, never seemed to understand that it must someday reach the sea. He passed laws that left us no clear avenue to refuse *any* act of magic that would improve the general well-being.

"Our first act was to give homes to the homeless folk of Atlantis. Thousands of architects, wizards, supervisors from the court, created housing across one whole mountain range: the Gift of the King. They needed *everyone.* For the first time in my life, I had enough money to live, money even for a few luxuries. I began seeing a girl. *Ah.*"

"Ah?"

"I just realized. It's been thirty years and I just . . ." Morth blinked, sipped wine, started over.

"Whandall, what the King intended would use the same manna that was keeping us above the waves. To use too much was the doom of Atlantis. *It's so simple.* How could the best wizards in the land be unable to explain what was *wrong* with the Gift of the King? I only *just* realized that we weren't trying very hard. The Gift of the King was employment for everyone. Wizards would get rich, architects would get rich, every court-appointed supervisor had a nephew who needed work."

"You weren't actually one of the best wizards, were you, Morth?"

"What? No. I served the southeast coast fishing industry. The mers catch all the fish; they herd them into nets to be pulled aboard boats. The men bring the fish in and store them; other men distribute them. We're needed to make weather magic and command the elementals, and the spell that floats a ship above the water sometimes needs re-working. It's all spelled out in books a thousand years old. Doesn't pay much. The Kingsmen didn't offer a choice, mind, but they offered twice what I was getting.

"Where was I? We built the Gift of the King. Along the north Atlantis loop a few farms drowned, some docks and warehouses slid beneath the water. But the homeless now had homes, more than they could ever use, we thought. And when a homeless person got in some citizen's way, or a thief, he or she was conveyed to the Estates.

"In the Estates a criminal class evolved within, it seemed, hours. Rape, armed theft, extortion, casual murder, all flourished in the shadows and corners. Bad enough, but the people of the Estates didn't stay there! Their hunting grounds expanded to all who lived nearby.

"The King couldn't have that! He ordained that there be light. Whandall, I would have lost my home without these magical projects. Glinda would have left me. I kept my mouth shut. I participated in the spell that caused every outside wall in the Estates to glow."

"Sometimes I have trouble thinking like a kinless," Whandall confessed. "Why did the King think that light would stop a gatherer?"

"Thieves, rapists, killers—*Lordkin*," said Morth, "don't commit their crimes in daylight if they think they'll be seen and punished. But the King stopped the punishments. He would cause no pain to his subjects. It was part of the Gift of the King.

"The Estates taught them that they did not need darkness to do whatever they wanted. This lesson they practiced the length and breadth of Atlantis, retreating to the Estates before anyone could hamper them.

"The King couldn't have that!"

"Calmly, Morth."

"Sometimes I miss my home." Morth fished the wine flask out of Whitey's hand and drank.

"It's under water, I take it."

"Taken for taxes. The King paid slowly. He couldn't collect taxes fast enough, and of course if we did get paid, some of it went for taxes; we never touched it. The mers used to pay in fish, but at least I got to eat the fish! The King's men who paid us also wanted to tell us how to do our jobs! And write down everything we'd done in crazy detail! And wait for payment until each and all were satisfied!

"I was ashamed to see Glinda. With all my heart I wished I'd never taken money from the King! It was too late. We were in thrall. And now the King had another idea.

"We were summoned for one massive, magnificent spell: a compulsion of novice's simplicity, but of huge effect.

"Every violent criminal—*not* every thief. One courageous wizard rightly pointed out to the King's advisor that no spell can make the subtle, vague distinction between a thief and a tax collector. On a good day, I honor him. On a bad day, I wish that the thieves and tax collectors had all been ensorcelled together."

"You're rambling."

"But that would have been fun." Morth handed the wine flask to Green Stone and drank from the water bucket. "We cast the spell, Whandall. On a morning nine days before the Lifting of Stone, every violent lawbreaker went to the City Guard to make his confession. And on that morning it was as if all Hell had let out for a holiday.

"Every guard station was surrounded. The criminals of the Estates outnumbered the guards forty to one. No natural inclination could have brought them together in any such cooperative venture, but they were here, and there was nothing to drink or eat or steal, but none who would dare interfere with them. The screaming of confessions alone drowned any cry for help. When they had satisfied their compulsion, they did what they felt like . . . and their will was to tear down the doors and murder the guards.

"At dawn any pair of guards found themselves surrounded by a score of . . . of *Lordkin* who first shouted their crimes in gory, hideous detail, more bragging than confessing. A guard told me that. *He* escaped by being a better climber than any burglar. By afternoon there was not a living City Guardsman outside the Guard stations themselves.

"The King was very angry with the wizards." Morth picked up the flask of wine with exaggerated care and drank.

"Was that when you left?"

"How could we leave? We had to collect the money the King still owed us. But first we had to correct the ill we had done. The King's men didn't have but the vaguest idea how that might be done, but they'd know it was done when the King showed himself satisfied. Then again, the Lifting of Stone was only six days away, and the Achean navy was preparing an attack—"

"Any Lordkin would have left *right then!*"

"I did."

"You did?"

"Do I look *stupid?*"

"Ask me if you look *drunk.*"

"I could see what was coming. We couldn't ever satisfy the King, but any wizard who wasn't seen trying would be axed. Seen trying had to mean something even a King's councilor could see, using manna we couldn't spare. The Lifting of Stone takes manna. The manna would be gone and the wizards would be exhausted. This year the Lifting of Stone just wasn't going to work.

"They'd taken my house and I didn't have anything to save except Glinda. I went to visit; I hinted at what I had in mind. Her brothers threw me out. She didn't stop them.

"I went down to the dock. Finding work was easy; all the other wizards were working for the King. The *Water Palace* had been sitting in dock for weeks—"

"A ship?"

"Right, one of the old ships that floats above the water. That style can cross land and ride above the big waves, but there are windows and cargo hatches on the underside, so it can't go anywhere at all without the occasional blessing. Over four days I convinced Captain Trumpeter to keep me aboard and get himself gone ahead of the Achean navy. I'd bless the ship at sea. We'd have been gone and free if the Acheans had been a little faster. I was half a world away before I knew what the priests had done to me."

Over many days they all exhausted their fund of stories. Communities were sparse and tiny and the tales they told were local gossip. A few memories stood out:

Farmers roasting a pit-killed mammoth and a harvest of spring vegetables. They were eager to share. By the smell of it, the meat had gone pretty high. Morth told them they were wizards cleansing themselves for a ritual. None could eat meat, except for (at his request) their driver. Watching Whitecap Mountain devour a mammoth kidney, Whandall thought that Puma must be part scavenger.

An elk challenged their wagon. They killed it, then wrestled it into the wagon bed. That afternoon they presented it to a loose cluster of a hundred farmers. By nightfall a meat and vegetable stew was ready to serve. A widow told of her late husband's year-long duel with what was believed to be a werebear. Lilac traded children's stories with the old wives' clique. Whandall told the tale of Jack Rigenlord and the Port Waluu woman.

It was a long, lazy time for Whandall. Responsibilities were bounded. At one town Whandall was tempted by a woman's offer. Dream of Flying was lovely by firelight, but he pictured Green Stone wondering where his father was sleeping, and then going to ask Lilac . . . and he told Dream that his wife was a powerful shaman and a mind reader too. She said that many husbands were sure of that; he agreed; the moment passed. The next morning he learned that offers had been made to each of them.

A good place to come back to.

On another night Whitecap Mountain told how the town of Fair Chance came to be deserted . . . and he found that all of the locals wanted to help him tell it. The tale went to babbling, then became a kind of throw-and-catch game . . .

They dug a pit to trap a mammoth.

They dug it well away from the town. No mammoth would come near dwellings, and if it did, there was no telling what damage it would cause.

They dug it big enough to hold such a beast and deep enough that the fall would kill it, and they covered the pit with redwood boughs and went home.

But before dawn they heard monstrous noise and felt the ground shake. When they spilled out to look, Behemoth itself had wedged its foot in the hole!

Houses were falling as the mountainous beast tried to tear loose. It saw the crowd arrayed to look, and it turned and bellowed at them. Its nose reached out and out, a day's walk long, and flung villagers left and right, windward and lee.

They ran in a tumble of falling houses, and they never came back, said Whitey. Two boys went back to look, another said. The company argued about what they found.

These farmers entertained guests rarely. Wizards were rarer still. They pulled Morth's story out of him, of how he had crossed the continent . . .

"We were safe at sea when the sea roared and sent a wave under the *Water Palace*'s windows. When we reached land there was no shore where men still lived. Making landfall where that monstrous wave had killed so many would not be prudent.

"The *Water Palace* sailed inland. We traveled for many days and ultimately set down at the town of Neo Wraseln, along a southward-facing shore. We rested less than a day before I stole the *Water Palace.*"

A murmur rose from the farmers. "Gathered," Whandall said.

"No, I saved them all! I saw a wave of mist coming out of the ocean, and perceived an iceberg within the mist, and the elemental within the ice. I ran for the ship. I didn't have time to stop for any of the crew. I took it west to lure the elemental away from the town, then north, inland.

"At least I had someplace to go. In a dream I'd seen a tremendous wave smash the old Attic to rubble and roll onto the land, left and right as far as I could see. I recognized the Attic from the mers' description—"

Whandall said, "You sent word. Rordray told me."

"You'll be thinking I should have guessed the rest? But I can't foresee my own paths. The sinking of Atlantis took me completely by surprise. But I dreamed where Rordray would settle at Great Hawk Bay, and I sailed there. Ultimately they guided me to the Burning City, where magic doesn't work and a water elemental can't survive."

"And a wizard can't either," Whandall said, but Morth only shrugged.

CHAPTER

57

On the evening of the twenty-eighth day they camped in reach of a stream narrow enough to step across.

The water elemental had not shown itself since a waterfall followed Morth down Mount Carlem. "It prefers the sea, I think," Morth said. "Its time within the mountain must have been uncomfortable."

They had been approaching a range of hills for several days now. Whandall recognized this stretch. They would pass north of those hills. Another eight to twelve days, they'd be home. Now they were close enough to make out the spires that gave the place its name.

At night the Stone Needles glowed with manna, the wizard said, but only he could see it.

They moved at first light, Whandall driving.

Morth stirred. He scrabbled about in the wagon bed. Wrinkled around the eyes, white beard, gray-white hair, until he reached into the cold iron box. Then . . . well, nothing much changed. The talisman he'd made on Mount Carlem must be fading.

Around midmorning Lilac suddenly gasped, "Behemoth!" and pointed into the Stone Needles. The distant, misty heights ahead and right showed nothing.

Morth's head popped into sunlight. "What are you looking for?"

"I saw him! Behemoth!" Plaintively Lilac said, "I never saw him before."

Whitecap Mountain, strolling alongside the driving bench because it seemed to make the bison walk a little faster, was looking back down the road. "Wagonmaster, you may want to see this too."

Whandall stood up on the bench to look over the hood.

Dots in their wake, seven or eight men scattered across the road were watching the bison-drawn wagon. Now two jogged off in opposite directions.

"Could be farmers going about their business," Whitey said. "Could be bandits. A lone wagon makes a tempting target."

They were too distant, too slow to be seen moving, but dust in the air showed that they were following the wagon.

"They'll be a while catching up, won't they?"

"Oh, yes. They'll take their time. Sunset. We don't have any food, Morth."

They couldn't hunt with bandits about.

Whitey asked, "You know something of bandits, don't you, Whandall Feathersnake?"

"Yes, Whitecap Mountain. The first rule is, never separate the wagons or let them be separated."

"Better skip to the second rule."

Whandall stood to look back along the road. Men followed, far back and in no hurry. Those others who went jogging off would be bringing reinforcements or weapons or some stored magic, maybe a lurking spell.

"Never make half of a war," he said. "What do you think? If a Puma wearing a backpack and a man hideously scarred by a mad wizard's tattoo came loping back to meet them, would they run? Could we deal with them before anyone else comes? Kill them, frighten them, buy them off?"

Whitey said, "I think they can probably run almost as fast as you. If I run ahead, it's just me and them. Together we wouldn't catch them before nightfall, and if they've got friends they'd be right there to meet us. And if they sent friends ahead, who would defend the wagon?"

"All right. My third plan is, when they get close enough, I'll take off my shirt."

"Oh, *that* should scare them . . . you know, it might," Whitey acknowledged. "They might have heard of you."

Morth spoke. "Get me to the Stone Needles before they get to us, then leave the rest to me."

"That'll be tight," Whandall said.

"Try."

* * *

By noon the five had become a dozen. Whitecap Mountain drifted into the brush and was gone. Any bandits circling round might meet a Puma where it was least wanted. But a Puma could not attack a dozen farmers!

By midafternoon Stone Needles wasn't ahead anymore, it was a sixth of a circle rightward. The band following the wagon numbered around twenty. They were close enough that Whandall could make out hoes and scythes and less identifiable farm implements.

There was time to discuss it. If they turned off the path now, despite the rougher ground, it would tip bandits to where they were going. If the bandits broke into a run, attacked short of the Stone Needles, arrived panting and breathless, and fought in daylight—bad practice, but they'd win.

Lilac was driving. Whandall, watching the bandits, heard her say, "I saw it again!"

Morth exclaimed, "So do I!" and Whandall's head snapped around.

Behemoth, blurred by mist and distance, stood halfway up the Stone Needles. Mountains should have collapsed under it. Behemoth was even bigger than Whandall had seen it twenty-two years ago, all crags and angles, as if it had not fed well. Tusks to spear the moon. The shaggy hair that hung down everywhere was snow white, not piebald.

"That's not the same Behemoth," Whandall said. "There *must* be two. At least two."

Morth said, "I don't sense a god. Some lesser being."

It stood steady on legs like buttes, studying the tiny wagon. The long, boneless arm of its nose lifted in greeting or acknowledgment.

Lilac turned the bison straight toward Behemoth.

Whandall watched her do it. She didn't look at any of her companions, didn't invite comment.

Whandall stood up on the driving bench. He stripped to the waist and stood for a time, visible above the wagon's hood, in the near horizontal afternoon light.

The bandits were black shadows well beyond fighting range. Body language showed them in excited conversation, but they were still coming.

Whandall sat down. "I believe you have a family secret," he said to Lilac. "And that's fine, but does it threaten us?"

She said, "No."

Whandall let his eyes half close. He could relax for just a little longer.

Lilac said, "But we might be safer if I could tell someone."

"Speak."

Nothing.

"Does Whitecap Mountain know?"

"He might. He's of a different family. We haven't spoken of it," she said. "But I could tell my husband."

Green Stone jumped as if stabbed. "If you have a husband, I—"

"No! No, Stone."

Stone collected his tattered wits. "Should I be driving?"

Lilac shook her head violently.

"Green Stone, I believe I should speak for us now," Whandall said. "Lilac, would you accept my son as your husband? As wagonmaster I can declare you mated."

"Yes, subject to trivia related to dowry."

"Before we deal with *that* . . . are you taking us where you want us?"

Lilac smiled. Dimples formed. She hadn't looked back; she couldn't know exactly how close the bandits were. She was steering straight up into the mountains. "I thought Behemoth might frighten them off. *You* tried that."

Whandall stood to look back. "Well, they might be slowing down. You have a dowry?"

"It's mostly in goods, of course. We're not wealthy, Wagonmaster." She described possessions worth the price of a pair of good bison and a one-horn. "If you were to add"—about three times as much—"we could buy a wagon with that."

"Or I could buy a wagon for Green Stone. If you left him you'd still have enough to live on."

"But I wouldn't have a wagon," she said coolly.

On the mountain above, Whandall had marked out an imaginary line. Cross that line and he would be where Behemoth could crush his tiny wagon in one step, but they hadn't reached it yet.

"Our *children* and I wouldn't have a wagon," she mused.

He said, "Lilac, it's not easy to set a price on your family secret until you describe it. As for the rest, do your other suitors have families so eager as mine? We'll be at Road's End in twelve days or so. You could ask around. The wagons won't return from the Firewoods for another fifty, but you might get some sense of what offers await you. Come to me then."

He didn't say, *Have you other suitors?* He didn't say, *And we'll see what the one-horns say.*

But Lilac was glaring. "Does it strike you that a one-horn might improve *my* bargaining position?"

The truth was, it hadn't. Whandall sensed how much Green Stone wanted to speak. He did not look at his son. "I can mate you under two oaths. One or the other will bind us all, depending on what the one-horns say."

"Have we *time* for this?"

Big as he was, Behemoth shifted uneasily. The wagon had crossed that imaginary line and was within his range. Whandall stood up for a quick look back. The bandits had stopped in the road.

He asked, "Do you understand the term *glamour?* Appearance altered or enhanced by magic? Some women cast a glamour by instinct, with no training at all. Others are accused unjustly. It's why lovers don't bargain for themselves if they have family."

"You know I've cast no glamour! After seventy days' traveling? Look at me!"

Lilac was a good-looking woman, and no illusion, with the road's dirt under her nails and in her hair. If they hadn't all been so afraid of water these past forty days . . . curse! They'd all have been better traders!

"Suppose I just suggest," he said, "that mammoths also can cast a glamour. Hugeness is theirs, but they cast an appearance even more vast. Dead, they lose that power. A live mammoth trapped in a pit might seem to be Behemoth struggling to free his foot—"

She stared straight ahead, her face set like stone.

"But a mammoth could still crush this wagon, and if he's as close as he seems distant . . . Did you say something?"

"Where are the bandits?"

He stood and looked back. "Just watching." And ahead. "So's Behemoth. Lilac, I accept your terms." After all, it wasn't an argument he wanted to win. The Feathersnake wagons could not afford to look cheap! "I'll buy you a wagon. Your family can buy the team. You are a fine trader." *Even though you haven't fooled Feathersnake!*

"Thank you." She smiled: dimples again. Behind them, Green Stone whooped.

"But now I'd *really* like to extend the trade route. There are getting to be just too cursed many of us."

Morth jumped down from the wagon. "We're high enough." He straightened and was taller than he had any right to be. Behemoth backed up a step, then cocked an ear to whatever Morth was bellowing in throaty Atlantean speech.

Then the god-beast's arm uncoiled, reached out and over the wagon and down.

The farmer-bandits scattered, tripping over each other. Their piping screams rose up the mountain.

Morth was dancing on the hillside. "Yes! See that, you apprentice bandits! I'm a wizard again!" He saw his companions staring. He said, "I persuaded the beast that those rural Lordkin are bushes covered in cranberries."

The vast rubbery arm rose up and coiled back across the sky holding . . . a bush torn up by its roots, or the illusion of one. Not some luckless sodbuster-turned-bandit. Those were scattered the width of the path and further, running west.

Behemoth fed itself, chewed, found nothing in its mouth, bellowed, and reached again after the running bandits.

Something called from far above: a distant trumpet plaintively played by a madman.

Behemoth turned to answer. Whandall slammed his hands over his ears. A madman's trumpet screamed inside his head, the sound of the end of the world, or the end of all music. Behemoth turned away, toward the peak, and started to climb.

CHAPTER 58

There was water, but no stream was close enough to be a danger. It seemed a reasonable place to make camp.

Morth opened one of the talisman boxes and took something out, faster than Whandall could shield his eyes. "Used up," he said. "I can't even reenchant it."

Lilac was looking too. The doll was crude, of barely human shape. It had a wild white beard and long white braided hair, blue beads for eyes, and something like Morth's color.

Whandall asked, "Does it lose magic if too many people see it? Is that why you didn't want to show it?"

Morth didn't answer.

"Or were you just embarrassed?"

Morth laughed. "I'm no artisan." He tossed it away. "I'll make another tomorrow."

Around sunset an animal stalked the camp half seen; and then Whitecap Mountain stood among them.

"You're in time," Whandall said, and among the company assembled, Whandall Feathersnake declared Green Stone Feathersnake mated to Lilac Puma. At this time he exercised his first wish, and Morth wove a blessing of good luck on the marriage.

Afterward he told Whandall, "You know the spell won't work except in the most barren of places."

"Then they'll know where to go when things go wrong. If Willow and I had known *that*, that first year . . ."

* * *

Morning. Morth bounded from his blanket, lean and bony and agile as a contortionist, and howled in joy. Whitecap Mountain snapped awake with a hair-raising snarl. Green Stone and Lilac came running to see what the commotion was. They'd made their bed in a thicket last night.

"No problems," Whandall shouted. "Just Morth—"

"Whandall! See this? Rosemary." Morth pointed out the plant he meant.

Lilac shouted, "We'll collect some, Father-found!" and they ran off.

Morth said, "I'm going up. Climb with me. Maybe we'll find thyme too."

Whandall looked up. The mountain seemed to rise forever, and this time there would be no magic to make it easier. "How high?"

"Not far. Manna's blazing all over this mountain. I'll be back before noon." Morth was bouncing around like a happy ten-year-old. As a hiking mate he would be a pain.

"If you find thyme, tell us. I'll pick what's here."

The wizard began running. Whandall shouted, "Hold up, Morth," and pointed to a plant. It seemed to be growing everywhere, knee high and pallid white. "What's this? How can a plant live if there's no green to it?"

"I don't know it." Morth picked a leaf and nibbled the edge. "It's nothing Rordray would want, but I taste magic."

Whandall half filled a pack with rosemary. No need to keep spices in a talisman box. He didn't doubt Green Stone and Lilac would collect more in their copious free time. Maybe he'd try it in his cooking. They'd have more than Rordray needed.

From time to time he ran across a stone spire. They were all over the place, growing thicker uphill.

Noon, and Morth wasn't back.

This wasn't the wild magic that drove Morth crazy. No gold around here. Was there? It didn't *look* like places where he had seen gold.

Whandall began climbing. Morth might have gotten lost or stepped on.

The view was wonderful. The breath in his lungs was clean and rare. Stone pillars stood about him. This was heady stuff even for a man with no magical sense.

He shouted, "Morth!" and "Morth of Atlantis, are you lost?" but never with real concern. He didn't think that anything here could hurt a wizard in his full power . . . except that any other magic thing would be in *its* full power. Behemoth, say, or last night's trumpeter, which might be another Behemoth.

A thousand huge stone spires protruded through the ground. They didn't look like natural formations. Here and there stood a stone ridge looking almost like the rib cage of something ages dead. Bone-white primitive-looking scrub grew everywhere. Sage and rosemary grew too. Whandall picked some sage.

Once he looked down and was shocked at how high he'd climbed. Yet the peak pulled him on.

The way grew more difficult. Then insanely difficult. Whandall kept climbing. It just didn't occur to him to turn back. The mountain grew more wonderful as it rose. Now he was finding steps in the most difficult places, stairs hacked at seeming random into the naked rock. No, not hacked: rock had *flowed.*

A man was watching him from high above.

The sun had burned him black . . . like Morth on the mountain, Whandall thought, though his beard and hair were wild gold and he wasn't wearing any clothes at all. The Stone Needles Man watched in silence, and Whandall wondered what he would sound like.

"Thyme," he called up. "There's a plant called thyme, but I don't know what it looks like."

"Who are you?" The Stone Needles Man sounded raspy and unpracticed, a voice unused for a long time.

Whandall started to tell him. His mere name didn't seem adequate, so he told more; but wherever he tried to start his story, something earlier was needed—Morth, the Hemp Road, the caravan, the Firewoods—until he was babbling about kinless woodsmen in the redwoods around Tep's Town. He climbed as he spoke, and that had him gasping. The man watched and listened.

Even close, Whandall couldn't guess his age, wasn't even sure he was human. Something odd about his nose, or his scowl. Maybe he was were.

"Thyme," the old man said, "there," and pointed with his nose. "All through that patch of dragon nip."

"That's the white stuff?" Whandall had to go back down by a little to reach it.

"Um. I could call it mammoth nip; they like it too. Thyme is grayish green stuff, grows low to the ground. Yes, that. Rub a leaf in your fingers and sniff. Never forget *that* smell."

"Nice."

"I used it in the stew. Come eat." The old man started to climb higher yet. He turned once and said, "I want *your* lunch."

"Agreed."

"Um. I get tired of goat. Keep changing the spices—it's still goat. What've you got?"

"Nothing."

The man turned on him a look of baffled rage. Whandall felt ashamed. "I didn't know I was going to keep climbing," he said, and that led him to wonder, *Where do they think I went?* He should do something about that. The wagon was a fantastic distance below him, and the sun was halfway down the sky.

But they'd climbed to the top of the world, and here was a small neat garden and a fireplace and an animal skin shelter set on poles. Stew was simmering. Whandall was suddenly ravenous.

Morth lay by the fire. He looked dead.

The Stone Needles Man pulled the stew off the coals. "Don't try to eat yet. Burn yourself."

"Morth?" Whandall knelt by the wizard. Morth was snoring. Whandall shook him. It was too much like shaking a corpse.

"What happened to him?"

"Got curious. You got a bowl? Cup? Good." He took Whandall's cup and scooped stew into it. Whandall blew to cool it. Tasted.

"Good!" Meat, carrots, corn, bell pepper, something else.

"Sage and parsley, this time. It's always the same except for the spices. I have to grow the parsley. The rest is all around us." And the old man chuckled.

"Feels like I've known you forever," Whandall said. "I was trying to remember your name."

"Born Cath—no, *Catlony*. Barbarians called me Cathalon. Later I called myself Tumbleweed. Just kept rolling along, following the manna. Wound up here. Call me Hermit."

"I was Whandall Placehold, and Seshmarl. Now Whandall Feathersnake. What happened to Morth?"

At the sound of his name, Morth rolled out of his sleep. "Hungry!" he said. He scooped a bowl of Hermit's stew. Whandall tried to talk to him, but Morth paid no attention.

Hermit said, "Came up here this morning. We talked. He's a braggart."

"He's got a lot to brag about."

"You know, I may be the safest man in the world. The oldest love spell in the world is parsley, sage, rosemary, and thyme. I grow the parsley and the rest of it covers the whole mountain. You're inside a love spell."

Whandall looked around him in surprise. "Great view too!"

"I never learned to talk to people. Reason I kept moving. Never liked anyone I met. They never liked me. Anyone who can reach me up here, he's welcome."

"I'm lucky you didn't send me back down for your lunch," Whandall said. "I'd have gone."

The old man's face twisted. "Idiot. You'd starve on the way! And be climbing in the dark!"

"Hah. You're inside a love spell too!"

The Hermit stared, horror widening his eyes. Whandall laughed affectionately. He asked again, "What happened to Morth?"

"Hungry!" said Morth. "Burm my mouf. Curf!" He went on eating.

"Morth of Atlantis wanted manna," the Hermit said. "And food. I *did* eat *his* lunch, so I started some stew. But he wanted manna, so I said, 'Climb one of the fingers and touch the tip. Get yourself a real dose.' "

"Fingers?"

Hermit waved at a stone pillar twelve feet tall. "Morth heaved himself up to the top of that. When he floated down I could perceive the manna blazing up in him. He said, 'Yes! There's a god in there. Under. Feel a little sleepy.' And he curled up and stayed that way till now."

"Fingers? What's going on?" Suspicion . . . wouldn't come.

"Giant with ten thousand fingers. I've tried to feel its thoughts, but I can't. Too self-centered. I was that way when I came up here, and it's been so long. If I lost touch with the manna hereabouts, I'd dry up like an Egyptian corpse."

"But there's a god under the ground?"

"Feathersnake, did a god touch you? There's a trace in your aura."

"Yangin-Atep and Coyote both."

"So another touch wouldn't kill you."

A giant under the ground?

Suspicion would have made sense, but the Stone Needles Man wouldn't let him hurt himself, would he? He couldn't believe it. Whandall climbed the stone finger and laid the palm of his hand on top.

The land was in a coma of starvation.

Once these expanses of narcotic white weed had lured dragons out of the sky, down to the ridges where they could feed. Then stone fingers closed on them and they were lost. The bones of dragons remained, ossified stone ribs.

But dragons were gone now. Ten thousand huge fingers poked from the ground, questing for prey gone mythical. Flesh alone was not enough to feed a near god. Mammoths were big enough and had magic too, but they ate the dragon nip and avoided the fingers. A mammoth's long nose was perfect for that.

The Giant had been dying for ages, in a sleep as deep as death.

"Sleepy," Whandall said, stumbling back to the fire. "Hungry," as a whiff of stew reached him. He scooped more stew from the pot, working around Morth's hand, barely aware that they were both burning themselves. He ate and then slept.

"I remember when dragon nip grew taller," Hermit said. It was morning, and he wasn't likely to be interrupted. Morth and Whandall were eating. "Thousand years ago. I think it learned to grow shorter than what dragons could pull up. Plants do fight back, you know."

The pot was clean. Whandall licked his bowl. He wondered if he was being rude, but the Hermit was amazingly rude, and so what?

Morth asked, "What did you tell them, down there?"

"Nothing," Whandall said.

"They'll be going crazy. I'd better send a message."

The rainbow-colored crow came at his call. It settled on his shoulder, listened to a whispered message, then winged away.

Morth said, "We should be going too." He didn't stand up.

Hermit picked up a hollowed-out ram's horn. He asked, "Want to ride down?"

"Ride?"

The Hermit blew into the horn. Morth and Whandall winced away from a blast of sound, the sound of Behemoth screaming. Faintly an echo rose from below. No, wait, that wasn't . . .

From behind a granite mass too small to hide him, Behemoth stepped into view, and *reached*. Whandall threw himself flat beneath nostrils big enough to swallow a wagon. "I believe I'll walk—"

"Yes, indeed," Morth babbled, "but thank you *very* much—"

"Come visit any time," Hermit said. "People *do* visit. They never hurt me or rob me. It's getting rid of them, that's the trick. They taught me to be rude."

"They did not," Morth said immediately.

The Hermit snickered. "Well. No, but I get tired. The cursed *language* changes every few years and I have to learn to talk all over again. I do get lonely, though. Come again."

The wagon was in sight, and Green Stone was closer yet and climbing. Morth said, "It wasn't just different customs. He's crazy."

Whandall smiled. "Likable, though. He keeps giving things away.

Anyone who comes here for the spices will *have* to climb, I think, and be glad he did."

Then Green Stone, gasping too hard to speak, was nonetheless demanding where they'd been for two days and nights.

Three bison-drawn wagons were in view, way off down the road.

When Whandall's wagon reached the flats, they were closer yet. His own bison were glad to stop and graze while they waited. Whitey loped off west to make contact.

Feathersnake's other wagon and two Puma wagons pulled up around sunset. Carver told him, "We were worried. A talking bird isn't a message we could verify."

"Did bandits give you any trouble?"

"No. This last village, there wasn't anyone in it. You didn't—"

"I never touched them! They just ran away. Must have thought you'd bring Behemoth down on them."

CHAPTER 59

The two Puma wagons rolled past the New Castle's gate. The Feathersnake wagons stopped. Green Stone helped Lilac down. Whandall waved Morth back before Morth could join them. Where was everyone? "We sent the cursed bird," he said.

"We'll take care of it," Green Stone said. "Go on, Father."

"Tell Willow that I have brought Morth of Atlantis and will take him to Road's End. He will not be coming in."

"Right."

Whandall set his own wagon moving and looked behind to see Carver's wagon following. They had left considerable cargo in Green Stone's care. He didn't intend to pay storage and tax on all of this!

Every wagon fit to roll was gone from Road's End. The two Puma wagons were on their sides, stripped of their covers and their wheels. Puma guarded stacks of cargo. Carver went searching for the repair crew. Chief Farthest Land's men had to be found to open the warehouses—

"I could do that," Morth said.

"Better if they don't know it. Hello, that's . . ." Whandall called, *"Twisted Cloud!"*

"Whandall Feathersnake!" Twisted Cloud made her way toward them, but she was limping. Two boys ran ahead of her. "You're back in good time!"

"Yes, but why aren't you with the caravan?"

"I broke an ankle. Patch of mud wasn't dry yet. It's almost healed, but I couldn't stand at all when the caravan rolled. I had to send Clever Squirrel." Her daughter, Coyote's daughter. Whandall's daughter, some would say. An obligation if Twisted Cloud cared to make it one, but she never had, beyond the wagon Whandall had bought for her daughter. "The wagon's hers, and she's old enough now."

"She was born old enough. Twisted Cloud, this is Morth of Atlantis, of whom you've heard tales. You're both wizards—"

"Yes, I can see the glow," Twisted Cloud said.

"And you, there's a familiarity. Like Whandall. A god has been in you?"

She blushed. "Well . . . yes."

The boys watched and listened with interest. Boys would not be introduced until they discovered their names . . . as Green Stone found malachite in a cave, or as his father's tales of the Black Pit shaped Saber Tooth's dreams.

"Did you come to join the caravan?" Twisted Cloud asked.

Morth said, "Yes, to reach the Burning City."

Whandall said, "I fear Morth has been sniffing raw gold—"

"Whandall, I can't tell you more! Your mind is open to too many gods, and the gods of fire and trickery all seem to be related."

Twisted Cloud said, "But the wagons are all gone!"

Whandall said, "Yes. Morth, they left when we did, as soon as the Hemp Road became passable. You'll be here until spring. That gives you most of a year to come to your senses!"

"And then the caravan goes only as far as the Firewoods," Twisted Cloud said.

"Curse," Morth said. "I'd lose all the power I gained on the mountain."

Whandall noticed that the band around the Puma wagons had grown. "I need to do some business," he said.

"I'll scrape up a meal for us," Twisted Cloud offered.

"Here, I brought back some spices."

Chief Farthest Land's men made meticulous records as Whandall stored his gatherings. They took a percentage of the estimated value. It was worth it to most traders, and to Whandall too, up to a point. The New Castle was the only hold in these parts that could be called safer than the Chief's safehouse.

Then again, like the Spotted Coyotes, or the Toronexti in Tep's Town, Chief Farthest Land *insisted.*

No doubt the Chief knew—*very* likely his clerks knew—that not everything Whandall brought home came this far. He had never made a point of it, and Whandall didn't abuse the privilege.

Whandall completed arrangements for repairs on his own wagons. Puma had arrived first; their wagons would be repaired first. Give them Morth's preserving box full of Whandall's spices to carry to Great Hawk Bay. They'd be back before the autumn rains.

He returned to Twisted Cloud's fire and a rosemary-flavored bison stew.

Morth's youth, restored in the Stone Needles, had gone to hale middle age. Twisted Cloud had put on some weight since their encounter with Coyote, and birthed six children too, four still alive. Still a good-looking woman, she had a round face made for laughter.

"The tribes just don't get it," she chortled. "They think I should have seen it coming and walked around the mud patch!"

"It's like looking at the tip of your own nose," Morth agreed. "Your own future is all blurred. I saw the great wave from the sinking of Atlantis and missed the sinking itself!"

"Got clear, though."

"Lucky. Fated. Whandall told you? But there are things he couldn't have known. . . ."

There were three guesthouses at Road's End: low pits with tents over them. Rutting Deer and Mountain Cat ran these and lived in one. In the absence of her wagon, Twisted Cloud was using one. Her boys had moved Morth's baggage into the third while he took care of some business matters.

Now the wizards were verbally dancing around each other, each trying to learn what the other knew, hoarding secrets for later trade. Whandall tried to follow their talk, feeling more and more left out. Presently he went off to his travel nest to sleep.

CHAPTER
60

Without a wagon and team it was only a four-hour walk home. Whandall and Carver didn't hurry. Evening fell, and a long twilight. It might be the last peace they saw in some time.

The pile of goods was gone from the New Castle's gate. They parted there. Carver went on to the Ropewalk. Whandall went in.

The New Castle was a household disrupted by sudden marriage. Willow had put Green Stone and Lilac in the guesthouse. Stone's room wasn't enough to house two, and the noise . . . well, newly-weds were *expected* to be noisy. It was hours before Whandall and Willow could retire.

The bird had returned to Willow. "He's a good messenger," she said, "but next time, *you* speak the messages. I still flinch from Morth's voice."

"I will. And we have a wish coming." Whandall grinned in the dark. "Yes, we have a wizard's boon. There were two, but I used one. You awake?"

"Tell it."

He launched into his story. "Morth blessed Lilac and Green Stone's marriage," he concluded. "Now we've reached Road's End, so he owes us a second wish. He'll find someone to take him to Tep's Town. He'll die there, I think. We should collect before he goes south, but that won't be before spring."

"What shall we wish for?"

"Something for Saber Tooth? If he was affianced I wouldn't even hesitate, but we've got a married daughter now. We can give the wish to Hawk In Flight, or her firstborn. Too bad we'll never get our third wish."

"*Our* lives are perfect?"

"Yeah."

"Just asking." Willow stirred in his arms. "I thought of asking Morth to leave our family alone forever."

"That's easy magic."

"A waste. Some gift for our children's children? Ask him if he can do that."

Hawk In Flight had never been happier than when planning her own marriage. Now, seven weeks a wife, she entered the field as an expert. She and Willow began planning a formal wedding for Lilac and Green Stone when the caravan returned.

The celebrants were seen only at mealtimes.

Whandall kept himself occupied.

The bison had been well kept, but they needed exercise. The men who worked the New Castle had complaints they could not bring to Willow. He must hear them out and make judgments. Two must be married. Two needed a shaman's attention (and six *thought* they did). A woman must be put on the road. Her man went with her, and now they'd need a new blacksmith.

Whandall went up to the graveyard by day to pull weeds and tend flowers. Willow visited the hives nearby. Whandall didn't go with her. Willow must keep treaty with the queen bees; they didn't deal well with men.

"But you didn't get stung?"

"No," said Willow. She showed him bees still exploring her hands.

"Well, rumor says the Tep's Town bees are above First Pines this year. They mate with local queens, and then all the worker bees grow little poison daggers. Twisted Cloud calls them *killer bees.*"

He went to the graveyard again at midnight to keep his peace with the dead, lest they grow restless. It was always freshly surprising, how the dead accumulated over a man's lifetime. Old friends; two children; no other family, and that was rare.

Whandall talked to them, reminiscing, while they hovered around him. It was hard to tell their thoughts from his own.

The twisted ghosts from Armadillo Wagon had raged at him for years after that business at the Ropewalk. Tonight they were not to be seen. Ghosts did fade . . . or perhaps the fools had tired of his jeering.

Three days of that, and then Lilac joined her prospective mother and sister. The servantwomen were drawn into that circle. The servantmen and Green Stone showed the same sense of abandonment that Whandall could feel nibbling at his own composure.

"The magic goes away," he told Green Stone. They were where the women couldn't hear. "It's the great secret of the age."

Green Stone said, "The honeymoon, we tell each other it fades. Father, it happened too soon."

"Maybe you started early? I'm not asking," Whandall said, "only musing."

Green Stone was silent.

"Hey, this place will survive without us. I should supervise repair of the wagons. Three days. Want to come along?" He could exercise the bison too. Hitch all six to one wagon.

The Puma wagons were upright again, looking almost new and ready to go. There were no bison about, nor Puma tribesmen either. They would be out finding fresh bison to catch and tame.

Two of the repair crew were about. He'd expected to find more. They tried to rag him about hitching six bison to one wagon. Whandall made up a story about a troll sometimes seen on the road. The troll was willing to bargain, a bison for two men. This time they'd missed him. Might meet him coming back.

Whandall spent several hours inspecting his wagons and arranging repairs, taking it as an opportunity to teach Green Stone.

Then he and Green Stone made their way toward White Lightning's workshop. Lightning wouldn't be awake in daylight, but it was near sunset and the days were getting long.

Most boys found their own names, but White Lightning had been named for the lightning blast that left his pregnant mother blind and deaf for nearly a year. The baby she bore had skin as white as snow. He was a good glassworker, strong and skilled, but he couldn't travel. The sun would burn him badly.

White Lightning was peering into a white-hot coal fire through the slits in a soaked leather mask. Stone and Whandall closed the door flap and waited, standing well clear. White Lightning pulled a gob of glowing glass out of the fire on the end of a long tube. He blew into the tube to make a globe, stretched it, twisted it. Now he had two lobes joined by a narrow neck. Lightning set it gently in a box of black powder and rolled the powder over it. Then he picked up the black double bottle with wooden paddles and danced it into an oven that was cooler, darker than the fire he'd been using, and closed the door on it.

"Dexterous," Whandall said. "You look good."

Lightning turned without surprise. "I never felt better in my life. Hello, Whandall Feathersnake. Ah—"

"Green Stone is now a married man."

"Boy, you all grow faster than I can catch up. Feathersnake, what's your need?"

"Lamps. Twenty, if you'll give us the quantity discount."

Lightning doffed his mask. His face was chalk white, but there weren't any sores, and his eyes looked good. "You need them before fall?"

"No."

"Then, sure, take eight for seven."

"Oh, *all* right, make twenty-four. What are you making now?" Whandall saw Lightning hesitate. "Don't tell me secrets—"

"He didn't say so. One bottle, but it has to be perfect. Glass glazed with iron. Wizards! But he's a *great* medicine man." Lightning stretched on tiptoe. "Every joint doesn't hurt! I can see again too!"

"He wants a *black* bottle?"

"Come see it after I've fired it. I'll get two this way. He can take his choice."

Rocks burned in a circle of rocks. Morth of Atlantis sat with his back to a small fire so that he could face Twisted Cloud. The medicine woman sat so far back that her face was in darkness. It looked awkward. Stone and Whandall joined Morth, backs to the fire.

Whandall asked, "Gold?"

"Right," Twisted Cloud said. "For years they've been paying me in river gold. Time comes when wild magic is needed; it's good to have, I suppose, but what can I do with it otherwise? Finally comes a man who can refine it for me."

"A pleasure," Morth said.

Whandall couldn't exactly ask after Coyote's daughter. When he had the chance he asked Twisted Cloud, "How's the wagon holding up?"

"That was Mountain Cat's work, wasn't it? Eight years, and we've only had that one broken axle, and twice a wheel. It's Clever Squirrel's first time out alone, but she'll be fine too. She's been running the wagon since she was fifteen," her mother said. "I just go along for the ride.

"It's *her* wagon. Her dowry, given by Whandall," Twisted Cloud said to Morth, "though she's Coyote's daughter. Feathersnake, I don't think she'll marry."

"Oh, she'll find her man," Green Stone said. Coyote's daughter was his weird half-sister; his tone was proprietary. "She's just—exploring. He'll have to be someone who doesn't listen to unicorns. He'll need courage, too."

Morth asked, "Wagonmaster, have you settled on a wish?"

"Not yet. Where can I find you when I do?"

Morth glanced at the shaman. "I'll be in the guesthouse while I take care of some business here. Then back to the Stone Needles. Plenty of manna there. I'll take things for the Hermit, make myself welcome."

"Fascinating place, it sounds like," Twisted Cloud said. "Maybe I'll visit."

"You'll *love* the Hermit."

Twisted Cloud laughed. "But he's very accommodating, you say."

"I'll wait there for spring," Morth said. "Travel with the caravan, leave them at the Firewoods, go on into Tep's Town. I'd like it if you came, Whandall."

Whandall shook his head. "I promised Willow, long ago. Promised myself too."

"Weren't you telling me," Morth asked, "that you want to extend the trade route? Find more customers, peddle more exotica, hire everybody's children . . . ?"

"I'm looking around, that's true. But my children are able, Morth. We raise them that way. They'll find another path, or make one." Whandall didn't look at Green Stone, but the boy was listening.

Morth said, "Puma holds the path to Rordray's Attic. No room for you. But the Lords in Tep's Town, what've they got that's worth having?"

Whandall held his arms straight out. The left was shorter than the right and a little crooked. "I'm not wanted in the Lordshills," he said, "and they did this to prove it."

"That was then. You'll go back as a looker—"

"I've heard this tale before."

"More than a looker. You have a reputation. After twenty years and more of ships carrying tellers, the tales are bound to have reached the ears of Lords and kinless too."

"Kinless won't deal with a Lordkin!"

"Then again, do *Lordkin* have anything worth trading?"

"Well, yes, if you'll allow that some kinless is carrying it for us, but you still can't think that Wolverines or Owl Beaks or Water Devils will deal with a man from Serpent's Walk!" Whandall didn't speak of the deaths in his own family, the ruin that had dogged Morth. Morth *knew* those dangers. Whandall couldn't yet believe the wizard was serious. "I'd be crazy to go back. You too. Get away from that—" He gestured behind him at the fire of gold ore. "Get your head right. Think it over then."

"Are you enjoying your return to domesticity?"

"Very much."

"All the same, didn't you leave debts behind you in Tep's Town?"

"Nothing I could ever pay," Whandall said.

Green Stone spoke for the first time. "What's it like?"

Morth spoke of running a shop among kinless and Lordkin. Somehow Whandall found himself telling of how he'd played with the ghosts in the Black Pit. Then Morth again. . . . Whandall's family knew his tales of Tep's Town, and had heard Willow's tales too, but Morth was speaking secrets he'd never known.

It was late before they slept.

CHAPTER 61

The next day Mountain Cat and three more repairmen were all at work on Puma wagons. Whandall and Green Stone watched for a bit, talked to them a bit. Then they worked on the Feathersnake wagons. They left both wagons on blocks, each with missing wheels.

Whandall had bought three new wheels to replace the old, not because they were ruined, but to show Green Stone how to dismount and then mount a wheel. Green Stone had to know this stuff!

But they'd mount the wheels tomorrow. If the mad wizard took it into his head to run for Tep's Town *tonight*, he would not ride a Feathersnake wagon.

It was rare that Whandall Feathersnake remembered Tep's Town. What would his brothers say, watching him make repairs ahead of a band of kinless so he wouldn't have to pay them as much?

Enough of the day was left for hunting. Hunting was better while the wagons were gone from Road's End. They bagged a deer and some onions and brought it all back to become the evening's dinner. Twisted Cloud and her boys and Rutting Deer set potatoes, corn, and bell peppers to roasting too.

Dinner would be late. It took time to roast a deer. They told stories of Tep's Town while they waited.

"Lookers blame the fire god," Morth said. "Kinless blame the gatherers, and a natural human lust for what others have. I believe the curse on Tep's Town is a pattern of habits, rather than the baneful presence of a moribund fire god."

Green Stone asked, "What do you do to break patterns?" When nobody had an answer, he asked, "What does it look like? Lordkin all stand around waiting for someone to set a fire?"

"Come and see," Morth said to him. Then to Whandall, "Was there treasure you couldn't carry away with you? Enemies who couldn't touch a caravan master? If there ever was a chance to set things right in Tep's Town, this is your *best* chance. You'd go with a wizard. You'll carry refined gold."

This was beginning to make Whandall uncomfortable.

"I'll invest some gold with you myself," Twisted Cloud said. "I like the trade possibilities."

"I bet you do, Coyote's woman." Her attitude had Coyote's touch! Any risks would belong to Morth and Feathersnake, but new trade routes would be shared by Bison Clan and every wagon served by the Road's End shaman. Whandall asked, "Gold refines itself in Tep's Town, doesn't it, Morth?"

"Yes—"

"The wild magic leaks away? And your wizardry won't work either. Whatever you have in mind, try to remember that. Dinner's starting to smell wonderful, Cloud—"

When Rutting Deer and the boys went to retrieve the food, some glowing lizard thing leaped at them out of the burning rocks.

Whandall Feathersnake got his blade between them and the threat. Something like a Gila monster stood up four feet high and screamed at him, and as it came at him Whandall wondered if he'd finally bitten off more than he could chew. But it tried to eat his knife, and died.

"I never saw a thing!" Rutting Deer cried. "Oh, curse—" A quarter of deer lay in the dirt.

"Something changed by the gold. A lizard, maybe," Twisted Cloud said. "Deer, it's not your fault."

Whandall thought of work to be done tomorrow. If he went to bed now he could rise early.

Whandall woke before dawn. Green Stone was not in his blanket. Voices from Twisted Cloud's dying fire—wood, for the gold had run out—suggested that they'd been talking all night.

For White Lightning it would be near bedtime.

He was still up. With pride he showed off a black glass bottle. Another firing had glazed it. There were rainbow highlights in the black finish. He'd made a glazed glass stopper in the same fashion.

"So, and this one is second best?"

White Lightning laughed. "Yes, second best for Morth! He chose the other one. Why, are you thinking of buying it?"

"Never crossed my mind."

The smith settled for a bit of gold half the size of his thumb.

By examining this thing, Whandall might learn Morth's purpose. What was Morth hiding from Whandall? The only certainty was that this bottle was intended for magical use.

Glass in a cold iron glaze. What would Morth perceive? To a wizard this would be a hole, a blank spot. Hide it under gold—even refined gold—and a wizard would see only gold.

Morth and Green Stone were packing one of the Puma wagons.

"I thought you were staying longer," Whandall said.

"I had a notion," Morth said. "It might be worthless. Fare you well, Whandall Placehold. When you decide what you want, I'll be in the Stone Needles, growing strong again."

"Time we went home too. Green Stone, come."

The sky darkened as they traveled. Cloud drew itself across the sky, but there was no smell of rain. The wind made a strange crying sound.

Green Stone understood first. He didn't warn Whandall. He casually traded away his place on the driver's bench and crawled under the roof to sleep.

White dung began to rain down.

There was no way to hurry bison. Whandall could hear muffled laughter from under the wagon cover. The wagon, bison, and driver were covered in white when the bison plodded through the New Castle gate in a sunset sky dense with passenger pigeons.

Everywhere outside of the Burning City, elders remembered when evening's dinner could be *summoned*. Where civilization grew dense, surviving animals learned to avoid people. Some learned to fight back. In these days of dwindling magic, seeking meat became an adventure. Meals were often vegetarian at the New Castle. But twice a year, birds would overfly the land. . . .

There was nobody to greet Whandall's return. Men, women, children were all over the landscape, all swinging slings, sowing a hail of rocks and reaping birds. Green Stone and Whandall arrived in time to share the plucking.

The evening was spent stripping feathers and roasting and eating pigeons. Everyone gorged. They all reached bed very late.

*   *   *

Late breakfast was cold roasted pigeons. Whandall and Willow spoke of mundane matters.

Green Stone had been days away from his new bride. No need to disturb *them*. As for the wedding, plans had firmed up; most of the arguing had stopped. With the caravan away, not much could be done to prepare. If only Hawk In Flight would stop blurting out new ideas!

Morth would be no bother until next spring. "He'll be on a mountain," Whandall said. "If we can pick a wish . . ."

"Something?"

"Mm?"

Willow said, "You were talking and you just trailed off."

"I can find him 'when I decide what I want,' Morth said. *Maybe* he meant the wish he owes us. *Maybe* he still thinks I'll come with him."

"You wouldn't."

She looked so worried that Whandall laughed. "He's off to fight a water elemental on *my* home turf, but that's okay, he's got a *plan,* only he can't tell *me* because the fire god won't like it!"

"So you won't—"

"But if I'm willing to make the effort, I could be standing *right next to him* when it all happens!"

"—won't go."

"Dear one, I will not go. A Lordkin's promise. Now, what shall we wish for? Something a magician can reasonably be expected to accomplish? Nothing outrageous."

"We have most of a year—"

"I don't think so. There was something in his voice. Willow, he won't wait. He's thought of something. Maybe Stone knows."

"Why would he tell Green Stone?"

"Well, we generally ate with Morth and Twisted Cloud, and told stories."

"We'll catch him at dinner," Willow said. "And now, Lordkin, will you go to encourage the kinless at their work?"

"In my dreams," Whandall said. He went out naked. It was appropriate for the work, and the weather was warm.

Where passenger pigeons had passed, every human hand was needed to clean the droppings from every human artifact. Women worked inside, men outside. Whandall Feathersnake in his youth had learned to climb. He spent the day scraping roofs alongside those few who didn't fear heights.

The New Castle men and boys spent day's end in the pond, trying to get each other clean.

But Green Stone wasn't there.

CHAPTER
62

The household was in an uproar again. Whandall's impatience died when he saw his wife's face, and Lilac's.

"I almost followed him alone," Lilac said. "We have bison and another wagon, why not? But I don't know enough. He tried to tell me it was for the children! I called him an idiot, and he packed and left. Father-found, what happened at Road's End?"

"For the children? *What* for the children?"

"He's off to see the wizard! Morth of Atlantis is going to the Burning City, and Green Stone will go with him!"

"Whandall," Willow demanded, *"what happened at Road's End?"*

"Ah."

He must sound like he'd been punched in the gut, the way they looked at him. And now the hard part was admitting his mistake.

"Green Stone was with me the whole time. Morth wants *me* to go with him back to Tep's Town. Didn't I leave anything there? Unfinished business, family, debts, grudges, buried treasure, live enemies? Some crying need for what a trader's wagon can carry? He can't tell me why he needs me. Can't tell me any of his plans. I am to take some wagons into Tep's Town and find a way to get rich, and Morth is to come along. *Right.*

"Willow, I've been an idiot. He was talking to Green Stone!"

Lilac said, "We'll get him back!"

"He's a grown man, you know." He was still speaking to Willow. "If I force him to stay, he's a kinless."

"What could Morth have offered him?"

Think! "At Road's End he learned enough to firm up his plans. *Then* he tried to get me involved. . . . Stay here. I want to show you something."

He needed a lantern by now.

The droppings-covered roof had been stripped off the wagon and was soaking. There was no trapdoor in the wagon's floor, but with the wagon empty, the boards would slide out. Whandall set aside the bags of gold in the hidden well to reach the glazed black bottle and stopper, then brought it inside.

"Cold iron," he said. "It must be for holding something magical. The one Morth took is just like it."

They looked at it, and him.

"He went to Road's End. He needed a glassblower. I have *no* idea why he wants it. All right, let's just *guess* that Morth also wants *me*. Thirty years ago he saw lines in my hand. He looked at Stone's hand too—"

Lilac's hard hand closed on his wrist. *"What did he see?"*

"Early marriage, twin girls, then nothing. A blur."

Her grip tightened. "Twins? But why would Stone's future fuzz out? Is that *death?"*

"No! No, Daughter-found. A wizard can't see a lifeline that's tangled up with his. Curse! He really is going . . . or else he's going to handle raw gold. That can screw up a prediction too."

You have less magical talent than anyone I ever met, Morth had told Whandall. Could *that* be why the wizard wanted him?

"All right. Morth has my son. Is that because I might go along to protect him?"

"Dear, you have to," Willow said.

"Haven't I heard that song sung with different words?"

"Whandall Feathersnake!"

"I know. *Curse* Morth!"

"Why are we standing here? We have to *catch* him!"

"Wait now, Lilac. It's too dark to load a wagon and take off. Did any kind of dinner get made?"

"We roasted another batch of pigeons," Willow said. "Last night."

" 'Course you did. So we can't leave until morning, Lilac, and that puts Stone a day ahead of us, but *that* doesn't matter, because Stone's on foot. He'll catch Morth. Morth is *two* days ahead in a wagon drawn by bison. You don't expect to *run* after them? Well, bison move at only one speed. We'd still be two days behind when our wagon gets to the Stone Needles."

They went behind the big house, to the stream, where an army of roasted pigeons had been buried in mud.

They talked as they ate. Presently Whandall said, "I think we shouldn't chase him at all."

The women waited.

"Let's give Green Stone's mind a chance to work. He's deserted his wife of, what, twenty days? A marriage blessed by a wizard. He's got fifty, sixty days to think about that, and then everyone he knows comes home and finds out what he did. You're pregnant, Lilac, and if he hasn't guessed that, Morth can tell him.

"Whatever Morth has in mind for Tep's Town, if he can't tell me, he'll *have* to tell Stone. Give Stone a few days to give Morth's intentions a hard look. They may be plain idiotic.

"In particular, I want Green Stone to feel good sense rushing back into his mind as he leaves a mountain-size love spell. It's unforgettable. On the mountain with Morth he'll be accepting everything he's told, but as soon as he gets to where they left the wagon . . . *heyyy!* Lilac, you've been there."

"Yes, Father-found. I didn't realize. I just felt . . . like, we'd been married about a day. Making love in a scent of crushed spices," Lilac said with a wonderfully lascivious grin that faded even as they smiled back. "But you try to share a blanket with him, when he rolls up there's nobody in there *but* him. And you'd have given me more than just a wagon, Father-found."

Willow asked, "Lilac, is Whandall talking sense?"

"That part."

"One more thing," Whandall said. "We can talk to them. We've got the bird." Whandall lifted an arm; the bird settled. Whandall said, "We should work out what we want to say."

"Anything to get them back here!"

"My hope lies in your shadow," the bird said.

CHAPTER
63

Every message was sent after considerable argument. It helped that Willow could write.

"I don't want them *afraid* to come here," said Willow, "with all of us waiting to jump him."

"Let's not make it too easy. Curse it, the boy betrayed me too. Let's just leave it that Green Stone is on a journey and we need to work out details. And keep it *short.*"

"Dear one, does it bother you that he doesn't obey?"

Whandall stared at his mate, then laughed immoderately. "Willow, can't you see I still have trouble saying 'My son'? No, Saber Tooth is a *good* wagonmaster, and I can't break up the Feathersnake wagons unless I've got two directions to send them! So what is there for my second son? He'd *better* be able to find his own directions."

She smiled. Then, "Does it bother you that he chose the Burning City?"

"Yes."

"You do all the talking, then, and you talk only to Morth, right? We women aren't speaking to Green Stone. We're furious. You, you're talking business."

Seshmarls, carry my words. Morth, my son is in your care. We need to know what you intend. Will you leave for Tep's Town this year? Message ends. Seshmarls, go.

* * *

The bird returned two days later with Morth's reply: *We hope to.*
Whandall sent: *Return before his autumn wedding?*

Three days later: *Hope to.*
Stop at the New Castle. The boy's wife and mother are concerned.

Four days later: *I've lost my transport! May wait for spring. Will come to New Castle whatever happens.*
"That's good!" Willow exclaimed, and made the bird repeat it.
Whandall said, "Let's keep up the pressure."
I remind you, you blessed this marriage. Disrupting that spell could be perilous.
"Dear, couldn't he take that as a threat? Oh, you mean *magic!*"
"I meant *both,* curse him!"

Four days later: *Understood. What we intend will make Green Stone and Lilac's children safe for a hundred years. Stone says Behemoth is on the Hemp Road?*

"I saw Behemoth once," Willow said. "But why does the wizard want to know about Behemoth? And the Stone Needles Behemoth, it was *white*?"
"That idiot. That utter idiot. Ah, *curse.*" The women were staring. Whandall said, "Lilac, Stone won't turn back now."
Shall we assemble provisions? Can you grant a second wish?

The bird returned in three days. They must be in transit. *I can't prepare your second wish if you can't describe it. We need . . .* There followed a brief list of provisions.
Whandall said, "Morth is keeping the weight down."
"Tell him to give us back our man!"
"If we wanted a kinless we could have raised one, Lilac. Son and husband, but not slave. Green Stone stands by his own decisions."
"Then carve out a wish that keeps him safe until we see him again!"
"Spells don't work in Tep's Town—"
"They can, you know," said Willow. "You saw ghosts in the Black Pit! And there's magic along most of the Hemp Road—"
"Try this, then: *Cast good fortune for travelers under the Feathersnake sign.*"

Done. Expect us in six days.

* * *

"There's one more thing I can try," Whandall said, "but we can't count on it. Willow, if Stone goes anyway, shall I go with him?"

"Yes!"

The wagon was in sight a good hour before it arrived. Morth and Stone stopped just under the Feathersnake sign, and there they prepared a brief ritual. As soon as Whandall realized he was watching magic, he went behind the house and waited until he heard the gong.

Green Stone guided the bison through the gate. Whandall made no move to stop or welcome them. This had been the topic of much discussion. But when they were firmly on his land, Whandall lifted the black glass bottle and silently showed it to Morth.

Green Stone reacted with wild laughter. *"Yes!* Father, it was wonderful! You should have seen it! Morth said you didn't know—"

Morth said, "I should have bought both bottles. Curse, why not? One might break!"

"Well, yes, but what is it? But if it's a good story, save it for the women." Whandall led them behind the house, to a table and chairs set under a great tree. Willow and Lilac were waiting there, and servants had laid out a lunch.

Willow could think of no way to talk to her son without letting Morth of Atlantis onto New Castle land. But he wasn't to come inside!

Whandall set the bottle on the table, waited until Morth was seated, and sat down himself. Green Stone was still standing, looking at Lilac. Lilac looked back.

"I *had* to wonder why you came to Road's End," Whandall said to Morth. "Nobody but White Lightning can make anything like this bottle. My guess is, you want to carry magic. Something like a talisman, in a cold iron glaze so nothing godlike can leach it out."

Morth said, "Very good—"

"Father, we've got a whole wagon load of them!" Green Stone caroled.

Morth swallowed a snarl. Green Stone saw that . . . but Morth waved, *Tell it,* and Green Stone did.

"Father, we set up camp by the stream, on a nice wide beach of clean white sand, on the eighth night. In the morning the wizard went up the mountain. I waited for two days—"

"I wanted to borrow Behemoth," Morth said. "The Hermit would have given him up, but I saw that the white Behemoth is the Hermit's only friend."

Lilac dropped her staring contest. *"Borrow* Behemoth?"

"I couldn't do that to him," Morth told her. "But at least I could deal with the bottles—"

Green Stone broke in. "Morth brought a chunk of cast iron with him, shaped like a heart with lumps around the rim, and *heavy*. We half buried that in the sand and he set the bottle on it. Then we went back to the wagon.

"Night came. We'd left Morth's bottle behind a stand of bushes. Lights made scrollwork in the sky above it, curving out like a thousand whirlpools. Morth wouldn't let me go and look. When we went back in the morning there were bottles, more than I could count. They weren't all the same size. They trailed off in arcs and spirals and little knots, getting smaller and smaller, no bigger than sand grains at the tips. We left most of them. I don't know how Morth picked which ones to take."

Morth shrugged. "I took the biggest."

"The iron was all gone. There was just a pit shaped like a lumpy heart."

"So," Whandall said, "you need a *lot* of . . . what?"

"Virgin gold," Morth said.

"*Wild* magic?"

"I can't tell you any more. I wish you didn't know as much as you do! But I can't go near raw gold, so I'll need help to collect it."

"Yes. Well," Whandall said, "I've examined that bottle. Then I wondered what you might not want me thinking when *Yangin-Atep* looks in there."

"You'd come?"

He let his eyes flick toward Green Stone. "I'd have to." Let the boy work out the rest.

"How often have you felt the touch of the fire god?" Morth asked.

"Yangin-Atep left me about the time you did. Just that once. I think." Earlier? The madness with Dream-Lotus? Easy to blame that on the god, but he knew better. "Just that once, with Yangin-Atep. A season later, Coyote had me for some hours. Both did me more good than harm."

"We should hire you out as an inn. All gods welcome at the Sign of the Winged Serpent."

So there it was. Taking Whandall into the Burning City might tell the fire god too much. If Morth refused to carry Whandall, he might leave Green Stone too . . . and Whandall saw now that that wouldn't work. He dared not let Green Stone go alone.

He said, "If rumor of the Feathersnake sign has reached Tep's Town, you'll be safer with me along."

"Yes, if you can go as a legitimate merchant! Your son and I have spoken of this. The caravan must be nearly to the Firewoods already. We'll meet them and assemble a few wagons. *That* will be easier with you along. . . ."

They'd finished eating. This would have been the time to invite Morth to stay the night, but of course that wasn't going to happen. "I'll ask some men to load your wagon," Whandall said.

"Good. Whandall, taking you into Tep's Town might be too dangerous now."

"Sorry."

"But I need you to persuade . . . curse. Curse! Come. We should get on to Road's End. We may not have much time."

Lilac said, "I'll come that far. Stone and I should talk. I'll walk back."

"Take the bird," Willow said.

They walked into the house to get the bird. Willow asked, "What's *your* intent?"

"As Morth says. Get some wagons from the caravan, and anyone who wants to come along, and goods to sell to the Lords in Tep's Town. Come back with tar for your brothers, if nothing else."

"You're going, then."

"Don't you see? Morth offered Green Stone a ride on the Piebald Behemoth! *No* boy of nineteen could turn that down."

She said, "Nor can a boy of forty-three." Seshmarls walked onto her arm and across her shoulder to Whandall's. "Let me know what's happening."

"I will."

PART TWO

Gold Fever

CHAPTER
64

Whandall drove with Morth beside him. Lilac and Green Stone talked in the back, and whatever they babbled of persuasions and recriminations was lost. Blue in the distance, a shape from the world's dawn ambled toward them.

Morth said, "Behemoth must be close to Road's End by now. I wish I could have warned Twisted Cloud."

"You know, this is the craziest thing I've ever done," Whandall said.

"*I'm* not crazy. Crazy would be waiting for a water elemental to find me. I don't know what the sprite is doing. I've *never* known how far it can come inland. I've got to keep *moving.*"

Repairs, loading, rebuilding of warehouses, all had stopped while Twisted Cloud and four of the chief's men watched Behemoth come. The men gaped in awe. Twisted Cloud was wild with laughter and delight.

The shaman caught sight of Morth. "Wizard, is that yours? The beast should be here by morning."

"I wish it were sooner."

"Wizard's flattery?"

"Medicine woman's sarcasm? I feel the elemental's cold wet breath on my neck."

Behemoth drifted toward Road's End like a storm cloud. Twisted Cloud watched. "He looks to be covering a league with every step, but he isn't. Wizard, how does one summon Behemoth?"

"Like summoning a rabbit for dinner. You must know the prey in your mind. I have Green Stone's stories of Behemoth and his description of a dead mammoth. As you see, they were enough."

Lilac and Green Stone would have their chance to make peace, Whandall thought, in one of the guesthouses tonight. The magicians would have to share another. Rumor told that Twisted Cloud had given up men years ago. But she seemed to get along with Morth, and Whandall wondered. . . . Well, after all, who wouldn't?

By dawn light it was as if Road's End huddled at the foot of a small hairy mountain. Behemoth was still a morning's walk uphill and would come no closer.

Morth's bottles, and a parsimonious few of the goods Whandall had sequestered, rode in the wagon with Lilac, Twisted Cloud, Morth, Whandall, and Green Stone. The bison ambled straight toward the great beast. Behemoth's illusion was too *big* to worry them.

As they neared Behemoth, he seemed to dwindle.

When they stood beneath him, he was a living image of a mammoth. Not small! He stank like a whole herd of wild bison. His trunk took Morth's proffered hand, and Morth spoke Atlantean gibberish. Then the beast lifted Morth into place.

Morth sang and danced on its back. The point of that became clear when dead things began raining out of its hair: parasites in wild variety, from mites too small to see up to crustaceans the size of a thumb joint. Morth brushed more from under the beast's great flapping ears.

Under Morth's direction they girdled the beast's torso with the fishnet they'd carried from Great Hawk Bay.

The beast picked up the travelers one by one. Whandall managed not to scream. Green Stone lifted his arms and *hugged* the beast's trunk. It lifted their cargo up to them and they tied every item carefully in the fishnet, while the bird fluttered wide around them, screaming curses. Lastly Morth summoned the bird with a gesture. Behemoth turned toward the hills.

The beast climbed steadily up a ravine, brushing aside knee-high bushes and trees, until it reached the ridge line. This high, the wind was cold. Whandall imitated Morth: he huddled prone against the beast's back, gripping the net. It was like riding a furnace.

Compared to wooden wheels bouncing on a rutted road, this ride was wonderfully smooth. Their motion was barely felt. Whandall savored the awe and the thrill of riding a moving mountain, if not as master, at least as a guest. Was this anything like what Wanshig had felt aboard a ship?

Was this thing any faster than a bison team?

Traveling above the Hemp Road made landmarks hard to find . . . but *that,* already behind them, was Chief Farthest Land's high peak and lookout point, as the caravan first saw it coming home. Landscape drifted by much faster than it ever would at a bison's pace. Behemoth was *fast.*

Morth asked Green Stone, "Have you any idea where we might find gold? There must be rivers all along . . ."

Green Stone was shaking his head.

"I know a hillside covered with virgin gold," Whandall said, "if we can find it, if it hasn't been mined out. I went up it in the dark. Came down with Coyote in my head. But it's south of First Pines. Now you tell me, will we pass close enough to First Pines to know this place? Stone, you've actually seen First Pines more often than I have."

"I'll ask Behemoth." Morth crawled forward to speak into the beast's ear.

Green Stone waved to the south. "Those are the pines, there where the land starts to dip. It looks like Behemoth wants to go above them."

Morth returned. He said, "Behemoth believes that he goes where he will, but he's wrong. He can't *see* places low in manna. They're holes in his map. He won't go near towns."

"Just as well."

Green Stone said, "So when we run out of pines we just walk on down and get the gold, yes, Father? We've covered a daywalk already, two wagon-days. Morth, were you going to travel at night?"

"Better not."

They camped on the crest. Pines ran from the frost line right down into the canyon, hiding the canyon and the Hemp Road.

Morth summoned a yearling deer to roast. The bird hunted his own dinner. Behemoth ate the tops of young trees and pushed down older ones to get at their top foliage.

Next afternoon they ran out of pines. Now they could see down into the canyon. A beige trace was the Hemp Road, running almost parallel to a stream's blue thread, but higher. The ragged slope of the far hill, and the stream that ran down the gorge, were familiar. The caravan passed twice a year, but Whandall had never been impelled to climb that hill again.

Huddled up against the forest was the town of First Pines.

Morth and Whandall were lowering cargo from the mammoth's back. Green Stone looked from the chaparral-covered hillside across from them, down into the canyon, then at Morth's bags of bottles. He said, "You want *all* of these filled with *gold?*"

"Yes."

His son hadn't quite imagined the size of this job! Whandall grinned. "We're far enough from town, locals won't bother us. Bandits might. We've been attacked here more than once. We can take a first pass this afternoon. Camp tonight at the caravan campground, watch for bandits—"

"No! Come back up. Sleep here," Morth said. "Bandits won't bother Behemoth."

Sleep with Behemoth—sure, that sounds safe. "Couple of days, then, if there's any gold. Twisted Cloud has known about this place all along. She might have told anyone."

"How do I know gold?" Green Stone asked. "How do I know wild from refined?"

Whandall wasn't sure he would either. Gold ore wasn't always bright smooth yellow. He said, "You coming, Morth?"

Morth was torn. "You've seen what I'm like when I've touched wild gold. Do you really need me?" Hopefully. Resisting.

Whandall said, "I can't sense it, you know."

"Don't I just. *Ah!* Take the bird," Morth said. "Watch Seshmarls."

CHAPTER
65

Stone and Whandall set out with the bird wheeling above them. They'd half filled their packs with empty bottles. Those didn't weigh much, but they'd be heavy coming back.

The rising wind was to Seshmarls' taste. The rainbow crow flew with motionless wings, pretending to be a hawk. He had to flap more often than a hawk would.

Without that bird they might have come and gone unnoticed.

They reached the floor of the canyon in a ring of older children all chasing around under the bird, demanding to know whose it was, or swearing it must belong to Whandall Feathersnake.

Whandall introduced himself and his son and the bird. When he asked where they were from, they pointed up the valley toward First Pines.

They crossed the valley floor, and the stream, in a circle of children and a flood of questions. While they climbed, Whandall told tales of the bandit attack and of Coyote's possession.

A few of the smallest couldn't keep up and dropped out. An older girl went with them, complaining bitterly of the excitement she would miss. Green Stone apologized. "We can't stop. We have to finish before dark."

Now ten remained of the original fifteen.

He just couldn't tell. These might be from First Pines, the children of customers and friends. They might be bandits' children, or First Pines might include part-time bandits. Then again, it was a fine day for

walking uphill in a gaggle of babbling tens and twelves, with bright
noon light to guide them around malevolent plants that had ripped
half his skin off one black night.

"Oh, look!" cried a black-haired boy, and he pointed up.

The bird was arguing territory with a hawk. What had the hawk so
confused, what had excited the boy, was the brighter-than-rainbow
colors flashing across Seshmarls' feathers. It hurt the eyes to look.

"Wild magic," Whandall murmured, and Green Stone nodded.
They took note of where they were and continued to climb.

The stream ran to their right. The children's chattering had dwindled, but one boy—thirteen or so, with straight black hair and red skin
and an eagle's nose—urged them on. Whandall spun them a tale
about an Atlantis magician in flight from a magical terror. He did not
speak of gold. He let the bird's display guide him up the hill.

Gold would not be found where Seshmarls kept his accustomed
colors. Where colors rippled across the bird in vibrating bands and
whorls, hurting the eyes . . . well, it seemed they were tracking a
flood that might recur once or twice in a man's lifetime. Gold followed
the flooding.

"Oh, look now!"

The bird sank toward the stream, darkening as he fell. The children
ran.

Greenery thickened, blocking passage. Stone and Whandall forced
their way through. And there in the water, with eight children all
around it, sat the skeleton of a man. Seshmarls perched on his skull,
jet black.

Whandall said to them, "Here rests Hickamore, shaman to Bison
Clan, lost these many years."

"Gold," Green Stone said, and picked up two yellow lumps as big as
finger joints. He put one in his pouch and gave the other to the oldest
boy. "Here," he said, and pointed out more dully glowing bits of gold
for the children to collect, until every child had a bit of gold and they
were scattered all up and down the streambed. Green Stone and
Whandall tried to find gold in places a child would miss, and thus
filled their belt pouches.

Day was dimming. Whandall gave a tiny black glass bottle to the
oldest girl. "Wait three days," he said, "then show it to your folk and
tell them where to find Piebald Behemoth the shaman."

They all trooped down to the valley floor and parted there.

Whandall and Green Stone followed the last sunset light up toward
the crest and Behemoth. "That was clever," Whandall said.

"Thank you, Father. I wasn't sure."

"No, it was brilliant! This isn't what Morth needs; it's refined. Valuable, of course, but Coyote used up all the manna in it. But it'll draw them."

Morth heard their tale, then asked, "Will the children wait?"

"Don't know. We still don't know if those are First Pines children or bandits. It doesn't matter. It doesn't matter if they tell their parents or go themselves. The way to get the refined gold around the shaman's skeleton is to go up the river. We'll cross lower down tomorrow and get the wild gold on the slopes. We know where it is now."

The bird settled on Morth's arm. "Reminds me," Green Stone said. "Keep the bird with you tomorrow, Morth. He attracts too much attention . . . oh, that'll do," as the bird on Morth's forearm turned glossy black.

CHAPTER 66

They crossed the valley at dawn. A lone black crow wheeled above them. They saw no children.

They filled some bottles with water. Water going up, gold coming down. They panned a little gold in the stream. It was only a powder here. They stopped again at the bottom of the ancient mud flow. Whandall thought he saw color in the mud, not yellow, but the odd tints of gold salts.

And he felt the pressure of a lurk's eyes.

They kept climbing. Whandall looked about him, taking it all in, letting his mind find patterns. He didn't look for a face among weeds. That was not how you spotted a lurk.

The bird wheeled above them . . . and suddenly blazed with colors.

Vegetation was low and sparse, leaving little cover to hide a man. Flooding had left whole river bottoms sprawled across this slope; then years of rain had washed away the lightest particles of silt, leaving what was heaviest; and that must have happened over and over. Gold was everywhere.

Following the firebird's path, Whandall began collecting nuggets. Green Stone couldn't perceive gold until they'd been at it awhile, but then he caught the knack.

Seshmarls flapped uphill in a wide spiral. He was black again. Was he seeking the mad magic in gold, or just his dinner? The bird dwindled until they almost lost him. Then they saw his rainbow flare and followed.

Now Whandall had no thought for watching eyes, nor for anything but gold. When their belt pouches were full they emptied the gold into their packs. By sunset every muscle was screaming. Their empty bellies cried for food.

A half-moon gave them little light. It was good they'd brought water, but that was gone now. Unable to see to collect more gold, they began sifting the gold sand into bottles in the dark.

By moonset most of the bottles were full. There was no gold left in the packs, and no light at all.

Green Stone hefted his pack. "That's heavy!"

"Put it down. We can't walk in the dark."

"It'll still be heavy tomorrow. I'm cold, hungry. Father, what are we doing here?"

"Gold fever. We should have been on our way hours ago. Now we'll be here the night." With their gold sealed in cold iron, Whandall was having second thoughts. He thought his sanity had returned.

Green Stone said, "I wish Morth were here. He'd summon something to eat."

"Gold drives Morth crazy! We don't dare build a cook fire anyway."

"Well, we got his gold for him."

"Why does Morth want it?"

"I'm not supposed to tell."

"Not Morth's plans, no, but do *you* have a plan? Or did you come just to ride Behemoth?"

"Maybe I can find my fortune in Tep's Town, or earn it. Maybe it's my blood calling to me."

"Let me tell you about your blood," Whandall Feathersnake said, "and about *Morth.*"

And they talked.

Whandall had first seen Morth of Atlantis from Lord Samorty's balcony, when he was learning how to lurk. . . .

One night during the trek to find Morth, Green Stone had crawled into Lilac's blanket and gotten himself a long and heated lecture involving one-horns, rumor, custom, and the rights of parents. Lilac was still ticked at his father for suggesting otherwise. So was Green Stone. . . .

Whandall's father had died robbing Morth of Atlantis. The Placehold men had died because . . .

When the gold fever really did ease off, hours later, Whandall tried to remember the long mad night of laughter and horror. How much of this had he actually *said?* Things he'd *never* confessed.

But he *had* told his son how the Placehold men died while Whandall stayed to gather a kinless woman and mutilate the man who tried to strangle her. Told him about ruling the Placehold until Mother came home with Freethspat. How Mother's lover made him a murderer. How Whandall made Freethspat carry garbage . . . like a kinless . . . and why that was funny . . .

Green Stone was snoring gently.

Whandall wriggled around until his back was to his son's, head to foot, separated by backpacks stuffed with bottles. Dozing, he suddenly remembered a sense of being watched.

He swept an arm wide around, just above the packs. His hand smacked hard into a thin forearm, and closed. The arm tried to pull away. He followed through on the sweep, reached across, letting go to avoid a possible knife thrust, and had the other hand with a knife in it. Then Green Stone was twisting the intruder's head.

"Don't kill him," Whandall said quickly. The struggling shape went rigid.

Whandall took the intruder's knife. "Let me speak first," he said. "You're a very good lurk. We'll speak more on this. We need this gold for ourselves, but I can offer you something you'll *never* refuse. But I'm just not sure I want you yet. Let him speak, Stone."

A boy of twelve or thirteen cried out in anger and terror. *"Who have you killed?"*

"What?"

"You're Whandall Feathersnake!"

"Your face," Green Stone told his father. "It's glowing."

"That's wrong. I haven't killed anyone in six years!"

"Must be the raw gold," said Green Stone.

"Yes. I don't kill lightly, boy. What's your name?"

Silence.

"Make one up. Never mind; we'll call you Lurk. Are you a bandit?" He didn't say *bandit's son.* Give the boy his dignity.

The boy said, "Yes. Do you need all of those bottles?"

"If the wizard would just *talk* to me, I might have an intelligent answer. Green Stone?"

"Father, Morth doesn't *know* how many he needs."

"Stay with us, Lurk," Whandall said. "I'm going to let go. In the morning we'll talk. If we don't need you, I'll send you home with the smallest of these bottles and a tale to make you famous. But if we need you, you'll ride Behemoth with us. I'm letting go now."

He let go.

The boy went to his belly and backed away. Whandall had expected that; he could have caught him. The boy backed under a stand of thorns and was gone.

Again Whandall and his son stretched out head to foot and back to back. Green Stone said, "He heard everything."

"Yes."

"I'm not sure what you said. I must have dreamed some of that. Gold fever. Did you ever tell Mother any of that?"

"No! You don't either, right?"

"Right. Why do you want Lurk?"

Whandall wondered if the bandit boy was still out there. "I've been thinking. If ever we hope to trade in Tep's Town, we have to do something about the Toronexti. . . ."

By late afternoon they had carried those fearsomely heavy packs up to Morth and Behemoth. They slept the rest of the day and most of the night.

Then up and off at first light, down to the river and up the far hill before Seshmarls' colors flared. Gold madness had them again. They'd have carried more gold, and saved a smidgen of weight, by piling gold sand loose in their packs. Whandall convinced Green Stone that it would drive them mad: they would try to carry a mountain's weight of gold, and it would kill them.

Again darkness caught them, and again they filled bottles by moonlight.

The moon sank. They curled back to back with the gold between them.

From the darkness, from beyond a knife's reach, came the voice of Lurk. "I think you lie about riding Behemoth."

"As you like," Whandall said.

"He's not so big as all that," Lurk said, "but he could crush a man with his foot, or his nose."

"How close did you get?"

"I touched his hind foot." When they didn't answer immediately, Lurk added, "His skin is rough. His smell is very strong. He opened one eye, and I smiled at him, and he watched me back away. You've wrapped his belly in—"

"Why did you touch him?"

"I got that close. Isn't that what you want?"

That was perceptive. "I need a man who sees all and is never seen. Did Morth see you?"

"No. You didn't see me either." Lurk laughed. "When you think you're safe, you sleep on your back, feet apart, your arms for a pillow. Do you have trouble breathing?"

"No, but I did once." Story for story, Whandall spoke his memory aloud: "I was healing from what the Lordsmen did to me. Broken ribs, broken arm, bruises everywhere . . . knees, kidneys . . . they smashed my nose and cheek and some teeth. Had to breathe through my mouth. I'd try to sleep on my side and wake up suffocating, and when I tried to roll over, everything hurt. So I learned to sleep on my back. You listening, Green Stone? I tried to go where I wasn't wanted. It's *dangerous* in Tep's Town. Lurk, it's *dangerous*. You could stay here and be safe."

"What are you offering?"

"You'll serve the Feathersnake wagons."

"That's *all?*"

"What do you have now? If you like what you have, what you are, then go home."

In the morning Lurk was there. They knew him: a thirteen-year-old boy, the oldest of the children on the hill. Straight black hair, brown eyes, red-brown skin, nose developing a hawk's prow. He wouldn't pass for Lord or Lordkin or kinless.

Lurk carried his share of gold-filled bottles as they made their way across the valley and up. By and by Lurk asked Whandall, "What are the Tornex to you?"

"Toronexti. They're gatherers who place themselves between me and what I want, between me and the Burning City." Whandall told him what he remembered. He could paint a verbal map of the Deerpiss, the Wedge, the guardhouse at the narrows. But the Toronexti . . . "If the Spotted Coyotes never gave anything for what they took, if they took whatever they wanted and there was no way around them, that's the Toronexti. None of us knew them well. I think it's always been one family, like the Placehold . . . my family. They walked and talked like Lordkin. But Lordkin don't have their own wealth. Where do they shop? Where do they get their mates? It isn't a Lordkin who rises from his blanket and goes to a guardhouse because it's *time*. Be he sleepy, or horny and a woman nearby, be his throat sore and his nose running and some fool waiting to yell in his face, a kinless goes because his Lord expects him. Lords do that too. A boy on a roof does that when the bugs are on the plants, and so does a Toronexti guard. They're weird. Lurk, I need someone to spy on them."

"And why should I come with you?"

"That's if Morth accepts you. You say Behemoth already has?"
Lurk waited.

"If you live, you will have stories your tribe will never believe and never forget. You ride Behemoth's back with Whandall Feathersnake. A fire-colored bird wheels above you and waits to carry your messages. You learn what Whandall Feathersnake can teach. You'll watch me destroy the most powerful bandit tribe in the Burning City with your badly needed help. You'll help the last wizard of Atlantis destroy a water elemental. You'll get rich too, if everything goes right. I have never seen everything go right. You coming?"

CHAPTER

67

Lurk gripped the fishnet like a dead man in rigor mortis. His face was buried deep in a patch of lank and matted brown hair. But Behemoth's ride was smooth, and by and by he looked up.

By and by he was sitting upright. Then he was pointing out landmarks.

When they stopped that evening, Lurk vanished.

Whandall set about making camp. He tried to think like a Hemp Road bandit. He wished he knew how far they had traveled. They'd come a good way . . . *maybe* farther than a bandit's child might find allies. Did bandits still fear Whandall Feathersnake? Or was he legend going myth?

It wouldn't matter. Whatever the truth of the stories, whether First Pines harbored bandits in exchange for a share of their loot, none would risk robbing Whandall Feathersnake without assurance that the tale would never be told.

But Lurk returned unseen bearing rabbits and a fat squirrel, and a coyote that was only stunned. "Some folk hold to a coyote totem," he said.

Good point. "Let it go," Whandall said. The beast limped away.

Morth summoned. Raccoons came. Watching raccoons skin the other creatures cost Lurk his appetite, but it surged back with the smell of broiling meat.

* * *

"Languages," Whandall said. "If we are to trade in Tep's Town, we need more who can speak the language. Morth, can you teach Green Stone and Lurk?"

"Yes, but to what point? Magic doesn't work in Tep's Town. The knowledge would fade like dreams."

"But if you teach them here, and they practice here? They'll remember what they practiced, even when the magic goes away."

Morth nodded sagely. "Well thought. That should work. We need a safe place."

"Safe?"

"All three of you must sleep," Morth said. "Understand, there may be effects we do not know. They may gather some of your memories as well as your knowledge of the language."

"You know the language," Whandall said. "Use yourself as model."

"Never, and for the same reason."

"Oh." Whandall thought on it. "So be it."

And afterward, on the journey south, they spoke only the language of Tep's Town, but curiously, not as Lordkin and not as kinless. They sounded like Lords . . . almost.

Stone and Lurk were speaking as an eleven-year-old Whandall Placehold understood Lords to speak. "Your mind does not accept that these two are Lordkin," Morth speculated. "Hah! But can they pass?"

"Not for Lords, not for kinless, not for Lordkin. Lookers. Lurk, Green Stone, you know enough to trade, or you might even pose as tellers. In a pinch, talk Condigeano."

The ridge had descended, but the company perched on Behemoth's back still had a god's-eye view of Firewoods Town.

Several new houses had appeared since Whandall Placehold came out of that forest. Sixty houses, half adobe and the rest wood, all built for mass and durability and looking much alike, like an art form, *planned,* were strung along three parallel dusty streets. Fenced yards. Flower gardens. All very impressive to a Lordkin boy.

All the townpeople were gathered at the north end of town, around and among fifteen big covered wagons drawn in a wide circle. There were tents. A hundred hands were pointing up, up at Behemoth.

Lurk whispered, "Do you think they see *us* as giants?"

Whandall said, "Morth?"

"I don't know. Ask."

The Firewoods Wheel was turning.

It was not much more than a wide flat disk mounted horizontally. Twenty children crowded onto it. Adults and older children were pushing it around.

"The first go-round wheels ran themselves," Morth said.

"But what's it for?" Lurk asked.

"Altered state of consciousness," said the wizard. "In the old days *anyone* could sense magic. It was everywhere, talking animals, gods in every pond and tree. Stars and comets would shift position to follow events on Earth. Our ancestors missed that sense, so they invented wine and stage magic and the powders and foxglove I used to sell in Tep's Town, and the go-round wheel. Now too much of the magic is gone. It only makes us dizzy."

They watched. The folk below watched back; the wheel slowed. Green Stone said, "Nobody's coming up to help us move this stuff, are they?"

The wheel had Whandall mesmerized. He could almost remember. . . .

He shook himself. "Morth, stay here with Behemoth. We'll go down and get someone to carry."

A crowd of merchants and townsfolk watched them come. The wheel slowed with their inattention.

Whandall shouted, "This is Lurk. He's with me." He moved through the crowd a little faster than anyone could talk to them, he and Green Stone bracketing Lurk. They jogged to catch up with the rim of the wheel and began to push. Lurk caught a handhold and pushed too.

Children piled on and crawled inward to reach the padded handles. Others took the easy way, crawling under the wheel, emerging in the hole near the hub. They sought to hang on, if only to each other, to resist being thrown off onto the grass, until they got too dizzy or the adults were worn out.

Whandall ran and pushed, showing off his strength. *Forty-three, but not frail.* But a memory came flooding back with a terrible sadness, and he said, "There was one of these in Tep's Town. . . ."

He told it in gasps. *Whandall and others of Serpent's Walk arrived while Lordsmen were anchoring the wheel. Kinless were already there. Lordsmen used bulk and muscle to start the wheel turning. Children surged onto it. The armored Lordsmen went back to guarding while older children and parents ran round and round the outside of the wheel.*

Now Serpent's Walk children bent their efforts to picking purses, be-

cause it would go hard for them if they didn't. But the day wore on, and the kinless were careful of their purses, and the wheel looked like fun.

It happened all in a surge: the Lordkin children moved in and piled on and chased the kinless children off the wheel.

And the wheel slowed and stopped.

"I wasn't *really* confused here," Whandall panted. The Firewoods Wheel was turning nicely. "They were pushing it." Townsfolk were still looking uphill toward Behemoth, but a few were starting to push again. "The Lords let us think that—magic was turning the wheel, and hey—I was just a little boy. But the kinless wouldn't push if there weren't any kinless on it. If nobody pushes, it stops! We barely had time to feel what it was like. So we went back to picking pockets—and the kinless took their children and went away."

There were plenty of hands turning the wheel now. From those who had run out of breath and dropped out, Whandall picked out a big woman from the Feathersnake wagons. "Hidden Spice, where's Saber Tooth?"

She wanted to talk. He insisted. She pointed.

That was Saber Tooth . . . and everyone wanted to talk. Hard to guess which had more of the crowd's attention: Behemoth, or Whandall Feathersnake sprung up suddenly in their midst, or the bandit boy. They forged a path through the crowd.

Above the noise, Saber Tooth demanded, "Father, how did you get here? *Why?*"

"I'm here to protect your brother. Green Stone is here following Morth of Atlantis. My son, what the wizard's doing is the really interesting part. But . . . you've heard me talk about new markets? I think I've finally got a handle on that."

"Father, you can't mean what I think you mean."

"We'll talk. Maybe I'll come to my senses. Maybe your brother will too. Meanwhile, Saber Tooth, I need some muscle," he said. "About six of your men to go up the hill to where you see Behemoth. They're to do what a red-haired wizard tells them. They'll be coming down with heavy loads. I need those bottles protected. They're glass, and what's inside is dangerous, so don't bounce them. Then we can talk, but this is urgent, and those bottles are valuable."

"I'll go myself."

"Thank you. And where's Clever Squirrel?"

Saber Tooth waved. "See the one-horns?"

"Right." The one-horns had all drifted into one corner of the corral. "I should talk to her. Lurk, Green Stone, come with me."

* * *

"The one-horns don't want to be near her." Green Stone laughed. "See, Lurk, this is *Coyote's daughter.* Special. As a little girl she got to know the one-horns. The young colts, they thought she was their older sister. One morning when she was fifteen—she's a season older than Saber Tooth, two years older than me—she went out to the corral and the one-horns freaked. She stormed right back at them. She's got them cowed. They don't like it, but if she had to ride one, he'd carry her. *Hi, Squirrelly!*"

"Stones! Have you been riding Behemoth? Father-found, I'm not surprised, but Stones?"

"I can ride Behemoth and you can't!" Green Stone cried. They hugged each other hard, then the girl turned to the others.

"Clever Squirrel, meet Lurk," Whandall said.

"My name is Nothing Was Seen," the bandit boy said shyly.

Clever Squirrel had deployed her travel nest, with her dowry wagon for one wall and boxes of trade goods for the rest. She even had a little fire going, and she set a teapot on it, with Lurk trying to help.

They found each other interesting, Whandall thought. Should he be protective? They should at least know something of each other.

So. "Squirrelly, he wouldn't tell *us* his name. Nothing Was Seen, how did you find your name?"

"I became the best lurk in Red Canyon Tribe." He told Squirrel how he had spied on Whandall Feathersnake and the wizard who rode Behemoth. He told a minimum of what he had heard that first night. Whandall was glad of that.

Squirrel asked, "Father-found, what are you *doing* here?"

"Waiting for Saber Tooth and Morth of Atlantis, just now. We're going into the Burning City to see if we can kill a water elemental and set up a trade route." She lit up and he said, "No, I *can't* deprive the caravan of their medicine woman, and I *have* a wizard."

"Mother-found Willow will kill you."

"We talked."

She had to raise her voice above a rising background murmur. Her travel nest must be surrounded by most of the caravan and half the townsfolk, all asking each other what Whandall and Green Stone Feathersnake were doing *here* riding *Behemoth!* "Back into the Burning City? With Stones and not *me?*"

"Sorry. If I can really get a trade route going—"

"Show me your hand. Curse! Stones? *Curse!* The lines all disappear!"

"Then we're really going!" Green Stone was jubilant. He must have had his doubts.

"Well, then, what is it like to ride Behemoth, Stones?"

Green Stone said, "You never feel a bump."

"We had to stop off to collect wild gold," Whandall said. "I have no idea why the wizard wants that, but what bothers me is, why was it still there? Your mother has known where that gold is since the night you were conceived."

In the roar of rumor outside the wall of cargo boxes, Clever Squirrel didn't even drop her voice. "I'll answer if you'll tell me about that night. *All* about that night."

"Done."

She laughed. "Mother tells everyone else she never found the place again. She was outside her mind with ecstasy. The gold wasn't there anyway. The whole story's fiction."

"She told me different. She's tried to refine raw gold. She gets some in payment for a cure or a prophecy. But she never learned to block the flow of . . . chaos manna?" Whandall nodded, Lurk merely listened, and she went on. "Gold fever does things to Mother. She always winds up getting laid."

Whandall said, "That—" and his memory felt his wife's fingertips brushing his lips closed.

Too late. Coyote's daughter laughed and said, "Yes, that explains how I come to have five sibs! Five times she's refined gold, five children plus me. A woman who *knows* can take a man without getting a child, but not around gold, not Mother! Even during her time of blood, the gold changes her. That's how she got Hairy Egg. After Father went away—"

Nothing Was Seen was staring at Whandall.

Clever Squirrel laughed. "No, no, not Father-found," she said. "I mean Stag Rampant. He knew Mother had conceived me before they were married. No one dared put horns on him for Coyote's child! But my other sibs were too much for him. And after he left, Mother gave up men entirely.

"Can you guess what would happen if Mother led a man up that gold-covered hill? There are stories only the men tell, but *I* know them. Now tell me of my siring."

"I first saw that hill in black night with your mother pulling me along at a dead run," Whandall began. *Are you listening, Lurk? I will not answer for advice not taken. She's Coyote's daughter and Feathersnake's too! Treat her well and warily.*

CHAPTER
68

Saber Tooth and five strong men came down the mountain carrying heavy bags. Morth was with them. They brought the bags into Clever Squirrel's tent, and then Saber Tooth sent them away.

Above the village Behemoth came to his senses, shook his great head, and turned back to the mountains.

"Father, you'll have to talk to them," Saber Tooth said. No need to explain who he meant. The crowd outside was larger than ever.

"How long have you been here?" Whandall asked.

"We came in yesterday morning."

High noon now. "You were just setting up the market?"

Saber Tooth nodded.

"Good. Finish doing that, set up the tightrope and get your sister ready to perform, and set up a stage to talk from. Tell everyone to come in two hours. Morth, can you show them Behemoth again?"

"Show? Yes, of course," Morth said. "As long as no one wants to ride him!"

"Good. One more thing, I doubt anyone would try to steal from Clever Squirrel . . ."

She grinned. There were tales from when she was five and six and eight.

"But just in case, have a couple of reliable men sit right here, next to those bags. Squirrel, can we meet here for supper? Good. As soon as the market closes. Now let's give these rubes a show."

"But Father, what will you tell them?" Saber Tooth demanded.

"I'm not going to tell them anything," Whandall said. "You're going to tell them how you brought them the greatest show ever."

"But what will you do?" Saber Tooth asked.

"Why should I do anything? It's your wagon train and your show," Whandall said. "Tell you what. I'll catch for your sister. I'm still strong enough for that. You do the rest."

Burning Tower had grown in the months since Whandall had last seen her. The terror bird costume Willow had made for her was tighter, and what it revealed was no longer a little girl. Whandall stood beneath her tightrope, a rope set higher than Willow had ever dared, and hoped she wouldn't fall. He was aware of the stares of all the young men, wagoneers as well as townsfolk.

They were going to need more jobs! No question about it.

Her mother had taught her well. Forward somersaults, back flips, and a grand finale that involved spiraling down the left-hand pole to land on one foot, back arched, high kick to her forehead. Then she was away to the changing tent.

Morth appeared on the platform in a cloud of fog. He gestured to the hills. Behemoth came over the brow of a hill far away, bigger than the hill, as large as the mountain beyond. He reared high, then stood on one leg, kicking high with the other in a hilarious imitation of Burning Tower's finale. The crowd went wild. . . .

Supper was local jackrabbit stewed with spices from Stone Needles. Whandall insisted they finish eating before they talked. Then he sent out all but family members, Morth, and Lurk.

Saber Tooth was relaxed and smiling. "I don't think we ever made this much profit at Firewoods," he said.

Burning Tower grinned. "We'll sell them more tomorrow when they come back to find out which story we told today is true. . . ."

"If any," Lurk said.

Whandall stood. Carefully he opened one of the bags and spread black glass bottles out with his fingers. Clever Squirrel gasped.

"You can tell what's in them?" Morth demanded.

"The iron is thin on *that* one," Squirrel said. She set it aside. "And I saw how heavy they were."

Morth looked worried.

"What are they, Squirrel?" Saber Tooth demanded.

She laughed. "Gold! Wild gold aflame with magic and chaos!"

"Gold?" Saber Tooth looked at the bags. "All of that? No wonder my arms ache! Father, this is more than we'll make in two years! Three, if the Leathermen keep moving their wagons ahead of ours! Gold!" He reached for the flawed bottle.

"No, son," Whandall said. "Listen first. I have a tale to tell." He laughed and said, "And I don't know the ending yet! I don't even know what the wizard intends with these cursed bottles, and you can't tell me, can you, Morth? We'll have to *make* an ending.

"But I need Lurk. I need the wizard, and he needs *all* of these wonderful bottles."

"What can you do that's worth three years' profits?" Saber Tooth demanded.

"A new trade route," Whandall said.

Saber Tooth frowned. "Like the one to Quaking Aspen?"

Whandall laughed. "I grant you that was costly, but we'll make it back."

"In about seven years," Saber Tooth muttered. "So where this time?"

"To the Burning City."

At least Green Stone had the wit to keep unspoken his *I'm going and you're not!* while Saber Tooth thought that through. "Wow. Are we taking the whole caravan?"

"Not worried about the profits?" Burning Tower asked innocently.

Saber Tooth struggled with his dignity before putting his tongue out at his sister.

"I can't risk taking the whole caravan," Whandall said. "Not this time. I need four wagons, and son, I can leave you refined gold to hire more, but I'll need the best traders and fighters you have . . . no, not quite the best. The most ambitious."

"Same people, curse you."

"We need trade goods, anything that can't get to Tep's Town by ship. Terror bird feathers. Grain. Cooking pots. Nothing magical, not for Tep's Town. We'll pick as many Miller and Ropewalker kids as we can get, because they've got relatives in there. I have more refined gold, and that's a lot more valuable in Tep's Town than out here."

"But what do the harpies have that we need?" Saber Tooth demanded.

Burning Tower giggled. "We're harpies too, brother!"

Saber Tooth grinned at her. "Sure, but it's still a good question."

"I don't know," Whandall said. "Whatever we buy, we'll have storage after we get rid of Morth's bottles. . . ."

After that, they all talked at once.

CHAPTER
69

Late that night Whandall dismissed the others and went to Saber Tooth's travel nest. They sat on ornate carpets in a wagon den of polished wood.

"You'll be wanting this wagon, of course," Saber Tooth said.

"Well—"

"It's yours, Father. I have my own."

"Who's in that?"

"Hammer Miller."

"Is his wagon here?"

"Yes, it's loaned to one of his wife's relatives." Hammer had married a girl from a town in Paradise Valley and was content to be a wagoneer foreman.

"Complicated," Whandall said. "Think Hammer would like to come to Tep's Town?"

"I think you would have to tie him to a wagon tongue to keep him out."

"And you as well?"

Saber Tooth didn't say anything.

"Son, I would rather have you with me," Whandall said, realizing that it was true. "But Feathersnake can't spare you. It can spare me—"

"Father!"

"It can, so long as you're in charge," Whandall said. "And you know it. You're a better trader than I will ever be."

Saber Tooth didn't answer. They both knew it was true.

"So I can be lost, and Green Stone can be lost, and Feathersnake goes on. Your mother will grieve, but she won't starve, and neither will your sisters and their kin. Number One, we need you out here."

Saber Tooth was a long time answering. Finally, "Father, I'll take the caravan on to Condigeo. Having a new opportunity doesn't make an old one less worthwhile. I've always wanted to be the Feathersnake wagon boss. Most never see their dreams in old age, let alone as young as me." He sighed. "I've always wanted to see Tep's Town, too, but that can wait. You go in. We'll travel light to Condigeo, and we may be back here when you come out. If not, you can wait here for us."

"Good plan. What are you carrying to Condigeo?"

"Marsyl poppy seeds. Gorman hemp. Some bad carpets that will still be better than anything they have that far south."

Whandall nodded to himself. The Feathersnake wagons didn't go all the way south unless they had cargo Condigeo would pay for, and time to reach Road's End before the snows. Storms chopped off the Condigeo leg two years out of three.

"And civet cat glands," Saber Tooth said. "Two jars."

"I want one," Whandall said.

"Did your nose die of old age? Or do they make perfume in Tep's Town?"

"Not that I heard," Whandall said. "Just an idea. I won't need a whole jar; two cups of the juice will do. Be sure it's sealed tightly."

Saber Tooth's nose wrinkled. "Don't worry about that!"

"So," Whandall said. "It's my wagon, and Hammer Miller's, and who else do I take?"

"Four, you said?"

"Four wagons if I can get 'em."

Saber Tooth poured tea. Sipped. "Not Fighting Cat Fishhawk," he said. "His mother's getting pretty old now; she'll expect to see him."

"How is she?"

"Sorry she retired, I think," Saber Tooth said. "But she was too damn old to be on the road!" He brooded, thinking of the first hard decision he'd had to make as a wagonmaster. Beaching one his father's oldest friends. The worst of it was that Whandall should have done it years before and hadn't.

"So who?"

"Insolent Lizard," Saber Tooth said positively.

Whandall nodded. Kettle Belly's fourth son. Reliable and skilled, if a bit of a smart-ass. "One more, then."

"You'll need a blacksmith," Saber Tooth said. "I can hire another for a while. Take Greathand. He'd follow you anywhere."

Starfall Ropewalker's brother, not her father. The son took the father's name when the first Greathand died six years ago, a skilled giant to his last day. He wasn't blood, but he was kin. "Good. I'll talk to them after we've left this town behind."

Saber Tooth nodded agreement. The less the townfolk knew of family affairs, the better he liked it.

"Sure you'll be all right letting me have this wagon?"

"Truth is, Father, I like my own better. This is the nicest travel nest on the Road, but—"

"But you designed and built yours," Whandall finished for him. "Yup. All right, now for supplies."

"This is going to be like herding snakes. We have to cut out four wagons, take all the Condigeo cargo off them, put anything you want for Tep's Town onto them, and get it done out of town without making camp before the damn Leathermaster caravan catches up and sees us!"

"No doubt you are competent—"

Saber Tooth took on a cagey look. "This will be tricky, and tricky is expensive."

"Never knew I'd have to bargain with my own son," Whandall said.

"Sure you did." Saber Tooth looked thoughtful. "It's Morth who needs the gold in those bottles."

Whandall nodded.

"I do not exactly see why we need Morth."

"There's me and there's Morth, and nobody else on this expedition knows a cursed thing about Tep's Town."

"And we need him that much? I could sell everything we have and not come up with that much gold."

Whandall sighed. "Son, it's wild gold. Unrefined."

"But contained. There are wizards in Condigeo who would be more than pleased to refine it for us."

"It's not mine. Morth helped gather it. It's a matter of our word," Whandall said.

"Oh. I take it this is entirely a Feathersnake enterprise?"

"Yes, if we can keep it that way."

"Do that," Saber Tooth said.

CHAPTER
70

Every wagon owner expected to call at Whandall Feathersnake's wagon den, to present respects and get a glass of the best wine or tea or both, to meet the wizard who was Whandall's guest, to learn why Whandall Feathersnake kept a boy from a bandit family as guest, to test bargaining skills. Had Whandall Feathersnake gone soft from living in town?

Fighting Cat Fishhawk hailed Whandall with a glad cry. Ruby Fishhawk's son was four years older than Whandall, a touch of his mother's kinless ancestry in the ears.

"Give my warmest respects to your mother," Whandall said.

"Won't you see her yourself?"

Curse. "Perhaps not. I will not go farther than the Springs this trip," Whandall said. "Tea or wine?"

"Both, please, but little of the wine. The Springs? So you believe the stories of gold in the hills above?"

"Lurk, make us some tea." Whandall had taught him how. It was best to have something to do to cover a social gaffe. And Burning Tower was eager to be hostess for her father, but Whandall had sent her on errands. She wanted to help, too much.

"Condigeo is getting soft," Fighting Cat said. "I sold a Marsyl carpet, used, for seven sea turtle shells."

"Good price. Are sea turtles so common now?"

Fighting Cat grinned. "No more common than ever."

Whandall sensed a story. "How?"

"I don't talk so much."

Whandall grinned and waited . . . and Fighting Cat grinned back. Whandall said, "*Ex*cellent!" and they moved on to what Whandall needed, which was two repaired wheels, water jars, root vegetables, and dried meat.

When Fighting Cat left, Whandall told Lurk, "My first trip, the caravan had just found out we had a wagonload of refined gold. I'm passing Fighting Cat's wagon, he pulls me into his travel nest by the arm. Shows me a necklace that would look wonderful on Willow. I admired it. He wanted nine thumbweights of gold. Far too much, but it really was a beautiful necklace, and I was—I wanted very much to please Willow. He showed me each turquoise, blue to match Willow's eyes, tiny gold flecks. He pointed out the absence of cracks, that there was no yellow or green, which are flaws, but I didn't know it then.

"I kept looking. It was clear I wanted it, but the gold wasn't all mine—we hadn't divided it yet—and I wasn't saying anything. He told me its history. Offered me three Shambit figurines to go with it, still nine thumbweights. Y—" Lurk wasn't listening closely, getting bored.

Some things you say because they'll be understood later. "I already knew nobody could force me to buy without actually drawing a knife. So I was entertained. He showed me everything he had, and I smiled and admired and watched him go from nine thumbweights to two and a half. Willow loved it. And I told Fighting Cat what he'd done wrong a year later."

PART THREE

The Year of Two Burnings

CHAPTER
71

They left Firewoods Town at dawn of the third day. At noon they came to a side road that led steeply downhill and off to the west.

A score of locals had been overjoyed to find there was suddenly employment in the Feathersnake wagon trains. Where the road forked, they watched in astonishment as four wagons were separated out.

Fallen Wolf had been hired to replace a guard who was going with Whandall. "That's where you came up from the river, twenty years and more ago," he said. "You'd felled some trees. Big ones."

Whandall remembered. Two trees had blocked the wagons. It had taken all day to cut them, and he'd been much younger and stronger then. "I'd hate doing it again," he said.

"My Uncle Badwater found them," he said. "You'd already started a road in. Uncle logged them out, and that's been a logging road ever since."

Whandall frowned. "Does it go all the way to Tep's Town, then?"

"Great Coyote, no!" Fallen Wolf was horrified. "Down and along the stream, up the other side of the hill, then the creepers start. Creepers and vines, and stuff that wants to kill you!"

"And no one has explored farther?"

Fallen Wolf looked from Whandall to Saber Tooth and back. Thinking. "Okay, you hired me, you hired what I know. When I was about sixteen, maybe nine years ago, there was a lot of smoke out of the

Valley of Smokes. A lot more than usual. Me and three friends put on leather stuff, took axes and food, and tried to get in.

"The creepers were bad enough; they'll be worse now. We hid from three armored men who were coming out. Four days we cut our way through, chopping tangled crap you'll be glad to find gone. Then we saw a wall. Big stone house. Masked men in leathers, spears. Saw them just in time. We ran. They came after us. We brushed some stuff we'd avoided going in. Got away, but I sure wouldn't want to go back! We were a month getting over the itch."

"Want to come with us now?" Whandall asked.

"You all going?"

"Just four wagons," Whandall said. "With me."

"So it's true."

"What's true?" Saber Tooth demanded.

"Crazy old woman in town, babbling that Whandall Feathersnake is going home," Fallen Wolf said. "Look, all my life I wanted to work in the Feathersnake wagon trains, but if it's all the same to you, I'll stay with the main wagon train. I'd hate to get killed my first trip out!"

Fighting Cat's wagon came by. "Not going farther than the Springs?" he called. "I see you haven't lost your skill."

"Farther *south*. Thank you."

"And good luck. Wish I were going in with you; Mother would love to know."

"I'll visit her afterward."

Fighting Cat went on. He wasn't expecting Whandall back. He'd heard about Tep's Town all his life.

Of thirty-one volunteers, Whandall rejected five. That gave him twenty-eight fighters counting himself and Green Stone, one spy—he'd better not count on Lurk to fight—and one wizard.

They had four wagons. He took leathers, axes, long poles to make severs. Morth gathered herbs to make remedies against touch-me and thorns.

They carried weapons, but not to sell. A mixed bag for trade goods, a sampling of things based on old memories. Memory said that clay and metal pots would be best, but they had few because there were good markets for those along the Hemp Road. Mostly they had anything that should have sold somewhere but hadn't.

Saber Tooth stood by as Whandall's band turned off down the logging road. "Farewell. Good trading."

Whandall waved. Then all his attention was taken with guiding the bison down the old road. When he looked back, Saber Tooth and the Feathersnake wagon train were gone.

They reached the stream by evening and made camp high. "It reached you in three days last time," Whandall told Morth. "How long until it finds you?"

Morth shook his head. "There's no knowing. But I wouldn't stay here very long."

"I don't intend to."

At dawn he sent Lurk and Hammer Miller ahead to scout out the old route up the hill, then a crew with axes and brush hooks to clear the way. They were moving up the stream by noon, the wagons jouncing along the old streambed.

"A big flood cleared out many of the boulders," Whandall said. "I suppose that was your flood, Morth?" There was no way to know, but bison moved up the streambed as fast as the boneheads had taken them down. By nightfall they were ready to climb up the embankment, and Whandall had torches lit. He would not let them camp until they were high above the water.

And he remembered what he had learned while he was eldest in the Placehold: everyone complains to the Lord, and they do it all the time.

They found the first of the touch-me creepers just over the brow of the hill. The trail Whandall had burned through the forest was clear of big trees, but vines had grown into it. One rustled slightly as the bison approached it. The bison stopped. Could it sense danger? Or did it feel Whandall's thoughts?

But the way didn't seem too bad. There was more creeper than anything else. Here and there were the bright flowers of lordkin's-kiss and the duller lavender of creepy-julia, but the plants mostly defended the big trees. The road they would take wound through those. A few redwoods had sprouted up and were now a dozen years and more tall, still small among the giants. Small armies grew around their bases.

It would be tedious but not impossible.

Whandall halted the wagon train and drew everyone around.

"I've told you of touch-me before. This is what it looks like."

"Does it strangle you?" Lurk asked.

"No, but the poisons can make you wish it had," Whandall said. "And it doesn't just lie there; it can come after you. That's lordkiss over there. Stay away from it. Lizard, serve out the tools, and lash blades to the poles we brought. I'll show you how to deal with lordkiss.

"All of you, I don't know what this stuff will do to a bison, but I don't think we want to find out. We certainly don't want to brush up against a bison who's got the oils on his coat. Remember that when you're clearing the path.

"This"—whack, his palm against a slim trunk—"is an apple tree.

You can eat the fruit. There's other stuff you can eat, trees and bushes and patches of brambles, but most of them are poison. Ask Morth or me. Morth can see poison."

"Yes, Father—"

"Burning Tower, you were supposed to go on with Saber Tooth!"

"Did I say I would?"

Of course she had never agreed, and it was too late to send her back now. Whandall looked into her triumphant smile, remembering Willow's nightmares.

That first year he'd grown used to waking in Willow's grip. Coming out of a nightmare, she would wrap herself around him for reassurance. *Yes, you're here; I'm out of the city, I'm free.* The nightmares faded over the second and third years . . . and she faced the old terrors when she named her third child.

If something happened to Burning Tower, Willow would be long getting over the loss. So would he.

"Use rakes," Whandall said. "Never touch it with your hands, and use the yellow blankets we brought to clean tools. Wear leathers, and don't touch the leathers when you're taking them off or putting them on. When you do begin to itch, see Morth, and don't put that off."

"Don't forget, we may want to come out fast, with heavy loads and enemies behind," Green Stone reminded them. "So make the way smooth *now*. Now let's get to it."

It felt good, at first, to swing an ax again. He left the creeper to the younger men and women, and took Greathand to attack the first tree to bar their way. It was a small redwood, no more than ten years old, perhaps less. They used severs to clear away the defending brush. Greathand stepped forward with his ax.

"Wait," Whandall said. He approached the tree and bowed. "I'm sorry you're in our way," he said. He bowed again. "Now."

Greathand chopped through the arm-thick trunk in one blow.

When Burning Tower found a patch of redberry brambles, she called him. He was unspeakably relieved. "Drop all your weapons here," he told the assembled workers. "Yes, the knives too. Now go look." They walked cautiously closer to the brambles. Then the magic reached them and they surged forward. They gorged, fighting like children for the berries, and left only twigs.

Hours later he held them back from a darker bramble patch. "Poison," he told Burning Tower, raising his voice so others would hear. "The creepers'll wind around your ankles and hold you while you die. They want your body for fertilizer. The only thing that can eat those berries is à kind of bird. Those." Little and yellow, with scarlet wings, fluttering among the brambles. "Watch for the flushers. Flushers and thornberries, they made a deal, long ago. The flushers swallow the seeds and carry them—"

"Father? How do you know?"

What *was* he remembering? "Coyote," he said. "Coyote made the bargain. He can eat thornberries too." Would that protect Whandall? Not bloody likely, he decided.

They made camp in the wagons, in a wider area they had cleared. It was not wide enough to allow them to unload the wagon boxes. Whandall was hungry. Chopping wood and vines was harder work than he was used to.

But dinner was delayed.

"Father!" Burning Tower called. "All the fires are out! I can't light the brazier."

"Curse. Of course you can't," Whandall said. He called for Greathand. "You'll have to strike fire for us. Keep it outside. From here on, fire won't burn inside a house or a home, and our wagons must seem too much like houses to Yangin-Atep."

"It may be more than that," Morth said.

"You have a vision?"

"No. But does Yangin-Atep? I've lost most of my perception, Whandall."

The Toronexti were waiting for them.

Just after first light on the fifth day, the wagon train rounded a curve to see a thick wedge of grass cleared of creeper and brush, leading like a funnel to a brick gatehouse. Seven men in leathers, wearing fancy hats with tassels perched ridiculously above their leather masks, stood in a line in front of the brick gatehouse. More were on the roof, and Whandall thought there were others concealed in the thick chaparral on both sides of the road. The seven were armed but their weapons were sheathed. Whandall couldn't see the men in the gatehouse. Beyond the gatehouse four men tended a big cook fire with an iron pot suspended over it.

As the last wagon rounded the bend, Lurk dropped away from the wagon train.

"Sure you can find us?" Whandall asked.

"I know the language. How can you hide a wagon train?" Nothing Was Seen asked reasonably. "Tonight or tomorrow."

"I don't remember their acting like this," Hammer said. He had come up to walk beside Whandall as others drove their wagons. His sling was barely concealed and he had a bag full of rocks.

"Nor I. Don't show our strength yet."

The Toronexti seemed to be engaged in a ritual. One came forward holding a leather strip. Something was wrong with the hand that held it. Two fingers were missing right to the wrist.

Because he was hidden beneath the masks and leathers, there was no other way to identify him at all.

He unrolled the leather strip and held it in front of him as he spoke. "Greetings, strangers to our land. This is Tep's Town. We are the Toronexti, spokespeople and servants to the Lord's Witnesses of Lordshills, Lord's Town, and Tep's Town. You are welcome here. Your trade goods are safe here.

"We regret that there is a small charge for this protection, and another for passage through our territory. Our inspectors will assess the charges depending on what goods you are carrying.

"Do you submit to the authority of the Lord's Witnesses?"

"You have some proof of your authority?" Morth asked dryly.

The Toronexti spokesman beamed. "We do! We have a charter from the Lord's Witnesses."

"Ah." Morth seemed boundlessly amused. "May I see it?"

"Whatever for?" Whandall demanded.

Morth shrugged.

Half Hand turned to his colleagues. They huddled. Finally the spokesman emerged and said, "One of you may approach the charter. It is kept inside the gatehouse."

"Inside," Whandall said to Morth. "So it won't burn? I'm guessing."

"A reasonable guess," Morth said. "Note the cook fire, to placate Yangin-Atep." Louder he said, "I will approach. I am Morth of Atlantis, wizard to the wagon train of Whandall Feathersnake, whose fame is known to the four winds."

Morth went inside. Whandall conferred with Hammer and Insolent Lizard. "Did anyone see them last night?"

Lizard said, "I thought I heard something up the road, but nobody came close, and I'd swear no one came through the forest."

"So they knew wagons were coming, but not how many," Whandall said. "Maybe they didn't bring their whole strength—"

Greathand was shouting. "Hey, harpy!"

The wagon train boiled with activity. Every armed man turned out. The women slammed the wagon covers closed. Hammer and Insolent Lizard were already running toward Greathand's wagon before Whandall could react to the traditional shout of a wagonman for help.

Two Toronexti stood menaced by Greathand and his hammer. Four more had drawn swords, and another held a spear. Greathand was shouting, the Toronexti were shouting, and no one understood a word . . .

"What is this?" Whandall demanded.

"We are Toronexti inspectors, and this man is resisting," one of the Toronexti said.

"Hold off, Greathand," Whandall said. "If you please." To the Toronexti: "Our wizard is inspecting your documents. Surely you can wait for this? Please go back to your guardhouse for instructions from your officers!"

Interestingly, they did.

"Not Lordkin," Hammer said. "Not as I remember Lordkin, any-way."

"It's an old puzzle." Lordkin wouldn't acknowledge any authority of officers and wouldn't worry about charters in the first place. But he knew Toronexti only from the Lordkin's viewpoint.

Whandall drew his wagon owners around him. "This could be tricky. Watch me, and be careful. We *do not* want to fight. Stone, go see what's keeping Morth."

Green Stone returned a few minutes later. "He's looking at an enormous pile of parchment," Stone said. "They won't let him touch it, but one of them, a crazy-looking guy in a robe and a funny hat, is spreading out the stuff on a table. One of the sheets has huge writing that says 'witnesseth' and then some other stuff I wasn't close enough to see."

"You can read it?" Greathand asked.

Willow had taught all the children to read the languages of the Hemp Road, but—

"Sure, it's in that language Mother and Dad use when they don't want us kids to understand them," Stone said. "Morth taught me that speech. And the letters are the same as we use."

"Did Morth say how long he'd be?"

"He said give him a quarter hour, but it wouldn't make much differ-ence. Whatever that means. Dad, there was something else scrawled across the ceiling in big black letters. 'I killed Sapphire my wife. I burned my house to hide her corpse, but Yangin-Atep's rage took me and I burned more. Fire surrounded and killed me. But I am not Yangin-Atep's! I am kinless!' "

Some old memory was knocking at his skull, demanding entry, but there just wasn't time. "All right. Time to get ready. We'll have to let them inspect the wagons," Whandall said. "The only thing we have to hide is gold, and that's hidden as well as it can be."

"Those bottles aren't hidden," Hammer said. "A whole wagon-load!"

"Leave those to me."

Morth returned chuckling. "It's a charter all right. And regulations. What they can collect, what they can't. In theory they're limited to one part in ten, except they can collect up to nine parts in ten of any tar being imported."

"No one would bring tar into Tep's Town," Whandall protested.

Green Stone said, "One part in ten isn't all that bad—"

"Then there are the exceptions," Morth said. "Whandall, that document seems to have grown over the fifty years or so when there was still trade from outside into Tep's Town."

"I don't remember there ever being any land trade," Hammer protested.

"Neither do they, nor does anyone living," Morth said. "But there are still regulations and rules, and what it amounts to is they can take anything they want if they read it all closely enough."

"And they're sure to have read it," Whandall said.

"Well, no, they haven't," Morth said. "They can't read. Except for that one, the odd one with the robe, who keeps babbling about old crimes. Egon Forigaft."

"Forigaft." A Lordkin name. Again, the old memory would not come.

"He appears to be their clerk. They treat him with an elaborate respect that he does not deserve, but Whandall, he is the only one of them who can read. They don't care what that charter says, I think. They will take what they believe is in their best interest."

"Maybe that's why these costumes, and showing us the charter," Whandall mused. "They've never seen foreign trade. Let's find out."

He strolled rapidly up to the gatehouse. "Noble Toronexti," he said. He'd learned long ago flattery was cheap goods. "We are the first of our kind in many years. Others will come, bearing many goods, cook pots, pottery of the finest make, skins of exotic animals. Furs and feathers and gems to adorn your women, all this can we bring, but none will come if we do not return happy."

The Toronexti officer grinned behind his mask. "And what do you bring this time?"

"Little of value, for this is an exploration. But we do have these, as gifts for your officers." He waved, and one of the boys brought a cheap carpet, laid it down, and unrolled it. Three bronze knives lay there, with half a dozen showy rings with glass stones, the kind that Whandall was accustomed to giving Hemp Road children as trinkets.

The Toronexti scooped them up eagerly, carpet and all. The officer eyed Whandall's knife. "Yours is even more elaborate—"

"Take it if you like." The Toronexti was already stepping forward as Whandall said, "That's how I got it."

The Toronexti officer stopped. He eyed Whandall's ears, then his tattoo. "You have been here before."

Whandall said nothing.

"A good way to get a knife," the Toronexti said. "What more have you brought?"

"There will be more of value when we leave," Whandall said.

"If you trade well."

"We will." Whandall sighed. "I show you the most valuable thing we have." He waved again, and Green Stone brought another cheap carpet. *Curse,* Whandall thought. *I should have realized they have no real carpets here. They'll all want them!*

Stone unrolled the carpet. Twelve black glass bottles were nested in wood shavings.

"I know the people of Lord's Town will pay well for these," he said. "Let's think, now. The Lord's Town kinless will give me more for these bottles than they'd give you. A *lot* more. Because I don't work for the Lords." Whandall watched the tax man's face: was that still an insult? And would the man see past it, to see that Whandall was right?

"With," the tax man said. "Work with. Show me those two." He pointed to the smallest bottles.

"The little ones?"

"They're finer work."

Whandall's face didn't change as he realized the Toronexti had nothing like glass bottles. They were common enough outside, but he had never seen a glass bottle in Tep's Town! They must not be in the sea trade.

And they liked the smallest ones. Whandall remembered Green Stone's tale of the spirals of bottles made by Morth's magic. They'd left *thousands* of bottles smaller than these! What might they be worth here?

Later. Carefully Whandall lifted out the two tiny bottles. As he put one in the Toronexti's hand, he winked at Morth.

The wizard did nothing Whandall could see, but the bottle broke into a paste of sand and putrid liquid that ran on the officer's fingers.

"Curse!" Whandall exclaimed.

"Curse indeed. What *is* that?" the Toronexti demanded.

"Extract from civet cat glands," Whandall said. "It is used to make perfume."

"Perfume? That?" He reached for the other bottle. It too broke into putrescence.

Whandall stared, bug-eyed, and cried out as if strangling. Then he put a third bottle in the tax man's limp hand. Again the glass crumbled into sand and stinking liquid. The Toronexti flung it away with a curse. The other tax man broke into wild laughter. "Magic? Magic doesn't work here, you fool!"

Morth said, "I'm sorry, Feathersnake! These magic bottles will disintegrate at the touch of anyone in this cursed town. They'll have to be emptied over a basin!"

"You say the kinless of Lord's Town will pay for this? To make perfume?" the Toronexti officer demanded.

"Well, they do in Condigeo!"

"Then let them do it! We certainly don't want that stuff. The bottles now—"

"Another time," Morth said. "They can be made without magic. I had not realized the backwardness of this place."

"Backward? *Us?*" But the Toronexti guard was laughing. "So what else do you have?"

"Little, for we thought those the best things to sell."

"Why'd you think that?" the Toronexti asked craftily.

"We speak to ship captains," Whandall said. "We learn. What, would you know all the secrets of a master trader?" He smiled broadly.

Behind him his wagoneers had arrayed themselves. Greathand leaned on a two-handed sword, point down. Hammer and some of the younger kinless idly held slings and rocks. Green Stone held an ax and wore a big Lordkin knife. They all smiled and listened to their wagonmaster. And stood with weapons ready.

Whandall had no trouble reading the Toronexti leader's thoughts. The wagoneers might be telling truth—there were more and richer trains to come if this one came out whole. There were thirty armed men, more than the strength the Toronexti had brought today. The wagon train would be more valuable coming out than going in, and it would come at a time when they could bring their entire strength.

"Do you have more of those rings?"

"A dozen, as a gift," Whandall said.

"Food?"

Whandall threw down a box of dried bison meat.

The Toronexti grinned. "Pass, friends."

CHAPTER
72

The trail crossed the Deerpiss a final time. "Now," Whandall told Green Stone. "We'll see Tep's Town as soon as we've got around this grove."

The town lay ahead, down a gentle slope. Thirty men armed and wearing Lordsmen armor blocked the road. They stood to attention, not menacing, but there was no way around them.

"Bandits," Green Stone shouted.

Whandall stood on the driving bench and gestured violently at the following wagons, both hands out, flat, empty, pushing down. *Put down your weapons!* Green Stone saw the urgency in his father's face. He rushed back to the others, urging calm.

Whandall dropped from the wagon. He stepped forward, the big engraved knife prominently sheathed. "Hail."

"Hail." The spokesman was elderly, his face hidden in the Lordsman helmet and armor, but the voice sounded familiar. "Whandall Feathersnake. We have heard the stories." He turned to speak to someone behind him, a man hidden by the ranks of guardsmen. "It's him, Lord. Whandall Placehold, returned." He turned back, looked at the caravan, and turned again. "Come back rich, he has."

"Peacevoice Waterman," Whandall said.

"Master Peacevoice Waterman to you, sir!" There was some amusement and no malice in the voice. "Not surprised you remember me. Sir."

"Is that Lord Samorty in command, then?"

"No, sir, Lord Samorty is dead these five years, sir."

Somehow he was surprised. But Lords *did* die; they only seemed to live forever. "May we pass? We come to trade," Whandall said.

"Up to the commander, sir!"

With patience, Whandall said, "Then let's talk to the commander—"

Waterman's face didn't change. He turned and shouted, "Whandall Placehold wishes to speak with the commander, Lord!"

The hidden Lord said something in a low voice. "Lord says a quarter hour, Master Peacevoice!" a guardsman shouted.

"Quarter hour, sir!" Waterman said. He returned to a position of rigid attention. When it was clear he wasn't going to say or do anything else, Whandall went back to the wagons.

Morth was grinning. "Interesting."

"Why?" Whandall demanded.

"Look." Morth pointed. A small cart drawn by one of the big horses the Lords used had pulled up behind the ranks of guards. Three workers had taken a small tent from the wagon and were busily setting it up. Another set a charcoal burner down. It was clear from the way he handled it that it held a live fire, and sure enough, he put a tea kettle on top of it. Another worker brought a table, then two chairs, went away for a while, then returned with a third chair.

The kinless workers were dressed all in yellow and black shirts. Whandall remembered Samorty's gardeners, but those weren't the same colors. Morth frowned. "Quintana," he said.

"Say?"

"Those are Quintana's colors," Morth said. "And it appears from his age that that's Lord Quintana himself. He must be seventy years old now, and no magic to help. And he came himself. Whandall, they are certainly taking you seriously."

"Is this good?"

Morth shrugged.

A corporal came up to them. "Whandall Feathersnake, Lord Chief Witness Quintana requests your company at tea," he said formally. "And asks that you permit the sage Morth of Atlantis to accompany you."

Morth's grin turned sour, but he said, "We will be delighted. Come, Whandall."

It was Whandall's turn to grin.

A servant stood behind Quintana and held his chair as Quintana stood. "Whandall Feathersnake, I am delighted to meet you. Morth of

Atlantis, it is good to see you again. You look younger than the last time we met."

"Indeed, I am younger, Lord Quintana."

Quintana smiled wryly. "I don't suppose you can sell me anything that will do the same for me?"

"Not so long as you insist on living in that blighted area you call the Lordshills," Morth said.

"Ah. But elsewhere?"

"Nowhere short of the distant mountains," Morth said. "I've found a *wonderful* place half a hundred days' walk west by north—"

Quintana nodded. "Hardly surprising. Please be seated, Wagonmaster, Sage. I can offer you tea."

Weak hemp tea with a smoky flavor of tar. Morth sipped and made appreciative noises. Whandall smiled: the Lord wasn't trying to drug him.

"May I be blunt?" Quintana said. "Wagonmaster, what are your intentions?"

"We bring trade goods," Whandall said. "Some fit for Lords. If we have reason, we will send in more wagons with more goods. I had hoped to make camp at Lord's Town."

"There is no suitable accommodation for all of you there," Quintana said. "We can offer lodging for you and the Sage in Lord's Town, but there is no place for all of you, and I am certain you would prefer to remain together."

"Oh, yes." Get separated, *here?*

"So. Welcome back to Tep's Town," Quintana said.

Morth chuckled.

"You are amused, Sage?"

"Mildly so," Morth said. "And curious as to why the chief witness would come personally to greet a trader."

Quintana's expression didn't change. "We are not often visited by wealthy caravans."

"Even so, I would wager this is the first one you have met."

"It is also the first I have seen, as you must know. And I grow old; I grow bored." Quintana said. He stood abruptly. "I grow frail. Master Peacevoice Waterman will escort you to a suitable camping ground. Perhaps I may visit you there. Welcome to Tep's Town."

Whandall invited Waterman to ride on the wagon with him.

"Don't mind if I do, sir," Waterman said. "Not getting any younger."

"Beaten up any boys lately?" Whandall asked conversationally.

"A few," Waterman said. "Comes with the job. Didn't fancy you'd have forgotten. Sir."

"Truth is," Whandall said, "that was nicely judged. Here." He pulled the sleeve from his left arm. "I can't forget, no, but I can still pick things up. I wonder if you've seen the teller Tras Preetror lately?"

"Not for ten years. He doesn't come to Lord's Town, of course, but I keep track. Why?"

Whandall told the tale as they drove. "So I've been on both sides of that fence, Master Peacevoice."

They drove in silence for a few minutes. "There was something Lord Quintana wasn't saying," Whandall said.

"Yes, sir, there was," Waterman said readily enough. "You're still not welcome in Lordshills."

"But—Lord Samorty's dead?"

"Oh, yes."

Waterman—Quintana—the Lords were keeping a promise made to a dead man. Because he was dead, the order could never be changed. Lords were strange. Whandall had not guessed how strange.

"Them Toronexti," Waterman said.

Huh? "What about them?"

Waterman said nothing. Why had he brought up the subject at all? "Do you work for the Toronexti?" Whandall prompted.

Waterman sucked air through his teeth, an ugly sound. "Why ask that?"

"Not to offend. The Toronexti had to send you a runner," Whandall said. "He must have waited just long enough to see"—he brushed his tattooed cheek—*"me,* and then run like the wind. And you came. With Lord Quintana and most of your army."

"Not most," Waterman said. "Some. As to the Toronexti, what you think you know about them is likely wrong."

"Please do go on. We like to trade stories."

"And it's my turn?" Waterman grinned. "Most Lordkin think they're just another band. A few think they work for the Lords."

"Don't they?"

"Used to," Waterman said. "Used to collect taxes, and keep some, of course. They kept the kinless from running away, looked after trade stuff for the Lords. But my father's father told me trade stopped coming through the woods, and then there were *more* Toronexti, and they kept more of what they took." Waterman spat over the side. He said, "Gathered. I guess maybe they still keep to some of their tasks. Some goods get through from the forest. They did send a runner to tell us about your wagons. But mostly they work for themselves now."

"We never knew where they lived, how they lived, what they did with all that wealth. Who their neighbors were. If they were Lordkin, where's their turf? If they're kinless . . . are they kinless?"

"I know how they started," the Master Peacevoice said. "Our forebears burned their way through the forest and took Tep's Town. You know that. But Lords and Lordkin didn't want to live together. When things had settled down, there were . . . I'm told . . . exactly sixty boys and girls who had a Lord for a father and a Lordkin for a mother."

"Never the other way around?"

"No."

Silence could often be the essence of tact.

Waterman said, "A place had to be found for them. They were set to guard the way through the forest. Kinless must not escape, you see; they might bring allies. But the tax men lived on site and built their homes along the Deerpiss. It was their duty."

"No homes there now," Whandall remembered. "Just that guardhouse and the barrier. That big center section is stone; must have been built by kinless. The wings are crude work, more recent. They *didn't* become kinless."

Waterman said nothing.

Whandall asked, "What do you wonder, when you wonder about the Toronexti?"

They'd passed the edge of town and were moving through Flower Market territory. The streets looked empty until Whandall's mind adjusted. Then . . . here was the snapdragon sign crudely painted on a crumbling wall. Motion along a roof: a clumsy lurker . . . a whole line of them. Motion in window slits. An audience was watching the parade.

Waterman hadn't answered.

Whandall asked, "Why tell me?"

Waterman stared straight ahead.

They rolled along in a silence that might have been companionable. Whandall waited. Some secrets must be hidden, but some may be traded. . . .

The caravan skirted the edge of Serpent's Walk, along the road between Serpent's Walk and Flower Market. Whandall remembered the road. Lordkin came out of houses to stare at them. No one was going to try gathering from wagons escorted by marching Lordsmen.

Over there was an empty lot. A large square building must have covered that, and another behind it, now both gone. Ahead was a ruined wall, remains of a burned out building, and ahead of that—

A field, once paved with cobblestones. Grass and mustard stalks grew among the stones. All the walls around the field were ruins, buildings long burned out.

A fountain stood in the center. Water trickled from it—

"But this is Peacegiven Square!" Whandall shouted.

Waterman nodded, his expression unreadable, amused? Wry? Whandall couldn't tell. "That is it. Sir. It's where Lord Quintana said you was to make camp. Good roads from here, room to set up a market, not much water but more than most places. He thought it would be a good place."

Whandall stared at the ruins. "All right, he has a point. This will do. Master Peacevoice, it strikes me that you could have told me about *this*. Where we're to set up our market, and why, and what happened here in the twenty-two years I've been gone. But you decided to talk about the Toronexti. Was *I* supposed to know something? I never came anywhere near the Deerpiss until—"

Until Wanshig got involved in making wine.

There's a question; he's waiting for it. Whandall asked, "Did Lord Quintana ask you to mention Toronexti?"

"Wouldn't say yes; wouldn't say no," Waterman said.

"What would the Lords do if the Toronexti just . . . disappeared one day?"

"Find someone to take their place," Waterman said. "Someone more reasonable, and a lot fewer. I think me and ten men could do their job."

"Sons? Nephews?"

"There's a notion."

CHAPTER
73

Whandall raised his hand above his head and brought his arm around in a wide circle. "Circle the wagons," but with only four they made a square.

There were wagons—small flatbeds, with no roofs, in the kinless style—at the far end of the square. Waterman went over to them. Whandall was just unhitching the bison when Waterman returned leading a young man. He was shaven clean, no tattoos, and no more than twenty, perhaps less. It was difficult to tell his age because of his clothing. He wore a dark robe and a close-fitting cap that came down over his forehead and was low enough to cover his ears.

"Witness Clerk Sandry," Waterman said. "I present you to Wagonmaster Whandall Feathersnake. Wagonmaster, Clerk Sandry is here to assist you. Any questions you may have, any requests, he'll help you."

"Thank you, Master Peacevoice." As Waterman went back to his troops, Whandall inspected the younger man. He was taller than Whandall remembered any Witness Clerk as being, and of course Whandall had been younger and shorter then. Most of his body was hidden by the loose robe, but where his arms showed they were more muscular than any clerk's. His cap wasn't new, but it didn't fit him very well. Whandall's expression didn't change. "Welcome, Clerk Sandry."

"Just Sandry will do, sir."

"Very well. I presume you can read."

"Yes, sir, I can read and calculate."

"Good. Find us a place to corral the bison. Then find where we can buy fodder for them. Bison eat a lot, Clerk Sandry. More than you would expect. We'll want a full wagonload of hay or straw."

"As you wish, sir," Sandry said. He inspected the trickle of water from the fountain. "Might I also suggest a water wagon? Sir."

"What will that cost us?"

"I'll find out, sir. But not so much if it's river water. Only for animals, of course."

Whandall remembered the stinking water of the rivers in Tep's Town. He'd been glad enough of it at one time. Now he was used to better, and the memory of that water choked him. The fountain water wasn't good, but it had to be better than river water.

"Please arrange it."

"Yes, sir."

Green Stone came up to watch Sandry walking across the square. Whandall explained.

"Who do you think he is, Father?" Green Stone asked.

Whandall shook his head. "I never knew that much about the Lords and Witnesses and their clerks. He may be just what he says he is, but I doubt it. Remember that he can read. Don't leave anything around he shouldn't see."

"I never do," Stone said.

"Of course you don't."

"Handsome boy," Burning Tower said from behind him.

"Too old for you, Blazes," Green Stone said.

"Well, maybe," Burning Tower said. "And maybe not."

"Don't you two have work to do?" Whandall Placehold Feathersnake asked.

At the far end of the square kinless workmen set up a camp for Waterman and his Lordsmen guards. One of the kinless, a boy about fifteen, came over to Whandall. He took off his cap and shuffled from one foot to the other. Whandall stared in confusion, then embarrassing memories returned. A kinless who wanted to speak to a Lordkin but was afraid.

"Talk to me."

"Master Peacevoice Waterman said I was to ask if you need workers to help setting up camp."

"No, thank you. We're used to doing it ourselves."

The kinless boy watched as Whandall's people unloaded wagon boxes. He seemed astonished.

Of course. There was Green Stone, with a Lordkin's ears, carrying a box with one of the Miller boys. The Millers all looked kinless, except for those who looked like Bison tribesmen, and Mother Quail, daughter to a Bison man and the younger Miller girl, an exotic mix whose beauty edged the supernatural. Burning Tower looked like a slim young Lordkin girl. And they all worked together.

"Firewood," Whandall said. "We'll pay for firewood."

The kinless boy nodded. "We can get you some." He seemed hesitant.

"Spit it out, lad," Whandall said.

The boy flinched.

"Come on—what is it?"

"My name is Adz Weaver."

"Weaver. Ah. You'll be kin to my wife, then?"

"It's true? You *married* Willow Ropewalker?"

"More than twenty years now," Whandall said. "Stone," he called. "Green Stone is our second son. Stone, this is Adz Weaver. He'll be some kind of cousin."

Stone held up his hand in greeting. Whandall nodded approval. It was a Hemp Road gesture not used in Tep's Town, but then in Tep's Town there wasn't any gesture a Lordkin would use to greet a kinless.

Adz Weaver glanced around, obviously aware that a knot of Lordkin were watching from the Serpent's Walk side of Peacegiven Square. "You're welcome here," Whandall said. "But it might be best if you come back after we have the walls up. No sense in gathering Lordkins' attention. And we do need firewood."

"Yes, sir," Weaver said. Whandall smiled to himself. Adz Weaver had used the tone that kinless used when addressing an older relative, not the more obsequious falling tone used to address Lordkin.

Progress.

Well before the Lordsmen guards' camp was up, the wagon boxes had been offloaded, carpets unrolled, awnings erected, and the bison corralled in a nearby vacant lot. Sandry appeared with kinless driving a wagonload of hay and another wagon with a water tank. Whandall recognized one of the fire prevention wagons kinless used. More kinless brought firewood. When Stone offered a kinless the smallest fleck of gold they had for a heap of wood, it was obvious that they'd paid far too much. Whandall negotiated for shells and was pleased: they bought several bags of shells, too many to count, for one gold nugget.

Trading would be good here.

Whandall's travel nest was divided into two rooms. The inner was more ornate than most, as befitted a wealthy merchant prince. Willow worried about that, so the outer sides of Whandall's wagon boxes were scarred and unfinished, and the outer room was plain. In the inner room the wood was polished, rubbed with the shells of laq beetles until it shone. Two mirrors hung so that they faced each other, making a magical display the children never tired of. Wool for his carpets came from highland sheep sheared after a hard winter, and his cushions were filled with wool and down. Outside was poverty, but inside the nest everything said "I can afford to ignore your inadequate offer."

Dinner was locally bought chicken stewed with local vegetables. Between what the Toronexti took and what they'd sold here, there wasn't any more bison jerky or fruit. Whandall had just filled his bowl for a second helping when Stone came into the nest. "There's an old man wants to see you."

"You should be specific," Whandall said. "Kinless, Lordkin, Lordsman. Witness. Lord even. Not just man."

"I can't tell," Stone said patiently. "He has a knife."

"Lordkin," Whandall said. "Old?"

"A lot older than you, Father. No teeth, not much hair."

"I'll come out."

Old described him. The Lordkin still stood erect and proud and wore his big Lordkin knife defiantly, but Whandall thought he'd better have sons with him if he wanted to walk far in Tep's Town.

Whandall held out his hand, Lordkin to Lordkin. They slapped palms. The old man's eyes twinkled. "Don't know me, do you, Whandall?"

Whandall frowned.

"Know anything about wine?"

"Alferth!"

"That's me."

"Come in; have some tea," Whandall said. He led him into the outer nest. No point in giving too much away—

Alferth looked around and laughed. "Tarnisos said you took a kinless wagon, and I heard you married a kinless. Now you live like one?" He grinned. "You must be rich."

"I am," Whandall admitted. "How is Tarnisos?"

"Dead. Most everyone you knew is dead, Whandall."

Lordkin killed each other. Even men who lived here forgot.

"Something I've wondered about all these years," Alferth said. "Tarnisos said you really were possessed by Yangin-Atep. Burned a torch right out of his hand! Was he lying?"

"No, I did that." Whandall tried to remember that time. Alferth and the others beating a kinless man—Willow's father!—into something unidentifiable. The rage that filled his mind and flowed through his fingers . . . was gone. "I burned our way through the forest."

"I always hoped it was true," Alferth said. "Never happened to me. I mocked Yangin-Atep, pretended to be possessed when I wasn't." He shrugged. "Too old now, I think. Why would Yangin-Atep be interested in an old man?"

He looks twenty years older than me, Whandall thought. *But it can't be more than five.*

"Hungry?" Whandall asked.

"Nearly always," Alferth admitted.

Whandall clapped his hands. "Stone, please ask Burning Tower to bring dinner for my friend. Alferth, this is my son, Green Stone."

Alferth stared.

Son, Whandall thought. *I said son, and Alferth isn't kin.*

Alferth came to himself and nodded greeting. He'd been studying Green Stone's ears. Of course he would. Well, the Lordkin could just damned well get used to it!

Burning Tower brought in a pot of stew. Alferth took a carved wooden cup from his belt and held it out. She filled it, not bothering to hide her curiosity about this strange man who sat as a friend in her father's nest.

"Things have not been good?" Whandall asked.

"Not good, not since the year we had two Burnings."

"In one year?"

"Yeah. Nine years ago now. First Burning, that was *fun,* but the second was bad. We burned things we needed. That's when Peacegiven Square went, with half the city."

"How did it start?"

Alferth shrugged. "I never did know, Whandall, because I never really believed in Yangin-Atep. But that time, that second Burning, *everyone* was possessed! They ran around pointing and fires roared up, and we all went damn near mad gathering. I went right into a fire and came out with an armload of burning bath towels! Took me half a year healing from the burns. I'll never have a beard again, this side. Pelzed smelled roasting meat and ran into a burning butcher shop and staggered out hugging a side of ox. His heart quit."

"Lord Pelzed is dead, then?" Whandall wasn't much surprised.

"Sure—hey, Whandall, your brother is Lord of Serpent's Walk now."

"Shastern?"

Alferth's face wrinkled. "Shastern? Oh, him, naw, he's been dead what, fifteen years? No, the old one, Lord Wanshig, he's Lord of Serpent's Walk now. Matter of fact that's why I'm here—be sure it's really you."

And see how the land lies, Whandall thought. "Tell my brother—tell Lord Wanshig I'm delighted. And I would like to see him again, here or anywhere he'd like."

Alferth's face twisted into a grin. "Thought you would be." He looked around the plain boxes. He leaned close and dropped his voice. "I could help you find a better place to feed him."

Whandall stood. "Let me try first," he said. He pushed aside a tall man's height of boxes that turned out to be nailed together, and led Alferth into the inner nest.

"Yangin-Atep's eyes! You do live fancy," he said. "So those stories are all true—you went off and got rich!"

"There's a lot more," Whandall said. He gestured eastward. "Out there. I can bring more in. Except I can't."

"Hmm?"

"Toronexti. They took a lot of what we brought. They'll take more going out." Testing, Whandall said, "I'd kill them all if I could." Alferth had felt that way once.

"Thought of it myself," Alferth said. "I hired Toronexti to guard Lord Quintana's grapes and move his wine that he put in my charge. They let some Lordkin gather one of our wagons, *just* what they was supposed to stop, and two of them dead and the rest screaming *at me.* That was you and Freethspat, wasn't it, Whandall?"

"Sure."

"And we all took our lumps, Quintana and the Toronexti and me, and let it go. But, you know, strong as they were supposed to be, they shouldn't let go so easily. I should have known. But I kept my Toronexti guards, and paid them high out of what I was getting, and when that *wave* of gatherers came out of Tep's Town, they ran. They let that mob into the vineyards and the vats. Some of 'em were in the mob! Quintana had a price on my head for a year, and he never spoke to me again. Sure I'd like to kill the Toronexti, but you can't fight Lords."

"Lords protect Toronexti? *Which* Toronexti?"

"All. Whandall, everyone knows that. They *collect* for the Lords. Well, maybe you don't know it," Alferth conceded. "But everyone who ever tried to make anything of himself knows it. If you nose around their territory, the Lords take a big interest in you."

"Toronexti have a *territory?* Is this something everyone knows too? We only knew—"

Alferth held out his empty cup. Whandall clapped and waited for Burning Tower to fill the cup again. He said, "We only knew about the Deerpiss and the gatehouse. We never knew where they lived."

Alferth said, "They don't talk. But I *knew* they had a territory. They *must*. They hide their faces. The leathers they always wear, that must hide a band mark. There *had* to be a way to hurt them. What else could I think about while I hid? I asked around, and I thought. Then the search got hotter and I had to stop looking. I had to leave Serpent's Walk. I live on the beach at Sea Cliffs, and nobody knows anything there."

"That sounds—"

"But before they shut me down, I learned some. Foot of Granite Knob. That's theirs."

"Them? Alferth, no. The Wolverines don't live near the Deerpiss."

"I'd bet my patch of dry sand on it, against the rest of this stew."

Not a heavy bet. Whandall thought back. He'd never been on Wolverine turf. Children were told to avoid it. It was over toward the forest, backed up against a chaparral-covered granite hill, not isolated but easily defended, near two hours' walk from the Deerpiss. No one ever went there uninvited, and there weren't many invitations.

You saw Wolverines raiding, but rarely, and in big packs. Funny, nobody ever wondered . . . nobody but a merchant *would* ever wonder how bands that big could gather enough to share. Like they did it just to fight, just for practice. . . .

Wolverine territory. "You're pretty near guessing," Whandall said.

"Whandall, do you remember those crazies who could *read?* At your party they got too much of your powder—"

"Got into a graveyard. Heads full of ghosts. Pelzed traded them to the Wolverines for a wagonload of oranges. That used to *itch* at me. How did he get anyone to take them at all?"

A slow grin, four teeth in it. Alferth asked, "Why would Wolverines want readers too crazy to remember secrets?"

"Forigaft."

"Right."

The brothers Forigaft. Egon was the youngest, sold to the Wolverines and now clerk to the Toronexti! I owe you, Alferth. "Have an orange? Show your belly some variety."

"Yeah!"

"Does my brother live in Pelzed's old house?" Whandall asked.

"He let Pelzed's women keep it," Alferth said. "Lord Wanshig lives in that big stone place you come from. I think his lady Wess didn't want to move."

Wess. Whandall felt a twinge in his loins. Wess was alive. She'd be the first lady of the Placehold. Alferth wouldn't know about that.

They talked until well after dark. When Alferth left, Whandall noticed that four young Lordkin were waiting under a torch. He merged with them; they doused the torch and all merged into the shadows.

Then one of the shadows became Lurk.

Lurk glided in almost supernatural silence, but slowly, sideways and twisted over. One arm was swollen into a red pillow streaked with purple. Whandall knew those marks. He didn't touch them. He set him down on a burlap sheet and sent for Morth.

Morth looked ancient, worse than Alferth. He came leaning heavily on Sandry's arm. The wizard examined Nothing Was Seen without touching the boy. He muttered words in a language none of them knew. They watched, fearing to interrupt.

Morth snarled, "I sold ointments for plant poisons for near thirty years! Now I'll have to make more on the spot! Clerk Sandry, I need *any* breed of belladonna. Tomato, bell pepper, potato, chilis—"

Sandry was slow to react . . . as if he weren't used to taking orders. Then, "At once, Sage."

They could hear him speaking rapidly to someone outside. Morth moved them out of the nest. Under the awning outside he tended a firepot, set water to boiling, added chipped dried roots and some leaves from the forest, soaked a clean shirt. "Wash yourself, if you can stay awake. What were you doing in the chaparral, boy?"

Lurk looked to Whandall. *Speak in front of the wizard?* Whandall said, "Go ahead."

"Whandall set me to watch the tax men." Lurk's voice was slurred. "A wagon came out of those low woods, a tiny wagon with a tiny pony driving it. I tried to follow it home. They went straight into the woods. There was just a trace of path. I *know* that wagon was wider than I am, and *it* got through, but it wasn't trying to hide too." He scrubbed his arm, tenderly. "When my arm swelled up I was deep in the woods and getting dizzy. Here, something scratched me here too before I could get out." Three puffy parallel lines along his hip. "I swear it *reached out.*"

"Wash that too, idiot!" the wizard snarled. "Get your clothes *off.* We'll have to bury them."

Whandall said, "They reach. You remember what I told you going through the forest? It's the same stuff. It *wants* to kill you. You were smart not to go in very far."

"Lucky, too," Lurk said. "But I lost them." He sounded disgusted.

Sandry was back with a double handful of bell peppers. Morth went to work.

"They were carrying a big pile of stuff, that stack Morth was looking at in their gatehouse," Lurk said. "They loaded it in that wagon, and maybe ten of them went with it, like it was the most valuable thing they had."

"What did they do with it?" Whandall asked.

"Don't know. I told you. Got away." Lurk's voice was fading fast.

"What do you think they were doing, Clerk Sandry?" Whandall asked.

Sandry's face was a mask to match Whandall's trading face. "No idea, sir. None at all."

"I see." Whandall turned back to Lurk and said, softly, "Maybe I found them at the other end."

Lurk looked less puzzled than dizzy. But Whandall was making maps in his head. Do it on parchment later, check it out. . . .

No one had ever walked it, really, but it must be near two hours from Alferth's grape fields down the Deerpiss and across to Wolverine turf . . . by the streets. Those streets curved around a knob of hill covered with chaparral thickening to dwarf forest. But as the crow flies—

How could he have seen Staxir's armor and Kreeg Miller's leathers and never made the connection? *They go into the woods. Kinless woodsmen can do that, and so can I. The Toronexti have to, to move what they take!*

"Which way did they go?" Whandall asked. "Show me on a map." He called for lamps and parchment.

While they waited, Morth wrapped paste-covered cloths around puffy red blotches on Nothing Was Seen's arm and lower belly. "And drink this."

Lurk sipped. He protested, "Man, that's *coffee!*"

"Sorry. If I had honey . . . oh, just drink it."

"I will send for honey," Sandry said.

And we were speaking Condigeo, which Sandry hasn't admitted knowing, Whandall thought. "Thank you."

With Stone and Morth and Sandry at his elbows, Whandall drew maps of Tep's Town. Whandall gave his attention to Wolverine turf and the Deerpiss, and the streets that curved around a peninsula of forest. Through the forest was much shorter, but slower too if a man didn't want to die horribly.

But Morth was concentrating *his* efforts from the Black Pit west toward the sea, sketching in detail on a path that evaded the Lords-hills, otherwise following the lowlands.

When Sandry refused to help them work on Lord's Town, Morth protested. "These have to be accurate. I'll need them later. And at least twenty of your Lordkin, Whandall—"

"I tire of your hints. Maps won't help," Whandall said. "Morth, no Lordkin knows maps." He turned to the kinless boy huddled at the outer edge of the band. "Adz Weaver, do you understand maps?"

"No, sir; I never saw anything like that," the young kinless said. "But I've been watching; I think I have the idea. You're making a picture of where we are?"

Whandall was startled. "Yes! Come here; help us mark this."

They watched Adz draw detail into kinless territory.

And it was all filling in nicely. "If he can learn that quickly, so can others," Morth said.

Whandall nodded. If kinless could learn, Lordkin could learn. Lordkin were smarter than kinless. He said, "Nothing Was Seen."

Lurk stood with difficulty. He leaned on his arms above the map. "Is this the big stone gatehouse that blocks the way to the forest? They went along here, up the Deerpiss. About here they went off the road and uphill, and I last saw them here, bush getting thick—"

Whandall grinned. "Good."

"Good? I lost them!"

"Up and across!" Whandall's fingertip ran through the mapped forest to the suburb of Granite Knob.

"I'll go see."

"Wait for dawn."

"No," Lurk said.

Stone would have stopped him, but Whandall shook his head. It would be a matter of pride with Lurk. Let him go. . . . *"Not* into the forest, understand? I only want to know where they come out."

Lurk nodded, then faded.

They worked on maps all night.

CHAPTER
74

Master Peacevoice Waterman and two men came to Whandall's wagon when the sun was an hour high. "Message, sir!" Waterman said. "Lady Shanda wishes to see you, here, at the sixth hour today, sir."

Shanda. "Who is Lady Shanda, Master Peacevoice?"

Waterman's expression changed only slightly. "First lady of Lord's Town, sir."

"She's married to Quintana?" Whandall asked.

Waterman was shocked. "No sir. She is married to Lord Quintana's nephew, and Lord Quintana being a widower, she is the official hostess for his household, sir." His voice held reproach, as if Whandall should know better.

"You like her, don't you, Master Peacevoice?"

"Everybody likes Lady Shanda, sir. That right, Corporal Driver?"

"Yes, Master Peacevoice."

Interesting. Sixth hour. Five hours from now. She must be partway here already. "Please send word to Lady Shanda that we will be delighted to have her join us at the sixth hour," Whandall said. A conventional phrase, but he found that he meant it. Shanda.

They set up the market before noon. A tightrope, high the way Burning Tower liked it. Hammer Miller and a kinless boy stood under to catch. Neither Lordkin nor Lord would do that in Tep's Town, and for the moment it was better if Whandall Feathersnake kept his dignity, even if he didn't like it.

Nothing went wrong. Burning Tower's act was flawless. And Clerk Sandry stood, mouth open, watching her in fascination as she wheeled and spiraled halfway down the pole, then deftly climbed, feet on the pole, back up it again.

"Smitten," Whandall heard Green Stone say behind him. "With my sister."

"And well he might," Whandall said softly.

"With Blazes? But all right, she's good on that rope."

"That wasn't the entire reason I had in mind," Whandall said.

It was only after Burning Tower finished her act and went to the changing tent that Sandry went to negotiate for another wagonload of hay and another of water for the bison. As Whandall had guessed, no one in Tep's Town would have dreamed that animals could eat so much.

Or make so much waste for the kinless to clean up . . .

Shanda arrived in a small wagon drawn by four Lord's horses. A teenage girl rode with her. Two chariots, one in front and one behind, clattered along with her. Each chariot held an armored man. If they were trying to convince him that Shanda was important, they succeeded.

He knew she was younger than he was, but she looked Whandall's age. He would not have recognized her. The self-assurance he remembered was there, but the little girl had become regal, desirable, attractive rather than beautiful, but extremely so. She wore a short skirt of thin wool, belt with ornate silver buckle, a brooch with blue and amber stones. Her hair was coiled atop her head, and although she must have been traveling all day in a wagon, she looked cool and fresh.

The girl with Shanda carried a large pine cone. Shanda smiled faintly. "What's it like outside?" she asked.

It took Whandall a moment to remember. "Don't they let you go outside yet?" he asked.

She laughed. "You do remember." She pointed to the pine cone. "And keep your promises too."

"Is that really the same one?"

"No, of course not," she said. "This is my daughter, Roni. Roni, greet Whandall Placehold Feathersnake, merchant prince and a very old friend of your mother's."

Whandall bowed. "And this is Green Stone, my son, and Burning Tower, my daughter. I think the girls will be about the same age. Will you come in, Lady Shanda? We have tea." He led her into the inner nest.

Shanda marveled. "You have done well. Two mirrors! And I'd love to know the secret of how you get wood to shine like that." She stared admiringly at the carpets. "You have done well indeed, Whandall Feathersnake."

"Thank you, Lady. And have things been well for you?"

"Not as well as we would like," Shanda said, serious for a moment before her smile returned. "But well enough."

"Did you ever finish the new aqueduct?"

Her smile faded again. "Not yet. We keep hoping."

"Peacegiven Square," Whandall said. "I was shocked."

She nodded, waited until Burning Tower poured tea, sipped, and nodded again. "Thank you. Whandall, it shocked us all, that second Burning."

"What happened?"

"Lord Chanthor always hoped to buy dragon bones," Shanda said.

"I remember. We were hiding on Shanda's balcony," Whandall said to his son. Green Stone and Burning Tower knew the story, but Roni *looked* at her mother. "Some captain sold Chanthor rocks in a fancy box. He had the man killed."

"Yes. And another promised but couldn't deliver, but he didn't take any money. Chanthor kept trying. One day it came. Dragon bones! In an iron box. Terribly, terribly expensive.

"We really couldn't afford them, but, well, we planned to do so much for the people!" Shanda said. "Make rain in just the right places to clear out the waterways, wash all the filth out to sea. Repair buildings. Heal the sick. Finish the aqueduct! It would have been worth what we paid." She was talking as much to Green Stone as to Whandall. Maybe it was the ears? Green Stone could absolve her, speaking for the kinless? Forgive her for the crushing weight of taxes to buy this disaster.

Resalet had opened a cold iron box. . . .

"Back there, at that building, the Witnesses had an office." Shanda pointed through the doorway to where no building stood. Dark ground, charred. "Lord Chanthor brought the box there to be registered. Then they set up by the fountain for the ceremony," she waved at the fountain, blackened and split by heat and near waterless, "with our wizard. We tried to find Morth of Atlantis. He'd gone like smoke in a Burning. Years later we were told he left with you, Whandall! So we hired the wizard from the ship that brought the dragon bones, and on the fountain he opened it . . ." She fell silent.

"And the last thing his eyes ever saw?"

She stared.

"Yangin-Atep took the magic," Whandall prompted.

Shanda's daughter Roni jumped. "Yes!" she said. "He's right, isn't he, Mother? We were home waiting. Mother was so excited, all the good we could do, and she was watching for dark storm clouds, for rain, and suddenly black smoke was pouring up everywhere. Burning," Roni said. "We'd just *had* a Burning!"

"It was horrible, Whandall," Shanda whispered. "They burned so much! The square, the new ropewalk we'd paid so much to build after we lost the Ropewalker family! To you, they told me! You took the Ropewalkers out of Tep's Town. I don't think I ever quite forgave you for that."

"I didn't know who they were when we started through the forest," Whandall said. "Or what Ropewalkers do. But, Shanda, I'd have freed those children anyway."

"What? Yes. Yes, of course," Shanda said, and blushed violently. "Whandall, I almost went outside. My stepfather thought of marrying me to a Condigeo merchant prince, and I'd have lived in Condigeo. But he didn't—maybe the man lost his nerve—and then I met Qu'yuma." Her voice and expression changed and for a moment Whandall envied Qu'yuma.

Green Stone asked, "Yangin-Atep took the dragon bone manna to himself. Like with new gold?"

"And came violently awake," said his father. "And possessed whoever he could."

"And the city has never been the same," Roni said.

He thought, *Really?* He remembered better than that.

Shanda brightened. "But now you're here! You can help."

"How?" Whandall asked.

"Trade. We can use more trade," Shanda said.

"It's hard for wagons to compete with the sea captains," Whandall said.

Roni started to say something, looked to her mother, and kept silence. Whandall let the silence stretch on. It was painful, but he was Whandall Feathersnake, and his son was watching. Better to win the bargain and then be generous than to let anyone think he could be cozened.

"There aren't so many ships, now," Shanda said, trying to keep it light. She sipped weak hemp tea. "They came for the rope, of course," and the words were escaping, slipping free. "It was *all* that brought them. Father explained it to me. When the Ropewalk disappeared, we had to import another system, and that evil captain screwed us against a wall—sorry. Sorry. But he took every coin we could find, and then the Ropewalk was gone in the two Burnings! Ships still come for tar, but now the harbor is silting up," she said. "It's hard to get in, and worse, we don't have as much to trade as we used to. There's only the little Ropewalk now, so there's not much rope for the ships."

"Tar," Whandall said. "Tar is always valuable."

"And we have lots, yes," Shanda said. "But I may as well be honest. They found tar somewhere south of here, some lagoon between here and Condigeo. It's hard to get to, but if we charge what we need, the ships will go there instead. But you'll help, won't you?"

"Why should he?" Green Stone demanded.

Whandall gestured. This was not the time to play roles in the game of negotiation. Was it?

"It's his home," Shanda said simply.

"No, Lady," Green Stone said. "Not anymore. Whandall Feather-snake lives in the New Castle at Road's End. Everyone along the Hemp Road knows that!"

Burning Tower looked admiringly at her brother.

And it's all true, but this was *my home,* Whandall thought. *Good or bad, it was my home.* "I'll do what I can," Whandall said. "We'll look to see what's plentiful here and valuable on the Hemp Road. There must be something. And however easy or hard these new tar fields are to get to by ship, this place is easiest for me. Decide what's your price for tar. It'll tell me whether I come back."

A pony nickered outside. Whandall's expression didn't change as he thought how valuable a bonehead pony grown into a one-horn stallion would be. He said, "Ponies, maybe; there are places along the Hemp Road that might buy a pony. There must be other such things, magical items and animals stunted by Yangin-Atep. We'll look.

"But there's a problem," Whandall said. "The Toronexti make it very difficult for traders."

"We've spoken to them about that," Shanda said. "But I'm afraid they go their own way, much as the Lordkin do. And they have a charter."

"Scraped-off skins?" Whandall asked. "Covered with black marks?"

"I never saw it," Shanda said. "Writings, yes, witnessed by Lords in every generation, granting them privileges. Promises made long ago."

"By dead men."

She shrugged. "Still promises, written and witnessed. Written and witnessed."

Summon them up and ask . . . but this is Tep's Town. "If they lost that charter?"

Her eyes twinkled, just a touch, like the young girl he'd known deviling her governess. No one else saw it. "They'd never do that. It would be like—like it never was, wouldn't it?"

"How is Miss Batty?" Whandall asked suddenly.

"She married a senior guard," Shanda said. "But I didn't know for years. Samorty dismissed her after we . . ." She glanced at her daughter, then said it anyway. "Spent the night in the forest."

"They keep a shop in Lord's Town," Roni said. "Her daughter is learning to be a governess. For my children after I'm married." Roni was very serious.

"And Serana?"

Roni smiled. "She's chief cook, which means she doesn't do any work and orders everyone around."

"Even me," Shanda said.

"Good. Tell her I remember her puddings. Wait. Here . . ." He found it tucked under an Owl Tribe basin. Rosemary in a little parchment bag. "Tell her to crush this and rub some on red meat before roasting. Bison or goat or terror bird. And I'll send her some spices with the next caravan I send in here."

"Oh, good. You will be back?" Roni asked.

"If this works out. Shanda, I will need some help. Chariots. I'll need at least two—three would be better—with drivers. Lord's horses, not ponies! If I send my clerks around to look for trade goods, I want to know they can outrun gatherers." And because he'd seen Morth mapping out a path a daywalk long!

"I'll send for drivers," Shanda said. "The kinless hire out, but it will be better if your people are with a Lordsman. Fewer problems—I know. Roni, your cousin Sandry and his friends. Do you think they'd like to do this?"

"Sandry?" Whandall asked.

"We know a Sandry," Green Stone said. "Master Peacevoice Waterman brought him. To assist us. Said he was a clerk."

Shanda smiled thinly. "I hope you're not angry?"

Whandall grinned. "I'd guessed he was more than a clerk," he said. "What of the others? Will they be drivers?"

"Sandry will," Roni said. "I'm not sure about all the others."

"We'll send several," Shanda said. "Whandall can choose those he likes best. I'll have them here in the morning. And I'll speak to Master Peacevoice Waterman about deceptions."

And what will you say to him? "Be more clever next time?" "Thank you. Now, who sells me tar?"

"Us," Shanda said. "The Black Pit belongs to the Lords. A kinless family takes care of that for us. Roni, see to that, please. Find out how many jars Whandall will want, and arrange for them to be filled and sealed and brought here. It's time you learned some of that aspect of city management, I think."

"It's a man's job, Mother."

"Of course it is, but if women don't understand these things, how can we make sure the men do them right?" She grinned at Whandall, the old Shanda again for an instant. "I'm sure our merchant prince understands," she said.

"And if I don't, Willow will explain. My wife," he said, in case she'd missed it earlier. Both of us married, with children. Right? Right.

He was ready for bed when Morth came in. "I walked up Observation Hill," he said. "I used to go there a lot. Those ruins at the top, that was an old kinless fort. I can see the ocean from there, way off. I couldn't *see* anything, but with my talisman I perceived the elemental."

"Talisman. Another doll?"

"Yes. It won't last long. Whandall, the elemental perceived *me*. I should go out to look for myself. Sea Cliffs."

"Take a fast chariot. I'll have chariots tomorrow."

CHAPTER
75

Two hours after daybreak, seven chariots clattered into Peacegiven Square and drew up in a line in front of the Lordsman camp. An earnest young driver in Lordsman armor stood beside each one. One was Sandry, no longer wearing a clerk's cap. The horses were big grays, matched pairs at each chariot. They were well groomed and well fed. The chariots would hold two adults. In each chariot was a leather sheath holding a long thrusting spear and two shorter throwing spears ready to hand between driver and passenger.

They were smaller than Whandall remembered. He'd imagined Lords' chariots big enough to hold half a dozen men. They looked that big coming at you, but of course that was silly. Not even the big Lord's horses could pull such a load.

Master Peacevoice Waterman walked up and down the line examining each horse and driver. He muttered something and one of the drivers flicked dust off his gleaming armor. Another tightened the harness of his horse. When Waterman was satisfied, he strode briskly to Whandall's tent. "Chariots and drivers waiting inspection, sir!"

Morth and Whandall crossed the square to the waiting line. Whandall moved closer to Waterman. "I'm not used to chariots," he confided.

"Not surprised at that," Waterman said. "Trick is to spread your feet out, brace one against the sidework. There's a brace built into the floor to wedge your other foot against. Bend your knees so there's some spring in them; otherwise, you'll bounce right out when you hit a bump. Chariots are fast, but they tire the horses fast too."

"Are these horses tired?" Morth asked.

"Not too bad, sir; they led these in at first light, no load. The horses that pulled the chariots here from Lord's Town are resting up. They'll all be fresh come tomorrow morning."

"Good. Who's the best driver?"

"For what purpose, sir?"

Morth considered.

Finding the right questions wasn't easy here. "Speed. Distance," Whandall said. "We might have to cross most of the city. Maybe fighting."

"Best *fighting* driver would be young Heroul there."

Whandall regarded the charioteer. Young, clear eyed. Armor polished. He stood impatiently. "Is he reliable?"

"Depends on what for," Waterman said. "He'll take orders just fine. And he's got the fastest horses in the corps."

"Who for just speed and distance and a passenger who can't fight?"

"That's not Heroul. He likes to *win,*" Waterman said. "You can depend on young Sandry there. Lord Samorty's grandson, he is, and best officer cadet in the corps."

"Lord Rabblie's son?"

Waterman looked at him oddly. "Reckon they called Lord Rabilard something like that when he was a lad. Yes, sir, that's his father."

And the Lords still talk about family to strangers. Brag, even. Not like Lordkin. Like *us.*

"He'll be steady, then?"

"I'd trust him," Waterman said. "You needn't tell him I said that. Cadet's head doesn't need more swelling."

"Thanks. You won't need to introduce us."

"Reckon I won't, sir," Waterman said.

"Morth, you take Sandry, then—"

"No, I want speed," Morth said. "You said that one is fastest?"

"Yes, sir."

"I'll take Heroul. And put some handhold lashings in that chariot. If you don't know how, I do. I had one of these in Atlantis."

Whandall stood uncertainly in Sandry's chariot. It was hard enough keeping his footing on streets. The potholes rattled him around inside this bucket on wheels. It would be a lot harder going across country. If Sandry noticed Whandall having difficulty keeping his footing, he didn't say anything about it.

"Can you carry an old man in one of these?" Whandall asked.

Sandry nodded. He needed all his attention to avoid a young Lord-kin who had darted into the street. Then he answered. "Yes, Wagonmaster. We can strap a chair where you're standing, strap a man into the chair. But you're doing fine." *For a beginner,* he didn't add.

"Not me," Whandall said. "Morth."

"He didn't seem that old."

"He can get older fast."

"Oh. Aunt Shanda says she's known you a long time," Sandry said.

"Yes, more than thirty years." He looked at Sandry and made a decision. "Did you ever know of a servant girl named Dream-Lotus? Kinless, from the Ropewalk area."

"No, but I can ask," Sandry said. "Is it important?"

"Not very. I'd just like to know. Turn right just ahead there."

The streets were in worse repair, and there were more burned buildings than Whandall remembered. "Now left." Ahead lay the Serpent's Walk meetinghouse. Curse, it had a roof now! And a new fence. Oversize cactus plants grew against the fence. Two kinless were raking the yard, although it didn't appear to need raking. *Neat,* Whandall thought. *Wanshig always was neat after he came back from the sea.*

The Placehold looked neat too. In Whandall's time there was a half-ruined house down the block. That was gone, its lot planted with what looked like cabbages tended by kinless, and a small cottage stood behind the cabbage patch.

Whandall pointed to the front door of the Placehold. "Stop just there and wait for me. You won't be allowed inside."

Sandry nodded. He looked glad of the armor he wore. "Sure you'll be welcome?"

"No," Whandall said.

"What's the best way out of here?" Sandry asked.

Whandall chuckled. "Straight ahead, left at the end of the block. And stay in the middle of the street."

"You know it."

Boys lounged at the doorway. That hadn't changed. "Tell Lord Wanshig that Whandall wishes to speak with him." He lowered his voice so that Sandry wouldn't be able to hear. "Whandall Placehold."

Two of the boys ran inside. Another stayed in the door staring at Whandall's tattoo.

The doorway stood invitingly open. Whandall grinned to himself. At least one, probably several armed Lordkin adults would be in there, one behind the door waiting for anyone to come in uninvited—

A girl about fifteen came to the door. She wore a bright dress, too fancy for housework. "Be welcome, Whandall," she said, loud enough that everyone near would hear.

"Thank you—"

"I'm Firegift, Uncle Whandall. My mother is Wess."

And calling me Uncle says I'm accepted as one of the men of the Placehold, not that she's Wanshig's daughter, Whandall thought. She could be, but she won't claim that. Just her mother. The Lordkin ways were coming back to him, but as a half-remembered dream.

"Lord Wanshig is waiting upstairs."

Wanshig sat at one end of the big meeting hall. It seemed full of people, none Whandall could recognize. Except Wess. She stood in the doorway of the corner room. The room that was his, with her, for a while, when Whandall Placehold was the eldest man in the Placehold. A lifetime ago.

She was still pretty. Not as pretty as Willow, but to Whandall no woman ever had been. But Wess was a fine woman still! Firegift went to stand by her mother. They looked more alike, side by side, than they had when they were apart.

"Hail, brother," Wanshig said.

"Lord Wanshig."

Wanshig laughed hard. Then he got up and came to Whandall, slapped hands, hugged him in a wiry embrace that showed Wanshig hadn't lost his strength. Neither had Whandall, and they stood half embracing and half testing for a minute.

"Been a long time," Wanshig said.

"That it has. You've come up in the world."

Wanshig looked at the ornate knife Whandall wore. "So have you."

"That's nothing," Whandall said. He took off the knife and sheath, revealing a plainer and more functional blade underneath. "A present," Whandall said, and held out the ornately decorated knife. "Among others. I'm rich, brother."

"That's nice—"

"I can make the Placehold rich," Whandall said. "I'll need help doing it. Actually, I'll need Placehold and Serpent's Walk together."

"After lunch you'll tell me," Wanshig said. He gestured, dismissing the men and women who had crowded around. "You'll all meet Whandall later," he said. "Give me time to talk with my brother."

Brother. We had the same mother. Not necessarily the same father, and in our case certainly not the same. Lordkin!

The others went away or settled in corners of the big room.

"We'll eat in here," Wanshig said. He led Whandall into the big corner room. A table had been set up, and Firegift was bringing food and tea. "You'll remember Wess. She's my lady now. First lady of the Placehold," Wanshig said.

Whandall didn't say anything.

"What? Ah. That's right; you'll remember Elriss," Wanshig said.

"And Mother."

Wanshig nodded. "Dead, brother. Dead together, with Shastern. Fifteen years ago—"

"Sixteen," Wess said. "Firegift is fifteen."

"Sixteen years ago. The Burning started by Tarnisos."

"Tarnisos killed our family?"

"No, he started the Burning. It was a Mother's Day; the women had gone to Peacegiven Square. The Lords still gave Mother's Day presents there. You remember?"

"Yes."

"Shastern went with them. They had collected the gifts, were coming back, when the Burning started." Wanshig shook his head. "We went looking for them. Found them dead, two Bull Pizzles dead with them. Everything they had was gathered, of course. Later Pelzed and Freethspat went looking for Pizzles to settle the score, but the Pizzles claimed their people were killed helping Shastern. Could have been, even. Could have been."

"Who did they say?" Whandall demanded.

Wanshig's expression was bleak. "You think you'll get even, now, after sixteen years when you weren't here, little brother? You think I haven't tried?"

"Sorry. Of course you did."

Wanshig nodded grimly.

"What happened to Freethspat?"

"He tried too. Mother was his woman; he was really close to her. Closer than I was to Elriss by then, I think. He went looking one day. Never came back."

"And Wanshig became eldest in the Placehold," Wess said. And didn't say that Firegift was born a few months later, but that was clear enough.

"So. How can we help you, little brother?" Wanshig asked.

"Two ways, if you can work with me," Whandall said.

"It's possible," Wanshig admitted. "What two ways?"

"First, burn out the Wolverines."

"That's hard, little brother. Hard. You know who they are?"

"I hope I do. I've got no quarrel with the Wolverines. But Alferth says they're the Toronexti. I have reasons to think he's right."

"So do I," Wanshig said. "And the Toronexti work for the Lords." He looked thoughtful. "And you? You have a chariot and a Lordsman driver. Have the *Lords* told you you can burn out the Toronexti?"

"Pretty close," Whandall said. "They won't help, but if it happens they'll be happy enough to take credit. There won't be a blood war. If there's a blood price, I can give it back to you."

"I need to think on this. What's your other task?"

"Morth of Atlantis needs help. We'll explain later. But it needs reliable people. He needs a truce with Sea Cliffs, at least to take a chariot there. And Wanshig, I can use some help outside, out of Tep's Town, if there's anyone who wants to go."

Wanshig stared at him. "Out?"

"There's a whole world out there."

"Twenty years ago I'd have come with you," he said. "Not now, and I need all the men I have, in Placehold and in Serpent's Walk. These are hard times, little brother."

"We like it here," Wess said possessively. "But I have a son, Shastern." She nodded at Whandall's look. "Named for your younger brother. He's a wild boy. I don't think he'll live long here. Take him with you."

"How old?"

"Ten," Wess said.

"He can come. But Wess, if he comes with us, he won't be a Lordkin anymore. He'll learn different ways. I doubt he can ever come back."

"You did," Wess said.

"Whandall, there are some who'd like adventure," Wanshig said. He sighed. "And I'm still Lordkin, and they'll never let me go to sea again. Unless you own ships, little brother?"

"That's not the route I took. Let me show you, big brother. Did you learn maps while you were sailing?"

"Maps? We knew about maps. Never saw them. They were locked up in the captain's cabin."

"The idea is to make a picture of where you are and where you want to be and things you see on the way. Landmarks." Whandall began drawing on the table. Tep's Town as a little black blotch, Firewoods in dried chili seeds, the Hemp Road in charcoal. Wess watched the mess being made, looked at Wanshig, and decided not to interfere.

"This is where we went, me and a wagon with children hidden like wine. Wildest battle of my life, *here.* My tattoo lights up when I kill, out there where there's still magic." By First Pines, he'd run out of room. "I have to draw it smaller."

"So that's how it works."

"May I teach this? In the courtyard? It would be something to give back," Whandall said. Anyone who worked the caravans would have to learn maps eventually. Who could he take? Best find out who had the knack! Best find out—

"Big brother, do you remember when I tried to teach you about knives?"

Wanshig grimaced. "Yes."

"May I try again? Teach them all? Tomorrow. Maps today."

Wanshig looked into his face.

"You're older and smarter. I'm a better teacher. Line up your best knife fighters. Watch me. Watch them. This time you'll get it."

"You meant it."

Whandall made no answer.

"Yes. I want to watch that," Wanshig said. "We'll listen to your wizard and I'll send a gift to Sea Cliffs. Give me a day or so to get the word out—Whandall of Serpent's Walk is back and is welcome at the Placehold. Your woman too, of course."

"She's not here." Whandall thought of Willow coming into a Lordkin castle. "She's outside."

They returned to Peacegiven Square to find Morth raving.

"He's a madman!" Morth shouted. He pointed to Heroul, who stood grinning on his chariot. It looked odd with no horse hitched to it. Then Morth turned jubilant. "But it's *there!*"

"The wave."

"Heroul drove me out to Sea Cliffs. The wave stood up and came at us, way too low, of course. Hit the cliff hard enough to shake our shoes! Then this maniac drove us right down into the lowlands!"

"Heroul, are you all right?" Sandry asked.

The young charioteer's grin was wide. "It was wonderful!" he burbled. "The water just humped itself and came right at us! Real magic! Nothing like Qirinty's dancing cups—"

"And this madman *toyed* with it!" Morth said. "He stayed just ahead of it, all the way—"

"—along Dead Seal Flats. It slowed when it started up the ridge," Heroul said. "I could see it was slowing, and I didn't want to founder the horses! So *I* slowed, and it came on almost to the top. Then it slumped and ran back down toward the ocean. Ran like water, I mean, not fled."

"You were teasing it!"

"Maybe a little, sir. And we still exhausted the horses." Heroul waved to indicate two chariot horses being groomed by some of Waterman's men. "I'll get new ones for tomorrow, let these rest up a day."

"Not for me, you won't, you maniac!" Morth said.

Whandall grinned. "Younglord Heroul can drive me tomorrow," he said. "Sandry, if you please, shepherd this ancient wizard around the city."

"Certainly, sir."

Morth gave them a sour look. "That water sprite has chased me half my life, and today was as close as it ever came to catching me."

"But it didn't," Heroul said. "Sir."

PART FOUR
Heroes and Myths

CHAPTER
76

At dawn the next morning a half dozen kinless came to Peacegiven Square and began work on the ruins of an adobe house at one corner. Whandall remembered the house as belonging to a Bull Pizzle Lordkin. Or was it Flower Market? But the big Lordkin who came with the kinless wore a serpent from left eye to left hand.

In an hour they had cleared out the front yard and set up a cook fire. In another they had set out tables and chairs and hung up a sign painted with a cup and roasted bird's leg. A tea shop, at Peacegiven Square. Another sign went up: a serpent, but this was set at the edge of the lot, right at the corner. The sign in front of the shop bore a palmetto fan to indicate peace, all welcome.

Pelzed had dreamed of taking another side of Peacegiven Square, but he had never dared. Of course now it wasn't worth as much. . . .

Whandall went over to inspect. Sandry—Younglord Sandry—followed. The kinless waitress was in her thirties, well dressed, elaborately polite. "Yes, Lords. Welcome."

Whandall lifted his hand in greeting. It was a useful gesture, a way to be polite without losing status. The big Serpent's Walk Lordkin came out of the house. He was young and hadn't had the tattoo long. "Lagdret," he said. "You'll be Whandall. Welcome." He pointed to the back of the house. "I'll be living here until the Bakers here get the house next door fitted up. Lord Wanshig says if you need me, call." He went back into the shop without waiting to be introduced to Sandry.

"Polite," Whandall said.

Sandry looked the question.

"He hasn't anything to say to you, and he won't take up your time. He came out here to tell me only because Wanshig asked him to. His job—never say *job;* it's just what he's agreed to do—is to protect this place. What he gets out of it is a new house kept up by the kinless he protects." Whandall smiled thinly. "Probably his first house; now he can attract a woman of his own."

"I should learn more about Lordkin," Sandry said.

Whandall smiled. "Our custom, it is, to swap information and stories."

"Ah."

"I never knew much about Lords," Whandall said. "No more than I could learn watching from a distance."

"Sometimes you were closer," Sandry said. "What do you want to know?"

"There are bandits on the Hemp Road. Sometimes enough of them get together to set up a town and collect tolls. Now, all towns collect tolls, one way or another, but most of them give something back. Keep the roads up, provide dinners, drive away gatherers, keep a good market square open. Bandit towns just take. When that happens, all the wagon trains get together and go burn them out.

"Sandry, your Aunt Shanda wants us to bring wagon trade into Tep's Town."

"We all do."

"So tell me about the Toronexti."

Sandry looked surprised. "I distinctly remember Lord Quintana telling Waterman to talk to you about the Toronexti."

"Maybe he didn't tell me enough."

"They have a charter," Sandry said. "Promises made over the years. Some of them were bad promises, stupid promises, but they've kept the decrees, every one of them, and if we try to do anything about them they can produce a promise, signed and sealed, saying we can't do that."

"Lords are big on keeping promises?"

"Formal, written, signed, and sealed? Of course."

"Did you promise to help them?"

"Against all outside enemies," Sandry said.

"Not against Lordkin?"

"No! They'd never ask. At least they never have, and if they did now, well, it would take three full meetings of all the Lords even to consider extending the Toronexti charter. But it wouldn't happen. The charter says *they* protect *us* against revolt."

Whandall sipped tea. It was good, root tea, not hemp. The shop wanted three shells a cup, a high price, but prices always went up when the wagon train was in town. "Sandry, are you afraid of Master Peacevoice Waterman?"

"Wouldn't you be?"

"Well, maybe, but by that light I should be afraid of Greathand the blacksmith," Whandall said. "But Waterman's a Lordsman and you're a Lord."

"Younglord," Sandry corrected. "Apprentice, if you like to think of it that way. Waterman would take my orders, if I were dumb enough to talk back to him. Then it would get back to my father. Wagonmaster, you tell your blacksmith what to make, but you don't tell him how to make it."

"I wouldn't know how."

"And I wouldn't know how to train men."

"Or get them to fight," Whandall said.

"That part's easy. It's called leadership," Sandry said, and blushed a little. "Getting them to fight together, to do things all of them at once, not one at a time, that's hard."

Like learning knife fighting, Whandall thought. *But if you learn one thing at a time, you can put it all together.* He thought about battles they'd had with bandits. Kettle Belly had taught him to get as many men together as you can, make them stay together and fight together. Twenty on three always won, and usually with none of the twenty getting hurt.

And the Lords knew all that, and the Lordkin didn't, and—

"So what shall we do today?" Sandry asked.

"I'll send you with Morth, but hold up a breath or two." Whandall considered. "You can't tell me how to fight the Toronexti." He got a confirming nod. "But what can you tell me about dealing with the Wolverines under Granite Knob?"

Sandry smiled. "I asked about that after last night. Fights between Lordkin are not my concern. I won't help you fight them, but I can tell you anything you want to know about Wolverines."

And Whandall was sure, now. The Toronexti were the Wolverines. But what good did it do to know that?

It was known that he intended to take a few people out of Serpent's Walk, out of Tep's Town. Some were willing to help him choose.

Several Lordkin tried to extract promises from him. Take my

nephew, he doesn't fit in . . . my daughter, she's sleeping with the wrong men . . . my son, he's murdered someone powerful . . . my brother, he keeps getting beaten up. Whandall didn't promise. Nobody can force you to buy without actually drawing knife . . . and that happened only once.

Fubgire was one of Wanshig's guards, in his late twenties, brawny and agile. Whandall retreated from the room where Fubgire confronted him, into the courtyard, and there he turned it into a knife fighting lesson.

Kinless and Lordkin came to him, driven by distaste for the ways of the Burning City. He would make an offer to a few of these. He set some of the kinless to working on maps.

Yesterday the courtyard had been covered with maps sketched in sawdust. Today Morth and Wanshig and a few visitors from other turf were making maps inside.

Lured by the fight with Fubgire or by Wanshig's wonderful new knife or by rumor and curiosity, nearly forty men waited at dawn to be trained in knife fighting by Whandall Placehold. Too many by far, of course. One was Fubgire, older than most of these, but bandaged and determined to learn from his mistakes. Try him on maps too?

Whandall began to teach. More drifted up, until there were sixty in the Placehold courtyard.

Many felt that they already knew how to fight, that no outsider had anything to teach them. They spoke this truth, or it showed in their sneers. They began to drift away.

Some stuck to it. Some stayed to laugh at the rest, and they had a point. That was why he had practiced in secret, because it did look funny. When Wanshig finally emerged around noon, the numbers were down to thirty.

The essence of knife training, as Whandall taught it, was to practice each of several moves separately until the mind turned to jelly. Whandall looked for those who could stick to it for an hour, perfecting one move, and move on to the next, and end the day without screaming in anyone's face.

To them, and to those who could work with maps and still not scream in anyone's face, he would make an offer.

There were too many. He had no confidence in most of them. The cursed trouble was that you could not set tests for a Lordkin, because he wouldn't put up with it. You learned what a Lordkin was made of by watching him, sometimes for years.

Whandall didn't have years.

* * *

His bed was waiting, but so was Morth. The wizard asked, "How are you feeling?"

"Worn out. I've been training Lordkin in knife fighting. How would you feel? Want some tea?"

"Yes, please. Whandall, do these Lordkin make you angry? You've been away a long time."

"Embarrassed. I used to *be* them. I kept my temper all day."

"I expected you to lose your temper with the Toronexti."

"Morth, it's a dance. They're clumsy at bargaining. That bottle trick was fun."

"Has anything made you angry lately?"

"Is this about anger, Morth?"

"Yes."

Whandall considered. "Not angry. Shocked. This . . . wilderness was Peacegiven Square. It wasn't just the place where our mothers gathered what our families needed to live. It was . . . order. Order where we lived, like the houses in the Lordshills."

"You're shocked but not angry."

"Well, I—"

"I wasn't asking. Whandall, Yangin-Atep hasn't even looked at you these three days, not a flicker, I can *tell,* and that's why. You don't get angry. If I threw a calming spell at you, I'd have to tell you about it later. But can you keep it up?"

"Merchants don't get angry, Morth. Good merchants don't even fake it."

"Then . . . it could work. Here's what I need."

Whandall listened. Presently he asked, "Why?"

And presently he asked, "Why should I?"

"Oh, make up your own cursed motives. What has a water elemental ever done for you?"

"It gave me water to drink when I was a boy."

"I thought that was me, but all right. Yangin-Atep?"

"Burned . . . burned my family. Yes, I see. Morth, this is the craziest idea I've ever heard, even from you, but I . . . I think I see how to use this. I mean, for the caravan. For my family. For Feathersnake. If you'll do it *my* way."

"Yes?" And Morth listened.

The next day's mapmaking went on in the dining hall behind locked doors. Whandall spent some time in the courtyard supervising knife fighters at their practice, and some time with the map.

The Gulls at Sea Cliffs hadn't seen Morth dancing on the cliff above them. They knew only that a tremendous wave stood up and smashed four houses before it washed against the cliff. Three housed kinless, but in the biggest house three or four Lordkin lived in every room. Two were killed. Nine were homeless.

Now came word from Wanshig of Serpent's Walk. Their people were drowned, their stronghold smashed and washed away, by a water demon. Wanshig's runners told the Gulls what had hurt them, and who could kill it, and what was needed.

The sprite's route inland would begin there.

"So we hold Sea Cliffs, and they brought in those that hold Dead Seal Flats. Now, you want to put people all along here," Wanshig said. "If you don't want them attacked, nobody had better know what you're giving them, and we still need truce for the whole length. This is Ogre turf here. They're crazy. We can't get truce and we couldn't trust it. Why not go around?"

"We'd never get a moving wave up here. Too high."

"Lord Wanshig?" That was Artcher, one of Wanshig's entourage, likely a nephew. He'd shown some skill with maps. Now he asked, "What if we ran the line along here? It's Long Avenue. The road runs this way because deer followed the low route, and it's Weasel turf from here all the way to here. They keep their truce too."

"They take cursed big gifts to make truce!"

"I think I hear my secret name," Whandall said. An ornate knife, some glass jewelry, honey candy, and half their route was secured right there.

As they nailed down the route, Wanshig sent out runners. The blades Whandall had brought for Lords were all going to Lordkin, but that was all right. The Lords wanted him much more than he had expected.

"That's a nice low run. Dark Man's Cup?"

"Bull Pizzles," Wanshig said.

"Don't tell me that!"

"Freethspat was good, little brother, but he didn't keep other people's promises. It's a garbage dump again too. Look, Dark Man's Cup is perfect if those Pizzles will trust me not to snatch it back."

"Offer to scour it clean for two coils of hemp. Say we've got a wizard. If they've heard the rumors, they'll know it's true. Say they can pay on delivery."

Runners began flowing in with answers. Long Avenue was under truce. Bull Pizzles would deal if Serpent's Walk would wait half a year for the hemp. Now send a credible messenger to get the kinless out of

Dark Man's Cup. No details could be given, as they might leak, but *get out!*

Dirty Birds were easy, still allies after all these years.

Silly Rabbits would not make truce. They *had* to have that stretch. Send another offer, but count on sending guards to protect Whandall's chosen.

That evening Whandall gathered his chosen in the banquet room, now map room. He spoke briefly, and he passed out bottles.

"Anyone who wants to leave Tep's Town: here is a cold iron-glazed bottle. Don't open it tonight!"

Knife training and mapmaking gave him men who could keep their temper. Millers and Ropewalkers he gave special consideration. This woman could read. This one cooked a stew from random gatherings. Green Stone watched children pulling weeds on the Placehold roof garden, and chose three. Freethspat's boy, Whandall's last half brother aged thirty, was worth a look. He'd rejected the maps and the knife practice, but he got a bottle.

Any of his chosen might take a mate when they left.

None were told what would be done. Yangin-Atep might take anyone's mind.

Back in Peacegiven Square, Whandall went to Morth's quarters to choose his running gear. "Pick something colorful, something distinctive. Don't you have anything that isn't gray or black, Morth?"

"I've seen your motley crew. None of them dress like any other! Those Flower Market Lordkin make Seshmarls look diffident! And you want distinctive?"

Whandall sighed. "Sandry, doesn't your cousin Roni know a seamstress?"

"Likely enough, sir."

"Green Stone, write. 'Roni, Morth must have a wizard's robe by *tomorrow night*. Something anyone can see from a mountaintop on a cloudy day. Please carry my word to your seamstress. This is her price.'" Whandall chose a swath of the finest cloth in the caravan, lavender with highlights in it, then sheets of bright green and bright gold. "And this for Morth."

CHAPTER
77

The bottles had been given out the previous evening. This day was given to more knifeplay and mapmaking. After dinner all gathered to be given their final instructions.

Morth wore robes in blazing green patched with huge golden stars. Whandall stared. The cursed robe was perfect, just perfect. From a mountaintop on a cloudy day. He'd said that. It would be bad to laugh, but . . . "Morth, you *really* look like a *wizard,* Morth."

"Oh, shut up!" Morth hurled the pointed cap at the floor. "How was that supposed to *stay* on? Did you think—"

"This is Morth!" Whandall bellowed, and waved grandly. *"Look at him! Know him when you see him again!"* There was laughter, none of it muffled. These were Lordkin. "Good. Morth, now I need you to ferret out every bottle that has been opened."

Laughter died as Morth moved among the giggling horde and pointed, pointed. Wanshig's musclemen moved after him and saw to it that certain men and women went away.

"I only had it open for an instant!"

Morth took the stopper off. "Nothing. Refined. Keep it, but go."

Another complained. Morth pulled the stopper out and back fast. "Still some power left. How long did you have this open?"

"Long enough for Tarcress to finish cooking sand dabs. Just time to pour a bit out, to think that that was gold and . . . put it back."

"Keep your place." Morth opened another bottle. "No gold. Fool! Keep the bottle and get out."

"Gathered by my brother!"

"Fool!"

Wanshig asked above the noise, "You're sure? They keep the bottles?"

"If they go quietly. Fifteen of my heroes are clean missing, bottle and all, but these came," Whandall said.

"I count eleven missing."

Morth tapped five in a clump of six. The sixth boy watched them depart. Whandall asked him, "What happened?"

"We all live in a room at the Placehold. Last night Flaide opened his bottle and poured out a handful of gold. He told the rest of us."

"Why didn't you open yours?"

Silence.

"Good. Your name? Sadesp, were you all six stationed next to each other? Curse. Whandall, all of these other bottles stayed closed."

"Hold up, Morth. I don't know some of these people." Fifteen gone but four replaced by strangers. The woman was looking at him. "Did I give you that bottle?"

Pride and terror. "No, Feathersnake. I'm taking Leathersmith Miller's place."

"Where is he?"

"Smitty slept beside me last night. I'm Sapphire Carpenter, and I know more about love than any woman in the inner city."

Wanshig said, "She speaks the truth. Sapphire, you're *leaving*?"

"Morth, look her over."

"She's clean. No diseases, no curses. A few fleas. She's left the bottle stopped. Sapphire, can you throw?"

"Yes. Smitty showed me his place. I have his map."

She'd kept the bottle unopened for several hours.

"Take your place," Morth said. "And, Sapphire, if you think you know every pleasure that may pass between a man and a woman, we should talk."

Three more carried black bottles Whandall hadn't given them. Three men had backed out, or gotten high or drunk, or—face it— been killed for their places. Too late to tell. Whandall sent one away, with a gold nugget and no bottle, because he didn't like his look. He would risk the others.

He nodded to Wanshig. Wanshig unbarred a door and they trooped in. "Watch your step," Whandall called, then followed with Green Stone.

They had been all day working on this map, using charcoal and props.

Whandall said, "Green Stone, take over." The boy had been familiar with the general plan for months. He believed, where Whandall didn't quite. And—Whandall should not fully concern himself. A curious fire god might still look into Whandall's mind.

Traders were trained to project their voices above rushing rivers, storms, bandit raids. Green Stone used his caravan voice. "You're the chosen. In your lives you have seen just enough magic to know that it's real. You are going to witness and be part of the most powerful wizardry this city has ever seen. Those who stay behind will never see the like again. Play your part and you will leave Tep's Town and see sights you've not yet had the wit to dream.

"Those of you who understand maps will recognize what's going on here. This," Wanshig's gold saltbox, gathered long ago, long emptied, "is the Placehold. Here, the Black Pit"—a dark pool on the floor, ancient blood. They'd started their map there. "Here, the Lordshills. Forest. Deerpiss and the Wedge, and the Toronexti here"—a brass coin.

"These jagged lines way out here are shoreline, here at Sea Cliffs, here at Good Hand Harbor. We got some help on these from a Water Devil. We don't know what's between them. More shore.

"Off beyond Sea Cliffs is ocean and a water elemental. Morth of Atlantis can tell you more about it. It's been trying to kill Morth since Atlantis sank.

"Morth intends to kill it. That has never been done before.

"The elemental will show itself as a mountain of water. It will chase Morth. Morth—see these paired lines? One red, one green, all the way across the map? Morth will follow the green line from Sea Cliffs across Dead Seal Flats, uphill here, down along Long Avenue to Dark Man's Cup—see? And on inland. The wave will follow the lowlands. We'll be strung out all along the red line, above it all, watching.

"We want to throw bottles ahead of the wave. When Morth is past, take the stopper out and throw the black bottle. Throw it at something hard, like a rock! It has to break!" Take the stopper out *or* break it—both would work—but these were Lordkin; they might forget.

"Yangin-Atep takes the magic, all in an instant, if they break too soon. You—Sintothok?—you opened your bottle, but not long enough for Yangin-Atep to gather all the manna in the gold. But break it just in front of the wave, the elemental will take it.

"And that's the point of all this. The wave will sink and flow back to the ocean if we don't give it the power to go on. The wild magic will keep it moving until it gets *here. Here* at the Black Pit is where Morth will trap it, with no manna to move it and no way to get more, and here Morth will kill it.

"Afterward, gather at Peacegiven Square. . . . Questions?"

Lordkin don't raise their hands and wait. They bellow. Green Stone pointed and said, "Hey! Hey! You."

"I've seen waves. They're fast. Your wizard is *nuts.*"

"Morth can outrun lightning. I've seen it. You will too. If you miss it you'll regret it the rest of your life. *You—*"

"You want to move the wave *uphill?*"

"Here and here we'll have the wave going uphill, yes. I'll bunch you up a little there, because we'll *really* need the gold."

And because some of these won't throw, Whandall thought, *but you can't tell them that some of them can't be trusted.* "Corntham? What?"

"How do you kill a water elemental?"

Morth said, "That's the tricky part."

Green Stone said, "Morth has made gifts to us for our part in this. Our gifts to you will be freedom from Tep's Town, just as you've been promised. You'll have a place in the caravans on the Hemp Road, or you may find better lives than that. Whandall Placehold was one of you. What he is now brought him back as greater than a Lord. My father." Green Stone watched them flinch at that word, and he grinned.

CHAPTER
78

Some of the bottle throwers, those with the most distant posts, must be sent off that night in a protected band. Sea Cliffs would house them.

The rest dossed down in the Placehold for what remained of the night. The caravan would have to take care of itself. Whandall and Green Stone needed their sleep.

The sale at Peacegiven Square would have nearly emptied out the kinless quarters. Lordkin who knew nothing of Morth's plan wouldn't be interfering with Morth's route. They'd be burgling empty houses while the kinless were away, or trying to profit from the fair . . . or so Whandall hoped.

Morth and Whandall boarded their chariots behind Sandry and Heroul.

Wanshig hadn't caught the hang of mapping, and at his age, no wonder. Two sisters' sons had. They rode Wanshig's chariot, placing bottle throwers from Dark Man's Cup southeast to the Black Pit.

Whandall moved west.

His chosen were not standing beside friends to hold them steady. Each could just see the next to either side, not too far for a voice to carry. Except . . . that yawning gap. Five of six boys gone, and Sadesp standing alone. Whandall slowed to space them more regularly.

Now Morth was far ahead. His chariot slashed through the weeds that lined Dark Man's Cup, while Whandall and Heroul followed him along the ridge. Whandall couldn't see deep enough into the chaparral to pick out kinless houses or the warrens of the hemp growers. They'd been warned. They'd got out, or they hadn't.

The beach was in sight. Sandry stopped his chariot on the ridge above Dead Seal Flats, and Morth got out and went on.

The last runner, a woman of Sea Cliffs, had slowed to a walk and was checking her map to find her place. Her man had already taken his. Whandall had Heroul pull up between them. He walked to the edge.

He would have driven on to the bluff above Sea Cliffs Beach. He'd see it all from there. From here, Morth was already out of sight. But Whandall's chariot would need the head start, if what he remembered was no hallucination.

A wave rose up and rolled forward, crested in white, climbing as it came. Where was Morth? Already gone?

There, a green and gold dot, unmistakable—*look* at that man *move!* The wave came after him too slowly, losing ground, but higher every second. *Throw,* Whandall thought, but he wouldn't speak. This was how he would know his own, if they threw or if they didn't.

Whandall jumped aboard. "Go. Go!"

Heroul used the reins. Horse, then chariot lurched into motion.

Delirious laughter rose above the wave's roar, and Whandall wondered why the sound was so delayed when Morth was halfway to the first rise.

The woman threw. Her man threw too. Bottles arced down and shattered, and a mountain of water rolled past, raising thunder and spume just below Whandall's whirling wheels.

The big horse looked terrified. Heroul was elated. The wave so far down was no threat to them. Morth was nearly out of sight, disappearing in chaparral, where Dead Seal Flats rose uphill.

Morth stopped as if he'd hit a wall.

The wave rolled on. Whandall rolled past an elderly kinless man curled up with his hands over his ears, crying, bottle abandoned. Wrinin of Flower Market hurled her bottle; it bounced unbroken and rolled but left a trail of yellow gold. Sapphire Carpenter waited until she was in his full view, then threw beautifully; the bottle smashed just under the wave.

Morth was in a tottering run, and the wave was closing. Bald scalp, thin white fringe. Teeth showed in a snarl of effort as he turned back, just for an instant, and grinned at the showers of gold and glass splinters. And the wave rose to hide him, but Sandry was waiting with the chariot and was helping Morth to board.

Now the wave was moving uphill, losing water, losing mass. Whandall's chariot was pulling ahead of it. Below, the wizard and Sandry came back into view. The Lord's son drove like White Lightning twisting a gob of molten glass, carefully, aware of danger, not hurrying, doing his job.

Swabott's mother was first lady of Flower Market. They'd *needed* truce with Flower Market to post their bottle throwers. Whandall had prepped him. Swabott knelt with bottle in hand, the stopper already out, as the wave came toward him.

Even from far away, Whandall could see him shaking with terror. When he stood to throw, the bottle jittered in his hand and gold showered all about him. The wave was ahead of Whandall here . . . and now it was passing Swabott, and he hadn't thrown.

He turned toward Whandall, and a serene joy was in his face. He wasn't shaking at all. He took it all in; his smile widened to a manic grin. . . .

Before Whandall could twitch, Swabott was running alongside Whandall's horse! The horse was running full out, but when Swabott swung onto its back the horse screamed and surged faster. Swabott dug his heels into its sides and yelled. Whandall was ready to jab a spear into him when he threw.

The bottle dropped neatly in front of the wave and smashed.

Whandall turned the spear around and rapped Swabott smartly on the back of his head. "Get off my chariot!" Swabott leaped from the horse, rolled, and was on his feet and running, laughing like a madman. Gold fever . . . and he'd earned his place.

The low path turned here and became Dark Man's Cup.

Padanchi the Lop still had one good arm. His bottle shattered ahead of the wave. Then the wave turned to follow Morth's chariot, and the foamy crest slapped Padanchi off the cliff.

Kencchi of the Long Avenue froze at the sight. He didn't hear his woman screaming at him to throw. Nor did Whandall; he only saw her wide mouth, straining throat. But when the time came, she threw. Kencchi didn't.

Decide later.

Morth's properly terrified horse was pulling him nicely through Dark Man's Cup, following its own trail of smashed vegetation. The wave rolled on, no less monstrous, feeding on the wild magic in the smashed bottles.

Here several of his chosen were missing . . . the wave began to slump . . . and there was fighting ahead.

Four of Whandall's bottle throwers had managed to reach each other and were fighting back to back against six men of the North Quarter. North Quarter had broken truce! Whandall signaled Heroul, who pulled toward the ring of Lordkin around the four survivors.

They saw him coming. Running wouldn't help; his first target braced himself to duck aside. Whandall outguessed him and punched his blade deep into the man's torso. His grip on the long haft twisted the man halfway around, and then Whandall could pull the blade free, all in a background of screaming. The ring of gatherers was broken and running. Whandall reached out with the long shaft and stabbed another.

Heroul was looking for another target.

"Keep it moving," Whandall shouted. The wave was gaining on Morth. Its dark green face had crosscurrents in it, interference patterns.

The ground leveled off ahead. Whandall's advantage of altitude was dwindling. He had no reason to think that this mindless water elemental would take an interest in him, but . . . *but*. Whandall's path had grown rougher; the wave was past him; behind him he could see its wake of black wet ground.

Morth might die in this crazy project. Whandall would not mourn long. His promise bound him, but this was also his chance to choose whom he might rescue from the Burning City. *If* Whandall could survive. He might *die* rescuing the idiot wizard.

Morth was almost under the wave, already beyond rescue.

Morth opened a black bottle and showered gold all over himself. Sandry turned in surprise. Morth's hair flashed brick red and he was *moving*.

The chariot was left behind, horse and all, swallowed by foam in the next instant. But Morth was running on the vertical cliff with the charioteer held wriggling above his head. He dropped Sandry on the lip of the crest and veered back into the valley, leaving a wake of mad laughter.

The charioteer was on hands and knees, coughing, then vomiting. Whandall waved at Sandry but didn't slow. Then the horse stumbled and Heroul *had* to slow.

Horse and driver, he'd get no more out of either.

Whandall jumped out and ran, wobbling from the beating his sense of balance had taken. Heroul followed, shouting, "Where? Sir, where are we—?"

"Follow Morth!" He was passing the last bottle carrier—Reblay of Silly Rabbits, sitting spraddle-legged, his bottle thrown. Running on flat land now, past a broken chariot and three men on their backs gasping for air. Wanshig and his two nephews—

Those weren't the nephews he'd started with.

Whandall ran. If he lived, he'd hear the story. The Black Pit was ahead. Whandall could see its ripple and gleam: water covering black tar, a death trap shining in the sun.

Morth was slowing again, gray with fatigue. He looked back, and from the look in his eyes, what he saw was his death.

Manna in raw gold had energized the water sprite and driven it mad. The wave had followed Morth, and a trail of wild magic, deep into the heart of the Burning City. Now it was stranded in a place where the magic was gone; and now there was nothing behind it but refined gold. It still stood higher than any building of that age. White-crested, with weird ripples rolling across its green face, it rolled toward the staggering, gasping wizard.

Reblay was *not* the last bottle carrier. *Here* was where Freethspat's son should have been, where lay a black bottle no bigger than Whandall's fist. Whandall scooped it up and kept running. He neared Morth, pulled the stopper and threw.

Gold and glass sprayed around the wizard's feet. Morth whooped and ran, over the fence in a leap, across the dark water too fast to sink into it, to the far side of the Black Pit and over the far fence.

A mountain of water rolled into the Black Pit, absorbed the pond water, and grew.

The tar burst into flame.

Whandall barely felt his hair and eyebrows singed to ash. For an instant that seemed to last forever, he perceived what Yangin-Atep perceived. . . .

CHAPTER
79

Yangin-Atep, Loki, Prometheus, Moloch, Coyote, the hearth fires of the Indo-European tribes, uncountable fire gods were one and many. He, she, they had the aspect/powers of bilocation and shared minds. Pleasure or pain seeped from lands where a lord of fire and mischief might be worshipped or tortured.

Every cook fire was a nerve ending for Yangin-Atep. Whandall could feel the god's shape, the terrible freezing wound at his heart, the numb places where parts of the city were abandoned and no fires were lit, the long, trailing tail through the Firewoods. He felt sensation where Lord and Lordkin armies had passed, the path of Whandall's escape and return.

Yangin-Atep stirred rarely. It was only his attention that moved . . . but where Yangin-Atep's attention fell, things happened. Fires went out when Yangin-Atep took their energy. He put out forest fires. Cook fires he allowed to burn. If he snuffed them too early, they were of no use.

Fires indoors went out. Yangin-Atep in Whandall's mind remembered why. An ancient chief had bargained with Yangin-Atep, had woven a spell to prevent his nomad people from settling in houses.

Cook fires gave him his life.

But there was not enough magic even in fire. Every several years, Yangin-Atep fell into deathlike sleep. Then fires raged unchecked, even indoors. Yangin-Atep's famine-madness would fall on receptive worshippers, and people called that the Burning. In his coma Yangin-

Atep might not respond to the Burning for days, yet his chosen would feel the easing of his hunger, his growing strength. Their own grief was eased by the fires.

When Yangin-Atep revived it was all in a surge. He took fire where it was hottest, and though some fools might continue to throw torches, the Burning was over.

But now the trickle of life in Yangin-Atep was trickling away, and a line of bleeding emptiness crawled toward him from the sea. It was water, water come to challenge him. The manna that kept a water elemental alive was the life of Yangin-Atep.

The fire god's attention moved across the Burning City and centered on the Black Pit.

Tar and oil.

The pond water that covered the Black Pit had been rolled up into the greater mass of the sprite. Tar lay naked and exposed. Yangin-Atep's attention set it afire. Flames cradled the sprite. The sprite danced like a bead of water on a skillet, trying to withdraw from the fire.

Ancient dead animals played in the flames. Sabertooth cats pawed at the air, swatting at the water above them. Great flaming birds circled. A mastodon formed, then *grew* until it loomed above the sprite. Behemoth stamped down with both forefeet . . . and was gone, and the sprite was unharmed.

The child Whandall had seen these ghosts as holes in fog. Now they were flame . . . but Whandall's perception saw more. Yangin-Atep was summoning them to absorb their manna. The fire god was eating the ghosts.

Morth lay limp on the far side of the Pit. Whandall made his way around the fence toward Morth, his haft and blade forgotten in his hands. It was a long way around. He could barely see, hear, feel, with the fire god's senses raging in his head.

The elemental knew what it wanted, and Yangin-Atep felt it too. Yangin-Atep raised fire to block the elemental from its prey, from Morth of Atlantis. The elemental countered with a blast of wild magic, gold magic, nearly its last. If Whandall couldn't feel magic, the fire god could. Yangin-Atep's attention snuffed out, then snapped back.

And Morth, half dead beside the Black Pit fence, snapped awake and strong, awash in manna. He spilled his pack, stripped to the waist, and smeared his arms and chest with white paint, all in great haste. He faced the Pit and his arms began to wave.

To Whandall it looked like he was conducting music or a dance. Indeed, fire-beasts danced in response, even as they winked out one by one.

The war was half seen, half felt, half hidden. Whandall wasn't perceiving it all. In flashes of clarity he made his way to Morth.

Morth's back was turned. "Just stay clear," he said without turning around. Gold rings glittered on every finger.

"Can't I do something?"

"Clear!" Morth danced on.

Then Whandall's only senses were Yangin-Atep's.

Water wanted to cool fire. Fire wanted to burn water. Yangin-Atep wrapped the elemental like an eggcup around an egg. Water sizzled. Fire dimmed. Both were dying.

Some power remained in the Black Pit to feed the ghosts of the ancient animals, and that power was being used now. Yangin-Atep reached out for more and was blocked at the fence. But there was enough.

The sprite died in a blast of live steam.

Whandall covered his face with his arms and fell to the tarry ground. Heat scalded his hands. Morth's arms never missed a beat, but Whandall heard his howl.

Yangin-Atep hunted. If there had been a trace of the water elemental, Yangin-Atep would have eaten the manna in it. But the water thing was dead, myth, gone. Yangin-Atep reached farther.

There was *nothing* outside the Black Pit.

Now Whandall felt claustrophobic terror, a sudden shrinkage. From occupying the valley's vastness, enclosed by forest and sea, fed by cook fires, Yangin-Atep was numb and paraplegic beyond the border of the Black Pit. Some enemy was weaving—*had* woven—a wall!

Yangin-Atep twitched to the rhythm of the spell and sought a new enemy, and found him too late. Whandall recognized Morth of Atlantis, his dancing arms and fingers, but the wall was complete and Morth was outside, untouchable. Manna streamed thinly from the stars, but Yangin-Atep couldn't feel it. Morth had woven a lid to the box.

Yangin-Atep pushed against it. Whandall heard Morth's bellow of agony, dimly, but he *felt* the fire god's agony. The magical barrier was pitifully thin, but it was water magic.

Yangin-Atep hunted with the ferocity of a Lordkin, and found . . . a Lordkin.

Then Whandall and Yangin-Atep were two aspects of the fire god. The fire god reached down and picked up his haft and Lordkin blade.

Whandall Feathersnake let it fall.

Yangin-Atep stooped to pick up the spear, stooped and reached, bent his knees and reached, desperate to make this body move. *Move! Why wouldn't the Lordkin move?*

Morth danced like a marionette, his back turned. Whandall Feathersnake stood at peace with himself and the god raging in his mind. Whandall was familiar with the hard sell. Every merchant in the world thinks he can make you buy, but he can't. Listen, nod, enjoy the entertainment. Offer tea. At the right price, buy.

Whandall felt the fire fill him, running down his arms. Little flames licked his fingernails. Fire lit his mind. *The Toronexti! We'll burn them out! Houses, gatehouse, forest paths, men, we'll burn them all! Take the children hostage to hold the women. Next, the Bull Pizzles—*

What you offer has value, of course, but how can I risk so much? If I lose, my people starve, my family, all who trust Feathersnake. No, your price is too high.

Flame licked his fingertips. *Rage!*

Frivolously high. Fire, you can't be serious.

Burn!

Control. Relax. Stand. Smile. *Breathe.*

There was no manna left. Yangin-Atep faded to a dying spark.

Not here on the surface, but deep down beneath the tar where no wizard could ever have been, the last trace of the fire god found a last spark of manna. The fire god sank, faded, and was myth.

Yangin-Atep was myth.

Whandall's face hurt. Clothing had covered the rest of him, but his hands and the left side of his face and scalp were hot with pain. His hand found no eyebrows, no lashes, no hair on that side.

Morth was a stick figure, bald as an egg. Clothing charred black across the front of him, and his arms waved, conducting unseen musicians. Whandall dared not interfere. There was no trace of ancient animal ghosts now, and every fire was out.

Morth lowered his arms, bowed, and fell on his face.

Whandall rolled him over. Morth's eyes were half open, seeing nothing.

Whandall said, "The sprite is dead, Morth."

Morth sucked air. *Alive.* "Can't know that."

"Morth, I strangled it myself and ate every trace of it. It's *dead.* Excuse me, did I say? I was being Yangin-Atep."

"Feathersnake Inn."

"All gods welcome. I want no more of it, Morth."

"Won't happen again. What's left of Yangin-Atep, I wove deep into the tar. Whatever the fire god has been doing to this town, it's over. Ten thousand years, maybe more, maybe forever, Yangin-Atep sleeps below the tar. Maybe you can make something of that. I'm burned. Get me to the sea, for the manna. Wash me with salt water. Wait. You sure the sprite is—"

"*Dead.*"

"Good."

PART FIVE

Feathersnake

CHAPTER
80

Sandry and Burning Tower clattered up, horses lathered. Heroul was just behind him with Green Stone.

"Father!" Burning Tower shouted.

"I'm all right."

His children began to inspect him. They looked to be caught between horror and laughter. Whandall said, "It's Morth who needs help. Sandry, can you get him to the sea?"

"He doesn't look strong enough to ride in a chariot," Sandry said.

"I'll get a wagon," Heroul said. "Coming?" he asked Green Stone.

"See to it," Whandall said. "Get Morth *into* the water."

"I will," Heroul shouted. He wheeled away and lashed the horses, dashing across the uneven ground.

"We'll stay with you," Whandall said.

Burning Tower knelt beside the aged wizard.

"Stay there," Morth said. "Some say there's magic in a young girl's smile. Whandall! We did it!"

Heroul was back with a kinless in Quintana colors driving a four-horse wagon. Whandall and Green Stone lifted the wizard into the wagon and laid him on the blankets that filled it.

Whandall demanded, "Morth, how long?"

Morth smiled with no teeth. "Get me into the sea," Morth said distinctly. "The sea is magical everywhere. Quick enough, I might live."

The wagon moved away with Heroul's chariot as escort.

"Shouldn't we go with him?" Burning Tower asked.

"He's in good hands," Whandall said. "I'm more worried about the caravan now. Sandry, can this thing carry three?"

"If one is as light as she is," he said.

"I can ride the wagon tongue," Burning Tower said. "See!"

"Blazes—Burning Tower, that isn't safe," Sandry said.

"Safer than a tightrope. You just drive."

It was the final-day sale for the caravan. Pitchmen were shouting it. "Last day. Everything goes! Never be lower prices."

Burning Tower leaped from the chariot before it stopped. She raced to the sign outside Whandall Feathersnake's market pitch, snatched up a charcoal from the fire, and began to scrawl huge black letters across the neatly scribed sign. Nothing Was Seen came out of the nest to stare as if he could read.

"Lurk, are you all right?"

The bandit boy looked nearly healed but still swollen in spots. "Feathersnake, they're working me like a kinless." He must have learned that from a customer. *See, I speak your language!* "You look half fried, and where's the wizard? Tell me a story!"

"Later. Back to work." Sandry was half strangling on his own laughter. Whandall had never seen him do that. He demanded, "What does it say?"

Sandry looked at Whandall. It was clear what he was seeing: a tattooed man with every hair of his body singed off, burn spots and blisters on his arms and hands and on one cheek. Sandry struggled with laughter and lost. "Sir, it says *FIRE SALE.*"

"I should never have let her mother teach her to read," Whandall growled. "I want a new shirt. Then let's see if I can sell something."

The sale was a roaring success, kinless and Lordkin alike come to see what the traders from Outside had brought, what they could buy.

Heroul and Green Stone returned in late afternoon. Whandall was selling a carpet out of his own travel nest. He'd run out of stock early. Two Lordsmen were paying a manweight of tar and some jewelry; the Lord waited silent behind them. Whandall asked, "Is the wizard dead?"

"Morth is well," Green Stone said.

Whandall looked around. "You left him alone?" Abandoning an ally was much different from leaving one's dead.

"He's not alone." Though it was half killing them, they both waited for Whandall to complete the sale. Then Green Stone babbled, "We ran straight to Good Hand Harbor. Some Water Devil gatherers would have stopped a wagon, but not Heroul's chariot. They followed us. There's a boat bigger than *all* the boats we saw at Lion's, and there were seamen all about. But there's a beach. We didn't want to move him, so we ran the wagon right down into the water. I got in and held Morth's head up.

"There were seamen and Water Devils all wanting our story. They saw the same thing we did. Morth lay there looking drowned, grinning with no teeth and bragging in a guttural whisper about what we'd done. He's got deep burns, meat burns, but some blisters healed while we watched. He grew some hair, just stubble in patches where he was burned least, but it's *red* stubble. He grew teeth. He started to laugh."

Heroul said, "Last I saw him, he was up to his neck in sea water asking the crew for food. Said he could pay. Wants to know if the ship needs a wizard. A crewman was going for the captain."

"A wizard in his element," Whandall mused. "Did he say when he was coming back?"

"Father, he won't even try to stand up," Green Stone said. "He said he can't leave the sea, not for weeks."

"We can't stay weeks!"

"Father, he's done his part!" Green Stone said.

"You look worried," Burning Tower said.

"Oh, Stones is right, Blazes, but now we have to fight our way out past the Toronexti without a wizard!"

"Oh. But we've got Sandry."

"We'll escort you out," Sandry said.

Burning Tower caught his tone. "Sandry? You won't *fight?*"

"We can defend ourselves if they attack us. *Maybe* they're that stupid."

"And maybe that will be enough," Whandall said.

Green Stone was looking out at the crowd. "Good business," he said.

"Yes, but Stones, none of them seem to know," Burning Tower said. "Yangin-Atep's gone mythical and they don't know!"

"Morth said it would take a while," Green Stone said. "Manna is low, and there aren't any wizards. They've been gone for centuries. How will anyone know magic works here?" He rubbed his hands together. "Father. We get out. We join up with Saber Tooth and come back with Clever Squirrel and every shaman we can hire! Think what they'll pay here just for rain! We'll clean up."

"You're thinking like Saber Tooth," Burning Tower told her brother.

"About time," Whandall said.

Peacegiven Square buzzed like a hive, and trade was brisk. A few Lordkin were to be expected, and Whandall had counted twenty or so. They were looking, not gathering much. The merchants must have educated them early . . . but Whandall was keeping his eye on a cluster of Lordkin, seeing them as trouble, wondering when they'd split up and begin gathering.

Serpent's Walk would have *filtered* in, not come in a bunch. Others had noticed. Merchants and customers were all beginning to bristle.

Whandall wondered if it might make sense to pay off the Toronexti. Get out, then return in two weeks with weapons and magic . . . and plant poison rubbed on sever blades . . .

No. Too late in the year. After the tax men stripped them, they wouldn't have wealth to show outside. They wouldn't get enough fighting men to bring back, and winning a few battles wouldn't help if they had to stay the winter. *No*.

The knot of a dozen Lordkin he'd been watching had crossed the square to Hammer Miller's wagon. They began gathering goods. When Hammer came out to collect, one backhanded him with a laugh.

"Hey, harpy!"

The whole square glittered for a moment. The cry of "Hey, harpy!" rose in a chorus. Whandall jumped the counter, knife in hand.

He was surprised to see Sandry and Heroul wheel their chariots around and leave the fight, rolling at top speed toward the Lordsmen camp. But the rest of the action was familiar.

Kinless took cover.

Most of the Lordkin decided it wasn't their business and took cover too. A few, enraged at having their fun interrupted, readied to fight. But the harpies were behaving like Wolverines: clustered back to back in the open square, giving themselves room to fight, allowing nobody near.

Caravaners armed themselves and moved toward the gatherers at a trot. The flurry of slingshot missiles surprised the harpies. They didn't notice what else was going on among the Lordsmen. Whandall barely saw it himself, but, running to test his knifework against Tep's Town harpies, he slowed.

Waterman had been watching. As the two chariots neared the camp, they were joined by three more.

"Riders mount up!" Waterman shouted.

Men ran from their tents to take places beside the charioteers. "Go get 'em! Sir!" Waterman shouted.

Sandry waved toward the knot of harpies. "At a walk! At a trot!"

He took the long spear in his right hand. The other drivers were doing the same. The riders held short spears at the ready.

"Charge!"

Five chariots in line hurtled across the square. "Throw!" Five short spears arched out, and four of the intruding Lordkin fell. The others ran, dropping their loot, dropping everything else they carried. Only one turned to raise his Lordkin knife in defiance. He got Heroul's spear dead in his chest for his effort. The charioteers came to a halt.

Across the square Waterman was still forming up his infantry troops, but there was no need. Heroul set his foot on a corpse and wrenched his spear loose. Three of the gatherers were dead. Two others probably wouldn't live, not if *that* was the care they were getting.

Whandall went to a dead harpy and turned him over with a foot.

A stylized long-nosed animal was tattooed on the upper arm. The style had changed in twenty-two years, but—"Wolverines," Whandall said.

"Glad that's over," Burning Tower said. She stood half fascinated by the dead men, every now and then glancing up toward Sandry. Sandry looked both pleased with himself and astonished that all his training had paid off—it worked just the way his teachers had said it would. . . .

"It's not over," Whandall said. He pointed.

Lagdret of Serpent's Walk lay dead in front of the Miller tea shop. The pretty waitress behind him was bleeding from a knife wound to her shoulder.

Wanshig arrived half an hour later. He sent two of his Lordkin to wrap Lagdret's body. "Carry him home," he said.

Wanshig inspected the dead Wolverine. "These?"

Whandall said, "These, or the ones that got away. Wolverines, anyway."

"Doesn't matter."

"No?" Whandall was astonished at his brother's cold voice.

"Doesn't matter," Wanshig said again. "Wolverines killed my man. Killed a Placeholder on neutral ground. Never make half a war. Whandall, is it true? We've put *Yangin-Atep* to sleep?"

"Yes."

"I had to try it. I took a torch indoors. Of course that would work . . ." Wanshig looked around him; Lordkin and kinless were coming out from cover, watching each other warily. Wanshig said softly, ". . . during the Burning."

"Ten thousand years, Morth said."

"But a torch burns indoors, and the Wolverines don't know it," Wanshig said. "Well, they'll know it soon enough. By noon tomorrow every damn one of them will know it."

"Do you have enough men to attack the Wolverines?" Whandall asked. "They're strong."

"So are we," Wanshig said. "Whandall, I've done my best to stay out of wars. Build alliances. Do favors. Now I'm calling in every favor I have coming. Flower Market and Bull Pizzle won't want to send anyone, but they can't keep me from asking, from spreading the word that we're going to gather in rich territory, got room for anyone who wants some loot.

"Can I tell them the Lordsmen fought Wolverines when I talk about gathering?"

"They fought *here,* yes, but they may not carry it farther. Don't promise anything. We'll be leaving in the morning," Whandall said. "The Toronexti are sure to be watching. We can't get to their gatehouse before noon."

"They'll want a lot of their strength there," Wanshig said. "You'd be rich pickings. Like nothing they've seen in their lifetimes! And they won't expect me to be looking for them right away. They sent a man to offer blood money."

Whandall looked at his brother.

Wanshig grinned. "Never found me. Can't find me. He went to the Serpent's Walk clubhouse. At the clubhouse, they said I was gone back to the Placehold; Placehold will send him to Pelzed's old place. He's always just missed me. Curse, you did. bring some excitement, Whandall! I never quite found the right time to take back Dark Man's Cup. But I contracted to clean it, right? It's as clean as a river bottom! And the Bull Pizzles don't want to pay."

"So when will you go into Wolverine territory?" Whandall asked.

"Was planning on first thing in the morning, but it's even better at noon. About the time they see you, their turf will be burning." Wanshig laughed. "Never fight half a war. I taught my people—"

"I taught mine."

"Whandall, Wess will bring her boy over in the morning. You take care of him."

"I will. Wanshig? The gold is still down there, you know, under the water, all along the Long Avenue."

"Ah." Wanshig stood. "It's been instructive, Dall. And maybe I'll see you again, maybe not."

"You too, Shig. I'll be back."

"I think you will. Maybe I'll be here too."

CHAPTER 81

It was barely light when Wess came. Wess's son looked nothing like Shastern. He was a small boy, big eyes, a thoughtful look. "Like I remember you were," Wess said. "But he's smaller than you were. Take care of him, Whandall."

"Things will be different here," Whandall said. "Maybe—"

"Not that different that soon," Wess said. "Please."

"He can come with us, Wess, but we have to get past the Toronexti. If that goes bad—" He thought for a moment. "If that goes bad I'll send him home with one of the Lordsmen. Sandry has been to the Placehold. He'll take him."

"All right." Wess kissed her son. He stared with big eyes at her, then at Whandall. "Good-bye." She turned and ran.

"Burning Tower, this is Shastern," Whandall said. "Keep him out of trouble. Shastern, you stay with her." *And just maybe,* Whandall thought, *that will keep both of you out of the fight.*

Thirty-seven of Whandall's tested bottle throwers came at dawn. Ten were kinless. All carried large sacks, all the possessions they would be taking outside. They chattered eagerly of a new life.

"Who's missing?" Whandall asked. "I thought everyone would come."

Fubgire had endured the knife lessons and thrown his bottle. He said, "Wanshig was persuasive. They went to gather at Granite Knob. The rest of us are here, Lord."

"I'm not a Lord. We have no Lords. I'm Wagonmaster."

"Close enough for me, Lord." But Fubgire was laughing.

"All of you, stay together," Whandall said. "Green Stone will tell you what to do."

A couple of the Lordkin muttered.

"Get used to that!" Whandall snapped. "Working with us means following instructions. The way to win in a fight is to stay together and act together. Green Stone knows your language. Listen to him!

"I ask you to walk alongside the last wagon. Keep your weapons ready, don't hide them, but don't threaten anyone. If you have to raise a weapon, use it. We're going to see if the Lords can talk us past the Toronexti. I don't expect them to do it."

"We'll have to fight, then?" Hammer Miller asked.

"I think so, Hammer. Don't you?"

"Yes." He turned to the ten kinless who were coming out with them. "You all have your slings." It wasn't a question, and they all did: the ceremonial nooses around their necks came off quickly.

"Be sure you have a good supply of rocks."

The Lordkin frowned. Kinless without nooses, kinless with weapons.

The wagon train left as soon as it was light enough to see, but Waterman had his men on the road first. The Lordsmen marched on ahead. Whandall glimpsed Lurk and Shastern in the last wagon and thought no more of it. He had larger concerns.

There were seven chariots, Sandry and his friends. Every chariot held a driver and a spear thrower. The charioteers tried to stay with the wagon train, but horses hated to match a bison's pace. They learned to hang back, then dash ahead to catch up.

It was enough of an escort that no one wanted trouble. Word had spread: Wolverines had attacked the wagons, and the Lordsmen had killed Wolverines. Leave the wagon train alone! Even the stupidest of Lordkin could understand that. The bison moved at their slow pace through streets deceptively quiet.

Near noon, an old man hobbled out of the shade of the biggest tree. He leaned heavily on a giant. The giant was elderly, gone to fat, and his smile was more goofy than challenging. Still, a giant. They approached without fear. Bent and twisted as the master was, Whandall wondered at his equally goofy grin. Like a Lordkin springing a trap?

Then Whandall recognized him. "Tras!"

"Whandall Feathersnake. Always surprising. I much prefer this to your last surprise."

"I—"

"Shall I tell you how I got myself off your land alive? After I crawled back into the crypt, I fainted. When my man Hejak—"

"Hold up, Tras. Arshur?"

"Arshur the Magnificent," the giant confirmed. "Not sure I remember you. Got a drink?"

"I was with Alferth when you got your first drink here. You getting beaten up, that started the Burning twenty-odd years back. I thought you'd be leaving on the next ship."

"I like it here."

They rounded the last bend. The Toronexti were ahead.

The caravan moved toward them. Whandall's merchants moved to the tailgates, ready to jump down. The new recruits huddled around Green Stone. They would be at the gatehouse in minutes.

Hobbling along with his stick in one hand, the other on Arshur's arm, Tras was still keeping up with the burdened bison. "Hejak gave up on me and was leaving when I crawled out, but I—"

Whandall said in some haste, "Tras, I'm just too busy right now, but can you climb a tree?"

Tras Preetror gaped. "Do I look—?"

"He can climb a tree," Arshur said. "Or I can throw him up a tree. Should I do that?"

"Both of you." Watchman had pounded Arshur's head with sticks. The treatment seemed to have done some permanent damage.

Now Tras Preetror saw the armored Toronexti ahead. "That officer—I know how he hurt his hand."

"I've stopped caring."

"Three Lordsmen wanted out of Tep's Town, with their armor. The tax men tried to stop them. They wanted one suit of armor."

"Tras, you two are about to see a really good story happen right in front of you."

"They're more careful now. Do you mean . . ." Tras was finally seeing the danger. "Story. May I call it 'The Death of Whandall Feathersnake'?"

"If that's what you see, that's what you tell, but see it from a height, Tras, and in hiding. If you live, *you owe me.*"

The kinless bonehead ponies were getting larger, horns growing as they approached the forest. That hadn't happened this close to Tep's Town last time, Whandall remembered. Yangin-Atep was myth. Whoever saw the implications first would make fortunes.

Waterman was ahead of them, his band grown to nearly fifty men drawn up in three ranks. An officer's tent was set up behind them. Whandall didn't recognize the Lord, but Sandry rode up alongside the wagon. "My father," he said. He whipped up his horses to go to his father's tent.

The wagons reached the Toronexti gate.

The big Toronexti officer with the injured hand was waiting. There were more of the masked and armored tax collectors, fifty that Whandall could see, more in the tollgate building, probably some behind the building. Whandall waited.

Sandry brought his chariot up. "Let them pass."

"Now why should I do that?" Half Hand demanded.

"Orders from the Lord Chief Witness. This wagon train passes without taxes."

"Now does it? Chief Clerk!"

The shuttered door on the second floor of the brick gatehouse popped open. There stood Egon Forigaft, and a glimpse of dark ancient tapestries behind him. He leaned far out over the ten-foot drop to put daylight on the sheet of parchment in his hands. A Toronexti guard held his sash.

"Decree of Lord Chief Witness Harcarth: the Toronexti shall have the right of taxation on all goods departing through the forest. There is more."

"Enough, I think," the scarred officer said. "Younglord, we have a charter. Witnessed and signed, Younglord. Witnessed and signed."

Sandry shrugged helplessly. Toronexti moved forward.

Whandall said, "Hey, harpy!"

The fighting men of the wagon train leaped down to join the Lordkin and kinless walking alongside the wagons. Together they made a formidable band. Women took over the reins, closed the gaps in the wagon covers.

"You want our goods? Come and take them!" Whandall shouted.

"A decree!" Egon Forigaft shouted. "The Lords will assist the Toronexti when they are attacked by outsiders."

"Who's an outsider?" Whandall jumped to a wagon roof and stripped off his shirt. "I am Whandall of Serpent's Walk! Who dares say I am not Lordkin?"

No one moved. Sandry laughed. "What does it say about Lordkin, Clerk?"

Egon found it. "The Toronexti shall protect the Lords and their agents from civil unrest."

Sandry said, "We owe you no protection from Lordkin. *You* protect *us,* you misbegotten goblins!"

One of the Toronexti threw a stone. It struck Sandry's spearman in the stomach. The spearman bent over, retching.

Sandry gave a wide grin and lifted his spear.

"A proclamation of Lord Qirinthal the First!" Egon shouted from his upper story. "There shall be truce between Lords and Toronexti so long as this charter endures. If Toronexti shall strike a Lordsman, that Toronexti shall be liable for double the injury in blood, two eyes for an eye, two limbs for a limb, two lives for a life, and this be paid, the truce shall endure!"

"We pay!" the Toronexti officer shouted. "Bring me that man!" He pointed to the window, though the man who had thrown the stone had vanished. Two Toronexti dragged him over. The officer hit him in the stomach with all his strength, then again. "Do the Lords demand another man be punished?" he shouted.

Sandry turned away in disgust.

"It's that stack of old parchments, isn't it?" Whandall said.

Sandry nodded.

"What if it were to burn?"

Sandry grinned.

"Go! Stone! Distract them while I get that paper!" Whandall shouted. The Toronexti wouldn't understand the language of the Hemp Road.

Stone led his band toward the Toronexti. Whandall charged forward to dash inside the gatehouse, but someone inside saw what he intended. The gatehouse door slammed shut with a crash.

"Greathand! Break the door!"

Greathand had a sword in one hand and a hammer in the other. He ran forward. Whandall ran with him, his cloak wrapped around his arm to protect them both. He blocked a slash, felt his cloak yield to a sharp blade. A Toronexti moved toward them, then fell to Hammer Miller's sling. Now a dozen slingers were in action, and stones fell among the Toronexti. They held up their arms to protect their heads. Two more fell.

Twenty of the tax men came around the building. They held shields and moved in behind them in a rattle of stones from the kinless slings. They got between the other Toronexti and the slingers.

Whandall's Lordkin stalwarts rushed forward, but despite all Stone could do, they didn't stay together. They came in ones and twos, and in ones and twos they were cut down. Whandall saw a dozen of his men on the ground to half that many enemies.

"Smoke!" One of the Toronexti gibbered and pointed. A black cloud of smoke rose over Granite Knob. "Smoke! That's our *homes!*"

Whandall smiled grimly.

"We have to protect our homes!"

"Stand fast!" Half Hand shouted. "It's a trick! It's just smoke to draw us away! Stand fast!"

Greathand pounded on the door with his hammer. The door did not yield. "I need an ax!" he shouted.

Hammer Miller ran to a wagon and got an ax. He ran toward Greathand with a tax man behind him. Hammer swung the ax. The Toronexti ducked and lashed out with his Lordkin knife. Hammer fell in a shapeless heap.

"See, Younglords, how we protect you!" The Toronexti officer gestured to send ten armored men to face Whandall, Greathand, and four others at the door. One of the newcomers took the ax from Hammer Miller, started forward, and went down under a Toronexti knife. Greathand shouted defiance and moved toward the ax. The battle surged around him. Four men charged. Greathand turned and struck two men with his hammer before he was beaten to his knees. More Toronexti moved toward Whandall, moving together, carefully and slowly—

Whandall's wagon curtain opened, and Burning Tower ran out.

Right. Whandall had foisted Shastern on her, but she'd passed the boy on to Nothing Was Seen, and now she was free to run at the Toronexti line with a torch in her hand. She leaped onto the back of one of the bison, over his head, and down to the ground. Before laughing Toronexti could catch her, she reached the flagstaff in front of the building and climbed it. From the top she leaped across to the open doorway where Egon Forigaft stood. She waved her torch in triumph.

The Toronexti officer roared in laughter. "Torches inside, here, on Yangin-Atep's spine!" His laughter turned to horror as Burning Tower put her torch to the thin parchments Egon Forigaft was holding. They blazed. She whirled the torch about, and ancient ceremonial tapestries were burning, flames everywhere.

"There!" she shouted. "Where's your charter now? Read it now!" She kicked blazing parchment out of the doorway. "It's gone. Sandry!" Then she was out of the doorway, climbing toward the roof, two Toronexti chasing her.

Sandry shouted. "Waterman!"

"Sir!"

"Clean out these vermin!"

"Sir! Lock shields! Spears high! Forward!"

The line of Lordsmen moved toward the Toronexti.

Sandry grabbed the throwing spear from his crippled spearman. It arched high. The Toronexti on the roof screamed and fell. Burning Tower stood on the roof and shouted. "Good throw, Sandry!"

And six more chariots were charging the Toronexti line. Javelins flew, and now there was only Whandall and the Toronexti leader with the ruined hand. Half Hand backed away. Whandall feinted high, then drove his knife point just below the line of the man's leather armor. It went in to the hilt.

He turned to see everyone staring at him.

"Your face," ten-year-old Shastern said in awe. "It lit up!"

"For the last time," Whandall said. "I hope." What did they *see?*

There were eleven dead, four from the wagon train. "Six more probably won't make it," Green Stone said. "Three times that if we don't get out to a healer pretty quick. Too bad we don't have Morth."

"We'll go," Whandall said. "The way's clear. Get loaded up."

"Shall I come with you?" Sandry asked.

"Aren't you needed here?"

Sandry looked at the piled bodies. "It will all be different now. Yes, sir, I may be needed. But—"

"She'll be back," Whandall said. "In a year. If you still remember her—"

"He will," Burning Tower said from behind him. "I will!"

"We'll know that next year," Whandall said. "Stone, are we loaded?"

"We are."

"Move them out." Whandall looked back. Tep's Town wasn't visible from here, but there was dark smoke over the hill below Granite Knob. Not many of the Toronexti would be going home to defend Wolverine territory.

Smoke rose elsewhere too. Wanshig hadn't done that, and the time of Yangin-Atep's Burning was over. But . . .

Tep's Town was only now discovering that fires would burn indoors.

Given their lack of faith in the fire god, kinless didn't have the habit of leaving flammable trash about. Lordkin did. Sailors didn't. A few days from now, the Placehold might be the last stronghold unburned.

And it wasn't Feathersnake's problem. "Move them out, Stone. It's your wagon route. Not too soon for you to take charge of it. I'm going home."

AFTERWORD

Over millennia the Hemp Road spread from Condigeo south through the isthmus and deep into the southern continent. When the caravans died out, the feathered serpent remained a symbol of civilization.

The "Native" Americans who invaded the American continents from Siberia fourteen thousand years ago found that they could use the native mammoths and horses as meat. These creatures they ultimately exterminated. When the Americas were later invaded from Europe, there were no suitable riding beasts from which to fight.

The *Los Angeles Times* says, ". . . redwood fossils discovered in Pit 91 [of the La Brea Tar Pits] indicate that the big trees, now generally seen only in the mountain forests of Northern California, grew along what is now Wilshire Boulevard" (July 28, 1999).

When the redwoods were gone, the truce of the forest died too. California chaparral has lost much of its malevolence, but some plants still maintain their blades, needles, and poisons. Hemp still soothes, distracts, then strangles its victims at any opportunity.

The killer bees of Tep's Town ultimately armed every hive on Earth with poisoned weapons. Bees no longer negotiate worth a damn.

* * *

Foxglove—digitalis—has lost much of its power. The pretty little flower is still a euphoric and a poison.

The madness that comes of touching river gold is still remembered in Germany, in *Die Nibelungen,* and in the United States, in such movies as *The Treasure of the Sierra Madre.*
The legend of a madman's lost gold remains current.

Parents continued to tell the tale of a charismatic man who contracted to resolve a town's infestation of vermin. When the Lords refused to pay him, he led away not just the vermin but all the youth of the town. Ultimately his tale became that of the Pied Piper of Hamelin.

The story of Jispomnos's murders, which spread with the tellers from Tep's Town to Condigeo and then returned to Tep's Town as an opera, spread farther yet. Ultimately it fell into the hands of the playwright William Shakespeare, to become *Othello.*

Yangin-Atep lay mythical for nearly fourteen thousand years, entombed in petroleum tar, until two men came to dig for oil in the La Brea Tar Pits.
Their names were Canfield and Doheny. Yangin-Atep's call and the lust for precious metal played a resonance with the gold fever in their brains. At the La Brea Tar Pits they tried to dig an oil well with shovels! They didn't stop until they were one hundred and sixty-five feet down, a few inches above death by asphyxiation. Bubbles of unbreathable gas crackled under their shovels. Fumes made them dizzy and sick. At last they went to find a partner who knew about pipes; and then they woke the fire god and built an empire on petroleum.

In 1997 the authors found Pinnacles National Park to be exactly as described. Sage, rosemary, thyme, and pallid dragon nip still grow there, and the giants' fingers and dragons' rib cages are still in place.

Yangin-Atep feeds the fires that move a billion automobiles and a million airplanes everywhere in the world.
Not cook fires alone but also automobile and diesel motors are each a nerve ending for Yangin-Atep. The god's nerve trunks reach along

freeways, paths that once ran through forest, then and still Yangin-Atep's tail. From time to time the fire god's attention shifts, and then the Burning comes again.

Some people like to play with fire.

I hated going to the beach—no bathing suits for me!—and with arthritis in my hands and knees, it was tough to do any physical activities. That was until I met Dr. Gerry Mullin and learned about the Gut Balance Revolution.

I lost 40 pounds following the Gut Balance Revolution program, and I look and feel 15 years younger! I went from a size 10 dress down to a 0! The weight loss makes me feel terrific.

Before the program, I was plagued by debilitating irritable bowel syndrome symptoms, fatigue, joint pain, and brain fog. I also had allergies and skin problems. Every one of these symptoms has been resolved. I feel like a new person!

So many people ask me what I've done to look and feel so great. I can't believe that this simple program—it really is a simple way of eating—can transform your life. The Gut Balance Revolution is an easy way to lose weight, eat healthy, and curb carb cravings. I strongly recommend this program to everyone!

–*Terri*

Before the Gut Balance Revolution, I wasn't able to climb a flight of stairs without being short of breath. On this program, I've lost 19 pounds, I am down a couple sizes in my clothes, I feel great about myself, and I look fantastic! Now I can handle the stairs with no problem and breathe normally when I reach the top.

I have tried many programs before, and some worked for the time I was on them. But this one not only worked for me while doing it but it made me feel so good afterward that I am compelled to continue on it for a life change so that I not only lose weight but remain healthy. It's a mind-set thing. I am now determined to be healthy and beautiful at the same time and am loving life! I would recommend anyone to just try it. The results speak for themselves.

Dr. Gerry, thank you so much! I appreciate people like you taking the time to care for others and to help us be what God intended us to be in the first place: healthy! I have learned that to be healthy, it doesn't mean you have to stress about it or be sad. Be happy in what you are doing, which is bettering your body, mind, and well-being. Thank you for helping me get on the right track. Now I am able to help others. For you have to partake first and be an example to show that it really works.

From my heart, I thank you so much! My body is grateful for your program.

–*Bernadette*

I lost 20 pounds on the Gut Balance Revolution! I can't tell you how much better I feel. I'm not tired all the time like I used to be. I sleep better. My clothes fit better and aren't as tight. I feel great!

This program is different because it teaches you which foods will help you feel better and lose weight.

I am still going through the program now and probably will continue it for the rest of my life. It's so easy to follow. And I know if I go back to eating like I was eating before, I will not feel like I do now.

–*Stephanie*

On the Gut Balance Revolution, I lost 10 pounds. I don't get sick or have a bulging stomach after I eat anymore (which is the best part!). My clothes fit again. I feel energized, healthy, and clean. My cholesterol levels even went down. I changed my mood, my bowels are working regularly, and I am no longer fatigued. Now if I even try to cheat, I get sick. My body has changed. It doesn't recognize processed unhealthy foods anymore. I don't have cravings or get the 3:00 p.m. hunger headache anymore. It's great!

It's a real learning experience to see all of the "bad" in the food you used to eat, and it makes you ask, "How am I not 300 pounds?"

–Jennifer

Originally, I went on the Gut Balance Revolution program, because I was plagued with digestive issues. I struggled to find a solution to the constant gut distress. It really limited my life. I was exhausted all the time and constantly worried about what I could eat–and where the bathroom was. But all that changed when I went on the Gut Balance Revolution.

Within 6 weeks, my symptoms were nearly gone. And there was an unexpected bonus. My husband, Scott, who'd been trying to lose weight for years, went on the diet with me and dropped 19 pounds. Both of us began feeling so much better just by eating healthy foods and getting rid of all that processed stuff.

Now when I travel to conferences, the business lunches are no longer a nightmare. And Scott and I can enjoy having dinner with friends, take in a movie, and even go to football parties.

Our world has opened up again.

–Cindy

I've gone on lots of diets over the years. I tried everything from Weight Watchers to Jenny Craig. But nothing really worked until this program. In 8 weeks, I lost 12 pounds–and I felt so much better.

–Monique

THE
GUT BALANCE
REVOLUTION

THE

GUT BALANCE REVOLUTION

BOOST YOUR METABOLISM, RESTORE YOUR INNER ECOLOGY, and LOSE THE WEIGHT FOR GOOD!

GERARD E. MULLIN, MD

Associate Professor of Medicine at The Johns Hopkins University School of Medicine

RODALE.

Published by Rodale Inc. as *The Good Gut Diet*, a direct mail hardcover, in 2014.

© 2015 by Gerard E. Mullin, MD

Exercise illustrations on pages 223–233 © 2014 Rodale Inc.

Rodale books may be purchased for business or promotional use or for special sales. For information, please write to:
Special Markets Department, Rodale Inc., 733 Third Avenue, New York, NY 10017

The content on pages 200 and 202 to 209 is reprinted by permission from SAGE Publications: Bernstein A BJ, Ehrman JP, Goulbic M, Roizen MF, *American Journal of Lifestyle Medicine* (vol. 8, issue 1), pp. 33–41, Copyright © 2014 by SAGE Publications.

The following recipes are reprinted courtesy of Stone Mill Bakery: Greek Village Salad, page 280; Wild Rice and Turkey Soup, page 314; and Dr. Gerry's Super Salmon Salad, page 317.

Printed in the United States of America
Rodale Inc. makes every effort to use acid-free ♾, recycled paper ♲.

Illustrations by Karen Kuchar
Book design by Christina Gaugler

Library of Congress Cataloging-in-Publication Data is on file with the publisher.

ISBN 978-1-62336-401-4   trade hardcover

2   4   6   8   10   9   7   5   3   1   trade hardcover

We inspire and enable people to improve their lives and the world around them.
rodalebooks.com

To the loving memory of my parents,
Frances R. Magnanti Mullin and Gerard V. Mullin Jr.

To my family and loved ones for their unwavering support

To those who struggle with weight-related problems, the
clinicians who care for them, the researchers looking for a cure,
and the organizations and individuals who promote awareness
and research

To Drs. Anthony Kalloo, Myron Weisfeldt, Linda Lee, my
colleagues and friends, administrators, and staff who support
my work at Johns Hopkins

CONTENTS

INTRODUCTION:
IT'S NOT YOUR FAULT!

T he year was 1977. A 17-year-old high school student and his mother walked into a new doctor's office for the first time looking for answers to a recent and inexplicable sore throat, loss of appetite, fatigue, and fever. The esteemed doctor was referred by a leading physician in their small community of Wayne, New Jersey. The physician was fresh out of training in endocrinology and metabolism and was beginning his practice in the region's top multispecialty group.

When the doctor walked into the room wearing his white coat, he gazed up and down at the boy, shot him a dismissive frown, then looked over at the boy's mother with disapproval in his eyes.

In the few minutes allocated for the visit, the doctor stated he was certain that this young man had mononucleosis and ordered confirmatory blood tests. As he was leaving the room, the boy's mother asked, "Doctor, he has a difficult time eating. Do you have any suggestions?"

The physician turned around with an angry scowl and sharply rebutted, "Ma'am, if he didn't eat for a week, it wouldn't hurt him. Given his size, it may make a healthy dent!" With that, he stormed out of the room. The chill that followed was like a blast of arctic air. The boy and his mother were momentarily frozen by the doctor's painful words.

This young man was 293 pounds the day he visited that doctor, and his shame about his weight was immense. If you haven't guessed by now, the young man in that doctor's office was me.

Unfortunately, that doctor was more interested in assigning blame than he was in offering solutions. We now know that this type of stigmatizing and shaming approach toward overweight people is counterproductive and can actually cause weight gain.[1] In fact, blame, shame, and lack of support are feeding directly into the obesity epidemic.[2] But after all these years, I now realize that doctor did me a favor. He gave me an example of what *not* to aspire to as a physician. Doctors are healers who are bound by the Hippocratic oath to provide empathetic care to those in need.[3] That man broke the spirit of his oath.

Though disappointed and hurt by my first encounter with this physician, I went back for another visit to be cleared for return to school following my bout of mononucleosis. The illness had been more severe than usual, and I had lost 12 pounds in only a few weeks. When I walked into the office, the doctor remarked, "I'm glad that the illness was therapeutic," and smiled.

As he looked over my chart, he noted that my high school football team was ranked as number one in the state and asked me what I was studying at DePaul High School. "I'd like to be a doctor," I replied. That's when he dealt the final blow. He chuckled, looked me up and down once again, and said, "Not looking like this, you won't." Our relationship ended.

Despite the doctor's rudeness, he communicated an important and sobering message to me: "Physician, heal thyself." If I wanted to be a doctor, I should first look at my own body and take care of it. Back then, the prevalence of obesity was low and most doctors were thin. So a morbidly obese person aspiring to be a doctor was being unrealistic. I needed to lose the weight if I wanted to be a physician.

That's when my own weight-loss journey began.

HOW I ALMOST DIDN'T BECOME A DOCTOR

Shortly after my visit to that physician, I graduated from high school and entered college. I was morbidly obese, and it quickly became plain that I wasn't living up to my potential academically. I was strongly advised by the head of the university's preprofessional committee to consider another profession–such as podiatrist or physician assistant–since I wouldn't be recommended for medical school. That's when I hit rock bottom. My life's dream had been to become a doctor, and it looked like I wouldn't achieve it.

That Christmas, I spent some time at my brother Tim's house. The movie *Rocky* was on television. That's when I had my aha moment. All I had to do was figure out what steps I needed to take to make it happen, as Rocky did in the movie.

I had a vision of myself as an empathetic doctor who would help others who struggled to lose weight, but I knew that first I had to find my own path to health. I found my inspiration and my focus. I spent hours in the library researching diet programs and the effects of different foods on human metabolism. I tested several "diets" and failed at many, but I was committed to succeeding. I knew that if I searched hard enough, I could find an answer to my weight problem.

At the checkout counter of my local grocery store, I came across a book about the health benefits of fiber. I purchased it and read it over winter break. The author explained why fiber was important for maintaining a healthy weight–and it dawned on me that my own diet had always been fiber poor. I realized that the diets I'd attempted–like the "grapefruit diet," popular in the late 1970s–were futile because they contained little or none of this critical substance.

So I decided to create my own diet plan, one that was rich with fiber. One of my staples was oat bran (to bolster my fiber intake) with plain low-fat yogurt, sweetened with a pinch of molasses, pure maple syrup, or raw honey. I also began to switch my protein sources to mainly seafood and away from red meat. I used olive oil and nuts as my principal sources of fat.

I went for long walks across campus or rode a bicycle during study breaks for exercise. In no time, I was dropping weight and feeling fantastic. My energy skyrocketed, and so did my mental clarity.

After losing my first 50 pounds, I began running and lifting weights and engaging in a number of athletic activities with my brothers Patrick and Tim, along with my friend Chris Houlihan. It was like *Rocky* come to life.

By the end of 1979, I got down to 175 pounds—a result that rivals gastric bypass surgery. My aptitude and scholastic performance dramatically improved. A year later I was accepted into medical school. Today, I am an academic gastroenterologist among an elite group of doctors at one of the leading hospitals in the nation. I'm not sure I could have achieved all this had I not been able to drop the weight and *persevere.*

But how did I make the change when so many others can't? Why did the diet plan I developed on my own actually work?

20/20 HINDSIGHT

I now realize that I'd developed a way of eating that restricted foods that promote inflammation and spike blood sugar and fat-forming insulin. I was also supporting the growth of friendly bacteria in my gut with prebiotic fiber-rich foods and live yogurt cultures. As you'll learn in this book, this may be the key reason the diet worked. We know today that the trillions of bacteria housed in our digestive tract have a significant influence on our ability to gain or lose weight. I'll explain more about this in a moment.

First, I want to share another key discovery I made during this time.

I realized that it wasn't my fault that I was so large. I hadn't been eating lots of junk food. I was just unknowingly eating the wrong foods that were promoting inflammation, reducing the diversity of microbes in my gut, and leading to fat accumulation.

If you're overweight, it's likely not your fault either. Nobody wants to be overweight, but it happens to many despite their best intentions.

We live in a world where obesity is a global epidemic, and it didn't come about because people are lazy or stupid. Something else is at work. At one time, just getting enough to eat was the most basic problem of survival. Now we face the opposite problem.

Seventy percent of Americans are overweight and 36 percent are obese.[4] Globally, 1.5 billion people are overweight and half a billion are obese. Today, one-third of all women and one-quarter of all men in America are on a diet. In the United States alone, more than $60 billion is spent on weight-loss products per year.

Studies estimate that up to two-thirds of those dieting will gain back more weight than they lost when they stop their diet programs. You've probably seen popular celebrities and even former contestants from *The Biggest Loser* regain weight months after successful dieting. In fact, most Americans can only sustain a behavioral-modification-diet lifestyle program for 3 to 6 months before falling off and rebounding. And amazingly, one-third of those who undergo gastric bypass obesity surgery regain the weight because the underlying problem was not fixed.

Obesity has crippling effects on health and well-being, shortens life expectancy, hinders quality of life, and adversely impacts the economy. Treating obesity and obesity-related conditions costs billions of dollars a year. By one estimate, the United States spent $190 billion on obesity-related health-care expenses in 2005–double previous estimates.[5] Looking ahead, researchers have estimated that by 2030, if obesity trends continue unchecked, 50 percent of America will be obese, and obesity-related medical costs alone could rise to $66 billion a year. Obesity is a major driver of Medicare costs and contributes to our growing federal debt.

HOW DID THIS HAPPEN?

I blame the food industry's promotion of processed foodlike substances that I call "ingestibles" and rich proinflammatory and disease-promoting crops that become affordable junk food. We rely on a "food industry" to promote our health, while our health-care industry fails to promote the role of sound nutrition in healthy living and disease prevention. The "food industry" does an excellent job of designing and selling tasty and addictive products that make consumers continuously buy and eat more than what they need. Big Food knows all too well how to make its products appealing, tasty, irresistible, and cheap, so that people keep coming back for more–despite the consequences. Americans now consume 150 pounds of sugar sweeteners (cane and beet sugar and corn sweeteners)[6] a year–about 22 teaspoons daily–and the food industry is partially to blame. Historically, our sustenance came from foods high in nutrition and low in calories, but the products designed by food conglomerates today are low in nutrition and high in calories. Most Americans are overfed yet nutritionally starving. As government continues to subsidize the food industry's mass production of fast-food staples such as wheat, dairy, and soy over real food, we're likely to see these trends continue.

But we cannot put all the blame on the food industry and the government subsidies it receives. The behavior, mind-set, and lifestyle of the present generation are a vital part of the dynamics of obesity and weight-related illness. We need to look at the greater ecosystem of biological, microbiological, sociological, and psychological influences that lead to weight gain to find a solution to this problem.

They teach us in medical school–in the few hours devoted to the subject–that weight gain and weight loss are merely a reflection of total caloric consumption, metabolism, *and nothing else.* But this concept doesn't explain why people can't drop weight despite eating less food. Why are so many people gaining weight, and what can we do to help them lose it?

That's what this book is about.

THE REAL REASON FOR THE OBESITY EPIDEMIC

The truth is that you gain or lose weight for multiple reasons. We now know that glycemic control, insulin spikes, inflammation, and even hormones that regulate metabolism are all factors that determine your weight. Obesity is a complex disorder resulting from a combination of genetic, behavioral, lifestyle, and psychological factors that influence food choices and activity.

Sure, overconsumption of calories may be part of the reason people gain weight. But why are these folks overconsuming food in the first place? There are many reasons. If you trace only one possible biochemical chain of causality, you get something like this: Overeating stems from imbalances in the network of brain biochemicals called neurotransmitters (like dopamine), along with gut-derived hormones that regulate satiety and short-term appetite (like ghrelin) and control our urge to eat. As we overconsume calories and become inactive, our fat cells continue to grow and become insensitive to insulin. This results in diabetes, atherosclerosis, cardiovascular disease, and a number of other complications.

But there are *many* other ways to gain weight. Science is now showing us that obesity can result from a number of imbalances in the body, from inflammation to endocrine and metabolic dysregulation. The story of weight loss is much more nuanced than most of modern medicine would have us believe.

Fascinating new research points to yet another contributing factor I've long known played a role in the weight-loss drama–the gut microbiome, the ecosystem of flora in your intestines. Research is showing that it's the balance and diversity of these microbiota in your gut that may ultimately determine the fate of your weight.

In retrospect, this is the precise reason I was able to drop the weight that had plagued me for so many years–I rebalanced the flora in my gut. In 1979, I was ahead of my time in forming my own blueprint for weight-loss success. Impressed with my results, friends and family started asking for dietary advice. Although only a junior in college, I was counseling people about diet and weight loss, and I've done so ever since. Even then, I found that my approach allowed people to eat more, weigh less, and feel more vibrant. Over the years, I've refined this plan based on my education and experience as a doctor. But you'd be surprised how much of my approach is the same as it was in the '70s.

Why? Because the diet I developed happened to focus on improving gut microbial balance and diversity. My original vision of becoming a doctor was to help others lose weight once I found a system that worked. What I didn't know was that my mission to help people would come to fruition through serendipity.

My accidental discovery has now been borne out by two new major areas of research that have revolutionized our understanding of why people gain weight. Both point to a disordered digestive tract as playing a central role.

First, the human gut microbiota have been found to play a pivotal role in weight maintenance because of their influence on food metabolism, appetite regulation, energy expenditure, endocrine regulation, gut barrier integrity, inflammation, and insulin resistance. Distortions in the composition of normal, healthy intestinal flora have been found to contribute to obesity.

Second, weight gain has recently been linked to chronic low-grade systemic inflammation in the gut that results from the seepage of gut-derived bacterial toxins through a porous intestinal lining into the bloodstream. This further drives problems with insulin resistance and fat accumulation.

When people address these two core systemic processes by focusing on rebalancing the flora in their gut, the results are often miraculous. I've witnessed the turnaround of patients who have followed the same program you'll learn in this book. I've observed many patients in my clinic lose as much as 10 to 15 pounds every 4 weeks. They were able to burn fat and keep it off for the long term. They were succeeding on my plan even though other diet programs had previously failed them. With my plan, their weight loss has been seamless and sustained. And miraculously, many of their chronic digestive symptoms disappeared as well.

ONE UNFORGETTABLE CASE

A woman named Rose came to see me after being treated by several other doctors for troubling gas and bloating. Despite her search, Rose couldn't find relief and was eventually diagnosed with irritable bowel syndrome (IBS). Although she "starved herself," Rose gained weight, and no doctor could find a metabolic cause.

I suspected that Rose's gas, bloating, and abdominal discomfort after meals were due to the rapid fermentation of foods by an overgrowth of bacteria in her small bowel. This condition is called small intestinal bacterial overgrowth (SIBO). My suspicion was confirmed by lactulose hydrogen breath testing. I placed Rose on the Gut Balance Revolution and treated her with antimicrobial herbs to help kill off the overgrowth of gut bugs in her small bowel.

Six weeks after her initial visit, Rose came in for her follow-up. Repeat lactulose hydrogen breath testing showed the SIBO was gone, and Rose no longer had gas, bloating, or abdominal discomfort. Plus, she was proud of her new figure—she'd lost 20 pounds in 6 weeks, though she'd never dropped a single pound on one of her many previous diets.

Why did Rose lose weight on this program when so many others had failed?

Gut bugs. That's right. Gut bugs.

Around the same time I treated Rose, the science behind the role of gut microbes in weight gain, obesity, and diabetes had begun to explode. Research showed that lean mice can be made overweight by simply transferring gut microbes from obese mice. Likewise, the transfer of gut microbes from lean mice into obese mice improves diabetes.

In this book, I'll tell you more about exactly how a healthy balance of gut flora holds the key to maintaining a healthy weight. I'll also outline a complete program that will allow you to overcome your struggle with sustained weight loss. When you follow the plan, you'll likely find that you not only lose weight but also feel energized and vibrant, and many of your chronic health complaints may simply disappear.

Diet plays a special role in fostering the growth of microbes that favor obesity or feed bacteria that promote a lean metabolism. By tilling the soil of your gut microbiome, reseeding your gut with good fat-burning bacteria, fertilizing these friendly flora with special foods like prebiotics, and enhancing the overall biodiversity of your inner ecosystem, you can easily reboot, rebalance, and renew your health. I'll give you all the steps to do that. Along the way, I'll provide step-by-step meal plans, shopping lists, restaurant guides, recipes, recommendations on dietary supplements, stress-reduction techniques, exercise programs, and more.

The gut microbiome appears to be the mysterious factor that may drive weight gain despite our best efforts. Yet no other program has approached weight loss by rebalancing the gut flora. After seeing the success stories in my clinic, I felt it was time for me to share with the public the program I've been developing for decades.

If we take an integrative, whole-systems approach to health, healing, and weight management—when we learn to balance our body ecology and think about the species that live within us—we have greater hope for long-term success with weight loss and health outcomes.

By remapping your gut ecology, you can shed weight, rejuvenate your health, and feel vibrant. That's what the Gut Balance Revolution and this book are all about.

THE
GUT BALANCE
REVOLUTION

CHAPTER 1

The Hidden Secret to Weight Loss

WEED, SEED, AND FEED YOUR INNER GARDEN

Eat less and exercise more.

We've all heard it–from our doctors, on TV, on the Internet, in magazines, from friends and family. At one time or another, most of us have even tried it. But let me ask you: How has this recipe for weight loss worked for you?

It seems like such a simple formula–it matches our understanding of the physical principles of the universe. Energy in, energy out. What we don't spend, we store. It's common sense. It *must* be right.

There's just one small problem. It doesn't tell the whole story of why people gain weight. And it doesn't tell us how to lose it.

The calories in/calories out theory of weight loss is outdated. Modern science has proven beyond any shadow of doubt that your weight and your health are dependent on much more than how many calories you consume. You'll learn about some of this evolving science in this book. However, common sense and personal experience tell us that if weight and health were all about the amount of calories you consume each day, you could eat 1,800 calories of Oreos and Diet Coke and stay fit and healthy. But, of course, we all know that doesn't work. The food you eat has a far greater influence on your body than solely the amount of energy it provides. It has wide-ranging effects on numerous biochemical and physiological processes. While it's true that most of us could afford to eat a little less, and reducing total caloric intake is necessary to a certain point to incur weight loss, the quality of the calories you consume is far more important in the long run.

That's especially true if you want to burn fat and keep it off for good. Anyone can go on a starvation diet, burn out the treadmill, and drop a few pounds. You might even lose a couple of pants sizes or notice that you look a little better in your bathing suit. But the sad reality is that most of the pounds you drop will be water weight, and some fat-burning muscle to boot. Without altering your lifestyle and eating habits, revisiting your relationship to food, and systematically enhancing the overall quality of the calories you consume, your diet is doomed to fail in the long run.

In fact, research has shown that the vast majority of calorie-restricted diets fail long term. A study conducted at the University of California in Los Angeles showed that people who go on calorie-restricted diets typically lose 5 to 10 percent of their body weight within 6 months–but regain everything they've lost within 4 to 5 years.[1]

And this yo-yo effect causes downstream biological complications that make it even more difficult to lose weight in the long run. Your body is a complex ecosystem (actually, an ecosystem *within* an ecosystem, as we'll see shortly), and all complex biological systems have mechanisms in place to maintain homeostasis. The dictionary defines homeostasis as "the maintenance of relatively stable internal physiological conditions (as body temperature or the pH of blood) in higher animals under fluctuating environmental conditions." It's easy to see why this is important. If you didn't have a built-in biological mechanism for maintaining basic physiological processes such as body heat, survival would be far more complicated.

What does this have to do with weight? Well, the rate of your metabolism and the amount of fat you carry are tightly regulated by a complex array of homeostatic internal processes. Some doctors call this internal thermostat your "body weight set point," and it's influenced by a number of factors such as hormones, neurotransmitters, intestinal peptides, your gut microbiome, and more.[2, 3]

Several studies have shown that your body weight set point remains fairly constant, maintaining your body weight in a stable range despite minor changes in energy intake (calories in) and expenditure (calories out). It's also been shown that your body is very efficient at holding on to weight during periods of caloric deprivation. That's because your body set point has shifted downward and is telling your body that your metabolism needs to be slowed to minimize weight loss during periods of caloric deprivation. This provides a clear survival advantage but demonstrates how low-calorie diets that are based solely upon energy deprivation have short-term efficacy as the new set point limits ones weight loss. Your body weight set point will also try to keep you from gaining weight when you eat too much by burning more calories, but this effect is short lived. Overall, it's harder to lose weight than it is to gain weight–an experience many of us are all too familiar with. Yo-yo dieting is a very common result of weight-loss programs and causes one to ultimately weigh more. Yo-yo dieting has been shown to raise the body's set point, which is your brain telling your body "Hey, we ought to now weigh more to reach this new equilibrium" and sending control signals throughout your body to slow metabolism so you gain body weight and fat mass–the new normal. Thus, you weigh more than before with each failed energy-deficit diet program and it becomes harder and harder to lose weight as the set point is raised each time a weight-loss regimen fails.[4]

To effectively lose weight and keep it off, you need to strategically alter your body weight set point. Emerging evidence suggests that bariatric surgery, particularly gastric bypass, may work in part by helping the body establish a new set point by altering the physiology governing body weight.[5] And that's the real problem with yo-yo dieting–every time your weight rebounds, your set point gets pushed higher, so your body acclimates to the new body weight set point as "the new normal." Hormonal and metabolic adaptations now make it more and more difficult to lose weight.[6]

Calories in/calories out doesn't work for the masses, because it *can't* work. It can't work, because simply reducing the amount of food you consume and spending more energy exercising doesn't necessarily influence your body weight set point. Sure, there are some people out there who can lose weight by eating less and jogging 100 miles a week, but they're the exception. We may admire (or even be a little jealous of) them, but they don't point the way for the majority of us to lose weight and stay healthy.

So if eating less and exercising more isn't a realistic, sustainable way to lose weight, what is?

This is where things get interesting. When you talk behind closed doors to doctors or scientists who specialize in metabolism, they'll reveal that we aren't 100 percent certain *why* there is an obesity epidemic in this country in light of the fact that we are consuming fewer calories as a nation.

Yep, you read that right. We are getting fatter, even though we are taking in fewer calories than we did a decade ago. A new study published in the *American Journal of Clinical Nutrition* shows that the average daily caloric consumption of Americans fell by 74 calories between 2003 and 2010. Despite this shift, obesity rates among women have stayed at a whopping 35 percent, and for men they continue to increase.[7]

This finding confused the authors of the study. "It's hard to reconcile what these data show, and what is happening with the prevalence of obesity," said coauthor Dr. William Dietz, former director of the division of Nutrition, Physical Activity, and Obesity at the Centers for Disease Control and Prevention.[8] The data simply don't bear out the whole calories in/calories out concept.

But there's no question we're in trouble. The constellation of obesity, metabolic syndrome, and type 2 diabetes is arguably the greatest single health-care challenge in the industrialized world, and it's rapidly spreading to less-developed nations. Until a few decades ago, obesity was rare. Now the people who are obese or overweight outnumber those suffering from malnutrition. This is an unprecedented state for our species.

And it's spawned an industry of celebrity "experts," each of whom claims to have found "the single most important reason America is overweight." These people will try to convince you their special method can help every person drop many pounds overnight. Many will hype an exotic food-based supplement that no one has heard about except on celebrity talk shows, while others talk about detoxing, juicing, and bizarre rituals that grab our attention based on pure sensationalism. More evidence-based health experts deliver the message that stabilizing insulin resistance and blood sugar is key, while others focus on reducing inflammation. Other authorities tell us about the importance of balancing our hormones. Then there's the "Paleo" prophets and the vegan aficionados, and a million others.

So which of them is right? None of them and all of them.

There are *many* factors that lead to weight gain and weight loss. There's no question insulin resistance and blood sugar balance play a vital role, and they may indeed be one of the core reasons so many of us are overweight, exhausted, and unwell. They are the key factors in metabolic syndrome and type 2 diabetes. We also know that low-grade systemic inflammation and creeping weight gain, especially around the belly, are intimately linked. In fact, the adipose tissue that collects around the belly is inflammatory and leads to a cycle of hormonal imbalance and further weight gain. Do hormones play a role? Absolutely. Insulin, leptin, ghrelin, thyroid, and other hormones are all pieces of the weight-loss puzzle.

Recent research has even linked certain environmental toxins, such as persistent organic pollutants (POPs), to weight gain. These chemical substances—often referred to as obesogens—persist in the environment, bioaccumulate through the food web, and pose a risk of causing adverse effects to human health and the environment. POPs mimic hormones like estrogen that encourage your body to put on weight, and they block cellular docking stations that trigger weight loss.

Genetics plays a role, too, and so does your community—people who have good social support networks tend to weigh less and live healthier, longer lives. Yes, calories play a role and how much you eat does seem to matter, but it's not the whole picture.

And there is one, until now largely unrecognized factor that connects many of these pieces. . . .

New research is showing us that this factor has a far more profound impact on long-term weight-loss results and overall health than anybody expected. Medical scientists are beginning to find that when you balance this area of your health, weight tends to drop off more easily and your results last longer. My extensive experience as a leading digestive health specialist and medical nutritionist at The Johns Hopkins University School of Medicine bears out what this cutting-edge science is now revealing. Your gut microflora—the vast ecosystem that lives in your intestines—is a crucial factor in weight gain and illness and holds the key to permanent weight loss and vibrant health.

THE HUMAN GUT MICROBIOME: THE GARDEN OF LIFE AND KEY TO HEALTH

As human beings, we do not live in isolation. We are part of a complex social network of people who collectively interdepend on one another for just about everything. Whether it's food, mail delivery, energy to run our homes, or whatever else we want or need, we're reliant on tens of thousands of people to optimally live our lives. Modern industrialized society has evolved to a highly sophisticated synchrony of symbiosis.

The human body is not so different. It's not a sterile island but a complex network of trillions of microorganisms. These tiny beings surround us and lie deep within us, and we are utterly dependent on them for our health and well-being.

This may be difficult to fathom, since we're taught that we need to get rid of germs and maximize our hygiene to optimize our health. In fact, at the first sign of any apparent illness in childhood, we're doused with antibiotics, though medical science has little idea and virtually no research regarding the long-term consequences of these treatments.

We didn't evolve in a glass bubble, and we don't live in a germ-free world today. Nor would we want to. As you'll learn in this chapter, these microorganisms are crucial for the development of a healthy immune system and play a role in many other vital functions.

Living deep in your lower intestines is a complex ecosystem of microorganisms—a veritable garden of life. This magnificent orchard is composed of viruses, bacteria, and fungi, all of which collectively constitute what's called the human gut microbiome. When we care for this garden and nourish our flora, our health flourishes. But when we feed these microorganisms poorly and treat them poorly, the biodiversity of this ecosystem plummets and our health is compromised.

The modern movement of "going green" has taught us a lot about the importance of developing practices that support environmental sustainability. Each of us participates in a larger ecosystem, and our actions influence the health of that ecosystem. If we want our world to be healthy, we have to act in ways that help make it healthy.

But what about the ecosystem inside of you? It's something few of us think about. Just as our actions influence the ecosystem around us, they influence our ecosystem within. Balance and biodiversity in this ecosystem create health—imbalance and reduced diversity in the ecosystem create illness. There are many mechanisms by which microbes can protect us from disease or make us sick, help us lose weight or pack on the pounds, and we'll discuss many of them throughout this book. Indeed, the most important lesson is that the solution to your weight problem as well as many of the diseases we face today may never be found if research remains focused on you, the host. We must pay due attention to the host-environment interface—the complex set of relationships that constitute the human–gut microbiome connection.

The average human being has about 100 trillion of these organisms at any given time. Although most are located in your lower intestines, you're literally bathed and surrounded by microbes. Despite the best hygiene, we carry billions of microbes that hide under fingernails, lounge between teeth, stick to our skin, coat our eyes, hang out in our hair. There are more than 600,000 bacteria living on just 1 square inch of skin. The same holds true at internal passages: your respiratory system, genitourinary system, eustachian (ear) tubes, and much more. Just like in the 1999 sci-fi movie *The Matrix,* the naked human eye sees only an altered reality. It's incapable of seeing the trillions of microbes that constantly surround us. How would you feel if you could see every one-celled organism?

The microflora in your gut alone weigh about 3 to 5 pounds. These microbial cells outnumber your own human cells by a factor of 10 to 1, and microbial DNA outnumbers your human DNA by 100 to 1. Take a moment to think about what that means. Inside your body, there are more bacterial cells and DNA than human cells and DNA. Do you think this might have an impact on your health?

While we haven't yet identified all the strains of human gut microflora, the Human Microbiome Project, a collaboration led by Dr. Jeffrey Gordon of Washington University School of Medicine in St. Louis, made substantial advances in accomplishing this incredible feat. With $173 million in funding from the National Institutes of Health, this project's mission was to comprehensively characterize and analyze their role in health.[9, 10]

So far, they've isolated 1,000 species across dozens of different phyla–an astounding variety of microbes. There are few ecosystems on the planet that are as complex as the one inside of you. The species density and biodiversity of the human large intestine is nearly equal to that of the Amazon rain forest.

Our relationship with this ecosystem is symbiotic. We house our flora and provide them with food. In turn, these organisms serve us in a number of ways. They:

- **Break down complex carbohydrates**. Humans lack the enzymes to do this. You wouldn't be able to properly digest a single fruit or vegetable without your gut microflora.

- **Produce vitamins and nutrients**. You'd otherwise be unable to manufacture these on your own, including vitamin K, vitamin B_{12}, niacin, pyridoxine, and others.[11]

- **Produce short-chain fatty acids (SCFAs)**. We'll spend a good deal of time in the next chapter on what these are and why they're important, but for now, be aware that they're involved in regulating immunity, healing, and combatting inflammation, and they may protect you against cancer and other diseases.[12]

- **Protect against pathogens**. Your gut microflora are your first line of defense against foreign invaders.

- **Help train the immune system**. Bacterial genes send signals to your gut's immune system that control local and systemic inflammation and play a role in determining whether you develop allergies and autoimmune diseases.[13]

- **Support detoxification**. When you metabolize your food, toxic metabolites (including carcinogens) are formed in your liver and carried by your bile into your digestive tract for elimination. Your gut flora degrade these potentially harmful biochemicals so they can be safely eliminated.

- **Modulate the nervous system**. Emerging research shows a connection between your gut microbiota, your digestive system, your nervous system, and your brain that may affect everything from appetite regulation to behavior to mood.[14]

For all these reasons–and many more–your gut microbiome has a profound impact on your weight, your health, and the quality of your life. Balance in this ecosystem leads to health and optimal weight. Imbalance contributes to weight gain and a plethora of diseases including type 2 diabetes,[15] irritable bowel syndrome,[16, 17] inflammatory bowel disease,[18-23] cardiovascular disease,[24] allergies,[25, 26] mood disorders,[27] and many others.

How Does the Gut Microbiome Get out of Balance?

There are lots of ways.

Consider, for instance, where your founding populations of intestinal bacteria came from–their origin impacts your weight and health. When you're in the womb, your intestines are relatively sterile. Babies acquire their gut microbiota from their mothers while passing through the birth canal and via breastfeeding.

When babies are born by Caesarean section (C-section) or bottle-fed, their gut flora aren't as fully developed. Several studies have shown that babies who were breastfed appear to be protected against the development of childhood obesity,[28] and that being born via a C-section puts young people at higher risk for developing this condition.[29] In Chapter 2, you'll learn more about these studies. I'll go into greater detail about the importance of early exposure to flora and explain how our hygiene-obsessed culture may be setting the stage for illness and weight gain by killing off our friendly gut microbes.

Obviously, you have no control over how you were born or whether you were breast-fed. But the good news is that there are plenty of other factors you do have control over that influence the balance of your gut microbiome. For example, your diet.

As Dr. Stig Bengmark explained in his article "Nutrition of the Critically Ill–A 21st-Century Perspective": "Diet has the most powerful influence on gut microbial activity."[30] Everyone knows the saying "You are what you eat." Dr. Sanjay Gupta went a step further when he wrote: "If we are what we eat, then Americans are corn and soy."[31] His sobering report shows how ubiquitous these disease-promoting, proinflammatory food commodities are in our bodies. Dr. Gupta actually had a strand of hair analyzed by Dr. Todd Dawson from the University of California, Berkeley, revealing that 69 percent of the carbon in that sample was derived from dietary corn. Our bodies are reflections of our dietary choices—all food is ultimately digested then metabolized by our gut flora, so it's actually more accurate to say "You are what *they* ate!"

Increasing evidence shows that how you feed your gut microbiome is a critical factor in your health and weight. Eating a diet rich in high-fat, sugary, processed foods reduces the overall biodiversity of your gut microbiome. These changes can happen in as little as 24 hours, and growing evidence shows that when the diversity of your gut microbiome is altered, you pack on pounds. A review paper published in the journal *Future Microbiology* that looked at the role of the gut microbiome in weight gain and obesity stated, "The gut microbiome's influence on obesity is likely to involve a microbial-dietary interaction."[32]

Diet isn't the only factor that affects the health and biodiversity of the gut microbiome. The unnecessary use of antibiotics also plays a role in the balance of the gut microbiome, as highlighted by Dr. Martin Blaser's new book, *Missing Microbes*.[33] We give antibiotics to children at record rates. In the United States, the average child now receives one course of antibiotics per year and has received 10 to 20 courses of antibiotics by the age of 18.[34] While antibiotics can be useful medications, they're overprescribed, and they have a detrimental long-term impact on the human intestinal microbiome. This may be one reason for the skyrocketing of childhood obesity rates. Indeed, a recent report showed that infants given broad-spectrum antibiotics before the age of 2 have a higher chance of becoming obese while children.[35]

That's to say nothing of the hidden antibiotics we're exposed to every day. Our meats are loaded with detectable levels of antibiotics, which adversely impact the balance and biodiversity of our gut microbiome.

Is this overuse of antibiotics and its impact on our gut microbiome responsible for the boom in obesity rates? It's obviously not the sole factor, but growing evidence is showing that it may be an important—and until now underrecognized—contributor to the obesity epidemic in this country. I'll explain more about why and how in the next chapter.

Other factors contribute to an out-of-balance gut microbiome, including stress, physical inactivity, and personal relationships. Each has an important influence on your health that can positively or negatively impact the symbiotic helpers in your gut.

So how do you keep the friendly flora happy and healthy? You become a good gut bug gardener.

Becoming a Good Gut Bug Gardener: Weeding and Seeding Your Inner Flora

By now you may be thinking, "Okay, I've heard some of this before. I know there are bugs in my gut. Don't I just need to eat some yogurt or kefir or take probiotics to keep them healthy?"

It's a lot more complicated than that. Yogurt, kefir, and probiotics can be very helpful, and each is an important part of this program, but these alone aren't enough. Just as you can't support a rain forest by dropping a few pine seeds or spreading some nitrogen fertilizer, a couple cups of store-bought yogurt a day won't provide your gut microflora the complete nourishment they need to thrive.

You have trillions of tiny beings living inside of you—an ecosystem so complex human science has yet to understand it fully. As you live and eat, so does your gut microflora live and eat. When you're healthy, the ecosystem is healthy. Perhaps the most important mark of a healthy ecosystem is biodiversity—the more types of species present, the healthier the overall ecosystem is likely to be.

As with all ecosystems, different species constantly vie for power and superiority. When one gets a strong enough foothold and starts to outcompete the others to the point of extinction, the health of the overall ecosystem plummets. Imagine what happens if a species of predators hunts its prey to extinction. This can create obvious problems: The predators, for example, now have nothing to eat. But these changes in species can have effects that reverberate throughout the ecosystem in ways we may not expect, because all the species in an ecosystem are dependent on one another in numerous ways.

The same is true of your inner ecosystem. When certain strains of gut bugs get too strong a foothold, they can outcompete their counterparts, with broad effects throughout your gut microbiome and your body. Some bugs are flat-out bad actors. Salmonella, shigella, and others will make you sick even if they are found at low levels in your gut. Other strains can cause problems only if they predominate. You may gain weight, develop chronic illness, and experience other difficulties. As we'll see in Chapter 2, there are at least seven pathways that lead from gut microbiome imbalance to weight and health problems—and science is discovering more connections every day.

On the other hand, there are trillions of gut microbiota that are commensals (friendly microbes typically found in healthy humans), which we know play a role in supporting proper weight regulation and are important for optimal health and well-being. These include bifidobacteria, some strains of lactobacillus, and many others.

The number and type of bugs throughout your gut are also important. The vast majority of your gut microbiome is located in your large intestine, and that's where the vast majority should be. However, there are relatively smaller quantities of bacteria throughout your small intestine and the other parts of your gut as well. This is normal. Problems can arise if too many bacteria begin to inhabit your small intestine, leading to a condition called small intestinal bacterial overgrowth (SIBO), which we'll discuss later.

Of course, you want to have plenty of the commensal flora or good bugs in your large intestine, but you *always* have strains of potentially helpful and noxious bacteria in your inner ecosystem. Indeed, some species seem to have positive effects under some circumstances and negative effects in others. The name of the game isn't "eliminating bad bugs"–you couldn't do that even if you wanted to without extensive and counter-productive collateral damage (though it's imperative in the event of a gastrointestinal infectious illness). Instead, medical science is showing us that the basic biological laws governing the ecosystem around us also apply to the one within. It's the overall bal-ance and biodiversity of your inner ecosystem that's important, and the Gut Balance Revolution program is designed to help you enhance your gut's biodiversity and regain balance.

To achieve this, I've created a three-phase diet and lifestyle change system based on the best research current science has to offer. It's supported by my personal experience as well as my experience as a clinician. I have treated hundreds of patients (some of whom you'll meet along the way) using the methods in this book with positive results. Here's how it works.

- **Phase 1: Reboot.** In this phase, you'll till the soil of your gut microbiome, setting the stage for a lush garden to flourish. It's a 30-day higher-protein, ketogenic, low-glycemic-load, low-FODMAP diet (if you don't know what those terms mean, don't worry–you'll learn along the way). It's designed to enhance your digestive health, speed up your metabolism, reduce inflammation, improve insulin sensitivity and blood glucose bal-ance, burn fat and help you lose weight and keep it off for good, enhance your mood, and set the stage for the resolution of many chronic illnesses.

- **Phase 2: Rebalance.** Once you've tilled the soil of your gut, you're ready to plant seeds and fertilize them so your inner garden will flourish. In this phase, I'll teach you how to strengthen and diversify your inner ecosystem by fertilizing it with special foods and supplements that are like Miracle-Gro (or compost, if you prefer an organic gar-dening analogy) to your good gut bugs. These include prebiotics, probiotics, and other foods that help them thrive.

- **Phase 3: Renew.** Once you've completed Phase 2, your gut microflora will be properly balanced, biodiversity will have returned to your inner ecosystem, and you'll natu-rally lose weight and feel more energetic. You may find feelings like depression and anxiety evaporate and make tremendous strides in overcoming chronic illness. Now your job will be to integrate a long-term, flexible, sustainable eating plan that will help you keep the weight off. This is where the vast majority of diets fail and why so many studies show that diets don't work. Many programs can help you lose weight for a little while– 6 months to a year–then your body weight set point slows metabo-lism and gradually induces weight gain, as we've already learned. But I want you to have the tools to achieve and maintain optimal weight, health, and gut microbiome balance *for life*. That's what you'll learn to do in Phase 3.

As you walk down this path toward a healthy, thriving personal ecosystem, I will provide you with the tools and information that you need to rebalance your gut microbiome, optimize your nutrition, exercise more effectively in less time, live a less stressful and more fulfilling life, achieve optimal health and weight, vitality, and more. You will discover:

- Superfoods that will support your gut microflora, help you lose weight more effectively, and may protect you from a wide variety of chronic illnesses (eat these and you will see your health bloom as your waistline shrinks)

- Foods to avoid to keep your gut microbiome balanced for life

- A complete eating program—including delicious menus and recipes—that will keep your gut bugs happy and healthy

- When you should include fermented foods in your diet and when to avoid them (eat them at the wrong time and you send your gut microbiome further out of balance)

- How stress adversely impacts your gut microbiome and how one special relaxation technique may help nourish the friendly flora within

- Why getting the right amount of sleep is critical if you want your inner garden to thrive

- Simple, effective, quick exercise routines you can do at home that will amp up your metabolism

- The truth about supplements for weight loss: which ones work, and which are absolute bunk (I will also teach you what to look for in a high-quality probiotic)

- And more . . .

I'm eager to get started and share more about the surprising ways your gut microbiome impacts weight and health. But before I get to that, I want to address one critical question you may be asking yourself right about now.

IS THIS PROGRAM FOR ME?

You may be a little skeptical about this program, and I want to be honest and let you know it's not for everyone. There's no one-size-fits-all diet that works for every person. Despite what many experts might tell you, humanity has thrived on a wide variety of diets. From the Maasai, whose diet largely consisted of blood and yak milk, to the Pima, who ate acorns and cactus, one thing is clear: Homo sapiens is an adaptable species.

As we learn more about human biology, we move ever closer to a truly personalized model of medicine where specific interventions are developed for specific individuals. I believe that at some point in the future, we may be able to develop diet and lifestyle recommendations tailored to every person's specific requirements.

But we're still a long way from that, so for now we have to take what we know of the science today and apply it in a way that makes the most sense for the general population. That's what I've attempted to do with this program.

It's highly likely your gut microflora are not optimally balanced. If you've struggled to lose weight or keep it off; if you had several courses of antibiotics in your youth or have undertaken a course of them in the last year; if you suffer with digestive discord; if you struggle with a chronic illness (one-third of Americans do); if you have allergies or asthma; or if you're coping with depression, anxiety, or other mood disorders, it's highly likely that your gut microbiome is not in optimal condition–and it may be *way* out of balance.

You have nothing to lose in learning more about your gut microflora and trying this program. The good news is that the same things that support your inner ecosystem optimize your entire biology. So the worst-case scenario is that you'll learn to eat and live in a way that supports your body, reduces inflammation, rebalances your hormones, enhances insulin sensitivity, and reestablishes a lush garden in your digestive system. Plus, you'll likely learn a few things you didn't know about your digestive health along the way.

But honestly, I think you'll get a whole lot more than that out of this program. Most of my patients who have tried this diet have lost at least 10 to 12 pounds in a matter of weeks, felt more energized than they had in years, and watched many chronic symptoms simply fade away.

THE GUT BALANCE REVOLUTION SUCCESS STORIES
Ted, 79

Ted, a 79-year-old gentleman from Iran, came to see me accompanied by his daughter. He presented with metabolic syndrome, severe cardiovascular disease with two cardiac stents and subsequent angioplasty, type 2 diabetes, and hypertension, and he was morbidly obese. He came in to my office because he had started suffering from bloating, abdominal swelling, excess gas, and he was exhausted. He began to wonder if something in his gut may be the core of many of his health problems.

Ted ate a standard American diet (SAD)—high in inflammatory fats and processed carbohydrates and low in omega-3 fatty acids, fruits and vegetables, and fiber. I realized immediately that Ted's gas, bloating, and sudden abdominal distention after meals is typical of small intestinal bacterial overgrowth (SIBO), which could easily be the outcome of how he was eating and living. SIBO occurs when gut bacteria overpopulates the small intestine. In SIBO, the bacterial counts in the small intestine are markedly elevated and are imbalanced with the enrichment of anaerobes. This leads to a host of metabolic complications that you will learn about in the next chapter.

To confirm my suspicion of SIBO, I ran a lactulose hydrogen breath test, the standard test for the condition, in which the patient drinks a sugary solution. The bacteria present in the gut ferment the sugar, producing gases that are diffused into the bloodstream and exhaled into a tubelike breath analyzer.

Teds test was off the charts for SIBO. I placed him on a diet low in a category of fermentable foods called FODMAPs (fermentable oligo-, di-, monosaccharides and polyols) to starve out the heavy burden of bacterial overgrowth in the small intestine. To further weed out these bugs, I advised Ted to take some antimicrobial herbs for an additional month while he continued on the diet.

After 60 days, Ted felt like a new person. He lost 27 pounds and felt more energetic than he had in years. His gas and bloating after meals disappeared, and his metabolic syndrome improved.

Ted then returned to Iran. I advised him to begin fertilizing his flora with pre-biotic and probiotic foods like kimchi, miso soup, pickled foods, asparagus, and homemade yogurt. After another 30 days of fertilizing his inner garden, he lost another 10 pounds, and every symptom he entered my clinic with disappeared. Ted was a new man.

Ted, like many of my patients, lost weight while healing his gut and rebalancing his intestinal flora. I invite you to join me on the same journey that he took: to go where no weight-loss book has gone before. We'll travel deep inside your gastrointestinal system, where an array of flora lives that rivals even the most fecund rain forest. Along the way, you'll learn how these bacteria support your health and how you can support them. You'll learn to live in balance and harmony with your gut microflora. And by doing so, you will lose weight, feel better, and be happier than you have in a long time.

To begin the journey, let's take a more careful look at the ways your gut microbiome influences your health. I want you to understand some of the basic biochemical pathways that connect the flora in your gut to the rest of your body. This will help you realize just how powerful these microscopic organisms are and give you the knowledge you need to better care for them so that they can better care for you.

CHAPTER 2

Dysbiosis—
Gut Microbe Imbalance

SEVEN PATHWAYS TO WEIGHT GAIN AND ILLNESS

Strange but true: Growing research suggests that the bugs in your gut send messages to your brain causing the release of hormones that make you feel full and satisfied and help you lose weight. Your gut flora also influence the chemical pathways that help regulate blood sugar and insulin balance. And your gut microbiome teaches your immune system how to function correctly and even helps regulate how fast–and how well–your metabolism works.

Your gut flora represent a highly diverse ecosystem whose composition is as unique as your fingerprint. The more diverse it is, the healthier you are. Your gut ecosystem is also delicately balanced between many friendly symbiotes and a limited number of potentially harmful pathogens that are prevented from gaining a foothold and triggering an aggressive immune response.

There are times, however, when your gut's garden gets out of balance, resulting in an overabundance of pathogens and/or a deficiency of beneficial bacteria. This is called dysbiosis–a state of microbial imbalance related to your gut ecosystem, your skin, your inner ear, or any of the other communities of microbes in your body. The scientific literature is quite robust in connecting dysbiosis of human ecosystems to adverse health outcomes.

But the key news is this: We're beginning to understand that your gut microbiome has a far broader impact on your health and weight than scientists originally knew. The influence appears to be so strong that some researchers refer to the gut microbiome as a "hidden organ" whose health is a strong indicator of your long-term weight and well-being.

In this chapter, I'll review seven ways your gut microbiota influence your health and weight. We'll take a journey into the fascinating relationship between your brain and your gut bugs, and we'll look at how your gut flora influence your metabolism. We'll

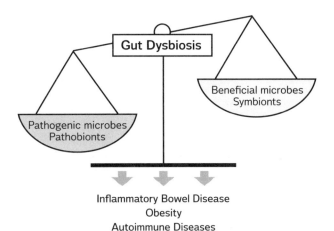

Inflammatory Bowel Disease
Obesity
Autoimmune Diseases

GUT DYSBIOSIS—CONSEQUENCES

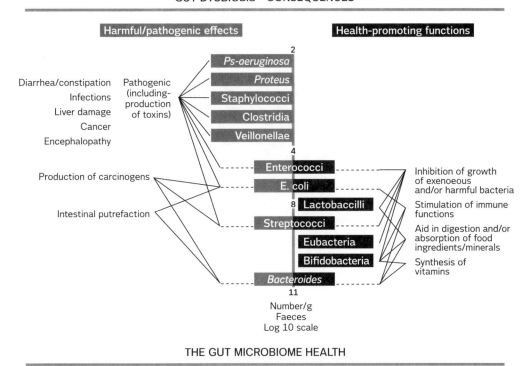

THE GUT MICROBIOME HEALTH

even talk about how these commensals (friendly microbes) communicate with your genes to influence your health. Along the way, we'll review some of the most recent, cutting-edge research in the fields of gastroenterological well-being and metabolism that demonstrates just how powerful these tiny symbiotic microbes are.

The take-home message: *The type of flora in your gut profoundly influences your weight.* But how? What do these bugs do in your body to tell it to store fat or drop it?

Could a Poo Transplant Help You Lose Weight?

Scientists at the Center for Genome Science and Systems Biology at Washington University in St. Louis asked themselves a simple question: Does gut flora influence weight gain? To find the answer, they designed an interesting experiment.[1] They took two groups of mice whose digestive tracts had been sterilized. In the first group, they colonized the mice's intestines with the fecal flora from an obese cage mate. In the second group, they colonized the intestines with gut flora from a lean mouse. They then fed these two groups of mice the same diet for 2 weeks. At the end of 2 weeks, the mice that were inoculated with feces containing gut bugs from the obese mice had gained more weight than the mice exposed to the lean mouse's gut microbiome, despite equivalent food intake and activity.

This experiment shows that there are specific types of gut flora that cause you to gain fat—and other types that lead to weight loss. The type that's dominant will dictate how much fat you accumulate.

There are more recent and compelling fecal transplant experiments that further illustrate the importance of the gut flora in determining body weight. For instance, there is a study that examines the gut flora of pregnant women. In pregnancy, maternal gut microbes shift to a mix that favors fetal growth in the 3rd trimester of pregnancy which is associated with accelerated growth of the unborn and metabolic alterations in the mother such as insulin resistance and inflammation. The study found that fecal transfer from 3rd trimester pregnant women into germ-free mice causes obesity whereas 1st trimester donors remain lean.[2]

Another series of fecal transplant experiments provide further insights into the therapeutic potential of fecal transplants to treat obesity. Again, investigators from Washington University led by Dr. Jeffrey Gordon transplanted the feces from human twins that were discordant for body weight into the colon of germ-free mice. Mice receiving feces from the obese twin became obese while mice who were fecal recipients from the lean mice stayed lean. In the second part of this experiment these mice (lean and obese) were co-housed resulting in the exchange of fecal material. The scientists knowing how diet influences the gut microbiome then fed these co-housed mice either a high fat, low fiber or a low fat, high fiber diet. The obese mice receiving the low fat, high fiber diet lost weight and had the thin twins gut bacteria take over their flora while those fed the high fat, low fiber diet remained fat. These experiments are the first in humans to show that leanness is transferrable but only in the presence of a diet that promotes the growth of healthy flora.[3]

There have been interesting preliminary human trials using fecal bacteriotherapy (FBT)—the transfer of intestinal flora from one individual to another to establish a healthy gut microbiome in the recipient. In other words, these "poo transplants" take the feces of someone with a healthy microbiome and introduce it into someone who lacks one.

Most of the FBT studies so far have been conducted to determine whether this intervention would be an effective way to fight recurrent *Clostridium difficile* infection (CDI), which is usually seen after the use of antibiotics. Once successfully treated with antibiotics, CDI has a high recurrence (greater than 25 percent), since these antimicrobials generate dysbiosis that is characterized by a reduced diversity of the microbiota and the favoring of the growth of pathogenic species. CDI is a highly contagious diarrheal illness that is increasingly common in hospitals and can be lethal. Of the more than 400 cases of recurrent CDI that have been treated with FBT so far, the cure rate is over 90 percent for those with a potentially life-threatening infection that is resistant to all other aggressive medical therapy protocols. This is a powerful model for showing how dangerous dysbiosis can be and how rebalancing the gut ecosystem by infusing a healthy mix of gut microbes can produce dramatic results. There is even new research showing that swallowing a capsule of strained feces from a donor (poop pill) also works for recurrent *C. difficile*.[4] While other scientists are working on a synthetic stool solution.[5]

The million-dollar question: Are poo transplants an effective intervention for weight problems? Though they're not a cure for obesity, they appear to be capable of shifting one toward a lean metabolism.

In 2010, a randomized, double-blind, controlled trial on the use of FBT for diabetes and obesity was conducted in 18 male subjects.[6] Half received fecal material from lean male donors; half were implanted with their own feces. After 6 weeks, those who received fecal transplants from lean donors saw a marked reduction in fasting triglyceride levels and significant improvement in insulin sensitivity. This is a small test group, but the results were replicated in a similar follow-up study by the same researchers, so the science is promising.

Does that mean you'll be able to walk into your doctor's office in the near future and ask for a poo transplant to improve diabetes or lose weight? Not likely. The safety of fecal transplantation has never been formally investigated long term, and clinicians have expressed concerns about FBT "opening up a can of worms after 4 of 77 patients developed a de novo autoimmune disease after FBT."[7] Furthermore, the FDA limited the practice of FBT to those with CDI-associated diarrhea that failed to respond to conventional medical therapy, provided donors are properly screened and patients are informed that fecal transplants are still experimental.[8]

This is an exciting area of research. The Johns Hopkins University School of Medicine and its dean, Dr. Paul Rothman, have formed a microbiome interest group led by Drs. Cynthia Sears and Glenn Treisman to set priorities and to collaborate and pool resources. I'm fortunate to be working with this distinguished team of investigators. Dr. Linda A. Lee* leads the Johns Hopkins FBT program. Research on FBT may pave the way for more targeted, safer interventions for obesity, irritable bowel syndrome, inflammatory bowel problems, metabolic syndrome, and more.

---

* Dr. Lee is a pioneer and leader in the field of integrative gastroenterology and director of the Johns Hopkins Integrative Medicine and Digestive Center and is clinical director for the division of gastroenterology at The Johns Hopkins Hospital.

What implications does this have for your health? And most important, what can you do about it?

This book will guide you in shedding inches and pounds and gaining health and vitality by rebalancing your gut flora using an inside-out approach. But I've found that people have the most success in programs like this when they know *why* the interventions work.

So let's look at some of the ways imbalanced gut microbiota set the stage for weight gain. Then, in the remainder of this book, I'll explain precisely what you can do to rebalance your gut microbiome. What you're about to read is by no means a comprehensive review of the scientific literature on this subject. Instead, I've focused on key discoveries to give you a sense for how important your gut microbiome is for your weight and health.

First, let's look at how the bugs got in your gut in the first place and how this early inoculation may set the stage for your lifelong health.

PATHWAY 1: ORIGIN—WHERE YOUR GUT BUGS CAME FROM IS IMPORTANT

In your lower intestines is an ecosystem as complex as a rain forest. How did those bugs get there? Remember that the intestines are sterile *in utero*—there were no bugs in your gut when you were in the womb. You got them from the environment. So the first place most people acquire flora is via the birth canal. The female vagina is one of the few places besides the gut that harbors a significant population of microflora. Some vaginal fluid is almost always swallowed at birth, so the flora in it contain the first bugs that colonize the infant's gut.

The next significant influence on your gut microflora is breast milk, which contains bifidobacteria, a powerful probiotic we'll look at later in this book. It also appears that breast milk enhances the growth of biofilms—layers of friendly flora that adhere to and line our gastrointestinal tract, protecting against pathogens and infection.[9]

Growing data show that these early influencers on the gut microbiota may have long-term health impacts. A new study has found that C-sections and formula-feeding disrupt the development of intestinal microbial communities in infants. Researchers evaluated the composition of gut microbes of 24-month-old infants. When compared to vaginally delivered children, infants delivered by C-section were deficient in a specific genus of gut bacteria called *Bacteroides*, which helps break down complex molecules in the intestine, and in some studies appears to protect against obesity.[10]

In addition, researchers found significant differences between the gut microbes of infants who were strictly formula fed and those who were breastfed. For example, formula-fed infants had higher levels of the pathogenic organism *Clostridium difficile*, which can potentially cause an aggressive course of diarrhea.

Researchers have also proven that children born via C-section start life with fewer

THE GUT BALANCE REVOLUTION SUCCESS STORIES
Brenda Davis Gandy, 52

Back in the day, Brenda was a skinny kid and a slender, active teenager. But soon after college, that effortlessly slim girl became a stress eater and began to pack on the pounds. "For some reason," she says, "I'd go for the rice and pasta and bread whenever I was anxious—the stress would just make me want to eat everything in sight." Diets? Brenda tried them all. She'd drop a few pounds, then go off the program and gain the weight back.

But by February 2014, she'd gone up to a size 18 and was having trouble walking up a flight of stairs without getting short of breath. "I decided that I needed to do a complete life change," she recalls. "I didn't want to die young because of health problems—I wanted to change my lifestyle. Even if there were stressful situations that I had no control over, I realized that I could control what I put into my mouth." That's when she decided to try the Gut Balance Revolution.

For Brenda, the program was simple. "I liked that there were foods to favor, foods to have a few of, and foods to just forget about," she says. "Before, my diet consisted mostly of carbs—bread was really my weakness—but now I can go through a whole meal without having a slice of bread. My cravings haven't gone away completely, but I've tamed them quite a lot. And I've also found better ways to deal with stress." A surgical technician who works in the operating room, assisting the nurses and doctors, Brenda would often come out of a lengthy session filled with anxiety and grab a candy bar to calm her down. Now? "I just have a cup of yogurt and some fruit," she says. "It makes me feel better than a Snickers bar ever did, and it's way better for my health."

And now that she's lost 20 pounds—in just 6 weeks—a lot of things are better for Brenda. She's gone from a size 18 to a size 12, and she's had fun shopping for new clothes. Reluctant to exercise when she was heavier, she's now taken up Zumba and she's not afraid to rock a bathing suit. She sleeps better, too, and her acid reflux is pretty much a thing of the past. And, best of all, she has a brand-new sense of confidence. "I love all the compliments," she says. "I feel good, I look good, and it feels great to have my self-confidence built up."

healthy microbes in the gut, resulting in a higher risk for developing serious disease,[11] that these microbial imbalances may last up to 7 years after delivery,[12] and that Caesarean birth is a risk factor for allergies, asthma,[13] inflammatory bowel disease, celiac disease, type 1 diabetes, and autoimmunity.[14] It even predicts which babies will develop colic.[15] Additional studies show that babies born by Caesarean delivery are at higher risk for developing obesity, while those who are breastfed are more likely to be lean during childhood.[16, 17]

The rate of Caesarean births has steadily increased in recent decades. In 1965, the national Caesarean birth rate was 4.5 percent.[18] Today, nearly 32.8 percent of babies are born via C-section.[19] During this same time, the rate of childhood obesity has steadily increased. Correlation doesn't equal causation–that these two trends took place at the same time doesn't necessarily mean that an increase in C-sections is leading to increased rates of childhood obesity. But the coincidence invites the question: Are the two connected?

That's *not* to say that C-sections and formula-feeding are wrong. In many cases, Caesarean birth is the safest delivery method for mother and baby, and some women have difficulty breastfeeding. The point here is to illustrate how important our gastrointestinal flora are to our long-term health. One of the outcomes of studies like these is that medical researchers are now looking for ways to provide babies born by Caesarean, as well as formula-fed babies, the critical food for the gut microbiota.

But even if a baby is born by C-section or isn't breastfed, its gut microbiome can be rebalanced over time. That's because as we age, our environment, our lifestyle, and our diet continue to influence what kinds of bugs are in our guts and where they live.

In Chapter 10, we'll examine lifestyle factors like diet, exercise, and stress, but for now, let's take a moment to look at the ways we continue to acquire bugs through our childhood and learn about some of the specific challenges our children face in a world riddled with agents that kill these friendly flora.

Some of My Best Friends Are Germs: The Hygiene Hypothesis

Remember when your grandma told you that playing in the dirt would give you bugs? Well, she was right, but the bugs you collected were probably not the kind she referred to.

After vaginal birth and breastfeeding, the next place your gut bugs come from is the environment around you. Playing in the dirt, being around other children, even snuggling with the family pet provide important species of flora that help fill out our inner ecosystem. There's accumulating evidence that the intestinal bacteria acquired in postnatal development play an important role in "training" our immune system to function properly.

The prevalence of allergic disease sufferers has increased from 15 million in 1998 to 25.7 million in 2010.[20] The highest proportion is among children ages 5 to 14. Gut microbiome balance may hold one of the keys to unlocking the mystery of why we see this sudden increase in immune system imbalance.

Research has shown that children raised in rural environments, where playing in the dirt and being around farm animals are more common, have lower incidences of allergies and other autoimmune conditions.[21] Why? Well, these kids have a different relationship to the bugs in their environment.

In her fascinating book *Farmacology*, family doctor Daphne Miller investigates this relationship between rural environments—specifically small family-owned sustainable farms—and health. The book is a beautiful view of how the soil truly feeds us. One of the recurring themes in the book is that the microbial biodiversity of the soil breeds the diversity of our gut microbiome and impacts our health in a variety of ways. First, there is the simple fact that people who live on farms have more exposure to a broad array of microbes—from the soil, from the dung of farm animals, from the milk products of ruminants, and more. This exposure to a diverse microbial environment offers health benefits.[22] The amount of exposure children have to other kids also makes a difference, because they're exposed to more microbes. Scientists at the University of Arizona examined the incidence of asthma in 1,035 children and the prevalence of frequent wheezing related to the number of siblings or whether the children attended daycare.[23] They found that having older siblings protected against the development of asthma, as did attendance at daycare during the first 6 months of life. That's because increased germ exposure early in life confers protection against the future development of asthma. Since people who live and eat on farms are exposed to even more bugs, it's reasonable to assume that they receive further health benefits. Indeed, a study recently published in the *New England Journal of Medicine* showed that children raised on farms had lower incidences of asthma than those raised in urban environments; exposure to a broader array of microorganisms is the probable cause.[24]

But the relationship between microbes, farms, and health goes deeper. As Dr. Miller explained, the soil in sustainable organic farms has a broader biodiversity of microbes, which assimilate nutrients from the earth. The plants grown in this soil are more nutrient rich than their conventionally grown counterparts. Animals that eat these plants or humans who eat this nutrient-rich food acquire health benefits. One study revealed that organically farmed soils have higher biodiversity and that fruits grown in this rich microbial environment have higher levels of antioxidants, phenolics, and ascorbic acid.[25] Organic gardening has been shown to improve soil biodiversity and protect plants against harmful soilborne pathogens.[26] (This is a core principle of the organic movement, for which my publisher, Rodale, has long been an advocate.) In contrast, soil "treated" with antibiotics and pesticides results in reduced soil microbiome diversity and the selection of antibiotic-resistant microbes whose genes eventually are conferred to the gut microbiome of consumers. Farm animals add yet another link in the chain. As they eat and digest the nutritionally enriched food on sustainable farms, they fertilize the soil with manure that's chock-full of a diverse array of microbes, which in turn feed the soil, which feeds the plants we eat, and so the cycle continues.

These connections between microbial diversity of the soil, the nutrient profile of foods that results, and the microbial diversity of humans are profound, and we're only beginning to understand them.

"The impact of the gut microbiome on our health is very much like the influence of the soil microbiome on plant nutritive composition and its health," said Dr. Miller. In a sustainable model whereby human stool compost is used as plant fertilizer, our fecal microbiome enriches the soil microbiome biodiversity, establishing a symbiotic cycle between the soil and human microbiome and leading to improved health outcomes.

Concepts like these and the studies highlighted here have led to growing support for a theory known as the hygiene hypothesis,[27] which suggests that living in an oversterilized environment where early vaccination is commonplace and antibiotic use is prevalent may set the stage for the epidemic of allergies, asthma, autoimmunity, type 1 diabetes, and obesity and the growing problem of inflammatory bowel conditions in children.[28, 29]

Originally proposed by Dr. David P. Strachan in 1989, when he noticed an inverse correlation between family size and incidence of hay fever,[30] this theory has gained traction in medical circles over the last 2 decades and was updated by Professor Graham Rook as the "Old Friends" theory.[31] The premise: Our "old friends"–the microorganisms that we are exposed to in early life and that eventually inhabit our gut–coevolved with us, and over time they've come to play an essential role in helping us establish healthy immune function. Our immune systems, through exposure to these friendly organisms, learn how to properly recognize ally or intruder and are trained to attack the right invaders. According to Dr. Rook, "the rise in allergies and inflammatory diseases seems at least partly due to gradually losing contact with the range of microbes our immune systems evolved with, way back in the Stone Age. Only now are we seeing the consequences of this, doubtless also driven by genetic predisposition and a range of factors in our modern lifestyle–from different diets and pollution to stress and inactivity."

According to the "old friends" theory, children who aren't exposed to the diverse array of these immune-educating microorganisms early in life have a reduced biodiversity of commensals in their gut. The result is that the underdeveloped gut immune system is overreactive to foreign invaders, resulting in harmful inflammatory responses that become sustained and lead to chronic allergic and inflammatory disease.

Today, children receive antibiotics at record rates. The average child in the United

States and other developed countries receives 10 to 20 courses of antibiotics by the time he or she is 18 years old, antibacterial soaps adorn many bathroom sinks, and there's a bottle of sanitizing gel in every home–if not every room.[32] How do all these sterilizing agents affect our body's microbiome, and what are the long-term consequences on our health? What happens when we are consciously killing off our "old friends"?

Researchers have begun looking for answers to that question, and what they're finding isn't pretty. Even a short 5-day course of a common antibiotic like ciprofloxacin has been shown to kill up to one-third of the gut microbiome, resulting in an unbalanced and reduced biodiversity of the gut microflora. While some of these bugs recover once the patient goes off the antibiotic, scientists have found that many species remain dormant for up to 2 years after treatment.[33] What's more concerning is recent evidence suggesting every course of antibiotics may produce *permanent* and unfavorable alterations in the composition of our gut microbiome.[34]

So is avoiding overuse of prescription and over-the-counter antibiotics enough to reverse this trend toward a permanently altered gut microbiome? Unfortunately, the answer is no.

Our meat supply is loaded with detectable levels of antibiotics that adversely impact the balance and diversity of the flora in our gut. The FDA has estimated that the livestock industry now uses 20 million pounds of these antibiotics annually.

These drugs were originally dispensed to keep infection down in the horrific conditions that used to be called feedlots and are now known as CAFOs (concentrated animal feeding operations), where animals are kept for more than 45 days in extremely confined areas that produce no vegetation. But farmers noticed something interesting–antibiotics not only kept infection at bay, they also seemed to fatten up the livestock. That's why, since the 1950s, antibiotics have been used in low *nontherapeutic doses* to increase the body weight of cows, sheep, pigs, and chickens.[35]

Are the antibiotics used to "beef up" our meat actually fattening up America? A study at New York University Medical Center sought to answer that question. Dr. Ilseung Cho and his colleagues administered antibiotics commonly used in livestock to weaning mice at doses similar to those used in agriculture, and the conclusion was that these drugs may well be a contributing factor to the obesity epidemic in this country.[36]

The team found that antibiotics led to significant changes in the composition of the gut microbiome, resulting in modifications and copies of key genes involved in the metabolism of carbohydrates to short-chain fatty acids. This is a key finding, because short-chain fatty acids govern how much energy we harvest from carbohydrates. Increases in colonic short-chain fatty acids meant more energy was extracted from the foods these mice ate, which led to increased weight gain. After about 6 weeks, the study mice had gained approximately 10 to 15 percent more than their untreated counterparts, despite being fed the same diet. Other important metabolic changes included alterations in the metabolism of lipids and cholesterol by the liver. Disrupting the finely balanced ecosystem of the gut microbiome through the use of antibiotics clearly has consequences. It disrupts metabolism and leads to weight gain.

Does this mean that overuse of antibiotics and the resulting disruption in *your* gut ecosystem lead to weight gain? The evidence seems to point in this direction. Does it mean that the antibiotics used to fatten up livestock are also fattening up many of us who consume significant quantities of these livestock? Probably. There's no question antibiotics kill off our gut microflora and that this has an effect on our health.

Could altering our gut microbiome and changing our relationship to our "old friends" be part of a cycle of ill health that leads to increased inflammation, which leads to even more weight gain and poorer health in a spiral that spins ever further out of control? To answer that question, we need to discuss the next pathway and look more carefully at the relationships between gut microflora, inflammation, and weight.

PATHWAY 2: INFLAMMATION—YOUR SYSTEM ON FIRE

One of the keystone discoveries of modern medicine is the relationship between systemic inflammation and a host of chronic illnesses, including cardiovascular disease, dementia, gastrointestinal disorders, type 2 diabetes, weight gain, and more. Virtually all specialties in the medical sciences recognize inflammation as a major player in the development of chronic disease states.

Inflammation is important, but in some ways it's gotten a bad rap. It's not inherently good or bad. It's about balance–yin and yang; acute versus chronic; controlled versus uncontrolled. You hear a lot about how important it is to "cool down" or "turn off" the inflammatory response, and for most Americans, that's essential. But to properly moderate inflammation, you need to know what it is, how it works, and how you got so inflamed in the first place. And, as we'll see, the gut microflora are important actors.

When Your Immune System's Sprinkler System Fails

Our immune systems are cellular forces that have evolved to protect us from infectious elements. When you get a splinter and the area turns red, swells, and becomes warm–that's your immune system at work. When you have a fever and you feel like you're about to burn up as you try to fight off a cold, it's a sign your immune system is mounting a healthy response to clear the infection.

Your immune system involves a lot of inflammation because immune and inflammatory reactions are basically the same thing. Virtually every aspect of your health operates on a spectrum from optimally balanced to completely out of control. Weight is like this–you could be a few pounds too big to look supersexy in this summer's bikini, you could be morbidly obese, or you could be somewhere in between. The numbers on the scale (and your lab tests) creep in one direction or the other, depending on where you fall on this spectrum. And your gut controls your body curves. If you want to look sexy outside, start fixing the inside.

Your immune system exists on the same kind of spectrum. When it's optimally balanced, the immune system releases cells that attack foreign invaders when needed, but otherwise it rests. When it's out of balance, it's constantly sending cellular messengers that say "attack," and in the worst cases, these cellular protectors turn on your body and start to beat up your own cells. This is called systemic inflammation.

The condition may sound familiar. We talked about how the incidence of allergies, asthma, and other autoimmune (*auto* means "self," so the term means "self-immune") conditions is on the rise. Inflammation is at the very core of this process. Inflammation also leads to weight gain. Here are a few highlights illustrating the connection between runaway systemic inflammation and fat accumulation.

- **Insulin resistance.** Inflammatory cytokines block insulin receptors, reducing your sensitivity to the hormone. As you become more resistant to insulin, your body has a more difficult time converting the calories you consume into energy. Instead, you pack on fat. That's why metabolic syndrome, type 2 diabetes, and obesity are intimately interwoven conditions.

- **VAT.** Visceral adipose tissue, also known as belly fat, is metabolically active and encourages further inflammation in the body. So fat makes you inflamed, which causes you to gain more fat in a vicious cycle.

- **Leptin resistance.** Inflammation of the hypothalamus leads to resistance to leptin, the chief hormone that makes you feel full. When you've eaten enough, your body senses this and sends this hormone to your hypothalamus to tell you to stop. When you become resistant to leptin, you feel hungry more often and it's difficult to satiate that hunger, so you eat more and you gain weight.

Remember, the flora you're exposed to when you're young train your immune system to differentiate friend from foe. If you don't have the right bugs in your gut at an early age, the stage is set for immune imbalance, inflammation, and thus weight gain. But what if your immune system *was* properly trained when you were young? Is it still possible for your immune system to swing out of balance?

Absolutely. There are many dietary, lifestyle, and environmental factors that can lead to inflammation. Too much sugar in your diet (Americans eat about 150 pounds per person yearly—way too much), too little or too much exercise, stress, environmental toxins, food sensitivities, and more can all lead to chronic systemic inflammation.

However, one overlooked player in this cycle of inflammation, weight gain, and disease is your gut microflora. In Chapter 1, we talked about the consequences of failing to support the healthy bugs in your gut. Under normal circumstances, the gut flora

Can Bad Bugs Make Your Liver Fat?

The production of endotoxins by bugs in your gut doesn't only set off systemic inflammation, it also makes your liver fat. Nonalcoholic fatty liver disease (NAFLD) is a condition characterized by fatty infiltration of the liver in people who don't drink excessive alcohol. In NAFLD, 5 to 10 percent of your liver turns to fat, impacting its function in a number of ways. Lipid and glucose metabolism are affected, and you have a more difficult time detoxifying your blood. It's estimated that from one in three to one in four people have a fatty liver, and it's clear that the condition is linked to overweight/obesity, metabolic syndrome, and diabetes.[37]

While many physiological processes drive the condition—including inflammation, insulin resistance, and oxidative damage—new evidence suggests that endotoxins from gut bacteria are involved in the development of NAFLD.[38, 39]

Dysbiosis may weaken the tight junctions that are the glue holding together the cells of your intestinal lining, allowing bacterial toxins to enter the liver. These endotoxins then foster an increase in free fatty acid uptake and production by the liver, ignite inflammation, and promote insulin resistance—a harmful trifecta that injures the liver.

People with NAFLD also have a higher prevalence of small intestinal bacterial overgrowth[40] (SIBO—a condition we'll discuss later in the chapter). Ironic though it may be, the organ meant to detoxify your body may be dramatically impacted by gut-derived bacterial toxins that result from dysbiosis. Probiotics have been shown in laboratory animals to prevent and treat NAFLD by rebalancing the gut flora and restoring gut barrier integrity.[41]

represent a tremendous variety of species (500 to 1,000). The biodiversity in your intestines is a marker of health. This is actually a primary law of all biology: The greater the diversity of an ecosystem, the greater its health.

A sudden shift away from a healthy mixture of bugs reduces the biodiversity of our microbial friends and diminishes our ability to adapt. In the case of your gut microbiome, as biodiversity diminishes, the preponderance of pathogenic species of bugs tends to increase.

This can be problematic, because certain strains of bacteria produce endotoxins (toxins generated inside your body) that, if absorbed into the bloodstream, can be harmful to human health. Among the many endotoxins microbes can produce, lipopolysaccharide (LPS)—an essential component of their cells—is among the worst, because it triggers a powerful immune response that when left unchecked can develop into chronic systemic inflammation.

Your body doesn't like LPS, so it primes your immune system to go after LPS with all its might. It sends cytokines into action—powerful immune messengers that stimulate several classes of cells, including macrophages, monocytes, dendritic cells, and others. This begins the inflammatory process. And that's the issue with having an underdeveloped immune system with a faulty braking mechanism that permits inflammation to go unimpeded like a runaway train.

Intestinal inflammation loosens the adherence of your gut lining cells at critical junctions, creating breaches in this lining–which allows LPS and other bacteria-derived toxins to enter your bloodstream.[42] Some label this situation the *leaky gut syndrome*. When your immune system senses that these toxins are leaking into the bloodstream, it cranks up the inflammatory response even more in a vain attempt to beat back the LPS.

Systemic inflammation from gut bacteria–derived LPS has been implicated as an early driver of obesity and insulin resistance, and this process is probably the reason.[43] Plasma levels of LPS are higher in people with obesity and type 2 diabetes, and increased levels of a powerful inflammatory molecule induced by LPS called serum amyloid A proteins are found in obese people.[44, 45] Associations between serum levels of LPS and serum levels of insulin and triglycerides were reported in patients with type 2 diabetes and obesity.[46] And researchers have shown that subcutaneous infusions of LPS can cause weight gain and insulin resistance in mice.[47] Short-term antibiotic administration that kills off the intestinal bacteria that produce LPS in obese mice has been shown to decrease weight and body fat.

How does your gut become overrun with bugs that set off this inflammatory chain reaction? Well, many factors are involved, but your diet–specifically the amount and type of fat you eat–is probably the most important. Eating too many inflammatory fats induces changes in the gut microbiota that lead to endotoxemia and the resultant inflammation.[48] Investigators have demonstrated that a high-fat diet leads to detrimental changes in flora that set off the exact kind of LPS-driven inflammation we just reviewed. We also know that when you get this inflammation under control, the weight naturally drops away.

Fats aren't necessarily evil. The *type* of fat you eat is what's critical. In Chapter 4, I'll explain exactly what kinds of fats you should focus on and which you should avoid to reverse and avoid the intestinal inflammation that can lead to weight gain.

Supplements may help protect you from this process, too. Augmenting levels of bifidobacteria in the gut, either with probiotics or prebiotics, has been shown to reduce inflammation and improve glucose tolerance.[49] Replenishing bifidobacteria has also been shown to reduce gut leakiness, allowing less inflammatory LPS to pour into your bloodstream.[50] We'll review how to use supplementation to support your weight-loss efforts in Chapters 4 and 11.

However, before we get to all that, we need to complete our exploration of the ways in which imbalance in your gut microbiome can lead to weight gain. So let's talk about how the overall profile of your flora may be the best indicator for how likely you are to gain or lose weight.

PATHWAY 3: TYPE—HOW YOUR GUT BUG "FINGERPRINT" AFFECTS YOUR WEIGHT

Could you have a "gut microflora type" like you have a blood type? Emerging science is showing that different people have gut microbial combinations that are as specific to them as their fingerprints. And we're beginning to learn that the type of bacteria that is dominant in your gut–your personal floral fingerprint–may have a dramatic impact on your weight and health.

The overall consensus is that obesity and weight gain are characterized by an over-abundance of a class of bacteria belonging to the phylum Firmicutes, which many doctors now call "fat-forming bugs." While there's some variation in the findings, most of the studies show that a preponderance of bacteria from the phylum Bacteroidetes correlates with leanness.[51]

Scientists at the Washington University School of Medicine are leaders in this field of research. To begin determining whether or not a gut floral fingerprint could have an impact on weight, they analyzed the gut microbiota of genetically altered mice (the genes that control the appetite-regulating hormone leptin production were rendered inactive or were "knocked out"). You may remember from earlier in the chapter that leptin governs satiety–the feeling of fullness. Mice without these genes are constantly hungry, so they eat all the time and get fat. When the scientists looked at the gut microbiome of these obese mice, they found that they had more bacteria from the Firmicutes phyla of bacteria and less from Bacteroidetes.[52] Their lean mice counter-parts showed exactly the opposite floral fingerprint.

Excited by these findings, these scientists conducted follow-up research in humans that demonstrated similar microbial patterns. In one study, 12 obese participants were ran-domly assigned to either carbohydrate-restricted or fat-restricted diets. Both groups lost weight and both groups had a reduction in Firmicutes and an increase in Bacteroidetes.[53]

To confirm these findings, these investigators, looking for patterns between micro-bial clustering and leanness or obesity, compared the fecal microbial communities between adult female twin pairs and their mother. The twins who were obese showed reduced bacterial diversity, fewer Bacteroidetes, and more Firmicutes, just as predicted. Similar to the results found in mice, lean twins showed the opposite pattern–enhanced biodiversity, a greater number of Bacteroidetes, and fewer Firmicutes.

Why are Firmicutes associated with overweight and obesity? It appears these bugs have an impact on carbohydrate and lipid metabolism. They may actually be *too* efficient at extracting energy from the food you eat, which may explain the reason a Firmicutes fingerprint is associated with weight gain.[54] We'll discuss this further in Pathway 5 (page 32).

Studies have also shown that the burden of Firmicutes in obese people decreases after weight loss, even after gastric bypass surgery. [55] The improvement in gut microbial balance appears to occur soon after gastric bypass surgery and may contribute toward the rapid improvements in insulin sensitivity after the procedure prior to any substansive changes in weight. In fact, some researchers are now suggesting that the weight-loss results of this surgery may result to a certain extent from a change in gut microflora.[56, 57]

Understand that the aforementioned Bacteriodetes-Firmucutes story is more consistently observed in mice than in humans and that there are other organisms that may influence obesity. For instance, methane-producing bacteria, such as Methanobacter smithii,[58] is felt to increase the risk of obesity by speeding up the breakdown of food, boosting the production of fatty acids, and leading to the formation of fat, which over time, results in obesity.[59] In contrast, others such as A muciniphilia, and H. pylori and *Christensenellaceae minuta*[60] appear to be protective and favor being lean. Ultimately, the combination of genetics and diet determine which bacteria are more predominate in our gut. Overall, a balanced, robust, and diverse community of gut flora are the key to good health and a lean metabolism.

Again, we see the powerful influence that gut bugs have on your ability to create a lean metabolism. Now you may be asking yourself, "Hmm, how can I get a fat-burning floral fingerprint that will help me lose weight?" The answer brings us to Pathway 4 and diet.

PATHWAY 4: DIET—THEY ARE WHAT *YOU* EAT

You know the old saying "You are what you eat." But when we eat, we're feeding more than ourselves—we're feeding an entire ecosystem. What you feed your gut bugs determines a great deal about what species of bugs predominate at any one time. And as you now know, the balance of bugs in your gut has a tremendous impact on your health and weight. What you feed your gut microbiome—how you fertilize your inner garden—may be the key determinant in whether you are able to lose weight.

It's repeatedly been shown that the standard American diet (SAD)—high in inflammatory fats, high in processed carbohydrates, and low in fiber—negatively impacts gut flora in several ways.

First, animals and humans experience unhealthy shifts in both bacterial and metabolic profiles when fed a high-fat, high-sugar, low-fiber diet. The SAD diet shifts the relative balance of bugs in your gut toward the Firmicutes phylum—the fat-forming bugs.[61] It appears that a dramatic shift to these fat-forming bugs can occur in as few as 24 hours[62] after consuming a high-fat meal. That an alteration in gut microbiota can happen this quickly is an astounding finding, revealing what a powerful influence diet has on health.

If you want to have a fat floral fingerprint, just keep eating in a SAD way. But if you want to fertilize bugs in your gut that will help you lose weight, then you should cut back on inflammatory fats, dramatically reduce your sugar intake, and increase your levels of fiber. But you need to do this in a specific order or you may inadvertently encourage the wrong bugs to grow in the wrong places in your gut. (Learn details about the steps you need to take in the chapters that follow.)

Then there's the diet-inflammation-gut microbiome link we began discussing earlier in this chapter. Foods you eat have a dramatic impact on how much systemic inflammation you experience—there's no longer any question about that. Inflammatory saturated fats and high-glycemic-index carbs spark the fires of inflammation. When this conflagration creeps into your intestines, like a forest fire within, it devitalizes the gut's terrain so that bad bugs can proliferate.

As you learned when we talked about Pathway 2, these bad gut bugs may produce harmful metabolic by-products that further increase inflammation, promote fat accumulation, and increase insulin resistance. Left unchecked, this process can punch holes in your gut, causing it to become porous—which only serves to exacerbate this cycle of inflammation, poor health, and weight gain.

The answer is deceptively simple. You just need to stop eating foods that set your system on fire and start eating the foods that cool it down. I'll give you all the details in the next chapter.

Finally, the foods you eat impact your genetic expression, and your gut microflora may be one of the primary means by which this occurs. Let's take a step back and discuss the difference between your genotype, your phenotype, and how your gut microbiome "talks" to your genes.

Genotype, Phenotype, and Genetic Cross Talk

It was once thought (and many people, including some doctors, still believe) that your genes are unchangeable. In some respects, this is true. Unless we learn how to genetically modify humans, the color of your eyes, your height, the shape of your face, and many other fundamental aspects of who you are won't change no matter how powerful the environmental influence. Similarly, we have genetic predispositions toward the amount we weigh, what diseases we're prone to, and more. These "hard-coded" aspects of your physiology are known as your genotype.

However, your genotype tells only part of the story about who you are and who you will become. Environmental influences *do* impact the expression of certain parts of your genetic code. Diet, exercise, stress levels, toxins, and more can trigger receptors in your genes that will alter the messages they send your body. That means what you do, what you eat, how you exercise, how much stress you have, and how you behave every day actually affects you at the deepest possible biological and physiological levels. These environmental influences can reprogram the translation and/or expression of the genes that control your body systems. The ability of environmental influences like these to alter your genes is called epigenetic modification. While we don't have control over our geno-type, we can influence the expression of our genes to alter health outcomes.

One of the key influencers of epigenetic modification is diet. The foods you eat send messages to your genes. A new branch of science called nutrigenomics has been devel-oped to uncover how the foods you eat modify genetic expression of body physiology. As it turns out, the gut microflora play an important role.

The bugs in your gut have a special superpower–they can communicate geneti-cally. This is called "quorum sensing,"[63] and your gut flora use this power to commu-nicate with one another and with you, their human host. Bacteria can actually "swap" DNA with one another by sending signals that alter the genetic pattern of their neigh-bors. A fascinating study conducted at the University of Victoria in Canada provides an example of how this occurs.[64, 65] Scientists sought to discover why Japanese people extract more nutritional value out of nori* (the seaweed in sushi) than other folks do. As it turns out, genetic cross talk between microbes is at the very center of the story.

Zobellia galactanivorans is a bacterium that lives on several species of seaweed, including those used to make nori. When people eat seaweed, they unwittingly consume this microorganism that has hitchhiked onto the plant and then takes up residence in the gut microbiome of the host. Once there, *Z. galactanivorans* sidles up to its bacterial counterparts and says, "Hey, check this out. I can digest seaweed better than you. Want a piece of this action?" The surrounding bacteria engage in "horizontal gene transfer," stealing the genes that allow *Z. galactanivorans* to get more nutrients out of the seaweed. Once that happens, they can digest seaweed just as well as the ocean-based bacterium can. It's almost like a magic trick.

Overall, gut bugs communicate with your DNA by emitting proteins that impact receptors on the gene. These alterations in genetic expression may drive fat accumula-tion and change the way you process sugar. So the foods you eat impact the kind of flora in your gut, which then send messages to your DNA telling it to pack on fat.

The key takeaway is pretty straightforward: What you eat affects your gut flora, which in turn send messages to your body to either pile on fat or burn it off. To have a lean metabolism, you need to rebalance your gut microbiome to help you lose weight.

In the next chapter, we'll discuss how to make the needed changes in your diet to shift your microbiome back to a balanced state. For now, let's look at a few more ways that disruptions in the gut ecosystem and a reduction in the diversity of the gut micro-biota can cause you to pile on the pounds.

---

* Nori is the Japanese name given to various types of edible seaweed and algae. Nori's origin dates back to ancient China and Japan, around the 8th century. It is usually used as a wrap for sushi, in miso soup, or just eaten plain. Nori has a high content of minerals, fiber, and many different types of vitamins.

PATHWAY 5: METABOLISM—THE IMPORTANCE OF SHORT-CHAIN FATTY ACIDS

The role of the gut microflora in metabolic function is now well recognized. The amount of energy you harvest from the foods you eat is largely determined by the type of bugs you have in your gut. Let's look at what this means and why it's important.

Eating is an interesting process. As you chew your food, salivary enzymes are added to it, turning it into a substance called chyme. This is then swallowed, and the chyme moves down to your esophagus and drops into your stomach, where it's exposed to hydrochloric acid and additional enzymes that pull it apart into its chemical constituents. These are delivered to your small intestine, where most of the nutrient absorption in your body occurs. What's left over drops into your large intestine, where the vast majority of your gut microflora live. Then your bugs have a feast.

One of their favorite foods is fiber. Human beings can't digest fiber without the help of our flora. That's why a certain amount of fiber simply passes through us—what our bugs don't eat comes out in our poo. This is one among many reasons fiber is such an important dietary substance. Without enough fiber in your diet, your flora starve, biodiversity plummets, and dysbiosis can set it.

As your gut flora eat fiber, they break it down into short-chain fatty acids (SCFAs), which are extremely important to human health. SCFAs increase the gut's absorption of water, regrow gut cells, and may provide defenses against colon cancer, inflammatory bowel disease, and more.[66]

The amount of SCFAs your gut bugs produce is incredibly important—as usual, balance is the key. Too few SCFAs and you don't get their protective benefits. Too many and weight gain, glucose imbalance, and increased triglyceride production may result.

As their name indicates, SCFAs are fatty acids that are energy dense and calorie rich. The more short-chain fatty acids you produce, the more calories in your diet. In normal humans, SCFAs provide from 80 to 200 calories per day, depending upon the amount of daily dietary fiber intake.[67] However, certain species of your gut microflora overproduce SCFAs from carbohydrates, so there is interspecies variation in the efficiency of the fermentation of fiber to SCFAs. Remember the Firmicutes bacteria from our discussion about gut bug fingerprints? They're thought to be fat-forming gut microflora by most scientists today, and the SCFA connection tells us why.

A shift of either 20 percent more Firmicutes or 20 percent fewer Bacteriodetes results in more SCFAs extracted from fiber and absorbed to provide a gain in caloric energy. Why do the Firmicutes bacteria produce more SCFAs? They overdigest the fiber you eat. That means less is left undigested as fiber that comes out in your poo and more SCFAs are absorbed and turned into energy in your body. What happens with the additional energy you can't use? It gets stored as fat by a complex mechanism that we discuss later on in this chapter, but this is likely the reason SCFAs trigger increased triglyceride production in your liver.

But this isn't the only way that Firmicutes influence your metabolism. A new study[68] shows that this class of bacteria encourages your body to also *absorb* more of the fat you consume in your diet, creating a double whammy of increased SCFA production and increased dietary fat absorption that has been concretely associated with weight gain.

These facts alone show that the calories in/calories out diet approach is hopelessly out of date—there's no way for you to accurately track how many calories your gut bugs are harvesting for you. It also shows that the type of food you eat is probably much more important than the amount.

Does this mean you should eat less fiber, so your food won't be converted into SCFAs? No! As we've already learned, when you eat a high-fat, low-fiber diet, your gut bug profile swings toward Firmicutes and ultimately turns into fat. Once these fat-forming bugs take over, what little fiber you do eat is overdigested and turns into more fat—all of which is another step in the wicked cycle of weight gain. Fiber is not your enemy. In fact, it's one of your dearest dietary friends. You just need to balance it with proper amounts of healthy fats, high-quality protein, and low-glycemic carbs so that it can do its job correctly.

As if runaway Firmicutes and the problems associated with it weren't enough cause for concern, studies have now shown that your gut microbiota govern another important regulator of lipid metabolism called angiopoietin-like protein 4 (ANGPTL4), also known as FIAF (fasting-induced adipose factor).[69] ANGPTL4 helps regulate the proportion of triglycerides deposited in your adipose tissue (your fat). When too little of it is floating around in your body, more triglycerides are sequestered as fat. Research on ANGPTL4 is in its early days, but studies show that the type of bugs in your gut seems to influence how much of the protein is in your blood.[70, 71] This may be another mechanism by which your flora impact your metabolism and your ability to gain or lose fat.

This is all more evidence that your gut flora have a significant impact on your ability to lose weight. As you'll learn in Chapter 3, you can create a lean metabolism by feeding your gut bugs right and changing your lifestyle to support theirs.

But for now, let's look at two more pathways leading to weight gain. You see, it's not only the type of bugs in your gut that's important, but where they live.

PATHWAY 6: PLACEMENT OF GUT BUGS—THE SIBO EPIDEMIC

Under normal circumstances, most of your gut microbiota live in your large intestine, closer to the end of your digestive tract, an oxygen-poor environment inhabited predominantly by anaerobic bacteria. The small intestine, where most of the nutrients from your food are absorbed, is a relatively sterile and better oxygenated environment that favors the growth of aerobic bacteria under controlled circumstances. The growth of gut bugs in your upper digestive tract is limited by the suppressive actions of stomach acid, digestive enzymes, bile, the sweeping movement of peristaltic waves, and more.[72]

In some cases, however, gut bugs either crawl up into your small intestine from the large intestine or aren't cleared from it properly. When this happens, these gut bugs disrupt the way the small intestine functions. This is called small intestinal bacterial overgrowth (SIBO), and it can be a serious problem. SIBO is defined as having more than 100,000 bacterial organisms per milliliter of fluid in the small intestine. Compare this to the small intestine's normal low levels of a mix of aerobes and anaerobic bacteria at a concentration of 1,000 to 10,000 organisms per milliliter of fluid, and you can see the problem.

SIBO symptoms typically include gas, bloating, and flatulence after meals but can include loose stools, constipation, abdominal distention, and abdominal pain. SIBO has also been associated with chronic fatigue syndrome, fibromyalgia, rosacea, restless leg syndrome, and more. Many patients say that when their SIBO is finally resolved, chronic symptoms disappear and they feel more vibrant and energetic than they have in years. Irritable bowel syndrome (IBS) has been shown in many studies to be associated with gut dysbiosis,[73] including SIBO. Systematic reviews of the research have revealed that the majority of patients with IBS suffer from this condition.[74, 75] Furthermore, individuals with obesity have been reported to have a higher prevalence of functional gastrointestinal disorders such as IBS.[76] This connection of obesity, SIBO, IBS, and dysbiosis further supports the foundation for the Gut Balance Revolution approach for Ted, whose story you read in Chapter 1.

I have felt that SIBO was a factor in weight gain for a long time. I've observed that when patients are treated for SIBO, they seem to naturally lose weight while gaining energy (weight down = energy up). Ted's story is a perfect example. When we resolved his dysbiosis and treated him for SIBO, he lost weight and his energy skyrocketed. Recall that Ted was originally referred to me for assistance managing his IBS, not his obesity. Observations like this are part of what drove me to write this book. The weight gain/weight loss story is more complicated than most people think, and my gut instincts convinced me that the intestinal microbiota play a role. My clinical observations (and my gut instincts) are finally being borne out by research.

A provocative study was recently conducted that shows SIBO leads to increased intestinal permeability–an issue we discussed earlier in this chapter–which allows more gut bacteria–derived endotoxins into your bloodstream, setting off the cascade of events highlighted in Pathway 2. Researchers analyzed 137 morbidly obese individuals who had been referred for bariatric surgery and 40 healthy controls for SIBO by glucose hydrogen breath testing (the standard test for the condition) and liver biopsy (to assess liver injury). These investigators reported that SIBO was more common in obese than lean participants. The obese subjects testing positive for SIBO also had more severe liver problems, suggesting that the condition contributed to fat accumulation in the liver.[77] There are many other scientific studies in laboratory animals that demonstrate how

SIBO weakens the integrity of the intestinal lining, permitting bacterial toxins to escape into the liver and cause injury.[78]

These findings have been confirmed by a recent study showing the results of hydrogen breath tests can accurately predict whether you have too much body fat and whether or not you're at risk for weight gain and obesity. Dr. Ruchi Mathur and colleagues showed that participants with higher concentrations of methane and hydrogen in their breath—sure signs that the small intestine has been overgrown with *Methanobrevibacter smithii*—had a higher body mass index (BMI).[79] Dr. Mathur, director of the outpatient diabetes treatment center at Cedars-Sinai Medical Center, stated, "It's possible that when this type of bacteria takes over, people may be more likely to gain weight and accumulate fat. . . . Obesity is not a one-size-fits-all disease."[80] More proof that calories in/calories out is far from the whole story.

Does this mean if you're overweight you definitely have SIBO? Not necessarily. However, if you've tried many diets but the fat is still stubbornly on your body and you suffer from the typical symptoms of SIBO, there may be bugs in the wrong part of your digestive system.

Antibiotics that kill these bugs are presently the gold standard of medical practice to treat this condition, but they can be problematic. For one thing, they don't selectively kill the misplaced anaerobic colonic flora that have found their way into your small bowel. They simply wreak havoc on your entire gut microbiome, as all antibiotics do. There is extensive collateral damage that can last for years. In my experience, and that of many of my colleagues, SIBO tends to reappear quickly if the root causes (such as poor diet, poor digestive function gut movement, and structural abnormalities in the gastrointestinal tract) are not addressed, which leads to recurrent courses of antibiotics. Seems like a catch-22, doesn't it?

Fortunately, diet has been found to play a prominent role in treating this condition. Less severe cases of SIBO can often be improved by "starving out" the overpopulation of microbes in the small bowel with a change in diet. In mild to moderate cases, I've been able to combine herbal preparations designed to suppress the growth of these bugs with diet to eliminate SIBO.[81] In persistent cases, antibiotics may be the only option. If this is the case for you, it's still best to take a careful look at the underlying causes driving the condition and optimize your diet and lifestyle to reduce the risk of SIBO recurring. So the Gut Balance Revolution is most certainly for you.

Now let's turn our attention to the last pathway leading from an imbalanced microbiome to weight gain and disease: the ways bugs talk to your brain and the rest of your body.

PATHWAY 7: COMMUNICATION—HOW YOUR GUT TALKS TO YOUR BRAIN

It's long been known that your gut communicates with your brain. In fact, the connection is so profound that it inspired author Dr. Michael Gershon to call the human digestive tract "the second brain."[82] Your gut tells your brain when you've had enough to eat and when to send messages to the pancreas to release insulin. It has a dramatic impact on your mood and so much more.

One of the most rapidly expanding areas of research is around gut-brain-microbe communication. We now know that hormones and neurotransmitters in your gut aren't alone in talking to your brain but that your intestinal flora have a conversation with your head, too.

A number of biochemical pathways lead from your gut to your brain, and several are affected by flora. But let's focus on the most important of these: your hypothalamic-pituitary-adrenal (HPA) axis, because as far as gut-brain communication is concerned, your HPA axis is an interstate freeway.

The HPA Axis: A Freeway of Information

The hypothalamic-pituitary-adrenal axis is a complex set of interactions between the hypothalamus in your brain; your pituitary gland, which controls several hormones in your body; and your adrenal system, which governs your stress response. It's the major freeway of information in your neuroendocrine system responsible for a wide variety of physiological processes including stress, digestion, immune function, energy storage, appetite and expenditure, mood, and sexuality.

Gut bugs may play a role in the development of your HPA axis. It's been shown that a healthy microbiota early in life is critical for the proper development of the HPA axis in rats.[83] If this turns out to be true of humans as well, we'll know that your microbiota have a far wider influence over your health than we originally thought. Improper development or dysregulation of your HPA axis can lead to an exaggerated stress response, impaired cardiac function, alterations in neurotransmitters and brain hormones, and increased caloric intake. This may be one of the reasons why mood disorders such as depression and anxiety and even autism have been tied to dysbiosis and why administering probiotics helps improve these conditions.[84, 85]

The gut uses the HPA axis to communicate with your brain through enteroendocrine cells. These cells are regulated by your gut microbiota and thus influence them in important ways.[86] They impact the secretion of incretin hormones, including glucagon-like peptides 1 and 2 (GLP-1 and GLP-2). A series of studies has shown a close connection between gut microbes and levels of both GLP-1 and GLP-2.[87]

These two hormones are important because they stimulate the release of insulin from the pancreas, slow gastric emptying, promote satiety (the feeling of fullness), promote insulin sensitivity, and reduce gut permeability—all of which counter obesity.[88, 89] For example, if there's too much GLP-1 in your blood, your pancreas will release more insulin that can, over time, lead to insulin resistance and weight gain. But if you don't have enough GLP-1, your stomach will empty more quickly, dumping sugar into your blood, causing insulin resistance and weight gain.

GLP-1 and GLP-2 also decrease your appetite. So if you have too little of them, you will be hungrier and likely to eat more. The way your gut talks to your HPA is critical. When that communication goes haywire, you're much more likely to pile on the fat.

As always, balance is key. How is optimal hormonal balance obtained? With diet—by eating plenty of nondigestible carbohydrates, specifically oligofructose, found in fruits and vegetables like bananas, onions, Jerusalem artichokes, asparagus, leeks, and others. This class of fiber is so important because your gut bugs *love* to eat these fiber-rich and fermentable carbs, and when they get them, they send out "happy" messages encouraging your body to produce these chemicals in the right amounts. That's why this class of fiber has been found to help people lose weight, reduce hunger, moderate caloric intake, and balance insulin and glucose.[90] But as I mentioned earlier in this chapter, we will take a systematic approach toward rebalancing your gut microflora and weight loss by recommending food groups in discrete phases.

LOOKING AHEAD

All this science is showing us that the human body is an ecosystem. And ecosystems are complex entities requiring attention and care to remain healthy. Most of the one-dimensional formulas for weight loss on the market today fail to take this fact into account. We've been led to believe that the number of calories you consume is the decisive factor in weight loss. I hope this chapter has illustrated that this idea is simply false.

So what's the solution? You can change your diet in ways that will help your gut bugs tell your body to burn fat. You can weed, seed, and feed your inner garden and help a lush orchard to grow within. You just need to know which foods to eat, which to avoid, and how to design your meals for each phase of this program so you can create a lean metabolism. In the chapters that follow, I'll show you how.

CHAPTER 3

The Gut Balance Revolution Overview

You are about to embark on a journey–one that will take you deep into the Amazon rain forest that lives inside your gut. On this journey, you'll have some unexpected adventures and be confronted by strange, counterintuitive facts–for example, that you can eat more (not less) and still lose weight, and that you can burn fat and rebalance your gut microbiome by simply relaxing.

You'll also meet a host of odd creatures that cause you to gain fat and others that help you burn it off. You'll be introduced to bugs like bifidobacteria[1] and lactic acid bacteria.[2] Some of these creatures will be your friends on your weight-loss journey. Others will be your foes.

During your trip, something profound is going to happen. You will revolutionize your understanding of weight loss, health, and the nature of the human body. You will restore your metabolism so you can experience a lifetime of great health and vitality. You will create a new relationship with the complex ecosystem that lives inside you.

Welcome to the Gut Balance Revolution.

At this point, I hope I've convinced you that the reason why you pack on fat or burn it away is far more complex than the old calories in/calories out story you've been told for decades. As I described in Chapter 1, weight loss is about much more than simply eating less and exercising more. The factors that lead to weight gain and weight loss are far reaching and include genetic predisposition, phenotypical influences (like diet, lifestyle, and stress), blood sugar and insulin balance, hormone regulation, inflammation, energy metabolism, and more.

And as you've learned, your gut microbiome–your inner garden, the rain forest you're about to journey into–is a key player in the story of weight loss and health that has been largely ignored.

Until now.

You see, despite all of the complexities of the science of why people gain weight, there's a wonderfully simple approach you can take to shedding pounds and rebalancing your health. All you have to do is eat and live in a way that makes your gut bugs happy. You need to become a good gut bug gardener.

By focusing on rebalancing your gut microbiome and taking a community-based ecosystems approach to the whole puzzle of weight loss, you cut through the junk science, the late-night infomercial claims of "automatic weight loss," and instead go right to the heart of weight gain and the obesity epidemic that haunts this country.

Eating in a way that supports your gut microbiome means you're also eating in a way that avoids the primary drivers of unwanted weight. When you feed your flora the foods they love, when you till the soil of your inner garden and then seed your gut with friendly

Can Gut Bugs Regulate Hunger?

Leptin and ghrelin are the two primary appetite-regulating hormones in your body. Leptin, made by your fat cells, sends signals of fullness and satiation. Its counterpart, ghrelin, made predominantly in your stomach, sends signals of hunger to your brain. When either one is out of balance, or when your cells become resistant to their messages (as happens in cases of leptin resistance), your appetite (and your weight-loss attempts) can go haywire.

But the bugs in your gut affect your appetite. Ghrelin is suppressed by *Helicobacter pylori*.[3] More ghrelin in your blood means you feel hungrier more often.

Nobel Laureate Barry Marshall, MD, has shown that *H. pylori* is connected to heartburn, acid reflux, and ulcers, and he developed an antibiotic regimen to treat these conditions by killing off *H. pylori*. But what if this sends the gut microbiome out of balance? Could treating patients with antibiotics that eliminate *H. pylori* make them hungrier and cause them to gain weight?

Maybe. One study has shown that 92 veterans treated with antibiotics for *H. pylori* gained significant weight compared to their untreated counterparts. That's because when the *H. pylori* was killed off, levels of the appetite-regulating hormone ghrelin increased sixfold—a profound change. The physiological expectation is that the resultant increase in appetite would lead to significant weight gain.

It's been noted that *H. pylori* has virtually disappeared in our children due to multiple courses of antibiotics, with only 6 percent of kids showing evidence of this strain of flora in their guts. Could our escalating obesity rates be connected to the reduction in *H. pylori* due to these treatments? Could *H. pylori* be at times a commensal (friendly microbe) in disguise while at other times a pathogen? It's too early to say for sure whether *H. pylori* is a "Dr. Jekyll and Mr. Hyde" bug, but some scientists are suggesting that treating *H. pylori* infections may have opened up a Pandora's box.[4]

flora, you not only rebalance your gut microbiome and optimize all the pathways high-lighted in Chapter 2, you also:

- Rebalance blood sugar and insulin levels, in many cases reducing or reversing insulin resistance.

- Cool off chronic systemic inflammation—one of the major contributors to all chronic illness.

- Reestablish optimal levels of appetite-regulating hormones like leptin and ghrelin.

- Reverse damage done to your body by a high-sugar diet.

- Rev up your overall metabolism so you can keep fat off long term.

This all happens automatically when you shift your focus to eating and living in a way that's good for your friendly flora of gut bugs. Remember, the commensal microbes in your gut thrive on the same things you thrive on, and vice versa. Eating in a way that makes sense for your gut bugs means eating in a way that makes sense for you.

That's why, starting right now, I invite you to think of yourself as more than an individual person. Instead, think of yourself as an entire ecosystem. The digestive tract is the inner core of your body's ecosystem, and these microbial communities have a powerful influence on your fat-burning machinery—your metabolism—as well as your overall health and well-being. Your job is to keep your gut microbial ecosystem balanced and strong in order to obtain optimum health.

Here's how you do it.

WEEDING , SEEDING, AND FEEDING YOUR INNER GARDEN: AN ECOSYSTEMS APPROACH TO WEIGHT LOSS

The Gut Balance Revolution is a three-phase program designed to reduce dysbiosis, reseed your gut microbiome with friendly flora, and then fertilize that inner garden so it stays healthy for a lifetime.

This isn't some gimmicky crash diet that leads to yo-yo dieting, poor long-term results, and a harmfully raised metabolic body weight set point, as we discussed in Chapter 1. Instead, it's a science-based program designed to help you restore a healthy metabolism and enhance the vigor of your life by reestablishing a robust inner ecology.

To achieve this, you have to address what I call the Three Rs:

- **Reboot** your inner ecology. This is a time of renewal when you "till the earth" to set the stage for a healthy garden in your gut while priming your fat-burning metabolism.

- **Rebalance** your flora. After you've weeded your inner garden, you rebalance your gut microbiome by seeding your gut with healthy bacteria and fertilizing those bugs with the right foods.

■ **Renew** your health for life. This is the ongoing, long-term, lifestyle change part of the plan, where you integrate the healthy habits you've learned into a manageable program that fits your personal needs.

By following these Three Rs, you'll burn off fat and rebalance your gut microbiome. And you'll feel more energetic and happier than you have in a long time.

The program is simple—though that doesn't always mean it will be easy! Here's how it works.

Phase I: Reboot—Weed Your Inner Garden and Rev Up Your Metabolism

The first 30 days of the program will help you reestablish a healthy relationship with food. For most of you, this will naturally lead to accelerated weight loss. Many of you will lose 10 to 15 pounds (or more!) during the first month of the program, and you'll do this by making a few dietary and lifestyle modifications that starve out the bad bugs in your gut, reduce systemic inflammation, and rebalance your blood sugar.

The key to this phase is a low-carbohydrate, moderate-fat, higher-protein ketogenic diet that specifically reduces a class of highly fermentable carbohydrate-rich foods called FODMAPs.

FODMAPs is an acronym for "fermentable oligo-, di-, and monosaccharides and polyols." I know that's a mouthful, but don't worry—you don't have to remember all of those terms. What it really refers to is a class of carbohydrates that contain short-chain sugars that gut bugs can readily ferment, which promotes their growth and leads to a host of digestive symptoms including gas, pain, bloating, and more.

By limiting these foods and dramatically reducing your intake of starchy and highly processed carbs, you'll remove from your diet the primary food sources that sustain the imbalance in the microbial communities in your digestive tract.

Reducing these carbs and focusing on lower-glycemic-load meals also has the happy benefit of rebalancing your blood sugar, reversing insulin resistance and fat accumulation, and reducing overall systemic inflammation (a process that's further enhanced in this phase by eliminating inflammatory oils from your diet).

Instead of eating inflammatory, sugary foods that lead to imbalance in your gut microbiome, you'll focus on fat-burning superfoods (like blueberries, green tea, and chile peppers) that will rev up your metabolism while supporting the community of your gut's beneficial bacteria. In fact, I'll provide you with a list of my top 10 fat-burning superfoods to include in your diet—all of which are also featured in the delicious, gut-bug-balancing meal plans and recipes you'll find in Chapter 11.

By the end of Phase 1, you will:

■ Lose up to 15 pounds (or more)

■ Set the stage for a rebalanced gut microbiome

- Improve your blood sugar balance and reduce systemic inflammation
- Reduce any digestive complaints[5, 6]
- Enhance your energy levels
- Improve your mood and cognition

You may notice that, barring a few exceptions like the reduction of FODMAPs, this reboot phase of the program parallels a few highly successful low-carb healthy eating plans that are proven to be effective[7-14]—at least in the short term. That's intentional. I wanted to leverage the best of all the weight-loss science that exists for this program.

Unfortunately, though, other weight-loss programs do poorly long term[15] because they're difficult to stick to—and because they also kill off some good gut bugs that sustain our health (like bifidobacteria) and are important for a lean metabolism.[16, 17] That's why, with this system, I want to take things a step further. I want to provide you with all the tools you need to rebalance your metabolism, burn fat, and reestablish a healthy gut microbiome. I'll do that by teaching you how to seed and fertilize your inner garden and achieve inner ecological harmony for life. That way, this program will be the last, best diet you'll ever need!

That is what Phase 2 is all about.

Phase 2: Rebalance—Seed and Fertilize Your Inner Garden to Restore Ecological Harmony

After 30 days of rebooting your gut microbiome and revving up your metabolism, it'll be time to shift your focus toward rebalancing your inner flora by fertilizing the friendly helpers that support your health. Now that you've weeded your inner garden, it's time to seed and feed it.

In Phase 2, you will be increasing your carb intake. Our focus will be on healthy, whole-foods carbohydrates that are packed with fiber and healthy prebiotic fibrous foods that feed your fat-burning friendly flora, instead of the junk carbs that got you into trouble with your weight in the first place. Specifically, we'll do that by reintroducing into your diet some key fibrous, complex carbohydrates—fruits and vegetables that are high in insoluble fiber that your human digestive tract can't break down but that are the perfect fuel for fat-burning bugs. Burn, baby, burn! I'll add plenty of fermented foods that are filled with the healthy bacteria your gut microbiome needs to flourish.

Low-carb diets have their place, particularly when you're starting out in the reboot part of this program. Many popular diets have proven—and the research has shown—that reducing your overall carbohydrate intake is important for rebalancing blood sugar, reducing inflammation, losing weight, and generally improving your health. I'm with them on that.

However, maintaining these programs doesn't usually work. In the long run, low-carb diets have a high "recidivism rate," which just means people tend to fall off the wagon and regain everything they've lost—and then some.

One of the reasons these diets may not work in the long run is that they tend to kill off certain species of friendly bacteria in your gut. For example, recent studies have shown that a gluten-free diet can cause a reduction in key species of healthy beneficial gut microbes such as lactobacillus and bifidobacteria.[18, 19] Long-term energy-restricted diets, which form the foundation for the vast majority of weight-reduction programs, are also associated with a decrease in bifidobacteria.[20] Why is this important?

Remember the bifidobacteria from Chapter 2? That little bug appears to support a lean metabolism.[21] Children who maintain a normal weight have been reported to have higher stool bifidobacteria counts than those who become obese.[22] Studies have linked low levels of bifidobacteria to obesity in adults.[23, 24] And it's not just your waistline that suffers when these species of friendly flora are killed off. Bifidobacteria, one of the primary probiotics found in places like mother's milk, has a broad range of health effects. Low levels of bifidobacteria in the digestive tracts of infants have been linked to an increased risk for allergy, asthma, autoimmune disorders, and, yes, obesity.[25] This may be one reason why feeding infants breast milk, which is loaded with prebiotics and even bifidobacteria, prevents the future development of childhood obesity.[26, 27]

Your metabolism doesn't like long-term low-carb eating. Your inner garden doesn't like it. And your waistline doesn't like it. The results of low-carb diets are, unfortunately, very predictable: People fall off the wagon, they regain weight, and, often, they pack on even more pounds than they had before. As you know, the more yo-yo dieting you do, the higher your body weight set point is raised and the more weight you're liable to gain—it's a horrible rebound effect.

We're going to take a different approach on this program. One that will rejuvenate your inner garden *and* provide you with long-term weight loss. And it all comes from taking that ecosystems approach to eating I mentioned earlier.

Phase 1 has been designed to "reboot" your metabolism by basically hitting the proverbial reset button. You will be eliminating foods that are high in sugar, promote inflammation, and sustain an unhealthy and imbalanced gut ecosystem. These bacterial communities are interacting to slow down your metabolism, accumulate fat, and hold on to weight. In Phase 1, the fat-burning machinery is turned on by cutting out the unhealthy refined carbs that got you into trouble while shifting the gut microbial communities to a more healthy mix that favors a lean metabolism. In a sense, you are tilling the garden in preparation for the planting of new life. In Phase 2, you fertilize your inner garden with healthy foods to support the growth of commensal flora that shift the microbial communities in your gut ecosystem back to health and promote a lean metabolism. So in this phase, I ask you to increase your intake of fermented foods such as sauerkraut, kimchi, yogurt, kefir, and miso. These foods help seed your gut with good bugs that will rebalance your gut microbiome. Then we'll feed these good bugs with prebiotics–a special class of fiber-rich, very filling carbohydrates such as oat bran, artichokes, Jerusalem artichokes, and others that the good bugs in your gut love to feast on.

By doing this, you'll increase your high-quality carb and fiber intake over the course of Phase 2. This will not only set the stage for a rebalanced gut microbiome–one that will help you kick your metabolism into high gear–but will also curb your appetite and help avoid the kinds of hormonal and metabolic adaptations that can lead to trouble.

As long as you're on Phase 2, you can expect a sustained weight loss of about 5 to 10 pounds of excess body weight per month. I want you to stay on this phase until you achieve your goal weight. You'll find that it's a healthy plan for long-term eating, and you can certainly remain on it as long as you like.

In the rebalance phase, you can expect:

■ Enhanced energy as your mind and body become accustomed to this new way of eating and living

■ A renewed sense of well-being

■ If your doctor checks your blood chemistries, an ongoing reduction of inflammation and continued rebalancing of your blood sugar and insulin levels

You may want to make this way of living and eating your lifelong path. If you do, that's fine. Or perhaps you'd like to reintegrate a few more foods and even allow yourself a treat every once in a while (I know I do!). That's where the last phase of the program comes in.

Phase 3: Renew—Keep Your Friendly Flora—and You—Healthy for Life

Once you achieve your goal weight, you'll feel renewed, your gut microbiome will be rebalanced, and you'll have set the stage for long-term health and optimal weight.

When you reach this point, you'll have the metabolic flexibility to integrate more foods into your diet and even eat off the plan once in a while. Here's a key point to remember: The dose makes the poison. As long as your gut microbiome is healthy, your metabolism is balanced, and you focus on real foods, small amounts of comfort food–even a little pasta or dessert from time to time–will not pack on the pounds. The human body is designed to eat a wide variety of foods, and when it's operating optimally, it still has resilience.

You'll find that some foods have a larger impact on your weight and health than others. Everybody is different, every metabolism is different, and every gut microbiome is different. Remember that the flora in your gut are as specific to you as your fingerprint. No one else has quite the same mix of gut bugs as you do. Little wonder that we all respond to dietary and lifestyle influences so differently.

That's why I designed this phase to provide you the flexibility to create your own ideal, personalized eating plan for life. I'll teach you how to identify foods that support you and your gut microbiota and eliminate foods that don't. This will give you the secret key to unlock the door of lifelong health and optimal weight.

I created this part of the program with real people in mind, people who live busy, hectic lives–just like you do. You see, another problem I have with most of the diet programs out there is that they set up an impossible standard and then get judgmental when you can't meet it. For example, I've met precious few people who eliminate all processed sugar for life. Sure, reducing it is a great idea. But are you really *never* going to have a scoop of ice cream or fresh homemade cookies again? When the holidays hit, are you really going to skip the pumpkin pie or the cookies? I doubt it. Even if you could, who would want to? There's no point in being healthy and thin if you can't have fun so relax and enjoy life! Why set impossible goals like these as the standard? It just doesn't make sense.

More to the point, unless you have very specific health problems, you don't have to stick with a severely regimented eating program for the rest of your life to maintain a healthy weight.

That's why during the renew phase you're going to take holidays off (you deserve it!) and rest from your diet on the 7th day (if you want to). Once you achieve your goal weight, as long as you stick to healthy real foods most of the time, limit sugars and processed substances, and remain mindful of the foods you know don't nourish your body or your gut microbiome, you'll be able to maintain your weight effortlessly for life.

During the renew phase, I'll teach you how to do that. I'll also explain what to do when the program is over (it's actually never really "over"; you just keep eating healthy for life).

LOOKING AHEAD

Okay, that covers the basics. Now it's time to roll up your sleeves. We will begin like any good gardener does by tilling the soil and preparing your inner garden for all the goodness to come. In the next chapter, you'll discover how to mitigate the dysbiosis that is sending your inner ecosystem out of balance by improving the biodiversity of the microbial communities in your gut.

I will also explain how to limit foods in your diet that could be disrupting your gut microbial balance and causing a wide range of uncomfortable symptoms (i.e., bloating and flatulence). I will teach you how to replace these foods with healthy, satiating, anti-inflammatory alternatives that will support your health inside and out.

Finally, you'll learn about my top 10 superfoods for Phase 1. If you don't believe food can be used as medicine, I have a feeling I will change your mind once you read about these amazing nutritional superstars.

That's all coming up in Phase 1. Ready to dive in?

CHAPTER 4

Phase I: Reboot

WEED YOUR INNER GARDEN
AND REV UP YOUR METABOLISM

Imagine a patch of ground overgrown with weeds. The soil is hard, dry clay. The only plants that grow are invasive species of weeds–hardy and durable, but hardly the type of plants you'd want in a lovely, healthy garden.

Now let's pretend you want to start a garden on this piece of untended land. What's the first thing you'll do? Clear out the weeds and prepare the soil, right?

Well, the steps are not so different when it comes to preparing the "soil" of your gut for the healthy ecosystem of gut microbiota you wish to plant in it. You want to increase the overall biodiversity of this inner ecosystem, shifting it toward a robust set of microbial communities that work together in a symbiotic way to support your health and help you achieve an optimal weight.

That's precisely what Phase 1 is designed to do. During the first 30 days of this program, you'll focus on weeding your inner garden and tilling the soil of your gut. You'll do this by:

1. Rebooting your gut ecosystem

2. Reestablishing good eating patterns

3. Revving up your metabolism

Here's how it works.

REBOOTING YOUR GUT ECOSYSTEM: TILLING THE SOIL IN YOUR INNER GARDEN

Living deep in your lower intestines is a complex ecosystem of microorganisms that constitutes a garden of life. This magnificent orchard is composed of trillions of highly diverse organisms that have evolved to a sophisticated synchrony of symbiosis. When we care for this garden and nourish our flora, our health flourishes. But when we feed our friendly gut bugs poorly and treat them poorly, the diversity of gut microbes is diminished and our health is compromised. Just as your stockbroker advises you to diversify your portfolio, my goal is to teach you to biodiversify your gut microbiome to improve your overall health and promote a lean metabolism. As with our own communities, reduced diversity results in stagnation and decay. We all need a diverse and balanced community of microbes whose functions complement one another, producing the symphony of good health. Abundant data support the importance of biodiversity in health, and its loss causes various inflammatory conditions, including asthma, allergic and inflammatory bowel diseases, type 1 diabetes, liver disease, obesity, and much more.[1, 2] I'll go into greater detail about why this is the case later this chapter when I explain why inflammatory foods, in particular, tend to lead to weight gain and digestive symptoms for so many. To reverse dysbiosis (the imbalance of microbial communities we discussed in Chapter 2), we need you to restrict highly refined inflammatory foods from your diet. Doing this will rebalance your gut ecosystem, cool off systemic inflammation, and help rebalance your blood sugar, insulin levels, and more.

Remember that the type of gut microbiota predominating in your gut is strongly influenced by what you eat. In fact, in a study recently published in the journal *Nutrition*, scientists stated that "diet has the most powerful influence on gut microbial communities in healthy human subjects."[3] The Western diet is a master manipulator of the intestinal microbiota and villain of friendly flora.[4] "About 75 percent of the food in the Western diet is of limited or no benefit to the microbiota in the lower gut," according to Stig Bengmark, MD, PhD, honorary visiting professor in the division of surgery and interventional science, University College London. "Most of it, comprised specifically of refined carbohydrates, is already absorbed in the upper part of the GI tract, and what eventually reaches the large intestine is of limited value, as it contains only small amounts of the minerals, vitamins, and other nutrients necessary for maintenance of the microbiota."[5] Radical amounts of unhealthy inflammatory fats and sugary foods adversely impact the profile of gut microbial communities very quickly.[6] The Western diet has been shown to promote dysbiosis and disrupt gut barrier function, permitting the seepage of gut bacterial–derived toxins into the circulation, thus causing systemic inflammation.[7] Western diets also reduce microbial diversity, a common thread in many chronic inflammatory diseases including obesity, metabolic syndrome, Crohn's disease, nonalcoholic fatty liver disease, and more.[8-10] Diets rich in proinflammatory omega-6 polyunsaturated fatty acids found in conventionally raised corn-fed red meat (which as we'll see are particularly high in the Western diet) are linked to intestinal dysbiosis and systemic inflammation.[11] Likewise, safflower oil, rich in omega-6 proinflammatory fats, decreases the Bacteroidetes phylum–a microbial shift associated with obesity in many studies.[12] A pivotal study showed that giving omega-3 fatty acids such as fish oil together with the omega-6-rich proinflammatory fats *prevented* dysbiosis and diet-induced weight gain.[13] These data (and more) bolster one of my cornerstone arguments: You can take the Western diet and toss it in the trash can!

The good news: By changing your diet, you change the overall terrain of your inner ecosystem, a crucial step in your progress toward weight loss and spectacular health.

There's only one slight downside to this approach—"collateral damage." We don't yet have a way to pinpoint and eliminate *only* the strains of gut bugs contributing to your weight gain and ill health. Despite the work in animals and humans, science still hasn't provided insight into the specific organisms that *consistently* cause weight gain. Yes, there are trends and patterns, and dysbiosis is clearly a critical factor in fostering weight gain—but we as a scientific community currently lack the ability to selectively target a phylum or species of dysbiotic organisms with antimicrobial interventions. Intense efforts continue to map the human gut microbiome, yet, for now, we lack the ability to identify which organisms are responsible for metabolic dysregulation in a given individual. For instance, the ecosystem of gut microbes of an individual may have an overpredominance of a certain bacteria in the phylum Firmicutes, which is associated with obesity in mice and in some human studies. However, the specific species of gut microbes and their metabolites (the chemicals they make) that contribute to weight gain may differ from person to person. Although technologies exist to identify bacterial metabolites—this field of study is called metabolomics—scientists still lack the sophistication to identify or deliver targeted therapies to eliminate "the community of bad bugs" causing weight gain.

The fact is that some of your healthy flora will die off during Phase 1. There's no way around that. Your flora are composed of a matrix of communities of commensal "friendly" organisms and potential pathogens, all of which are fed by what you eat. Research has taught us that fat-forming bad bugs tend to thrive on inflammatory fats and sugary foods. That's why we'll limit these foods in this phase. However, when you're dealing with ecosystems as complex as your gut microbiome, changes like these can have broad effects across the numerous microbial populations in the ecosystem. As we discussed in Chapter 1, the gut ecosystem includes fungi and viruses (outnumbering bacteria by 10 to 1), whose contribution to health, let alone obesity, is unknown. Dietary patterns alter the intestinal microbiota both functionally and ecologically—that means the communities change, their activity in the body changes, and the biochemicals they make also change. Remember, for example, that gluten-free diets can reduce the amount of bifidobacteria—a healthy strain of bacteria—in your gut. Yet I'll ask you to go gluten free on Phase 1. Why would I recommend a diet for 30 days that may put at risk some of the friendly flora at home in your GI tract? Well, there are several reasons.

First, you'll be cutting off the food supply of microbes that thrive on sugary proinflammatory foods, which helps shift the communities of your gut ecosystem away from dysbiosis. Less dysbiosis means the good strains of friendly flora in your gut can reclaim their proper place in the gut microbiome and do their job of promoting a lean metabolism more easily and efficiently.

On Phase 2 of the Gut Balance Revolution meal plan, I'll show you how to expand these populations of friendly flora once we've tilled the soil. Of course, this is only one example. Many other strains of detrimental microbes depend on foods we'll limit in this phase, so you're looking at an overall upgrade, diversification, and rebalancing of your gut microbiome.

Second, it's important to rev up your metabolism during Phase 1 by reducing the glycemic load of the foods you eat. This has a broad array of important metabolic effects—some of which we've already discussed, some of which we'll examine in greater detail in this chapter.

For example, if you're eating the Western diet or the standard American diet (SAD), radically reducing your sugar intake is a critical step to achieve optimal weight and life-long health. Most Americans eat what some doctors have called "pharmacological doses" of sugar, wreaking havoc on the body by setting off a cascade of negative biochemical effects leading to systemic inflammation, blood sugar imbalance, insulin resistance, metabolic syndrome, and, ultimately, type 2 diabetes and many other chronic illnesses. Phase 1 will help you begin to address these kinds of problems.

Finally, when it comes to rebalancing and diversifying the gut microbiome, there are just three possibilities.

1. **Change the way you eat and live.** This is the best way I know to rebalance your gut microbiome, and it starts with tilling the soil of your gut, creating a "clean slate" in which healthy flora can be planted. This is our objective during this phase of the program.

2. **Add in tons of prebiotic and probiotic supplements and/or foods and hope they outcompete the weight-retaining microbes.** Probiotics are great for some individuals but not all, and once the soil of your gut is ready for them, they can be an excellent adjunct to this type of program. But just eating a bunch of probiotic foods or taking supplements tends not to work nearly as well as tilling the soil and setting the stage for this "reseeding."

3. **Prescribe antibiotics that kill off bacteria.** These medications do exist, but they're like the nuclear option for gut microbiome health problems. They're only necessary (or even desirable) when no other options are available, and there are consequences that must be carefully considered when going this route. These medications kill off massive quantities of bacteria—not bothering to differentiate friend from foe. Antibiotics of any kind (especially ones this powerful) have negative long-term consequences for gut microbiome health and raise concerns for causing obesity, as we saw in Chapter 2. For some health conditions, antibiotics may be necessary, but it's always best to try more benign interventions first.

I strongly prefer option 1 in most cases. Yes, there will be *some* collateral damage. Yes, you'll kill off a few health-promoting microbes along the way. But remember that we're

The Three Fs That Help
Your Friendly Flora Flourish

Most diets take a fairly one-dimensional approach to what you eat, insisting that you "eat this, not that." But a healthy diet for humans can contain a very broad array of foods, and cultures all over the world have flourished on everything from acorns, mesquite, and fish (the Pima) to goat's milk and blood (the Maasai), so there's no magic formula for how every human should eat.

But there *are* some "foods" traditional human cultures simply didn't have access to, and we really shouldn't be eating them either. These are the sugary, starchy, highly processed foodlike substances that make up the majority of the Western diet and take up most of the real estate in your local supermarket. So we'll forget these on this program, as I'll explain in a moment.

Putting aside these obvious foodlike substances that send our metabolism out of balance (Coca-Cola and Cracker Jack, anyone?), I do have guidelines regarding what will help you and your friendly flora flourish under various circumstances. These aren't as black and white as the "eat this, not that" advice commonly reported in the news, but they're a good benchmark for how to eat in order to lose weight and get healthy. That's why on this program I decided to take the "Three F" approach to eating:

- **Favor.** These are the healthy, whole foods that will support your inner garden. They'll constitute the majority of your diet in a given phase.

- **Few.** You can simply reduce your intake of certain foods; you don't have to eliminate them entirely. So for each phase, I've called out the foods you will want to limit but not necessarily exclude.

- **Forget.** Some foods you want to omit entirely, at least until you get to Phase 3 and allow yourself an occasional break. Even then, you'll want to stay away from some things we call "food" that simply aren't, and you may find you don't want to eat these products anymore even on your days off from the program.

It's important to note that the Three Fs change from phase to phase. Pay special attention to the charts on pages 241–256, where all this is outlined in detail, especially if you decide to make your own meals during the program.

The Gut Balance Revolution meals have been built on these principles, so you can just follow the appropriate meal plan exactly as designed and easily stay on the program. I'll talk more about the meal plans, the foods lists, and how to use them in Chapter 11. We've managed to create some *spectacularly* delicious recipes while sticking to precise nutritional guidelines. I think you're going to love them.

preparing the soil for the good flora for your garden. When you till a piece of land to prepare it for a crop, a few good plants may get dug under, but you accept this sacrifice for the greater good of the garden you're creating. The same holds true for your inner garden.

To prepare the soil of your gut, we'll *forget* certain foods altogether and eat *fewer* of a class of foods that causes gastrointestinal distress to flourish and may lead to further dysbiosis if your inner ecosystem is out of balance. We'll *favor* the healthy, whole foods your good gut microbes and your body prefer.

Now let's dive into more details about what's allowed in Phase 1, what you need to reduce, and what to eliminate altogether. It's easier to start at the end and talk about what foods you'll want to forget for the next 30 days, so we'll begin with that.

Forget Foods That Promote Dysbiosis, Inflammation, Blood Sugar Imbalance, and Insulin Resistance

During Phase 1, we'll omit a number of foods that cause disruptions and imbalances in your gut ecology, cause your blood sugar to spiral out of control, set off inflammation

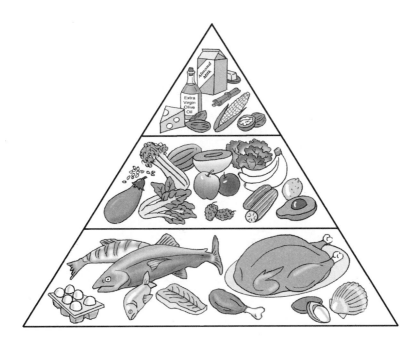

The Gut Balance Revolution Phase 1 Food Pyramid: This figure prioritizes the foods to eat during Phase 1, the reboot phase. Foods that are limited are at the top of the pyramid (i.e., gluten- containing foods and oils). Fruits and vegetables that have a relatively low to moderate FODMAP content (greens, squash, cucumber, berries) are placed in the middle of the pyramid. High-protein foods such as poultry, eggs, and fish, which are to be eaten in abundance, are at the base of the pyramid.

throughout the body, and generally wreak havoc on your metabolism, your waistline, and your overall health. Eliminating these foods is your first and most important step in tilling the soil of your gut and rebooting your metabolism.

You'll find the complete list of foods to eliminate in the Forget column of the Phase 1 food plan, starting on page 241. For now, let's review a few of these foods to highlight exactly how detrimental they are to your health.

Sugar

The average American eats 150 pounds of sugars (total caloric sweeteners) annually. In 2000, 66 pounds of beet and cane sugar and 87 pounds of corn sweeteners were consumed by Americans.[14, 15] That's a lot of sugar. To get a sense of just how that stacks up, consider that before the Industrial Revolution, humans consumed about 20 teaspoons of sugar per person per year; in Paleolithic times, that amount was as little as 2 teaspoons.[16, 17] Recent reports by the World Health Organization (WHO) and the Centers for Disease Control and Prevention (CDC) find that Americans currently consume an average of 15 to 20 percent of their daily calories from added sugars–that's about 300 to 400 calories a day based on a 2,000-calorie diet.[18, 19] This is particularly problematic in light of the fact that the WHO now recommends that no more than 5 percent of our daily calories should come from added sugar.[20] This means the average American eats three to four times more sugar than he or she should every day. These new WHO recommendations came on the heels of research attributing increased risk of cardiovascular disease mortality to excessive sugar consumption.[21] The American Heart Association concurs with the WHO and recommends that women consume no more than 100 calories a day from added sugars and men no more than 150 calories a day (1 teaspoon of sugar = 17 calories).[22]

Researchers at the Division for Heart Disease and Stroke Prevention of the CDC examined the National Health and Nutrition Examination Survey database, which contains information on some 11,733 individuals who, between the years 1988 and 2010, consumed 25 percent of total calories from sugar.[23] They found that this excessive sugar consumption *tripled* the participants' risk of cardiovascular disease mortality compared to those who consumed less than 10 percent of their calories from sugar.[24] Prior linkages have connected high sugar intakes to type 2 diabetes, obesity, fatty liver disease, stroke, and other adverse health conditions.[25] The study's researchers stated: "Our findings indicate that most US adults consume more added sugar than is recommended for a healthy diet."

Can anyone say "understatement"?

What are considered added sugars? Just cruise down the middle aisles of your local grocery store and look at the labels of processed foods–they are loaded with added sugars. The following list* provides some samples. Understand that these sugars and syrups are *added* to foods or beverages when they are processed or prepared. This does not include naturally occurring sugars such as those in milk and fruits.

- Anhydrous dextrose
- Brown sugar
- Confectioners' (powdered) sugar
- Corn syrup
- Corn syrup solids
- Dextrose
- Fructose
- High-fructose corn syrup (HFCS)
- Honey
- Invert sugar
- Lactose
- Maltose
- Malt syrup
- Maple syrup
- Molasses
- Nectars (e.g., peach nectar, pear nectar)
- Pancake syrup
- Raw sugar
- Sucrose
- Sugar
- White granulated sugar

*Source: choosemyplate.gov/weight-management-calories/calories/added-sugars.html

It's quite a list—and it doesn't even cover every possible form of sugar you'll find in your supermarket. No wonder some doctors say we're consuming pharmacological doses of sugar in amounts that impact our biochemistry. But how does it affect us?

1. **It imbalances our blood sugar.** When we consume immense doses of sugar, our blood glucose levels become elevated. Stable blood glucose is a hallmark of good health, so this by itself is reason enough to limit sugar intake.

2. **It leads to insulin resistance.** In response to all this sugar, our pancreas releases a substantial amount of insulin to usher the sugar into our cells, where it can be metabolized and converted into energy or stored as fat. When the influx of sugar exceeds metabolic needs, that sugar is packed away as fat on your butt, hips, thighs, tummy, and everywhere else you don't want it. As the fat cells grow, they become resistant to insulin's effects over a long period of time. Your body then requires more insulin to properly maintain blood sugar levels and provide cells with energy. This is a key component of metabolic syndrome and can eventually lead to type 2 diabetes.

3. **It inflames the body.** Sugar in significant quantities is inflammatory, and systemic inflammation is intimately related to chronic illness and fat gain.

4. **It promotes glycation.** When your blood glucose is elevated for long periods of time, the excess glucose irreversibly binds to proteins in your body, which then clump together into advanced glycation end products (AGEs). These molecules can lead to neuropathy and other health problems.

5. **It upsets gut microbial balance.** Harmful microbes such as clostridium, enterococcus, and other species in your gut *love* sugar.[26] Plus, inflammatory fats, so high in the

Western diet, work as a partner in crime with sugar, creating even more disruptions in gut microbial balance.[27] When you eat too much of these foods, noxious bacteria thrive, which can lead to gastrointestinal dysbiosis and all the problems that come with it.

The bad news about sugar doesn't end there. Another recent study found that eating large quantities of fructose rapidly leads to gut-derived endotoxemia and liver damage, even in the absence of weight gain.[28] This is particularly interesting to our discussion here for several reasons. To understand why, you need to know something about fructose.

Fructose is a kind of sugar that used to be found most often in fruit. It's a monosaccharide–a simple sugar–and some people are intolerant of it even in fruit, as we'll see when we discuss the FODMAPs group of highly fermentable foods.* For most folks, however, fruit is a perfectly safe way to consume this sugar. Fruit isn't the culprit. In fact, there are loads of studies showing that a diet rich in fruits and plants prevents many chronic diseases and cancers. Whole fruit is also loaded with fiber, which slows the release of monosaccharides into the bloodstream without the massive surge in insulin release triggered by other forms of added sugars. We're seeing concurrent epidemics of nonalcoholic fatty liver disease (NAFLD) and obesity worldwide, with excessive consumption of refined sugars (not fruit) as the leading cause.[29] So who's the bad actor in this drama of sugar, weight gain, and the far-reaching health consequences that come along with it? Enter the dragon–high-fructose corn syrup (HFCS).

HFCS: No Worse Than Table Sugar—Or Is It?

For decades, there's been a raging controversy about high-fructose corn syrup.† On one side stands the National Corn Growers Association, claiming that HFCS is no worse than table sugar. On the other side stand doctors and scientists concerned that this supersugar may adversely impact human health more severely than table sugar.

Evidence is mounting that there's real cause for concern about HFCS. Fructose consumption has increased in recent decades, especially due to increased consumption of sweetened beverages and processed foods with added fructose.[30] In fact, from 1980 to 2000 the consumption of cane sugar stabilized while the consumption of corn sweeteners has increased more than 50 percent during the same time period.[31, 32] HFCS intake has been associated with pathologies such as NAFLD.[33, 34] In fact, a recent study has

---

* For this reason, we will be limiting the types of fruits allowed in Phase 1. It's not because they are unhealthy; rather, it's because they are high in FODMAPs that are highly fermentable by gut bacteria, causing uncomfortable digestive symptoms, and some may cause imbalances in the composition and biodiversity of the gut microbiome. See all the details in the section on FODMAPs on page 61.

† Plain corn syrup can be used to enhance the appearance of foods, but it's often combined with white table sugar because it's not very sweet due to a large composition of glucose. The addition of "unbonded" or "free" fructose to corn syrup gives it an incredibly sweet taste so there's no need to add table sugar.

shown that individuals with NAFLD who were placed on low-fructose/low-HFCS diets experienced improved liver function, more balanced liver chemistry, and enhanced cardiometabolic markers.[35]

A meta-analysis of 3,102 articles linked HFCS intake to features of metabolic syndrome: high resting blood sugar, hypertension (high blood pressure), and abnormal cardiovascular lipid profiles.[36] These and other studies about the impact of fructose on liver health are only a few in a growing body of research that suggests HFCS, like table sugar, is detrimental to our health and our waistline. But why?

As its name suggests, HFCS is corn syrup chemically altered so that it is particularly high in *free* fructose and glucose monosaccharides, which are readily absorbed into the bloodstream. In contrast, table sugar has *equal* fructose content to HFCS, but the fructose is bound to glucose as sucrose, a disaccharide that requires enzymes to break it apart before it can be absorbed into the bloodstream. The free fructose form is what gives HFCS a supersweet taste and allows food chemists to use much smaller quantities of it than they would table sugar to achieve the same level of sweetness. This provides food companies a low-cost way to add sweetness to food, pushing their profit margins higher, along with your blood sugar level and waistline.

It's this trait–intense sweetness for a fraction of the cost–that's led to HFCS being a popular additive in processed foodstuffs the world over. Since 1975, it's found its way into everything from soda to bread to breakfast cereals to canned beans, condiments, "yogurt," and even some commercial pickles–potentially detracting from their health-promoting probiotic effect (recall that some gut pathogens thrive on sugar). The result: Most Americans are eating a high-fructose diet. Could this be one of the reasons the national waistline has ballooned out of control since the 1970s despite an overall lower caloric intake?

While there's ongoing debate and a ton of finger-pointing between the table sugar and HFCS camps, the truth is that they're both capable of causing a metabolic storm of inflammation and obesity when overconsumed. Head-to-head studies show that they're similarly noxious to our body and need to be limited in our diet.[37] Sugar-sweetened beverages are problematic because they're a source of many of our ills and account for a large portion of calories in today's youth–in a dose-response fashion, the more youngsters consume, the more problems they have.[38] One study reported that nearly 94 percent of children ages 3 to 5 years consumed sweetened milk products, 88 percent consumed fruity drinks, 63 percent consumed sodas, and 56 percent consumed sports drinks and sweet tea.[39] Remember, the dose makes the poison. When dealing with a poison, keep the dose down!

How does all this sugar impact the gut microbiome and intestinal health? It isn't pretty. Back in Chapter 2, we discussed endotoxemia, the process by which gut-derived bacterial toxins find their way into your bloodstream. Certain gut bugs produce lipopolysaccharide (LPS), a critical component of their cell walls but a substance that isn't very good for us. You see, your immune system is particularly sensitive to LPS. We don't

What About Diet Sodas?

The first thing people ask me when they hear my take on sugar is, "What about diet sodas and artificial sweeteners? They're okay, right?" In a word, no!

Evidence has been piling up against artificial sweeteners in general and diet sodas in particular for some time now. For example, a new study out of The Johns Hopkins Bloomberg School of Public Health shows that overweight people who drink diet sodas tend to consume *more* calories overall—approximately 194 additional calories daily.[40] This research confirmed the observations of scientists at the University of Toronto's Department of Nutritional Sciences, who observed 3,682 overweight participants in a study recently published in the journal *Obesity*.[41]

How could this be? Well, people who make the switch to diet drinks appear to eat more to compensate for the caloric deficit, as if their body weight set point has been moved upward. But why? A possible reason is that diet sodas may trigger appetite. It appears that the combination of carbonation and aspartame synergizes and elicits powerful signals from reward centers in the brain. This increased activation of reward regions may trigger hunger responses, as we discussed with sugar.[42] Research out of Salerno, Italy, demonstrated that the presence of carbonation itself reduces the neural processing of sweetness perception, which could lead to the consumption of *more* sugar.[43] Carbonation and its adverse impact on digestive hormonal reflexes, along with taste signals in the gut and brain elicited by aspartame, may all be involved in the increased caloric consumption associated with diet sodas.

To make matters worse, there have been questions about aspartame and other sweeteners since their creation, including some concerns that they may be carcinogens.[44] A study with profound implications recently published in the journal *Nature* linked the use of noncaloric artificial sweeteners (NASs) such as saccharin, sucralose, and aspartame to the development of diabetes—the condition that they were designed to avert and combat—thus their use for "weight control" is now fraught with deep concerns. Interestingly, these scientists linked the underlying root cause of the deleterious effects of the NASs on blood sugar dysregulation resistance to disruption of the gut microbiome. They were even able to confer glucose intolerance to otherwise healthy, germ-free mice via fecal transplants and normalize blood sugar via antibiotics.[45] In fact, there's evidence that aspartame disrupts the stability of the gut microbiome, another reason to advise caution.[46]

Glucose, on the other hand, reduces postconsumption hunger and increases satiety signals by inducing gut hormones that make you feel full while reducing the appetite-stimulating hormone ghrelin.[47] My suggestion: Stay away from artificial sweeteners. They aren't good for you, and you won't find them on this program.

know exactly why, but we do know that when it senses LPS, the immune system sets off a massive inflammatory reaction.

Excess fructose consumption in primates has been linked to gut-derived endotoxemia. The LPS released by the gut bugs in this process is eventually absorbed into the liver's circulation, injuring the hepatic tissues and causing fat accumulation,[48] which may be the causal link between HFCS consumption and NAFLD. This is the same mechanism we discussed in Chapter 2, where we learned that when high-fat Western diets were fed to animals, gut-derived endotoxemia, type 2 diabetes, and inflammation-related metabolic diseases emerged.[49]

Whether we blame HFCS or table sugar, they are *both* overconsumed in the form of highly refined carbs and junk food, which have in large part created the diabetes and obesity epidemic. HFCS and table sugar have been shown to drive hyperinsulinism, increased fat accumulation, excess belly fat, obesity, and related diseases. Both HFCS and table sugar increase appetite while free glucose reduces appetite![50] These sugars also work on the reward-pleasure centers in the brain via the release of dopamine, suggesting they may be addictive.[51, 52]

What a win for the fast-food industry. They fill us up with supersize sodas loaded with table sugar and/or HFCS. We become hungrier, consume more high-fat junk food filled with HFCS, and unknowingly become addicted. All this goes to show that the interrelationships between what you eat, gut microbial imbalances influenced by your diet, and the resultant systemic inflammation (which leads to weight gain) are a profound set of interlocking puzzle pieces that need to be addressed to lose weight and to address the obesity epidemic in our society.

If you're interested in learning more about excess sugar consumption, I recommend *Fat Chance* by Dr. Robert Lustig, one of the premier experts on the problems with fructose, and *Salt Sugar Fat* by Michael Moss, a journalist who has exposed why the food industry dumps obscene quantities of sugar, salt, and fat into virtually all the food it makes. The bottom line: We eat way too much sugar, and we need to kick the habit to reboot our gut microbiome, rev up our metabolism, lose weight, and get healthy. You won't find much sugar on this program, and it will be particularly limited in Phase 1.

Starchy Carbs

Sugar isn't the only dietary demon in the American way of life. A close second is sugar's cousin: refined starchy carbs. This includes bread, bagels, pasta, cereal, crackers, cookies, and cakes made from refined grains depleted of fiber and nutrients; white potatoes (think french fries); white rice; and just about any processed food in the middle aisles of your supermarket. These foods are sugar in disguise. Your body barely knows the difference–they're converted almost immediately to sugar after you eat them, and they set off all the same biochemical and gut microbial reactions.

This is why, especially in Phase 1, I ask you to keep your total carb load very low: no more than 50 grams a day. But don't *count* carbs or calories (as you would in most other weight-loss programs); that's not necessary as long as you follow the food charts and meal plans in Chapter 11. But you do need to be aware of why I'm asking you to make this change.

Fifty to 60 percent of the standard American diet is carbohydrates—and I'm not talking veggies here, folks. I'm talking chips and soda—starchy carbs and sugar. Low-carb diets have been shown to burn fat in the short term, likely because reducing your carb load helps rebalance your hormones (especially insulin), reduces inflammation, and starves out dysbiotic bugs in your gut—all very good things when it comes to getting rid of unwanted weight. On the flip side, traditional low-carb diets nonselectively "starve" good gut microbes, including fat-burning bifidobacteria—leading to the aforementioned collateral damage. As you will see, the Gut Balance Revolution keeps the carb count low during Phase 1 while expanding the biodiversity of the gut microbiome and minimizing collateral damage to the good gut microbes.[53]

Other low-carb plans put you in a state called ketosis, which means that certain cells in your body begin to use ketones (or ketone bodies) as their primary fuel source. I mention this because some folks worry that going into ketosis is dangerous—quite the opposite. Research has shown that ketogenic diets are a very effective method for kicking off weight loss and are safe for healthy individuals for up to 6 to 12 months (and perhaps longer, although they are unsafe for people with preexisting kidney problems).[54] The mechanisms underlying the effects of ketogenic diets on weight loss are still a subject of debate, but they may include the following:[55, 56]

■ Dr. Robert Atkins's original hypothesis suggested that weight loss was induced by losing energy through excretion of ketone bodies, which are appetite suppressants. More recent science supports the principle that protein increases satiety and reduces appetite, meaning you naturally eat less overall.[57, 58]

■ As you eat more protein, energy production shifts toward protein oxidation, which is inefficient. It is "more expensive" for the body to burn protein than sugar or fat for energy. This means more calories are burned as you metabolize your foods.

■ Ketogenic diets seem to have an impact on the appetite control hormones leptin and ghrelin.[59]

■ Fat production (lipogenesis) is reduced while fat-burning (lipolysis) is increased, and the overall efficiency of your fat-burning machinery is enhanced.[60]

■ To get the glucose it needs, your body shifts to gluconeogenesis (which just means it creates glucose from the protein you consume). This has a higher "metabolic cost" than eating straight carbs or sugar, meaning your body burns more calories (even at rest) when you shift into ketosis.[61, 62]

Furthermore, low-carbohydrate diets can improve insulin resistance and glucose levels, reduce hemoglobin A1c, and improve glucose uptake in people who are overweight and/or suffer from type 2 diabetes.

There's even evidence that ketogenic diets can reduce small-particle LDL (one of the more dangerous types of cholesterol), lower triglycerides, and increase HDL ("good" cholesterol)–all wonderful effects for cardiovascular health.[63]

While some people experience an initial period of fatigue and lethargy (typically lasting a few days up to a week), these diets ultimately help improve cognitive impairment, mood, and energy in people who are overweight.[64, 65] And ketogenic diets are increasingly being shown to have therapeutic value for uncontrolled seizure disorders and possibly brain tumors.[66, 67]

In the long run, these generic super-low-carb ketogenic diets do have some problems, as we discussed in Chapter 3. They tend to lead to an increased body weight set point and yo-yoing if you stay too low carb for too long. However, I designed the Gut Balance Revolution program so that you won't stay in ketosis for more than 30 days. The overwhelming majority of people are perfectly safe going into ketosis for this amount of time or even longer, and the research clearly indicates that going into ketosis for this time period supports weight loss and may have other benefits such as anticancer and neuroprotective effects and improved sports performance.[68] Additionally, ketogenic diets have not been shown to promote osteoporosis or liver dysfunction, a concern that some people have about these types of diets.[69]

One caveat: If you have kidney problems, doing Phase 1 as outlined in this book isn't for you. In this case, I recommend you work with a physician in your community who is familiar with the concepts in this book and who can help you adapt the diet to your needs.

For the rest of you, eating low carb for the first month of the program will reignite your metabolism and help rebalance your blood sugar levels and gut microbiome. It's healthy and safe, and there are loads of delicious low-carb foods (see the recipes in this book if you don't believe me!). So get the sugar and starch out of your diet and see how you feel.

Later, when we get to Phase 2, we'll selectively reintegrate some of these foods and strategically increase your carb load gradually. In other words, you don't need to stay on this low-carb part of the program forever–just long enough for your body to reset itself using the healing power of whole foods.

Inflammatory Fats

Fats have long been a vexing issue in nutrition. For many years, we were taught, incorrectly, that fats are intrinsically evil and that low-fat diets were the holy grail of weight loss and wellness. Over time, this "low-fat" view has come under increasing scrutiny, and the fat myths most of us once believed have been dispelled by research. For example, a pivotal randomized clinical trial recently observed that a moderate-fat diet was an effective part of a weight-loss plan and was associated with improved lipid-related risk factors and fasting insulin levels.[70] In a meta-analysis published in 2010, scientists reviewed data from 21 studies that included nearly 348,000 participants and came to the conclusion that "there is no significant evidence for concluding that dietary saturated fat is associated with increased risk" of coronary heart disease or cardiovascular disease.[71]

So it's clear: Myths about fat simply don't hold up under scrutiny. Fat is not inherently bad. In fact, it's necessary for your survival. You could live without carbohydrates—you wouldn't be happy, but you would be alive. Without any fat in your diet, you'd perish. We need fats for optimum cellular membrane health and for a healthy nervous system. Your brain is 65 percent fat. The complications of essential fatty acid deficiency are legion.[72] Why would you deprive yourself of something so essential?

The simple answer is that you shouldn't. But that doesn't mean you should go out and eat fat with abandon. The real story about fat is too complicated for sound bites, and we scientists don't know as much about it as we'd like to think. What's the optimal intake of fat for the human body? What are the upper limits we can eat while still remaining healthy? What *types* of fats should we focus on? Which should we avoid? This is where the water gets muddy. However, there are a few things we are reasonably certain about.

Fat comes in basically two flavors: inflammatory and anti-inflammatory. You've probably heard a lot about omega-3s, omega-6s, omega-9s, and so forth. These distinctions are important enough to explore a bit. What the numbers represent is the carbon atom on which a double bond is formed. Omega-3 fats such as alpha-linolenic acid (ALA), eicosapentaenoic acid (EPA), and docosahexaenoic acid (DHA) are fundamental to human health. Omega-6s are mainly (though not entirely) inflammatory fats, extremely prevalent in the Western diet, as we'll explore shortly. Omega-9s are anti-inflammatory in nature but less common. They can be found in foods like avocado, squid, olive and sunflower seed oil, almonds, and several others.

A few foods contain only one type of fat—fish, high in omega-3s, are a good example. For other foods, the story is more nuanced. Some omega-6s, such as those in borage oil, black currant seed oil, and evening primrose oil, are healthy anti-inflammatory fats.[73] Others, such as corn oil, are unhealthy inflammatory fats. Should you avoid *all* foods that contain omega-6s? Not necessarily. What you really want is to have a good balance between inflammatory and anti-inflammatory fats. You can't eat food and eliminate *all* the inflammatory fats—it just won't happen. It's the ratio between the two that's important. And it's this ratio that is wildly out of balance in the modern Western diet.

The ideal ratio between inflammatory and anti-inflammatory fats is a perfectly balanced 1 to 1. Currently, we eat a diet that's 20:1 to 50:1 in favor of inflammatory fats.[74] By now, I'm sure you realize why that's a problem.

Where did all of these inflammatory fats come from? From the hydrogenated oil, soybean oil, cottonseed oil, corn oil, "vegetable" oil (a combination of the others), and other

What About Animal Fat?

Research on animal fat is lagging. On the one hand, it's been shown that diets high in conventionally raised red meat contribute to weight gain, cardiovascular issues, and certain cancers. We now know that this is likely due to the high levels of inflammatory fats in these animals—plus the fact that conventionally raised red meat is laced with antibiotics in sufficient levels to alter the gut microbiome and contribute to obesity. Studies in mice have shown that when given equivalent amounts of antibiotics as are found in our meat supply, mice become fat. Could this be one reason humans are facing an obesity epidemic? More research is needed.

On the other hand, grass-fed animals raised on pasture are more widely available than they used to be, and some evidence suggests that these animals are higher in healthy, anti-inflammatory fats than their conventionally raised counterparts. Unfortunately, no research has been done proving whether or not shifting from conventionally raised to pastured animals impacts long-term weight, the gut microbiome, or health.

Based on evidence, I've elected to keep red meat to a minimum on this program and focus on lean protein sources that we know support optimal weight and health, including seafood, skinless white meat chicken, and vegetable sources such as tofu.

If you're going to eat red meat, stick with pastured sources, as they may be higher in healthy fats, and they're typically free of antibiotics.

---

inflammatory fats poured into all of the processed foods we eat. These poor-quality fats set off systemic inflammation, causing you to pack on fat and setting the stage for every chronic disease in the book. And remember the many experiments in mice and humans we reviewed in Chapter 2 showing how a Western diet high in inflammatory fats shifted the gut microbiome toward a less diverse and less healthy ecological community. We'll dramatically limit these inflammatory fats in this program, and for good reason: They're bad for your inner ecology and overall health.

At the end of the day, it's not how *much* fat we consume that gets us into trouble (I'm including myself–remember I was nearly 300 pounds as a teenager!), it's those high glycemic proinflammatory foods that wreak havoc on your blood chemistry and gut microbiome.

EAT FEWER FODMAPS

Possibly the most important class of foods we'll address in Phase 1 is FODMAPs. Remember that FODMAP is an acronym for fermentable oligo-, di-, and monosaccharides and polyols. Reducing your intake of these foods is critical to the success of this program.

Saccharide is simply another word for sugar. So oligosaccharides, disaccharides, and monosaccharides are all forms of sugar. They're short-chain carbohydrates. Monosaccharides have one sugar molecule; disaccharides have two sugar molecules, and so forth. Polyols are sugar alcohols–a sugar molecule with a molecule of alcohol appended to it. Sugar alcohols can be found naturally in some foods, but the place they're most commonly found is in certain artificial sweeteners, such as xylitol, mannitol, and sorbitol.

These foods are highly fermentable, and they're not well absorbed in the small bowel–they pass from your stomach through your small intestine and into your large intestine mostly undigested and unabsorbed. The degree to which they're digested varies from person to person. For example, some people don't produce enough lactase–the enzyme needed to break down lactose (a disaccharide) in milk products. Other people have fructose (an oligosaccharide) transport defects, causing malabsorption of this sugar and creating a feast for their gut bugs. Fructans and galacto-oligosaccharides are polymers of sugars (fructose and galactose, respectively) that require bacterial enzymes for their digestion, so they're usually processed in the large bowel unless you have an overgrowth of bacteria in the small bowel (aka SIBO–more about this later). Because these highly fermentable foods pass to the large bowel either undigested or only partially digested, they can cause several problems.

First of all, your gut microbiota *love* to eat FODMAPs–they're like fast food for your flora. They gobble them up, ferment them, and produce gases like hydrogen, carbon dioxide, and methane. Gas is bad enough, but FODMAPs can lead to more serious problems. You see, your body naturally tries to dilute small, concentrated doses of undigestible

Where's the Fiber?

No question about it: Fiber is one of the most important foods you need for long-term health and optimal weight. It helps you feel full, it's fabulous food for your flora, it helps with stools, and it "scrubs" your intestines. Most health organizations recommend getting at least 25 to 35 grams of fiber a day. Unfortunately, Americans aren't getting anywhere near this much fiber in their diet—their average intake is only 15 grams per day, and only 5 percent of Americans consume the daily recommended intake.[75]

Despite this, I'm recommending that you limit your fiber intake during Phase 1. We'll enhance fiber intake in Phase 2, along with prebiotic foods (foods that selectively feed your friendly flora) to diversify your inner garden once you've tilled the soil and it's ripe for planting the seeds of a healthy gut microbiome.

carbohydrate molecules by forcing water into your GI tract. This can lead to a host of uncomfortable symptoms, including gas, bloating, pain, loose stools, and more.

This is compounded if you suffer from a condition called small intestinal bacterial overgrowth (SIBO), which occurs when the microbial communities in your small intestine are overabundant and harbor a mix of gut bugs that resembles the flora in your colon. This can happen for many reasons, such as when the valve separating your colon and your small bowel doesn't close properly[76] or if gut bugs aren't being cleared from the small bowel from lack of small intestinal movement, lack of stomach acid or pancreatic enzymes, and many other reasons.

You can imagine why this may cause problems. When you have SIBO and you eat lots of FODMAPs, the gut microbes now in your small intestine feast on these carbs and cause even more gastrointestinal distress from gas and bloating.

In my experience–remember Ted's case history from Chapter 1?–there's an intimate relationship between gut dysbiosis (including but not limited to SIBO), weight problems, gastrointestinal symptoms, and chronic conditions like irritable bowel syndrome (IBS). And I've noticed that obesity seems to predispose people with these conditions toward a poorer prognosis.[77] I've treated many patients for SIBO using a revolutionary low-FODMAP diet, which improves the condition.[78] In patients who have SIBO and who are also overweight to obese, weight loss has been a bonus on this diet. My personal experience parallels the research.

Science has demonstrated a link between SIBO and obesity.[79-82] A recent study noted that 41 percent of obese patients suffered from SIBO.[83] A 2008 study revealed that SIBO prevalence is higher in obese patients than in the normal population, concluding that "in morbidly obese patients, bacterial overgrowth prevalence is higher than in healthy subjects and is associated with severe hepatic steatosis."[84-86] It's been accepted for a decade that GI symptoms like gas, bloating, and flatulence are more prevalent and intense in overweight people.[87-89]

Another study reported a positive association between body mass index (BMI), abdominal pain, and diarrhea.[90] And it's been shown that factors that directly impact the gut microbiome (such as diet, physical activity, and body weight) influence the propensity of digestive symptoms. These observations were later corroborated by a study done on children, in which exercise, diet, and weight loss helped reverse IBS symptoms in those who were overweight.[91] Taken together, these reports confirm the higher prevalence and severity of functional digestive symptoms in overweight individuals. And they linked the observed higher prevalence of SIBO in the overweight to abnormalities in small bowel transit. Surprisingly, gastric transit has been found to be accelerated in overweight people, meaning carbs are dumped quicker into the bloodstream and there is little time for the body to send satiety signals from the gut to the brain to stop eating.

This has led Dr. Anthony Kalloo of Johns Hopkins to strategically apply intragastric Botox injections to slow down the hurried stomach in the overweight.[92]

Studies have also illustrated a complex interrelationship between SIBO and type 2 diabetes. Remember that imbalances in your gut microbiome can contribute to the development of type 2 diabetes–and vice versa. For example, diabetic neuropathy can adversely impact the nerves in the small bowel that govern your whole gut transit time– the time that it takes food to move through your GI tract (aka your "gut clock" and "cleansing wave," which we'll discuss in more detail in Chapter 10).[93]

Does this mean that if you're overweight you definitely have SIBO and/or a gut movement disorder? Not necessarily. But if you experience flatulence, gas, and bloating after meals–particularly high-starch or sugary meals–you may well have the condition. Even if you don't, it's highly probable that your gut microbiome is out of balance if you're overweight.

In either case, reducing your FODMAP intake helps reduce these symptoms.[94] By limiting these highly fermentable short-chain carbs and sugary foods that your gut bugs love to eat, you'll severely limit the food supply of these misplaced microbes and reduce their infestation of the small intestine, leaving your inner garden freshly tilled and ready to be seeded and fertilized in Phase 2.

It's important to understand that not all FODMAPs are inherently bad for us. In fact, some FODMAPs–like asparagus and artichokes–are superfoods in the right contexts, as they selectively feed the beneficial bacteria that bolster our metabolism. But if you suffer from weight problems or SIBO–or *both*–you need to initially *reduce* your intake of these foods for a short time, which will improve digestive symptoms.

For this program to be effective, you need to *reduce–not eliminate*–FODMAPs. Feeding with a limited amount of healthy gut microbiome–friendly FODMAPs has been shown to improve biodiversity.[95] The amount of FODMAPs you can consume and still remain healthy is individual, and over time you may experiment with the amount of these foods in your overall diet. For Phase 1, I recommend consuming a diet that is low in FODMAPs, as this plan will fit the most people. See the Phase 1 food plan on page 241 for my specific guidelines on what to leave out of your diet during this part of the program. Or, to make it easy on yourself, just follow my delicious, gut-balancing daily meal plan: It has been specifically tailored to optimize your FODMAP intake.

If you're interested in a more detailed discussion on SIBO, check out my book *The Inside Tract.* If you want to know more about FODMAPs, I strongly recommend *The Complete Low-FODMAP Diet* by Sue Shepherd, PhD, and Peter Gibson, MD. They're the leading world experts on the science of FODMAPs, and the book is a treasure trove of information on these tricky sugars.

Next, two special FODMAPs we'll leave out of Phase 1: gluten and dairy.

Gluten

Technically, gluten isn't a FODMAP. It's a protein found in many high-FODMAP grains, including wheat, rye, and barley, which are a special kind of oligosaccharide called fructans. Fructans are chains of fructose molecules with a glucose molecule at the end. As mentioned earlier in this chapter, these molecules cannot be digested by the human body. Only your gut flora can help you eat them, and they're a rich source of food for gut bugs. When your gut microbiome is imbalanced or gut bugs are misplaced (i.e., in the small intestine), overeating these foods can exacerbate these problems—so we'll limit them in Phase 1.

Even if you don't follow the health section of the newspaper or aren't up on the latest in nutritional science, you've certainly seen the growth of the gluten-free section in your supermarket. We're inundated with antigluten messages, and for some people gluten *is* a problem. But the story about gluten is more complex than the media would have you believe.

I've seen many people come through my clinic with adverse reactions to gluten. As a GI specialist, I'm well aware of the problems gluten causes to the inside tract—especially the small intestine—for people who have an all-out autoimmune reaction (celiac disease) or a sensitivity to the substance. About 3 million Americans are diagnosed with celiac disease, though some research suggests it may be more common than this. Dr. Peter Green, an expert on the disorder, has called it a "hidden epidemic." The data on gluten intolerance are more difficult to ascertain, as it can present as a host of symptoms that people may not connect to diet. Suffice it to say, millions of Americans have problems with gluten. I'm pleased to see a growing awareness about these problems, as it offers people who suffer from these issues much-needed affirmation.

That said, gluten isn't the one and only cause of chronic illness and weight gain in America. Not everyone is sensitive to it. And there are *no data* proving that going off wheat or gluten itself for the long term will assist with weight loss. Going off cookies, crackers, bread, and pasta—yes, this is associated with weight loss. Going off gluten, not so much. After all, there is plenty of unhealthy gluten-free junk food (refined and processed grains such as cookies, crackers, bread, pasta, and so on) on the market! And a long-term gluten-free diet presents challenges in maintaining adequate niacin, folic acid, calcium, zinc, and fiber intake.[96] Plus, there's some evidence that eliminating gluten from your diet if you're not sensitive to it could have adverse effects on your gut microbiome—particularly your levels of bifidobacteria, which foster a healthy, lean metabolism.[97, 98]

Finally, remember that at the end of the day, gluten-free cookies, crackers, cakes, bread, and pasta are still just cookies, crackers, cakes, bread, and pasta. Eating them in excess isn't healthy, doesn't do your gut microbiome any favors, and doesn't substitute for the whole, healing foods you need to achieve optimal weight and thrive.

Dairy

Milk products are high in calcium and most are enriched with vitamin D, two critical cofactors for a strong skeletal structure. They also appear to support weight loss–a number of studies show an association between calcium, vitamin D, and dairy intake and maintenance of a healthy weight.[99-102]

Fermented dairy products are high in the friendly flora you need to rebalance your gut microbiome. As you'll see in Phase 2, I'll encourage you to add plenty of probiotic-rich dairy that helps diversify the mix of friendly flora in your gut microbiome. Foods like yogurt and kefir are critical in that part of the program. If you tolerate dairy well, these can be among the most healing and helpful foods in your diet.

On Phase 1, however, we'll eliminate dairy because it's high in FODMAPs, and the sugar it contains may be rapidly fermented by gut bugs, causing gas, cramping, and even fertilization of these nasty critters. In Phase 2, we'll reintroduce dairy, mainly in a highly therapeutic probiotic form to help you reverse dysbiosis and lose weight.

Calcium and Lactose Intolerance

Dairy is the most bioavailable form of calcium in our diet. So how can you get adequate calcium if you're lactose intolerant? This can be tough, but here are some nondairy sources to consider.

Green vegetables, such as the superfoods kale, Swiss chard, and greens, are loaded with calcium. So are beets, almonds, beans, buckwheat, figs, kiwifruit, miso, potatoes, cocoa, soy, sesame seeds, and tahini. But you need to eat a lot of these foods to receive enough calcium to meet the Dietary Reference Intakes (DRIs) recommended by the USDA and the Institute of Medicine.[103] And foods that are high in fiber—or, more critically, those high in dietary phytates and phosphorus—may block calcium absorption (important to remember if you are trying to get adequate calcium from nondairy sources).

Take spinach, for example, one of the vegetables highest in calcium. One cup of cooked spinach has about 245 milligrams of calcium,[104] but not all of it is absorbed, since spinach (like many of the foods listed) is high in oxalic acid, which binds dietary calcium, preventing its absorption in the gut. You'd need to eat 5 to 6 cups of spinach daily just to meet the DRIs for calcium. That's more or less true for the rest of the veggies mentioned above.

So if you're lactose intolerant, increase the amount of these veggies in your diet and consider a high-quality calcium supplement. Dr. Sue Shepherd, who discovered the low-FODMAP approach, recommends supplementing calcium (see page 340 for specific guidelines) for those on the diet for more than 30 days.

Some people are intolerant to dairy, which contains several components that people can be sensitive to—the most common culprits are lactose, a FODMAP, and casein. Lactose is the only disaccharide in the diet that causes people problems, and the reason comes down to how much lactase (the enzyme that digests lactose) you make. If you make too little lactase, you can't digest lactose properly and are "lactose intolerant." However, this is a pretty one-dimensional term, as levels of lactase expression and the degree of intolerance vary widely. Remember, the dose makes the poison. Someone with lactase production deficiencies may tolerate a low dose of lactose products such as Cheddar cheese but become ill when eating whole milk or ice cream.

Casein is a protein in dairy products that produces symptoms in some people in similar ways gluten does. Tolerances vary, so discovering what works for you and your body is key to any long-term healthy eating plan.

As with gluten, reactions to dairy are highly individualized. And as always, the dose makes the poison in lots of cases. Some can't handle any at all. Others may be able to consume a little dairy. And for still others, dairy may not present a problem. It all depends on you. One final word: If you're dairy sensitive or intolerant, don't worry. There are plenty of nondairy probiotic-rich foods to focus on in Phase 2.

FAVOR FOODS THAT REV UP YOUR METABOLISM

So far, we've discussed lots of foods you *can't* eat during this phase of the program. At this point, you may be wondering what you *can* eat during Phase 1! Don't worry—there are plenty of delicious, healing, whole foods we'll focus on for this phase.

Talking about these healing, whole foods is my favorite part of the plan. As disciplined as this style of eating may seem, it's actually *not* about deprivation at all. It's about honoring your role as caretaker of the ecosystem inside of you and nourishing that inner garden with foods that will help it heal. When it heals, you heal, and you lose weight along the way as a perk. So reward yourself with the gift of good health by favoring these foods on Phase 1.

Appetite-Reducing Protein

Looking for a delicious appetite-reducing food that naturally builds fat-burning machinery in your body without causing huge surges in your blood sugar and insulin levels? Protein is precisely such a food. When you stick to sources free of inflammatory fats, it's among the healthiest foods you can eat. Here's why.

Lean, high-quality protein (such as wild, line-caught salmon or cod or American farm-raised tilapia; skinless poultry; eggs; wild game; and healthy vegetable sources like nuts and tofu) is extremely satiating—it naturally reduces your desire to eat. Studies have repeatedly shown that people who increase their protein intake reduce their overall caloric consumption due to protein-induced satiety.[105-108] Protein is by far the most satiating macronutrient,[109] making it a perfect place to start improving your diet for a weight-loss program like this.

This has been proven by studies at Maastricht University, which showed that increasing dietary protein promoted weight loss by increasing energy expenditure and inducing satiety.[110-112] It's likely one reason higher-protein, lower-carb diets tend to work so well, especially in the induction phase—they make you feel full longer and help you burn more calories. Here are more specifics on how it works.

Eating protein affects fullness-related hormones and gut peptides, including ghrelin, glucagon-like peptide 1, insulin, cholecystokinin, and peptide YY.[113] It also increases thermogenesis—the amount of calories you burn just by digesting your food. It takes *a lot* of energy to break down and oxidize protein, and even more to convert protein to sugar through the process called gluconeogenesis. So eating protein increases your overall metabolic rate while at rest. You burn more calories even while sitting around as your body spends energy to break down the protein in your diet.

The scientists at Maastricht demonstrated this in a groundbreaking study in which 113 people consumed a very low-energy diet for the 4-week induction, resulting in a 5 to 10 percent loss of excess body weight. Then these subjects were followed for 6 months postdiet to see if they could maintain their reduced weight. The subjects were randomly assigned to groups receiving a standard diet or a diet containing 30 grams of additional protein a day.

Both groups lost a similar amount of weight during the low-energy portion of the induction phase of the program. But the group who ate more protein in the maintenance phase (after the low-energy induction phase) preserved more weight loss and kept more inches off their waist. These people lost 7.5 percent of their body weight and were able to keep it off longer than the nonprotein group. Researchers concluded that these results could be explained by increased satiety, enhanced thermogenesis, increased sleeping metabolic rate (the rate at which you burn calories in your sleep), and improved fat oxidation.[114] Similar findings have been replicated many times in different trials by other scientists.[115, 116, 117]

The takeaway: When it comes to weight loss, maintenance is where it's at. That's what distinguishes this program. Many diets allow you to lose a few pounds for a while, but when the diet is over, you're more likely than not to gain them back and then some—pushing your body weight set point ever higher. Increasing your protein intake appears not to have this rebound weight-gain effect, an impressive fact indeed.

The type of protein you eat may produce different effects on appetite, satiety, and metabolism. Two types seem to stand head and shoulders above the rest in terms of their ability to reduce appetite: fish and whey protein.[118] Fish appears to have this effect by increasing blood levels of tryptophan, an amino acid that's a precursor and signaling molecule for serotonin (the "happy and full" neurotransmitter), which is involved in satiety.[119] And whey protein apparently not only has an impact on appetite hormones but also produces superior insulin responses and provokes a lower rise in blood glucose than other forms of protein.[120] Dairy and eggs can also be highly satiating.[121, 122]

Consider the recent meta-analysis comparing high-protein–low-carbohydrate diets, like Atkins, with high-carbohydrate–low-fat diets, such as the plan of Dr. Ornish.[123] Weight loss was significantly greater with the high-protein diets in studies lasting up to 6 months, although the differences *weren't* significant in studies spanning 12 months. There are many reasons why these effects are short lived–compliance, compensatory mechanisms, effects on the gut microbiome, and more. This further supports the fundamental precepts on which the Gut Balance Revolution is built: a short-term ketogenic diet followed by a gradual shift toward a more Mediterranean style of eating. The rationale is clear: Ketogenic diets help induce weight loss in the short term. In the long term, they are hard to maintain and may have some negative effects on the gut microbiome depending on which carbs are being permitted. Thus, gradually shifting from a very low-carb diet to a more Mediterranean style of eating (Phase 3) seems to be the key for long-term sustainable weight loss, as we'll discuss in Chapter 8.

Where's the Beef?

Given all this positive news about protein, you may be wondering why there's no red meat in the meal plans. Unfortunately, there's ample evidence that red meat (at least the hormone- and antibiotic-laden and GMO-corn-and-soy-fed type commonly found in the American marketplace) and processed meat products (like hot dogs) are associated with weight gain. Numerous studies have associated increased red meat consumption with obesity and reduced intake with improved adiposity, body weight, markers of metabolic syndrome, and inflammatory markers.[124-129] These foods are loaded with inflammatory fats (conventionally raised animals are much higher in omega-6 fatty acids) and antibiotics–which, at doses present in meats, can lead to weight gain in mice and possibly in humans.[130]

The Gut-Heart Connection

Red meat and processed meat products have also been associated with colorectal cancer–which has been increasingly linked with gut dysbiosis as a risk factor.[131] Furthermore, profiles of metabolic by-products of gut bacteria have been recently reported to help identify those with colorectal neoplasia.[132] Recent evidence also shows that disruption of gut microbiome balance caused by diets high in animal protein may be the hidden link between red meat and cardiovascular disease.[133-135] How could gut microbiome imbalance impact your heart health? To figure this out, Dr. Stanley Hazen from the Cleveland Clinic took a novel approach. He bought a George Foreman grill and started cooking up steaks and giving them away for free to hungry students. He then measured

Protein: How Much Is Too Much?

The Gut Balance Revolution is a *short-term* higher-protein ketogenic diet (Phase 1) coupled with measures to resolve dysbiosis (Phase 2) and maintain optimal weight, gut microbiome balance, and total health for life (Phase 3).

Tempted to maintain a high-protein diet for 6 months or more? There may be consequences. Groundbreaking research reported in the journal *Cell Metabolism* linked protein intakes with age and mortality in 6,381 Americans over the course of an 18-year study conducted in the United States and Italy.[136] Those ages 50 to 65 who reported a high protein intake had a 1.5-fold increase in overall mortality (analogous to the risk imposed by cigarette smoking as an independent risk factor) along with a fourfold increase in cancer death risk in the following 18 years. Among those whose protein source was heavily plant based, including nuts and legumes, the risk of death from cancer or any cause was negated. These data, along with other mounting evidence, support my recommendations about limiting antibiotic- and hormone-laden red meats, which have many cancer-related associations.

Mouse studies were performed in tandem to correlate findings in humans to mechanisms involving the growth hormone receptor (GHR)/insulin growth-factor-1 (IGF-1) involved in cell repair and proliferation, which also has the potential to support tumor cell progression, obesity, and aging. The study reported that high-protein diets in mice promoted progression of breast cancer and melanoma through GHR/IGF-1 signaling. In humans, those having high levels of GHR/IGF-1 further increased the risk of cancer and all-cause mortality in the high-protein group. The science offers a clear caution to those whose weight-loss and maintenance solution is a long-term high-protein diet.

Some doctors have expressed concern about the theoretically detrimental effect of high-protein diets on calcium balance and bone health. According to the acid-ash hypothesis, eating meat (especially red meat) creates an acidic environment in your blood, sending your pH out of balance and causing your body to "steal" minerals from your bones to buffer the acid in the meat and balance your blood pH. While it's theoretically plausible, evidence doesn't yet support it. In fact, the data paradoxically show that dietary protein increases bone mineral mass and reduces incidence of osteoporotic fracture due to calcium repletion.[137-139] So this isn't a factor I'm concerned about, especially on a 30-day ketogenic diet program.

One legitimate concern is that heavy consumption of sulfur-containing amino acids can cause a loss of nephron mass, an indicator for renal failure. That's why people with kidney insufficiency or failure shouldn't follow this diet but should consult their physician to adapt this program to their individual needs.

the students' blood for levels of a compound called trimethylamine N-oxide (TMAO). High levels of this compound correlate with an increased risk of atherosclerosis and cardiovascular events. Based on previous research he'd done in this area, Dr. Hazen guessed that these students had higher levels of TMAO because they were meat eaters. Why would meat eaters have higher levels of TMAO? It seems that those who eat meat regularly become very efficient at converting the L-carnitine in red meat to TMAO. But how did he know this metabolic shift had anything to do with changes in gut microbial balance?

To find out for sure, he took a group of the original volunteers and asked them to take a broad-spectrum antibiotic for 2 weeks and then repeat the test. On follow-up, the amount of TMAO in the group that took the antibiotic was much lower. His conclusion, corroborated in follow-up studies: Eating lots of red meat led to a *proliferation of gut bugs*, creating chemicals that increase the risk of heart disease.

On the flip side, those on a strict vegan diet, who eat no red meat for at least a year, do not produce TMAO, perhaps because this prebiotic-rich diet favorably shifts the gut microbiome away from production of TMAO and cuts down on one of its sources, L-carnitine. Another possibility is that red-meat eaters tend to consume other unhealthy foods (aka junk food) as part of the Western diet that cause dysbiosis, thus providing a source of TMAO, and underconsume items that improve gut microbial biodiversity and are prebiotic in nature (like nuts, fruits, veggies).

This idea that the Western diet can rapidly *and* adversely shift the gut microbiome has now been reproduced and published in the journals *Science* and *Nature*–two of the most highly regarded scientific publications.[140, 141] Exactly which bugs proliferate varies from study to study. But the core point here is simple: The way to someone's heart is through the gut microbiome.[142] Eating junk is like putting a dagger through the heart!

The research is clear: Eating too much conventionally raised red meat pumped full of antibiotics and high in proinflammatory omega-6 saturated fats imbalances your gut microbiome. For all these reasons and more, I've elected to eliminate conventionally raised red meat from Phase 1. You don't have to keep it under wraps forever–pasture-raised lean red meats are reintroduced in Phase 2. For now, though, shift your attention to healthy sources of protein such as eggs, fish, whey, and poultry raised without antibiotics or hormones.

Anti-Inflammatory Fats

The low-fat dietary dogma of the 1980s and '90s is being questioned. Reducing your total fat intake isn't nearly as important as balancing the types of fats you eat. The Gut Balance Revolution is not a low-fat diet. It's a *low–inflammatory fats* diet. There's a big difference.

Instead of the inflammatory oils that constitute most of the fat Americans consume, we will focus on anti-inflammatory alternatives that fight chronic illness and help you lose weight. The two most important fats we will focus on in this program are:

1. **Extra-virgin olive oil (EVOO).** It's hard to overstate the health benefits of EVOO. A 2010 Spanish study found that the cardiovascular protective effects and other health benefits of the Mediterranean diet may largely be due to olive oil.[143, 144] Investigators looked at individuals who were genetically prone to inflammation and cardiovascular disease and provided them either no dietary intervention or the Mediterranean diet with a high intake of EVOO or nuts. After 3 years, those who followed the Mediterranean diet program with EVOO had the greatest reduction of body weight. What in EVOO provides its benefits? One of the active ingredients is oleocanthal, which has been found to have similar anti-inflammatory effects to nonsteroidal anti-inflammatory medications such as ibuprofen.[145] This is one reason EVOO is a staple of the Gut Balance Revolution. There's also solid data for the use of the Mediterranean and even the Baltic Sea diet for overall health and for weight maintenance–see details in Chapter 8.

2. **Canola oil.** This unsaturated fat is higher in omega-3s and healthy omega-6s than any of the other commonly used cooking oils in the Western diet. Studies show that the aminolevulinic acid in this oil may reduce your blood pressure, balance cholesterol, and fight off inflammation.[146] Canola oil not only improves cardiovascular risks (blood lipids, inflammatory markers) but also improves insulin sensitivity.[147] The only downside: Much of the canola oil on the market is genetically modified, which I typically recommend avoiding. In any event, it should only be used in high-heat cooking, which you won't be doing much of during Phase 1.

These and the other fats allowed on this program will fend off the inflammation that keeps your gut microbiome out of balance, causes pounds to pile up, and leads you down the road to chronic illness. These healing fats are a core part of this program, and I encourage you *not* to do a "low-fat" version of this diet. The total amount of fat you consume will be well within healthy limits, and it will help cool off your body while melting away pounds. This is one reason low-fat diets are *not* successful in the long term. You are starving your body of the very essential anti-inflammatory fats that you need to fight inflammation and prevent disease. Yes, the calories in/calories out approach to weight loss makes it look attractive to cut calorie-expensive fat from the diet, but in the long term, this is counterproductive.

Healing Carbs

Carbohydrates are among the healthiest foods on the planet. I'm not talking about cookies, cakes, crackers, rice, potatoes, and their ilk. I'm talking about low-glycemic fruits and vegetables packed with healthy phytonutrients that heal your body and nourish your gut microbiome. There may be no easier way to improve your overall health than to increase the amount of fruits and vegetables you eat each day. Good evidence shows that increasing your intake of veggies reduces your risk of heart attack, stroke, and more. For example, the Harvard-based Nurses' Health Study–one of the largest and longest nutrition studies ever–shows that people who ate more than eight daily servings of vegetables were 30 percent less likely to have a heart attack or stroke.[148] No one ever became overweight or ill by eating too much kale and raspberries. In fact, these are highly therapeutic superfoods included throughout this program.

There's only one tiny caveat to the "fruits and veggies are the healthiest foods on the planet" argument: Some fruits and veggies are high in FODMAPs. Remember, that doesn't mean they're unhealthy. They're highly fermentable and help bacteria grow–and some are selective for friendly flora (called prebiotics), which we'll discuss in Chapter 6. Suffice it to say that we need to minimize these whole foods–based FODMAPs for a short time while your inner garden is being rebalanced.

On this phase of the program, we'll load up on the veggies and some fruits, but we'll stick to those that are lower in FODMAPs. As long as these low-FODMAP vegetables aren't breaded, creamed, or fried, they're allowed on the program. But we'll especially favor low-FODMAP fruits and veggies that nourish your body while giving your gut microbiome a chance to *reboot* itself. For details on which fruits and veggies to favor and which to eat fewer of, see the Phase 1 food chart starting on page 241.

A Few Other Dietary Tips for Phase I

Just a few more notes, then you're on your way to tilling the soil of your gut microbiome and losing weight.

Soups

I love soup, and not only because it reminds me of home. Good data show it supports weight loss because it increases satiety.[149] To understand why, you need to know about a concept called energy density.

The energy density of foods is defined as the amount of energy per unit weight of food. Adding water to foods influences energy density, because it adds weight without calories. Soup has quite a lot of water but very few calories (unless it is cream based), so it's low on the energy density scale. This is important, because low–energy density foods have been shown to reduce weight, lower BMI, and reduce overall caloric consumption. Scientists now believe this is why eating a salad or a soup before a meal tends to reduce your overall food intake. The low–energy density soup or salad satiates you without adding too many calories, so you consume less food over the course of the meal, particularly when the soup includes a vegetable puree.

In one study, scientists covertly added pureed veggies into various soups, then compared the energy intake of those who got the veggie puree against a control group who ate the same soup without the puree. The vegetable puree group naturally ate about

202 fewer calories daily than their peers who ate the puree-free soup. Good news for those who want to lose weight.

Warm, filling, nourishing soups will keep you satisfied for hours, so you'll find many outstanding soup recipes in the meal plans in Chapter 11. I encourage you to indulge in these nourishing, comforting, healing, weight-loss-supporting dishes.

Water

The average human is 60 to 75 percent water. Every one of the cells in your body depends on water for life and health—yet many of us don't drink enough. Make sure you're hydrated by drinking a minimum of 64 ounces of water daily. Carbonated beverages shouldn't replace water, as they may lead to the consumption of more food. So avoid carbonated water and stick with plain, flat, filtered tap water.

There's evidence that increased water consumption benefits weight-loss efforts. Investigators at the Berlin School of Public Health systematically analyzed the world's literature on this subject and found that 11 studies met their strict criteria for review.[150] Those dieters who consumed more than 1 liter of water a day were found to lose more weight than those who drank less. And those who drank 2 cups of water before a meal lost 4 pounds more than those who didn't. The mechanisms by which water consumption improves weight loss are unclear.

The School Nutrition Association in 2010 reported that in the United States a stunning 30 to 40 percent of daily calories is consumed as beverages, with 144 calories of high glycemic soft drinks and fruit juices.[151, 152] A can of regular soda contains about 140 calories of added sugar—about 7 percent of total daily energy needs, based on a 2,000-calorie diet. The report showed that water accounted for only 35 percent of US beverage consumption. Swapping zero-calorie water for high-calorie, sugary beverages is a good way to jump-start weight loss.

Snacks

Developing a healthy relationship with food means eating when you're hungry. Sometimes, that means having a meal; other times, it means having a snack. Tune in to your hunger signals and try to follow them to guide your eating. I've incorporated snacks into the meal plans, but to give you a better sense of how and when to snack, here are some guidelines.

1. **Eat three meals and two snacks**. This is a good guideline, not a hard-and-fast rule. The key is to keep your appetite and blood sugar from moving wildly up and down like a roller coaster. Most of us can do this by sticking with three squares and one or two snacks in between.

2. **Don't graze**. Snacking and grazing are different things. It's fine to have a small snack between meals to stabilize your blood sugar and reduce your appetite. Eating small amounts of food all day long is *not*. This just keeps your blood sugar and

insulin levels elevated throughout the day, setting off negative hormonal and metabolic effects. So snack, but don't graze.

3. **Go for a handful of low-FODMAP nuts and fruits.** Here's how to make the easiest, most nutritious gut-microbiome-balancing snack in the world: Consult the Phase 1 food charts on pages 241–256. Select your favorite low-FODMAP nuts (mine are walnuts). Grab a piece of your favorite low-FODMAP fruit (I love blueberries). Enjoy!

Alcohol

The question comes up in my clinic all the time: *Can I drink alcohol? Just a little red wine?* No doubt a little alcohol can be one of the joys of life, and good data have clearly shown that red wine, in particular, can help people live healthier[153] and longer.[154, 155] But add a little more and all kinds of negative consequences occur, including an imbalanced gut microbiome.[156] So avoid alcohol for 30 days in Phase 1. We'll add it back in during Phase 2.

Coffee

More than 60 percent of Americans drink coffee, most for that early-morning boost or to overcome the afternoon slump. But does the beverage have any health benefits? *Yes.* There are so many health benefits that coffee is now recognized by many as a superfood. In fact, I list coffee as a superfood for Phase 3, where I discuss all the latest research about its health benefits.

This is good news, because most of us don't want to give up our morning cup of joe, but it doesn't quite tell the whole story about the coffee bean. While there's evidence that coffee is healthy, excessive amounts may lead to significant problems, including acid reflux and other GI symptoms, insomnia, anxiety, aggregate arrhythmias, and high blood pressure.

So if you keep coffee in your diet, drink it in moderation—no more than one or two cups daily. Skip the cream and sugar and opt for a dash of anti-inflammatory and fat-burning cinnamon, cocoa powder, or nutmeg instead. Organic decaf is okay, too, if you prefer it. The organic processing averts exposure to potentially harmful organochemical solvents.[157]

One final note on coffee: If you rely on it to get through your day, you may want to rethink this policy. In many cases, coffee is used to compensate for a sleep debt, and as we'll see in the lifestyle section in Chapter 10, lack of sleep is strongly associated with–and is a possible cause of–weight gain, obesity, and a host of health problems. We shouldn't need stimulants to get through the day, and you'll find you don't need to when you rebalance your gut microbiome.

There's quite a bit to digest in this chapter (yes, the pun is intended). But there's a way to make it easy on yourself: Just stick to the Gut Balance Revolution meal plans and recipes in Chapter 11. These meals follow rigorous nutritional guidelines, they're easy to make (most take as little as 15 minutes), and they are so scrumptious you can even invite your foodie friends over to partake. Losing weight and getting healthy have never been more delicious.

What You Can Expect During Phase I

Phase 1 is designed to help you till the soil of your gut microbiome and kick-start your metabolism. Follow these steps to lose weight and feel healthier. It won't happen overnight, but it will happen. This phase will begin the process of rebalancing your gut microbiome, reduce systemic inflammation, help rebalance your blood sugar, banish chronic symptoms you've experienced for years, renew vigor, and set the stage for lifelong vibrant health.

The first few days may be hard. That's normal. Some people experience "withdrawal symptoms," including irritability, grumpiness, fatigue, headaches, and possibly others. This is more likely to be a problem if you've been eating a lot of carbs and drinking lots of coffee and if your inner garden is more like a cesspool. If that's the case, you have the most to gain by sticking with this plan. For most people, these symptoms begin to fade after a few days, and from there on out their energy increases, their symptoms decrease, and they lose weight.

No one can guarantee how much weight you'll lose in the first 30 days of any diet as individual responses will vary. I'm comfortable saying many of you may lose as much as 15 pounds after the first month on the Gut Balance Revolution. It could be more for some, less for others. Everyone is different. Biochemical individuality and personalized medicine will, in my opinion, be the hallmark of 21st-century medicine. The goal is not to lose as much weight as fast as you can. Programs that promise that tend to fail in the long run. It's far more important to achieve a slow, sustained burn, where you see a steady drop in weight, an increase in energy, and a reduction in symptoms over time.

So don't focus too much on the numbers. I'm all for weighing yourself, but don't obsess about it. Focus instead on how your clothes fit, how your belly feels, and how energetic you feel. Pay attention to symptoms that disappear and how your overall body and brain perform. These are the real signs that your gut microbiome is healing. The weight loss will come.

LOOKING AHEAD

That covers all the dietary basics for your first 30 days on the program. But before we move on to Phase 2, I want to take all of this a step further by teaching you about a few superfoods that will supercharge your success on Phase 1. That's what the next chapter is about.

CHAPTER 5

Rev Up Your Metabolism with Dr. Gerry's Top 10 Superfoods for Phase I

"**L**et medicine be thy food, and food be thy medicine." These words of Hippocrates, the father of Western medicine, are as true today as they were when first spoken more than 20 centuries ago. In fact, growing evidence shows that certain "superfoods" support weight loss and optimal health, while other foods (like sugar and processed carbs) are metabolic poisons that hamper weight loss and contribute to chronic illness. While there's no standard definition of a superfood, most agree that they constitute special, nutrient-rich foods that provide disease-fighting properties and are especially good for overall health and well-being.

I not only want you to lose weight on this program. My dream for you is much bigger than that. I want you to achieve optimal health, rebalance your gut microbiome, build resilience, and protect yourself from the chronic illness epidemic that ravages America today. That's why on each phase of the program, I ask you to focus on integrating into your diet some key superfoods that will rev up your metabolism, help you heal your body, and nourish your inner ecosystem. For each of the three phases of the Gut Balance Revolution, I'll highlight my top 10 favorite superfoods, plus award some honorable mentions. These foods are featured in the gut-balancing meal plans in Chapter 11. In Chapter 4, I provided a Phase 1 food pyramid to help you visualize the preferences and priorities of foods and in your diet. I'll do this for each phase. Favor these superfoods, and your gut microbiome (and your health!) will thank you for it.

I. EGGS

No food has gotten such an undeservedly bad reputation as eggs. Fear of this food evolved in the 1980s, when doctors were concerned that the cholesterol in eggs might increase overall cholesterol levels in the body. As it turns out, this idea was never founded on scientific principles; it became a myth that was perpetuated for decades.

The effect of dietary cholesterol on blood cholesterol has never been clear. The kind of cholesterol found in eggs is different from that in the human body, so it's entirely possible eggs have zero effect on your cholesterol levels. Even if they did, we now know that the story behind cholesterol is far more complicated than we previously realized–raising total cholesterol isn't nearly as important a risk factor in heart disease as raising low-density lipoproteins (LDL) and a subclass of LDL called LDL pattern B. These lipoproteins contain relatively high amounts of cholesterol and are associated with an increased risk of atherosclerosis and coronary artery disease.

Eggs are actually a superprotein. They contain all nine of the essential amino acids your body needs to thrive. It's been shown repeatedly that people who eat eggs for breakfast feel fuller longer, reduce their overall daily caloric consumption, and lose weight. A study published in the *Journal of the American College of Nutrition* reported that overweight women who ate eggs rather than bagels for breakfast had greater feelings of satiety and a reduced appetite and consumed fewer calories throughout the day and for the next 36 hours.[1]

Two compelling studies from St. Louis University show that an egg breakfast is superior to a caloric and energy density–matched bagel breakfast. The first study, reported in 2005, compared egg (18.3 grams of protein) and bagel (13.5 grams of protein) breakfasts. The egg breakfast increased satiety and reduced energy intake at lunch, with no rebound increase in energy intake in the 24-hour period following.[2] In the second study, reported in 2008, scientists provided two groups of obese participants with an isocaloric breakfast consisting of either two eggs or a bagel for at least 5 days per week for 8 weeks. The egg breakfast group showed a 61 percent greater reduction in body mass index (BMI), a 65 percent greater weight loss, a 34 percent greater reduction in waist size, and a 16 percent greater reduction in percent body fat.[3]

A 2010 study, looking at blood chemistry, confirmed these findings in a randomized crossover design in which subjects served as their own controls. The results were shocking! Participants consumed fewer calories after the egg breakfast compared with the bagel breakfast, which carried over for the next 24 hours. Bagel consumers were hungrier and less satisfied 3 hours after breakfast compared with egg eaters. The bagel eaters had higher levels of blood glucose, ghrelin (a hunger-stimulating hormone), and insulin.[4] These findings suggest that eating eggs for breakfast results in stabilized glucose and insulin, a suppressed appetite (due to the ghrelin response), and reduced energy intake.

Think skipping breakfast is the solution? Think again! A study published in the *American Journal of Clinical Nutrition* looked at this issue to see if skipping breakfast was associated with alterations in appetite, food motivation and rewards, and snacking behavior in overweight girls. A 6-day randomized crossover study was performed on 20 overweight young women with an average age of 19.1 years. For their morning meal, they ate a high-protein breakfast or a normal-protein breakfast or none at all. On the 7th day, participants underwent biochemical testing and responded to questionnaires. The high-protein breakfast was associated with appetite suppression, lowered ghrelin, raised peptide YY (which lowers appetite), and even decreased evening snacking.[5] The normal-protein breakfast, while associated with better satiety than breakfast skipping, didn't alter appetite hormones as did the high-protein breakfast. The takeaway: Eggs are a superbreakfast loaded with protein and nutrients. Bagels are empty calories—bad carbs that turn quickly into sugar and spike insulin levels, which drives fat accumulation.

Studies consistently show that eating a protein-rich breakfast lowers appetite throughout the day. Your best bet is to eat more calories while you are physically active—so that egg breakfast offers a perfect combination.[6]

Do eggs have a role in the lunch menu? You bet! Eggs are an all-star protein source to consider at any meal or snack, as you'll see in your meal plans for all three phases. A 2011 study analyzed the results of eating three different lunches—an omelet, a baked potato, and a chicken sandwich. The omelet was found to be more satiating than the potato or chicken meal, and the energy intake at dinner was not significantly different between the three—there was no rebound increased consumption at dinner after a greater satiety response at lunch.

But the benefits of eggs aren't reserved to weight loss alone. They also support cardio-vascular function and brain health and protect your liver due to the high levels of choline and phosphatidylcholine they contain. Eggs are also good for your eyes, since they're high in two superstar eye nutrients, zeaxanthin and lutein. So embrace the lowly egg and reintroduce it to its proper place as a staple in your diet.

2. CHIA SEEDS

Looking for a plant food packed with healthy anti-inflammatory fats, high-quality protein, and fiber to help you feel fuller longer? Something loaded with antioxidants to protect against heart disease and type 2 diabetes, lower blood lipids, and possibly ease the inflammation of arthritis?[7, 8]

Look no further than the humble chia seed. Chia has been used as a medicinal food in Central and South America and across many cultures to prevent diabetes, obesity, and cardiovascular disease. Many studies support these traditional uses.[9-11] The chia seed is rich in omega-3 and anti-inflammatory omega-6 fatty acids, flavonols, and phenolic acids, which provide many health benefits. Chia oil is particularly high in polyunsaturated fatty acids (omega-3s), which account for its potent cholesterol-lowering effect.[12] A mere tablespoon of this powerful plant food packs a walloping 2,500 milligrams of omega-3 fatty acids, 4.5 grams of fiber, 3 grams of protein, and a boatload of phytonutrients. And it's one of the few seeds considered low FODMAP, so it's a perfect fit for Phase 1–yet it still has relatively high levels of soluble fiber, making it a top food for Phases 2 and 3 as well. Use ground chia in your morning shakes to up your intake of healthy fats. Sprinkle it on salads to add a little crunch at lunch. Chia is the gluten-free gem that's been used as a superfood to bolster the health benefits of breakfast bars, yogurts, cereals, salad dressings, and other products in the food industry.

3. CINNAMON

This beloved zero-calorie medicinal spice comes with a bevy of healthy benefits pertinent to weight control and the complications of being overweight.[13] One USDA study showed that as little as $1/4$ teaspoon of cinnamon daily lowered blood sugar, cholesterol, triglycerides, and LDL in type 2 diabetics.[14, 15] It's also a fat-burning powerhouse that boosts metabolism and has been proven to help your body block the absorption of glucose and enhance the action of insulin to clear sugar from your blood.

Cinnamon is one of the most powerful antioxidant spices and an anti-inflammatory agent that counteracts the effects of obesity. It's been shown to slow gastric emptying, which stabilizes blood sugar by slowing its transit into the small intestine, its principal site of absorption. Remember that overweight and obese people often have poor satiety mechanisms and faster gastric emptying of food, so they tend to dump loads of sugar into the bloodstream, inducing a surge of insulin release by the pancreas, which facilitates fat accumulation. So cinnamon is a clear winner for these folks. Research also shows that cinnamon slows the rate of gastric emptying and stabilizes aftermeal blood glucose in healthy subjects.[16] Adding 6 grams of cinnamon to rice pudding significantly delayed gastric emptying and lowered blood sugar levels after the meal–one reason cinnamon is an excellent addition to the diet for overweight individuals.[17-19]

Cinnamon is also a powerful antimicrobial agent that works against a number of pathogenic gut microbes, making this a top spice as a Phase 1 superfood.[20] So add cinnamon to your daily cup of coffee or sprinkle it on the low-FODMAP fruits allowed in Phase 1 for a tasty snack or luscious dessert.

4. BERRIES

Berries are my favorite sweet treat for Phase 1. They're powerful foods rich in disease-fighting polyphenols such as anthocyanins, flavan-3-ols, procyanidins, flavonols, ellagitannins, and hydroxycinnamates.[21] These compounds provide many cardiovascular protective benefits, including improved endothelial function, reduced blood lipids, decreased arterial stiffness, and reduced blood pressure.[22] These effects are particularly notable in cranberries, strawberries, and blueberries. Fermented blueberry products such as wine are strongly anti-inflammatory (enjoy it in limited amounts in Phase 2).

Blueberry juice has been shown to prevent obesity in mice due to the heart-healthy anthocyanins just mentioned.[23, 24] Blueberries are also low on the glycemic index, strongly anti-inflammatory, and even fight cancer![25, 26]

Blueberries can help you lose weight, too. A study with obese rats found that blueberry peel extract reduced body-weight gain and inhibited fat accumulation in these animals.[27] This had nothing to do with reduced food intake but rather occurred by downregulating fat-influencing genes–factors that included a key adipose cell transcriptional regulator (read: fat-maker signaling molecule) called perixosome proliferator-activated receptor.[28] So a few blueberries can actually send your cells and your genes messages that say, "Let's stop making so much fat."

Blueberries also inhibit fat cell growth and differentiation.[29] When rats with metabolic syndrome from eating high amounts of fructose (sound familiar?) were fed blueberry pomace, they lost weight and their leptin levels were reduced more than control groups'.[30] These effects are further supported by studies showing blueberry phenols have anti-diabetic effects and improve insulin sensitivity in obese, nondiabetic, insulin-resistant people.[31, 32] A similar antidiabetic effect has been described for bilberry extracts.[33]

Another perk of berries is their ability to favorably alter gut microbiome balance. They selectively inhibit the growth of some ferocious pathogens such as salmonella, staphylococcus, and listeria.[34] In particular, blueberry husks have a prebiotic effect–their fermentation by our friendly flora becomes particularly important for Phases 2 and 3. In fact, blueberries are a superfood for all phases. They are low in FODMAPs and have a low-glycemic impact, yet they're extremely anti-inflammatory, making them perfect for Phase 1. Their antimicrobial effects and prebiotic power make them awesome for Phase 2. And they're insulin sensitizing while stifling the growth of fat cells–and that's what we want in Phase 3.

Raspberries are another example of a low-FODMAP plant food that's high in fiber and phytonutrients while being rich in flavor. One cup of raspberries contains an amazing 8 grams of fiber–a dose your friendly bacteria will love. They're packed with vitamins and nutrients like calcium, magnesium, phosphorus, potassium, and vitamin C.

The anthocyanins that give the berries their beautiful color are COX-2 enzyme inhibitors–powerful anti-inflammatories shown to fight systemic inflammation, reducing C-reactive protein (a primary marker of inflammation) levels. The anti-inflammatory effects are so strong that a beneficial biochemical called ellagic acid found in red raspberries was able to protect animals from chemical-induced colitis (an inflammatory bowel disorder).[35] Raspberries also reduce blood sugar and insulin response when consuming other starches.[36] This gives you an edge in your fight against heart disease, type 2 diabetes, and weight gain. Try berries sprinkled with cinnamon and a little crushed chia seed for a spectacular superdessert or as part of the Blueberry Protein Smoothie on page 276.

5. GREEN TEA

After water, tea is the most frequently consumed beverage in the world. It's produced from the leaves of the *Camellia sinensis* plant, typically classified by degree of fermentation. Black tea (fermented) is predominantly consumed in Western countries. Oolong tea (partially fermented) is primarily consumed in southern China and Taiwan. And green tea (unfermented) is mainly consumed in Asia. All types of tea are rich in flavonoids. Catechins are the main flavonoids in green tea, while black tea mainly contains chemicals called theaflavins and thearubigins.[37] The polyphenols in green tea, such as epigallocatechin gallate (EGCG) and epicatechin gallate, which are responsible for its beneficial effects (including its antioxidant potential and antimutagenic capacity), are converted into thearubigins and theaflavins during the fermentation process that creates black tea.

Many studies link green tea to enhanced weight loss, plus a number of health benefits worth mentioning.[38] Green tea—along with another superfood, cocoa, and the new kid on the superfood block, coffee—provides cardiovascular protective properties including stroke prevention. The flavonoids and polyphenols in green tea improve endothelial function and lower total and LDL cholesterol as well as decrease the risk of stroke.[39, 40] Green tea extract reduces blood pressure, inflammatory biomarkers, and oxidative stress; stabilizes blood sugar; and improves parameters associated with insulin resistance in obese hypertensive patients.[41, 42]

When it comes to weight loss and fat-burning, green tea has a number of benefits that make it and black tea and coffee attractive superbeverages for a lean metabolism. The caffeine in green tea enhances energy expenditure and fat oxidation by activating the sympathetic nervous system, while the polyphenols counteract the reflex decrease in the resting metabolic rate that usually accompanies weight loss.[43]

Two meta-analyses evaluated 49 studies for the effect of green tea and its extracts on weight regulation. Overall, caffeinated green tea was found to promote and maintain weight loss.[44, 45] A third meta-analysis that evaluated 15 studies with 1,243 patients confirmed that caffeinated green tea was associated with enhanced weight loss, reduced waist circumference, and lower body mass index (BMI).[46]

How much tea should you drink for these effects? My recommendation: Shoot for two to three cups of caffeinated green tea daily.

Green tea appears to have a prebiotic effect, too—it helps support the growth of the fat-burning friendly flora. Green tea powder in combination with a single strain of *Lactobacillus plantarum* promoted growth of lactobacillus in the intestine and attenuated high-fat diet-induced inflammation.[47] Green tea catechins also decrease fat absorption and affect short-chain fatty acid production—by-products of fermentation that improve the health of your GI tract in a variety of ways and are involved in the regulation of satiety hormones, energy expenditure, and fatty acid oxidation.[48-50] In a clinical trial of 14 healthy volunteers, 1.3 cups of green tea was shown to improve satiety.[51]

Now, I'm not saying it's okay to have a Big Mac with fries—and a cup of green tea to neutralize your (un)happy meal. But I encourage you to use superbeverages like green tea, black tea, and even coffee as therapeutic drinks to melt the fat away. They have a powerful thermogenic effect, revving up your body's fat-burning machinery.

6. GINGER

Zingiber officinale, commonly known as garden ginger, is an important spice with myriad health benefits. This piquant spice has been used in Ayurvedic and traditional Chinese medicine since the inception of those therapies. Ginger is often referred to as the "universal remedy." What ancient medical practitioners knew instinctively about ginger is now being borne out by science.

Evidence suggests that ginger consumption has anti-inflammatory, antihypertensive, glucose-sensitizing, and stimulating effects on the gastrointestinal tract.[52] The rhizomes have been used for centuries for the treatment of arthritis, rheumatism, sprains, muscular aches, pains, sore throats, cramps, hypertension, dementia, fever, infectious diseases, catarrh, nervous diseases, gingivitis, toothache, asthma, stroke, and diabetes.[53] The anti-inflammatory and antioxidant effects of ginger are very strong—as powerful as common nonsteroidal anti-inflammatory medications (NSAIDs).[54, 55] The antioxidant activity of ginger extracts lasts even after boiling for 30 minutes at 212°F, indicating that the spice's constituents are resistant to thermal denaturation. So you can cook with ginger and still receive health benefits.[56]

The anti-inflammatory effect of ginger as a first-line agent in the treatment of rheumatoid arthritis (RA) was suggested in an animal model of RA. In the study, a ginger-turmeric rhizomes mixture was found to be superior to the drug indomethacin against RA severity and complications.[57]

You probably realize why this is important: Inflammation leads to weight gain and is a major contributor to just about all chronic illness. So cooling down the fire-promoting enzymes and biochemicals is priority number one for optimal weight and health.

Ginger may also reduce your body weight! The structural composition of gingerols is similar to the molecular composition of capsaicin (see Cayenne Pepper, page 86, suggesting it may have similar effects on weight loss. When gingerols are injected into the paws of animals, increased thermogenesis occurs,[58] probably because gingerols, like capsaicin, activate our "fight-or-flight" sympathetic nervous system that, in turn, increases thermogenesis and fat oxidation.[59] One study found that giving men grains of paradise, a species of the ginger family, activated brown adipose tissue and increased whole-body energy.[60] This is a critical point, as brown adipose tissue is one of two types of fat (the other being white adipose tissue) that is metabolically active, with white tissue supporting inflammation and insulin resistance and brown tissue supporting enhanced thermogenesis and energy loss by boosting metabolism. So the fact that ginger activates brown adipose tissue is a major perk.

An intriguing study from the Institute of Human Nutrition at Columbia University assessed the effects of a hot ginger beverage on energy expenditure, feelings of appetite and satiety, and metabolic risk factors in 10 overweight men in a randomized placebo-controlled crossover trial.[61] The results were impressive. Investigators reported ginger significantly increased the thermic effect of food (the process of heat production and release in the body—a form of energy expenditure), lowered hunger, lowered prospective food intake, and increased feelings of fullness. Additional studies are needed to confirm these findings.[62]

A recent study evaluated changes in body composition, blood pressure, lipid profile, and testosterone in 49 faculty, staff, and students participating in a 3-week low-energy dietary intervention (women ate 1,200 to 1,400 calories; men 1,600 to 1,800 calories).[63] The program consisted of a green drink superfood blend. In the second week of the study, a "cleanse" supplement loaded with anti-inflammatory nutrients was added.* This was replaced with prebiotic and probiotic supplements in week 3. The group lost an average of 8.7 pounds and as much as 14.2 pounds—well beyond that expected with a low-energy diet alone—yet another reason to give up the calories in/calories out rhetoric of the past. Even more important, total cholesterol, LDL cholesterol, and blood pressure were reduced, while both waist and hip circumferences diminished. Overall, the 13 men in this study also experienced an increase in testosterone. This study raised some eyebrows about the possible connections between accelerated weight loss, improvements in serum cholesterol, improved male sex hormone levels, and how all of this may be connected to the anti-inflammatory, gut microbiome restorative nature of the program.

Another interesting study compared the efficacy of ginger and orlistat on obesity management in male albino rats.[64] Orlistat is an FDA-approved medication used for promoting weight loss in obese individuals by interfering with the activities of the fat-digesting enzyme lipase made in the tongue, stomach, and pancreas. Inhibiting lipase causes fat to be excreted from the body instead of absorbed and stored, leading to weight loss but also to foul-smelling stools and other possible complications. In the study, ginger was shown to have a greater ability to reduce body weight than orlistat without inhibiting lipase. Ginger supplementation was also reported to significantly raise heart-healthy HDL cholesterol. In fact, ginger had a greater effect in increasing HDL cholesterol than orlistat. The ginger provided all of the benefits and none of the side effects.

---

* The "cleanse" contained magnesium, chia seed, flaxseed, lemon, camu camu, cat's claw, bentonite clay, turmeric, pau d'arco, chanca piedra, stevia, zeolite clay, slippery elm, garlic, ginger, peppermint, aloe, citrus bioflavonoids, and fulvic acid.

There are many gastroprotective effects of ginger worth mentioning, since many people who are overweight tend to suffer from digestive distress (refer to Chapter 4). Scientific studies have validated that ginger can be used as a home remedy to improve many of these digestive complaints, including constipation, dyspepsia, belching, bloating, epigastric discomfort, indigestion, and nausea. Ginger has also been shown to be effective in preventing gastric ulcers induced by NSAIDs.

In my digestive health practice, I've found ginger to be a wonderful tool for managing upset stomach and other digestive complaints. If you suffer from these symptoms, try adding a little ginger to your stir-fry. Or steep it in a cup of hot water for a delicious ginger tea. It will calm your stomach as it helps you burn fat.

7. AVOCADO

Avocados are one of the rare foods containing high amounts of healthy anti-inflammatory fats, a decent amount of protein, tons of healing phytonutrients, and a magnificent amount of fiber (11 to 17 grams per avocado!)—all in one convenient package, keeping you feeling fuller longer than many other foods.

Avocado oil is especially high in monounsaturated fatty acids (MUFAs) and very low in saturated fats. This superfood is particularly rich in an omega-9 fat called oleic acid, a MUFA that has been shown to quiet hunger. Additionally, MUFA-rich diets help protect against abdominal fat accumulation and diabetic health complications.[65] Clinical studies conclude that avocado consumption supports cardiovascular health in a number of ways, most prominently by its beneficial effects on serum lipids. Avocados can fit into a heart-healthy dietary pattern such as the Dietary Approaches to Stop Hypertension (DASH) diet plan and the Mediterranean diet, as emphasized in Phase 3. A randomized single-blind crossover study showed that as little as half an avocado a day may reduce hunger and increase overall levels of satisfaction. Scientists asked overweight adults to add approximately one-half a Hass avocado to their lunch meal,[66] which was found to significantly enhance postmeal satisfaction and reduce the desire to eat for up to 5 hours. Avocados also have a beneficial effect on blood cholesterol levels, likely due to the fruit's high beta-sitosterol levels, a chemical that blocks cholesterol absorption. Plus, they've been proven to benefit eye health because they're high in leutin and zeaxanthin, and the strong antioxidant content protects against skin wrinkling.[67, 68]

Probably the main reason people don't think of avocados as a weight-loss food is due to their caloric content. This idea is founded on the calories in/calories out theory of weight loss, which we now know is obsolete. When people eat avocados, they tend to consume *fewer* calories throughout the day because they feel fuller—a net gain. Spend a few calories on avocados and you'll save more calories in the long run. Mix up some guacamole or cut an avocado in half and add a little salt, pepper, and lime juice for a perfect flora-friendly snack.

8. QUINOA

Pronounced KEEN-wah, this helpful whole grain is underused (and unknown by many) in this country. Interestingly, it's been around since the time of the Incas, who called it the "mother of grains"—a name it no doubt deserves based on its nutritional profile. It's got a good dose of fiber (5 grams per serving) and has a low-glycemic impact. Quinoa is high in magnesium, which is a key regulator of energy and promotes good blood sugar control. It's also rich in potassium and iron, along with other key nutrients involved in energy production, such as riboflavin and manganese.

Gluten-free quinoa is one of the few whole grains low in FODMAPs, which is one of the reasons I've included it in this phase. This healing whole grain is also high in protein, another reason for its inclusion here. Another perk: It's filling. A study at the University of Milan showed that quinoa has a satiating effect—the highest among the gluten-free grains.[69]

Two cautions: First, quinoa is coated with saponin, a potentially toxic, bitter-tasting chemical.[70] So rinse it thoroughly before cooking—rinsing doesn't diminish the nutritional benefits of quinoa.[71] Second, be aware that this superfood is high in oxalates, which could be a problem for folks who tend to form oxalate kidney stones.

Throughout this program, I've tried to focus on "normal" foods you can find in any supermarket. Quinoa takes us a little off the beaten path, but it's becoming more widely available. Try adding it to your diet to replace other whole grains during this phase. Unless kidney stones are an issue for you, I recommend that you include this filling, wholesome grain in your Phase 1 meal plans and beyond.

9. CAYENNE PEPPER

Cayenne pepper is a member of the *Capsicum* genus of vegetables, along with chile peppers and bell peppers. This spicy pepper adds zest to tasty meals mainly through a family of compounds called capsaicinoids. The compound responsible for this hot taste is known as capsaicin. The amount of capsaicin in the chile pepper directly correlates with the sensation of heat—more capsaicin results in a hotter chile pepper. It also means a healthier chile pepper.

Capsaicin has loads of health benefits due to its anti-inflammatory and antioxidant capacity. Many studies document its cardiovascular benefits—it can lower triglycerides and cholesterol, decrease platelet aggregation, and enhance the body's ability to break up small blood clots.[72, 73] However, two studies show high doses in pill form may lead to myocardial infarction.[74, 75] Stay away from capsaicin supplements—take it in its wholefoods form instead. Again, the dose makes the poison!

Although many think of hot pepper as a cause of stomach ulcers, capsaicin actually prevents their formation. It's also an inhibitor of a molecule called substance P, which mediates pain in nerve endings.[76, 77] Studies have shown that topical application of capsaicin ointment improves pain relief in diabetic neuropathy, postherpetic neuralgia, and neuropathic pain.[78] Despite the popular use of capsaicin as a topical application for arthritis, there are conflicting data regarding its efficacy.[79] Capsaicin has also been reported to have anticancer properties.[80]

Chile pepper has long been associated with weight loss, and the data show that a little can help you burn away unwanted pounds.[81] Capsaicin lights up your fat-burning metabolism as few other spices can, in part because it triggers your stress hormone response system. When your sympathetic nervous system (also known as the fight-or-flight response) is activated, hormones called catecholamines, such as epinephrine and norepinephrine, are released into the bloodstream. This process increases thermogenesis, whereby fat is oxidized more effectively. That means your fat becomes fuel for your metabolic fire in as few as 20 minutes after eating cayenne.[82] Just eat a little chile pepper and, 20 minutes later, you're burning fat like a champ. This thermogenic effect isn't unique to capsaicin. As you may recall, we discussed enhanced thermogenesis and fat-burning when we talked about caffeinated green tea. The same is true for ginger, as well as a few supplements such as bitter orange and guar gum.[83, 84] Capsaicin also seems to promote satiety.[85] What a perfect combination for weight loss—burn more fat calories while feeling less hungry!

A recent meta-analysis identified 68 studies evaluating the potential role of capsaicin in weight management.[86] An impressive 13 of 15 trials reported an increase in postconsumption energy expenditure, 7 of 11 showed increased lipid oxidation and decreased fat stores, and 5 of 7 trials confirmed capsaicin's effect on suppressed appetite. However, the most impressive evidence for capsaicin's effects on weight loss showed an increased energy expenditure of at least 50 calories daily when cayenne pepper was used as an accent spice—that adds up to 5 to 7 pounds of fat loss a year just by adding a dash of this spice to one meal daily!

10. WHEY PROTEIN

Have you ever seen whey protein on a list of superfoods? Probably not. This food is undervalued by many, which is a shame. It's a superprotein if there ever was one.

Whey is a lactose-free milk-derived protein, typically well tolerated by those with lactose intolerance. It's also free of casein, the other dairy component that many are sensitive to. (Dairy product proteins are typically 80 percent casein and 20 percent whey.) This makes whey a safe form of protein for most folks who are dairy sensitive. But if you're one of the rare few who is sensitive to the whey component of dairy (or you simply don't like it), you might try a rice, hemp, or pea protein substitute.

Compared with other foods, whey protein contains the highest concentrations of branched-chain amino acids, especially leucine, which preserves fat-burning muscle for a lean metabolism.[87, 88] Administration of either an amino acid mixture or leucine alone has been shown to suppress food intake for up to 24 hours.[89] Studies in the elderly show that whey supplementation was associated with a decrease in adiposity (fat) and preservation of lean muscle mass.[90, 91]

Whey is a high-quality protein that promotes a sense of fullness and satiation after meals and decreases further food consumption. Whether it's more satiating than other protein sources is a matter of debate; there's literature in favor of and against its superiority.[92-95]

Whey protein also doubles as an immune system regulator because it's rich in anti-inflammatory chemicals called glycomacropeptides and beta-glucans. This is why whey-enriched formulations have been shown to improve the outcome of Crohn's disease in children.[96-98] When given to adult patients with Crohn's disease, whey improved intestinal barrier function as evidenced by diminished small intestine permeability.[99] As we learned in Chapter 2, many overweight people have imbalances in their gut microbiome associated with defects in gut barrier function similar to Crohn's disease. When these defects are serious enough, toxins from enteric bacteria can "leak" into your circulation, inciting a systemic inflammatory response, insulin resistance, and fat accumulation.[100] Whey protein heals the gut lining and cools down the inflammation, helping to reverse this problem.

All this raises a much larger discussion about dairy and its role in weight management. In the next chapter, I'll discuss how yogurt and kefir help you get and stay slim by seeding your gut microbiome with fat-burning flora. Whey protein can also be fermented to become a probiotic that repopulates the gut microbiome. Interestingly, a novel probiotic product has recently been developed based on a traditional dehydrated wafer once used in a Mexican dessert. To make it, they take sweet goat whey and ferment it with *Bifidobacterium infantis* or *Lactobacillus acidophilus*.[101]

There's no doubt about it. Whey is a superfood to keep in mind as a high-protein supplement that offers a host of health benefits and promotes slimness.

LOOKING AHEAD

After 30 days on Phase 1, it'll be time to reintegrate some of the foods we eliminated, seed your gut with the good bugs you need to thrive, and fertilize your inner garden so it can flourish again. This is what we'll do in Phase 2. That phase of the program is designed to reincorporate foods that are high in prebiotics and probiotics. These special foods will reinoculate your gut with healthy bacteria and further diversify your microbiome. Scientific evidence has connected probiotics and prebiotics to positive long-term weight and health outcomes. In the next chapter, we'll review these data, and I'll explain exactly how to add these foods back into your diet so that you can fully balance your inner ecosystem.

CHAPTER 6

Phase 2: Rebalance

RESEED AND FERTILIZE YOUR INNER GARDEN

Close your eyes for a moment. Picture a lush field of green populated with an endless array of beautiful wildflowers in every color imaginable. The flowers sway gently in the breeze as far as the eye can see. As you envision this scene, you touch on a deep quiet within, and a sense of profound peace washes over you. You feel relaxed, whole, and healthy.

This field is your inner garden, the ideal vision of the ecosystem deep within your gut. The grass and flowers that live there are the flora we'll plant in your gut during this phase of the program. Now that we've prepared the soil in Phase 1, it's time to reestablish a thriving gut microbiome that will help you achieve your ideal weight and optimal health. We'll do that by seeding and fertilizing your inner ecosystem during this part of the program. To do this, there are two simple but extremely important steps.

1. **Reseed your inner garden.** During this phase, we'll incorporate fermented foods such as yogurt, kefir, sauerkraut, kimchi, and others that are rich in healthy microbiota such as bifidobacteria. These probiotics have been shown to promote healthy gut microbiome balance and weight loss.

2. **Fertilize the friendly flora.** Your friendly intestinal flora need something to eat for your gut microbiome to thrive. That's why in Phase 2, I want you to add a class of fiber-rich, highly satiating complex carbohydrates called prebiotics into your diet. These foods are like Miracle-Gro for the friendly bacteria in your inner garden; they'll help reestablish harmony in your inner ecosystem.

Reseeding your gut with friendly bacteria and fertilizing them with prebiotics has a broad range of biochemical and metabolic effects that help you develop the lean metabolism you desire. The science increasingly shows that rebalancing your gut microbiome using the approach we'll take during this phase supports long-term weight loss.

I recommend that you stay on Phase 2 until you achieve your desired weight. By following this plan, you can expect a sustainable loss of 5 to 10 pounds of excess body weight per month as long as you are on Phase 2. Plus, inflammation will continue to be reduced throughout your body, your blood sugar and insulin levels will stabilize further, and you'll experience focused energy that lasts all day.

Okay, let's get started.

RESEEDING YOUR INNER GARDEN

Your first task: to cast seeds that will bloom in the lush, diverse inner ecosystem you need to achieve optimal weight and health. We'll do that by integrating numerous probiotic-rich foods into your diet.

Probiotics are live microorganisms that when consumed in adequate amounts have been shown to confer health benefits on the host. Growing research points to the important role of probiotics in favorably altering gut microbiome balance by increasing health-promoting bacteria such as lactobacillus, bifidobacteria, and others. This is critical, because your microbiota influence numerous biological systems that regulate the availability of nutrients, energy storage, hunger, fat mass, inflammation, and insulin sensitivity—which all play an important role in weight and health.

Research in this area has exploded in the last few years. More than 10,000 publications have reviewed the potential health benefits of probiotics. The vast majority of these were published after 2008, so we're in the midst of a gut microbiome renaissance—there's clearly enough data to strongly suggest that you should integrate probiotic-rich foods as a critical component of Phase 2 if you want to achieve long-term weight loss and lasting health.

We'll do this by diversifying the species of your gut microbiome instead of focusing on specific species or phyla of bacteria. In contrast to popular belief and television marketers, there's no single strain of bacteria, fungi, or yeast that works as a magic bullet to completely rebalance your inner garden and permanently shift you toward a lean metabolism. There are a few favorable species that seem to enhance overall health. But the data are varied, and the benefits are often strain specific.

For example, at least 200 studies have been done on humans and animals on the use of different lactobacillus species for weight loss alone.[1] This species is part of the phylum Firmicutes—the fat-forming bugs that took most of the blame in the early studies linking gut microbiome balance to obesity. It appears the story is a little more complicated than these early studies suggested.

In a recent meta-analysis of the lactobacillus data, scientists learned that different strains of lactobacillus seem to have different effects on weight regulation and overall health. For instance, in 13 studies that included 3,307 subjects (897 of whom were human), scientists found that *Lactobacillus acidophilus* seems to cause weight *gain*.

Do All Probiotics Help with Weight Loss?

◆ Myth: All probiotics will promote weight loss.

◆ Fact: Some probiotics work better than others. Be careful with single strains of lactobacillus for weight regulation. *Lactobacillus gasseri* (LG2055), *L. plantarum*, and *L. paracasei* promote weight loss.

In contrast, another well-designed study showed that consumption of fermented milk containing *Lactobacillus gasseri* (LG2055) was associated with significant weight loss, a lower waist and hip circumference, reduced subcutaneous and abdominal visceral fat, and improvement in metabolic markers compared to consumption of fermented milk without additional bacteria.[2] Fermented milk has many health benefits and helps shift the balance of your inner garden to support a lean metabolism.

Studies on *Lactobacillus plantarum* and *L. paracasei* show that these strains may shrink fat cells and reduce total body fat.[3, 4] Additional research has shown that various strains of lactobacillus decrease fat mass, reduce the risk of type 2 diabetes, and help mitigate insulin resistance.[5, 6] And these studies account *only* for research on one species of probiotics.

Hundreds of other studies have shown that modulating the gut microbiome using probiotics has a wide range of health effects that include:[7]

■ Improving blood lipid patterns

■ Reducing risk for hypertension

■ Enhancing intestinal health and reducing risk of inflammatory bowel disorders

■ Supporting the immune system

■ Reducing risk of allergies and/or their symptoms

■ Synthesizing and enhancing the bioavailability of nutrients

While there may be some relationship between specific strains of bacteria and health outcomes—such as the link between *L. gasseri* and weight loss—the important message is that the community of bacteria and their interaction are what produces health outcomes. Diversity is the key to inner ecosystem health—so that will be our goal in Phase 2. Animal studies in this area lend further support to the idea that rebalancing your gut microbiome by using probiotic-rich foods can lend a powerful helping hand in your journey to optimal weight. These studies have shown that simply administering probiotics without other dietary changes leads to weight loss, reduction in adipose (fat) tissue, reduced blood glucose, increased insulin and leptin sensitivity, and more.[8, 9] This has been my clinical experience as well. Consider Josephina, whose stubborn weight wouldn't budge until she tried probiotics.

THE GUT BALANCE REVOLUTION SUCCESS STORIES

Josephina

Josephina is a health-care provider in her mid-forties who found herself gaining weight uncontrollably. When she maxed out at 320 pounds, she could hardly carry on with her job and care for her family. She developed type 2 diabetes and experienced labored breathing whenever she exerted herself.

Desperate for help, she underwent gastric bypass surgery. Although she recovered well and looked and felt much better, she lost only 70 pounds, 41 percent of her excess body weight—but she knew she should've lost much more. (Data from seven studies and 1,627 patients undergoing this surgery show that the mean first-year weight loss is 67.3 percent.[10]) Josephina was disappointed that her results were so far below average.

That's when she began looking for help. I asked her some questions that led me to believe she was experiencing a common complication of gastric bypass surgery—small intestinal bacterial overgrowth, or SIBO. Remember from Chapter 4 that SIBO is a common result of obesity—that's why I recommend a low-FODMAP diet to curb symptoms and help shift the microbial terrain in the gut during Phase 1. Josephina's case was a little different. The altered anatomy from her surgery resulted in what doctors called a "blind limb"—a part of the intestine that diverts digested materials away from the digestive tract and into a short one-way tube. This part of the intestine lacks flow and is stagnant, and SIBO is a common outcome.

This reminded me of a game-changing study in which morbidly obese patients undergoing gastric bypass surgery were consequently diagnosed with SIBO through breath testing.[11] Researchers at Stanford University School of Medicine explored whether probiotics could accelerate weight loss in those who developed SIBO resulting from gastric bypass surgery. Forty-two subjects were randomly assigned to receive either 2.4 billion colonies of an undisclosed lactobacillus species or a placebo daily. The lactobacillus supplement resulted in a loss of 10 percent more excess body weight at 3 months, and the trend continued at 6 months of therapy. A significant reduction in SIBO was also observed. I shared the outcome of this study with Josephina and recommended she take a probiotic product with a mix of lactobacillus and bifidobacteria species. In a month, she lost 10 more pounds without changing her diet or level of physical activity and noticed that her gastrointestinal symptoms had improved markedly.

Choose the Right Chicken!

Remember that conventionally raised poultry is infused with antibiotics to pro-mote growth by disrupting the birds' gut microbiome? A study on conventionally raised broiler chicken compared weight gain in those birds fed either antibiotics or probiotics or no additive to their diet.[12] Each of these three groups was sub-divided into three more groups by whether their fat source was soybean oil (proinflammatory), free fatty acids (mix of pro- and anti-inflammatory fats), or standard feed.

The results are compelling. The birds fed antibiotics gained more weight than either the probiotics- or standard-fed birds. In fact, the probiotics made the birds lose weight. Plus, the type of fat used made a difference. The group that was fed proinflammatory soybean oil gained the most weight compared to those fed free fatty acids and standard feed. The birds that gained the *most* weight were in the group raised on *both* antibiotics and soybean oil, showing a synergistic interac-tion. That's why I recommend antibiotic-free poultry and grass-fed over corn- and soy-fed cattle.

We'll talk more about the specific ways probiotics tend to effect these changes later in the chapter, when I explain which of these foods to focus on during this phase. But first, let me introduce you to another class of foods to integrate in Phase 2: prebiotics—the fertilizer for your inner garden.

FERTILIZING YOUR FRIENDLY FLORA

When you plant a garden, you don't just throw some seeds down and hope they'll grow. You tend the garden, adding fertilizer as necessary so the plants can flourish. The same is true of your inner garden: You must be attentive to it and provide the food it needs to make it a healthy, diverse ecosystem.

One of your gut bugs' favorite foods is prebiotics. These are foods your human metab-olism cannot digest but your good gut bugs absolutely adore. They're a class of soluble fibers that help your gut microbiome thrive. Many of these foods are the FODMAPs we reduced during Phase 1 of the program to help reverse any gut dysbiosis you may have been suffering from. Now that we've mitigated this gut dysbiosis by tilling the soil of your gut microbiome, it's a good idea to reintegrate some of these foods, enhance your fiber intake, and give your bugs the foods they need to thrive.

As with probiotics, prebiotic-laden foods correlate with weight loss and health gains. In a series of Belgian studies, researchers showed that giving people 5 to 20 grams of prebiotics per day altered gut microbial balance and led to reduced blood sugar, increased satiety, decreased hunger, and reduced fat mass.[13]

Yet another double-blind, placebo-controlled trial put one group on oligofructose (a prebiotic in the FODMAP family) and gave the other group a calorically equivalent placebo. The group receiving the prebiotics lost 2.2 pounds of body weight in 12 weeks without any other changes in diet.[14] Most of this weight was fat mass lost from the trunk of the body. (You know that belly fat you want to target? Well, this is how you do it!) The placebo group *gained* weight.* Both groups had the same amount of calories added to their diet, but the *type of calories*–the prebiotics–made the difference.

Need more proof? In a groundbreaking study, researchers provided a group of type 2 diabetics only 8 grams of the prebiotic inulin daily for 4 weeks, with no other changes to their diet. The group taking the inulin saw a "statistically significant reduction in blood glucose"–a stunning finding that reveals just how effectively food can be used as medicine. Indeed, data are emerging that suggest prebiotics should be considered as a treatment for metabolic syndrome.[15]

Why do prebiotics have such a powerful impact on weight and health? One of many reasons is that they influence the production of peptide (small protein) hormones in the gut called glucagon-like peptide 1 and 2 (GLP-1 and GLP-2), which are thought to play an important role in appetite, satiety, gut motility, insulin function, and many bodily functions. We'll go into more detail about GLP-1 and GLP-2 later in this chapter, but the short story here is that when you feed your gut microbiome the right way, they cause the gut to produce these peptide hormones that support your overall health–a pretty big score for prebiotics.

The best news: Providing prebiotics and probiotics at the same time, which is what we'll do in this program, may have even more profound health benefits. Studies have shown that taking prebiotics and probiotics together (aka synbiotics) produces a favorable metabolic profile of short-chain fatty acids (SCFAs) in addition to the other health benefits listed above.[16] These anti-inflammatory fats help your gut absorb water, help regrow healthy gut lining cells in the colon, and may provide defenses against colon cancer and inflammatory bowel disease. This is an important though not surprising finding. Seed your gut microbiome with health-promoting gut microbes–aka "friendly flora"–while providing them with their favorite foods so they can thrive, and you end up with a plethora of benefits as well as weight loss. The power of this ecosystems approach to eating never ceases to amaze me. I discovered this as a teen light-years ahead of the data, and it helped me *lose more than 120 pounds and keep them off for good!*

So how do you get these health benefits? Simply focus on the right foods in Phase 2 and forget or eat fewer of the foods that don't support the lean metabolism you deserve. Here's how to do that.

---

* The placebo contained maltodextrin, which comes from treated grain starch, primarily corn or rice starch. It can also come from wheat and potatoes. Though not a sugar, it still has a glycemic index of 130 by itself (table sugar is only 65). This starchy, high-glycemic "sweetener" in the placebo caused weight gain despite not adding more caloric energy.

FORGET FOODS THAT SEND YOUR INNER ECOSYSTEM OUT OF BALANCE

During Phase 1, you did a lot of work to remove from your diet junky foods that send your gut microbiome and your metabolism out of balance. We got rid of sugar (in all of its subversive forms), starchy carbs (bread, pasta, potatoes, and so on), and unhealthy inflammatory oils (soy, corn, vegetable, and others). You learned why these substances are unhealthy and read about studies showing that the overconsumption of these products is correlated to weight gain and poor health.

In Phase 2, to achieve your health and weight-loss goals, I want you to continue abstaining from the most harmful forms of these foods. So continue avoiding the following:

■ **Sweeteners.** As you'll see in the following section on the foods you can add back into your diet, during this phase of the program you may have limited quantities of certain sweeteners. However, I want you to continue avoiding the most egregious ones.

  ● High-fructose corn syrup (HFCS).

  ● Agave–it's high in FODMAPs.

  ● Artificial sweeteners, including but not limited to the sugar alcohols: mannitol, xylitol, and sorbitol, which are also high in FODMAPs. Note that some "all natural" yogurts–a food critical in this phase–are allowed by the FDA to include artificial sweeteners, so make sure you read labels carefully.

  ● Refined honey, which is among the top most insidious sweeteners of all time. It's high in fructose (a FODMAP) and it's overused. Steer clear of any refined honey, though raw honey is a different story. Good data show that a teaspoon or less per day of raw honey has positive effects on gut microbiome health–thus earning an honorable mention in the Phase 2 superfoods list. Don't overdo it, but if you're looking for something sweet in your coffee or whey protein shake, a little raw honey is just the ticket.

- **Sweet drinks.** This includes soda, fruit juices (they spike blood sugar and insulin levels and rate high on the glycemic impact index), vitamin waters (full of added sugars), and their ilk.

- **White flour and potatoes** (including products made with them). Avoid pasta, bread, cookies, crackers, cakes, and so on, as they're all high on the glycemic impact index and spike blood sugar and insulin.

- **Inflammatory oils.** While my restrictions on these are fewer than they were in Phase 1, you should still stay away from corn oil, lard, hydrogenated oil, palm oil, safflower oil, and a few others.

- **Gluten.** Barley, wheat, rye, and other grains that contain gluten are high in FODMAPs. Many people are sensitive to them, and you can use other less harmful whole grains to support your gut microbiome instead (such as quinoa). For now, stay away from foods high in gluten. Oats are another great option; they are high in prebiotics and benefit the gut microbiome, so their benefits outweigh the potential for gluten cross-contamination, which is a result of being processed in the same mill as gluten-enriched grains.

Depending on how much weight you have to lose, you may need to remove these foods from your diet for a few weeks, a few months, or even longer. After you've completed your weight-loss journey, arrived at your goal weight, and are in maintenance mode, you'll shift to Phase 3, when you can indulge in the occasional sweet treat, potato chip, or french fry without too many adverse consequences. Look for more details in Chapter 8.

But aside from an occasional treat, most of these products have no place in the human diet, and I recommend that you limit all of them for the long term. The preponderance of these foods is one of the leading causes of the overweight and obesity epidemics. If you want to embrace the Gut Balance Revolution and take a stand against the imbalanced food environment in which we live, I ask you to avoid these products during this phase. As with Phase 1, you'll find all the specifics on what to avoid in your Phase 2 food charts on pages 246–251.

ADD BACK A FEW OF YOUR FAVORITE FOODS

Phase 2 isn't all discipline and deprivation! You'll have much more flexibility in this phase than you did on Phase 1. The restrictions on FODMAPs are dramatically reduced, you can now have a little lean red meat and pork, and some select prebiotic-rich whole grains have been included due to their wonderful fertilizing effects on the friendly flora. Even the occasional pint of beer, glass of red wine, chunk of dark chocolate, and a few select sweeteners are allowed.

The Gut Balance Revolution Phase 2 Food Pyramid: This figure prioritizes foods in Phase 2, the rebalancing phase. Foods that are limited are at the top of the pyramid (i.e., lean red meats, butter, coffee, extra-virgin olive oil). Nuts, seeds, beans, green tea, and gluten-free whole grains are placed in the middle of the pyramid. Fruits, vegetables, fish, poultry, vegetable poultry soups, wild game, and fermented foods (such as pickled vegetables, sauerkraut, kefir, miso soup, yogurt, and kimchi) are at the base of the pyramid.

I specifically designed this part of the program in a way that would enable you to stick with it for longer periods of time without feeling deprived. This will allow those of you who have substantial weight to lose the dietary flexibility to achieve your weight-loss goals without falling off the wagon. So let's look at some of these delicious foods you can eat in moderation during Phase 2.

FODMAPS: THE DOSE MAKES THE POISON

During Phase 2, we reintegrate many, though not all, of the FODMAPs we eliminated on Phase 1. We'll keep out some of the major offenders like high-fructose sweeteners, high-FODMAP fruits (mangoes, pears, and others), gluten (like wheat, rye, barley), and a few other sources (sugar alcohols, for example). This will allow you to reduce your overall FODMAP consumption while still taking advantage of foods that provide health benefits but technically qualify as FODMAPs. A few of these FODMAP-rich foods–specifically, those high in prebiotics–are critical during Phase 2, and it's important to understand the relationship between prebiotics, fiber, and FODMAPs to fully recognize the rationale behind this program.

Many prebiotics qualify as FODMAPs. Of these, the fructans (inulin in particular) and oligosaccharides (such as fructooligosaccharides and galacto-oligosaccharides) are probably the most important. These foods are high in fiber, especially soluble fiber, which cannot be digested by the human gut alone–your gut microbiota must break these foods down for you. The good news: Your friendly flora absolutely love to eat this fiber. So once your gut microbiome is rebalanced, fiber-rich foods like these are a wonderful food source for your inner garden–a type of fertilizer that helps it flourish.

Fiber and the prebiotic effects of these foods have a wide range of health and weight-loss benefits as well. First, insoluble fiber is highly satiating. Because it dissolves in water and becomes a kind of gel in your gut, it gives you a feeling of fullness and reduces over-all hunger.[17]

The benefits of insoluble fiber show even more brightly, however, when we analyze them in terms of what they do for our inner garden and how this impacts our health and weight. These fibers are readily fermentable, so your good gut bugs love to feast on them. Research has shown that adding prebiotics to your diet increases the growth of commen-sal species like bifidobacteria, lactobacillus, and others. In fact, in order to be a prebiotic, these fibers by definition are required to stimulate the growth of bifidobacteria–called "the prebiotic effect."

For example, one study showed that increasing inulin-type fructans enhanced levels of bifidobacteria and lactobacillus in only a few days. These improvements in overall gut microbial balance disappeared in as little as a week after removing the prebiotic inulin from the diet.[18, 19]

Scientists have also demonstrated that prebiotics like oligofructose can alter as many as 102 different types of gut bugs in obese type 2 diabetic mice. These alterations were associated with reduced fat mass, increased lean muscle, improved glucose and lipid metabolism, reduced systemic inflammation, and more.[20] It's a long way from mice to men, but these finding are impressive, and they clearly illustrate that what we eat influ-ences our inner ecosystem–which in turn impacts our health.

In fact, it's been repeatedly shown that prebiotics alter the overall terrain of the gut micro-biome and lead to a reduction in inflammation, improvements in intestinal barrier function, and improved insulin sensitivity in both human and animal models.[21, 22] Why is this?

Many mechanisms are at play, but gut peptides are important actors connecting the pieces of the puzzle. We discussed two of these gut peptides in Chapter 2–glucagon-like peptides 1 and 2 (GLP-1 and GLP-2). A growing body of research shows that the release of these two gut peptides (along with a few others like peptide YY and ghrelin) is highly influenced by your gut microbiota. We think this has to do with the way your gut bacteria "talk to" your brain.

The amount of research about the bidirectional communication between the gut and the brain is rapidly expanding. These data are showing us that gut microbes are not only involved in the regulation of our metabolism but also trigger behaviors that ultimately influence our food choices. [23, 24]

Ultimately, when you feed your inner ecosystem prebiotics like inulin, oligosaccharides, and others, it seems to shift the overall balance of your gut microbiome in a positive way that leads to an increased release of peptides like GLP-1 and GLP-2—and that affects insulin levels, feelings of fullness, and more.

This has been well documented in the research. For example, in a recent Belgian study, scientists took a group of healthy volunteers and fed them 16 grams of inulin-type fructans a day for 2 weeks. GLP-1 and GLP-2 increased, the volunteers reported feeling fuller, they naturally ate less, and their glucose levels after meals (postprandial glucose) were reduced. But one of the most mind-blowing aspects of this study has to do with genetic expression.* These foods actually *reprogrammed* the body to reduce the size of fat cells in the volunteers involved in the study.[25]

Back to the Belgian study: Could it be that the prebiotics enhanced levels of healthy bacteria that then "talked to" the volunteers' DNA, saying, "Hey, would you mind reducing the size of this guy's fat cells?" More research needs to be done to tease out all the relationships, but this is a distinct possibility. (For a review of bacterial gene swapping, turn to pages 16–17 in Chapter 2.)

The bottom line: We need prebiotics to achieve optimal weight and health. In the previous phase, I asked you to dramatically reduce your intake of FODMAPs and soluble fiber. This was done to mitigate dysbiosis and reduce digestive symptoms such as gas and bloating to improve your quality of life as you shift the microbial terrain toward balance. Now that you've tilled the soil in Phase 1, it's time to refeed your gut microbiome with these healthy foods to rebalance your inner ecology and produce a lean metabolism. By enriching the biodiversity of microbial species in your gut, this new healthy network of symbiotes (go team microbes!) will provide a wide range of biochemical and metabolic benefits that support long-term weight loss and better health.

Remember that when it comes to FODMAPs, the dose makes the poison. Some folks can handle more than others, so listen to your own body and fine-tune this program to your needs. But the following guidelines for reintegrating FODMAPs in your diet should help.

■ *Favor* **vegetables and beans high in prebiotics.** We'll talk more about these later. They include lentils, chickpeas, asparagus, artichokes, Jerusalem artichokes, and others.

---

* Inulin-like fructans are fermented by good gut bacteria into short-chain fatty acids, which activate cells via G-protein-coupled receptors (GPRs) such as GPR_{41} and GPR_{43}. The Belgian study showed that people eating this prebiotic-rich diet actually induced the expression of a gene called GPR_{43}, which is involved in determining how big fat cells are.

- **Eat a *few* whole grains and nuts.** More details to follow, but the short story here is that nuts–packed with omega-3 fats as well as prebiotics–are among the healthiest snacks you can eat, and there are good data showing select gluten-free whole grains (in moderation) support gut microbiome health and help you lose weight.
- **Forget high-FODMAP sweets, fruits, sugar alcohols, and glutinous grains.** This will reduce your overall FODMAP intake and eliminate foods that spike blood sugar and insulin levels and produce bothersome digestive symptoms.

Whole Grains for Health

Whole grains have a long history of inclusion in health programs and have been a dietary staple in many traditional cultures for millennia. But as Dr. William Davis describes in his best-selling book *Wheat Belly*, the source, digestibility, and gluten content of wheat has radically shifted over the years, creating a crisis of gluten overload and intolerance, with negative health effects.[26]

Wheat Belly is part of a cultural revolution telling us how we can add to our health by subtracting wheat from our diet–a sort of addition by subtraction approach. Dr. Loren Cordain's best-selling book *The Paleo Diet* delves into the history of Paleolithic hunter-gatherer people who didn't have access to the grains available today and explains how we can promote health by going back in time to the high-fiber anti-inflammatory diet of humanity's ancestors.

There's quite an audience for these low-grain diets. *Wheat Belly* had been a *New York Times* bestseller for 133 weeks as of the time of this writing. Furthermore, the *New York Times* best-selling book *Grain Brain* by Dr. David Perlmutter summarizes compelling data regarding how gluten-containing grains may begin a cascade of events in the gut, leading to a variety of neurobehavioral impairments and neurodegenerative processes.[27] And another researcher, Dr. Alessio Fasano, has published studies showing how gluten may break down the gut barrier defenses to initiate a chain reaction of downstream inflammatory events, possibly leading to autoimmunity.[28]

However, there are many critics who disagree with these folks and tell us that wheat and other gluten-containing grains are perfectly safe. So what's the real story?

The concerns of the low-carbers may have more than a grain of truth in them.

I was recently on Dan Rodrick's radio show on Baltimore's NPR affiliate, WYPR, discussing high-protein diets in weight loss and health.[29] Many of the callers were happy about their success with limiting grains and carbs, at least in the short term. This made sense to me, as the data show that low-carb ketogenic diets work in the short term, as discussed in Chapter 4. That's why I designed Phase 1 of this program as I did.

I agree that we're seeing more convincing data that there's a large population of people who are intolerant to wheat, and it's clear that for them, gluten can trigger a host of digestive symptoms.[30] In the gastroenterology literature, when wheat is given in the form of a capsule, it provokes symptoms in those with irritable bowel syndrome (IBS), and when it's restricted from the diet, symptoms improve.[31] Furthermore, glutinous grains are rich in FODMAPs and provoke symptoms in those with SIBO.

We're living in an era of consumer-driven gluten-free living, and science is trying to understand why so many benefit from gluten restriction. But much of the gluten-free dogma–and the products this new market has created–is misguided. After all, gluten-free cookies and cakes aren't healthy and don't deserve a place in your diet any more than their gluten-packed counterparts do.

For these reasons, I elected to keep gluten-rich grains out of Phase 1. A very low-carb program with limited grains for the first 30 days will help resolve SIBO, improve gut symptoms, and balance the microbial terrain. Unfortunately, there may be some collateral damage, as data show that a gluten-free diet can reduce the amount of important species of microbes like bifidobacteria, which play a critical role in gut immune function and weight regulation.[32] However, as previously cited, Halmos et al. reported that a diet low in FODMAPs enhanced gut microbiome biodiversity.[33] Thus, cutting out the junk and keeping some of the prebiotic FODMAPs will limit any compromise to the gut microbiome during Phase 1.

Now in Phase 2, we're reestablishing more healthy communities of gut microbes and refeeding them with prebiotic foods that help them thrive. Once this is achieved, most people can gradually introduce a modest amount of gluten-free whole grains in their diet without adverse consequences. In fact, these fibrous foods can be highly satiating and provide an important source of prebiotics (oligosaccharides). In the meal plans, you'll find nonglutinous whole grains for this purpose. As you'll see in the Phase 2 food charts on pages 246–251, amaranth, brown rice, buckwheat (also known as Japanese soba; not actually a form of wheat), popcorn, oat bran, quinoa, and teff* are all options for this phase.

Does that mean you should scarf down multiple bowls of brown rice or oat bran? Certainly not. Eating too many gluten-free whole grains can be problematic, as it can raise blood glucose levels. But in my experience, brown rice, quinoa, and the other gluten-free whole grains that I include in this phase aren't the type of foods people binge on.

As we'll see when we get to Phase 3, some of the best data we have show that diets that support long-term health and weight loss include some fiber-rich whole grains. So stick with the science and include a limited few healthy whole grains in Phases 2 and 3.

Go Nuts!

Aside from vegetables, it's hard to think of a group of foods more touted for its health benefits than nuts. These tiny, shelled tree fruits do indeed offer a bevy of benefits, not the least of which is their effect on your gut microbiome.

---

* Be careful with ordering teff when dining out, as many eateries (such as Ethiopian restaurants) do not make their own teff, and many vendors mix wheat with the teff. When in Washington, DC, or Baltimore, ask the owner of the restaurant Dukem (dukemrestaurant.com) for gluten-free teff 1 day in advance of your visit and she will oblige.

Nuts are probably most famous for their high level of healthy fats, especially the omega-3s. These fats may be one of the reasons people who eat nuts have such impressive health improvements. For example, an analysis of two massive health studies–the Nurses' Health Study and the Health Professionals Follow-Up Study–reviewed data on over 118,000 participants and found that the frequency of nut consumption was inversely correlated with all causes of mortality.[34]

Some nuts clearly demonstrate medicinal potential when added to your diet. For example, a study from India recently showed that people with metabolic syndrome who added a daily serving of pistachios reduced body fat, improved overall cholesterol levels, reduced inflammation markers, and even seemed to see a positive effect on fat-storing hormones like adiponectin.[35] All this from a simple nut–pretty impressive, right?

The positive health benefits don't stop there. A recent cutting-edge study shows that almonds and almond skins have a powerful prebiotic effect. Forty-eight volunteers were divided into two groups.[36] One group was given 56 grams of almonds (about 40 nuts) a day. The other group was given 8 grams of a commercial fructooligosaccharide supplement as a control. The group who ate the nuts saw a significant increase in bifidobacteria and lactobacillus and a reduction of other, potentially harmful species, such as *Clostridium perfringens*. A few nuts a day seem to help rebalance your inner ecosystem.[37]

Nuts have a number of health benefits that include promoting weight reduction. I will expand on the discussion of the health and weight-loss benefits of nuts in Chapter 9, when I discuss superfoods for Phase 3.[38] In the meantime, include plenty of nuts during Phase 2. One caveat: Don't go completely nuts on nuts–a little goes a long way. I kept a lid on nuts for Phase 1 since they have a relatively high carb load. Include them on Phase 2 and beyond, but be aware that overeating these healthy foods may undo your attempts to lose weight since they are energy dense. Keep it to one or two handfuls per day.

Where's the Meat?

A little lean, pasture-raised, grass-fed beef, bison, wild game, or lamb or some pastured pork can be a healthy addition to your diet. But look at all the modifiers in that sentence and compare it with the typical consumption of meat in this country. That may give you some sense of why I asked you to eliminate these foods during Phase 1 and why I strongly encourage you to limit them during the remainder of this program.

Americans eat way too much meat. If you've grown accustomed to 24-ounce rib eyes and half-pound burgers, don't go back to those habits now. A "little meat" means two to three weekly palm-size servings. Eating more meat than this has consistently been associated with weight gain, cardiovascular issues, and many other health problems. Recent evidence also shows disruption of gut microbiome balance caused by diets high in animal protein.[39]

Stick to a couple of small servings a week and you'll be fine. I *strongly* suggest you choose grass-fed and pastured sources. They're more expensive, but that will just motivate you to eat a little less. Animals raised conventionally in concentrated animal feeding operations (or CAFOs–another term for feedlots) are lower in healthy omega-3 fats and are pumped full of antibiotics that have serious detrimental effects on your gut microbiome and that recent data strongly suggest lead to weight gain.[40]

A TOAST TO YOUR MICROBIOME

I'd like to raise a toast to your gut microbiome, and in Phase 2, you can join in with a glass of beer or wine. These beverages, which have literally been with us since the beginning of recorded history (recipes for beer are among the earliest written documents), are perfectly healthy additions to the Phase 2 diet. As long as you keep your consumption to no more than one glass of beer or wine per day, these fermented beverages may even have some health and weight-loss benefits.

It appears that people who drink a light to moderate amount of alcohol have smaller waists than people who don't drink at all.[41] It's also been illustrated that moderate drinkers tend to gain less weight over time and have less abdominal fat specifically.[42, 43]

Red wine in particular is one of those foods that targets belly fat. We think it has to do with its relatively high levels of the antioxidant resveratrol, which modulates fat storage and may act directly on the fat cell itself.[44] A study published in the *Journal of Clinical Nutrition* concluded that resveratrol reduces the amount of fat cells generated by your body. That means it could be an excellent weapon in the battle of the bulge.

Some studies indicate drinking red wine with a fatty meal prevents the rise in blood lipids because the polyphenols in the wine block lipid absorption, improve cardiovascular metabolic markers, lower blood lipids, and prevent the activation of inflammatory pathways.[45] These same polyphenols also seem to have prebiotic effects–moderate red wine consumption may support gut microbiome diversity.*

Of course, you can't slam down a bottle of wine or drink multiple pints with your buddies. High alcohol intake (three or more glasses a day or more than eight in a week) has clearly been associated with weight gain and health problems. Chronic alcoholism shifts the healthy community of bacteria in the gut microbiome to a state of dysbiosis, which disrupts gut barrier function and can lead to endotoxemia and its legion of harmful consequences.[46, 47] On the flip side, moderate red wine consumption–one glass nightly–prevents endotoxemia and promotes the growth of bidifobacterium–another reason I've included it in Phase 2 and beyond.[48] Again–the dose makes the poison.

As long as you stick with these guidelines, I encourage you to enjoy a glass of this nectar that's been with us since ancient times. One final caveat: Drop hard liquor–it's been associated with increases in abdominal fat.[49]

---

* A glass of red wine contains only 1 milligram of resveratrol, and its health benefits may also be derived from its prebiotic influence on promoting microbial diversity.

FAVOR FOODS THAT DIVERSIFY YOUR GUT MICROBIOME: PROBIOTICS AND PREBIOTICS

Biodiversity is the hallmark of any healthy ecosystem. That's why, during this phase, you'll favor foods that enhance the biodiversity of your inner garden, rebalance your gut microbiome, and encourage the growth of bacterial communities that support your health. Specifically, we'll focus on foods with prebiotic and probiotic effects.

Foods containing probiotics will seed your inner garden with the friendly flora that help you thrive. Prebiotics are the fertilizer that helps seeds flourish, turning them into rich gut microbial communities that nourish and support you.

In the pages that follow, I'll discuss prebiotics in more depth, focusing specifically on prebiotic-rich vegetables. These are the foods you'll want to focus on as the fertilizer for your good gut bugs.

But first, let's talk a little about those gut bugs and how you can enhance and diversify them with fermented foods–the number one source of probiotics.

What Is Fermentation and Why Is It Important?

From a culinary point of view, fermentation is the act of transforming and preserving foods through the use of bacteria, fungi, and enzymes. Human beings have been fermenting foods for a very long time. Pottery shards from more than 9,000 years ago show residues of alcohol, suggesting that the tradition of fermenting foods is older than government, the written word, and possibly even civilization itself.

Virtually every culture in the world has a fermentation tradition, and it's easy to see why: Before refrigeration, fermentation was one of very few ways to preserve food. Of course, humans didn't invent this process–we stole it from nature. From a biological point of view, any process by which nutrients are converted to energy in the absence of oxygen (anaerobic metabolism) is considered fermentation. The outcome of this process is a combination of gases (like the bubbles in beer), acids (like lactic acid), and alcohol (all alcoholic beverages are fermented).

Fermentation is occurring inside you all the time. It's what your inner flora do. They take the sugars, carbohydrates, and soluble fiber you eat, ferment these substances, and convert them into other chemicals, from short-chain fatty acids to vitamin K and more. When we ferment foods, we're sort of "predigesting" them, changing their chemical composition before they've entered our bodies. We're also creating an environment in which probiotics–friendly flora that provide us with health benefits–can flourish.

It's interesting to consider that before microbiology even existed, cultures the world over had been actively "farming" bacteria by fermenting foods. (The word *culture* even refers to the act of intentionally cultivating living materials like bacteria, like a culture with which you inoculate yogurt, as well as to the beliefs, customs, arts, etc., of a society.) Humans have been practicing a rudimentary form of this science by actively encouraging the growth of particular strains of bacteria in their food for eons. Though primarily a method of preservation, by so doing these societies were garnering the health benefits of probiotics without even realizing what bacteria were or how they were involved in our health.

It's difficult to overstate the health benefits of eating fermented foods. They've been shown to regulate immunity, improve digestive function, and reduce inflammation. Recent evidence also indicates that they improve weight-loss outcomes and enhance metabolism in a variety of ways. And as you will learn, increasing your intake of fermented foods reduces your risk of chronic illness, including cardiovascular disease, type 2 diabetes, certain types of cancer, Alzheimer's disease, and more. They may even affect conditions like arthritis and allergies. We now know that these effects are largely due to the fact that probiotic-rich foods encourage the growth of healthy microbial species in your gut.

The health effects of lactobacillus and bifidobacteria–two of the more common strains of commensals found in fermented foods like yogurt, sauerkraut, and others– have been well documented. It's now well accepted that these friendly species of bacteria modulate processes like insulin resistance and inflammation that lead to weight gain.

For example, in one study, researchers took 45 people with glucose intolerance, gave half of them 10 billion colony-forming units (CFUs) of lactobacillus and the other half a placebo for 4 weeks. Those who got the lactobacillus showed a reduction in insulin resistance and inflammation.[50, 51]

In obese people, the administration of a single strain of lactobacillus has been shown to decrease fat mass and the risk of type 2 diabetes. This was illustrated in a study published in the *Journal of Pediatric Gastroenterology and Nutrition*.[52] In the study, 12 billion CFUs of *Lactobacillus rhamnosus* or a placebo was assigned to obese children for 8 weeks. Researchers noted that the probiotics ameliorated the progression of obesity and diabetes.

Exactly how these friendly flora achieve these effects is still being researched. However, some of the mechanisms we know are involved include:

- **Reduction in blood glucose and insulin, and increased insulin sensitivity.** These effects have been shown in study after study. One of the major players in this are the gut peptides GLP-1 and GLP-2.[53] Other factors may include alteration in satiety (meaning people who consume probiotics may eat less), the influence of probiotics on inflammation, and more.

- **Gut flora's interaction with the immune system and inflammation modulation.** We know your gut microbes "train" your immune system and thus have substantial influence on systemic inflammation. For a detailed discussion, see Chapter 2.

- **Reduction of leptin levels and increased leptin sensitivity.** Probiotics seem to influence hunger hormones like leptin and ghrelin–so when your gut microbiome is balanced, you tend to feel fuller and eat less.[54]

- **Altered activity in appetite centers of the brain (hypothalamus).** Your gut flora "communicate" with your central nervous system by enticing your intestines to release hormones that travel to your brain with peptides like GLP-1, GLP-2, peptide YY, and others, sending messages of fullness and satisfaction. The use of prebiotics in the treatment of neuropsychiatric disorders promoting mental health via the gut-brain axis is presently the subject of much research.[55]

- **Production of short-chain fatty acids.** Certain strains of bugs seem to produce more SCFAs than others. These important fats reduce systematic inflammation, help heal and repair the gut, and have other important health effects.

- **Absorption of lipids.** Remember from Chapter 2 that the amount of energy you harvest from your food and how fat is stored on your body are determined in part by your gut microbiome. When your inner ecology is in balance, fat absorption and deposition are managed more effectively.

- **Genetic influences that determine adipocyte size.** As we already learned, it appears that certain gut microbial communities "talk to" your genes, telling them how big your fat cells should be.

- **Increased production of conjugated linoleic acid (CLA).** This one is a little controversial. CLA is a healthy fat found in mammals. Certain strains of microbes (*Lactobacillus plantarum*, for example) produce more CLA. Substantial evidence links the production of this fatty acid to overall weight reduction in animal models.[56] To date, the human literature on this subject is mixed. But it still may be a mechanism by which gut microbes influence weight and fat gain.

These are only a few of the ways probiotics influence your ability to lose weight. There are many other connections, some of which are still being discovered by researchers. The bottom line is this: Probiotics have a profound influence on weight and health, and you can get more of these friendly bacteria by eating more fermented foods.

When you add more fermented foods to your diet, you don't need to pay too much attention to the exact species of bacteria you're ingesting. There is a broad range of probiotics in fermented foods, and focusing on any one of them simply isn't necessary. Remember, the name of the game is balance and biodiversity. Simply include more fermented foods in your diet and this is virtually guaranteed.

Learning how to ferment your own foods can be fun. It connects you to ancient traditions just as it offers a deeper understanding of the ecological relationships between you, your flora, and the world around you. That's why I've included recipes in Chapter 11 that will teach you how to ferment your own food. You'll learn how to make yogurt, kefir, sauerkraut, kimchi, and more.

You can purchase substitutes from the market if you don't have time to ferment your own foods, but please follow my recommendations on choosing the right types of foods. The "pickles" you buy in the store may not be "pickled" in the traditional sense. So make sure you read the next sections carefully if you are unable to cultivate your own ferments.

Even if you can't keep batches of fermented foods going all the time, I strongly encourage you to try making some of them from scratch. Cultivating probiotics in your home that you then consume to support your flora will create a more meaningful and profound relationship between you and your good gut bugs. It's a wonderful illustration of ecosystems at work, and it brings to light our multifaceted and nuanced relationships with the various ecosystems within and around us. Seeing these relationships will, I believe, give you further encouragement to keep your inner ecology balanced for life.

In the meantime, here are important notes to keep in mind when choosing fermented foods at the market. These foods come in two varieties: fermented veggies and fermented dairy products.

Fermented Veggies

Traditionally pickled vegetables are among the healthiest foods you can eat. They're packed with fiber and phytonutrients; because they're "predigested" their nutrients are more bioavailable;[57] and, of course, they're teaming with probiotics.

Unfortunately, the word *pickles* doesn't mean what it once did. Traditional pickles are prepared very simply: Take some veggies like cabbage, beets, or cucumbers. Shred, chop, or simply leave them whole. Add salt or brine (salt plus water). Drop in a little seasoning (dill, garlic, ginger, cayenne pepper, or just about any other spice you like). Cover them and let them sit in their own brine for 1 to 3 weeks or–in the case of kimchi or miso pastes–months or years. Bacteria from your hands and on the veggies themselves thrive in the anaerobic environment created by the brine, multiply like crazy, and transform the raw vegetables into pickles in the process. This is known as lactic acid fermentation; it's among the simplest and oldest forms of pickling on the planet. Sauerkraut, one of the simpler lacto-ferments, has been around for more than 2,000 years.

However, in our microbephobic culture, the word *pickles* is almost universally associated with vegetables drowned in mixtures of sugar, water, and vinegar and heated to high temperatures to kill off any bacteria. The result is a soggy, floppy product inferior in almost every way to the traditional pickle.

If you don't make your own pickled veggies at home, look for versions in your supermarket or health food store that were recently fermented and contain live cultures. These products will most likely be found in the refrigerated sections of your grocery store. Avoid the canned versions that have been sitting on the shelves and have long since lost any live probiotics. There are lots of pickled vegetables to choose from. Some examples are listed on the next page.

- Sauerkraut
- Cucumber pickles
- Pickled beets
- Pickled corn relish
- Pickled radishes

- Kimchi (which is a veritable superfood–see Chapter 7)
- Natto
- Miso
- Tempeh

These foods add a novel and delicious flavor to almost any meal. They can be eaten with omelets in the morning, as a substitute for salad in the afternoon, and as a delicious accompaniment to many dinners. For more ideas on how to use these pickles in your personal cuisine, check out the recipes and meal plans in Chapter 11.

Fermented Dairy Products

These are far more popular in America than fermented veggies. And of the fermented dairy products on the market, yogurt is king. On the surface, this seems great. After all, yogurt usually contains multiple strains of probiotics, including lactobacillus and bifidobacteria, both of which occur naturally in the milk of pastured animals like cows, goats, and sheep. So it can be a wonderful source of these friendly healing microbes.

Unfortunately, the yogurt in your grocery store has suffered a similar fate as many of the once healthy and delicious foods co-opted by modern food processing. First, it's *loaded* with sugar. You can hardly find a yogurt these days that doesn't come with an inch-thick disk of jelly buried in it. Many brands even contain HFCS and other powerful sweeteners that aren't good for your gut microbiome or your health. Many so-called "all-natural yogurts" are loaded with aspartame and other artificial sweeteners that have been associated with weight gain and other health problems.[58] All the sugar and artificial sweetener poured into most modern yogurt likely undo any health benefits brought about by the powerful probiotics it contains.

Another irony of modern yogurt production is that it's usually made from milk that's been put through ultra-high-heat pasteurization, which heats milk to 275°F, eradicating every microbe in the milk by sterilizing it completely. This bacteria-free milk is then inoculated with cultures of microbes like lactobacillus so that it can ferment into yogurt.

On the surface this seems crazy–kill off the bacteria only to add them back in? Well, the rationale goes back to the process of pasteurization. Milk, especially when it comes from cows raised in CAFOs, may contain microbes harmful to human health such as salmonella, E. coli, listeria, and others. Pasteurizing milk, especially at high temperatures, eradicates these bacteria.

Because of these issues, raw milk from local sources has become increasingly popular. Raw milk from grass-fed cows has been shown to have a higher content of omega-3 fatty acids (anti-inflammatory fats) and even CLA–which may promote weight loss.[59] At Johns Hopkins, a colleague surveyed a raw milk–buying community to determine whether raw milk consumption mitigated digestive symptoms provoked by pasteurized milk. The survey, completed by 153 of 265 members, showed that more than 20 percent reported gastrointestinal discomfort when drinking pasteurized milk, but 99 percent were able to consume raw milk without discomfort.[60] Those selling raw milk and the estimated 10 million American consumers of this controversial drink have come under tremendous scrutiny. Selling raw milk is actually illegal in half of the United States, so you may not be able to readily access it even if you want it.

In a recent report, the CDC notes that the rate of raw milk-associated illness quadrupled in 2007–2012 (13 annually) when compared to 1993–2006 (3 annually). These outbreaks mainly occur in states that are legally permitted to sell raw milk and their products (for example, cheese).[61] Among the dairy product–associated outbreaks that occurred between 1998 and 2011, 79 percent were due to raw milk products, and *most of those affected were children*, according to the CDC. For this reason, the CDC says that unpasteurized milk is 150 times more likely to cause foodborne illness than pasteurized products.[62]

Raw milk does have its dangers–I'm not a raw milk evangelist. However, the debate over raw milk illustrates our shifting attitude toward the bacteria around and within us. Consider the rates of *C. difficile* in hospitals as a counterpoint to these concerns about raw milk. In the last 10 years, rates of this potentially fatal form of infectious diarrhea have exploded, with 2.2 *million* cases recorded between 2001 and 2010.[63] Nearly 68 percent were contracted while a patient was in the hospital or under medical supervision–largely associated with antibiotic usage. Furthermore, antibiotic overusage has led to resistant strains called *superbugs*. There is a state-to-state national debate about whether or not we should be drinking raw milk while until recently there was barely a peep about a raging *C. difficile* epidemic that is becoming more resistant to treatment, along with superbugs threatening our health.* What is the number one cause of *C. difficile* infection? What is the number one overprescribed medication in the United States? You guessed it: antibiotics, which also appear to contribute toward our obesity epidemic.

For all these reasons, I encourage you to make your own yogurt if you can. You'll find recipes to fit your needs in Chapter 11. If you choose to buy yogurt, go with an unsweetened (plain) version. Look for local sources if you can. Definitely select yogurt from

---

* The Obama administration released a national 5-year strategy calling for a new presidential advisory council to make specific recommendations to the White House by February 2015. This strategy calls for a 50 percent reduction in the overall incidence of *Clostridium difficile* and in the number of methicillin-resistant *Staphylococcus aureus* (MRSA) infections by 2020. In addition, the president's Council of Advisors on Science and Technology (PCAST) released a 78-page report detailing practical steps the government can take to both track resistant germs and develop novel antibiotics to treat bacterial infections.

100 percent grass-fed animals if possible. I personally love White Mountain Bulgarian yogurt, which contains more than 90 billion CFUs of live cultures per serving.

You can also try alternative options like goat's and sheep's organic milk yogurt. And review the labels to make sure the product you choose contains live cultures (at least 1 million colony-forming units or CFUs per gram) and be careful about yogurts doused with added sugar. You can always add a little sweetener like maple syrup if you like.

The other major fermented dairy product in the American marketplace is cheese, which accounts for more sales than yogurt, although many Americans don't seem to realize it's a fermented product. Maybe that's because the American cheese standard–called American cheese–doesn't contain live bacteria. It's hardly cheese at all.

Cheese making is an ancient art, dating back at least 5,000 years and thought to have originated from nomadic herdsmen who stored their milk in sacks made from the stomachs of goats and sheep. The bacteria naturally occurring in the milk reacted with the lactic acid and rennet in the stomach linings, coagulated, fermented, and turned into cheese. Though it has been refined into a high art today, cheese makers still use this same basic set of processes to create cheese (though none that I am aware of store milk in stomachs!).

This kind of cheese–what we now call artisan cheese–is rich in probiotics. In fact, a brick or round of cheese is kind of a living thing that changes over time, its flavors becoming more complex as the bacterial communities it contains develop. Cheese makers are bacteria herders practicing a kind of microbial husbandry. And like fermented vegetables and yogurt, cheese making (and eating!) is a tantalizing example of what happens when the culture around us meets the cultures within.

However, "American cheese" is not such a product. In fact, it was intentionally developed to kill off the microbial communities in cheese. In 1912, a cheese peddler, James

What About Milk and Other Forms of Dairy?

Aside from fermented milk products, the only other dairy allowed in Phase 2 is butter—a healthy, delicious fat you can freely add to your diet at this stage. In fact, ghee is a probiotic form of butter that we highly recommend! Butter from grass-fed cows is best. Choose it if your budget allows. In turn, I'd like you to stay away from milk, cream, half-and-half, custard, and a few other forms of dairy. This will help keep your overall FODMAP count low and has the added benefit of eliminating a set of foods that many people are sensitive to. All the details on what forms of dairy are favored in Phase 2—and which forms you should forget—are in the Phase 2 food charts on pages 246–251.

Lewis Kraft, seeking to make cheese more "shelf stable," created a cheese that would keep for long periods so he could maximize his profits and minimize his losses from cheese spoilage. In the years that followed, food industry entrepreneurs would seek solutions for these problems in their own basement laboratories, just like Kraft.

After conducting experiments, he found that cooking cheese at high temperatures while stirring it constantly emulsified the fats within the cheese and created an easily pourable mixture that he could put into tins, seal, and keep long term. The key reason this "cheese" didn't spoil as quickly was precisely because he'd killed all the microbes by cooking it at high heat. Kraft cheese was born, and it became the flagship product for what would eventually be one of the biggest food conglomerates the world has ever seen.[64]

Today we see "cheese" in millions of processed food products the world over. Powdered cheese, cheese in a can, liquid cheese to shoot inside pizza crusts–the list goes on. These products aren't what I'd call cheese, and they're not what I recommend you include in your diet.

Instead, try adding artisan cheeses. These contain live cultures and are more readily available in supermarkets across America than they've ever been. Experiment with Edam, feta, fresh mozzarella, Brie, blue cheese, ricotta, fromage fraise (fromage blanc), and others. The options are virtually limitless, and these living foods not only add more probiotics to your diet but also enhance the flavor of a broad variety of dishes. So, say cheese! But steer clear of the processed type so typical in the standard American diet.

Of course, cheese and yogurt aren't the only fermented dairy products. You can also try kefir (a superfood I'll discuss in Chapter 7), sour cream, and others. Enjoy these fermented dairy products as a treat, and include them in Phase 2 to help rebalance your inner ecosystem.

Favor Prebiotic Plant Foods

We've already reviewed data showing why prebiotics are such an important part of your diet. They're the fertilizers your gut microbiome needs to flourish, and their benefits have been proven repeatedly in study after study. One question remains: Which prebiotics should you focus on?

Remember that you can include some gluten-free whole grains in your diet. Most of these have prebiotic effects, but don't overdo it, as they're high in carbs and can raise blood sugar–and that has myriad negative downstream metabolic effects. The same is true of nuts, some of which have prebiotic qualities.

So the prebiotics that I want you to favor most during this phase are fruits and veggies high in soluble fiber, plus legumes, a rich resource of prebiotics. These include but are not limited to:

- **Cherries.** Go for sour cherries if you can. They have a lower glycemic load, higher anti-inflammatory activity, and plenty of prebiotic fiber.

- **Berries.** You've already been eating these in Phase 1. Keep it up. Blueberries, raspberries, and others not only contain high levels of antioxidants but also have plenty of soluble fiber like pectin, which your gut bugs love to eat.

- **Bananas.** They're high in resistant starch and are prebiotic, so they feed beneficial bacteria. Try a firm, greenish banana—it tastes a little different and it's slightly higher in fiber and less sugary.

- **Asparagus.** This Phase 2 superfood is packed with healthy fiber your good gut bugs go mad for. See more on the amazing asparagus in Chapter 7.

- **Jerusalem artichokes.** Little known in America, this root vegetable is packed with inulin—the fructan that's been associated with so many impressive effects on the gut microbiome. Steam, peel, mash, and add a little butter to Jerusalem artichokes for a delicious prebiotic-rich alternative to mashed potatoes. Mashed cauliflower with a little butter is another wonderful alternative to potatoes, which leads me to the next class of prebiotics you should include in your diet . . .

- **Cruciferous veggies.** These include broccoli, cauliflower, collards, bok choy, Brussels sprouts, mustard, and kale. Cruciferous veggies are packed with prebiotic dietary fiber, shown to have significant influence on microbial communities in the gut.[65] They also contain a comprehensive profile of nutrients that support the liver, are high in antioxidants, and more. So go green and add plenty of these healthy veggies to your diet.

- **Beans.** The magical fruit. How come the more you eat of these superfoods, the more you toot? It's because your gut bugs are feasting on the galacto-oligosaccharides in them, fermenting the fiber, and releasing gas as a result. Beans are wonderful for the gut microbiome, they enhance satiety, they're easy to prepare, they're packed with phytonutrients, and they have many other health benefits we'll dive into in Chapter 7. Don't worry, you don't have to end up feeling embarrassed by including this magical fruit in your diet. There are ways to prepare beans that reduce their gaseous effects—I'll explain more later.

These are only a few of the all-star options of plant foods that are high in prebiotics. See the Phase 2 food charts on pages 246–251 for more ideas, and make sure to try the delicious prebiotic-rich recipes in Chapter 11.

That's all you need to know to succeed during Phase 2. Remember, if you want to make the program easy on yourself, just follow the meal plans and make the delectable recipes in Chapter 11. Your good gut bugs will absolutely love them. Your palate won't be disappointed either.

WHAT YOU CAN EXPECT DURING PHASE 2

This phase should be substantially easier than Phase 1, and that's a good thing because you're liable to remain on it longer. Any withdrawal symptoms you may have experienced in Phase 1 should be well behind you, and you'll be reintegrating enough foods in this phase to keep the diet interesting enough to keep you on the wagon. I designed Phase 2 this way because I want you to stay on it until you've achieved your desired weight.

You can expect a sustained weight loss of 5 to 10 pounds of excess body weight a month during Phase 2, so you may be on this phase for quite a while if you have substantial weight to lose. That's not a problem at all. Phase 2 is a healthy eating plan you can stick with as long as you like. If you ate this way for the rest of your life, you'd be getting all the healing foods you need to keep your body healthy and balanced. Since Phase 2 encourages the consumption of fermented dairy products, calcium supplementation to compensate for lack of intake of this mineral is not required.

Remember, the name of the game in Phase 2 is diversifying your gut microbiome and providing the fertilizer it needs to thrive. Of all the foods we've discussed in this chapter, pay special attention to the prebiotics and probiotics. These will nourish your inner ecosystem, empowering it to help you lose weight and stay healthy.

Once you've achieved your goal weight, you can transition to Phase 3, a more Mediterranean-style diet that allows you to indulge in the occasional treat while still helping you maintain your weight loss for the long haul. Look for details on how this works in Chapter 8.

LOOKING AHEAD

Now that you understand the principles of Phase 2, it's time to look at our superfoods for this phase. As you can probably guess, lots of them are the prebiotics and probiotics you need to seed and fertilize your inner garden. But I have a few surprises in store for you, including a fermented dairy beverage whose name literally means "good feeling," an ancient Indian spice that will help you burn fat and turn down systemic inflammation, and a fermented condiment from the ancient Near East. Include these superfoods in Phase 2 and your inner garden will flourish like never before.

CHAPTER 7

Dr. Gerry's Top 10 Superfoods for Phase 2

The superfoods for Phase 2 are filled with prebiotics and probiotics, though I have thrown in an anti-inflammatory spice and a pungent fermented condiment for good measure. No doubt a few of these will be familiar to you, but I think you'll be surprised by some of them. Include plenty of these foods in your Phase 2 eating plan and you'll burn more fat while enjoying the benefits of a health-promoting biodiverse gut microbiome.

1. OATS

Oats are the most nutrient-rich superstars in the cereal kingdom. The bran of oats is particularly high in fiber and is a good source of protein. One serving–just $^1/_4$ cup–of oat bran contains 4 grams of protein and 3.6 grams of dietary fiber.[1] Although the carb content appears high at 15.6 grams per $^1/_4$-cup serving, the rich, nonabsorbable fiber content keeps the *net* absorbable carb content to just 12 grams. The benefits of satiation, along with the prebiotic effects, make oats a weight-loss superfood. A serving of oats contains nearly the entire Recommended Dietary Allowance (RDA) of manganese–a trace mineral involved in bone health, blood sugar regulation, and more–and a good dose of vitamin B$_1$, copper, biotin, and other nutrients. One of the key features of whole grain oats is their negligible impact on blood sugar levels and gentle stimulation of insulin. It's a good carb to include in your weight-loss arsenal!

Oats originated in Asia, and the modern oat is a descendant of the wild red oats that were classically grown there. In Asia, oats were used medicinally. When they were brought to the West, they were thought of only as food for animals, specifically horses. Indeed, whole oats can't be digested by humans and are used solely as animal fodder.

Hulled oats, cleaned and toasted–called oat groats–are a wonderful food source for people. The Scots were among the first Europeans to add oats to their diet, and steel-cut oats (which I strongly recommend) are sometimes called Scotch oats to this day. Steel-cut oats are simply oat groats cut into several pieces. They retain more of the bran than rolled oats, and the bran is where the action is when it comes to the prebiotic effect of this superfood.

Oat bran is a powerful prebiotic. Bran is the part of a whole grain from which fiber comes. Oat bran is special because it contains a particular kind of fiber called beta-glucan, shown to reduce cholesterol levels and risk of cardiovascular events.[2, 3] This relationship between increased dietary fiber and reduction in heart disease has been repeatedly corroborated. For example, in one study, researchers followed 10,000 people over 19 years and found that those who ate the most fiber had 12 percent less heart disease and 11 percent less cardiovascular disease.[4] A meta-analysis published in the *American Journal of Clinical Nutrition* showed even more impressive results–those with the highest fiber intake suffered 29 percent less cardiovascular disease compared to those with the lowest.[5]

The effects of oats on blood sugar levels, type 2 diabetes, and obesity have also been studied. Oats are digested slowly, so they keep blood glucose more stable over time. Their fiber also helps you feel full, leading to your eating less–and if you have them for breakfast, you'll feel full later into the day. This effect goes back to beta-glucan, which is a soluble fiber, so it soaks up water and creates a kind of gel in your intestines.

Oat bran is high in magnesium, a mineral that plays a role in blood sugar control and insulin secretion. An 8-year trial involving 41,186 women showed a fascinating relationship between oat intake, magnesium levels, and incidences of type 2 diabetes.[6] Women who ate whole grains rich in magnesium had a 31 percent lower chance of developing type 2 diabetes compared to those who had a magnesium-poor diet.

Oats seem to enhance immune response,[7] they may protect against breast cancer,[8] and they can help prevent and reverse childhood asthma.[9] Some doctors even suggest that their health-promoting activities are equal to or greater than those of fruits and vegetables.

Oats are gluten-free grains, although conventionally grown and processed oats have problems with cross contamination and may contain some gluten–which may become problematic if you are known to have gluten intolerance or celiac disease. If so, I am recommending you continue to avoid gluten and consume certified gluten-free, organic, steel-cut oats. For those without a gluten sensitivity, the issue of potential cross contamination is less crucial; if you can afford the additional cost, purchase the organic steel-cut oats, as they are free from gluten cross contamination.

Oats have helped me tremendously on my own weight-loss journey. Here's a tip that's worked for me: Cook some steel-cut oats, add a little unsweetened (plain) yogurt or kefir and a dab of 100% pure maple syrup or raw honey, and you've got a powerful gut microbiome-balancing superbreakfast that will help you burn fat (and protect your heart, immune system, and more) all day long.

Honorable Mention: Raw Honey

I asked you to avoid honey in Phase 1 due to its rich fructose content (38.5 grams per 100 grams of honey) and high glycemic impact. As a general rule, I ask you to *limit* raw honey in Phase 2 as well. Keep it to about a teaspoon at a time, and don't use it as a sugar substitute—use it in precious limited quantities as a superfood. But ample evidence shows that raw honey has positive effects on gut microbiome health.

There is also evidence that honey has antimicrobial effects against gut pathogens such as *E. coli* O17:H7, *Pseudomonas, Proteus, Enterobacter,* and other bugs we want to keep in check for a healthy gut microbiome. Raw honey, a prebiotic due to its rich oligosaccharide content that promotes the growth of bifidobacteria,[10] also limits growth of pathogenic biofilms. Honey has anti-inflammatory, antioxidant, immunoregulatory, and antitumor properties.[11, 12] It both contains and raises levels of nitric oxide in tissues, which improves healing, enhances antibiotic functions, and protects the nervous and cardiovascular system.[13] In addition, it has antibiotic effects[14] and positive effects on:

- Allergies[15]
- Bone health[16]
- Burns[17]
- Common cold[18]
- Diabetes[19]
- Leg ulcers[20]
- Skin care[21]
- Wound healing[22]

You may wonder why we're devoting so much time to discussing honey if it's so restricted in the meal plans. Remember the mantra—the dose makes the poison! Treat honey as a superfood, not a sugar substitute. Use it in tiny amounts in tea or coffee or as a sweetener for your shakes.

Note that high heat inactivates the propolis (waxy resin) and hence the antimicrobial activities of honey. True raw honey retains these properties and is often available at farmers' and organic markets. Look for organic or wild, nonpasteurized honey for all the gut-balancing benefits that will help melt those calories away.

You can also try manuka honey, made in New Zealand from the nectar of manuka flowers (*Leptospermum scoparium*). In 2007, the FDA approved a medical-grade manuka honey, sold as Medihoney, for treating wounds and skin ulcers.

An important note: **Don't feed infants honey.** On rare occasions, honey products may be contaminated with *Clostridium botulinum* spores and toxins, toxic to infants.

2. ASPARAGUS

Asparagus is the weight-loss tree of choice. Its small thin stalks, considered a delicacy for more than 2,000 years, are shoots that, left uncut, would grow into a small tree. Mature asparagus is inedible, but the delectable immature shoots are packed with health benefits.

For starters, asparagus is high in inulin—the prebiotic fructan we've been discussing throughout Phase 2. So it's an ideal food source for healthy microbial communities like bifidobacteria, lactobacillus, and others. The other major inulin contenders are Jerusalem artichoke and chicory root, both of which are more difficult to find in the American marketplace.

Its prebiotic effect alone is enough to recommend asparagus for this program,[23] but its benefits don't end there. It's rich in saponins, a class of phytonutrients repeatedly shown to possess a variety of biological properties, such as being antioxidant, antihepatotoxic, antibacterial, anti-inflammatory, immunoregulatory, and anticancer agents.[24-26] They also reduce blood pressure, balance blood sugar, and reduce body fat levels. Natural medicine clinicians often recommend asparagus to reduce ankle swelling.[27]

Asparagus, an antioxidant powerhouse,[28] is one of the few foods besides cruciferous vegetables containing a meaningful amount of glutathione—a powerful antioxidant that reduces fat-promoting inflammation and oxidative stress throughout the body. One serving provides the RDA of vitamin K, substantial amounts of folate and vitamin B_1 (which play a critical role in the regulation of homocysteine, an amino acid that can increase the risk of cardiovascular problems when it gets too high), vitamin C, vitamin E, and many other health-promoting nutrients.

The best thing about asparagus? It's easy to prepare. Steam it, grill it, roast it. Add a little olive oil, salt and pepper, and lemon. You and your good gut bugs will enjoy a feast!

3. BEANS

Beans are among the few foods that receive the support of virtually every major health and wellness organization on the planet. The American Diabetes Association,[29] the American Heart Association,[30] and the American Cancer Society,[31] to name a few, recommend two to three servings of beans weekly to reduce the risk of a wide variety of chronic illnesses, from type 2 diabetes to cardiovascular disease to cancer.[32,]

What makes beans such a powerful superfood? One element is their combination of fiber and protein. One serving provides about 15 grams of protein and between 11 grams (kidney beans) and 17 grams (adzuki beans) of fiber per cup.[33] This one-two punch of protein and fiber has a wide range of health benefits.

First, they stabilize blood glucose levels. Fiber and protein move through your digestive tract slowly, so they're converted to sugar slowly, which is precisely what you want to lose weight and get healthy. Fiber also reduces the uptake of cholesterol, and high-fiber diets have been associated with a reduction in both cholesterol and heart disease.[34] The gut microbiota may play a role in determining the risk of cardiovascular disease, so the prebiotic properties of soluble fibers in beans may protect against heart disease by favoring the growth of good gut bugs.[35]

Additionally, the fiber in beans is a wonderful food source for your good gut bacteria. When your friendly flora eat the mixture of fiber in beans, they seem to produce more butyric acid, which the cells in the lining of your colon use for various activities. This keeps the lower part of your digestive tract healthy and supports a perfect environment for a thriving inner ecosystem.

Beans are also rich in important antioxidant and anti-inflammatory compounds, yet another reason researchers believe they protect against chronic illness.[36] They contain high levels of saponins, just as asparagus does, and they also have three important anthocyanin flavonoids: delphinidin, petunidin, and malvidin–phytonutrients with both anti-inflammatory and antioxidant properties.[37] Their anti-inflammatory properties are so powerful that they can increase healthy colonic biomarkers and attenuate experimental colitis.[38]

These extraordinary plant foods even contain alpha-amylase inhibitors, chemicals that reduce the activity of the alpha-amylase enzyme (aka starch blockers).[39] That's important because this enzyme is involved in the rapid breakdown of food into simple sugars. By slowing down its activity, beans give you another edge against the blood sugar roller coaster you need to avoid to achieve long-term health and optimal weight. But is there proof that these firecracking leguminous plants can help you lose weight?

A 2014 study determined that a bean-rich diet that was high in fiber while low in absorbable carbohydrates enhanced satiety and promoted weight loss.[40] In the study, 173 obese women and men were randomized into either a high-fiber bean-rich diet providing 35.5 daily grams of fiber for women and 42.5 grams for men, or a low-carbohydrate diet. After 16 weeks, the difference in weight loss between the two groups (bean-rich 9 pounds, low-carb 11.4 pounds) was not statistically significant. However, the low-density lipoprotein (LDL) cholesterol and total cholesterols (atherogenic lipids) were significantly lower in those on the bean-rich diet compared to the low-carb diet. Another study in 2011 evaluated 32 obese subjects randomly assigned to one of two calorically equivalent, energy-restricted diets for 8 weeks: a legume-free diet or a legume-based diet.[41] The legume-based diet involved 4 weekly servings of lentils, chickpeas, peas, or beans. The legume-rich diet was associated with a significantly greater weight loss than the legume-free diet. Plus, the high-legume diet was associated with reduced proinflammatory markers and with improved cardiovascular profile (lipid profile and blood pressure).

These studies blow a hole in the low-carb-for-life approach to keeping the weight off. Our body needs good fibrous carbs to thrive–the survival of our friendly flora that sustain our livelihood requires fiber.

There *is* a downside to beans. They may increase flatulence. To avoid this problem, simply soak dried beans for a few hours, which has been shown to reduce two of the components that lead to gas: raffinose and stachyose.[42]

Canned beans are fine if you're tight on time. Rinse them well before eating and make sure you stick with salt-free versions—salt them to taste yourself. Presalted beans tend to be very high in sodium. I prefer cooking with presoaked dried beans, as the flavor and texture are better, and there's evidence they may retain higher quantities of the important phytonutrients that protect your health and your waistline.

4. KALE

Along with its cousins broccoli, bok choy, cabbage, mustard, Brussels sprouts, and collard, kale is the descendant of a wild cabbage plant that originated in Asia Minor. These plants are all called cruciferous vegetables, from the Latin word for "cross-bearing," which makes sense if you've ever seen the yellow cross-shaped blossoms these plants produce.

Cruciferous vegetables are a superfamily of foods, so powerful that some doctors recommend eating as much as four or five 2-cup servings weekly. And though it's hard to choose just one of these superveggies, recent research suggests that kale deserves a special place of recognition among its brethren. That's because it contains 45 different flavonoids—phytonutrients known for their anti-inflammatory properties. This is a stunning variety of flavonoids in a single food, and I'm not aware of any other vegetable containing as many. Of the flavonoids in kale, kaempferol and quercetin hold the spotlight.

A hundred calories of kale also provides 350 milligrams of alpha-linolenic acid, a healthy omega-3 fat contributing to the plant's anti-inflammatory properties. And it has more than 1,180 percent of the RDA of vitamin K, a key nutrient deeply involved in regulating the inflammatory process. That's a lot of anti-inflammatory muscle for one plant.

Research shows that kale may mitigate your risk of colon, breast, bladder, prostate, and ovarian cancer, probably due to its high levels of glucosinolates, a set of compounds that provide anticancer activity.[43] Kale also reduces blood levels of cholesterol, supporting heart health. The mechanisms by which it does this have been well documented. Bile, made in the liver using cholesterol as one of its primary building blocks, is needed to digest fat in the foods you eat. Once it's made, it's released from the liver and stored in the gallbladder. The gallbladder then delivers bile as needed to help you digest fat. Nutrients in kale bind to these bile acids in the gut, allowing them to pass through the digestive system and out through your bowel without binding to fat, forcing the liver to tap into your cholesterol store to make more bile, thus lowering overall cholesterol levels.

Kale lowers cholesterol so effectively that it was recently compared with a cholesterol-lowering prescription medication called cholestyramine, which reduces serum cholesterol using the same method outlined above. Steamed kale was found to be 42 percent more effective than the drug cholestyramine.[44]

5. MISO

Miso is made by steaming soybeans, mashing them, adding salt, and then inoculating them with *koji*—a traditional Japanese rice-based starter culture that typically contains high levels of the fungus *Aspergillus oryzae*. This mixture is then allowed to age and ferment for a few months to a few years. The resulting paste is a microbial paradise that you can use to rebalance your inner ecosystem by adding it to soups, salads, and stir-fries. Made from soybeans, miso provides many of the health benefits you get from beans while packing a probiotic punch at the same time—a spectacular one-two combination for gut microbiome health.

The Salt Problem and Obesity

Most everyone knows that too much sodium is a bad thing for cardiovascular health. Keeping sodium consumption in check is one of the biggest challenges facing those of us who dine out for work-related or social functions, because restaurants are notorious for adding salt to optimize food taste and create thirst to spike beverage sales.

Too much sodium in your foods can translate to big-time health problems, and lowering consumption to the CDC's and American Heart Association's recommended guidelines of 1,500 to 2,300 milligrams daily lowers blood pressure, stroke risk, cardiovascular risk, and mortality from ischemic heart disease.[45, 46] "Nearly everyone benefits from reduced sodium consumption," said Janelle Gunn, a public health analyst in the CDC's division for heart disease and stroke prevention. "Ninety percent of Americans exceed the general daily recommended sodium intake limit of 2,300 milligrams, increasing their risk for high blood pressure, heart disease, and stroke."[47]

So if this is a book about your gut and weight loss, why all the sodium coverage? Well, believe it or not, high sodium intake in adolescents has been linked to—you guessed it—being overweight! In a study reported in the journal *Pediatrics,* adolescents' sodium intake was as high as adults' and more than twice the guidelines of the American Heart Association.[48] High sodium intake was correlated with adiposity and inflammation independent of total caloric intake and sugar-sweetened soft drink consumption. And some data link sodium intake to heightened levels of inflammatory conditions, such as tumor necrosis factor-alpha.[49,50] High-salt diets have been linked to tissue inflammation and worsening of autoimmune disease. Sodium-restricted diets have been shown to lower inflammatory markers prior to changes in blood pressure.[51]

Ultimately, what does all this mean? Sodium intake appears to be linked to inflammation, which has been strongly linked to obesity. In putting together a program to reduce inflammation and promote weight loss and good health, I took the CDC's dietary guidelines for sodium content into account.

One criticism of miso has been that it's high in salt, and excess sodium can be a contributing factor to high blood pressure and cardiovascular conditions. But recent Japanese studies may indicate that there's nothing to fear from miso. In one study, researchers fed one group miso and a second group an equivalent amount of table salt. These two dietary alterations had very different effects. The high-salt diet increased blood pressure. The diet that included the same amount of sodium in the form of miso had no effect at all. Some studies have shown that miso may have a cardioprotective effect; in one large trial involving 40,462 participants, intake of miso reduced the risk of cerebral infarction, a major type of stroke.[52]

The process of miso fermentation seems to further enhance the nutritional profile of this superfood. For example, isoflavones in soy have come under recent scrutiny due to their impact on estrogen levels and the resulting health consequences that may ensue. The primary fungus used in miso fermentation, *Aspergillus oryzae*, seems to break down two of the more dangerous of these isoflavones: daidzein and genistein. The fermentation process also appears to create antioxidant compounds such as ferulic, coumaric, and kojic acids (among others), which may provide this food's anticancer activity.

Traditionally, of course, miso is made into soup, and no doubt this is among the most delicious ways to consume it. There's only one downside to eating miso as soup: You kill off some of the good bacteria by heating it. One way to minimize this is to avoid boiling miso soup, which most chefs recommend anyway simply to retain its nuanced flavors. Try to keep the soup below 120°F to retain its microbial cultures, though this is difficult without monitoring the pot with a thermometer.

A different approach is to add fresh, uncooked miso to salad dressings. This is a delicious way to incorporate the fresh miso paste that will give your inner garden the seeds it needs to flourish.

6. YOGURT

Fermenting milk to make yogurt was first done by Balkan nomads in the Middle East, who used this technique to preserve the milk from their animals as they roamed. Yogurt can be made from the milk of any ruminant animal, including sheep, goats, and cows. Cow's milk yogurt is by far the most popular in this country, but I encourage you to try yogurt from sheep and goats as well–they all have a different flavor and texture.

One of the best probiotic foods is live-cultured yogurt, especially handmade at home–it can contain up to 100 times as many live cultures per serving as store-bought varieties. I especially like goat's milk yogurts and cheeses, as they are particularly high in probiotics like *Streptococcus thermophilus*, *Bifudus*, *Lactobacillus bulgaricus*, and *L. acidophilus*. Your good gut bugs are telling your brain, "Yum–please make some for us to feast!"

Yogurt containing live cultures has been shown to decrease total cholesterol while increasing HDL, the healthy cholesterol you want more of. In one study, Iranian women

Honorable Mention: Other Fermented Soy Foods

While we're talking about fermented soy products, let's take a moment to bring some other soy-based superfoods to your awareness and palate.

Tempeh is a probiotic food derived from fermented soybeans. The primary probiotic in tempeh is *Rhizopus oligosporus,* which produces a natural antibiotic against enteric pathogens (pathogens produced inside the body), as well as phytase, an enzyme that helps break down phytate acid, which increases the absorption of minerals. Fermented soy paste reduces visceral fat accumulation.[53] Plus, since tempeh isn't salted, it's suitable for people on a low-sodium diet.

Natto is made from fermented soybeans; it contains the bacterial strain *Bacillus subtilis*, which gives this food its characteristic stringy consistency. In addition to being a probiotic source containing soy, natto contains the enzyme nattokinase, which dissolves dangerous blood clots.[54] The protein and other nutrients in soybeans become more digestible after they're broken down by bacteria or mold, and that's why fermented bean products like tempeh and natto don't cause the flatulence associated with beans.

Soy itself may impart an antiobesity benefit. Several nutritional intervention studies in animals and humans indicate that soy protein consumption reduces body weight and fat mass in addition to lowering plasma cholesterol and triglycerides.[55] In animal models of obesity, soy protein limits or reduces body fat accumulation and improves insulin resistance, the hallmark of human obesity.[56] In obese humans, dietary soy protein also reduces body weight and body fat mass in addition to reducing plasma lipids. A head-to-head trial of calorically equivalent soy milk to cow's milk showed that there was no difference in the weight-reducing benefits.[57]

who consumed 10 ounces of yogurt a day for 6 weeks saw total cholesterol drop while HDL increased.[58] Researchers feel the reason may have to do with sphingolipids–healthy fats naturally occurring in yogurt that play a key role in cellular signaling. A recent study from India also showed that 2 cups of yogurt weekly reduced the risk of hip fracture.[59] The healthy bacteria in yogurt also help metabolize food more efficiently and produce higher levels of short-chain fatty acids–those healthy fats that are important for proper intestinal functioning.

These benefits only scratch the surface. The list is constantly expanding, especially since the first global summit on the health effects of yogurt was held in 2013.[60] For example, cultured milk and yogurt have been linked to a reduced risk of developing colorectal cancer and to preventing antibiotic-induced diarrhea,[61] improving digestive symptoms,[62] improving dental health,[63] preventing osteoporosis, lowering the risk of heart attack, and decreasing blood pressure.[64]

Studies have also shown that regular consumption of yogurt can reduce your risk of developing type 2 diabetes.[65] A recent analysis compared 11 years' worth of food journals from 3,502 people and found that those who regularly ate yogurt were 28 percent less likely to become diabetic.[66] Most scientists agree this is related to two components in yogurt: protein and probiotics. Yogurt is relatively high in protein, which is digested slowly, helping keep blood sugar stable over time. Greek yogurt is thicker and particularly high in satiating protein. A word of caution for those with a known sensitivity to casein–Greek yogurt is nearly 100 percent casein, as the whey is strained out to enhance thickness. While I couldn't find any head-to-head studies of Greek yogurt to conventional yogurt regarding satiety, metabolic parameters, or weight loss, I do recommend this form to patients who desire an appetite-curbing snack. Try it with berries, such as highly fibrous raspberries, and some nuts. There are now manufacturers of organic Greek yogurt.

The healthy probiotics in yogurt seem to further support its blood glucose balancing effects. The microbes in yogurt regulate the passage of food through your gut. Steady digestion is important for blood sugar regulation, as it keeps food from being digested too quickly (which can spike blood sugar and insulin) or too slowly (causing blood sugar and insulin to dip too swiftly after meals).

Studies suggest that dairy in general supports weight loss, and fermented dairy seems to be particularly useful in this regard, probably because the whey protein in dairy regulates satiety. Although the energy intakes for yogurt and other fermented dairy products such as cheese and milk are similar, yogurt produced the greatest suppressive effect on appetite.[67] Some interesting proof: A study of 212 Korean women found that those who consumed at least one daily serving of yogurt weighed less.[68] Another Korean study demonstrated that consumption of a specially formulated yogurt (NY-YP901) improved blood lipids and cardiovascular markers and induced weight loss in obese individuals with metabolic syndrome.[69] In yet another study, yogurt consumption was found to decrease body weight and postmeal hunger. Investigators found that those consuming yogurt had higher levels of the gut-derived hormone glucagon-like peptide 2, which suppresses appetite.[70] Other research shows that substituting the same quantity of calories of yogurt for other foods preserves lean muscle mass while augmenting fat loss, improving waist circumference, and reducing fat gain.[71]

One of the most compelling studies on the influence of yogurt on weight comes from Spain, where many people consume yogurt as a dessert. Investigators from Seguimiento Universidad de Navarra evaluated 8,516 men and women prospectively during a 2-year period as to yogurt consumption and outcome. Those who consumed more than seven servings (125 grams per serving) per week of yogurt (full fat) were associated with a lower incidence of overweight or obesity in comparison to those whose consumption was low (less than two servings weekly).[72] Moreover, this association was even stronger in those who were regular fruit consumers–typical of the Mediterranean lifestyle that forms the foundation for our Phase 3. The fruit likely provided a prebiotic effect to bolster the probiotic weight-reducing effect.

These effects seem to span age ranges from young to old, so most everyone can benefit from yogurt. One study attempted to improve constipation in elderly individuals by feeding them yogurt. While the yogurt didn't appear to improve constipation, it did help the participants lose significant body weight.[73]

I have a bias toward the probiotic cultures in yogurt, which are a big part of what makes it a superfood for weight loss because it restores your gut balance. But the healthy bacteria in this fermented milk product are not the only things that provide health benefits, so let's look at a few other important components of yogurt.

Yogurt is loaded with calcium and vitamin D. There are data showing that calcium and vitamin D may influence weight balance. In one study, women burned more fat and calories when they had 1,000 to 1,400 milligrams of calcium per day. And in a study of 218 obese-to-overweight postmenopausal women with vitamin D insufficiency, those who supplemented with vitamin D and attained sufficient serum levels lost more weight, reduced their waist circumference, and dropped more body fat.[74] So it's certainly possible that vitamin D and calcium provide fermented dairy products with additional weight-loss prowess.

Remember that today's milk is far from perfect because it contains antibiotics, hormones, pesticides, and other foreign substances or potential contaminants. We avoided milk products in Phase 1 due to their high FODMAP content and the fact that the fatty acid profile of conventional milk products is on the proinflammatory side. So why bring milk products back into Phase 2 and beyond?

Well, unless you're lactose intolerant, fermented milk products promote a healthy gut microbiome and appear to facilitate weight loss. It's also interesting to note that yogurt is lower in lactose than milk. As milk is fermented by these friendly bacteria, they digest part of the lactose. Even those who are lactose sensitive can eat yogurt in some cases–more so if it is homemade. Experiment with it, tune in to how your body reacts, and see if it works for you.

Not only does consumption of dairy products and their milk proteins increase satiety and reduce food intake, but it decreases blood glucose response when consumed alone or with carbohydrates.[75] And the fatty acids found in these products, particularly the conjugated linoleic acid (CLA), may support weight-loss attempts. (Refer to page 106 in Chapter 6 for a refresher on CLA.)

Remember that most industrial yogurt is first pasteurized and then inoculated with specific strains of bacteria–a process that works but that may produce suboptimal amounts of "live" probiotics. That's why I recommend you make your own yogurt and other fermented milk products. Use organic milk whenever possible, as it's typically

What About Fat-Free Dairy Products?

Is fat-free, or skim, milk as good as whole milk for reducing appetite? That controversy continues to rage in the medical literature. Even nutrition experts from Harvard say that there's a quicker blood sugar response to fat-free milk, as the fat in whole milk slows down the entry of milk sugar (lactose) into the small intestine, where it's absorbed.[76] There is ample evidence that fat-free dairy provides no additional benefit for a healthy weight status over regular-fat products.[77, 78]

If you've been convinced that fat-free milk products are healthier, you may think me mad for suggesting whole milk over fat-free in your tea and cereal. You may wonder if whole milk increases the risk of cardiovascular disease.

A recent study put things in perspective. Investigators examined the association between the type of dairy and the risk of having a myocardial infarction (heart attack). Bottom line: Overall, milk, cheese, and yogurt are inversely associated with cardiovascular disease (CVD) risk.[79] A meta-analysis of more than 600,000 multiethnic adults found no difference between full-fat or low-fat dairy consumption (less than 200 grams/daily).[80] This dose-response meta-analysis of prospective studies indicates that milk intake is not associated with total mortality but may be *inversely* associated with overall CVD risk. A Dutch study that was prospective and observational confirmed these retrospective conclusions about total dairy intake lowering CVD risk in those without preexisting hypertension and noted that only those who consistently consumed ice cream and butter lost this protective effect. These investigators also reported that only fermented dairy products are to be associated with a lower risk of stroke.[81]

antibiotic free and may be higher in healthy fats. Grass-fed cows have higher levels of CLA and more anti-inflammatory fat profiles.

There are now machines that make it simple to prepare your own yogurt at home. These can be a convenient addition to your kitchen. You'll find an easy recipe for yogurt in Chapter 11.

If you choose to purchase yogurt, look for brands containing live cultures with at least 1 million CFUs (colony-forming units).[82] The National Yogurt Association developed a Live & Active Culture seal to help consumers identify products that meets its standards for significant amounts of live and active cultures. Refrigerated yogurt products containing at least 100 million cultures per gram and frozen yogurt products containing at least 10 million cultures per gram at the time of manufacture may bear the seal. The store-bought yogurt with the highest cultures, according to New York City nutritionist Dr. Loren Marks, is White Mountain organic Bulgarian yogurt, containing 90 billion CFUs per serving (whitemountainfoods.com/Products.html). It goes wonderfully with fresh Turkish or Mission figs (not dried, which is loaded with sugars)—a nice prebiotic!

7. KEFIR

The word *kefir* derives from the Turkish word *keif,* which denotes the good feeling one has after drinking this fermented milk product.[83] Kefir looks like a runny yogurt or thickened milk and has a slight sour taste and smell. It originated in the Caucasus Mountains between the Caspian and the Black Seas. The people there seem to have preferred fermenting camel's milk to make kefir. Today, it's most commonly made from cow's and goat's milk.

Kefir is among the simplest fermented products to prepare at home. All you do is find a few kefir grains, drop them in milk, store the mixture out of direct sunlight for 1 to 2 days, stirring it occasionally–and, voilà, you have kefir.

The kefir grains themselves are one of the most fascinating microbial communities around. They are a SCOBY–an acronym that stands for "symbiotic colony of bacteria and yeast." The kefir SCOBY is an ecosystem in its own right that involves at least 10 to 20 different strains of bacteria and yeast, including lactobacilli, *Leuconostoc, Acetobacter,* and *Saccharomyces.*[84] During fermentation, the grains increase in size and number and are either left in the fermented milk or recovered and reused.

Multiple studies have shown that kefir has a wide range of health benefits.[85] Several studies demonstrated that kefir and its constituents have antimicrobial, anticancer, and immune regulation activities[86] and many others.[87] It improves gut microbiome balance through its powerful probiotic effects. This is probably one of the reasons it's known to protect against gastrointestinal diseases. For example, bacterial strains from kefir cultures reduce intestinal inflammation and ameliorate symptoms in those who suffer from colitis.[88] It also appears to help with lactose digestion in adults who suffer from lactose intolerance.[89]

The anti-inflammatory properties of kefir are impressive. Studies have revealed that it reduces cytokine production, mitigates mast cell degranulation, and reduces the production of IgE in people who suffer from allergies.[90] So if you suffer from the spring sneezes, drink up! Plus, preliminary evidence in animal models shows that it may be a key agent in the fight against cancer due to its antitumor properties.[91]

Historically, kefir has been recommended for the treatment of digestive conditions, hypertension, allergies,[92] and heart disease.[93] This superfood may even block cholesterol assimilation, reducing overall blood levels.[94] Kefir has anti-fat-forming effects that may, in part, explain the benefit of fermented milk in fighting obesity in one clinical trial.[95]

Kefir is high in vitamin K_2, thiamin, B_{12}, calcium, and a host of other vitamins and minerals–each of which adds to its superstar status among fermented dairy products.

Try making kefir at home and adding it to cooked steel-cut oats with a few blueberries for a delicious breakfast your inner flora will thank you for.

8. KIMCHI

Kimchi, the iconic food of Korean culture, is a natural but powerful probiotic. It's made in homes and restaurants across the country and served as a side dish with virtually every meal. The result is a mind-boggling array of kimchi in the world. If you've ever been to a Korean restaurant and been presented with dozens of small dishes filled with wonderful ferments of every shape, size, color, and consistency, then you may have some sense of how many different kinds of kimchi Korean culture has produced. But even for those of us who are fans of this cuisine, it's stunning to consider that 167 distinct styles of kimchi have been documented, and there may be even more, given regional and household differences in recipes.

The health effects of kimchi would take up a book in their own right.[96] So here we'll focus on *baechu*, a spicy Korean sauerkraut made from Chinese cabbage. The same fermentation process–lactic acid fermentation–is used for both sauerkraut and *baechu*, but unlike sauerkraut, *baechu* typically incorporates radish, red pepper, ginger, garlic, and a host of other vegetables and spices. This amalgamation creates health benefits greater than the sum of the parts.

Baechu is high in vitamin C, the B-complex vitamins, and minerals like sodium, calcium, potassium, and others. It typically has lots of capsaicin–the healthy, anti-inflammatory constituent of peppers we learned about in Phase 1.

A good deal of research has been done on the effects of kimchi on weight loss, and the results are stunning. In rats, kimchi normalized and sustained a healthy body weight.[97] How is that possible? Well, kimchi is actually like a superfood *within* a superfood! It contains Korean red-pepper powder or *kochukaru*, a thermogenic that may be partially responsible for kimchi's fat-burning effect.[98] Remember when we discussed the fat-burning effects of peppers in Chapter 5? Well, the capsaicin is almost certainly one of the reasons for the fat-burning potential of kimchi.

Rats aren't the only creatures that lose weight when kimchi is added to their diet. It works on people, too. In a study of obese women, one group engaged in 1 hour of exercise per week. The second group exercised and took a kimchi supplement (3 to 6 grams of freeze-dried kimchi daily). Those who took the kimchi capsules lost an impressive amount of weight–approximately 22 pounds over the course of 12 weeks. They saw significantly greater improvement in their body mass index (BMI), visceral fat, and triglyceride levels compared to the women who didn't receive the kimchi.[99]

Another study showed that fresh, fermented kimchi (not freeze-dried) has even more powerful effects. In this study, researchers encouraged overweight and obese subjects to eat kimchi regularly. When participants did so, they not only had a reduction in weight and BMI but their overall body fat percentage dropped, they experienced a decrease in waist-to-hip ratio, blood glucose stabilized, fasting insulin dropped, and leptin levels improved.[100] These researchers concluded that adding kimchi to the diet may reduce the risk of metabolic syndrome, cardiovascular disease, and type 2 diabetes.

There's also good evidence kimchi improves cholesterol profiles. In a recent study, researchers reviewed the effects of daily kimchi consumption on the lipid parameters of 102 adult Korean men between the ages of 40 and 64.[101] They found that eating kimchi increased HDL and reduced LDL; the preference for hot taste correlated with a reduction in systolic blood pressure, indicating that the capsaicin in the red pepper has antihypertensive properties.

Additional research suggests that kimchi may have anticancer properties[102] and modulate immune system function.[103] Kimchi has impressive antimicrobial activities against bad bugs such as *Bacillus subtilis*, *Escherichia coli*, *Salmonella enteritidis*, *S. paratyphi* and *S. typhi*, *Staphylococcus aureus*, and *Shigella boydii* and *S. sonnei*. Overall, kimchi is the one-stop superfood for protecting your health.

You can make your own kimchi at home or buy it at the supermarket. If you choose to purchase it, select a brand containing live active cultures. The jar should fizz when you open it, a sure sign that the friendly microbes you desire are alive and well.

9. TURMERIC

Turmeric, along with the other spices discussed throughout this book, may provide the best model for the food-as-medicine approach to halting the vicious cycle of obesity and inflammation. This bright yellow spice is most well known as one of the primary ingredients in curry. Americans are probably more familiar with it as the agent that makes ballpark mustard a bright yellow. Turmeric has an exotic floral fragrance, which may be why it was used as a perfume in biblical times.

Turmeric has long been used in Chinese and Indian medicine systems to treat ailments ranging from flatulence to chest pain to menstrual difficulties. Modern science is showing that it does, indeed, have some serious pharmacological capabilities. In fact, its primary active agent, curcumin, has anti-inflammatory properties as strong as prescription medications like hydrocortisone and over-the-counter painkillers like ibuprofen.[104] But while these medications can lead to ulcer formation and liver damage, curcumin has no such adverse effects.

Its anti-inflammatory action makes curcumin an excellent adjunct to treatment for a broad range of inflammation-based illnesses such as osteoarthritis, nonulcer dyspepsia (abdominal discomfort), inflammatory bowel disease, and rheumatoid arthritis; it may also be useful in preventing cancer and heart disease.[105, 106] As we discussed in Chapter 2, chronic low-grade inflammation may underlie much of the pathology contributing to the health risks associated with obesity. Given the amount of information on turmeric's health benefits, let's look into its potential for helping you keep the weight off and why I chose it as a superfood for the Gut Balance Revolution approach to a lean metabolism.

Curcumin has been shown to reduce intestinal inflammation, improve gut barrier function, and decrease the translocation of harmful bacterial by-products from the gut into systemic circulation (endotoxemia). Plus, it calms down the inflammatory and immune responses–important to a number of intestinal conditions as well as obesity.[107]

In fact, a number of studies performed on laboratory animals support the contention that curcumin improves the loss of body weight, increases basal metabolism, blocks adipogenesis (fat creation), facilitates the regression of fat cell mass, and reduces inflammatory markers.[108–110]

Inflammation is one of the villains driving the overweight and obesity epidemics in this country. It disrupts critical pathways involved in energy metabolism and injures a vast array of systems, producing many complications throughout the body.[111] Therapies that reduce inflammation can help derail the vicious cycle of weight gain and chronic illness.

Fat cells, of course, aren't simply innocent bystanders when you gain weight. They not only grow in size but produce and release proinflammatory, fat-forming molecules called adipokines (fat cell–derived cytokines) that have a broad array of deleterious effects on metabolism. They also influence the hormones leptin and adiponectin, which are directly involved in energy metabolism.

Leptin is secreted by your fat cells; circulating levels of it are directly proportional to the amount of body fat you have. When you become obese, your body becomes resistant to the actions of leptin (a condition called leptin resistance), which leads your fat cells to secrete even more of it. This not only causes you to feel hungrier (leptin stimulates appetite) but also further inflames your body. Studies demonstrate that leptin has proinflammatory effects that promote obesity,[112] and it's also been recently linked to disruptions in the intestinal barrier, already compromised in the development of obesity. Put simply, gaining fat sets off a vicious hormonal cycle encouraging your body to pack on ever more fat. Not a pretty picture.

What does all this have to do with turmeric? In cell cultures, curcumin prevents the damage to the intestinal barrier by leptin.[113] Curcumin supplementation lowers leptin levels while raising serotonin and tryptophan, all of which enhances satiety and lowers appetite.[114] Curcumin improves insulin resistance[115] by increasing adiponectin. Adiponectin, involved in insulin sensitivity, lessens inflammatory responses and influences numerous other metabolic pathways. When you're overweight or obese, you're most likely deficient in adiponectin because inflammation inhibits its secretion by fat cells. This contributes to insulin resistance. In obesity-engineered mice, adiponectin intervention can reverse insulin resistance. That curcumin increases your blood levels of this important hormone naturally is an impressive feat indeed. Additionally, curcumin blocks a key pathway in the inflammatory cascade called nuclear factor kappa B, or NF-κB. NF-κB controls the transcription of DNA involved in regulating immune responses, inflammation, infections, and other related processes.

But the good news doesn't end there. Curcumin prevents the damaging effects of blood sugar on tissue systems called glycation (the process by which glucose binds to proteins and interrupts enzyme systems and/or lipids and can compromise the integrity of cellular membranes).[116] Curcumin regulates key factors involved in fat cell gene expression, signaling, proliferation, and differentiation; fat cell programmed death (called apoptosis).[117, 118] (By the way, ginger–a Phase 1 superfood–has similar effects to curcumin on a cellular level, which is why these two related spices are primo to use for fat-burning.[119])

Curcumin is also good for cardiovascular health, and it helps modulate lipid metabolism. In fact, it acts much like statin medications–with none of the risks. It inhibits lipid synthesis and storage and stimulates fatty acid degradation. It also lowers bad cholesterol.[120] There's evidence that long-term intake of curcumin suppresses the growth of atherosclerotic lesions just as well as the statin medication lovastatin in mice fed a high-cholesterol diet.[121]

Similar findings can be seen in trials on humans. A study published in the *Indian Journal of Physiology and Pharmacology* gave 10 volunteers 500 milligrams of curcumin a day for 7 days. After only a week, their blood levels of oxidized cholesterol (one of the primary markers of later heart disease) dropped a whopping 33 percent.[122] Meanwhile, their overall cholesterol dropped 11.63 percent and their HDL increased by 29 percent.[123] Turmeric may also protect your brain. Studies have shown that it boosts immunity in Alzheimer's patients, removing amyloid plaques that are indicative of the disease.[124]

Perhaps the best thing about this healing spice is that it's so easy to incorporate in your diet. Buy a bottle of turmeric and experiment. Add it to whole grains and eggs; sprinkle it on chicken or pork before sautéing. You can even mix it with yogurt and make a delicious basting sauce for meats. This spice knows no bounds in terms of culinary applications, and its healing properties should ensure its place in your spice cabinet.

10. VINEGAR

The first writings referring to vinegar date back to about 5000 BC, when the Sumerians of Babylonia used ferments from unattended grape juice as a cleaning agent. If they hadn't let it sit so long, they could have had a nice glass of wine instead! Over the ages, historical figures have found clever uses for this strongly acidic fermentation by-product.[125] The first medicinal use of vinegar was ascribed to Hippocrates, the father of modern medicine, who used vinegar beginning around 420 BC to sterilize wounds, and he advocated that patients drink it for medicinal benefits. Drinking vinegar is mentioned in both the Bible and Talmud. During the Black Plague in Europe and on the battlefields of World War I, vinegar was used to clean wounds and save lives. In traditional medicine, vinegar has been used to treat a wide range of disorders from dropsy to poison ivy, from croup to stomachache and even diabetes.[126]

In a recent study published in *Diabetes Care*, vinegar was shown to have positive effects on insulin sensitivity in folks with insulin resistance.[127] Researchers found that vinegar may have physiological effects similar to the medication metformin, a drug given to diabetics to increase insulin sensitivity. There's also some evidence that the acetic acid in vinegar slows the passage of food down your digestive tract, making you feel fuller longer.

From the French *vin aigre* for "sour wine," vinegar is the result of alcohol (or other solutions of fermentable sugars) being exposed to oxygen, allowing the growth of *Acetobacter*, which ferments the alcohol into acetic acid. It was once believed that real vinegar couldn't be made without a mother of vinegar–a SCOBY not unlike the one in kefir (though it more closely resembles the disklike SCOBY of kombucha). While a mother of vinegar will expedite the process, it isn't needed. Simply leave wine, cider, sake, or any one of a number of other concoctions out on the counter and you'll eventually end up with vinegar. Wine produces wine vinegar, cider produces cider vinegar, and so forth.

Vinegar, like the other probiotic superfoods we've considered, is a paradise for healthy bacteria. Unpasteurized vinegar (that's what you want to look for) contains a great number of vitamins and minerals. In fact, some vinegars may have as many as 50 critical nutrients, including those that come from the original fruit or wine from which they were fermented.

In the 1970s, apple cider vinegar was promoted as a popular weight-loss agent, especially among bodybuilders, though there were no formal studies showing its efficacy. Other cultures have adopted the practice of using vinegar as a weight-loss agent. North African women, for example, have used apple cider vinegar to achieve weight loss for generations.[128] However, a recent report of a Moroccan 15-year-old female with dental erosion from the daily consumption of a glass of *undiluted* apple cider vinegar raises a red flag for the injudicious use of this ferment.

But it's not just North Africans who use vinegar to control weight. *Kurozu*, black vinegar produced from unpolished rice, is a popular weight-loss product in Japan, where fermented rice vinegar is also used for hyperlipidemia and even cancer.

There may be something to this folk tradition. Research reported in the journal *Lipids in Health and Disease* found this traditional fermented beverage blocked lipid absorption from the gut by inhibiting the pancreatic enzyme lipase.[129] These investigators showed that kurozu shrinks fat cells. A Japanese-based study showed similar results. Vinegar intake at both 1 or 2 tablespoons daily was shown to reduce body weight, body fat mass, and serum triglyceride levels in obese subjects.[130]

A recent study from the University of Malmö in Sweden provides some clues as to why vinegar may improve satiety and facilitate weight loss. Doctors there developed a well-designed study in which diabetics with gastroparesis–slow stomach emptying– drank very diluted vinegar (2 tablespoons in a glass of water) for 2 weeks, then switched to plain water for another 2 weeks. The results showed that the vinegar further delayed gastric emptying. As we learned in Chapter 4, gastrointestinal motility abnormalities have been observed in those with obesity.[131] And it's been observed that obese individuals experience accelerated gastric emptying, which hastens the delivery of sugars from food into the bloodstream—stimulating more fat-forming insulin. Vinegar, by delaying and slowing down gastric emptying, may promote a sense of fullness for longer periods and help balance blood sugar. Only a clinical trial, however, will verify this observation.

Another study that may support the folk-medicine use of vinegar for weight loss comes from a recent report in the journal *Food Chemistry*. It showed vinegar produced by tomatoes suppressed fat cell differentiation and fat accumulation in obese rats.[132]

As a side note, the acetic acid in vinegar may play a role in facilitating weight loss above and beyond its probiotic effect.[133]

Go for oil and vinegar on salads (or make some of the delicious salad dressing recipes you'll find in Chapter 11), drizzle it on steamed veggies, or even add it to fish or meat. You can learn how to make vinegar sodas called shrubs—they're delicious gut-healing tonics.

Add plenty of these 10 superfoods in Phase 2, and you'll give your gut microbiome that extra boost it needs to help you develop a lean metabolism, lose weight, and remain healthy for life. Don't forget, we've added lots of these foods to the recipes for this phase, and I definitely encourage you to try some of them out.

LOOKING AHEAD

You'll be done with Phase 2 when you've achieved your goal weight. For some of you, that may mean sticking with this part of the program for a month or two; for others, it may be longer. Whatever the case, Phase 2 is a healthy long-term eating plan designed to help you achieve optimal weight by rebalancing your gut microbiome. The superfoods you learned about in this chapter will help you do that.

Once you've achieved your weight-loss goals, it will be time to shift to Phase 3. The nutritional program in that phase is designed to help you sustain optimal weight for life while providing the flexibility to indulge in the occasional treat. At the heart of Phase 3 are the Mediterranean and Baltic Sea diets—arguably the two best-studied diets for long-term health and weight loss.

CHAPTER 8

Phase 3: Renew

KEEP YOUR FRIENDLY FLORA— AND YOU—HEALTHY FOR LIFE

What is the best way to help a garden thrive? Does it take around-the-clock vigilance? Incessant watering? Aggressive fertilization with chemicals? Loads of herbicides and pesticides to kill weeds and pests?

None of the above! When it comes to gardens, sustainability is the name of the game. The ecological systems that succeed in the real world for the long term—whether it's a micro ecosystem like the vegetable garden in your backyard or a gigantic ecosystem like the Amazon rain forest—don't require massive work, chemical inputs, or constant vigilance to maintain. They thrive when nature's own strategies are used to sustain them—natural fertilizers, biodiversity to keep pests under control, periodic strategic watering, a little weeding, and some gentle nurturing are far more effective ways to sustain ecosystems.

The same is true of your gut microbiome and the larger ecosystem of your body. Trying to stick to an unsustainable dietary discipline won't keep you healthy and fit, just as massive doses of antibiotics and other medications won't cure the chronic illness epidemic we're facing in this country. These practices are unsustainable. We need a different approach to health and weight maintenance, one that's gentler, more realistic, and more applicable in our daily lives.

The Gut Balance Revolution isn't just about losing weight for swimsuit season and gaining it back around the holidays, it's about keeping it off for life while enjoying a diet that's sustainable for the long term. It's about seeking out a way of life that will help you achieve optimal health for good.

The problem with many popular diets is that they focus only on short-term weight loss—lose 7 pounds in 7 days. I know that sounds like an oxymoron—after all, why else would you go on a diet if you didn't want to lose a few pounds ASAP? But hear me out.

There are a million ways to drop a few pounds in the short term. You could restrict calories or carbs. You could fast. You could only drink liquids. You could try diet pills. You could even try one of the more bizarre fad diets like the grapefruit juice or cabbage soup diet that were popular in the 1980s. The cabbage soup diet limits food choices to veggies, fruits, and cabbage soup, so dieters lose water weight, then quickly rebound, creating a higher body weight set point, as discussed in Chapter 1. This means your body's metabolism is adjusted to maintain a higher weight than prior to dieting–a rebound phenomenon seen with yo-yo dieting. The grapefruit diet, which has been around since the Great Depression, also permits some nonstarchy veggies, emphasizes high protein intake with fish and some meats, and restricts sugars and carbs–it's a modified Atkins diet with grapefruit, eaten with every meal, as the main carbohydrate. The hypothesis–that grapefruit is fat-burning–has no science to support it. Instead, the low-calorie (800 kilocalories a day) and ketogenic aspects of the diet drive weight loss.[1] So barring the obviously ridiculous (the Twinkie diet or the beer and ice cream diet–yes, these are real), you can shed a few pounds using any number of popular diets. Dropping a few pounds for a couple weeks or even a couple of months is achievable for most people. You probably know this from experience.

The problem isn't weight loss. It's *weight maintenance.* That's precisely what this phase of the program is all about. By the time you come to Phase 3, you should be at your goal weight. So the big question is, how do you keep the weight off for the long term?

MOST DIETS DON'T WORK BECAUSE THEY *CAN'T* WORK

Most diets are unsustainable. That word gets bandied about a lot, so let's be clear about what it means. If something's unsustainable, it literally *cannot* be maintained forever. You cannot fast forever. You cannot drink grapefruit juice and exclude other wholesome foods that feed your good gut flora and expect to be healthy. You know from Chapter 4 that very low-carb diets (under 50 grams of carbs daily) tend not to work for most people in the long run, so you can't call them sustainable. And indefinitely keeping your caloric intake too low will cause your body to (1) respond with powerful hormonal and biochemical messages that make it nearly impossible to resist eating and (2) lower your metabolism so you burn *fewer* calories. Neither of these options keeps the weight off for good.

The approach of this book is different. It leverages the best data we have on what helps people lose weight and keep it off for life. I specifically designed it as a three-phase system to take advantage of this science, and I walk you through a sequence of steps that allow you to lose weight and recondition your gut microbiome in a healthy, achievable way. As you'll learn, this multiphasic approach is beginning to be tested and has shown excellent early success.

Now that you're in Phase 3, a brief recap will help you see my logic for building this program the way I did. Phase 1 was designed to be a 30-day low-carb, low-FODMAP, higher-protein ketogenic induction that would rapidly reduce inflammation, balance blood sugar, and till the soil of your inner garden while facilitating weight loss. I decided on this approach because ketogenic diets are an excellent way to jump-start weight loss, and reducing FODMAPs has been shown to facilitate a reduction in digestive symptoms (especially small intestinal bacterial overgrowth, or SIBO) and improve gut microbiome biodiversity. Unfortunately, this diet is difficult to maintain for long, and it may lower your intestine's bifidobacteria counts if you remain on it for extended periods. Phase 2 was developed to gradually enhance your healthy carb intake while diversifying your gut microbiome by focusing on pre- and probiotic foods packed with healthy bacteria. This critical step to weight loss is validated by the scientific literature, though it's been largely overlooked in popular diet books to date.

My mission with Phase 3 is to present you with a way of eating that allows you to maintain your weight loss for life. To do this, I dove into the scientific literature and found that such a diet is possible—and I discovered *tons* of scientific evidence proving its benefits, including weight loss and better health. In this chapter, you'll learn all about it. It's a traditional, flexible eating program filled with mouthwatering health-promoting foods to boot. First, I want to dig into this issue of weight maintenance a little more.

WEIGHT MAINTENANCE: THE NAME OF THE GAME

When you began the Gut Balance Revolution, you were probably more interested in weight loss than weight maintenance. That makes sense—you most likely had some pounds to lose. But by the time you start Phase 3, you will have achieved your goal weight. The next step is keeping the weight off, and that's where the real challenge begins.

How do we know if a diet works? Although there's no universally accepted definition of successful weight-loss maintenance, we all agree that the benchmark for a successful program isn't about short-term weight reduction. Losing a few pounds is nice, but keeping the weight off is the goal, and there are very little data about how successful popular diets are in the long run.

A Danish systematic review looked at 898 studies on weight-loss programs published between 1931 and 1999.[2] They defined successful dieters as those who kept all their weight off or maintained a minimum weight loss of 20 to 24 pounds for 3 years or more. One-third of the studies originally slated for review had to be thrown out because they didn't follow people this long. Of those that remained, few were designed well enough to provide meaningful data. At the end of the day, only 17 studies—a mere 2 percent of the total—held up to the Danish researchers' scrutiny and were included for analysis, although only 3 of these were well-designed randomized trials. What did these 17 studies show? Of the 3,030 participants, only about 15 percent—about 450 people—were considered successful dieters. Important indicators for success: Those who combined diet with group therapy had the best results for long-term weight maintenance, with a success rate of 27 percent. And those who were actively followed by their clinics experienced a higher success rate (19 percent) than those who weren't (10 percent). Behavior modification also appeared to have a positive effect on weight maintenance. (I'll explore this concept of connection, support, and behavior modification and more in Chapter 10.)

Another group of scientists from the University of Kentucky took a different approach to studying the efficacy of long-term weight-loss programs. Rather than identifying success or failure rates of dieters, they completed a meta-analysis of 29 studies done in the United States in which participants were guided through a structured weight-loss program for more than 2 years. Their objective was to determine the average weight loss a person might experience on one of these programs.[3]

They found that after 5 years, the average overweight or obese person would keep off an average of 6 pounds using the protocols studied. This may not seem like much, but, as the authors pointed out, people *not* on a diet program like this may gain weight. One of the control studies used showed that the average person gained 14 pounds over 5 years.

Think these criteria of long-term weight loss are too stringent? Some scientists would agree with you. A growing constituency of medical professionals believes that a good definition of successful weight loss/maintenance would be losing 5 to 10 percent of your body weight on purpose and *keeping the weight off for at least 1 year.*[4] Why 5 to 10 percent? Because in overweight or obese people, dropping 10 percent of body weight results in significant reductions in their risk for type 2 diabetes and cardiovascular disease.[5]

But this isn't as easy as it sounds. For example, if you're 165 pounds, dropping 10 percent of your body weight will mean losing 16.5 pounds. That's a lot of weight to lose. Keeping it off for a full year is no easy feat in the best of circumstances. To do it, you have to change your body weight set point as we discussed in Chapter 1. You have to reset the metabolic control mechanisms to be *balanced* at 148 pounds instead of 165. Your body at 148 pounds should leave you with an appetite to consume an amount of energy equal to your adjusted metabolic rate. When you try to do this with the latest unsustainable instant-weight-loss fad diet, it's all but impossible. You know what happens–you've probably experienced it. You lose a combination of muscle and water and perhaps some fat, but your percentage of body fat doesn't fall significantly–in fact, you look more flabby! Then you fall off the wagon, because these diets are impossible to maintain–your appetite is driving you to eat more so you weigh 165 pounds again. You yo-yo, moving your body weight set point and consequently your appetite even higher and making weight loss that much more difficult the next time around. And the cycle continues.

This may sound like grim news. On some level it is, but not in the ways you might think. What these studies really tell us is that we need more good research in the fields of nutrition and weight loss. The fact that only 1.8 percent of the 898 studies done over the course of 6 decades were of sufficient quality to be included by the Danish researchers in their systematic review is testament to a sad truth: Much of the research in the field of weight loss is suboptimal. Most of us working in this field would like to see a sequence of large randomized controlled trials comparing diets over long periods of time. Unfortunately, this is easier said than done. Studies like this are expensive and difficult to conduct; the compliance rate is often low and the dropout rate is high as people inevitably tire of the eating regimen they've been assigned.

We also need realistic expectations. Participant compliance has been a limiting factor in past studies. After all, if people who have agreed to be part of a scientific study won't stick to the diet, how likely is it that average Americans will? Probably not likely at all. To move the needle on the obesity epidemic, we must develop realistic eating programs that are *actually* sustainable, and we need to think about providing support through behavioral change, social intervention, and lifestyle alteration–factors repeatedly shown to influence weight and health outcomes.

We don't know what the perfect diet is for every person on the planet. (There probably isn't one.) We don't know, with 100 percent certainty, which of the thousands of diets work best for long-term weight loss. We don't know exactly how much weight the average person will lose on any given diet program. That may seem like a lot of uncertainty, but there are *many* things we do know.

We know that some diets don't work because they *can't* work. They can't work because they aren't sustainable. That's because (1) they don't provide your body and your gut microbiome the nutrients they need to maintain optimal health and weight, and/or (2) they don't provide the needed flexibility that allows you to follow the diet in your everyday life–and to enjoy the food you eat. And I believe that enjoyment is important in order to maintain a healthy diet.

We also know that the obesity epidemic is a relatively recent phenomenon, corresponding with the advent of highly processed foods packed with sugar, starch, inflammatory fats, and salt. Of course, correlation doesn't equal causation, but here the correlation is close enough to raise an eyebrow, which leads me to my next point.

For millennia, human beings thrived on a wide variety of diets, and obesity in most cultures across the world was rare or unknown. What can we learn from these traditional styles of eating that we can apply in our modern lives to mitigate our weight problems and the chronic illnesses associated with them? As it turns out, there is a lot we can learn. Some of the best-researched diets for long-term health and weight loss also happen to feature traditional patterns of eating that remained relatively stable until about the last 60 years. These are the diets we need to turn to in our quest to find a flexible way of eating–not a diet–that will allow us to keep weight off for the long term, reduce our risk of chronic illness, and provide the delicious foods we crave to keep body and soul together.

THE HERITAGE OF THE HUMAN DIET

The diets with the best data supporting long-term health and weight maintenance are what are sometimes called "heritage diets." The two that I'll focus on here (primarily because the data on them are excellent) are the Mediterranean and Baltic Sea diets, but there are many heritage diets in cultures from Africa to Asia to South America and beyond. These diets constitute centuries-old traditional ways of eating long associated with spectacular health and optimal weight. The beauty of heritage diets doesn't end there. These diets not only improve health but offer a way of eating that's delicious, enjoyable, socially connected, and relaxed. They bring pleasure to the experience of food.

A fascinating nonprofit organization called Oldways has been promoting heritage diets (and the Mediterranean diet, or MedDiet, in particular) as a healthy way of eating for more than 2 decades. Back in 1993, Oldways teamed up with the World Health Organization and the Center for Nutritional Epidemiology at the Harvard School of Public Health to review the implications of traditional diets for public health. (We'll look at some of the data they collected.) One of their objectives was to develop a series of food pyramids reflecting the dietary patterns of cultures around the world. The food pyramids you found in Phases 1 and 2 were inspired by these. For Phase 3, Oldways inspired

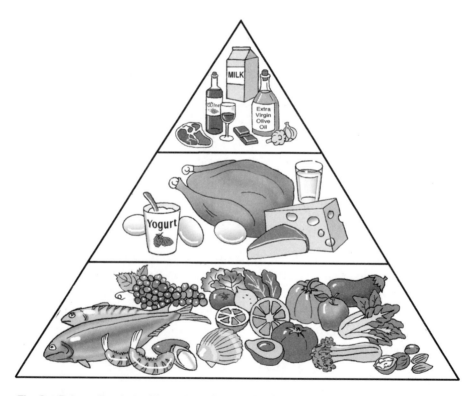

The Gut Balance Revolution Phase 3 Food Pyramid: This figure prioritizes foods in Phase 3, the renewal phase. Foods that are limited are at the top of the pyramid (i.e., alcoholic beverages—beer, wine—lean red meats (wild game preferred), coffee, dark chocolate, milk, and extra-virgin olive oil. Cheeses, yogurt, kefir, eggs, and poultry from the middle of the pyramid. Nuts, seeds, beans, green tea, herbs and spices, fruits, vegetables, seafood, wild fish, and vegetable poultry soups are at the base of the pyramid.

my adaptation shown opposite of their Mediterranean Diet Pyramid from that conference. It illustrates the basic principles of this healthy way of eating.

This is among the best graphic representations of a healthy human diet–far superior to the old US Food Pyramid or the new ChooseMyPlate initiative. For one thing, it's far simpler. For another, it organizes foods into meaningful groups and illustrates a reasonable way to eat–placing vegetables and whole grains at the bottom, fish and seafood right above them, chicken and dairy products (especially fermented dairy) in the next tier, and topping the pyramid with lean red meats (wild game preferred) and sweets–foods we should eat less of overall.

Oldways has published heritage diet pyramids for African, Asian, and Latino eating as well. Each is interesting in its own right, and I respect each of these traditional ways of eating. However, I wanted everything in the Gut Balance Revolution to have a strong foundation in science and clinical application, so I elected to build Phase 3 on two of the best-studied heritage diets around: the Mediterranean diet and the Baltic Sea diet. In the remainder of this chapter, we'll review the science supporting these diets and the similarities between them (and other traditional nutrition plans). Then I'll explain what foods you should forget, eat fewer of, and focus on in Phase 3.

Let's take a look at the most scientifically validated diet for long-term health and weight maintenance.

THE MEDDIET

The MedDiet isn't really a "diet" per se. Rather, it's a pattern of eating embraced by many people in olive-growing areas throughout the Mediterranean, including those in Greece, Crete, Italy, southern France, and Spain. Granted, these eating patterns have become less common in the last 60 years, thanks to the advent and worldwide influence of the modern, highly processed Western diet. And different studies focus more on the dietary patterns in specific geographical regions. But taking a broad overview of the area, we find the following are consistent, healthful trends.

- Abundant plant foods, including fruit, vegetables, bread, other forms of cereal grains, potatoes, beans, nuts, and seeds
- Fresh fruit as the typical daily dessert
- Olive oil as the principal source of fat
- Cheese and yogurt as the principal dairy products–these sources come from a wide array of animals including goats, sheep, and cows
- Fish in moderate to high amounts
- Poultry as the primary source of animal protein in moderate to small amounts
- Weekly consumption of eggs

- Low to moderate red wine intake
- Occasional inclusion of lean red meat (wild game preferred)
- Occasional sweet treats
- Overall, minimally processed, seasonally fresh, locally grown foods

Another factor important in the Mediterranean way of eating is the social and environmental context of meals. Delicious, artfully prepared meals are eaten slowly and enjoyed with friends and family, offering a relaxing respite from the workday and providing the social connections on which we thrive. Lunch is typically followed by a siesta, offering another opportunity for rest and relaxation and optimal digestion. These connections between lifestyle, diet, stress, and the overall health of the mind, body, and spirit are largely missing from today's world. We no longer connect the way we eat with the way we live. It's been my experience (and the data support this) that this disconnection between how we eat, interact, and live is a major contributing factor to the epidemic of weight gain and chronic illness in the Western world. We'll explore these connections more in Chapter 10, when we discuss how to live a healthy, gut-balancing lifestyle.

Exercise was also a key component of this traditional way of eating and living. Before the 1960s, those in this region were engaged in farm or kitchen work.[6] The exercise they received doing their daily chores was another contributing factor to the healthy Mediterranean way of life.

The data prove that the health outcomes of eating and living this way are spectacular. In fact, when Oldways in partnership with the Harvard School of Public Health developed the Mediterranean Diet Pyramid, they found that people in Crete, much of the rest of Greece, and southern Italy who ate this way had some of the highest adult life expectancies in the world, with relatively low rates of coronary heart disease, certain cancers, and a few other diet-related chronic illnesses. The MedDiet is clearly associated with big improvements in cardiovascular health. Notable studies, such as the PREDIMED (Prevención con Dieta Mediterránea) trial and the Lyon Diet Heart Study,[7-9] confirm that the MedDiet provides cardiovascular benefits and decreases all-cause mortality.

For example, in the PREDIMED trial, a randomized controlled 5-year study conducted in Spain, researchers assigned 7,447 people ages 55 to 80—more than half of them women—to one of three diets: a regular Western diet, the MedDiet supplemented with olive oil, or the MedDiet supplemented with nuts.[10] Originally scheduled for 10 years, the scientists elected to stop the study halfway through because their data were so powerfully in favor of the MedDiet that there were ethical concerns about keeping the control group on the regular Western diet. The groups on both versions of the MedDiet were 70 to 72 percent *less likely* to have a heart attack or stroke or to die from any other cause than the Western diet group.

A meta-analysis conducted by the Cochrane Collaboration reached similar conclusions.

Scientists reviewed 11 trials that included data on 52,044 participants and found that those eating a MedDiet saw reductions in total cholesterol, LDL, and blood pressure.[11]

While there are many reasons the MedDiet supports heart health, we know that one key component is olive oil—one of the Phase 3 superfoods you'll learn more about in the next chapter. Olive oil has been shown to enhance vascular endothelial function (cardio-vascular disease oftentimes commences with dysfunction of the cells that line the vas-culature, aka endothelium) and reduce blood lipids as well as the risk of atherosclerosis. Plus, the phytochemicals in olive oil have numerous anti-inflammatory, antioxidant, hypolipidemic properties.[12] You'll find more details in the next chapter, but for now suf-fice it to say extra-virgin olive oil (EVOO) is among the healthiest foods for your heart.

The MedDiet has also been shown to profoundly improve metabolic syndrome and type 2 diabetes. In another Spanish study, researchers randomly divided 3,541 people into three groups—they ate a MedDiet supplemented with EVOO, a MedDiet supple-mented with nuts, or a standard low-fat diet.[13] The folks on the MedDiet did not alter their physical activity in any way. The conclusion? Both groups on the MedDiet had a reduced risk of developing type 2 diabetes. Another study from the Department of Nutritional Sciences at the University of Connecticut reviewed recent data on a wide variety of diets and their impact on metabolic syndrome—a cluster of symptoms includ-ing central obesity, hypertension, high fasting glucose, and increased inflammation that puts people at increased risk for heart disease, type 2 diabetes, and other chronic illnesses.[14] They concluded that the MedDiet, coupled with regular exercise, had the biggest impact on metabolic syndrome. Other studies have demonstrated that the Med-Diet reduces inflammatory markers including those generated by fat cells (adipokines) in those with metabolic syndrome, even in the absence of weight loss.[15, 16] Of course, the effect is even greater in those who *do* lose weight. The MedDiet has been shown to improve nonalcoholic fatty liver disease; in a recent study, adherence to this diet was associated with lower abdominal fat gain.[17, 18]

There's mounting evidence that the MedDiet has a positive impact on the health of your gut microbiome. A small study working with nine overweight/obese men and women revealed that utilization of the MedDiet for 2 weeks decreased serum triglyceride levels by 14 percent and LDL by 12 percent while increasing the overall gut microbiome biodiversity and richness.[19] Little wonder—the MedDiet is rich in fermented milk prod-ucts packed with probiotics and has tons of prebiotic foods and fiber that feed a healthy gut microbiome.

The MedDiet also has powerful anti-inflammatory benefits and is packed with pre-biotics that enrich the diversity of the gut microbiome. It's not surprising that evidence suggests the MedDiet alleviates chronic diseases associated with inflammation and gut dysbiosis. It appears to provide protection against diseases associated with chronic inflammation, including metabolic syndrome, atherosclerosis, cancer, diabetes, obesity, pulmonary diseases, and even cognition disorders.[20] The gut microbiome has a strong influence on mood and behavior; dysbiosis has been linked to autism, mood and behavior disorders, and more.[21] The MedDiet has decreased depression in high-risk people with chronic lung disease.[22] Likewise, the PREDIMED study showed that the MedDiet supplemented with nuts could reduce risk of depression in patients with type 2 diabetes.[23] There is some preliminary evidence to suggest that the MedDiet may improve cognition and protect against senile dementia due to its anti-inflammatory properties and its biodiversifying influence on the gut microbiome.[24, 25]

But more to the point of this book, a number of studies indicate that the MedDiet helps facilitate weight loss and maintenance. Canadian researchers, for example, evaluated 77 women, who were randomly assigned to one of two diets (the MedDiet or a standard diet) for 12 weeks and attended seven individual sessions with a dietitian. Small but significant decreases in body weight and waist circumference were observed after the study's completion. Increased consumption of legumes, nuts, and seeds and decreased consumption of sweets were significantly associated with decreased waist circumference. As part of a Med-Diet program, an increase in consumption of legumes, nuts, and seeds and a decrease in the consumption of sweets were associated with some beneficial changes across the board.[26]

In another study, 31 overweight-to-obese participants took part in the Spanish Ketogenic Mediterranean Diet (SKMD), which incorporated extra-virgin olive oil as the principal source of fat; moderate red wine, green vegetables, and salads as the main carbohydrate sources; and fish as the main protein source.[27] What made this study noteworthy? The SKMD was an *unlimited* calorie program. Participants were allowed to eat as much as they wanted; they were simply asked to follow the SKMD program. The result? An *extremely* significant reduction in body weight, body mass index, systolic blood pressure, diastolic blood pressure, total cholesterol, and glucose. There was a significant reduction in triglycerides and LDL cholesterol and a significant increase in HDL, the good cholesterol. The SKMD promoted weight loss, improved lipid profiles, lowered blood pressure, and decreased fasting blood glucose levels.

The bottom line: When it comes to sustainable diets that show improved health in the long run, few diets compete with the eating patterns long embraced by the people in the Mediterranean. There are similarities between these eating patterns and the diets of many traditional cultures. The historical evidence, scientific data, my clinical experience, and common sense all point to this way of eating–one that focuses on real, healthy whole foods–as the way human beings were meant to eat.

PROOF FOR THE GUT BALANCE REVOLUTION METHOD OF PERMANENT WEIGHT LOSS

Following the MedDiet in Phase 3 will not only help you cultivate a rich and biodiverse gut microflora but will also deliver a host of health benefits for a long, healthy life. Growing evidence confirms my weight-loss method of using the ketogenic diet (Phase 1) to induce weight loss, followed by gut microbiome restoration (Phase 2) and then a MedDiet (Phase 3) for maintenance and continued health promotion. This combination is the best approach for long-term weight loss and maintenance while providing numerous health benefits.[28] A recent study at the University of Padua saw magnificent long-term weight and health outcomes using a diet similar to the one found in this book. Though the study was small (only 89 subjects were followed over a period of 12 months), the results were extremely impressive. Over the course of 1 year, the average participant experienced:

- Significant decrease in weight–an average of 33 pounds
- 10 percent loss of body fat
- Reduction in blood pressure–systolic blood pressure was down 7 points, diastolic 4 points
- Decreased LDL and increased HDL–the good cholesterol
- Reduction in triglycerides
- Reduction in blood glucose

In addition, there was 90 percent compliance with the diet (unheard of with any diet program) and 88 percent of participants maintained for 1 year. The poststudy analysis found that those who didn't achieve successful weight loss hadn't complied with the program and went back to eating high-glycemic junk foods.

The magnitude of change, and the fact that people maintained their weight loss for a year after the study was completed, is compelling. Few studies have shown these kinds of results in as few as 12 months.

The science is beginning to prove what I've seen in my practice: A multiphasic approach to weight loss may be the way of the future. My only beef with the study? They didn't measure effects of their program based on gut microbiome health!

The Baltic Sea Diet

The other heritage diet we'll look at, the Baltic Sea diet, also has sound data to support it, and a validated tool called the Baltic Sea Diet Score (BSDS) has been developed by scientists to help judge adherence to the diet. The BSDS is based on the following nine dietary factors:

1. High intake of Nordic fruits like apples, pears, and berries
2. High intake of Nordic veggies like tomatoes, cucumbers, leafy vegetables, roots, cabbages, peas
3. Low-fat and fat-free milk
4. Nordic cereals like rye, oat, and barley

5. Nordic fish–salmon and other freshwater fish

6. Balanced ratio of polyunsaturated fats to saturated and trans fats

7. Low intake of red and processed meat

8. Moderate total fat percentage

9. Low to moderate alcohol intake

You may notice that this diet looks much like the MedDiet except for the use of low-fat and fat-free dairy products and an increased focus on specific groups of fruits and vegetables. Nevertheless, scientists have found that this diet, like the MedDiet, has a profound influence on health.

For example, in one study, researchers looked at food journal data from 4,579 people ages 25 to 74 and scored them based on their adherence to the Baltic Sea diet.[29] After adjusting for factors like age, socioeconomic status, length of education, and other lifestyle factors, they found that those who adhered to the diet most carefully had:

- Increased levels of adiponectin–more adiponectin in the blood is associated with reduced body fat percentage

- Reduced levels of inflammatory markers like interleukin 6 and C-reactive protein

These are the precise kinds of changes that lead to lower weight and lower risk for inflammatory and weight-related health concerns such as type 2 diabetes and heart disease. It appears that increased fruit, vegetable, and whole grain intake and reduced red meat intake associate most clearly with the reduction in inflammation. Moderate alcohol intake also seemed to be a primary dietary factor for reducing inflammation.[30] However, it's important to be aware that alcohol can cause gut dysbiosis and disrupt precious gut barrier function, so it's best to limit your moderate alcohol consumption to Phases 2 and 3 when your gut function is fully restored and you can benefit from some of the beneficial properties of alcoholic beverages.

A Finnish study showed that adherence to the Baltic Sea diet is associated with lower rates of abdominal obesity.[31] Researchers assessed the diet of 4,720 people between the ages of 25 and 74. Their findings were extremely straightforward: The closer participants adhered to the Baltic Sea diet, the less likely they were to be overweight and the less likely they were to carry belly fat. The effect seemed to be slightly stronger in younger age groups. The dietary factors that appeared to have the most effect were Baltic whole grain cereals and moderate alcohol consumption. How can carbs foster weight maintenance? It may be that low-carb dieting decreases your gut bifidobacteria and that whole grains are prebiotic and feed your good gut flora. These are the likely reasons that Baltic whole grain cereals help maintain weight, since they support the fertile soil of your gut's garden of life and promote a lean metabolism. As for alcohol, remember that "the dose is

What's the Real Story with Alcohol?

Alcohol has been villainized as a bad actor in society as abuse can lead to reckless behavior, lethal accidents, and numerous adverse health consequences. However, abundant data show that moderate alcohol consumption (150 milliliters of red wine a day) acts as a drug to improve blood lipid profiles, decrease chances of forming potentially lethal blood clots, increase coronary bloodflow, reduce blood pressure, improve insulin sensitivity and immunity, and decrease serum markers of inflammation.[32] But is it the alcohol itself that provides benefit or some other special properties in alcoholic beverages? Although the jury's still out, we do know that alcoholic beverages have identifiable plant-based nutrients (phytonutrients) that provide clear health benefits. Wine and beer contain many nutrients not related to alcohol, including soluble fiber that feeds your good gut bugs, minerals and vitamins, and polyphenols—which all help you combat disease. Specifically, red wine contains the polyphenol resveratrol, which improves immune function, prevents cancer, and cools down inflammation to help prevent disease. Likewise, beer has the polyphenol xanthohumol, an anti-inflammatory flavonoid regulating the immune system.[33] The more alcohol that a person drinks, the higher the risk of developing digestive tract cancers (mouth, pharynx, larynx, esophagus, colon-rectum, liver) but also female breast.[34] Moderate alcohol consumption may place women at higher risk for breast cancer (10 percent lifetime increased risk and may be related in part to alcohol's effects on estrogen metabolism or even subclinical folate insufficiency as folate requirements are higher in those who consume alcohol).[35]

the poison," but in certain cases, the poison can also be the remedy, depending on the dose. This yin-yang of alcohol reminds me of a process that I learned from Dr. Patrick Hanaway.* He brought to light the term "hormesis," which signifies how a stress to the body at low doses can cause a positive adaptive response but is harmful in higher doses.

The point isn't to determine whether the Baltic Sea diet or the MedDiet is superior. As we've discussed throughout this book, humans have thrived on a wide variety of diets for millennia. In fact, assessment tools like the Baltic Sea Diet Score[36] were developed because we've found that these diets don't always see the same success when they cross over into different cultures. The reasons for this are still obscure, but they likely include genetic predispositions and lifestyle and cultural factors that make adherence to these diets less likely when they are exported to other countries.

---

* Patrick Hanaway, MD, is the medical director, Cleveland Clinic Center for Functional Medicine (IFM)—an organization designed to promote the application of whole-systems practices to prevent and treat chronic disease by emphasizing nutrition and lifestyle-based interventions. Patrick, myself, Dr. Thomas Sult, and Dr. Elizabeth Lipski teach the GI Module at IFM-based symposia and elsewhere. To learn more about IFM, visit functionalmedicine.org.

Can You Stress Your Body to Health?

There's evidence that periodically indulging in low to moderate amounts of harmful substances (such as alcohol) may improve health in the long run. This idea is called hormesis. Gently stressing the body with these substances from time to time puts stress on your cells' power plants—the mitochondria—forcing them to adapt and making them stronger over time. We will discuss in Chapter 10 how interval training results in the division and expansion of fat-burning mitochondria in muscles. Since your mitochondria are your body's energy-producing factories, doing this may generate more energy in the long run. So periodic but limited indulgence can be a good thing. Substances such as curcumin (the curry in Indian food), even in low doses, have hormetic effects and are worthwhile in small amounts.[37] Homeopathy is another classical example of this concept. In homeopathy, "poisons" are given at infinitely low doses to stimulate a healing response.

Alcohol appears to operate according to hormesis as well.[38] Researchers explain it this way: One drink of red wine, beer, or stout provided equivalent increases in plasma antioxidant activity. Three drinks of red wine, beer, or stout provided equivalent increases in plasma prooxidant activity. This may explain, at least in part, the decreased risk of cataract and atherosclerosis from daily consumption of one drink of different types of alcoholic beverages, as well as the increased risk from daily consumption of three drinks of alcoholic beverages. The plasma prooxidant activity appears to be due to ethanol metabolism, whereas the antioxidant activity may be due to the absorption of polyphenols in the beverages. Hormesis may be one factor involved in this dichotomy of alcohol's effects—a true Jekyll and Hyde phenomenon.

In analyzing these data, it's more useful to come to consensus about what a healthy diet might look like for people in the long term.

Is There an Ideal Diet for Humans?

There's probably no one-size-fits-all diet perfect for every person on the planet. But by reviewing the data and comparing the heritage eating styles, we *can* come to a consensus about what dietary factors are involved in weight loss and health. I've identified 10 principles that should be the foundation for a healthy long-term eating program, and I've designed Phase 3 around these principles. Understand them and you'll be on your way toward creating a sustainable, lifelong, healthy eating plan to keep you at your optimal weight. (For more scientific details, refer to the article "Search for the Optimal Diet" that I wrote several years ago for *Nutrition in Clinical Practice*.[39] I was a guest editor for that issue, which discussed the holy grail of health diets and my no-spin-zone analysis and bottom line of what works and what to avoid.)

1. Nutritional Ketosis Works Short Term—Not Long Term

The data make it fairly clear that very low-carb, higher-protein diets that induce nutritional ketosis work as a short-term induction to weight loss. But these diets are difficult to sustain for long, and they may have a negative effect on the gut microbiome if maintained for too long.

Instead, a biphasic (or, as in this book, triphasic) approach seems to work best. By moving from a ketogenic diet in the short term to a Mediterranean/Baltic diet in the long term, you can lose weight and keep it off more effectively while improving many health outcomes. And if you start to backslide and regain weight, you can always go back to a 30-day ketogenic diet and work your way back through Phases 1 through 3.

2. Diets High in Sugar and Processed Carbs Don't Work

One of the problems with the low-fat dogma that has been dominant in our culture since the 1980s is that, in most cases, fat has been replaced with carbohydrates. Though I'm not a proponent of long-term, extremely low-carbohydrate plans, it's clear that carbohydrates—specifically, processed carbohydrates and processed, refined sugar—are the most prevalent dietary demons in the modern Western way of eating. Inflammatory fats run a close second.

While my reading of the data suggests that the inclusion of some low-glycemic-load whole grains in your diet can be part of a healthy way of eating for the long term, I want to be 100 percent clear that I *am not* encouraging you to overdo these foods, and I'm not condoning the overconsumption of carbohydrates.

Rather, it's been my experience clinically—and the data agree—that whole grains can be part of a long-term healthy diet for many. Healthy whole grains are a core part of both the Baltic Sea diet and the MedDiet, and they can be found in other healthy ways of eating the world over. Remember, when it comes to whole grains, portion control is important—the dose makes the poison or the remedy. However, whole grains are not typically the kinds of foods people binge on, so most of you will benefit from adding foods like oat bran, quinoa, and other healthy whole grains to your diet. They increase satiety, your gut bugs love to eat them, and, in moderation, they're a delicious addition to a well-rounded eating plan.

As we'll discuss later in the chapter, you can even "go off your plan" and indulge in an occasional dessert or pizza from time to time once your gut microbiome and metabolism have been rehabilitated and you've achieved your goal weight. I will give you all the details when we talk about taking a "rest" from the program and giving yourself permission to indulge in (but not binge on) your favorite foods from time to time.

The bottom line: Eating processed carbs can be a slippery slope. They can be addictive, and eating too much will upset gut microbioial biodiversity, lead to blood sugar and insulin imbalances, cause the fires of inflammation to burn once more, and set you up to regain weight and lose health. I don't like saying any food is bad, but of the many foods in the typical Western diet, processed carbs are among the most dangerous and insidious. Be wary of them.

3. Prebiotics and Probiotics Play an Important Role

Foods like live-culture yogurt and goat cheese are considered core components of the MedDiet. Little wonder why. These probiotic powerhouses are a wonderful way to balance the gut microbiome and keep your weight down, and good evidence suggests fermented milk products may reduce your risk of a wide variety of chronic illnesses. Vegetable ferments play a less prominent role in Mediterranean cuisine than in some other cultures (Korean and Japanese cuisine, for example), but they still exist. *Giardiniera* is a classic fermented Italian pickle that includes carrots, cauliflower, peppers, and other veggies. Cucumber pickles are known in both Greece and Italy. While probiotic-rich foods may not feature as prominently in the data on the Baltic Sea diet, many Nordic traditions were rich in fermented foods—including *surströmming*, a fermented Baltic herring that is a staple of traditional northern Swedish culture.

Plus, both diets are rich in vegetables and whole grains that have a prebiotic effect on the gut microbiome—and combining probiotic-rich foods with prebiotic vegetable foods is the one-two punch needed to maintain inner ecosystem balance for the long haul. Both these traditional dietary patterns include these types of foods.

4. Focus on Whole Foods

One of the most obvious and profound consistencies among traditional diets like the MedDiet and the Baltic Sea diet is the focus on real, whole, healing foods, not the processed junk food that dominates the modern Western diet. More than any of the other healthy elements of traditional eating, this may be the key differentiating factor.

Science has repeatedly shown the importance of whole foods. For example, a clinical study of 120,887 individuals who were nonobese and free of chronic disease were followed over 20 years to determine the dietary factors associated with weight maintenance and gain.[40] The findings, reported in the *New England Journal of Medicine,* showed that yogurt was the food best associated with maintaining a healthy weight.[41] The consumption of vegetables, whole grains, fruits, and nuts—all superfoods that feed our fat-burning friendly flora—was associated with maintaining healthy weight in ascending order of magnitude. In contrast, eating potato chips, potatoes, sugar-sweetened beverages, unprocessed red meats, and processed meats predicted long-term weight gain in descending order of magnitude.

A proper whole-foods-based diet rich in phytonutrients and pre- and probiotics, along with an active healthy lifestyle, is the best way to maintain a healthy weight. Other lifestyle factors independently associated with weight change in the study above included physical activity, moderate alcohol use (one 3-ounce glass of wine; one can, bottle, or glass of beer; or a 1-ounce shot or drink of hard liquor per day), quitting smoking, good sleep quality, and reduced television watching. The data on the influence of moderate alcohol consumption on weight change appear to vary in studies, perhaps because of technical measures, but I recommend that you wait until Phases 2 and 3 before enjoying an occasional alcoholic drink with your main meal and perhaps more on special occasions. There's little research on the potential benefits of distilled spirits.

The heritage diet of human beings is a whole-foods diet. After all, until about 60 years ago, there was nothing else. Remember that Oldways, the not-for-profit organization whose mission is "to guide people to good health through heritage," has developed food pyramids for traditional African, Asian, and Latino diets in addition to the MedDiet pyramid in this book.[42] While the data don't yet support these diets as a way to maintain health, it's easy to see the similarities between them when you compare these heritage-based diet pyramids. In fact, many of the key factors are the same across the board: lots of fruits and vegetables, moderate whole grains, seafood as a primary protein source, lots of probiotic-based foods like cheese and yogurt, little red meat, and few sweets.

What did these traditional cultures know that we don't? Good question, but it might actually be a matter of what they *didn't know*. Remember that these traditional ways of eating developed in the cradle of civilization, ages before food processing as we know it today existed. Ample evidence shows that when sugary, starchy, processed foods are introduced to these cultures, they begin to experience an explosion of weight gain and chronic illness similar to ours.

Modern food production has its advantages—it's fast, convenient, and accessible. We shouldn't sacrifice this entirely and go back to grinding our grain by hand with a stone mortar and pestle. But in our quest for convenience, we've lost our connection to fundamental truths about what it means to be a biological organism that consumes other biological organisms to live. We're no longer connected to the food we eat or the environment in which it is grown. Divorced from this outer ecology, it's no wonder we've lost contact with our inner ecology. The outcome: imbalance inside and out, driving an epidemic of weight gain and chronic illness.

Looking at traditional ways of eating offers us a connection back to our past that helps us understand and embrace real, whole foods once again. Whether you're in the Paleo crowd, love the MedDiet, or are interested in other traditional eating patterns, one thing is clear: Our ancestors didn't eat Doritos. Ever. Those comestibles were simply unknown. Our forebears wouldn't have recognized as food much of what fills the shelves of your local supermarket.

This transition from a cultural dietary paradigm of healthy whole foods to one built on highly processed foodlike substances has happened *extremely* quickly. Your grandparents and great-grandparents wouldn't have known what Lunchables are, but I'd bet my life your kids do. Even if you never buy those processed-food lunch kits, their friends at school eat them, and your children see commercials for them during afternoon cartoons.

That transition from a world where processed food is unknown to one where it's one of the predominant sources of calories has correlated with the worldwide rise of overweight, obesity, and chronic illnesses such as cardiovascular illness, type 2 diabetes, and more. A mere coincidence? I think not.

I'm not a food extremist. I won't tell you never to buy a can of soup again. But be aware that most of those cans contain your Recommended Dietary Allowance for sodium and then some, as well as a nice dose of sugar and/or HFCS to boot. The more you become aware of the foods you eat, and the more you choose to cook and eat real, whole, healing foods–organic and locally grown when possible–the healthier you'll be and the deeper the connections you will make between who you are, how you feel, and what you eat. This awareness supports your inner ecology as well as the broader ecological system of planet Earth.

Whether it's Mediterranean, Baltic, African, Asian, Latino, or some other traditional food culture, what you'll find at its base is the same: real food. That's the big difference between heritage ways of eating and the modern Western diet. Be aware of it.

5. Add More Fruits and Veggies

Increasing your intake of fruits and vegetables is an easy and delicious way to enhance your health. Studies have shown eating eight servings of veggies daily reduces your risk of heart attack and stroke by as much as 30 percent–and that's only the beginning of the health benefits these phytonutrient-packed plant foods provide. (Phytonutrients are plant-based natural products that provide disease-fighting health benefits.) Other studies have shown that increased fruit and vegetable consumption is associated with a reduction in all-cause mortality,[43] and health benefits directly correlate with an increased consumption of fruits and vegetables.[44] Those studies about the Baltic Sea diet and MedDiet corroborate this. The data are clear. Fruits and vegetables must be at the root of a healthy diet, so visit your produce section first on your next trip to the grocery store.

6. Try Lean Protein and Don't Overdo Red Meat

We've already reviewed why protein is an important part of your diet: It increases satiety, reduces fat production, has thermogenic effects, builds fat-burning lean muscle, and more. Recall that the type of protein you choose is essential. A little lean red meat from time to time is fine. I allow it on Phase 2, and you can keep it in your Phase 3 eating plan. But too much red meat, or too many fatty cuts, is unhealthy. It increases your risk of cardiovascular disease, upsets gut microbiome balance, and creates other problems, as we've discussed in earlier chapters. The Baltic Sea diet, the MedDiet, and *all* of the heritage diet pyramids created by Oldways to date keep red meat to a minimum.

But don't reduce your protein intake overall. In fact, many people should eat *more* protein. Remember that healthy protein sources like fish and chicken are just above fruit, vegetables, and whole grains in the Mediterranean Diet Pyramid. The point isn't to reduce protein, it's to focus on healthier protein options. Two standouts in terms of their satiating effects are whey protein and fish.[45] Fish is not only filled with high-quality, appetite-reducing protein but is also high in omega-3 fats, another critical component of a healthy diet. Whey protein has been used for millennia–Hippocrates, the father of Western medicine, prescribed it to help patients strengthen muscles and enhance their immune function,[46] purposes for which it's still used today.

7. Do Not Fear Fat

The amount of fat in the MedDiet is extraordinary by modern standards, ranging from 28 percent of total calories in southern Italy to as much as 40 percent in Greece. While the Baltic Sea diet may not contain quite as much fat, moderate amounts are still considered key. Those in the Baltic Sea region and those in the Mediterranean don't fear fat, and you shouldn't either.

Of course, the focus must be on healthy fats like olive oil, the main fat source of the MedDiet, not the trashy, inflammatory omega-6 fatty acid–rich fats of the modern Western diet. These inflammatory fats run a close second to processed sugary carbs in my list of dietary demons. The ratio of inflammatory to anti-inflammatory fats is way out of balance in America today, and it's not doing any good to the national waistline or our chronic illness epidemic.

So what fats can you eat? Extra-virgin olive oil (EVVO) is my number one choice. It's one of the key factors leading to the health outcomes we see from the MedDiet, and it's a veritable superfood. It should be your go-to oil for dressing salads and other veggies, sautéing, and other forms of medium-heat cooking. Other healthy fats include canola oil (for high-heat cooking) and coconut oil, avocado oil, and sesame oil (in limited quantities). Naturally, there are the fats in the fish you consume and in healthy plant foods like avocado, chia seeds, flaxseeds, and more. These types of fats should be the ones you focus on, and it's easy to do that by sticking to a whole-foods diet and avoiding overindulging in processed foods, which tend to be loaded with inflammatory fats.

8. Add Plenty of Fat-Burning Herbs and Spices

While herbs and spices aren't a focus in the research on the Mediterranean, Baltic Sea, or other heritage diets, I'm convinced they should be considered. These undervalued, phytonutrient-filled health helpers have nutraceutical properties that modern science is only now beginning to understand. You may remember that in earlier chapters I talked about superfood spices like cinnamon, ginger, cayenne pepper, and turmeric and the extraordinary health benefits they provide. I encourage you to add plenty of spices to your diet. They make food taste better and more enjoyable—and many of them support your fat-burning efforts and your overall health.

The Gut Balance Revolution recipes are packed with these and other healing spices. If you're not sure how to integrate them into your cooking, or if you're looking for delicious recipes that include these healing foods, try out the meal plans and recipes in Chapter 11.

9. For Many, A Little Alcohol Is Your Friend

In the studies we reviewed above on the Mediterranean and Baltic Sea diets, low to moderate intake of alcohol was not only healthy, it was among the most important factors correlating with reduced inflammation and increased health. Fermented beers and red wine have been part of the human heritage for millennia. In fact, in *Beer, Bread, and the Seeds of Change*, Thomas and Carol Sinclair argue that it was the production of beer, *not* bread, that led to the advent of agriculture.[47] We can never know whether or not this is true, but a little alcohol has been repeatedly correlated with a wide range of health benefits with the exception of breast cancer. This excess risk, though, may be reduced by consuming enough folate.[48-50]

So in Phases 2 and 3, enjoy a glass of wine or beer occasionally with your main meal. These fermented beverages nurture your body and your gut microbiome as they relax your spirit.

10. Enjoy Your Food—That's More Important Than You Think

This final point is critically important, yet it's tremendously undervalued by the medical community and, arguably, American society in general. Food is far more than a vehicle for energy and nutrients, though you'd never know this by reading scientific studies about diets that focus only on its nutrient composition and calories.

Food is one of the fundamental joys of life and a foundational element in human civilization. Richard Wrangham, the biological anthropologist from Harvard University, suggests that cooking food was not only critical to the development of human society as we know it but to the evolution of our species. Consuming calories is a necessary activity for all living things, but cooking and eating food are distinctly human. As with other human activities, there's a profound joy, a spiritually nutritive substance to food that goes beyond the vitamins it contains or the kilocalorie of energy it's worth.

Match this fundamental joy of eating with the vital social aspect of human existence, and what you have is the family meal—an institution unfortunately dying in the West. One of the essential features of the MedDiet (and many other heritage diets) is the slow, artfully prepared meal enjoyed with family and friends. Using meals as an opportunity to relax and connect adds another dimension to food's medicinal nature. Food is more than its constituent nutrients. Our way of eating is at the very heart of our species' development. So sit down and enjoy your food with friends and family. It's a wonderful way to deepen the connections between the community of microbes in your gut, the community of friends and family who surround you, and the nourishing food that feeds them both.

These 10 principles are what a healthy human diet is founded on. I'll share exactly what you should favor, what you should eat fewer of, and what you should forget in Phase 3. But all you really need to do is think through these 10 principles as you plan your meals day to day and week to week. There's great flexibility within these parameters. Some people might like to eat a little more animal protein; others may be vegetarians. For some, a higher dose of anti-inflammatory fat like olive oil may satiate hunger and satisfy a craving for rich foods; others may prefer a little less fat. Some may thrive on a few more servings of whole grains weekly than others. Just use these basic rules and tune in to what works for you and what doesn't.

How will you know? Your body will tell you. If you start regaining weight, that's a sign something has gone haywire and it's time to reevaluate your diet. If you begin to experience symptoms (such as digestive upset, joint pain, brain fog, mood imbalances, and others) that disappeared on previous phases, that's another sign. Medical tests like blood pressure, blood glucose levels, and C-reactive protein levels provide additional information. Together, these and other factors indicate how healthy or unhealthy you are and provide a benchmark for manipulating your diet to create optimal health. Pay attention to how the food you eat influences your weight and health and consciously make choices that help you thrive. Stay away from foods that diminish your health, lead to mood and energy imbalances, or cause you to gain weight. The particular foods will change, to some extent, day by day, but as long as you abide by these general criteria, you'll thrive and keep the weight off. There's truly no such thing as a "perfect diet"—any diet that helps you thrive is perfect for you. If you're honest and attentive to the signals your body provides, you'll find that the best diet for you fits somewhere inside these 10 principles through Phase 3 and beyond.

However, for those of you who want a little more detail, let's look more carefully at what you should favor, what you should eat fewer of, and what you should forget on Phase 3.

Don't Just Forget Foods

On Phase 3, you don't technically have to "forget" any foods. One key aspect of this phase is that you can eat off the program from time to time. Indulging in a dessert or having a little pizza once in a while shouldn't affect your weight or long-term health once you've rehabilitated your metabolism. In fact, the guilt some of us associate with "cheating" when eating foods like chocolate cake may actually cause us to gain weight. A fascinating study published in the journal *Appetite* appropriately titled "Chocolate Cake. Guilt or Celebration?" sought to determine if those who feel guilt about their eating behaviors (such as indulging in chocolate cake) actually lost weight and kept it off. The question these scientists asked: Do these guilty feelings have a positive or negative effect? After all, guilt has the potential to motivate behavior change, but it can also lead to feelings of helplessness and loss of control.

Researchers conducted an interesting experiment.[51] They examined whether feelings of guilt or celebration when eating chocolate cake were related to differences in attitudes, perceived control, and intentions to maintain a healthy lifestyle. Then they looked at weight-loss outcomes as they were associated with these feelings over a 3-month and an 18-month period. They found that guilt provided no motivation for healthy living—those who experienced guilt when eating chocolate cake felt they were less in control of their eating habits than their counterparts who felt eating chocolate cake was a celebration. At both the 3- and 18-month marks, people who felt guilt were less likely to achieve and maintain their weight-loss goals. Guilt had no positive benefits.

Our attitudes toward eating need a major overhaul. Food is a celebration, but that doesn't mean we should overindulge. We just need to keep things in perspective. That's why in Phase 3, I encourage you to "rest on the 7th day"—once a week, you can eat whatever you want—and you can take a break from this program on holidays, birthdays, and other special occasions. On these days, you aren't strictly forbidden from any foods. Taking a break and resting from your eating plan from time to time is essential to maintaining a healthy diet for life. After all, why bother to be fit and healthy if you can't periodically enjoy the good things in life, like a rich steak or a luscious piece of cheesecake? Our favorite foods are part of what makes life worth living.

First, remember that highly processed foods or those filled with substances toxic to the human body don't nourish you mentally, physically, or spiritually. If you tune in to your body and focus on what you truly enjoy, you'll find that you naturally shy away from foods such as:

- Overcooked, heavily breaded, creamed, or deep-fried foods
- Processed foods filled with hydrogenated oils and other unhealthy fats
- Highly processed meats and cheese—which are different from traditionally cured meats and cheese
- Highly processed soy and legume foods like "vegetarian cheese" or "chickpea chips"
- Foods filled with starch, like doughnuts, bagels, and muffins
- Soda and other sugary beverages
- Artificial sweeteners, high-fructose corn syrup, and other sugary substances made in labs but not found in nature

These are not food. We just don't have another appropriate word to define them. I referred to them as "ingestibles" in my book *The Inside Tract*,[52] and that seems fitting because they're products that can be ingested but they don't provide nutritional value. Even these foodlike substances aren't strictly forbidden in Phase 3, but I advise you to stay away from them. There are plenty of other options to satiate your cravings that don't poison your metabolism and decimate your gut microbiome.

Second, remember that periodic indulgences should be just that, periodic. Taking a break from healthy eating occasionally is fine. In fact, it can actually make you healthier! It's not the occasional treat that impacts health and causes weight gain. It's the daily assault of nutritionally vacant calories, sugary processed foods, inflammatory fats, stress, lack of exercise and sleep, and toxic exposure that deprives us of health. Enjoy a treat once in a while. Then get back to your healthy lifestyle the next day.

This leads me to my final point. Some foods may lead you down a slippery slope to overindulgence. You know who you are, and you know which foods do this for you. My recommendation: Stay away from these foods until you're confident they won't trigger bingeing or other unhealthy behaviors.

Foods You Should Eat Less Of

The foods you should eat fewer of in Phase 3 should be relatively clear. They include everything in the Forget section, as well as any that don't fit into the 10 principles mentioned above. However, there are a few "dishonorable mentions" to point out in this category, because though they're often considered healthy, they can be problematic unless consumed with caution—in moderation at best.

- **Store-bought fruit juices.** Juicing at home using whole fruits and vegetables is a great way to enhance your intake of healing plant foods. But store-bought juices are almost universally made of juice concentrate, high in sugar and stripped of the fiber and phytonutrients that make fruits and vegetables so healthy. They're basically sugar in disguise, so don't overdo them. For instance, while waiting in the checkout line at Baltimore's Mount Washington Whole Foods Market, I noticed some juice options in the refrigerator case. Naked Juice Company's Green Machine, with "no sugar added," caught my attention. An 8-ounce serving had 33 grams of carbs and 140 calories—and it came in a 16-ounce bottle. Most people will drink the entire bottle and pour 66 grams of carbs into their bloodstream, quickly setting off a strong insulin response. Even the Protein Zone smoothie, with 16 grams of protein, contains 220 calories per 8-ounce serving, due to the very high natural sugar content in the fruit juices used. I sampled it—one swig brought on an instant sugar rush. (Note that there was a class action settlement against Naked Juice Company for claiming their juice was "all natural." The suit also demands proof of the non-GMO status on the product label; see nakedjuiceclass.com.) And the organic, kosher, non-GMO Suja

Green Supreme drink, with kale, apples, and lemon, provides a whopping 110 calories per 8-ounce serving–plus a sugar rush. There are suitable choices available, if you go the purchased juice drink route. Some Suja products have as few as 35 calories per serving (Twelve Essentials, for example) and are rich in disease-fighting and fat-melting organic greens. The organic "Greens" drinks from BluePrintJuice have 110 calories and 24 grams of carbs–but contain more romaine lettuce and cucumber than any other greens with kale toward the bottom of the ingredient list. Another favorite brand is Evolution Fresh Organic Sweet Greens with either lemon or ginger (evolutionfresh.com/en-us/juice/organic-sweet-ginger). It contains 50 calories and 11 grams of carbs per 8 ounces–I highly recommend this product. The problem with some of these store-ready veggie juices is the lack of pasteurization, thus rendering them susceptible to contamination and foodborne illness. Otherwise, make your own fresh juice using greens that you hand-pick and wash thoroughly.

■ **Dried fruit, applesauce, etc.** In moderation, dried fruit is a fine occasional snack, but be aware that drying fruit or making fruit sauces breaks down the fiber and concentrates the naturally occurring sugars–a little goes a long way in terms of total sugar intake.

■ **Dairy.** Fermented dairy products like artisanal cheese, yogurt, kefir, and others are on the foods to favor list. But other forms of dairy such as cow's, goat's, and sheep's milk; custards; ice cream; and a few others should be kept to a minimum, mostly because they're higher in sugar than other forms of dairy and they cause adverse symptoms for many. Use them in moderation and watch to see how they affect you.

■ **Gluten.** I am not 100 percent antigluten. Unless you're sensitive or allergic, a few servings of whole grains like barley, rye, spelt, and whole wheat are okay. Whole grains have some positive impacts on gut microbiome diversity. However, gluten-rich grains shouldn't be the predominant whole grains in your diet. Instead, focus on options with a lower glycemic load and higher protein content, such as amaranth, brown rice, quinoa, teff, chia, millet, and others. See the Phase 3 food charts on pages 251–256 for details.

■ **Red meat and dark meat poultry.** These are associated with poor health outcomes and weight gain.

■ **Sweeteners.** You can now reintroduce into your diet a few natural sweeteners, such as agave syrup, blackstrap molasses, stevia extract, and raw honey. However, these should be used as a condiment–a teaspoon in your coffee or morning shake is fine, but more really isn't healthy.

There are a few other foods to keep to a minimum, but we've covered most of them. For further detail, see the Phase 3 food charts on pages 251–256.

Foods to Favor

Once you've fine-tuned your Forget and Few lists, the foods you favor in Phase 3 will be everything else. Choose from the broad rainbow-colored array of fruits and vegetables in your produce section. Ask your butcher for lean cuts of red meat and chicken, and ask about available fish. Stock up on whole grains in the bulk section of your supermarket. Include a little goat's milk kefir or cow's milk yogurt (make it at home if you can) and a few delectable artisanal cheeses. Buy properly fermented vegetables or make your own ferments at home using the recipes in Chapter 11. The rich palette of healing whole foods is now open to you. Embrace them. Enjoy them with family and friends. And relish the foods that feed your inner ecology as well as your body, mind, and spirit.

I've included a Phase 3 meal plan and recipes in Chapter 11. These recipes represent quintessential Mediterranean dishes. They're exquisite, and I encourage you to try them. Use them as inspiration for your own creations. And as you dive deeper into this healthy way of eating and living, seek out more delicious recipes that fit the parameters of this program. The options are endless and include a broad array for cuisines from across the world. *Bon appétit!*

What You Can Expect During Phase 3

Phase 3 is a lifelong healthy eating plan built on heritage diets, especially the Mediterranean and Baltic Sea diets. It's a sustainable way of eating that will keep you trim and support optimal weight for life. Phase 3 never ends. It's not a diet—it's your lifelong eating plan, a way of eating and living in harmony with your inner ecology and the broader ecology around you.

What can you expect during this phase? Well, life is complicated, and it's hard to say what any individual will encounter. But my deepest hope is that this way of eating and living offers you a path toward reclaiming your human birthright: delicious food, slowly prepared meals enjoyed over a glass of wine with family and friends, optimal weight, excellent health, hope, happiness, and mental, physical, and spiritual nourishment.

LOOKING AHEAD

This chapter represents both an end and a beginning. You now understand what you need to know to create a healthy pattern of eating for yourself. The formal part of the program is complete. From here, it's up to you to decide which foods you'll favor, which you'll eat fewer of, and which you'll forget. I hope my guidelines offer you a road map to make nutrition decisions that will nourish you inside and out.

But there's always more to learn about healthy living. We're discovering more every day, adding nuance to what we already know. Now you have the tools you need to take control over your own health and become a full-fledged member of the Gut Balance Revolution club. That means you'll constantly be seeking new and innovative ways to support the garden of life inside and all around you.

The next step on your journey is to learn about the superfoods to include in Phase 3 for even more health benefits. After that, in Chapter 10, I'll explain how to take your progress toward healthy living to another level by creating a gut-balancing lifestyle. Then, in the Appendix, I'll give you the inside scoop on a highly controversial subject–the use of dietary supplements to support weight loss.

THE GUT BALANCE REVOLUTION SUCCESS STORIES
Monique Hendrix, 29

When your employer is the United States Army, keeping fit goes with the territory. Just ask Monique Hendrix. Her official job description may have been operating room technician at a base hospital, but, like all soldiers, she needed to stay in shape, too. "It was enforced that you exercise all the time," she explains. "I'd lift weights and run 3 or 4 miles, so you'd think I'd be pretty slim. But the problem was, I'd run right to McDonald's and grab a quarter-pounder. My diet wasn't healthy, and I really started to put on weight."

Even though her military career had come to an end, her unhealthy eating habits continued—but her exercise habits didn't. Little by little, she noticed that her clothes were getting tighter and she was having trouble catching her breath when she climbed up a flight of stairs. That's when she took the Gut Balance Revolution for a test drive.

"I've gone on lots of diets over the years," recalls Monique, a mother of four young children who's studying to become a registered nurse. "I tried everything from Weight Watchers to Jenny Craig. But nothing really worked until this program. In 8 weeks, I lost 12 pounds—and I felt so much better."

CHAPTER 9

Dr. Gerry's Top 10 Superfoods for Phase 3

The superfoods for Phase 3 are those you want to include in a healthy diet for life. Some were allowed in previous phases, as they constitute a healthy part of just about any nutritional program. I elected to feature them as superfoods in this phase for a few reasons. First, I want to highlight the types of foods to focus on as you move into this lifelong way of eating. They represent the broad range of choices now available to you. A few also feature prominently in the Mediterranean diet–another reason I feature them here. Finally, these foods are medicinal powerhouses that, when consumed regularly, can protect your health and waistline for years to come. So without further ado, here are my top 10 superfoods for Phase 3.

1. SALMON

The easiest way to increase your anti-inflammatory fats: Switch out red meat for salmon as much as possible. Try to consume this amazing superfood at least a couple times weekly. Salmon is chock-full of omega-3s–the healthy fats that reduce your risk of heart disease; enhance insulin sensitivity; support brain health, cognition, and mood; and help you burn fat. However, there are two important points to consider when adding this superfood to your diet.

Salmon has an outstanding ratio of omega-3 to omega-6 fats (5:1)–the opposite direction of the standard American diet ratio 1:14 to 1:25.[1] To maximize these anti-inflammatory omega-3 fats in your fish, go for wild, line-caught salmon–it's vastly healthier than farmed salmon, which has a higher content of the omega-6 inflammatory fats you're trying to avoid by adding fish to your diet. Why the difference between wild and farmed? For one thing, farmed salmon is fed genetically modified proinflammatory-rich soy and corn, given antibiotics, and contaminated with toxic chemicals such as dioxin and PCBs, which cause cancer and retard brain development *in utero* and in infants.[2]

Wild salmon, on the other hand, is extremely rich in health-promoting omega-3 fats while providing less toxic exposure.[3] These fats can even help protect you from Alzheimer's disease, the number three killer in America, according to Dr. David Perlmutter's bestseller *Grain Brain!*[4]

Leading the pack for wild-caught salmon are Alaskan salmon—my favorite is king (sometimes called chinook) salmon, but I also enjoy sockeye, coho, pink, and Kodiak. Whichever species you prefer, I encourage you if possible to pay the premium for wild salmon to maximally support your health. You get what you pay for, so buy the good stuff.

Aside from the beneficial anti-inflammatory fatty acids, salmon contains bioactive peptides that regulate several hormones in the body that support cartilage and fight arthritis and may help prevent colorectal cancer.[5] Salmon is moderately high in purine, a food chemical that may flare gout in those who are susceptible, so if you have gout or are susceptible, beware.

But has salmon consumption been associated with weight loss? We've already discussed fish as one of the most satiating sources of protein—research shows that fatty fish can modulate hunger hormones and inflammation in overweight folks. During an 8-week intervention, salmon consumption modulated fasting insulin, as well as ghrelin and leptin, and lowered inflammatory markers.[6, 7] Varying the fish source has been demonstrated to improve compliance in those who favor fish as a protein source for weight loss.[8] Remember the Baltic Sea diet we discussed in Chapter 8? Rich in omega-3-fatty acid from fish, it's associated with weight loss and improved cardiometabolic markers.[9]

That's one reason I recommend that as you move into this lifelong journey toward health, you place fish on your menu often. Have fish as your main protein source two or three times weekly to cool inflammation. Use this high-quality protein source to regulate blood biochemistry and metabolic, satiety-controlling hormones. There are many varieties of fish to choose from and endless ways to prepare them. Some, like omega-3-rich Pesto Baked Cod (page 282), are included in your Gut Balance Revolution meal plans. In fact, a European study showed that consumption of cod increases weight loss in men and has other positive health effects.[10] A compelling study out of Iceland (which is in the Baltic region) reported a dose-response relationship between cod consumption and weight loss during an 8-week energy restriction diet.[11] Participants in the study ate diets consisting of one of these three seafood sources.

- Diet 1: 150 grams of cod five times per week

- Diet 2: 150 grams of cod three times per week

- Diet 3: No seafood

Those who consumed 150 grams (5.3 ounces) of cod five times weekly were found to have lost 1.7 kilograms (3.7 pounds) more than those who ate the same amount of calories without seafood.

Of course, other varieties of seafood may benefit weight loss by virtue of satiation and omega-3 content, or, like cod and salmon, they may have other properties that provide weight-loss benefits. However, not all fish of the same species are equally healthy—a wild salmon from the Pacific Ocean, for example, is different in many ways from a farm-raised salmon. The farm-raised salmon is much higher in cancer-causing organochemicals and lower in health-promoting omega-3 fatty acids and astaxanthin (a carotenoid pigment with powerful anti-inflammatory properties). In the Gut Balance Revolution recipe section, fishes high in astaxanthin, rich in omega-3 fatty acids, and low in mercury are favored.

Seafood Formerly Known as Healthy

Larger fish species like tuna (albacore, yellowfin, bigeye, ahi), swordfish, marlin, bluefish, grouper, halibut, orange roughy, skipjack, and shark were once among the healthiest foods on the planet but are no longer safe to eat in large quantities due to environmental mercury contamination.[12] That's because this toxic metal bioconcentrates up the food chain—small fish are exposed; medium fish eat the smaller, doubling their exposure; larger fish eat the medium fish—and they all end up with more mercury in their bodies, all the way up the food chain.

To reduce your mercury exposure, limit yourself to no more than one serving of albacore or yellowfin tuna weekly and avoid larger fish like shark, swordfish, king mackerel, or tilefish altogether. Limit fish with moderate mercury content to about one serving weekly. These include striped bass, carp, Alaskan cod, halibut, lobster, mahimahi, monkfish, perch (freshwater), sablefish, skate, snapper, tuna (canned chunk white, skipjack), and weakfish (sea trout).[13] The Crunchy Almond Tuna Salad in the recipe section (page 285) calls for chunk *light* tuna, which is lower in mercury.

I recommend consuming seafood that's low in mercury and organochemical pollutants, rich in omega-3 fatty acids content, and wild or fresh-caught in local waters. Examples include Atlantic or Pacific (US) cod, anchovy, butterfish, catfish, canned light tuna, flounder, haddock, herring, ocean perch, mussels, oysters, plaice, pollack, rainbow trout, rockfish, sardines, scallop, sea bass (black), shad (US), shrimp, sole, spiny lobster, striped bass, tilapia, trout (freshwater), wild eastern oyster, whitefish, and whiting. Pollack, rockfish, and black sea bass are threatened in certain waters; for more information, visit drweil.com/drw/u/ART02049/facts-about-fish.html. In general, farm-raised tilapia is loaded with antibiotics. The United States and Ecuador maintain the best practices for farming, and certain supermarket chains carry antibiotic- and hormone-free tilapia as an affordable whitefish option.[14]

A key superfood, seafood is underconsumed in the United States. The Dietary Guidelines for Americans suggest that everyone eat fish twice weekly,[15] but only about a third of Americans do. As you'll see in the meal plans, I recommend consuming safe seafood several times weekly during each phase. The health benefits are numerous—and you're worth it!

2. OLIVE OIL

I've highlighted the health benefits of olive oil throughout this book, but I decided to add it as a superfood in Phase 3 because it's the predominant source of fat in the MedDiet. Olive oil is, arguably, the healthiest oil on the planet, not only packed with monounsaturated fats but also containing high levels of phenols—antioxidants that play a role in heart health and fight chronic disease. The MedDiet features foods high in monounsaturated fatty acids (MUFAs), which may provide a nice perk to facilitate weight loss. Nuts, avocados, and olive oil, loaded with MUFAs, are anti-inflammatory superfoods. While many diet plans designed for short-term weight loss promote a low-fat approach, the Gut Balance Revolution favors foods that quench the fire of inflammation and improve satiation—that is what leads to a lean metabolism and weight loss. We need to move away from thinking that all fat-rich foods are evil and focus instead on eating fats that are anti-inflammatory. [16]

Another taboo is that energy-dense high-fat foods such as those high in MUFAs should be severely restricted. But this kind of thinking is based on the outdated calories in/calories out theory. While olive oil does contain 125 calories and 14 grams of fat per tablespoon, there's far more to health and weight than how many calories you consume. I'm not suggesting that you guzzle olive oil, but it has unquestionable therapeutic value and supports long-term weight maintenance.

A recent study published in the *European Journal of Clinical Nutrition* compared three diets: a low-fat diet against two slightly different MedDiets (nut rich versus olive oil rich as the prime source of fats). The MedDiets supplemented with virgin olive oil or nuts improved glucose metabolism as much as the typical low-fat diet. But unlike the low-fat diet group, both MedDiets groups lost significant body weight.[17]

What can explain these results? One reason: olive oil's effects on satiety. All fat enhances satiety to some extent, inducing gut hormones that make you feel full. However, there's a clever way that olive oil induces satiety: The scent of olive oil itself provokes a sense of fullness. A study published in the *American Journal of Nutrition* showed that spiking low-fat yogurt with the scent of a fat-free olive oil extract improved satiety and enhanced brain activity typically associated with fat consumption and reward.[18] Olive oil has special properties that profoundly impact satiety—its scent alone hits receptors in the brain promoting the sense of fullness.[19, 20] (There's even an ice creamery in Baltimore (Taharka Brothers, taharkabrothers.com) that developed an olive oil and sea salt flavor—a good way to feel more profoundly full with less ice cream!)

By now you know that fighting inflammation is a vital element of this program. Olive oil, especially extra-virgin olive oil (EVOO), is a strong anti-inflammatory compound with myriad health benefits.[21] EVOO has a very high polyphenol content and is considered a COX-1 and COX-2 inhibitor–the same class of anti-inflammatory as powerful medications like ibuprofen.[22]

These anti-inflammatory powers are important for cardiovascular health in particular. Anti-inflammatory fats are less likely to be involved in the oxidation of LDL that leads to coronary artery disease and atherosclerosis.[23, 24] Substituting carbohydrates for a calorically equivalent amount of olive oil has been shown in some studies to increase the good cholesterol–HDL–while having no effect on LDL. That's another excellent reason to incorporate more olive oil into your diet.[25] Olive oil is also high in oleic acid, which reduces the risk of blood clots, and it's a decent source of vitamin E–1 tablespoon contains 12.9 percent of the RDA. [26, 27]

Many people gain weight through a process called "emotional eating" in which they binge on food during periods of turmoil. Many factors can influence a binge eating disorder (BED), though good nutrition can help control this destructive impulsivity. A recent study showed that consumption of EVOO and nuts as part of the MedDiet decreased the risks of BED.[28] Compliance with the MedDiet was associated with a lower prevalence of BED, while the consumption of creams, butter, cakes, sweets, and baked desserts was a trigger for it.[29]

But what about weight loss? You guessed it. Olive oil probably helps you lose weight, too. A study on weight loss in 44 overweight breast cancer survivors used an olive oil-based diet, since studies have shown an association of olive oil consumption with a decreased risk of breast cancer development.[30] In the 44-week study, participants were randomly assigned to either an olive oil–enriched plant-based diet or a calorically equivalent diet from the National Cancer Institute (NCI). Their total fat intake was greater than 15 percent but less than 30 percent of the calories they consumed. Twenty-eight people completed the clinical trial. The olive oil–based diet proved to be more effective for weight loss, lowering serum triglycerides and raising high-density lipoproteins (good cholesterol), than a standard NCI low-fat diet. Significantly more women lost 5 percent or more of their body weight on the olive oil–based diet than on the NCI diet.

What other health benefits does olive oil confer on women aside from weight control and cancer protection? Olive oil has been shown in laboratory animals to protect female rats who have undergone surgically induced menopause against bone loss.[31]

Mediterranean people have used olive oil as their primary fat source for millennia, with no evidence of harm. In fact, it seems to be one of the key dietary factors in the long, relatively disease-free lives of those living in this region. So stick with EVOO as your main source of oil. It will keep the pounds off as it keeps your heart (and the rest of you!) healthy.

3. APPLES

According to researchers from the School of Food Science at Washington State University, an apple a day can literally keep the doctor away. These scientists evaluated the gut microbiome profiles of obese and lean laboratory rats before and after the consumption of apples and found that ingestion of apples normalized the maldistributed gut flora of the obese rats, making them similar to those of the lean ones. Several different varieties were tested, with all showing this benefit; however, the Granny Smith apple was found to provide the best protection against the development of obesity by promoting a healthy gut flora. The Granny Smith apple is highest in nondigestible fibers (gut flora food!) and anti-inflammatory natural products.[32]

These superfruits, cultivated in temperate zones the world over, have been around for nearly 3,000 years. Apple seeds are heterozygous–if you remove the seeds from the apples you buy in the store and plant them in the ground, four different types of apples will grow. This has several implications. One is that there's a virtually endless variety of apples. Unfortunately, few of them are the sweet, delicious fruit you're used to. Each of those store-bought varietals has been carefully cultivated by farmers, in some cases for centuries. Every apple in your local supermarket comes from a grafted tree. Some heirloom strains of apples have been passed down (and eaten!) by humans for hundreds of years. It's a good thing, too, as this superfruit comes with some real health benefits.

One reason we think apples are so healthy is their high levels of phytochemicals like flavonoids, carotenoids, and phenolics, plus powerful antioxidants like quercetin, catechin, phloridzin, and chlorogenic acid (the latter is also found in the weight-loss-promoting green coffee bean). This powerful combination of phytonutrients plus their soluble fiber–called pectin–and their relatively high amounts of vitamin C make apples a nutritional powerhouse that can reduce your risk of a wide variety of chronic illnesses. The anti-inflammatory activity, coupled with the feeding of the friendly flora by its pectin, makes apples a superfood for overall health and weight maintenance. For example, regular consumption of apples reduces your risk of heart disease. The Women's Health Study, which followed 40,000 women for nearly 7 years, showed that those with the highest consumption of flavonoids had the lowest risk of heart disease. Intake of apples and broccoli specifically further reduced the risk of cardiovascular events. Women who regularly consumed apples saw a 13 to 22 percent reduction in cardiovascular events[33]–a correlation that's been replicated in many studies.[34-37]

The antioxidant and anti-inflammatory chemicals in apples are one of the reasons they're so healthy for your heart. However, another factor is that apples seem to lower blood lipids. Remember that fiber has a powerful effect on blood lipids. While apples are reasonably high in fiber, the amount they contain doesn't seem to account for their overall effect on blood lipid levels. A group of French scientists designed a clever experiment to solve this mystery. They fed three groups of rats as follows:[38]

- Group 1 got apple pectin (the primary source of fiber in the fruit).

- Group 2 got a freeze-dried apple (in which the fiber was reduced) that was high in polyphenol content.

- Group 3 got both.

Guess which group had the lowest blood lipids? Group 3. It appears that apples (like many foods) are more than the sum of their parts. It's not just the pectin *or* the polyphenols that have this effect on blood lipids. It's the unique combination of these powerful phytochemicals and fiber that makes apples a superfruit.

These effects on heart health and blood lipid levels would be enough to recommend apples. But the benefits don't stop there. Apples have repeatedly been shown to have cancer-protective effects, especially against lung cancer. The Nurses' Health Study, involving 77,000 women and 47,000 men, showed that women who consumed one serving of apples or pears a day had a reduced risk of lung cancer.[39] In a study out of Hawaii, scientists sought to find out just how powerful this anti–lung cancer effect was. They took two groups of patients—582 with lung cancer and 582 without it—and compared their smoking history and food intake. Those with the highest consumption of apples, onions, and white grapefruit had a 40 to 50 percent reduced risk of developing lung cancer compared to those with the lowest intake of these foods.[40]

Apples appear to enhance pulmonary health in the absence of lung cancer. They seem to decrease the risk of asthma, reduce the severity of asthma attacks, and decrease bronchial hypersensitivity.[41] They also appear to enhance overall lung capacity. In a Welsh study, the lung capacity of 2,512 middle-aged men between ages 45 and 59 was assessed using a tool called forced expiratory volume (FEV), which measures how much air you can push out your lungs.[42] Scientists found that those who ate more apples weekly had better FEV scores, almost certainly due to high levels of flavonoids—especially quercetin—found in apples.

Not only do apples support heart and lung health, but they also seem to help people reverse type 2 diabetes and lose weight. In a Finnish study, the dietary history of more than 10,000 men and women was reviewed. Researchers found that increased apple consumption was associated with a reduced risk of type 2 diabetes.[43] Higher intake of quercetin, one of the major flavonoids in apples, was associated with a further reduced risk.

The bottom line for weight loss? The mighty apple helps you shed pounds and stay slim. A study conducted at the State University of Rio de Janeiro in Brazil randomly assigned 411 women to supplement their diet with one of three interventions: an apple, a pear, or an oat cookie snack three times daily. The women who ate one serving of apples three times daily lost 2.6 pounds in a 12-week period while lowering triglycerides and total cholesterol.[44]

Animal studies show similar results. An interesting controlled study in diet-induced obese rats demonstrated improved lipid profiles and loss of body fat and weight when these animals were fed either apple pomace (the residue after the juice extraction process) or apple juice concentrate (both having a high concentration of polyphenols and flavonoids as well as soluble fibers) *while consuming a Western diet high in saturated fat.* So what does this mean? Rats who become obese by consuming a diet high in saturated fats (aka diet-induced obesity) can reverse their obesity just with apple products.[45] The potential mechanisms of body-weight- and fat-loss-promoting benefits of apple products in this study include the soluble fiber blocking the absorption of cholesterol and bile acids, soluble fiber promoting healthy bacteria to improve metabolism, and the anti-inflammatory effects of the polyphenols in the apple products. A recent study confirmed that clear apple juice devoid of prebiotic pectin and lower in polyphenolics does not provide these benefits.[46]

These fascinating findings clearly demonstrate the healing power of this superfruit. But one other study brings home why superfood apples are especially suited to the Gut Balance Revolution. Scientists have recently shown in animal models that regular consumption of apples enhances the biodiversity of the gut microbiome.[47] Animals whose diet was supplemented with pectin (the primary fiber in apples) experienced a twofold increase of butyric acid–the primary fuel for cells in the large intestine, changes that didn't occur in controls or in animals fed apple puree, pomace, or juice. So go ahead and have an apple a day.

4. DARK CHOCOLATE

Chocolate is derived from tropical cocoa beans from the genus *Theobroma*, a word that translates as "food of the gods"–a name it deserves not only for its rich, luscious flavor but also for its health effects.

Chocolate contains two types of flavonoid: flavanols, made up of molecules called epicatechins and catechins, which are also found in tea; and procyanidins, longer flavanol molecules. Studies have shown that cocoa and some types of dark chocolate are higher in polyphenols, flavonoids, and antioxidant activity than many of the other superfoods highlighted here. Indeed, dark chocolate outscores acai, blueberries, cranberries, and pomegranates in each of these categories.[48] Fascinating information–but the real question remains: Do these increased levels of healthy phytochemicals in chocolate correlate with improved health outcomes? The data show that they do.

Much of the research on chocolate and health has revolved around its impact on cardiovascular disease, cholesterol oxidation, and hypertension. This superfood performs extremely well in each of these areas. Back in 2004, a coalition of scientists from the Netherlands, Belgium, and Australia joined together to identify dietary interventions to help people reduce their risk of heart disease.[49] To find out what this healthy meal would consist of, they reviewed data from the Framingham Heart Study and its Offspring Study (two of the largest studies ever conducted to determine the factors leading to heart health or disease). The scientists created the Polymeal–a diet that if eaten daily would decrease the risk of cardiovascular events by as much as 76 percent, a vastly better outcome than any existing medication, with no side effects. The meal consisted of fish, dark chocolate, fruits, vegetables, garlic, and almonds. Sound familiar? The researchers found that 100 grams of cocoa-rich chocolate alone could reduce risk of cardiovascular events by as much as 21 percent.

These are impressive findings and interesting dietary recommendations right in line with the Mediterranean Diet I recommend for Phase 3. But how does dark chocolate have such a profound effect on heart health? We don't have all the answers, but several mechanisms seem to be at play.

First, the high phenolic content of dark chocolate has both anti-inflammatory and antioxidant properties. In one study, an amino acid called clovamide and two phenolic extracts from roasted and unroasted cocoa beans were tested for their effects on proinflammatory cytokines and NF-κB gene activation (two primary markers for inflammation).[50] All three reduced these inflammation markers, and the clovamide also enhanced PPARγ activation, which is a key factor in reducing systemic inflammation. As systemic inflammation plays a key role in heart disease, these effects suggest that consuming dark chocolate may mitigate your risk.

Another study showed that the antioxidant activity of dark chocolate may play an even more powerful role in cardiovascular health. Scientists at the University of Pennsylvania sought to determine how dark chocolate influenced heart health.[51] They divided 23 healthy subjects into two groups, giving one a standard Western diet and the other the same diet supplemented with 22 grams of cocoa and 16 grams of dark chocolate daily. The results? The dark-chocolate group experienced far less oxidation of LDL cholesterol–critically important because cholesterol oxidation is *the* leading factor in cardiovascular disease and heart attacks. It's also been shown that regular consumption of dark chocolate reduces blood pressure and enhances endothelial function, which seems to hold true both in healthy populations and in people with essential hypertension (high blood pressure with no known cause).[52, 53] We think that this effect on blood pressure has to do with the fact that the flavonoids in chocolate influence an important vasodilator called nitric oxide, important in regulating blood pressure. Dark chocolate is also high in oleic acid, the heart-healthy monounsaturated fat found in olive oil–perhaps another reason for its heart-protective effects.

Mounting evidence also suggests that dark chocolate may improve insulin sensitivity. A recent study in the *American Journal of Clinical Nutrition* revealed that healthy subjects who ate 100 grams of dark chocolate daily saw a significant increase in insulin sensitivity compared to those who ate a calorically equivalent amount of white chocolate. Plus, a decrease in systolic blood pressure was also observed.[54] British studies showed that higher consumption of flavones (found in berries and dark chocolate) was associated with a lower risk of diabetes, obesity, cardiovascular disease, and cancer. Higher flavone intake was also associated with improved insulin sensitivity.[55, 56]

This delectable superfood, rich in polyphenols that fight inflammation and improve insulin sensitivity, also turns out to be a prebiotic.[57] Investigators from Louisiana State University reported that fibers in dark chocolate are fermented by good obesity-fighting gut microbes, such as bifidobacteria and lactic-acid bacteria, which in turn make even more anti-inflammatory compounds, which benefits cardiovascular health and weight regulation.[58] So dark chocolate has prebiotic properties that make it a suitable Phase 2 or Phase 3 superfood.

Could something considered a sweet treat facilitate weight loss? Yes! Researchers from the University of Granada in Spain reported a European study involving 1,458 adolescents ages 12 to 17 showing that more chocolate consumption was associated with lower levels of total and central fat.[59] How can that be? A new study published in the *Journal of Agriculture and Food Chemistry* points to a possible answer.[60] It appears the flavanols in chocolate, especially the oligomeric proanthocyanidins (OPCs), are active obesity-preventing agents. Scientists fed mice a high-fat diet and then gave them a variety of flavanols found in chocolate. After 12 weeks, the mice receiving the OPCs were best protected against weight gain, fat mass accumulation, impaired glucose tolerance, and insulin resistance.

Please note that we're talking about *dark chocolate*, which is very different than the majority of chocolate you'll find in your local supermarket. When buying chocolate, look for products that are at least 70 percent cacao and not filled with sugar—that usually means paying a premium for specialty brands. Avoid milk chocolate and white chocolate (they're chock-full of sugar), and stick with the richest, darkest varieties.

Though I'm an advocate of dark chocolate, don't eat too much. Even dark chocolate has sugar in it. Enjoy a few servings—usually a couple of squares—three or four times weekly. More than this probably won't provide additional health benefits, and the sugar may indeed harm your health and your waistline if you overindulge. As long as you enjoy dark chocolate in moderation, you can (and should!) make this "food of the gods" part of your long-term eating plan.

5. GREENS (LEAFY GREENS, SALADS)

Leafy greens constitute a broad class of vegetables including but not limited to:

- Spinach
- Swiss chard
- Kale (this was a superfood for Phase 2, so I won't reiterate those points here)
- Mustard greens
- Collard greens
- Leaf lettuce

While these foods don't all possess the same health benefits or even come from the same plant family, it's useful to classify them together for one simple reason: Incorporating leafy green vegetables of *any* variety into your diet has a broad array of health benefits. Prepare them as salads, braised greens, or any of the other myriad ways—they're a relatively simple, low-cost, low-labor, delectable way to enhance your health. For ease, let's divide this immense group of veggies into salads and leafy greens. First, let's look at some of the data on leafy greens. Then we'll talk about the supermeal called salad.

Leafy Greens

One group of vegetables I haven't talked about at length is the Chenopodiaceae family, which includes spinach, Swiss chard, beets, and quinoa. The health effects of these foods are increasingly being celebrated because they contain a set of phytochemicals that confer cancer-protective effects. These protective plant chemicals are called carotenoids; a specific subset of these, called epoxy xanthophylls, seems to inhibit the proliferation of cancer cells. Spinach and Swiss chard both have high levels of these epoxy xanthophylls, which may be one reason these foods have been shown in repeated studies to protect against cancer.[61]

That's a big claim, so let's look at some of the studies backing it up. In animal models, it's been shown that the carotenoid neoxanthin stops the proliferation of prostate cancer cells.[62] A recent study published in the *International Journal of Cancer* analyzed the association between the intake of five common flavonoids and ovarian cancer incidences in the 66,940 women who took part in the Nurses' Health Study. They found that high intakes of the flavonoid apigenin–particularly high in spinach and parsley–was associated with lower rates of ovarian cancer. Kaempferol, an important flavonoid found not only in spinach but also in cruciferous vegetables, including leafy greens like collards and mustard, also seems to play a critical role.[63] Additionally, spinach consumption appears to reduce the risk of breast cancer. A study at the National Institute of Environmental Health Sciences reviewed health and food intake data from 3,543 women diagnosed with cancer and compared it to 9,406 controls. Their findings? Those who ate spinach and carrots twice weekly were 56 percent less likely to develop breast cancer than those who didn't eat these foods at all. Not only does spinach appear to mitigate cancer proliferation, but it also has antimutagenic properties (meaning it reduces the rate of cellular mutation). One study found that 13 chemical constituents of spinach acted as antimutagens in the human body.[64] And though the evidence isn't yet conclusive, it appears that increasing your spinach intake may decrease your risk of aggressive prostate cancer (stages III and IV).[65]

What about Swiss chard? Though fewer studies have been done on this vegetable, it stands to reason that Swiss chard has similar effects, since it contains many of the same specialized, cancer-fighting carotenoids as spinach.

Does this mean that you if you add a little spinach or chard to your diet you will be magically cured from cancer or remain cancer free for life? Certainly not–no one can promise that. Nevertheless, the growing research supporting the use of these foods in the fight against cancer is extremely compelling.

The health benefits of these leafy greens do not stop with their cancer-fighting properties. Spinach may reduce blood pressure. It's likely to have positive effects on eye health due to its relatively high levels of lutein and zeaxanthin, two carotenoids known to support eye health and mitigate macular degeneration.[66] Swiss chard, on the other hand, may help you fight high cholesterol levels and colon cancer and may protect liver function in type 2 diabetics.[67, 68]

No food is a magical cure-all. But taken together, the data suggest that a diet high in these leafy greens will protect your health on multiple fronts.

What about collards, mustard, kale, cabbage, and other leafy greens in the cruciferous vegetable family? Actually, this entire family of vegetables has medicinal properties and contains some of the healthiest foods you can consume. There are a few all-star players like kale (a Phase 2 superfood) and broccoli (part of the cruciferous family, with many of the same health benefits—and then some). You can't go wrong adding more crucifers to your diet—each is full of phytochemicals that can protect you from a wide variety of chronic illnesses. So let's take a few minutes to look at how cruciferous foods perform overall in terms of health outcomes.

Crucifers may have even more profound cancer-protective effects than those reviewed for spinach and Swiss chard. Though the evidence is mixed, over the last few decades epidemiological studies have shown an inverse correlation between cruciferous vegetable consumption and the risk of gastric, breast, lung, prostate, colorectal, bladder, and other cancers.[69-73] The correlation seems to be best illustrated for lung, gastric, and colorectal cancers,[74, 75] and most scientists now agree that eating more cruciferous veggies will help protect some of us from these three forms of cancer—and perhaps others as well. But which people are protected and why?

One reason these supergreens have cancer-protective effects is that they're a rich source of glucosinolates—unique phytonutrients metabolized in the body and turned into other chemicals called isothiocyanates (ITCs), which seem to have the powerful anticancer effect. They enhance elimination of potential carcinogens from the body, increase the transcription of proteins that suppress tumor formation, block enzymes used on carcinogen activation, and trigger cancer cell apoptosis (cell death).[76, 77] However, these effects appear to be somewhat dependent on individual predispositions. People with a gene called glutathione S-transferase M1 (GSTM1) don't seem to get the same protective effects from these greens. That's because this gene is involved in the urinary transport of ITCs, so those people pee out much of the goodness they get from cruciferous veggies. Thus, the cancer-protective effects you get from these veggies depend, to some extent, on your genetic makeup. How do you know if you have the GSTM1 gene? Well, you could get personalized gene testing to help determine if eating more greens may protect you from cancer, but it probably isn't worth the expense, as crucifers have plenty of other health benefits that justify their place in your diet.

Another area where these veggies shine is in their effect on blood lipids and cardio-vascular disease. In Chapter 7, I described the process by which eating kale enhances levels of bile acids that bind to cholesterol, allowing you to excrete it and lowering your overall blood levels of cholesterol. Kale isn't the only vegetable that accomplishes this. All crucifers can, and some are even better at it than kale—collards come in first place, and mustard isn't far behind. Cabbage is also a winner.[78] So if you want to lower choles-terol naturally, include plenty of cruciferous veggies in your diet. There's also some evi-dence that the same ITCs that may protect against cancer also have cardioprotective effects.[79] Again, the presence or absence of the GSTM1 gene appears to impact this effect.[80]

But how do cruciferous vegetables influence weight gain and type 2 diabetes? While there's little evidence that crucifers have a direct impact on type 2 diabetes and weight, increasing your overall intake of fruits and vegetables is inversely correlated with these con-ditions.[81] What's more, the phytochemicals in these leafy greens have anti-inflammatory and antioxidant effects, so they may indirectly influence type 2 diabetes and the complex of symptoms involved in metabolic syndrome. Of course, more research is needed to tease out all the relationships, but it's logical to conclude cruciferous vegetables don't have any nega-tive impact on these conditions—and they may improve them. So eat your greens—they're good for you.

Salads

It's difficult to ascertain the exact health benefits of salads for one main reason: They're all so different. A spinach salad is different from a mesclun mix, and both are different from a Cobb salad. But one thing's certain: As long as you avoid inflammatory fats (con-tained in many commercial salad dressings) and sugar (in candied nuts or in sweet dressings), you can't go wrong with a salad. It's not a superfood, it's a supermeal with health benefits more than the sum of its parts.

Since we're talking about greens, let's discuss the most common salad green of all: lettuce. There are hundreds of varieties of lettuce, and all of them are healthy except, perhaps, iceberg lettuce, which has zero nutritional value. Lettuce is universally low in calories, and most varieties are high in vitamins A and C as well as iron and calcium. Some lettuce varieties, like romaine, are also high in vitamin K (romaine contains 100 percent of the RDA for vitamin K) and folate. Research has shown that red and green leaf lettuces contain anthocyanins that are COX-1 and COX-2 inhibitors (the same class of chemicals as NSAID medications), and they mitigate lipid peroxidation—the process by which free radicals steal oxygen molecules from fat cells, causing oxidative stress that can contribute to cardiovascular damage and other conditions.[82]

There's also evidence that some types of lettuce have relatively high levels of the fla-vonoid quercetin[83]—the same antioxidant molecule contained in apples and onions. Both red and green lettuce have strong antioxidant and anti-inflammatory activities that vary by phenolic composition according to the type of lettuce. Higher amounts of phenolics, including anthocyanin, found in berries and present in red lettuce, may indicate that consumption of red lettuce provides better health benefits than green lettuce.[84] So it's logical to assume lettuce may have similar health effects to these foods, and increasing your intake of vegetables is one of the easiest ways to protect your overall health. And that's as easy as making a quick salad. Consider the overall potential health benefits of the following salad.

- Red leaf lettuce
- Spinach
- Baby chard
- Nuts
- Avocado
- Fresh feta cheese

Drizzle with olive oil and red wine or balsamic vinegar and you've got a supermeal if ever there was one. Every one of these ingredients is a superfood. The dish contains healthy protein, high-quality fat, a good amount of fiber, and probiotics all in a meal that takes you about 5 minutes to prepare. Want more protein? Add canned salmon or cooked chicken breast. Don't like feta? Shred fresh Parmesan instead. Not in love with the taste of chard? Replace it with baby kale. The variations are endless.

There's evidence that consuming salads as a preload facilitates weight loss.[85] "Preload" refers to a small meal eaten just before the main meal to curb appetite and ultimately lower caloric intake of the main meal so that the energy consumption of both meals combined is lower than from the main meal alone. A team of doctors demonstrated that salad preloading resulted in lower body weight, waist circumference, triglycerides, total cholesterol, and systolic blood pressure. The preload concept has been demonstrated to facilitate weight loss in a program called Volumetrics.[86] It involves eating low-energy-density foods as appetizers, which promote satiation and reduce appetite during the meal itself. Salads are popular preload appetizers shown to be effective, but others include soups[87] and even higher protein snacks.[88] That's why I view soup and salads as prime preload superfoods for weight control in Phase 3. As you'll see in the meal plans for recipes for this phase, I feature a Minestrone Soup (page 316) that has prebiotic and potent antioxidant properties to fight inflammation and add good bacteria to your inside tract.

One way preloading diminishes appetite is by slowing stomach emptying. The form and thickness (viscosity) of soup may alter the efficacy of the preload.[89] For example, pureed vegetable soup decreases gastric emptying time, slows down digestion, and gives a sense of fullness, but it also increases the insulin response (high glycemic response due to its predigested form and rapid absorption) and increases diet-induced thermogenesis (energy burning during digestion) compared to when the solid vegetables in soup are consumed with a glass of water. Eating soup can have gastrointestinal, endocrine, and metabolic consequences that may influence food intake and satiety, and the form of soup may influence these responses.

Eating soup regularly can reduce energy intake, enhance satiety, and promote weight loss.[90] A recent study reviewed epidemiological data from more than 10,500 adults who participated in the National Health and Nutrition Examination Survey.[91] Compared with non-soup eaters, those who ate soup had lower body weight and lower waist circumference. Soup consumption was associated with a lower dietary energy intake, independent of whether data on beverage or water consumption were included. Diet quality was significantly better in soup consumers as well–they ate less saturated fat and ate more protein and dietary fiber as well as several vitamins and minerals.

Soup appears to help you maintain a healthy weight in a number of ways, but the real key may ultimately be that it feeds your good gut bacteria to induce a lean metabolism and reduce your intake of energy-dense foods.[92] A word of caution: In this study, soup was also associated with a higher intake of sodium, which portends cardiovascular risks.

Epidemiological studies have revealed that soup consumption is associated with a lower risk of obesity. Moreover, intervention studies have reported that soup consumption aids in body-weight management. In 2013, researchers based in the University of Iowa looked at the US-based National Health and Nutrition Examination Survey (NHANES) that took place from 2003 to 2006[93] after reviewing health and dietary data on 4,158 participants. Their results were similar to a UK-based study: Non–soup consumers were at a higher risk of being overweight or obese and had a higher prevalence of reduced HDL cholesterol. The frequency of soup consumption was inversely associated with body mass index and waist circumference. Scientists concluded that "there is an inverse relationship between soup consumption and body weight status in US adults, which support laboratory studies showing a potential benefit of soup consumption for body weight management." A subsequent publication by these investigators using the NHANES database from 2003 to 2008 reported that soup consumers had a lower body weight, a lower waist circumference, and a trend toward a lower total energy intake.[94]

Several studies worldwide show that eating soup negatively correlates with body mass index, serum cholesterol and triacylglycerol levels, and blood pressure.[95, 96] So soups and salads are primo superfood appetizers for the Gut Balance Revolution weight-loss plan. Ultimately, the gut controls your figure, and just choosing the right foods that work with your gut physiology can help you lose fat in all the right places and keep your curves.

By now you should be aware that I have included many soups and salads in the recipes and meal plans in this book. Each is a supermeal in its own right. But don't stop with these. Use the recipes to inspire your own creations. The possibilities are endless when it comes to making supermeal salads.

6. FLAXSEED

Flaxseed has been with human beings a long time. It was known in the Stone Age, cultivated in Mesopotamia, has a long history of use in India, and was popular in Rome until the empire fell. Unfortunately, flax fell into obscurity until the modern era. In the 20th century, flaxseed was primarily used to produce linseed oil, a common ingredient in paints, varnishes, and other industrial chemicals.

It wasn't until the 1990s that flaxseed's health benefits became known to the public at large again. First off, it's one of the richest plant-based sources of omega-3 fats around, containing 132.5 percent of the DRI of these anti-inflammatory fats. Flaxseeds also contain extremely high levels of antioxidant polyphenols. Among 100 of the most common sources of polyphenols in the American diet, flaxseeds rank ninth, beating out such antioxidant powerhouses as blueberries and olives.[97] Researchers now consider flaxseeds to be *the* highest source of a unique type of fiber-related polyphenol called lignans, with seven times more of these important phytochemicals than their closest runner-up—sesame seed. These lignans are one of the key reasons flaxseeds are so good for us, and they only become bioactive when broken down by gut bacteria in a conversion process involving a wide mix of gut bacteria including those from the genera *Bacteroides, Bifidobacterium, Butyribacterium,* and *Eubacterium.* It's another glimpse into the important web of relationships between what you eat, the biodiversity of your gut microbiome, and your health.[98]

Another unique feature of flaxseeds is that when they're ground and mixed with water, they create a gel that seems to reduce appetite and overall food intake.[99]

This combination of factors—high omega-3 fat content, high polyphenol content, high lignan content, and a fiber that becomes gelatinous in water—is probably why their use produces such powerful, positive results in metabolic syndrome, insulin resistance, type 2 diabetes, and heart disease.[100]

The Importance of Lignans

Lignans are important fiber-related polyphenols. They:

- Are disease-fighting, plant-derived chemicals found in plants, seeds, whole grains, legumes, fruits, and vegetables.[101]

- Are precursors converted to other polyphenols by bacteria that normally colonize the human intestine, providing a weak estrogenic effect.

- May help prevent hormone-associated cancers, colon cancer, osteoporosis, and cardiovascular diseases.

- May improve menopausal symptoms and protect against breast cancer.[102]

Flaxseeds are the richest dietary source of lignan precursors. Sesame seeds are another rich source, followed by brassica vegetables, then grains (barley, oat, wheat, and rye).

For instance, a study at North Dakota State University randomized a group of obese, glucose-intolerant people, giving one group 40 grams of flaxseed and another group 40 grams of wheat bran baked bread. Each group took the prescribed supplemental fiber for 12 weeks. The group receiving the flaxseed saw reduced inflammatory markers, reduced blood glucose and insulin levels, and a 20 percent reduction in the prevalence of metabolic syndrome.[103]

Another study sought to determine whether or not flaxseed had an impact on cardiovascular disease risk in healthy menopausal women–a group whose number one risk of death is heart failure. The study investigators enrolled 199 women who were divided into two groups and assigned either 40 grams of flaxseed daily or 12 grams of a wheat germ placebo for 12 months.[104] After a year, those who took the flaxseed had increased levels of omega-3 fatty acids and reduced risk factors for cardiovascular illness including LDL, C-reactive protein, and blood glucose. This effect of flaxseed on LDL levels has been replicated several times. In one study, scientists found that LDL was reduced by as much as 12 to 15 percent with flaxseed supplementation, while fat excretion from the body was increased.[105] Another study showed that supplementation with flaxseed lignan for 12 weeks reduced cholesterol levels in men with moderately high cholesterol while decreasing liver disease factors.[106]

But can flaxseeds give you back your figure? Get this: Dietary flaxseed oil has been shown to reduce *fat cell size* and inflammatory mediators in obese insulin-resistant rats.[107, 108] In an interesting study, scientists induced obesity in rats by turning on inflammatory responses and appetite centers in their brains (the hypothalamus). They then showed that diet-, pharmacological-, and gene-based approaches could reverse this weight gain.[109] To do this, they used fire-quenching anti-inflammatory oils. They reported that either *partial substitution* of dietary omega-3–rich flaxseed-derived oil or omega-9–rich monounsaturated olive oil reversed hypothalamic inflammation and corrected the molecular mediator involved in inflammation in the first place. This intervention also helped rebalance hormones like insulin, leptin, and others. There are several important lessons from this study.

1. Bad diet can lead to inflammation in the brain, stimulating the appetite and leading to increased energy intake and insulin resistance.

2. This process is *reversible* with a healthy anti-inflammatory prebiotic diet.

In fact, researchers injected these anti-inflammatory oils directly into the hypothalamus and were able to emulate the dietary effects on appetite, metabolism, and body weight.

In a study of 115 women conducted by Laval University in Quebec, those with a higher consumption of lignans were healthier and thinner. They had a lower average body mass index (BMI), and those who ate the most flax had 8.5 kilograms (nearly 18 pounds) less body fat. Simply put, higher intake of lignans was associated with lower BMI and body fat mass and improved insulin sensitivity.[110]

So while I emphasize eating more olive oil through the Gut Balance Revolution, remember that ground flaxseed is a nice source of lignans that are prebiotic and whose oils are anti-inflammatory–a one-two punch to fight body fat.

You can grind flaxseeds and add them to baked goods, one of the typical methods they're administered in studies. But that's not the only way to enjoy them. Grind and add them to your morning shake, try them as a crust on broiled chicken, or add them to plain live-cultured yogurt with a little raw honey and blueberries for a superdessert. I love to stir a decadent blend of ground flaxseeds and chia seeds, cocoa, and coconut into a mixture of plain Greek and White Mountain yogurt (for a probiotic colony boost) and top it with berries and sliced almonds or walnuts. That's a superfood weight-loss-promoting healthy snack to be sure!

7. NUTS

Can a calorie-rich food packed with fat help you lose weight, lower your risk of type 2 diabetes and heart disease, and reduce your risk of mortality from all causes? That food does exist–it's the tree nut.

Nuts have basked in a lot of glowing press over the last decade, and for good reason. The data show that regular consumption of nuts has a wide array of health benefits, from the prebiotic effects of almonds to the cholesterol-improving, anti-inflammatory effects of pistachios. But that's only the beginning of the story about this superfood. Nuts in all forms–almonds, macadamias, pistachios, cashews, Brazil nuts, and others–have impressive effects on health and can help you lose and keep weight off. Let's go to the science that proves it.

A recent study published in the *New England Journal of Medicine* reviewed data from the Nurses' Health Study and the Health Professionals Follow-Up Study, which together included 118,962 people.[111, 112] Scientists found that nut consumption was inversely correlated with mortality from all causes–the more servings of nuts people ate per week, the less likely they were to die over the course of the studies. The researchers also noted that significant inverse associations were observed between nut consumption and risk of cancer, heart disease, and respiratory illness.

The long-studied correlation between nut consumption and reduced risk for cardiovascular disease has been replicated so many times that it's well accepted that nuts reduce your risk of cardiovascular disease and death from heart attacks for many reasons. We initially became aware of this correlation in 1992 with the completion of the Adventist Health Study, one of the first to show that nut consumption correlated with a reduced risk of cardiovascular illness.[113] This was quickly followed by another study published by the same group of scientists, revealing that eating walnuts reduced serum cholesterol levels and blood pressure in healthy men.[114] These two seminal studies kicked off what has now been more than 2 decades of research on the health effects of nuts.

A meta-analysis of four of the largest of these studies (Adventist Health Study, Iowa

Women's Health Study, Nurses' Health Study, and the Physicians' Health Study) showed that the risk of cardiovascular illness is 37 percent lower in people eating nuts four or more times per week.[115] Of the four studies reviewed, the Physicians' Health Study is of particular interest because the inverse correlation between nut consumption and cardiovascular illness was primarily due to a 47 percent reduction in sudden cardiac death and lowered total coronary heart disease mortality.[116] In each of these studies, there was a dose-response relationship between nuts and cardiovascular risk independent of gender, age, BMI, alcohol use, other nutritional characteristics, or other cardiovascular risk factors. That means simply eating more nuts–without changing anything else–may dramatically reduce your risk of heart disease.

Why do nuts have such a powerful influence on heart health? Most likely because they reduce cholesterol, inflammation, and oxidation, and they're also rich in fiber, which feeds your good gut bacteria, providing a wide array of benefits.

In a pooled analysis of 25 intervention trials in which nuts were given to participants, it was shown that on average 67 grams of nuts eaten daily reduced LDL cholesterol by 5 to 7 percent.[117] Again, nuts had this effect in a dose-response relationship independent of all other risk factors. Similar results were found in a meta-analysis of 13 studies done on walnuts.[118] When compared to control diets, walnut-enriched diets reduce LDL cholesterol by an average of 6.7 percent. In both these analyses, nuts had no influence on HDL. On the surface this sounds insignificant, but it's actually critically important. By reducing only LDL while having no effect on HDL, nuts improve the overall ratio of these different types of cholesterol in the body–very desirable for heart health.

Several studies have also revealed that eating nuts reduces systemic inflammation in the body–a primary risk factor for cardiovascular disease (as well as for weight gain, type 2 diabetes, and other chronic illnesses). One analyzed data from 6,000 participants in the Multi-Ethnic Study of Atherosclerosis in an attempt to uncover a relationship between nut consumption and inflammatory markers in the blood.[119] The results were astounding. People who ate nuts had reduced levels of C-reactive protein, interleukin 6, and fibrinogen–a powerful indication that nuts reduce inflammation. Other studies have come to similar conclusions.[120, 121] No doubt these effects are due to the fact that nuts are high in anti-inflammatory omega-3 fatty acids.

Growing evidence also shows that the tocopherols and polyphenols in nuts reduce lipid oxidation–another risk factor for heart disease. Studies in both animals and humans confirm this effect.[122]

The health benefits of nuts continue: They reduce your risk of metabolic syndrome, type 2 diabetes, and obesity. A recent study from the School of Public Health at Loma Linda University found that nut consumption had an inverse relationship to metabolic syndrome and obesity.[123] The data showed that people who ate the most nuts had a lower average BMI–they typically weighed less than their non-nut-eating counterparts.

How could it be that people who eat more calorie- and fat-rich nuts actually weigh less? It's likely because the protein, fiber, and fat in nuts reduce appetite and increase satiation.[124] A study from the School of Pharmacy and Medical Sciences at the University of South Australia showed that daily consumption of almonds reduced blood glucose, appetite, and the desire to eat.[125] This suggests that although nuts are a relatively energy-dense snack, they satiate hunger–when you eat them, you're likely to consume fewer calories over the course of your day. A number of studies have indicated that nuts induce satiation by eliciting the secretion of gut-slowing hormones that also act on the brain, such as cholecystokinin and peptide YY.[126, 127] Avoiding nuts because they're high in calories may be pennywise but pound foolish. The net result of eating nuts as a snack is overall daily caloric reduction that comes with a massive host of very well-documented health benefits.

Nut consumption has been firmly linked to a lean metabolism, a lower risk of obesity, and improved weight maintenance. Epidemiologic and clinical studies suggest that moderate consumption of nuts may provide people an enjoyable way to control their weight.[128-134] Most notable and widely cited throughout this book is the analysis performed by Harvard researchers led by Dr. Walter Willett,* who prospectively evaluated three separate cohorts,† including 120,877 US women and men who were free of chronic disease and who weren't obese at the beginning of the study.[135] Overall, those who increased the daily serving of nuts lost an average of 0.57 pound over a 4-year period of time, independent of many other dietary factors. In the Nurses' Health Study II, increasing nut consumption in women translated to a 1-pound weight loss per 4-year period, equaling yogurt as the two most prominent foods that help maintain body weight in women.

Although there are many choices for healthful and weight-loss-promoting nuts, there are interesting data about pistachios.[136] The pistachio is a nutrient-dense nut that promotes heart-healthy blood lipid profiles with potent antioxidant and anti-inflammatory activity. It enhances glycemic control while maintaining endothelial function.[137] When consumed in moderation, pistachios may help control body weight, because they signal satiety in the brain and have relatively few calories. In fact, those who eat nuts requiring removal of the shell actually consume fewer pistachio nuts compared to those who eat unshelled nuts–

---

* Dr. Willett is the Fredrick John Stare Professor of Epidemiology and Nutrition and the chair of the department of nutrition at Harvard School of Public Health. He is also a professor of medicine at Harvard Medical School and is the principal investigator of the second Nurses' Health Study, a compilation of studies regarding the health of older women and their risk factors for major chronic diseases–which was part of the analysis cited above. He has published more than 1,000 scientific articles regarding various aspects of diet and disease and is the second most cited author in clinical medicine. (hsph.harvard.edu/walter-willett/)

† The Nurses' Health Study (NHS) is a prospective study of a cohort of 121,701 female registered nurses from 11 US states who were enrolled in 1976. The Nurses' Health Study II (NHS II) is a prospective study of a cohort of 116,686 younger female registered nurses from 14 states who were enrolled in 1989. The Health Professionals Follow-Up Study (HPFS) is a prospective study of a cohort of 51,529 male health professionals from all 50 states, enrolled in 1986.

either from visual cuing and/or from the extra time and labor involved in eating more mindfully, which slows the process of eating.[138, 139] One study with subjects in a weight-loss program demonstrated lower BMI and triglyceride levels in individuals who consumed pistachios compared with those who consumed an isocaloric pretzel snack.[140] I strongly recommend that you incorporate pistachios into your diet–just beware that the pistachio is relatively rich in the FODMAP xylitol and may not be suitable for the Phase 1 diet plan.

Overall, nuts aid weight management by virtue of their strong effects upon satiation, the inefficiency of absorption of fats, and an elevation of energy expenditure and fat oxidation.[141] But given their high energy density, don't go totally nuts on nuts. It's easy to overeat them, and the effects can be deleterious. Two cups of nuts equals about 1,600 calories. I'm not a big calorie counter, but that's a lot of calories for not much food. My recommendation: Stick to a handful or two of nuts daily. Most of the studies have people consuming somewhere between 60 and 100 grams (around 30 to 50 nuts) daily–more than many of you will need to tide you over between meals. I strongly encourage you to include this crunchy, delicious snack in your daily diet–in moderation. There are few foods with such comprehensive data illustrating that they're truly medicine.

8. COFFEE

Almost everyone is surprised to find coffee on my list of superfoods, yet the data increasingly show that this ancient beverage, dating from 15th-century Ethiopia, has a plethora of health benefits, as long as you drink the right type of coffee in moderation and consider your personal health status while doing so. Let's address some of these issues.

The "right type of coffee" is most definitely *not* a grande frappucino from Starbucks. Coffee as a health food means the classic beverage brewed from ground coffee beans. It is the coffee, *not* the milk and sugar, that provides health benefits. If you prefer your coffee in the form of a milkshake, it won't benefit your health or your waistline. Plain old black coffee–possibly with a little cream (or almond milk if you're dairy sensitive) and a teaspoon of a stevia sweetener or raw honey, or a few sprinkles of cinnamon–is the way to go. Caffeinated or decaf are both fine, though caffeinated coffee may have slightly better health benefits. However, be careful about decaf, which is mainly processed using organochemical solvents (such as methylene chloride and ethyl acetate).[142] Decaf is also more acidic than regular coffee and can raise serum lipids levels, which raises cardiovascular risk.[143]

The key to coffee is moderation. Studies show that health benefits occur by consuming one to four 8-ounce cups daily. Less than this and you probably won't receive the same health benefits; more and you're liable to run into acid reflux, insomnia, and anxiety. Up to four cups may sound like a lot of coffee, but remember–that's a maximum of 32 ounces of coffee a day.

If you're anxious or have hypertension, minimize or eliminate your caffeine intake. Data show that drinking caffeinated coffee raises blood pressure–a primary risk factor for cardiovascular disease and heart attack—so if you have hypertension, I strongly encourage you to limit coffee or go for decaf and have your doctor monitor your blood pressure.[144] With these caveats in place, let's look at the research that supports the use of this superbeverage for supporting health and weight outcomes.

Perhaps the most profound evidence in favor of coffee as a superfood comes from a study published in the *New England Journal of Medicine*[145] that reviewed the data from 229,119 men and 173,141 women who participated in the NIH-AARP Diet and Health Study. Inverse associations between coffee consumption and deaths due to heart disease, respiratory disease, stroke, injuries and accidents, diabetes, and infections were observed. Put more simply: Coffee was correlated with a reduction in all-cause mortality.

As long as you don't have high blood pressure, there's strong evidence that regular coffee consumption *reduces* your risk of heart failure. Researchers at Harvard Medical School dug up studies on the relationship between cardiovascular disease and coffee consumption conducted from 1966 through 2011 and found five independent prospective studies including 140,220 participants. They performed a meta-analysis of this data and discovered that those who drank four cups a day had a significantly lower risk of heart failure than those who consumed no coffee. On the other hand, those who consumed more than four cups daily had a potentially higher risk of fatal heart attacks.

Coffee appears to have similarly powerful effects on type 2 diabetes. Researchers at the City University of New York conducted a meta-analysis of 20 epidemiological studies focusing on coffee consumption and type 2 diabetes risk. These studies include data on more than 300,000 people followed between 6 and 23 years. Seventeen of the 20 studies found evidence that coffee consumption can reduce the risk of type 2 diabetes. The other three showed no correlation; none of the studies showed that coffee had a negative effect. On the surface, this seems at odds with other data from the Netherlands that have shown a rapid intravenous infusion of caffeine over 15 minutes can raise blood glucose by reducing insulin sensitivity by 15 percent, at least in the short term.[146] Bear in mind this is likely because the caffeine shock induced by infusing the blood with so much at one time raised plasma stress hormones such as epinephrine and norepinephrine, which promote insulin resistance and inflammation. Still, how could drinking coffee reduce the risk of type 2 diabetes yet raise blood glucose in the short term? It doesn't seem to make sense. Well, one small study (this one had only 12 participants) may not completely emulate real life. Food eaten with the coffee and/or cream in the coffee would delay gastric emptying and the absorption of caffeine. Plus, noncaffeine compounds in coffee mitigate the blood sugar–raising effects over the long run, and research on such compounds is limited. However, there are three chemicals in coffee that show promising results in this area.

The first is chlorogenic acid, which is also a phytonutrient in apples. A study conducted at the University of Surrey in the United Kingdom showed that chlorogenic acid altered caffeine absorption rates and reduced blood glucose.[147] The researchers took three groups of people and gave them 25 grams of glucose in either water, regular coffee, or decaffeinated coffee. As expected, caffeinated coffee spiked blood glucose more than decaf or water. But here's where it gets interesting. Both coffee groups experienced a change in gut hormones directly responsible for insulin secretion and glucose absorption. This was not seen in the control. It appears that chlorogenic acid in coffee delays glucose absorption in the gut so that less ends up in the bloodstream. By the same token, less insulin is released, indicating enhanced insulin sensitivity. This is one mechanism scientists now feel is responsible for the relationship between regular coffee consumption and reduced risk of type 2 diabetes.

The second all-star player in coffee is quinidine. Animal models have shown that quinidine reduces liver glucose production, and we think the same thing may happen in humans.[148] Finally, there's the magnificent mineral magnesium. Coffee has relatively high amounts of magnesium (about 7 milligrams per cup, according to the USDA), and we know that magnesium enhances insulin sensitivity, reduces the risk of type 2 diabetes, and improves the metabolic profiles of those with metabolic obesity.[149, 150]

These effects on blood sugar, as well as caffeine's thermogenic effects and its positive impact on satiety, may be why coffee helps people keep weight off for the long term.[151] A prospective study of 18,417 men and 39,740 women who were followed for 12 years showed that those who drank more coffee gained less weight.[152] And a recent study out of the New York Obesity Research Center found that men who drank a beverage infused with mannooligosaccharides from coffee for 12 weeks lost more weight and visceral fat (that flab around the belly we all want less of) than did their counterparts who received a placebo.[153]

Since Phase 3 is all about weight maintenance, this makes coffee a particularly useful superfood for this phase. Coffee drinkers also seem to have lower rates of melanoma, depression, stroke, Parkinson's disease, cognitive decline/Alzheimer's disease, colorectal cancer, liver disease, gallstones, and vision loss.[154-161]

All that from a cup of coffee. Don't listen to the naysayers. Coffee's a superfood—no doubt about it. Just don't overdo it, avoid those sugar-laden coffee drinks, and choose lighter roasts—there's evidence that these retain more of the chemicals that help you burn fat.

9. BROCCOLI

The word broccoli comes from the Italian word for "cabbage sprout," and for good reason. Broccoli is a member of the cruciferous family of vegetables, and all these plants are derived from the same common, ancient ancestor. You'd never know it by looking at them in the produce department, but all crucifers—from bok choy to broccoli rabe—are a result of human selection occurring over the thousands of years these foods have been cultivated.

This makes it easier to understand why they have similar nutritional profiles and impacts on health. Like the other crucifers, broccoli is loaded with vitamins K and C and folate. It has the same power to bind to bile acids as its cousins, so it can reduce your cholesterol levels; it helps diversify your gut microbiome, as all the cruciferous veggies do; and studies have shown that eating crucifers may reduce your risk of cancer.[162]

Given all these similarities, why would I call out broccoli as a superfood?

Two reasons. The first is practical. Few people are aware that broccoli is in the same family as cabbage and kale. It's not intuitive, since they don't look much alike. So it made more sense organizationally to separate broccoli from the crowd. But the more important reason is that broccoli has special health benefits that other cruciferous vegetables don't.

Broccoli appears to have a powerful effect on prostate cancer. While all cruciferous vegetables seem to reduce the risk of cancer, few foods protect your prostate the way broccoli does, especially against more aggressive forms of prostate cancer. A study led by Dr. Victoria Kirsh and colleagues at Cancer Care Ontario's Division of Preventive Oncology in Ontario, Canada, reviewed data from 1,338 patients with prostate cancer and found that intake of cruciferous vegetables reduced the risk of aggressive stage III or stage IV prostate cancer.[163] Broccoli had the most powerful effect. People who ate more than one serving of broccoli per week were 55 percent less likely to develop aggressive prostate cancer than those who ate less than one serving monthly. A few servings of broccoli a week kept cancer at bay.

Why does broccoli, in particular, have such a powerful impact on prostate cancer? While more research needs to be done, scientists have tracked down a few of the biochemical properties that we think lead to these effects.

The first is that consuming broccoli appears to modulate the GSTM1 genotype—which is involved with inflammation and carcinogenesis in positive ways. Broccoli "tells" your genes to turn down inflammation and tumor production. Recent research showed that men who ate a broccoli-rich diet showed precisely these kinds of changes in gene expression.[164]

What is it in broccoli that produces these changes in gene expression? Broccoli, like all of those in the Brassica family, is particularly rich in the anti-inflammatory, antioxidant glucosinolates; in particular, it has high levels of glucoraphanin, gluconasturtiin, and glucobrassicin.[165] Scientists believe these chemicals may pull epigenetic triggers that mitigate the progression of prostate cancer. These three glucosinolates also happen to support various steps in the body's detoxification process, including activation, neutralization, and elimination of unwanted contaminants. So your detox system benefits from broccoli and the Brassica family of vegetables such as broccoli rabe.

As much as broccoli is an antioxidant-rich superfood, it's got plenty of soluble fiber to feed your good gut bacteria and induce a lean metabolism. Broccoli also has potent anti-inflammatory activities[166] and directly affects your fat cells, causing them to shrink into oblivion. For instance, the indole-3-carbinol (I3C) in broccoli and other cruciferous vegetables targets a specific receptor on fat cells to block their proliferation.[167] One study demonstrated that I3C—when given to mice with diet-induced obesity via a high-fat diet—improved blood lipid profile, reduced inflammatory markers, decreased the expression and levels of proinflammatory mediators, and modulated genes that control leptin and adipocyte protein 2 expression. This suggests that I3C has the potential to prevent obesity and metabolic disorders via multiple mechanisms, including decreased fat storage, reduced inflammation, and enhanced thermogenesis.

These phytonutrients appear to be most bioavailable when you lightly steam broccoli, though you can get them from raw broccoli as well. Don't overcook this vegetable, as some of its anticancer properties may be diminished if you do. I recommend preparing broccoli simply: Cut the florets into pieces and lightly steam for 3 to 5 minutes, or until just tender. Dress with olive oil, salt and pepper, and a splash of vinegar if you like. Broccoli rabe is a bold member of the Brassica family with a slight bitterness that is wonderful on the taste buds. Steam it and serve with olive oil, lemon juice, and a dash of salt–a Dr. Gerry favorite! Enjoy this delectable dish knowing you're fighting cancer, optimizing your fatty acid balance, and supporting excellent health all at the same time.

Honorable Mention: Broccoli Sprouts Powder

Broccoli sprouts are rich in antioxidants and have been tested for their ability to attenuate type 2 diabetes in humans in part by reducing oxidative stress and inflammation-induced insulin resistance.[168] Eighty-one patients were randomly assigned to receive either 10 grams daily of broccoli sprouts powder, 5 grams daily of broccoli sprouts powder, or a placebo for 4 weeks.[169] After 4 weeks, consumption of 10 grams daily of the powder resulted in a significant decrease in serum insulin concentration and improved insulin sensitivity. Broccoli sprouts may improve insulin resistance in type 2 diabetic patients.

Two marvelous scientists at Johns Hopkins put broccoli sprouts on the map: Dr. Paul Talay and Dr. Jed Fahey.[170] In fact, after their discoveries of the anticancer benefits of broccoli sprouts, the sales of these sprouts in the United States doubled. Thanks to these doctors, research has further elucidated the many health-promoting benefits of broccoli sprouts.

10. ARTICHOKES

We end the list of Phase 3 superfoods with a prebiotic edible thistle that has been with humanity for eons and was prized by Romans as a food of nobility. Artichokes are high in inulin–the prebiotic fiber that feeds your gut microbiome. These kingly foods share their name with two other foods they aren't related to: Jerusalem artichoke (also known as sunchoke) and Chinese artichoke. Don't get confused. The thistle with hard leaves that looks like a bulb is the one I'm referring to here.

Insulin is a natural oligomer of fructose that, following ingestion, is fermented by the bifidobacterial population of the colon, increasing its growth. Inulin added to food may prevent diabetes and obesity. Artichokes contain a special type of inulin called very-long-chain inulin (VLCI). In fact, artichokes have the longest chains of inulin of any vegetable,[171] and studies are showing that VLCI may have special effects on your gut microbiome.

A recent randomized, double-blind, placebo-controlled study (the gold standard in science) took two groups of people and gave them either 10 grams daily of VLCI derived from artichokes or maltodextrin.[172] The folks who took the VLCI supplement (remember, this is the same type of inulin found in artichokes) had significantly higher levels of bifidobacteria and lactobacilli and a reduction in pathogens such as species of *Prevotella* bacteria.[173] The health benefits of this superfood don't stop with its fertilizing effect on your gut microbiome. Artichokes may reduce LDL cholesterol, increase HDL cholesterol, and improve certain metabolic parameters in overweight people.[174, 175]

Most of the studies done in these areas have focused on the use of artichoke leaf extract, a supplement containing the phenolic compounds, flavonoids, and other protective compounds in the leaves of artichokes. While you'd have to eat a boatload of artichoke leaves to get the same amount in the supplements, it's logical to assume you'll still get some of the same positive effects by sticking with the whole-food version.

Artichokes may also balance blood sugar and improve other metabolic parameters associated with weight gain and type 2 diabetes. Research at the University of Paiva in Italy showed that supplementation with artichoke extract helped people reduce their fasting blood glucose, HA1c was reduced (meaning glycated hemoglobin in the blood was lowered), the patients' hyperlipidemic patterns improved, and patients saw improvements across several other metabolic pathways.[176]

To top it off, artichokes couldn't be easier to prepare. Just snip off the spiky ends of the leaves, drop the bulb in water, and simmer until tender. Then pull the leaves away and enjoy. Of course, don't skip the delectable heart.

LOOKING AHEAD

"Let medicine be thy food, and food be thy medicine." Hippocrates' words are more valuable today than ever. The superfoods I've highlighted in this book illustrate the profound healing power that food–real, whole food–can have. None of them individually will cure illness. But together they offer broad health-protective effects that may indeed shield you from chronic illness while keeping your waistline slim and trim.

So many people don't eat what I'd call food. The modern Western diet, filled with "ingestibles"–highly processed foodlike substances–is a poor excuse from both a health *and* a flavor perspective compared to the real, whole foods humanity evolved to eat.

The Gut Balance Revolution emphasizes superfoods found in your pantry to promote slimness by melting away your excess fat. Your pantry should be filled with items that can improve your metabolic fat-burning furnace. Remember that spiced foods and herbal drinks can lead to greater energy loss by thermogenesis, oxidizing fat and in some cases increasing satiety. These herbs have a wide range of effects that can upregulate the body's built-in weight-loss mechanisms. Capsaicin, black pepper, ginger, green tea, black tea, and caffeine have the potential to raise your metabolism and help you lose weight automatically just by incorporating these healthy functional foods into your repertoire.[177]

Adding the superfoods in this phase (and those from previous phases) back to your diet will provide not only a bevy of health benefits but also an opportunity to reconnect with the food that nourishes you and to experience a way of eating and living that's been part of the human experience for generations. When you do this, your gut microbiome will thank you, your health will thank you, and your waistline will thank you.

Another important step on the path to good health is learning how to reduce stress, exercise optimally, sleep better, and live a gut-balancing, health-promoting lifestyle. In the next chapter, I'll explain how to do that.

THE GUT BALANCE REVOLUTION SUCCESS STORIES
Stephanie Gittens, 37

Piling on the pounds might be easy, but as Stephanie Gittens knows, taking them off—well, that's another story. Over the years, she'd been on more diets than she could count. She'd quickly trim off a couple of pounds but gain them all back—and then some—even faster. Meanwhile, the number on the scale kept creeping up.

"When I reached my highest weight of 317," Stephanie recalls, "it definitely slowed me down, and I knew I had to try something else." When the Gut Balance Revolution came along, Stephanie realized she'd finally found a totally new eating plan that would work for the long haul. "I really liked learning about the connection between weight and the good and bad bugs in the gut," Stephanie says. "And I loved the ease of the plan—with the charts that showed us which foods to favor and which ones to forget, it was such a simple, effective diet."

Stephanie filled up her pantry and fridge with the Gut Balance Revolution foods and got started with the plan. And it worked—in 8 weeks, she'd lost 20 pounds. As it turns out, the other things she lost were even better. "I noticed that my moods were getting brighter," says Stephanie, who's a front desk receptionist at a surgeon's office. "I was so much happier, and I seemed so much more energized. And it was fantastic being able to go outside and play with my children. Everyone seems to notice that I've changed for the better!"

CHAPTER 10

Living a
Gut-Balancing Life

Creating a healthy, sustainable ecosystem inside and out is about more than how we eat. Certainly, what you feed your gut microbiome is at the foundation of good health–it's the first step you need to take to rebalance your inner garden, lose weight, and remain healthy for life. However, taking an ecosystems approach to weight loss means looking not only within our bodies but also at the broader picture of our lives and figuring out how to live in a way that supports our health, weight, and inner ecology. It's about learning how to live with the natural rhythms of life in a sustainable way that fits us for the long term.

Most of us don't live this way today. We're overworked and stressed out; we sleep too little and worry too much. We take our lunch at our desks because "we don't have time to eat," and we rarely make the time for activities that nourish us inside and out. We live in a world out of sync with the natural rhythms of day and night, work and rest.

We also have a bizarre relationship to exercise. We either exercise way too little or way too much. The most recent data from the Centers for Disease Control and Prevention reveal that 79 percent of Americans don't get the minimum recommended amount of exercise[1]–for adults, at least $2^1/_2$ hours of moderate-intensity aerobic exercise weekly or $1^1/_4$ hours of vigorous-intensity activity or a combination of both types. Those least likely to engage in physical activity were age 65 and older (nearly 16 percent of exercisers). Adults should also engage in muscle-strengthening activities like lifting weights or doing pushups at least twice per week. Research has shown approximately 25 to 35 percent of US adults are physically inactive,[2, 3] which translates to 40 million to 50 million Americans.

On the other side of the equation are those who overdo it at the gym, trudging for hours on the treadmill, hoping beyond hope (or reason) that if they exercise *a little more* they'll burn off the fat on their belly, butt, and hips. Those "weekend warriors" who are inactive all week, then overcompensate on weekends with high-intensity exercises, are exposing themselves to an increased risk of cardiovascular events.[4]

Put simply: Our lives are out of whack, and this impacts our health and our gut microbiome in surprising ways. Stress, sleep, exercise, the way you eat, when you eat, and other factors affect hormonal balance, metabolism, and the health of your inner garden.

That's why I want to provide you the tools you need to live a lifestyle that helps maintain balance inside and out. The Gut Balance Revolution is about more than changing your diet and reestablishing a relationship with the friendly gut symbiotes that keep you healthy and happy. It's about revolutionizing the way you live and relate to the world so that you can live in harmony with the broader ecology inside and around you.

Let's start by taking a close look at one of America's most unhealthy national pastimes–chronic stress–and review the ways it sends your life, your health, and your gut microbiome spiraling out of balance.

STRESS: THE UNHEALTHIEST PASTIME IN AMERICA

America is at a critical crossroads when it comes to stress and our health.

—Norman B. Anderson, PhD, CEO,
American Psychological Association

Americans are a stressed-out people. A staggering 40 million of us over the age of 18– that's 18.1 percent of the adult population–have an anxiety disorder, costing the United States more than $42 billion per year.[5, 6] Forty-four percent of American adults report that their stress levels have increased over the last 5 years.[7] Unfortunately, it appears that the younger generations are getting hit the hardest. According to the American Psychological Association's report *Stress in America*, millennials (people who came of age during the 2000s) are the most stressed-out generation.[8] How come? Everything from money problems to work issues, from family troubles to personal challenges.[9] Stress is not just compromising our quality of life, it's also contributing to our chronic disease epidemic–and it's not doing any favors to our waistlines, either. Among the physical consequences of stress:

- It increases the amount of belly fat you have, makes it easier for you to store fat, and reduces your ability to burn fat.[10-12]

- It sets off a fire of inflammation in your body that can lead to metabolic syndrome, type 2 diabetes, weight gain, and other health problems.

- It increases your incidence of cardiovascular disease, especially among lower socioeconomic classes.[13, 14]

- It may lead to a 400 percent increase in the risk of developing hypertension.[15]

- It raises your blood sugar, makes it harder for sugar to get into your cells, and makes you less insulin sensitive, putting you at increased risk for type 2 diabetes.[16]

- It causes you to crave sugary foods and can set off emotional eating.[17]

- It leads to imbalance in your gut microbiome, causing a decrease in *Bacteroides* and an increase in *Clostridium* species. These imbalances may set off a downward spiral of continued stress and disrupt the harmony of the gut microbiome, since your intestinal flora has a significant impact on your mood and eating behavior, leading to a vicious cycle.[18, 19]

This is just the short list of detrimental effects of chronic stress, and it doesn't account for problems like lack of life satisfaction and relationship issues. For an in-depth look at the full host of health problems that can arise from chronic unrelenting stress and the underlying biochemistry that drives them, I recommend the book *Why Zebras Don't Get Ulcers* by Dr. Robert Sapolsky, one of the premier stress researchers in the country.[20]

Why does all this stress happen, and what can we do about it? Let's reach back to our caveman past to unearth the biochemical underpinnings of the stress response.

FIGHT OR FLIGHT: STAYING ALIVE IN CAVEMAN TIMES

Our stress response is an ancient survival mechanism easiest understood by considering why it likely evolved over time. Imagine you're a prehistoric man or woman out happily gathering and munching on berries. Behind you, in the brush, you hear a low growl, panting, and twigs snapping. What happens next is familiar to anyone who's been in a frightening or life-threatening situation: Your stress response–also known as the fight-or-flight response–is triggered, setting off a sequence of biochemical events that prepare you to either run like crazy or fight like a demon. Three primary chemicals are released into your bloodstream: epinephrine, norepinephrine, and cortisol. These chemicals trigger the physiological responses needed to prepare you for the imminent attack by the monster that wants to eat you. Your eyes dilate slightly so you can see more clearly, your blood is shunted toward your lower appendages so you can move more quickly, and your nonessential biological processes (digestion and the reproductive system, for example) are downregulated, conserving energy for the important work of staying alive.

This response is what gives you a fighting chance in life-threatening situations. Without it, humans very likely wouldn't be on the planet because most of them would have become dinner for stronger, faster predators. You can thank your stress response for saving you if you've ever been in a near-miss car accident or have accidentally stepped off the curb in the path of an oncoming bus only to quickly reel back onto the sidewalk before getting flattened. In fact, all these situations are examples how the stress response is *supposed* to work. An explosion of powerful biochemicals temporarily turns you into a superhuman so you can stay alive during trying circumstances. These chemicals are then rapidly ushered out of your bloodstream, your stress response cools down, and you go back to your regular, relatively relaxed way of life.

But there's one major problem in the modern world: The average life is not "relatively relaxed." Your body doesn't know the difference between perceived stressors and real, life-threatening stressors. It responds as though you're about to be eaten by a wild beast anytime something shakes you up. So if you're under heavy deadlines at work, your boss yells at you, you're stuck in traffic, you're having relationship problems, you don't sleep enough, your nutrition is poor, you don't exercise enough, or you exercise too much, your body will react to all these and the million other stressors you encounter daily as though you're in real, life-threatening danger. Physiologist Hans Selye, who coined the term "stress" in the 1950s, defined it as "the nonspecific response of the body to any demand made upon it." Decades of research since show that this definition is accurate. And it's this fact that has brought America to the "critical crossroads" Dr. Anderson was talking about in the quote earlier in this chapter.

Chronic, unremitting pathological stress is what most of us are facing today, and this form of stress is contributing to the chronic illness, weight gain, mental health problems, and general malaise so many people suffer from. Constant stress is like having the pedal to the metal all day, every day. Eventually, your engine begins to break down. The outcome? You gain weight, you're unhappy, you get sick–and your gut microbiome suffers.

So what's the solution? Most books will tell you to practice activating your relaxation response, and there's something to this. Your stress response is wired into your sympathetic nervous system, so you literally have no control over it–it's triggered by what stresses you out, period. However, we have a built-in antidote to this sympathetic stress response, known as the relaxation response. It's built into your parasympathetic nervous system–the part of your neurology you *do* have some control over. You activate a healing cascade when you make a conscious effort to deeply relax your body through activities like meditation, prayer, yoga, deep breathing, mindful eating, and progressive muscle relaxation.

Studies have shown that learning relaxation and stress-reduction strategies may be a key component of any effective long-term weight-loss program. Researchers at the University of Kentucky divided a group of 26 participants in half. They taught one group stress management techniques but provided no dietary intervention. Instead, they met with these participants for 75 minutes twice weekly for 7 weeks. They taught the other 13 participants an intuitive eating-based dietary intervention that encouraged them to tune in to hunger signals and only eat when hungry. At the end of 7 weeks, the group that learned stress management lost 17 pounds, a loss they sustained at their 14-week follow-up. Those who learned intuitive eating did not lose significant weight.[21]

There's been a recent explosion of research in this area. The Academy of Nutrition and Dietetics has published a position paper supporting the application of mindful eating and intuitive eating as part of nutrition interventions in those with eating disorders.[22] The organization has dedicated dozens of articles in its journal to this topic, demonstrating its efficacy for eating disorders and obesity management.[23-25] These and many other studies demonstrate the powerful tool of integrating mindful and intuitive eating practices into behavior and lifestyle modification plans.

Dr. Michelle May, who runs mindful eating workshops, notes in her programs that "many of the habits that drive overeating are unconscious behaviors that people have repeated for years, and they act them out without even realizing it. Mindfulness allows a person to wake up and be aware of what they're doing. Once you're aware, you can change your actions."[26]

Learning to relax is likely to improve your weight loss, and it's a central part of this program. Later in this chapter, I'll provide some relaxation exercises to integrate into your life. That's a good first step. However, recent research shows that to deal more effectively with stress, we need to do more than simply counter stress with relaxation. We need to develop resilience.

WHAT IS RESILIENCE—AND WHY IS IT IMPORTANT?

Dr. Mehmet Oz talked about resilience and reserve being vital elements to healthy aging at the Integrative Healthcare Symposium in 2013, which inspired me to research this topic and share its importance with you. Resilience is the ability to rebound from an illness, challenge, or life event without developing a maladaptive chronic stress response. Some people have that ineffable quality to be knocked down by life and come back stronger than ever. The more resilient you are, the less you become physically or emotionally compromised by life's stressors and more able to rebound when a setback occurs. After all, stress isn't going away anytime soon. You can reduce your life stressors and learn to relax more—important parts of becoming more resilient—but you won't eliminate all anxiety. In fact, as many as 90 percent of people will experience a traumatic event in their lifetime.[27] Even if you're one of the lucky ones who don't, you probably won't walk through life stress free—nor would you want to. We create deadlines, pressure ourselves to succeed at work, and have family responsibilities for good reasons. Though they can sometimes be stressful, they encourage us to engage with life in a meaningful and productive way. Other stressors–like exercise, which by definition puts stress on your body–are necessary for health and well-being.

Remember the concept of hormesis, which advocates that the human organism copes with a wide variety of harsh environmental conditions by acquiring physiological adaptive mechanisms that improve survival.[28] Exercise is the perfect example of a hormetic process that forces your body to adapt by acutely stressing the body, releasing catecholamines and other biochemicals that transiently alter cardiovascular and systemic physiology. When you overdo exercise or exercise in inappropriate ways, you unduly overstress your body and set off an alarm response with inflammation and other negative physiological reactions. However, when you exercise appropriately, inflammation is lessened. Some scientists think that hormesis is one of the ways by which inflammation is better managed when you exercise regularly.[29] Yet again–the dose makes the poison!

When it comes to stress, more is at stake than initially meets the eye. For example, it's not just the events in your life but the way you perceive and react to them that may make them stressors. In some cases, we may perceive something as a threat when it's really not. If these maladaptive thoughts are recurrent, then the stress response becomes chronic, eventually causing pathophysiological consequences. But if we perceive genuine stressors as a test of our tenacity and our ability to adapt and persevere, they may have a hormetic effect that only makes us stronger. Remember the old saying: What does not kill us makes us stronger.

As always, the key is balance and the ability to bounce back when adversity inevitably hits. That's what resilience is. How do we develop this useful trait? It's clear there are a few important factors that help. Here's what most experts in the field of resilience say you need to do to bounce back from adverse events more effectively.[30]

1. **Have a strong community and solid social support.** Friends, family, and loved ones provide the foundation we need to make it through the tough times.[31]

2. **Keep perspective and maintain a positive attitude.** Looking at the glass as half full instead of half empty seems to have a significant impact on our ability to manage stress.[32] Data from the Women's Health Initiative linked optimism to healthier eating.[33]

3. **Take care of yourself and maintain a positive self-image.** Developing self-confidence and trusting in your ability to overcome difficult challenges helps build resilience.[34] This is a key attribute to perseverance and success.

4. **Confront your fears.** The psychological literature increasingly shows us that avoidance isn't a successful strategy for managing adversity. Exposing yourself to what you fear helps you overcome it.[35]

5. **Accept that which you cannot change**. Change and trauma are a part of life. Ignoring this fact will not help you adjust to the difficulties you face. There is, perhaps, no better embodiment of this truth than the Serenity Prayer, which reads: God, grant me the serenity to accept the things I cannot change, the courage to change the things I can, and the wisdom to know the difference.[36]

6. **Rely on the spiritual**. Meditation and spiritual practices have been shown to help people cool off the stress response and recover more effectively.[37]

7. **Exercise regularly**. Those who exercise regularly tend to bounce back more effectively when confronted with acute stressors.[38]

How do we develop resilience? Some methods are fairly straightforward. Getting more exercise, for example, means setting a routine that makes sense for you–and then doing it. Later in this chapter, I'll outline several different routines based on your needs and fitness levels. Other attributes take time and personal exploration to develop. If you don't have a strong social support network, for instance, going out and meeting friends or reconnecting will take some effort and maybe even personal coaching or professional intervention. For some folks, creating a meditation or spiritual practice may seem difficult. For others, confronting their fears may feel impossible.

There's no one-size-fits-all prescription for resilience–you need to seek your own path, experimenting, testing, and keeping what works, rejecting what doesn't. Take the

Resilience and My Journey to Johns Hopkins: Ode to Dr. Tony Kalloo

If you've read my first book, *The Inside Tract*, you may remember that at one point I was sidelined by a bizarre series of medical mishaps resulting in disability. But as the old saying goes, "What doesn't kill you makes you stronger."

I returned to my roots of natural medicine and faith-based self-healing, and the rest is history. My family and close friends, old and new, rallied around me, and I defied another doctor to use the word *can't*. (After all, one of my favorite movie lines is from a Rocky movie, when Mickey, the trainer, tells Rocky, "Can't, there is no such thing as can't.") I fired my nay-saying doctors, and in due time, I grew stronger. Self-belief, motivation, and community are so important. They give people a reason to succeed, a reason to go on. Nature is smarter than people think.

time to tune in to your own needs and find ways to reduce the overall burden of stress in your life. Become more resilient so that when the inevitable stressors come your way, they won't take such a heavy toll on your weight, health, and life.

In the remainder of this chapter, I'll provide tips on how to build resilience. They include relaxation, mindful eating, improved sleep hygiene, exercise, and more. These techniques have been useful in my own life and with my patients, and the research supports them. This chapter is by no means a comprehensive program for reducing stress or building a more resilient character—it's a primer to introduce you to some valuable basics. If you integrate these steps into your life, I virtually guarantee the quality of your life and health will improve, you will lose weight more easily, and you'll be less likely to regain any weight you do shed. Consider what you're about to read as a beginning. Once you've added these steps into your life, then reach into the vast literature on stress reduction and resilience building on your own, tap into your personal resources, and seek out ways to better balance your life in a way that makes sense for you. You only live once. Enjoy the life you have and make the most of it. You deserve it!

Now let's learn how to relax and bounce back a little more effectively. It all starts with the breath.

LEARN TO BREATHE

Sometimes, all it takes to gain a new perspective on a stressful situation is to take a time out and a few deep breaths. Deep breathing is a simple, powerful, effective,

For me, this was a story of resilience, the ability to "take the hits in life and keep going." A year or so after starting my job at Johns Hopkins, my director, Dr. Anthony Kalloo, stopped by my office and looked at the poster of Rocky on my wall—a bit unusual for this academic workplace. Tony knew my story and was willing to gamble on hiring me—I was his first hire when he became chief of gastroenterology at The Johns Hopkins Hospital. When he looked at my poster, he said, "You need to see the movie *Rocky Balboa*.[39] There's a quote in it that will resonate with you." It was about resilience, which separates those who succeed from those who blame others for their failures. Here's the quote.[40]

> *You, me, or nobody is gonna hit as hard as life. But it ain't about how hard you hit. It's about how hard you can get hit and keep moving forward; how much you can take and keep moving forward. That's how winning is done!*

easy-to-learn relaxation activity you can take with you everywhere you go. It's been shown to reduce blood cortisol levels and improve heart rate variability—primary indicators of a more relaxed physiological state.[41, 42] You can do it anytime, anywhere, and it only takes a few moments. There are *many* deep breathing practices out there. Try this one and adapt it to your needs. Do this for 1 to 2 minutes to experience deep and immediate relaxation.

1. **Get comfortable.** Lie down on your back, sit comfortably in your chair, or just stand where you are with your arms loose and dangling at your sides. If you can, loosen any tight clothing.

2. **Inhale slowly through your nose for a count of 5.** As you slowly draw your breath down with your diaphragm, count 1-2-3-4-5. If you can't breathe through your nose, it's okay to breathe through your mouth.

3. **Exhale through your mouth to a count of 5.** Exhale as slowly as you inhale, counting 1-2-3-4-5.

Repeat the process five times anytime you're stressed, and you'll find the tension slowly fade away.

When you begin practicing deep breathing, I usually recommend doing it three to five times a day. Do this every day you're on this program. After you've integrated the practice into your life, you'll find yourself using it naturally when you're feeling tense or anxious.

Some people feel lightheaded or slightly dizzy when they begin this practice. For most, that fades away after a few times, but if it doesn't, discontinue the practice, use the relaxation techniques that follow, and check with a physician to see if you have an underlying medical problems causing this.

EAT MINDFULLY

It may be hard to believe that eating in a particular way can reduce stress and help you take life a little more lightly, but I assure you this technique will not only help you relax, it will revolutionize your relationship to what you put in your mouth.

Mindfulness is the state of simple, attentive awareness of what's going on around you moment by moment. In our fast-paced society, our mind races from one activity to the next with some seemingly simultaneous, chaotic, uncontrollable chatter. We think about the future ("What are we going to eat for dinner tonight?"), we think about the past ("Why did my boss say that to me?"), we tune in to our devices to check e-mail or work or play games at all hours of the day and night. During waking hours, life becomes a symphony of constant multitasking. Rarely do we take a step back, recenter ourselves, observe our own mind and surroundings, and connect with the inner peace and deep quiet within.

There are times when moving quickly to accomplish tasks is justified. In my job as a medical professional, for example, it's often absolutely necessary. Deadlines, benchmarks, and goals are all put in place as a way to encourage us to accomplish what we need to in a timely manner. But most of us are rushing from the moment we wake up until the moment we pass out at night, and this isn't healthy. It's stressful. It's exhausting. And perhaps most significantly, it diminishes the quality of our life.

So how do we beat the rush, step out of the rat race (at least for a moment), slow down, relax, and take the pause we need to reconnect with our inmost selves? There are lots of ways to do this, but one of my personal favorites is eating mindfully. This simply means putting aside other distractions, eating, and paying careful attention to food. It's about becoming attentive to your present experience and tuning in to what you're ingesting, how it tastes, and how it makes you feel. It's not difficult–it's actually very enjoyable–and doesn't take much time. Here's how.

1. **When you eat, just eat.** Don't take meals at your desk, in front of the TV, or while surfing the Internet. Just sit and eat, either alone or with family and friends. This allows you to be more attentive to the experience of eating. When I find myself finishing a fast-paced treadmill-like workday, rather than just running to the next task, I take a Stone Mill Bakery timeout to eat a simple meal (outdoors when possible).

2. **Acknowledge the food.** Before you begin eating, take a quiet moment to acknowledge the food and be grateful for the nourishment it brings.

3. **Pay attention as you eat.** Bring your full attention to the act of bringing the food to your lips, placing it in your mouth, and chewing. Pay attention to the flavors, consistency, taste, and smell of the food.

4. **Take your time.** Throughout the meal, take breaks. Just sit and breathe and enjoy your company (if you have any), the scenery, or the quiet time you're spending alone. Don't rush to gobble your food as quickly as you are otherwise programmed to do.

Eating this way not only allows you to relax and take a break, it also helps you draw the full nutritional value from the foods you eat. The first stages of digestion begin before you even put food in your mouth, so when you slow down and pay attention to what and how you eat, you take advantage of the full digestive process. And you're also likely to eat healthier, more nourishing foods and consume fewer calories overall.[43] When you bring your attention to the taste, feel, and flavor of what you eat, you will find that some foods you once thought delicious (like sugar) don't please you as they did, and others (like veggies) are actually more satisfying than you imagined. And by paying more attention to your hunger signals and feelings of fullness, you're likely to eat less.

Mindful eating has health benefits. Chewing food well helps regulate digestion and create a link between the digestive tract and the brain, improving satiety and tricking your brain into thinking you ate more food than you actually did. Plus, the simple act of enjoying food improves satiation. Mindful eating also helps keep digestion parasympathetic dominant by slowing the process down and providing adequate time for satiation signals to reach your brain. If you eat when you're stressed out, you don't digest as well since your body attenuates digestion in times of stress. When we gulp down our food, we don't give our body time to send signals to our brain telling us we're full. There is lag time between the moment food hits our stomach and when satiety signals are released. When we eat more slowly, we allow more time for those signals to travel to our brain and tell us we are full. So eating mindfully and slowly translates to eating less.

Mindful eating may positively impact type 2 diabetes. A 2012 study from Ohio State

Confucius Says: Eat Less, Weigh Less (or Digest Better)

Another principle worth discussing is one called *hara hachi bu*. Derived from the teaching of Confucius, this instructs a person to eat until he or she is about 80 percent full. Okinawans apply this principle rigorously. They have a typical BMI of around 20 (compared to the United States, where 67 percent of the population is overweight and/or obese with a BMI of 26 or greater) and are among the longest-living cultures in the world.[44] The practice of *hara hachi bu* trains the brain to sense satiety sooner and feel quite satisfied with less food. Similarly, Ayurveda and traditional Chinese practices espouse that a meal be eaten in a peaceful setting and until two-thirds full to promote healthy digestion—and never consumed late at night (a time of cleansing) lest small bowel overgrowth and gut dysbiosis ensue.[45, 46] All of these principles promote a relaxed parasympathetic-dominant state at the time of eating to maximize the enjoyment of the dining experience—and requiring less food to boot!

Are You an Emotional Eater?

The impulse to guzzle chocolate ice cream after a stressful day at work is understandable but unhealthy. We get trapped in this kind of impulsive eating because we're unconsciously seeking foods that satisfy reward centers in our brain. That's why the chocolate cake looks mighty tempting when you're feeling anxious or blue. This is called emotional eating, and some people engage in it to avoid or mitigate emotional stress, boredom, anger, fear, sadness, or anxiety.[47] The hunger emotional eaters experience isn't physical—your body doesn't need the calories or nutrients—it's emotional. So the question isn't "What are you eating?" but "What's eating you?"

While virtually all of us have experienced the psychological release that comfort foods bring from time to time, when emotional eating gets out of control it can become dangerous and lead to binge-eating disorders, bulimia nervosa, and more. If you're concerned that you may have an eating disorder, seek the help of a psychotherapist experienced in treating eating disorders. In such a case, dieting is unlikely to help you achieve your health and weight-loss goals without psychological support. Most eating disorder treatment programs have a nutritional component to them as well, and many clinics have you meet with both a psychotherapist and a nutritionist. You can ask whether or not this program would be a useful adjunct to your treatment.

Emotional eating can be related to food addictions. Growing evidence suggests that high-calorie junk foods may be as addictive as smoking or drugs of abuse. In a study published in *Nature Neuroscience,* researchers showed that rats that regularly consumed high-calorie, sugary, fatty foods like bacon, sausage, cake, and chocolate showed a pattern of blunted reward centers in the brain very similar to those in humans addicted to drugs.[48] These rats had decreased levels of the same dopamine receptors reported in drug-addicted humans. And this reward desensitization lasted for 2 weeks after the rats were taken off the diet.

To take these findings a step further, these scientists decided to see if the rats would continue to eat these junk foods even if they knew it was detrimental— a hallmark of addiction in any species. To do this, they trained the rats to expect a painful shock when eating these foods. They found that the addicted, obese rats kept right on eating despite the pain.

Although more evidence is needed to correlate these findings to human food addiction and weight gain, it's still extremely compelling and provides scientific support for something that many of us are aware of instinctually: The fatty, sugary, processed junk foods on the market today are flat-out addictive.

Eating mindfully and engaging in relaxation or exercise rituals may help you better manage your emotional states so that you don't engage in emotional eating as often.

University found that eating mindfully led to weight loss and blood glucose control results that were similar to adhering to nutrition-based dietary guidelines.[49]

Eating mindfully may also reduce our risk of turning to comfort foods for emotional upset.[50] Stressors and distractors can lead to emotional overeating, which in its most severe forms can turn into a binge-eating disorder (see "Are You an Emotional Eater?" on page 197). Becoming more mindful of the food we eat, and really tuning in to our hunger signals and our experience, can lessen this problem and return us to a more balanced relationship with food.

MEDITATE

Meditation is an ancient practice that includes a broad range of techniques from seated mindfulness meditation to moving forms of meditation such as yoga, tai chi, and qigong. Studies have shown that each of these techniques can help you feel more balanced and at peace and diminish your stress response; some have been directly shown to help you lose weight.

For example, a meta-analysis of 18,753 citations for mindfulness-based studies, which included 47 trials, was performed by my colleagues at Johns Hopkins. They found that regularly engaging in a mindfulness meditation program led to improvement for chronic conditions such as anxiety, depression, and pain.[51] Another study, which included 47 overweight or obese women, found that those engaging in mindfulness practices had reduced anxiety, better eating habits, and reduced abdominal body fat.[52] One study suggests that these effects may be increased when mindfulness is practiced in group settings.[53] A clinical trial under way now aims to identify how mindfulness-based stress reduction alters the gut microbiome in the context of irritable bowel syndrome.[54]

Yoga may have even more powerful results. Researchers at the Fred Hutchinson Cancer Research Center in Seattle reviewed data on 15,550 adults ages 53 to 57 who were recruited to the VITamins And Lifestyle (VITAL) Cohort Study. They found that practicing yoga lessened weight gain.[55] Those who were healthy and normal weight and practiced for 4 or more years were 3.1 pounds lighter than their nonpracticing counterparts. But here's what's really cool: Overweight participants who practiced yoga weighed 18.5 pounds less than those who didn't practice.

Indeed, the idea that yoga may lead to weight loss has been corroborated by a meta-analysis recently published in the *American Journal of Lifestyle Medicine*.[56] Scientists reviewed existing studies to find out if yoga could help you lose weight. Even though they found that the studies have some weaknesses such as small sample sizes, short durations, and lack of control groups, they still concluded that yoga likely leads to weight loss. According to these scientists the possible mechanisms were about more than the fact that you burn calories in yoga sessions. They include:

- Reducing joint and back pain, allowing for more exercise outside of yoga sessions

- Heightening mindfulness, improved mood, and stress reduction, all of which may reduce food intake

- Helping people feel more connected to their bodies, perhaps leading to an enhanced awareness of satiety and the discomfort that comes with overeating

While studies like these haven't been done on qigong or tai chi, we have every reason to believe they would work the same way, as these practices relax the mind and create balance in the mind, body, and spirit.

How to get started? You can look for local classes, which offers the additional benefit of putting you in a community of like-minded individuals where you're likely to make friendships. You might also try some of the many yoga, tai chi, and qigong resources online. And give my mindful eating exercise a chance. You can also experiment with the mindfulness meditation that follows.

I think that the institution of these practices may be helpful in your succeeding to control your weight and remain structurally sound. The figure on page 200 depicts the benefits of incorporating yoga as part of your weight-loss plan. I practiced tai chi for my first 2 years at Johns Hopkins and found it useful in my recovery. For others, qigong may be quite useful and effective. The key is to move, balance the healing life force, or chi, and improve health in mind, body, and spirit.

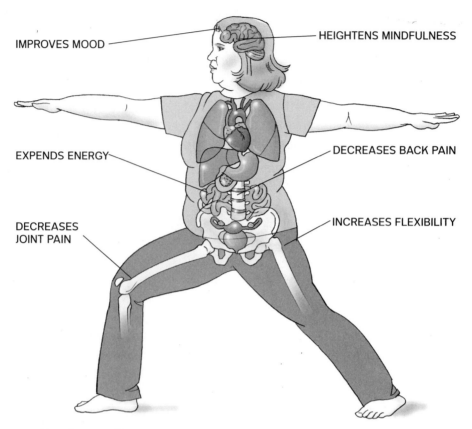

IMPROVES MOOD

HEIGHTENS MINDFULNESS

EXPENDS ENERGY

DECREASES BACK PAIN

DECREASES JOINT PAIN

INCREASES FLEXIBILITY

How Yoga Reverses Obesity: Yoga may improve flexibility, decrease joint pain, and enhance mobility, which facilitates energy expenditure. Yoga also helps attenuate stress, depression, anxiety, insulin resistance, hypertension, and dyslipidemia.[57] By improving mindfulness, yoga is felt to diminish emotional eating behaviors, improve satiety, and make one more immune to the influence of external stimuli to the ear.[58] Studies have shown that yoga as a lifestyle intervention decreased body fat, body mass index, and body weight while improving lean body mass by building muscle.[59, 60] Regular yoga (1 to 2 times per week, 45-minute sessions weekly) has been associated with lower cortisol levels, a stress hormone that promotes obesity. Yoga practice has been associated with a decrease in inflammation, which improves cardiovascular function and insulin resistance.[61] Bernstein et al recommend 3 months of instructor-led yoga (45- to 60-minute sessions one to two times per week), with 25 minutes of independent practice where there are no formal sessions (5 minutes of meditation, 15 minutes of poses, 5 minutes of rest).[62] Those with cardiopulmonary disease should consult a physician before engaging in yoga. Musculoskeletal pain is the most common adverse event, which should be reported to the instructor.

THE GUT BALANCE REVOLUTION SUCCESS STORIES

Terri Meekins, 58

Arthritis, tummy troubles, weight gain—just a couple of years ago, Terri Meekins chalked it all up to aging. When her hands were too stiff to knit, she figured that arthritis went with the territory. When she started to pile on pounds and suffer from anxiety and depression, she figured it was menopause. And when the digestive issues from IBS—which had plagued her for years—started to worsen, she figured that now that she was in her fifties, this was just a normal way of life.

"I always tried to eat healthy foods," Terri recalls, "and I made it a point to choose small portions. But nothing seemed to help, and I just kept gaining weight. I hated going to the beach—no bathing suits for me! And with arthritis in my hands and knees, it was tough to do any physical activities." That is, until she met Dr. Gerry Mullin and learned about the Gut Balance Revolution.

About to undergo a series of serious surgeries, her doctor sent her to Dr. Gerry for a checkup in June 2013. That's when she learned that the root of all her health concerns was small intestinal bacterial overgrowth—SIBO—and that, with Dr. Gerry's help, she could feel better once and for all.

Terri was a willing patient, and she followed the doctor's orders to a T. "When Dr. Gerry told me that what I was suffering from was abnormal, and that it could be improved," she says, "I was willing to do anything to feel better." So she went on the low-FODMAP eating plan, and in a matter of weeks, her life began to change. "It was like a fog lifted," she recalls. "Many of my symptoms got better or just went away."

Now, a year and a half later, she's 40 pounds lighter and feeling better than ever. She's outside every day, going for her "run-walk," and she's been knitting sweaters for her grandchildren—and for herself. The headaches she experienced daily? Now that she's eliminated processed foods from her diet, they're a distant memory. "My skin looks better, and I have so much more energy," Terri says. "People tell me that I look younger. This new way of eating has changed my life."

YOGA POSES IN THE MANAGEMENT OF OVERWEIGHT AND OBESITY

1 **SEATED POSITION:** Sit at the edge of your chair and keep your feet flat, under the knees; lightly rest your palms on your upper legs and keep your spine straight. (This is the alignment for all seated postures.)

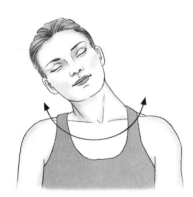

2 **NECK ROLL:** Sit straight and with your eyes closed. On an inhalation, drop your chin to your chest; on the exhalation, roll your right ear to your right shoulder. Return your head to center, then switch sides.

3 **SHOULDER ROLLS:** Sit straight and, on the inhalation, gently lift your shoulders to your ears and gently roll your shoulders around and back, squeezing your shoulder blades together and dropping them away from your ears.

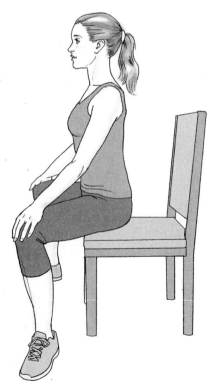

4 EASY SPINAL TWIST: Sitting at the center of your seat, with your spine straight, place your right hand on your left knee and lightly rest your left hand on the edge of the seat or the back of the chair for support, keeping your shoulders parallel to ground. Inhale and twist, looking over the left shoulder. Return to center, then switch sides.

5 GROIN STRETCH: Sitting at the center of your seat, with your spine straight, gently open your legs as far apart as possible, keeping your feet flat on the ground and pointing in the same direction as the knees. Lightly rest your palms on the upper legs and ensure the knees are directly above the ankles.

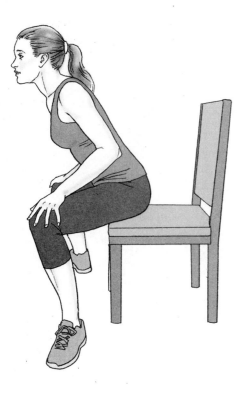

6 **LEANING GROIN STRETCH:** Keeping your spine straight, with your hands on the upper legs, inhale and lean forward with your chin and chest pointing forward.

7 **NUMBER 4 STRETCH:** Keeping your spine straight and your left leg at a 90-degree angle, bring the outside of your right ankle above the left knee. Lightly place your right hand on the inside of the right upper leg and your left hand on your right ankle. Inhale and lean slightly forward. Repeat on the other side.

8 **LIFTED HAMSTRING STRETCH WITH DEEP FOOT FLEX:** Return to the center of your seat, with your knees at a 90-degree angle and your spine straight. Holding a yoga strap with both hands, loop it over the arch of the left foot and, on inhalation, lift and straighten the left leg, using the yoga strap for support. Exhale and slowly lower your leg. Repeat on the other side.

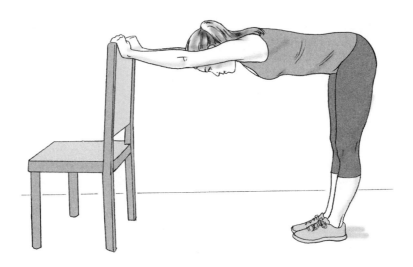

9 **TABLE POSE:** Stand up and walk around the chair; put your hands on the back of the chair and walk backward. With your spine straight, lean forward until your body forms a table position and your arms are straight; keep the hips over the feet and the feet slightly apart. On exhalation, tuck your chin to your chest and slowly roll up and walk back toward the chair.

10 MOUNTAIN POSE: Stand with your feet slightly apart, your hips over the feet, your shoulders over the hips, your chin parallel to the ground, and your weight evenly distributed.

11 EASY BACK BEND: In Mountain pose, clasp your hands behind your head and pull your elbows back. Inhale and pull your abdomen in, gently look up, and slowly bend back.

12 RULER POSE: From Mountain pose, inhale as you gently lift your arms toward the ceiling (your arms should be perpendicular to the floor and parallel to each other) and tuck your shoulder blades under. Exhale and, slowly lowering your arms, return to the center position.

13 PRESS-UPS: From Mountain pose, focus your eyes straight ahead. Pressing your toes into the ground, lift your heels up and down three times and, on the fourth, hold, then come down.

14 WARRIOR 1: Face the side of the chair with the seat back on your right side. Start in Mountain pose with parallel feet, then gently lift and place your right foot on the chair seat, your knee in a 90-degree angle. Lean slightly forward, keeping your left leg straight, and press your left heel down, taking care to keep the foot at a 45-angle from your spine. Gently lift your arms toward the ceiling (your arms should be perpendicular to the floor and parallel to each other). Step slowly back into Mountain and switch sides.

15 WARRIOR 2: From Mountain pose, step your feet about hip-width apart and stretch out your right arm straight in front of you. Turn your gaze and look toward your right fingers as you slowly bend the right knee, making sure you're able to see your first toe when your knee is bent. Return to Mountain and switch sides.

16 TREE POSE: From Mountain pose, focus your eyes straight ahead. Slowly shift your weight slightly onto the left foot and bend your right knee. Draw your right foot up and place the heel against the inner left shin, keeping your left leg as straight as possible. Put your hands together, close to your chest, and hold. On an exhalation, lower the right foot. Repeat on the other side.

17 HIP CIRCLES: From Mountain pose, move your feet about hip-width apart. Keeping your knees and ankles loose, gently move your hips in a circular motion using the balls of your feet.

18 RELAXATION POSE: Lightly rest your palms, facing up, on your upper legs. Keeping your spine straight, close your eyes and rest, concentrating on breathing.

Meditation: Watching Your Thoughts

One of the hallmarks of mindfulness meditation is becoming aware of your thoughts, feelings, and bodily sensations *without doing anything to change them.* The objective isn't to change your world or your experience but to become more deeply aware of and attentive to that experience. By a lucky, but tricky, set of cognitive, behavioral, and emotional human tendencies, when you become more aware of your own internal experience, that experience tends to shift on its own. You become less stressed and more at peace simply by paying attention to what's happening in your mind, body, and spirit. But be careful! Becoming mindful and meditating *because* you want to feel more peace may not work so well. If you sit down to meditate and think, "Don't stress out. Don't stress out," all that's likely to happen is that you'll become even more stressed. Instead, gently begin to notice what comes up for you emotionally, intellectually, and physically by following these guidelines.

1. Find a quiet, comfortable, distraction-free place to sit. Sit cross-legged on the floor with a pillow underneath you (a more traditional style of meditation) if that suits you, or simply sit in a chair with your back straight.

2. Take a few deep breaths using the deep breathing exercise on page 194 to enter a state of relaxation.

3. Just sit and breathe. As you do so, many thoughts, feelings, and bodily sensations are likely to arise. When they do, gently bring your attention to them and acknowledge them without trying to change them.

4. To help with this, you may want to label your experiences. For example, if you become aware of a slight pain in your ankle, you might label it "pain in the ankle." Or if you find yourself becoming anxious or angry, you could label these emotional experiences as such. The same with thoughts–you may find yourself getting distracted by the thought "I need to get to work." Just notice it. Label it. And let it be.

5. Float your experiences down the river of life. Thoughts, feelings, and bodily sensations tend to have an ebb and flow to them. Imagine standing next to a beautiful river, and as experiences come up, you write them on a leaf and watch them float away. For example, if you begin to feel tense, imagine yourself writing the word *tense* on a leaf. Then place the leaf on your river of personal experience and watch it float away.

Try this exercise two or three times a week for 10 to 20 minutes at time. As you grow more accustomed to meditating, explore it more often, for longer stretches of time. This simple exercise will put you in deeper touch with your personal experience and the array of thoughts, feelings, and sensations humans experience. It may affect you in unexpected ways. Answers to questions you've long struggled with may suddenly arise, no longer as challenging as they once seemed. When you tap into the deep inner wisdom of your own mind, body, and spirit, you'll be pleasantly surprised at what you find.

VISUALIZATION, GUIDED IMAGERY, AND HYPNOSIS

Take a moment to imagine you're relaxed. Close your eyes. Imagine yourself completely at peace. You might see yourself sitting on a quiet beach where the crystal blue water gently laps against long stretches of white sand. Or maybe you envision yourself walking slowly, meditatively, through an ancient redwood forest. Perhaps you find yourself in a cozy cottage where the delicious fragrances of home-cooked foods permeate the air. Simply visualize yourself at peace in your most cherished personal place. Go ahead: Close your eyes and do it now. Then come back to this book. How do you feel? I'd bet you feel more relaxed. Don't you? You just completed a very simple visualization exercise.

Our bodies respond to our thoughts. When you use your imagination, enter a state of absorbed and focused attention, and intentionally concentrate on specific images and ideas, you can help yourself relax, change mental and physiological processes, and enhance your belief in yourself and your goals. Hypnosis, visualization, and guided imagery are different techniques with this state of focused attention in common. Each has a broad range of ways to influence your mood, your weight, and your overall health. For example, they can help you:[63]

- Feel more relaxed, more positive, and less anxious, angry, or depressed

- Make better food choices

- Get motivated to exercise

- Uncover unconscious psychological barriers that may stand in the way of your health and weight-loss goals

- Increase your self-esteem and self-confidence

- Believe in your ability to stick to your health and weight-loss goals

Hypnosis can work as an adjunct for weight loss. In a recent study, 32 females and 5 males were recruited and divided into groups.[64] One-third were placed on a weight-loss plan with no other interventions. One-third were on a weight-loss plan and received cognitive-behavioral therapy (CBT) from a certified CBT therapist. The final group was on a weight-loss plan and got both CBT and hypnosis intervention. The group receiving hypnosis outper-formed both other groups in total weight lost. This is just one study with a small sample size, but it's an important finding that lends credence to the long-held belief those of us in the complementary and alternative medicine (CAM) community have embraced—mind-body medicine is an important piece of the weight-loss and antiobesity puzzle.

Give these techniques a try. You can get hypnosis, visualization, and guided imagery CDs or download electronic versions. One resource I like is healingwithhypnosis.com.

ACUPUNCTURE AND OTHER ALTERNATIVE TECHNIQUES

A growing base of research supports traditional medicine (such as traditional Chinese medicine and Ayurvedic medicine) for assisting with weight loss. Manual acupuncture (needling by hand), electroacupuncture (with an electronic device), and auricular acupuncture[65] (acupuncture delivered through the earlobe) all have evidence to support their use in the treatment of weight problems and obesity.

For example, a meta-analysis of 44 trials on acupuncture and 3 trials of combined therapy (Chinese herbs and acupuncture) that included 4,861 participants found that both acupuncture and the combined therapies were more effective than placebo or lifestyle modification for helping people lose weight.[66] The analysis stated that these methods work similarly to Western antiobesity drugs but with fewer adverse side effects. A similar study on auricular electroacupuncture that included 56 obese women randomly selected to receive electric stimulation or placebo found that the treatment group had a significant reduction in weight and BMI. Scientists think that acupuncture has these effects because it's known to:[67]

- Affect appetite
- Regulate intestinal motility–contractions that move food through your gut. This is important for reasons we will discuss later in this chapter.
- Speed up metabolism
- Increase neural activity in the hypothalamus (the command center of the brain that governs appetite and more)
- Increase serotonin levels and enhance mood
- Reduce stress

Preliminary evidence suggests that Ayurvedic medicine may also be a useful adjunct for long-term weight loss. Twenty-two women in a 3-month Ayurvedic treatment program for weight problems were encouraged to change their eating habits and activity patterns; improve self-efficacy, quality of life, well-being, vitality, and self-awareness around food choice; and manage stress more effectively. The results were positive–12 women completed the intervention as well as the 6-month and 9-month follow-ups. At the end of 9 months, each of these women had lost more than 10 pounds.

GET SUPPORT

Humans are social creatures–we need other people to survive and thrive. It could be argued that we depend on one another more today than we ever have, but we're ironically more isolated than we've ever been before. We rely on others for virtually everything in our lives, in ways we don't always realize. The water in your tap comes into your home because other people have built and managed an infrastructure of pipes to deliver that water to you. It's very likely that your home, your furniture, your car, your clothes, your computer, even your food was made by another person. And that only scratches the surface. Our cities, governments, and nations are the outcome of the interdependence of human beings. As I said in Chapter 1, our industrialized society has evolved to a highly sophisticated synchrony of symbiosis, so it's such a tragic irony that so many suffer in isolation today. Between 1985 and 2004, the number of people who said they had no one with whom they could discuss important matters tripled to 25 percent.[68] Computers, cell phones, instant messaging, e-mail, and social media allow us to connect in ways never before imagined, yet we feel more disconnected, more isolated than ever.

This isolation impacts our health and weight in distinct and disturbing ways. When scientists reviewed a sample of the women included in the Community-based, Heart and Weight Management Trial, they found that those with stronger social support groups and less perceived stress were more likely to engage in healthy behaviors and less likely to be obese.[69] And a systematic review that sought to determine the factors that worked in weight loss for men found that interventions delivered in social settings were far more likely to work and that group-based programs providing support for men with similar health problems were far more effective than interventions delivered in the clinical-care setting.[70]

Research also indicates that isolation leads to health problems and early death.[71] A 2014 University of Chicago study suggested that feeling lonely impairs executive function, sleep, and mental and physical well-being, all of which may lead to higher rates of morbidity and mortality, especially in older adults.

We humans need one another, and I encourage you to connect with others. It will improve your health, your weight-loss outcomes, and the quality of your life. Here are some ideas on how to do that.

- Ask a coworker or friend to do this program with you. This has many advantages, one of which is having an "accountability partner" to help you stick to the plan.

- Call an old friend you haven't talked to in a long time or, better yet, meet for lunch.

- Invite a coworker out to lunch.

- Join a support group, club, or gym.

- Go to a sporting event.

- Go on a date with your spouse or friend.

- Join a reading club.

- Create a game night with friends.

- Go for a walk or a hike with a buddy.

- Try team sports with a group of friends: baseball, softball, Ultimate Frisbee. Or go back to your childhood and try kickball or invite a friend to play catch.

The possibilities are endless. Get out and connect with real people in real life, away from electronic devices when possible. Facebook makes it seem like you have a thousand friends (and maybe you do!), but you'll get a lot more out of meeting people face-to-face. When it comes to human social interaction, there's nothing like seeing a real person in real life and giving them a handshake or a hug.

LIVING IN HARMONY WITH YOUR GUT CLOCK

It's not only what you eat and how you eat that can either stress out your body or relax it. *When* you eat is important, too. We're a culture that often eats until right before we go to bed. This can cause unnecessary physiological stress, weight gain, gastrointestinal distress, and an unhealthy, fat-forming gut microbiome. Here's why.

Your body operates on its own set of circadian rhythms—a kind of biological clock that helps you know, for example, when to sleep, when to eat, and when to release certain biochemicals. All animals have these internal clocks, but humans are the only ones who can consciously choose to ignore them. We stay awake after dark, eat whenever we want, and generally ignore our natural biological impulses.

But living this way can adversely impact our health if behaviors become too extreme. Sleep deprivation is a health epidemic, but many of us wear it as a badge of pride. We'll talk more about sleep and why getting too little can lead to weight gain and chronic health problems shortly. For now, let's focus on the circadian rhythms of your gut—your gut clock and the cleansing waves it sets in motion.[72]

Your gut clock determines when and how your gut contracts, a movement called gut motility—an extremely important part of your digestive health. These contractions occur with a certain regularity and become pronounced when your stomach is supposed to be empty (in between meals and during sleep). This is what I call the cleansing wave. It not only helps you digest food but helps keep bad bugs from getting a foothold in the wrong places in your gut, especially your small intestine. Remember when we talked about small intestinal bacterial overgrowth, or SIBO? Well, this cleansing wave is a critical part of preventing that condition.

These contractions happen outside your conscious control, but how and when you eat can affect them. Imagine you have a clock in your gut. If you eat a certain way, it sets an alarm that, when triggered, releases powerful cleansing waves that wipe away bad bugs and debris from your stomach and small intestine. But when you eat in a different way, the alarm is delayed and the waves become smaller and weaker. The technical name for the cleansing waves is the migrating motor complex (MMC), and it's strongest when you're asleep and fasting. In this state, the waves occur frequently and are quite vigorous. But when you eat late in the evening, the waves become weaker and less frequent. The later you eat, the less you'll clean out the small bowel, setting the stage for SIBO and all the problems that come along with it, including dysbiosis and weight gain as we mentioned on page 196 when discussing the practice of *hara hachi bu*, Ayurveda, and traditional Chinese eating principles.

Studies have shown that changes in gastrointestinal motility force your body to pack on the pounds.[73] I illustrated the connections between SIBO, GI distress, and weight gain more fully in Chapter 4. So remember that *when* you eat is nearly as important as how you eat. Here are some recommendations to help you live in harmony with your gut clock.

- **Eat your last meal earlier in the evening.** Stop eating at least 3 or 4 hours before bed; eating your last meal by 6:00 is ideal.

- **Drink water or herbal tea.** Instead of eating late into the evening, try drinking more water or a relaxing herbal tea like chamomile or peppermint.

- **If you're hungry, have a light snack.** Try to eat dinner by 6:00 p.m. If you're hungry later in the evening, have a light snack like a few nuts or plain Greek yogurt with a little raw honey–just enough to satiate your hunger.

You don't want bad bugs building up in the wrong part of your GI tract. To keep your inner garden healthy and radiant, keep the bugs out of your small bowel. Luckily, you have a built-in mechanism for doing this. So eat earlier and let the cleansing wave do the weeding for you.

Sleep Like a Baby

Americans seem to hate sleep. Unlike our Mediterranean counterparts, we don't have siestas, we don't take naps, and the less we sleep, the prouder we seem to be of ourselves, regarding our sleeplessness as proof of just how industrious we Americans are. The result? Forty million men and women in this country are chronically sleep deprived.[74] Think this doesn't affect your health and your waistline? Think again.

Disruptions in sleep, getting too little sleep, and having your circadian rhythms interrupted have all been implicated as contributing factors to type 2 diabetes and obesity.[75] This is likely due to the fact that not sleeping enough, even for one night, has negative impacts on your neuroendocrine system that cause you to feel hungrier and eat more as hunger hormones become altered–increasing ghrelin and decreasing leptin.[76] Restricting sleep to as little as 5 hours nightly reduces insulin sensitivity, sets off systemic inflammation, and puts you at increased risk of mortality by all causes.[77-79]

Scientists have learned that kids who stay up late to play video games are at an additional risk for obesity from the sleep deprivation itself.[80] A recent study concluded that compared with decreased sleep, increased sleep *duration* in school-age children resulted in lower reported food intake, lower fasting leptin levels, and lower weight. And other researchers recently observed that chronic sleep curtailment from infancy to school age was associated with higher overall and belly fat in mid-childhood–a fact further confirmed by yet another study.[81, 82] The potential role of sleep duration in pediatric obesity prevention and treatment warrants further study.[83, 84]

A 2010 study published in the *Annals of Internal Medicine* put all these data in perspective. Investigators at the University of Chicago demonstrated that insufficient sleep undermines dietary efforts to reduce overall body fat.[85] They conducted clinical trials in 10 overweight, nonsmoking adults who underwent 14 days of moderate calorie restriction with either 8.5 or 5.5 hours of nighttime sleep. Sleep curtailment decreased the portion that lost weight as fat and increased the loss of lean muscle mass. The scientists also found those who were sleep deprived experienced body weight set point adaptations that shifted them toward a state mimicking caloric deprivation: increased hunger and a relative decrease in fat oxidation. In fact, those who slept 8.5 hours burned twice as much fat as the 5.5-hour group. And over a year, the 8.5-hour group lost an average of 10 more pounds than the 5.5-hour group and preserved twice as much lean body mass.

There are no questions about it: Sleep deprivation compromises your efforts to lose weight. Your goal should be to get 7 to 9 hours of deep, restful sleep nightly. If you think you don't have the time to sleep that much, I suggest you rethink that position and make sleep a priority over other activities. Sacrificing sleep for the sake of productivity is seriously overrated. It's great to want to be more productive. But how much do you think you'll get done if your health suffers? Sleep deprivation has been linked to a number of adverse health conditions. Even evening shift workers have increased inflammatory markers portending adverse health outcomes,[86] and health-care shift workers aren't immune to these adverse effects of circadian rhythm disruption.[87] Whatever it is you're working on can wait a few hours.

On the other hand, if you have trouble getting or staying asleep at night, don't despair. Some simple interventions can improve the quality of your sleep and make it

The Adverse Health Effects of Sleep Deprivation

- Accidents
- All-cause mortality
- Alzheimer's disease
- Cardiovascular events
- Cognitive impairments
- Decreased quality of life
- Diabetes
- Gastrointestinal disorders
- Hypertension

- Impaired athletic performance
- Impaired work performance
- Increased colorectal cancer risk
- Memory loss
- Metabolic syndrome
- Osteoporosis
- Stroke
- Weight gain
- Worsening of mood disorders[88-95]

easier to fall asleep and stay that way. Most people with sleep problems are engaged in negative lifestyle or behavior habits prohibiting them from getting enough good sleep. You can change this by improving your sleep hygiene, and it isn't hard to do. Here are some tips to help you improve your sleep hygiene starting tonight.

- **Create a sleep ritual.** Doing the same thing before bed every night helps remind your body that it's time to go to sleep. You might change into pajamas, brush your teeth, turn out the lights, spread back the covers, or any other number of things. Just keep it consistent.

- **Relax before bed.** Try doing something relaxing every night 30 to 60 minutes before bed. You could try some deep breathing, mindfulness meditation, visualization, or even a little light, relaxing stretching.

- **Go to bed earlier.** If you need more sleep, it's probably best to go to bed earlier. Try climbing into bed 10 or 15 minutes earlier each week until you're enjoying 7 to 9 hours of shut-eye.

- **Don't stress before bed.** Getting stressed before you go to bed won't help you sleep better. Think of how many ways we amp up our stress hormones right before bedtime: watching the evening news or violent TV shows, surfing the Net, even checking e-mail. Try to make rational decisions about using electronic devices, and stay away from alcohol as well as caffeine and other stimulants.

- **Sleep in a completely dark room.** Light alters your circadian rhythms and may make it difficult to get or stay asleep—not just the lamps in your bedroom but also those little lights from phones, computers, TVs, DVD players, clocks, streetlamps, and more. Get blackout blinds for your windows if you need them. Turn your phone off and point your alarm away from the bed. If you have a computer, TV, or DVD player in your room, plug it into a power strip you can shut off easily before you go to bed. For millennia, humans went to sleep when it was dark. That ancient way of living is stenciled into our DNA. Respect your circadian rhythms and provide them the dark they need.

- **Experiment with naps (if you can).** For some, naps can actually improve nighttime sleep. For example, if you've learned to rely on a coffee at 2:00 p.m. to get through your day, you may find that a 20-minute nap does a better job of rejuvenating you without that jolt of caffeine. On the other hand, if you have a hard time sleeping already, napping during the day may not be the ticket. Try naps if you can and see if they work for you.

- **Drink a cup of tart cherry juice.** A small randomized clinical trial recently found that insomniacs who drank a cup of tart cherry juice twice daily (in the morning and evening) increased their sleep time by nearly 90 minutes.[96] The scientists hypothesize it's because the juice inhibits an enzyme that degrades tryptophan—an essential amino acid in your body's production of melatonin, the master circadian rhythm hormone. Speaking of which . . .

- **Try melatonin.** Supplemental melatonin can help put your sleep rhythms back on track and may provide support for people who either don't make enough or need to replete their levels. Try 1 to 3 milligrams 60 to 90 minutes before bedtime.

If you still have sleep problems, seek out the help of a sleep specialist. You may have undiagnosed sleep disturbances, such as sleep apnea, that can adversely impact your health and your weight. Don't take this lightly. Sleep apnea, in its worst forms, is a life-threatening condition. Even less severe forms of sleep apnea or other sleep disorders can compromise your health. Sleep is one of your most precious commodities. Don't short-change yourself by ignoring it.

EXERCISE MORE EFFECTIVELY IN LESS TIME

I cannot overstate the importance of exercise. It's a magnificent stress reducer that even enhances resilience. Movement reduces inflammation, makes you more insulin sensitive, improves your mood (exercise releases "happy" neurochemicals like serotonin), and builds lean muscle mass that enhances your fat-burning machinery by increasing the number of mitochondria (your body's fat-melting organelles).

It's too early to say whether or not exercise has a direct impact on your gut microbiome. A few studies, like one recently published in *Environmental Health Perspectives*, suggest that exercise may mitigate the damage done to your gut microbiome by environmental toxins and other factors.[97] However, even if exercise doesn't directly impact your inner garden, it indirectly impacts your flora by reducing inflammation. Exercise is one of the healthiest things you can engage in, and I would be remiss not to address it in a book about weight loss.

Our bodies were built to move. When we don't exercise enough, or when we live a sedentary life, our health breaks down. An Australian study looked at data from more than 220,000 people age 45 or older and found that those who sat more than 11 hours a day had a 40 percent increased chance of death from all causes.[98] Findings like these have been replicated by the American Cancer Society, the American College of Sports and Medicine, and other organizations.

Does that mean more is better when it comes to exercise? Well, yes and no. Certainly, most of us could afford to exercise more. But it doesn't necessarily follow that because an activity is healthy we should do it nonstop. Exercising too much or in the wrong way can lead to inflammation, injury, and metabolic adjustments that make it difficult to burn fat. This point is particularly important to keep in mind in light of our cultural addiction to the calories in/calories out theory of weight loss. We used to believe that if we burned more calories by exercising more and ate less, we'd lose weight. We used to believe this was the equation for weight loss. But we were wrong. The human body simply doesn't work this way. You gain or lose fat based on a wide variety of factors, including the health of your gut microbiome, your metabolic rate, hormonal balance, and more. All that plays a part in figuring how much–and how–to exercise.

The good news: You no longer have to spend long hours plodding on a treadmill to receive the many metabolic, neurochemical, and other advantages of moving your body.

The Health Benefits of Exercise

Exercise has so many health benefits, it's hard to catalog them all. These include but are not limited to:[99]

- Decreased risk of cardiovascular (heart) disease, high blood pressure, and stroke
- Decreased risk of colon and breast cancers
- Decreased risk of diabetes
- Decreased risk of osteoporosis
- Decreased risk of depression and dementia
- Decreased body fat

- Improved metabolic processes— the way the body breaks down and builds necessary substances
- Improved movement of joints and muscles
- Improved oxygen delivery throughout the body
- Improved sense of well-being
- Improved strength and endurance

Novel approaches to exercise have been developed in recent years, allowing us to exercise better and in less time and still achieve the results we want.

I'd like to share some of what I know about these breakthroughs. As you'll see, I've divided my exercise program into beginner, intermediate, and advanced options. Select the program that's right for you, and get moving!

Beginner: Walk

Walking may not be the most novel approach to exercise, but if you've been sedentary for a long time, it's the perfect place to start. There are dozens of studies that show walking as little as 15 to 45 minutes daily can reduce your risk of heart disease, stroke, type 2 diabetes, and more.[100-102]

If you don't exercise at all, you're out of shape, or you're injured, start with light walking. I recommend 15 to 45 minutes three to five times weekly, depending on your health status and conditioning. Why such a broad range? Because I want you to do what you're comfortable with. As the old saying goes, "The best kind of exercise is the kind you will do." If you set the benchmark too high, you'll resent and avoid your exercise routine, especially if you haven't been moving around much for a long time. Start where you can. If that means 15 minutes three times a week, great! If it means 30 minutes three times a week, great! If it means varying your routine based on what your lifestyle will allow, great! Just get moving–around the block, to the market, in the hills, on a trail, in the mall. I like getting outside in the fresh air and sunlight when I can, but for some folks, that's not possible. Bad weather, dangerous neighborhoods, and other factors may prohibit this. In that case, you can walk on a treadmill, use an elliptical machine, or climb stairs in your building.

Over time, you'll naturally feel yourself become accustomed to walking. When this happens, increase the amount of time you walk. You can also vary your routine by walking up stairs, walking up hills–or trying intervals. Here's how.

Intermediate: Walk with Intervals and Add Some Weight

Interval training allows you to get an excellent cardiovascular workout in less time, and some studies have shown it's a more effective way to burn fat and balance insulin than traditional cardio routines.[103-105] When doing interval training, you push as hard as you can for a set period of time, then you go at a more moderate pace, then you push again. One cycle of pushing and going slower is called an interval.

How long do you push, how long do you back off, and how many intervals are involved? That depends on the program or routine–there are many options available. Probably the most common interval sequence comes from the world of running. In this routine, runners sprint as fast as they can for 1 minute and run slower for 2 minutes. Six intervals are typically completed for a total workout time of about 18 minutes. That may not sound like very much exercise, but I can assure you the routine is extremely challenging (in fact, I don't recommend you do it for the intermediate routine). It also provides the same or better cardiovascular and metabolic benefits as a 60-minute jog, with less wear and tear on the joints. I encourage you to give intervals a try. They can give you a better workout in less time, and they make exercise more fun.

Intervals: Where to Begin?

If you're at an intermediate level of exercise, or if you've worked through the beginner's program and you're ready to try intervals, here's what I recommend.

Plan to exercise five times a week for 20 to 30 minutes. You may do a little less on some days, a little more on others. Two days a week, you'll walk with intervals. The other 3 days, you'll do body-weight training (more on this in a moment). To integrate intervals into your walking, start with something manageable. Here is what I recommend.

TIME IN MINUTES	INTENSITY
0:00–5:00	Warm up with some slow, relaxed walking.
5:00–7:00	Walk at a moderate pace—quick enough to be a little difficult, but not to make you breathless. You'd be able to talk to a friend during this time.
7:00–8:00	Walk as quickly as you can without running. This should make you breathless, and you may feeling burning in your legs and arms.
8:00–10:00	Resume a moderate pace of walking for about 2 minutes, or until you're recovered.
10:00–25:00	Repeat minutes 5:00 through 10:00 for five intervals.
25:00–30:00	Cool down by walking at a slow, relaxing pace.

When you're ready to enhance the intensity of the routine, do more intervals—up to 8 or 10—and/or shorten your rest period. Here's an example.

TIME IN MINUTES	INTENSITY
0:00–5:00	Warm up with some slow, relaxed walking.
5:00–6:00	Walk at a moderate pace—quick enough to be a little difficult, but not to make you breathless. You'd be able to talk to a friend during this time.
6:00–7:00	Walk as quickly as you can without running. This should make you breathless, and you may feeling burning in your legs and arms.
7:00–8:00	Resume a moderate pace of walking for about 1 minute, or until you're recovered.
8:00–21:00	Repeat minutes 5:00 through 8:00 for seven intervals.
21:00–26:00	Cool down by walking at a slow, relaxing pace.

There are plenty of other options, so you can customize the routine to fit your personal preferences. Another possibility, for example, is to walk as fast as you can for as long as you can, rest when you need to, and walk fast again. Hills and stairs will further increase the intensity.

Integrate a routine like this into your schedule twice a week, and you'll be getting all the cardio you need. The other 3 days of the week, I want you to integrate body-weight exercises. Here's why.

Weight Training Using Your Own Body

Resistance training is an important part of any exercise program–possibly more important than cardio. It builds up your lean muscle mass, increasing your mitochondria, and is good for your skeletal structure as well. In fact, cardio and resistance training aren't actually different things. You can get a good cardio and resistance routine all in one go if it's structured correctly. The traditional wisdom that you need to exercise your aerobic and anaerobic systems separately is no longer considered valid. The systems are interrelated, and you can get far more benefits for far less work by weight training quickly a few times weekly.

So why do I suggest you divide the routines in the intermediate program? Mainly because working out this way is hard–too hard for a lot of folks. When you're building back up to your optimal fitness level, it's still useful to do weight training and interval walking on different days.

There are almost endless options for weight training, and I encourage you to seek a program that works best for you. I like body-weight training, possibly with light hand weights if needed. Most everyone can get a solid resistance workout with body weight alone, and you can do it anywhere. Here are two training routines I recommend.

WEIGHT-TRAINING ROUTINES

For the routines that follow, do all your 5 to 10 reps for each exercise in a row. This is one set. Take a 2-minute rest between sets, then repeat. The entire routine won't take more than 20 to 30 minutes, and if you do it correctly with good form, you'll feel like you spent an hour in the gym. When you're done, cool down with a walk and/or some full-body stretching.

WORKOUT I

Hinge and Row

A. Stand with your feet about shoulder-width apart. Hold a dumbbell in each hand in front of your legs, palms facing thighs.

B. Keeping your abs tight, bend forward from your hips, sliding the weights down your thighs. Slowly lower (about 4 counts) until your torso is almost parallel to the floor. If you notice that your back is rounding before that point, stop there. The dumbbells should be below your shoulders.

C. Bend your elbows toward the ceiling and pull the dumbbells up until your arms are bent at 90 degrees.

D. Straighten your arms. Do one more row, then slowly stand.

EASIER (OR IF YOU HAVE BACK PROBLEMS): Hold on to the back of a chair with one hand and do one-arm rows.

HARDER: Do one-legged hinges. Lift one leg behind you as you bend forward.

Plié Squat and Curl

A. Stand with your feet wider than shoulder-width apart, toes pointing out. Hold a dumbbell in each hand with your arms bent so your hands are by your shoulders, palms facing you.

B. Keeping your abs tight, bend your knees and lower yourself until your thighs are almost parallel to the floor. At the same time, straighten your arms and lower the dumbbells between your legs, palms facing forward.

C. Straighten your legs, squeeze your buttocks, and stand back up. Simultaneously, curl the dumbbells up toward your shoulders without moving your upper arms. Repeat.

EASIER: Don't bend your knees as far.

HARDER: As you stand up, raise one foot off the floor to do a side knee lift.

Lunge and Twist

A. Stand with your feet together. Hold a dumbbell with both hands and with your arms bent so the dumbbell is in front of your chest.

B. Keeping your abs tight, step back with your left foot about 2 to 3 feet and bend your knees. Lower yourself until your right thigh is parallel to the floor, keeping your right knee above your ankle. Your back heel will be off the floor. At the same time, rotate your torso to the right, bringing the dumbbell down by your right hip.

C. Press off your back foot to stand up as you rotate back to the starting position. Repeat for the recommended number of reps, then switch sides.

EASIER: Do stationary lunges, beginning with your feet apart and keeping them in that position the entire time.

HARDER: As you stand up, raise your back leg up in front of you to a knee lift.

Bridge with Flies

A. Lie on your back with your legs bent and your feet flat on the floor. Hold a dumbbell in each hand with your arms extended out to your sides, elbows slightly bent and palms facing up.

B. Squeeze your glutes and abs and lift your lower and middle back off the floor. At the same time, raise the dumbbells over your chest as if you were hugging a ball.

C. Lower your back and arms to the floor. Repeat.

EASIER: Lift into the bridge first, then raise your arms. Lower your arms and back separately or at the same time, whichever is easier for you.

HARDER: Hold in the up position and raise one foot off the floor. Hold for a second, then lower your foot to the floor. Then lower your arms and back to the floor at the same time. Alternate legs with each rep.

Kneeling Arm Raise

A. Get down on the floor on all fours. Hold a dumbbell in your right hand with your arm bent 90 degrees, your elbow by your hip, and your palm facing your thigh. Extend your left leg behind you and off the floor so you're balancing on your left hand and right knee. If your left wrist bothers you, hold a dumbbell so your wrist isn't bent.

B. Slowly straighten your right arm and raise the dumbbell behind you. Keep your abs tight and look at the floor a few feet in front of you to keep your head in line with your spine.

C. Slowly bend your arm back to the starting position. Your upper arm should remain still throughout the move. Repeat for the recommended number of reps, then switch sides.

EASIER: Keep both knees on the floor.

HARDER: Bend and straighten your leg as you bend and straighten your arm.

WORKOUT 2

Step and Extend

A. Holding the dumbbells at your shoulders, with your palms facing in, stand facing a staircase. Plant your right foot on the first step. (You can use the second or third step, depending on the height of the stairs and your fitness level.)

B. Press into your right foot and straighten the right leg while lifting the weights overhead. Tap your left toes on the step, then lower both feet back to the starting position. Complete a full set. Switch legs for your second set.

EASIER: Perform the move without the overhead press.

HARDER: Keep the foot you're stepping up with planted on the step throughout the exercise (lowering just the other foot to the floor).

Split Squat, Biceps Curl

A. Stand with your right leg 2 to 3 feet in front of your left leg. Hold a pair of dumbbells down at your sides.

B. Bend your right leg until your right thigh is parallel to the floor and the left leg is extended, with the knee bent and almost touching the floor. Be sure to keep your back straight, and don't allow your right knee to jut beyond your right toes. As you lower, bend your arms and curl the weights to your chest. Pause, then push back up to the starting position, lowering the weights as you stand. Complete a full set. Switch leg positions for your second set.

EASIER: Place one hand on a chair back for balance, and curl with only one arm at a time.

HARDER: Place the top of your back foot on a step.

Single-Leg Row

A. Stand with your feet about hip-width apart, holding the dumbbells down at your sides, with your palms facing in.

B. Bend forward toward the floor while extending your right leg straight behind you until your body forms a T (or as close to it as possible). Allow your arms to hang straight down toward the floor, with your palms facing each other.

C. Squeeze your shoulder blades together and raise the weights to either side of your chest. Repeat for half a set, then switch sides.

EASIER: Hold on to a chair back with one hand, and perform the rows one arm at a time.

HARDER: After rowing the weights to your chest, extend your arms straight back to add a triceps kickback.

Flamingo Lateral Lift

A. Stand with your feet about hip-width apart. Hold the dumbbells down at your sides, with your palms facing in.

B. Bend your right leg and lift your right foot off the floor as high as comfortably possible while maintaining your balance. Tighten your glutes and abs for support, then slowly lift the weights straight out to the sides until your arms are parallel to the floor. Lower your arms back to the starting position and repeat for a full set. Switch legs for the second set.

EASIER: Lightly place one foot on a step instead of suspending it in the air.

HARDER: Extend the lifted leg, holding it as high as possible while maintaining good form.

Dip and Crunch

A. Sit on the edge of a chair with your feet flat on the floor and your knees bent 90 degrees. Grasp the chair seat on either side of your butt. Walk your feet out slightly and inch yourself off the seat. Extend your right leg and plant the heel on the ground, keeping your foot flexed.

B. Bend your elbows straight back and dip your butt toward the ground while simultaneously contracting your abs and pulling your right knee toward your chest. Don't dip your elbows past 90 degrees. Return to the starting position. Complete a set (you may not be able to do 10 the first few times). Switch legs for the second set.

EASIER: Keep both legs bent while performing the move.

HARDER: Extend both legs while performing the move, bending the leg you bring to your chest.

Chest-Press Punch

A. Lie on your back on a mat or carpeted floor and bend your knees. Hold two dumbbells at either side of your chest, with the ends facing each other.

B. Contract your abs and curl your head, shoulders, and torso off the floor. As you come up, extend your left arm across your body to the right as though throwing a light punch in that direction. Return to the starting position. Repeat on the opposite side. Alternate for a full set.

EASIER: Perform the move without weights.

HARDER: Punch to each side before lowering back to the starting position.

Advanced: High-Intensity Intervals

Most of you will get extremely fit just doing the intermediate program. But if you want to take it to the next level, or you're already in super shape, I definitely have some options for you.

First, forget about splitting your cardio and weight-training days. Instead, just do the weight-resistance program on pages 223–233 three to five times a week, but do it *as fast as you possibly can while maintaining good form.* This will help you achieve failure. Yes, that's an oxymoron, but it's precisely accurate. Lifting to the point where you cannot lift anymore–which in weight-lifting circles is called "lifting to failure"–has a number of metabolic benefits to help you burn more fat and shape muscle. There are many ways to do this: You can go heavy and slow or fast and light. It doesn't matter for our purposes. You just want to get to the place where lifting more is very, very hard.

To do this with your own body weight, select three to five exercises (such as the routines on pages 223–233) that will hit all your major muscle groups and do three to five sets of 10 to 12 reps, moving as quickly as you can while still maintaining good form. If you hit failure before that point, you can either try a simplified version of the exercise, reduce the amount of reps and sets you do, or try fewer exercises at a time.

For most of you, that will be enough. Pumping through 30 to 50 Hinge and Rows, Pilé Squat and Curls, Lunge and Twists, Bridge with Flies, and Kneeling Arm Raises in 10 to 15 minutes is enough to keep you in amazing shape. And there's no question it will get your heart pumping. If you want to take it to the next level, reduce the amount of time you rest and/or add more weight.

If you really enjoy cardio and can't wait to get out for a run, try doing the classic high-intensity interval training (HIIT) running sequence, in which you sprint as fast as you can for 1 minute and rest for 2 minutes. Here's how to do that.

TIME IN MINUTES	INTENSITY
0:00–3:00	Warm up with a light jog.
3:00–5:00	Increase your pace. This should be quick enough to be a little difficult but not enough to make you breathless. You'd be able to talk to a friend during this time.
5:00–6:00	Sprint as fast as you can—you should be completely out of breath after your sprint.
6:00–8:00	Resume a moderate jog for about 2 minutes, or until you are recovered.
8:00–18:00	Repeat minutes 3:00 through 8:00 for two intervals.
18:00–20:00	Cool down by walking at a slow, relaxing pace.

As you improve, you can shorten your rest periods and increase your intervals as desired. Figure out what works for you.

Once you've mastered this, you'll probably be in the best shape of your life. This is an intense program, and no one needs more exercise than this to get fit and remain healthy. But if you love a challenge, there are always ways to take your performance to the next level. Just remember not to overdo it–too much exercise doesn't serve you any better than too little.

LOOKING AHEAD

You now have all the tools you need to optimize your nutrition, reduce stress, enhance resilience, and exercise optimally. If you do everything you've learned so far, you'll go a long way toward enhancing the health of your microbiome, losing weight, and getting healthy.

That said, there's one more subject I want to address–supplements to help you lose weight and diversify your gut microbiome. There's a lot of nonsense out there when it comes to this topic. A few supplements work to support weight-loss attempts. But most of them are bunk with little or no good scientific evidence behind them. In the Appendix I'll separate the wheat from the chaff and tell you the real truth about which supplements work, which don't, and how to integrate them properly into this program.

CHAPTER 11

THE GUT BALANCE REVOLUTION

FOOD CHARTS, MEAL PLANS, SHOPPING LISTS, RECIPES, AND OTHER TIPS ON HOW TO EAT ON THE PROGRAM

Food is medicine, and there's no better way to improve your health, lose weight, and rebalance your gut microbiome than to optimize your nutrition using the three-phase plan outlined in this book. This chapter gives you all the tools you need to do that.

I'll share more than 50 delicious anti-inflammatory, blood-glucose-balancing, fat-burning, gut-microbiome-diversifying recipes that I developed especially for this program. These recipes are something special. I worked extensively with a chef to create spectacular gourmet meals you can prepare on a budget and that follow the nutritional criteria for each phase of the program. They're easy to make–most take less than 30 minutes of prep and cook time–and they're tasty, and each and every one has the Dr. Gerry seal of approval. In fact, most of the recipes contain at least one (and in many cases more than one) of the superfoods in this book. I like to call these my WFMDs–weapons of fat mass destruction–because they'll blow the fat right off your body.

But I didn't stop there. For each phase, you'll also find a 2-week rotational meal plan to guide you on your way. I'll tell you more about how to use these in a moment. We also developed shopping lists to make your shopping experience a breeze.

If you don't want to make the recipes in this book every night, just use the Gut Balance Revolution food charts. These include the foods you should favor, eat fewer of, and forget altogether. Use these lists to create your own gut-microbiome-enhancing meals.

You'll also find tips on how to prepare foods ahead of time. You'll even find guidelines for eating out at restaurants, tips on how to prepare your pantry for the program, and more.

In short, you have all the information you need to lose weight, improve your lifestyle, and integrate the best-researched supplements for fat-burning into your daily routine.

Now it's time to put it all together, to get going with the program. And it all starts with preparing your pantry.

PREPARING A GUT-BALANCING PANTRY

The idea that the kitchen is the heart of our homes is an ancient concept that in modern times is often forgotten—it's disappearing from our culture so fast that some people see cooking as a lost art and wonder whether generations to come will have the skill set—let alone the interest—to cook. And that's something we should stand against. According to Michael Pollan in his recent book *Cooked*, each day the average American spends only 23 minutes preparing food in the kitchen and another 4 in the kitchen cleaning up. The USDA reports that the average American spends 78 minutes eating outside the home.[1] That's a real concern.

More to the point, evidence has begun to show that the amount of time you cook at home is inversely proportional to your risk of weight gain and obesity. In a study published in the *Journal of Economic Perspectives*, researchers looked at data on the correlation between obesity and home cooking across several cultures. Their findings? Cultures in which cooking at home was prominent had dramatically reduced rates of obesity.[2]

A big part of the Gut Balance Revolution is preparing your own meals. And that means reclaiming the kitchen and making it the center of family life once more. Doing this starts with setting up your kitchen and pantry with the foods you'll need to prepare (and eat!) the meals in this book. It also means cleaning out the junk food that may take up an enormous portion of the real estate in your cupboards, refrigerator, or freezer.

To prepare for the Gut Balance Revolution, here's what to do: Before Phase 1, go through your pantry (and your refrigerator) and throw out anything not allowed on the program. You can donate it if you'd like, but get it out of your house. That's because you're far more likely to eat junk food if it's around. When cravings strike, you can't give in if the food isn't there waiting for you.

Next, stock your pantry with weapons of fat mass destruction (WFMDs)—the ingredients to make the healing, gut-balancing recipes in this book. To do this, you can shop weekly for the items on the relevant shopping lists on pages 270–275. Make sure you have plenty of the superfoods for each phase on hand. And stock your spice shelf with the delicious, medicinal spices outlined in this book. Don't forget the extra-virgin olive oil (EVOO)! Consuming this good fat will help you feel satiated and actually burn fat.

Once you bring these foods into your home, organize them so they're easily accessible. Cooking in your kitchen should be an enjoyable experience. If you're scrambling around trying to buy ingredients at the last minute, or digging through the dark recesses of a disorganized dry goods cabinet, you're more likely to give up, go out, and eat off the program.

So take the time and prepare your pantry. I know it sounds like a chore, but do it. Don't underestimate this step. It will make sticking with the plan far easier, and it will set you up for long-term success.

DO-AHEAD GUIDELINES

Here are quick tips for preparing foods ahead of time to make cooking at home more convenient. The more preparation you do in advance, the more time you'll save, the easier your cooking experience will be, and the more likely you are to cook and eat at home. So strive to integrate these tips into your weekly routine.

Breakfast

Make a double batch of smoothies to freeze in airtight containers for a fast on-the-go breakfast that thaws in transit. Freezing yogurt or kefir doesn't kill their probiotics, but warming or heating in the microwave does. So let them thaw naturally.

Power Breakfast Bars (page 279) freeze well, too. Purchase a box of snack-size resealable bags–the perfect packing for individual servings–pop the bars in the bags, and toss in the freezer or fridge. Grab and go, or tuck one into your gym bag for an afterworkout meal.

You can also freeze the fully cooked Muffin-Size Frittatas (page 295) in sandwich bags. Use a permanent marker to jot down the freeze date. For a portable breakfast or a relaxing brunch entrée that's ready in minutes, thaw the frittata, unwrapped, in a 300°F oven for 10 minutes.

Lunch

Prep your greens up to 3 days in advance for fast cooking. Bok choy or Swiss chard, kale, romaine, and other mature greens can be trimmed, prewashed, and stored in large resealable plastic bags lined with paper towels to prevent wilting. Avoid washing baby greens that can easily rot, or opt for "prewashed" baby greens and tuck in a dry paper towel to keep them fresher long.

Prechop nuts and store them in the freezer to keep them from going rancid. No need to thaw them before use–just toss into salads and smoothies.

Soups freeze well and don't lose their nutrients. For Phase 1, make a double batch of the Spiced Pumpkin Soup (page 283) and Chicken Vegetable Soup (page 288). For Phase 2, prepare and freeze Cool Cucumber-Avocado Soup (page 296), Miso Soup (page 300), and Creamy Asparagus Soup (page 303). For Phase 3, rely on Wild Rice and Turkey Soup (page 314), Minestrone Soup (page 316), Turkey Chili (page 319), and Curried Red Lentil Soup (page 320), or mix and match the soups from other phases.

The Massaged Kale Salad (page 286) minus the toppings stores well in your fridge for up to 3 days. Use it as a base for any phase-appropriate protein from chicken to fish, beef, or turkey.

Prep salad dressings ahead and store in airtight containers in your fridge, like this tasty Greek Dressing for Phase 1 that you can use throughout the program.

Greek Dressing

MAKES 4 SERVINGS (2 TABLESPOONS EACH)

¼ cup extra-virgin olive oil

¼ cup lemon juice

2 teaspoons dried oregano

1 teaspoon Dijon mustard

⅛ teaspoon freshly ground black pepper

In a blender, combine the olive oil, lemon juice, oregano, mustard, and pepper and process until smooth. Transfer to an airtight container to store. Serve over the Greek Village Salad (page 280) or your own favorite medley of greens.

Dinner

Stock your freezer with frozen shrimp and place under cold running water to thaw in minutes. Similarly, if you don't have time to cook fresh shrimp, opt for cooked frozen shrimp (that's more economical) and thaw under cold running water.

Shop for a wide array of frozen berries as fast snacks to store in your freezer for up to 6 months.

Stock your pantry with low-sodium canned beans, such as chickpeas or black beans, and add this nutrient-dense prebiotic food to meals and snacks.

Both the Massaged Kale Salad (page 286) and the Greek Village Salad (page 280) will store in your fridge for up to 3 days and make perfect snacks or fast no-cook meals. Feel free to make them ahead or during the weekend.

Slow-cook your proteins to use for a quick-to-assemble supper. Cook boneless, skinless chicken breasts on low for 2 to 2½ hours with flavorings appropriate for each phase. Or cook salmon fillets (skin on) or raw shrimp on low for 1½ to 2 hours with flavorings appropriate for each phase.

Cook chicken breasts in batches. Cool and cube them, then store for up to 3 days in the fridge or freeze in 1-cup portions for fast weekday meals. See the recipe on page 240.

Buy items in bulk or family-pack sizes to save cash and trips to the store. For all phases, shop for low-sodium chicken or vegetable broth, tomato paste, kale, spinach, salad greens, frozen berries, eggs, and olive oil. Use baby or spinach greens within 5 days, but heartier greens will last up to 10, and so will eggs. For Phases 2 and 3, yogurt, kefir, lemons, avocado, and fresh ginger will store in your fridge for up to 2 weeks.

Have leftover tomato paste from a recipe? Freeze it in tablespoon-size portions in snack bags for future recipes.

Prechop celery, carrots, and garlic in a food processor for fast soup-batch cooking or for stew and salad prep.

Short on herbs for a particular recipe? Parsley and basil are all-purpose herbs that can make a tasty substitution.

Bulk Cooking Chicken

MAKES ABOUT 12 CHICKEN BREASTS

Cook chicken in bulk for fast mealtime salads.

4 pounds boneless, skinless chicken breasts

1 teaspoon salt (omit for low-sodium diets)

1 teaspoon salt-free garlic powder

1 teaspoon chili powder or mild paprika

½ teaspoon freshly ground black pepper

1. Preheat the oven to 400°F. Cover a baking sheet with foil and set aside.

2. Sprinkle the chicken with the salt (if using), garlic powder, chili powder or paprika, and pepper. Coat 2 large skillets with cooking spray and place over high heat for about 5 seconds. Place 3 or 4 breasts in each skillet without crowding them. Reduce the heat to medium and cook for 2 to 3 minutes, or until the chicken begins to brown. Turn the breasts and cook for 3 minutes. Transfer the chicken to the prepared baking sheet and repeat with the remaining breasts until the sheet is full.

3. Bake for 8 to 10 minutes, or until a thermometer inserted in the thickest part registers 165°F and the juices run clear. Let stand for 5 minutes before slicing. To store, allow the chicken to cool completely, then place in resealable bags. Store in the fridge for up to 5 days or in the freezer for up to 3 months.

Note: Cooking for just one or two? Cut the ingredient amounts in half and cook in a small skillet or use a loaf pan to bake in your toaster oven.

THE GUT BALANCE REVOLUTION FOOD CHARTS

Here are the food charts for each phase. Use these as a guideline for creating your own meals.

FOOD CHART	PHASE I

Baking Ingredients/Condiments

FAVOR

Baking powder (aluminum free)
Baking soda
Coconut, shredded
Flavor extracts, 100% (almond, orange, maple extract, etc.)
Mustard powder
Vinegars, clear
Wasabi powder (no colorings)

FEW

Arrowroot powder
Cocoa powder
Miso (gluten free)

Sea salt
Soy sauce (gluten free)
Tamari (gluten free)

FORGET

Condiments with unacceptable ingredients:
Chutney
Ketchup
Mayonnaise
Pesto
Sun-dried tomato paste

Beverages

FAVOR

Coffee
Teas: Emphasize green tea; black, white, and herbal teas
Water

FORGET

Apple cider
Chicory-based coffee
Fruit beverages and juice drinks or -ades
Sodas, regular and diet

PROTEIN/FAT SOURCES

Dairy

FAVOR

Butter
Cheese (Colby, Edam, feta, Gouda, Parmesan, Swiss)
Cheese, ripened (blue vein, Brie, Cheddar)
Fromage fraise

FORGET

Cheese, soft (cottage, ricotta, cream cheese, mascarpone, crème fraîche)

Cow's milk
Custard
Dairy desserts
Evaporated milk
Goat's milk
Ice cream
Milk powder
Sheep's milk
Sweetened condensed milk
Yogurt (cow's, sheep's, goat's)

Dairy-Free Alternatives

FAVOR

None

FORGET

See Dairy above

FEW

Almond, hemp, coconut, or rice nondairy
  beverages, plain and unsweetened
Coconut water

Fats and Oils

FAVOR

Canola oil (baking only)
Extra-virgin olive oil

Coconut oil, 100% palm oil (dairy-free,
  nonhydrogenated shortening)
Peanut oil

FEW

Almond, canola, flaxseed, grapeseed,
  olive, palm, pumpkin, safflower, sesame,
  sunflower, walnut oil, etc.
Canola oil

FORGET

Corn oil
Cottonseed oil
Lard
Shortening

Fish

FAVOR

Wild-caught favored over sustainably
  farmed seafood. Salmon, tilapia, Atlantic
  or Pacific (US) cod, anchovy, butterfish,
  catfish, canned light tuna, flounder,
  haddock, herring, ocean perch, mussels,
  oysters, plaice, pollock, rainbow trout,
  rockfish, sardines, scallops, sea bass
  (black), shad (US), shrimp, sole, spiny
  lobster, striped bass, trout (freshwater),
  wild eastern oyster, whitefish, and
  whiting.

FEW

Striped bass, carp, Alaskan cod, halibut,
  lobster, mahi-mahi, monkfish, perch
  (freshwater), sablefish, skate, snapper,
  tuna (canned chunk white, skipjack),
  and weakfish (sea trout), albacore or
  Yellowfin tuna (1 time weekly)

FORGET

Shark, swordfish, king mackerel, or tilefish

Meat (Organic, Pasture Fed and Raised)

FAVOR

Poultry (chicken, turkey, duck) without skin
Whole eggs, egg whites
Wild game

FORGET

Fatty cuts of meat (beef, pork, lamb)
Poultry with skin
Processed or aged meat and poultry
  products (hot dogs, deli meats, canned
  meat products, etc.)

FEW

Lean cuts of meat (beef, lamb, pork);
  grass-fed, organic favored

FOOD CHART   PHASE I

Fruits

FAVOR

Banana (green)
Blueberry
Cantaloupe
Cherries (sour)
Cranberries (whole)
Honeydew melon
Kiwifruit
Lemon
Lime
Passionfruit
Plums
Raspberries

FEW

Avocado
Grape
Grapefruit
Orange
Papaya
Pomegranate
Rhubarb
Starfruit
Strawberry

Tangelo
Tangerine
Tomato

FORGET

Apples
Applesauce and apple cider
Apricots
Blackberries
Boysenberries
Dried fruits (dates, figs, prunes, etc.)
Fruit beverages
Fruit juices or fruit concentrates (100%)
Fruits, canned in syrups
Mango
Nashi fruit
Nectarines
Peaches
Pears
Persimmon
Pineapple
Plantains
Tamarillo
Watermelon

Herbs and Spices

FAVOR

Fresh and/or dried herbs and spices:
  Cardamom
  Cayenne (ground red) pepper
  Cinnamon
  Cumin
  Ginger

FORGET

Herb or spice mixes or seasonings with
  unacceptable food ingredients

(continued)

Legumes (Vegetable Protein), Nuts, and Seeds

FEW

Almonds

Cashews

Chia seeds

Flaxseeds (linseed)

Hazelnuts

Natural nut butters made from almonds,
Brazil nuts, pecans, walnuts

Natural seed butters made from chia,
flaxseeds, hempseeds, pumpkin, sesame,
sunflower

Nut and seed beverages

Pistachios

Poppy seeds

Pumpkin seeds (pepitas)

Sesame seeds

Sunflower seeds

FORGET

Baked beans, bean sprouts, black-eyed
beans, borlotti beans, broad beans (fava
beans), chickpeas (garbanzo beans),
kidney beans, lentils, navy beans, peas,
split peas

Highly processed soy foods or legume
products (tofu hot dogs, soy chips,
garbanzo bean chips, etc.)

Highly processed vegetable protein
alternatives (Quorn, seitan)

Nut and seed butters made with
hydrogenated or peanut oils

Nut and seed products with unacceptable
toxic ingredients

Soybeans (edamame, tofu, miso, tempeh)

Tahini

Other

FAVOR

Garlic-infused olive oil

Ginger

Stevia

FORGET

Agave syrup

Brown rice syrup

Chocolate, cocoa products

Evaporated cane juice

Fruit sweeteners

Glucose

High-fructose corn syrup–containing
foods and beverages

Honey

Mannitol

Maple syrup, artificial

Maple syrup, 100%

Molasses, blackstrap

Sorbitol

Sucrose (table sugar)

Xylitol

Vegetables

FAVOR

Alfalfa sprouts

Bamboo shoots

Beans (green)

Bean sprouts

Bok choy

Butternut squash

Capsicum

Celery

Chard (Swiss)

Chives

Choy sum

Cucumber

Eggplant

Endive

Escarole

Greens (mustard, collard)
Kabocha squash (Japanese pumpkin)
Kale
Lettuce
Olives
Parsnip
Pumpkin
Radish
Silverbeet
Spaghetti squash (baked)
Spinach
Spring onion (green part only)
Squash (yellow, zucchini, butternut)
Turnips

FEW
Artichokes (globe and Jerusalem)
Asparagus
Beetroot
Broccoli
Brussels sprouts
Button mushrooms

Cabbage
Carrot
Cauliflower
Fennel
Garlic
Green peas
Leek
Okra
Onions (mature, cooking)
Shallots
Snap peas
Snow peas
Sweet corn
Sweet potato
Tomato juice (100%)
Vegetable juice (100%)

FORGET
All vegetables breaded, creamed, and fried
Overcooked tempura
Vegetable juices made with vegetables on
    Forget list
White potato

Whole Grains and Flours

FEW
Buckwheat
Corn
Gluten-free bread, cracker (plain,
    unseasoned), and cereal products*
Millet
Oat bran
Oats

Polenta
Quinoa
Rice
Sweet biscuit

FORGET
Barley-, rye-, and wheat-based bread,
    crackers, pasta, cereal, couscous, gnocchi,
    noodles, croissants, muffins, crumpets

All grain and flour-based products must be labeled gluten free.

FOOD CHART   PHASE 2

Beverages

FAVOR
Black tea
Ginger-herbal teas
Green tea
Water
Whey
White tea

FEW
Coconut water
Coffee
Fermented beers*

*Limit to 1 serving (glass) per day.

Kefir (variety of animal, seed, and nut milk
  sources)
Milk: 2% organic animal milk; nondairy (soy,
  almond, hemp), plain and unsweetened
Red wine*

FORGET
Fruit juices
Rice milk
Sodas
Sugar-sweetened beverages

Condiments

FAVOR
Arrowroot powder
Baking powder (aluminum free)
Baking soda
Cocoa powder
Flavor extracts, 100% (almond, orange,
  maple extract, etc.)
Mustard powder
Vinegars (clear)
Wasabi powder (no colorings)

FEW
Fruit-based condiments:*
  Chutney
  Ketchup
  Sun-dried tomato paste
Miso (gluten free)
Sea salt†
Soy sauce (gluten free)
Tamari (gluten free)

FORGET
Condiments with unacceptable ingredients:
  Mayonnaise
  Pesto

*High FODMAP
†High sodium

Fruits

FAVOR
Apples
Apricots
Avocado
Banana**
Berries (blue, black, etc.)
Cantaloupe

Carambola (star fruit)
Cherries (sour)
Cranberries
Figs
Grapefruit
Grapes (concord)
Honeydew melon

**Bananas are high in resistant starch and feed beneficial bacteria; it's best to eat a firm greenish banana.

Kiwifruit
Lemon
Lime
Oranges (tangelo)
Papaya
Passionfruit
Peaches
Pear (Asian)
Persimmon
Plums
Rhubarb

FEW
Grapes (green, red)

Mango
Oranges (navel, Florida)
Pears (Anjou, Bartlett)
Pineapple
Plantains
Watermelon

FORGET
Apple cider
Applesauce
Dried fruits (dates, prunes, etc.)
Fruit beverages
Fruit juices or fruit concentrates (100%)
Fruits, canned in syrups

Grains

FEW
Amaranth
Brown rice
Buckwheat
Oat bran
Popcorn
Quinoa
Teff

FORGET
Barley
Millet
Rye
Spelt
Wheat products

Oils

FAVOR
Canola (baking only)
Extra-virgin olive

FEW
Almond
Butter (from grass-fed cows)
Canola (baking preferred)
Coconut
Flaxseed
Grapeseed
Palm
Pumpkin

Safflower
Sesame
Sunflower
Walnut

FORGET
Corn
Lard
Margarine
Palm, hydrogenated
Safflower
Shortening

FOOD CHART   PHASE 2

Soups

FAVOR
Vegetable, bean, chicken (white meat, no noodles)

FORGET
Cream-based

Spices

FAVOR
Black pepper
Cardamon
Cayenne (ground red) pepper
Cinnamon
Cumin
Garlic
Garlic-infused olive oil
Ginger, fresh or ground
Herbs
Mustard
Turmeric

Sweet Additions

FAVOR
Stevia

FEW
Brown rice syrup
Chocolate (dark)
Cocoa products
Evaporated cane juice
Glucose
Honey, raw
Maple syrup (pure)
Molasses, blackstrap
Sucrose (table sugar)

FORGET
Agave syrup
Artificial sweeteners
Fruit sweeteners
High-fructose corn syrup (foods and beverages)
Honey, refined
Mannitol
Sorbitol
Xylitol

Vegetables

FAVOR
Alfalfa
Artichokes (globe and Jerusalem)
Asparagus
Bamboo shoots
Beans (green)
Bean sprouts
Bok choy
Brussels sprouts
Butternut squash
Cabbage
Carrots
Cauliflower
Chard (Swiss)
Chicory root, raw
Chives
Choy sum
Cruciferous vegetables
Cucumber
Dandelion
Eggplant
Endive
Escarole
Fennel

Garlic
Green peas
Greens (collard, mustard, turnip)
Kabocha (Japanese pumpkin)
Kale
Leek
Lettuce
Mesclun greens
Mushrooms
Okra
Olives
Onion
Parsnips
Pumpkin
Radish
Shallots
Silverbeet
Snap peas
Snow peas
Spaghetti squash (baked)
Spinach
Spring onion (green part only)
Squash (yellow, zucchini, butternut)
Tomato

Pickled foods:
Fermented tofu
Korean kimchi
Miso
Natto
Pickled beets
Pickled cabbage
Pickled corn relish
Pickled cucumbers
Pickled garlic
Pickled radish
Sauerkraut
Soy sauce
Tempeh

FEW
Beets (nonpickled)
Sweet corn
Sweet potato*

FORGET
All vegetables breaded, creamed, and
    fried
Overcooked tempura
Vegetable juices made with vegetables on
    forget list
White potato products

Baked with skin—highly satiogenic, high fiber, anti-inflammatory.

PROTEIN/FAT SOURCES

Dairy

FAVOR
Butter
Cheese (Colby, Edam, feta, Gouda,
    mozzarella, Parmesan, Swiss)
Cheese, ripened (blue vein, Brie, Cheddar)
Cheese, soft (cottage, ricotta, cream
    cheese, mascarpone, crème fraîche)
Fromage fraise
Greek yogurt
Yogurt (cow's, sheep's, goat's), home-
    made preferred
Yogurt, nondairy (almond, soy, coconut)

FEW
Lactose-free frozen yogurt
Sour cream

FORGET
Cow's milk
Custard
Dairy desserts
Evaporated milk
Goat's milk
Ice cream

(continued)

Fish

FAVOR

Wild-caught favored over sustainably farmed seafood. Salmon, tilapia, Atlantic or Pacific (US) cod, anchovy, butterfish, catfish, canned light tuna, flounder, haddock, herring, ocean perch, mussels, oysters, plaice, pollock, rainbow trout, rockfish, sardines, scallops, sea bass (black), shad (US), shrimp, sole, spiny lobster, striped bass, trout (freshwater), wild eastern oyster, whitefish, and whiting.

FEW

Striped bass, carp, Alaskan cod, halibut, lobster, mahi-mahi, monkfish, perch (freshwater), sablefish, skate, snapper, tuna (canned chunk white, skipjack), and weakfish (sea trout), albacore or Yellowfin tuna (1 time weekly)

FORGET

Shark, swordfish, king mackerel, or tilefish

Legumes

FAVOR

Chickpeas and other white beans (i.e., cannellini)
Kidney beans

Lentils
Mung beans
Soybeans

Meat

FAVOR

White meat poultry
Wild game (deer, buffalo, bison)

FEW

Lean meats (beef, lamb, pork), grass-fed, organic favored

FORGET

Dark meat poultry

Fatty cuts of meat (rib eye, lamb, duck)
Hamburger
Milk powder
Poultry with skin
Processed cheeses
Processed meats (hot dogs, deli meats, canned meats like Spam)
Sheep's milk
Sweetened condensed milk

Nuts

FAVOR

Almonds
Brazil nuts
Hazelnuts
Peanuts
Pecans
Pine nuts
Pistachios
Walnuts

FEW

Cashews
Macadamia nuts

FORGET

Processed nut and seed butters with hydrogenated oils and sweeteners

FOOD CHART PHASE 2

Other

FAVOR
Soy
Eggs (whole, whites)

Seeds

FAVOR
Chia seeds
Flaxseeds (ground)
Hemp seeds

Poppy seeds
Pumpkin seeds (pepitas)
Sesame seeds (tahini)
Sunflower seeds

FOOD CHART PHASE 3

Beverages

FAVOR
Black tea
Ginger-herbal teas
Green tea
Kefir (variety of animal, seed, and nut milk sources)
Water
Whey
White tea

FEW
Coconut water (without added sugar)

Limit to 1 serving (glass) per day.

Coffee*
Fermented beers*
Fruit juices
Milk: low-fat organic animal milk; nondairy (soy, almond, hemp), plain and unsweetened
Red wine*
Rice milk

FORGET
Any except for sodas, sugar-sweetened beverages, which are consumed rarely

Condiments

FAVOR
Arrowroot powder
Baking powder (aluminum free)
Baking soda
Cocoa powder
Flavor extracts, 100% (almond, orange, maple, etc.)
Mustard powder
Vinegars (clear)
Wasabi powder (no colorings)

FEW
Mayonnaise
Miso (gluten free)
Pesto
Sea salt†
Soy sauce (gluten free)
Tamari (gluten free)
Fruit-based condiments:††
  Chutney
  Ketchup
  Sun-dried tomato paste

†High sodium
††High FODMAP

FOOD CHART PHASE 3

Fruits

FAVOR

Apples
Apricots
Avocado
Banana*
Berries (blue, black etc.)
Cantaloupe
Carambola (star fruit)
Cherries (sour)
Cranberries
Figs
Grapefruit
Grapes (concord)
Grapes (green, red)
Honeydew melon
Kiwifruit
Lemon
Lime
Mango
Oranges (navel, Florida)

Oranges (tangelo)
Papaya
Passionfruit
Peaches
Pears (Anjou, Asian, Bartlett)
Persimmon
Pineapple
Plantains
Plums
Rhubarb
Watermelon

FEW

Apple cider
Applesauce
Dried fruits (dates, prunes, etc.)
Fruit juices or fruit concentrates (100%)
Fruits, canned in syrups

FORGET

None

Bananas are high in resistant starch and feed beneficial bacteria–best to eat a firm-greenish banana.

Grains

FAVOR

Amaranth
Brown rice
Buckwheat
Oat bran
Popcorn
Quinoa
Teff

FEW

Barley*
Millet*
Rye*
Spelt*
Wheat products (whole grain)*

FORGET

None except for white-flour-based
products, which should be limited: noodles,
croissants, muffins, crumpets, etc.

Those with celiac disease, nonceliac gluten sensitivity, and/or wheat allergy should avoid these grains.

Oils

FAVOR
Almond
Canola
Coconut
Extra-virgin olive
Flaxseed
Grapeseed
Palm
Pumpkin
Safflower
Sesame
Sunflower
Walnut

FEW
Butter (grass-fed)
Sesame

FORGET
None except for corn oil, lard, margarine, hydrogenated palm oil, safflower oil, shortening

Soups

FAVOR
Miso
Vegetable-based, legume-based, lean poultry with whole grains

FEW
Cream-based

FORGET
None

Spices

FAVOR
Black pepper
Cardamon
Cayenne (ground red) pepper
Cinnamon
Cumin
Garlic
Garlic-infused olive oil
Ginger, fresh or ground
Herbs
Mustard
Turmeric

FORGET
None

Sweet Additions

FAVOR
Chocolate (dark)*
Stevia

FEW
Agave syrup
Brown rice syrup
Chocolate (dark)
Cocoa products
Evaporated cane juice
Fruit sweeteners
Glucose
Honey
Maple syrup (pure)
Molasses, blackstrap
Sucrose (table sugar)

FORGET
None except limit (rare) artificial sweeteners, high-fructose corn syrup (in foods and beverages), mannitol, sorbitol, xylitol

*Dark chocolate should be 70% or greater cocoa and be limited to 2 ounces per day.

Vegetables

FAVOR

Alfalfa
Artichokes (globe and Jerusalem)
Asparagus
Bamboo shoots
Beans (green)
Bean sprouts
Beets (nonpickled)
Bok choy
Brussels sprouts
Cabbage
Carrots
Cauliflower
Chard (Swiss)
Chicory root, raw
Chives
Choy sum
Cruciferous vegetables
Cucumber
Dandelion
Eggplant
Endive
Escarole
Fennel
Garlic
Green peas
Greens (collard, mustard, turnip)
Kabocha (Japanese pumpkin)
Kale
Leek
Lettuce
Mesclun greens
Mushrooms
Okra
Olives
Onion
Parsnips

Pickled foods:
  Fermented tofu
  Korean kimchi
  Miso
  Natto
  Pickled beets
  Pickled cabbage
  Pickled corn relish
  Pickled cucumbers
  Pickled garlic
  Pickled radish
  Sauerkraut
  Soy sauce
  Tempeh
Pumpkin
Radish
Shallots
Silverbeet
Snap peas
Snow peas
Spaghetti squash (baked)
Spinach
Spring onion (green part only)
Squash (yellow, zucchini, butternut)
Sweet corn
Sweet potato*
Tomato

FEW

All vegetables breaded, creamed, and
  fried
Overcooked tempura
Vegetable juices made with vegetables on
  Avoid list
White potato products

FORGET

None

Baked with skin—highly satiogenic, high fiber, anti-inflammatory.

PROTEIN/FAT SOURCES

Dairy

FAVOR

Butter

Cheese (Colby, Edam, feta, Gouda, mozzarella, Parmesan, Swiss)

Cheese, ripened (blue vein, Brie, Cheddar)

Cheese, soft (cottage, ricotta, cream cheese, mascarpone, crème fraîche)

Fromage fraise

Greek yogurt

Sour cream

Yogurt (cow's, sheep's, goat's), home-made preferred

Yogurt, nondairy

FEW

Cow's milk

Custard

Dairy desserts

Evaporated milk

Goat's milk

Ice cream

Lactose-free frozen yogurt

Milk powder

Sheep's milk

Sweetened condensed milk

FORGET

None except for processed cheeses

Fish

FAVOR

Wild-caught favored over sustainably farmed seafood. Salmon, tilapia, Atlantic or Pacific (US) cod, anchovy, butterfish, catfish, canned light tuna, flounder, haddock, herring, ocean perch, mussels, oysters, plaice, pollock, rainbow trout, rockfish, sardines, scallops, sea bass (black), shad (US), shrimp, sole, spiny lobster, striped bass, trout (freshwater), wild eastern oyster, whitefish, and whiting.

FEW

Striped bass, carp, Alaskan cod, halibut, lobster, mahi-mahi, monkfish, perch (freshwater), sablefish, skate, snapper, tuna (canned chunk white, skipjack), and weakfish (sea trout), albacore or Yellowfin tuna (1 time weekly)

FORGET

Shark, swordfish, king mackerel, or tilefish

Legumes

FAVOR

Chickpeas and other white beans (i.e., cannellini)

Kidney beans

Lentils

Mung beans

Soybeans

FORGET

None except for highly processed soy and legume foods (tofu hot dogs, soy chips, garbanzo bean chips, lentil chips, etc.), which are rarely consumed

(continued)

FOOD CHART   PHASE 3

Meat

FAVOR

Lean meats (beef, lamb, pork), grass-fed, organic favored

White-meat poultry

Wild game (deer, buffalo, bison)

FEW

Dark-meat poultry

Fatty cuts of meat (rib eye, lamb, duck)

Hamburger

Poultry with skin

FORGET

None except for processed meats (hot dogs, deli meats, canned meats like Spam), which are rarely consumed

Nuts

FAVOR

Almonds

Brazil nuts

Cashews

Hazelnuts

Macadamia nuts

Peanuts

Pecans

Pine nuts

Pistachios

Walnuts

FORGET

None except for processed nut and seed butters with hydrogenated oils and sweeteners

Other

FAVOR

Eggs (organic; whole, whites)

Soy

Seeds

FAVOR

Chia seeds

Flaxseeds (ground)

Hemp seeds

Poppy seeds

Pumpkin seeds (pepita)

Sesame seeds (tahini)

Sunflower seeds

THE GUT BALANCE REVOLUTION SUCCESS STORIES

Cindy Lindgren, 49
Scott Lindgren, 50

Looking for Cindy and Scott Lindgren on a Saturday? In the not-too-distant past, you'd find them sitting at their kitchen table with a cup of coffee and a box of Pop-Tarts. These days, though, you'll have a tough time tracking them down. They might be visiting the farmers' market or exploring a park or hanging out with friends. "Nowadays, if we switch on the TV," Cindy says, "we'll look at each other and say, 'Let's not watch this.' "

For Cindy and Scott, life has been transformed. Cindy, plagued by digestive issues in the wake of gallbladder surgery, struggled to find a solution to the constant nausea and diarrhea. "It really limited my life," she recalls. "I was exhausted all the time and constantly worried about what I could eat—and where the bathroom was." But that changed when she started on the Gut Balance Revolution.

Within 6 weeks, Cindy's symptoms were nearly gone. And there was an unexpected bonus. Her husband, Scott, who'd been trying to lose weight for years, dropped 19 pounds. "Both of us began feeling so much better," Cindy says, "just by eating healthy foods and getting rid of all that processed stuff. Instead of relying on takeout, it's amazing how quickly you can fix a meal that's delicious and healthy—without turning your kitchen into a science project."

Lots of other things changed, too. For Cindy, a quality assurance executive for a nonprofit organization, the business lunches are no longer a nightmare. And she and Scott can enjoy having dinner with friends, take in a movie, and even go to football parties. "Our world has opened up again," she says.

Best of all, Cindy and Scott have adopted a beagle puppy named Gunnar. "Taking care of a puppy can be overwhelming," Cindy says. "Gunnar is so full of energy and intellect, and before, we would've been way too sluggish to be able to deal with him. But we take him to puppy kindergarten, and we go on adventures with him—there's no way you can just sit on the couch with a puppy in the house. The Gut Balance Revolution has completely reinvigorated us!"

THE GUT BALANCE REVOLUTION MEAL PLANS

Here are the Gut Balance Revolution meal plans. For each phase, I've provided 2 weeks' worth of menus. You can repurpose these week after week or mix up the meals within them as you choose. The other options are simple "no cook" meals you can make by

	BREAKFAST	LUNCH
Monday	Blueberry Protein Smoothie (page 276)	Spiced Pumpkin Soup with chicken (page 283)
Tuesday	Eggs to Go (page 277)	Raspberry Mesclun Salad with Green Tea Dressing with chicken or shrimp (page 284)
Wednesday	2 scrambled eggs or 4 ounces scrambled tofu with 2 cups steamed broccoli	Green salad: mixed greens, tomatoes, celery, cucumbers, sliced or shredded almonds, grilled chicken, olive oil vinaigrette
Thursday	Power Breakfast Bar (page 279)	Crunchy Almond Tuna Salad (page 285)
Friday	Vanilla Spice Quinoa Breakfast Cereal (page 278)	Greek Village Salad (page 280)
Saturday	2 poached eggs on 2 cups raw spinach or arugula	Massaged Kale Salad with chicken or shrimp (page 286)
Sunday	Breakfast Roll-Up: ½ chicken sausage link or ¼ cup chicken cooked with 1 egg rolled in 1 corn tortilla	Leftover Slow-Cooker Chicken Piccata

combining the ingredients listed. If you prefer some recipes over others, or if you need to switch a "no cook" option for a recipe or vice versa, feel free to make those changes as needed.

SNACK	DINNER
¼ avocado mashed with 2 tablespoons onion-free salsa served with celery sticks or lettuce leaves	Orange Salmon with bok choy (page 281)
Fat-Burning Tea: ⅓ cup protein shake mixed with 1 cup hot water with a pinch of cinnamon and cayenne (ground red) pepper	Spiced Pork Roast with Cauliflower Mash (page 289)
2 hard-cooked eggs or 10 walnuts or almonds with Cilantro Green Drink or Basil Green Drink (page 336)	Pesto Baked Cod with spaghetti squash (page 282)
2 tablespoons chia seeds mixed with ½ cup plain, unsweetened coconut milk and a drizzle of vanilla extract	Chicken Lettuce Wraps: cubed cooked chicken served in lettuce leaves spritzed with fresh lime juice and topped with 2 tablespoons unsweetened shredded coconut
Ginger-Crusted Kale Chips (page 290)	Broiled cod or shrimp with black pepper and fresh lemon served over salad greens
4 teaspoons almond butter spread inside celery sticks	Slow-Cooker Chicken Piccata (page 287)
Coconut Joy Pudding (page 291)	Grilled cod kabobs with cubed veggies served over ½ cup cooked quinoa tossed with herbs

(continued)

	BREAKFAST	LUNCH
Monday	Power Breakfast Bar (page 279)	4 ounces smoked salmon over baby greens or grilled zucchini, peppers
Tuesday	Blueberry Protein Smoothie (page 276)	Fast Gazpacho: 1 tomato, ½ cucumber, ½ green or red bell pepper blended with lemon or lime juice and a pinch of salt, topped with 1 cup cubed cooked chicken or shrimp
Wednesday	¼ cup dried quinoa flakes cooked according to package directions with ⅓ cup whey protein powder stirred in and a pinch of cinnamon or cloves	1 can spring-water-packed tuna, drained, mixed with olive oil and paprika, served with cucumber and red bell pepper wedges or over greens
Thursday	Coffee- or Tea- Flavored Smoothie: 1 cup cold coffee or tea blended with ½ cup berries, ⅓ cup whey protein powder	Crunchy Almond Tuna Salad (page 285)
Friday	Vanilla Spice Quinoa Breakfast Cereal (page 278)	2 cups low-sodium canned chicken and vegetable soup (no noodles) or leftover Chicken Vegetable Soup
Saturday	Blueberry Protein Smoothie (page 276)	½ dozen oysters with lemon juice, green salad with olive oil vinaigrette
Sunday	2 poached eggs on 2 cups steamed broccoli or 1 cup sautéed spinach	Chicken Vegetable Soup (page 288)

SNACK	DINNER
1 cup frozen edamame pods steamed and sprinkled with spices of your choice, such as black pepper, cumin, paprika, or hot chili powder	Steamed veggies and stir-fried chicken (no sauce)
⅓ cup whey protein powder blended with cold green tea	Take-out or homemade steamed veggies (such as broccoli, peppers, zucchini, or spinach) with chicken or shrimp (no sauce)
2 hard-cooked eggs with Cilantro Green Drink or Basil Green Drink (page 336)	Take-out egg drop soup with a side of steamed broccoli
Unsweetened Iced Coffee: 1 cup cold coffee; 2 tablespoons plain, unsweetened coconut milk; pinch of cinnamon; 2 tablespoons whey protein powder	Roast chicken (skin discarded) with a side of green beans topped with nuts or olive oil
Ginger-Crusted Kale Chips (page 290)	Orange Salmon with Swiss Chard (page 281)
¼ cup blueberries with 10 plain almonds or walnuts and ginger tea	Chicken breast cooked in the slow cooker for 2 hours on low, topped with freshly grated ginger, 1 tablespoon tomato paste, spices of your choice; served over cooked greens, such as bok choy
Satay Veggie Dip: 2 tablespoons almond butter mixed with 2 tablespoons plain, unsweetened coconut milk and a pinch of cayenne (ground red) pepper; served with celery, sliced bell peppers, or cucumber wedges	Spiced Pork Roast with Cauliflower Mash (page 289)

(continued)

	BREAKFAST	LUNCH
Monday	Pumpkin Pie Yogurt Parfait (page 293)	Chicken Tikka Masala (page 297)
Tuesday	Pomegranate Margarita Smoothie (page 294)	1 cup three-bean salad dressed with olive oil vinaigrette over 2 cups greens; add 1 cup cooked cubed chicken or shrimp
Wednesday	⅓ cup dry buckwheat porridge cooked according to package directions with 1 tablespoon ground flaxseeds, ¼ sliced banana, 10 pecans or slivered almonds	Leftover Ginger Fried Rice
Thursday	Muffin-Size Frittatas (page 295)	Fish sushi (brown rice only) served over green salad tossed with sesame oil
Friday	2 scrambled eggs with 2 tablespoons chopped kimchi or pickle of your choice	Leftover Sautéed Apples and Chicken Sausage with Sauerkraut
Saturday	Berries and "Cream": ½ cup berries topped with ½ cup unsweetened kefir or yogurt whipped with 2 tablespoons plain, unsweetened coconut milk and optional stevia or vanilla	Arugula Salad with Creamy Avocado Dressing (page 302)
Sunday	Salsa and Eggs (page 292)	Creamy Asparagus Soup with chicken or shrimp (page 303)

SNACK	DINNER
Savory Yogurt Dip: ½ cup plain yogurt mixed with a pinch of cumin, hot chili powder, and black pepper; serve with sliced green bell pepper and celery	Tangy Buffalo Burger with Pickles and Slaw (page 299)
3 tablespoons store-bought hummus with celery and cucumber wedges	Ginger Fried Rice with chicken or shrimp or tofu (page 301)
½ cup plain yogurt with a few berries, ground flaxseeds, unsweetened cocoa powder, and/or coconut	Miso Soup with Seaweed Salad and salmon (page 300)
12 pistachios and 1 ounce chopped 85% dark chocolate	Sautéed Apples and Chicken Sausage with Sauerkraut (page 304)
Coconut Banana: ½ banana, cut into chunks, dipped in yogurt and rolled in 2 tablespoons unsweetened coconut	Pistachio-Chia Salmon with butternut squash (page 305)
Creamy Strawberry Sorbet (page 308)	Kimchi Pork Lo Mein (page 307)
Dark Chocolate Nut Clusters (page 309)	Cajun Cod (page 306) with beans

(continued)

	BREAKFAST	LUNCH
Monday	½ cup cooked old-fashioned rolled oats topped with 2 table-spoons canned pumpkin or ber-ries or with 1 tablespoon nuts	Chicken Tikka Masala (page 297)
Tuesday	1 cup yogurt or kefir topped with ¼ cup fresh raspberries	1 cup three-bean salad dressed with olive oil vinaigrette over 2 cups greens; add 1 cup cooked cubed chicken or shrimp (oppo-site protein source from week 1)
Wednesday	Muffin-Size Frittatas (page 295)	Massaged Kale Salad (page 286) topped with 1 tablespoon chopped kimchi or pickles
Thursday	Pumpkin Pie Yogurt Parfait (page 293)	Leftover Zesty Lemon Chicken Salad
Friday	Salsa and Eggs (page 292)	Broiled shrimp or fish with grilled asparagus; Caesar salad (no croutons)
Saturday	½ cup cooked quinoa topped with ½ cup 2% plain kefir or yogurt, ½ teaspoon cinnamon	Creamy Asparagus Soup with chicken or shrimp (page 303)
Sunday	Pomegranate Margarita Smoothie (page 294)	1 cup shredded chicken with ½ cup cooked quinoa mixed with 2 tablespoons beans (any variety)

SNACK	DINNER
1 cup seaweed salad (homemade or store-bought)	Cool Cucumber-Avocado Soup with chicken or shrimp (page 296)
½ cup plain yogurt with a few berries, ground flaxseeds, unsweetened cocoa powder, and/or coconut	4 ounces extra-firm tofu sautéed in 1 tablespoon olive oil with ½ cup each broccoli florets and spinach; top with 1 teaspoon soy sauce or raw apple cider vinegar
2 tablespoons canned black beans mashed with 2 teaspoons olive oil and spices of your choice, served with celery and cucumber wedges	Zesty Lemon Chicken Salad (page 298)
1 cup leftover Cool Cucumber-Avocado Soup	Broiled cod with black pepper and fresh lemon served over salad greens
2 ounces store-bought spicy or mild seaweed chips	Grilled chicken with dill pickles over a plain salad
Frozen Berry Pops: ½ cup plain unsweetened kefir or yogurt blended with ¼ cup berries and optional stevia; freeze for 4 hours in ice pop molds or paper cups	Canned lentil soup topped with 1 cup cubed cooked chicken, shrimp, or tofu
10 macadamia nuts or hazelnuts and 1 ounce 85% dark chocolate	Pistachio-Chia Salmon with butternut squash (page 305)

(continued)

	BREAKFAST	LUNCH
Monday	Blueberry-Spice Waffles (page 313)	Quinoa Salad with Lemony Yogurt Dressing (page 315)
Tuesday	⅓ cup old-fashioned rolled oats cooked with 1 tablespoon flax-seeds and a pinch of cinnamon; stir in ⅓ cup whey protein powder	2 cups Minestrone Soup (page 316) sprinkled with Parmesan or Locatelli Pecorino Romano cheese
Wednesday	Fresh Cranberry-Spice Smoothie (page 311)	Dr. Gerry's Super Salmon Salad (page 317)
Thursday	Mediterranean Sunrise Surprise (page 310)	Leftover Turkey Chili
Friday	Lean Green Smoothie with Apple and Kale (page 312)	Smoked Salmon Salad (page 321)
Saturday	Leftover Blueberry Spice Waffles	Baked Zucchini Boats: zucchini, sliced in half lengthwise, each half topped with 2 tablespoons marinara and 2 tablespoons chopped cooked chicken, shrimp, or tofu
Sunday	Mocha Smoothie: 1 cup cold coffee blended with ½ cup 2% plain kefir or yogurt, ⅓ cup protein powder, 2 teaspoons unsweetened cocoa powder and optional stevia	Curried Red Lentil Soup with chicken or shrimp (page 320)

SNACK	DINNER
½ apple covered with 1 tablespoon almond butter and a pinch of cinnamon	Dr. Gerry's Super Salmon Salad (page 317), 1 cup Minestrone Soup (page 316)
Cucumber Salad: ½ thinly sliced cuke with 2 tablespoons yogurt or kefir and 1 tablespoon fresh lemon juice; add a pinch of spice	Zucchini Manicotti (page 325) with a side of tossed greens salad
½ apple with 1 square dark chocolate	Turkey Chili (page 319)
½ cup 2% plain Greek yogurt with berries and/or shaved dark chocolate	Salmon Cakes with greens (page 323)
Dark Chocolate Flourless Cake (page 326)	Roasted Parmesan-Kale Lamb Chops (page 324)
½ apple with almond butter and a sprinkle of ground flaxseed	Roasted Rosemary Chicken with Brussels Sprouts (page 322)
Leftover Dark Chocolate Flourless Cake	Sunday Stew (page 318)

(continued)

	BREAKFAST	LUNCH
Monday	2 poached eggs over raw baby kale or kale roasted at 400°F for 10 minutes with 2 teaspoons olive oil	Quinoa Salad with Lemony Yogurt Dressing (page 315)
Tuesday	Fresh Cranberry-Spice Smoothie (page 311)	Leftover Wild Rice and Turkey Soup
Wednesday	Lean Green Smoothie with Apple and Kale (page 312) **or** Mediterranean Sunrise Surprise (page 310)	2 cups Minestrone Soup (page 316)
Thursday	Fresh Cranberry-Spice Smoothie (page 311)	Greek Village Salad (page 280)
Friday	Blueberry-Spice Waffles (page 313)	Chopped Salad: chicken, avocado, cucumber, tomato, and egg (no cheese) over greens
Saturday	Lean Green Smoothie with Apple and Kale (page 312)	Soup: 1 cup cooked cubed chicken warmed in a saucepan with 2 cups store-bought broth, 1 cup baby spinach, and 1 cup finely chopped broccoli florets
Sunday	Eggs Benedict: 2 poached eggs over greens topped with ½ cup yogurt whipped with herbs and 1 teaspoon lemon juice	Dr. Gerry's Super Salmon Salad (page 317)

SNACK	DINNER
10 nuts (such as walnuts, almonds, or macadamias) and ¼ cup berries, any variety	Wild Rice and Turkey Soup (page 314) with a side of tossed greens salad
2 tablespoons store-bought hummus mixed with 1 tablespoon ground flaxseeds and served with veggie sticks	Surf and Turf: broiled shrimp and small filet mignon (no sauce) served with sautéed greens or plain grilled salad
Fast Artichoke Dip: 3 thawed artichoke hearts blended with ½ cup 2% plain Greek yogurt and a pinch of cayenne or garlic powder and served with raw veggies	Simple Chicken Parm: 1 cup cooked cubed chicken with 2 tablespoons marinara and 1 tablespoon grated Parmesan cheese; warm in the oven and serve over 2 cups baby spinach
½ cup 2% plain Greek yogurt with berries and/or shaved dark chocolate	Zucchini Manicotti with tossed salad (page 325)
2 zucchini strips thinly sliced lengthwise, topped with 1 tablespoon yogurt or kefir and 2 slices smoked salmon	Salmon Cakes with greens (page 323)
½ apple with almond butter and a sprinkle of ground flaxseeds	Surf and Turf: broiled shrimp and small filet mignon (no sauce) served with sautéed greens or plain grilled salad
Almond Yogurt: ½ cup 2% plain kefir or yogurt mixed with 2 tablespoons chopped almonds and ¼ teaspoon almond extract	Roasted Parmesan-Kale Lamb Chops (page 324)

THE GUT BALANCE REVOLUTION SHOPPING LISTS

These shopping lists go along with the meal plans on pages 258–269. Assuming you stick to the meal plans, all you have to do is buy the ingredients on these lists. I have broken these out into weekly shopping lists. Try to shop a couple of days before you start a new week on the program.

SHOPPING LISTS — PHASE I WEEK I

PRODUCE
2 pounds baby spinach
2 pounds kale, any variety
2 bunches romaine or butterhead lettuce
2 pounds mesclun greens
1 bunch watercress or ½ pound arugula
1 pound bok choy or Swiss chard
½ pound sprouts, such as alfalfa
1 head cauliflower
3 heads broccoli
1 bunch celery
4 tomatoes
4 cucumbers
1 red bell pepper
2 avocados, preferably Hass
1 head garlic
1 spaghetti squash (about 1 pound)
4" piece fresh ginger
1 bunch cilantro
1 bunch basil
1 bunch parsley
1 bunch chives (optional)
1 pint blueberries
1 small horseradish root (optional)
1 large orange
2 limes
3 lemons

DAIRY
3 dozen eggs or 3 packages (14 ounces each) extra-firm tofu
½ gallon plain, unsweetened coconut milk
1 piece (6 ounces) Parmesan cheese
4 ounces Greek feta cheese

MEATS/PROTEINS
1 pound lean pork loin
4 pounds boneless, skinless chicken breasts
1 pound thinly sliced raw chicken cutlets
2 pounds medium peeled, deveined shrimp (about 22 per pound)
2 pounds salmon fillets, skin removed
2 pounds cod fillets
1 package (6 ounces) low-sodium chicken sausages (optional)

FROZEN
1 bag (12 ounces) frozen berries (any variety)
1 bag (12 ounces) frozen raspberries

OILS, CONDIMENTS, SPICES
1 can (5 ounces) olive oil cooking spray
1 bottle (25 ounces) extra-virgin olive oil
1 jar (14 ounces) coconut oil
1 jar (16 ounces) almond butter
1 jar (8 ounces) Dijon mustard
1 container (26 ounces) salt
1 container (2 ounces) black pepper
1 jar (2 ounces) mild chili powder or paprika
1 jar (2 ounces) ground cardamom
1 jar (2 ounces) ground cumin or cumin seeds
1 jar (2 ounces) dried oregano
1 jar (2 ounces) Italian herbs or rosemary
1 jar (2 ounces) ground turmeric
1 jar (2 ounces) ground coriander (optional)
1 jar (2 ounces) ground cinnamon
1 jar (2 ounces) ground cloves (optional)

1 jar (2 ounces) garlic powder

1 bottle (2 ounces) pure vanilla extract

1 bar (4 ounces) 70% cocoa chocolate bar

1 box (50 count or less) stevia packets

1 jar (12 ounces) onion-free salsa

GRAINS AND DRY GOODS

8 tortillas, 100% corn (6" diameter)

1 box (12 ounces) quinoa flakes

1 box (12 ounces) quinoa

1 bag (16 ounces) chia seeds

1 bag (16 ounces) ground flaxseeds

1 bag (16 ounces) hemp seeds

1 bag (8 ounces) shredded unsweetened flaked coconut

1 bag (8 ounces) walnuts

1 bag (8 ounces) almonds

1 bag (8 ounces) pecans or hazelnuts

1 container (12 ounces) vanilla whey protein powder

1 container (12 ounces) plain whey protein powder

CANNED/JARRED GOODS

1 can (15 ounces) pumpkin

2 cans (5 ounces each) light spring-water-packed tuna

1 jar (3 ounces) capers

2 containers (10 ounces each) pitted olives, such as kalamata

1 container (32 ounces) low-sodium chicken or vegetable broth

1 tube (2 ounces) wasabi paste (optional)

SHOPPING LISTS   PHASE I WEEK 2

PRODUCE

1 pound mesclun greens

1 pound bok choy or Swiss chard

2 pounds kale, any variety

2 pounds baby spinach

2 heads broccoli

1 head cauliflower

1 bunch carrots

1 bunch celery

1 jalapeño chile pepper

1 zucchini

1 cucumber

2 red bell peppers

2 green bell peppers

1 bunch chives

1 bunch fresh rosemary (optional)

1 bunch cilantro

4" piece fresh ginger

2 lemons

1 lime

DAIRY

1 dozen eggs

½ gallon plain, unsweetened coconut milk

MEATS/PROTEINS

3 pounds boneless, skinless chicken breasts

4 bone-in chicken breasts

1 pound shrimp

1 pound lean pork loin

4 ounces smoked salmon

FROZEN

1 bag (10 ounces) frozen edamame pods

1 bag (12 ounces) frozen berries

1 bag (12 ounces) frozen blueberries

OILS, CONDIMENTS, SPICES

1 bottle (25 ounces) extra-virgin olive oil

1 jar (2 ounces) cayenne pepper or hot chili powder (optional)

GRAINS AND DRY GOODS

1 box (12 ounces) quinoa flakes

1 box (12 ounces) quinoa

1 container (12 ounces) vanilla whey protein powder

1 pound coffee, any roast

(continued)

CANNED/JARRED GOODS

3 cans (5 ounces each) light spring water–packed tuna

1 container (32 ounces) low-sodium chicken or vegetable broth

1 can (15 ounces) low-sodium chicken vegetable soup

1 can (5 ounces) tomato paste

PRODUCE

1 pound kale, any variety

1 pound baby spinach

2 pounds arugula

1 head broccoli

1 pound Brussels sprouts

2 pounds asparagus

1 head romaine lettuce

2 heads bok choy

1 head cabbage, such as red, savoy, or napa

1 bunch celery

1 bag carrots

1 bunch beets

1 green bell pepper

2 red bell peppers

2 bulbs fennel

1 small butternut squash (about 1 pound)

2 avocados

1 bunch cilantro

1 bunch parsley

2 cucumbers

1 lemon

1 lime

1 kiwifruit

2 bananas

1 apple

DAIRY

1 dozen eggs or 1 package (14 ounces) extra-firm tofu

1 container (35 ounces) 2% plain Greek yogurt

1 bottle (32 ounces) 2% plain kefir

1 container (8 ounces) plain or spicy hummus

1 container (8 ounces) low-sodium miso paste

4 ounces Greek feta cheese

MEATS/PROTEINS

2 pounds boneless, skinless chicken breasts

2 pounds shrimp or tofu

1 pound salmon, skin intact

1 pound salmon or cod fillets, skin removed

1 pound cod fillets

1 pound ground buffalo meat

1 container (14 ounces) extra-firm tofu

8 low-sodium chicken sausages

4 lean pork chops

FROZEN

1 bag (12 ounces) frozen blueberries

1 bag (12 ounces) frozen strawberries

1 bag (12 ounces) shelled edamame

OILS, CONDIMENTS, SPICES

1 bottle (6 ounces) sesame oil

1 bottle (16 ounces) raw apple cider vinegar

1 jar (2 ounces) pumpkin pie spice (optional)

1 jar or can (2 ounces) curry powder, such as Madras

1 jar (2 ounces) celery seeds or caraway seeds

1 jar (2 ounces) low-sodium Cajun spices

1 jar (2 ounces) low-sodium steak seasoning or grilling spices

1 bottle (10 ounces) reduced-sodium, gluten-free soy sauce or tamari

GRAINS AND DRY GOODS

1-pound bag short-grain brown rice
1 canister (18 ounces) old-fashioned
  rolled oats
1 box (12 ounces) buckwheat porridge
1 container (12 ounces) vanilla whey
  protein powder
1 container (12 ounces) plain whey protein
  powder
1 bag (16 ounces) red lentils
1 container (5 ounces) macadamia nuts
1 bag (16 ounces) chia seeds
1 container (8 ounces) unsweetened
  cocoa powder
1 package (8 ounces) dried seaweed or nori
1 jar (2 ounces) sesame seeds
1 bag (6 ounces) pistachios

1 bar (4 ounces) 70% cocoa chocolate
1 bar (4 ounces) 85% cocoa chocolate

CANNED/JARRED GOODS

1 bottle (8 ounces) unsweetened
  pomegranate juice
1 can (15 ounces) 100% pure pumpkin
1 can (5 ounces) tomato paste
2 cans (5 ounces each) light spring
  water–packed tuna
3 cans (15 ounces each) assorted beans,
  such as black or kidney, or chickpeas
1 can (15 ounces) kidney beans
1 jar (16 ounces) low-sodium sauerkraut
1 jar (16 ounces) kimchi
1 container (10 ounces) pitted olives, such
  as kalamata

SHOPPING LISTS   PHASE 2 WEEK 2

PRODUCE

2 pounds spinach
1 pound mesclun greens
1 pound kale, any variety
1 pound arugula
1 pound asparagus
3 heads broccoli
1 cucumber
2 red bell peppers
1 bunch cilantro
1 bunch mint
1 bunch basil
1 head garlic
2 avocados
3 kiwis
2 lemons
2 limes
1 honeydew melon
1 pint raspberries

DAIRY

3 dozen eggs
2 containers (35 ounces each) 2% plain
  Greek yogurt
1 bottle (32 ounces) 2% plain kefir
4 ounces Greek feta cheese

MEATS/PROTEINS

4 pounds boneless, skinless chicken breasts
1 pound cod fillets
2 packages (14 ounces each) extra-firm
  tofu

FROZEN

2 pounds shrimp
1 bag (12 ounces) frozen blueberries

OILS, CONDIMENTS, SPICES

1 bottle (6 ounces) sesame oil
1 bottle (16 ounces) raw apple cider
  vinegar
1 jar (2 ounces) pumpkin pie spice
  (optional)
1 jar or can (2 ounces) curry powder, such
  as Madras
1 jar (2 ounces) celery seeds or caraway
  seeds
1 jar (2 ounces) low-sodium Cajun spices
1 jar (2 ounces) low-sodium steak
  seasoning or grilling spices
1 bottle (10 ounces) reduced-sodium,
  gluten-free soy sauce or tamari

(continued)

GRAINS AND DRY GOODS

1 bag (8 ounces) almonds
1 bag (8 ounces) hazelnuts

CANNED/JARRED GOODS

1 can (5 ounces) tomato paste
1 can (15 ounces) low-sodium black beans

1 can (15 ounces) low-sodium chickpeas
1 can (15 ounces) low-sodium lentil soup
1 container (32 ounces) low-sodium chicken or vegetable broth
2 packages (2 ounces each) seaweed chips, mild or spicy

SHOPPING LISTS   PHASE 3 WEEK 1

PRODUCE

2 pounds baby spinach
3 pounds mesclun greens
1 pound Swiss chard
1 pound kale
2 pounds Brussels sprouts
4 parsnips
1 head romaine lettuce
1 head cabbage, savoy or napa
1 head cauliflower
1 head broccoli
1 pound green beans
1 bunch celery
1 bulb fennel
1 medium tomato
1 bunch radishes
1 red bell pepper
1 bunch fresh rosemary (optional)
1 jalapeño chile pepper
4" piece fresh ginger
1 head garlic
1 bunch basil
1 bunch chives
1 bunch cilantro
1 bunch mint
6 medium zucchinis
1 cucumber
2 lemons
1 lime
3 apples
1 bag (8 ounces) fresh cranberries
½ pint raspberries

DAIRY

1 container (35 ounces) 2% plain Greek yogurt

1 bottle (32 ounces) 2% plain kefir
½ gallon plain, unsweetened coconut milk
2 dozen eggs
8 ounces Greek feta cheese
4 ounces soft goat cheese
1 piece (6 ounces) Parmesan or Pecorino Romano cheese
½ pint heavy cream
½ pound unsalted butter

MEATS/PROTEINS

3-pound roasting chicken
1 pound ground turkey
1 pound boneless, skinless chicken breasts
1 pound thinly sliced raw chicken cutlets
8 ounces smoked salmon
2 salmon fillets, skin removed (4 ounces each)
1 rack of lamb (about 1 pound)
1 pound beef stew cubes

FROZEN

1 package (8 ounces) frozen artichoke hearts
1 bag (8 ounces) frozen peas

OILS, CONDIMENTS, SPICES

1 bottle (25 ounces) extra-virgin olive oil
1 jar (14 ounces) raw honey
1 jar (2 ounces) red-pepper flakes (optional)
1 can (5 ounces) olive oil cooking spray

GRAINS AND DRY GOODS

1 bag (16 ounces) ground flaxseeds
1 bag (8 ounces) unsweetened coconut

1 container (7 ounces) baking powder

1 container (12 ounces) vanilla whey protein powder

1 bar (4 ounces) 70% cocoa chocolate

1 jar (4 ounces) instant espresso powder

CANNED/JARRED GOODS

2 containers (32 ounces each) low-sodium chicken or vegetable broth

1 jar (28 ounces) low-sodium marinara sauce

2 cans (15 ounces each) low-sodium beans, such as pinto or kidney, or chickpeas

1 can (15 ounces) low-sodium chicken or vegetable broth

2 cans (5 ounces each) tomato paste

1 jar (8 ounces) unsweetened pomegranate juice

1 container (10 ounces) pitted olives, such as kalamata

1 jar (14 ounces) coconut oil

SHOPPING LISTS   PHASE 3 WEEK 2

PRODUCE

2 pounds kale

1 pound spinach

1 pound arugula

3 pounds mesclun greens

1 bunch bok choy

1 bunch Swiss chard

1 pound green beans

2 heads broccoli

1 bulb fennel

2 bunches celery

1 bunch carrots

1 bunch radishes

4 tomatoes

3 cucumbers

1 zucchini

1 green or red bell pepper

1 avocado

4" piece fresh ginger

1 bunch mint

1 bag (8 ounces) fresh cranberries

1 apple

DAIRY

1 container (35 ounces) 2% plain Greek yogurt

1 bottle (32 ounces) 2% plain kefir

2 dozen eggs

1 piece (6 ounces) Parmesan or Pecorino Romano cheese

4 ounces Greek feta cheese

1 container (8 ounces) plain or spicy hummus

MEATS/PROTEINS

1 pound ground turkey

1 rack of lamb (about 1 pound)

2 pounds boneless, skinless chicken breasts

1 pound salmon fillets, skin removed

4 ounces smoked salmon

FROZEN

1 bag (12 ounces) frozen berries

1 bag (12 ounces) frozen blueberries

1 package (8 ounces) frozen artichoke hearts

OILS, CONDIMENTS, SPICES

1 jar (2 ounces) nutmeg

1 bottle (2 ounces) almond extract

GRAINS AND DRY GOODS

1 box (12 ounces) quinoa

1 package (8 ounces) walnuts

1 bag (4 ounces) wild rice

CANNED/JARRED GOODS

2 containers (32 ounces each) low-sodium chicken or vegetable broth

2 cans (15 ounces each) low-sodium beans, such as pinto or kidney, or chickpeas

1 container (5 ounces) tomato paste

1 bottle (8 ounces) unsweetened pomegranate juice

Blueberry Protein Smoothie

Tender and nutrient dense, spinach is a mild-tasting green to sneak into your breakfast foods. Blueberries and sweet-tasting stevia will mask any slight veggie taste, making it a good option to share with family members who don't always eat their veggies.

For Phase 2, replace the coconut milk with 2% plain kefir or yogurt. Or for a flavor swap, use $1/2$ teaspoon almond extract in place of the cinnamon.

PREP TIME: 5 MINUTES ▪ TOTAL TIME: 10 MINUTES

1 cup leftover brewed green tea (cold)

1 cup plain, unsweetened coconut milk

⅔ cup plain or vanilla whey protein powder

½ cup fresh or frozen blueberries

½ cup raw baby spinach

2 tablespoons ground flaxseeds or chia seeds (or chia-flax flour)

1 tablespoon coconut oil

2 teaspoons stevia powder

½ teaspoon ground cinnamon

8 ice cubes

In a blender, place the tea, coconut milk, protein powder, blueberries, spinach, ground seeds, oil, stevia, cinnamon, and ice. Process until smooth. Divide evenly into 2 glasses and serve immediately.

MAKES 2 SERVINGS

PER SERVING (2½ cups): 261 calories, 20 g protein, 18 g carbohydrates, 14 g total fat, 9 g saturated fat, 0 mg cholesterol, 6 g fiber, 115 mg sodium

HEALTHY KITCHEN TIPS

Shop for coconut milk in the dairy aisle—it's much lower in fat than canned coconut milk and a perfect sub for all your favorite breakfast recipes. My favorite brands: So Delicious, 365, Silk, and Almond Breeze.

Make your own "power powder" by grinding ½ cup flaxseeds with ½ cup chia seeds. Always purchase ground flaxseeds or grind the whole seeds yourself in a coffee grinder. Store flaxseeds in an airtight container in the fridge.

Eggs to Go

Eggs are not only a nutrient-dense source of vitamins such as B_{12} and B_2 but they also deliver choline that protects your nervous system and may boost your mood. Shop for omega-3-fortified or pasture-raised eggs.

For Phase 2, replace 1 cup of the greens with $\frac{1}{2}$ cup beans, thinly sliced asparagus, or $\frac{1}{2}$ cup pickled veggies.

PREP TIME: 10 MINUTES ■ TOTAL TIME: 15 MINUTES

4 eggs

4 egg whites

3 tablespoons plain whey protein powder

$\frac{1}{4}$ teaspoon freshly ground black pepper

$\frac{1}{4}$ teaspoon paprika or a pinch of ground cloves

2 tablespoons extra-virgin olive oil, divided

2 cups chopped greens, such as spinach or kale

4 soft corn tortillas (6" diameter)

1. In a small bowl, whisk together the eggs, egg whites, protein powder, pepper, and paprika or cloves. Set aside.

2. Warm a large ceramic-coated or cast-iron skillet over medium-high heat and add 1 tablespoon of the oil. Add the greens and cook for 1 to 2 minutes, turning often, or until the greens wilt. Transfer the greens to a plate.

3. Return the skillet to medium heat and add the remaining 1 tablespoon oil and then the egg mixture. Cook for 2 to 3 minutes, stirring often, or until the eggs start to scramble. Add the greens and stir, cooking for 1 minute, or until the eggs are cooked through.

4. Set each tortilla on an 8" x 8" sheet of foil. Divide the eggs between the tortillas. Fold the tortillas and wrap the foil around them. Serve within 1 hour or store, refrigerated, until ready to eat.

MAKES 4 SERVINGS

PER SERVING (1 tortilla, 1½ cups eggs and greens): 220 calories, 14 g protein, 13 g carbohydrates, 12 g total fat, 2 g saturated fat, 186 mg cholesterol, 2 g fiber, 168 mg sodium

HEALTHY KITCHEN TIP

Can't do eggs? Scramble protein-rich tofu instead. Cook the vegetables until tender, then crumble the tofu into the pan and warm through. Flavor the tofu with dried herbs or anti-inflammatory spices from page 243.

Vanilla Spice Quinoa Breakfast Cereal

Quinoa is a nutritious gluten-free seed. It's high in potassium, fiber, protein, and a long list of strength-building nutrients. Shop for prewashed quinoa, since saponin, a bitter-tasting compound, covers the outside of the seeds and needs to be thoroughly rinsed away.

For Phase 2, replace ½ cup of the quinoa with ½ cup prebiotic dry old-fashioned rolled oats. For a flavor swap for Phase 2 or 3, swap out the berries listed and add in the same amount of strawberries, plus a pinch of cardamom.

PREP TIME: 10 MINUTES ■ TOTAL TIME: 40 MINUTES

- ⅓ cup dry quinoa, rinsed under cold running water
- 2 cups water
- ⅔ cup plain or vanilla whey protein powder
- ½ cup shredded unsweetened coconut
- ¼ cup hemp seeds
- 1 teaspoon pure vanilla extract
- 1 teaspoon ground cinnamon
- ¼ teaspoon ground cardamom
- 2 tablespoons ground flaxseeds or chia seeds or chia-flax flour
- 1 cup fresh or frozen raspberries or blueberries
- ¼ cup chopped walnuts

1. In a large saucepan, place the quinoa and water and bring to a boil over high heat. Reduce to a simmer and cook for 15 to 20 minutes, or until the quinoa is tender and the centers of the grains are translucent.

2. Stir in the protein powder, coconut, hemp seeds, vanilla, cinnamon, and cardamom. Stir in the flaxseeds or chia seeds or seed flour. If the mixture is too thick, add another ¼ to ½ cup water to reach the desired consistency. Divide the quinoa mixture into 4 bowls and top each with ¼ cup berries and 1 tablespoon walnuts. Serve immediately.

MAKES 4 SERVINGS

PER SERVING (1 cup): 233 calories, 15 g protein, 19 g carbohydrates, 11 g total fat, 4 g saturated fat, 0 mg cholesterol, 7 g fiber, 47 mg sodium

Power Breakfast Bars

Store-bought protein bars can be a hidden haven for sugar—as much as in a candy bar. This version contains good-quality protein, like quinoa (high in iron) and chia (high in plant-based omega-3s).

For Phase 2, replace $1/2$ cup of the quinoa with $1/2$ cup prebiotic dry old-fashioned rolled oats. For a flavor swap for Phase 2 or 3, swap out the berries listed and add in the same amount of strawberries, plus a pinch of cardamom, or chopped cherries with chopped 85% dark chocolate.

PREP TIME: 15 MINUTES ■ TOTAL TIME: 25 MINUTES

½ cup fresh or frozen blueberries

⅓ cup almond butter

2 eggs

2 teaspoons stevia powder

1 cup quinoa flakes

1 cup unsweetened grated coconut

⅔ cup vanilla whey protein powder

¼ cup ground flaxseeds

1 teaspoon pure vanilla extract

½ teaspoon ground cinnamon

¼ teaspoon ground cloves or cardamom

1. Preheat the oven to 400°F. Line an 8" x 8" baking dish with foil. Coat the foil with cooking spray.

2. In a large bowl, combine the blueberries, almond butter, eggs, and stevia. Mash gently with the back of a spoon. Add the quinoa, coconut, protein powder, flaxseeds, vanilla, cinnamon, and cloves or cardamom. Mash well with a fork until a thick, crumbly mixture forms.

3. Transfer the mixture into the prepared baking dish, pressing it into an even layer with a rubber spatula. Bake for 8 to 10 minutes, or until the top begins to brown and the edges are firm to the touch. Cool completely before cutting into 8 bars.

MAKES 8 BARS

PER SERVING (1 bar): 218 calories, 10 g protein, 16 g carbohydrates, 13 g total fat, 4 g saturated fat, 46 mg cholesterol, 5 g fiber, 42 mg sodium

HEALTHY KITCHEN TIP

Looking to burn calories more efficiently? Look no further than your spice rack for tasty ways to perk up healthy ingredients and boost antioxidants in your diet. Think of your spice rack as a flavor savior that also helps you to burn more fat faster. Go to pages 270–275 for lists of the top spices. Pumpkin pie spice, for example, is a tasty, antioxidant-rich addition to breakfast cereals, bars, or smoothies.

Greek Village Salad

This fresh, summery salad is adapted from one by Alfred Himmelrich, owner of Stone Mill Bakery and Café in Lutherville, Maryland–Dr. Gerry's favorite eatery in the Baltimore area. This delicious and filling salad was a collaboration by Alfie and the Skinny Chef and features a tangy dressing you'll get hooked on. Use leftover chicken or even salmon from other recipes to make this a quick dinner.

PREP TIME: 10 MINUTES ■ TOTAL TIME: 20 MINUTES

¼ cup extra-virgin olive oil

¼ cup lemon juice

2 teaspoons dried oregano

1 teaspoon Dijon mustard

⅛ teaspoon freshly ground black pepper

½ pound cooked cubed chicken or medium shrimp

2 medium tomatoes, cut into 1" slices and quartered

1 large cucumber, cubed

1 red bell pepper, seeded and diced

2 ounces feta cheese, cut into ½" cubes (about ½ cup)

¼ cup pitted olives, such as kalamata

In a blender, combine the oil, lemon juice, oregano, mustard, and black pepper until smooth. In a large bowl, add the chicken or shrimp, tomatoes, cucumber, bell pepper, cheese, and olives. Pour in the dressing, toss well, and serve.

MAKES 4 SERVINGS

PER SERVING (1½ cups salad): 344 calories, 27 g protein, 9 g carbohydrates, 22 g total fat, 4 g saturated fat, 91 mg cholesterol, 2 g fiber, 365 mg sodium

Orange Salmon

If you're a fan of salty with sweet flavors, you'll adore this unique orange-olive combination that gives plain salmon something to sing about. Citrus not only adds plenty of flavor but also cuts the scent of fish for those who are salmon newbies.

PREP TIME: 10 MINUTES ■ TOTAL TIME: 30 MINUTES

1 pound bok choy or Swiss chard, thinly sliced

4 salmon fillets (4 ounces each), skin removed

1 tablespoon extra-virgin olive oil

¼ cup black or green olives, chopped

½ teaspoon chili powder or ground coriander, mild or hot (optional)

½ teaspoon fennel seeds

1 large orange, peel grated, then thinly sliced

1. Preheat the oven to 400°F. In an 11" x 7" baking dish, spread the bok choy or chard and place the salmon on top.

2. In a small bowl, place the oil, olives, chili powder or coriander, fennel seeds, and orange peel and mash with the back of a spoon to combine. Spoon the mixture over the salmon and bake for 15 to 17 minutes, or until the fish is opaque and flakes easily. Top with the orange slices and serve immediately.

MAKES 4 SERVINGS

PER SERVING (1 salmon fillet, 1 cup greens): 307 calories, 25 g protein, 7 g carbohydrates, 20 g total fat, 4 g saturated fat, 62 mg cholesterol, 2 g fiber, 208 mg sodium

Pesto Baked Cod

Homemade pesto just takes minutes to whip together and tastes worlds above the jarred varieties. This basil pesto increases nutrition by 100 percent with the addition of spinach, a top superfood rich in vitamins A and C, folate, and fiber.

For Phase 2, replace 1 cup of the baby spinach with 1 cup fresh or frozen (and thawed) green peas.

PREP TIME: 15 MINUTES ■ TOTAL TIME: 45 MINUTES

2 cups baby spinach

2 cups basil leaves

½ cup grated Parmesan cheese

3 tablespoons extra-virgin olive oil

3 tablespoons walnuts

¼ teaspoon salt

4 cod fillets (4 ounces each)

1 spaghetti squash (about 1 pound), cut in half lengthwise

1. Preheat the oven to 400°F.

2. In a blender or food processor, combine the spinach, basil, cheese, oil, walnuts, and salt. Blend until a chunky mixture forms. Place the fish in an 11" x 17" baking dish. Spread the pesto in equal portions over each piece of fish. Bake for 15 to 18 minutes, or until the fish flakes easily.

3. While the fish is baking, prepare the spaghetti squash. Heat 4 inches of water in a large pot. Add a steamer basket and insert the squash. Steam for 10 to 15 minutes, adding ¼ cup water if the water level decreases, or until the squash is fork-tender. Transfer to a cutting board to cool. Remove the seeds and discard. Shred the flesh of the squash with 2 forks; you should have about 4 cups. Divide the squash between 4 plates, top each with a fillet, and serve immediately.

MAKES 4 SERVINGS

PER SERVING (1 cod with topping, 1 cup squash): 296 calories, 27 g protein, 10 g carbohydrates, 17 g total fat, 4 g saturated fat, 58 mg cholesterol, 3 g fiber, 402 mg sodium

HEALTHY KITCHEN TIP

Is your fishmonger out of cod this week? Then go for these two low-mercury choices: wild-caught pollack or freshwater trout. Both pollack and trout are sustainable fish and yummy!

Spiced Pumpkin Soup

It's easy to stick to your new eating plan when you feast on this velvety soup that's also appropriate for fall holidays. Rich-tasting, anti-inflammatory, fat-fighting spices like ginger, cinnamon, and coriander layer on serious flavor with hardly any calories and no sugar or salt.

For Phase 2, add ¼ cup old-fashioned rolled oats before blending, along with ¼ cup water to adjust the thickness.

PREP TIME: 10 MINUTES ■ TOTAL TIME: 40 MINUTES

2 tablespoons extra-virgin olive oil or coconut oil, divided

4 chicken cutlets

1 clove garlic, minced

2 teaspoons minced ginger

¼ teaspoon freshly ground black pepper

1 quart low-sodium chicken broth

1 can (15 ounces) 100% pure pumpkin

½ teaspoon ground cinnamon or ground cloves

½ teaspoon ground coriander or garlic powder

¼ cup cilantro or parsley leaves (optional)

1. Heat a large pot over medium-high heat and add 1 tablespoon of the oil. Add the cutlets and sprinkle them with the garlic, ginger, and pepper. Cook for 4 to 5 minutes, turning occasionally, or until the chicken browns and the juices run clear. Transfer to a plate.

2. Reduce the heat to low and add the broth, pumpkin, cinnamon or cloves, coriander or garlic powder, and the remaining 1 tablespoon oil. Cover and simmer, stirring occasionally, until the soup thickens and becomes fragrant. Divide the soup among 4 bowls. Shred the chicken and divide it between the bowls. Garnish with the parsley or cilantro, if using, and serve immediately.

MAKES 4 SERVINGS

PER SERVING (1¾ cups made with olive oil): 235 calories, 24 g protein, 12 g carbohydrates, 10 g total fat, 2 g saturated fat, 54 mg cholesterol, 3 g fiber, 172 mg sodium

HEALTHY KITCHEN TIP

To give this soup a spring or summer makeover, use 15 ounces fresh spinach or zucchini in place of the pumpkin. For a vegetarian option, add 14 ounces extra-firm tofu instead of the chicken.

Raspberry Mesclun Salad with Green Tea Dressing

Raspberries and green tea bring sweet-tart flavors along with fiber and antioxidants that can boost your calorie burn more efficiently. For serious gourmets, opt for the vanilla protein powder for a fragrant yet savory dressing.

For Phases 2 and 3, replace almonds with bright green pistachios, a fat-busting nut that also has visual appeal. Once you reach Phase 2, swap out the fresh radishes and cukes for the pickled equivalent.

PREP TIME: 10 MINUTES ■ TOTAL TIME: 40 MINUTES

6 cups baby mesclun greens

2 cups bean sprouts, such as alfalfa

1 cup thinly sliced radishes or cucumber

1 cup fresh or frozen raspberries, thawed

¼ cup chopped almonds

⅓ cup cold green tea

3 tablespoons plain or vanilla whey protein powder

3 tablespoons extra-virgin olive oil

1 teaspoon grated lime peel

2 tablespoons fresh lime juice

¼ teaspoon salt

12 ounces cooked chicken breast (2 breasts) or ½ pound cooked shrimp

1. In a large bowl, mix the greens, sprouts, radishes or cucumber, raspberries, and almonds.

2. In a blender, combine the tea, protein powder, oil, lime peel, lime juice, and salt. Blend until smooth. Drizzle over the greens. Top with the chicken or shrimp and serve immediately.

MAKES 4 SERVINGS

PER SERVING (2½ cups of salad with chicken): 288 calories, 25 g protein, 12 g carbohydrates, 16 g total fat, 2 g saturated fat, 54 mg cholesterol, 6 g fiber, 290 mg sodium

HEALTHY KITCHEN TIP

Save prep time but still get enough filling protein: Use 2 thinly sliced breasts of frozen cooked or grilled chicken without breading, added fat, or high amounts of salt. Or use 2 cups thawed cooked shrimp. For a vegetarian option, add 12 ounces drained tofu.

Crunchy Almond Tuna Salad

This crisp and refreshing tuna salad is made primarily from pantry staples that you'll have on hand. Look for light spring-water-packed tuna—it's lower in mercury levels.

For Phases 2 and 3, add ½ cup cooked quinoa or 1 cup pickled red cabbage.

PREP TIME: 10 MINUTES ■ TOTAL TIME: 15 MINUTES

2–3 teaspoons grated lemon peel

3 tablespoons fresh lemon juice

2 tablespoons plain, unsweetened coconut milk

2 tablespoons chia seeds

1 tablespoon coconut oil

¼ teaspoon salt

4 cups baby spinach or watercress, chopped

1 head broccoli, cut into florets (about 4 cups florets)

2 cans (5 ounces each) light spring-water-packed tuna, drained

¼ cup chopped pecans or hazelnuts

¼ cup chopped fresh chives (optional)

1. In a blender, combine the lemon peel, lemon juice, coconut milk, seeds, oil, and salt. Blend until smooth.

2. In a large bowl, place the spinach or watercress, broccoli, tuna, pecans or hazelnuts, and chives (if using). Drizzle with the dressing and toss well. Serve immediately.

MAKES 4 SERVINGS

PER SERVING (2½ cups): 244 calories, 24 g protein, 15 g carbohydrates, 11 g total fat, 1 g saturated fat, 21 mg cholesterol, 8 g fiber, 461 mg sodium

HEALTHY KITCHEN TIP

If you're on a low-sodium diet, omit the added salt in the dressing because tuna is naturally high in salt.

Massaged Kale Salad

Kale contains a world of nutrition, including incredibly high amounts of important anti-inflammatory nutrients like vitamins A and C. It also has lots of sulfur-based compounds that may combat several forms of cancers.

For a Phase 2 or 3 flavor swap, substitute the nuts with 3 tablespoons chia or sesame seeds. For a Phase 2 fiber boost, add 1 cup chickpeas, cooked lentils, or black beans.

PREP TIME: 10 MINUTES ■ TOTAL TIME: 1 HOUR 10 MINUTES

1 bunch (10 ounces) kale, sliced into 1" chunks

2 tablespoons extra-virgin olive oil

¼ teaspoon ground cumin or freshly ground black pepper or ½ teaspoon cumin seeds

¼ cup green or black olives

¼ cup walnuts or almonds

¼ cup crumbled feta cheese or thinly shaved Parmesan cheese

¼ cup diced avocado

2 cooked chicken breasts, cubed or sliced, ½ pound cooked shrimp, or 10 ounces firm tofu

1. In a large bowl, place the kale, oil, and ground cumin or pepper or cumin seeds. Using clean hands, rub the oil into the kale leaves, gently squeezing the leaves to soften them.

2. Sprinkle on the olives, nuts, cheese, and avocado. Cover and refrigerate for at least 1 hour. Top with the chicken, shrimp, or tofu and serve immediately.

MAKES 4 SERVINGS

PER SERVING (2½ cups): 298 calories, 23 g protein, 10 g carbohydrates, 19 g total fat, 3 g saturated fat, 62 mg cholesterol, 3 g fiber, 366 mg sodium

HEALTHY KITCHEN TIP

This Mediterranean-inspired salad, with tangy feta and savory olives, is high in anti-inflammatory ingredients like spices and olive oil that are a perfect fit for Phase 3. This filling salad gets its rich taste from three good-quality, and antioxidant-rich fat sources—olives, nuts, and avocado—that also help you feel full.

Slow-Cooker Chicken Picatta

Tangy picatta relies on two great low-cal ingredients—fresh lemon and capers—to give it savory flavor. This simple slow-cooker recipe is the perfect way to make a lean protein juicy.

For Phase 2, replace 1 cup of the lettuce with 1 cup sliced asparagus or cooked artichokes.

PREP TIME: 10 MINUTES ■ TOTAL TIME: 1 HOUR 30 MINUTES

2–3 teaspoons grated lemon peel

3 tablespoons fresh lemon juice

3 tablespoons extra-virgin olive oil

2 tablespoons capers, rinsed well under cold running water

¼ teaspoon freshly ground black pepper

1 teaspoon dried herbs, such as Italian seasoning, rosemary, or thyme

4 boneless, skinless chicken breasts

1 head romaine lettuce, thinly sliced

¼ cup thinly sliced Parmesan cheese

1. In a slow cooker, place the lemon peel, lemon juice, oil, capers, pepper, and dried herbs and stir well to combine. Add the chicken and turn to coat. Cover and cook on low for 1 to 1½ hours, or until a thermometer inserted in the thickest portion registers 165°F and the juices run clear. Transfer the chicken to a cutting board and cool for 5 minutes before slicing.

2. Divide the romaine between 4 plates and top each with 1 tablespoon of the cheese. Top with the chicken and juices from the slow cooker. Serve immediately.

MAKES 4 SERVINGS

PER SERVING (3 cups): 320 calories, 39 g protein, 5 g carbohydrates, 16 g total fat, 3 g saturated fat, 113 mg cholesterol, 2 g fiber, 406 mg sodium

HEALTHY KITCHEN TIP

Have limited space in your kitchen cabinets but still want to harness the flavor of herbs? Shop for premixed herbs such as Italian seasoning—a dried herb blend that's free of sugar and salt.

Chicken Vegetable Soup

Nothing is more soothing and nourishing than a hot bowl of soup, and this tasty version swaps out the customary onion for a gastrointestinal superfood, ginger. For a weekday shortcut, cook the veggies in the oil, then add shredded rotisserie chicken, the broth, and kale or spinach. Bring to a slow simmer, then serve.

For Phase 2, add $1/2$ cup prebiotic veggies such as asparagus. For Phase 3, stir in 1 cup cooked gluten-free brown rice noodles (al dente) or organic brown rice.

PREP TIME: 10 MINUTES ■ TOTAL TIME: 40 MINUTES

2 bone-in chicken breasts, skin on

¼ teaspoon freshly ground black pepper

1 tablespoon extra-virgin olive oil

4 carrots, peeled and cut into 1" chunks

2 ribs celery, thinly sliced

1 jalapeño chile pepper, seeded and finely chopped (optional), wear plastic gloves when handling

2 cloves garlic, finely chopped

1 (1") piece fresh ginger, finely chopped

1 teaspoon fresh or dried rosemary leaves

1 quart low-sodium chicken broth

2 cups chopped kale or spinach

1. Sprinkle the chicken with the black pepper. Heat a large pot over medium heat. Add the oil and chicken, skin side down. Cook for 1 to 2 minutes, or until the skin starts to brown.

2. Scatter the carrots, celery, chile pepper (if using), garlic, ginger, and rosemary around the chicken and cook for 5 minutes. Turn the chicken and stir the vegetables. Increase the heat to high and add the chicken broth. Bring to a simmer, then reduce the heat to low and cover. Cook for 10 minutes, or until a thermometer inserted in the thickest portion registers 170°F and the juices run clear. Turn off the heat. Let stand for 20 minutes.

3. Transfer the chicken to a cutting board and cool slightly for 5 to 6 minutes. Discard the skin and shred the meat. Return the meat to the soup along with the kale or spinach and cover for 5 minutes to wilt the greens. Serve immediately.

MAKES 4 SERVINGS

PER SERVING (1½ cups): 194 calories, 20 g protein, 8 g carbohydrates, 8 g total fat, 1 g saturated fat, 113 mg cholesterol, 2 g fiber, 294 mg sodium

HEALTHY KITCHEN TIP

Kids love soups. To make this a complete kid's meal, add ½ cup cooked whole grain pasta or quinoa to each bowl. Out of kale or spinach? For Phase 2 or 3, add broccoli florets or Swiss chard.

Spiced Pork Roast with Cauliflower Mash

Pork loin is a lean, tender cut that makes a perfect weekend roast for a family gathering. Serve leftovers over salad greens or use as a fast no-cook lunch.

For Phase 2, replace 1 cup of the greens with 1 cup sauerkraut, your favorite pickled vegetable, or a few teaspoons of jarred prepared horseradish.

PREP TIME: 10 MINUTES ■ TOTAL TIME: 50 MINUTES

2 teaspoons grated fresh ginger

1 teaspoon chili powder, mild or hot

½ teaspoon ground turmeric

2 tablespoons extra-virgin olive oil, divided

1 pound lean pork loin, trimmed of excess fat

½ head cauliflower, cut into florets (about 3 cups florets)

¼ cup chopped cilantro

2 tablespoons wasabi powder or grated fresh horseradish

1. Preheat the oven to 400°F.

2. In a small bowl, place the ginger, chili powder, turmeric, and 1 tablespoon of the oil. Mix well with a spoon or small spatula.

3. Place the pork in an 11" x 7" baking dish. Spread the oil mixture over the loin and bake, uncovered, for 25 to 30 minutes. Let stand for 5 minutes on a cutting board before slicing.

4. While the pork is baking, prepare the cauliflower mash. Heat 4 inches of water in a large pot. Add a steamer basket and insert the florets. Steam for 5 to 6 minutes, or until fork-tender. Transfer to a large bowl and mash with the cilantro, wasabi or horseradish, and the remaining 1 tablespoon oil. Serve immediately with the pork.

MAKES 4 SERVINGS

PER SERVING (1½ cups): 213 calories, 26 g protein, 6 g carbohydrates, 10 g total fat, 2 g saturated fat, 74 mg cholesterol, 2 g fiber, 162 mg sodium

HEALTHY KITCHEN TIP

Don't have a steamer basket? Just add the cauliflower florets directly to the pot and steam. Add additional water as needed, ¼ cup at a time.

Ginger-Crusted Kale Chips

Kale chips are all the rage. They have a wonderful flaky texture and crunch that any chip lover will enjoy. These are crusted with a superroot–a heavy hitter when it comes to quenching inflammation.

For Phases 2 and 3, add 2 tablespoons ground flaxseed to boost the fiber.

PREP TIME: 5 MINUTES ■ TOTAL TIME: 15 MINUTES

- 1 bunch (10 ounces) curly kale, stems trimmed
- ¼ cup chopped pumpkin seeds or pecans
- ¼ cup chia seeds
- 2 tablespoons finely grated fresh ginger
- ½ teaspoon chili powder or paprika
- ¼ teaspoon salt
- 2 egg whites

1. Preheat the oven to 400°F. Coat 2 baking sheets with olive oil cooking spray. Rinse the kale under cold water. Dry well with paper towels or a dry dishtowel.

2. On a sheet of waxed paper or a plate, place the pumpkin seeds or pecans, chia, ginger, chili powder or paprika, and salt. Mix well with your fingertips. It may clump slightly.

3. In a large bowl, whisk the egg whites with a wire whisk for about 10 seconds, or until foamy. Dip the edges of the kale leaves into the egg whites, then place on the prepared baking sheets. Sprinkle on the seed mixture. Spread the kale so the leaves don't touch. Coat the tops of the leaves with another spritz of cooking spray.

4. Bake for 10 to 12 minutes, or until the leaves are crisp and the seeds and nuts are golden. Cool for 2 minutes before serving.

MAKES 4 SERVINGS

PER SERVING (1 cup): 175 calories, 9 g protein, 13 g carbohydrates, 12 g total fat, 1 g saturated fat, 0 mg cholesterol, 4 g fiber, 212 mg sodium

Coconut Joy Pudding

No need to cook this sumptuous pudding, since protein-rich chia seeds swell when they come in contact with liquid. For a looser, creamier pudding, add an extra $1/4$ cup coconut milk to the oat and chia mixture before spooning into dessert dishes.

PREP TIME: 5 MINUTES ■ TOTAL TIME: 1 HOUR 5 MINUTES

1 cup plain, unsweetened coconut milk

⅔ cup plain or vanilla whey protein powder

⅓ cup chia seeds

1 cup cold water

¼ cup + 4 tablespoons shredded unsweetened coconut

4 tablespoons chopped or shaved 70% (or higher) dark chocolate

1. In a large bowl, whisk together the coconut milk, protein powder, chia seeds, water, and ¼ cup shredded coconut. Combine well. Set out 4 parfait glasses or 4 small airtight containers and add ¾ cup of the coconut mixture to each.

2. Sprinkle each with 1 tablespoon shredded coconut and 1 tablespoon chocolate. Cover the glasses with plastic wrap or close the container lids. Place in the fridge and chill for 1 hour before serving.

MAKES 4 SERVINGS

PER SERVING (¾ cup): 201 calories, 12 g protein, 14 g carbohydrates, 14 g total fat, 6 g saturated fat, 0 mg cholesterol, 8 g fiber, 161 mg sodium

HEALTHY KITCHEN TIP

Normally, saturated fat is a red flag for your health, but the saturated fat in this filling pudding comes from anti-inflammatory, heart-healthy sources like coconut and dark chocolate—so indulge!

Salsa and Eggs

This tangy lime-laced salsa not only adds flavor to eggs but also gives you a good dose of two prebiotic superfoods: kiwifruit and beans. Use leftover salsa (or double the salsa recipe) to top salads, grilled chicken, or fish.

PREP TIME: 10 MINUTES ■ TOTAL TIME: 20 MINUTES

2 kiwifruit, peeled and finely chopped

2 cups low-sodium canned black beans, rinsed and drained

¼ cup packed cilantro

1–2 tablespoons fresh lime juice

4 eggs

4 egg whites

⅓ cup plain whey protein powder

¼ teaspoon freshly ground black pepper

¼ teaspoon ground cumin

1 tablespoon extra-virgin olive oil

½ cup 2% plain Greek yogurt

1. In a medium bowl, combine the kiwi, beans, cilantro, and lime juice. Set aside.

2. In a small bowl, whisk the eggs and egg whites. Gently whisk in the protein powder, pepper, and cumin. Set aside.

3. Warm a large ceramic-coated or cast-iron skillet over medium-high heat and add the oil. Add the egg mixture. Cook for 2 to 3 minutes, stirring, or until soft curds form and the eggs are cooked through. Divide the eggs among 4 plates and top each with ¾ cup of the salsa and 2 tablespoons yogurt.

MAKES 4 SERVINGS

PER SERVING (2¼ cups: 1½ cups eggs, ¾ cup salsa): 247 calories, 22 g protein, 23 g carbohydrates, 9 g total fat, 2 g saturated fat, 187 mg cholesterol, 7 g fiber, 395 mg sodium

Pumpkin Pie Yogurt Parfait

Store-bought parfaits can be bursting with carbs and fat, since they're typically made from white processed carbs and sugar. But this easy, homemade version, which can double as a snack, provides a huge hit of hunger-calming protein along with other key nutrients.

PREP TIME: 10 MINUTES ▪ TOTAL TIME: 1 HOUR 5 MINUTES

2 cups 2% plain Greek yogurt

⅓ cup plain or vanilla whey protein powder

½ teaspoon pumpkin pie spice or ground cinnamon

¼ teaspoon ground cloves (optional)

2 tablespoons water

½ cup canned 100% pure pumpkin

¼ cup old-fashioned rolled oats

2 teaspoons stevia powder

1 teaspoon pure vanilla extract

1. In a medium bowl, place the yogurt, protein powder, pumpkin pie spice or cinnamon, and cloves, if using. Add the water and stir well. Distribute half of the yogurt mixture among 4 parfait glasses.

2. In a large bowl, place the pumpkin, oats, stevia, and vanilla. Stir well to combine. Divide half of the pumpkin mixture among the parfait glasses. Repeat with the yogurt and the pumpkin mixture. Cover each parfait glass with plastic wrap and refrigerate for at least 1 hour before serving.

MAKES 4 SERVINGS

PER SERVING (1¼ cups): 136 calories, 15 g protein, 13 g carbohydrates, 3 g total fat, 2 g saturated fat, 7 mg cholesterol, 2 g fiber, 54 mg sodium

HEALTHY KITCHEN TIP

For a flavor surprise, serve this healthy parfait topped with raspberries. For a spring version, substitute fresh or frozen berries in place of the pumpkin; in summer, try thinly sliced melon with fresh mint in place of the spices.

Pomegranate Margarita Smoothie

Blueberries and pomegranate make a strong anti-inflammatory pair, since antioxidants come from their vibrant color. You'll get hooked on the sweet-tart flavor of this delectable shake worthy of the name Margarita.

PREP TIME: 5 MINUTES ■ TOTAL TIME: 10 MINUTES

1 cup 2% plain Greek yogurt (or homemade yogurt, page 333) or kefir (or homemade kefir, page 334)

½ cup fresh or frozen blueberries

⅓ cup pomegranate juice

⅓ cup plain whey protein powder

2 tablespoons chopped macadamia nuts or walnuts

1 teaspoon grated lime peel

1–2 tablespoons fresh lime juice

2 tablespoons flaxseed, chia seed, or chia-flax flour

2 teaspoons stevia powder (optional)

½ cup water

8 ice cubes

In a blender, combine the yogurt or kefir, blueberries, pomegranate juice, protein powder, nuts, lime peel, lime juice, flaxseed or chia seed or chia-flax flour, stevia (if using), water, and ice cubes. Process until smooth. Divide into 2 glasses and serve immediately.

MAKES 2 SERVINGS

PER SERVING (1¼ cups): 272 calories, 21 g protein, 27 g carbohydrates, 12 g total fat, 3 g saturated fat, 8 mg cholesterol, 6 g fiber, 78 mg sodium

HEALTHY KITCHEN TIPS

Yearning for chocolate? Remove the lime juice and swap 2 tablespoons of 85% dark chocolate for the nuts.

Mix ½ cup pomegranate juice with ½ cup water and freeze in an ice cube tray. You'll love the convenience of using "pom cubes" for smoothies or in sparkling water, and you will have lowered calories and carbs by using the juice-water blend.

Muffin-Size Frittatas

Make these tasty frittatas in a muffin pan–they'll cook quickly and look elegant enough for a special brunch. Enjoy them at room temperature as finger food–they travel well, too.

For Phase 3, add a few teaspoons of salsa or add in ½ cup diced cherry tomatoes with 2 tablespoons finely chopped chives.

PREP TIME: 10 MINUTES ■ TOTAL TIME: 25 MINUTES

1 red bell pepper, seeded and thinly sliced

2 cups chopped spinach

¼ cup chopped fresh parsley and/or cilantro

¼ teaspoon dried herbs, such as thyme or rosemary (optional)

6 eggs

1 cup canned beans, such as black or kidney, rinsed and drained

¼ cup crumbled feta cheese

4 cups greens, such as arugula or dandelion greens

1. Preheat the oven to 400°F. Coat a 12-cup muffin pan with cooking spray and set it aside.

2. Coat a large skillet with cooking oil and place over medium heat. Add the bell pepper, spinach, parsley or cilantro, and dried herbs, if using. Cook for 3 to 4 minutes, stirring occasionally, or until the vegetables start to soften. Transfer to a plate.

3. In a large bowl, whisk together the eggs, beans, cheese, and cooked veggies. Pour the mixture into 8 muffin cups, filling them three-quarters full. Bake for 10 to 12 minutes, or until the eggs are firm and cooked through. Run a knife along the inside edge of each muffin cup and pull out the frittatas. Serve them over the greens.

MAKES 4 SERVINGS

PER SERVING (2 muffin frittatas, 1 cup greens): 218 calories, 16 g protein, 16 g carbohydrates, 10 g total fat, 4 g saturated fat, 287 mg cholesterol, 7 g fiber, 407 mg sodium

Cool Cucumber-Avocado Soup

Raw apple cider vinegar and kiwifruit give this creamy chilled soup a prebiotic boost. The perfect dish to take to your next cookout, serve it in paper cups for sipping or omit the water and use it as a dip for shrimp or thinly sliced raw celery and radishes.

PREP TIME: 5 MINUTES ■ TOTAL TIME: 10 MINUTES

1 large cucumber, peeled and quartered

1 ripe Hass avocado, peeled

1 kiwifruit, peeled and quartered

½ cup almonds

¼ cup fresh mint leaves or fresh dill

2 tablespoons raw apple cider vinegar

¼ teaspoon garlic powder or chili powder

1 cup cold water or cold green tea

1 pound frozen precooked shrimp, thawed

In a food processor, place the cucumber, avocado, kiwi, almonds, mint or dill, vinegar, garlic or chili powder, and water or tea. Pulse the mixture until smooth. Top individual servings with the shrimp and serve immediately or chill, covered, in an airtight container for at least 1 hour or up to 2 days.

MAKES 4 SERVINGS

PER SERVING (1½ cups with shrimp): 266 calories, 20 g protein, 12 g carbohydrates, 16 g total fat, 1 g saturated fat, 186 mg cholesterol, 5 g fiber, 649 mg sodium

HEALTHY KITCHEN TIPS

Stop at your local fish market or counter and ask for precooked cocktail shrimp to make this soup a no-cook feast.

All the sodium in this dish comes from the shrimp. You can decrease the sodium by decreasing the amount of shrimp, but note that the protein count will go down, too. For a low-sodium version, swap in chicken instead.

Chicken Tikka Masala

Tikka Masala gets its flavorful sauce from ginger, cilantro, and sweet-tasting tomato paste. Restaurants douse this dish in heavy cream, but this lighter version, with less sauce, adds more protein by swapping cream for yogurt.

PREP TIME: 15 MINUTES ■ TOTAL TIME: 40 MINUTES

2 boneless, skinless chicken breasts, cubed

4 ounces tomato paste (¼ cup)

½ cup chopped cilantro

1 clove garlic, minced

2 teaspoons curry powder, such as Madras

1 cup 2% plain Greek yogurt or kefir, divided

1 tablespoon coconut oil

1 head broccoli, cut into florets (about 4 cups florets)

¼ cup red lentils

½ cup water

1. In a resealable plastic bag, place the chicken, tomato paste, cilantro, garlic, curry, and ½ cup of the yogurt or kefir. Seal the bag and shake well to coat. Refrigerate for at least 30 minutes or overnight.

2. Heat the oil in a large skillet over medium heat. Add the broccoli. Cook for 3 to 4 minutes, stirring occasionally, or until the broccoli starts to brown. Reduce the heat to low. Add the chicken and marinade. Cook for 2 to 3 minutes, turning the chicken, or until it starts to brown around the edges. Add the lentils along with the water. Cover and cook for 6 to 8 minutes, stirring occasionally, or until the chicken is no longer pink and the broccoli and lentils are tender. Stir in the remaining ½ cup yogurt or kefir. Serve immediately.

MAKES 4 SERVINGS

PER SERVING (1½ cups): 254 calories, 29 g protein, 19 g carbohydrates, 7 g total fat, 4 g saturated fat, 58 mg cholesterol, 4 g fiber, 276 mg sodium

HEALTHY KITCHEN TIP

To make a cooling cucumber raita side dish: In the bowl of a food processor, place 1 small cucumber, cut in thirds, with ¼ cup cilantro and ¼ cup mint. Add 1 cup plain kefir or yogurt and a pinch of cumin. Pulse until a chunky mixture forms, then serve immediately with the Tikka Masala.

Zesty Lemon Chicken Salad

Herbs, citrus, and spices are your one-way ticket to flavor without packing on the sugar, fat, or salt. Miso is the secret probiotic flavor booster that gives normally bland-tasting chicken extra-zesty appeal. Look for miso in the dairy aisle of your local health food store.

PREP TIME: 1 HOUR 10 MINUTES ■ TOTAL TIME: 1 HOUR 40 MINUTES

4 boneless, skinless chicken breasts

¼ cup chopped cilantro

1 tablespoon extra-virgin olive oil

2–3 teaspoons grated lemon peel

3 tablespoons fresh lemon juice

¼ teaspoon freshly ground black pepper

¼ teaspoon ground turmeric

½ cup 2% plain Greek yogurt

1 tablespoon low-sodium miso paste

1 red bell pepper, finely chopped

2 tablespoons chopped almonds or macadamia nuts

6 cups mixed greens, such as mesclun and baby kale

1. In a resealable plastic bag, place the chicken, cilantro, oil, lemon peel, lemon juice, black pepper, and turmeric. Shake well to coat the chicken. Marinate in the refrigerator for at least 1 hour or overnight.

2. Heat a grill or grill pan over medium-high heat. Grill the chicken for 8 to 10 minutes, turning occasionally, or until a thermometer inserted in the thickest portion registers 165°F and the juices run clear. Set aside.

3. In a large bowl, whisk the yogurt and miso to combine. Add the bell pepper and nuts. Chop the chicken and add it to the bowl. Toss well to coat and serve immediately over the mixed greens.

MAKES 4 SERVINGS

PER SERVING (2½ cups): 297 calories, 43 g protein, 17 g carbohydrates, 8 g total fat, 2 g saturated fat, 111 mg cholesterol, 4 g fiber, 265 mg sodium

Tangy Buffalo Burgers with Pickles and Slaw

Dry steak seasoning or grilling spices, often found tucked in the back of your spice rack, are another way to flavor your burger with antioxidant-rich spices. Look for low-sodium options and mixes without MSG. If you can't locate ground buffalo (also known as ground bison), try ground chicken or grass-fed beef instead.

PREP TIME: 20 MINUTES ▓ TOTAL TIME: 40 MINUTES

Slaw

- 1 bulb fennel, trimmed and grated
- 4 carrots, peeled and grated
- ½ small red cabbage, grated (about 3 cups)
- 2–3 teaspoons lemon peel
- 3 tablespoons fresh lemon juice
- 1 cup 2% plain Greek yogurt
- 1 teaspoon celery seeds or caraway seeds

Burgers

- 1 pound ground buffalo meat
- ½ teaspoon dry steak seasoning or grilling spices
- ¼ teaspoon ground turmeric
- 1 avocado, sliced
- 8 thinly sliced low-sodium pickles or Pickled Cucumbers (page 331)

1. *To make the slaw:* In a large bowl, place the fennel, carrots, red cabbage, lemon peel, lemon juice, yogurt, and celery or caraway seeds. Toss well to combine and set aside.

2. *To make the burgers:* In a large bowl, place the buffalo meat, steak seasoning or grilling spices, and turmeric. Mix well and form into 4 burgers. Coat a large skillet or grill rack with cooking spray. Heat over medium-high heat and add the burgers. Cook or grill for 10 to 12 minutes, turning once or twice, or until the burgers are still slightly pink in the center.

3. Divide the slaw among 4 plates. Place a burger on top of each plate and top with avocado slices and 2 pickles each. Serve immediately.

MAKES 4 SERVINGS

PER SERVING (1 burger, 1 cup slaw): 284 calories, 31 g protein, 24 g carbohydrates, 9 g total fat, 2 g saturated fat, 56 mg cholesterol, 8 g fiber, 362 mg sodium

HEALTHY KITCHEN TIP

Buffalo meat is an excellent high-protein (and high-iron) substitution for corn-fed beef. Order it frozen online—try these sites: jhbuffalomeat.com, northstarbison.com, or wildideabuffalo.com.

Miso Soup with Seaweed Salad

You don't have to go to your favorite Japanese restaurant to enjoy a hot bowl of miso soup. Make this easy, protein-rich version at home that has the addition of fish.

PREP TIME: 15 MINUTES ■ TOTAL TIME: 40 MINUTES

Soup

- 8 cups water
- 1 tablespoon shredded nori or wakami seaweed
- 3 cups chopped greens, such as Swiss chard, kale, or bok choy
- ¼ cup low-sodium miso paste
- 1 block (4 ounces) firm tofu, cut into ½" cubes
- 4 salmon or cod fillets, cut into 1" cubes
- ¼ cup cilantro (optional)

Seaweed Salad

- 4 ounces dried seaweed
- 1 tablespoon raw apple cider vinegar
- 1 tablespoon sesame oil
- 1 teaspoon reduced-sodium soy sauce
- 1 tablespoon white or black sesame seeds

1. *To make the soup:* In a large saucepan, bring the water to a slow simmer and add the nori or wakami. Simmer for 5 to 6 minutes to flavor the water. Add the greens and cook for 1 minute. Reduce the heat to low and add the miso and tofu. Stir until the miso is well dissolved. Stir in the fish chunks and cilantro (if using), cover, and remove the saucepan from the heat. Let stand for 5 to 6 minutes, or until the fish is opaque and cooked through.

2. *To make the seaweed salad:* Put the dried seaweed in a large bowl and fill it with cold water. Soak for 10 to 12 minutes, or until tender.

3. Meanwhile, in a small bowl, whisk together the vinegar, oil, and soy sauce.

4. Drain the seaweed and use your hands to squeeze out excess water. Wipe out any water in the bowl, then return the seaweed. Add the dressing and sesame seeds. Toss well, then serve alongside the miso soup.

MAKES 4 SERVINGS

PER SERVING (2 cups soup, 1 cup seaweed salad): 340 calories, 29 g protein, 8 g carbohydrates, 21 g total fat, 4 g saturated fat, 62 mg cholesterol, 2 g fiber, 439 mg sodium

HEALTHY KITCHEN TIP

Carry the delicious seaweed salad into Phase 3 for a satisfying snack that gives you a fat-burning boost in the afternoon when the munchies strike.

Ginger Fried Rice

Take-out fried rice isn't only high in MSG, it's also made with white rice that can send your blood sugar skyrocketing. This version has plenty of vegetables and protein that can help anchor your appetite. You'll enjoy the base of brown rice, which is higher in fiber and has a pleasant, chewy texture.

PREP TIME: 10 MINUTES ■ TOTAL TIME: 15 MINUTES

½ cup dry short-grain brown rice

3 tablespoons coconut oil

2 boneless, skinless chicken breasts, cubed, or ½ pound shelled shrimp

1 head bok choy, chopped (about 4 cups)

2 cups frozen shelled edamame

2 tablespoons minced fresh ginger

2 cloves garlic, minced

½ teaspoon Chinese five-spice powder

¼ teaspoon ground turmeric

2 tablespoons reduced-sodium, gluten-free soy sauce or tamari sauce (optional)

1. Cook the rice according to package directions and set aside.

2. Heat a large skillet over medium heat. Add the coconut oil. Add the chicken or shrimp, bok choy, and edamame at once and increase the heat to medium-high. Cook for 3 to 4 minutes, stirring often, or until the chicken and vegetables begin to brown. Add the ginger, garlic, five-spice powder, and turmeric. Cook for 2 to 3 minutes, stirring well, or until the chicken is no longer pink and the juices run clear or the shrimp are opaque.

3. Reduce the heat to medium and stir in the rice and soy or tamari sauce, if using. Serve immediately.

MAKES 4 SERVINGS

PER SERVING (1½ cups): 376 calories, 28 g protein, 23 g carbohydrates, 16 g total fat, 10 g saturated fat, 54 mg cholesterol, 4 g fiber, 131 mg sodium

HEALTHY KITCHEN TIP

Top with probiotic Pickled Ginger (page 327) or serve ginger on the side.

Arugula Salad with Creamy Avocado Dressing

This salad has a one-two punch of superingredients—tangy kiwifruit and creamy avocado. Kiwi is low glycemic and a perfect prebiotic for the colon, while avocado, high in fiber, adds just the right kind of fat. For a vegetarian option, replace the tuna with 2 cups edamame.

PREP TIME: 20 MINUTES ■ TOTAL TIME: 25 MINUTES

Dressing

- 1 ripe avocado, cubed
- ¼ cup 2% plain Greek yogurt
- 1 kiwifruit, peeled
- 1 teaspoon garlic powder
- 1 teaspoon grated lime peel
- 2 tablespoons fresh lime juice
- 2 tablespoons water

Salad

- 1 teaspoon cumin seed
- 6 cups arugula
- 1 bulb fennel, shredded or thinly sliced
- 2 cans (5 ounces each) light spring-water-packed tuna, drained
- ¼ cup dry lentils, cooked according to package directions
- ¼ cup pitted olives, such as kalamata or Cerignola
- ¼ cup chopped almonds
- ½ cup Pickled Beets (page 328)

1. *To make the dressing:* In a blender, combine the avocado, yogurt, kiwi, garlic powder, lime peel, lime juice, and water until smooth.

2. *To make the salad:* Place the cumin in a small, dry skillet over medium-low heat. Toast the seeds in the skillet for 1 to 2 minutes, stirring often, or until the seeds are fragrant. Place the arugula and fennel in a large bowl or on a platter and scatter the seeds on top. Top with the tuna, lentils, olives, almonds, and beets. Drizzle with the dressing and serve immediately.

MAKES 4 SERVINGS

PER SERVING (3 cups with tuna): 264 calories, 24 g protein, 19 g carbohydrates, 12 g total fat, 1 g saturated fat, 22 mg cholesterol, 7 g fiber, 460 mg sodium

HEALTHY KITCHEN TIP

Trim your food budget by shopping for avocados in bulk. If your avocados aren't soft to the touch, store them on the countertop for 2 days to ripen, then transfer to the fridge to use throughout the week.

Creamy Asparagus Soup

Looking to make this soup more indulgent for Phase 3? Make your own Parmesan croutons. Preheat the oven to 400°F. Cover a baking sheet with parchment paper. Make 1-tablespoon mounds of grated Parmesan cheese on the baking sheet. Bake for 4 to 5 minutes, or until the Parmesan melts into crisp disks.

PREP TIME: 15 MINUTES ■ TOTAL TIME: 25 MINUTES

2 tablespoons extra-virgin olive oil

1 pound asparagus, trimmed and cut into 1" pieces

2 cloves garlic, minced

½ teaspoon ground cloves or ¼ teaspoon freshly grated nutmeg

¼ teaspoon freshly ground black pepper

32 ounces low-sodium chicken broth or vegetable broth

1 cup canned chickpeas, rinsed

¼ cup fresh basil leaves

2 cups diced cooked chicken or shrimp or 2 cups edamame

1. Heat a heavy stockpot over medium heat. Add the oil. Add the asparagus, garlic, cloves or nutmeg, and pepper. Cook for 3 to 4 minutes, stirring occasionally, or until the asparagus starts to brown lightly.

2. Add the broth and chickpeas. Bring to a simmer, then reduce the heat to medium-low. Cover and cook for 10 minutes, or until the asparagus is tender. Add the basil.

3. Using an immersion blender, puree the soup for about 1 minute, or until smooth. Alternatively, to puree in a standard blender, cool the soup for about 10 minutes, then work in batches. Puree half of the soup, transfer to bowls or an airtight container, then blend the remaining half. To serve, top with the chicken, shrimp, or edamame.

MAKES 4 SERVINGS

PER SERVING (2 cups): 242 calories, 22 g protein, 16 g carbohydrates, 11 g total fat, 2 g saturated fat, 36 mg cholesterol, 5 g fiber, 308 mg sodium

HEALTHY KITCHEN TIP

Buy whole nutmeg, with antioxidants still intact, for the freshest taste and the biggest nutritional punch. Grate it with a Microplane or on the fine grating side of a box grater.

Sautéed Apples and Chicken Sausage with Sauerkraut

Sweet, prebiotic apples pair perfectly with bok choy, another nutrient-dense fall food. Chicken sausages vary quite a bit in fat and sodium content, so double-check labels. If you can't find bok choy, substitute kale or spinach.

PREP TIME: 20 MINUTES ■ TOTAL TIME: 25 MINUTES

2 tablespoons extra-virgin olive oil

1 apple, thinly sliced

1 head bok choy, thinly sliced

½ teaspoon ground cinnamon

¼ teaspoon freshly ground black pepper

2 tablespoons white vinegar or raw apple cider vinegar

8 low-sodium chicken sausage links

8 ounces low-sodium sauerkraut, room temperature

1. Warm a large skillet over medium heat. Add the oil, apple, bok choy, cinnamon, and pepper. Cook for 4 to 5 minutes, or until the apple starts to soften and brown. Reduce the heat to low. Cover and cook for 2 minutes, or until the bok choy is very tender. Turn off the heat and stir in the vinegar.

2. In another skillet, add the sausage and cook over medium-high heat for 4 to 5 minutes, or until the sausage starts to brown. Reduce the heat to low and cover. Cook for 2 to 3 minutes, or until no longer pink. Serve immediately with the sauerkraut and apple mixture.

MAKES 4 SERVINGS

PER SERVING (2 sausage links, 1 cup apples with bok choy, ¼ cup sauerkraut): 254 calories, 24 g protein, 15 g carbohydrates, 12 g total fat, 2 g saturated fat, 40 mg cholesterol, 3 g fiber, 661 mg sodium

Pistachio-Chia Salmon

The pistachio is one skinny nut! Not only is it the lowest in calories, but new research shows that pistachios supercharge your body for weight loss while anchoring your hunger.

PREP TIME: 15 MINUTES ■ TOTAL TIME: 25 MINUTES

- 2 tablespoons shelled pistachios
- ¼ cup chia seeds
- 1 teaspoon fennel seeds or cumin seeds
- 4 salmon fillets (4 ounces each)
- ¼ cup dry quinoa, rinsed under cold running water
- 2 cups cubed butternut squash
- ½ teaspoon salt
- 3 cups water

1. Preheat the oven to 400°F.

2. In a food processor, place the pistachios, chia, and fennel or cumin seeds. Pulse 15 to 20 times, or until the pistachios are finely chopped.

3. Place the salmon in an 11" x 7" baking dish, skin side down. Coat each fillet with cooking spray. Sprinkle the pistachio mixture over the top. Bake on a bottom oven rack for 14 to 16 minutes, or until the fish is opaque.

4. While the salmon is baking, in a medium saucepan, place the quinoa, squash, salt, and water. Bring to a boil over high heat, then reduce to a simmer. Cover and cook for 20 to 25 minutes, or until the quinoa is tender and the squash is cooked through. Serve immediately with the salmon.

MAKES 4 SERVINGS

PER SERVING (1 crusted fillet, ¾ cup butternut-quinoa side dish): 364 calories, 27 g protein, 19 g carbohydrates, 20 g total fat, 4 g saturated fat, 62 mg cholesterol, 5 g fiber, 363 mg sodium

HEALTHY KITCHEN TIP

Many grocery chains are now peeling and cubing butternut squash and other squash for easy cooking. Ask your produce manager during your next grocery trip.

Cajun Cod

Cajun food often incorporates cayenne and black peppers as mainstay spices. Red bell pepper and celery are considered a must-have in Louisiana Creole cooking, and they make a flavorful addition to kidney or black beans.

PREP TIME: 10 MINUTES ■ TOTAL TIME: 30 MINUTES

4 cod fillets (4 ounces each)

1 teaspoon salt-free Cajun spice mix

1 pound asparagus, ends trimmed, cut into thirds

1 red bell pepper, seeded and chopped

2 ribs celery, chopped

2 cups canned kidney or black beans, rinsed and drained

2 tablespoons extra-virgin olive oil

2 tablespoons chopped cilantro or flat-leaf parsley

¼ teaspoon salt

1. Preheat the oven to 400°F.

2. Place the cod in an 11" x 7" baking dish. Sprinkle with the Cajun spice and coat the tops of the fillets with cooking spray. In a second baking disk, place the asparagus, bell pepper, celery, and beans. Drizzle with the oil and sprinkle on the cilantro or parsley and salt. Bake both dishes for 10 to 15 minutes, or until the fish flakes easily and the asparagus is tender.

MAKES 4 SERVINGS

PER SERVING (1 Cajun fillet, 1½ cups vegetables): 280 calories, 29 g protein, 24 g carbohydrates, 5 g total fat, 1 g saturated fat, 49 mg cholesterol, 9 g fiber, 538 mg sodium

HEALTHY KITCHEN TIP

Not a fan of spicy chiles? Start with just a pinch of pepper and work your way up to gradually build your tolerance for the hot stuff.

Kimchi Pork Lo Mein

Kimchi is a spicy pickled Korean cabbage that adds rich flavor to stir-fries and soups. Find it in your local health food store in the refrigerated aisle, where you'll also find miso.

PREP TIME: 10 MINUTES ■ TOTAL TIME: 30 MINUTES

- 3 tablespoons extra-virgin olive oil or coconut oil
- 4 lean pork chops, trimmed of excess fat, cut into thin 2"-long strips (about 12 ounces)
- 1 pound Brussels sprouts or cabbage, shredded
- ½ pound asparagus, thinly sliced
- 2 tablespoons reduced-sodium soy sauce
- ¼ cup kimchi, chopped
- 1 orange, peel grated, then thinly sliced

1. Heat the oil in a large skillet over medium heat. Add the pork strips. Cook for 2 to 3 minutes, stirring often, or until the pork begins to brown. Transfer to a plate. Reduce the heat to medium-low and add the Brussels sprouts or cabbage and asparagus. Cook for 2 to 3 minutes, stirring often, or until the sprouts or cabbage browns.

2. Return the pork to the skillet and add the soy sauce. Toss well to coat. Turn off the heat and stir in the kimchi and orange peel. Top with the orange slices and serve immediately.

MAKES 4 SERVINGS

PER SERVING (1½ cups): 265 calories, 24 g protein, 17 g carbohydrates, 12 g total fat, 2 g saturated fat, 40 mg cholesterol, 6 g fiber, 575 mg sodium

HEALTHY KITCHEN TIP

The traditional version of this recipe uses high-carb white noodles. Here, thinly sliced Brussels sprouts or cabbage takes their place, chopping calories by 75 percent and adding nutrients along the way. To make this a Phase 3 meal, add 2 ounces cooked soba noodles.

Creamy Strawberry Sorbet

Studies show that brightly colored vegetables and fruits reduce risk of chronic disease. But here's the really sweet news: Polyphenol-rich berries have even more antioxidant power when paired with dark chocolate, the perfect flavor mate.

PREP TIME: 10 MINUTES ■ TOTAL TIME: 4+ HOURS

2 pints fresh or frozen strawberries

½ cup pecans or walnuts

1 tablespoon coconut oil

2 egg whites or ¼ cup pasteurized egg whites from a carton

4 teaspoons stevia powder

1 teaspoon pure vanilla extract

¼ cup chopped 70% (or higher) dark chocolate (about 1½ ounces)

In a blender, combine the berries, nuts, oil, egg whites, stevia, and vanilla until smooth. Stir in the chocolate chunks. Transfer to an airtight container and freeze for at least 4 hours or overnight.

MAKES 8 SERVINGS

PER SERVING (½ cup): 101 calories, 2 g protein, 9 g carbohydrates, 7 g total fat, 3 g saturated fat, 0 mg cholesterol, 2 g fiber, 14 mg sodium

HEALTHY KITCHEN TIPS

If eating raw eggs concerns you, go for pasteurized egg whites from the carton for better food safety.

Berries and dark chocolate make an irresistible dessert pairing, but, since they're prebiotic, they're also a good match for your friendly gut bacteria.

Dark Chocolate Nut Clusters

Are you a fan of chocolate-covered pretzels or chocolate nut bark? Then these crunchy, high-protein nut clusters will hit the spot. Make an extra batch to take to parties or holiday events as the perfect hostess gift.

PREP TIME: 10 MINUTES ▮ TOTAL TIME: 40 MINUTES

2 egg whites

½ teaspoon ground cinnamon

½ cup assorted nuts, such as pistachios, macadamias, and almonds

⅓ cup plain or vanilla whey protein powder

2 tablespoons ground flaxseeds

¼ cup chopped 70% dark chocolate

2 tablespoons plain, unsweetened coconut milk

1. Preheat the oven to 300°F. Coat a baking sheet with cooking spray.

2. In a large bowl, whisk the egg whites and cinnamon until frothy. Add the nuts, protein powder, and flaxseeds and toss well. Spread on the baking sheet. Bake for 18 to 20 minutes, stirring once, or until lightly browned.

3. In a small saucepan over low heat, place the dark chocolate and coconut milk. Cook for 3 to 4 minutes, stirring often, just until the chocolate is melted and smooth. Drizzle over the nuts to cover. Cool for 4 to 5 minutes on a rack, then transfer to a plate and cool for at least 10 minutes before serving. Transfer to an airtight container and store, refrigerated, for up to 1 week.

MAKES 4 SERVINGS

PER SERVING (2 clusters): 177 calories, 11 g protein, 11 g carbohydrates, 12 g total fat, 3 g saturated fat, 0 mg cholesterol, 4 g fiber, 50 mg sodium

Mediterranean Sunrise Surprise

These herby eggs, flavored with fresh basil, make the perfect brunch treat served with a pot of green tea or black coffee. Are you a newbie at cooking eggs? Then this easy recipe is for you—the eggs cook directly in the sauce, with no expertise required.

PREP TIME: 10 MINUTES ■ TOTAL TIME: 20 MINUTES

---

1 tablespoon extra-virgin olive oil

4 medium tomatoes (about 1½ pounds)

1 large zucchini, thinly sliced

½ cup water

¼ cup chopped black olives, such as kalamata

8 eggs

¼ cup basil leaves

1. Heat a large skillet over medium heat and add the oil. Add the tomatoes and zucchini. Cook for 2 to 3 minutes, stirring often, or until the tomatoes give off their juices and the zucchini softens. Add the water and olives and stir well.

2. Crack the eggs on top of the vegetables. Reduce the heat to low and cover. Cook for 3 to 4 minutes, or until the whites of the eggs are cooked through. Scatter the basil leaves over the top, then serve immediately.

MAKES 4 SERVINGS

PER SERVING (2 eggs, ½ cup sauce): 215 calories, 14 g protein, 7 g carbohydrates, 14 g total fat, 3 g saturated fat, 372 mg cholesterol, 2 g fiber, 217 mg sodium

Fresh Cranberry-Spice Smoothie

Dried cranberries are high in sugar and carbs, so go fresh with fresh cranberries, available in the produce aisle during the fall holiday season. If you find yourself falling in love with this smoothie, prepare for the summer months and freeze fresh cranberries in a large resealable bag for 3 months or more.

PREP TIME: 5 MINUTES ■ TOTAL TIME: 10 MINUTES

1 cup 2% plain Greek yogurt or kefir

1 cup fresh cranberries (about 3 ounces)

½ cup pomegranate juice

⅓ cup plain or vanilla whey protein powder

¼ cup ground flaxseeds

2 tablespoons chia seeds

1 teaspoon ground cinnamon

1 teaspoon pure vanilla extract (optional)

4 teaspoons stevia powder

8 ice cubes

In a blender, combine the yogurt or kefir, cranberries, pomegranate juice, protein powder, flaxseeds, chia seeds, cinnamon, vanilla (if using), stevia, and ice. Blend until smooth. Serve immediately.

MAKES 2 SERVINGS

PER SERVING (1½ cups): 174 calories, 11 g protein, 18 g carbohydrates, 6 g total fat, 1 g saturated fat, 3 mg cholesterol, 5 g fiber, 58 mg sodium

HEALTHY KITCHEN TIP

For a summer twist, try substituting raspberries or strawberries for the cranberries.

Lean Green Smoothie with Apple and Kale

Minty and refreshing, this lean and green breakfast smoothie is a great way to get a dose of veggies fast. If you're not a mint lover, substitute a pinch of cinnamon.

PREP TIME: 5 MINUTES ■ TOTAL TIME: 10 MINUTES

1 cup plain, unsweetened coconut milk

1 cup 2% plain Greek yogurt

1 cup baby spinach

½ apple, cubed

½ cup fresh mint leaves

2 teaspoons stevia powder

2 teaspoons grated fresh ginger

½ cup cold water

8 ice cubes

In a blender, combine the coconut milk, yogurt, spinach, apple, mint, stevia, ginger, water, and ice. Blend until smooth. Serve immediately.

MAKES 2 SERVINGS

PER SERVING (1½ cups): 170 calories, 12 g protein, 21 g carbohydrates, 5 g total fat, 4 g saturated fat, 21 mg cholesterol, 3 g fiber, 76 mg sodium

Blueberry-Spice Waffles

These tender waffles will defy the notion that whole grain waffles have a tough texture. Make a double batch and cool them before freezing half for future fast, toaster-friendly breakfasts.

PREP TIME: 10 MINUTES ■ TOTAL TIME: 35 MINUTES

⅓ cup old-fashioned rolled oats

⅓ cup ground flaxseeds

⅔ cup plain or vanilla whey protein powder

¼ cup shredded unsweetened coconut

2 teaspoons stevia powder

½ teaspoon baking powder

1 cup plain, unsweetened coconut milk

2 eggs

1 cup blueberries

1. In a food processor, grind the oats and flaxseeds for about 10 seconds, or until you have a chunky flour. Transfer to a large bowl. Add the protein powder, shredded coconut, stevia, and baking powder. Stir well. Whisk in the coconut milk and eggs. Gently stir in the blueberries.

2. Heat a waffle iron according to manufacturer's directions. Coat with cooking spray. Add ½ cup of the batter and spread it with the back of a spoon. Close the lid and cook for 2 to 3 minutes, or until the waffle is firm and lightly browned. Repeat with the remaining batter. Serve immediately.

MAKES 4 SERVINGS

PER SERVING (1 waffle): 221 calories, 11 g protein, 21 g carbohydrates, 10 g total fat, 4 g saturated fat, 93 mg cholesterol, 6 g fiber 101 mg sodium

Wild Rice and Turkey Soup

You won't have to wait until Thanksgiving to make this delicious, filling soup that uses fall superfoods like turkey and wild rice. You'll find lean turkey breast cutlets in the poultry section of your meat department. Alfred Himmelrich, owner of Stone Mill Bakery and Café, serves up this hearty soup for hungry lunchtime patrons. You can enjoy it in your own kitchen. Shop for wild rice, or more affordable wild rice mixes, in the grain aisle.

PREP TIME: 10 MINUTES ■ TOTAL TIME: 30 MINUTES

2 tablespoons extra-virgin olive oil, divided

2 ribs celery, chopped

2 carrots, chopped

½ cup wild rice

2 cloves garlic, chopped

1 pound turkey breast cutlets (about 2 pieces), cubed

1 tablespoon paprika

1 teaspoon dried oregano or thyme

½ teaspoon freshly grated nutmeg (optional)

1 head broccoli, cut into florets (about 4 cups florets)

1 quart low-sodium turkey or chicken broth

1 can (15 ounces) no-salt-added diced tomatoes

1. Warm 1 tablespoon of the oil in a large pot over medium heat. Add the celery, carrots, wild rice, and garlic. Cook for 4 to 5 minutes to allow the veggies to soften.

2. Sprinkle the turkey with the paprika, oregano or thyme, and nutmeg, if using. Push the veggies to the side of the pot. Add the remaining 1 tablespoon oil. Add the turkey and increase the heat to medium-high. Cook for 2 to 3 minutes, turning the cubes, until they brown. Add the broccoli, broth, and tomatoes. Bring to a simmer, then cover. Reduce the heat to low and cook for 8 to 10 minutes, or until the turkey is cooked through and the broccoli is tender. Serve immediately.

MAKES 4 SERVINGS

PER SERVING (2½ cups): 324 calories, 36 g protein, 24 g carbohydrates, 9 g total fat, 2 g saturated fat, 70 mg cholesterol, 6 g fiber, 305 mg sodium

HEALTHY KITCHEN TIP

Don't toss the last of the Thanksgiving Day turkey! Shred it and add it to this soup. Just sauté your vegetables and add the turkey at the end, before serving.

Quinoa Salad with Lemony Yogurt Dressing

If you enjoy Greek salad or Mediterranean flavors, you'll be right at home with this lemony salad that has two high-quality protein sources–egg and quinoa. Pack the dressing separately if you transport this filling salad for a work or school lunch.

PREP TIME: 10 MINUTES ▪ TOTAL TIME: 40 MINUTES

4 eggs

2–3 teaspoons lemon peel

3 tablespoons fresh lemon juice

¼ cup crumbled feta cheese

2 tablespoons extra-virgin olive oil

6 cups mixed greens, such as watercress, mesclun, and baby kale

1 bulb fennel, shredded or grated

1 cup artichoke hearts

½ cup quinoa, cooked according to package directions

1 cup Pickled Radishes (page 329) or Pickled Cucumbers (page 331)

1. Place the eggs in a small saucepan and cover with cold water. Bring to a boil over high heat. As soon as the water comes to a boil, cover the pan, remove from the heat, and let stand for 15 minutes. Run the eggs under cold water and peel. Cut the eggs in quarters and set aside.

2. In a blender, combine the lemon peel, lemon juice, cheese, and oil until smooth. In a large bowl, place the greens, fennel, artichoke hearts, quinoa, and radish or cucumber pickle. Drizzle with the dressing. Toss well, top with the eggs, and serve immediately.

MAKES 4 SERVINGS

PER SERVING (2 cups): 232 calories, 11 g protein, 17 g carbohydrates, 14 g total fat, 4 g saturated fat, 194 mg cholesterol, 5 g fiber, 239 mg sodium

Minestrone Soup*

This hearty Italian soup will give you a prebiotic boost from the beans. Beans with red or black skins also boost your antioxidant levels—and provide a wonderful creamy texture.

PREP TIME: 10 MINUTES ■ TOTAL TIME: 40 MINUTES

2 tablespoons extra-virgin olive oil

2 cloves garlic, minced

2 teaspoons Italian seasoning or dried herbs

½ teaspoon red-pepper flakes (optional)

4 ribs celery, thinly sliced

2 cups thinly sliced cabbage or bok choy

2 tablespoons tomato paste

32 ounces low-sodium chicken broth

2 cups low-sodium canned beans, such as kidney or pinto, rinsed and drained

6 ounces Swiss chard, thinly sliced

¼ cup grated Parmesan cheese

1. In a large pot over medium heat, place the olive oil, garlic, seasoning or herbs, and red-pepper flakes, if using. Cook for 1 to 2 minutes, or until the garlic becomes golden. Add the celery and cabbage or bok choy. Cover and reduce the heat to low. Cook for 3 to 4 minutes, stirring often, or until the vegetables start to soften. Add the tomato paste and broth. Bring to a simmer, then reduce the heat to low.

2. Add the beans and the Swiss chard. Cook for 1 minute, or until the beans are warmed through. Sprinkle with the cheese and serve immediately.

MAKES 4 SERVINGS

PER SERVING (2 cups): 224 calories, 13 g protein, 24 g carbohydrates, 9 g total fat, 2 g saturated fat, 9 mg cholesterol, 6 g fiber, 587 mg sodium

HEALTHY KITCHEN TIP

For low-sodium diets, opt for no-salt-added beans. Kitchen Basics makes an all-natural, good-tasting, no-salt-added broth. Or make your own cooked beans by starting with sodium-free dried beans and cooking them in a slow cooker for 5 to 6 hours on low heat with water to cover.

*Also good for Phase 2 and for meal plans.

Dr. Gerry's Super Salmon Salad

This Phase 3 favorite is one of Stone Mill Bakery's most popular menu items. They slightly modified it for me and then made it part of the menu. I'm sharing this omega-3 fatty acid–rich, health-promoting, and weight-maintenance special recipe designed by Alfie Himmelrich and prepared by chefs Sarah Pigott and Toby Willse. This also serves as a nice Phase 1 low-carb, high-protein option.

PREP TIME: 15 MINUTES ■ TOTAL TIME: 25 MINUTES

1 medium cucumber, peeled and thinly sliced

2 tablespoons raw apple cider vinegar

2 tablespoons chopped dill, parsley, or basil

10 ounces salad greens, such as mesclun, baby spinach, arugula, or red leaf lettuce

4 ounces organic alfalfa sprouts (about 3 cups)

1 head broccoli, cut into florets (about 4 cups florets)

¼ cup extra-virgin olive oil + 1 tablespoon for grilling the salmon

¼ cup fresh lemon juice (from about 1 large lemon)

½ teaspoon salt

¼ teaspoon freshly ground black pepper

4 salmon fillets (4 ounces each), skin removed

1. In a medium bowl, place the cucumber, vinegar, and herbs. Toss well and set aside.

2. Chop the greens, sprouts, and broccoli florets. Place them in a bowl. Add the ¼ cup oil, lemon juice, salt, and pepper. Toss well.

3. Warm a grill or grill pan over medium-high heat. Rub the salmon fillets with the remaining 1 tablespoon oil. Grill the salmon for 6 to 8 minutes, turning once or twice, or until the fish is opaque. Divide the salad onto 4 plates and top each with a piece of salmon. Serve immediately along with the cucumbers.

MAKES 4 SERVINGS

PER SERVING (1 salmon fillet, 4 cups salad): 371 calories, 27 g protein, 11 g carbohydrates, 24 g total fat, 3 g saturated fat, 62 mg cholesterol, 4 g fiber, 467 mg sodium

HEALTHY KITCHEN TIP

For larger appetites, shop for 6-ounce salmon fillets, which add only 45 calories per serving.

Sunday Stew

Paprika is a flavorful Hungarian chili powder that comes in both "sweet" (mild) or hot varieties that you can find in the spice aisle. To protect the health benefits and flavor of spices, store them in a dark, cool drawer or cabinet, since heat and light can damage them.

PREP TIME: 10 MINUTES ■ TOTAL TIME: 4 HOURS

1 pound cubed beef stew meat

1 red bell pepper, finely chopped

4 ribs celery, chopped

2 tablespoons tomato paste

2 cloves garlic, chopped

1 teaspoon mild chili powder or paprika, sweet or hot

¼ teaspoon salt

2 tablespoons dry quinoa, rinsed under cold running water

1 cup frozen peas or edamame

4 cups salad greens, such as mesclun or baby romaine

3 tablespoons fresh lemon or lime juice

1. In a slow cooker, stir together the beef, bell pepper, celery, tomato paste, garlic, chili powder or paprika, salt, and quinoa. Cook on high for 3 to 3½ hours, stirring once or twice, or until the meat is tender. Stir in the peas or edamame and cover. Let stand for 5 to 6 minutes, or until the peas or edamame thaw.

2. Place the salad greens in a large bowl and sprinkle with the lemon or lime juice. Divide the stew into 4 portions and serve immediately with the salad.

MAKES 4 SERVINGS

PER SERVING (1 cup beef stew with 1 cup salad): 263 calories, 30 g protein, 21 g carbohydrates, 7 g total fat, 2 g saturated fat, 75 mg cholesterol, 7 g fiber, 354 mg sodium

Turkey Chili

Zesty turkey chili benefits from the tangy taste of seeded jalapeños that aren't overly spicy. If you have leftover chicken breast on hand, don't run to the store for ground turkey–just grind your chicken in a food processor for about 15 pulses until smooth.

PREP TIME: 10 MINUTES ■ TOTAL TIME: 40 MINUTES

1 tablespoon extra-virgin olive oil

1 pound ground turkey

2 tablespoons chili powder, mild or hot

2 teaspoons ground cumin

2 cloves garlic, minced

1 jalapeño chile pepper, seeded and chopped (optional—wear plastic gloves when handling)

3 ounces canned tomato paste

2 cups low-sodium chicken broth

¼ cup dry quinoa, rinsed under cold running water

½ cup water

4 cups chopped greens, such as spinach or kale

1 cup canned beans, any variety, rinsed and drained

1. Heat a large pot over medium heat. Add the oil and turkey and sear for 1 to 2 minutes without stirring, then sprinkle the chili powder and cumin over the meat. Add the garlic, jalapeño (if using), and tomato paste. Cook for 1 minute, stirring once or twice, or until the paste and garlic become fragrant.

2. Add the broth, quinoa, and water. Cover and reduce the heat to low. Simmer for 20 to 25 minutes, or until the quinoa is cooked through. Add the greens and beans and cook for 2 to 3 minutes, or until the greens are tender. Serve immediately.

MAKES 4 SERVINGS

PER SERVING (2½ cups): 333 calories, 31 g protein, 24 g carbohydrates, 13 g total fat, 4 g saturated fat, 80 mg cholesterol, 8 g fiber, 526 mg sodium

HEALTHY KITCHEN TIP

Sensitive to salt? Select no-salt-added beans and broth.

Curried Red Lentil Soup

Curry powder is an antioxidant-rich spice mix that powers up the flavor of healthy foods like lentils and cauliflower. Search out brands without added salt or sugar and with the superspice turmeric in the ingredient list.

PREP TIME: 10 MINUTES ■ TOTAL TIME: 40 MINUTES

- 4 thinly sliced chicken cutlets (about 1 pound) or 1 pound shrimp
- 2 teaspoons curry powder, such as Madras
- 1 tablespoon extra-virgin olive oil
- 1 tablespoon butter
- 2 cloves garlic, thinly sliced
- ½ cup chopped cilantro
- ½ head cauliflower, cut into florets (about 3 cups)
- ½ cup dried brown or green lentils
- 32 ounces low-sodium chicken broth or vegetable broth
- 2 tablespoons chia seeds

1. Sprinkle the chicken or shrimp with the curry powder. Warm the oil in a large pot over medium heat. Add the chicken or shrimp and cook for 4 to 5 minutes, turning once or twice, or until the chicken or shrimp starts to brown, the spices become fragrant, and the chicken is no longer pink and the juices run clear or the shrimp is opaque. Transfer the chicken or shrimp to a plate.

2. To the same pot, add the butter, garlic, and cilantro. Reduce the heat to low and cook for 1 to 2 minutes, or until the garlic becomes fragrant. Add the cauliflower and lentils. Add the broth and cook, covered, for 10 to 15 minutes, or until the lentils and cauliflower are tender. Shred the chicken and return it to the pot or add the shrimp. Sprinkle with the chia seeds and serve immediately.

MAKES 4 SERVINGS

PER SERVING (2 cups): 336 calories, 31 g protein, 26 g carbohydrates, 12 g total fat, 3 g saturated fat, 62 mg cholesterol, 7 g fiber, 201 mg sodium

Smoked Salmon Salad

Smoked salmon isn't just for brunch-time bagels, it also makes a protein-rich topping for this salad. You'll enjoy the sweet, tangy dressing that features chives in place of the scallions you'd normally pair with smoked salmon.

PREP TIME: 10 MINUTES ■ TOTAL TIME: 20 MINUTES

2 tablespoons extra-virgin olive oil

1 tablespoon raw honey

2 tablespoons chopped chives

2 teaspoons dried herbs, such as Italian seasoning

1 teaspoon chili powder or ⅛ teaspoon cayenne (ground red) pepper

¼ teaspoon freshly ground black pepper

6 cups salad greens, such as mesclun, baby spinach or kale, or romaine

½ head broccoli, cut into florets (about 2 cups florets)

8 ounces smoked salmon, thinly sliced

½ cup fresh goat cheese (about 2 ounces) or crumbled feta cheese

1. In a small bowl, whisk the oil, honey, chives, dried herbs, chili powder or cayenne pepper, and black pepper until smooth. Set aside.

2. In a large bowl, place the greens, broccoli, salmon, and cheese. Drizzle with the dressing and serve immediately.

MAKES 4 SERVINGS

PER SERVING (2 cups): 322 calories, 18 g protein, 25 g carbohydrates, 15 g total fat, 4 g saturated fat, 19 mg cholesterol, 6 g fiber, 555 mg sodium

Roasted Rosemary Chicken
with Brussels Sprouts

Nothing warms up the house–and your dinner guests–like a homey roast chicken. Coating your bird with tomato paste may seem novel, but you'll enjoy the sweet, savory flavor it lends to tender white meat.

PREP TIME: 15 MINUTES ■ TOTAL TIME: 1 HOUR 45 MINUTES

2 pounds Brussels sprouts, cut in half

4 parsnips, peeled and cut into 1" chunks

1 (3-pound) roasting chicken

1 tablespoon tomato paste

1 tablespoon extra-virgin olive oil

2 tablespoons chopped fresh rosemary

½ teaspoon garlic powder

¼ teaspoon ground turmeric

¼ teaspoon salt

1. Preheat the oven to 400°F. Place the oven rack at its lowest setting.

2. In an 11" x 9" baking dish, scatter the Brussels sprouts and parsnips. Rub the surface of the chicken with the tomato paste and oil, then sprinkle with the rosemary, garlic powder, turmeric, and salt.

3. Place the chicken on top of the vegetables. Cover loosely with a piece of foil. Roast for 1½ hours (stirring the veggies around the chicken once or twice), or until a thermometer inserted in a breast registers 180°F and the juices run clear. Let stand for 10 minutes before carving. Slice and serve immediately with the vegetables.

MAKES 6 SERVINGS

PER SERVING (½ pound chicken, 1 cup vegetables): 299 calories, 37 g protein, 25 g carbohydrates, 7 g total fat, 1 g saturated fat, 98 mg cholesterol, 8 g fiber, 276 mg sodium

Salmon Cakes

If you have a hankering for crab cakes, you'll dig this similar seafood cake made with omega-rich salmon. To prep ahead, simply bread the patties and chill them in the refrigerator for up to 3 hours before pan cooking.

PREP TIME: 20 MINUTES ■ TOTAL TIME: 35 MINUTES

2 salmon fillets (4 ounces each)

¼ cup old-fashioned rolled oats

2 teaspoons Dijon mustard

½ teaspoon Cajun spices or dried herbs such as thyme or rosemary

⅓ cup 2% plain Greek yogurt

½ cup ground flaxseeds or chia-flax flour

¼ teaspoon salt

4 cups greens, such as arugula, mesclun, or baby romaine

1. Coat the salmon with olive oil cooking spray. Heat a medium skillet over medium-high heat and add the fillets. Cook for 5 to 7 minutes, turning occasionally, or until the salmon flakes easily but is still slightly pink in the center. Transfer to a large bowl and let cool slightly.

2. To the same bowl with the salmon, add the oats, mustard, and spices or herbs. Toss to coat the salmon, breaking the fish into chunks. Add the yogurt and toss. Place the flaxseeds or chia-flax flour and salt on a plate and mix with your fingertips. Set aside.

3. Form the salmon mixture into 8 equal patties. Press each patty into the flax mixture and transfer to a baking sheet. Coat the tops of the patties with cooking spray and bake for 10 to 15 minutes, or until the patties are hot and the tops are crisp. Serve immediately over the greens.

MAKES 4 SERVINGS

PER SERVING (2 cakes, 1 cup greens): 338 calories, 25 g protein, 18 g carbohydrates, 18 g total fat, 4 g saturated fat, 127 mg cholesterol, 8 g fiber, 302 mg sodium

HEALTHY KITCHEN TIP

Mustard brings savory flavor to the fish in these cakes, and its spicy taste means it's thermogenic, helping you to burn more calories faster.

Roasted Parmesan-Kale Lamb Chops

This easy-to-prepare yet elegant meal will wow your family and friends even as you stick to your healthy-eating plan. Keep the recipe secret and feast on the compliments! For a splendid holiday or special-occasion meal, serve an additional vegetable side like roasted Brussels sprouts or the Massaged Kale Salad (page 286).

PREP TIME: 10 MINUTES ■ TOTAL TIME: 40 MINUTES

1 cup torn kale leaves

½ cup grated Parmesan cheese

1 tablespoon extra-virgin olive oil, divided

1 rack of lamb (about 1 pound), trimmed of excess fat

1 pound green beans, stemmed and cut into 1" pieces

1 teaspoon cumin seeds or fennel seeds

2 tablespoons chopped almonds

3 tablespoons ground flaxseeds

⅛ teaspoon salt

1. Preheat the oven to 400°F.

2. Place the kale in a food processor and pulse for about 20 seconds, or until finely chopped. Add the cheese and ½ tablespoon of the oil and process until smooth. Place the lamb in an 11" x 7" baking dish. Coat the top with the kale mixture. Bake, uncovered, for 40 to 45 minutes, or until a thermometer inserted in the center registers 145°F for medium-rare. Let stand for 10 minutes before slicing.

3. Meanwhile, warm the remaining ½ tablespoon oil in a large skillet over medium heat. Add the green beans and cumin or fennel seeds. Cook for 4 to 5 minutes, or until the beans start to brown and the seeds become fragrant. Add a few tablespoons of water and cover. Steam through for 1 minute. Remove the lid and toss in the almonds, flaxseeds, and salt. Serve immediately with the lamb.

MAKES 4 SERVINGS

PER SERVING (2 chops, 1 cup green beans): 355 calories, 31 g protein, 12 g carbohydrates, 20 g total fat, 5 g saturated fat, 81 mg cholesterol, 5 g fiber, 242 mg sodium

Zucchini Manicotti

Here's an Italian favorite redesigned to fit the new you. It still has the same flavors you long for, like marinara and Parmesan, but it ups the ante with fat-burning fuel like high-protein Greek yogurt and high-fiber spinach.

PREP TIME: 15 MINUTES ■ TOTAL TIME: 40 MINUTES

1 cup low-sodium jarred marinara sauce

1 pound zucchini, trimmed and thinly sliced lengthwise (about 2 medium)

1 cup 2% plain Greek yogurt

½ cup crumbled feta cheese or soft goat cheese

½ cup frozen peas, thawed

½ cup fresh basil (optional)

1 teaspoon garlic powder

½ cup grated Parmesan cheese

8 cups baby spinach

1. Preheat the oven or a toaster oven to 400°F. Spread ½ cup of the marinara sauce inside an 8" x 8" baking dish and set aside.

2. Heat a large skillet over medium heat. Pull the skillet off the heat and coat with cooking spray. Add the slices of zucchini, return the skillet to the heat, and cook for 2 to 3 minutes per side, or until the slices start to brown. Reduce the heat to low and cover. Cook for 2 to 3 minutes, or until the slices are tender. Remove the lid and let cool slightly while you prepare the filling.

3. In a large bowl, place the yogurt, feta or goat cheese, peas, basil, and garlic powder. Mix with a rubber spatula until smooth. Spoon 2 tablespoons of the yogurt mixture in the center of each zucchini slice, fold over, and place the pieces seam side down in the baking dish. Top with the remaining ½ cup marinara. Sprinkle the Parmesan over the top and bake for 15 to 20 minutes, or until the Parmesan is melted and brown. Serve immediately over the baby spinach.

MAKES 4 SERVINGS

PER SERVING (3 manicotti, 2 cups baby spinach): 224 calories, 17 g protein, 18 g carbohydrates, 9 g total fat, 5 g saturated fat, 30 mg cholesterol, 5 g fiber, 606 mg sodium

HEALTHY KITCHEN TIP

Shop for low-sodium or "sensitive formula" sauces that contain half the salt and no onions.

Dark Chocolate Flourless Cake

This cake is a protein burst in the guise of a tasty dessert. It is pretty enough for the grand finale of a dinner party or simply an end to a light meal of soup or salad.

PREP TIME: 5 MINUTES ■ TOTAL TIME: 30 MINUTES

¼ cup coconut oil

4 ounces 70% (or higher) dark chocolate, chopped

¼ cup stevia powder

1–2 teaspoons espresso powder (optional)

1 teaspoon pure vanilla extract

3 large eggs

⅓ cup plain or vanilla whey protein powder

¼ cup unsweetened cocoa powder

1 teaspoon baking powder

¼ cup heavy cream

¼ teaspoon ground cinnamon

½ teaspoon ground coriander

½ cup raspberries

1. Preheat the oven to 350°F. Lightly grease an 8" round cake pan. Cut a piece of parchment or waxed paper to fit, grease it, and lay it in the bottom of the pan.

2. In a microwaveable bowl, microwave the oil and chocolate for about 30 seconds, or until the chocolate is almost melted. Stir until the chocolate completely melts. Alternatively, place the coconut oil and chocolate in a small saucepan over very low heat and melt the chocolate, stirring often, for about 1 minute.

3. Transfer the melted mixture to a large mixing bowl and let cool slightly, for about 5 minutes. Add the stevia, espresso powder (if using), and vanilla and stir until smooth. Add the eggs, beating just until smooth. Add the protein powder, cocoa, and baking powder and mix just to combine. Spoon the batter into the prepared pan.

4. Bake for 7 to 10 minutes, or until the top forms a thin crust but is still soft to the touch in the center. Cool in the pan for 5 minutes. Loosen the edges of the pan with a butter knife and turn the cake out onto a serving plate.

5. Place the cream in a large mixing bowl. Add the cinnamon and coriander. Beat for about 2 minutes, or until fluffy. Stir in the raspberries. Spoon on the cake and serve.

MAKES 8 SERVINGS

PER SERVING (4" wedge with 1 heaping tablespoon whipped cream): 207 calories, 6 g protein, 10 g carbohydrates, 18 g total fat, 11 g saturated fat, 80 mg cholesterol, 3 g fiber, 39 mg sodium

Pickled Ginger

Use pickled ginger on cooked fish, chicken, or vegetables or blend it with olive oil to make a tasty dressing.

PREP TIME: 30 MINUTES ▪ TOTAL TIME: 3 TO 7 DAYS

1 teaspoon whole cloves

¼ teaspoon salt

½ pound fresh ginger, peeled and thinly sliced

1. Place the cloves and salt in an airtight glass container. Fill the container halfway with warm water and stir well to dissolve the salt. Add the ginger and add more water if necessary to cover. Leave 1" of space between the top of the water and the top of the jar.

2. Cover loosely with a kitchen towel or cheesecloth. Leave on your counter for 3 to 7 days. Check daily. The brine will begin to get cloudy and slightly bubbly. When the pickles taste tangy, cover tightly and refrigerate. Store in the fridge for up to 3 weeks.

MAKES ABOUT 2 CUPS

PER SERVING (2 tablespoons): 11 calories, 0 g protein, 2 g carbohydrates, 0 g total fat, 0 g saturated fat, 2 mg cholesterol, 0 g fiber, 38 mg sodium

Pickled Beets

Serve pickled beets with their flavor mates—nuts, greens, and even raspberries—over fresh greens. Pickled beets are also delicious with lean white meats like roasted chicken or roast pork.

PREP TIME: 30 MINUTES ■ TOTAL TIME: 3 TO 7 DAYS

1 teaspoon black peppercorns

1 teaspoon lavender blossoms or Italian herbs

½ teaspoon ground cardamom

¼ teaspoon salt

½ pound beets, peeled and thinly sliced

1. In an airtight glass container, place the peppercorns, lavender or Italian herbs, cardamom, and salt. Fill the container halfway with warm water and stir well to dissolve the salt. Add the beets and add more water if necessary to cover. Leave 1" of space between the top of the water and the top of the jar.

2. Cover loosely with a kitchen towel or cheesecloth. Leave on your counter for 3 to 7 days. Check daily. The brine will begin to get cloudy and slightly bubbly. When the pickles taste tangy, cover tightly and refrigerate. Store in the fridge for up to 3 weeks.

MAKES ABOUT 2 CUPS

PER SERVING (2 tablespoons): 6 calories, 0 g protein, 1 g carbohydrates, 0 g total fat, 0 g saturated fat, 0 mg cholesterol, 0 g fiber, 47 mg sodium

Pickled Radishes

Tangy pickled radishes are perfect paired with black beans or lentils, as a side dish for soups or stews, or incorporated into salsas.

PREP TIME: 30 MINUTES ■ TOTAL TIME: 3 TO 7 DAYS

- 1 tablespoon chopped fresh or dried rosemary
- 1 clove garlic, thinly sliced
- ½ teaspoon cumin seeds or fennel seeds
- ½ teaspoon crushed red-pepper flakes
- ¼ teaspoon salt
- ½ pound radishes, stems removed and quartered

1. In an airtight glass container, place the rosemary, garlic, seeds, red-pepper flakes, and salt. Fill the container halfway with warm water and stir well to dissolve the salt. Add the radishes and add more water if necessary to cover. Leave 1" of space between the top of the water and the top of the jar.

2. Cover loosely with a kitchen towel or cheesecloth. Leave on your counter for 3 to 7 days. Check daily. The brine will begin to get cloudy and slightly bubbly. When the pickles taste tangy, cover tightly and refrigerate. Store in the fridge for up to 3 weeks.

MAKES ABOUT 2 CUPS

PER SERVING (2 tablespoons): 3 calories, 0 g protein, 1 g carbohydrates, 0 g total fat, 0 g saturated fat, 0 mg cholesterol, 0 g fiber, 42 mg sodium

Pickled Horseradish

Served with lean turkey sausage links or even rack of lamb, pickled horseradish adds flavor with hardly any calories. Blend with low-sodium tomato juice for a healthful virgin Bloody Mary.

PREP TIME: 30 MINUTES ■ TOTAL TIME: 3 TO 7 DAYS

2 cloves garlic, minced

1 teaspoon mustard seeds (optional)

¼ teaspoon salt

½ pound horseradish, peeled and grated

1. In an airtight glass container, place the garlic, mustard seeds (if using), and salt. Fill the container halfway with warm water and stir well to dissolve the salt. Add the horseradish and add more water if necessary to cover. Leave 1" of space between the top of the water and the top of the jar.

2. Cover loosely with a kitchen towel or cheesecloth. Leave on your counter for 3 to 7 days. Check daily. The brine will begin to get cloudy and slightly bubbly. When the pickles taste tangy, cover tightly and refrigerate. Store in the fridge for up to 3 weeks.

MAKES ½ POUND

PER SERVING (2 tablespoons): 13 calories, 0 g protein, 2 g carbohydrates, 0 g total fat, 0 g saturated fat, 0 mg cholesterol, 0 g fiber, 37 mg sodium

Pickled Cucumbers

This low-sodium pickle recipe is an ideal swap for high-sodium jarred kosher or dill pickles. Use on meats, burgers, or alongside coleslaw.

PREP TIME: 30 MINUTES ■ TOTAL TIME: 3 TO 7 DAYS

2 tablespoons chopped dill

2 cloves garlic, minced

1 teaspoon mustard seeds (optional)

¼ teaspoon salt

½ pound cucumbers, any variety, trimmed and cut into ½" slices

1. In an airtight glass container, place the dill, garlic, mustard seeds (if using), and salt. Fill the container halfway with warm water and stir well to dissolve the salt. Add the sliced cucumbers and add more water if necessary to cover. Leave 1" of space between the top of the water and the top of the jar.

2. Cover loosely with a kitchen towel or cheesecloth. Leave on your counter for 3 to 7 days. Check daily. The brine will begin to get cloudy and slightly bubbly. When the pickles taste tangy, cover tightly and refrigerate. Store in the fridge for up to 3 weeks.

MAKES ABOUT 2 CUPS

PER SERVING (2 tablespoons): 3 calories, 0 g protein, 0 g carbohydrates, 0 g total fat, 0 g saturated fat, 0 mg cholesterol, 0 g fiber, 36 mg sodium

Sauerkraut

Homemade kraut has a fresher flavor than the canned version, and the caraway seeds give it a savory burst you'll love. Use red cabbage to cash in on the antioxidants found in plant pigments.

PREP TIME: 30 MINUTES ▪ TOTAL TIME: 3 TO 7 DAYS

2 cloves garlic, minced

½ pound cabbage (about ½ head), any variety, thinly sliced

½ teaspoon salt

1 teaspoon caraway seeds (optional)

1. In a large bowl, place the garlic, cabbage, salt, and caraway seeds (if using). Squeeze the cabbage with your fingers for 2 to 3 minutes to release some of its liquid. Transfer the mixture to a quart container. Press down on the cabbage occasionally with a spoon, pushing the cabbage under the liquid that it gives off. If it isn't covered with liquid after 24 hours, add ¼ cup water.

2. Cover loosely with a kitchen towel or cheesecloth. Leave on your counter for 3 to 7 days. Check daily. The brine will begin to get cloudy and slightly bubbly. Continue to press the cabbage beneath the liquid it generates. When the kraut tastes tangy, cover tightly and refrigerate. Store in the fridge for up to 3 weeks.

MAKES ABOUT 4 CUPS

PER SERVING (2 tablespoons): 3 calories, 0 g protein, 0 g carbohydrates, 0 g total fat, 0 g saturated fat, 0 mg cholesterol, 0 g fiber, 36 mg sodium

Homemade Dairy-Based Yogurt

Yogurt made at home has a superior flavor and a softer texture than store-bought. You'll savor its mild taste, which makes it an easier sell to kids.

PREP TIME: 30 MINUTES ■ TOTAL TIME: 6 HOURS 30 MINUTES

1 quart 2% milk, preferably from grass-fed cows

1 tablespoon raw honey

¼ cup store-bought low-fat plain yogurt or 2% plain yogurt (standard or Greek) with live cultures

1. In a heavy saucepan or 2-quart Dutch oven, heat the milk over medium-low heat for 6 to 7 minutes, or until it reaches 180°F and the milk is steamy and foamy. Do not let it boil. Stir the milk gently as it heats to make sure the bottom doesn't scorch. Add the honey and whisk well.

2. Let the milk cool for 12 to 14 minutes, or until it is just hot to the touch and measures 112° to 115°F. To speed the cooling process, fill a large bowl with ice and enough water to cover. Set the saucepan or Dutch oven into the ice water.

3. Pour about a cup of the warm milk into a small bowl and whisk it with the yogurt. Add the mixture to the warm milk.

4. Preheat the oven or toaster oven to 150°F for 4 minutes. Turn the heat off and allow the oven to cool for 5 minutes to drop the temperature to 112°F. Cover the top of the saucepan or the Dutch oven with foil, wrap in a clean dishtowel, and transfer to the warm oven, being sure the heat is off. Let stand, without turning the oven on, for 4 hours (for mild-tasting yogurt) to 6 hours (for tangier yogurt) to allow the bacteria to multiply. The texture should resemble a soft custard.

5. Remove the towel and secure the foil. Store the yogurt in the refrigerator for about 2 weeks.

MAKES 1 QUART

PER SERVING (½ cup): 78 calories, 5 g protein, 8 g carbohydrates, 2 g total fat, 1 g saturated fat, 9 mg cholesterol, 0 g fiber, 223 mg sodium

HEALTHY KITCHEN TIP

Homemade yogurt is definitely worth the 30-minute prep. It offers a mild taste and a silky texture, and once you've tried homemade you might not go back to store-bought. This low-sugar homemade recipe doesn't have the bitter tang of plain commercial yogurt. Flavor it with antioxidant-rich toppings like chopped 70% dark chocolate, dried cherries, or nuts.

Homemade Dairy-Based Kefir Made from Kefir Crystals

Shop for kefir crystals at your local health food store or online. While they're a little expensive, you'll save money in the long run by preparing your own kefir at home. And there isn't a simpler ferment you can make. Store unused crystals in a dark, cool cabinet until ready to use; they'll keep for a long time.

1 quart 2% milk, preferably from grass-fed cows

1 tablespoon kefir grains

Place the milk and the kefir grains in a glass jar and cover tightly. Set out at room temperature for 12 to 14 hours, or up to 24 hours, depending on the temperature of your home. Shake the jar gently a few times. When the kefir is ready, it will thicken. If the kefir grains coagulate on the top, strain the grains to use in the next batch. For a sourer, thicker kefir, let it ferment longer. For one less sour and thick, strain sooner. Experiment to see what works for you. Store the kefir, refrigerated, for 3 to 4 weeks.

Optional: There are many dairy-free kefir variations made by using other milks such as nuts (almond, walnut, and so on), coconut, rice, hemp, or organic, (non-GMO) soy, but the process of fermentation is less consistent than animal milks, which provide an ideal culture medium for the kefir grains to thrive and reproduce.

MAKES 1 QUART KEFIR

PER SERVING (½ cup): 68 calories, 5 g protein, 6 g carbohydrates, 2 g total fat, 1 g saturated fat, 9 mg cholesterol, 0 g fiber, 82 mg sodium

Dairy-Free Yogurt

Yogurt is one of the world's most popular fermented food. Store-bought yogurt is light on bacterial counts and just doesn't make a dent in restoring our gut flora. Homemade yogurt has billions of robust friendly flora to put us back into balance. Potent dairy-free yogurts are not commercially available.

2 cups cashew milk*

4 cups canned unsweetened coconut milk

1 tablespoon honey or coconut sugar

¼ teaspoon vanilla creme–flavored liquid stevia

1½ tablespoons gelatin or 1½ teaspoons agar powder dissolved in ½ cup boiling water

9 probiotic capsules containing 25 billion to 30 billion CFUs of any dairy-free probiotic

1. In a large saucepan over medium heat, place the milks, honey or coconut sugar, and stevia. Bring to a simmer. Watch carefully so it doesn't boil over. Once it begins to simmer, turn off the heat. Whisk in the dissolved gelatin or agar powder.

2. Pour the mixture into a large bowl. Put that bowl into a larger one of cold (but not iced) tap water and let the mixture stand until it cools to 92°F. If you used gelatin, you can whisk the mixture to cool it faster. Omit this step if you used agar powder, as whisking could make the agar powder lumpy.

3. When the mixture reaches about 92°F, add the contents of the probiotic capsules. Whisk them in well. Ladle into jars and keep warm for about 10 hours.†

4. If there is a clear pool at the bottom after 10 hours, secure the lids tightly and shake the yogurt to mix it in before refrigerating. (*Note:* For the agar option, shaking isn't necessary.) Refrigerate for 8 hours.

Optional: Put a drop or two of lemon extract on a spoon and stir into your jar of yogurt just before eating it.

MAKES 6 CUPS

PER SERVING (½ cup): 37 calories, 0 g protein, 4 g carbohydrates, 6 g total fat, 1 g saturated fat, 0 mg cholesterol, 0 g fiber, 29 mg sodium

* *Organic (non-GMO) soy and coconut are suitable substitutes while other milks such as hemp, rice, and nut milks have a consistency that is too thick.*

† *Keep warm with a yogurt maker or by putting it in a gas oven with a pilot light, in a cooler with warm water, or even into a hot tub.*

Cilantro Green Drink

Mojito lovers will adore this booze-free herb-y drink made with lime. It quenches your thirst with hardly any calories, a refreshing break from plain water. To make a whole pitcher, simply quadruple the ingredients and then store in your fridge for up to 3 days.

- 2 lime wedges
- 1 handful cilantro

- 2 cups filtered water
- 1 or 2 ice cubes (optional)

In a large glass, place the lime, cilantro, water, and ice (if using). Stir and serve immediately.

MAKES 1 SERVING

PER SERVING (2½ cups): 4 calories, 0 g protein, 1 g carbohydrates, 0 g total fat, 0 g saturated fat, 0 mg cholesterol, 0 g fiber, 0 mg sodium

Basil Green Drink

Ideal for those who don't love cilantro, basil is a fragrant flavor booster that pairs surprisingly well with lime. If fresh basil isn't available in your local grocery store, use mint instead.

- 2 lemon wedges
- 1 handful fresh basil

- 2 cups water
- 1 to 2 ice cubes (optional)

In a large glass, place the lemon, basil, water, and ice (if using). Stir and serve immediately.

MAKES 1 SERVING

PER SERVING (2½ cups): 5 calories, 0 g protein, 1 g carbohydrates, 0 g total fat, 0 g saturated fat, 0 mg cholesterol, 0 g fiber, 0 mg sodium

THE GUT BALANCE REVOLUTION SUCCESS STORIES
Jennifer Metevia, 37

What's normal, anyway? For Jennifer Metevia, it meant chronic sinus infections, constant courses of antibiotics, and tummy troubles that never seemed to go away. "I was continually getting sick," she recalls, "and after a while, I just figured that was how everybody felt—maybe it was just part of getting older." But swollen stomach that "freaked me out" and sent her on a late-night visit to the emergency room, and the eventual diagnosis of celiac disease, changed the way Jennifer looked at the world—and at her health. "I finally realized that living in pain wasn't normal, and I learned that there was something I could do to change it."

The solution? Though Jennifer had to take strong antibiotics to eliminate the overgrowth of the bacteria in the small intestine that were making her sick, an equally important part of her treatment was the eating plan of the Gut Balance Revolution. Within a few weeks, her symptoms began to disappear. And healing her gut came with a surprising side effect—the weight she'd been trying to lose for years began to literally melt away. Within just 2 weeks, she'd dropped 15 pounds.

Now, Jennifer insists, "I feel so much better, so much healthier. By eating differently, I'm noticing things about food that I'd never been aware of before. I used to crave sweets, but now I think my taste buds have changed—if I cheat a little bit and have a bite of cake, I can taste the chemicals and just spit it out. So I pretty much stay away from that stuff—I've learned that it's just not worth it."

Along with renewed health and a trim new figure, these days Jennifer has more energy than ever. Instead of coming home from work and crashing on the couch, she heads out to Zumba or takes a brisk walk. She had the fun of shopping for a new wardrobe, and her colleagues at work—she's an office manager—comment on her new appearance. "Everybody wants to know how I've done it," Jennifer says. "I've become a Gut Balance Revolution evangelist!"

CONCLUSION:
THE REAL SECRET TO WEIGHT LOSS

Before I close this book, I want to share the real secret to weight loss with you.

After reading hundreds of pages outlining the science behind good diet and gut microbiome health, you may be surprised that I would tell you there is yet another secret to weight loss. But there is, and it can be described in a single word.

Perseverance.

It's not sexy and it's not simple, but it's the truth. Despite the endless infomercials and advertisements that promise easy, dramatic results overnight, there are no magic solutions that will automatically and effortlessly cause you to lose weight. No single pill or supplement will allow you to burn away fat for the long term if you don't change what you eat and how you live. No one-size-fits-all diet will work for every person in every circumstance. Any claim to the contrary is simply a lie.

Of course, you probably already know this. If you've been on the path toward weight loss, if you've tried other diets and failed, if you've watched the pounds pile up around your waist yet can't figure out for the life of you why, then you know the real truth. Weight loss is not always easy. After all, life is challenging and it keeps on changing and moving forward. People fall off the diet wagon or get derailed due to life circumstances. They have difficulty changing their eating and exercise habits. Sometimes, medical issues, sleep disturbances, chronic stress, emotional problems, and other factors make it nearly impossible to lose weight.

Losing weight–and getting healthy–is not a bed of roses. It takes work. It takes persistence. It takes bravery to look yourself in the mirror, pull yourself up by your bootstraps, and get back to living a life that supports your weight and your health.

Lord knows I've been there. Losing 120 pounds was not easy for me, nor was recovering from a disabling illness. But through these experiences, I learned that when life knocks you down, you've got to pick yourself up and keep going.

If I can do it, you can do it.

Achieving your optimal weight and excellent health probably won't be a straightforward path. It may take twists and turns. You may have to dig in and do a little investigating, to see what works for you. Occasionally, sticking to your eating plan may be a challenge, and you may slip from time to time. But I'm living proof that you *can* lose weight and keep it off long term, *if* you persevere.

Winston Churchill, the famous British prime minister, was well known for statements like, "We shall never surrender," "Never give in," and "Withhold no sacrifice." After he finished his Upper Sixth Form (not the same thing as sixth grade here; more like high school) at Harrow, it took him three attempts to pass the entrance exam to the Royal Military Academy, Sandhurst, where he graduated 8th out of a class of 150, then ultimately rose to become one of the greatest wartime figures and speakers of the 20th century. Abraham Lincoln lost virtually every congressional election he ran in and was passed over as a vice presidential candidate. After he was finally elected president, his son Willie died less than a year after he took office. Despite his setbacks, he stands among the greatest American leaders in history.

I don't bring up historical figures like these for whimsy. On the contrary. These individuals have a lot to teach us about what it means to persevere–and succeed–in even the most trying circumstances. If Lincoln could lose nearly every election he ran in and then lose his son only 11 months after becoming president yet *still* rise to become one of our nation's finest statesmen, then you can lose the weight and find the health you deserve.

It may seem odd for a doctor to hang a poster of the movie character Rocky on his office wall, but it's there for a reason: Rocky represents the kind of mind and heart I believe it takes to succeed in the world *and* to be healthy. You have to be a fighter. Life will knock you down. But it's not about how many times you get knocked down, it's about how many times you get back up. Illness and weight gain are two of the most difficult setbacks we face as individuals and as a society. Yet we can fight against the tide of chronic disease in this country, just as we can battle against our personal bulge.

To do this, we must persevere.

So you get knocked off your diet. Get back on it. So life pushes you out of your exercise routine. Push back. Don't give up. Stay in the fight. As Rocky said, "That's how winning's done."

I know you can do it.

So go for it!

APPENDIX:

Common Dietary Supplements and Their Purported Mechanism of Action, Eefficacy, and Adverse Effects

The following easy-to-use table includes supplement names, proposed mechanism of action, adverse effects (if there are any), and other information where appropriate.

For the recommendations, I have applied an A through F grading system, just like in school. These grades were adapted from the levels of evidence and grades of recommendations used by the National Guideline Clearinghouse (guideline.gov), a public resource for evidence-based health-care practice guidelines. Here is what each grade means.

SUPPLEMENT (RECOMMENDED DOSE)	PROPOSED MECHANISM OF ACTION (IF KNOWN)	
Calcium*	• Causes fat cell death • Increases fecal fat losses	• Increases fat oxidation
Capsaicin	• Increases fat oxidation • Increases thermogenesis	
Carulluma fimbriata	• Suppresses appetite	
Chitin/chitosan	• Blocks dietary fat absorption • Improves satiety	• Lowers appetite • Lowers food intake
Chlorogenic acid	• Blocks fat cell formation • Is anti-inflammatory	• Enhances insulin sensitivity • Lipolytic—breaks down fat
Chromium picolinate	• Enhances insulin sensitivity • Enhances satiety	• Increases thermogenesis • Stabilizes blood sugar
Cissus quadrangularis	• Blocks dietary fat and carbohydrate uptake by inhibiting lipase and amylase enzymes • Reduces oxidative stress	
Citrus aurantium	• Adrenergic agonist—stimulates stress response • Decreases gastric motility and lowers food intake	
Coleus forskohlii	• Lipolytic—breaks down fat cells	
Conjugated linoleic acid	• Reduces fat synthesis • Increases fat oxidation	
Epigallocatechin gallate (EGCG: green tea extract)	• Increases energy expenditure • Increases fat oxidation • Suppresses the fat-making enzyme fatty acid synthetase	

Recommended dosage is 600–1,000 mg daily.

A–Evidence from meta-analysis of randomized controlled trials or evidence from at least one controlled study without randomization

B–Evidence from at least one controlled study without randomization or evidence from at least one other type of quasi-experimental study

C–Evidence from nonexperimental descriptive studies, such as comparative studies, correlation studies, and case-control studies

D–Evidence from expert committee reports or opinions, or clinical experience of respected authorities, or both

F–No evidence it works, and/or evidence it could harm your health

ADVERSE EFFECT(S)	RECOMMENDATION (A–F)
None reported	**Level A** when taken while maintaining sufficient 25-hydroxy vitamin D blood levels
Strongly pungent	**Level B** • Some evidence • Food-based source preferred
None reported	**Level F** • No known evidence • NOT recommended
Gastrointestinal discomfort and bloating	**Level F** • Some weak evidence • NOT recommended
None	**Level B** • Some evidence
Accumulation in the kidneys	**Level F** • Weak evidence • NOT recommended
None known	**Level F** • Weak evidence • NOT recommended
There are concerns that it may act like ephedra, but none reported to date	**Level F** • Weak evidence • NOT recommended
None reported	**Level F** • No evidence • NOT recommended
No known adverse effects	**Level D** • Uncertain • NOT recommended
No known adverse effects from tea. Herbal extracts can cause hepatotoxicity.	**Level A/B for tea** **Level F for extract as a supplement** • Some evidence • Recommended as a beverage (1–3 cups of tea per day) • NOT recommended for supplementation as an herbal extract

(continued)

Appendix: Common Dietary Supplements (CONT.)

SUPPLEMENT (RECOMMENDED DOSE)	PROPOSED MECHANISM OF ACTION (IF KNOWN)	
Fenugreek	• Lipolytic—breaks down fat cells or adipocytes • Is an antioxidant • Improves glucose tolerance	• Enhances insulin sensitivity • Improves blood lipids
Fish oil	• Blocks adipogenesis fat-making • Enhances insulin sensitivity • Increases fat oxidation	• Increases energy expenditure • Suppresses appetite
Garcinia cambogia	• Inhibits de novo lipogenesis—new fat cell production • Reduces appetite • Suppresses fatty acid synthesis	
Ginseng	• Delays fat absorption by inhibiting pancreatic lipase activity • Modulates carbohydrate metabolism	
Guar gum	• Blocks dietary fat absorption • Improves satiety	• Lowers appetite • Lowers food intake
Hoodia gordonii	• Is anti-inflammatory • Increases ATP production and decreases food intake • Inhibits de novo lipogenesis—new fat cell production • Suppresses appetite	
Konjac root fiber	• Blocks dietary fat absorption • Improves satiety	• Lowers appetite • Lowers food intake
L-carnitine	• Increases fat oxidation • Decreases fat synthesis	
Melatonin	• Is an antioxidant • Activates brown fat • Enhances insulin sensitivity	• Regulates leptin, ghrelin • Regulates sleep • Regulates stress
Phaseolus vulgaris	• Inhibits digestive enzyme alpha amylase and inhibits starch absorption	
Probiotics	• Are anti-inflammatory • Regulate appetite • Improve energy metabolism • Enhance gut barrier	• Improve dysbiosis • Improve SIBO • Enhance insulin sensitivity • Increase satiety
Psyllium	• Blocks dietary fat absorption • Improves satiety	• Lowers appetite • Lowers food intake
Resveratrol	• Is anti-inflammatory • Is an antioxidant • Enhances insulin sensitivity	• Increases fatty acid oxidation • Inhibits lipid formation in fat cells • Is a prebiotic
Vitamin D	• Unknown	

Table adapted from Poddar et al. with permission from Sage Publications.[6, 7]

ADVERSE EFFECT(S)	RECOMMENDATION (A–F)
Unknown	**Level B** • Some evidence
Burping Fishy taste, odor	**Level B** • Some evidence
No known adverse effects	**Level B** • Some evidence
None known	**Level F** • No known evidence • NOT recommended
Gastrointestinal discomfort and bloating	**Level F** • No evidence • NOT recommended
None known	**Level F** • No known evidence • NOT recommended
Gastrointestinal discomfort and bloating	**Level B** • Some evidence
No adverse effects	**Level F** • No evidence • NOT recommended
Drowsiness	**Level B** • Some evidence
None known	**Level B/C** • Some evidence
Bloating, flatus	**Level A/B** • Good evidence—appears to be strain specific
Gastrointestinal discomfort and bloating	**Level B/C** • Some evidence
None	**Level F** • No evidence • NOT recommended
Kidney stones at very high serum levels	**Level B** **Level A** when taken with 600–1,000 mg of elemental calcium daily

ACKNOWLEDGMENTS

As with every book, this one has its own story and its own unique journey. It encompasses all of those dedicated to educating and positively impacting the health and quality of life of you, the reader. I would like to acknowledge as many as possible of those who assisted and supported me during the creation of this book.

Two years ago, I was on the phone with Anne Egan of Rodale discussing *The Inside Tract*. At the tail end of our conversation–and well before the topic of gut microbiome health began making waves in the press–I pitched the notion that the Track 2 diet in that book was helping my patients lose weight and merited its own book. Unlike most publishers, Anne followed through and took a leadership role in moving this concept to the project level. Anne, many thanks for all you have done. Acquisitions Editor Nancy Fitzgerald of Rodale facilitated the proposal. Nancy has been a godsend and has my gratitude for her dedication in making *The Gut Balance Revolution* a reality. Jennifer Levesque from Rodale came onto the scene at the later stages of development, my deepest gratitude for your support. Chris DeMarchis, Brent Gallenberger, Evan Klonsky, and Emily Weber are absolute gems–brava! A big thank-you to Mary Ann Naples and to all the staff at Rodale for being a class act! I would also like to acknowledge Charles Frank Morgan of Baltimore for his counsel and guidance.

I would like to express my gratitude to the many experts whose exceptional contributions made this book possible: First and foremost, Spencer Smith for his outstanding developmental and editorial assistance. I cannot give him enough accolades–he's simply the best. Also, Jennifer Iserloh, the Skinny Chef, for her creativity and energy in helping to transform concepts into recipes and meal plans for this book.

The creation of a book takes long hours, and I've been blessed to have so many supporters to lean on. First, I drew inspiration from the loving memory of my parents, and I received continuing encouragement from my family–Patrick and Tatianna, Tim and Barbara, Maureen and Gwenn and their children. I am thankful to my godchild, Angela Girratano, whose energy and spirit brighten my life, and to Brian Veith though he actively posts anti–New York Knicks propaganda on Facebook. I'm grateful to Monsignors Arthur Bastress and Arthur Valenzano for their spiritual support and guidance, and to the staff at St. Alphonsus Church and the Basilica of the Assumption in Baltimore, Maryland.

I've been fortunate to have close friends who have been my backbone during the more-than-2-year odyssey of producing this book: Conchita, Miriam, and the Keena family, and the late Patrick Keena; Dr. Loren Marks, a cutting-edge nutritionist and integrative medicine expert in New York City; Dr. Christopher Houlihan, his wife Debbie, and their family; Dr. Laura Matarese, an international expert in nutrition support and a coeditor with me on many book projects, including *Integrative Weight Management*; plus so many good friends at Johns Hopkins. A special thank-you to Drs. Nina Victoria Gallagher in Fixby Park, Huddersfield, West Yorkshire, UK; Oxana Ormonova in Mount Shasta, California; and Mr. Abdul Aziz Al Ghurair of Dubai, United Arab Emirates, for their support and friendship.

Of course, I'd like to acknowledge everyone at Stone Mill Bakery, where I've spent many a lunch- and dinnertime nourishing my body and spirit with the wonderful food and kindred spirits I found there–thank you to Alfie and Dana Himmelrich, Sarah Pigott, Cris Janoff, Devin Adams, Toby Willse, and all the staff who make my food experience first-rate!

There are many people who have guided my career and sparked my interest in nutrition, integrative digestive health, and weight management, and I'd like to offer my gratitude to them as well.

Thank you to my mentors who have guided my career over the years, in particular Drs. Anthony Kalloo, Andrew Weil, and Victoria Maizes; and to the nutritionists whose collaborations have fostered career development and friendships, especially Drs. Carol Ireton-Jones, Mark DeLegge, Steve McClave, Kelly Tappenden, Jeanette Hasse, and Amy Brown. A special word of thanks to Kathie Swift, who coauthored *The Inside Tract* and introduced me to the FODMAPs–that was indeed a game changer for me. To Dr. Sue Shepherd and Dr. Peter Gibson, coauthors of the book *The Complete Low-FODMAP Diet* as well as many pivotal research articles that have revolutionized our approach to the role of food-based therapies in digestive health. Thank you to my great friend, colleague, and mentor in the area of weight management, Dr. Larry Cheskin, director of the Johns Hopkins Weight Management Center.

I would like to also thank my colleagues and friends at the Institute for Functional Medicine–a wonderful organization designed to promote the application of whole-systems practice to prevent and treat chronic disease emphasizing nutrition and lifestyle-based interventions. In particular, I would like to thank Dr. Patrick Hanaway, whose many inspiring lectures on the gut microbiome opened my mind to the mad, mad world of mighty microbes. Laurie Hofmann, Drs. Liz Lipski, Mark Hyman, David Jones, Dan Lukaczer, and support staff Sherrie Torgerson, Sally Priest, Wendy Baker, and so many more. I would like to acknowledge The Johns Hopkins administrative leaders in nutrition who have assisted me through the years, Sylvia McAdoo, Tiffani Hays and Susan Oh, for their collaboration over the years as we together advanced nutrition awareness at our institution.

Space prohibits me from naming everyone who has supported my clinical practice at Johns Hopkins, but among them I am grateful to my medical office assistant Julie McKenna-Thorpe; Erin O'Keefe and nurse clinicians Kimberly Kidd-Watkins, Julie Dennis, and Rose Fusco; administrators Lisa Bach-Burdsall and Nathan Smith; Eric Tomakin, Roseann Wagner, Jennifer Metevia, Helen McGrain, Dr. Lis Ishii, Christian Hartman, Kim Gerred, administrative director Tiffany Boldin and Dr. Linda A. Lee. Dr. Lee is the clinical director of the Johns Hopkins Division of Gastroenterology and Hepatology and director of the Johns Hopkins Center for Integrative Medicine and Digestive Health. Dr. Lee is a courageous and spirited champion of integrative medicine. To Dr. Myron Weisfeldt, chair of medicine at Johns Hopkins who, with Tony Kalloo, brought me to Hopkins to "reboot" my career and has nurtured me ever since–my heartfelt thanks.

Finally, to Dr. Paul Rothman, dean of the medical faculty; Dr. Ed Miller, dean emeritus; Mr. Ronald R. Peterson, president of The Johns Hopkins Hospital and Health System and executive vice-president of Johns Hopkins Medicine; Dr. Redonda Miller, Meg Garrett, Jeffrey Natterman, and the Johns Hopkins Medicine administration–thank you! You are truly the best of the best and the reason why Hopkins continues to be the world's leading medical institution.

Finally, I'd like to thank the great Sylvester Stallone for making the Rocky movies. They continue to inspire me to this day. I watched many a clip on YouTube during late nights writing this book to stay motivated. Thanks, Sly. You gave me the eye of the tiger.

–Gerard E. Mullin, MD
Baltimore, Maryland

ENDNOTES

Introduction

1   chicagotribune.com/health/sns-rt-us-girls-fattagreuters-com2014newsml-kbn0de1xq-20140428,0,6368122
    .story.

2   Kirk S et al. Blame shame and lack of support–a multilevel study on obesity management. *Qualitative Health Research* 2014;11:790-800.

3   You can see the Hippocratic Oath at nlm.nih.gov/hmd/greek/greek_oath.html. When we swear the oath as physicians, usually the first two paragraphs are omitted and we begin with "I will use those dietary regimens which will benefit my patients according to my greatest ability and judgment, and I will do no harm or injustice to them."

4   Flegal KM, Carroll MD, Kit BK, Ogden CL. Prevalence of obesity and trends in the distribution of body mass index among US adults, 1999-2010. *JAMA.* 2012;307:491-97. doi:10.1001/jama.2012.39.

5   Cawley J, Meyerhoefer C. The medical care costs of obesity: an instrumental variables approach. *Journal of Health Economics* 2012; 31:219-30.

6   usda.gov/factbook/chapter2.pdf

Chapter 1

1   Mann T, Tomiyama AJ, Westling E, Lew AM, Samuels B, Chatman J. Medicare's search for effective obesity treatments: diets are not the answer. *American Psychologist* 2007;62:220-33.

2   Farias MM, Cuevas AM, Rodriguez F. Set-point theory and obesity. *Metabolic Syndrome and Related Disorders* 2011;9:85-89.

3   Colmers WF. If there is a weight set point, how is it set? *Canadian Journal of Diabetes* 2013;37(Suppl 2):S250.

4   Ibid.

5   Farias MM, Cuevas AM, Rodriguez F. Set-point theory and obesity. *Metabolic Syndrome and Related Disorders* 2011;9:85-89.

6   Colmers WF. If there is a weight set point, how is it set? *Canadian Journal of Diabetes* 2013;37(Suppl 2):S250.

7   Ford ES, Dietz WH. Trends in energy intake among adults in the United States: findings from NHANES. *American Journal of Clinical Nutrition* 2013;97:848-53.

8   Dietz, quoted in Reuters News. reuters.com/article/2013/03/06/us-despite-obesity-rise
    -idUSBRE92518620130306.

9   Conlan S, Kong HH, Segre JA. Species-level analysis of DNA sequence data from the NIH Human Microbiome Project. *PLoS One* 2012;7:e47075.

10 Peterson J, Garges S, Giovanni M, McInnes P, Wang L, Schloss JA, et al. The NIH Human Microbiome Project. *Genome Research* 2009;19:2317-23.

11 Leblanc JG, Milani C, de Giori GS, Sesma F, van Sinderen D, Ventura M. Bacteria as vitamin suppliers to their host: a gut microbiota perspective. *Current Opinion in Biotechnology* 2013;24:160-68.

12 Layden BT, Angueira AR, Brodsky M, Durai V, Lowe WL, Jr. Short chain fatty acids and their receptors: new metabolic targets. *Translational Research* 2013;161:131-40.

13 Ivanov II, Honda K. Intestinal commensal microbes as immune modulators. *Cell Host and Microbe* 2012;12:496-508.

14 Rhee SH, Pothoulakis C, Mayer EA. Principles and clinical implications of the brain-gut-enteric microbiota axis. *Nature Reviews Gastroenterology & Hepatology* 2009;6:306-14.

15 Larsen N, Vogensen FK, van den Berg FW, Nielsen DS, Andreasen AS, Pedersen BK, et al. Gut microbiota in human adults with type 2 diabetes differs from non-diabetic adults. *PLoS One* 2010;5:e9085.

16 Weinstock LB, Fern SE, Duntley SP. Restless legs syndrome in patients with irritable bowel syndrome: response to small intestinal bacterial overgrowth therapy. *Digestive Diseases and Sciences* 2008;535(5):1252-56.

17 Jeffery IB, Quigley EM, Ohman L, Simren M, O'Toole PW. The microbiota link to irritable bowel syndrome: an emerging story. *Gut Microbes* 2012;3:572-76.

18 Stratiki Z, Costalos C, Sevastiadou S, Kastanidou O, Skouroliakou M, Giakoumatou A, et al. The effect of a bifidobacter supplemented bovine milk on intestinal permeability of preterm infants. *Early Human Development* 2007;83(9):575-79.

19 Patel RT, Shukla AP, Ahn SM, Moreira M, Rubino F. Surgical control of obesity and diabetes: the role of intestinal vs. gastric mechanisms in the regulation of body weight and glucose homeostasis. *Obesity (Silver Spring)* 2014;22(1):159-69.

20 Suez J, Korem T, Zeevi D, Zilberman-Schapira G, Thaiss CA, Maza O, et al. Artificial sweeteners induce glucose intolerance by altering the gut microbiota. *Nature* 2014;514;181-86.

21 nrdc.org/health/effects/mercury/guide.asp.

22 Hart AL, Hendy P. The microbiome in inflammatory bowel disease and its modulation as a therapeutic manoeuvre. *Proceedings of the Nutrition Society* 2014;1-5.

23 Ali BH, Blunden G, Tanira MO, Nemmar A. Some phytochemical, pharmacological and toxicological properties of ginger (Zingiber officinale Roscoe): a review of recent research. *Food and Chemical Toxicology* 2008;46(2):409-20.

24 Howitt MR, Garrett WS. A complex microworld in the gut: gut microbiota and cardiovascular disease connectivity. *Nature Medicine* 2012;18:1188-89.

25 Niers L, Martin R, Rijkers G, Sengers F, Timmerman H, van Uden N, et al. The effects of selected probiotic strains on the development of eczema (the PandA study). *Allergy* 2009;64:1349-58.

26 del Giudice MM, Leonardi S, Ciprandi G, Galdo F, Gubitosi A, La Rosa M, et al. Probiotics in childhood: allergic illness and respiratory infections. *Journal of Clinical Gastroenterology* 2012;46(Suppl):S69-72.

27 Neufeld KA, Kang N, Bienenstock J, Foster JA. Effects of intestinal microbiota on anxiety-like behavior. *Communicative and Integrative Biology* 2011;4:492-94.

28 Koletzko B, von Kries R, Closa R, Escribano J, Scaglioni S, Giovannini M, et al. Can infant feeding choices modulate later obesity risk? *American Journal of Clinical Nutrition* 2009;89:1502S-8S.

29 Li H, Ye R, Pei L, Ren A, Zheng X, Liu J. Caesarean delivery, caesarean delivery on maternal request and childhood overweight: a Chinese birth cohort study of 181,380 children. *Pediatric Obesity* 2014;19:10-16.

30 Bengmark S. Nutrition of the critically ill–a 21st century perspective. *Nutrients* 2013;5:162-207. doi:10.3390/nu5010162.

31 cnn.com/2007/HEALTH/diet.fitness/09/22/kd.gupta.column/.

32 Angelkais E, Armougom F, Million M, Raoult D. The relationship between gut microbiota and weight gain in humans. *Future Microbiology* 2012 Jan;7:91-109. doi:10.2217/fmb.11.142.

33 Blaser MJ. *Missing Microbes*. New York: Henry Holt & Co, 2014.

34 Sharland M. The use of antibacterials in children: a report of the Specialist Advisory Committee on Antimicrobial Resistance (SACAR) Paediatric Subgroup. *Journal of Antimicrobial Chemotherapy* 2007;60(Suppl 1):i15-26.

35 Bailey LC, Forrest CB, Zhang P, Richards TM, Livshïts A, DeRusso PA. Association of antibiotics in infancy with early childhood obesity. *JAMA Pediatrics* 2014; 168(11):1063-69.

Chapter 2

1 Turnbaugh PJ, Backhed F, Fulton L, Gordon JI. Diet-induced obesity is linked to marked but reversible alterations in the mouse distal gut microbiome. *Cell Host and Microbe* 2008;3:213-23.

2 Koren O, Goodrich JK, Cullender TC, Spor A, Laitinen K, Bäckhed HK, Gonzalez A, Werner JJ, Angenent LT, Knight R, Bäckhed F, Isolauri E, Salminen S, Ley RE. Host remodeling of the gut microbiome and metabolic changes during pregnancy *Cell* 2012 Aug 3;150(3):470-80. doi: 10.1016/j.cell.2012.07.008

3 sciencemag.org/content/341/6150/1241214

4 jama.jamanetwork.com/article.aspx?articleid=1916296

5 medicalnewstoday.com/articles/254864.php

6 Vrieze A, Holleman F, Zoetendal EG, de Vos WM, Hoekstra JB, Nieuwdorp M. The environment within: how gut microbiota may influence metabolism and body composition. *Diabetologia* 2010;53:606-13.

7 El-Matary W, Simpson R, Ricketts-Burns N. Fecal microbiota transplantation: are we opening a can of worms? *Gastroenterology* 2012;143:e19; author reply e-20.

8 cbsnews.com/news/fda-struggles-to-regulate-fecal-transplants/.

9 medicalnewstoday.com/articles/249584.php.

10 Azad MB, Konya T, Maughan H, Guttman DS, Field CJ, Chari RS, et al. Gut microbiota of healthy Canadian infants: profiles by mode of delivery and infant diet at 4 months. *CMAJ* 2013;185:385-94.

11 Dominguez-Bello MG, Costello EK, Contreras M, Magris M, Hidalgo G, Fierer N, et al. Delivery mode shapes the acquisition and structure of the initial microbiota across multiple body habitats in newborns. *Proceedings of the National Academy of Sciences of the USA* 2010;107:11971-75.

12 Salminen S, Gibson GR, McCartney AL, Isolauri E. Influence of mode of delivery on gut microbiota composition in seven year old children. *Gut* 2004;53:1388-89.

13 Negele K, Heinrich J, Borte M, von Berg A, Schaaf B, Lehmann I, et al. Mode of delivery and development of atopic disease during the first 2 years of life. *Pediatric Allergy and Immunology* 2004;15:48-54.

14 Bager P, Simonsen J, Nielsen NM, Frisch M. Cesarean section and offspring's risk of inflammatory bowel disease: a national cohort study. *Inflammatory Bowel Diseases* 2012;18:857-62.

15 de Weerth C, Fuentes S, Puylaert P, de Vos WM. Intestinal microbiota of infants with colic: development and specific signatures. *Pediatrics* 2013;131:e550-58.

16 Koletzko B, von Kries R, Closa R, Escribano J, Scaglioni S, Giovannini M, et al. Can infant feeding choices modulate later obesity risk? *American Journal of Clinical Nutrition* 2009;89:1502S-8S.

17 Taffel SM, Placek PJ, Liss T. Trends in the United States cesarean section rate and reasons for the 1980-85 rise. *American Journal of Public Health* 1987;77:955-59.

18 Li H, Ye R, Pei L, Ren A, Zheng X, Liu J. Caesarean delivery, caesarean delivery on maternal request and childhood overweight: a Chinese birth cohort study of 181,380 children. *Pediatric Obesity* 2014;9:10-16.

19 Hamilton BE, Martin JA, Ventura SJ. Births: preliminary data for 2010. *National Vital Statistics Reports* 2011;60:1-25. cdc.gov/nchs/data/nvsr/nvsr60/nvsr60_02.pdf.

20 Akinbami LJ, Moorman JE, Bailey C, Zahran HS, King M, Johnson CA, et al. Trends in asthma prevalence, health care use, and mortality in the United States, 2001-2010. *NCHS Data Brief* 2012:1-8.

21 Radon K, Windstetter D, Solfrank S, von Mutius E, Nowak D, Schwarz HP. Chronic autoimmune disease and contact to animals (CAT) study group. Exposure to farming environments in early life and type 1 diabetes: a case-control study. *Diabetes* 2005;54:3212-16.

22 Miller, D. *Farmacology: What Innovative Family Farming Can Teach Us about Health and Healing.* New York: Harper Collins Publishers, 2013.

23 Ball TM, Castro-Rodriguez JA, Griffith KA, Holberg CJ, Martinez FD, Wright AL. Siblings, day-care attendance, and the risk of asthma and wheezing during childhood. *New England Journal of Medicine* 2000;343:538-43.

24 Ege M. et al. Exposure to environmental microorganisms and childhood asthma. *New England Journal of Medicine* 2011;364:701-9.

25 Reganold J. et al. Fruit and soil quality of organic and conventional strawberry agroecosystems. *PLoS One* 2010;5:e12346.

26 Koberl M, Muller H, Ramadan EM, Berg G. Desert farming benefits from microbial potential in arid soils and promotes diversity and plant health. *PLoS One* 2011;6:e24452.

27 Sheikh A, Strachan DP. The hygiene theory: fact or fiction? *Current Opinion in Otolaryngology & Head and Neck Surgery* 2004;12:232-36.

28 Fung I, Garrett JP, Shahane A, Kwan M. Do bugs control our fate? The influence of the microbiome on autoimmunity. *Current Allergy and Asthma Reports* 2012;12:511-19.

29 Hviid A, Svanstrom H, Frisch M. Antibiotic use and inflammatory bowel diseases in childhood. *Gut* 2011;60:49-54.

30 Strachan DP. Family size, infection and atopy: the first decade of the "hygiene hypothesis." *Thorax* 2000;55(Suppl 1):S2-S10.

31 news-medical.net/news/20121003/e28098Hygiene-hypothesise28099-updated-to-e28098Old-Friendse28099-hypothesis.aspx.

32 Sharland M, SACAR Paediatric Subgroup. The use of antibacterials in children: a report of the Specialist Advisory Committee on Antimicrobial Resistance (SACAR) Paediatric Subgroup. *Journal of Antimicrobial Chemotherapy* 2007; Aug; 60(Suppl 1):i15-i26.

33 Jernberg C, Lofmark S, Edlund C, Jansson JK. Long-term ecological impacts of antibiotic administration on the human intestinal microbiota. *ISME Journal* 2007;1:56-66.

34 Dethlefsen L, Relman DA. Incomplete recovery and individualized responses of the human distal gut microbiota to repeated antibiotic perturbation. *Proceedings of the National Academy of Sciences of the USA* 2011;108(Suppl 1):4554-61.

35 Jukes TH, Williams WL. Nutritional effects of antibiotics. *Pharmacological Reviews* 1953;5:381-420.

36 Cho I, Yamanishi S, Cox L, Methe BA, Zavadil J, Li K, et al. Antibiotics in early life alter the murine colonic microbiome and adiposity. *Nature* 2012;488:621–26.

37 Henao-Mejia J, Elinav E, Jin C, Hao L, Mehal WZ, Strowig T, et al. Inflammasome-mediated dysbiosis regulates progression of NAFLD and obesity. *Nature* 2012;482:179–85.

38 Machado MV, Cortez-Pinto H. Gut microbiota and nonalcoholic fatty liver disease. *Annals of Hepatology* 2012;11:440–49.

39 Wigg AJ, Roberts-Thomson IC, Dymock RB, McCarthy PJ, Grose RH, Cummins AG. The role of small intestinal bacterial overgrowth, intestinal permeability, endotoxaemia, and tumour necrosis factor alpha in the pathogenesis of non-alcoholic steatohepatitis. *Gut* 2001;48:206–11.

40 Lichtman SN, Keku J, Schwab JH, Sartor RB. Hepatic injury associated with small bowel bacterial overgrowth in rats is prevented by metronidazole and tetracycline. *Gastroenterology* 1991;100:513–19.

41 Miyake Y, Yamamoto K. Role of gut microbiota in liver diseases. *Hepatology Research* 2013;43:139–46.

42 Cani PD, Possemiers S, Van de Wiele T, Guiot Y, Everard A, Rottier O, et al. Changes in gut microbiota control inflammation in obese mice through a mechanism involving GLP-2-driven improvement of gut permeability. *Gut* 2009;58:1091–103.

43 Ding S, Lund PK. Role of intestinal inflammation as an early event in obesity and insulin resistance. *Current Opinion in Clinical Nutrition and Metabolic Care* 2011;14:328–33.

44 Creely SJ, McTernan PG, Kusminski CM, Fisher f M, Da Silva NF, Khanolkar M, et al. Lipopolysaccharide activates an innate immune system response in human adipose tissue in obesity and type 2 diabetes. *American Journal of Physiology: Endocrinology and Metabolism* 2007;292:E740–E747.

45 Yang RZ, Lee MJ, Hu H, Pollin TI, Ryan AS, Nicklas BJ, et al. Acute-phase serum amyloid A: an inflammatory adipokine and potential link between obesity and its metabolic complications. *PLoS Medicine* 2006;3:e287.

46 Al-Attas OS, Al-Daghri NM, Al-Rubeaan K, da Silva NF, Sabico SL, Kumar S, et al. Changes in endotoxin levels in T2DM subjects on anti-diabetic therapies. *Cardiovascular Diabetology* 2009;8:20.

47 Cani PD, Neyrinck AM, Fava F, Knauf C, Burcelin RG, Tuohy KM, et al. Selective increases of bifidobacteria in gut microflora improve high-fat-diet-induced diabetes in mice through a mechanism associated with endotoxaemia. *Diabetologia* 2007;50:2374–83.

48 Cani PD, Amar J, Iglesias MA, Poggi M, Knauf C, Bastelica D, et al. Metabolic endotoxemia initiates obesity and insulin resistance. *Diabetes* 2007;56:1761–72.

49 Ma X, Hua J, Li Z. Probiotics improve high fat diet-induced hepatic steatosis and insulin resistance by increasing hepatic NKT cells. *Journal of Hepatology* 2008;49:821–30.

50 Stratiki Z, Costalos C, Sevastiadou S, Kastanidou O, Skouroliakou M, Giankoumatou A, et al. The effect of a bifidobacter supplemented bovine milk on intestinal permeability of preterm infants. *Early Human Development* 2007;83(9):575–79.

51 Okeke F, Roland BC, Mullin GE. The role of gut microbiome in pathogenesis and treatment of obesity. *Global Advances in Health and Medicine* 2014;3:44–57. doi:10.7453/gahmj.2014.018.

52 Ley RE, Turnbaugh PJ, Klein S, Gordon JI. Microbial ecology: human gut microbes associated with obesity. *Nature* 2006;444:1022–23.

53 Ibid.

54 Turnbaugh PJ, Hamady M, Yatsunenko T, Cantarel BL, Duncan A, Ley RE, et al. A core gut microbiome in obese and lean twins. *Nature* 2009;457:480–84.

55 Patel RT, Shukla AP, Ahn SM, Moreira M, Rubino F. Surgical control of obesity and diabetes: the role of intestinal vs. gastric mechanisms in the regulation of body weight and glucose homeostasis. *Obesity (Silver Spring)* 2014;22(1):159–69.

56 Zhang H, DiBaise JK, Zuccolo A, Kudrna D, Braidotti M, Yu Y, et al. Human gut microbiota in obesity and after gastric bypass. *Proceedings of the National Academy of Sciences of the USA* 2009;106: 2365–70.

57 Duncan SH, Lobley GE, Holtrop G, Ince J, Johnstone AM, Louis P, et al. Human colonic microbiota associated with diet, obesity and weight loss. *International Journal of Obesity* 2008;32:1720–24.

58 ncbi.nlm.nih.gov/pubmed/23712978

59 livescience.com/41954-gut-microbes-make-you-fat.html

60 cell.com/abstract/S0092-8674(14)01241-0

61 Turnbaugh PJ, Backhed F, Fulton L, Gordon JI. Diet-induced obesity is linked to marked but reversible alterations in the mouse distal gut microbiome. *Cell Host and Microbe* 2008;3:213–23.

62 Wu GD, Chen J, Hoffmann C, Bittinger K, Chen YY, et al. Linking long-term dietary patterns with gut microbial enterotypes. *Science* 2011;334:105–8. doi:10.1126/science.1208344.

63 britannica.com/EBchecked/topic/1368888/quorum-sensing.

64 Hehemann JH et al. Bacteria of the human gut microbiome catabolize red seaweed glycans with carbohydrate-active enzyme updates from extrinsic microbes. *Proceedings of the National Academy of Sciences of the USA* 2012;109:19786-91. doi: 10.1073/pnas.1211002109.

65 Hehemann JH, Correc G, Barbeyron T, Helbert W, Czjzek M, Michel G. Transfer of carbohydrate-active enzymes from marine bacteria to Japanese gut microbiota. *Nature* 2010;464:908-12.

66 sciencedaily.com/releases/2009/02/090205214418.htm.

67 Xu J, Gordon JI. Honor thy symbionts. *Proceedings of the National Academy of Sciences of the USA* 2003;100(18):10452-9.

68 Semova I, Carten JD, Stombaugh J, et al. Microbiota regulate intestinal absorption and metabolism of fatty acids in the zebrafish. *Cell Host and Microbe* 2012;12: 277-88.

69 Backhed F, Manchester JK, Semenkovich CF, Gordon JI. Mechanisms underlying the resistance to diet-induced obesity in germ-free mice. *Proceedings of the National Academy of Sciences of the USA* 2007;104:979-84.

70 Ibid.

71 Mandard S, Zandbergen F, van Straten E, Wahli W, Kuipers F, Muller M, et al. The fasting-induced adipose factor/angiopoietin-like protein 4 is physically associated with lipoproteins and governs plasma lipid levels and adiposity. *Journal of Biological Chemistry* 2006;281:934-44.

72 Quigley EM. Small intestinal bacterial overgrowth: what it is and what it is not. *Current Opinion in Gastroenterology* 2014;30:141-46.

73 Jeffery IB, Quigley EM, Ohman L, Simren M, O'Toole PW. The microbiota link to irritable bowel syndrome: an emerging story. *Gut Microbes* 2012;3:572-76.

74 Ford AC. Breath testing and antibiotics for possible bacterial overgrowth in irritable bowel syndrome. *Expert Review of Anti-Infective Therapy* 2010;8:855-57.

75 Pimentel M, Lembo A, Chey WD, Zakko S, Ringel Y, Yu J, et al. Rifaximin therapy for patients with irritable bowel syndrome without constipation. *New England Journal of Medicine* 2011;364:22-32.

76 Phatak UP, Pashankar DS. Prevalence of functional gastrointestinal disorders in obese and overweight children. *International Journal of Obesity* 2014 May 2. doi:1038/ijo.2014.67. [Epub ahead of print]

77 Sabate JM, Jouet P, Harnois F, Mechler C, Msika S, Grossin M, et al. High prevalence of small intestinal bacterial overgrowth in patients with morbid obesity: a contributor to severe hepatic steatosis. *Obesity Surgery* 2008;18:371-77.

78 Ilan Y. Leaky gut and the liver: a role for bacterial translocation in nonalcoholic steatohepatitis. *World Journal of Gastroenterology* 2012;18:2609-18.

79 Mathur R, Amichai M, Chua KS, Mirocha J, Barlow GM, Pimental M. Methane and hydrogen positivity on breath test is associated with great body mass index and body fat. *Journal of Clinical Endocrinology and Metabolism* 2013;98: E698-E702.

80 webmd.com/diet/news/20130326/breath-test-might-predict-obesity-risk.

81 Chedid V, Dhalla S, Clarke JO, Roland BC, Dunbar KB, Koh J, et al. Herbal therapy is equivalent to rifaximin for the treatment of small intestinal bacterial overgrowth. *Global Advances in Health and Medicine* 2014;3:16-24.

82 Gershon M. *The Second Brain.* New York: Harper Collins Publishers, 1999.

83 Sudo N, Chida Y, Aiba Y, Sonoda J, Oyama N, Yu XN, et al. Postnatal microbial colonization programs the hypothalamic-pituitary-adrenal system for stress response in mice. *Journal of Physiology* 2004;558(Pt 1):263-75.

84 Messaoudi M, Violle N, Bisson JF, Desor D, Javelot H, Rougeot C. Beneficial psychological effects of a probiotic formulation (Lactobacillus helveticus R0052 and Bifidobacterium longum R0175) in healthy human volunteers. *Gut Microbes* 2011;2:256-61.

85 Messaoudi M, Lalonde R, Violle N, Javelot H, Desor D, Nejdi A, et al. Assessment of psychotropic-like properties of a probiotic formulation (Lactobacillus helveticus R0052 and Bifidobacterium longum R0175) in rats and human subjects. *British Journal of Nutrition* 2011;105:755-64.

86 Cani PD, Possemiers S, Van de Wiele T, Guiot Y, Everard A, Rottier O, et al. Changes in gut microbiota control inflammation in obese mice through a mechanism involving GLP-2-driven improvement of gut permeability. *Gut* 2009;58:1091-103.

87 Cani PD, Hoste S, Guiot Y, Delzenne NM. Dietary non-digestible carbohydrates promote L-cell differentiation in the proximal colon of rats. *British Journal of Nutrition* 2007;98:32-37.

88 Reinhardt C, Reigstad CS, Backhed F. Intestinal microbiota during infancy and its implications for obesity. *Journal of Pediatric Gastroenterology and Nutrition* 2009;48:249-56.

89 Holst JJ. Glucagon and glucagon-like peptides 1 and 2. *Results and Problems in Cell Differentiation* 2010;50:121–35.

90 Parnell JA, Reimer RA. Weight loss during oligofructose supplementation is associated with decreased ghrelin and increased peptide YY in overweight and obese adults. *American Journal of Clinical Nutrition* 2009;89:1751–59.

Chapter 3

1   Di Gioia D, Aloisio I, Mazzola G, Biavati B. Bifidobacteria: their impact on gut microbiota composition and their applications as probiotics in infants. *Applied Microbiology and Biotechnology* 2014;98:563–77.

2   Tsai YT, Cheng PC, Pan TM. Anti-obesity effects of gut microbiota are associated with lactic acid bacteria. *Applied Microbiology and Biotechnology* 2014;98:1–10.

3   Francois F, Roper J, Joseph N, Pei Z, Chhada A, Shak JR, et al. The effect of H. pylori eradication on meal-associated changes in plasma ghrelin and leptin. *BMC Gastroenterology* 2011;11:37.

4   Chacko Y, Holtmann GJ. Helicobacter pylori eradication and weight gain: has it opened a Pandora's box? *Alimentary Pharmacology & Therapies* 2011;34:256.

5   Madrid AM, Poniachik J, Quera R, Defilippi C. Small intestinal clustered contractions and bacterial overgrowth: a frequent finding in obese patients. *Digestive Diseases and Sciences* 2011;56:155–60.

6   Clements RH, Gonzalez QH, Foster A, et al. Gastrointestinal symptoms are more intense in morbidly obese patients and are improved with laparoscopic Roux-en-Y gastric bypass. *Obesity Surgery* 2003;13:610–14.

7   Shai I, Schwarzfuchs D, Henkin Y, et al. Weight loss with a low-carbohydrate, Mediterranean, or low-fat diet. *New England Journal of Medicine* 2008;359:229–41.

8   Foster GD, Wyatt HR, Hill JO, et al. A randomized trial of a low-carbohydrate diet for obesity. *New England Journal of Medicine* 2003;348:2082–90.

9   Brehm BJ, Seeley RJ, Daniels SR, D'Alessio DA. A randomized trial comparing a very low carbohydrate diet and a calorie-restricted low fat diet on body weight and cardiovascular risk factors in healthy women. *Journal of Clinical Endocrinology and Metabolism* 2003;88:1617–23.

10 Gardner CD, Kiazand A, Alhassan S, et al. Comparison of the Atkins, Zone, Ornish, and LEARN diets for change in weight and related risk factors among overweight premenopausal women: the A TO Z Weight Loss Study: a randomized trial. *JAMA* 2007;297:969–77.

11 Yancy WS, Jr., Olsen MK, Guyton JR, Bakst RP, Westman EC. A low-carbohydrate, ketogenic diet versus a low-fat diet to treat obesity and hyperlipidemia: a randomized, controlled trial. *Annals of Internal Medicine* 2004;140:769–77.

12 Seshadri P, Iqbal N, Stern L, et al. A randomized study comparing the effects of a low-carbohydrate diet and a conventional diet on lipoprotein subfractions and C-reactive protein levels in patients with severe obesity. *American Journal of Medicine* 2004;117:398–405.

13 Nistal E, Caminero A, Vivas S, et al. Differences in faecal bacteria populations and faecal bacteria metabolism in healthy adults and celiac disease patients. *Biochimie* 2012;94:1724–29.

14 De Palma G, Nadal I, Collado MC, Sanz Y. Effects of a gluten-free diet on gut microbiota and immune function in healthy adult human subjects. *British Journal of Nutrition* 2009;102:1154–60.

15 Stern L, Iqbal N, Seshadri P, et al. The effects of low-carbohydrate versus conventional weight loss diets in severely obese adults: one-year follow-up of a randomized trial. *Annals of Internal Medicine* 2004;140:778–85.

16 De Palma G, Nadal I, Collado MC, Sanz Y. Effects of a gluten-free diet on gut microbiota and immune function in healthy adult human subjects. *British Journal of Nutrition* 2009;102:1154–60.

17 Nistal E, Caminero A, Herran AR, et al. Differences of small intestinal bacteria populations in adults and children with/without celiac disease: effect of age, gluten diet, and disease. *Inflammatory Bowel Diseases* 2012;18:649–56.

18 Nistal E, Caminero A, Vivas S, et al. Differences in faecal bacteria populations and faecal bacteria metabolism in healthy adults and celiac disease patients. *Biochimie* 2012;94:1724–29.

19 De Palma G, Nadal I, Collado MC, Sanz Y. Effects of a gluten-free diet on gut microbiota and immune function in healthy adult human subjects. *British Journal of Nutrition* 2009;102:1154–60.

20 Santacruz A, Marcos A, Warnberg J, et al. Interplay between weight loss and gut microbiota composition in overweight adolescents. *Obesity* 2009;17:1906–15.

21 Million M, Maraninchi M, Henry M, et al. Obesity-associated gut microbiota is enriched in Lactobacillus reuteri and depleted in Bifidobacterium animalis and Methanobrevibacter smithii. *International Journal of Obesity* 2012;36:817–25.

22 Kalliomaki M, Collado MC, Salminen S, Isolauri E. Early differences in fecal microbiota composition in children may predict overweight. *American Journal of Clinical Nutrition* 2008;87:534–38.

23 Schwiertz A, Taras D, Schafer K, et al. Microbiota and SCFA in lean and overweight healthy subjects. *Obesity* 2010;18:190–95.

24 Collado MC, Isolauri E, Laitinen K, Salminen S. Distinct composition of gut microbiota during pregnancy in overweight and normal-weight women. *American Journal of Clinical Nutrition* 2008;88:894–99.

25 Heine RG. Preventing atopy and allergic disease. *Nestlé Nutrition Institute Workshop Series* 2014;78: 141–53.

26 Owen CG, Martin RM, Whincup PH, Smith GD, Cook DG. Effect of infant feeding on the risk of obesity across the life course: a quantitative review of published evidence. *Pediatrics* 2005;115:1367–77.

27 Harder T, Bergmann R, Kallischnigg G, Plagemann A. Duration of breastfeeding and risk of overweight: a meta-analysis. *American Journal of Epidemiology* 2005;162:397–403.

Chapter 4

1 Haahtela T, Holgate S, Pawankar R, et al. The biodiversity hypothesis and allergic disease: World Allergy Organization position statement. *World Allergy Organization Journal* 2013;6:3.

2 Schnabl B, Brenner DA. Interactions between the intestinal microbiome and liver diseases. *Gastroenterology* 2014;146:1513–24.

3 Bengmark S. Nutrition of the critically ill–a 21st-century perspective. *Nutrients.* 2013;5:162–207.

4 Hold GL. Western lifestyle: a 'master' manipulator of the intestinal microbiota? *Gut* 2014;63:5–6.

5 Bengmark S. Nutrition of the critically ill–a 21st-century perspective. *Nutrients.* 2013;5:162–207.

6 Wu GD, Chen J, Hoffmann C, et al. Linking long-term dietary patterns with gut microbial enterotypes. *Science* 2011;334:105–8.

7 Pendyala S, Walker JM, Holt PR. A high-fat diet is associated with endotoxemia that originates from the gut. *Gastroenterology* 2012;142:1100–1 e2.

8 Hansen R, Russell RK, Reiff C, et al. Microbiota of de-novo pediatric IBD: increased Faecalibacterium prausnitzii and reduced bacterial diversity in Crohn's but not in ulcerative colitis. *American Journal of Gastroenterology* 2012;107:1913–22.

9 Martinez-Medina M, Denizot J, Dreux N, et al. Western diet induces dysbiosis with increased E. coli in CEABAC10 mice, alters host barrier function favouring AIEC colonisation. *Gut* 2014;63:116–24.

10 Devkota S, Wang Y, Musch MW, et al. Dietary-fat-induced taurocholic acid promotes pathobiont expansion and colitis in Il10-/- mice. *Nature* 2012;487:104–8.

11 Ghosh S, Molcan E, DeCoffe D, Dai C, Gibson DL. Diets rich in n-6 PUFA induce intestinal microbial dysbiosis in aged mice. *British Journal of Nutrition* 2013;110:515–23.

12 de La Serre CB, Ellis CL, Lee J, Hartman AL, Rutledge JC, Raybould HE. Propensity to high-fat diet-induced obesity in rats is associated with changes in the gut microbiota and gut inflammation. *American Journal of Physiology: Gastrointestinal and Liver Physiology* 2010;299:G440–48.

13 Ghosh S, Molcan E, DeCoffe D, Dai C, Gibson DL. Diets rich in n-6 PUFA induce intestinal microbial dysbiosis in aged mice. *British Journal of Nutrition* 2013;110:515–23.

14 usda.gov/factbook/2001-2002factbook.pdf.table 2–6, page 20.

15 usda.gov/factbook/chapter2.pdf.tables 2–6, page 20.

16 Cordain L, Eaton SB, Sebastian A, et al. Origins and evolution of the Western diet: health implications for the 21st century. *American Journal of Clinical Nutrition* 2005;81:341–54.

17 Cordain L. Implications for the role of diet in acne. *Seminars in Cutaneous Medicine and Surgery* 2005;24:84–91.

18 Yang Q, Zhang Z, Gregg EW, Flanders WD, Merritt R, Hu FB. Added sugar intake and cardiovascular diseases mortality among US adults. *JAMA Internal Medicine* 2014;17:516–24.

19 Schmidt LA. New unsweetened truths about sugar. *JAMA Internal Medicine* 2014;17:525–26.

20 usda.gov/factbook/chapter2.pdf.tables 2–6, page 20.

21 Yang Q, Zhang Z, Gregg EW, Flanders WD, Merritt R, Hu FB. Added sugar intake and cardiovascular diseases mortality among US adults. *JAMA Internal Medicine* 2014;17:516–24.

22 Johnson RK, Appel LJ, Brands M, et al. Dietary sugars intake and cardiovascular health: a scientific statement from the American Heart Association. *Circulation* 2009;120:1011-20.

23 Yang Q, Zhang Z, Gregg EW, Flanders WD, Merritt R, Hu FB. Added sugar intake and cardiovascular diseases mortality among US adults. *JAMA Internal Medicine* 2014;17:516–24.

24   Ibid.

25   Green AK, Jacques PF, Rogers G, Fox CS, Meigs JB, McKeown NM. Sugar-sweetened beverages and prevalence of the metabolically abnormal phenotype in the Framingham Heart Study. *Obesity* 2014;22:E157–63.

26   Turnbaugh PJ, Ridaura VK, Faith JJ, Rey FE, Knight R, Gordon JI. The effect of diet on the human gut microbiome: a metagenomic analysis in humanized gnotobiotic mice. *Science Translational Medicine* 2009;1:6ra14.

27   Ibid.

28   Kavanagh K, Wylie AT, Tucker KL, et al. Dietary fructose induces endotoxemia and hepatic injury in calorically controlled primates. *American Journal of Clinical Nutrition* 2013;98:349–57.

29   Nomura K, Yamanouchi T. The role of fructose-enriched diets in mechanisms of nonalcoholic fatty liver disease. *Journal of Nutritional Biochemistry* 2012;23:203–8.

30   Riveros MJ, Parada A, Pettinelli P. [Fructose consumption and its health implications; fructose malabsorption and nonalcoholic fatty liver disease]. *Nutrición hospitalaria* 2014;29:491–99.

31   usda.gov/factbook/2001-2002factbook.pdf.table 2–6, page 20.

32   usda.gov/factbook/chapter2.pdf.tables 2–6, page 20.

33   Nomura K, Yamanouchi T. The role of fructose-enriched diets in mechanisms of nonalcoholic fatty liver disease. *Journal of Nutritional Biochemistry* 2012;23:203–8.

34   Riveros MJ, Parada A, Pettinelli P. [Fructose consumption and its health implications; fructose malabsorption and nonalcoholic fatty liver disease]. *Nutrición hospitalaria* 2014;29:491–99.

35   Mager DR, Iniguez IR, Gilmour S, Yap J. The effect of a low fructose and low glycemic index/load (FRAGILE) dietary intervention on indices of liver function, cardiometabolic risk factors, and body composition in children and adolescents with nonalcoholic fatty liver disease (NAFLD). *JPEN: Journal of Parenteral and Enteral Nutrition* 2013 Aug 23. [Epub ahead of print]

36   Kelishadi R, Mansourian M, Heidari-Beni M. Association of fructose consumption and components of metabolic syndrome in human studies: a systematic review and meta-analysis. *Nutrition* 2014;30:503-10.

37   Ha V, Jayalath VH, Cozma AI, Mirrahimi A, de Souza RJ, Sievenpiper JL. Fructose-containing sugars, blood pressure, and cardiometabolic risk: a critical review. *Current Hypertension Reports* 2013;15:281–97.

38   Martin-Calvo N, Martinez-Gonzalez MA, Bes-Rastrollo M, et al. Sugar-sweetened carbonated beverage consumption and childhood/adolescent obesity: a case-control study. *Public Health Nutrition* 2014 Jan 31:1–9. [Epub ahead of print]

39   Nickelson J, Lawrence JC, Parton JM, Knowlden AP, McDermott RJ. What proportion of preschool-aged children consume sweetened beverages? *Journal of School Health* 2014;84:185–94.

40   Kavanagh K, Wylie AT, Tucker KL, et al. Dietary fructose induces endotoxemia and hepatic injury in calorically controlled primates. *American Journal of Clinical Nutrition* 2013;98:349–57.

41   Bleich SN, Wolfson JA, Vine S, Wang YC. Diet-beverage consumption and caloric intake among US adults, overall and by body weight. *American Journal of Public Health* 2014;104:e72–78.

42   Fowler SP, Williams K, Resendez RG, Hunt KJ, Hazuda HP, Stern MP. Fueling the obesity epidemic? Artificially sweetened beverage use and long-term weight gain. *Obesity* 2008;16:1894–900.

43   Sternini C. In search of a role for carbonation: is this a good or bad taste? *Gastroenterology* 2013;145:500-503.

44   Di Salle F, Cantone E, Savarese MF, et al. Effect of carbonation on brain processing of sweet stimuli in humans. *Gastroenterology* 2013;145:537–39 e3.

45   Soffritti M, Padovani M, Tibaldi E, Falcioni L, Manservisi F, Belpoggi F. The carcinogenic effects of aspartame: The urgent need for regulatory re-evaluation. *American Journal of Industrial Medicine* 2014;57:383–97.

46   Suez J, Korem T, Zeevi D, Zilberman-Schapira G, Thaiss CA, Mazo O, et al. Artificial sweeteners induce glucose intolerance by altering the gut microbiota. *Nature* 2014.

47   Wu GD, Chen J, Hoffmann C, et al. Linking long-term dietary patterns with gut microbial enterotypes. *Science* 2011;334:105–8.

48   Steinert RE, Frey F, Topfer A, Drewe J, Beglinger C. Effects of carbohydrate sugars and artificial sweeteners on appetite and the secretion of gastrointestinal satiety peptides. *British Journal of Nutrition* 2011;105:1320–28.

49   Piya MK, Harte AL, McTernan PG. Metabolic endotoxaemia: is it more than just a gut feeling? *Current Opinion in Lipidology* 2013;24:78–85.

50 Van Engelen M, Khodabandeh S, Akhavan T, Agarwal J, Gladanac B, Bellissimo N. Effect of sugars in solutions on subjective appetite and short-term food intake in 9- to 14-year-old normal weight boys. *European Journal of Clinical Nutrition* 2014;66(7):773–77.

51 Garcia-Caceres C, Tschop MH. The emerging neurobiology of calorie addiction. *eLife* 2014;3:e01928.

52 Malkusz DC, Banakos T, Mohamed A, et al. Dopamine signaling in the medial prefrontal cortex and amygdala is required for the acquisition of fructose-conditioned flavor preferences in rats. *Behavioural Brain Research* 2012;233:500–507.

53 Halmos EP, Christophersen CT, Bird AR, Shepherd SJ, Gibson PR, Muir JG. Diets that differ in their FODMAP content alter the colonic luminal microenvironment. *Gut* 2014 Jul 14. [Epub ahead of print]

54 Paoli A. Ketogenic diet for obesity: friend or foe? *International Journal of Environmental Research and Public Health* 2014;11:2092–107.

55 Ibid.

56 Paoli A, Rubini A, Volek JS, Grimaldi KA. Beyond weight loss: a review of the therapeutic uses of very-low-carbohydrate (ketogenic) diets. *European Journal of Clinical Nutrition* 2013;67:789–96.

57 Veldhorst M, Smeets A, Soenen S, et al. Protein-induced satiety: effects and mechanisms of different proteins. *Physiology & Behavior* 2008;94:300–307.

58 Westerterp-Plantenga MS, Nieuwenhuizen A, Tome D, Soenen S, Westerterp KR. Dietary protein, weight loss, and weight maintenance. *Annual Review of Nutrition* 2009;29:21–41.

59 Sumithran P, Prendergast LA, Delbridge E, et al. Ketosis and appetite-mediating nutrients and hormones after weight loss. *European Journal of Clinical Nutrition* 2013;67:759–64.

60 Veldhorst MA, Westerterp-Plantenga MS, Westerterp KR. Gluconeogenesis and energy expenditure after a high-protein, carbohydrate-free diet. *American Journal of Clinical Nutrition* 2009;90:519–26.

61 Fine EJ, Feinman RD. Thermodynamics of weight loss diets. *Nutrition & Metabolism* 2004;1:15.

62 Volek JS, Phinney SD, Forsythe CE, et al. Carbohydrate restriction has a more favorable impact on the metabolic syndrome than a low fat diet. *Lipids* 2009;44:297–309.

63 Volek JS, Sharman MJ, Forsythe CE. Modification of lipoproteins by very low-carbohydrate diets. *Journal of Nutrition* 2005;135:1339–42.

64 Lefevre F, Aronson N. Ketogenic diet for the treatment of refractory epilepsy in children: a systematic review of efficacy. *Pediatrics* 2000;105:E46.

65 Vining EP, Freeman JM, Ballaban-Gil K, et al. A multicenter study of the efficacy of the ketogenic diet. *Archives of Neurology* 1998;55:1433–37.

66 Thakur KT, Probasco JC, Hocker SE, et al. Ketogenic diet for adults in super-refractory status epilepticus. *Neurology* 2014;82:665–70.

67 Woolf EC, Scheck AC. The ketogenic diet for the treatment of malignant glioma. *Journal of Lipid Research* 2014 Feb 6. [Epub ahead of print]

68 Perez-Guisado J. [Ketogenic diets: additional benefits to the weight loss and unfounded secondary effects]. *Archivos latinoamericanos de nutrición* 2008;58:323–29.

69 Ibid.

70 Sacks FM, Bray GA, Carey VJ, et al. Comparison of weight-loss diets with different compositions of fat, protein, and carbohydrates. *New England Journal of Medicine* 2009;360:859–73.

71 Siri-Tarino PW, Sun Q, Hu FB, Krauss RM. Meta-analysis of prospective cohort studies evaluating the association of saturated fat with cardiovascular disease. *American Journal of Clinical Nutrition* 2010;91:535–46.

72 Lands B. Consequences of essential fatty acids. *Nutrients* 2012;4:1338–57

73 Cameron M, Gagnier JJ, Chrubasik S. Herbal therapy for treating rheumatoid arthritis. *Cochrane Database of Systematic Reviews* 2011:CD002948.

74 Galland L. Diet and inflammation. *Nutrition in Clinical Practice* 2010;25:634–40.

75 Palmer S. Fill in the fiber gaps—dietitians offer practical strategies to get clients to meet the daily requirements. *Today's Dietitian* 2012;14:40.

76 Roland BC, Ciarleglio MM, Clarke JO, et al. Low ileocecal valve pressure is significantly associated with small intestinal bacterial overgrowth (SIBO). *Digestive Diseases and Sciences* 2014;59:1269–77.

77 Bonilla S, Wang D, Saps M. Obesity predicts persistence of pain in children with functional gastrointestinal disorders. *International Journal of Obesity* 2011;35:517–21.

78   Halmos EP, Power VA, Shepherd SJ, Gibson PR, Muir JG. A diet low in FODMAPs reduces symptoms of irritable bowel syndrome. *Gastroenterology* 2014;146:67–75 e5.

79   Jouet P, Coffin B, Sabate JM. Small intestinal bacterial overgrowth in patients with morbid obesity. *Digestive Diseases and Sciences* 2011;56:615; author reply 616.

80   Sabate JM, Jouet P, Harnois F, et al. High prevalence of small intestinal bacterial overgrowth in patients with morbid obesity: a contributor to severe hepatic steatosis. *Obesity Surgery* 2008;18:371–77.

81   Madrid AM. Small intestinal bacterial overgrowth in patients with morbid obesity: reply. *Digestive Diseases and Sciences* 2011;56:615–16.

82   Madrid AM, Poniachik J, Quera R, Defilippi C. Small intestinal clustered contractions and bacterial overgrowth: a frequent finding in obese patients. *Digestive Diseases and Sciences* 2011;56:155–60.

83   Jouet P, Coffin B, Sabate JM. Small intestinal bacterial overgrowth in patients with morbid obesity. *Digestive Diseases and Sciences* 2011;56:615; author reply 616.

84   Ibid.

85   Madrid AM. Small intestinal bacterial overgrowth in patients with morbid obesity: reply. *Digestive Diseases and Sciences* 2011;56:615–16.

86   Madrid AM, Poniachik J, Quera R, Defilippi C. Small intestinal clustered contractions and bacterial overgrowth: a frequent finding in obese patients. *Digestive Diseases and Sciences* 2011;56:155–60.

87   Clements RH, Gonzalez QH, Foster A, et al. Gastrointestinal symptoms are more intense in morbidly obese patients and are improved with laparoscopic Roux-en-Y gastric bypass. *Obesity Surgery* 2003;13:610–14.

88   Foster A, Laws HL, Gonzalez QH, Clements RH. Gastrointestinal symptomatic outcome after laparoscopic Roux-en-Y gastric bypass. *Journal of Gastrointestinal Surgery* 2003;7:750–53.

89   Foster A, Richards WO, McDowell J, Laws HL, Clements RH. Gastrointestinal symptoms are more intense in morbidly obese patients. *Surgical Endoscopy* 2003;17:1766–68.

90   Levy RL, Linde JA, Feld KA, Crowell MD, Jeffery RW. The association of gastrointestinal symptoms with weight, diet, and exercise in weight-loss program participants. *Clinical Gastroenterology and Hepatology* 2005;3:992–96.

91   Ibid.

92   doctoroz.com/videos/botox-future-weight-loss.

93   Faria M, Pavin EJ, Parisi MC, et al. Delayed small intestinal transit in patients with long-standing type 1 diabetes mellitus: investigation of the relationships with clinical features, gastric emptying, psychological distress, and nutritional parameters. *Diabetes Technology & Therapeutics* 2013;15:32–38.

94   Staudacher HM, Irving PM, Lomer MC, Whelan K. Mechanisms and efficacy of dietary FODMAP restriction in IBS. *Nature Reviews Gastroenterology & Hepatology* 2014;11:256–66.

95   Halmos EP, Christophersen CT, Bird AR, Shepherd SJ, Gibson PR, Muir JG. Diets that differ in their FODMAP content alter the colonic luminal microenvironment. *Gut* 2014 Jul 14. [Epub ahead of print]

96   Kirby M, Danner E. Nutritional deficiencies in children on restricted diets. *Pediatric Clinics of North America* 2009;56:1085–103.

97   Nistal E, Caminero A, Vivas S, et al. Differences in faecal bacteria populations and faecal bacteria metabolism in healthy adults and celiac disease patients. *Biochimie* 2012;94:1724–29.

98   De Palma G, Nadal I, Collado MC, Sanz Y. Effects of a gluten-free diet on gut microbiota and immune function in healthy adult human subjects. *British Journal of Nutrition* 2009;102:1154–60.

99   Zhu W, Cai D, Wang Y, et al. Calcium plus vitamin D_3 supplementation facilitated fat loss in overweight and obese college students with very-low calcium consumption: a randomized controlled trial. *Nutrition Journal* 2013;12:8.

100 Tremblay A, Gilbert JA. Human obesity: is insufficient calcium/dairy intake part of the problem? *Journal of the American College of Nutrition* 2011;30:449S–53S.

101 Sun X, Zemel MB. Calcium and dairy products inhibit weight and fat regain during ad libitum consumption following energy restriction in Ap2-agouti transgenic mice. *Journal of Nutrition* 2004;134:3054–60.

102 Mozaffarian D, Hao T, Rimm EB, Willett WC, Hu FB. Changes in diet and lifestyle and long-term weight gain in women and men. *New England Journal of Medicine* 2011;364:2392–404.

103 Ross AC, Manson JE, Abrams SA, et al. The 2011 Dietary Reference Intakes for calcium and vitamin D: what dietetics practitioners need to know. *Journal of the American Dietetic Association* 2011;111:524–27.

104 Ibid.

105 Veldhorst M, Smeets A, Soenen S, et al. Protein-induced satiety: effects and mechanisms of different proteins. *Physiology & Behavior* 2008;94:300–307.

106 Lejeune MP, Kovacs EM, Westerterp-Plantenga MS. Additional protein intake limits weight regain after weight loss in humans. *British Journal of Nutrition* 2005;93:281–89.

107 Westerterp-Plantenga MS, Lejeune MP. Protein intake and body-weight regulation. *Appetite* 2005;45:187–90.

108 Westerterp-Plantenga MS, Lejeune MP, Nijs I, van Ooijen M, Kovacs EM. High protein intake sustains weight maintenance after body weight loss in humans. *International Journal of Obesity and Related Metabolic Disorders* 2004;28:57–64.

109 Westerterp-Plantenga MS, Nieuwenhuizen A, Tome D, Soenen S, Westerterp KR. Dietary protein, weight loss, and weight maintenance. *Annual Review of Nutrition* 2009;29:21–41.

110 Lejeune MP, Kovacs EM, Westerterp-Plantenga MS. Additional protein intake limits weight regain after weight loss in humans. *British Journal of Nutrition* 2005;93:281–89.

111 Westerterp-Plantenga MS, Lejeune MP. Protein intake and body-weight regulation. *Appetite* 2005;45:187–90.

112 Westerterp-Plantenga MS, Lejeune MP, Nijs I, van Ooijen M, Kovacs EM. High protein intake sustains weight maintenance after body weight loss in humans. *International Journal of Obesity and Related Metabolic Disorders* 2004;28:57–64.

113 Bowen J, Noakes M, Clifton PM. Appetite regulatory hormone responses to various dietary proteins differ by body mass index status despite similar reductions in ad libitum energy intake. *Journal of Clinical Endocrinology and Metabolism* 2006;91:2913–19.

114 Lejeune MP, Westerterp KR, Adam TC, Luscombe-Marsh ND, Westerterp-Plantenga MS. Ghrelin and glucagon-like peptide 1 concentrations, 24-h satiety, and energy and substrate metabolism during a high-protein diet and measured in a respiration chamber. *American Journal of Clinical Nutrition* 2006;83:89–94.

115 Batterham RL, Heffron H, Kapoor S, et al. Critical role for peptide YY in protein-mediated satiation and body-weight regulation. *Cell Metabolism* 2006;4:223–33.

116 Bowen J, Noakes M, Trenerry C, Clifton PM. Energy intake, ghrelin, and cholecystokinin after different carbohydrate and protein preloads in overweight men. *Journal of Clinical Endocrinology and Metabolism* 2006;91:1477–83.

117 Smeets AJ, Soenen S, Luscombe-Marsh ND, Ueland O, Westerterp-Plantenga MS. Energy expenditure, satiety, and plasma ghrelin, glucagon-like peptide 1, and peptide tyrosine-tyrosine concentrations following a single high-protein lunch. *Journal of Nutrition* 2008;138:698–702.

118 Holt SH, Miller JC, Petocz P, Farmakalidis E. A satiety index of common foods. *European Journal of Clinical Nutrition* 1995;49:675–90.

119 Uhe AM, Collier GR, O'Dea K. A comparison of the effects of beef, chicken and fish protein on satiety and amino acid profiles in lean male subjects. *Journal of Nutrition* 1992;122:467–72.

120 Pal S, Ellis V. The acute effects of four protein meals on insulin, glucose, appetite and energy intake in lean men. *British Journal of Nutrition* 2010;104:1241–48.

121 Rebello CJ, Liu AG, Greenway FL, Dhurandhar NV. Dietary strategies to increase satiety. *Advances in Food and Nutrition Research* 2013;69:105–82.

122 Douglas SM, Ortinau LC, Hoertel HA, Leidy HJ. Low, moderate, or high protein yogurt snacks on appetite control and subsequent eating in healthy women. *Appetite* 2013;60:117–22.

123 Hession M, Rolland C, Kulkarni U, Wise A, Broom J. Systematic review of randomized controlled trials of low-carbohydrate vs. low-fat/low-calorie diets in the management of obesity and its comorbidities. *Obesity Reviews* 2009;10:36–50.

124 Mozaffarian D, Hao T, Rimm EB, Willett WC, Hu FB. Changes in diet and lifestyle and long-term weight gain in women and men. *New England Journal of Medicine* 2011;364:2392–404.

125 Rosell M, Appleby P, Spencer E, Key T. Weight gain over 5 years in 21,966 meat-eating, fish-eating, vegetarian, and vegan men and women in EPIC-Oxford. *International Journal of Obesity* 2006;30:1389–96.

126 Cocate PG, Natali AJ, Oliveira AD, et al. Red but not white meat consumption is associated with metabolic syndrome, insulin resistance and lipid peroxidation in Brazilian middle-aged men. *European Journal of Preventive Cardiology* 2013 Oct 8. [Epub ahead of print]

127 Babio N, Sorli M, Bullo M, et al. Association between red meat consumption and metabolic syndrome in a Mediterranean population at high cardiovascular risk: cross-sectional and 1-year follow-up assessment. *Nutrition, Metabolism, and Cardiovascular Diseases* 2012;22:200–207.

128 Pan A, Sun Q, Bernstein AM, Manson JE, Willett WC, Hu FB. Changes in red meat consumption and subsequent risk of type 2 diabetes mellitus: three cohorts of US men and women. *JAMA Internal Medicine* 2013;173:1328–35.

129 Vergnaud AC, Norat T, Romaguera D, et al. Meat consumption and prospective weight change in participants of the EPIC-PANACEA study. *American Journal of Clinical Nutrition* 2010;92:398–407.

130 Cho I, Yamanishi S, Cox L, et al. Antibiotics in early life alter the murine colonic microbiome and adiposity. *Nature* 2012;488:621–26.

131 Jobin C. [Microbial dysbiosis, a new risk factor in colorectal cancer?]. *Médecine sciences* 2013;29:582–85.

132 cancerpreventionresearch.aacrjournals.org/content/7/11/1112

133 Wang Z, Klipfell E, Bennett BJ, et al. Gut flora metabolism of phosphatidylcholine promotes cardiovascular disease. *Nature* 2011;472:57–63.

134 Davidson S. Flagging flora: heart disease link. *Nature* 2011;477:162.

135 Ussher JR, Lopaschuk GD, Arduini A. Gut microbiota metabolism of L-carnitine and cardiovascular risk. *Atherosclerosis* 2013;231:456–61.

136 Levine ME, Suarez JA, Brandhorst S, et al. Low protein intake is associated with a major reduction in IGF-1, cancer, and overall mortality in the 65 and younger but not older population. *Cell Metabolism* 2014;19:407–17.

137 Thorpe DL, Knutsen SF, Beeson WL, Rajaram S, Fraser GE. Effects of meat consumption and vegetarian diet on risk of wrist fracture over 25 years in a cohort of peri- and postmenopausal women. *Public Health Nutrition* 2008;11:564–72.

138 Nicoll R, McLaren Howard J. The acid-ash hypothesis revisited: a reassessment of the impact of dietary acidity on bone. *Journal of Bone and Mineral Metabolism* 2014 Feb 21. [Epub ahead of print]

139 Calvez J, Poupin N, Chesneau C, Lassale C, Tome D. Protein intake, calcium balance and health consequences. *European Journal of Clinical Nutrition* 2012;66:281–95.

140 Wu GD, Chen J, Hoffmann C, et al. Linking long-term dietary patterns with gut microbial enterotypes. *Science* 2011;334:105–8.

141 David LA, Maurice CF, Carmody RN, et al. Diet rapidly and reproducibly alters the human gut microbiome. *Nature* 2014;505:559–63.

142 Tuohy KM, Fava F, Viola R. 'The way to a man's heart is through his gut microbiota'–dietary pro- and prebiotics for the management of cardiovascular risk. *Proceedings of the Nutrition Society* 2014:1–14.

143 Razquin C, Martinez JA, Martinez-Gonzalez MA, Fernandez-Crehuet J, Santos JM, Marti A. A Mediterranean diet rich in virgin olive oil may reverse the effects of the -174G/C IL6 gene variant on 3-year body weight change. *Molecular Nutrition & Food Research* 2010;54(Suppl 1):S75–S82.

144 Razquin C, Martinez JA, Martinez-Gonzalez MA, Salas-Salvado J, Estruch R, Marti A. A 3-year Mediterranean-style dietary intervention may modulate the association between adiponectin gene variants and body weight change. *European Journal of Nutrition* 2010;49:311–19.

145 Lucas L, Russell A, Keast R. Molecular mechanisms of inflammation. Anti-inflammatory benefits of virgin olive oil and the phenolic compound oleocanthal. *Current Pharmaceutical Design* 2011;17:754–68.

146 Wendland E, Farmer A, Glasziou P, Neil A. Effect of alpha linolenic acid on cardiovascular risk markers: a systematic review. *Heart* 2006;92:166–69.

147 Lin L, Allemekinders H, Dansby A, et al. Evidence of health benefits of canola oil. *Nutrition Reviews* 2013;71:370–85.

148 Hung HC, Joshipura KJ, Jiang R, et al. Fruit and vegetable intake and risk of major chronic disease. *Journal of the National Cancer Institute* 2004;96:1577–84.

149 Mattes R. Soup and satiety. *Physiology & Behavior* 2005;83:739–47.

150 Muckelbauer R, Sarganas G, Gruneis A, Muller-Nordhorn J. Association between water consumption and body weight outcomes: a systematic review. *American Journal of Clinical Nutrition* 2013;98:282–99.

151 usda.gov/factbook/chapter2.pdf.tables 2–6, page 20.

152 Nielsen SJ, Popkin BM. Changes in beverage intake between 1977 and 2001. *American Journal of Preventive Medicine* 2004;27:205–10.

153 Mullin GE. Red wine, grapes, and better health–resveratrol. *Nutrition in Clinical Practice* 2011;26:722–23.

154 Bertelli AA, Das DK. Grapes, wines, resveratrol, and heart health. *Journal of Cardiovascular Pharmacology* 2009;54:468–76.

155 Lekli I, Ray D, Das DK. Longevity nutrients resveratrol, wines and grapes. *Genes & Nutrition* 2010;5:55–60.

156 Wu GD, Bushmanc FD, Lewis JD. Diet, the human gut microbiota, and IBD. *Anaerobe* 2013;24:117–20.

157 coffeeconfidential.org/health/decaffeination/.

Chapter 5

1 Vander Wal JS, Marth JM, Khosla P, Jen KL, Dhurandhar NV. Short-term effect of eggs on satiety in overweight and obese subjects. *Journal of the American College of Nutrition* 2005;24:510–15.

2   Ibid.

3   Vander Wal JS, Gupta A, Khosla P, Dhurandhar NV. Egg breakfast enhances weight loss. *International Journal of Obesity* 2008;32:1545–51.

4   Ratliff J, Leite JO, de Ogburn R, Puglisi MJ, VanHeest J, Fernandez ML. Consuming eggs for breakfast influences plasma glucose and ghrelin, while reducing energy intake during the next 24 hours in adult men. *Nutrition Research* 2010;30:96–103.

5   Karra E, Chandarana K, Batterham RL. The role of peptide YY in appetite regulation and obesity. *Journal of Physiology* 2009;587:19–25.

6   Fallaize R, Wilson L, Gray J, Morgan LM, Griffin BA. Variation in the effects of three different breakfast meals on subjective satiety and subsequent intake of energy at lunch and evening meal. *European Journal of Nutrition* 2013;52:1353–59.

7   Vuksan V, Jenkins AL, Dias AG, et al. Reduction in postprandial glucose excursion and prolongation of satiety: possible explanation of the long-term effects of whole grain Salba (Salvia Hispanica L.). *European Journal of Clinical Nutrition* 2010;64:436–38.

8   Chicco AG, D'Alessandro ME, Hein GJ, Oliva ME, Lombardo YB. Dietary chia seed (Salvia hispanica L.) rich in alpha-linolenic acid improves adiposity and normalises hypertriacylglycerolaemia and insulin resistance in dyslipaemic rats. *British Journal of Nutrition* 2009;101:41–50.

9   Vuksan V, Jenkins AL, Dias AG, et al. Reduction in postprandial glucose excursion and prolongation of satiety: possible explanation of the long-term effects of whole grain Salba (Salvia Hispanica L.). *European Journal of Clinical Nutrition* 2010;64:436–38.

10 Chicco AG, D'Alessandro ME, Hein GJ, Oliva ME, Lombardo YB. Dietary chia seed (Salvia hispanica L.) rich in alpha-linolenic acid improves adiposity and normalises hypertriacylglycerolaemia and insulin resistance in dyslipaemic rats. *British Journal of Nutrition* 2009;101:41–50.

11 Vuksan V, Whitham D, Sievenpiper JL, et al. Supplementation of conventional therapy with the novel grain Salba (Salvia hispanica L.) improves major and emerging cardiovascular risk factors in type 2 diabetes: results of a randomized controlled trial. *Diabetes Care* 2007;30:2804–10.

12 Ayerza R, Jr., Coates W. Effect of dietary alpha-linolenic fatty acid derived from chia when fed as ground seed, whole seed and oil on lipid content and fatty acid composition of rat plasma. *Annals of Nutrition & Metabolism* 2007;51:27–34.

13 Ranasinghe P, Pigera S, Premakumara GA, Galappaththy P, Constantine GR, Katulanda P. Medicinal properties of 'true' cinnamon (Cinnamomum zeylanicum): a systematic review. *BMC Complementary and Alternative Medicine* 2013;13:275.

14 Bandara T, Uluwaduge I, Jansz ER. Bioactivity of cinnamon with special emphasis on diabetes mellitus: a review. *International Journal of Food Sciences and Nutrition* 2012;63:380–86.

15 Mullin GE. Nutraceuticals for diabetes: what is the evidence? *Nutrition in Clinical Practice* 2011;26:199–201.

16 Mullin GE, Clarke JO. Role of complementary and alternative medicine in managing gastrointestinal motility disorders. *Nutrition in Clinical Practice* 2010;25:85–87.

17 Hlebowicz J. Postprandial blood glucose response in relation to gastric emptying and satiety in healthy subjects. *Appetite* 2009;53:249–52.

18 Hlebowicz J, Darwiche G, Bjorgell O, Almer LO. Effect of cinnamon on postprandial blood glucose, gastric emptying, and satiety in healthy subjects. *American Journal of Clinical Nutrition* 2007;85:1552–56.

19 Mettler S, Schwarz I, Colombani PC. Additive postprandial blood glucose-attenuating and satiety-enhancing effect of cinnamon and acetic acid. *Nutrition Research* 2009;29:723–27.

20 Ranasinghe P, Pigera S, Premakumara GA, Galappaththy P, Constantine GR, Katulanda P. Medicinal properties of 'true' cinnamon (Cinnamomum zeylanicum): a systematic review. *BMC Complementary and Alternative Medicine* 2013;13:275.

21 Joseph SV, Edirisinghe I, Burton-Freeman BM. Berries: anti-inflammatory effects in humans. *Journal of Agricultural and Food Chemistry* 2014 Mar 17. [Epub ahead of print]

22 Rodriguez-Mateos A, Heiss C, Borges G, Crozier A. Berry (poly)phenols and cardiovascular health. *Journal of Agricultural and Food Chemistry* 2013 Oct 7. [Epub ahead of print]

23 Prior RL, S EW, T RR, Khanal RC, Wu X, Howard LR. Purified blueberry anthocyanins and blueberry juice alter development of obesity in mice fed an obesogenic high-fat diet. *Journal of Agricultural and Food Chemistry* 2010;58:3970–76.

24 Vuong T, Benhaddou-Andaloussi A, Brault A, et al. Antiobesity and antidiabetic effects of biotransformed blueberry juice in KKA(y) mice. *International Journal of Obesity* 2009;33:1166–73.

25 Vendrame S, Daugherty A, Kristo AS, Riso P, Klimis-Zacas D. Wild blueberry (Vaccinium angustifolium) consumption improves inflammatory status in the obese Zucker rat model of the metabolic syndrome. *Journal of Nutritional Biochemistry* 2013;24:1508-12.

26 Stoner GD, Wang LS, Seguin C, et al. Multiple berry types prevent N-nitrosomethylbenzylamine-induced esophageal cancer in rats. *Pharmaceutical Research* 2010;27:1138-45.

27 Song Y, Park HJ, Kang SN, et al. Blueberry peel extracts inhibit adipogenesis in 3T3-L1 cells and reduce high-fat diet-induced obesity. *PLoS One* 2013;8:e69925.

28 Ibid.

29 Moghe SS, Juma S, Imrhan V, Vijayagopal P. Effect of blueberry polyphenols on 3T3-F442A preadipocyte differentiation. *Journal of Medicinal Food* 2012;15:448-52.

30 Khanal RC, Howard LR, Wilkes SE, Rogers TJ, Prior RL. Effect of dietary blueberry pomace on selected metabolic factors associated with high fructose feeding in growing Sprague-Dawley rats. *Journal of Medicinal Food* 2012;15:802-10.

31 Roopchand DE, Kuhn P, Rojo LE, Lila MA, Raskin I. Blueberry polyphenol-enriched soybean flour reduces hyperglycemia, body weight gain and serum cholesterol in mice. *Pharmacological Research* 2013;68:59-67.

32 Stull AJ, Cash KC, Johnson WD, Champagne CM, Cefalu WT. Bioactives in blueberries improve insulin sensitivity in obese, insulin-resistant men and women. *Journal of Nutrition* 2010;140:1764-68.

33 Takikawa M, Inoue S, Horio F, Tsuda T. Dietary anthocyanin-rich bilberry extract ameliorates hyperglycemia and insulin sensitivity via activation of AMP-activated protein kinase in diabetic mice. *Journal of Nutrition* 2010;140:527-33.

34 Puupponen-Pimia R, Nohynek L, Hartmann-Schmidlin S, et al. Berry phenolics selectively inhibit the growth of intestinal pathogens. *Journal of Applied Microbiology* 2005;98:991-1000.

35 Rosillo MA, Sanchez-Hidalgo M, Cardeno A, de la Lastra CA. Protective effect of ellagic acid, a natural polyphenolic compound, in a murine model of Crohn's disease. *Biochemical Pharmacology* 2011;82:737-45.

36 Torronen R, Kolehmainen M, Sarkkinen E, Poutanen K, Mykkanen H, Niskanen L. Berries reduce postprandial insulin responses to wheat and rye breads in healthy women. *Journal of Nutrition* 2013;143:430-36.

37 Hodgson JM, Croft KD. Tea flavonoids and cardiovascular health. *Molecular Aspects of Medicine* 2010;31:495-502.

38 Mullin GE. Comment on: black and green tea consumption and the risk of coronary artery disease: a meta-analysis. *Nutrition in Clinical Practice* 2011;26(3):356.

39 Larsson SC. Coffee, tea, and cocoa and risk of stroke. *Stroke* 2014;45:309-14.

40 Larsson SC, Virtamo J, Wolk A. Black tea consumption and risk of stroke in women and men. *Annals of Epidemiology* 2013;23:157-60.

41 Bogdanski P, Suliburska J, Szulinska M, Stepien M, Pupek-Musialik D, Jablecka A. Green tea extract reduces blood pressure, inflammatory biomarkers, and oxidative stress and improves parameters associated with insulin resistance in obese, hypertensive patients. *Nutrition Research* 2012;32:421-27.

42 Suliburska J, Bogdanski P, Szulinska M, Stepien M, Pupek-Musialik D, Jablecka A. Effects of green tea supplementation on elements, total antioxidants, lipids, and glucose values in the serum of obese patients. *Biological Trace Element Research* 2012;149:315-22.

43 Hursel R, Westerterp-Plantenga MS. Catechin- and caffeine-rich teas for control of body weight in humans. *American Journal of Clinical Nutrition* 2013;98:1682S-93S.

44 Hursel R, van der Zee L, Westerterp-Plantenga MS. Effects of a breakfast yoghurt, with additional total whey protein or caseinomacropeptide-depleted alpha-lactalbumin-enriched whey protein, on diet-induced thermogenesis and appetite suppression. *British Journal of Nutrition* 2010;103:775-80.

45 Hursel R, Viechtbauer W, Westerterp-Plantenga MS. The effects of green tea on weight loss and weight maintenance: a meta-analysis. *International Journal of Obesity* 2009;33:956-61.

46 Phung OJ, Baker WL, Matthews LJ, Lanosa M, Thorne A, Coleman CI. Effect of green tea catechins with or without caffeine on anthropometric measures: a systematic review and meta-analysis. *American Journal of Clinical Nutrition* 2010;91:73-81.

47 Axling U, Olsson C, Xu J, et al. Green tea powder and Lactobacillus plantarum affect gut microbiota, lipid metabolism and inflammation in high-fat fed C57BL/6J mice. *Nutrition & Metabolism* 2012;9:105.

48 Hodgson AB, Randell RK, Jeukendrup AE. The effect of green tea extract on fat oxidation at rest and during exercise: evidence of efficacy and proposed mechanisms. *Advances in Nutrition* 2013;4:129-40.

49 Hsu TF, Kusumoto A, Abe K, et al. Polyphenol-enriched oolong tea increases fecal lipid excretion. *European Journal of Clinical Nutrition* 2006;60:1330-36.

50 Conterno L, Fava F, Viola R, Tuohy KM. Obesity and the gut microbiota: does up-regulating colonic fermentation protect against obesity and metabolic disease? *Genes & Nutrition* 2011;6:241–60.

51 Josic J, Olsson AT, Wickeberg J, Lindstedt S, Hlebowicz J. Does green tea affect postprandial glucose, insulin and satiety in healthy subjects: a randomized controlled trial. *Nutrition Journal* 2010;9:63.

52 Ali BH, Blunden G, Tanira MO, Nemmar A. Some phytochemical, pharmacological and toxicological properties of ginger (Zingiber officinale Roscoe): a review of recent research. *Food and Chemical Toxicology* 2008;46(2):409–20.

53 Haniadka R, Saldanha E, Sunita V, Palatty PL, Fayad R, Baliga MS. A review of the gastroprotective effects of ginger (Zingiber officinale Roscoe). *Food & Function* 2013;4:845–55.

54 Shobana S, Naidu KA. Antioxidant activity of selected Indian spices. *Prostaglandins, Leukotrienes, and Essential Fatty Acids* 2000;62:107–10.

55 Grzanna R, Lindmark L, Frondoza CG. Ginger—an herbal medicinal product with broad anti-inflammatory actions. *Journal of Medicinal Food* 2005;8:125–32.

56 Shobana S, Naidu KA. Antioxidant activity of selected Indian spices. *Prostaglandins, Leukotrienes, and Essential Fatty Acids* 2000;62:107–10.

57 Ramadan G, El-Menshawy O. Protective effects of ginger-turmeric rhizomes mixture on joint inflammation, atherogenesis, kidney dysfunction and other complications in a rat model of human rheumatoid arthritis. *International Journal of Rheumatic Diseases* 2013;16:219–29.

58 Eldershaw TP, Colquhoun EQ, Dora KA, Peng ZC, Clark MG. Pungent principles of ginger (Zingiber officinale) are thermogenic in the perfused rat hindlimb. *International Journal of Obesity and Related Metabolic Disorders* 1992;16:755–63.

59 Ibid.

60 Sugita J, Yoneshiro T, Hatano T, et al. Grains of paradise (Aframomum melegueta) extract activates brown adipose tissue and increases whole-body energy expenditure in men. *British Journal of Nutrition* 2013;110:733–38.

61 Mansour MS, Ni YM, Roberts AL, Kelleman M, Roychoudhury A, St-Onge MP. Ginger consumption enhances the thermic effect of food and promotes feelings of satiety without affecting metabolic and hormonal parameters in overweight men: a pilot study. *Metabolism: Clinical and Experimental* 2012;61:1347–52.

62 Henry CJ, Piggott SM. Effect of ginger on metabolic rate. *Human Nutrition Clinical Nutrition* 1987;41:89–92.

63 Balliett M, Burke JR. Changes in anthropometric measurements, body composition, blood pressure, lipid profile, and testosterone in patients participating in a low-energy dietary intervention. *Journal of Chiropractic Medicine* 2013;12:3–14.

64 Mahmoud RH, Elnour WA. Comparative evaluation of the efficacy of ginger and orlistat on obesity management, pancreatic lipase and liver peroxisomal catalase enzyme in male albino rats. *European Review for Medical and Pharmacological Sciences* 2013;17:75–83.

65 Paniagua JA, de la Sacristana AG, Sanchez E, et al. A MUFA-rich diet improves posprandial glucose, lipid and GLP-1 responses in insulin-resistant subjects. *Journal of the American College of Nutrition* 2007;26:434–44.

66 Wien M, Haddad E, Oda K, Sabate J. A randomized 3x3 crossover study to evaluate the effect of Hass avocado intake on post-ingestive satiety, glucose and insulin levels, and subsequent energy intake in overweight adults. *Nutrition Journal* 2013;12:155.

67 Nagata C, Nakamura K, Wada K, et al. Association of dietary fat, vegetables and antioxidant micronutrients with skin ageing in Japanese women. *British Journal of Nutrition* 2010;103:1493–98.

68 Cho E, Hankinson SE, Rosner B, Willett WC, Colditz GA. Prospective study of lutein/zeaxanthin intake and risk of age-related macular degeneration. *American Journal of Clinical Nutrition* 2008;87:1837–43.

69 Berti C, Riso P, Monti LD, Porrini M. In vitro starch digestibility and in vivo glucose response of gluten-free foods and their gluten counterparts. *European Journal of Nutrition* 2004;43:198–204.

70 Gomez-Caravaca AM, Iafelice G, Lavini A, Pulvento C, Caboni MF, Marconi E. Phenolic compounds and saponins in quinoa samples (Chenopodium quinoa Willd.) grown under different saline and nonsaline irrigation regimens. *Journal of Agricultural and Food Chemistry* 2012;60:4620–27.

71 Ruales J, Nair BM. Nutritional quality of the protein in quinoa (Chenopodium quinoa, Willd) seeds. *Plant Foods for Human Nutrition* 1992;42:1–11.

72 Raghavendra RH, Naidu KA. Spice active principles as the inhibitors of human platelet aggregation and thromboxane biosynthesis. *Prostaglandins, Leukotrienes, and Essential Fatty Acids* 2009;81:73–78.

73 Sayin MR, Karabag T, Dogan SM, Akpinar I, Aydin M. A case of acute myocardial infarction due to the use of cayenne pepper pills. *Wiener klinische Wochenschrift* 2012;124:285–87.

74 Ibid.

75 Sogut O, Kaya H, Gokdemir MT, Sezen Y. Acute myocardial infarction and coronary vasospasm associated with the ingestion of cayenne pepper pills in a 25-year-old male. *International Journal of Emergency Medicine* 2012;5:5.

76 Peppin JF, Pappagallo M. Capsaicinoids in the treatment of neuropathic pain: a review. *Therapeutic Advances in Neurological Disorders* 2014;7:22–32.

77 Sawynok J. Topical analgesics for neuropathic pain: Preclinical exploration, clinical validation, future development. *European Journal of Pain* 2014;18:465–81.

78 Peppin JF, Pappagallo M. Capsaicinoids in the treatment of neuropathic pain: a review. *Therapeutic Advances in Neurological Disorders* 2014;7:22–32.

79 Cameron M, Chrubasik S. Topical herbal therapies for treating osteoarthritis. *Cochrane Database of Systematic Reviews* 2013;5:CD010538.

80 Lin CH, Lu WC, Wang CW, Chan YC, Chen MK. Capsaicin induces cell cycle arrest and apoptosis in human KB cancer cells. *BMC Complementary and Alternative Medicine* 2013;13:46.

81 Whiting S, Derbyshire E, Tiwari BK. Capsaicinoids and capsinoids. A potential role for weight management? A systematic review of the evidence. *Appetite* 2012;59:341–48.

82 Kovacs EM, Mela DJ. Metabolically active functional food ingredients for weight control. *Obesity Reviews* 2006;7:59–78

83 Mercader J, Wanecq E, Chen J, Carpene C. Isopropylnorsynephrine is a stronger lipolytic agent in human adipocytes than synephrine and other amines present in Citrus aurantium. *Journal of Physiology and Biochemistry* 2011;67:443–52.

84 Davies IR, Brown JC, Livesey G. Energy values and energy balance in rats fed on supplements of guar gum or cellulose. *British Journal of Nutrition* 1991;65:41533.

85 Yoshioka M, St-Pierre S, Drapeau V, et al. Effects of red pepper on appetite and energy intake. *British Journal of Nutrition* 1999;82:115–23.

86 Whiting S, Derbyshire EJ, Tiwari B. Could capsaicinoids help to support weight management? A systematic review and meta-analysis of energy intake data. *Appetite* 2014;73:183–38.

87 Reidy PT, Walker DK, Dickinson JM, et al. Protein blend ingestion following resistance exercise promotes human muscle protein synthesis. *Journal of Nutrition* 2013;143:410–16.

88 Bowen J, Noakes M, Trenerry C, Clifton PM. Energy intake, ghrelin, and cholecystokinin after different carbohydrate and protein preloads in overweight men. *Journal of Clinical Endocrinology and Metabolism* 2006;91:1477–83.

89 Morrison CD, Xi X, White CL, Ye J, Martin RJ. Amino acids inhibit Agrp gene expression via an mTOR-dependent mechanism. *American Journal of Physiology Endocrinology and Metabolism* 2007;293:E165–E171.

90 Franceschelli A, Cappello A, Cappello G. [Retrospective study on the effects of a whey protein concentrate on body composition in 262 sarcopenic tube fed patients]. *Minerva medica* 2013;104:103–12.

91 Coker RH, Miller S, Schutzler S, Deutz N, Wolfe RR. Whey protein and essential amino acids promote the reduction of adipose tissue and increased muscle protein synthesis during caloric restriction-induced weight loss in elderly, obese individuals. *Nutrition Journal* 2012;11:105.

92 Hall WL, Millward DJ, Long SJ, Morgan LM. Casein and whey exert different effects on plasma amino acid profiles, gastrointestinal hormone secretion and appetite. *British Journal of Nutrition* 2003;89:239–48.

93 Veldhorst MA, Nieuwenhuizen AG, Hochstenbach-Waelen A, et al. Effects of complete whey-protein breakfasts versus whey without GMP-breakfasts on energy intake and satiety. *Appetite* 2009;52:388–95.

94 ——. A breakfast with alpha-lactalbumin, gelatin, or gelatin + TRP lowers energy intake at lunch compared with a breakfast with casein, soy, whey, or whey-GMP. *Clinical Nutrition* 2009;28:147–55.

95 Bowen J, Noakes M, Clifton PM. Appetite regulatory hormone responses to various dietary proteins differ by body mass index status despite similar reductions in ad libitum energy intake. *Journal of Clinical Endocrinology and Metabolism* 2006;91:2913–19.

96 Meister D, Bode J, Shand A, Ghosh S. Anti-inflammatory effects of enteral diet components on Crohn's disease-affected tissues in vitro. *Digestive and Liver Disease* 2002;34:430–38.

97 Polk DB, Hattner JA, Kerner JA, Jr. Improved growth and disease activity after intermittent administration of a defined formula diet in children with Crohn's disease. *Journal of Parenteral and Enteral Nutrition* 1992;16:499–504.

98 Benjamin J, Makharia G, Ahuja V, et al. Glutamine and whey protein improve intestinal permeability and morphology in patients with Crohn's disease: a randomized controlled trial. *Digestive Diseases and Sciences* 2012;57:1000–12.

99 Munukka E, Pekkala S, Wiklund P, et al. Gut-adipose tissue axis in hepatic fat accumulation in humans. *Journal of Hepatology* 2014;61:132–38.

100 Trujillo-de Santiago G, Saenz-Collins CP, Rojas-de Gante C. Elaboration of a probiotic oblea from whey fermented using Lactobacillus acidophilus or Bifidobacterium infantis. *Journal of Dairy Science* 2012;95:6897–904.

Chapter 6

1   Million M, Angelakis E, Paul M, Armougom F, Leibovici L, Raoult D. Comparative meta-analysis of the effect of Lactobacillus species on weight gain in humans and animals. *Microbial Pathogenesis* 2012;53:100–108.

2   Kadooka Y, Sato M, Imaizumi K, et al. Regulation of abdominal adiposity by probiotics (Lactobacillus gasseri SBT2055) in adults with obese tendencies in a randomized controlled trial. *European Journal of Clinical Nutrition* 2010;64:636–43.

3   Aronsson L, Huang Y, Parini P, et al. Decreased fat storage by Lactobacillus paracasei is associated with increased levels of angiopoietin-like 4 protein (ANGPTL4). *PLoS One* 2010;5.

4   Takemura N, Okubo T, Sonoyama K. Lactobacillus plantarum strain No. 14 reduces adipocyte size in mice fed high-fat diet. *Experimental Biology and Medicine* 2010;235:849–56.

5   Kadooka Y, Sato M, Imaizumi K, et al. Regulation of abdominal adiposity by probiotics (Lactobacillus gasseri SBT2055) in adults with obese tendencies in a randomized controlled trial. *European Journal of Clinical Nutrition* 2010;64:636–43.

6   Andreasen AS, Larsen N, Pedersen-Skovsgaard T, et al. Effects of Lactobacillus acidophilus NCFM on insulin sensitivity and the systemic inflammatory response in human subjects. *British Journal of Nutrition* 2010;104:1831–38.

7   Mullin GE. Integrative weight management. In: Bendich A, ed. *Nutrition in Health*. New York: Springer, 2014:71–106.

8   Lee HY, Park JH, Seok SH, et al. Human originated bacteria, Lactobacillus rhamnosus PL60, produce conjugated linoleic acid and show anti-obesity effects in diet-induced obese mice. *Biochimica et biophysica acta* 2006;1761:736–44.

9   Naito E, Yoshida Y, Makino K, et al. Beneficial effect of oral administration of Lactobacillus casei strain Shirota on insulin resistance in diet-induced obesity mice. *Journal of Applied Microbiology* 2011;110:650–57.

10 O'Brien PE, McPhail T, Chaston TB, Dixon JB. Systematic review of medium-term weight loss after bariatric operations. *Obesity Surgery* 2006;16:1032–40.

11 Woodard GA, Encarnacion B, Downey JR, et al. Probiotics improve outcomes after Roux-en-Y gastric bypass surgery: a prospective randomized trial. *Journal of Gastrointestinal Surgery* 2009;13:1198–204.

12 Sharifi SD, Dibamehr A, Lotfollahian H, Baurhoo B. Effects of flavomycin and probiotic supplementation to diets containing different sources of fat on growth performance, intestinal morphology, apparent metabolizable energy, and fat digestibility in broiler chickens. *Poultry Science* 2012;91:918–27.

13 Cani PD, Lecourt E, Dewulf EM, et al. Gut microbiota fermentation of prebiotics increases satietogenic and incretin gut peptide production with consequences for appetite sensation and glucose response after a meal. *American Journal of Clinical Nutrition* 2009;90:1236–43.

14 Parnell JA, Reimer RA. Weight loss during oligofructose supplementation is associated with decreased ghrelin and increased peptide YY in overweight and obese adults. *American Journal of Clinical Nutrition* 2009;89:1751–59.

15 Jakobsdottir G, Nyman M, Fak F. Designing future prebiotic fiber to target the metabolic syndrome. *Nutrition* 2013;30:497–502.

16 Arora T, Singh S, Sharma RK. Probiotics: Interaction with gut microbiome and antiobesity potential. *Nutrition* 2013;29:591–96.

17 Lawton CL, Walton J, Hoyland A, et al. Short term (14 days) consumption of insoluble wheat bran fibre-containing breakfast cereals improves subjective digestive feelings, general wellbeing and bowel function in a dose dependent manner. *Nutrients* 2013;5:1436–55.

18 Delzenne NM, Neyrinck AM, Cani PD. Modulation of the gut microbiota by nutrients with prebiotic properties: consequences for host health in the context of obesity and metabolic syndrome. *Microbial Cell Factories* 2011;10(Suppl 1):S10.

19 Delzenne NM, Neyrinck AM, Backhed F, Cani PD. Targeting gut microbiota in obesity: effects of prebiotics and probiotics. *Nature Reviews Endocrinology* 2011;7:639–46.

20 Cani PD, Osto M, Geurts L, Everard A. Involvement of gut microbiota in the development of low-grade inflammation and type 2 diabetes associated with obesity. *Gut Microbes* 2012;3:279–88.

21 Fallucca F, Porrata C, Fallucca S, Pianesi M. Influence of diet on gut microbiota, inflammation and type 2 diabetes mellitus. First experience with macrobiotic Ma-Pi 2 diet. *Diabetes/Metabolism Research and Reviews* 2014;30(Suppl 1):48–54.

22 Xiao S, Fei N, Pang X, et al. A gut microbiota-targeted dietary intervention for amelioration of chronic inflammation underlying metabolic syndrome. *FEMS Microbiology Ecology* 2014;87:357–67.

23 Ray K. Gut microbiota: microbial metabolites feed into the gut-brain-gut circuit during host metabolism. *Nature Reviews Gastroenterology & Hepatology* 2014;11:76.

24 Umu OC, Oostindjer M, Pope PB, et al. Potential applications of gut microbiota to control human physiology. *Antonie van Leeuwenhoek* 2013;104:609–18.

25 Cani PD, Joly E, Horsmans Y, Delzenne NM. Oligofructose promotes satiety in healthy humans: a pilot study. *European Journal of Clinical Nutrition* 2006;60:567–72.

26 Davis W. *Wheat Belly.* New York: Rodale, 2011.

27 Perlmutter D. *Grain Brain.* New York: Little, Brown and Co., 2013.

28 Fasano A. Zonulin, regulation of tight junctions, and autoimmune diseases. *Annals of the New York Academy of Sciences* 2012;1258:25–33.

29 wypr.publicbroadcasting.net/midday.html.

30 Biesiekierski JR, Peters SL, Newnham ED, Rosella O, Muir JG, Gibson PR. No effects of gluten in patients with self-reported non-celiac gluten sensitivity after dietary reduction of fermentable, poorly absorbed, short-chain carbohydrates. *Gastroenterology* 2013;145:320–8 e1-3.

31 Carroccio A, Brusca I, Mansueto P, et al. A comparison between two different in vitro basophil activation tests for gluten- and cow's milk protein sensitivity in irritable bowel syndrome (IBS)-like patients. *Clinical Chemistry and Laboratory Medicine* 2012:1–7.

32 Sanz Y. Effects of a gluten-free diet on gut microbiota and immune function in healthy adult humans. *Gut Microbes* 2010;1:135–37.

33 Halmos EP, Christophersen CT, Bird AR, Shepherd SJ, Gibson PR, Muir JG. Diets that differ in their FODMAP content alter the colonic luminal microenvironment. *Gut* 2014 Jul 12. [Epub ahead of print]

34 Bao Y, Han J, Hu FB, et al. Association of nut consumption with total and cause-specific mortality. *New England Journal of Medicine* 2013;369:2001–11.

35 Gulati S, Misra A, Pandey RM, Bhatt SP, Saluja S. Effects of pistachio nuts on body composition, metabolic, inflammatory and oxidative stress parameters in Asian Indians with metabolic syndrome: a 24-wk, randomized control trial. *Nutrition* 2014;30:192–97.

36 Liu Z, Lin X, Huang G, Zhang W, Rao P, Ni L. Prebiotic effects of almonds and almond skins on intestinal microbiota in healthy adult humans. *Anaerobe* 2014;26:1–6.

37 Ibid.

38 Tan SY, Dhillon J, Mattes RD. A review of the effects of nuts on appetite, food intake, metabolism, and body weight. *American Journal of Clinical Nutrition* 2014;100:412S–422S.

39 David LA, Maurice CF, Carmody RN, et al. Diet rapidly and reproducibly alters the human gut microbiome. *Nature* 2014;505:559–63.

40 Ray K. Gut microbiota: Adding weight to the microbiota's role in obesity—exposure to antibiotics early in life can lead to increased adiposity. *Nature Reviews Gastroenterology & Hepatology* 2012;9:615.

41 Tolstrup JS, Halkjaer J, Heitmann BL, et al. Alcohol drinking frequency in relation to subsequent changes in waist circumference. *American Journal of Clinical Nutrition* 2008;87:957–63.

42 Goldberg IJ, Mosca L, Piano MR, Fisher EA. AHA Science Advisory. Wine and your heart: A science advisory for healthcare professionals from the Nutrition Committee, Council on Epidemiology and Prevention, and Council on Cardiovascular Nursing of the American Heart Association. *Stroke* 2001;32:591–94.

43 Wannamethee SG, Shaper AG. Alcohol, body weight, and weight gain in middle-aged men. *American Journal of Clinical Nutrition* 2003;77:1312–17.

44 Fischer-Posovszky P, Kukulus V, Tews D, et al. Resveratrol regulates human adipocyte number and function in a Sirt1-dependent manner. *American Journal of Clinical Nutrition* 2010;92:5–15.

45 Pal S, Naissides M, Mamo J. Polyphenolics and fat absorption. *International Journal of Obesity and Related Metabolic Disorders* 2004;28:324–26.

46 Mutlu EA, Gillevet PM, Rangwala H, et al. Colonic microbiome is altered in alcoholism. *American Journal of Physiology: Gastrointestinal and Liver Physiology* 2012;302:G966–G978.

47 Mutlu E, Keshavarzian A, Engen P, Forsyth CB, Sikaroodi M, Gillevet P. Intestinal dysbiosis: a possible mechanism of alcohol-induced endotoxemia and alcoholic steatohepatitis in rats. *Alcoholism, Clinical and Experimental Research* 2009;33:1836–46.

48 Clemente-Postigo M, Queipo-Ortuno MI, Boto-Ordonez M, et al. Effect of acute and chronic red wine consumption on lipopolysaccharide concentrations. *American Journal of Clinical Nutrition* 2013;97:1053–61.

49 Riserus U, Ingelsson E. Alcohol intake, insulin resistance, and abdominal obesity in elderly men. *Obesity* 2007;15:1766–73.

50 Andreasen AS, Larsen N, Pedersen-Skovsgaard T, et al. Effects of Lactobacillus acidophilus NCFM on insulin sensitivity and the systemic inflammatory response in human subjects. *British Journal of Nutrition* 2010;104:1831–38.

51 Delzenne NM, Neyrinck AM, Backhed F, Cani PD. Targeting gut microbiota in obesity: effects of prebiotics and probiotics. *Nature Reviews Endocrinology* 2011;7:639–46.

52 Nagpal R, Kumar A, Kumar M, Behare PV, Jain S, Yadav H. Probiotics, their health benefits and applications for developing healthier foods: a review. *FEMS Microbiology Letters* 2012;334:1–15.

53 Yadav H, Lee JH, Lloyd J, Walter P, Rane SG. Beneficial metabolic effects of a probiotic via butyrate-induced GLP-1 hormone secretion. *Journal of Biological Chemistry* 2013;288:25088–97.

54 Kang JH, Yun SI, Park MH, Park JH, Jeong SY, Park HO. Anti-obesity effect of Lactobacillus gasseri BNR17 in high-sucrose diet-induced obese mice. *PLoS One* 2013;8:e54617.

55 Savignac HM, Corona G, Mills H, et al. Prebiotic feeding elevates central brain derived neurotrophic factor, N-methyl-D-aspartate receptor subunits and D-serine. *Neurochemistry International* 2013;63:756–64.

56 Chen SC, Lin YH, Huang HP, Hsu WL, Houng JY, Huang CK. Effect of conjugated linoleic acid supplementation on weight loss and body fat composition in a Chinese population. *Nutrition* 2012;28:559–65.

57 Katz SE. *The Art of Fermentation.* White River Junction, VT: Chelsea Green Publishing, 2012.

58 naturalnews.com/045791_all_natural_yogurt_aspartame_yoplait.html

59 Dhiman TR, Satter LD, Pariza MW, Galli MP, Albright K, Tolosa MX. Conjugated linoleic acid (CLA) content of milk from cows offered diets rich in linoleic and linolenic acid. *Journal of Dairy Science* 2000;83:1016–27.

60 Mullin GE, Belkoff SM. Survey of lactose maldigestion among raw milk drinkers. *Global Advances in Health and Medicine* (In press, August 2014).

61 cdc.gov/media/releases/2014/a1210-raw-milk.html

62 medpagetoday.com/MeetingCoverage/ICAAC/41531.

63 fda.gov/Food/ResourcesForYou/consumers/ucm079516.htm.

64 Moss M. *Salt Sugar Fat: How the Food Giants Hooked Us.* New York: Random House, 2013.

65 Li F, Hullar MA, Schwarz Y, Lampe JW. Human gut bacterial communities are altered by addition of cruciferous vegetables to a controlled fruit- and vegetable-free diet. *Journal of Nutrition* 2009;139:1685–91.

Chapter 7

1 fatsecret.com/calories-nutrition/usda/oat-bran?portionid=40316&portionamount=0.250.

2 Brown L, Rosner B, Willett WW, Sacks FM. Cholesterol-lowering effects of dietary fiber: a meta-analysis. *American Journal of Clinical Nutrition* 1999;69:30–42.

3 Kwiterovich PO, Jr. The role of fiber in the treatment of hypercholesterolemia in children and adolescents. *Pediatrics* 1995;96:1005–9.

4 Bazzano LA, He J, Ogden LG, et al. Dietary fiber intake and reduced risk of coronary heart disease in US men and women: the National Health and Nutrition Examination Survey I Epidemiologic Follow-up Study. *Archives of Internal Medicine* 2003;163:1897–904.

5 Anderson JW. Whole grains and coronary heart disease: the whole kernel of truth. *American Journal of Clinical Nutrition* 2004;80:1459–60.

6 van Dam RM, Hu FB, Rosenberg L, Krishnan S, Palmer JR. Dietary calcium and magnesium, major food sources, and risk of type 2 diabetes in U.S. black women. *Diabetes Care* 2006;29:2238–43.

7 Tsikitis VL, Albina JE, Reichner JS. Beta-glucan affects leukocyte navigation in a complex chemotactic gradient. *Surgery* 2004;136:384–89.

8 Suzuki R, Rylander-Rudqvist T, Ye W, Saji S, Adlercreutz H, Wolk A. Dietary fiber intake and risk of postmenopausal breast cancer defined by estrogen and progesterone receptor status–a prospective cohort study among Swedish women. *International Journal of Cancer* 2008;122:403–12.

9 Tabak C, Wijga AH, de Meer G, Janssen NA, Brunekreef B, Smit HA. Diet and asthma in Dutch school children (ISAAC-2). *Thorax* 2006;61:1048–53.

10 Al-Waili NS, Salom K, Butler G, Al Ghamdi AA. Honey and microbial infections: a review supporting the use of honey for microbial control. *Journal of Medicinal Food* 2011;14:1079–96.

11 Othman NH. Honey and cancer: sustainable inverse relationship particularly for developing nations—a review. *Evidence-based Complementary and Alternative Medicine* 2012;2012:410406.

12 Ansorge S, Reinhold D, Lendeckel U. Propolis and some of its constituents down-regulate DNA synthesis and inflammatory cytokine production but induce TGF-beta1 production of human immune cells. *Zeitschrift fur Naturforschung Section C: Biosciences* 2003;58:580–89.

13 Al-Waili NS. Identification of nitric oxide metabolites in various honeys: effects of intravenous honey on plasma and urinary nitric oxide metabolites concentrations. *Journal of Medicinal Food* 2003;6:359–64.

14 Wong D, Alandejani T, Javer AR. Evaluation of Manuka honey in the management of allergic fungal rhinosinusitis. *Journal of Otolaryngology, Head & Neck Surgery* 2011;40:E19–E21.

15 Israili ZH. Antimicrobial properties of honey. *American Journal of Therapeutics* 2013;21:304–23.

16 Kapoor S. Systemic benefits and potential uses of tualang honey in addition to its beneficial effects on postmenopausal bone structure. *Clinics* 2012;67:1345.

17 Pecanac M, Janjic Z, Komarcevic A, Pajic M, Dobanovacki D, Miskovic SS. Burns treatment in ancient times. *Medicinski pregled* 2013;66:263–67.

18 Fashner J, Ericson K, Werner S. Treatment of the common cold in children and adults. *American Family Physician* 2012;86:153–59.

19 Erejuwa OO, Sulaiman SA, Wahab MS. Honey—a novel antidiabetic agent. *International Journal of Biological Sciences* 2012;8:913–34.

20 O'Meara S, Al-Kurdi D, Ologun Y, Ovington LG, Martyn-St James M, Richardson R. Antibiotics and antiseptics for venous leg ulcers. *Cochrane Database of Systematic Reviews* 2014;1:CD003557.

21 Burlando B, Cornara L. Honey in dermatology and skin care: a review. *Journal of Cosmetic Dermatology* 2013;12:306–13.

22 Majtan J. Honey: An immunomodulator in wound healing. *Wound Repair and Regeneration* 2014;22:187–92.

23 Sabater-Molina M, Larque E, Torrella F, Zamora S. Dietary fructooligosaccharides and potential benefits on health. *Journal of Physiology and Biochemistry* 2009;65:315–28.

24 Gautam M, Saha S, Bani S, et al. Immunomodulatory activity of Asparagus racemosus on systemic Th1/Th2 immunity: implications for immunoadjuvant potential. *Journal of Ethnopharmacology* 2009;121:241–47.

25 Shao Y, Chin CK, Ho CT, Ma W, Garrison SA, Huang MT. Anti-tumor activity of the crude saponins obtained from asparagus. *Cancer Letters* 1996;104:31–36.

26 Negi JS, Singh P, Joshi GP, Rawat MS, Bisht VK. Chemical constituents of Asparagus. *Pharmacognosy Reviews* 2010;4:215–20.

27 Kumar MC, Udupa AL, Sammodavardhana K, Rathnakar UP, Shvetha U, Kodancha GP. Acute toxicity and diuretic studies of the roots of Asparagus racemosus Willd in rats. *West Indian Medical Journal* 2010;59:3–6.

28 Sun T, Powers JR, Tang J. Enzyme-catalyzed change of antioxidants content and antioxidant activity of asparagus juice. *Journal of Agricultural and Food Chemistry* 2007;55:56–60.

29 diabetes-guide.org/american-diabetes-association-diet.htm.

30 heart.org/HEARTORG/GettingHealthy/NutritionCenter/HealthyCooking/Bean-Benefits_UCM_430105_Article.jsp.

31 centralbean.com/beans-and-your-health/beans-and-cancer/.

32 Sarmento A, Barros L, Fernandes A, Carvalho AM, Ferreira IC. Valorisation of traditional foods: nutritional and bioactive properties of Cicer arietinum L. and Lathyrus sativus L. pulses. *Journal of the Science of Food and Agriculture* 2014 Apr 18. [Epub ahead of print]

33 nutritiondata.self.com/facts/legumes-and-legume-products/4284/2.

34 Riccioni G, Sblendorio V, Gemello E, et al. Dietary fibers and cardiometabolic diseases. *International Journal of Molecular Sciences* 2012;13:1524–40.

35 Hallikainen M, Halonen J, Konttinen J, et al. Diet and cardiovascular health in asymptomatic normo- and mildly-to-moderately hypercholesterolemic participants—baseline data from the BLOOD FLOW intervention study. *Nutrition & Metabolism* 2013;10:62.

36 Paper-behind-the-green-coffee-bean-diet-craze-retracted, washingtonpost.com/news/to-your-health/wp/2014/10/22/researchers-retract-bogus-dr-oz-touted-study-on-green-coffee-bean-weight-loss-pills/

37 Espinosa-Alonso LG, Lygin A, Widholm JM, Valverde ME, Paredes-Lopez O. Polyphenols in wild and weedy Mexican common beans (Phaseolus vulgaris L.). *Journal of Agricultural and Food Chemistry* 2006;54:4436–44.

38 Zhang C, Monk JM, Lu JT, et al. Cooked navy and black bean diets improve biomarkers of colon health and reduce inflammation during colitis. *British Journal of Nutrition* 2014:1–15.

39 Preuss HG. Bean amylase inhibitor and other carbohydrate absorption blockers: effects on diabesity and general health. *Journal of the American College of Nutrition* 2009;28:266–76.

40 Tonstad S, Malik N, Haddad E. A high-fibre bean-rich diet versus a low-carbohydrate diet for obesity. *Journal of Human Nutrition and Dietetics* 2014;27 Suppl 2:109–16.

41 Hermsdorff HH, Zulet MA, Abete I, Martinez JA. A legume-based hypocaloric diet reduces proinflammatory status and improves metabolic features in overweight/obese subjects. *European Journal of Nutrition* 2011;50:61–69.

42 Queiroz Kda S, de Oliveira AC, Helbig E, Reis SM, Carraro F. Soaking the common bean in a domestic preparation reduced the contents of raffinose-type oligosaccharides but did not interfere with nutritive value. *Journal of Nutritional Science and Vitaminology* 2002;48:283–89.

43 Higdon JV, Delage B, Williams DE, Dashwood RH. Cruciferous vegetables and human cancer risk: epidemiologic evidence and mechanistic basis. *Pharmacological Research* 2007;55:224-36.

44 Kahlon TS, Chiu MC, Chapman MH. Steam cooking significantly improves in vitro bile acid binding of collard greens, kale, mustard greens, broccoli, green bell pepper, and cabbage. *Nutrition Research* 2008;28:351-57.

45 Cook NR, Appel LJ, Whelton PK. Lower levels of sodium intake and reduced cardiovascular risk. *Circulation* 2014;129:981-89.

46 Whelton PK, He J. Health effects of sodium and potassium in humans. *Current Opinion in Lipidology* 2014;25:75-79.

47 consumer.healthday.com/public-health-information-30/centers-for-disease-control-news-120/cdc-salt-guidelines-too-low-for-good-health-study-suggests-686408.html.

48 Zhu H, Pollock NK, Kotak I, et al. Dietary sodium, adiposity, and inflammation in healthy adolescents. *Pediatrics* 2014;133:e635–e642.

49 Kleinewietfeld M, Manzel A, Titze J, et al. Sodium chloride drives autoimmune disease by the induction of pathogenic TH17 cells. *Nature* 2013;496:518–22.

50 Wu C, Yosef N, Thalhamer T, et al. Induction of pathogenic TH17 cells by inducible salt-sensing kinase SGK1. *Nature* 2013;496:513–17.

51 Rodrigues Telini LS, de Carvalho Beduschi G, Caramori JC, Castro JH, Martin LC, Barretti P. Effect of dietary sodium restriction on body water, blood pressure, and inflammation in hemodialysis patients: a prospective randomized controlled study. *International Urology and Nephrology* 2014;46:91–97.

52 Kokubo Y, Iso H, Ishihara J, et al. Association of dietary intake of soy, beans, and isoflavones with risk of cerebral and myocardial infarctions in Japanese populations: the Japan Public Health Center-based (JPHC) study cohort I. *Circulation* 2007;116:2553–62.

53 Lee M, Chae S, Cha Y, Park Y. Supplementation of Korean fermented soy paste doenjang reduces visceral fat in overweight subjects with mutant uncoupling protein-1 allele. *Nutrition Research* 2012;32:8–14.

54 Tai MW, Sweet BV. Nattokinase for prevention of thrombosis. *American Journal of Health-System Pharmacy* 2006;63:1121–23.

55 Jungbauer A, Medjakovic S. Phytoestrogens and the metabolic syndrome. *Journal of Steroid Biochemistry and Molecular Biology* 2013;139:277–89.

56 Torre-Villalvazo I, Tovar AR, Ramos-Barragan VE, Cerbon-Cervantes MA, Torres N. Soy protein ameliorates metabolic abnormalities in liver and adipose tissue of rats fed a high fat diet. *Journal of Nutrition* 2008;138:462–68.

57 Lukaszuk JM, Luebbers P, Gordon BA. Preliminary study: soy milk as effective as skim milk in promoting weight loss. *Journal of the American Dietetic Association* 2007;107:1811–14.

58 Fabian E, Elmadfa I. Influence of daily consumption of probiotic and conventional yoghurt on the plasma lipid profile in young healthy women. *Annals of Nutrition & Metabolism* 2006;50:387–93.

59 Cheng S, Lyytikainen A, Kroger H, et al. Effects of calcium, dairy product, and vitamin D supplementation on bone mass accrual and body composition in 10-12-y-old girls: a 2-y randomized trial. *American Journal of Clinical Nutrition* 2005;82:1115-26; quiz 47-48.

60 Donovan SM, Shamir R. Introduction to the Yogurt in Nutrition Initiative and the First Global Summit on the Health Effects of Yogurt. *American Journal of Clinical Nutrition* 2014;99(Suppl):1209S-1211S.

61 Jones K. Probiotics: preventing antibiotic-associated diarrhea. *Journal for Specialists in Pediatric Nursing* 2010;15:160-62.

62 Guyonnet D, Woodcock A, Stefani B, Trevisan C, Hall C. Fermented milk containing Bifidobacterium lactis DN-173 010 improved self-reported digestive comfort amongst a general population of adults. A randomized, open-label, controlled, pilot study. *Journal of Digestive Diseases* 2009;10:61-70.

63 Caglar E, Kargul B, Tanboga I. Bacteriotherapy and probiotics' role on oral health. *Oral Diseases* 2005;11:131–37.

64 Pala V, Sieri S, Berrino F, et al. Yogurt consumption and risk of colorectal cancer in the Italian European prospective investigation into cancer and nutrition cohort. *International Journal of Cancer* 2011;129:2712–19.

65 biomedcentral.com/1741-7015/12/215

66 O'Connor LM, Lentjes MA, Luben RN, Khaw KT, Wareham NJ, Forouhi NG. Dietary dairy product intake and incident type 2 diabetes: a prospective study using dietary data from a 7-day food diary. *Diabetologia* 2014;57:909–17.

67 Rebello CJ, Liu AG, Greenway FL, Dhurandhar NV. Dietary strategies to increase satiety. *Advances in Food and Nutrition Research* 2013;69:105–82.

68 Chung KH, Shin KO, Yoon JA, Choi KS. Study on the obesity and nutrition status of housewives in Seoul and Kyunggi area. *Nutrition Research and Practice* 2011;5:140–49.

69 Chang BJ, Park SU, Jang YS, et al. Effect of functional yogurt NY-YP901 in improving the trait of metabolic syndrome. *European Journal of Clinical Nutrition* 2011;65:1250–55.

70 Diepvens K, Soenen S, Steijns J, Arnold M, Westerterp-Plantenga M. Long-term effects of consumption of a novel fat emulsion in relation to body-weight management. *International Journal of Obesity* 2007;31:942–49.

71 Zemel MB, Richards J, Mathis S, Milstead A, Gebhardt L, Silva E. Dairy augmentation of total and central fat loss in obese subjects. *International Journal of Obesity* 2005;29:391–97.

72 Martinez-Gonzalez MA, Sayon-Orea C, Ruiz-Canela M, de la Fuente C, Gea A, Bes-Rastrollo M. Yogurt consumption, weight change and risk of overweight/obesity: the SUN cohort study. *Nutrition, Metabolism, and Cardiovascular Diseases*: NMCD November 2014, vol. 24, issue 11:1189–96.

73 Carlsson M, Gustafson Y, Haglin L, Eriksson S. The feasibility of serving liquid yoghurt supplemented with probiotic bacteria, Lactobacillus rhamnosus LB 21, and Lactococcus lactis L1A–a pilot study among old people with dementia in a residential care facility. *Journal of Nutrition, Health & Aging* 2009;13:813–19.

74 Mason C, Xiao L, Imayama I, et al. Vitamin D_3 supplementation during weight loss: a double-blind randomized controlled trial. *American Journal of Clinical Nutrition* 2014;99:1015–25.

75 Anderson GH, Luhovyy B, Akhavan T, Panahi S. Milk proteins in the regulation of body weight, satiety, food intake and glycemia. *Nestlé Nutrition Workshop Series Paediatric Programme* 2011;67:147–59.

76 Ludwig DS, Willett WC. Three daily servings of reduced-fat milk: an evidence-based recommendation? *JAMA Pediatrics* 2013;167:788–89.

77 Martinez-Gonzalez MA et al. Yogurt consumption, weight change and risk of overweight/obesity; Louie JC, Flood VM, Hector DJ, Rangan AM, Gill TP. Dairy consumption and overweight and obesity: a systematic review of prospective cohort studies. *Obesity Reviews*: an official journal of the International Association for the Study of Obesity 2011;12:e582–592.

78 aboutyogurt.com/Live-Culture.

79 Patterson E, Larsson SC, Wolk A, Akesson A. Association between dairy food consumption and risk of myocardial infarction in women differs by type of dairy food. *Journal of Nutrition* 2013;143:74–79.

80 Soedamah-Muthu SS, Ding EL, Al-Delaimy WK, et al. Milk and dairy consumption and incidence of cardiovascular diseases and all-cause mortality: dose-response meta-analysis of prospective cohort studies. *American Journal of Clinical Nutrition* 2011;93:158–71.

81 Dalmeijer GW, Struijk EA, van der Schouw YT, et al. Dairy intake and coronary heart disease or stroke–a population-based cohort study. *International Journal of Cardiology* 2013;167:925–29.

82 aboutyogurt.com/Live-Culture.

83 Lopitz-Otsoa F, Rementeria A, Elguezabal N, Garaizar J. Kefir: a symbiotic yeasts-bacteria community with alleged healthy capabilities. *Revista iberoamericana de micologia* 2006;23:67–74.

84 Margulis L, Sagan D, Thomas L. *Microcosmos: Four Billion Years of Microbial Evolution.* Berkeley: University of California Press, 1997.

85 de Oliveira Leite AM, Miguel MA, Peixoto RS, Rosado AS, Silva JT, Paschoalin VM. Microbiological, technological and therapeutic properties of kefir: a natural probiotic beverage. *Brazilian Journal of Microbiology* 2013;44:341–49.

86 Kabeerdoss J, Devi RS, Mary RR, et al. Effect of yoghurt containing Bifidobacterium lactis Bb12(R) on faecal excretion of secretory immunoglobulin A and human beta-defensin 2 in healthy adult volunteers. *Nutrition Journal* 2011;10:138.

87 Grishina A, Kulikova I, Alieva L, Dodson A, Rowland I, Jin J. Antigenotoxic effect of kefir and ayran supernatants on fecal water-induced DNA damage in human colon cells. *Nutrition and Cancer* 2011; 63:73–79.

88 Chen YP, Lee TY, Hong WS, Hsieh HH, Chen MJ. Effects of Lactobacillus kefiranofaciens M1 isolated from kefir grains on enterohemorrhagic Escherichia coli infection using mouse and intestinal cell models. *Journal of Dairy Science* 2013;96:7467–77.

89 Hertzler SR, Clancy SM. Kefir improves lactose digestion and tolerance in adults with lactose maldigestion. *Journal of the American Dietetic Association* 2003;103:582–87.

90 Furuno T, Nakanishi M. Kefiran suppresses antigen-induced mast cell activation. *Biological & Pharmaceutical Bulletin* 2012;35:178–83.

91 Liu JR, Wang SY, Lin YY, Lin CW. Antitumor activity of milk kefir and soy milk kefir in tumor-bearing mice. *Nutrition and Cancer* 2002;44:183–87.

92 Ishida Y, Nakamura F, Kanzato H, et al. Effect of milk fermented with Lactobacillus acidophilus strain L-92 on symptoms of Japanese cedar pollen allergy: a randomized placebo-controlled trial. *Bioscience, Biotechnology, and Biochemistry* 2005;69:1652–60.

93 Anderson JW, Gilliland SE. Effect of fermented milk (yogurt) containing Lactobacillus acidophilus L1 on serum cholesterol in hypercholesterolemic humans. *Journal of the American College of Nutrition* 1999;18:43–50.

94 Guzel-Seydim ZB, Kok-Tas T, Greene AK, Seydim AC. Review: functional properties of kefir. *Critical Reviews in Food Science and Nutrition* 2011;51:261–68.

95 Ho JN, Choi JW, Lim WC, Kim MK, Lee IY, Cho HY. Kefir inhibits 3T3-L1 adipocyte differentiation through down-regulation of adipogenic transcription factor expression. *Journal of the Science of Food and Agriculture* 2012;93:485–90.

96 Park KY, Jeong JK, Lee YE, Daily JW, 3rd. Health benefits of kimchi (Korean fermented vegetables) as a probiotic food. *Journal of Medicinal Food* 2014;17:6–20.

97 Yoon JY, Kim SH, Jung KO, Park KY. Antiobesity effect of baek-kimchi (whitish baechu kimchi) in rats fed high fat diet. *Journal of Food Science and Nutrition* 2004;9:259–64.

98 Choi SH, Suh BS, Kozukue E, Kozukue N, Levin CE, Friedman M. Analysis of the contents of pungent compounds in fresh Korean red peppers and in pepper-containing foods. *Journal of Agricultural and Food Chemistry* 2006;54:9024–31.

99 Ahn SJ. The effect of kimchi powder supplement on the body weight reduction of obese adult women [MS thesis]. Busan, Korea: Pusan National University, 2007.

100 Kim EK, An SY, Lee MS, et al. Fermented kimchi reduces body weight and improves metabolic parameters in overweight and obese patients. *Nutrition Research* 2011;31:436–43.

101 Kwon M J C, Song YS, Song YO. Daily kimchi consumption and its hypolipidemic effect in middle-aged men. *Journal of the Korean Society of Food Science and Nutrition* 1998;28:1144–50.

102 Park K. The nutritional evaluation, and antimutagenic and anticancer effects of kimchi. *Journal of the Korean Society of Food Science and Nutrition* 1995;24:169–82.

103 Kim KH, Park KY. Effects of kimchi extracts on production of nitric oxide by activated macrophages, transforming growth factor β1 of tumor cells and interleukin-6 in splenocytes. *Journal of Food Science and Nutrition* 2001;6:126–32.

104 Ngo ST, Li MS. Curcumin binds to Abeta1-40 peptides and fibrils stronger than ibuprofen and naproxen. *Journal of Physical Chemistry B* 2012;116:10165–75.

105 Asher GN, Spelman K. Clinical utility of curcumin extract. *Alternative Therapies in Health and Medicine* 2013;19:20–22.

106 Ginter E, Simko V. Plant polyphenols in prevention of heart disease. *Bratislavske lekarske listy* 2012;113:476–80.

107 Bereswill S, Munoz M, Fischer A, et al. Anti-inflammatory effects of resveratrol, curcumin and simvastatin in acute small intestinal inflammation. *PLoS One* 2010;5:e15099.

108 Ejaz A, Wu D, Kwan P, Meydani M. Curcumin inhibits adipogenesis in 3T3-L1 adipocytes and angiogenesis and obesity in $C5_{7/B}L$ mice. *Journal of Nutrition* 2009;139:919–25.

109 Yu Y, Hu SK, Yan H. [The study of insulin resistance and leptin resistance on the model of simplicity obesity rats by curcumin]. *Zhonghua yu fang yi xue za zhi* [Chinese Journal of Preventive Medicine] 2008;42:818–22.

110 Weisberg SP, Leibel R, Tortoriello DV. Dietary curcumin significantly improves obesity-associated inflammation and diabetes in mouse models of diabesity. *Endocrinology* 2008;149:3549–58.

111 Cao H. Adipocytokines in obesity and metabolic disease. *Journal of Endocrinology* 2014;220:T47–T59.

112 Ouchi N, Parker JL, Lugus JJ, Walsh K. Adipokines in inflammation and metabolic disease. *Nature Reviews Immunology* 2011;11:8597.

113 Kim CY, Kim KH. Curcumin prevents leptin-induced tight junction dysfunction in intestinal Caco-2 BBe cells. *Journal of Nutritional Biochemistry* 2014;25:26–35.

114 Mangge H, Summers K, Almer G, et al. Antioxidant food supplements and obesity-related inflammation. *Current Medicinal Chemistry* 2013;20:2330–37.

115 Jang EM, Choi MS, Jung UJ, et al. Beneficial effects of curcumin on hyperlipidemia and insulin resistance in high-fat-fed hamsters. *Metabolism: Clinical and Experimental* 2008;57:1576–83.

116 Tang Y, Chen A. Curcumin eliminates the effect of advanced glycation end-products (AGEs) on the divergent regulation of gene expression of receptors of AGEs by interrupting leptin signaling. *Laboratory Investigation* 2014;94:503–16.

117 Lee YK, Lee WS, Hwang JT, Kwon DY, Surh YJ, Park OJ. Curcumin exerts antidifferentiation effect through AMPKalpha-PPAR-gamma in 3T3-L1 adipocytes and antiproliferatory effect through AMPKalpha-COX-2 in cancer cells. *Journal of Agricultural and Food Chemistry* 2009;57:305–10.

118 Dagon Y, Avraham Y, Berry EM. AMPK activation regulates apoptosis, adipogenesis, and lipolysis by eIF2alpha in adipocytes. *Biochemical and Biophysical Research Communications* 2006;340:43–47.

119 Al-Suhaimi EA, Al-Riziza NA, Al-Essa RA. Physiological and therapeutical roles of ginger and turmeric on endocrine functions. *American Journal of Chinese Medicine* 2011;39:215–31.

120 Jang EM, Choi MS, Jung UJ, et al. Beneficial effects of curcumin on hyperlipidemia and insulin resistance in high-fat-fed hamsters. *Metabolism: Clinical and Experimental* 2008;57:1576–83.

121 Shin SK, Ha TY, McGregor RA, Choi MS. Long-term curcumin administration protects against atherosclerosis via hepatic regulation of lipoprotein cholesterol metabolism. *Molecular Nutrition & Food Research* 2011;55:1829–40.

122 Soni KB, Kuttan R. Effect of oral curcumin administration on serum peroxides and cholesterol levels in human volunteers. *Indian Journal of Physiology and Pharmacology* 1992;36:273–75.

123 Ibid.

124 Jaruszewski KM, Curran GL, Swaminathan SK, et al. Multimodal nanoprobes to target cerebrovascular amyloid in Alzheimer's disease brain. *Biomaterials* 2014;35:1967–76.

125 vinegarworkswonders.com/history.asp.

126 Johnston CS, Gaas CA. Vinegar: medicinal uses and antiglycemic effect. *Medscape General Medicine* 2006;8:61.

127 Johnston CS, Kim CM, Buller AJ. Vinegar improves insulin sensitivity to a high-carbohydrate meal in subjects with insulin resistance or type 2 diabetes. *Diabetes Care* 2004;27:281–82.

128 Gambon DL, Brand HS, Veerman EC. [Unhealthy weight loss. Erosion by apple cider vinegar]. *Nederlands tijdschrift voor tandheelkunde* 2012;119:589–91.

129 Tong LT, Katakura Y, Kawamura S, et al. Effects of Kurozu concentrated liquid on adipocyte size in rats. *Lipids in Health and Disease* 2010;9:134.

130 Kondo T, Kishi M, Fushimi T, Ugajin S, Kaga T. Vinegar intake reduces body weight, body fat mass, and serum triglyceride levels in obese Japanese subjects. *Bioscience, Biotechnology, and Biochemistry* 2009;73:1837–43.

131 Mushref MA, Srinivasan S. Effect of high fat-diet and obesity on gastrointestinal motility. *Annals of Translational Medicine* 2013;1:14.

132 Lee JH, Cho HD, Jeong JH, et al. New vinegar produced by tomato suppresses adipocyte differentiation and fat accumulation in 3T3-L1 cells and obese rat model. *Food Chemistry* 2013;141:3241–49.

133 Kondo T, Kishi M, Fushimi T, Kaga T. Acetic acid upregulates the expression of genes for fatty acid oxidation enzymes in liver to suppress body fat accumulation. *Journal of Agricultural and Food Chemistry* 2009;57:5982–86.

Chapter 8

1 webmd.com/diet/grapefruit-diet.

2 Ayyad C, Andersen T. Long-term efficacy of dietary treatment of obesity: a systematic review of studies published between 1931 and 1999. *Obesity Reviews* 2000;1:113–19.

3 Anderson JW, Konz EC, Frederich RC, Wood CL. Long-term weight-loss maintenance: a meta-analysis of US studies. *American Journal of Clinical Nutrition* 2001;74:579–84.

4 Lagerros YT, Rossner S. Obesity management: what brings success? *Therapeutic Advances in Gastroenterology* 2013;6:77–88.

5 Wing RR, Lang W, Wadden TA, et al. Benefits of modest weight loss in improving cardiovascular risk factors in overweight and obese individuals with type 2 diabetes. *Diabetes Care* 2011;34:1481–86.

6   Willett WC, Sacks F, Trichopoulou A, et al. Mediterranean diet pyramid: a cultural model for healthy eating. *American Journal of Clinical Nutrition* 1995;61:1402S–1406S.

7   Estruch R, Ros E, Martinez-Gonzalez MA. Mediterranean diet for primary prevention of cardiovascular disease. *New England Journal of Medicine* 2013;369:676–77.

8   Estruch R, Ros E, Salas-Salvado J, et al. Primary prevention of cardiovascular disease with a Mediterranean diet. *New England Journal of Medicine* 2013;368:1279–90.

9   Estruch R, Martinez-Gonzalez MA, Corella D, et al. Effects of a Mediterranean-style diet on cardiovascular risk factors: a randomized trial. *Annals of Internal Medicine* 2006;145:1–11.

10 Estruch R, Ros E, Martinez-Gonzalez MA. Mediterranean diet for primary prevention of cardiovascular disease. *New England Journal of Medicine* 2013;369:676–77.

11 Rees K, Hartley L, Flowers N, et al. 'Mediterranean' dietary pattern for the primary prevention of cardiovascular disease. *Cochrane Database of Systematic Reviews* 2013;8:CD009825.

12 Perona JS, Cabello-Moruno R, Ruiz-Gutierrez V. The role of virgin olive oil components in the modulation of endothelial function. *Journal of Nutritional Biochemistry* 2006;17:429–45.

13 Salas-Salvado J, Bullo M, Estruch R, et al. Prevention of diabetes with Mediterranean diets: a subgroup analysis of a randomized trial. *Annals of Internal Medicine* 2014;160:1–10.

14 Andersen CJ, Fernandez ML. Dietary strategies to reduce metabolic syndrome. *Reviews in Endocrine & Metabolic Disorders* 2013;14:241–54.

15 Richard C, Royer MM, Couture P, et al. Effect of the Mediterranean diet on plasma adipokine concentrations in men with metabolic syndrome. *Metabolism: Clinical and Experimental* 2013;62:1803–10.

16 Richard C, Couture P, Desroches S, Lamarche B. Effect of the Mediterranean diet with and without weight loss on markers of inflammation in men with metabolic syndrome. *Obesity* 2013;21:51–57.

17 Gotsis E, Anagnostis P, Mariolis A, Vlachou A, Katsiki N, Karagiannis A. Health benefits of the Mediterranean diet: an update of research over the last 5 years. *Angiology* 2014 Apr 27. [Epub ahead of print]

18 Funtikova AN, Benitez-Arciniega AA, Gomez SF, Fito M, Elosua R, Schroder H. Mediterranean diet impact on changes in abdominal fat and 10-year incidence of abdominal obesity in a Spanish population. *British Journal of Nutrition* 2014;111:1481–87.

19 Steinle N CS, Ryan K, Fraser C, Shuldiner A, Mongodin E. Increased gut microbiome diversity following a high fiber Mediterranean style diet. *FASEB Journal* 2013;27:1056.3.

20 Gotsis E, Anagnostis P, Mariolis A, Vlachou A, Katsiki N, Karagiannis A. Health benefits of the Mediterranean diet: an update of research over the last 5 years. *Angiology* 2014 Apr 27. [Epub ahead of print]

21 Bourlioux P. [Current view on gut microbiota]. *Annales pharmaceutiques françaises* 2014;72:15–21.

22 Olveira C, Olveira G, Espildora F, et al. Mediterranean diet is associated on symptoms of depression and anxiety in patients with bronchiectasis. *General Hospital Psychiatry* 2014;36:277–83.

23 Sanchez-Villegas A, Martinez-Gonzalez MA, Estruch R, et al. Mediterranean dietary pattern and depression: the PREDIMED randomized trial. *BMC Medicine* 2013;11:208.

24 Caracciolo B, Xu W, Collins S, Fratiglioni L. Cognitive decline, dietary factors and gut-brain interactions. *Mechanisms of Ageing and Development* 2014;136–137:59–69.

25 Otaegui-Arrazola A, Amiano P, Elbusto A, Urdaneta E, Martinez-Lage P. Diet, cognition, and Alzheimer's disease: food for thought. *European Journal of Nutrition* 2014;53:1–23.

26 Goulet J, Lamarche B, Nadeau G, Lemieux S. Effect of a nutritional intervention promoting the Mediterranean food pattern on plasma lipids, lipoproteins and body weight in healthy French-Canadian women. *Atherosclerosis* 2003;170:115–24.

27 Perez-Guisado J, Munoz-Serrano A, Alonso-Moraga A. Spanish ketogenic Mediterranean diet: a healthy cardiovascular diet for weight loss. *Nutrition Journal* 2008;7:30.

28 Paoli A, Bianco A, Grimaldi KA, Lodi A, Bosco G. Long term successful weight loss with a combination biphasic ketogenic Mediterranean diet and Mediterranean diet maintenance protocol. *Nutrients* 2013;5:5205–17.

29 Kanerva N, Loo BM, Eriksson JG, et al. Associations of the Baltic Sea diet with obesity-related markers of inflammation. *Annals of Medicine* 2014;46:90–96.

30 Nova E, Baccan GC, Veses A, Zapatera B, Marcos A. Potential health benefits of moderate alcohol consumption: current perspectives in research. *Proceedings of the Nutrition Society* 2012;71:307–15.

31 Kanerva N, Kaartinen NE, Schwab U, Lahti-Koski M, Mannisto S. Adherence to the Baltic Sea diet consumed in the Nordic countries is associated with lower abdominal obesity. *British Journal of Nutrition* 2013;109:520–28.

32 Ibid.

33 Ibid.

34 Rehm J, Shield K. Alcohol consumption. In: Stewart BW, Wild CB, eds. World Cancer Report 2014. Lyon, France: International Agency for Research on Cancer; 2014. worldcat.org/oclc/636655624/editions ?editionsView=true&referer=di

35 ncbi.nlm.nih.gov/pubmed/25505228

36 Kanerva N, Kaartinen NE, Schwab U, Lahti-Koski M, Mannisto S. The Baltic Sea Diet Score: a tool for assessing healthy eating in Nordic countries. *Public Health Nutrition* 2013:1–9.

37 Ali RE, Rattan SI. Curcumin's biphasic hormetic response on proteasome activity and heat-shock protein synthesis in human keratinocytes. *Annals of the New York Academy of Sciences* 2006;1067:394–99.

38 Prickett CD, Lister E, Collins M, et al. Alcohol: friend or foe? Alcoholic beverage hormesis for cataract and atherosclerosis is related to plasma antioxidant activity. *Nonlinearity in Biology, Toxicology, Medicine* 2004;2:353–70.

39 Mullin GE. Search for the optimal diet. *Nutrition in Clinical Practice* 2010;25:581–84.

40 Mozaffarian D, Hao T, Rimm EB, Willett WC, Hu FB. Changes in diet and lifestyle and long-term weight gain in women and men. *New England Journal of Medicine* 2011;364:2392–404.

41 Ibid.

42 oldwayspt.org/about-us/our-mission, #78494.

43 Oyebode O, Gordon-Dseagu V, Walker A, Mindell JS. Fruit and vegetable consumption and all-cause, cancer and CVD mortality: analysis of Health Survey for England data. *Journal of Epidemiology and Community Health* 2014;68:856–62.

44 Wise J. The health benefits of vegetables and fruit rise with consumption, finds study. *BMJ* 2014;348:g2434.

45 Holt SH, Miller JC, Petocz P, Farmakalidis E. A satiety index of common foods. *European Journal of Clinical Nutrition* 1995;49:675–90.

46 Langholf V. *Medical Theories in Hippocrates: Early Texts and the "Epidemics."* Berlin; New York: W. de Gruyter, 1990.

47 Sinclair TR SC. *Bread, Beer and the Seeds of Change: Agriculture's Imprint on World History* Wallingford, UK: CABI; 2010.

48 Larsson SC, Giovannucci E, Wolk A. Folate and risk of breast cancer: a meta-analysis. *Journal of the National Cancer Institute* 2007;99:64–76.

49 Zhang SM, Hankinson SE, Hunter DJ, Giovannucci EL, Colditz GA, Willett WC. Folate intake and risk of breast cancer characterized by hormone receptor status. *Cancer Epidemiology, Biomarkers & Prevention* 2005;14:2004–8.

50 Hamajima N, Hirose K, Tajima K, et al. Alcohol, tobacco and breast cancer–collaborative reanalysis of individual data from 53 epidemiological studies, including 58,515 women with breast cancer and 95,067 women without the disease. *British Journal of Cancer* 2002;87:1234–45.

51 Kuijer RG, Boyce JA. Chocolate cake. Guilt or celebration? Associations with healthy eating attitudes, perceived behavioural control, intentions and weight-loss. *Appetite* 2014;74:48–54.

52 Mullin GE, Swift KM. *The Inside Tract.* New York: Rodale, 2011.

Chapter 9

1 umm.edu/health/medical/altmed/supplement/omega6-fatty-acids

2 Matsumoto R, Tu NP, Haruta S, Kawano M, Takeuchi I. Polychlorinated biphenyl (PCB) concentrations and congener composition in masu salmon from Japan: a study of all 209 PCB congeners by high-resolution gas chromatography/high-resolution mass spectrometry (HRGC/HRMS). *Marine Pollution Bulletin* 2014;85:549–57.

3 Zacs D, Rjabova J, Bartkevics V. Occurrence of brominated persistent organic pollutants (PBDD/DFs, PXDD/DFs, and PBDEs) in Baltic wild salmon (Salmo salar) and correlation with PCDD/DFs and PCBs. *Environmental Science & Technology* 2013;47:9478–86.

4 Perlmutter D. *Grain Brain.* New York: Little, Brown and Co., 2013.

5 Fan YY, Ran Q, Toyokuni S, et al. Dietary fish oil promotes colonic apoptosis and mitochondrial proton leak in oxidatively stressed mice. *Cancer Prevention Research* 2011;4:1267–74.

6 Ramel A, Parra D, Martinez JA, Kiely M, Thorsdottir I. Effects of seafood consumption and weight loss on fasting leptin and ghrelin concentrations in overweight and obese European young adults. *European Journal of Nutrition* 2009;48:107–14.

7 Ramel A, Martinez JA, Kiely M, Bandarra NM, Thorsdottir I. Effects of weight loss and seafood consumption on inflammation parameters in young, overweight and obese European men and women during 8 weeks of energy restriction. *European Journal of Clinical Nutrition* 2010;64:987–93.

8 Thorsdottir I, Birgisdottir B, Kiely M, Martinez J, Bandarra N. Fish consumption among young overweight European adults and compliance to varying seafood content in four weight loss intervention diets. *Public Health Nutrition* 2009;12:592–98.

9 Poulsen SK, Due A, Jordy AB, et al. Health effect of the New Nordic Diet in adults with increased waist circumference: a 6-month randomized controlled trial. *American Journal of Clinical Nutrition* 2014;99:35–45.

10 Ramel A, Jonsdottir MT, Thorsdottir I. Consumption of cod and weight loss in young overweight and obese adults on an energy reduced diet for 8 weeks. *Nutrition, Metabolism, and Cardiovascular Diseases* 2009;19:690–96.

11 Ibid.

12 nrdc.org/health/effects/mercury/guide.asp.

13 Ibid.

14 seafoodwatch.org/cr/cr_seafoodwatch/content/media/MBA_SeafoodWatch_NationalGuide.pdf; wholefoodsmarket.com/blog/what%E2%80%99s-so-great-about-our-tilapia-we%E2%80%99ll-tell-you.

15 Benjamin RM. Dietary guidelines for Americans, 2010: the cornerstone of nutrition policy. *Public Health Reports* 2011;126:310–11.

16 Walker KZ, O'Dea K. Is a low fat diet the optimal way to cut energy intake over the long term in overweight people? *Nutrition, Metabolism, and Cardiovascular Diseases* 2001;11:244–48.

17 Lasa A, Miranda J, Bullo M, et al. Comparative effect of two Mediterranean diets versus a low-fat diet on glycaemic control in individuals with type 2 diabetes. *European Journal of Clinical Nutrition* 2014;68:767–72.

18 Frank S, Linder K, Fritsche L, et al. Olive oil aroma extract modulates cerebral blood flow in gustatory brain areas in humans. *American Journal of Clinical Nutrition* 2013;98:1360–66.

19 Alfenas RC, Mattes RD. Effect of fat sources on satiety. *Obesity Research* 2003;11:183–87.

20 Kozimor A, Chang H, Cooper JA. Effects of dietary fatty acid composition from a high fat meal on satiety. *Appetite* 2013;69:39–45.

21 Virruso C, Accardi G, Colonna Romano G, Candore G, Vasto S, Caruso C. Nutraceutical properties of extra virgin olive oil: a natural remedy for age-related disease? *Rejuvenation Research* 2013;17:217–20.

22 Martin-Pelaez S, Covas MI, Fito M, Kusar A, Pravst I. Health effects of olive oil polyphenols: recent advances and possibilities for the use of health claims. *Molecular Nutrition & Food Research* 2013;57:760–71.

23 Reaven P, Parthasarathy S, Grasse BJ, et al. Feasibility of using an oleate-rich diet to reduce the susceptibility of low-density lipoprotein to oxidative modification in humans. *American Journal of Clinical Nutrition* 1991;54:701–6.

24 Mensink RP, Katan MB. Effect of monounsaturated fatty acids versus complex carbohydrates on high-density lipoproteins in healthy men and women. *Lancet* 1987;1:122–25.

25 Ibid.

26 Ulbricht TL, Southgate DA. Coronary heart disease: seven dietary factors. *Lancet* 1991;338:985–92.

27 Willett WC, Sacks F, Trichopoulou A, et al. Mediterranean diet pyramid: a cultural model for healthy eating. *American Journal of Clinical Nutrition* 1995;61:1402S–1406S.

28 Bertoli S, Spadafranca A, Bes-Rastrollo M, et al. Adherence to the Mediterranean diet is inversely related to binge eating disorder in patients seeking a weight loss program. *Clinical Nutrition* 2014 Feb 14. [Epub ahead of print]

29 Ibid.

30 Flynn MM, Reinert SE. Comparing an olive oil-enriched diet to a standard lower-fat diet for weight loss in breast cancer survivors: a pilot study. *Journal of Women's Health* 2010;19:1155–61.

31 Puel C, Quintin A, Agalias A, et al. Olive oil and its main phenolic micronutrient (oleuropein) prevent inflammation-induced bone loss in the ovariectomised rat. *British Journal of Nutrition* 2004;92:119–27.

32 Condezo-Hoyos L, Mohanty IP, Noratto GD. Assessing non-digestible compounds in apple cultivars and their potential as modulators of obese faecal microbiota in vitro. *Food Chemistry* 2014;161:208–15.

33 Sesso HD, Gaziano JM, Liu S, Buring JE. Flavonoid intake and the risk of cardiovascular disease in women. *American Journal of Clinical Nutrition* 2003;77:1400–1408.

34 Knekt P, Jarvinen R, Reunanen A, Maatela J. Flavonoid intake and coronary mortality in Finland: a cohort study. *BMJ* 1996;312:478–81.

35 Knekt P, Isotupa S, Rissanen H, et al. Quercetin intake and the incidence of cerebrovascular disease. *European Journal of Clinical Nutrition* 2000;54:415–17.

36 Arts IC, Jacobs DR, Jr., Harnack LJ, Gross M, Folsom AR. Dietary catechins in relation to coronary heart disease death among postmenopausal women. *Epidemiology* 2001;12:668–75.

37 Hertog MG, Feskens EJ, Hollman PC, Katan MB, Kromhout D. Dietary antioxidant flavonoids and risk of coronary heart disease: the Zutphen Elderly Study. *Lancet* 1993;342:1007–11.

38 Aprikian O, Duclos V, Guyot S, et al. Apple pectin and a polyphenol-rich apple concentrate are more effective together than separately on cecal fermentations and plasma lipids in rats. *Journal of Nutrition* 2003;133:1860–65.

39 Feskanich D, Ziegler RG, Michaud DS, et al. Prospective study of fruit and vegetable consumption and risk of lung cancer among men and women. *Journal of the National Cancer Institute* 2000;92:1812–23.

40 Le Marchand L, Murphy SP, Hankin JH, Wilkens LR, Kolonel LN. Intake of flavonoids and lung cancer. *Journal of the National Cancer Institute* 2000;92:154–60.

41 Woods RK, Walters EH, Raven JM, et al. Food and nutrient intakes and asthma risk in young adults. *American Journal of Clinical Nutrition* 2003;78:414–21.

42 Butland BK, Fehily AM, Elwood PC. Diet, lung function, and lung function decline in a cohort of 2512 middle aged men. *Thorax* 2000;55:102–8.

43 Knekt P, Kumpulainen J, Jarvinen R, Rissanen H, Heliovaura M, Reunanen A, Hakulinen T, Aromaa A. Flavenoid intake and risk of chronic diseases. *American Journal of Clinical Nutrition* 2002;76:560–68.

44 Conceicao de Oliveira M, Sichieri R, Sanchez Moura A. Weight loss associated with a daily intake of three apples or three pears among overweight women. *Nutrition* 2003;19:253–56.

45 Cho KD, Han CK, Lee BH. Loss of body weight and fat and improved lipid profiles in obese rats fed apple pomace or apple juice concentrate. *Journal of Medicinal Food* 2013;16:823–30.

46 Ravn-Haren G, Dragsted LO, Buch-Andersen T, et al. Intake of whole apples or clear apple juice has contrasting effects on plasma lipids in healthy volunteers. *European Journal of Nutrition* 2013;52:1875–89.

47 Licht TR, Hansen M, Bergstrom A, et al. Effects of apples and specific apple components on the cecal environment of conventional rats: role of apple pectin. *BMC Microbiology* 2010;10:13.

48 Crozier SJ, Preston AG, Hurst JW, et al. Cacao seeds are a "super fruit": a comparative analysis of various fruit powders and products. *Chemistry Central Journal* 2011;5:5.

49 Franco OH, Bonneux L, de Laet C, Peeters A, Steyerberg EW, Mackenbach JP. The Polymeal: a more natural, safer, and probably tastier (than the Polypill) strategy to reduce cardiovascular disease by more than 75%. *BMJ* 2004;329:1447–50.

50 Zeng H, Locatelli M, Bardelli C, et al. Anti-inflammatory properties of clovamide and Theobroma cacao phenolic extracts in human monocytes: evaluation of respiratory burst, cytokine release, NF-kappaB activation, and PPARgamma modulation. *Journal of Agricultural and Food Chemistry* 2011;59:5342–50.

51 Wan Y, Vinson JA, Etherton TD, Proch J, Lazarus SA, Kris-Etherton PM. Effects of cocoa powder and dark chocolate on LDL oxidative susceptibility and prostaglandin concentrations in humans. *American Journal of Clinical Nutrition* 2001;74:596–602.

52 Faridi Z, Njike VY, Dutta S, Ali A, Katz DL. Acute dark chocolate and cocoa ingestion and endothelial function: a randomized controlled crossover trial. *American Journal of Clinical Nutrition* 2008;88:58–63.

53 Grassi D, Necozione S, Lippi C, et al. Cocoa reduces blood pressure and insulin resistance and improves endothelium-dependent vasodilation in hypertensives. *Hypertension* 2005;46:398–405.

54 Ibid.

55 Jacques PF, Cassidy A, Rogers G, Peterson JJ, Meigs JB, Dwyer JT. Higher dietary flavonol intake is associated with lower incidence of type 2 diabetes. *Journal of Nutrition* 2013;143:1474–80.

56 Wedick NM, Pan A, Cassidy A, et al. Dietary flavonoid intakes and risk of type 2 diabetes in US men and women. *American Journal of Clinical Nutrition* 2012;95:925–33.

57 Tzounis X, Rodriguez-Mateos A, Vulevic J, Gibson GR, Kwik-Uribe C, Spencer JP. Prebiotic evaluation of cocoa-derived flavanols in healthy humans by using a randomized, controlled, double-blind, crossover intervention study. *American Journal of Clinical Nutrition* 2011;93:62–72.

58 latimes.com/science/sciencenow/la-sci-sn-secret-to-dark-chocolates-health-benefits-20140318-story.html.

59 Cuenca-Garcia M, Ruiz JR, Ortega FB, Castillo MJ, group Hs. Association between chocolate consumption and fatness in European adolescents. *Nutrition* 2014;30:236–69.

60 Dorenkott MR, Griffin LE, Goodrich KM, et al. Oligomeric cocoa procyanidins possess enhanced bioactivity compared to monomeric and polymeric cocoa procyanidins for preventing the development of obesity, insulin resistance, and impaired glucose tolerance during high-fat feeding. *Journal of Agricultural and Food Chemistry* 2014;62:2216–27.

61 Asai A, Terasaki M, Nagao A. An epoxide-furanoid rearrangement of spinach neoxanthin occurs in the gastrointestinal tract of mice and in vitro: formation and cytostatic activity of neochrome stereoisomers. *Journal of Nutrition* 2004;134:2237–43.

62 Ibid.

63 Gates MA, Tworoger SS, Hecht JL, De Vivo I, Rosner B, Hankinson SE. A prospective study of dietary flavonoid intake and incidence of epithelial ovarian cancer. *International Journal of Cancer Journal* 2007;121:2225–32.

64 Edenharder R, Keller G, Platt KL, Unger KK. Isolation and characterization of structurally novel antimutagenic flavonoids from spinach (Spinacia oleracea). *Journal of Agricultural and Food Chemistry* 2001;49:2767–73.

65 Kirsh VA, Peters U, Mayne ST, et al. Prospective study of fruit and vegetable intake and risk of prostate cancer. *Journal of the National Cancer Institute* 2007;99:1200–1209.

66 Yang Y, Marczak ED, Yokoo M, Usui H, Yoshikawa M. Isolation and antihypertensive effect of angiotensin I-converting enzyme (ACE) inhibitory peptides from spinach Rubisco. *Journal of Agricultural and Food Chemistry* 2003;51:4897–902.

67 Lucarini M, Lanzi S, D'Evoli L, Aguzzi A, Lombardi-Boccia G. Intake of vitamin A and carotenoids from the Italian population—results of an Italian total diet study. *International Journal for Vitamin and Nutrition Research* 2006;76:103–9.

68 Ozsoy-Sacan O, Karabulut-Bulan O, Bolkent S, Yanardag R, Ozgey Y. Effects of chard (Beta vulgaris L. var cicla) on the liver of the diabetic rats: a morphological and biochemical study. *Bioscience, Biotechnology, and Biochemistry* 2004;68:1640–48.

69 Wu QJ, Yang Y, Wang J, Han LH, Xiang YB. Cruciferous vegetable consumption and gastric cancer risk: a meta-analysis of epidemiological studies. *Cancer Science* 2013;104:1067–73.

70 Liu X, Lv K. Cruciferous vegetables intake is inversely associated with risk of breast cancer: a meta-analysis. *Breast* 2013;22:309–13.

71 Wang LI, Giovannucci EL, Hunter D, Neuberg D, Su L, Christiani DC. Dietary intake of Cruciferous vegetables, Glutathione S-transferase (GST) polymorphisms and lung cancer risk in a Caucasian population. *Cancer Causes & Control* 2004;15:977–85.

72 Higdon JV, Delage B, Williams DE, Dashwood RH. Cruciferous vegetables and human cancer risk: epidemiologic evidence and mechanistic basis. *Pharmacological Research* 2007;55:224–36.

73 Tang L, Zirpoli GR, Guru K, et al. Consumption of raw cruciferous vegetables is inversely associated with bladder cancer risk. *Cancer Epidemiology, Biomarkers & Prevention* 2008;17:938–44.

74 Higdon JV, Delage B, Williams DE, Dashwood RH. Cruciferous vegetables and human cancer risk: epidemiologic evidence and mechanistic basis. *Pharmacological Research* 2007;55:224–36.

75 Kim MK, Park JH. Conference on "Multidisciplinary approaches to nutritional problems." Symposium on "Nutrition and health." Cruciferous vegetable intake and the risk of human cancer: epidemiological evidence. *Proceedings of the Nutrition Society* 2009;68:103–10.

76 Higdon JV, Delage B, Williams DE, Dashwood RH. Cruciferous vegetables and human cancer risk: epidemiologic evidence and mechanistic basis. *Pharmacological Research* 2007;55:224–36.

77 Clarke JD, Dashwood RH, Ho E. Multi-targeted prevention of cancer by sulforaphane. *Cancer Letters* 2008;269:291–304.

78 Kahlon TS, Chiu MC, Chapman MH. Steam cooking significantly improves in vitro bile acid binding of collard greens, kale, mustard greens, broccoli, green bell pepper, and cabbage. *Nutrition Research* 2008;28:351–57.

79 Angeloni C, Leoncini E, Malaguti M, Angelini S, Hrelia P, Hrelia S. Modulation of phase II enzymes by sulforaphane: implications for its cardioprotective potential. *Journal of Agricultural and Food Chemistry* 2009;57:5615–22.

80 Cornelis MC, El-Sohemy A, Campos H. GSTT1 genotype modifies the association between cruciferous vegetable intake and the risk of myocardial infarction. *American Journal of Clinical Nutrition* 2007;86:752–58.

81 Liu S, Serdula M, Janket SJ, et al. A prospective study of fruit and vegetable intake and the risk of type 2 diabetes in women. *Diabetes Care* 2004;27:2993–96.

82 Mulabagal V, Ngouajio M, Nair A, Zhang Y, Gottumukkala AL, Nair MG. In vitro evaluation of red and green lettuce (Lactuca sativa) for functional food properties. *Food Chemistry* 2010;118:300–306.

83 Becker C, Klaering HP, Schreiner M, Kroh LW, Krumbein A. Unlike quercetin glycosides, cyanidin glycoside in red leaf lettuce responds more sensitively to increasing low radiation intensity before than after head formation has started. *Journal of Agricultural and Food Chemistry* 2014;62:6911–17.

84 Mulabagal V, Ngouajio M, Nair A, Zhang Y, Gottumukkala AL, Nair MG. In vitro evaluation of red and green lettuce (Lactuca sativa) for functional food properties. *Food Chemistry* 2010;118:300–306.

85 Azadbakht L, Haghighatdoost F, Karimi G, Esmaillzadeh A. Effect of consuming salad and yogurt as preload on body weight management and cardiovascular risk factors: a randomized clinical trial. *International Journal of Food Sciences and Nutrition* 2013;64:392–99.

86 Rolls BJ. Dietary strategies for weight management. *Nestlé Nutrition Institute Workshop Series* 2012;73:37–48.

87 Flood JE, Rolls BJ. Soup preloads in a variety of forms reduce meal energy intake. *Appetite* 2007;49:626–34.

88 Ma J, Stevens JE, Cukier K, et al. Effects of a protein preload on gastric emptying, glycemia, and gut hormones after a carbohydrate meal in diet-controlled type 2 diabetes. *Diabetes Care* 2009;32:1600–1602.

89 Marciani L, Hall N, Pritchard SE, et al. Preventing gastric sieving by blending a solid/water meal enhances satiation in healthy humans. *Journal of Nutrition* 2012;142:1253–58.

90 Rolls BJ, Roe LS, Beach AM, Kris-Etherton PM. Provision of foods differing in energy density affects long-term weight loss. *Obesity Research* 2005;13:1052–60.

91 Zhu Y, Hollis JH. Soup consumption is associated with a lower dietary energy density and a better diet quality in US adults. *British Journal of Nutrition* 2014;111:1474–80.

92 Rolls BJ, Roe LS, Beach AM, Kris-Etherton PM. Provision of foods differing in energy density affects long-term weight loss. *Obesity Research* 2005;13:1052–60.

93 Zhu Y, Hollis JH. Soup consumption is associated with a reduced risk of overweight and obesity but not metabolic syndrome in US adults: NHANES 2003-2006. *PLoS One* 2013;8:e75630.

94 ———. Soup consumption is associated with a lower dietary energy density and a better diet quality in US adults. *British Journal of Nutrition* 2014;111:1474–80.

95 Kuroda M, Ohta M, Okufuji T, et al. Frequency of soup intake is inversely associated with body mass index, waist circumference, and waist-to-hip ratio, but not with other metabolic risk factors in Japanese men. *Journal of the American Dietetic Association* 2011;111:137–42.

96 ———. Frequency of soup intake and amount of dietary fiber intake are inversely associated with plasma leptin concentrations in Japanese adults. *Appetite* 2010;54:538–43.

97 Perez-Jimenez J, Neveu V, Vos F, Scalbert A. Identification of the 100 richest dietary sources of polyphenols: an application of the Phenol-Explorer database. *European Journal of Clinical Nutrition* 2010;64(Suppl 3):S112–S20.

98 Woting A, Clavel T, Loh G, Blaut M. Bacterial transformation of dietary lignans in gnotobiotic rats. *FEMS Microbiology Ecology* 2010;72:507–14.

99 Ibrugger S, Kristensen M, Mikkelsen MS, Astrup A. Flaxseed dietary fiber supplements for suppression of appetite and food intake. *Appetite* 2012;58:490–95.

100 Khan MI, Anjum FM, Sohaib M, Sameen A. Tackling metabolic syndrome by functional foods. *Reviews in Endocrine & Metabolic Disorders* 2013;14:287–97.

101 Adlercreutz H. Lignans and human health. *Critical Reviews in Clinical Laboratory Sciences* 2007;44:483–525.

102 Sturgeon SR, Heersink JL, Volpe SL, et al. Effect of dietary flaxseed on serum levels of estrogens and androgens in postmenopausal women. *Nutrition and Cancer* 2008;60:612–18.

103 Rhee Y, Brunt A. Flaxseed supplementation improved insulin resistance in obese glucose intolerant people: a randomized crossover design. *Nutrition Journal* 2011;10:44.

104 Dodin S, Lemay A, Jacques H, Legare F, Forest JC, Masse B. The effects of flaxseed dietary supplement on lipid profile, bone mineral density, and symptoms in menopausal women: a randomized, double-blind, wheat germ placebo-controlled clinical trial. *Journal of Clinical Endocrinology and Metabolism* 2005;90:1390–97.

105 Kristensen M, Jensen MG, Aarestrup J, et al. Flaxseed dietary fibers lower cholesterol and increase fecal fat excretion, but magnitude of effect depend on food type. *Nutrition & Metabolism* 2012;9:8.

106 Fukumitsu S, Aida K, Shimizu H, Toyoda K. Flaxseed lignan lowers blood cholesterol and decreases liver disease risk factors in moderately hypercholesterolemic men. *Nutrition Research* 2010;30:441–46.

107 Baranowski M, Enns J, Blewett H, Yakandawala U, Zahradka P, Taylor CG. Dietary flaxseed oil reduces adipocyte size, adipose monocyte chemoattractant protein-1 levels and T-cell infiltration in obese, insulin-resistant rats. *Cytokine* 2012;59:382–91.

108 Fukumitsu S, Aida K, Ueno N, Ozawa S, Takahashi Y, Kobori M. Flaxseed lignan attenuates high-fat diet-induced fat accumulation and induces adiponectin expression in mice. *British Journal of Nutrition* 2008;100:669–76.

109 Cintra DE, Ropelle ER, Moraes JC, et al. Unsaturated fatty acids revert diet-induced hypothalamic inflammation in obesity. *PLoS One* 2012;7:e30571.

110 Morisset AS, Lemieux S, Veilleux A, Bergeron J, John Weisnagel S, Tchernof A. Impact of a lignan-rich diet on adiposity and insulin sensitivity in post-menopausal women. *British Journal of Nutrition* 2009;102:195-200.

111 Bao Y, Han J, Hu FB, et al. Association of nut consumption with total and cause-specific mortality. *New England Journal of Medicine* 2013;369:2001-11.

112 Bao Y, Rosner BA, Fuchs CS. Nut consumption and mortality. *New England Journal of Medicine* 2014;370:882.

113 Fraser GE, Sabate J, Beeson WL, Strahan TM. A possible protective effect of nut consumption on risk of coronary heart disease. The Adventist Health Study. *Archives of Internal Medicine* 1992;152:1416-24.

114 Sabate J, Fraser GE, Burke K, Knutsen SF, Bennett H, Lindsted KD. Effects of walnuts on serum lipid levels and blood pressure in normal men. *New England Journal of Medicine* 1993;328:603-7.

115 Kelly JH, Jr., Sabate J. Nuts and coronary heart disease: an epidemiological perspective. *British Journal of Nutrition* 2006;96(Suppl 2):S61-S67.

116 Albert CM, Gaziano JM, Willett WC, Manson JE. Nut consumption and decreased risk of sudden cardiac death in the Physicians' Health Study. *Archives of Internal Medicine* 2002;162:1382-87.

117 Sabate J, Oda K, Ros E. Nut consumption and blood lipid levels: a pooled analysis of 25 intervention trials. *Archives of Internal Medicine* 2010;170:821-27.

118 Banel DK, Hu FB. Effects of walnut consumption on blood lipids and other cardiovascular risk factors: a meta-analysis and systematic review. *American Journal of Clinical Nutrition* 2009;90:56-63.

119 Jiang R, Jacobs DR, Jr., Mayer-Davis E, et al. Nut and seed consumption and inflammatory markers in the multi-ethnic study of atherosclerosis. *American Journal of Epidemiology* 2006;163:222-31.

120 Mantzoros CS, Williams CJ, Manson JE, Meigs JB, Hu FB. Adherence to the Mediterranean dietary pattern is positively associated with plasma adiponectin concentrations in diabetic women. *American Journal of Clinical Nutrition* 2006;84:328-35.

121 Salas-Salvado J, Garcia-Arellano A, Estruch R, et al. Components of the Mediterranean-type food pattern and serum inflammatory markers among patients at high risk for cardiovascular disease. *European Journal of Clinical Nutrition* 2008;62:651-59.

122 Lopez-Uriarte P, Bullo M, Casas-Agustench P, Babio N, Salas-Salvado J. Nuts and oxidation: a systematic review. *Nutrition Reviews* 2009;67:497-508.

123 Jaceldo-Siegl K, Haddad E, Oda K, Fraser GE, Sabate J. Tree nuts are inversely associated with metabolic syndrome and obesity: the Adventist health study-2. *PLoS One* 2014;9:e85133.

124 Rebello CJ, Liu AG, Greenway FL, Dhurandhar NV. Dietary strategies to increase satiety. *Advances in Food and Nutrition Research* 2013;69:105-82.

125 Tan SY, Mattes RD. Appetitive, dietary and health effects of almonds consumed with meals or as snacks: a randomized, controlled trial. *European Journal of Clinical Nutrition* 2013;67:1205-14.

126 Cassady BA, Hollis JH, Fulford AD, Considine RV, Mattes RD. Mastication of almond: effects of lipid bioaccessibility, appetite, and hormone response. *American Journal of Clinical Nutrition* 2009;89:794-800.

127 Pasman WJ, Heimerikx J, Rubingh CM, et al. The effect of Korean pine nut oil on in vitro CCK release, on appetite sensations and on gut hormones in post-menopausal overweight women. *Lipids in Health and Disease* 2008;7:10.

128 Mattes RD. The energetics of nut consumption. *Asia Pacific Journal of Clinical Nutrition* 2008;17(Suppl 1):337-79.

129 Mattes RD, Dreher ML. Nuts and healthy body weight maintenance mechanisms. *Asia Pacific Journal of Clinical Nutrition* 2010;19:137-41.

130 Mattes RD, Kris-Etherton PM, Foster GD. Impact of peanuts and tree nuts on body weight and healthy weight loss in adults. *Journal of Nutrition* 2008;138:1741S-45S.

131 Casas-Agustench P, Lopez-Uriarte P, Bullo M, Ros E, Cabre-Vila JJ, Salas-Salvado J. Effects of one serving of mixed nuts on serum lipids, insulin resistance and inflammatory markers in patients with the metabolic syndrome. *Nutrition, Metabolism, and Cardiovascular Diseases* 2011;21:126-35.

132 Mozaffarian D, Hao T, Rimm EB, Willett WC, Hu FB. Changes in diet and lifestyle and long-term weight gain in women and men. *New England Journal of Medicine* 2011;364:2392-404.

133 Bes-Rastrollo M, Sabate J, Gomez-Gracia E, Alonso A, Martinez JA, Martinez-Gonzalez MA. Nut consumption and weight gain in a Mediterranean cohort: The SUN study. *Obesity* 2007;15:107-16.

134 Bes-Rastrollo M, Wedick NM, Martinez-Gonzalez MA, Li TY, Sampson L, Hu FB. Prospective study of nut consumption, long-term weight change, and obesity risk in women. *American Journal of Clinical Nutrition* 2009;89:1913-19.

135 Mozaffarian D, Hao T, Rimm EB, Willett WC, Hu FB. Changes in diet and lifestyle and long-term weight gain in women and men. *New England Journal of Medicine* 2011;364:2392–404.

136 Dreher ML. Pistachio nuts: composition and potential health benefits. *Nutrition Reviews* 2012;70:234–40.

137 Ibid.

138 Kennedy-Hagan K, Painter JE, Honselman C, Halvorson A, Rhodes K, Skwir K. The effect of pistachio shells as a visual cue in reducing caloric consumption. *Appetite* 2011;57:418–20.

139 Honselman CS, Painter JE, Kennedy-Hagan KJ, et al. In-shell pistachio nuts reduce caloric intake compared to shelled nuts. *Appetite* 2011;57:414–17.

140 Li Z, Song R, Nguyen C, et al. Pistachio nuts reduce triglycerides and body weight by comparison to refined carbohydrate snack in obese subjects on a 12-week weight loss program. *Journal of the American College of Nutrition* 2010;29:198–203.

141 Tan SY, Dhillon J, Mattes RD. A review of the effects of nuts on appetite, food intake, metabolism, and body weight. *American Journal of Clinical Nutrition* 2014;100:412S–22S.

142 berkeleywellness.com/healthy-eating/food/article/decaf-healthy-choice.

143 health.harvard.edu/fhg/updates/update0406c.shtml.

144 Steffen M, Kuhle C, Hensrud D, Erwin PJ, Murad MH. The effect of coffee consumption on blood pressure and the development of hypertension: a systematic review and meta-analysis. *Journal of Hypertension* 2012;30:2245–54.

145 Freedman ND, Park Y, Abnet CC, Hollenbeck AR, Sinha R. Association of coffee drinking with total and cause-specific mortality. *New England Journal of Medicine* 2012;366:1891–904.

146 Keijzers GB, De Galan BE, Tack CJ, Smits P. Caffeine can decrease insulin sensitivity in humans. *Diabetes Care* 2002;25:364–69.

147 Johnston KL, Clifford MN, Morgan LM. Coffee acutely modifies gastrointestinal hormone secretion and glucose tolerance in humans: glycemic effects of chlorogenic acid and caffeine. *American Journal of Clinical Nutrition* 2003;78:728–33.

148 Greenberg JA, Boozer CN, Geliebter A. Coffee, diabetes, and weight control. *American Journal of Clinical Nutrition* 2006;84:682–93.

149 Rodriguez-Moran M, Guerrero-Romero F. Oral magnesium supplementation improves the metabolic profile of metabolically obese, normal-weight individuals: a randomized double-blind placebo-controlled trial. *Archives of Medical Research* 2014;45:388–93.

150 Rodriguez-Moran M, Guerrero-Romero F. Oral magnesium supplementation improves insulin sensitivity and metabolic control in type 2 diabetic subjects: a randomized double-blind controlled trial. *Diabetes Care* 2003;26:1147–52.

151 Kovacs EM, Lejeune MP, Nijs I, Westerterp-Plantenga MS. Effects of green tea on weight maintenance after body-weight loss. *British Journal of Nutrition* 2004;91:431–37.

152 Lopez-Garcia E, van Dam RM, Rajpathak S, Willett WC, Manson JE, Hu FB. Changes in caffeine intake and long-term weight change in men and women. *American Journal of Clinical Nutrition* 2006;83:674–80.

153 St-Onge MP, Salinardi T, Herron-Rubin K, Black RM. A weight-loss diet including coffee-derived mannooligosaccharides enhances adipose tissue loss in overweight men but not women. *Obesity* 2012;20:343–48.

154 Lucas M, Mirzaei F, Pan A, et al. Coffee, caffeine, and risk of depression among women. *Archives of Internal Medicine* 2011;171:1571–78.

155 Kokubo Y, Iso H, Saito I, et al. The impact of green tea and coffee consumption on the reduced risk of stroke incidence in Japanese population: the Japan public health center-based study cohort. *Stroke* 2013;44:1369–74.

156 Sinha R, Cross AJ, Daniel CR, et al. Caffeinated and decaffeinated coffee and tea intakes and risk of colorectal cancer in a large prospective study. *American Journal of Clinical Nutrition* 2012;96:374–81.

157 de la Figuera von Wichmann M. [Coffee consumption and hepatobilliary system]. *Medicina clinica* 2008;131:594–97.

158 Derkinderen P, Shannon KM, Brundin P. Gut feelings about smoking and coffee in Parkinson's disease. *Movement Disorders* 2014;29:976–79.

159 Freedman ND, Everhart JE, Lindsay KL, et al. Coffee intake is associated with lower rates of liver disease progression in chronic hepatitis C. *Hepatology* 2009;50:1360–69.

160 Molloy JW, Calcagno CJ, Williams CD, Jones FJ, Torres DM, Harrison SA. Association of coffee and caffeine consumption with fatty liver disease, nonalcoholic steatohepatitis, and degree of hepatic fibrosis. *Hepatology* 2012;55:429–36.

161 Saab S, Mallam D, Cox GA, 2nd, Tong MJ. Impact of coffee on liver diseases: a systematic review. *Liver International* 2014;34:495–504.

162 Ambrosone CB, Tang L. Cruciferous vegetable intake and cancer prevention: role of nutrigenetics. *Cancer Prevention Research* 2009;2:298–300.

163 Kirsh VA, Peters U, Mayne ST et al. Prospective study of fruit and vegetable intake and risk of prostate cancer. *Journal of the National Cancer Institute* 2007;99:1200–1209.

164 Traka M, Gasper AV, Melchini A, et al. Broccoli consumption interacts with GSTM1 to perturb oncogenic signalling pathways in the prostate. *PLoS One* 2008;3:e2568.

165 Steinbrecher A, Linseisen J. Dietary intake of individual glucosinolates in participants of the EPIC-Heidelberg cohort study. *Annals of Nutrition & Metabolism* 2009;54:87–96.

166 Bahadoran Z, Mirmiran P, Azizi F. Potential efficacy of broccoli sprouts as a unique supplement for management of type 2 diabetes and its complications. *Journal of Medicinal Food* 2013;16:375–82.

167 Choi Y, Um SJ, Park T. Indole-3-carbinol directly targets SIRT1 to inhibit adipocyte differentiation. *International Journal of Obesity* 2013;37:881–84.

168 Bahadoran Z, Mirmiran P, Hosseinpanah F, Hedayati M, Hosseinpour-Niazi S, Azizi F. Broccoli sprouts reduce oxidative stress in type 2 diabetes: a randomized double-blind clinical trial. *European Journal of Clinical Nutrition* 2011;65:972–77.

169 Bahadoran Z, Tohidi M, Nazeri P, Mehran M, Azizi F, Mirmiran P. Effect of broccoli sprouts on insulin resistance in type 2 diabetic patients: a randomized double-blind clinical trial. *International Journal of Food Sciences and Nutrition* 2012;63:767–71.

170 pages.jh.edu/~jhumag/0408web/talalay.html.

171 Lopez-Molina D, Navarro-Martinez MD, Rojas Melgarejo F, Hiner AN, Chazarra S, Rodriguez-Lopez JN. Molecular properties and prebiotic effect of inulin obtained from artichoke (Cynara scolymus L.). *Phytochemistry* 2005;66:1476–84.

172 Costabile A, Kolida S, Klinder A, et al. A double-blind, placebo-controlled, cross-over study to establish the bifidogenic effect of a very-long-chain inulin extracted from globe artichoke (Cynara scolymus) in healthy human subjects. *British Journal of Nutrition* 2010;104:1007–17.

173 Ibid.

174 Rondanelli M, Giacosa A, Opizzi A, et al. Beneficial effects of artichoke leaf extract supplementation on increasing HDL-cholesterol in subjects with primary mild hypercholesterolaemia: a double-blind, randomized, placebo-controlled trial. *International Journal of Food Sciences and Nutrition* 2013;64:7–15.

175 Barrat E, Zair Y, Ogier N, et al. A combined natural supplement lowers LDL cholesterol in subjects with moderate untreated hypercholesterolemia: a randomized placebo-controlled trial. *International Journal of Food Sciences and Nutrition* 2013;64:882–89.

176 Rondanelli M, Opizzi A, Faliva M, et al. Metabolic management in overweight subjects with naive impaired fasting glycaemia by means of a highly standardized extract from Cynara scolymus: a double-blind, placebo-controlled, randomized clinical trial. *Phytotherapy Research* 2014;28:33–41.

177 Kovacs EM, Lejeune MP, Nijs I, Westerterp-Plantenga MS. Effects of green tea on weight maintenance after body-weight loss. *British Journal of Nutrition* 2004;91:431–37.

Chapter 10

1 cbsnews.com/news/cdc-80-percent-of-american-adults-dont-get-recommended-exercise/.

2 americashealthrankings.org/all/sedentary.

3 sciencedaily.com/releases/2009/08/090810024825.htm.

4 Mons U, Hahmann H, Brenner H. A reverse J-shaped association of leisure time physical activity with prognosis in patients with stable coronary heart disease: evidence from a large cohort with repeated measurements. *Heart* 2014;100:1043–49.

5 apa.org/news/press/releases/stress/2011/final-2011.pdf.

6 Kessler RC, Chiu WT, Demler O, Merikangas KR, Walters EE. Prevalence, severity, and comorbidity of 12-month DSM-IV disorders in the National Comorbidity Survey Replication. *Archives of General Psychiatry* 2005;62:617–27.

7 Kessler RC, Demler O, Frank RG, et al. Prevalence and treatment of mental disorders, 1990 to 2003. *New England Journal of Medicine* 2005;352:2515–23.

8 apa.org/news/press/releases/stress/2012/generations.aspx.

9 apa.org/news/press/releases/stress/2011/final-2011.pdf.

10 Morton NM, Seckl JR. 11beta-hydroxysteroid dehydrogenase type 1 and obesity. *Frontiers of Hormone Research* 2008;36:146–64.

11 Black PH. The inflammatory consequences of psychologic stress: relationship to insulin resistance, obesity, atherosclerosis and diabetes mellitus, type II. *Medical Hypotheses* 2006;67:879–91.

12 Peeke PM, Chrousos GP. Hypercortisolism and obesity. *Annals of the New York Academy of Sciences* 1995;771:665–76.

13 Huang CJ, Webb HE, Zourdos MC, Acevedo EO. Cardiovascular reactivity, stress, and physical activity. *Frontiers in Physiology* 2013;4:314.

14 Redmond N, Richman J, Gamboa CM, et al. Perceived stress is associated with incident coronary heart disease and all-cause mortality in low- but not high-income participants in the Reasons for Geographic and Racial Differences in Stroke study. *Journal of the American Heart Association* 2013;2:e000447.

15 Bacon SL, Campbell TS, Arsenault A, Lavoie KL. The impact of mood and anxiety disorders on incident hypertension at one year. *International Journal of Hypertension* 2014;2014:953094.

16 Whitworth JA, Williamson PM, Mangos G, Kelly JJ. Cardiovascular consequences of cortisol excess. *Vascular Health and Risk Management* 2005;1:291–99.

17 Ventura T, Santander J, Torres R, Contreras AM. Neurobiologic basis of craving for carbohydrates. *Nutrition* 2014;30:252–56.

18 Bailey MT, Dowd SE, Galley JD, Hufnagle AR, Allen RG, Lyte M. Exposure to a social stressor alters the structure of the intestinal microbiota: implications for stressor-induced immunomodulation. *Brain, Behavior, and Immunity* 2011;25:397–407.

19 Cryan JF, Dinan TG. Mind-altering microorganisms: the impact of the gut microbiota on brain and behaviour. *Nature Reviews Neuroscience* 2012;13:701–12.

20 Sapolsky RM. *Why Zebras Don't Get Ulcers*, 3rd ed. New York: Holt Paperbacks; 2004.

21 news.ca.uky.edu/article/uk-researcher-finds-stress-management-may-contribute-weight-loss.

22 Mathieu J. What should you know about mindful and intuitive eating? *Journal of the American Dietetic Association* 2009;109:1982–87.

23 Schaefer JT, Magnuson AB. A review of interventions that promote eating by internal cues. *Journal of the Academy of Nutrition and Dietetics* 2014;114:734–60.

24 Kidd LI, Graor CH, Murrock CJ. A mindful eating group intervention for obese women: a mixed methods feasibility study. *Archives of Psychiatric Nursing* 2013;27:211–18.

25 Godsey J. The role of mindfulness based interventions in the treatment of obesity and eating disorders: an integrative review. *Complementary Therapies in Medicine* 2013;21:430–39.

26 May M. *Eat What You Love, Love What You Eat: How to Break Your Eat-Repent-Repeat Cycle: Am I Hungry?* Austin, TX: Greenleaf, 2011.

27 Breslau N. The epidemiology of trauma, PTSD, and other posttrauma disorders. *Trauma, Violence & Abuse* 2009;10:198–210.

28 Lopez-Diazguerrero NE, Gonzalez Puertos VY, Hernandez-Bautista RJ, Alarcon-Aguilar A, Luna-Lopez A, Konigsberg Fainstein M. [Hormesis: What doesn't kill you makes you stronger]. *Gaceta medica de Mexico* 2013;149:438–47.

29 Nunn AV, Guy GW, Brodie JS, Bell JD. Inflammatory modulation of exercise salience: using hormesis to return to a healthy lifestyle. *Nutrition & Metabolism* 2010;7:87.

30 apa.org/helpcenter/road-resilience.aspx#.

31 Southwick SM. *Resilience: The Science of Mastering Life's Greatest Challenges*. New York: Cambridge University Press; 2012.

32 Hughes V. Stress: the roots of resilience. *Nature* 2012;490:165–67.

33 Hingle MD, Wertheim BC, Tindle HA, et al. Optimism and diet quality in the Women's Health Initiative. *Journal of the Academy of Nutrition and Dietetics* 2014;114:1036–45.

34 Sarkar M, Fletcher D. Psychological resilience in sport performers: a review of stressors and protective factors. *Journal of Sports Sciences* 2014;32:1419–34.

35 Martin AS, Distelberg B, Palmer BW, Jeste DV. Development of a new multidimensional individual and interpersonal resilience measure for older adults. *Aging & Mental Health* 2014:1–14.

36 cptryon.org/prayer/special/serenity.html.

37 Gard T, Taquet M, Dixit R, et al. Fluid intelligence and brain functional organization in aging yoga and meditation practitioners. *Frontiers in Aging Neuroscience* 2014;6:76.

38 Childs E, de Wit H. Regular exercise is associated with emotional resilience to acute stress in healthy adults. *Frontiers in Physiology* 2014;5:161.

39 imdb.com/title/tt0479143/.

40 samplage.com/movie-quotes/it-aint-about-how-hard-you-hit/.

41 Dawson MA, Hamson-Utley JJ, Hansen R, Olpin M. Examining the effectiveness of psychological strategies on physiologic markers: evidence-based suggestions for holistic care of the athlete. *Journal of Athletic Training* 2014;49:331–37.

42 Prinsloo GE, Derman WE, Lambert MI, Laurie Rauch HG. The effect of a single session of short duration biofeedback-induced deep breathing on measures of heart rate variability during laboratory-induced cognitive stress: a pilot study. *Applied Psychophysiology and Biofeedback* 2013;38:81–90.

43 Shah M, Copeland J, Dart L, Adams-Huet B, James A, Rhea D. Slower eating speed lowers energy intake in normal-weight but not overweight/obese subjects. *Journal of the Academy of Nutrition and Dietetics* 2014;114:393–402.

44 okinawa-diet.com/okinawa_diet/hara_hachi_bu.html.

45 nhlbi.nih.gov/guidelines/obesity/prctgd_c.pdf.

46 Johnson PM, Kenny PJ. Dopamine D2 receptors in addiction-like reward dysfunction and compulsive eating in obese rats. *Nature Neuroscience* 2010;13:635–41.

47 Mantzios M, Giannou K. Group vs. single mindfulness meditation: exploring avoidance, impulsivity, and weight management in two separate mindfulness meditation settings. *Applied Psychology Health and Well-being* 2014;6:173–91.

48 clinicaltrials.gov/ct2/show/NCT01619384?term=bowel&recr=Open&cntry1=NA%3AUS&rank=69.

49 Goyal M, Singh S, Sibinga EM, et al. Meditation programs for psychological stress and well-being: a systematic review and meta-analysis. *JAMA Internal Medicine* 2014;174:357–68.

50 Daubenmier J, Kristeller J, Hecht FM, et al. Mindfulness intervention for stress eating to reduce cortisol and abdominal fat among overweight and obese women: an exploratory randomized controlled study. *Journal of Obesity* 2011;2011:651936.

51 Kristal AR, Littman AJ, Benitez D, White E. Yoga practice is associated with attenuated weight gain in healthy, middle-aged men and women. *Alternative Therapies in Health and Medicine* 2005;11:28–33.

52 Bernstein A BJ, Ehrman JP, Goulbic M,Roizen MF. Yoga in the management of overweight and obesity. *American Journal of Lifestyle Medicine* 2014;8:33–41.

53 Gurgevich S. *The Self-Hypnosis Diet Book.* Boulder, CO: Sounds True, 2009.

54 sleepandhypnosis.org/pdf/15_1_1.pdf.

55 Yeo S, Kim KS, Lim S. Randomised clinical trial of five ear acupuncture points for the treatment of overweight people. *Acupuncture in Medicine* 2014;32:132–38.

56 Sui Y, Zhao HL, Wong VC, et al. A systematic review on use of Chinese medicine and acupuncture for treatment of obesity. *Obesity Reviews* 2012;13:409–30.

57 Bernstein A BJ, Ehrman JP, Goulbic M, Roizen MF. Yoga in the management of overweight and obesity. *American Journal of Lifestyle Medicine* 2014;8(1):33–41.

58 Rioux J, Thomson C, Howerter A. A pilot feasibility study of whole-systems Ayurvedic medicine and yoga therapy for weight loss. *Global Advances in Health and Medicine* 2014;3(1):28–35.

59 Bernstein A BJ, Ehrman JP, Goulbic M, Roizen MF. Yoga in the management of overweight and obesity. *American Journal of Lifestyle Medicine* 2014;8(1):33–41.

60 Sarvottam K, Yadav TK. Obesity-related inflammation and cardiovascular disease: efficacy of a yoga-based lifestyle intervention. *Indian Journal of Medical Research* 2014:139(6):822–34.

61 Ibid.

62 Sui Y, Zhao HL, Wong VC, et al. A systematic review on use of Chinese medicine and acupuncture for treatment of obesity. *Obesity Reviews* 2012;13:409–30.

63 Cabyoglu MT, Ergene N, Tan U. The treatment of obesity by acupuncture. *The International Journal of Neuroscience* 2006;116:165–75.

64 jstor.org/stable/30038995.

65 Cho JH, Jae SY, Choo IL, Choo J. Health-promoting behaviour among women with abdominal obesity: a conceptual link to social support and perceived stress. *Journal of Advanced Nursing* 2014;70:1381–90.

66 Robertson C, Archibald D, Avenell A, et al. Systematic reviews of and integrated report on the quantitative, qualitative and economic evidence base for the management of obesity in men. *Health Technology Assessment* 2014;18:1–424.

67 Cacioppo JT, Cacioppo S. Social relationships and health: the toxic effects of perceived social isolation. *Social and Personality Psychology Compass* 2014;8:58–72.

68 Konturek PC, Brzozowski T, Konturek SJ. Gut clock: implication of circadian rhythms in the gastrointestinal tract. *Journal of Physiology and Pharmacology* 2011;62:139–50.

69 Fu XY, Li Z, Zhang N, Yu HT, Wang SR, Liu JR. Effects of gastrointestinal motility on obesity. *Nutrition & Metabolism* 2014;11:3.

70 sleepfoundation.org.

71 Schmid SM, Hallschmid M, Schultes B. The metabolic burden of sleep loss. *Lancet Diabetes & Endocrinology* 2014 Mar 25. [Epub ahead of print]

72 Schmid SM, Hallschmid M, Jauch-Chara K, Born J, Schultes B. A single night of sleep deprivation increases ghrelin levels and feelings of hunger in normal-weight healthy men. *Journal of Sleep Research* 2008;17:331–34.

73 Copinschi G. Metabolic and endocrine effects of sleep deprivation. *Essential Psychopharmacology* 2005;6:341–47.

74 Depner CM, Stothard ER, Wright KP, Jr. Metabolic consequences of sleep and circadian disorders. *Current Diabetes Reports* 2014;14:507.

75 Ferrie JE, Shipley MJ, Cappuccio FP, et al. A prospective study of change in sleep duration: associations with mortality in the Whitehall II cohort. *Sleep* 2007;30:1659–66.

76 Gilbert-Diamond D, Li Z, Adachi-Mejia AM, McClure AC, Sargent JD. Association of a television in the bedroom with increased adiposity gain in a nationally representative sample of children and adolescents. *JAMA Pediatrics* 2014;168:427–34.

77 Taveras EM, Gillman MW, Pena MM, Redline S, Rifas-Shiman SL. Chronic sleep curtailment and adiposity. *Pediatrics* 2014;133:1013–22.

78 Fisher A, McDonald L, van Jaarsveld CH, et al. Sleep and energy intake in early childhood. *International Journal of Obesity* 2014;38:926–29.

79 Hart CN, Carskadon MA, Considine RV, et al. Changes in children's sleep duration on food intake, weight, and leptin. *Pediatrics* 2013;132:e1473–80.

80 Nedeltcheva AV, Kilkus JM, Imperial J, Schoeller DA, Penev PD. Insufficient sleep undermines dietary efforts to reduce adiposity. *Annals of Internal Medicine* 2010;153:435–41.

81 Khosro S, Alireza S, Omid A, Forough S. Night work and inflammatory markers. *Indian Journal of Occupational and Environmental Medicine* 2011;15:38–41.

82 Malmberg B, Kecklund G, Karlson B, Persson R, Flisberg P, Orbaek P. Sleep and recovery in physicians on night call: a longitudinal field study. *BMC Health Services Research* 2010;10:239.

83 Ibid.

84 Palma JA, Urrestarazu E, Iriarte J. Sleep loss as risk factor for neurologic disorders: a review. *Sleep Medicine* 2013;14:229–36.

85 Ruggiero JS, Redeker NS. Effects of napping on sleepiness and sleep-related performance deficits in night-shift workers: a systematic review. *Biological Research for Nursing* 2014;16:134–42.

86 Ali T, Choe J, Awab A, Wagener TL, Orr WC. Sleep, immunity and inflammation in gastrointestinal disorders. *World Journal of Gastroenterology* 2013;19:9231–39.

87 Noguti J, Andersen ML, Cirelli C, Ribeiro DA. Oxidative stress, cancer, and sleep deprivation: is there a logical link in this association? *Sleep & Breathing* 2013;17:905–10.

88 Palma JA, Urrestarazu E, Iriarte J. Sleep loss as risk factor for neurologic disorders: a review. *Sleep Medicine* 2013;14:229–36.

89 Ruggiero JS, Redeker NS. Effects of napping on sleepiness and sleep-related performance deficits in night-shift workers: a systematic review. *Biological Research for Nursing* 2014;16:134–42.

90 Ali T, Choe J, Awab A, Wagener TL, Orr WC. Sleep, immunity and inflammation in gastrointestinal disorders. *World Journal of Gastroenterology* 2013;19:9231–39.

91 Noguti J, Andersen ML, Cirelli C, Ribeiro DA. Oxidative stress, cancer, and sleep deprivation: is there a logical link in this association? *Sleep & Breathing* 2013;17:905–10.

92 Palagini L, Bruno RM, Gemignani A, Baglioni C, Ghiadoni L, Riemann D. Sleep loss and hypertension: a systematic review. *Current Pharmaceutical Design* 2013;19:2409–19.

93 Wiebe ST, Cassoff J, Gruber R. Sleep patterns and the risk for unipolar depression: a review. *Nature and Science of Sleep* 2012;4:63–71.

94 Cassoff J, Wiebe ST, Gruber R. Sleep patterns and the risk for ADHD: a review. *Nature and Science of Sleep* 2012;4:73–80.

95 Wolk R, Somers VK. Sleep and the metabolic syndrome. *Experimental Physiology* 2007;92:67–78.

96 Pigeon WR, Carr M, Gorman C, Perlis ML. Effects of a tart cherry juice beverage on the sleep of older adults with insomnia: a pilot study. *Journal of Medicinal Food* 2010;13:579–83.

97 Choi JJ, Eum SY, Rampersaud E, Daunert S, Abreu MT, Toborek M. Exercise attenuates PCB-induced changes in the mouse gut microbiome. *Environmental Health Perspectives* 2013;121:725–30.

98 nytimes.com/health/guides/specialtopic/physical-activity/print.html.

99 van der Ploeg HP, Chey T, Korda RJ, Banks E, Bauman A. Sitting time and all-cause mortality risk in 222 497 Australian adults. *Archives of Internal Medicine* 2012;172:494–500.

100 Jeon CY, Lokken RP, Hu FB, van Dam RM. Physical activity of moderate intensity and risk of type 2 diabetes: a systematic review. *Diabetes Care* 2007;30:744–52.

101 Oguma Y, Shinoda-Tagawa T. Physical activity decreases cardiovascular disease risk in women: review and meta-analysis. *American Journal of Preventive Medicine* 2004;26:407–18.

102 Gregg EW, Gerzoff RB, Caspersen CJ, Williamson DF, Narayan KM. Relationship of walking to mortality among US adults with diabetes. *Archives of Internal Medicine* 2003;163:1440–47.

103 Trapp EG, Chisholm DJ, Freund J, Boutcher SH. The effects of high-intensity intermittent exercise training on fat loss and fasting insulin levels of young women. *International Journal of Obesity* 2008;32:684–91.

104 Teixeira-Lemos E, Nunes S, Teixeira F, Reis F. Regular physical exercise training assists in preventing type 2 diabetes development: focus on its antioxidant and anti-inflammatory properties. *Cardiovascular Diabetology* 2011;10:12.

105 DiPietro L, Dziura J, Yeckel CW, Neufer PD. Exercise and improved insulin sensitivity in older women: evidence of the enduring benefits of higher intensity training. *Journal of Applied Physiology* 2006;100:142–49.

Chapter 11

1   Hamrick K, et al. How much time do Americans spend on food? Economic Information Bulletin No. 86 (EIB-86), November 2011.

2   Cutler D, Glaeser E, Shapiro J. Why have Americans become obese? *Journal of Economic Perspectives* 2003;17:93–118.

INDEX

Appetite *(cont.)*
   hormones and, xv, 14, <u>39,</u> 58, 78
   ketogenic diets and, 58
   reducing
      nuts for, 178
      preloading for, 172
      probiotics for, 106
      protein for, 67–69
      yogurt for, 123
   sugar consumption and, 57
Apple cider vinegar, 131
Apples
   benefits of, 164–166
   Lean Green Smoothies with Apple and
      Kale, 312
   Sautéed Apples and Chicken Sausage
      with Sauerkraut, 304
Arrhythmias, 75
Arthritis
   capsaicin creme for, 87
   ginger for, 83
   turmeric for, 128
Artichokes
   benefits of, 64, 183–184
   Quinoa Salad with Lemony yogurt
      Dressing, 315
Artificial sweeteners
   in diet sodas, <u>56</u>
   sugar alcohol in, 62
Artisan foods, 111
Arugula
   Arugula Salad with Creamy Avocado
      Dressing, 302
Asian foods
   Ginger Fried Rice, 301
   Kimchi Pork Lo Mein, 307
   Miso Soup with Seaweed Salad, 300
Asparagus
   as prebiotic food, 112
   benefits of, 64, 117
   Cajun Cod, 306
   Creamy Asparagus Soup, 303
Aspartame, <u>56</u>
Asthma
   apples for, 165
   bifidobacteria levels and, 43
   children and, 20, 22
   oats for, 115
Atherosclerosis, 69, 71, 78, 177
Attitude, stress and, 191

Autism, 142
Autoimmunity
   bifidobacteria levels and, 43
   children and, 20, 22
Avocados
   Arugula Salad with Creamy Avocado
      Dressing, 302
   benefits of, 85
   Cool Cucumber-Avocado Soup, 296
Awareness, mental, 210–211
Ayurvedic medicine, <u>196,</u> 212

B

Bacillus subtilis, <u>122</u>
Back bend stretch, **206**
Bacteria. *See* Gene transfer of bacteria
Bacteroides, 18, 28, 188
Baechu, 127
Baked goods, gluten-free, 65
Baking ingredients, food rules for, <u>241</u>
Baltic Sea diet, 72, 137–138, 143–146
Bananas, 112
Bariatric surgery. *See* Gastric bypass
      obesity surgery
Bars
   Power Breakfast Bars, 279
Basil
   Basil Green Drink, 336
Beans and legumes
   as prebiotic food, 99–100, 112
   benefits of, 117–119
   Cajun Cod, 306
   Chicken Tikka Masala, 297
   Creamy Asparagus Soup, 303
   Curried Red Lentil Soup, 320
   food rules for
      phase I, <u>244</u>
      phase II, <u>250</u>
      phase III, <u>255</u>
   Minestrone Soup, 316
   Muffin-Size Frittatas, 295
   Salsa and Eggs, 292
   Turkey Chili, 319
Beef. *See also* Meat
   Sunday Stew, 318
Beer
   benefits of, 103, <u>145</u>
   hormesis and, <u>146</u>
   recommendations for, 152

Breast cancer, <u>70</u>
Breastfeeding, 7, 18, 43
Breathing, 193–194
Bridge with flies exercise, **226**
Broccoli
    benefits of, 181–183
    Crunchy Almond Tuna Salad, 285
    Dr. Gerry's Super Salmon Salad, 317
    Smoked Salmon Salad, 321
    Wild Rice and Turkey Soup, 314
Broccoli sprouts powder, 183
Brown adipose tissue, 83–84
Brussels Sprouts
    Kimchi Pork Lo Mein, 307
    Roasted Rosemary Chicken with
        Brussels Sprouts, 322
Buffalo meat
    Tangy Buffalo Burgers with Pickles,
        299
Bulk buying, 239
Bulk cooking, 240
Burgers
    Tangy Buffalo Burgers with Pickles,
        299
Butter, <u>110</u>

C

Cabbage. *See also* Cruciferous vegetables;
    Kimchi; Sauerkraut
    kimchi, benefits of, 127–128
    Kimchi Pork Lo Mein, 307
    Minestrone Soup, 316
    Sauerkraut, 332
    Sautéed Apples and Chicken Sausage
        with Sauerkraut, 304
Caesarean section births, 7, 18, 20
Caffeine, 75–76
CAFOs, 23, 103
Cajun foods
    Cajun Cod, 306
Cakes
    Dark Chocolate Flourless Cake, 326
Calcium
    in dairy products, 66, 124
    lactose intolerance and, <u>66</u>
    low-carb diets and, <u>70</u>
    supplements of, <u>66</u>

Caloric intake
    diet sodas and, <u>56</u>
    nuts and, 179
    protein and, 67–68
    weight loss and, xiv–xv, 1, 3
Calorie-restricted diets, 2
Cancer. *See also specific types*
    prevention of
        apples for, 165
        broccoli for, 182
        kale for, 119
        kimchi for, 128
        leafy greens for, 169–171
        lignans for, <u>174</u>
        olive oil for, 163
        yogurt for, 122
    red meat consumption and, 69, <u>70</u>
Canola oil, 72, 151
Capsaicin, 127–128. *See also* Cayenne
    pepper
Carbohydrates
    digesting, 6
    energy from, 23
    FODMAPs foods, 41
    inflammation and, 29
    metabolism of, 28
    processed, dangers of, 147–148
    recommendations for, 57–59, 72–73
Carbonated beverages, <u>56,</u> 74
Carcinogens, <u>56</u>
Cardiovascular disease
    canola oil and, 72
    coffee and, 179–180
    full-fat dairy and, <u>125</u>
    hypothalamic-pituitary-adrenal
        (HPA) axis and, 36
    inflammation and, 24
    ketogenic diets and, 59
    preventing
        apples for, 164
        chocolate for, 166–167
        flaxseed for, 174
        leafy greens for, 164
        nuts for, 176–177
        vegetables for, 73
    red meat consumption and, 69, 71
    saturated fats and, 60
    sugar consumption and, 52
Cardiovascular exercises, <u>234,</u> 234–235